PRAISE FOR DAVID ADAMS CLEVELAND'S PREVIOUS NOVEL, *TIME'S BETRAYAL*

"How are our lives unknowingly motivated by our ancestral past? In its scope, artistry, and depiction of the interlinked cause-and-effect patterns spanning more than a century, Cleveland's (*Love's Attraction*, 2013) third novel raises the bar for multi-generational epics. At its heart is one man's quest to uncover the truth about his late father, John Alden III, who disappeared behind the Iron Curtain in 1953 for reasons unknown. Peter Alden's recollections begin with his own 1960s youth at the Etonesque Massachusetts prep school cofounded by his abolitionist great-grandfather; a place where his father's reputation as a star athlete, archaeologist, and war hero looms large. The expansive yet tightly controlled narrative, in which numerous mysteries are compellingly unearthed, spins out to encompass post-WWII Greece, the race to decipher the ancient Greek script known as Linear B, the Vietnam War, the Berlin Wall's dismantling, and a Civil War battle's aftermath. The writing is gripping throughout, incorporating both haunting lyricism in its characters' yearning to recapture a lost golden age and a high-stakes tension evoking the best Cold War thrillers. Cleveland is particularly strong in presenting the complicated entanglements of love and betrayal and the barrier between freedom and oppression that each generation contends with. While its length may appear daunting, this unforgettable tour de force is well worth the time."

—***Booklist***, Starred Review

"This is a literary page-turner with many philosophical themes running throughout. It is a worthwhile read for anyone who loves to lose themselves in a big book and willing to make the investment in time and effort."

—**Janice Ottersberg**, Historical Novel Society

"With this monumental work David Cleveland has achieved nothing less than the disinterment of the various skeletons of the American psyche from the Civil War to Vietnam and beyond, and the painting of a multi-generational portrait of a pedigreed American family whose own skeletons not only refuse to stay buried, but actively haunt its progeny. There will be those who, captivated by the author's brilliant insights into the inner workings of the CIA, KGB and MI6, and by a canvas that stretches from New England to Prague and Greece to Southeast Asia, will describe *Time's Betrayal* as an international spy novel, which it is, if only in the sense that *Moby-Dick* is a yarn about a big fish and *Huckleberry Finn* a tale of a boy on a raft. But this is not Ludlum, folks, nor is it LeCarre. It is in a league of its own and a class by itself. *Time's Betrayal* is a large-hearted American epic that deserves the widest possible, most discriminating of readerships."

—**Bruce Olds,** Pulitzer Prize–nominated author for
Raising Holy Hell and *The Moments Lost*

"*Time's Betrayal* is a vast, rich, endlessly absorbing novel engaging with the great and enduring theme of literary art, the quest for an identity. Moreover, it seamlessly expands that quest beyond the individual to the family, to the nation. *Time's Betrayal* achieves a rare state for massively ambitious novels: it is both complex and compelling. David Adams Cleveland has instantly taken a prominent place on my personal list of must-read authors."

—**Robert Olen Butler,** Pulitzer Prize–winning author of
A Good Scent from a Strange Mountain

"It is an oddity of history that the early CIA—a world of deceit and betrayal—was dominated by New England prep school grads whose chief cultural values, supposedly, were decency and fair play. In *Time's Betrayal*, David Cleveland takes us into this world in his sweeping, ambitious novel. With drama and flair, he follows the true, if crooked path, of the human heart. It makes for a compelling and provocative read."

—**Evan Thomas,** author of *The Very Best Men:*
The Early Years of the CIA

"This is the best book I've read all year, and I've read many excellent ones. It's also the longest novel I've read, ever, but, after reading the first 100 pages, I was hooked and eagerly looking forward to the next thousand. I took a week off in mid-August, planning to catch up on work around the house and read maybe 100 pages a day so I'd have it finished by the deadline. Instead, I spent a good part of the week with this book and don't regret it. (It does move quickly.) . . . there's so much more that could be said. I could also note that there are two strong and multi-faceted female characters, and multiple complicated love affairs, and that the storyline delves deeply into the real-life history of the Cambridge Five spy ring who passed secrets to the Soviets up through the 1950s. I never considered Cold War thrillers to be my type of book, but this novel was. What to compare it to? For the family saga aspect and mysteries related to it, it would appeal to Kate Morton's fans, although it's more ambitious than even her novels. It should be on the radar of readers of spy thrillers, obviously. It's also a moving coming-of-age tale. Best of all is seeing how the multiple story lines, characters, and time periods come together. The book arrived with glowing blurbs from Robert Olen Butler and Bruce Olds, the latter of whom had said, among other things, 'It is in a league of its own and a class by itself,' which is true. I can't think of another novel quite like it."

—**Sarah Johnson,** Reading the Past

ALSO BY DAVID ADAMS CLEVELAND

NOVELS

Love's Attraction

With a Gemlike Flame

Time's Betrayal

ART HISTORY

A History of American Tonalism: 1880–1920
Crucible of American Modernism

Intimate Landscapes: Charles Warren Eaton
and the Tonalist Movement

Ross Braught: A Visual Diary

Ralph L. Wickiser: The Reflected Stream
The Abstract Years 1985–1998

Paul Balmer: Cityscapes

DAVID ADAMS CLEVELAND

GODS OF

DECEPTION

A NOVEL

GREENLEAF
BOOK GROUP PRESS

This is a work of fiction. Although some of the characters, organizations, and events portrayed in the novel are based on actual historical counterparts, the dialogue and thoughts of these characters are products of the author's imagination.

Published by Greenleaf Book Group Press
Austin, Texas
www.gbgpress.com

Distributed by Greenleaf Book Group

For ordering information or special discounts for bulk purchases, please contact Greenleaf Book Group at PO Box 91869, Austin, TX 78709, 512.891.6100.

Design and composition by Drew Stevens and Greenleaf Book Group
Cover design by Jason Booher
Cover Images: ©Getty Images/stefko; ©Getty Images/Bettmann; ©Alamy/Heritage Image Partnership Lt
Interior images:
Title page: Heritage Image Partnership / MPWX20 / Alamy Stock Photo
Figure 3: Everett Collection Historical / KWCNR4 / Alamy Stock Photo
Figure 7: Panther Media / J66D73 / Alamy Stock Photo
Figure 16: Retro AdArchives / FKCE81 / Alamy Stock Photo
Figures 17, 13, 34, 45, and 48: GRANGER
Figure 53: TX4EH8 / Alamy Stock Photo
Figure 58: Robert Carner / BPT9HJ / Alamy Stock Photo
Figure 66: Steve Bloom Images / A97F58 / Alamy Stock Photo
Figure 69: D. Trozzo / B5NH3K / Alamy Stock Photo
Figure 70: Rivera Photography
Excerpt from "Two Tramps in Mud Time" by Robert Frost from THE POETRY OF ROBERT FROST edited by Edward Connery Lathem. Copyright © 1969 by Henry Holt and Company. Copyright © 1936 by Robert Frost, copyright © 1964 by Lesley Frost Ballantine. Reprinted by permission Henry Holt and Company. All Rights Reserved.

Publisher's Cataloging-in-Publication data is available.

Print ISBN: 978-1-62634-918-6

eBook ISBN: 978-1-62634-919-3

Part of the Tree Neutral® program, which offsets the number of trees consumed in the production and printing of this book by taking proactive steps, such as planting trees in direct proportion to the number of trees used: www.treeneutral.com

Printed in the United States of America on acid-free paper

22 23 24 25 26 27 28 29   10 9 8 7 6 5 4 3 2 1

First Edition

For the temper of Stalin's mind requires a strategy of multiple deceptions, which confuse the victim with the illusion of power, and soften them up with the illusion of hope, only to plunge them deeper into despair when the illusion fades, the trap is sprung, and the victims gasp with horror, as they hurtle into space.

—Whittaker Chambers

ALGER HISS FOUND GUILTY

Alger Hiss Convicted Of Perjury

Jury Decides
He Spied
For Communists

NEW YORK, Jan. 20, (UP) — Alger Hiss was found guilty of perjury by a Manhattan Federal Court jury which decided he betrayed his country to a Communist spy ring when he held a post of trust in the State Department.

The jury of eight women and four men reached a verdict 23 hours and 38 minutes after it went out in this second trial of the 45-year-old "career man" who through the Government...

Alger Hiss Convicted of Two Perjury Counts

Alger Hiss Is Found Guilty By Jurors in Perjury Case

BY DAN HARRISON

NEW YORK, Jan. 20, (UP) — Given a moment's respite, Edward lifted his gaze to the dull liquid January light flooding the fantail window...

Verdict Brands Him as Red Spy

NEW YORK, Jan. 21 (AP) — Associate counsel for the Edward Denock, summer tan attractively faded beneath...

Alger Hiss Guilty of Perjury

Former Federal Official Convicted Of Two Charges

Jury Finds Hiss Lied When He Denied Stealing Secrets In 1938 For Delivery to Chambers; Eight Women, Four Men On Jury Deliberated 9 Hours, 13 Minutes

(By H.D. QUIGG)

New York—Alger Hiss was found guilty of perjury yesterday by a Manhattan Federal Court jury which decided he betrayed his country to a Communist spy ring when he held a post of trust in the State Department.

The jury of eight women and four men reached a verdict 23 hours and 38 minutes after it went out in this second trial of the 45-year-old "career man" who had risen through the Government to a post of advisor to President Roosevelt at Yalta.

They found him guilty on both perjury counts—that he had lied when he denied he served a Communist network in the New Deal 1930s by handing over to spy courier Whittaker Chambers secret documents from the State Department, that he lied when he said he had not seen Chambers after January, 1937.

The conviction means that Hiss faces a possible maximum sentence of 10 years in prison and a $4,000 fine.

Continued in Bail

Judge Henry W. Goddard set the time for sentencing to 10:30 a.m. He continued Hiss at liberty in $5,000 bail until that time.

Hiss' attorney, Claude B. Cross, announced the conviction "certainly will be appealed."

Alger Hiss was convicted on two counts of perjury by a federal jury today. Hiss is shown above accompanied by his wife Priscilla Hiss.

ALGER HISS

...urors' ...t Hailed ...mbers

Federal... Find Alger Hiss Guilty of Perjury

Judge will Sen...

Alger Hiss Is Convicted On Two Perjury Counts

NEW YORK —(AP)— Alger Hiss was found guilty of perjury yesterday by a Manhattan Federal Court jury which decided he betrayed his country to a Communist spy ring when he held a post of trust in the State Department.

Judge Henry W. Goddard set the time for sentencing to 10:30 a.m. He continued Hiss at liberty in $5,000 bail until that time.

Hiss' attorney, Claude B. Cross, announced the conviction "certainly will be appealed."

Hiss took the verdict without so much as a twitch of a facial muscle...

1
Perjury

We are caught in a tragedy of history.

—Whittaker Chambers

JANUARY 21, 1950

ASSOCIATE COUNSEL FOR the defense Edward Dimock, summer tan attractively faded beneath his chestnut hair, sat forward at the defense table as he inspected the twelve jury members filing back into the federal courtroom templed above Foley Square. He cocked his head, squinting, like the expert birder he was, off-blue eyes attentive to any telltale clues in the rapt faces of the eight women jurors, finding himself relieved at the serious, if not severe, freshly lipsticked frowns telegraphing from the oak-paneled jury box. He checked his watch and then the brass wall clock above the jury room entrance: 2:46—twenty minutes since lunch break. (A configuration of hands, an angle of 165 degrees, to be exact, that would forever become annealed in his mind's eye.) He nodded mechanically, as if a switch in a finely tuned mechanism had been tripped. Forty-three years old, now at the height of his powers, a few gray strands in the upturned flourish of his eyebrows for gravitas, he pensively rested his jaw on his fist.

No, certainly not much in the way of indecision on display, and even less in the forthright stare of jury forewoman Mrs. Ada Condell, who waited grimly in her seat for the judge to inquire as to their verdict. These and other portents of disaster caused Edward to glance down the defense table to where his client, Alger Hiss, sat with stoic determination next to his wife, Priscilla. Her familiar upturned nose

1

and quivering, compressed lips caused Edward's pulse to quicken, and he ground his fist against the sharp angle of his chin, repressing the urge to gasp out a warning, while bracing himself for the worst. Below, the vague tremor of traffic or the rattle of a subway train vibrating the floor. On the mocha plane of his half-drunk coffee, a ripple moved. Yet another avatar of cosmic cataclysm, which Judge Henry W. Goddard seemed to savor: what the newspapers already heralded as the trial of the century, even a century only half done. Goddard paused again, absorbed in his own little drama of shuffling papers on his bench, perhaps girding himself for the sure-to-come uproar in the aftermath of this four-week ordeal, a thing anticipated by the hundreds of reporters stacked to the coffered ceiling of his courtroom, peering forward as one with pens raised, breath suspended . . . while grave Fortuna, coiled catlike, ready to spring in the left front corner of the jury box, awaited her moment on history's stage.

Given a moment's respite (shuffle, shuffle), Edward lifted his gaze to the dull liquid January light flooding the fantail window above the jury box, thirteen stories above Foley Square and the teeming metropolis where he and his father before him had mightily prospered. Yet there was nothing in that cloudy gray to give him pleasure, except thoughts of escape on ardent wings to Hermitage, his Catskill retreat—now, today, in an hour or less, with Annie and the girls and Teddy (all still on Christmas break, the girls from Chapin and Teddy from Yale). Closing his eyes for an extended tattoo of heartbeats, he sought to rally the moral gravitas and professional competency that Groton, Yale, Harvard Law, a treasured clerkship with Oliver Wendell Holmes, his position as top gun at Beekman-Morris, and three years on the War Production Board in Washington had long instilled, the experience and finely honed instincts that now prompted him to abandon his longing gaze for the sullen emptiness of the witness box. He sighed as he contemplated one final time that stage setting, where, only days before, he'd deployed the unctuous theories of psychopathic personality disorder and unconscious motivation against the prosecution's star witness, onetime ex-Communist and *Time* magazine editor Whittaker Chambers, with the ghastly results to be confirmed momentarily.

That afterimage still pressed on his guilty soul: Chambers seated in his unpressed trousers, dirty shirt collar curled over his seedy jacket, scuffed shoes. Those deep-set sleepless eyes, sad and tortured yet brimming with the wisdom of the solid earth . . . a man of sorrows, a prophet of doom, who now invisibly inquired of his persecutor about the sad fate of the artist, one George Altmann, on Christmas Eve, a short four weeks before. Chambers's testimony had craned the necks of jurors and judge alike: hushed, reticent, searching, laconic; a voice that would haunt Edward Dimock all his days, living on to captivate him in years to come from the pages of Chambers's best-selling autobiography, *Witness*.

Edward Dimock's beleaguered inspection of the witness box deepened with regret as he recalled yet again the ineptitude and inquisitorial overreach he'd foolishly undertaken at Alger Hiss's promptings and assurances—if not vague threats, something his mentor Justice Holmes would have severely chastised him for. "Son, once a man's reputation is besmirched, threats or no . . ." Edward winced with the pain of one who had disregarded his betters, if not his better instincts, thereby trashing what little remained of his, much less his profession's, pretension to a moral code.

He reached to the heavy briefcase by his leg, if not for assurance, possibly in prayer that he might be spared the full implications, if not deployment, of what lay concealed within.

A cough, a clearing of the throat, and Edward, starting from reverie, looked to the acanthus-carved bench where, papers finally shuffled, the experienced and respected Honorable Henry Goddard prepared to proceed, arraying his silver-bespectacled aquiline profile to full effect, only to begin a quick inventory of the rapt congregants crowding his oak-paneled courtroom.

A wave of relief washed over Edward that the thing was now out of his hands: that twelve ordinary Americans would do their duty and pronounce a verdict that might contradict the expectations of some of the finest legal minds and savvy commentators of his generation—august public servants and gilded pundits all—and, in turn, repudiate the most astute lawyering money and reputation could buy (the like of which he'd never dreamed possible), thus shifting or at least sharing the blame for his egregious and smarmy psychiatric hucksterism employed at Chambers's expense. Hadn't all the Harvard boys on the defense team signed off, in the end? Hadn't their outrageous ploy been indulged by Judge Goddard? Even if only to even the score by allowing the prosecution to call ex-NKVD agent Hede Massing as a witness, and so fingering Alger dead to rights.

Petite, doe-eyed, redheaded Hede, so Edward assured himself, with her warm and melodic Viennese cadences, had surely sunk them anyway, along with the Hisses' black maid, Claudia Catlett, and the irrevocable evidence of the purloined secret State Department papers copied on the Hisses' Woodstock typewriter. Surely the facts, as facts always do, would, in the fullness of time, extract the barbed hook of infamy from a career now in dire jeopardy.

Edward concentrated once again on Alger and Priscilla Hiss, as if for a final reckoning—and for Alger it would be the last time—before history weighed fully, if ambiguously, in the scales of justice. That agile kitelike face (yellow-billed), rigid with righteous indignation, with an air of detached concentration—expensive winter suit, starched shirt with French cuffs always discreetly hidden, soft, becoming tie, and shiny black shoes—swept Edward back to the day only two months before when Alger strode into his Beekman-Morris office to make the case for accepting the role of associate defense counsel (slated for one singular task) in his second perjury trial, equally cajoling and flattering and so, so subtly threatening. Even pressing Priscilla into the act—and it had always been a paired-horse marriage—at their rendezvous in Riverside Park. The still lovely though desperately anxious Pross on her lunch break from Dalton, taking his hand tenderly and pleading the good cause with tear-verging blue eyes, those same strong and so agile fingers—touching his for quick moments—that had clandestinely cantered across the keys of the green Woodstock typewriter, which, even now, stared back like some bleak totemic object of the industrial age from the evidence table next to the jury box.

The thought of all those top-secret State Department documents made for another moment of serenity, a half-smile as Edward loosened his tie: damning evidence produced like a conjurer's trick by Whittaker Chambers and thus, truth be told, dooming their case from the get-go. With the testimony of that mysterious Red pixie Hede just the icing on the cake, along with the Hisses' Negro maid. Edward sighed as he again scrutinized the rapt face of the jury forewoman: a final confirmation that, professionally speaking, he'd done the necessary—defending his family—and canny thing in face of insuperable obstacles, even as those damned Altmann sketches had blindsided him. And with this bit of self-assurance, he reached under the defense table to his leather attaché case once again and gave it a reassuring pat that his insurance (nine portrait sketches by the recently deceased artist George Altmann) would not now, not ever—thank God!—require deploying.

So, let history be his judge and jury. Even if the brass clock over the door to the jury room seemed to have barely moved. Even if his wife, Annie, had barely spoken to him in a month, after dutifully sitting in on the first day of the trial. Even if his beloved son, Teddy, had avoided him all Christmas, preferring to spend his time with his Yale roommates in the city. Time and sunlight were the final disinfectant of one's integrity.

Lengthening his focus just above Alger's cleanly parted hair, he caught a glimpse of his opponent at the prosecution table, Assistant U.S. Attorney Thomas F. Murphy, formidably tall even when seated, his dark mustache flexing optimistically as he stared down at the number-two pencil in his hand with the unshakable confidence of one who'd already caught the glint of the executioner's raised ax.

The rest of the defense team, Cross and McLean, remained rigid, perspiring, having read those twelve faces as well as he had.

Judge Goddard nodded at the court clerk, who leaped to his feet as if from a jack-in-the-box and demanded the verdict.

"How find you?"

Ada Condell didn't wait a beat, thus heralding in the chaotic world that would become the Red-baiting McCarthyite decade of the 1950s. In a choked, then clearing high-pitched voice, she declared, "We find the defendant guilty on the first count and guilty on the second count."

Oddly, Edward wanted to reach out a steadying hand to Alger, his onetime Harvard Law confrere and fellow birder, but found him rigid, with arms folded, stiffened brows and clenched lips impervious to time as well as to history, as one hundred-plus pens in the press gallery swept across acres of spiral notepads. Priscilla barely blinked, her traumatized gaze flashing to the wintery space of light from the fantail window, her prim shoulders bent, hands crossed limply in the silk folds of her lap. If he could have spoken to her, this was the query that hovered on his lips like an incantation out of time itself: *Oh, my dear Pross, how far from Handytown now?*

And with that, he gave his attaché case yet another relieved pat.

Of the following fifteen minutes of instructions to the jurors not to blab about their deliberations, and a quick to-and-fro over the five-thousand-dollar bail, Edward found in later years that he remembered almost nothing. Only a final image of Alger grabbing Priscilla's hand, whispering in her ear, "Keep your chin up," and leading her quickly out past the horde of snarling reporters.

With that verdict of dishonor and ruin, Alger exited Edward Dimock's life, as if he'd never been, which, upon deeper reflection, might indeed have been the case.

For as Edward would remember until his dying day, his thoughts at that moment flowed along these lines: A man who lies so expertly, so convincingly, who threatens with the merest inflection of voice, rarely treads the boards of this life, and then only in pursuit of his spectral shadow. Or as his grandson would put it to him some fifty years later: "Judge, it was as if you inhabited two different stages, two parallel universes; and I'm not entirely sure, even now, if you know the difference."

2

Landscapes Transcendent

♦

GEORGE DIMOCK ALTMANN swiveled on his heels to make a last check of the hanging in Dark Matter, his four-year-old Chelsea gallery. Last dance, last chance for a profitable show to keep his gallerist gig above water after a disastrous post-9/11 year. Against all advice, against the odds in a contemporary art world more and more obsessed with the next wunderkind out of a prestige art school, he'd bet on a dead white male artist—George Altmann, no less, his grandfather and namesake. George surveyed his arrangement of Altmann's late abstract landscapes from his Woodstock years, 1939 to 1949. LANDSCAPES TRANSCENDENT. The title was emblazoned in hemlock green on the wall opposite the entrance, where a crowd of well-dressed and grunge-chic fashionistas was just filtering in. The living, breathing reality check—even worse, he thought, sighing, than a peer-reviewed paper.

After long months of planning—selecting, cleaning, framing— George would have to introduce himself to and glad-hand potential collectors, and elevator-pitch *his* grandfather's artworks. (How could one even feign the pretense of objectivity?) To intercept a panic attack that had lain in ambush all day, he fixed his eyes on the showcase canvas facing the entrance: a shear-faced rocky escarpment, seething horizontals of milky-quartz tones, strips of jittery pigment describing a 430-million-year-old sedimentary conglomerate only recently revealed by the last ice age. This, the stunning cover image of his scholarly catalog, cropped to dramatize the masterful paint handling. But instead of experiencing pride, even ecstatic joy, he might as well have been dangling from that rock face by his fingernails as the knot in his gut expanded upward to compress his windpipe. And so he beat a hasty retreat into his office, holding up his cell phone and signaling to his assistant, JJ, standing at the entrance handing out catalogs, that he had an important call to take.

Clozapine, 1 mg. Take one every twelve hours for generalized anxiety.

He stared at the prescription bottle neatly tucked into the side of his desk drawer for emergencies, his heart doing a spiky tango, a bloom of sweat turning his blond hair dirty brown, chewed fingernails hovering. He grabbed two Listerine tabs instead and crammed them into his mouth, then rushed over to the single tall window of his book-crammed office, there to savor a vertical slice of teeming Eleventh Avenue from eight stories up. Where, in the distance beyond the careening buzz of evening traffic, interspersed with a nervous blur of Juicy Fruit light bars from phalanxes of parked police cars, two huge beams of diaphanous white sliced majestically into the night sky. He leaned into the plate glass, drawn to those ghostly beams, even as his thirty-two-year-old pathetic paunch and the click of his too-tight belt buckle thwarted a closer inspection—along with a bizarre yearning to merge with such a potent photon stream, and so scattered to the solar winds, his soul released in some quantum approximation of his essential self, minus the constant hassles and crippling uncertainty that had plagued him in recent years.

Like Einstein, he preferred a universe that played by the rules, where the twin towers still stood tall and proud and regal, perhaps where infinite inflation found them still aglow in some faraway morning's early light, and Joe Santiago, still on his client list, waiting, even now, in his gallery for a tour of Altmann's exhibition.

Fat chance, he thought, sighing. Anyway, what could alien eyes possibly make of those twin points of light coming from some random exoplanet in a backwater of an undistinguished galaxy: a desperate stab at contact; a cry of distress from a civilization embarked on wanton self-destruction; a celebration of endurance against all the odds? A hope, if even that, rendered meaningless by a faster-than-the-speed-of-light expansion of the visible universe, so that by the time such a feeble signal might be registered by some extraterrestrial intelligence, the culture that produced it would have long succumbed to suicide or been blown to smithereens by a meteor strike, with an exhausted sun for a sucker-punch finale—the Trade Center attack a firefly flicker in the cosmic void. Seven years analyzing luminosity and spectrum analysis of Cepheid variable stars in distant galaxies in the Princeton Astrophysics Department had more than convinced him of the pointlessness of such pitiful conjectures, given such vast soul-crushing distances. Just another pathetic thought experiment—past anxieties only fueling present anxieties—that he tried to put out of his mind. Even as he pressed his flattened palms against the glass in solidarity, full of guilt and anger that he hadn't even had the guts to attend the memorial service of a few days before. Much less watch Bush at the U.N. yesterday demand that the world do something to stop Saddam Hussein from developing weapons of mass destruction, or the United States would.

—

Just a year ago, like yesterday, with the bubble-wrapped painting tucked safely under his arm, he'd ascended the subway steps into that perfectly blue sky above the plaza, delighted to be personally delivering the artwork as promised to Joe Santiago, partner at Cantor Fitzgerald. Joe had spent a precious half hour in Dark Matter, away from the trading desk, picking out the perfect gift for his wife's birthday.

"She—Jean—loves the kids, of course; her garden, especially the azaleas and hollyhocks; our black Lab, Chewbacca—kids, you know—get it . . . yeah, chews the shit out of the furniture. Mykonos she picked out for our honeymoon—lots of gay guys, you know; they have their own nude beach. And Danielle Steel is her favorite author. Did I mention she studied art history at Bard? A woman, don't you agree, Mr. Altmann, always knows what she loves; they always have an opinion—always. Trust me, it's part of my job to know such things."

Joe had finally settled on a still life of yellow roses and tiger lilies in a crystal vase, eggplants on a blue platter, against a backdrop of a red-checkered tablecloth.

"Like you say, George—can I call you George?—a hint of Cézanne—for sure. The warm sunlight and those purples will make her happy—absolutely guaranteed. She's big into moussaka—see, her Greek mom, but hey . . . George, it's all about happiness with the small things in a marriage—trust me. Love comes and goes; endearments, like memories of happy times, last forever."

The crystalline blue of the sky at the top of the concrete stairs, the sweetness of Joe's Brooklyn accent, the nasal vowels and his excitement at the perfect gift of happiness—now cradled in his arm—all conspired against the scene of mayhem that greeted George in the plaza. Stink of jet fuel, the inferno belching fiery smoke and swirling paper geysers from the gaping wound in the vertical skin of glass and steel—so impossibly high above the churning chaos below. Mesmerized onlookers in gesticulating groups of two or three, some lingering, some running, on cell phones or snapping photos. He simply refused to believe his eyes. He had the floor number, the suite number, the telephone number—on a Post-it note affixed to the bubble wrap, the gift: all he needed to conclude an act of goodness. He'd promised Joe the painting for his wife's surprise birthday party at a Greek restaurant in Nutley, New Jersey, that evening. He called on his cell phone. No answer. One hundred and first floor. Idiotically, he began counting the floors below the smoke-bellowing wound of the north tower, clutching the wrapped canvas to his chest like a scared child. Somehow his absolute belief in Joe's gift, the deliberations of a busy man that had gone into this act of loving consecration, of solidarity with a kinder universe—much less that agreed upon delivery date, September 11, Jean's birthday—belied what his eyes were witnessing. He remained rooted, willing time to retreat, the belching flames and acrid smoke to retreat and order reassert itself and so cancel out such hellish confusion.

Then the falling bodies began to hit the pavement, the first a hundred yards away . . . a dull thud thrown up from a pink mist. Then closer. People screamed. Then a shadow, followed by a splash of brilliant fiery red against the blue as the second 767 sliced into the south tower, followed by the roar of jet engines. He began to move off, disoriented, unsure whether he should retreat to the subway or head north on the West Side Highway. Then he caught sight of a black-suited figure on the concrete of the plaza. Perhaps he had tripped and needed help; perhaps it was Joe, who had rushed out to find him, to grab his offering of sanity and hope in the nick of time and find his way home. But as he approached, he found only the flattened shadow of a man's suit, his innards, a pink mush, sprayed ten feet in all directions.

———

Six months later, he'd finally summoned the nerve to track down Joe's widow. It was spring then in Nutley. Blooming azaleas dotted the cul-de-sac of modest faux half-timbered Tudor-style homes. Dogs barked. Scent of newly mown grass. Through her tears and dark bagged eyes, Jean Santiago, her two children hovering behind in the foyer, embraced him on her doorstep, embracing the canvas as well, holding him tight for over a minute, as if some part of her missing husband—his body was never recovered or identified—had returned home. She was still young, but her long brown hair was streaked with mourning gray, her gray-green eyes, red-veined and dark-circled, sunken. The children had been kept home from school. They shook hands when introduced but remained speechless. Chewbacca came and sniffed his shoes, then his hand, and then the wrapped painting. The dog began whining and wagging its tail. The children broke into tears that almost did him in.

When she unwrapped the painting, she, too, broke down in tears, rushing it to the living room, where Joe's favorite La-Z-Boy remained extended full length, holding the painting up to the window, where the sunlight made the colors dance. Her kids, a girl eight and a boy six, stood on either side and reached to the canvas, first to the swelling swirls of pigments that formed flowers, then to the purples and blues of the eggplants. The three of them walked from room to room to room, trying to decide where to hang Daddy's painting. When George left, it was still undecided. Even now, Jean Santiago texted at least once a week, with questions about exactly what Joe had said at the exhibition, about the artist, about her—why he'd chosen this particular painting for her, which she'd rehung a dozen times, as if some different configuration might yet reveal something she'd missed.

He found himself caught up by her constant inquiries, feeling compelled to fill in details about their honeymoon in Mykonos as told him by Joe: about eggplants he'd admired in the marketplace, sold by an old Greek woman; about the nude beach where Joe liked to proudly show off his new bride; how the morning light in her auburn hair against the pillow in their hotel room had made him fall in love all over again . . . same light as in the painting. He'd even read Danielle Steel, to indulge some parallel universe, so as to savor something of her longing.

He'd never cashed Joe's check.

—

"Your mother just called," said JJ, sticking her head in the door of his office. "She found a parking spot on Nineteenth Street and will be here with your aunts in ten minutes." JJ held up her clipboard in a victory salute. "And we just sold seven paintings, including the one on the catalog cover and the one inside the cover—that's almost half the show."

"No fucking way—seriously?"

"Like, how do you say—pancakes?"

"Hotcakes."

"Yes"—she tapped the clipboard—"very hot."

"Who bought the cover one and the one inside the cover, someone on our client list or mailing list?"

"New, never heard of him," said JJ. JJ was a tall, striking Chinese woman whose exquisitely made-up face accented her green eyes. She spoke near-perfect English and perfect Mandarin, and was a canny saleswoman of prodigious conviction when moving the merch. "Just sailed in, Armani suit, black silk turtleneck, spent five minutes walking around with the checklist, picked out the two most expensive pieces and didn't even negotiate on price."

"The review," he intoned.

"Yes, he had folded page in his pocket."

"Thanks, JJ, I'll be out in a moment."

———

George, digesting the sales report, felt as if a pall of disaster had lifted, replaced by a surge of confidence. He grabbed the rave *New York Times* review of that morning off his desk and let his pale blue-gray eyes luxuriate one more time: "a rediscovered genius . . . Rothko before Rothko . . . avatar of abstraction from nature in the line of Inness, Marsden Hartley, and Avery . . ."

Committing pithy excerpts to memory, George adjusted his silver-gray suit jacket, and the thin *moiré* stain of a tie that barely showed against his black shirt—hipster uniform for the contemporary art scene, acquired on JJ's advice—and drifted out into the gallery. A huge crowd jammed his tiny three white cubes of exhibition space. The din was low and respectful. Instead of standing around, oblivious, in chatting clusters, consuming his cheap chardonnay, singletons and couples, catalogs in hand, were actually looking at Altmann's abstract landscapes as if ardently absorbing their hypnotic splendor. Even the usual suspects, artists and their groupie hangers-on in deftly torn jeans and paint-stained plaid shirts, were exchanging heated opinions. He smiled. The good artists were always intent on stealing anything worth stealing. George immediately began sorting the crowd, spotting the admixture of potential well-heeled upscale buyers, as if a long year in the doldrums of panic and grief was quite enough, thank you. For an instant, he indulged the corollary fantasy that his George Altmann revival was the catalyst to celebrate the end of a city's and a nation's mourning and a return to normalcy—that beauty, like the spectacle of a supernova (the end of a world), could trump tragedy. And with that delicious notion, the prospect of sales, of commerce, eased up a smile of pride and relief on George's pudgy but not entirely unhandsome face as he began convincing himself that his harebrained plan to give up astrophysics for the art world was finally paying off; that he'd had the aesthetic moxie to look under his nose and take a risk on his grandfather's forgotten work; that judicious restoration and cleaning would make all the difference, not to mention the simple yet sumptuous and expensive—slightly distressed—oak frames he'd chosen.

"Yes!"

Altmann's genius was so blindingly clear: how his grandfather had taken the bone and gristle of Woodstock's hills, and the conglomerate Palisades along the Shawangunk Ridge, and transposed their underlying patterns and color tonalities into masses of scintillating paint marks—brushed and scumbled and scraped and flattened and translated with bravura handling to reveal the metamorphic qualities of rock and foliage—the essence of the land. For the first time in his young life, he felt his grandfather's awe (a man dead decades before he was born) as his own: nature's timeless recrudescence.

"My God . . . the love . . ."

With an airy spring in his step, George began to mingle, luxuriating in his anonymity for just another moment as he listened in on the chatter. How he relished seeing his own words from the catalog imprinted boldly on the gallery walls: "Moments of rapture in the act of creation . . . a one-man battle against the drift into chaos. An artist taking the raw chaotic data of the universe and ordering it on a more human scale. Soul's antidote to a new age of fanaticism and murderous hatred."

George winced at the hyperbole. And yet . . . and yet some irrepressible yearning in him sought to make convincing that causal connection between tragedies past and present—now buttressed by the proof—like a perfect algorithm that dismissed all competing conjectures. He nodded to himself. A man with such a magnificent talent could not have killed himself, somehow slipped or fallen onto the ice from the Sawkill Bridge, Christmas Eve, 1949. Everything—the sheer creative energy on the surrounding walls gave the lie to that oft-rumored suicide that had plagued the family for three generations. The burden of fifty years lifted by the simple glory of paint applied to canvas . . . and so cauterizing that even more terrible impact of human breakage at terminal velocity.

—

"Well, baby love . . ." Cordelia Dimock Altmann embraced her son with an amused smile, brushing her hand along the side of his head, as if approving the tidy haircut, the shimmer of mousse that gave his dirty-blond hair a fifties look and feel. "My baby love, my Kookie, my one and only." Her once-fashionable Indian batik dress was accessorized with silver moonstone jewelry, dripping from wrists, neck, and ear-lobes, marketing tool for the handcrafted trinkets she sold to tourists coming through Woodstock in search of some authentic 1960s karma.

"Kookie?"

"Before your time, dear." She patted his cheek. "I can't believe you really and truly pulled this off! Not just did it but actually succeeded in doing it." Cordelia looked around with genuine incredulity, tears spark-ing her sea blue eyes beneath hay-colored bangs as her earrings of lapis lazuli jingled like temple bells. "I can't believe these dumb old paintings have been kicking around in our damn barn for over fifty years and . . . well, presto—here they are, big as life, as if by magic."

George nodded judiciously at his mom's loopiness. "A lot of elbow grease. Amy, my restorer, performed her magic on the craquelure. And I think I got the lighting right and the frames—do you like the frames?"

She touched her son's arm and bent to kiss his cheek. "You're the magic—my magic, Georgie."

"Not here, Mom. It's George."

"It's like they've been transformed"—she laughed, and resisted doing a little jig (something of her sadly shortened career with New York City Ballet still embedded in muscle memory)—"washed in the Redeemer's blood and cleansed of sin—hallelujah!" George grimaced at heads turned in their direction. "I guess having them underfoot and all the bad vibes from Jim about his childhood . . . well. And, God knows, I did try to sell a few of 'em after Jim walked out. Couldn't give them away."

"We've already sold half the show. That means we're profitable." George glanced over at JJ, who was standing, checklist in hand, expec-tantly fingering a sheet of red stickum dots, before another power couple, by the looks of the shoulder pad–assisted wingspan of the two-button pinstripe jacket and the slinky obsidian sable dress.

Cordelia followed his gaze with a wry smile.

"It's like, well . . . the Trade Center never happened."

"I know, I know—a little spooky, isn't it?"

"Life must go on, up or down, inside out, or just twisted into granny knots." Cordelia, at fifty, the youngest daughter of Edward Dimock, the afterthought in family lore, smiled gamely, swiping fingers at her face as if in hopes of dispersing age lines, and so recapturing something of the flower-child glamour that had once graced the New York State Theater and then *Life*'s Woodstock coverage in 1969. "First time I've been back in the city since the attack." She shook off a hint of anxiety and smoothed down the wrinkles in the reticulated blue-green pattern of her dress. "I mean, I don't really own a somber dress, and nothing in black, which seems de rigueur these days for evening events." She gripped her son's shoulder. "Not to put a damper on things, but Felicity called this morning. The Judge has stopped eating. She says he's decided it's time; seems he doesn't want to go on anymore."

"The Judge isn't eating?"

"Not for two days. '*Starve* himself out of life,' as Felicity put it."

"He can't do that!" said George indignantly. "Not when I'm finally getting things going here."

"Oh, George, you know him better than anyone. He doesn't care about you or *this* or the family or anything anymore—if he ever did. The only thing that mattered was his career and legacy. He's so out of touch. He's ninety-five. And I think the Trade Center bombing really shook him up, as well."

"Did I ever tell you he called me that day to see if I was all right?"

"Well, that's a lot more than he bothered to do for Martha, much less for Erich or Karen or their kids."

"But his mind's all there; at least it was this summer when I was up at Hermitage."

"I was going to drive over to Hermitage tomorrow, but I've got to open the bookstore, and I can't find anybody to replace me for the day."

"I can drive up. And anyway, I've got to stop by Woodstock this weekend and get some more works out of the barn—while the show's hot."

"Who's hot?" George's aunt Alice barreled through the crowd to give him a peck on the cheek, sloping a glass of wine in an outstretched hand.

"Aunt Alice!" he exclaimed, a little giddy. "Thank you for coming. And Stan," he added, shaking hands with her elderly screenwriter husband, who seemed more than a little amused with the goings-on. "Oh my God, you're all here." He turned and kissed his aunt Martha and her grown children, his first cousins, older by ten years, Erich and Karen, as they made their way over to him.

"A mini Dimock reunion—how could we miss *your* opening?" said Alice, the eldest at sixty-eight, the tallest and certainly the thinnest of the three Dimock sisters. The onetime radical Bay Area lawyer, now teaching politics and law at SUNY New Paltz, had instantly taken the measure of the gilded gathering. "And where did you find all these fat cats?" She swiveled her once-handsome face, a thin compact bone structure neatly expressing her piercing gray-green eyes, auburn hair gone to gray in places and cut short for convenience, as she always insisted. "The place reeks with nouveau riche real estate money."

"Look at the paintings, for heaven's sake, Alice," scolded Cordelia with a hint of pride as she glared at her sister (older by almost twenty years) and her stylish four-button black jacket over matching trim trousers, the flaring lace collar of her white blouse setting off the thicket of tendons in her long neck and a discreet layering of pearls.

"Is this the real you?" asked his aunt Martha, a little spacey, now drawing into the circle around George, plucking at the sleeve of his jacket. Of the three, Martha, second eldest, doyen of the Upper West Side psychiatric profession, seemed the worst for wear: overweight, her face fleshy, dyed brown hair falling in ringlets to her shoulders. "I can't remember the last time I saw you out of jeans and a Princeton Astrophysics Department T-shirt."

"Such sartorial splendor," offered cousin Erich. "You've put on weight, cuz."

"So salesmanly, Georgie," said Martha's daughter, Karen, who was closely examining any unattached men under forty.

Martha whispered in his ear. "You know, my appointment calendar is quite open these days."

"Whatever happened to Good Will Hunting, the brainiac kid?" said Erich, tall, angular, a little sheepish now that he found himself dressed only in worn corduroys and a plaid button-down.

"Or Luke Skywalker." Karen laughed, as if diligently shuffling back in time for the earliest, most steadfast image of her younger cousin. "*Curious George.*" She had her mother's compact build and earnest humor, an instinct to probe for weakness.

"These people," said Alice. "Seriously, what smarmy depths did you stir them up from? Look how they flaunt their chic duds, as if they're more on display than the pictures. And my God, just a year ago this town was in shock and mourning."

George smiled sheepishly under the onslaught, always the baby, always the butt of some complaint or snarky observation. "Hey"—he waved a hand as if easily dispersing a bad stink—"the *Times* reviewed the show."

"A fabulous review," said Cordelia, nudging Alice protectively. "And nice pearls." She fingered her sister's velvet jacket. "And you're hardly out of place, Alice."

"Just as long as their checks don't bounce," said George.

"But do they really buy art?" asked Martha. "Or do they just display with the art—art as fashion accessory? There can't be much left after the Prada bill."

"Oh Martha," said Cordelia, defending her son, "we can't all be sophisticated Upper West Siders with Zabar's charge accounts."

"Zabar's long ago gave up charge accounts, and their bagels—I have to go across the street to H&H now—are just dreadful. I just find it fascinating, the flaunting of wealth, as if the Trade Center never happened—goodness."

"The art," reminded Cordelia. "What do you all think about George's grandfather's paintings? I think they're really super."

"Well, you would," said Alice. "Maybe you'll finally extract some loot out of the estate of your no-good two-timing ex-husband."

Cordelia frowned at her sister. "You mean my 'blue-collar alcoholic bum,' as you and Daddy always called him. And I guess all these crappy paintings are just . . . well, so much blue-collar trash, handmade to boot, nothing so exalted as the fabled Dimock exaltation of the *law*."

"You do jingle, dear," said Alice, eyeing Cordelia's left earring.

"I think it's rather brilliant of George," said Martha with a dreamy smile, "upstaging his own deadbeat dad, the man who neglected him, and so cannily appropriating his grandfather's legacy for his own." She molded the air for emphasis. "Editing out the father and so becoming his own man."

"Bravo, Mom," said her daughter, Karen, in her tight pencil dress, neatly displaying a bulge of décolletage. "Freud could turn that into a theory, or, even better, a how-to book on solving one's oedipal conflicts by airbrushing the problematic generation."

"Speaking of the working class," piped up Alice while grabbing a refill of chardonnay off a passing tray, "I always thought George Altmann did murals for the WPA, figurative stuff celebrating the exploited factory workers and so on."

"That was in the thirties," said George, "when he was famous for his American scene painting."

"You mean social realism," replied Alice, "all that pinko 'workers of the world unite' crap. And wasn't he a court sketch artist at some point? I seem to remember he covered the Alger Hiss trial for the *Herald Tribune*—no? In fact"—she held up a long, crooked finger with a perfectly manicured pink nail and wagged it—"he gave me a sketch of our famous papa as a souvenir when I attended the opening day of the Hiss trial—that travesty of a judicial circus!"

"Who's Alger Hiss, again?" asked Erich.

"Oh my God!" exclaimed Alice. "Not another one of the walking brain-dead; I have enough of those in my constitutional law class."

"For goodness' sake, Alice," said Martha, "not all of us like to chew over ancient history—lost causes—every day in seminar."

"I thought chewed-over memories were your stock-in-trade, dear sister. Or the unconscious, the dark recesses of the mind, the pathologies of everyday life, those so delicious recovered memories and whatnot."

"Sketches?" asked Cordelia vaguely. "That's how I met Jimmy in the first place; Daddy insisted I drive his red Merc to Woodstock to return a bunch of George Altmann's sketches to Jim."

George cocked his head at his mother, as if something had slipped past him.

Karen broke in: "Freud is, as they say, so-o-o yesterday—even for Mom."

Martha looked uneasily at her daughter, as if she'd lost the sense of the conversation.

"*Your* grandfather," said Alice to Erich, including George and Karen in her fierce glance, "our illustrious Judge, failed to defend Alger Hiss in the trial of the century. He let Nixon and the fascist FBI run roughshod over his client, an innocent man, a progressive champion of the New Deal, who ended up in jail because of his complete fuckup. Right, little sister? Especially his spouting all that psychobabble—right, Martha?—about that lying right-wing stooge, Chambers." She tugged on the tweedy sleeve of her husband, who was admiring a nearby gaggle of young women in stiletto heels. "Stan got it in the neck, too, a year in Danbury for contempt of HUAC. You kids have no idea."

"Oh, his poor wife, Priscilla," clucked Martha. "Alger treated her so badly; for years she came to me for help—"

"Mom," warned Karen, "really, you know you shouldn't be talking about clients."

George bent to his mother's ear and asked sotto voce, "What sketches, Mom?"

"Speaking of the Judge," said Cordelia, "I just heard from Felicity this morning that he is refusing to eat, that he's made up his mind he wants to die."

"Well," snorted Alice, "that sounds like the best idea he's had in a long time."

"Don't be so cruel," scolded Cordelia.

"Oh, how sporting of you, Cordelia, considering you were his first victim. That is, until Karen was old enough to get the full lecher treatment."

"Oh, that," said Karen with a distracted wave, squinting as she continued to seek out any hopes of male company. "We were just kids messing around. In fact, I sort of miss him—well, you know, Hermitage."

"Listen," said George, "I've got to drive up to Woodstock tomorrow anyway, so why don't I stop by Hermitage on the way and get the lay of the land. He probably just needs a little company to cheer him up now that all the summer people have left."

"Good for you, George," Alice laughed. "I'm sure the old buzzard will be delighted to hear how his latest investment in the art world is going. Which is hell of a lot more than he's done for my offspring. Cecily, by the way, may be heading east for medical school."

"Okay, that's settled," said Cordelia. "If Dad will listen to anyone, it will be George."

"Darth Vader," said Erich, laughing.

"And don't forget your lightsaber." Karen smirked, edging off on her own hunt.

—

George continued to circulate as the crowd thinned, taking over the sales clipboard from JJ, making a few last pitches to latecomers, totaling up the numbers, visualizing the gaps on the walls where replacement works would be needed for those sold. For a brief moment, he pondered the ethics of breaking up the exhibition ensemble before the end of the show with new works . . . but commerce was commerce. And the extra cash would get Dark Matter through the year.

About to hand over closing duties to JJ and the cleanup crew and join his family for dinner, he noticed a young woman still lingering in the main gallery. She intently eyed an unsold canvas. He realized he'd seen her earlier. Tall, athletic, long reddish blond hair gathered in a blue barrette. Something about her face was vaguely familiar, perhaps the long nose with its slight upward tilt, which revealed more cartilage than classic beauty demanded, an elegant structure that read ambiguously, if strongly, in various lights. She wore a tight-fitting sleeveless gray dress that came to just above the knee, with pleats down the center bracketed by a strip of white on either side, a band of brilliant red as a collar. As he drew closer, he realized that the vertical pleats weren't pleats, but a kind of smocking, subtle variations of light and darker gray, with similarly patterned panels on the sides from hip to hem.

"Hi, can I help you with anything about the artist or the work?"

She turned a beaming smile his way. "Oh, no need to sell me. I bought that one over there"—she pointed to a landscape of horizontal cliffs—"half an hour ago."

"Good choice." He could not help admiring the elegant tailoring of her dress, how the two white verticals over the bust narrowed at the waist, squeezing the gray verticals into tapering ends—an understated design that showed off her tensile figure and small breasts.

"I was just wondering if I can still afford another before they're all gone."

He glanced at his checklist and smiled in the affirmative. "I'm glad you like the work. I'm George Altmann, by the way, director of the gallery. And, I probably shouldn't tell you, but no rush; there are plenty more where these came from."

"As good as these?"

"Hard to tell. I tried to pick out the best, but the canvases were so dirty that it was impossible to see the real colors until they were cleaned."

She shot out a hand and looked at him forthrightly in the eye. Hers were slate blue and her handshake strong, the palm roughened with blisters.

"Wendy, Wendy Bradley. I'm delighted to meet you. And congrats on the exhibition and the catalog." She held up the catalog with an admiring sideways tilt of her head, an aspect that showed off her long, delicate nose and expressive lips touched with perfectly applied copper-rose lipstick. "I've been reading your essay; it's got me hugely pumped."

"Did you see the *Times* review?" He noticed the ropy muscles in her arms, Band-Aids on both elbows, not an ounce of fat anywhere, mid-to-late twenties: How could she afford to be buying art?

"That's what caught my eye, the Shawangunk."

"Yeah, well, I worked pretty hard at identifying his painting grounds in the essay."

"I don't need to tell you: He—your grandfather, right?—was so ahead of his time." She walked him over to the long horizontal painting of cliffs and sky she'd bought, caressing the red dot on the exhibition label. "This in 1943, with only the barest hints of the tree line, or clouds; even the rock face is only a blurred suggestion, and not a single paint mark depicting a form—but it's all there, embedded in the pigment just the same, in the shape and energy—the gesture of the stroke." The fingers of her right hand, prancing, twirling, mimicking the movement of the brush, a kind of digital duet across fifty years of time and space. Her nails were raw, broken, cuticles stained, her palms rough and dusty pale, as if she just stepped away from a dough board. "Rothko wasn't even close to this kind of abstraction in 1943."

He brought his face close to the canvas. "Can I hire you?" He indicated the area of pigment she had mentioned. "The sense of energy flux in the paint, as if seeking to replicate itself, building a stable structure . . . order and permanence out of nature's chaos."

She looked at him intently, as if intrigued by his words, her eyes seeming to hold him prisoner with their fascination. Her nose, again, familiar, maybe less for its forthright bone structure than the way it projected the passionate liquid blues of her eyes, something of an aura of unswerving confidence, demanding as a warning shot across his bow.

"Yes," she replied, sighing, "and I know *exactly* where this is."

"Exactly?"

"It's the Shawangunk, a section known as the Trapps. I've climbed it more times than I can count."

"I'll be damned, the Shawangunk. I don't know it well enough to pinpoint the exact location, even though I grew up in Woodstock." His gaze lowered to her knotted calves and a purple bruise on her right shin. "You're a climber?" Strappy black high-heeled sandals. He sucked in his gut.

"You see"—she pondered for a moment, ignoring his question—"it's not the place so much as the fact he's caught the spirit, the mood, the very atmosphere—damn spooky. I can feel it in the hairs on the back of my neck."

"So . . ." he murmured, repeating, not a little enchanted, "you're a climber?"

"Among other things." She shrugged.

"Then I'm really glad you bought this painting. That it will bring you joy, happiness."

"I could mate with this painting." She looked him straight in the eye with a half-smile that in no way diminished the seriousness of her remark. "But I'm curious—the name of your gallery, Dark Matter: It strikes me as a little cold, even a little uninviting."

"You're not the first to have asked. It's a term we use in astrophysics; it refers to the invisible substance that actually controls the formation of galaxies and stars, the ordinary matter that we see in the night sky, the stuff under our feet."

"But it's invisible?"

"Undetectable, and yet it forms a much larger part of our universe than ordinary matter. It kind of reinforces the gravitational attraction that keeps everything from flying away. It's critical to star formation, galaxies, like the sun—light. We wouldn't be here without it . . . just utter chaos."

"So it's invisible and undetectable, but it's essential—to what, the structure of the universe—paint on canvas?"

"To life itself—order, if you like."

"So . . . the name of the gallery."

"Art is essential."

"Oh, I love it, that's so, so, so hot."

"Well, in *that* case, why don't you have dinner with me—and my mother and aunts and cousins. They've got a table waiting at Franico's, across the street."

She seemed slightly taken aback, hesitant. "Your family?"

"I know, believe me, it's asking a lot . . . to be saved."

"Ah, to be saved . . . but who do I come as, exactly?"

"Why, Mondrian, of course."

"Mondrian?"

He looked her up and down admiringly, emboldened by the sudden buzz of renewed self-assurance, of appreciation for his work, his bloodline, and cash in the coffers . . . a new client! For a moment their eyes locked, and in the frozen instant of her amused stare he felt as if he caught sight of something more, something depthless and invisible, if not terrifying, a fiery quantum essence that knew no bounds and took no prisoners.

As if reading his mind, she raised her honey-blush eyebrows and smiled graciously and laughed like a girl.

"You like it—so, Mondrian it is."

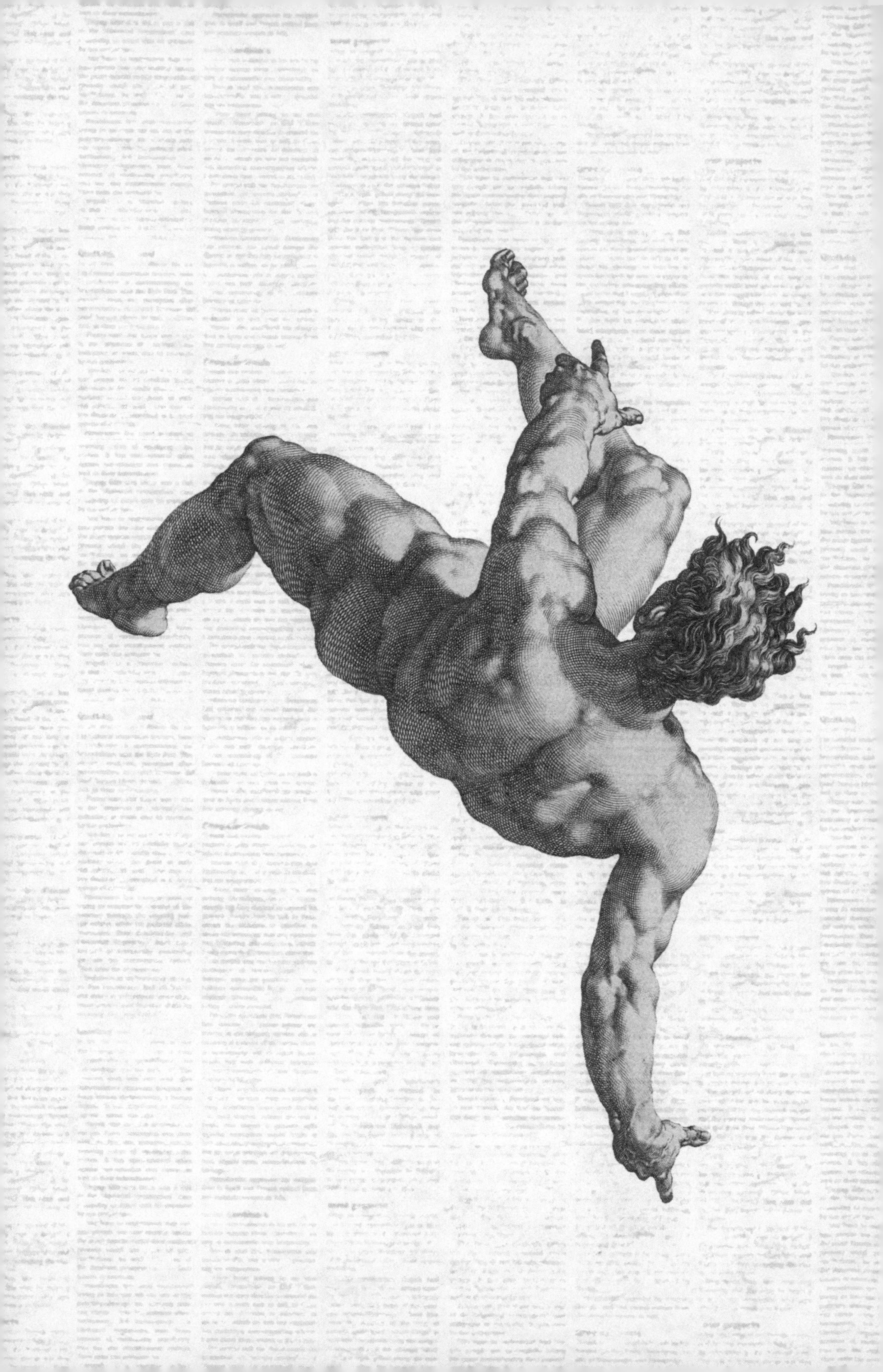

3

De l'Infinito, Universo E Mondo

*My children, as long as you live, the shadow of the Hiss
case will brush you. In every pair of eyes that rests on you,
you will see pass, like a cloud passing behind a woods in
winter, the memory of your father—dissembled in friendly
eyes, lurking in unfriendly eyes.*

—Whittaker Chambers

GEORGE EASED HIS blue Tahoe along the narrow gravel drive behind
the sprawling Shingle Style cottage overlooking the lake, sidling up to
a massive woodpile across from the kitchen's back door and the wing
that had once been the servants' quarters. ("In Dr. Dimock's day, the
Irish maids got a dollar a week and were glad of it.") He unloaded his
bags of groceries, including a ten-pound standing rib roast picked up at
Citarella, and a bottle of Veuve Clicquot and a vintage Medoc to celebrate a nearly sold-out exhibition and, more spectacularly, the successful
revival of George Altmann's reputation, something George thought the
Judge might appreciate, since he and the artist were nearly the same
generation. Indeed, as even Aunt Martha had suggested, wouldn't the
revival of such a stellar career do much to perhaps amend—"airbrush
out"—the embarrassing existence of Jimmy Altmann, George's father,
the ex-son-in-law the Judge detested so unreservedly? Breathing
deeply of the damp, loamy scent of rotting leaves and newly split oak
logs, George found his mood brightening as he left his bags by the
kitchen stairs in his eagerness to indulge his return to the "Dimock
homestead," in the Judge's nostalgic usage.

He was halted in his tracks by the now rarely driven red 1965 Mercedes 280 SL coupe tucked into the old carriage house. Something about its squared-off headlights and sleek-starred grille struck a discomforting note, like a slightly sinister, if debonair, smile. "The Judgemobile," so dubbed by his cousins as youngsters. The sleek contours drew his curious touch (something in the tone of his mother's story from the night before), and he gently ran a palm over the sensuous curve of the hood, this sporty, near-mythic presence out of his childhood, with its cute yet chic pagoda roof and sumptuous burgundy leather interior, bone white steering wheel, powered by a 2.5-liter engine, which, on the few occasions the Judge had let him drive it in recent years, still went like the wind. Lovingly maintained by a team of mechanics down the Delaware River in Matamoras. Still a dazzling ruby luster, as if this foxy lady had only just stepped off the showroom floor. How many Friday nights in July had the cousins waited, hungry with anticipation, for the lusty purr of the red Merc along the winding dirt road by the lake, each downshift a predatory growl of pleasure, signaling the return of their lord and master from his court on Foley Square, just in time for their delayed dinner and jockeying for attention. But not before that tall, imposing figure—his shock of hair gone mostly gray and off-white—had parked the Merc in the carriage house, then made his way with a huge black attaché case in hand and dark suit jacket over one arm to the veranda steps, where, depositing his worldly cares with a deep breath, he was off to the boathouse, disappearing for a few agonizing minutes more. "What's he doing down there?" a nine-year-old George had once asked his older cousins. "Peeing off the dock," said Karen, snickers all around. "A ritual blessing," added Aunt Alice's daughter, Cecily, laughing. "Once a boy always a boy," retorted Karen as they now moved to the great room in preparation for the Judge's grand entrance.

"My one extravagance, my one vanity," the Judge had acknowledged some years before when George would take his grandfather for a spin in the red Merc along the back roads as far as Monticello, or down to Glen Spey and the Hawk's Nest along the Delaware, with the Judge eagerly pointing out where the Delaware and Hudson Canal had once hugged the rocky shore of the great river before turning east at Port Jervis and heading up the Rondout Valley for the Hudson River.

But now, something else nagged at George, that offhand comment of his mother's the night before at the gallery and then again at dinner, something about being conscripted to return a bunch of Altmann portrait sketches to the artist's son and heir, bribed with a chance to drive the red Merc—"scene of the crime," as she'd put it laughingly at dinner. Presumably, the circumstances of her first meeting, at the tender age of seventeen, with Jimmy Altmann, in Woodstock.

"No Merc, Georgie, no you—ha-ha!"

The kind of inanity a parent drops in a moment of careless ine-briated candor, which turns out to be a depth charge—as indeed it would—into her son's muddled, unhappy past.

As he turned now to the glittering lakefront, he couldn't quash a sense of foreboding—or was it paradox?—at the rumored imminent demise of one grandfather while another had, literally overnight, seem-ingly risen from obscurity to incipient fame. This convergence, this entanglement through time and space had him spooked. Every twitter and rustle out of the dappled tree shadows whispered ominously. He found himself stalking the gray-green clapboard wings of Hermitage overhung with beetling gables and panels of green pebbledash, glanc-ing up at the eavesdropping bays of leaded-glass windows. As he approached the threshold of the sprawling front veranda overlooking the lake, he rattled the bottle of Xanax in his pocket for luck. He paused, listening—the silence after the city, eerie—hoping the scents of sum-mer's end might settle his nerves. To better get his bearings, he began an inventory of any threatening signs of change: the spiky ferns turned a yellow-dun, uncollected chanterelles hiding in rooted nooks—a nasty brain-shaped false morel sulking in the roots of an ancient stump near the boathouse path, spindly maples shot through with mottled scar-lets, the acorns, crunching underfoot, gathered by swirling gray gusts of near-crazed squirrels, incredulous at the sudden bounty. His brows fur-rowed at the complex geometries of the boathouse roof, silhouetted by the placid stillness of the lake, disquieting spectral glints of lilac-green in the boathouse windows, translating the fathomless pale blue of the sky into luminous portals under the sloping eaves.

Maybe that was all, just the overnight change in the weather. Most of September had been damp and dreary, until this morning, when the leading edge of a Canadian high came barreling through, bringing sunny, crisp skies and lower humidity, the first real hint of fall. Too much like those splendid cloudless days surrounding 9/11 of a year before. The very thought of which somehow dampened his carefully formulated game plan to humor the Judge and so cajole him out of any catastrophic ideas of ending his life.

He slapped his bejeaned knee impatiently. "You've got to be fucking upbeat for the old guy, George."

With this injunction, he turned to fully absorb the faltering history at his elbow and find ways to turn it to his advantage in talking around the Judge. The inviting, even homey Shingle Style cottage had been built by his great-grandfather, Dr. Clement A. Dimock, obstetrician, gynecological surgeon, and cancer specialist to New York society's 400. For decades around 1900, Dr. Dimock delivered the "million-dollar babies"—so touted in the press—of the Astors, Fishes, Roosevelts, Vanderbilts, Goulds, and Strongs. The famous "Dr. D.," as he was called by the upper reaches of Fifth Avenue society and Newport's Bellevue crowd of the superwealthy, made a very handsome living, enhanced by insider advice on stocks to buy and hold, which had fabulously paid off when, in 1895, he'd employed the foremost architectural firm of the day, McKim, Mead & White, to build his Catskill retreat: "It shall be called Hermitage, a functional and understated woodland abode for my family and friends." He'd insisted on employing local materials and workmen, and eschewing the ostentation of "Lenox and the hideously overwrought European extravagances of Newport" for an American vernacular cottage that serenely made itself at home with the outdoors. "Yes, but a bitch to heat in cold weather," the Judge had commented when others gasped in admiration at the great room with its famous ship's keel ceiling.

The two-story façade of gray cedar shingle with generous green trim was located on a gentle rise above the lakeshore, a view made readily accessible from the indoors by plentiful bay windows; high pocket doors let one space glide unimpeded into the next, while skylights with plate and blown glass in decorative configurations invited pine-filtered sunlight—tinctured, toned, and transmuted—to play freely across polished fruitwood surfaces, an effect both dazzling and restful to the eye—"meditative," according to Stanford White, who'd handpicked many of the decorative artifacts for the interior on his European buying trips—an ensemble of simmering chiaroscuro that gave the whole an otherworldly weightless charm. As the Judge liked to laconically put it, "Hermitage was my father's escape from the disasters of the operating theater, which, in the days before penicillin and chemotherapy, were many and disheartening. And not being a religious man, he believed in getting one's taste of heaven in the here and now."

The generous piazza, wrapped from fore to aft around the sprawling lakeside façade, offered the less intrepid bird-watching from the comfort of high-backed wicker chairs and porch swings. George smiled to himself, fingering the two granite snubbing posts, rope-scarred relics of the Delaware and Hudson Canal (which had once passed eight miles to the south), presiding like archaic totems on either side of the piazza stairs. Placing two hands on the weathered brow of the tallest, he vaulted himself onto the creaking pine flooring as he had as a kid. Happily locating his favorite chair, a huge pea green fan-shaped wicker monstrosity with battered cushions, he lowered himself, pulled up his feet, and curled down into its enveloping arms, only lacking some good science fiction to re-create a beloved childhood moment. Safe in the arms of the past, he looked out beyond the hip roof and rough-hewn columns. As his eyes adjusted to the shade, he found himself indulging the mosaic of light apertures hovering within the scrim of pine, oak, and black birch, and lower down, nearer the shore, the rich sunbursts refracted from the lake surface blew into the leafy understory of mountain laurel, rhododendron, and high-bush blueberry, at least six shades of green on the visible spectrum, to his astrophysicist's eye. Here and there the splayed fingers of glittering goldenrod and amethyst steeplebush added to the delightful constellation, while a few small cedars cowered in their sylvan lairs.

Even in the darkest of his Princeton years, struggling to prepare for his orals and defense of his astrophysics Ph.D. dissertation, this same creaky wicker chair had provided a kind of sanctuary from the days and weeks and years of staring into the outermost reaches of the visible universe—infinite spaces, unimaginable distances, and numbers uncountable that had finally sunk him into a black hole of depression. The very thing, his wide-eyed youthful curiosity about things big and small, those tantalizing telltale patterns that had so galvanized his adolescence, become a weighty incubus of uncertainty.

"Hung by your own petard, young man," the Judge had consoled. "It happens to the best of us. How many lawyers in their fifties regret their trade. Step away for a few years—yes, try the art business if you like—and then return to that Ph.D. defense refreshed."

It sometimes seemed, if not for the Judge's calm certainties about all matters human and terrestrial, he would have totally lost it. As if the old man and Hermitage constituted his last enduring refuge of faith in an increasingly unintelligible universe, where dark matter and dark energy reigned, where infinite expansion dazed the soul, where tall buildings tumbled like matchsticks, taking thousands with them.

Where had the wonder gone? The splendor of a tiny blue planet, the glory of being human . . . so he had once assured himself, of a human scale just the right size—just big enough to make cosmic conscious-ness possible. He gripped the sturdy armrest. Bigger than the wayward inconstant particles of the quantum world, smaller than the infinite clustering of galaxies, so enabling a functioning three-pound brain to form thoughts—and the ability to make such observations in real time! Something, so he'd argued in his dissertation, denied any galactic-wide intelligence limited by the speed of light to thousand-year transmis-sions of information across the vastness of space-time. Holding fast to the padded armrests like some intrepid Captain Kirk, he felt flickers of his old confidence return—time and space for the supernovas to produce their heavy elements, time for a lowly solar system and a stray exoplanet to find a sanguine orbit around a warming star, a moon to regulate the tides . . . the woods and the lake and sheltering sky, and a comfortable chair and books, a place where the complexity of our brains and the age of the universe coalesced as one . . . and so offering humankind the possibility of discoverable truths, for the universe to know itself as being alive and sentient—"and, yes, so fucking beautiful!"

He pumped his fist: "Yes, yes, yes . . ."

Now on a roll, George found himself—or at least the avatar of his teenage self—almost convinced that he personally had been put on this tiny blue terrestrial speck, if not to connect with life in outer space, at least to save the old man and Hermitage from ruin. As he had the reputation of another old man, one he'd never even known, the art-ist George Altmann. A genius who now shone all the brighter in the scintillating blue eyes of Wendy Bradley, who had quieted last night's dinner table as Aphrodite a brawling squall.

This destiny, embrace it you must.

At this small voice, this recrudescence out of earliest childhood, George laughed, happy to embrace the safety of order and good hab-its ("Annie's rules" or "Annie's way," as the Judge had always described her path to Handytown, a defunct, overgrown homestead deep in their woods). A flash of color, a flurry of wings confirmed this happy thought in a sudden assault by bands of purple buntings, nuthatches, blue jays, goldfinches, and a wayward scarlet tanager on the nearby line of bird feeders. Summer's last holdouts. Scrunching deeper into the cushions, his cozy time machine responded to its navigator with plumes of scented pine pollen accented with the acidic notes of bat and mouse droppings, perennial oblations to faltering summer, and these, for good measure, dipped and simmered in a consommé of warmed and sun-weathered shellac emanating from the beadwork paneling above and the pine floorboards at his feet. Dead moths fluttered like distant schooners marooned in the cobwebs under the eaves. While from somewhere a temple bell—Cordelia's addition when the Judge retired full-time to Hermitage—rang sweetly, herald of that Canadian high. He could feel the slippage of the sun in every mobile shadow across the lake, in the drooping rat tails of the ferns, harbinger not just of winter but possibly much worse.

God knows, he told himself, at ninety-five the Judge can't last much longer anyway, nor his world. The Judge's finances remained a mystery to everyone. He still paid all his bills, kept all his investment and pension accounts locked in his desk. Some years he seemed more flush than others. "On the way to the poorhouse" was his constant refrain when asked how things were going. More than once he'd told George, "When the money's gone, so goes Hermitage. Why"—a wicked smile—"I keep my revolver ever handy in my bedside drawer."

Only a year before, when the Judge had spent days glued to the coverage of the Trade Center attack on his satellite TV, Felicity, the Judge's longtime housekeeper and nurse, had removed his Smith & Wesson .38 snub-nose from his bedside table drawer and deep-sixed it in the lake. "Precautions," as she put it.

His phone vibrated in his pocket, a rarity in these parts, with the closest cell tower in Monticello thirteen miles away, although the thinning trees, he speculated, might enhance reception.

Loved your show and dinner! Class moved back. Now gets out at the Gunks at 4:00 p.m. See ya, W.

He smiled and shook his head, as if still not quite believing his luck. Wendy Bradley, the improbable Wendy, who had proved a brilliant and charming raconteur the night before at dinner with his family. Full of disarming toughness and thrilling insights into the professional climbing fraternity, and barely twenty-six! A maturity for her age that put his fumbling thirty-two to shame. Better yet, a feisty protectress shielding him throughout the meal from the worst his mother and aunts and cousins could dish out. Even cynical Aunt Alice hung on her every word, especially her saga of climbing Everest and making it though the dead zone, avoiding a surprise blizzard. Of course, nothing quite added up: a climbing instructor with money enough to buy not one but two expensive paintings, and somehow just a little too much in the know about the art scene for comfort. But, hey . . .

And then there was the chaste but meaningful lingering kiss as they parted, and plans to meet after her climbing class at the Gunks, with Wendy enthusiastically volunteering to help him pack the replacement paintings in the barn at Woodstock.

But more than the chemistry, or the delicious mystery, was something she'd said at dinner that stuck with him.

"You survive by training, meticulous preparation, and airtight procedure under pressure: the body—muscle memory, instinct—in an emergency, takes over from the mind."

With that admonition, words that had been in reply to someone else at the table, but clearly directed his way, he sensed the arrival of an intrepid wingman grounded in common sense and experience, which, as a "science kid," had always proved an attractive trait in the opposite sex. Gorgeous, if not a slightly intimidating, force of nature.

So fortified with good vibes, George sprung up to seek out his quarry, locked and loaded for his mission to get the old man back on track and save the day.

—

The massive Dutch door swung open noiselessly into the mote-swarming space of the great room, the inner sanctum of a century's summers. His bewitchment as a child again hovered before his eyes—there, in the richly paneled walls, the subtle inlaid patterns of lozenge and herringbone, enhancing the amber radiance like a thing alive. He almost feared another infusion of childlike delight, another sensual high with a letdown if too fully gratified, as if memory overload might leave him floundering. For a moment more, he fingered the brass spiral handle of the huge double-hung door, drawn to the familiar radiating checkerboard pattern of pine end grain in the upper panel, each cube tempting one's fingertips to the dendrological evidence of a hundred—no, a thousand growing seasons!

Muscle memory, instinct, takes over from the mind.

"Yeah, baby . . ."

So prompted across the threshold, he found himself christened in the familiar blue-gold aura—awash in a pale luminescence saturated with a fusty, if delicious, scent of beeswax and wood polish. He raised his eyes, blinked, and sighed in recognition of having again safely breached the hallowed sanctuary of the household gods. This just one of the many spells cast by Hermitage's famous ship's keel ceiling, especially when ashimmer with lake-reflected sunlight, and doubly so in the early fall, when the red and white oaks were baring their souls, the maples shed their yellow-orange plumage, and the sun swooned lower through the bay window. The ship's keel ceiling in the great room was Hermitage's pièce de résistance, an original Renaissance beamed structure ca. 1590, possibly the masterpiece of some obscure Venetian boatwright and equally obscure artist. Such cryptic anonymity only added to its aura.

This extravagance of Renaissance building arts had somehow been secured by Stanford White—snatched, stolen, bribed, desecrated, and absconded with, depending on the historian—under the noses of the Italian authorities. A bona fide Italian national treasure by any measure, on a par with the ship's keel ceiling of Venice's Church of Santo Stefano. "Saved," according to White, from a crumbling palazzo near Padua (rumored to have offered sanctuary to Giordano Bruno when he was fleeing the Inquisition). In 1893, the individual sections had been painstakingly disassembled by skilled carpenters and numbered, packed in straw and burlap and crated, and surreptitiously shipped from Trieste to New York, and then meticulously reinstalled in the great room at Hermitage in 1895 by specialist Italian woodworkers employed by White. This acquisition of a unique example of Paduan/Venetian craftsmanship for his renowned client, Dr. Dimock, was considered one of White's greatest coups, and celebrated as such in all the books and scholarly articles on the architect, a subject of enduring interest as well to architectural historians of the Italian Renaissance and scholars of Giordano Bruno, who read much into the complex iconology of the painted beam work.

The square hand-hewn beams were set on the horizontal, supported by five massive crossbeams, giving the impression, in certain casts of sunlight, of a shimmering expanse of pastel blue sky, or possibly rippling waves retreating to the fieldstone backdrop above the mantel. Much of the enchanting effect was due to the undulating warping of the beam work, adorned with subtle patterns depicting geometric fractals (various scholarly articles claimed the Flower of Life patterns were derived from Giordano Bruno's *Articuli centum et sexaginta adversus huius tempestatis mathematicos atque philosophos*, published in Prague in 1588). Woven into this complex three-dimensional cosmic tapestry were various groupings of gods and astrological imagery, some boldly displayed on the underside of the beams or tucked into the shadowy recesses of the ceiling above, where, like a supernova appearing out of the interstellar gloom, fantastic jewel-like personages—moon faces appearing in a dozen phases—peaked from beneath the aged varnish. These starry denizens seemed, upon closer inspection, to be engaged in an elaborate courtly dance, or perhaps a phantasmagoria choreographed to some infinitely faint change ringing, all in celebration of their blissfully ordered cosmos.

Staring upward as he circled the great room, George found himself again slipping back to long-ago reveries of childhood, intrigued then as now by the unspooling sacred geometries interlaced over every surface like some visionary *Goldberg Variations*. From various vantage points, depending on the quality and angle of light, more intertwined circles and spirals might emerge from under the honey-rose varnish, repeated patterns mimicking the contortions of the scaly ouroboros prominently displayed on the underside of a central beam. This schematic snake- or dragonlike geometric figure twisted in upon itself as if to swallow its tail, symbol of the cycles of life, of the cosmos's eternal renewal. Not a day had passed over his childhood summers when the ouroboros with its attendant gods—especially the buxom Ariadne, Europa, and Aphrodite—and their wandering seven planets had not inflamed his imagination.

One might have thought, for a brilliant astrophysicist, such an archaic sky chart would long ago have paled in relevance, given the past century's advancements in cosmology, much less a love-struck adolescence drawn to the vivid fantasies of the *Star Wars* franchise. To which the stellar revelations of the Hubble telescope had only multiplied wonders even more fantastic. And yet George, massaging his neck, found himself as enamored as ever precisely because of the consoling Ptolemaic vision—like his long-ago summers at Hermitage, snugly preserved behind varnish.

For all its fame and speculations about the various artists' hands (Titian, follower of Titian, workshop?) detected by scholars in the figures, the ship's keel ceiling was esteemed within the Dimock clan for entirely different reasons. Nobody could quite put his finger on it, although many engineers and historical architects had tried. Certainly, this phenomenon had never crossed Stanford White's mind—a thing he would surely have boasted of if it had. The acoustics of the ceiling and surrounding paneled walls for piano or small ensemble were nothing less than astonishing, transcendent, a benefit that had gone entirely unrecognized during Hermitage's first forty years of existence, and were only revealed by Annie Dimock, the Judge's wife and a professional pianist, who first played at Hermitage in 1933. Annie considered the acoustics of the great room—for Mozart, her specialty—to be better than anything she'd ever encountered in the concert halls of Europe or the United States. Her ecstatic reaction had often been proudly recycled by the Judge: "Better than Salzburg's Mirabell Palace or the Scuola Grande di San Rocco in Venice. It must be that the seasoned wood absorbs the sound waves, giving the music just that extra clarity, warmth, and evenness of texture—it's a marvel, a miracle, a treasure."

Only a few years before, Hermitage had been added to the National Register of Historic Places. And so, hopefully, preserved for posterity, even as the life, much less the resources of its lord and master, now hung precariously in the balance.

As George, casting a timorous glance at the Steinway concert grand lurking in the corner, drifted over to the hearth in a half daydream, he found himself continuing to ponder the sad epitaph for Giordano Bruno, emblazoned on the central support beam, where a fiery-orbed Helios figure gazed around—narrow face, fringe of curly hair, lips pursed as if to whisper a curse or blessing, blazingly sharp and intelligent blue-gray eyes—this figure rumored to be nothing less than a portrait of Giordano Bruno himself. The gold-lettered inscription underneath the fiery orb read *De l'Infinito, Universo e Mondo*. This, just one of the many charges—"claiming the existence of a plurality of worlds and their eternity"—leveled at Bruno by the Papal Inquisition, for which he was hanged upside down and burned alive at the stake in Rome's Campo de' Fiori.

Unhappy thoughts of sizzling human flesh caused George to reach a steadying hand to the surround of blue Delft tiles that framed the fireplace with its bald eagle brass andirons. The charming ranks of dancing peasants in the tiles returned a smile to his face, an earthier, more intimate companion piece to the gods above. Flanking the fireplace, about four feet high and carved out of bog oak, twin angels of medieval vintage stood sentry duty. The architect, Stanford White, had picked out the pair for Dr. Dimock as a housewarming present for his wife, Elsie. One faced heavenward, while her twin gazed ominously downward, either to Hell or its approximation in the leaping flames of the hearth. These spirit guardians were exquisitely carved with

delicately detailed wing feathers, streamlined and tucked in close, giving them—at least to once-young eyes—the aspect of compact missiles
yearning to launch. Each played a whimsical mandolin with clumps of
schematic fingers pressed into the frets and strings. Mysterious, even
troubling, the carved angels had long been subjects of some consternation in George's boyhood, due to the Judge's enigmatic questions
posed at cocktail hour, often variations on a theme, such as "If our two
angels could be birds, what species, do you think, George, would they
choose to be and why?" Or "If our angels could speak, what secrets of
their celestial realm would they impart?" George had known it was a
test and so had struggled mightily for the right answer, one that forever
eluded him. Pensively, he let his fingers linger over the reticulated pattern in the tapering wings of the angel on the right, then moved to her
upturned face, pocked with wormholes. He traced her chubby cheeks
and sensual parted lips, her eyes, slanted wide and bearing an otherworldly expression that was, curiously, if anything, a swoon of ecstatic
release. An entirely unholy swoon of pleasure echoed in the bowed face
of her sister, as well. Precocious cousin Karen, to his preteen consternation, had always referred to them as "our orgasmic twins." Arriving
at the breakfast table and turning to her cousin Cecily, she would say,
loudly enough for the boys to hear, "I had two last night, just to keep
up with our orgasmic twins."

"Wormholes in space," he muttered, as if only now chancing
on the right answer. Stepping back, his gaze lifted to the Chinese
blue-and-white ginger jars—echoing the pastel blues of the Delft
tiles—that ballasted the slate mantel, chiseled with the famous lines
from Whitman's "When Lilacs Last in the Door-yard Bloom'd." At
the fulcrum point of this ensemble stood an antique clock, a Louis
XVI green onyx crystal regulator, whose spear-point hands, neatly
skewering the II and resting on the IX, were stopped in perpetuity
at forty-six minutes after two. When inquiries had been made about
this glaring irregularity in a home that proudly ran like clockwork, the
Judge had many explanations, from admitting nonchalantly that he had
lost the winding key, to explaining there was a broken mechanism—a
penurious shrug—that was too expensive to have a clockmaker fix, to
declaring with a wry smile, "The hour Louis lost his head," to offering, in a more wry mood, "In memory of Louis the Sixteenth's golden
hour with his favorite mistress." Now tantalized by this uncharacteristic
anomaly from the perspective of years, George reached up and pried

open the oval glass cover and stood on tiptoe to peer more closely at the face. He fingered the brass hands, only to realize they had been crudely bent down, flattened against the enamel like moribund shadows, thus forever thwarting adjustments. This discovery, not unlike the indeterminate quirkiness of the quantum scale, left him more than a tad uneasy. Causing a reflex motion, his eyes turned heavenward, where he caught sight of a doomed Phaeton tumbling backward through space.

Pressing a palm through his dirty-blond hair, his pounding heart nudging his windpipe, he surveyed the great room again for other telltale minutiae that might have escaped him. The Inness landscapes in their gilded frames hung as ever, bathed in silvery light from an inglenook. The worn Persian rugs, a fully stacked woodpile, four Tiffany lamps . . . until his gaze settled on the Judge's Stickley armchair, where a morocco-bound copy of Emerson's essays caught his attention. Or more precisely, a familiar-looking bookmark peeking from its pages. He picked up the volume and opened it, to find the invitation, printed on heavy card stock, to his George Altmann retrospective: "Landscapes Transcendent." Not that he'd expected the Judge to come. But the invitation was creased, the edges rubbed, smudged with much handling, as if the thing had, at the very least, provoked a reminder of something, an occasion to be mulled over, perhaps even fretted about. Sparking a vague memory of the Judge's disdainful reaction when he'd left Princeton's Astrophysics Department and first broached the idea of starting an art gallery, only, a day later, to reverse himself, even encouraging the project. "Take some time off from the infinite for your gallery idea and in a few years finish up that Ph.D."

Transcendental landscapes for a transcendentalist, he mused, returning the invitation to the page it had marked.

In the shadows of the far corner, as yet untouched by the afternoon sun, the huge Steinway grand still held pride of place, an aloof, even awe-inspiring, if infuriating, presence since earliest childhood. Seeming monstrously huge to him at six, even sixteen, it still struck him as huge, even for so large a room. This was the infernal machine upon which his adolescent pride had been repeatedly broken. Now, so it occurred to him, more like a portable altar where an array of silver-framed photos of the Judge's wife, Annie, had been neatly arranged. "Worth a king's ransom, but the cost for running the damn humidifiers is ruinous," the Judge had liked to comment, but he fooled nobody. His eyes shined with pride at the Steinway that Annie, a teenage prodigy, had played in Carnegie Hall, which he had subsequently bought secondhand as a birthday present for his wife in the depths of the Depression. Annie had died of cancer in the spring of 1969. As children, one of the cousins would be designated each week for the sacred duty of opening Annie's well-thumbed and fingered Chopin score on the piano stand first thing before breakfast. On Friday evenings in summer, as soon as the Judge arrived from the city, the five cousins (including Billy, Alice's dead son) played their weekly recital. An excruciating experience, since George, the youngest, was always last and always the worst, and the butt of groans and hissing from the audience of five teens—hungry for dinner—as he murdered the music. The Judge would preside from an inglenook, listening while looking out at the lake or a nearby bird feeder, while Caterina, stern and tyrannical taskmaster, a Romanian phenom studying at Juilliard, driven up once a week for the lessons, loomed from behind the keyboard, clucking disapproval as she turned pages.

The Judge had a standing bribe to all his grandchildren: ten thousand dollars to anyone who could play through, "with competency and musicality," the complete Chopin Etudes by age eighteen. Only Cecily, Alice's daughter, had managed the trick at seventeen, grabbing the cash and heading off to Stanford, never to return. George tapped middle C and listened as the note echoed sweetly back from the ship's keel ceiling. Still perfectly in tune . . . He then went to the pile of music in a leather-lined brass box on the floor and dug out the Paderewski edition of the Etudes, replete with Annie's penciled fingerings, and left it open to the fourth, *Torrent*, which had forever stumped him, after the third, *Tristesse*, which he had adored.

Caterina: "*Legato . . . legato*, little Georgie. And work the pinkie a little harder to bring out the inner voices—yes. Next week you work on the sixths—for sure."

The Judge: "Adequate, George—barely, but adequate."

George winced as he reviewed the silver-framed studio and publicity portraits of Annie playing, her high forehead and long nose—barest hint of an upturned tip—bent to the keys, her eyes flexed tight at the corners, agile fingers a phantom blur, and her parted full lips expressing (it always seemed to George) an unnerving profundity of feeling sadly lacking in her grandson.

Returning to the center of the room, where four Stickley leather easy chairs of worn red leather were placed in an open circle facing the hearth, he flopped into the one next to the Judge's and fingered an Arts and Crafts book table stuffed to overflowing with a century's residue of "intelligent"—the Judge's singular criteria—reading matter. All the regulars were still nosed up to the bar—the moldy volumes of Burroughs's writings on the Catskills, Quinlan's *History of Sullivan County*, various nature references to the local flora and fauna, memoirs of fishing along the Neversink, histories of the D & H Canal, the Erie Lackawanna, and the Port Jervis & Monticello—except now there was an empty space among the volumes of Emerson's essays. A pang of imminent abandonment swelled his chest. Who cared? Did anyone care? Did he still care? He grabbed a random volume, a Burroughs first edition, which the author had inscribed to Dr. Dimock in 1901, and raised the yellowed pages and cracked leather binding to his nose and breathed in its sere aroma. Scents of lake water and foxing, beeswax, pollen spores, and, flattened between the pages, a stray trillium and crushed blackflies. With a sigh of intoxicated relief, he replaced the volume, detecting as he did a more recent effluvium emanating from the bottom shelf, stacked with board games: Monopoly, Clue, Risk, and Scrabble, impregnated with the faint odor of stale beer, bubble gum, greasy potato chips, cigarette smoke . . . and the fugitive boredom of rainy afternoons.

George proceeded to the dining room, pausing a moment at the entrance, where a rotund brass gong incised with an elaborate Chinese character—a Double Happiness symbol, according to the Judge—was suspended on a wrought-iron frame, poised throughout his childhood to summon the cousins to meals. Five minutes and one second after the second gong sounded and you went without. He tapped gently on the hammered concavity, shimmering a dusty bluebird blue, the ripples of sound, those deliciously agitated electrons, providing a soft meditative murmur, causing him to move his palm across the shallow dips and peaks in the brass, like tiny impact craters on some hidden moon; and in the somber decay of sound, another unnerving whisper as to the fragility of all things, how death, whether of three thousand or even one old man, could mean the hollowing out of a world, or, at least, the world as he'd known it and loved it.

"My God, George, you have no idea: just the upkeep on top of the extortionate Port Jervis school taxes—death and taxes, whichever comes first."

He shrugged. As if one could halt the solar winds or prevent that Canadian high, brewing in the west, from sweeping summer away.

"Change, George, is the only thing you can bet your bottom dollar on; that from my mentor, Oliver Wendell Holmes, who fought in the Civil War, which took the best in his generation, then lived to see the Great War take the best of that generation, only to survive into the Great Depression, which hollowed out the land he loved."

What arguments could he deploy against change—or a well-timed death? Much less change a mind not amenable to correction? George spent a few moments more pondering his strategy, searching for telling arguments amid the spacious alcove beneath the broad central staircase that rose to the second floor. Here numerous old photos were arrayed like votary offerings in a side chapel, shades of shades deployed to keep memories alive. Yet these, too, would be doomed once the old man was gone. Who in the family gave a fuck? Even if he did give a fuck, his George Altmann retrospective was a last gasp attempt to keep his gallery alive, and, even if successful, unlikely to generate the kind of income to keep Hermitage going. He viewed the familiar images of a white-gowned Dr. Dimock at his surgery, a formal portrait study of the founder of the American Cancer Society, Memorial Hospital (now Memorial Sloan-Kettering), and the Harvard Club of New York. But he passed quickly over these familiar tokens of family pedigree for more nostalgic fare: the informal Kodaks of the bewhiskered doctor hiking down the railroad to the Neversink, or walking the canal path of the Delaware and Hudson Canal in black coat and tie, where he spent his summer weekends treating, gratis, the boatmen and their families. As the Judge always put it, Dr. Dimock "was not a little obsessed with the old canal in its dying days before the turn of the century; the thing stirred some obscure longing in his romantic soul, a thing crushed by three years sawing off limbs in field dressing stations." Here, too, resided blurry visions of the canal towns and locks, of canalboats piled with Pennsylvania coal, stacked with quarried bluestone, lumber, and tanned hides. Along the dirt towpaths, small barefoot boys in oversize straw hats rode or led the donkeys with wicker feed baskets hung over their snouts. Lovingly collected, these and similar antique images, blurred and sunstruck, preserved glimpses of life in the quiet canal towns of the 1880s: repair yards, feed stores, skaters in winter on the Port Jervis canal basin . . . gone, gone, with only the names lingering, carefully inscribed in block letters: Huguenot, Godeffroy, Cuddebackville, Westbrookville, Brown Haven, Graham's Dock, Wurtsboro, reaching as far as Summitville and Ellenville—about the limit of a day's excursion for Dr. D.'s two-horse buggy.

"The children were the worst," the Judge liked to relay to his grand-children in the Victorian cadences playing like yesterday in his mind, "their bare feet cut up and snakebit from leading the mules along the canal path. The section around Ellenville was the most dangerous, when in the summer drought, the rattlers, like Beelzebub's own minions, slithered down from the Shawanagunk and the farmers couldn't even get the harvest in for fear of being bitten."

For George, the canal names were like a refrain from a child-hood nursery rhyme; he could repeat them by heart, just as they were inscribed on brass plaques on the upstairs bedroom doors.

Pride of place went to the long horizontal photograph of Roebling's Neversink aqueduct, completed in 1851 (predating his Brooklyn Bridge by thirty years), marvel of its age, engineered for elegant func-tionality, lifting the D & H Canal on massive cut-stone abutments and steel cables over the broad rapids of the Neversink River just above Cuddebackville. Over all the long summer days of his childhood, those looming stone abutments—all that remained of this grand achieve-ment—marked the storied goal of their Neversink hikes for picnics and trout fishing.

George made one last oblation. In a corner nook hung a framed gold-matted black-and-white photo, a faded portrait, mottled and ghostly, of a steely-eyed young man, hair parted smartly, with a long chin and a handlebar mustache. Printed on the gold matting was the following: "A man said to the universe, 'Sir, I exist.' 'However,' replied the universe, 'the fact has not created in me a sense of obligation.'" The portrait was of Stephen Crane, whose father, a minister in Port Jervis, was a close friend of Dr. Dimock's. Stephen had written *The Red Badge of Courage* in a cottage nearby, and had spent many an hour on the veranda of Hermitage listening to Dr. Dimock's tales of Civil War battlefields, where he had served as a military surgeon for almost three years. A letter from Crane, affixed in plastic on the back of the frame, thanked Dr. Dimock for sharing his reminiscences, many of which had appeared in slightly altered form in the novel.

Moving at last to the dining room and the kitchen beyond, George found something unsettling about the long table of pale sandalwood, where three pairs of extravagant silver candelabra—gaping-jawed brown trout rising and swirling the stems—glittered defiantly like never before, as if beacons to some inextinguishable feminine virtue: Annie's way.

Faithful Felicity, even facing the end . . .

And it was August again, when the Judge took his vacation and the cousins abandoned the kitchen table for the dining room and dinner with their grandfather. Sitting at the head, his luxuriant eyebrows standing out like lopsided exclamation points above his eyeglasses, he took pains to correct table manners—a backhanded dig at his daughters' parenting skills—while eliciting intelligent conversation about various issues of the moment. Or, after two or three glasses of wine, rehearsing stories of his own youth, and tales of the early settlers passed down in the cadences of Dr. Dimock, as the Judge referred to his own father. His older cousins, by nearly ten years, had all balked under that exacting, faultfinding, faintly sarcastic gaze, but there was no denying, at least for George, the comfort of a male authority figure who preserved a living link with the past, *and* a place, as much an embodiment of time as his youthful mind could reasonably fathom. While Erich and Karen, Cecily and Billy, all squirmed with adolescent irritation, George hung on the Judge's every word with rapt attention, assured of the veracity of the pearls of worldly wisdom being dispensed. Often the Judge would pick a controversial subject in the headlines and assign two teams made up of the four older cousins, one to support the proposition and the others to attack it, while he adjudicated—paying lip-service to George as a fellow jury member—the worthiness of the arguments. Always to the end of hammering home his core convictions.

"Why is tribalism bad? Answer: violence and war. Just look at our inner cities and the drug trade."

"What is central to the development of European culture, and thus Western culture—and so America's? The concept of the rule of law. Meaning? The ruler is not sovereign: Law is sovereign. The king is accountable to the law. This system allows for a strong ruler but one always subject to institutional restraint. Children, that is what your grandfather does for a living: I am the institutional restraint and take my marching orders from the Constitution. Upon which all our freedoms rest. That and the First Amendment. Now, what's for dessert?"

Moving on to the mudroom stacked and hung with dilapidated fishing and camping gear, George reviewed yet another photo gallery, this of more recent vintage. Among them were a group portrait of the Judge's Yale class of 1927, his *Harvard Law Review* section of 1930, and a signed photo of the Judge standing with his mentor, Supreme Court justice Oliver Wendell Holmes, on the porch of Holmes's summer home at Beverly Farms, for whom he'd clerked in 1930–1931. The family chronology continued with a wedding photo of his marriage to Annie Davenport in the fall of 1932. Then the children: a beaming, handsome Theodore, their first child, posed in a canoe in the boathouse slip: the family's golden boy, Theo to the Judge, Teddy to his sisters. He died in Korea in the battle of the Chosin Reservoir during the disastrous marine retreat below the thirty-eighth parallel. Then came George's aunts, Alice and Martha, pictured as young girls, playing the piano in the great room, hiking the trails, legs dangling from the abutments of the Neversink aqueduct, picnicking at Handytown, a sylvan glade on the property with a spring of wonderfully clear water. His mother, Cordelia, was shown in dance class at the School of American Ballet; lovely Cordelia, the miracle late child to replace Teddy. And then, with a wall to herself, a series of photos of Annie, the Judge's tall, talented, disciplinarian wife, playing piano in Carnegie Hall, canoeing with her daughters, sitting reading on the piazza with a pair of binoculars ever ready at her elbow.

He thought of something his mother, Cordelia, had always said: "You know, it's really Annie's house; her spirit reigns everywhere." Could it be so? He'd never known Annie, his maternal grandmother, nor his paternal grandmother, for that matter; both had died before he'd been born. George found himself intrigued, sensing the Judge's hand everywhere, even as he excused his tyranny as simply enforcing "Annie's rules," or referring to the setting at the dinner table opposite the head as "Annie's place," or her favorite walk to Handytown as "Annie's way" (a backhanded acknowledgment of her love of Proust), as in "Children, let take Annie's way today; there's not enough time—it may rain anyway—to do the entire Neversink hike."

Contemplating this echo, this lingering of a beloved's name, George was reminded of something his Princeton doctoral adviser had drummed into his head: "All we can hope to do, George, as astrophysicists, is connect up our consensus reality with external reality, the mathematical universe that was here long before we managed to show up—and will be after we return to interstellar dust. As for people's subjective reality, yours, mine, the man in the moon's, well, let's just leave that messy brew of hope and faulty memory to the cognitive scientists to go figure—or, better still, to the imagination of poets and artists."

George reached to straighten the framed photograph of Annie seated in his favorite fan-shaped wicker chair, a book—most likely her

Proust or a birding guide—open on her lap. As Einstein suggested, change is an illusion and time simply another dimension in unchanging space-time . . .

"Well, I thought it might be you." Housekeeper, cook, and now nurse-companion to the Judge, Felicity, appeared from the swinging door to the kitchen and swept a hand through her flyaway white hair. She inspected the youngest Dimock cousin for a moment and embraced George.

"I came as soon as I heard."

"Oh"—she waved dismissively—"I've just got his highness down for his nap."

"So what's the story? Is he really refusing to eat?"

"Not a bite for three days." She fingered a small crucifix around her neck, her bright, slightly bloodshot eyes examining George intently. "He'll take water and orange juice, for now, but that's it."

"You think he's serious?"

"As serious as the Day of Judgment." She untied her apron, where a pair of latex gloves dangled from a pocket. "He had his last will and testament amended a week ago, and then picked up by FedEx for delivery to his lawyer in New York. He's made arrangements with the local undertaker and a funeral home on Madison Avenue. And this letter is for you." She handed him an envelope with his name scrawled in blue block letters. He frowned, weighing it, detecting an object inside.

"What's this about?"

"Key to his office upstairs and, I think, instructions about what do with all his stuff."

He tore open the envelope, took out the key, frowned again, and quickly read the letter.

"He wants *me* to edit his memoir for publication?" George gave Felicity an incredulous look and bent again to the page: "Distribute my law and history books to local libraries; the ones on natural history, first editions on ornithology to the Anglers' Club in New York; and the rest, anything of literary merit, to family members who want them."

"'Battening down the hatches,' as he calls it."

"And Hermitage?" She shrugged at his inquiring look. "Is he still paying the bills?"

"Like clockwork: The bills and bank statements come in and I mail out the checks every second week without fail."

"What about his investment accounts?"

"They arrive every month from J. P. Morgan private banking and every month he's regularly on the phone to his financial adviser."

"Does he seem concerned about money?"

"Always—you do when you're his age."

"Is he slipping mentally?"

"Ditto. He's ninety-five."

"When was the last time he was in his office, Summitville?"

"He hasn't been up there for at least five years, not since he fell and couldn't make the stairs any longer. I give it a dusting once in a while, but he told me to leave everything exactly as is. That was his engine room, you know, after he retired, how he remained connected to the world. Now"—she shrugged—"I don't know."

"Does he still read the *Times* and the *Journal*?"

"Pokes around."

"The Yankees?"

"He was spending an hour now and then if it was a Red Sox game."

"So what's gotten into him—what prompted this decision to *die*—now?"

"Like I said, he's ninety-five, George. He tires easy and even just getting around the place on his walker exhausts him. The Trade Center attack last year didn't help his mood any. Of course, your quitting Princeton before that didn't help, either."

"Oh, thanks a lot."

"He liked to brag to his old buddies on the phone about his brilliant grandson in the Astrophysics Department at Princeton. Now they're all dead and gone, as well."

"I spent a couple of weeks around here this summer; he didn't seem the worse for wear."

Felicity scissored her lips, as if faced with a delicate quandary.

"Well, your invitation to the opening at your gallery for that artist, when it arrived a few week ago . . . well, it kinda shook him up."

"Shook him up—my George Altmann exhibition!—how?"

"He kept the invitation by his chair in the great room. I'd catch him picking it up, staring at it, fingering it, folding it, then putting it down. Lost his appetite, began sleeping late, wind kinda knocked out of his sails. Then three days ago, he announced he's done, not to bother fixing him meals."

"Jesus, he never even acknowledged the invitation—not that I really expected him to come or anything. But not even a phone call."

"A man, a name outta his past—your name to boot. Seemed a little spooked, confused."

"And the Yankees—headed for the play-offs."

"I turn the games on for him, but it bothers him that he can't remember the names of the players like he used to."

She made a face of tired resignation, which, to George, suddenly added years to her once-ageless demeanor. He figured she had to be nearing sixty. "The indignities of age, you don't want to know. His heart's not what it used to be." She put a palm over the name Sparrow Bush Fire and Rescue on her green sweatshirt. A knowing look further compressed the crow's-feet bracketing her blue eyes. "He's lonely. As he never ceases to remind me, he's buried everyone in his generation. He said he wasn't interested in seeing through another winter."

"Up here, in the Catskills—who can blame him?" George looked into Felicity's exasperated face. "You really tossed his pistol?"

"Oh that—off the dock. As far as I could heave the wicked thing."

"So, you were worried?"

"Always a temptation . . . when he had a spot of pneumonia last winter. Where I come from, a mortal sin." Felicity brought a finger to her lips. "Cussed me out—'damn fool woman.'" She smiled. "Asked how he was supposed to protect himself now that I'd left him defenseless."

"From what?"

"As he always says, a judge makes lots of enemies."

"Up here, retired at Hermitage—it's been years?"

"Oh, in the old days, he used to get plenty of crank calls and threatening letters."

"Threats on his life?"

"He took the Trade Center attack quite personally."

"Well . . ." George rolled his eyes. "How long is he down for his nap?"

"A couple of hours."

"Okay, I tell you what. I've brought up a super expensive rib roast, the kind he always liked for Sunday dinners. I'll go bring it in, and why don't you put it in the oven so that it smells up the place when he wakes. Then, when you go get him, tell him I'm here to celebrate a successful show at my gallery, a celebration that includes some of his favorite champagne. And please, Felicity, plan to join us at the table. I've got some ideas about getting him a condo in Florida for the winter."

Felicity flashed a delighted smile. "Florida?"

"Could you go?"

"Are you kidding? Winter, *here* . . . I may not still fit into my bikini, but I'm still good for the beach."

"Jinx" Sign Is Being Hanged on Espionage Probe

Three Persons W...
Nam...

Duggan-Field Link May Be Clue To Seven Unsolved Disa... ...ances Or D... Following R... ...er Hiss C...

Washington Merry-Go-Round

Seven Mysterious Deaths Have Followed Hiss Case

By Drew Pearson

PEARSON

FRANKFORT—The most talked about unsolved mystery in America and Europe is the sudden vanishing act of four American men involved in the Noel Field case. Whittaker Chambers fingered Fields as a member of the underground Communist cartel in the U.S. State Department. For the first time, this case is being linked to the strange death of Laurence Duggan—another unsolved mystery in the United States. Duggan's body was found in a sidewalk snowbank 16 floors below his New York office window. Duggan, too, was named in the State Department investigation, although he was cleared of wrongdoing by the Justice Department.

It is amazing that a total of seven people to date involved in the Alger Hiss case have suddenly died or mysteriously disappeared following revelations in the case. Noel Field disappeared first on May 10, 1949 while visiting Czechoslovakia. Next Field's brother Herman mysteriously vanished August 22, 1949 while flying between Warsaw and Prague. Mrs. Noel Field then disappeared in Prague while searching for her husband. A year later a friend of the Fields', Erica Wallachs, ventured into Berlin's Russian zone in search of the couple and never came back. All of these disappearances occurred at around the same time that three people involved in the Hiss case died under mysterious circumstances. The three are:

Death No. 1—Harry Dexter White reportedly died of heart failure on August 16, 1948, mere hours after testifying before the House un-American Activities Committee. Former assistant secretary of the Treasury, White was charged by Elizabeth Bentley as being a member of an elite Communist group installed inside the government. Announcement of White's death was withheld for a time and his body was buried hastily. It was later discovered that the real cause of White's death was not heart failure, but an overdose of digitalis.

Death No. 2—Walter Marvin Smith, whose body was found crumpled at the bottom of a Justice Department stairwell where he had either jumped or fallen on October 20, 1948, a day after the House un-American Activities Committee investigated his notarization of the transfer of the title of a Ford Model A belonging to Alger Hiss to one William Rosen, accused by the Committee as a Communist organizer. According to Whittaker Chambers, Hiss insisted on turning over the car to Rosen. The only actual witness to the transfer was Smith.

Death No. 3—Laurence Duggan, the most mysterious of all three deaths. The former State Department official, "while putting on his overshoe to go home," fell through the window of his New York office. Only a few days earlier, Duggan had been questioned by the Committee regarding Communist Spies in the State Department. Insurance investigators believed it unlikely that a... would commit suicide while putting on his... shoes and paid his widow non-suicide bene...

Bad Luck Strikes Figures in Probe

By EDWARD V. ROBERTS
United Press Staff Correspondent

Washington, Dec. 22—(UP)—Such a de... ultory project was the last thing he wa... ...ed or needed. Much less the disposi... ...maybe a thousand...

House Spy Committe... Shows Signs of Jinx

WASHINGTON — (UP) — They are beginning to hang the "jinx" sign on the house un-American activities committee's investigation of alleged communist espionage within the government.

Three persons whose names have figured in the case have died since the inquiry opened last summer.

The chairman of the commi... Rep. J. Parnell Thom... been indi...

Two Repub...
committee we...
vember electio...
Whittaker Cha...
munist whose c...
case into the ope...
resign his $25,00...
Time magazine. ...
Al...

[left column fragments]
h...
on...
ga...
ic...
riag...
scin...
age.
nearl...
a nea...
weighe...
knew, a...
ticulous...
modus ...
ful arran...
for his be...
George). V...
upper lip, ...
the cover c...
Whittaker C...
thickness of...
the autobio...
enced in the l...
swivel office ci...
to go through t...
tained many i...
marginal annota...
ry reading confi...
ways heard about...
tion for a felicitou...
prose style in his ...
and dissents.

Nevertheless, suc...
project was the last t...
or needed. Much less ...
of hundreds, maybe a ...
books! He made a cur...
the ugly green m...
the lines of gunr...
cabinets (any law ...
packed with offi...
ence and printed ...
dissents going back...
ory search brought ...
is attention, unlike t...
eatly typed labels, ...
he Judge's distinctive ...
RISCILLA. A relative ...
ontaining some twenty ...
tters from the early ti...
te seventies. All signe...
ions of "Love R...

4

Snappers

The party's problem is a practical one: 1) to protect the threatened apparatuses; 2) to reassure the loyal underground workers whose morale is bound to be shaken by a defection. It is necessary to demonstrate that the apparatus moves swiftly to safeguard them, and that no one can defy it with impunity.

—Whittaker Chambers

GEORGE, BACKPACK SLUNG over his shoulder, mounted the familiar switchback of stairs to his bedroom, Cuddebackville, named, like the rest of the bedrooms in Hermitage, after villages along the D & H Canal. The brass plaque on the door inscribed in florid engraving had been polished to such a sheen (another Hermitage tradition maintained by Felicity) that he could clearly see his reflection. He made a face and tipped his Princeton Astro-P cap in mock greeting, noting with dismay the thickening along his chin remarked upon by both Karen and Erich the night before. He tossed his backpack onto the bed in the corner. Pinned on the wall above was a blue-and-white banner: YALE CLASS OF 1953. Teddy's class. Teddy's room. The Judge's firstborn and eternally beloved only son. George shrugged and made a brief inspection before going to open the window. Cuddebackville (the town named after a Revolutionary War hero) had been awarded to the four-year-old George when he first arrived at Hermitage, or that was as far back as his first memories went. Whether it was remarked upon at the time, he couldn't say, but in later years it had been noted to him more than a few times, and with significant eyebrow raises, by his aunts and cousins that

"Teddy's room"—as it was still called by Alice and Martha—had been left vacant for almost twenty-four years, and that even Cordelia, as a child, had not been given Teddy's room. This delicate question of pro-tocol, whether to do with status or pecking order or perhaps the waning of grief for its onetime occupant was largely lost on young George, but over time, he came to fully appreciate that he occupied another's space, his room filled with artifacts not be moved or tampered with in any way. He was simply a placeholder, undertaking a trial run to see if he measured up—if he fit the Dimock mold. "Spooky . . . you know it's haunted," teased his older cousins. "Teddy's ghost roams the upstairs hall at night." How many terrifying nights had he started awake to a screech owl in the moonlit shadows, or a knocking-scratching-baying at his door (giggles and scamperings in the hall). Even worse, the older cousins soon began calling him "Cruddyback" or the "Cruddyback Kid"—"Crudhead" for short, until later, when various mocking *Star Wars* monikers were substituted, a spigot of humiliation only relieved with the mass abandonment of Hermitage in the catastrophic summer of 1981, when cousin Cecily, abetted by Karen, almost managed to burn down the boathouse while setting off a fireworks display. His aunts, Alice and Martha, in the subsequent brouhaha, accused the Judge of fooling with their pyromaniac daughters, and then, for good measure, dredged up his supposed molestation of Cordelia as an adolescent. Soon followed a barrage of accusations, countercharges, and denials that resulted in the Judge ostracizing his family from Hermitage. All except George (with Cordelia's brokered dispensation), who returned summer after summer to work odd jobs around the place, splitting firewood, and later fixing plumbing, a handyman running errands into town. Only Cordelia, of the three daughters, showed on special occasions when she could get away from managing the bookstore in Woodstock.

Now, as he surveyed Cuddebackville after the triumph of the night before, George found himself not a little aghast at his pusillan-imous acquiescence to living in another's shadow for so many years, this war hero, this champion oarsman at Groton and Yale, winner of numerous academic prizes in school, slated to attend Harvard Law, and, like his father before him, voted by his Yale class, in a posthu-mous gesture, the most likely to have served on the Supreme Court. George gazed up at the glittering shelves of Teddy's rowing trophies from Henley, Quinsigamond, and various Olympic tryouts; a lower shelf was devoted to his school yearbooks and college texts; another shelf held Joseph Conrad first editions, given by his doting parents for birthdays and Christmas; another housed his collections of arrowheads, birds' nests, a tattered album of bird feathers, and a couple of dozen rusty iron spikes pried loose from the abandoned ties of the defunct Port Jervis & Monticello Railroad. Even the closets still contained some of Teddy's fishing gear and waders, which the Judge had encouraged George to put to good use once he'd grown into them. What little remained of George's summer sojourns had to be squeezed in around the edges: some Princeton astrophysics texts, Ray Bradbury sci-fi novels, all of Carl Sagan, and a slew of more recent art history books, and a couple of dog-eared issues of *Penthouse* stuck into bottom drawers. All pathetic reminders of a half-life of near misses, certainly in the Judge's eyes.

George took down a small framed photograph of Teddy in khaki uniform at Camp Lejeune posed with his comrades. Blond hair shorn to reveal that confident face and wide-apart eyes and set jaw—so reminiscent of a younger Judge. A marine hero, a first lieutenant killed in Korea over fifty years before, awarded posthumously a Bronze Star and a Silver Star, beloved by his unit, his Yale class, his family . . . "One fucking hell of a guy."

Strangely, something in Teddy's face, his forthright stance, arms akimbo, reminded him of Wendy Bradley's gaze from the night before: her forceful chin raised to him when they parted on Twenty-third Street, the intrepid silver-blue of her eyes as she indicated, once again, the catalog and his splendid essay held up in her hand (marred by one conclusion to which she'd vehemently objected), the way she squeezed his arm as she bent for that chaste, lingering kiss on the cheek. A replayed moment that again stirred a welcome boost to his faltering self-worth.

He moved to the window and the waning throb of summer's last cicadas, detecting the distant honking alarm of Canada geese disturbed on the lake. Rare in his childhood, now pests in their multitudes, even as they were attacked on every front: by eagles from above, by foxes and coyotes from the shore; raccoons and skunks eating their eggs; and the huge mossback snappers rising from the muddy gloom, grabbing a leg and dragging down their flapping, protesting victims to their doom. Even the bass joined the genocide, taking the goslings every spring—a 70 percent attrition rate, while the hunters harvested the survivors in the fall. And still they came to the killing ground year after year after year.

"Snappers—ugh!" A knowing nod to himself, chortling, "*Et in Arcadia ego.*"

Surprising himself, he spun around and went and loosened the four rusted thumbtacks and let the moth-eaten Yale banner slough to the bed, where he ceremoniously folded it and stowed it in a bottom drawer with a ten-year-old copy of *Penthouse*.

Perhaps it was time—even if change was an illusion—to assert his claim, in the nick of time, before everything went to hell in a hand-basket anyway.

George headed for the Judge's office but found himself waylaid by the open door of the spacious master bedroom, Graham's Dock, directly overlooking the lake, once the bedroom of Dr. Dimock and his wife, Elsie, and then of the Judge and Annie, and later the Judge alone after Annie's death of uterine cancer in 1969. Now abandoned, like his office, five years before, when the Judge, his arthritic legs giving out, had been forced to move into what had once been a servant's bedroom on the first floor, off the kitchen. "Where the scullery maids once slept. What would my father think?"

Standing in the doorway, he was struck by the air of quietude, the seeming weightless otherworldliness of a sanctuary, perhaps due to the pale afternoon light, the aqueous reflections from the lake pouring through the antique panes of the twin bay windows. And by the simple adornments—her "Shaker simplicity," according to the Judge—insisted upon by Annie, who found much of Hermitage cluttered with Victorian monstrosities. Here, in her retreat, she'd had the beadboard walls painted a cream white, along with the furniture, all of simple Arts and Crafts design, with a single curly-maple framed mirror over her dressing table, still laid out with her brushes and combs. Much of the bedroom was given over to bookshelves, painted an off-white as well, containing yard upon yard of Annie's favorite authors: Jane Austen, Trollope, Hardy, Brontë, Elliot, Conrad (which she read to her firstborn, Teddy), and her beloved Proust, in the original French Pléiade editions, and the Moncrieff English translation. The Judge in recent years had spoken fondly of his old bed in Graham's Dock as "a thing of magic and enchantment": All except Teddy (their Venetian miracle) had been conceived by *moonlight*: all August conceptions and May births.

As he turned to leave, George noticed a beam of sunlight falling on an oil painting of Annie seated at her Steinway grand. The painting was by Raphael Soyer, dated 1947, at the height of her fame. Under his wistful gaze, the prismatic light seemed to penetrate the varnish and pigment, activating the surface of the canvas, so popping the blue and turquoise tones in Annie's dark gown, while the honey highlights in her long hair glowed with lucent depths, deftly focusing the viewer's eyes on the delicate yet agile white of her curved fingers poised over the slashing paint marks of black and white. Her face was bowed to the keyboard in concentrated rapture, a diamond brooch glittering below the strap of her low-cut gown, eyes showing hints of aquamarine . . . so alive—such an irrepressible, vital presence. Her long nose with a slight upward tilt, the aching arch of her eyebrows, a single ecstatic furrow bisecting her brow. George touched the warm canvas, as if reminded of something, drawn to some quantum entanglement across time and space lingering in the artist's gestural response to a woman of such talent and beauty. He smiled to himself: perhaps a goddess who could just as well have found her way to the ship's keel ceiling as to the hand of Raphael Soyer. Soyer, he mused, who, in the early thirties, had once taught with his grandfather, George Altmann, at the Art Students League, perhaps friends—who knows—until Altmann had given up figuration in 1939 for his late abstract landscapes.

—

Next door was the Judge's private office, Summitville, which had been strictly off-limits to the cousins. A lair from which the Judge would emerge bleary-eyed on weekends in July, or most afternoons in August for hikes and swimming, or a dash to the Neversink for trout fishing before dinner. To be summoned to Summitville, whether for disciplinary offenses or just a good talking-to, was always cause for much trepidation among the kids. Everyone tiptoed past the closed door—clatter of typing echoing down the hall—for fear of disturbing the Judge "in his chambers," as his aunts called it, when, even in August, he labored over his opinions for the Second Circuit Court of Appeals, or was under deadline for a prestigious law journal.

George slipped the key into the lock, resisting the instinct to hold his breath. He blinked in the intense sunlight coming in through the single window and tried to get his bearings as the warm air, hermetically sealed like some pharaoh's tomb (walls lined with framed sheepskins), assaulted him, the yet-to-be-decanted aroma of a thousand musty volumes. His gaze immediately went to the archaic Underwood typewriter, the carriage-return lever a gleaming silver

scimitar, long an antique of a bygone age. Nearby, on the sprawling but nearly empty mahogany desk, was a neat stack of pages,
a typescript weighed down by a thick tome. He knew, as if he'd
always known—meticulous preparation was the Judge's modus operandi—that the purposeful arrangement had been conceived for his
benefit (loyal George, gullible George). With a cynical twist of his
upper lip, he went over and touched the cover of the book, *Witness*,
by Whittaker Chambers. He noted the thickness of the typescript
beneath, the autobiography-memoir referenced in the letter, and so
sat in the swivel office chair for a few minutes to go through the
pages, which contained many inked-out lines and marginal annotations. Even a cursory reading confirmed what he'd always heard about
the Judge's reputation for a felicitous and plainspoken prose style in
his rulings—opinions and dissents.

Nevertheless, such a desultory project was the last thing he wanted
or needed. Much less the disposition of hundreds, maybe a thou-
sand-plus books! He made a cursory review of the ugly green metal
bookshelves, the lines of gunmetal gray filing cabinets (any law office
circa 1950) packed with official correspondence and printed opinions
and dissents going back decades. A cursory search brought only one
file to his attention, unlike the others with neatly typed labels, this
labeled in the Judge's distinctive precise hand: PRISCILLA. A relatively
thin folder containing some twenty handwritten letters from the early
thirties to the late seventies. All signed with variations of "Love, Pross."
He brought the file and its contents to his nose and breathed in the distinct scent of a woman's perfume. If a secret lover or mistress (rumors
in the family had always run rampant), there seemed little attempt to
have hidden the evidence. He returned the file to its cabinet and turned
to the functional metal shelving filled with the standard legal references in uniform bindings. The remaining shelves contained the Judge's
favorite volumes, reference books galore on natural history, fishing,
birding, anthologies of Burroughs, Muir, Emerson and Thoreau, the
Romantic poets, Conrad, Shakespeare in both a leather-bound set and
dog-eared paperbacks, Gibbon's *Decline and Fall*. In pride of place were
the writings of the Judge's mentor, Oliver Wendell Holmes, including
his magisterial *The Common Law*. Like Justice Holmes, the Judge had
always prided himself, and had been justly praised, for the directness
and intellectual elegance of his opinions, to which these well-thumbed
volumes had certainly given wing.

George took down a volume of the writings of Learned Hand, whom the Judge had replaced as chief judge on the Court of Appeals for the Second Circuit in 1951. Inscribed on the title page in a tight blue script was the following: *Liberty lies in the hearts of men and women; when it dies there, no constitution, no law, no court can save it; no constitution, no law, no court can even do much to help it. Learned Hand. Good luck on your new appointment—you will need it. Court of Appeals, 1951.*

Framed on the back wall was the Judge's Harvard Law School degree and a dozen other citations for meritorious service from various bar associations. Interspersed, sunstruck black-and-white photos of a young Edward Dimock standing next to Oliver Wendell Holmes on the porch of his Beverly Farms summer home; posed with a seated Franklin Roosevelt at a signing ceremony in the Oval Office when he worked for the War Production Board; and another ten or so empty hooks—Presidents Truman through Reagan—denizens of the Judge's power wall—now exiled to his tiny bedroom beside the kitchen.

Confronted with the evidence—the tools, artifacts, and commendations of such an esteemed and exceptional life and career—George just shook his head, perplexed at the executor's role being pressed upon him. He gazed down again at the title page of the Judge's draft memoir: *A Life in the Law and Out.* What the fuck did he know about editing, especially things legal? Surely, the Judge's daughter Alice, a lawyer and renowned scholar in her own right, would be better qualified to take on this duty. Not that the Judge would ever trust his "radical left-wing firebrand" with such a responsibility. On second examination, the inclusion of Whittaker Chambers's *Witness* confounded him even more than the typescript. Knowing the Judge's fondness for intellectual puzzles and misdirection to elicit the results he favored, George immediately suspected this blatant juxtaposition with the typescript had some enigmatic, if not self-serving, purpose. He picked up the book and walked with it to the window—throwing open the double leaded-glass panels to finally let in some cool air—and to better inspect the black-and-white photo on the cover.

There was something vaguely ominous in the beefy-faced shadow beneath a broad fedora, and not a little creepy—those sorrowful, deep-set, plum-dark baggy eyes: a weight, a sorrow, a hard-won wisdom. The pages were heavily underlined and dog-eared. And he thought he detected at least two hands in the different underlining and marginalia, some in pencil, some in ink. A precise inked *P* in block letters next to passages mentioning Priscilla Hiss, along with extensive underlining and annotations, and not a few question marks and exclamation points. Curious, he turned again to the jowly face on the cover to further ponder the drooping, heavy jaw, world-weary—if not a wary expression . . . a man of spiritual depths and skeptical, knife-edged intelligence. Turning the book over, he began reading the back-cover copy, phrases jogging vague memories of Dimock family lore and long-forgotten conversations as a child: *trial of the century . . . Alger Hiss's accuser . . . witness to the Soviet underground's penetration of the U.S. government . . .*

Whittaker Chambers, he now remembered, was the crucial witness for the prosecution in the Alger Hiss case: the man Edward Dimock, as assistant defense counsel, had been hired to destroy.

George shook his head in consternation and opened to the frontispiece, where he found an inscription: *To the beloved Annie, a fellow pilgrim soul embarked on life's fraught journey. May your talent and decency and love—after your recent tragic loss—allow the remainder of your journey to be smooth and trouble-free. Whittaker Chambers, 1954.*

Annie, he thought, clearly one of the hands, the annotations, had been Annie's.

Not a little perplexed at this personal note (the loss of Teddy) in the inscription to his wife of a man the Judge had hounded in court, he carefully placed the copy of *Witness* with the memoir in his backpack and prepared to leave, when he noticed a large corkboard turned to and leaning up against the rear wall. He wiped away cobwebs and dust and tipped the corkboard back, peering down, to discover the thing chock-a-block with pinned papers. With a hand on either edge, he walked the corkboard into the light, leaning it against the desk to better examine its contents. He stood staring for minutes, first mystified and then mesmerized . . . incredulous.

"No fucking way."

Nine pencil sketches, portrait heads, were attached to the corkboard with thumbtacks (instantly bringing to mind his mother's careless refrain: "No Merc, Georgie, no you—ha-ha"). These had to be the detailed portrait studies by his grandfather, George Altmann, mentioned by Cordelia: two at the top, four in a line beneath, and then a final line of three. One woman, eight men. All but the top two sketches included stick-pinned note cards inscribed with names and lines of data carefully annotated in the Judge's hand. All were skillful, assured renderings, the supple line work and delicate crosshatching perfectly catching the character of the sitters. These drawings were almost certainly from the thirties, when Altmann had first made his reputation as one of the most important social realist artists of the day. All seemed done from life, all animated by a similar quality of ambient light. Even the poses and expressions of the subjects had a family resemblance: pensive, reflective, as if listening avidly to a speaker. He noted their similarity to studies Altmann had done for various mural projects at the peak of his fame in the mid-thirties, when he was summoned to Washington to head up the mural division of the Federal Art Project.

Pinned beneath the sketches were groupings of blurry black-and-white photos, carefully clipped from newspapers or magazines: jostling crowds on courthouse steps, suspects confronted by reporters, caught in the glare of a flashbulb—frightened, some with distressed expressions, grimaces, hemmed in or protected by burly police officers; harried men in fedoras with clipped mustaches and glinting spectacles; women displaying heavily lipsticked looks of alarm, wearing calf-length sober dresses, their hair bobbed in tight waves. There was an air of almost palpable paranoia. By the look of the clothes and cars in the background, he figured these were mostly from the late forties or early fifties, at the height of the Red Scare.

More disconcerting were the captioned photographs of crime scenes: a tall façade on Forty-fifth Street with a dotted line and arrow describing the passage of a falling body from a sixteenth-story window to the street below; another taken from the top of a spiraling stairwell in the Justice Department, with a graphic X marking the spot in the marble-floored lobby where the body hit; and finally a spare white-clapboard farmhouse overhung by twisted oak branches in Fitzwilliam, New Hampshire, scene of a dramatic death or suicide.

A thick envelope labeled TRIAL, containing even more clippings, was pinned to the bottom corner of the corkboard.

He touched the headline on the largest clipping (DUGGAN: SUICIDE LEAP OR FOUL?), tracing the trajectory of a falling body past the mullioned windows of a skyscraper to a snow-banked sidewalk on Forty-fifth Street. The image made him almost physically sick. For a minute or two, he sat in the desk chair, face in hands, until his nerves had calmed and he resumed his examination of the corkboard.

The first pair of Altmann sketches he recognized immediately: Alger and Priscilla Hiss. The three-quarter profile of Alger Hiss was striking: dark eyes gleaming—crisply intelligent—hair perfectly groomed, chin and nose and curve of his right cheekbone executed with a single heavy stroke of lead to emphasize a decisiveness of character, an incisive spirit unyielding to human frailty. His lips were poised, as if he had just finished speaking or was just about to speak. While Priscilla's expression was more withdrawn, thoughtful, her eyes seemingly focused on her husband, her hair tight against the back of her head; prim, composed . . . attractive, not beautiful, in the way a highly intelligent, forthright woman can exude a certain kind of electric sex appeal. Reminding him, not a little, of a similar electricity in the Soyer portrait of Annie.

"Where the hell did these come from?" he muttered over and over again. Almost a mantra to calm his mind as he realized the coincidence: these the very same sketches referred to by his mother the evening before, the cause of what turned out to be her wild escapade to the town of Woodstock in the red Merc, meeting her husband-to-be, Jimmy Altmann, and disappearing for two weeks, only to be finally located by a half-crazed Judge in the muddy aftermath of the Woodstock festival.

He tried to step back, calm his mind, and rationally decipher the patterns, the faces, the crime scenes, the panicked expressions, all the cryptic data on the note cards. What in God's name was the Judge trying to elicit in this display, which had once clearly hung across from his desk, where George now detected the sunstruck afterimage of the corkboard on the wood paneling? What methodology was being employed? Surely that of a highly rational and organized mind trying to penetrate some mystery by the physical juxtaposition of evidence, as if to decipher a series of causal relationships between seemingly disparate and random suspects and events. But what narrative, what story was the Judge attempting to uncover? He could feel his own ingrained habits of thought being engaged: analyzing seemingly random patterns, attempting to establish order out of chaos, transforming randomness into possibilities, coincidences into cause and effect.

He reached to the note card held in place by a red pin that separated the twin portraits of Alger and Priscilla Hiss from the seven faces beneath: a précis in blue ink that seemed to best explain the purpose of the corkboard and the obscure fate of its denizens.

Key Conspirators and Potential Witnesses Against Alger Hiss Either Silenced, Eliminated, Disappeared, or Placed Beyond the Reach of the U.S. Government.

Harry Dexter White (Died Before Trial)

Harvard, senior official, Treasury, anti-Japanese before Pearl Harbor. Anti-Chiang by 1943. Pro–Red Chinese 1943 on. Cut off monetary aid to Nationalists 1944. Helped develop Morgenthau Plan, Operation Keelhaul, key points of Yalta, in consultation with Hiss. (Chambers's and Bentley's lists.) Murdered or possible suicide by overdose of digitalis at his summer home in Fitzwilliam, New Hampshire, August 1948.

Laurence Duggan (Died Before Trial)

Harvard, State Department. (Chambers's and Bentley's lists.) Headed South American division of State in late thirties. Close to Hiss both professionally and socially. Pushed or fell to his death out of sixteen-story building at 2 West 45th Street, December 1948.

Marvin Smith (Died Before Trial)

Attorney, Justice Department, friend of Hiss beginning in 1933, AAA; notarized the transfer document on Hiss's Ford. Like Duggan, pushed or fell to his death. Fell down stairwell at Justice Department, October 1948.

William Remington
(Died After Trial While Hiss in Prison)

Dartmouth, State Department. (Bentley's list.) Admitted spying, then denied it, convicted of perjury. Murdered in Lewisburg prison by fellow inmate when Hiss was still incarcerated there. KGB warning to Hiss just before his release?

Lauchlin Currie (Unavailable as Witness in Trial)

Harvard, White House, personal representative of FDR and deputy head of Foreign Economic Administration 1943–1944. Intimate with FDR, Harry Hopkins, Eleanor Roosevelt. (Chambers's and Bentley's lists.) Fled to Colombia 1950 and so unavailable to testify.

Noel Field (Unavailable as Witness in Trial)

Harvard, State Department. (Chambers's list.) Arrested in Prague by KGB in 1949, held in Budapest prison for five

years on orders of Soviets, and so unavailable to testify in
Hiss trial. Living in exile in Czechoslovakia.

Anonymous

Unidentified figure.

"Harvard," he muttered, noting how the word had been emphati-
cally underlined in every case with a slash of blue ink. The note cards
looked to be of more recent vintage than the sketches or clippings, the
paper fresher, maybe from the late seventies or eighties, when, presumably, the Judge had first embarked on his memoir as retirement loomed.

"Or something out of his past had him by the throat."

Just hearing this conjecture in his own voice had the odd effect
of intensifying his visceral attraction to the sketches, to these people he'd never known but who had been known to his grandfather,
the artist—some or all, presumably, to the Judge, as well. Something
about the intimacy and delicacy of touch, full of vibrant and febrile
human emotion, drew his disoriented gaze to their intent faces, his
fingers hovering, caressing the fine laid paper in a mute attempt to
fathom these lives, even if they existed only in a kind of spectral
limbo before his eyes. He found himself speaking their first names
like a familial incantation: "Alger, Priscilla, Harry, Laurence, Marvin,
William, Lauchlin, Noel . . ."

The echo of his voice in the sunlit confines of the Judge's office
snaked a shiver down his spine, as if the spoken names invoked an
unwanted intimacy, calling out to the more obscure recesses of his
soul, an estrangement beset by odd fragments of troubling memories
that had reemerged over the last days and hours: vague, unsettling,
frustrating. Triggering, in turn, lurking feelings of despondency and
doubt from years past—but of joy as well, a multiplicity of coeval pasts,
whether hanging out at Hermitage or walking to Handytown or staring into the transfixing heart of galaxy clusters, his eyes bathed in the
pulsing light of distant worlds, vast, unimaginable, inscrutable. That
numberless past, shadowless and cold, placing the creation of these
sketches a mere blink of an eye ago, with an immediacy that trumped
the fleet-footed decades. He licked his lips, dry as doubt itself, of time's
rancid aftertaste.

There was a quality in these sketches not found in other Altmann
studies of the period, which tended to the bombastic, mostly idealized

subjects for the artist's Depression-era murals: brave and stalwart workers with brows of steel and jaws of iron. And it suddenly dawned on him that through all his research for the Altmann catalog in the artist's barn studio, over all his rambling Woodstock youth, he'd never come across anything quite like these sketches, nothing so personal, not even of Altmann's family members, his wife, his young son—nothing. As if some slate of family memory, much less love, had been wiped clean. Leaving these portraits of strangers as his first real glimpse of his grandfather's love—if it could be so dignified—of humanity. (Altmann's abstract landscapes were full of love, but of a different order and dimension.) Here, preserved on faded sunstruck paper, was a human depth, a record of passionate attachment that offered a poignant rejoinder to whatever crimes or follies or sad fate these people had endured. A transcendent vitality writ glowingly in the luminous portrait of Priscilla Hiss: some indefinable allure in her shining eyes and soft lips, a sensuous winsomeness that verged on a depiction of the beloved.

Tantalized, he unpinned the sketch of Priscilla Hiss, took it over to the window, and held it up to the sunlight. And as he did he noticed in faint pencil at the bottom of the sheet an address: 3415 Volta Place, September 7, 1937.

"Volta Place," he intoned, shaking his head in wonderment.

And, as if in need of an answer to this parallax vision merging past and present, he glanced from the sketch into his backpack at Chambers's *Witness* and the typescript of the memoir that only moments before had seemed a thankless, if not impossible, task he'd planned to get out of: now a key, an anchor to windward, both in terms of this enigmatic woman's stare returning his and his own troubled life.

For a few minutes more, he busied himself with photographing the contents of the corkboard, many of the clippings crumbling at the touch, then removing the sketches and storing them carefully in a manila envelope. Halfway through shooting the fifty-year-old headlines, he suddenly realized the inchoate dread that filled him: the ambiguous fate of his own grandfather, George Altmann, over the Christmas break during the Hiss trial.

> *The Red Trail of Death by Violence . . . Probe Death Plunge of Key Spy Witness . . . Widow of Marvin Smith Denies Fall from Staircase Suicide . . . Where Duggan Plunged to Death . . . Drew Pearson: Duggan-Field Link May Be Clue to Seven Unsolved*

Disappearances or Deaths Following Revelations in Alger Hiss Case . . . Duggan Widow Denies Sixteen-Story Plunge Was Suicide . . . Widow of Harry Dexter White Says Husband Had Weak Heart . . . Not Suicide.

Now working in a frenzy, he photographed the contents of the envelope containing clippings from the Hiss trial:

Harvard Expert Says Chambers Mentally Ill; Hiss Expert Claims Chambers Has "Psychopathic" Ailment; Eisler's "Ex" Pins Hiss as Commie Ring Boss; Hede Massing Testimony Seals Hiss's Fate in Trial of the Century; Prosecutor Murphy Makes Mincemeat of Edward Dimock's Expert Witnesses Against Chambers: Psychiatrists Binger and Murray—Fools All; Dimock and Harvard-Columbia Shrinks Humiliated by Prosecution Cross-Examination; Hiss Convicted on Two Counts of Perjury; Hiss Sentenced to Four Years; Alger Hiss— Symbol of a Mad Period; Hiss's Society Supporters, Dean Acheson and Others Still Can't Accept Guilt; A Generation on Trial . . .

Finally, placing the envelope containing the nine sketches in his backpack, he paused at the door before hightailing it for Handytown and an hour's solitude and sanity before the Judge woke from his nap. He stared back at the not so empty office . . .

Ghosts.

Chambers Went 'Underground' on Orders of Russian Agents

False Names Helped Him Lose Identity

Not Even Party Friends Knew Where He'd Gone

This is the fifth of 14 installments of a condensation of the book, "Seeds of Treason," just published by Funk & Wagnalls, New York.

It is the first orderly, factual account of the events that brought Whittaker Chambers and Alger Hiss face to face — sensational trials of

By Ralph de Toledano and Victor Lasky

FROM WRITER TO SPY

When Whittaker Chambers walked out of the Daily Worker office in 1929, he still believed firmly in the Bolshevik seizure of power and the dictatorship of the proletariat.

The right instruments to bring about the revolution would come in time. They would be schooled and dedicated young men, and he would be one of them. In the meantime, he would write.

Chambers knew that he could easily earn more than his Daily Worker salary by doing literary translations. Since the middle twenties, when he had translated the best-selling "Bambi" by Felix Salten, his reputation in that field had been high. And he could continue to write the poems which were common in their reflection

was at once grandiose and practical: he wanted to create the Bolshevik as a figure in American literature. It was this character who dominated the short stories he began to write.

During this relatively calm and productive period in his life, Whittaker Chambers married Esther Shemitz. He had seen her for the first time when he was covering the 1926 Passaic textile strike for the Worker.

The police had surrounded a hall in which strikers were gathered. Suddenly the doors burst open and the strikers marched out to meet the police. They were led by a slender, dark-haired girl.

The girl, a labor organizer, was arrested in the struggle that followed. Chambers learned then that her name was Esther Shemitz, but it was not until years later that he met her again.

Neither a party member, Esther was one of the multitude of sympathizers in party organiza...

Whittaker Chambers -- Eye of a Storm

...GROUND included Hiss and Nathan ...s testifies before House probers.

ON THE STAND — Before House probe group he fires accusations at Hiss.

Spy Witness Quits Post with 'Time'

NEW YORK, Dec. 10 (AP)—...taker Chambers, central figure ...probe of alleged Communists ...Friday quit his job as a senior ...of Time magazine.

His resignation was an...suddenly by his attorneys a...bers waited at the federal ...to testify before a federal g...whose investigation he re...this week.

Offer Accepted

Chambers said in a pre...ment his offer to quit an...tance of the offer "becar...when I recently began"...

Three Decisions by Chambers, Produc... Of Disillusionment, Led to Hiss Tri...

Rejection of Suicide, Joining Reds, Later Break With Them Built Powerful Drama.

By JOSEPH DRISCOLL
National Correspondent of the Dispatch

WHITTAKER CHAMBERS made three important decisions in his life.

1. Not to commit suicide.
2. To join the Communist party.
3. To break with the Communist party.

The three decisions, taken in sequence were to build up to a

They were to throw a spotlight backward on the Washington of yesterday, when the official policy of the United States Government was pro-Soviet— and some of the American behaved more Russian than the Russians.

Back to Lost Generation

And the spotlight went even further back to the aftermath of World War I, when the failure of the world's peacemakers contributed to the disillusionment of the younger generation— and made the college campuses of the nation fertile recruiting fields for Communist agents.

Communism, as has been pointed out before, thrives on disillusionment, and disillusionment is one commodity which the younger generations (and the older, too) never have found in short supply. Before Chambers joi...

leading was bankrupt, and tha...to find another solution to the ...of life and death.

Chambers's younger brothe...of whom he was very fond, pro...way out. Dick said the two of the ...gentle people incapable of cop...the world," and invited his ...join him in a suicide pact.

Brother Kills Self.

Whittaker Chambers thought ...might be another way out, a via ...rosa that led toward Moscow. B...younger Richard was stubborn ...killed himself with illuminating g...the age of 22.

For several months after his br...death, Whittaker Chambrs, by his ...testimony, was "immobile."...

5
Judicial Review

As men's prayers are a disease of the will, so are their
creeds a disease of the intellect.
Things are in the saddle/And ride mankind.

—Ralph Waldo Emerson

THE SMELL OF wood smoke drifted his way and he looked up from the trail, to detect a silver plume through the trees rising from the tallest of the redbrick chimneys into the thinning blue. He sighed with longing, knowing it was too chilly for the Judge to be out on the piazza and that, indeed, fall, with winter not far behind, had come to Hermitage.

He took another few steps and paused again, thunderstruck at how nothing had changed and everything had changed.

Entering the great room from the piazza, he closed the large door quickly, with barely a sound, before the Judge could complain about a draft. The old man sat in bowed profile with an open book in his lap, ensconced in his favorite Stickley chair on the right flank of the cozy horseshoe ensemble nearest the fire, orange juice at his elbow, his walker parked within easy reach. Four colorful Tiffany lamps blazed out like miniature suns, enchanting, sumptuous, kaleidoscopic, providing, as ever, a festive mood around the roaring hearth. George found himself instantly transported back to childhood, when he and his older cousins would gather at bedtime before the fire to be read to by the Judge. Always August, always Conrad, when he would sit listening, transported to the antipodes while mesmerized by the intense glow of the stained-glass lamp shades replete with serpentine vines of emerald and olive green, ruby dragonfly wings, bluebirds on the wing, and the delicious pinks of blooming lotus flowers. While the ship's keel ceiling, even absent its afternoon luster, still cast its spell, here and there faded to a turbid bronzy green in the lamplight, moody, ghostly, like an antique mirror blackened with age; but for a child, gazing into the arching carapace of carved and painted beams, a thing alive, glittering in the firelight, an enchanted woodland pool out of which fleshy gods and goddesses materialized like goldfish rising from the murk. George took a deep breath, re-anchoring himself in the present as he gave the ceiling a final glance—Jesus, just the allure, the age: to think it had endured five hundred sweltering summers and frigid winters.

At the squeak of a floorboard, the Judge's large head and prepossessing brow rose from the pages in his lap, white hair neatly barbered, his flaring brown-tipped eyebrows like miniature whitecaps above the black frames of his reading glasses. He wore his usual cocktail hour/dinner attire of a blue button-down Brooks Brothers oxford-cloth shirt, khakis, and, given the chill, a hunter green herringbone jacket with kid-leather collar. As George came forward to greet his grandfather, he was pleased to find the aroma of roasting beef mixing happily with that of burning oak logs, dry and seasoned like the voice greeting him.

"You're back, Tiger."

"Yes, sir, time traveling like crazy."

George squeezed his grandfather's liver-spotted hand, a bit frail and cold to the touch, and held on for a moment longer than usual. His face appeared thinner, jowls with a sere looseness, yet the baggy eyes, magnified by the reading glasses, still held a luster sparked by flame. He took a seat opposite, where a glass and bottle of chardonnay awaited on the inlaid top of the revolving book table, backlit by the lush effusions of the Tiffany lamp shade.

"Your hand is cold. So, how was our fair Handytown?"

"The Handy tombstones still stand; the hermit thrush were silent; the birch growing out of the cellar hole has gone canary yellow . . . the spirit of fall is upon us."

The Judge removed his glasses and carefully folded them into his jacket pocket.

"So, Felicity tolled my demise and it's you who shows up." The Judge nodded appreciatively, bending forward to examine his grandson's face. "You've gained weight."

"You knew I'd come, Judge."

"I'll miss our conversations most of all, George. I always felt we were very much on the same page." And he leaned farther still, as if to impart a confidence. "I am such an admirer of the scientific method, which, as you know, I feel is very much akin to the empirical tradition of the common law: experience rather than theory."

"Dependable George." He smiled gamely. "And we need theories to jump-start research."

"If overly earnest—one of your most redeeming features." The Judge leaned back, fiddling with the hearing aid in his left ear, the better to hear his grandson above the snap of the oak logs.

"Mom had to open the bookstore this morning; I'm sure Alice and Martha will follow up."

"Not before the undertaker. I haven't seen hide nor hair of those two in over a decade. So, tell me more of Handytown."

"Annie's way . . ." He smiled, more a question than a statement. "Beautiful as ever. The maples have already turned, even if the silence was quite deafening. The morels are out in force and it's a bumper crop for acorns."

"I can't tell you how I miss my walks. First to go was the Neversink, then Handytown; now with help from Felicity I totter down to the boat-house on occasion." He tapped the cover of the book in his lap. "I must now content myself with Emerson or"—he looked up at the ship's keel ceiling, as if some glimmering fancy had caught his eye—"Mr. Burroughs sauntering in the Catskills before I was born, seeing the birds through his eyes . . . our woods chock-a-block with striped hemlock trunks—heca-tombs felled like skittles to the greed of the tanneries. The 'bark-peelers,' he called them." He cocked his head toward the fading sunset in the windows behind the piano. "First evening I haven't sat out on the porch this summer. Feels like a Canadian high coming through."

"Yes, so says the weatherman." George grabbed his wineglass, let-ting his impatience get the better of him. "So, what's all this bullshit about, anyway?"

The Judge looked to the angel with the upturned gaze closest to where he sat, where the firelight flickered on her pocked face. He rubbed his hands together to warm them, grimaced with a weary sigh, as if exasperated at the repetitive nature of the various health crises of the last decade.

"Nobody pretends old age is a bed of roses. I watched old Justice Holmes struggle in his last years, and God knows I never expected to get *that* old—and now I've surpassed Ollie. But without the exercise, the fresh air pumped through your lungs, blood to the brain, the joy fades as the energy recedes. And birds don't behave the same on a feeder. And the best songsters keep to themselves in the depths of the woods."

"Well, that roast beef sure smells good. Felicity must be working her magic."

"George, you'd never make it as a lawyer—thank the Lord: Your well-intentioned stratagems wouldn't fool a jury of third graders."

George laughed, held up his glass of chardonnay in salute, and drained it.

"What, my celebration—I did send you an invitation—of George Altmann's triumphant return to the New York art scene after half a century of neglect." George stole a quick glance at the Emerson essays where his gallery invitation still peeked from the pages. "Perhaps you saw mention in the *New York Times*; they gave my show a rave review. And we sold ten paintings at very good prices. And better still, there's plenty more where those came from, stored in the barn at Woodstock."

"Ah, yes, your namesake, no less." The Judge held up his palm like a prizefighter and then returned it to his lap as if to begin an examination of the ragged life lines writ there. "So, after everything, you've become a successful art dealer." He went on disparagingly, turning his troubled red-rimmed eyes on George. "A wheeler-dealer."

"You say that with almost the same snide cutting edge as Aunt Alice and Aunt Martha."

The Judge smiled at the apt riposte.

"Best education money can buy, summa from Princeton, and you drop out of the Astrophysics Department with your Ph.D. dissertation completed, lacking only a defense. How utterly asinine is that—a terrible waste."

"Judge, the show was my Hail Mary after a disastrous last year—for everybody in the New York art world. And I'm sorry you wasted your money. But as you know, I could have done the whole Princeton boat on scholarship."

"That wouldn't have been right. Not as long as I *had* the money. And that scholarship presumably went to some worthy kid who really needed it, even if it was to Princeton's benefit. God knows where my meager gifts to Yale go these days."

"I'm still in your debt on the gallery, but with any luck we'll be profitable this year—after last year's disaster—and I can pay you back in full. I expect you to stick around for repayment of that debt."

"And I wish to offer you an apology."

"Apology?"

"For all those years ago putting you in Teddy's room."

"Well . . ." George offered a guilty shrug.

"There was only the guest room left, of course, after your four cousins, but I was tempting—or perhaps bribing fate, letting you contend with such expectations, and so young. The truth is, I needed to wean myself from going in there to remember, to dwell on the thing."

"You still miss him, I'm sure."

The Judge's eyes deepened, a quiver in the lined chin, and then a tentative smile.

"Did I ever tell you the day I caught him in here—gosh, he couldn't have been more than six or seven, and he had the line of his fly rod tangled in the beam over there, where the golden Pisces shimmers. Seems he'd been practicing his casting, trying to land his fly on Pisces, as if casting his line into the heavens above. Well, the line had gone right over the beam and the fly had snagged and he was pulling on it with all his might. I scolded him awfully for such a stupid thing. Had to get up on a ladder to extract the fly with a pair of pliers. Left an awful scratch. Annie was beside herself. You can still see the scratch mark in the beam if you look closely."

George rose from his seat and squinted upward where the Judge had pointed. He found himself smiling again at a pensive angelic Virgo with her filigree dragonfly wings spread wide like a shy maiden her lavender skirt as she curtsied at court; and nearby Gemini's adorable cherubic twins propelled by gaseous farts; and the intertwined golden carp of Pisces nibbling each other's scaly tails (much beloved of the Judge, who said they reminded him of the Pisces figure on the Torre dell' Orologio in St. Mark's Square); a fleet-footed Hermes of the winged sandals with erection at full mast (always fascinating to cousins Karen and Cecily); and defiant Icarus trailing feathers as he tumbled through space, blond hair ablaze—how his adolescent alter ego, Luke Skywalker, identified with poor Icarus and his genius father!

"I think we all, the cousins, felt a little in awe of Teddy." George shivered as he regained his seat, the tumbling figure of Icarus now evoking a disturbing unease.

"Oh my. . . the beauty of his line, the artistry of his casting; I sometimes dream of his fluid form in the dappled sunlight, wading in the Neversink."

George sighed and stared over his glass at the fire.

The Judge raised an admonishing finger. "Nobody can replace another, nor should anyone try. Funny, I sometimes thought of you in a similar way, casting your line into the universe in search of that perfect star."

"Hah—planet—a failure at that, too."

"Hardly. All I care about is that at least one of my progeny actually makes something of his life. You know, I found myself quite enamored of your search for order and symmetry, that elusive glimmer—heh"—he gestured royally with outstretched arms, as if to encompass the ceiling above, where the firelight picked out their audience of stars and planetary gods—"an intelligible structure, some predictability amid the primordial chaos. Oh, how I enjoyed those conversations, George. I thought we shared that, you and I, your love of symmetry—that theory of everything you used to go on about. I couldn't help but feel it echoed something of my long-ago conversations with Justice Holmes, when we hashed out the best means of bringing order and justice to an unjust and messy world."

"Oh," George cried out, waving facetiously to the ship's keel ceiling, "before Galileo went and spoiled it all, when we only viewed the stars through naked eyes, that homely, if serene, cosmos of interconnected spheres in which everything had its place, God's clockwork of perfect order—like your court, like Hermitage."

"Something bothering you, son?"

George tossed his head. "Aren't you being a little tough on Cordelia, Alice, and Martha, much less my cousins?"

"Shall we go down the list of broken, unhappy marriages and useless jobs?"

"Well, I guess that includes me—now . . . I mean, who the fuck needs art anyway?"

"Intellectual accomplishment is the gold standard"—he motioned with a significant squint at the bookshelf nearest the wooden armrest of the Stickley chair where his grandson's hand rested—"that and the pursuit of values that contribute to and uphold the common good."

George, worried if the Judge's omniscience now included his sacrilege of deep-sixing Teddy's Yale banner, reached over to the floor beside the revolving shelf where he'd left his backpack.

"A high bar, sir." He glanced up into the looming rafters as if for emphasis and pulled out a copy of his Altmann catalog and handed it to his grandfather. "But here's a little housewarming gift, a contribution. I'll take credit for the essay. And choosing my restorer, framer, and one hell of a talented photographer and designer. Funny, how this genius, the grandfather I never knew, seems to have been hiding in plain sight all these years."

The Judge, listening intently, a flicker of unease in the crinkled corners of his chapped lips, put on his reading glasses and flipped the pages of the catalog.

"I didn't know Altmann painted things like this—landscapes, aren't they? I somehow thought of him as a portrait artist, a court sketch artist, if memory serves."

"Ah." George refilled his glass, eyeing the old man intently. "There you go, a perfect example of how a consensus reality gets a foothold and the truth—the true reality—is lost." He gestured, followed by a glance in the direction of the flaming portrait of Giordano Bruno on the huge central beam just behind where they were seated. "Very abstract, very cutting-edge for the 1940s—who knew, who remembered? I think reviving Altmann's reputation—not that his figurative work from the thirties wasn't excellent—and making a case for his genius, an artist far ahead of his time, has its value in the scheme of things." He drank and savored his wine for a moment. "Wasn't it you who always told me a man's reputation is everything?"

"As I understand it—correct me if I'm wrong"—his atrophied hands fumbled to turn the pages of the catalog—"the team you were on at Princeton was doing fundamental research into the origins of the universe. The possibility of life elsewhere—important questions: Nobel Prize material."

"I wouldn't go *that* far, so to speak."

"It's one thing to have your gifts wasted by a careless upbringing, another to have those gifts in abundance and properly shepherded—not that Cordelia helped you a damn—and then just give up at the final hurdle."

"There is no final hurdle—no final frontier—not out there." George again swept a frustrated hand upward at the constellations in the flame-lit imperium, brought up short by a vague memory occurring to him of a similar conversation years before when he'd abruptly left Princeton, and the Judge had made some facetious remark to the effect: Well, you could always go off and sell your grandfather Altmann's paintings. "Let's save the infinitudes of astrophysics for dinner, when I've had the chance to down a few more glasses of this fine chardonnay. Besides, I think your stranded angels"—he nodded right and left of the hearth—"are quite enjoying our company after a long summer hiatus—cozy, aren't they?"

"Annie found them troubling, you know; she called them 'our weird sisters.' Not that she liked much that Stanford White—*'fussy, eclectic womanizer*—managed around here," he added, startling George for a moment in imitation of his wife's tone. "Except for the ceiling of course, the acoustics . . . ah, Annie's acoustics, but alas without her genius to make them sing." He shrugged, glancing over at the piano and placing the catalog on his side table. "Not that I can hear much or taste damn all at this point, wine or anything else, for that matter."

"Well, I'm planning to celebrate my success with you tonight with a hunk of roast beef that would put Gallagher's to shame. And, listen, this place was never meant for winter living. Why don't we arrange a Florida condo for five months, someplace nice, overlooking the beach—plenty of bikinis . . . well, maybe not on Felicity."

"George, I admire the effort." He waved a hand dismissively. "What makes you think I could afford such a thing? That I can afford to save this goddamn ship's keel ceiling and everything else? Besides, do I strike you as a snowbird ready for winter warehousing in an oldster's mausoleum?"

"Hey, they got pythons and monitor lizards down in the Everglades now, to go along with the alligators—you'll fit right in. Perched on the beach with a pair of binoculars for company and all the herons and ibises and pelicans your heart desires. It almost gets me a hard-on."

"I'm happy to die in my own bed, in my own home, in my own woods—in my own time—fall suits me, thank you. And I'm well past my sell-by date. I've outlived Dr. Dimock, who lasted till ninety-four. Besides, my world has gone extinct: colleagues, friends, my Yale class-mates—they've all rejoined their fathers . . . There's nothing left for me here. And to tell you the truth, the World Trade Center attack left me somewhat despondent."

"I was there . . ."

The Judge rattled on: "That there are people willing to commit such horrors in the name of religion is—I was going to say 'beyond me,' but of course it's not. The minute the religious get their hands on power, they saddle up their dark minions to destroy the nonbelievers. Thank God—who had nothing to do with it—we have a Constitution that keeps the snake-oil purveyors of organized religion from getting their megalomaniacal hands on the powers of the state. What enrages me . . . after we helped them, the Muslims, in Afghanistan against the Soviets, in Bosnia against the Serbs, in Kuwait against Saddam Hussein?" He flung a hand in disgust and reached for a sip of orange juice. "I thought with the defeat of fascism, the demise of communism, the world was finally safe, at least for a generation, from fanatical ideologies. Now it looks like you're going to be saddled with something even worse, a kind of ubiquitous apocalyptic violence that has no bounds and knows only one end: the end of civilization as we know it. Back to the dark days"—and he waved at the coruscating depths of the ship's keel ceiling above—"of poor Giordano Bruno."

"Auto-da-fé wasn't it? You always asked us to define it."

"Yes, yes, charges leveled at our Bruno by the Roman Inquisition, for which he was hung upside down and burned at the stake in Rome's Campo de' Fiori."

"Well, now we've got the end of history, right?" George raised his glass in a mock toast to the martyr's portrait over their heads. "And while we're on the subject of George Altmann, the artist, that is," and George reached again into his backpack for a manila envelope and slipped out the contents, handing the sketches to the Judge, "imagine my surprise when I found these sketches by Altmann pinned on the abandoned corkboard in your office. I've got to say, finding these sketches—your rogue's gallery, whatever—was quite a jolt. Mom was going on about them just last night at dinner."

The Judge put on his reading glasses once again and examined the first two sketches, those of Alger and Priscilla Hiss, holding them admiringly up to the lamplight.

"Goodness gracious . . . forgot about these." The Judge nodded appreciatively. "I guess Felicity—that was pretty quick—gave you my instructions for the office." He nodded at the sketch of Priscilla Hiss: pensive young face, soulful eyes with luxurious brows, hair swept back in a bun. "Long, long time ago I was in love with her. And now she's gone as well, predeceased Alger by twelve years." He motioned as if to fling the sketches on the fire. "I suppose I should have burned these," he said, nodding, "a *long* time ago."

"Why, when they were obviously important to you? And where the hell did they come from in the first place? They look as if they were done from life . . . What was George Altmann doing sketching these people"—he paused, searching for the accurate term—"these spies or whatever?"

The Judge began to go through the other sketches in his lap.

"Ghosts," he murmured. "Ghosts before they were ghosts."

"Ghosts?"

"Who would have believed it possible—it still doesn't seem possible, even if I lived through it. And what will your generation or future generations make of these fine intellects: Treasury official, White House adviser, State Department brass . . . the best minds Harvard could produce?"

"And what's with Volta Place?"

"Volta Place?" The Judge's voice rose as if mystified.

"An address with a date, very faint in pencil on the bottom of the sketch of Priscilla Hiss."

The Judge held up the sketch to his lamp and squinted and shook his head in frustration.

"My eyes aren't what they used to be."

George took the sketch and raised it to his face, squinting. "3415 Volta Place, September 7, 1937."

The Judge waved his hand as it was nothing. "The home of Alger and Priscilla in Washington." He sighed. "A long way back."

"I don't get it, Judge—what's all this ancient history about, and why me? The Altmann sketches, the newspaper clippings, the note cards—data points? Is this a matter of causality or correlation? And if cause and effect, about what, exactly? What's the gist of the thing? From what I remember—not that you ever talked about it much—I thought you defended Alger Hiss."

The Judge smiled gamely, as if a trifle uncertain of this fact.

"Ah, that's more like it: You're beginning to sound like a scientist again. What did you once tell me . . . what did you call all that stuff that's supposed to be holding the universe together—how I enjoyed those chats—but we can't see it? Your gallery's name, black something?"

"Dark matter."

"That's right, the stuff that keeps the whole shebang going."

"Well," George said, filling his glass once again, then holding it up to the firelight, pondering the dance of refracted photons, "there's both dark matter and dark energy. Between them, we figure, making up something like ninety-six percent of the mass of the universe, even if the stuff's invisible, or, worst luck, undetectable. Dark matter, an adjunct to gravity, acts to form galaxy clusters, while dark energy does just the opposite, kind of acts to disperse things—cosmic expansion—infinite expansion—a little unnerving, believe me. You might say that dark matter shapes ordinary matter into—this." He waved his hands toward the fire, where Annie's weird sisters watched with bated breath. "While dark energy is the dynamic force—change, I suppose—that keeps everything"—and he gestured extravagantly to the watching figures in the ceiling above—"rolling along even as it blows things to hell."

"Yes, yes, invisible, isn't that just a tad paradoxical? The world we think we know—heh?"

"Gravity is invisible as well, so is the electromagnetic force and the strong and weak interaction. Let me tell you: Seeing is not believing. We don't see the radio-wave part of the spectrum. Hell, if we could see microwaves, the whole sky would be luminous with the remnant of the cosmic microwave background. But at least dark matter is measurable in the way it dominates a galaxy's net mass. It guides the concentration of ordinary matter in the construction of the stars and planets that make up the Milky Way—you and me—everything we see and touch, including those damn sketches in your lap."

The Judge smiled gaily, his eyes touched with the happiness of memory. "This is like old times, when you were still in college." He held up a considered hand. "So, your dark matter is our friend, the creator of worlds. While dark energy is the destroyer of worlds . . . of me," he said with a wink.

"Like most things . . . over time, it takes a little of both for our friend Giordano's infinite realms to prove true."

"Then," and the Judge held up the sketch of a thoughtful, intense face in three-quarter profile, as if facing a jury, "perhaps my Alger is our dark energy, our invisible destroyer of worlds."

George bent forward in his chair as the wine went to his head. "Judge, just what are you getting at? Why am I here? Not that I'm not happy to see you. Where did the fucking sketches come from? And what am I supposed to do—me—with your memoir?"

"About fifteen years ago, nearing retirement from the bench, having failed to get the Supreme Court nomination that had been promised me by more than one administration, as I began researching my promised memoir, I realized that hidden in its pages was a potentially monstrous conspiracy, of which I may have been oblivious, or, worse, abetted or condoned." He gave a knowing tilt of his lush eyebrows. "Perhaps your invisible reality . . ."

At this, George reacted with exasperation, reaching for his backpack again. He withdrew the typescript and the volume of *Witness*, weighing them in his hands for emphasis.

"Tuning in gamma rays, we'd see titanic explosions all over the universe. So maybe it's just as well we don't. Rather than go crazy."

"A judge has no choice in the matters that come before his court."

"Okay, okay—Alger Hiss, the man you defended, right? Who was convicted of spying?"

"Convicted of perjury, to be precise, for lying about passing top-secret government documents, lying about when he knew Whittaker Chambers. When he died six years ago, some forty years after his perjury conviction, he was still trying to overturn that conviction, mocking the very judicial system he'd sworn to protect and defend." The Judge raised his chin, eyeing the manuscript in his grandson's hands. "Like I said, I just ran out of steam."

"Because of the stairs, or because Hiss was dead? Or a consensus reality beginning to slip from your grasp? Or even, common as dirt, payback? Isn't that why most people write memoirs—to get even?"

"*Entropy*—isn't that the right word?—you once told me, is the second law of thermodynamics. My mentor, Justice Holmes, was a stickler for the bon mot. A running down of energy and fading interest in my illusive quarry."

"You've had second thoughts about your client, Mr. Hiss?"

"Second—ha! How about third, fourth, and fifth!"

"But where does Altmann come into this—the sketches? Where did you find them?"

"I believe he gave them to me"—he motioned to the manuscript—"look it up in the memoir. Everything I know, or I should say *knew*, is in there, as of five years ago."

"So, that's where I come in, the editing part . . . what, a transfer of new energy? But I'm not an editor, certainly not a lawyer, and I still don't get it: You defended him and lost. Alice and Martha were just bitching last night at my opening about how you screwed up Hiss's defense. Are you having reservations about—what?—him, your strategy, your performance?"

"How loyal, my own daughters—condemning *me* in public for incompetence."

At this, George raised his eyebrows, the lines in his brow tightening.

"Let Alice do your editing—she's a lawyer, a scholar."

The Judge fixed him pointedly. "You have no idea of what she's capable."

George settled the pages in his lap. "Those people in the sketches—they're all dead and gone. Their world—I'm sorry—is dead and gone, too . . . long, long before I was even born. I know next to nothing about it—not my thing."

"And yet that didn't stop you from writing your catalog on George

Altmann, your namesake—your legacy—much less investigating the origins of the universe. A feat of time travel far beyond what I'm suggesting."

George replied with a sarcastic pout, "Judge, I don't know—who are these fucking people, and how come George Altmann sketched them back in 1937 at Volta Place?"

The Judge held up his catalog. "Your flesh and blood, to my great chagrin. The world you inherited whether you like it or not."

George, as if challenging his opponent, held up the copy of *Witness* and flipped the pages for emphasis. "And Whittaker Chambers?"

"*Your* reality check . . . to the memoir." The Judge smiled, as if delighted at the proceedings, the game at which he was a master. "My alter ego."

"Alter ego?"

"If Alger was innocent, *Witness* is close to a total fabrication, perhaps a work of brilliant fiction. If Alger was guilty, *Witness* speaks to an Alger and a Priscilla with an intimacy and love I never even imagined. A parallel universe—isn't that what you used to call it?—hidden to us all. Art or experience—heh?"

"Seems you made a fool of yourself attacking Chambers. So why are you still fucking around with my head?"

"For perjury, Alger served forty-four months. And then spent the next forty years trying to establish his innocence, if not in the eyes of the law, certainly in the eyes of public opinion."

"So, what's it to you, at this point?"

"It's nothing to me—not now at least, in a week or two or however long it takes."

"Well, that's damn generous of you, dumping whatever it is in my lap."

"It's what one doesn't know, George." A facetious glare. "As a *one-time* scientist, certainly you can understand. For some, I championed the defense of an innocent man; for others, I am a betrayer of liberalism and progressive values, the man who let the government, Hoover and Nixon, destroy the reputation of one of the finest New Deal patriots of his generation."

"But he *was* convicted—right? You lost the case—big deal. Isn't that enough?"

"Not if the thing is invisible, don't you see," and he waged an accusing finger, "like your dark energy."

"What, this—this Communist conspiracy? But surely, with the fall of the Berlin Wall over ten years ago, there's nothing left to conspire about."

"Except the truth—your consensus reality—which changes everything, just as with your George Altmann, the artist you're now proclaiming to the world as a lost genius."

"Sorry, the past doesn't change, even in Einstein's space-time."

"Everything." The Judge gestured broadly and held up the sketches with a knowing look.

"Okay, I get it," George slurred. "You're looking for some kind of reproducible thought experiment, a theory perhaps, or even a smoking gun? Or is it a new data point, some variable that can be plugged into an algorithm that will ease you into your grave?"

The Judge smiled as if mightily pleased now that his grandson had grasped the nettle. "There was something ten years ago, when the Soviet Union collapsed, access to KGB files, but nothing conclusive came of it. The uncertainty, you see, the doubt about one's life story, about not being able to quite trace the path you followed with any confidence." He shook his head and reached to take sip of his orange juice. "It sometimes feels like I've lived two different lives."

George grunted and turned a pensive stare to the faces of the carved angels, holding up his vertical palm, tipping left and then right.

"Two paths, parallel universes separated by a question mark—a flip of a coin."

"If Alger Hiss was indeed a spy, it is a very different world from the one where he was an innocent man. And I sometimes I feel I lived through both"—he smiled knowingly—"a difficult, even curious, proposition to manage when facing the grave."

"But you knew him, you defended him. Surely if anyone on the planet would know the truth, it would be you—right?"

"But that's just the point, don't you see. Those closest to him were the ones who were most blinded by the brilliant light of his talent and dedication as we thought we knew it. I went to Harvard Law with him, we both clerked for Oliver Wendell Holmes, and when he sought me out, he insisted that Oliver would have wanted me to join his defense team on his second trial. 'A matter of loyalty,' as he put it. And it's still no clearer to me, now, if he was what we supposed him to be—a man of surpassing virtue, or one of the greatest con artists of all time. An actor of protean power. A man with a peculiar brilliance, able to keep thousands, if not millions, of people under his dreadful spell, a harbinger of chaos, to literally blow up our world." The Judge tapped the sketch. "A fiendish mimic holding up the mirror of your heart's desire, with charisma to burn. And yet if that jury was right: a traitor to friends and country, a Beelzebub intent on destroying the very civilization of which he portrayed himself its most luminous incarnation."

George sat up, head cocked, not unmoved at the vehemence of this outpouring.

"Or, to hear Alice tell it last night at dinner: a martyr to that great right-wing conspiracy headed by Hoover's FBI and Richard Nixon."

"Don't mention that man's name in this house."

"Hoover or Nixon?"

"One a bungler, the other a scoundrel of the first rank."

"Well, the FBI sure messed up on the World Trade Center. But what about all the other Altmann subjects? Conspiracy theories give me the creeps," George mumbled between sips of wine.

"Why would a man so convicted, who lost all appeals, spend the rest of his life trying—destroying the sanity of his wife—to overturn the jury's decision and bring the world around to his view? By the seventies and eighties, certainly in leftist circles, he was a conquering hero again, a paragon of virtue and martyred symbol of everything that was wrong with America."

"But I still don't get it. *You* defended him."

"I failed him."

"Did you really believe him when you defended him? Not that it matters in *your* line of work, I guess."

The Judge laughed, nodding, his weary gaze drifting off. "Alger wined and dined me on his innocence, his assertions that Whittaker Chambers was a psychopath, that the FBI had rigged all the evidence, that the Republicans were in cahoots to destroy all that had been gained by the New Deal. And I believed him. Well, part of me *wanted* to believe . . . There was always something about Alger that was unfathomable."

"So, he lied to you—is that it?" George flipped the pages of the memoir in his lap. "And your memoir is your way of payback, to get you off the hook—*your* reputation?"

"The least of his sins, even if the jury convicted him of lying. We didn't have much of a case. The physical evidence, the stolen top-secret State Department documents that Chambers produced, was irrefutable. And yet, Alger walked out of that court and never spoke another word to me, all the while maintaining he'd been framed, telling everyone I'd been too stupid to make the case for his acquittal. Behind the scenes, throughout the appeals process and later, he blamed his defense team."

"So, I get it: He played you for a fool and you're still pissed off at him."

"Oh, I was shunned for years: by his supporters for failing him, by his opponents for defending him in the first place—including my own son. The Left proclaimed Alger the first victim of McCarthy's and Nixon's depredations, their attack on progressive virtue. They blamed me, too, of course, for insisting we put a psychiatrist—two of them, in fact—on the witness stand. *That* was at Alger's insistence. I did everything in my power to destroy the good name of the prosecution's star witness, Whittaker Chambers. For my troubles, I was made a laughingstock in the courtroom, but I did what I was hired to do. Even as it devastated my family. But I didn't dwell on it; I had a career to follow, a family to support. I was content to let time settle old scores and history tell the truth. Alger, if he really was a spy, part of an insidious network, a conspiracy to destroy our country, well . . . one had to figure that over time, as the decades passed, in all probability, someone or something was bound to shake loose, tell all. Or some conclusive evidence turn up, somebody—something had to give . . ."

"And did it?"

"You can read Hiss's *Times* obituary of six years ago: still a controversial figure, an unproved case of spying, 'a division of opinion to this day.' I believe his son is still out there pleading his innocence."

"And so . . ." George held his glass up to the fire as an alchemist might, to examine the delicate precipitant of gold, through which the prismatic flames offered a hypnotic counterpoint to their echoing voices in the rafters above. "Dark energy, huh"—he shrugged, searching—"change—what?—friend or foe, or maybe just a big badass black hole ready to swallow all who venture beyond its event horizon."

"Ah, how I loved those conversations from your Princeton days." The Judge smiled nostalgically, his voice rising. "George, one owes this life something . . . order against chaos. What I struggled to give you and your cousins, much less my own children."

"Mozart played to perfection . . . or was that Annie—Annie's way?"

The Judge stared intently into the fire, his haggard, lined, once-so-handsome face drooping now as he searched among the embers.

"Perfection . . . How I miss her."

"I know you do."

"I neglected her and I hope to make amends in the memoir and see that she gets her due—even her recordings are now unavailable." He nodded. "I want you to promise me that."

George tapped the cover of Whittaker Chambers's *Witness*, as if in acknowledgment of the inscription to Annie within. He opened the cover to the frontispiece, about to read, but something held him back.

"If you'll have dinner with me."

The Judge sank back into the red leather of his chair.

"For years I was too busy on the bench to think much more about the Hiss affair. Oh, I suppose I kept a vague half-open eye cocked to the past. But as I neared retirement, as younger scholars asked me about the case, as I was encouraged to write my memoir . . . I kept getting stuck. As if some cog had jammed and nothing in my life quite made sense. Instead of putting it behind me, I found myself haunted by the faces in these sketches: all connected to Alger, many who died under mysterious circumstances—suicides, falls from windows or staircases— or those who conveniently disappeared south of the border or behind the Iron Curtain and so were unavailable to testify."

"You're talking about a massive cover-up?"

"Crimes, and maybe much worse, that went unrecorded and unpunished. Like your dark energy—gods of deception: invisible but shaping the reality we lived through."

"So, this is not just, well, personal . . ."

"Of course it's personal: to enlist your wife, Priscilla—to drive her to despair and separation—and later enlist your only son in your lies— your flesh and blood—and then tour college campuses to enlist a new generation to your cause, to continue on your path of deception after everything—when the world has moved on. Why not just let the world forget? Why persist unless you're a maniac or a monster . . . unless there is something bigger—like you suggested, your *consensus reality*—that lie—which at all costs must be sustained." The Judge cocked his head as he once might have at the bench, questioning the admissibility of evidence. "Perhaps he had no choice in the matter."

"Unless he was really innocent," George replied.

"Anything is possible."

"You don't know how true that is, how truly scary that is when glimpsed on a cosmic scale." George shook his head, thinking. "And the *something bigger*?"

"Call it your dark energy."

"And your memoir?" Again George hefted the pages.

"Remains unfinished and unavailing to time without any new evidence in the matter of Alger Hiss."

"But the sketches, George Altmann's sketches. Did Altmann know these people?"

"Your grandfather, George Altmann, worked as a court sketch artist during the Hiss trials. He handed me the sketches at the beginning of the second trial. I assumed he was giving them to me as some kind of souvenir. Frankly, I didn't pay much attention at the time; there was simply too much going on."

"But according to your corkboard, your rogue's gallery: Alger Hiss, Priscilla Hiss, Harry Dexter White, Laurence Duggan, Lauchlin Currie, and the others were all possible spies?"

"So it has been suggested—mostly by right-wing crazies like Joe McCarthy—over the years, *and* as the circumstantial evidence piles up, but again, without the necessary proof that would hold up in court."

"The sketches seem all of a piece, as if they were done at the same sitting."

"Your grandfather was probably in the Communist Party, like so many artists in the thirties. And he worked in Washington—as I'm sure you know—in the late thirties for the WPA, a top administrative role to support worthy artists during the Depression with mural commissions and the like. I mention him in the memoir, something about a sketch of the Hisses' child at their home on Volta Place. Perhaps he did the sketches on a whim, in some kind of Party meeting or study group."

George examined the Judge's worn face with wary skepticism.

"Now wait a minute. I just did a show and catalog and biography on my grandfather, and nowhere—no way—did I find anything about his being a Communist."

The Judge smiled. "So shocked, young man—you of the invisible world."

"If I didn't know you so well, I'd almost suspect you've had this new data point up your sleeve for some time—a long time." The Judge only offered another enigmatic smile, much enjoying the give-and-take. "So, you're accusing George Altmann, my grandfather, of being a Communist?"

"Don't look so appalled, common as dishwater back in the day. Well," the Judge said, holding up the sketches, "he clearly had some kind of contact with Alger and Priscilla Hiss and their Washington circle. Check the memoir."

"Something . . . aren't you being just a bit cagey? Or is this just your way of seeing to it that I edit the damn thing?"

"Trust me, my mind ain't what it used to be. And I'm a little loath to put something into the hands of my publisher that hasn't been vetted by someone I trust."

"Judge, I appreciate your confidence, but, as I said, I found nothing about his being a Communist."

"Well, now your sleuthing"—a wicked grin—"just turned up these sketches—evidence." He cocked his head with an expression of long-suffering tribulation, sighing. "By the late forties, they were all covering their tracks."

"George Altmann died in 1949, on Christmas Eve." George swished the wine in his glass, pondering. "Come to think of it, wouldn't that have been slap-bang in the middle of your Hiss trial?"

This seemed to go unheeded or unacknowledged.

"It was never against the law to be a member of the Communist Party. By 1939, after the Nazi-Soviet pact, he probably saw the light and gave it up. The smart ones, the good people did."

"But the sketches, at least as a group, *are* proof—"

"Of nothing." The Judge's voice rose in unaccustomed alarm. "They could have been done anywhere at any time. And, like I said, being a member of the Communist Party was not in itself a crime, although it often as not led in that direction. But without context or intent, inadmissible in court."

"But why would Altmann have given them to you, the defense lawyer for Alger Hiss?"

"It's all down there in my memoir." The Judge waved his hand dismissively as he caught his grandson's squint of annoyance. "I think I buried them in the defense files. Perhaps the evidence burdened Altmann in some way."

"Why give them to you? Why didn't he just destroy them?"

"Perhaps he wanted someone to know he'd given them up for safekeeping. A comradely gesture."

George noted the slight upward shift of the Judge's left eyebrow, which in mere mortals might be interpreted as a note of guilt.

"My grandfather Altmann fell off the Sawkill Bridge, froze to death on Christmas Eve." George grimaced, as if strangely disbelieving his own sad, dreamy voice.

"We were in the middle of the trial. I don't think I had any idea at the time."

"It wasn't widely reported. He was an alcoholic walking back from his favorite bar in Woodstock when he slipped on the ice and fell off the bridge into Sawkill Creek. Some in town thought he'd committed suicide; the family preferred to call it an accident. That's about as much as I ever got from Mom, or my father."

The Judge looked down at the sketches in his hand.

"Do you ever hear from your father?"

"Never."

The Judge shook his head. "Well, one thing for sure: George Altmann was unavailable as a witness for the prosecution."

George shot back, "Okay, okay—now you've got my attention. So what am I supposed to make of that?"

"Check on page sixty-five of that book you've been so casually fingering in your lap, where I've underlined."

George opened the Judge's copy of *Witness* and scanned the page.

"Let me paraphrase," continued the Judge. "Any idiot can commit murder, but it requires an artist to pull off a good natural death."

"Any fool," George corrected, now reading the original. "What the fuck does that mean?" he exclaimed, not a little impressed with the old man's ability to recall things when he wanted to.

"It was something of a specialty of the KGB, according to Chambers. At least four of the people who knew Hiss, either in connection with his perjury charge or as a possible Soviet agent, and who could have testified at the trial, met ambiguous ends. These four," he said, handing George the sketches one by one: "White by an overdose of digitalis; Duggan in a fall from a sixteen-story window; Marvin Smith, a friend of Hiss's in the Justice Department, who signed a crucial piece of evidence, an automobile-transfer document, fell to his death in a Justice Department stairwell; and William Remington, a convicted spy, was later murdered in Lewisburg prison." The Judge glanced again at the open pages of *Witness* in his grandson's lap. "As Chambers wrote, the Party has two critical problems: to protect its underground apparatuses and prevent defections. Defections shattered the morale of loyal underground workers and so had to be punished swiftly. No one, it seems, got away with defying the Party with impunity."

George now nervously fingered the sketches, trying to steady a slight tremor.

"Are you suggesting that George Altmann, because he might have been a Communist, a potential witness against Hiss, could have been in danger, as well?"

"Anything is possible."

"You're not suggesting he was a spy?"

"Hard to believe that of an artist working for the WPA. But you're his grandson; you just wrote an outstanding essay about his life and work, claiming his genius for the ages. How did you explain his untimely death?"

George shuffled the four sketches in his lap, holding them out one by one to the firelight, staring intently at the flame-lit faces so beautifully rendered in his grandfather's hand. The wine, the ambiguity, and now the dreaded specter of doubt began to claw at his chest.

"You were on Alger Hiss's fucking defense team; how would you have liked to have George Altmann testifying for the prosecution about these sketches?"

The Judge smiled. "I like that—your instinct is to defend him."

"Damn right, and I've done more than that. I've revived his reputation; I've brought him back to life. While so many of his contemporaries—like Raphael Soyer—stuck with their insipid social realism, falling by the wayside, while he persevered with a new abstract style, reinventing himself and forging a modernist canon that will stand the test of time, even as he was vilified and dismissed in the forties by his fellow artists, critics, and dealers."

A look of sheer delight flickered on the Judge's face.

"Perhaps you've answered your own question."

"And what question is that? I'm not sure I need any of this."

"You can tell a lot about a man by the enemies he makes."

"You're not—you can't be suggesting that somebody tried, that he was . . . pushed?" His voice broke as he struggled to get the words out.

"At the very least, he must have broken with the Party."

George reared up with sudden indignation. "And who, exactly, are *your* enemies?"

The Judge laughed, clearly enjoying the spirited exchange.

"Do you mean Time? I mean, who's left besides my loyal daughters?" He laughed again. "Time—what say you? In the historical record, in the transcript of the trial, I defended Alger Hiss, and tried to destroy, by any means, the prosecution's star witness." He glanced at the book in George's lap. "That's how I will be remembered by history. Possibly overshadowing my record of opinions for the Second Circuit."

"And if I agree to edit your memoir, keep it out of Aunt Alice's hands—isn't that what this is really all about?—do I take it verbatim, at face value, or do I assume it is purely self-serving, perhaps a score-settling final testament?"

"You're really asking what's in it for you."

"Me?"

"George, I've known you for over thirty years. A true scientist is only interested in one thing."

"I'll tell you one *thing* I'm not into: conspiracy theories! Especially ones long dead."

The Judge flicked his eyebrows, his eyes sparking, mouth twisted with a hint of cruelty or a matter-of-fact tediousness.

"It is unfinished, or perhaps that is the wrong word. Let's say incomplete. There is a provision in my will to compensate you handsomely for your trouble. For the memoir may describe a world that really didn't exist if the underlying premise is all wrong."

"If Alger Hiss was truly part of a wider conspiracy?"

The Judge sat back, his hand shaking. "The ambiguity of the thing is almost too terrifying to contemplate."

"I'm sorry, you're tired. I didn't mean to press you on the subject."

"No, you're right. That is how a scientist should respond, with skepticism until proven correct. Or is it curiosity—I loved that about you—that drives the greatest scientific minds?"

"Guilty as charged," said George, now trying to lighten the moment.

"Ah, but who cares. Alger is dead, Priscilla is gone, and Chambers— they're all dead, and I'm soon on my way to join them." He bowed his head and placed his hand over his heart. "And Annie . . . here with me."

George hastened to fill his glass, to gird himself for the fight.

"That's so unlike you: the man who preached the importance of truth, of service to mankind, who explained to us kids the nobility of a legal system that protected the rights and freedoms of every man, woman, and child, that evolved from the people, from the common law—'the genius of the generations' I think you called it: a thing unplanned but embodying the accretions of law and the successful and practical customs of ordinary men over time. Laws based on precedent and adversarial argument, genteel competition and natural selection of the tried-and-true." George raised his glass in salute. "How did I do?"

"Did I really tell you all that? Goodness, you always were an apt listener. Perhaps I should have encouraged you to go into law instead of paying for you to become a world-class physicist."

"Astrophysicist. The going was pretty good except for a few wrinkles like quantum weirdness, dark matter and dark energy . . . that invisible world. With infinite expansion as a kicker."

"So," the Judge said, bending forward and eyeing his grandson, "unless time can be reversed or even revisited, what's done is done." He slipped back in his chair with a sigh, as if he'd quite played out his hand. "You needn't bother with the memoir—just forget it."

The silence swam between them, filled with the urgent crackle of burning logs.

"Unless you believe, like my Princeton doctoral adviser, that the cosmic dials are always being nudged, or Einstein, who claimed that the distinction between past, present, and future is only a stubbornly persistent illusion. I would say that there's still plenty of room to allow for some experimental uncertainty. That the internal reality, really the subjective reality in our head, must ultimately be dependent on the consensus reality, which we share with the universe." George stood and walked to the fire, tossing in another log, then resting his weight on the head of the bowed angel. "You see, Judge, there *is* a measurable external reality, the world of mathematical descriptions, but suffice it to say, the consensus reality—you, me, and our two twisted sisters here—is a stubborn beast, often unyielding to proof positive: We fail more often than not to put a premium on experimental reliability and repeatable evidence." He caressed the head of the angel. "So, when was the last time *you* dipped into the data pool?"

"My head may still be attached, unlike that of poor Louis Seize"— he gestured to the frozen clock hands on the mantel—"but right now you've got it spinning. My clipping services went out of business years ago. I'm down to the *Times* and the *Journal* on my better days."

"No television news, no computers, no Internet or Wi-Fi—it's what I always liked about Hermitage: Nothing ever changes here."

"It does for me. The body goes, the memory goes, and with it the reason to go on."

"You really should have been keeping up with the Yankees. They're on the way to the play-offs and Jeter is having a great season."

"Tedious. They all have such strange names—*Jeter*—these days."

George laughed.

"Before we go in to dinner, let's try a little thought experiment. What, precisely, would it take to affect our consensus reality?" He held up his mobile phone toward the lake and the extinguished sunset, toward the ceiling, where, in the firelight and the soft glow of the Tiffany lamps, the figure of Phaeton hung suspended in space, trailing flaming embers. "Hey, a miracle, I have one bar. Let's tap into some of the cosmic microwave background in the way of a Google search." He paused. "Alger Hiss . . . Soviet spy . . . new . . ." He typed on his phone's keypad with a theatrical flourish and waited.

"What's this *Google* thing?"

George held up his hand with one finger raised, as if the cosmos might indeed be at his beck and call.

"Hey . . ." He squinted at his phone. "A controversial new book published a few years ago by Random House, *The Haunted Wood*, by Allen Weinstein and Alexander Vassiliev, containing new information from Soviet archives, and relying on recently declassified Soviet decrypted cable traffic from the forties, points conclusively to Alger Hiss as an agent of influence for Soviet military intelligence. Conclusive proof, as well, according to the authors, that after Yalta, Alger Hiss was briefly in Moscow, where he received the Order of the Red Star from the head of Soviet intelligence."

The Judge, his blue-gray eyes sparked with flame, stared, a little bewildered, at his grandson.

"Allen . . . Allen Weinstein, you said?"

"Do you know him, the author?"

"Familiar, somehow . . ."

"Hey, he's the archivist of these here United States."

The Judge still appeared bewildered. "Oh, can't be the same person."

George snapped his phone shut with the satisfied grin of a chess master who just deployed his queen for the coup de grâce.

"Don't know about you, but I'm starved," he said. "I have a feeling that a grand dinner celebrating the life and work of George Altmann might just give us a chance to get better acquainted. Not to mention how you bribed my mother with the red Merc to deliver these sketches to Woodstock—and my fucking father, which is—how fucked-up a parallel universe is that—why, come to think of it, I'm even here at all." He went to the entrance to the dining room and banged the gong, pausing as the sweet reverberations filled the ship's keel ceiling like a whispering breeze across invisible sails. Then coming back to where the Judge sat, not waiting for Felicity, he maneuvered the walker over to help his grandfather up. Withdrawing his outstretched hand for a cautionary moment, he delivered a sharp glance of knowing suspicion and smiled icily. "But I'll bet I'm not telling you anything you don't already know."

6

The Neversink Way

IN A MORNING daze, George navigated the winding back roads of Hermitage, heading for the Kingston highway and Woodstock, with an eagerly anticipated stop at the Gunks to pick up Wendy Bradley. Sleepy and not a little hungover, after staying up half the night reading the Judge's memoir and a sampling of his many underlinings in Whittaker Chambers's *Witness*, he found himself utterly bewildered. More than once he'd been awakened, as he had as a child, by a persistent screech owl and the honking alarm of geese on the lake: "Fucking snappers . . ." At the dinner table, it was just like old times, the Judge eating heartily while assaulting his grandson with jocular insinuations as if over a high-stakes poker game while they negotiated the disposition of the memoir.

"No, Alice isn't to get her hands on it until Norton publishes the damn thing—with your expert guidance and final say. I've told my editor—a nice fella—there as much *and* it's in the contract."

—

Opening the Tahoe's windows and sunroof, he sought the lustrations of the forty-degree morning air, shivering as he inhaled the sobering sunlight flooding the crimson canopy overhead.

Even scenes of home ground, overgrown pastures of second-growth forest hemmed in by stone walls, failed to lighten his mood as he tried to process the seeds of uncertainty the Judge had so deftly sown: "So, at least you're curious about the Altmann sketches—heh—that's always a good start." As if life was just one long journey of deceit and disaster—and he better damn well get used to it. He slowed, studying the delicate mosaics of moss-capped bluestone walls—"ghost walls," they called them as kids—wondering which of the early settlers had so painstaking exhumed the rocks and set them with such loving care. "I've included much about Handytown in the memoir, certainly for Annie's sake, her favorite place—who else in the family will pass on the stories if not you?" The Judge had relished telling tales about the dirt-poor first settlers during their hikes, a duty passed down from Dr. Dimock—retold with a priestlike intoning, if not the Apostles' Creed recited in a sylvan nave—that something of their humble shades might be kept alive.

"Children, we are their blood offering." A dramatic pause. "Go look it up, George—don't they teach you the *Odyssey* at Woodstock High? Why your damn mother insists on keeping you in such a rural slum, I cannot fathom."

Every spring, as a young man, the Judge had walked the woods with Dr. Dimock on expeditions to repair the old walls, when all they still corralled were stalwart mullions (cowboy's toilet paper, so he'd joshed the cousins with a smile), wild aster, milkweed, thistle, faded meadowsweet, grizzled goatsbeard, dowdy Queen Anne's lace, and, in the fall, as in the present moment, the first scattering of barberries, flecks of brilliant red against a blur of mauve shadow.

More than ever, George felt the merging of all these perennial pasts, just as the naming of names had linked him to the visible universe, as the Judge had taught him how to identify birds and their songs, the names of wildflowers, their colors, petal configuration, patterns, the very thing that had drawn him to the patterns and colors of the constellations, as if the ship's keel ceiling had, all along, been the sacred keystone to his visual memory.

As the woodland meadows gave way to the deeper shadows of a hemlock glade, he found himself systematically replaying snatches of dinner conversation. He couldn't escape the feeling that the Judge, back in classic form, had thoroughly sandbagged him. Recalling his mother's admonition: "Just remember one thing about your grandfather: He's not *just* smarter than you; he's *way* smarter than you can even imagine. He covers his tracks better than any Lenape ever could."

Even if his mind was clearly going—a perfect excuse to ignore or finesse inconsistent or inconvenient facts.

"You'll find it in the memoir or, if not, we'll consult and put it in there."

George shivered and sped on, as if to escape the sharp blades of serried sunlight slicing and dicing the hemlock gloom that led to the main road.

How had his ruse of a celebratory dinner at Hermitage to save the life—at least for a time—of one grandfather been confounded by the possible murder of another? Mention of which he'd found nowhere in the memoir, at least not on a quick inspection.

A possibility that also pointed up the ineptitude of his catalog essay on George Altmann, which clearly failed to get the most basic biographical details straight. A Communist Party member in the thirties? Possibly eliminated by a KGB hit team on a bitterly cold Christmas Eve in 1949? A possibility, something of a KGB specialty, noted time and again in the Judge's underlined passages of Chambers's *Witness*, which had taken on a harrowing immediacy in his untutored mind. Such things really had happened back in the thirties, forties, and fifties! Chambers, so it seemed, had only escaped a similar fate by the skin of his teeth.

He cringed, shivering with cold at the Judge's repeated refrain.

"Order of the Red Star . . . Order of the Red Star, well I'll be." At which a wicked yellow glint flared in the Judge's blue-gray eyes, as if he'd caught sight of the inferno itself in the crackling dining room fireplace, further fueling that laboring but still canny lawyerly mechanism behind the extravagant eyebrows. Eyes relishing the silver trout pole-dancing on the candelabra. "Well, Dr. Dimock spent his winters in Palm Beach, after all. So why not a migration to warmer climes."

For George, the meal was an extended ordeal of agonized doubt, as if he was being forced to watch a deliberate reshuffle of a well-worn tarot deck, but these with unfamiliar faces and unfamiliar names in unfamiliar sequences—in patterns he couldn't conceptualize, with implications he couldn't yet visualize or categorize in his mind. Instead of a celebration for the revived reputation of George Altmann the artist, he found that a stone had been removed from the Judge's solonic heart, enough to enable him to preside at a grand jury inquiry of one into the death of George's namesake.

"Listen, Priscilla was obviously his first victim." And the Judge held up his glass of Veuve Clicquot, where the bubbles swam in amber flame. "She was such a vivacious live wire on our birding walks in Riverside Park. Her arguments were always vehement on issues of social justice, but nothing beyond romantic New Dealism. Clearly, Alger drew her in deeper and deeper, and in the end drove her to despair, mental illness, and an early death. Rotten bastard . . . unforgivable." Switching to his Medoc, he swirled the rich reds, reflected in the white pallor of his cheek, as he examined the dregs like an alchemist of old. "As to the fate of the others: White, Duggan, Smith, and Remington—and now I suppose your grandfather Altmann—your guess is as good as mine."

And when George had pressed him on Chambers, he said, "A deluded creature who awoke from the depths of degeneracy—escaping Dante's eighth circle—personal and ideological, but brought with him profound insights into the political and existential morass we found ourselves in during those dark times. My attacks on him in court are, of course, unforgivable, an ineradicable stain on my reputation." Fork raised, impaled pink beef hovering, he pointed it at George's heart. "That's where you come in."

Pressed for more details on George Altmann's sketches—the circumstances of his possession of them in the first place—the Judge continued to plead vagueness or faulty memory, sticking to his story about having had them dumped in his lap sometime before the trial began. "Perhaps on the street or the steps outside the courthouse on Foley Square; it was all a rush, a blur. Whatever the case, it awaits you in the memoir, George. And yes, yes, years later, I dug them out of the defense files and foolishly tried to get Cordelia to return them to Altmann's son after Annie's death: a misbegotten point of honor, I suppose."

As family lore would have it, it was August 1969, when the innocent seventeen-year-old Cordelia, the most beautiful of the Dimock girls, had run off with the Judge's red Mercedes coupe, disappearing for a two-week assignation with the crazy, drug-addled Jimmy Altmann, electrician and soundman, hired by Jock Roberts and Joel Rosenman to build the electrical and sound systems for the concert stage on Max Yasgur's dairy farm.

"So, there you have it, George. I guess the nine sketches are your birthright, so to speak. Enough that you'll have to at least read the damn memoir—and Chambers where you find him a help—and let the chips fall where they may. I leave it up to you to lay me low where I've been unfair or gone astray or not told the truth, the whole truth, and nothing but the truth. That's all that matters—now that we *know* . . ." The old man took a deep breath and closed his tired, watery eyes, as if savoring the moment of clarity. "I trust you to do the right thing . . . for Hermitage, of course." A cryptic smile. "In truth, dear George, the money dwindles. The proceeds from my apartment in the city is almost exhausted, the principal of my stock portfolio is well-invaded, and my pension is my pension, and the property taxes on Hermitage, not to mention the maintenance for this dinosaur, have almost tripled in the last decade." He swished his glass of wine as if again exploring for portents of doom among the dregs. "You're the only one who would want to take it on, who cares—but you'll never make enough of a living to keep it going. Even if I left it to you, to sell, perhaps, the others would only resent you more than they already do."

"Well, thank God for small blessings."

"Oh don't go sulking on me. None of my children could afford it, either, so no need to feel bad. But I have a responsibility, damn it, for that ship's keel ceiling, if nothing else—for Annie's sake. I've explored with Yale the possibility of the art museum's taking it on, as a retreat for scholars or the like. But for all I know, they'd break the agreement and take the ceiling and reassemble it in the new addition to the museum they're planning."

"It wouldn't be the same," George pleaded, displaying visceral horror at the idea.

"Damn right it wouldn't. If only you could have heard your grandmother Annie play in the great room." He shook his head with pained wonder. "I owe it to her, you know; she still inhabits . . ." His voice fell away, as if exhausted.

Transfixed by this awkward communion of wine and bloodred beef and flickering candlelight, George felt the rumble of shifting tectonic plates, or was it the rusty gears of the Judge's traplike brain . . . the terrible glow of a distant supernova, seeding interstellar space with the makings of yet another undreamed life?

George had held up his nearly empty wineglass in mocking salute.

"To the right fucking thing . . ."

In that moment, so George would realize three months later, walking the beach at Siesta Key—and confirmed seventeen years after that with the first detection of gravitational ripples in the fabric of space-time—the Judge, like Einstein, had cagily entrapped him: set in motion the underlying dynamic of space and time in his soul. How the past inexorably catches one up, like a hidden current sweeping one out, a riptide bending one's floundering soul along time's curving rack, and so merging the eternal present inextricably with the calamities of the past that first gave it life.

—

George blew on his fingers, clutched the steering wheel as if for dear life, while stoically keeping the windows wide as he picked up speed on Route 7 south and began snaking his way out of the Catskills. With the wind and cold in his face, he felt more at one with the passing landscape, with the whispered flow of the Bush Kill on his right, where, on the hillside above, cloaked in dew-spangled mountain laurel and hemlock, scattershot of yellow and orange maples elbowing their way in the sunshine, the defunct roadbed of the Port Jervis & Monticello Railroad descended the mountain. This the navelike trail of so many childhood hikes to the Neversink aqueduct. And then, as if memory invoked, the bright obsidian back of the Neversink, fresh from the peaks of the upper Catskills, careened in from the left, passing under the road bridge to reappear in foaming white rapids along his route south. Once the companionship of the Neversink along this winding stretch of road had soothed his end-of-summer blues as he faced a return home to detested Woodstock, which had barely felt like home, not since his father had left when he was eight, and the miseries of high school commenced at twelve, where a science whiz kid, president of the astronomy and math club, was an object of ridicule and bullying. The popular kids' parents had been mostly artists or musicians—the famous ones—while techies like Jimmy Altmann—a cuckold dumped by his adulterous wife—were on the lowest rung of the social totem pole.

"Then again, maybe we should be thankful—what say you, George? Without Alger Hiss . . . I guess you wouldn't be here."

With that cryptic smirk of paradox and a histrionic "Goodnight, my dear Horatio," the Judge had signaled to Felicity, who had then led him, wobbling, off on his walker to his bedroom, cracking out orders as he went.

"Enough!" George banged the steering wheel, closed the windows, and turned the heater on high.

Thawing, he gazed out at the spume-scarred back of the Neversink, surging through doglegs and weirs of massive boulders . . . bringing to mind careless days of childhood and first learning to cast among the quieter eddies and pools where the river slowed as it neared the abutments of Roebling's aqueduct.

"Fuck, fuck, fuck." George continued banging the steering wheel to jog his brain to a higher pitch. How had the Judge managed to put the kibosh on almost an entire year of researching his Altmann catalog essay? He had scoured the artist's papers and files, meticulously building a biographical context for the paintings, a neatly constructed silver lining to the artist's alcoholism, depression, and suicide. Redemption for his tragic death in the genius of the late abstract landscapes.

It was Christmas Eve, 1949, a wintery night, cold and unfor-
giving. George Altmann had worked the whole day in his
studio barn. Even with the ice on the roads, he told his beloved
wife he'd walk the mile into town to pick up some groceries and
have a drink with his cronies—"a quick celebration with the
fellas"—at the local tavern, which had been his habit for years.
His friends said he lingered longer than usual, downing glasses
of Christmas cheer. Some said two or three whiskies; some said
five or six. Some said he seemed pleased, if frustrated, with his
current work. Frustrated that he had to spend much of the week
in New York, earning a living as a court reporter, sketching
trials for the Tribune. *Some said he seemed a little depressed,*
uneasy, fidgety, and maybe a tad apprehensive of the lonely
walk home in freezing weather as he fortified himself against
the cold with a last tumbler. He never made it home that night
after leaving the tavern. Two hours later, his half-crazed
wife and son found his frozen body lying facedown under the
Sawkill Creek Bridge. The police report and the coroner's indi-
cate that, sufficiently inebriated, he might have slipped and
somehow fallen over the bridge's guardrail. The family accepted
the verdict of accident, but for years the rumors in Woodstock
persisted of depression and suicide.

That—damn it—was still the truth as best he knew it.

Even as those rumors of suicide had taken on a life of their own, persisting like a jarring dissonance throughout his father's childhood, if not poisoning his own embittered and chaotic adolescence.

Except now, that fatal phrase—"Order of the Red Star"—gleaned from the ether, taking wing on the Judge's lips, bronze medal of an armed cadre dangling from a red ribbon, had taloned his mind like a double dose of Adderall (an addiction kicked only in his last year at Princeton): If Alger Hiss was a spy, an agent of influence seated at Roosevelt's right hand at Yalta, member of an underground cell, as suggested by George Altmann's sketches, then the KGB might well have done everything in its power to protect their main man—certainly if Chambers was to be believed.

An eventuality that the Judge had musingly alluded to, as if the thing was only coming clear in his own mind after fifty years, when George pressed him.

"Now you see, George, the defense team—not that I grasped this fully at the time—and I got hired late in the game—had assiduously cleared the decks of everybody who might prove a threat, neutralizing—now that you bring it up—all those in Altmann's sketches who survived—Laughlin Currie and Noel Field—or who might have testified for the government. All with the exception of one, Hede Massing, a beautiful redhead, a Comintern apparatchik, who knew a passel of the KGB's Washington agents, including, so she testified, Alger Hiss. Lovely Hede, like her fellow KGB operative, Whittaker Chambers, would never have allowed a likeness of herself to be done, much less of her agents— and certainly not in a group setting. For that matter, hard to believe that Alger Hiss would have allowed such a foolhardy thing, unless Pross somehow finagled it. The defense team in the first trial had scuttled Massing's testimony by appealing to a sympathetic judge. But prosecutor Murphy and the government managed to sneak her by our judge—Judge Goddard, who presided at the second—and sink us. A quid pro quo, I might add, for allowing the defense to call two psychiatric experts to disparage the sanity, if not morals, of Chambers, much to my horror and shame. How she—dear Hede, a turncoat—survived, is beyond me. And Chambers, as *Witness* makes clear, survived by subterfuge and meticulous planning, and only because he'd taken precautions by hiding the incriminating top-secret State Department documents—his lifesaver— threatening to reveal Hiss's stolen papers if he or his family were harmed. Later, he became too well known to the public and press to be physically eliminated. Although, as he makes clear in *Witness*, he kept a loaded gun at home close at hand."

"Is that why you kept that Smith & Wesson?"

"Snappers."

———

Glancing out his side window at the Neversink, George sought to absolve himself from possible accusations of sloppiness—something his Princeton dissertation adviser, Donald Spier, would have severely upbraided him for. Truth be told, he'd embraced the family lore and purposely narrated his catalog essay along tragic lines: how Altmann's struggle with alcoholism and depression, along with his rejection by his more conventional colleagues and the art establishment, had led his melancholic mind to seek escape and inspiration in radical new forms of expression; how the late abstract canvases were "both constructs of natural symbols and abstract projections of the quantum world . . . dazzling intimations of the hidden wonders of the universe detected in the quotidian experience. A rapturous distillation of form and color to heal the artist's despair."

Okay, so maybe he'd overdone it with the geeky physics stuff, but the catalog essay had certainly grabbed the attention of the *New York Times* reviewer—and sold paintings. But now the Judge's new information cast much into doubt. As a scientist, he might be disgraced for using false or misleading data, almost as bad as faked or bogus experiments that failed the most basic test of reproducibility—an unsupported hypothesis. What if what he wrote turned out to be a sham? Even if he hadn't come across an iota of evidence about the artist's connection with the Communist Party. On the other hand, he'd failed to interview his father, whom he hadn't spoken to in over twenty years. (A touchy subject: Who might legally assert ownership of the paintings?) And Cordelia's recollections of Altmann family scuttlebutt, jaundiced at best, were all secondhand, and thus suspect. Not that the Judge's regular disparagement during his childhood hadn't shaped his narrative: "What news of your good-for-nothing, ne'er-do-well, wife-deserting, alcoholic, deadbeat father?"

Then there were his own dark moods . . . and his mother's leery eye: that something of her alcoholic husband's darksome gene pool had infected her only child.

His consternation was further abetted by the sudden sensation of Wendy Bradley's grip on his arm the night before last as they had parted, when she had sweetly but firmly offered her considered opinion.

"George, I just can't buy the depression and bitterness thing: suicide." Her eyes had tightened on his meaningfully. "The paintings, George, are filled with wonder and love—sheer exhilaration at being alive! At least for me they are, and I prefer to listen to the art . . . if not the artist." And, to hammer home her point, that lingering kiss on his right cheek and an even firmer squeeze to his left shoulder.

"Fucking hell!"

At the intersection of 209, instead of taking the turn east on the Kingston Road for the Gunks and Woodstock, he turned right for Cuddebackville (loathsome name), in hopes a short, nostalgic detour might restore his peace of mind. Just as he parked, his cell phone, five bars showing, rang. Aunt Alice . . . she'd probably already heard from Felicity. He let the call go to voice mail and abandoned his phone in the Tahoe.

As he climbed the winding path through the sparse riparian woodland, his eyes lit up at the chanterelles, which would be within easy reach upon his return to the car. At each step, the gentle flow of the river grew more distinct. He paused often to take in the view of sunlight glinting on the rocky pools sheltering along the south shore of the Neversink, favored spots—easy pickins—where the Judge had once taken him for his first fly-fishing lessons.

How the Judge had relished figuring the probabilities: "Bait selection should always be attuned to the selective feeding option—when your chances are greatly improved by providing the one seasonal insect, the one fly that will surely get the attention of the three-pound brown trout hiding under his favorite rock." Remembering that voice booming out from where the Judge had stood on the abutment, pointing out pools (too unsteady on his feet to enter the river himself), criticizing his casts, George found himself attuned to yet another obscure corner of space-time, where his paternal grandfather, George Altmann, still stood at the railing of the Sawkill Bridge on that bitterly cold Christmas Eve in 1949 . . . a fate indeterminate.

"That son of a bitch—talk about bait selection!—knew damn well I'd probably turn up those Altmann sketches," George muttered.

Reaching the upper section of the massive stone abutment, all that was left of Roebling's 1851 aqueduct, where it faced its northern twin on the far bank, George waited, brooding, simmering, line adrift, breathing in the crisp mineral scents of the Neversink as if for answers. He retreated a few steps to where the six massive rusted iron eye loops remained anchored in the concrete footings of the abutment, relishing their endurance; there, he sat for a spell, tempted to curl up and take a nap and let the river wash away the accumulating sediment of doubt. The morning sunlight was sleepy and warm.

"It soared, boys and girls." (The Judge had been dressed in his splendid Abercrombie & Fitch regalia, gesturing with his hickory walking stick as he tried to bring to life a lost world to a rabble of Pac-Man-jaded grandchildren.) "Oh how it soared, as if on eagle's wings, to girdle the Neversink and so provide safe passage for the coal boats on their way from the coal mines of Honesdale and along the Delaware and down the Rondout Valley to the Hudson River and all the way to tidewater and the docks of New York. Imagine, if you will, the splendor of such a wonder of engineering in a primitive landscape, in a still primitive age, before even the advent of the railroads. Energy, power to fuel the growing nation. And you see, *he* learned it all right here, our good Mr. Roebling, that is: solved all the engineering and design problems that were required to build the Brooklyn Bridge . . . Think about it, you lazyheads; try to picture the thing: the iron cables, nine and a half inches wide, carrying thousands of tons of water, timber, and steel over a hundred and sixty feet! Oh, a thing of such lovely fictile proportions . . . fictile, George, what does *fictile* mean?"

Some hours later, George started awake from his nap, rising out of nonexistent time at the lower regions of the Planck scale to the rapid-fire scolding of two titmice amid the tattered yellow leaves of a maple bough. Still half-asleep, he returned to where the stone siding of the abutment dropped to the river. Staring out across the murmuring waters, listening as if for an echo, George found his waning nostalgia now tinged with suspicion, where garlands of hazy sunlight were draped across the beautifully patterned stonework of the far abutment, where, as if slipping through time's looking glass, he found his younger self staring blankly into space, a pathetic preteen version stranded forever on the far shore of memory: chubby-cheeked, cowlicks of blond hair sticky with bubble gum, torn *Star Wars* T-shirt emblazoned with the sultry smile of Princess Leia (his first love), blaster pistol secreted in the pocket of his chinos, armed with nothing more than Teddy's pathetic old hunting knife, a sad last-minute substitution for his beloved lightsaber, which the Judge had insisted he leave behind.

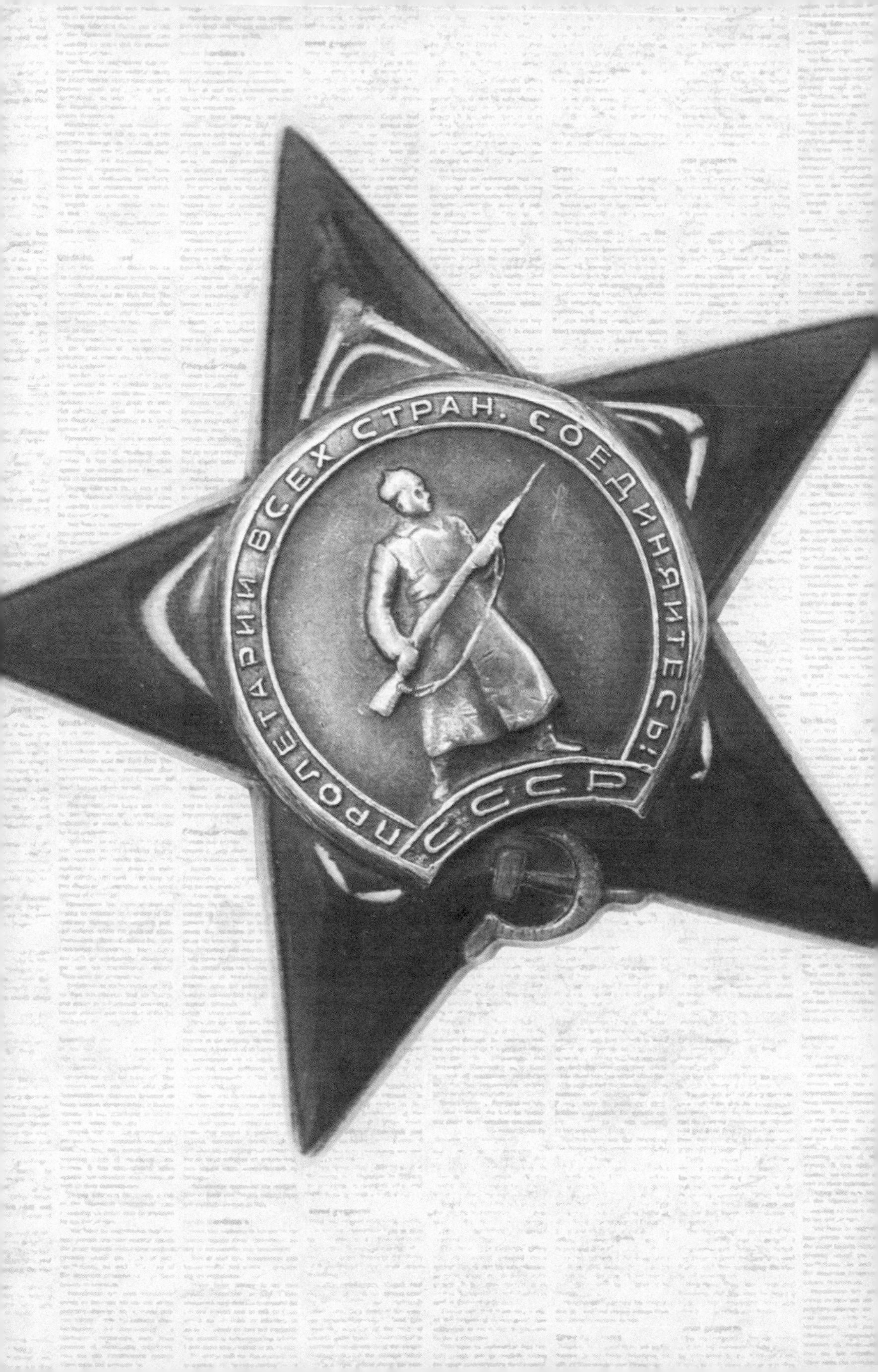
ПРОЛЕТАРИИ ВСЕХ СТРАН, СОЕДИНЯЙТЕСЬ!
СССР

7

A Life in the Law and Out: Introduction

HOW MANY TIMES over the years have I been asked, "When will you write a memoir?" What people really mean is, When will you tell us the truth about the Hiss treason trial? As if Hiss's conviction on two counts of perjury is not self-evident. As if my scores of opinions—all but one upheld by the Supreme Court—are matters of only passing interest. Any discussion of the Hiss trial is, of course, subject to the constraints of attorney-client privilege, and as long as Alger Hiss remains alive, I must bow to the legal protocols, at least in the details. But two points I feel warrant stressing. First, I was brought on for the second trial at very short notice. I did it as a favor to Alger because of our long acquaintance—mind you, not friendship, as many have described it in the press. Friendship is reserved for a relationship of candor and trust, and by any measure we never enjoyed such confidences. I was, in effect, a relief pitcher brought in at the bottom of the ninth with the bases loaded, charged with striking out the top of the order, because that was what was needed to win acquittal after the near-death experience of the hung jury in the first trial. The Hiss team in the first trial had benefited by a very inexperienced (or sympathetic to the defense) judge, Samuel Kaufman, who restricted the evidence allowed to be introduced, while giving Hiss's chief defense counsel, Lloyd Paul Stryker, wide latitude to run roughshod over the jury, besmirching Whittaker Chambers by every means allowed and disallowed, employing innuendo, slander, verbal abuse—allusions to leprosy and uncleanness among Stryker's favorite metaphors—not to mention low-down, nefarious, and numerous filthy allusions to a variety of sexual perversions—all to prove him a liar and pervert, and so not to be believed in claiming a long-running friendship with Alger and Priscilla Hiss.

Stryker, under the inept handling of Judge Kaufman, had sown just enough confusion to squeak by with a hung jury. We were not to be so lucky in the second trial. Alger discarded Stryker—with the dirty work done—figuring he needed a higher tone, "a scientific dissection of Chambers's pathologies," second time around, and so hired me to "raise the discourse," as he put it, by putting professional psychiatrists in the witness box. Our defense was based on three legs: a reputational defense of Mr. Hiss; dismissal or at least undermining the undeniable credibility of the physical evidence—the purloined State Department papers that had been typed on the Hisses' Woodstock typewriter, much less the summaries of other documents written in Alger Hiss's hand; and the character assassination of the prosecution's star witness, Whittaker Chambers, who had testified, now multiple times, that Hiss had acted as a spy for the Soviet Union in the late 1930s. My role, I found out after I accepted the position, was the demolition job on Whittaker Chambers—Stryker redux, but in a more genteel, objective manner, or, to put it more plainly, to smear Mr. Chambers's character by the use of the most tendentious expert psychiatric testimony then available. Why I agreed to this shameful strategy, in retrospect, I can't say, except—at the time—a compelling case was made to me by Mr. Hiss in our preliminary discussions concerning the malevolent and twisted personality of Chambers that these handpicked experts would do the trick.

Dr. Binger, our lead defense psychiatrist, something of a hero in my daughter Martha's pantheon, turned out to be an interesting case in his own right. Initially, Binger had been allowed to participate in the first trial; he sat throughout the hearing, then was allowed to take the witness stand, whereupon Stryker launched into a foul-minded antihomosexual tirade against Chambers, which resulted in Judge Kaufman dismissing Binger from the witness stand before he could answer Stryker's first rhetorical question. I failed to take note of this farcical episode in my initial background preparation for my own folly, and only found out later, much to my astonishment, that Binger was a personal friend of the Hisses, and so provided his services gratis. Alger's faith in the efficacy of a psychiatric hatchet job, an evaluation based purely on the observation of the subject on the stand, along with his testimony and writings—without benefit of a personal interview or close questioning of any kind—relying solely on the practitioner's sub-jective judgment of human character, pathological or otherwise, now seems almost laughable. But Alger was convinced that this disciple of Herr Freud would do the trick and that my fresh face captaining the psychiatric defense, coupled with my establishment credentials, might indeed save the day.

"Your credibility and integrity and reputation for fair play when contrasted with that vile liar Chambers will prove his insanity." And Alger placed a knowing hand on my shoulder. "Trust me, you will quickly see what I've been up against over the last year."

I was promised complete access to the defense files, which stretched back almost two years from the initial investigations by HUAC, the civil complaint for defamation filed by Hiss against Chambers, the grand jury inquiry, and the first trial for perjury by the government against Mr. Hiss. Those files were split between Mr. Marbury's firm in Baltimore and Mr. McLean's firm in New York, and my access, so it turned out, was limited and selective, mostly to do with the dirt turned up by the defense investigators on Chambers's personal life, material, I should add, largely provided by Communists and ex-Communists, who either detested Chambers for his defection or were, interestingly, avid supporters of the patriotic Alger Hiss: odd bedfellows, I always thought. Full and complete access to the defense files, I suspect, would have painted a far different picture of what I was getting myself into—namely, that the reputational defense of Mr. Hiss was coming apart at the seams, while the physical evidence for conviction was all but irrefutable. And so my relief role—perhaps more like the knuckleballer brought in at the eleventh hour in the dead of night to face an unknown batter in a ballpark where he'd never pitched, with teammates—and a client!—who were full of more secrets than professional competence, and motivated by assumptions that still remain a mystery to me.

Thank the Lord for Judge Henry W. Goddard, who skippered our second trial; without his experienced and fair hand on the scale, I would have made a bigger fool of myself than I did. He allowed the latitude of evidence that brought in the clowns, Drs. Binger and Murray, to testify to Chambers's multiple psychiatric disorders, but they were literally laughed out of court by the scorching cross-examination of the lead prosecutor, Assistant U.S. Attorney Thomas Murphy. And the testimony of ex-Red agent, Hede Massing—excluded from testimony by Judge Kaufman in the first trial—who put the knife to Alger good and deep.

I deserved the shellacking I got in the press and professional circles.

—

The final chapter to this whole bizarre debacle has been most strange, in that it never seems to end, while the ground keeps shifting with every change in the wind. And although my physicist grandson assures me that change is ubiquitous on both the quantum level and that of everyday reality—whatever that means—I still find myself buffeted by unseen forces, nameless yet ubiquitous. In the fifties, in the years immediately after the trial, I thought I'd gotten away with my shirt; I was celebrated in progressive circles as a hero for having stood up to the reactionary McCarthyite forces unleashed on the land and having fallen nobly on my sword to save the New Deal in defending Hiss. Rewarded, in fact, during the Truman administration by being nominated for a judgeship on the Second Circuit Appeals Court. As the fifties turned into the sixties, as I made a name for myself with many crucial civil rights decisions, I was increasingly disparaged by the Left and faulted for having failed miserably in my defense of Alger Hiss— this as Hiss, out of jail, mounted his campaign for vindication, trashing his defense team for ineptitude and for being bulldozed by the FBI, Hoover, and Nixon. By the seventies, with Nixon in the White House and Alger's drive for redemption gaining steam, I was talked about behind my back as actually having been in league with the government in the trial against my own client, perhaps a stooge of Hoover's FBI planted to disparage Hiss and get a conviction at any cost.

As the Vietnam War raged and the streets filled with protestors and bombs went off in federal facilities and the inner cities burned, as Alger Hiss toured college campuses to nostalgic acclaim and support for the anti-imperialist Communist cause in North Vietnam, my "reactionary views" on the Second Circuit Appeals Court were described, ex post facto, as yet a further explanation for the unfair conviction of Hiss. I was condemned as a reactionary ideologue in the pay of the military-industrial complex—and much of this calumny from the lips of my own daughter, Alice, from the radical barricades of the Bay Area.

And then by the Reagan eighties, with Nixon dismissed as a criminal, I was suddenly kosher again, perceived as a Democratic moderate, the judge everybody could work with, whose opinions were overwhelmingly upheld by the Supreme Court. All of a sudden I was seen as the golden boy, striking the right balance between the Constitution and the practical adjustments required by a just society, the man who had seen that Alger Hiss got a fair trial but was not beholden to forces on either the Left or the Right. With Nixon long gone, as Alger Hiss's flame finally began to wane once more with the faltering of the Soviet Union, I was, so the White House assured me, on the short list for the next Supreme Court vacancy. My stock was rising as Hiss's flickered and fell. Alas, mine fell short as the Clinton years commenced and my retirement loomed. And so I find myself marooned on an unquiet shore, my life and career indelibly stamped by the enigma of Alger Hiss, his place in history unresolved in the minds of those who knew him best, while a symbol of treachery or honor to those who knew him least, who still care to remember.

Whatever the malevolent fallout from the Hiss trial on the country during the Cold War, it was the grievous toll on my immediate family that I most regret, especially that on my beloved wife, Annie.

And, I must admit, I can never forgive Alger for trying to divorce Priscilla in 1958, when she simply couldn't take it anymore. He abandoned her for other women who would hold his flag high, while she, poor thing, was left isolated and scorned by his growing legion of admirers. Even her son by Alger became distant. We met and spoke and sometimes wrote in those last years, but never once did she admit anything or say a bad word about Alger. Loyal to a fault. The moment Priscilla died, in 1984, Alger remarried a woman he'd been living with for many years.

8

Muscle Memory

STILL FUMING, GEORGE pulled into the Mohonk Preserve's West Trapps parking lot. Half an hour before, he'd given in to his aunt Alice's demand that he make a detour to her home in New Paltz.

"George, I need a full debrief on the Judge, and I want it today. Dinner at six. Be there."

So much for a brief stop at Woodstock to gather replacement works. He wondered how the change in plans might affect Wendy's eagerness to engage in this road trip, which would now include an overnight stay at his mother's.

As instructed in Wendy's last text—she was running late—he took the Undercliff Road, a wide gravel walking trail accessing the best climbing routes. Passing him in the other direction were returning groups of climbers of all ages weighed down with backpacks, helmets, huge foam pads, coiled multicolored nylon ropes, and jangling unidentifiable gear hanging off impressive waist harnesses. Clearly a fraternal microculture of which he'd been oblivious—like so much else. His fascination with the sweaty climbers and the tools of their trade faded as each turn in the path revealed more panoramic scenes of early fall across the Rondout Valley, an inland sea awash with green waves flecked with silvery scarlet and yellow breaking against the battlements of the Shawangunk Ridge, which rose higher and higher over his left shoulder, like some hull of a titanic ship docked against the sky. More than odd, almost chilling, was the sense of déjà vu . . . how well he knew these places from Altmann's abstract landscapes; how the artist had caught the very essence of the thing, the raw abrasions of geologic time scribbled across the cliff face, balancing on thin air, and all done with only the merest suggestive paint marks and color saturations. Again, as earlier in the day, he scolded himself for his negligence in not having reconnoitered this painting ground, when he knew full well from the penciled titles on the stretchers and the artist's record book that Altmann had made excursions to the Shawangunks. As if needing to do penance for yet another careless oversight, he moved to the cliff face, running his hands over the rough pebbly surface, astounded at the uncanny correspondence to Altmann's rugged, scumbled paint surfaces.

The sun-warmed surface of the sedimentary conglomerate stirred an even deeper wonder: the sheer age of the sandstone—on closer inspection, quartz, lots of quartz, tiny white pebbles with black striations, rounded and worn smooth, as if carried for hundreds of miles over millions of years in some prehistoric river, perhaps polished by the waves of some ancient sea, finally marooned, embedded for—what?—300, maybe 400 million years in a Silurian waste. A mere speck of time in a fourteen-billion-year-old universe, a kindergartener's sandbox compared to that starry abyss into which he'd spent more years staring than he cared to remember.

With an involuntary shudder, he withdrew his hand and wiped his palm on his jeans, settling his gaze on the welcoming lushness of the Rondout Valley and the sanguinities of a more human time scale etched in the patchwork of farms and wooded acres and the merest hint of a ninety-mile-long abandoned ditch bisecting the autumnal splendor of the valley. He saw the silver-gray cliffs of the Shawangunk through the eyes of the D & H Canal boatmen as they passed through nearby Ellenville, gazing out day after sultry and meandering day over the slow summer boating season, a chalky outcropping above the corn and barley distance, a familiar landmark floating past to the hum of crickets as they moved toward or away from the vast sea, perhaps a comforting halfway point in a boatman's precarious life.

When he reached her climbing station, he found a loyal remnant of Wendy's class staring up at their instructor. She seemed to skitter across the cliff face, literally hanging by her fingertips from the transverse sheets of conglomerate. At first glance he missed her rope, due to the reflected glare of the lowering sunlight. He held his breath as he watched her long-legged, orange-helmeted figure continue to glide across and up the cliff face. Standing with their gear, avid students craned their necks as she demonstrated the movement and grip placements, calling out each move in a loud but unhurried voice, her agile and adept transfers of weight effortlessly executed. For a moment, she lay marooned flat against the stone, carabiners on her harness glinting, clinging like a bent spring as she prepared the next move. She was wearing blue spandex tights, a sports bra, and gray climbing shoes, her outstretched fingers dusted in white chalk. Every tendon and muscle showed in long, tensile lines across her arms, shoulders, and back as she reached far up and sideways, seeking a hold, testing, swinging up and over, adjusting limbs as she mastered the equilibrium point for the next advance skyward: ten thousand years in every reach. Moving closer for a better view, he was relieved as her rope became visible, a thin blue lifeline attached to a harness on her waist. His initial apprehension was calmed by the rapt appreciation of her students below as they absorbed the technical details on offer. An older climber stood at the base of the cliff, holding her belay line. Once at the top, she gave a wave and quickly, expertly rappelled herself down to the climbers below, high-fiving the men and hugging the women—clearly the alpha female in the pack. Then everyone began to gather up their gear and move off toward the gravel carriage road and parking area.

Only then, as she was gathering up her stuff and policing the area, did Wendy realize she still had company. A palm over her eyes to shield the glare out of the west, she looked at her watch, then smiled and came forward to give him a sweaty kiss on the cheek.

"You found me," she said, letting out a sigh as she caught her breath. "Sorry if I kept you waiting."

"My legs are shaking. I didn't see the rope at first."

"This is kindergarten, a cakewalk; I could free-climb it with my eyes closed."

"I think it's terrifying."

"My dad took me climbing when I was eight on much tougher terrain than this. But the Gunks are pretty cool—best rock climbing in the east, certainly the best teaching courses."

As she looked up from her backpack, holding a bottle of water to her lips, the slanted sunlight caught the blue of her eyes, the honey streak in her ponytail, the quivering, shapely ridge of her long nose. Her muscled body, caked with sweat and rock dust, smelled of dirt and leaves . . . and fall.

"You and Altmann," he said with a hint of chagrin, something about her—the upturned tip of her nose, her long, agile fingers—reminding him of someone. He felt not a little bewildered at her seeming transformation from two nights before.

"Ah, so you get it now"—she pointed to where he stood with a hand braced against the cliff face—"the fissures, the lichen patterns, the shadings of striations in the sandstone—and just fourteen thousand years ago the last retreating glacier polished them up for us and your grandfather."

"I feel pretty stupid that I never bothered to check this all out."

"The moment I walked into your gallery, I knew. Like an old friend . . . the feel of this place. I was just blown away."

"Expensive friend, dropping forty thou like that."

"Cheap!" She snapped her fingers. "What price for the timeless." She arched her chalk-stained eyebrows. "And you don't have to worry: My check won't bounce. I'm a long-term investor."

"You are the dream—ah, Duveen, right, priceless?—client. A triple threat: enthusiasm, connoisseurship"—he was going to say "money" but then thought better of it—"and an offer to schlepp paintings. What's not to like." He gazed at her, a tad nervous. "Fraid to say, there's been a slight hitch in plans."

"I know, I had to take on an extra class and we ran late."

"My aunt Alice—you met her at dinner—insists I stop by for dinner tonight."

"That's cool."

"Means we'd have to stay over at my mom's tonight."

"Cordelia. I absolutely loved your mom."

She smiled, seemingly embarrassed at her undue enthusiasm, and so returned to a diligent survey of the climbing route to make sure everything was shipshape. He noticed sketch pads held by rubber bands next to her backpack, and one that lay open, a pastel and ink rendering of a rock face.

"You sketch, too, while you climb?"

"Oh, these," she said, coming over. "Just noodling around when there's time to kill."

He picked up the open pad, a Penguin paperback of Jane Austen's *Persuasion* beneath, and began flipping through the pages: pencil sketches and pastel renderings of the rocks, lush color-saturated studies of the cracks and crevices and patterns in the grain. He paused, staring at a drawing of a nude figure gripping a rocky overhang. "Geest," he said, looking up at her, "is this your work? Did you do this, too?"

"Yup, like I said, scratching around."

He couldn't hide his indignation. "You've been fucking with me. These are really good, professional-caliber."

"Just as well you have a good eye," she replied with a bemused, endearingly goofy expression.

"So, I don't get it. You're an artist who teaches climbing, or a climber who does art on the side—while buying expensive paintings for kicks?"

"Actually, I'm a professional climber with sponsors. And I don't need to tell you: Only a few contemporary artists make a living at what they do. Not unless they're in bed with Gagosian or Glimcher or part of the celebrity art circus."

"So, you've been fucking with me."

"I hadn't gotten around to that yet."

"You never said boo at the opening or dinner."

"Listen," she said, an indignant flush in her cheeks, "that was *your* celebration for your *genius* grandfather. It wasn't my place to butt in and go on about myself—another contemporary artist pushing her shit."

"You're hardly a shrinking violet."

"With your family clamoring like hungry beasts, what else was I supposed to talk about *except* my climbing?"

"They thought you were a rock star." He kept flipping through the sketch pad. "Is this what you do, the nudes against the cliff background?"

"Stone nudes, self-portraits. It's my thing, my signature style—you know how it is."

He stared at a delicately sketched nude woman, upside down, clinging to a ledge by hands and feet, every sinew and tendon stretched, the line of her backbone echoing the horizontal creases in the escarpment above.

He shook his head, exasperated. "Paintings?"

"Yes, paintings."

"How *big* are the paintings?"

"Some life-size, some smaller, some *mucho* bigger. It's all about the color and texture—stone and skin tones, the patterns of line in the rock and the body—real formal issues." She glanced at him as he closed the sketchbook and handed it to her. "Listen, this isn't about my pimping myself for your gallery, if that's where this conversation is leading."

"You have representation?"

"Not exactly. A few group shows here and there, lots of private clients, especially in the climbing fraternity—it's tough starting out."

He smiled, his head perched at a jaunty angle on his wide shoulders. "But you'll let me do a studio visit?"

"We'll do an exchange. I'll help you move your grandfather's stuff—get a gander at the estate—first pick, shall we say—and then I'll grant you the visit. And you don't even have to sleep with me."

"God forbid. Do you work from sketches or photographs?"

"Both." She held up her phone, which she'd been checking for messages. "Photographs, which I work up into sketches, and sketches, which I photograph and then work up into paintings, abstracting and teasing out the formal relationships as the process unfolds."

"You have a professional do the initial photography?"

"Nope, can't afford professionals; just friends, colleagues. People like you. Here, I'll show you—if you're game, if it won't embarrass you."

"Try me."

"Help me get my crash pad positioned underneath the overhangs there. Just keep your eyes peeled; I saw a copperhead around here last week."

9

A Life in the Law and Out:
Teddy and Alice

THERE IS ANNIE, blond hair in a bun, sitting in her favorite wicker chair on the piazza as she nurses tiny Teddy, her white breast swollen with milk, her contented face dappled in leafy sunshine on this late-spring day. She is humming to her firstborn, humming a lullaby over the breeze rippling the lake, humming in time to the song of the Blackburnian warbler, orange-throated fellow just returned from the South—rudely interrupted by the redheaded drumbeat of a pileated woodpecker—her warm breath mixing with the scent of pine and damp moss and the nearby woodpile of aging oak logs.

Why is it that sometimes this image, this timeless maternal image, should strike such a sinister note in my soul? As if Annie held a viper to her breast. I recoil from the thought, realizing that perhaps the Hiss trial has branded my heart with a cruel streak of cynicism: that good can so easily be transformed into evil. That the goodness of my son could prove the downfall of my family.

Is such a metamorphosis possible—even likely—and for a child so early introduced to the goodness and healthy life of the woods, the woods he came to love, and so made his own? A child who came under the spell of the ship's keel ceiling, where Annie would place him in his infant bassinet and later his playpen for naps while she played Saint-Saëns's *Carnival of the Animals* or some dreamy Debussy or Satie, soothing him with evocations of clouds and sea and the early-morning mists over the lake of which she was so fond. All in forlorn hopes of encouraging an attachment to the piano that might sprout wings in his young heart. As she also did with the girls—obtaining equally meager results.

Even at three or four, there would be little Teddy, toddling down to the lake along the rooted path with a huge pair of binoculars like an

anchor weighed around his neck to spy on his "birdies," his blond hair
tousled, knees scraped. He'd spend hours staring up at the boathouse
rafters, where the barn swallows made their nests and shuttled to and
fro, feeding their young. Or he'd fish off the dock for bass, waiting for
the bald eagles to glide into view, a mating pair that had taken up residence on the tallest white pine down the lake—Annie's sunlit steeple of
Saint-Hilaire. That boy had the patience of Job—unlike his father—the
way he could sit and watch, waiting for their mating dance, for their
frolicking pinwheeling through space like tiny white angels, as he often
said. Or perhaps white-robed gods escaped from their lair in the ship's
keel ceiling to sport among the clouds, as he later, already a teenage
heartthrob, fancifully described another pair of eagles to me. Teddy
grew by leaps and bounds from summer to summer—butternut-tanned,
agile, ropy-muscled—and, unlike most first children—delighted at the
advent of his sisters, Alice and Martha, mostly because they distracted
Annie and so left him free to roam.

And roam he did in realms of gold, both past and present. For when
he wasn't birding or fishing or exploring Handytown (avoiding piano
practice), he'd be huddled with John Burroughs and Jack London by the
hearth. Before he was ten, first encouraged by Annie (bored with children's literature), he immersed himself in Joseph Conrad, who seemed
to stir some far-flung adventuring spirit in his soul. In the pages of
that exiled Polish author he encountered a congenial band of courageous misanthropes and duty-bound natural philosophers. Often he'd
quote at dinner—drawing on his near-photographic memory—whole
paragraphs of Conrad's alter ego, whether Marlow or the narrator, who
insisted on man's duty to persevere in the face of an unrepentant, uncaring nature—the cruel yet enchanting sea that tested men relentlessly.
One troubling quote that Teddy repeated more than once stays with
me: "Few men realize that their life, the very essence of their character,
their capabilities and their audacities, are only an expression of their
belief in the safety of their surroundings." Was Teddy, in this line from
An Outpost of Progress, slyly acknowledging the efficacy of the Bill of
Rights to his lawyer father? I think not. For Teddy seemed innately
attuned to natural laws, if not nature red in tooth and claw. As a boy
and youth, he found in the mastering of any adversity or challenge
our woods might pose a kind of inner serenity, a oneness—perhaps a
completeness (as Annie did with her music and books), which fueled
the audacious escapades of his short but glorious life. Looking back, I

can almost see him as a Lord Jim, striking out on his own, exiled by his dreams and ambitions to prove himself worthy in the eyes of Marlow (God forbid his father), living up to some intuited code of conduct while testing his limits when faced by the forces of chaos. So I was not surprised when he joined the marines. I suspect he felt as safe in the competency of his will to survive as he did in the company of like-minded comrades who shared a common fidelity to a code of honor.

All of which Annie dismissed as balderdash.

"Teddy, Conrad was an artist, not a philosopher. Read his *Nigger of the 'Narcissus,'* where he writes of art as something transcending wisdom, which speaks—how did he put it?—to 'our capacity for delight and wonder, to the sense of mystery surrounding our lives; to our sense of pity, and beauty, and pain; to the latent feeling of fellowship with all creation . . .' That's why you need to keep practicing, to feel the music, the timelessness of Mozart at your fingertips—that's what binds us together. As your Conrad put it, 'the dead to the living and the living to the unborn.'"

How often Annie and I feared for Teddy's safety when he failed to return from a hike until after dark. Or when he took to rowing his racing shell in the middle of the night, sprinting like a demon under the quicksilver moonlight, when an unseen root or stump could prove disaster. A boy, a youth, strong and determined, with a will that both disarmed and charmed his disciplinarian mother, a boy whose natural talent and physical skills at the keyboard often drove her to distracted tears. Teddy could effortlessly put pages of music to memory in one or two practice sessions. Of all my children and grandchildren, he was the only one who genuinely cared about the sorry fate of the old D & H Canal and the early settlers, as if drawn to their sad unstoried past, these phantoms who had once peopled Hermitage's woods, their tiny hardscrabble farms, now just pine-clad clearings, scattered like so many tattered prayer rugs over the endless foothills, where phantom walls appear and disappear like despoiled chthonian altars. He loved nothing better than hunting out artifacts of their desperate lives, digging up old bottles and rusted bits of farm implements, repairing walls in places I'd never laid eyes on. Perhaps he saw these "invisibles," as he liked to call them, as yet more Conradian figures lost to time, revenants inscribed in their tumbled fieldstone walls.

Teddy was hardly a solitary dreamer. He loved company, especially that of girls, who would flock his way, not just because he was good-looking and could play anything by ear on the piano, or because of his outrageous

sense of humor and happy-go-lucky high jinks, but for his essential kindness. And, too, they were drawn to his wildness—his daring outrages (if
Alice is to be believed), a kind of romantic deviltry that fed some need of
letting go in the fair sex, a break with the ordinary—a freedom, a daring,
the allure of risk-taking that, oddly enough, produces in some a feeling of
safety. So unlike his circumspect father, who bored the young women of
his youth to tears with briefs on history and the law. Or was it that he'd
absorbed so much of his mother's spiritual grace, and so saw in a woman's pensive smile a reflection of his own deepest yearnings, and they an
abiding competency and love in his seductive arms?

What can a father say about a child who is not only different from
his parent but who, in youth, had already bested him in most of what
he'd been taught, blessed, too, with an innate temperament that both
disarmed those who knew him and effortlessly earned their love? Dare
I say it: a temperament not unlike that of Alger Hiss, who so deftly
deployed his charm and expertise as to effortlessly win over his detractors to his cause, and turn friends into loyal minions.

My dear wife, Annie, were she still here, would accuse me of being
in awe of my own son, as she often did, or worse, of giving into his every
whim, of being too aloof, of refusing to discipline him. Of the same
laxity of character, if not judgment, that allowed Alger to manipulate
me and so doom our son.

"My God, Edward, I do believe you are jealous of your own son.
When you're not competing with him, you're egging him on to disaster
or worse."

Annie claimed I pretended to rule the roost with my logical mind,
setting goals and standards, but always turning a blind eye to Teddy
and the girls with a busy shirk, while, needless to say, ignoring their
deeper needs. Not that Annie wasn't a little overawed by Teddy's physical prowess at the keys. Annie was an artist, a musician, a believer in
the imaginative glory of music and literature, and so felt that raising
children required only firm but empathetic fellowship—leading by
example and meticulously laying down the law—to solve everyone's
problems. Like her beloved Proust, she believed that art and abiding
memory, compacted in a book or a Mozart sonata, were all children
required to ground them in the sustaining heart of life.

If only it were so.

If only the Hiss case could have been resolved by everyone just
sitting around and calmly talking things through, finding common

ground, agreeing on a verdict—instead of destroying our marriage, for which Annie blamed me. She accused me of holding things back, of not confiding in her, "in the marriage bed," as she put it. As if professional ethics condoned such a thing or courts upheld the sharing of such secrets. And God only knows, there were secrets aplenty—attended by the gravest of fears. Secrets that to this day haunt my worst nightmares surrounding the Hiss case, suspicions that still wake me in the middle of the night in a cold sweat.

Perhaps it was just as well Annie abandoned our marital bed after Teddy's death.

Whether the Hiss case was the cause of the slow crack-up of our marriage and the alienation of Alice and Martha, or whether our family was simply another casualty of the paranoia and distrust that haunted the Red-hunting fifties—that eerie maelstrom of fear and deceit—is a question I hope to explore herein.

A case in point, Teddy's sister: Alice.

Alice, the elder daughter, in the early firmament of our marriage got the full brunt of Annie's iron discipline. Teddy, being the firstborn, could do no wrong and so got away with murder, at least in his sister's eyes. While Martha, a year younger than Alice, watched us all from another planet. Alice revolted early against her mother's strictures, and later railed against mine, both personal and professional. But I can't help feeling that Teddy, a year her senior, had more to do with her choices in life than her parents' sins, real or imagined. Teddy, our human dynamo, had his sister in thrall from infancy, when he used to peer into her crib and make spooky birdcalls or wave his toys just out of her reach. My most lasting memories are of Alice as a young gangly thing, tall, like her mother, with narrow and hungry features, ever determined, even at age four, to keep up with Teddy on our hikes down the railroad tracks to the Neversink aqueduct. They competed endlessly to harvest the iron spikes still embedded in the abandoned ties that littered the old railroad bed. Sometimes little Alice would throw herself bodily on a rotted tie to prevent Teddy from stealing her prize. Exhausted, dragging, stumbling, she still refused my offer to pick her up and carry her. And Teddy all the while egging her on, teasing her about being a weak little muffin—"Blueberry," he called her.

As the children grew, Teddy's magnetic personality cast its spell over his awestruck siblings. He was not just an older brother but a pathfinder, able to charm, defy, and cajole his parents. Fearless. Intrepid.

Teddy was the only one who could distinguish the song of the common thrush from that of the hermit thrush. He located and identified birds I'd never discovered. His love of birds would later prove a queasy reminder of the way Alger Hiss would sometimes eagerly talk about sightings during breaks in our pretrial meetings. But I think it was Teddy's fearlessness that in some uncanny way had the deepest hold on Alice. Teddy loved nothing better than wading into the lake and hauling out a huge snapper to show off in front of the girls. He'd corral the beast on the boathouse dock and wave his hand in front of its ugly snout, daring them to do the same. Alice was always tempted to take him up on the dare, going so far as to touch its shell, while Martha fled, screaming, to Annie. And when Annie caught wind of this, she'd dash down to the boathouse, grab a paddle, and heave it off the dock.

Teddy saved his most outrageous stunt for a family hike down to the Neversink. He must have been fifteen or sixteen at the time. We were brought up short by a telltale rattle. There in the middle of the old railroad right-of-way was a huge coppery-black timber rattler sunning himself on a cool August morning. Black head coiled to strike, tail erect and shaking like a tiny buzz saw. Although this was not a common occurrence, we all knew enough to give the creature a wide berth. Not Teddy. He picked up a sturdy stick and deftly pinned the rattler and then grabbed it behind the head and lifted its writhing four-foot-plus body into the air, taking up its tail and extending it full length to better display the creature to Annie and the girls.

"Isn't he a beaut," exalted Teddy, his face alight with a kind of mystic rapture at his prize.

Annie screamed at him. Alice and Martha shrieked and kept their distance as he approached them. I was aghast but not a little spellbound, realizing in that instant that this was not the first time Teddy had so deftly managed this trick. His wrangling of the rattler, his sheer aplomb, seemed almost second nature. My God, I thought, all those days off alone in the woods, he's been doing crazy stunts like this! Teddy, his jaw firmly set, stood admiring his captive, his blue eyes softening with something approaching the peaceful bliss of a mother with babe in arms, that silenced tail firmly in his grip.

Annie shoved my shoulder. "Do something."

"Teddy," I demanded. "Stop this foolishness and get rid of the damn snake before you or someone else gets bitten. We're over two hours away from medical help."

"Isn't he magnificent?" His admiring eyes glittered with a curious awe as he struggled to fully stretch out the snake's writhing coils of tan and coal gray streaked with bits of white, its white-fanged mouth gaping wide, black forked tongue flickering.

"For God's sake, Teddy," Annie screamed, "now stop it this second. Obey your father and get rid of it."

"Come on, Allie," Teddy said, grinning at Alice, egging her on. "Don't you at least want to touch it, pet him, stroke him? I think he'd be thrilled. Come and count his rattles for me; I think there must be at least thirteen—just about your age."

Alice stood agog, Martha cowering behind her, hand pulling on the belt of Alice's jeans. Alice pushed Martha away and took a step toward her brother, her intent eyes flashing between Teddy's goading grin and the gleaming coiled muscle stretched between her brother's powerful hands. I could see she was terrified, but no power on Earth was going to let her show it—not now, not once Teddy had challenged her. He took another few steps toward Alice, his bare arms almost completely stretched, as if pulling a bow, eyes intent on his sister's. Martha shrieked and retreated farther away. Alice held her ground and reached out a brave hand and touched the scaly coils and then jerked her fingers away.

"Enough, damn it," I shouted. "Teddy, put that thing away this moment or we'll dock your allowance for six months."

Teddy turned toward Annie and me and, with a dreamy look of awed fascination, struggled to work the tail of the rattler around toward its head, in effect twisting it into a circle as he approached us. There was a distinct musky smell in the air, the strong sunlight bringing out a yellow tone in the rattler's skin, its diamond-patterned scales glinting in the sunlight as if freshly varnished.

"What do you think, Dad: our ouroboros? Don't you think him a fine fellow to be keeping us company in our woods? Why, didn't you know he slithers down from the ship's keel ceiling every morning to sun himself and returns every night to curl up for sleep? Really just one of the family."

He laughed insouciantly at his mother's near panic and then released the snake near where we stood, watching it quickly glide down into the gully beside the right-of-way and disappear under a pile of rocks. Then, without further ado, Teddy picked up his fishing gear and waved us onward, as if it had all been just another day at the office.

Good and evil, life and death: a hairbreadth apart.

Where Alice felt she could prevail was at the piano. At some point that summer, right about the time of our run-in with the timber rattler, Teddy, fed up with Annie's constant badgering, simply refused to practice anymore. No threats or entreaties by Annie could dissuade him. At this juncture, a gleeful Alice threw herself into practicing as if her life depended upon it. Teddy had all the physical gifts, Alice the "touch" and talent, and Martha neither. Poor Annie. I remember her lying next to me in bed, fretting about the waste. "If I had Teddy's hands, his strength, his reach, his agility, I could be as good, if not better, than Rubenstein or even Horowitz."

As a struggling young New York lawyer during the Depression and later working for the War Production Board in Washington in the forties, I was hard-pressed to spend much time with the children, and perhaps Alice felt I spent what little family time I had with Teddy. I fear it is a law of nature that the firstborn boy always gets the lion's share of attention from his father. And Teddy, if he was anything, was a charmer. Along with the knack of inspiring others: captain of crew and football and senior prefect at Groton. "He has you wrapped around his little finger" was Annie's lament to me. But Alice and Martha never wanted to go to a Yankee game, nor did they care much for fly-fishing on the Neversink. Did I favor Teddy, my only son? What father can resist the handsome, intrepid image of his own youth? His fly-fishing technique was a thing of instinct and art; to watch his graceful movements, like those of a young Nureyev, brought tears to my eyes—even as Annie dismissed my infatuations as bad for the boy and worse for his sister's sense of self-esteem. Yet when Teddy was killed in Korea, I think, in some respects, it took more out of Alice than any of us. I was hollowed out, bereaved, and then beset by Annie's grief, which soon turned into blind rage at my failures as a father and my defense of Alger Hiss, the two sins merging as one. For which she never forgave me. While Martha's response was to withdraw from everyone into her studies and then, later, medical school and a psychiatric practice in which she plied her patients with the same nostrums that had proved so useless in taming Teddy's—her first love's—wildness. What I believe she referred to as his "total lack of self-awareness." Alice's reaction was of a different order: Her lodestar, her intellectual companion, her indomitable competitor was out of the fray. Two weeks after the funeral, she announced to the world that she, too, was going to be a lawyer. And damned if, years later, she didn't get herself into the University of Chicago Law

School after graduating from Vassar. She simply walked away from her budding concert career, for which Annie always berated her, and washed her hands of her summa in French literature and music. Her husband once told me she didn't touch the piano for ten years.

I've never understood what prompted her radical streak. Perhaps something of Teddy's equanimity had sunk its barbs, his Conradian belief that all men share an unspoken faith in our common humanity, our better angels: that time and unremitting patience will bring about a better world. Echoing the conviction of my mentor, Oliver Wendell Holmes, that the law and the courts provide the forum for the evolutionary churn toward a better world. Or as he put it to a young clerk, presiding from his oversize wicker chair on the back porch at Beverly Farms, "Sonny, the law is there to provide the forum for the clash of social interests, a gridiron on which the struggle can take place within prescribed boundaries, and so limit the damage to the commonweal."

But Alice only looked for the worst in people and, above all, lacked the necessary patience—she was always in a rush—and faith in the fundamental soundness of our sometimes plodding system of law.

My first real inklings of the firebrand Alice was when she began to circulate in the poor neighborhoods of Chicago in the early days of the Kennedy administration, at first doing charity work and then pro bono legal work on behalf of the black residents. I admired her greatly for her commitment to social justice and later for her fight to end racial discrimination and segregation in the South. Alice was one of the first Freedom Riders, and she worried us sick. She marched with Martin Luther King Jr. in Selma. I was proud that she had somehow absorbed the abolitionist fervor of her forebearers on Annie's Davenport side. She said she was marching to honor Teddy, because Teddy was the only one in the family who would've had the guts to march. Perhaps true, as far it went, as far as King's fundamental message that all men, black and white, deserve to be treated equally, to live in harmony, and be loved as God's children.

For a few years in the late sixties, Alice and I seemed to be on the same page, fighting for desegregation and voting rights. But for Alice, change was always too tepid, and came too slowly. Annie frustrated Alice because, though always willing to contribute lavishly to her daughter's causes, Annie remained too absorbed by her work with George Balanchine, while looking after Cordelia, our miracle child, born in 1952, to do more than pay lip service to the "movement," as

Alice always called it. More than once, Alice reminded me of a young Priscilla Hiss as I knew her before the war: same indignation at privilege and visceral hatred of injustice. It is something of a riddle in my life that I seem to love and be drawn to powerful women, forever impatient that time will not yield them some fugitive prize or give them their just due.

The rift between Alice and Annie only grew in the years before Annie's death.

When Alice set up her law firm in Oakland in the late sixties, she seemed to slip beyond the pale of what I considered responsible legal stewardship. Every other foul word out of her mouth seemed about condemning the "pigs" or the "fascist FBI" or the "exploitive capitalist system"; she denounced the Johnson administration as warmongers and racist bigots, and then, with Nixon, she seemed to lose all hold on reality. She could have been one of the most brilliant defense lawyers of her generation if her radical politics and rhetoric hadn't gotten her in trouble with judges and juries. The methodology, which she developed to a fine art, of raising bogus political issues to frame her clients' cases, defending the indefensible, first stirred up resentment among her peers and then trouble among her dangerous clients. I couldn't help but feel there was a screw loose in her character—whether tilting with the ghost of Teddy or sticking a finger in my eye. She seemed to lack that elusive sense of balance, proportion, and good judgment that is so critical to the well-tempered legal mind. She eventually became obsessed with her criminal clients: if there might be some legal maneuver she'd failed to try, some angle in the judicial system she hadn't yet exploited, perhaps a technical error in a judge's instructions to a jury that, on appeal, might have gotten her client off. It didn't matter, if the trial dockets are any record, that the cold-blooded killers she defended would go right out and murder again. In one case, a policeman shot in the head during a traffic stop, or, most famously, a black prostitute with a three-year-old daughter murdered in cold blood with a shot to the chest.

As Annie always liked to tell me, the Bay Area may have gotten Alice about as far from me and my court as geography allowed, but the specter of Teddy's daring a little girl to put her finger in front of the snout of a snapper never left her—and it almost got her killed. Driven by her rage at what she perceived to be society's injustice, she defended an unwholesome breed of black murderers and political con artists, too often turning clients into friends and allies—and, disastrously, lovers.

If I dared give her advice, it was not to mix up her work life and personal life. I told her that passion for a cause is fine, but the law is about drawing fine distinctions and rational arguments, not using polemics to confuse and intimidate. I can still see her turning on me, her face ablaze with purple rage, fulminating with the filthiest language as she stomped out of the great room at Hermitage, even as, summer after summer, she left her children, first Cecily and then Billy, in my care. Little did I realize the reason: Her family was being threatened by rogue elements of the Black Panthers back in Oakland.

I always hoped that marrying Stanley, an older, hopefully wiser Hollywood Ten veteran, might settle her. And again, when she fled east to a teaching position at SUNY New Paltz, that this new start might provide her a second chance to calm her demons. Yet her untamed restlessness remained. With Annie and Teddy gone, she could never stand to spend more than a few days at Hermitage in the summers with her children. There was always something that took her away, a conference, a protest—work. If she wasn't blaming me for a recent opinion on the Second Circuit, it was "Annie's rules" that I was inflicting on her children, or her niece and nephews, over summers at Hermitage. She showed almost no interest in Cecily and poor Billy when they were young, only when they were old enough to share in her politics, and by then she'd become a broken record. She'd wander around Hermitage like a lost, tormented soul. I'd catch her just standing in the great room, staring up into the glittering spaces of the ship's keel ceiling, moving slightly, searching from a different angle, as if something of Teddy lingered there. As children, they all had their favorites among the gods and goddesses, seeing in their various attributes powers for which they yearned, or stories to inspire their dreams. Every so often I'd hear Alice seated at Annie's Steinway, sounding a few notes, playing a few phrases, and listening for those distinctive glorious sonorities echoing as if out of heaven itself. There'd be tears in her eyes—was it a road not taken?— and then she'd rush off on the trail to Handytown or a hike to the Neversink, or just spend time by herself in Teddy's old room, reading though his notebooks or his yearbooks, the latter signed by his adoring friends and girlfriends—still arguing with his ghost, as far as anybody could make out, over God knows what. Only when young George took over Teddy's room did she stop making her pilgrimage there.

As Stan once told me, "You have to understand. She's actually come to believe her own rhetorical excesses: the efficacy, if not necessity, of violence to bring about social charge, that the system needs to be dis-mantled from the bottom up, one case, one precedent at a time."

Well, her legacy is there for all to see and ponder: Stokely Carmichael and later the Black Panthers took to her rationalizations about the effi-cacy of revolutionary violence to smash the fascist system like mother's milk, exploiting her rhetorical and maximalist excess to their own mis-begotten ends. Injustice was always society's fault, while the guilty were to be excused their crimes as victims of a degrading system, their own victims merely the roadkill on a journey to a better, more just world. Denying individual responsibility, due process, presumption of inno-cence, as I always pleaded with her, is a form of narcissistic insanity that leads to hell, or something like the gulag . . . And in Alice's case, to a dark, smelly corner of the visitor's room of San Quentin, a Dantesque cesspool—or is it a windstorm—if there ever was one.

I think it is fair to say that Alice has had her revenge on me, about as close a direct knife thrust to the system as she ever managed. I heard more than once through the grapevine that no one in the Reagan White House really gave a damn about the Hiss trial, but the antics of my radical daughter—her very public disparagement of some of my most celebrated opinions—and her plead-the-Fifth husband definitely put the kibosh on my nomination for the Supreme Court.

10

Catwoman

EXHAUSTED FROM A hard day's teaching, Wendy quickly fell asleep along the way to New Paltz, lulled by the winding, hilly roads. Dusk seemed to catch them unaware, a stealthy outrider to the cooler weather. While the outskirts of the town, the fields and copses where many of the SUNY faculty had their homes, had been translated to soft blurs under a last blush of nacreous sky. Aunt Alice and Uncle Stanley's split-level white rambler, a peaked roof and dormer added at some point, was the last house on a dead-end road. Though small, even by faculty housing standards, the home was situated on a sprawling chunk—Stanley's word—of ten rural acres, comprising lawns that merged with untended meadows, bordered on two sides by a state park, where stands of stately spruce and spindly oaks jostled the sky. The property was set off from the road by a substantial mortared stone wall, a remnant of some bygone estate, which corralled rambling meadows, now mostly populated by the brittle silver husks of milkweed pods presiding over the tarnished brass of the fallen.

As he turned into the rutted drive, George's gaze was captured by the swooping shadows of red-tailed hawks gleaning the unmowed meadows for a last squirrel or chipmunk before turning the killing fields over to the owls. Nearer the house, three crows were perched on a bird feeder, three scimitar beaks turning to the sound of interlopers. Aunt Alice always had a thing for crows, admiring their intelligence and adaptability, a source of constant argument decades before with the Judge, who hated "ravens and their devilish ilk, the mafia of the bird world," so described because of how the sly beasts harassed and stole from every other species. As a child, Alice had raised a pair of pet crows, which she delighted in feeding out of her hand.

"Black chaos on the wing," he muttered to himself, echoing the Judge's pithy phrasing.

He pulled up in front of the open garage, illuminating his aunt's sensible Audi and a lovingly maintained 1973 Porsche 911 T Targa, which his uncle drove only to and from the university. He turned an anxious gaze toward the interior light coming from a wide bay window: the abode of two intellectuals, two academics, both now tenured professors nearing retirement, with good pensions and storied pasts on the West Coast. Children . . . gone, gone, gone.

—

He turned to his still-sleeping passenger in the seat beside him, her sweat-stained face composed, relaxed, looking more like that of a young girl, somewhat lonely, he thought, vulnerable, even lost.

"Oh!" Wendy exclaimed as he switched off the ignition. "Br-r-r, it's cold." She rubbed her thighs under her blue climbing tights and pulled her skimpy fleece vest tight around her shoulders.

"Where were you?" he asked.

She looked at him, blinking, brow furrowed, as if caught off guard. "Monster Rock, Texas, with my dad. On the summit, as the stars appeared, he always liked to recite Shelley's 'Ode to the West Wind.'"

"Well . . . low forties tonight," he said with an apprehensive stare. "Are your loins girded for battle?"

"I thought your aunt was perfectly charming at dinner the other night." Her voice had modulated back to its forthright tone as she turned to his distracted face in the half-light from the bay window, which framed a wall of bookshelves, the checkerboard of shadow from the six-over-six sashes spilling across the windshield.

"You sprinkled fairy dust."

"My oh-so-fatal charm," she pronounced in a Texas drawl, and then started at the sharp report of cawing as dark wings and dangling clenched talons moved off and merged with the night.

"Damn crows."

"You don't look pleased."

"No, it's nothing, really. Only, last time I was here, it was for a memorial service for their son, Billy. He died on his twenty-ninth birthday. A heroin OD on a perfect spring evening in his apartment in Poughkeepsie. He used to come down to Princeton and we'd hang out in the Astrophysics Department, looking at stars, getting high."

"How sad for Alice and Stan."

"When we were kids, my cousin Billy was the life of the party—kept everyone in stitches. Every joke I hear, I think, How would Billy have told it? He did an imitation of Skip Wilson—well, more like channeling Skip Wilson."

"Alice mentioned her daughter at dinner, Cecily, isn't it? Married to some world-famous surgeon."

"Flew the coop over twenty years ago. She was as beautiful as she was kind, my favorite cousin, escaped to Stanford, never to return. Didn't even show for Billy's memorial service."

"No . . ." She peered with compressed eyebrows toward the lighted bay window and the cozy bookshelves on the interior, as if trying to visualize the possibility of such a thing. "Empty nest—and some."

"Sorry to drag you into this—wasn't part of the plan."

"There's no such *thing*," she replied in a searching but assured voice.

"Well, just keep sprinkling the pixie dust, 'cause I'll need it tonight."

"Her husband didn't seem to have much to say at dinner."

"Stan likes watching. He was a screenwriter in Hollywood in the forties and was nominated for an Academy Award. A lot of noir 'B' thrillers. He teaches film and theater at the university. He knew everybody—and he's drawn to beautiful artistic women, so you should provide the perfect distraction."

She laughed and struck a runway pose as she got out of the car. "Well, I always wanted to be in pictures."

"You'd be perfect for a remake of *North by Northwest*—what's her name . . ."

"Eva Marie Saint."

"Eva, dangling from Mount Rushmore."

"Like snot from Washington's nose until Mr. Thornhill saved me."

———

As the front door opened, a huge Siamese scooted in between their legs.

"Catch her, Stan. Mickey's got a mouse and it's still twitching."

"Got 'er," said Stan, struggling with a buzz saw of fur and feet. "Gangway, folks."

Stan, still agile in his eighties, held the cat outstretched in front of him, its claws shredding air, and marched outside to release the field mouse.

Alice, in sneakers, tight slacks, and a rose-colored blouse, finally managed a greeting, ushering in her nephew and his guest. Stan followed with Mickey, who was still wildly hissing and protesting the loss of her latest victim.

"No wonder your crows were freaking out," offered George.

"You little monster." Stan panted. "She damn well caught a crow last week." He tossed the cat on a nearby sofa, then apologized and came over to shake hands. He was taller even than his wife, with a leonine mane of white hair swept back from a brow of sun-damaged skin. He wore a kitchen apron emblazoned with a film poster for *Babette's Feast*, where the silhouetted figure of woman in a long dress was holding a small square basket while bending to pick herbs from a garden.

"Let's keep her inside tonight, Stan; there's going to be a frost."

"She fucking bit me," said Stan, holding up his bleeding palm.

"Put some Neosporin on it, my bathroom cabinet, bottom shelf, on the left."

"I'm afraid I'm like something the cat dragged in, too," said Wendy apologetically. She flipped back her ponytail and made motions of presenting a more well-groomed face. "I thought we were going to grab some paintings out of a dirty old barn and head straight back to the city."

"Sorry about the detour, dear," apologized Alice, studying Wendy with a curious squint, as if not quite able to match the fashion plate of two nights before with the scrappy Amazon who had now appeared. "But George and I have a little catching up to do."

"You're very sexy like that," Stan assured her, holding his hand as he eyed the blue tights, as if mystified as well by the transformation. "Like you're auditioning for Catwoman."

"Chanterelles, George!" exclaimed Alice as she accepted an outstretched Baggie from George. "Stan, chanterelles from Hermitage."

"Precious as gold," said Stan.

"And, dear, girls today don't want to hear compliments from an old fart like you. That's why he's always getting himself in trouble with his students," she added, turning to Wendy.

"Oh," said Wendy, "I'm perfectly okay with Catwoman, except I forgot the kinky mask and those adorable ears. But if quartz dust in every pore, sweat"—she wrinkled her nose—"chalk"—she held up her hands contritely—"and plenty of good old-fashioned dirt turns you on, I'm your babe."

"Simone Simon!" exclaimed Stan. "I knew I'd seen you somewhere."

"Who's that, Uncle Stan?" asked George with raised eyebrows directed at Wendy, but glad for any subject except the one that was on the docket.

"*Cat People*, 1942. I did the rewrite for Jacques Tourneur. Simone Simon played Irena Dubrovna, who turns into a black panther when stirred by love's passions. A kiss"—and Stanley blew a kiss at his wife—"will do it."

"Enough already, Stan," scolded Alice, shifting back her mane of graying auburn hair.

"But don't you agree? She's got those same mysterious eyes and aristocratic nose and enchanting French smile."

"Well, *this* Simone Simon would love to grab a shower before dinner, if you can spare a bathroom."

"Of course you can, dear. Stan, don't fucking bleed on the guests—and show Simone to Cecily's bedroom and bathroom. Make sure there are fresh towels in there. And, Wendy, feel free to grab some warm clothes in the bureau by the bed; Cecily will never miss them."

Alice took George's arm and led him though the living room, its built-in bookshelves packed to the faux-wood beams lining the plaster ceiling. The little remaining wall space was hung with vintage Hollywood posters of Stan's films, a writing credit for *The Big Sleep*, *Night and the City*, and *Double Indemnity* signed by director Billy Wilder with a note of appreciation to Stan, along with others from the late forties and early fifties. A beat-up baby grand with no name he could recognize was squeezed into a corner.

The moment they made it to the kitchen and out of earshot of the others, Alice was all business.

"So what's with you and the old bastard? Felicity said he ate all his dinner *and* then some." Steadying herself with an outstretched arm on the granite island counter, she turned to examine him from head to toe, sweeping back unruly strands of hair, gray-green eyes focused in a skeptical squint, as if he might try to escape at any moment. "Beer, wine?" She turned to the refrigerator. "I'm having chardonnay to start."

"I'll take a Corona if you've got it." George snapped his fingers. "Nastassja Kinski did the remake—right?"

"What was that?"

"Nothing."

"With a lime, right? All Stan's theater students take it that way."

"Sounds good."

"Come on, out with it. You two are thick as thieves." She pulled out a frosty bottle of white wine. "Here, pull the cork, will you? My hands aren't as strong as they used to be."

"Same old, same old. Nearly impossible to know exactly what's on his mind."

"Felicity says he's suddenly perky as can be. So how come he no longer wants to off himself?"

"He wants me to edit his memoir."

"You—his memoir?" Alice shot her face forward and squinted, inspecting his face in disbelief. "What kind of a memoir, exactly?"

"I've only dipped into it . . ." George shrugged, pretending to be preoccupied with the cork. "Four-hundred-page typescript of his life and times, Second Circuit Court judgeship, the Hiss trial—"

"Hiss? What about the family?"

"That, too, I suppose."

"Does he have a publisher?"

"He mentioned an editor at Norton."

"And what, exactly, does he expect *you* to do? You don't know squat about the law."

"He described it as unfinished. He stopped work on it five years ago. Maybe it needs a little trimming or updating."

"From you?"

George looked up from where he'd been turning the corkscrew, giving his reply with as much sincerity as he could muster.

"I suggested you'd be better qualified."

"Damn right. I suppose touting his obscurantist hidebound record on the Second Circuit. My whole life, my whole damn career—like an albatross having him there, having to always explain him away."

"Actually, the legal stuff takes up only a brief section." George popped the cork. "As he pointed out to me, his opinions and dissents are already on the record."

"George, don't pretend to be so guileless with me. What's he up to? Goddamn it, you're practically a physics Ph.D."

"Astrophysics."

"Out with it, Jedi knight."

"The Hiss trial does seem to play a central role in the narrative."

Alice grunted as she continued to concentrate fiercely on slicing a lime on a cutting board.

"You know the Judge is a legal Houdini. He used his role in the trial to pacify his pals on the Left and suck up to the establishment on the Right—all to grease the skids on his Second Circuit appointment by the Truman administration a year later."

"Aunt Alice," he replied, popping the cork, "that was long before I was even born."

"Damn right it was, and that's why you'd better listen to me and turn the manuscript over this minute."

"I always listen to you."

"What's really going on? Is he finally going bust? Felicity says he's slowly losing his marbles."

"He's holding on or holding out; I'm not sure which. But the one thing that seemed to get his motor running was when I Googled a recent book that claims to prove that Alger Hiss *was* a spy."

"Oh Christ, George, spare me." She popped the top of the Corona. "Do you have any idea how long this shit has been going on? Look at me: your aunt Alice, the sixty-eight-year-old woman who now stands before you with bad knees and arthritis." After drying her hands, her fingers strayed to a necklace of white marble beads with interlocked silver *C*s. "And a sagging chin like Methuselah's." She twisted the necklace as if to collect her thoughts. "Listen, I attended the Hiss trial when I was a teenager, eager to see *Daddy* at his masterful best. Of course, I thought he was Clarence Darrow. But so what if Hiss may have passed on a few documents to the Soviets in the thirties." She began struggling to force the lime slice into the neck of the bottle. "And now we're best pals with the Russians. But his screwups"—she handed the Corona to her nephew—"his failure to attack the system and get his client off, nothing will change that."

George grimaced, brows furrowed, as he tipped the bottle to his lips.

"You see, there's new information from deciphered Soviet cables from the forties and recently opened KGB files. It seems Hiss flew to Moscow in early 1945, after Yalta, where he met with the Soviet deputy commissar of foreign affairs, Andrei Vyshinski, and was given the Order of the Red Star. That little factoid lit up the Judge like a supernova."

Alice laughed hysterically and downed her first glass.

"So he thinks his tarnished reputation has been saved from the dustbin of history—because of that! *P-a-l-e-a-se*, as my grad students say. He allowed the system to ride roughshod over Hiss—Hoover and Nixon and their scaly minions. His psychiatric attack on Chambers left

him a laughingstock in the profession. Don't tell Martha I said that."
She refilled her glass. "So, how about turning over the typescript to
your favorite aunt?"

"I promised him I'd handle it."

"Bullshit, George. Even Jedi knights know when they're out of their
depth. And he doesn't need to know."

"Just lose the Jedi thing."

"You were so damn cute in that T-shirt, waving around that
thingummy."

"I'm sorry, he trusts me."

"George, you don't know shit about the law, and, like you said, you
weren't even—hell, your mother, my baby sister, wasn't even born until
after the Hiss trial." She drained her half-filled glass, hand shaking.
"You have to understand: He manipulates everyone and everything,
if not with his rulings on the Second Circuit, his fucked-up opinions,
then by emotional blackmail in the family around Hermitage. He put
my mother, Annie, through hell with all his affairs. Messed with my
daughter *and* your mother," she spat out. "And now, now he's playing
you, too."

"Go ask him yourself. I don't really give a shit."

"George, you're lying to me about something." She put a hand on his
shoulder. "I once made my living reading jurors' faces; I got hardened
criminals and killers acquitted." He could feel the tremor of repressed
rage in her body. "Law, George, case law, opinions, descents . . . they
live on, they survive or fail, prosper or gather dust, and go on to wreak
terrible damage, like defective genes passed in the blood." She closed
her eyes for a moment. "The *damage* that man has done."

"Go have this conversation with him. I'm sure he'd be delighted to
see you."

"It's the system, George." Her eyes widened, flashing gray-green.
"The Judge, you see, wasn't the only defense counsel; Hiss had, I don't
know, eight or nine of the finest legal minds in the country defending
him at one time or another, all part of their Harvard Law School mafia.
And they raised hundreds of thousands in legal fees for his defense
fund—from the old-boy establishment or God knows where. As far
as I know, none of those big swinging dicks ever told the real story
about how they fucked up so badly and why—and they all must be
dead by now. The establishment tried to save itself by sacrificing one
of its own. So if the Judge is coming clean, trying to resurrect his bona

fides"—Alice's eyes quieted a moment, reflective, a quiver of her lower lip—"that's quite a story for . . . well, a law journal article at least . . . something I could do justice to, George."

"I'm sorry, Aunt Alice. His instructions are actually in a letter, a *legal* document, witnessed and notarized."

"That fucking monster. How much is he paying you?"

"There was a fee mentioned in the letter but not an amount. That's probably in his will. And I couldn't care less about the money; I've got *bigger* issues to deal with anyway."

Alice smiled at this, squinting, fingering her glass hungrily.

"Did you see his will?"

"Felicity said he revised it and FedExed it to his lawyer in New York last week."

"Oh, spare me. So the whole starving himself thing was just a ploy to summon his boy Friday to his side. You're almost as much a conniver as he is, Georgie. Always sneaking around for handouts from the Judge. For four years at Princeton, too, I bet, when he wouldn't pay a red cent for Cecily at Stanford."

"You said she got a scholarship . . . and she got the Judge's Chopin prize."

"She damn well did, thank you."

"Listen, why don't we just skip dinner; I've got a lot to do, getting replacements for the paintings that have sold."

"No, stick around; dinner's almost ready." She went over and stirred Stan's stew. "Where is the cook anyway? Stan," she called, and picked up the Baggie of chanterelles and put them in a colander to rinse. "And I like your girlfriend—perhaps a little young; she reminds me of Cecily at that age in some ways. She'll be good for you, George—you need a tough broad in your life."

"She's not my girlfriend."

"So," she went on, arranging the chanterelles on a cutting board and beginning to slice them carefully, "what was the name of this recent book on Hiss you mentioned?"

"*The Haunted Wood*, by Allen Weinstein and some Russian guy."

"Weinstein, Weinstein—oh my God . . . not *Allen* Weinstein?" She rinsed her hands and dried them. "Come along, *mon cher*." She led him through the compact dining room, past the Arts and Crafts table set for dinner, and back to the cozy living room. She scanned her bookshelves, which were crammed with uniform editions of legal reference books, volumes of French literature, rows of cookbooks and Hollywood memoirs, and cassettes of Stan's films. "Hold on." She took out a pair of reading glasses from the pocket of her slacks. "Here it is." She pulled out a well-worn volume, weighing it in her hands. "Allen Weinstein's *Perjury*, an exhaustive examination of the Hiss trial, published back in the late seventies. Impressive scholarship. I'm sure I sent Daddy a copy. If memory serves, Weinstein started out being a big fan of Hiss's and then, after years of research into the defense and FBI files, turned the tables on his man. Got a lot of old lefties all upset—*betrayed*, I think, is the operative term." She tapped the cover and gave a snort. "As I remember, dear Daddy comes off a gullible fool and, worse, an inept and sleazy bully of Whittaker Chambers. Of course, the Judge refused to be interviewed by Weinstein. Which figures: His seat on the Second Circuit Court was safe by then and he was gunning for the Supreme Court, and so he just pretended to be above it all. Somehow I can't see Weinstein now in Daddy's corner."

"I believe Weinstein is *now* the archivist of the United States."

"Allen Weinstein! Unbelievable. Ain't that the way of the world. All the old lefties have drifted into the safe and comfortable pockets of the establishment." She turned as Stan came back from his bedroom to check the lamb stew. "Isn't that right, Stan, all you old lefties have retreated into the embrace of the establishment or academia?"

Stan turned, distracted, a large Band-Aid on the back of his hand.

"Sorry, I just got a distress call from our Blanche DuBois about her stressed vocal cords." He wiped his hands on his apron, which was covered in silver-brown fir.

"Allen Weinstein has written another book on Hiss. And get this, Bush seems to have appointed him archivist of these here United States."

"Allen who?"

"Turn your goddamn hearing aids on. That's why we bought the damn things. Allen Weinstein."

"Oh, the guy who fucked over Hiss—right." His soft brown eyes found George's and then his wife's. "Hate to tell you, my dear, we *are* the establishment, or haven't you heard? Dinner should be ready in ten, and I hear the hair dryer going in Cecily's bathroom."

"Hey, Stan." Alice handed George the well-thumbed copy of *Perjury* and returned to the kitchen to retrieve her wineglass. "George's got a terrific idea for a screenplay with a fantastic final twist: Alger Hiss turns out to be a Soviet spy after all, and his great defender, Edward E.

Dimock, that Harvard bad boy, turns out to have been hoodwinked by his own client. Or better still, a KGB agent himself. How's that for a nifty twisty ending?"

"How do you want to cook the chanterelles?"

"Sauté them in butter and olive oil, a touch of tarragon, a squeeze of lemon, salt and pepper, then, near the end, a splash of wine. That's how Annie always prepared them."

As George followed her into the kitchen, flipping through the pages of *Perjury*, he noted the name Dimock heavily circled throughout. Toward the back he came upon a folded piece of heavy paper. He opened it, to discover a George Altmann sketch of the Judge seated at the defense table, staring defiantly off under prominent eyebrows, jaw shot forward in determined concentration.

"Where did you get this?" asked George, holding out the sketch.

"A souvenir—oh, there it is—from your great genius and namesake. He was sketching the trial the opening day. He gave it to me as a present when I went to congratulate Daddy after court was adjourned."

George examined the sketch. A thing of energetic but deft strokes, it wonderfully captured the likeness and quick intelligence of the fortyish defense attorney. He carefully examined the signature and date: G. Altmann 11/17/49.

"After adjournment?"

"How young he looks," said Stan, looking over George's shoulder. "What a ravishing profile, like Atticus what's his name in *To Kill a Mockingbird.*"

"Finch," said George.

"Gregory Peck." Alice sighed. "What a dreamboat."

"Greg is a true gentleman," noted Stan. "He signed a letter condemning HUAC's witch hunt of the film industry. I helped out on some rewrites for *Twelve O'Clock High,* and he told me his greatest passion had been for Ingrid Bergman—*Spellbound,* you know."

George held the sketch under the lights over the kitchen counter. "You were really there," he said dreamily, as if struggling again to connect the phantom swirl of data points inundating his mind.

"Bright-eyed, dewy-eyed innocent Chapin girl with a crush on one of Teddy's Yale friends, whom I was praying would show up for New Year's Eve at Hermitage."

"Ah," murmured Stan, stirring away, "how I wish I'd been that boy and had known you then, Alice dear."

Alice scowled. "You were happily married to airhead Samantha. Remember the pug-nosed starlet with the big tits?"

George glanced at his uncle, who only shrugged and gave him a faint smile.

"You know," said George, brow flexed in thought, "it's weird, but when I went into the Judge's office to get his typescript, I found nine finished sketches by George Altmann pinned to an old corkboard. Nothing like this dashed-off caricature, but all exquisite renderings from the thirties, executed in beautiful detail, like portrait studies. They were of Priscilla and Alger Hiss and a bunch of guys who, according to the Judge, either died mysteriously or were conveniently out of the country and unavailable as witnesses for the prosecution."

Alice looked at him with a curious flicker of her penciled eyebrows. "Really . . . from the thirties? Where'd the old man come by them?"

"He told me, in fact, that it's in his memoir; Altmann gave them to him on the first day of the trial, on the steps of the courthouse."

Alice now looked at him pointedly with a hint of incredulity as she took hold of his arm, her voice pitched in a stern prosecutorial tone.

"Gave them to him? Now why would he have wanted to do that?"

"The Judge suggested last night that they might depict a gathering of important government officials in Washington, all with connections to the Communist Party or the KGB. A Party cell or a secret caucus."

"Oh George"—a frisson of raw emotion lit up her eyes—"per usual, he's fucking with your mind."

"Well," piped up Stan, "in the old days we caucused a couple of times a month in the hills, talked scuttlebutt, the latest Party literature in the *Daily Worker* or *The New Masses*. Planning the revolution— doncha know."

"You were hardly accused of spying," his wife shot back, impatiently.

"The Judge had them all carefully arranged with their names and bio data, like a police lineup."

At this, Alice seemed to go quiet, a look of momentary uncertainty, or a vague memory she was trying to summon.

"Have you got 'em? Show 'em to me, George."

George took out his phone and pulled up his photos, first of the intact corkboard and then the individual sketches. Alice grabbed the phone, put on her glasses, and examined each one closely. "Hard to make out the faces, but I recognize Alger and Priscilla Hiss. Who are the others?"

George went through them one by one: "Harry Dexter White, Laurence Duggan, Marvin Smith, Lauchlin Currie, William Remington, Noel Field, and one guy the Judge couldn't identify."

"Duggan was that poor fellow who jumped out the window after HUAC got their claws into him," noted Stan from the stove.

"Four died under mysterious circumstances," said George. "Two or three weren't available to testify."

"The plot thickens, nicely, along with my stew," said Stan. "HUAC accused White, too, of being a Commie. Heart attack—wasn't it, poor guy."

Alice returned the phone and brought her face close. "George, I was there, from before the opening gavel to adjournment on the first day. Daddy was seated at the defense table, surrounded by his colleagues; there's no way Altmann could have just waltzed up to him and handed him nine sketches."

"They were in a manila envelope," noted George, sensing something in his aunt's voice, "according to the Judge."

"Ah," and Alice raised a wagging finger, "always the telling detail . . . What is he up to this time?" And she cast a knowing glance at Stan. "What's he got up his sleeve?"

"Don't be so hard on George, dear," offered Stan. "And hardly a matter you need concern yourself with."

"Did he tell you"—Alice stepped back, assuming a prosecutorial pose—"exactly when your namesake turned over these sketches in the manila envelope on the first day of the trial?"

"Does it matter?"

"Of course it does. If he was given those sketches before the start of the trial, in the discovery phase, any evidence pertaining to the perjury charges must be shared by the defense with the prosecution, and vice versa. After the discovery phase has ended and the trial has started, if the defense comes upon or is offered evidence that harms their case, they are no longer bound to share said evidence—well, it's a little ambiguous—with the prosecution."

George locked eyes with his aunt and held out the Altmann drawing of the Judge. "You said Altmann handed you this after adjournment."

Alice smiled icily and nodded.

"We were all gathered around Daddy to celebrate. Altmann rushed up to Annie, nervous as a jaybird, like a worshipper in her fan club, and tried to put this sketch of handsome Papa into her hands—an offering, a gift, a souvenir, I suppose. But our usually gracious mama would have nothing to do with him; she shook her head vigorously and literally held up a palm to fend him off. At which point, his face fell and, looking around, a little panicked, he offered it to me. Well, I was thrilled, better than a foul ball in Yankee Stadium. I took the sketch and thanked him profusely—polite little dutiful daughter that I was. Daddy was right beside me, in fact, saying good-bye, since we weren't sure we could stay in the city for dinner—Teddy was already long gone, having left in disgust after the lunch break." With this, her face suddenly deepened with memory, eyes blurring, head ever so slowly nodding. "Then he, Altmann, just barged in front of me like a panicked animal and pressed an envelope into Daddy's hands—a manila envelope, muttered something in his ear, and disappeared back into the press gallery." Alice remained frozen in place, as if a little spellbound by the vividness of this forgotten moment. "I'll be damned."

"So," George now prompted, "the trial had officially started; they were out of the discovery phase?"

Alice cackled. "What a cool fucking customer." She took her nephew's arm and squeezed it for emphasis. "And he lied to you about this, too. You said it happened on the steps of the courthouse."

"It was fifty years ago; his mind is going."

"Poor Daddy." She maintained her hold on his arm. "Legally speaking, if defense counsel receives a physical item implicating the client in criminal conduct during the discovery phase, he or she must—and it's required by federal law—deliver such evidence to law-enforcement officials, or in this case the FBI. But once the trial is under way, defense counsel is only required to return the item to the source from whom he received it, with advice as to the legal implications, or consequences, possession or destruction of the item might result in. On the other hand"—a smile of quiet pleasure came over her face—"defense counsel may retain the item for a reasonable amount of time if he intends to return the item, or fears its return will result in its destruction, or has reasonable fears that the return of the item will result in the physical harm of someone, or"—she raised a finger along with her voice—"if defense counsel intends to test, examine, inspect or use the item in the defense's case to the benefit of the client." Alice sighed with the delicious effort of recall. "Well, that's more or less the statute—drugs and weapons require different handling. But bottom line: Once discovery has been completed, protection of the client's interest would be paramount."

"In the memoir—what I've read so far—he writes he was preoccupied, and only examined the sketches briefly and—I think the phrase he used was 'absence of mind'—buried them in the defense files and promptly forgot about them, until digging them out years later."

At this, Alice erupted with indignation. "What a master—that's at least three lies he's told. Any defense counsel worth his salt would have immediately checked out such a thing and examined the sketches in detail, either for the advantage or damage they might pose to his case. Clearly, he was making damn sure those sketches were never introduced as evidence in the trial—ha, talking about disappearing witnesses."

"So he did the right thing, legally speaking?"

Alice just shook her head and took a spin around the kitchen, coming to rest at the stove with a serving dish for Stan's stew.

She smiled to herself, as if trying to keep her cards close, muttering, "If he indeed shared the evidence with his colleagues and his client, Alger Hiss, about the disposition of—the implications—of such evidence appearing out of the blue from the hand of a panicked alcoholic—like father, like son, wouldn't you say?"

"The Judge told me that, in retrospect, he figured George Altmann had probably once been a member of the Communist Party."

"Hey, Stan, hear that? You're our in-house expert."

"Almost all the artists and writers—the good ones—I knew back *dans le temps* were in the Party."

"Well, there you go." Alice left Stan with the serving dish and refilled her glass. "So where are the sketches now?"

George looked into her eager eyes and, without compunction, lied straight to her face.

"Oh, I left them where I found them, pinned on the corkboard in Summitville."

Alice intently inspected her nephew's face over the top of her glass. "Really . . ."

"George Altmann died a month after the trial began . . . slipped or fell off the Sawkill Bridge on his way back from town on Christmas Eve."

"How delicious," murmured Stan, tasting his stew. "Sounds like a promising elevator pitch for my next film."

Alice placed a steadying hand on her nephew's shoulder, affectionate, half-flirting. "Sorry, George, you may have gotten the Judge's brains but not his looks. Maybe Cordelia's eyes—what do think, Stan?"

"Beats me, Allie." He smiled at George and winked. "Take the brains, dear nephew—looks fade. And the Judge is one purebred IBM."

"Now that Wendy of yours, I like her; she reminds me of somebody: the nose, the eyes, the expressive strong hands." Alice gazed at her arthritic right hand with a sorry pout. "Who does she remind you of, Stan?"

"I told you, Simone Simon . . . a dream, a shape-shifter, a panther with a taste for her lover's blood."

Alice rolled her eyes in annoyance. "No, no, the nose is all wrong." Then, head canted with a hint of incredulity, her eyebrows lifted, she said, "Annie . . . a young Annie. In her early publicity shots—don't you think, Stan?—on the piano at Hermitage."

"Ah!" exclaimed Stan, spoon raised. "Your slave driver, your mommy dearest—my poor little traumatized girl." He stepped over and gave his wife a kiss.

"Keep it," said Alice to George, seeing how her nephew's eyes kept returning to the sketch of the handsome defense counsel, "maybe it'll be worth something someday if you can keep priming the art pump. We'll call it a trade for the other nine sketches."

Distracted, George continued talking about Altmann: "The police called it an accident, but most people, including his wife and son, assumed it was suicide. Frustration, a career stalled . . . depression, you know."

Alice, watching her nephew's face intently, now nodded sympathetically.

"Don't take it too much to heart, George. I mean the gene thing, if that's what's bothering you. Highly overrated. And for what it's worth, I could smell the booze on Altmann's breath that day in court, BO, too—like I said, a very nervous fellow."

"He'd been drinking, you think?"

"Anyway, such evidence—your enigmatic sketches—if it can be so dignified, without a witness, without corroborating testimony, is virtually worthless."

"But then . . ."

"Besides, I'm sure Cordelia must have told you after all this time."

"Told me what?"

"Listen, I handled the divorce case for her. When we first contacted Jimmy Altmann with the complaint about his desertion—no child support and all those back taxes owing—he wrote back that Cordy had admitted to him that he wasn't the father of her child. Some guy, some famous rock star, who used Dylan's Woodstock studio for a recording session. Lives out in L.A. He wrote that greatest-hits-of-all-time love song about Cordy—she's always humming it."

George remained rooted, staring at the sketch.

"What song?"

"Surely, Cordy told you, George. Talk about ancient history."

"For Christ's sake, Allie," scolded Stan, untying his apron. "What a shitty thing to throw out like casual gossip. Don't listen to her nonsense, George. People say the damnedest things in divorce cases. My first wife, as you, Alice, well know, accused me of everything short of murdering the Black Dahlia. And Cordelia may be your sister, but she's still your client, and that's privileged information, among other things. *You*, of all people . . ."

———

Dinner, as George feared (his life further turned upside down by his aunt) descended into a fun house of distorting mirrors. Both Alice and Stan, seated at either end of the table, were thoroughly dazzled, if not mesmerized, by Wendy, as was George, albeit for different reasons, while Wendy, although not exactly relishing being the center of attention, seemed more intent on deftly deflecting inquiries so as to elicit more details about her interrogators than she provided about herself.

"That's what I like to see," said Alice to Wendy, who was sitting on her left, "a hungry woman, a fearless woman, a street fighter—just look at those broken nails, will you! I love it."

"Simone Simon would be aghast, I guess," said Wendy, looking up from her plate. "I've had broken nails since I was eight. And I've missed out on the whole nail parlor thing."

"Christ," said Alice, "my best girls in constitutional law, I swear they spend half their leisure time getting pedicures and the other getting their pubes waxed."

"You, Steinem, Betty Friedan, and Hugh Hefner stormed the barricades for the resurrection of Barbie." Stan held up his glass in mock salute. "So old farts like me can sit back and admire the result. That blue sweater, by the way, looks stunning on you, Wendy."

"You don't think Cecily would mind my borrowing it?" she asked between bites.

"Cecily would be more than honored to share with a soul sister," said Stan. "Here, have some more chanterelles."

"Who's Hugh Hefner?" she asked.

"*Playboy*," said George, who had been quiet for most of the meal, "he founded the magazine."

"A pig," said Alice, "objectified airbrushed women—airheads."

"Half the women in my film class aspire to do female porn," said Stan. "Like you said, they airbrush themselves."

"Don't you think porn has liberated women, Alice?" asked Wendy. "There are some really talented women directors who have learned how to shoot human flesh with nuance and flare, bringing out the abstractions of the female body, of women alive to the pleasures of their flesh."

"Oh, your generation! Spare me the details," said Alice, waving as if to disperse a bad smell.

Stan laughed and saluted his guest with a broad smile. "You're such a cut above, dear, so refreshing from the complainers in your generation." He examined his gnarled hands. "And to think I once had my manicurist at the Pink Lady do my nails once a week, meet up with all the other fellas." He pressed his lips into a wistful pout.

"Stan," offered Alice sweetly, "you're still my Tinseltown big deal."

"How exciting," said Wendy, "all the actors you worked with."

"You know, Wendy, what really saddens me, how the kids today have no memory or exposure to the theater greats of the past—they're barely names, if that. Take Boris Karloff; they don't even know his horror films. As a stage actor, Boris, with that unforgettable face and eyes and slight baritone lisp, was in a class of his own, like a musical instrument onstage. And the kindest man I've ever known; we who knew him and worked with him loved him. Remember, Alice, we saw him with Julie Harris in *The Lark*. I took you backstage. Of course, you only had eyes for Joan of Arc, always looking for a pyre to build around yourself. Who remembers any of the greats like Katharine Cornell or my soul mate Lillian Hellman?"

"Oh, save it Stan. You old Reds are pathetic."

"Or Ruth Chatterton, still the epitome of grace and glamour for me—a true star."

"My father was a big movie buff," said Wendy. "Took me to see all of Fellini, Truffaut, Vittorio De Sica—*The Garden of the Finzi-Continis* was my favorite of all time, along with Zeffirelli's *Romeo and Juliet*. I know it by heart."

Stan said with a serene smile, "A romantic—but as an artist, you would be."

"What do you think, Wendy?" asked Alice. "Your generation . . . I mean, I've never seen so many overindulged, pampered, touchy-feely children, afraid to offend, afraid of a misstep, to be politically incorrect, and just plain terrified to take their cause to the streets. They're such a bunch of moaning sheep terrified to push down the walls of their pen."

"Aunt Alice," said George, with an exasperated glance across the table, "Wendy is hardly a spokesman—spokeswoman—for her generation."

"What would you know, Georgie, mooning away at the sky. Your generation might be too late for the street fight, but you're all happy to grab the benefits handed to you on a silver platter."

"Is that why Cecily hightailed it for Stanford?" shot back George. "For all the street fighting?"

Alice paused, her wineglass raised to her lips, squinting with a half-smile, very much enjoying the jousting.

"You have to forgive your aunt, George. We just heard from Cecily yesterday that she's divorcing her husband of eight years."

"Stan, stop feeding the cats." Alice kicked at something under the table.

"I'm not, I swear," he replied with a repressed smile.

"A wonderful black man." Alice sighed. "A world-famous surgeon, beloved by patients and colleagues at Stanford University Hospital—a tribute to his race."

"Dear, we first need to hear her side."

"Cecily was my favorite cousin," said George, now with a pointed look at his aunt, "along with Billy, of course."

This seemed to bring about a momentary truce in the conversation.

"What about your mom and dad?" asked Alice.

"I lost my parents when I was thirteen," said Wendy, meeting the eyes of all at the table, as if this revelation meant nothing. "You might say I pretty much had to make it up as I went along. I mean, growing up in a suburb of Houston is like coming from the dark side of the moon."

"I'm sorry to hear that," said Alice. "Dixie, how rotten for you."

"Jesus, what happened?" asked George.

"A climbing accident." She raised her glass, swirling the red wine, her lips pressed inward as she swept back hair from one side on her face and then the other. "I don't really like to talk about it."

"Like I said, Stan"—Alice shot a knowing look at her husband—"even the perseverance of Annie, given her rotten childhood."

"Who's Annie?" asked Wendy.

"My God," said Stan, "and yet you went right back to climbing? Everest, even. What a fearless young lady. My hat's off to you. I really do wish—if ever you think about changing professions . . . Well, you've certainly got the acting chops—pathos, pathos is the glittering prize."

"Oh, enough Stan—really."

"People accuse me of being an exhibitionist—for my work, my self-portraits—but I'm actually quite shy. Staring at myself, my body, is a real struggle."

"She paints nudes," explained George, not a little fascinated.

"That's what I mean!" exclaimed Stan. "That's your strength; that's where real pathos comes from—the damaged soul, the lost childhood—and very few actors have that, pathos. The great ones know all the tricks, staying at odds with their surroundings, doing the unexpected or unsettling, capturing just the right glint of light in their eye—a sudden entrance, a sudden dazzling vocal speed, reaching for a voice from the past, or just milking the poetry for full effect. But pathos, that's inborn. Olivier could fake it, but he didn't have it. Only Ralph Richardson and, in my generation, Brando had it—don't you agree, Alice?"

Alice waved a dismissive hand at her husband. "What I want to know about are the men in the climbing profession—do you call it a profession? Do they respect you, or treat you like a second-class citizen?"

Wendy shrugged, sighing, her reddish blond hair glistening in the candlelight where it fell across her shoulders against the soft blue of her "soul sister's" sweater. "There's really no place for that kind of stuff when everybody's life is on the line. My father instilled that in me that from the first day he taught me to climb. He was a stickler on safety. He believed in the purity of climbing. When you're on the rock face, it's all about balance and technique, not brute strength. As long as you can lift your own weight, the men really don't have an advantage. And my height does give me an advantage in terms of reach, at least compared to that of other women climbers. I tell my young girls, climbing is all about mastering your fate. Once you've planned everything out, taken all safety precautions, checked equipment twice over—you're in charge."

"I always liked take-charge women," said Stan, cocking his head at his wife.

Alice spread the fingers of her free hand, intently examining the polished nails. "Reach, reach . . . my brother, Teddy, had the most extraordinary reach on the keys."

"So did Billy," put in Stan as a tender reminder.

"Do the *men*," asked Alice, glaring at Stan, "the guys who run the climbing school, give you equal billing with students? Will guys take instruction from you, or are they humiliated by a strong woman?"

"The school is owned and run by a woman. Guys often feel the women are more patient and less critical. They figure, If a girl can do it, why can't I? On a professional level, the guys are pretty competitive—with themselves most of all. I mean, I'm not really into FAs—first ascents—that kinda thing . . . like my mother. A lot of guys are into that." She flashed an inquisitive look at Alice. "Bet you've seen a lot of that in your legal world."

"Well, in my day," said Alice, with a proud nod to Stan, "Bernadette and I kept the bully boys on their toes without any help from Hefner." She shrugged and smiled at Stan. "In the Bay Area courts, it was always a slog for respect: You had to fight twice as hard and be three times as good."

Stan turned eagerly again to Wendy, who was finishing off her second helping of his lamb stew. "But I have to say—today, I mean—such courage. Still climbing after what happened . . . the twin towers . . . those poor people forced to burn or jump?"

Alice rolled her eyes. "Don't go fishing for a screenplay idea, Stan."

"Jesus, Uncle Stan," said George, "let's not go there."

"My apologies, George, I forgot about you."

Wendy shot a searching look across the table at George, and seeing something in his troubled eyes, she switched tack. "I do it because I love it." She sipped her wine. "And if I didn't, I'd obsess . . . I'd probably, you know, after what happened, go into a corner and curl into a fetal position and freeze up. The first weekend, you know, after . . . I just had to hightail it out of the city and spend the day solo climbing."

"I love brave women—it's why I married your aunt," Stan intoned with a wink at George.

Wendy gave a tentative smile. "If you don't face your fears, they consume you. You set your protection and you move on."

"Tough way to make a living, though," said Alice, looking skeptically at Wendy, as if trying to fathom the range of emotions flickering across her face.

"Wendy is a fine artist," said George, trying to short-circuit the subject. "An even tougher way to make a living."

Alice shook her head and caught her husband's eye. "Uncanny, she's even got Annie's no-nonsense savoir faire."

"Annie?"

"Sorry, dear," apologized Alice. "You remind me of my mother. She was a world-class concert pianist."

"The celebrity artist rat race," Wendy offered, giving George an exasperated glance. "So much for purity—huh, George?" She turned back to Alice. "Annie, she was that good?"

"Played Carnegie Hall. She recorded for RCA in the thirties. A hard act to follow as a daughter."

"Ah," said Stan, gazing fondly at his guest, "that explains how we met you at George's opening."

"I'm totally in awe of George Altmann's work."

"So much so, she bought two of his paintings," said George, looking pleased to throw out another tantalizing data point to keep the pot stirred.

"Pricey," said Stan.

Alice shoved a bottle of wine that required opening to her husband and fixed her stare on George.

"Odd, George, such an albatross around your neck—you and Cordelia, abandoned by her ne'er-do-well *alcoholic* husband, a barnful of unsellable paintings, back taxes to pay—three, four years' worth . . . Did that make it into the Judge's memoir, George? How he paid off those taxes and kept his lovely Cordelia in her rural slum of a home? When he could just as easily had you two back in his apartment in New York. Why'd he do that, George?"

Stan cleared his throat and flashed a warning look down the table at his glowering spouse.

"Dear—"

"Altmann is a genius and, yes, full of pathos," noted Wendy to Stan with a melting smile, a look of rapture in her blue eyes.

Alice chortled. "Come to think of it, Stan, what was it the Judge popped off about at Cordelia's wedding? Something about George Altmann being a washed-up old Communist—like you, honey."

"Of course, dear—a badge of honor. Like I said, all the good artists, directors, creative people were Communists back in the thirties." Stan continued in a tone of avuncular assurance. "Anybody in the arts—it was pretty much de rigueur."

"Why Communists?" asked Wendy.

"My dear Simone," said Stan, bending forward to pat her hand, "during the thirties and forties, the Communist Party in America led the way in the fight against fascism, and the battle for Negro—as it was called then—rights, and social justice for the workers."

Alice snorted. "You and George Altmann . . . two Jews, and Alger Hiss, the Party's token WASP—if Mr. Weinstein is now to be believed."

"One thing for sure," and Stan raised a straight finger, "Hiss was never a member of the Communist Party. And I have than on good authority."

Alice laughed and bent toward her husband, raising a jousting finger in reply, as the Judge was wont to do when making a critical point from the bench.

"Because, ipso facto, he wasn't a Jew."

Stan laughed as he eased out the cork on the bottle Alice had pushed over to him. "In facto, I always got on terrifically with your father. We understood each other just fine." He offered a wry smile to George. "Like he always told me, 'I got to hand it to you Jews: Hollywood, finance, now law—you people own the works.'"

"Right, Stan." Alice made a grab for the bottle. "Just like he went around moaning at Cordy's wedding: 'How is it I ended up with three kikes for sons-in-law?'"

"What I heard was, 'Scratch a Communist and a Jew bleeds.'"

"Who's Alger Hiss?" asked Wendy in all innocence.

"Hasn't George told you about the skeleton rattling the family closet?" slurred Alice as she examined the label of the bottle skeptically. "After all, the great man has appointed, so it seems, his youngest grandson to whitewash—or is it airbrush?—his memoir."

"We really need to get going," said George.

"To answer your question, Stan, this bottle stinks. Wendy," said Alice, waving her glass and slopping wine, "a long, long time ago, in a galaxy far, far away"—she nodded, smiling, at George—"there was a trial, a famous trial: the trial of the century. So they called it. Standing room only. The OJ trial pales in comparison; trust me on this, kiddies, not even close. This trial changed the course of American history. Isn't that right, Stan? Certainly changed yours. You'd never have been blacklisted if Daddy had saved Hiss's ass, or served time in Danbury. Not that Daddy really blamed you for being blacklisted, only that you'd—'in a moment of self-righteous insanity'—pleaded the Fifth. Isn't that how he put it: 'Stan, why didn't you just tell them you made a mistake as an idealistic young man, a mistake you regret, and give 'em a few names of friends—fellow travelers like you, who have long since seen the light and rejected the Party.' Isn't that how he put it to you, Stan?"

Stan smiled gamely. "When God wants to punish an unbeliever, he gives him a pious wife."

She raised her glass along with her eyebrows and drank deep. "Daddy was our god, our way of righteousness entitlement, our belief in a benevolent system . . . as our mother, Annie, with all her rules, was our way of being . . . *ladies*."

"Annie," said Stan, sighing, his eyes glittering with memory, "radiant as the sun and moon. I feared crossing her more than the old man any day."

"Annie gave him hell for taking on the Hiss trial. Never forgave him—never."

"Why would she do that?" asked Wendy. "Her husband."

"She didn't like Alger Hiss for beans. My God, you should've seen it: Alger Hiss never looked more confident and splendidly attired, his face compact and intent as he eyed his accusers at the prosecution table. I remember feeling like we were at the epicenter of history. You could have cut the tension in that courtroom with a gilt-edged knife. The soul of the country was being wagered: whether to believe a slovenly and deceitful ex-Communist, Whittaker Chambers, or a paragon of Harvard Law, the State Department, and president of the Carnegie Endowment for International Peace. Virtue and progressive charm incarnate. I was so proud of Daddy that he was there to save the day."

"And your mother?" pressed Wendy.

"My mother did not seem to share my pride; she bristled and complained and seemed totally out of sorts. I'd never seen her so nervous as that first day in court, just wanting the thing to be over. While Teddy, my brother, groomed to follow in Daddy's footsteps, called it a 'freak show,' as did all his right-wing pals at Yale. *Alger Hiss, that rotten traitor.* And perhaps they were right, George . . . Perhaps Teddy *was* right." For a moment, Alice faltered and fell silent, looking away from her jury of three while wiping a stray tear or two from her olive green bloodhound eyes. "You see, in that moment, that jury of twelve, eight women and four men, still held the future—the Red Scare of the fifties and McCarthy's depredations—the fate of one Edward Dimock and family—in their hands. After that Christmas break at Hermitage, we would never all be together again. And George, for the record, when your namesake, with his black beret and ratty goatee, handed me that sketch at the end of that first day, his breath *did* stink of cheap whiskey . . . Like father, like son—huh? So maybe, Jedi, he was already well on his way to that fall. A tragic end—yes, I read your catalog—to, conveniently, supercharge his posthumous reputation."

Stan leaned down the table, glaring. "What a terrible thing to say, Alice; you're really in top form tonight."

"Nothing but the truth, boys and girls."

"Ah," said Stan, and held up his glass in a toast. "As my old granny always liked to say, 'Every ass likes to hear himself bray.'"

"No way it was suicide," spouted Wendy with sudden conviction.

Alice, oblivious, leaned forward. "I hate to tell you this, George: In this world, my world, the only one—where the rules are made—that really counts, the Judge will always be the man who defended Alger Hiss—and lost. And nothing—trust me—you can do will change that."

11

A Life in the Law and Out: Cordelia

LOVELY CORDELIA, HER early life bookended by tragic deaths.

It never leaves my mind, that humid night, late August of 1951—eighteen months after the Hiss trial, eight months after Teddy was killed—in our bedroom at Hermitage, when her journey began. Annie and I lay on top of the bed, blankets thrown back, windows thrown wide to the moonlight over the lake, hoping for a cooling breeze to gather us into sleep. Why was Annie here? She had not spoken more than two words to me for eight months, not since we had gotten the telegram confirming Teddy's death back in December. She blamed me. She blamed my defense of Alger Hiss—for a lot of things. Already, she had shifted her attention to the ballet world around Balanchine, playing as soloist onstage for his new ballets. When I was confirmed that June to my appointment to the U.S. Second Circuit Court of Appeals, she wrote me a sarcastic note of congratulations and slipped it into my briefcase: "Now you've been paid in full for defending Hiss, for sacrificing Teddy—your blood offering to ambition." From day one, she had called me a hypocritical scoundrel for taking the defense job in the Hiss trial. She said I only did it to make a name for myself. Or worse, because I was still in love with Priscilla Hiss. She never forgave my attack on Whittaker Chambers. No matter how I pleaded innocent on all counts, she saw Priscilla as the fiendish manipulator of our sad fate. Something she may have picked up from rumors among the defense team, who speculated that it was Priscilla who had been the spy, sneaking secret papers out of her husband's briefcase and copying them and turning them over to Chambers on the sly. The Irrational: Thy name is woman.

In New York, she'd moved into our guest bedroom. At Hermitage, she'd taken to sleeping in Cuddebackville, Teddy's room. But on this night, she'd suddenly returned to our marital bed after midnight. I remember, as we lay there in the moonlight, naked, sweating, listening to the chirp of the last of the summer cicadas punctuated by the hungry call of a screech owl, being impressed with the whiteness, the sparseness of our bedroom, which had all been Annie's doing. After we were married, she made a clean sweep of Dr. Dimock's heavy Victorian leavings, replacing them with simpler Shaker-style furnishings, painted white to go along with the white walls and ceiling. To clear her mind for sleep, she always said. To go along with all those white shelves containing rank upon rank of the English novels in which Annie so loved to lose herself, as if drifting back to some prelapsarian Anglican arcadia. And her beloved Proust, of course, in both French and English editions. She often said she enjoyed Proust's Combray childhood more than her own.

I glanced at the Raphael Soyer portrait across the room that I had commissioned for her fortieth birthday, which had always seemed to capture so serenely in paint her inner beauty, the effortless motions of her body translated into the inspirational power of her music. And then I turned for a glimpse of her forty-two-year-old body, still as slim and tough and purebred against the sheet as the first night of our marriage, like one of those tomb carvings discovered by Tess D'Urberville, white marble faces polished by the awed touch of generations. If we hadn't spoken in eight months, we hadn't touched one another sexually for at least a year, as the venomous notoriety from the trial spread, as Hiss fired his lawyers and hired a new team to mount his appeal. Insult to injury, Annie would sneer. Even on the street, she bemoaned, she'd be assailed by some total stranger who called me a traitor for defending Hiss.

And yet that night, she had returned silently to our bed. I sensed she was still awake, and I could make out her breasts gently rising, gently falling, as they had in the early years of our marriage when she would slip down early in the morning and practice in the nude, head held high to her musing gods in the ship's keel ceiling, her playing filling Hermitage, as if the very walls breathed something of her soul. I asked if she might like me to read to her—perhaps some Trollope, as we had often done in the early days when we couldn't sleep. I expected silence. Then I saw her hands lift from the sheet and come to rest on her white thighs for a moment, and then the fingers begin to play upon her pubic bones, across her womb, as if practicing the fingerings of some favorite encore from her repertoire, or imploring her dormant sensuality. I could hear her humming under her breath. Sometimes she would do this to put herself to sleep. On the white beadboard ceiling, the shimmer of the moonlight off the lake undulated like a luffing sail seeking a following wind.

"I'm going to divorce you, Edward. But I think that it only right to give you a last chance to redeem yourself. A sporting chance, as you might have it, for Teddy's sake. I was spotting this week, so there is still a chance, though a slim one. Make—no . . . I was going to say 'Make love to me,' but that is an inappropriate term. Fuck me, like a beast in the field. Breed with me, if you will. If you can get me with child and he lives, I will try to forgive you, for the child's sake, for Teddy's sake . . . for the girls. Those, I think, are the very best terms I can offer. You see, Edward, you are like a character out of Dante: You never change . . ."

I think she said this as an act of cruelty, to break me, to break my spirit and so set herself free. Coming from a long line of Unitarians, she did not believe in miracles, only in the search for truth and ameliorating the lot of our fellow men with good works. That and the consolations found in her music and books. She would not kiss me or touch me or encourage me in any way, but simply spent a few minutes touching herself and then spread her legs for the sacrifice. A woman who in the early days of our marriage had displayed such heights of ecstatic passion in the act of congress that I feared she might lose her mind. Since Teddy's death, Annie had moved to another plane of detached quiescence, and there she remained during the act, as if to thwart me. And so I managed to make love, but not to my wife, not to the woman I loved, the mother of our children, but to some fantasy goddess who had appeared out of that moonlit night transformed, perhaps a succubus with the call of the screech owl on her bloody lips. For at the end, as I reached completion, she bit deeply into my ear, so deep that I had to abandon our bed for a washcloth and bandage. When I returned, she was gone, back, I suppose, to her dead son's bed.

The pregnancy changed her, gradually, and as the pregnancy took hold, we returned to speaking terms. For she did acknowledge the miracle of the pregnancy, confirmed by her doctor, who had warned her after the birth of Martha and the resulting complications to avoid further pregnancies. Only when Cordelia was born, and not without a rush to the emergency room and a cesarean delivery, was something of the companionship of our early days reclaimed. We had longed for and expected a boy, but any miracle to be credible must come with a

twist to shatter expectations—a changeup requiring not just an adjustment in the timing of your swing but the power of that swing. Cordelia
came packaged with her own laws of aerodynamics, something indeed
of Teddy's good nature and physical prowess, but utterly unlike either
Alice or Martha. Or maybe we were just different parents. A year after
Cordelia was conceived (a name Annie chose, as if to upbraid Alice and
Martha for their aloof neglect after Teddy's death), lying in our bed
at Hermitage nursing, having recovered much of her strength, Annie
opened up to me suddenly, as if overcome by a revelation blown to her
on the pine breezes from across the lake. She tenderly took my hand
and offered a pledge, and announced new ground rules for our second
chance, that we might yet survive as a family.

"I'm going to give up the concert career, Edward, and concentrate
on my students. No more travel, no more months of preparation for
a recital. And I'm going to take the position offered me as rehearsal
pianist with Mr. Balanchine. I vow I will spend more time with my
daughter. I will be a better mother. I will not require she take piano;
in fact, I will discourage her from doing so. I will not lay expectations
on her of any kind in terms of her life's goals. And neither will you. I
will let her be herself and find her own level. And you should just be a
father to her, a friend, not an authority figure, not an aloof patriarchal
presence like your father, or Justice Holmes. You have your clerks for
that. You do not need to awe her. We must let her discover her own
personality in her own time. And you must promise me to keep Mr.
Freud away from her at all times. And she must never, never be given
Teddy's room; Cuddebackville—or is it Groton and Yale?—must
remain unoccupied."

And so Cordelia came into our lives, a happy golden girl, with some
of Annie's height and much of Teddy's, as we couldn't help remarking,
intrepid physical talents. She laughed at everything, ran like the wind,
and was scared by nothing. We never mentioned Teddy, never made
comparisons, swore her elder sisters to the same: to keep her innocent
of any expectations concerning the brother she never knew. And yet it
was uncanny how she was drawn to the lake and the woods and even
fishing, as if Teddy somehow hovered over her shoulder, called to her
in the song of the hermit thrush. Of course, she became fascinated
by his room, filled with all his—to her—exotic boy things, his books
and trophies and fishing gear. Sometimes we'd find her in the morning
hidden away in Cuddebackville, curled up in his bed, as if dreaming

in some abandoned specter of his unlived life. She was a tomboy for most of her early years. Annie doted on her but did not try to influence her or enfold her in her Juilliard or School of American Ballet life in any way. I tried to spend as much time with her as I could, having her much to myself, especially over the summers at Hermitage, as Alice and Martha had long become preoccupied with their own lives. We spent time birding together, as I had with her siblings, until she knew all the songs by heart. We would walk to Handytown in the dusk and listen for the hermit thrush. We reset the fallen stones in the farmers' walls. And fished on the Neversink and the lake with barbless hooks, since she didn't like to harm the fish. Our best times were on our long hikes down the defunct railroad right-of-way to the Neversink aqueduct, when I did my best to impart the lore of the D & H and the early settlers. Like Teddy, she loved nothing better than scavenging the anchor spikes from the rotted ties abandoned along the roadbed.

Against all expectation, the more distance Annie kept professionally, the more Cordelia was drawn to her musical world, to the hints of glamour and the adoring students and public who still lingered from Annie's concert days. Juilliard still insisted she give recitals for her fans and their top students, even as most of her friends and perhaps her lovers were now firmly from the ballet world. And so, as if competing with her shadow, Cordelia insisted on piano lessons with one of Annie's Juilliard colleagues and began studying like a demon. Perhaps it was the spell of Hermitage, the ship's keel ceiling, which her mother sounded like the harp of the winds: her daughter's first memories. As a little girl, she danced in circles in the great room, staring upward into the heavenly host of strange and bewitching figures as her mother played. Is it any wonder that Cordy wanted some of that magic for her own? Sadly, she had neither the physical aptitude—the strength and reach of Teddy—nor Alice's innate musicality and touch. Longing for success and acclaim in her own right, and Annie's approval, if not glamour, Cordelia began to tag along to her mother's rehearsals at New York City Ballet, turning the pages and watching the dancers go through their paces. And this is where she found her métier, where Annie's height and Teddy's leg strength and fearlessness took flight. Within four years at the School of American Ballet, Cordelia was one of Mr. B.'s top students, a natural. Annie and I would attend her student recitals and find that our girl had turned into a striking beauty and a fast and agile dancer, no less determined than her mother to make her mark. And with Mr. B.'s eyes firmly focused on her development as he groomed his protégée for ballets as yet unchoreographed.

One makes accommodations in this life, one anticipates the unseen, but there is always something . . . something, as Pope put it so well:

> That something still which prompts the eternal sigh,
>
> For which we bear to live, or dare to die,
>
> Which still so near us, yet beyond us lies . . .

I remember the moment distinctly, her first triumph, watching Cordelia's debut as Clara in the City Ballet's *Nutcracker* and thinking, How wonderful, how free she is, how lucky she has escaped—untouched by the sad tragedy of Teddy, much less the political turmoil that had almost destroyed our family in the early fifties. But strangely, weirdly, there on that darkened stage set with a glittering Christmas tree and presents, the creeping shadow of Alger Hiss roused me once more, in this instance—oh, how strange—in the guise of Herr Drosselmeyer, a specter of adult psychosexual pathologies looming over that huge stage set where my little Clara, a fully blossoming adolescent, scampered across a Christmas Eve ballroom in search of her lover, the Nutcracker prince. Somehow that scene, that oddly poignant fable of the precarious nature of childhood joys and the unseen threat of a longed-for future, here in the guise of a malevolent shape-shifting adult, stirred a buried memory, an indistinct but nagging anxiety. It took me a few days of deep thought over many tedious hours presiding on the bench to unpack what it was that disturbed my sleep, like those fitful dreams that keep escaping one's embrace upon waking.

—

Beyond the magical world of Christmas and *The Nutcracker*, the late sixties was already at our throat. With the Vietnam War at its peak, with protests up Broadway at Columbia, and just months after Annie was diagnosed with her fatal cancer—eighteen years after the Hiss trial, the dead hand of the past touched my family once again. I had been aware that certain historians were now beginning to poke around the smoking embers of the Hiss trial in earnest for the so-called real story, the untold story, and the tales of conspiracy that would surely explain the conviction of an innocent man: "the truth" that so rankled left-wing intellectual circles in New York of the day. There had been plenty of crazy books on the trial in the fifties and early sixties, most based on pure speculation and nothing in the way of new facts. Controversy about Hiss's conviction simmered like a pocket of molten lava, threatening to erupt, refueling many of the ideological battles between supporters and detractors of Hiss, between the old Left and the new, who had long broken with their father's adoration of Stalinism, and yet found Ho Chi Minh a sympathetic figure, if not a champion for their anti-imperialist cause and every other cause in its wake. As if flushed out of the shadows, Alger Hiss began his campaign to overturn his conviction and blame the unjust verdict of history on a sinister conspiracy by the government—"forgery by typewriter," he called it—indicting HUAC, the FBI and Hoover, and Nixon, especially as Nixon's political prospects rose once again. Unsaid but implied were the failures of his defense team, which were whispered about with the most cutting and snide innuendo. With Hiss's blessing, an eager young historian was anointed by his camp followers to begin picking over the bones of the trial; Freedom of Information requests were filed for the FBI files on Hiss and others, along with access to HUAC and grand jury files, and the various defense team files housed in law firms in Baltimore and New York. The man of the hour was a meticulous academic, Allen Weinstein, whom Hiss had encouraged to go forward and so, at long last, prove his innocence.

Weinstein brazenly invited himself to my office on Foley Square and sat himself down in front of my desk. He had a roundish face, with a narrow, hard mouth and piercing eyes behind round steel spectacles: an earnest face, a determined face, a prepossessing brow harboring a quick intelligence. Surely a man of the Left out to make mincemeat of that travesty of injustice in which I'd played my benighted role. Would I talk? He asked. Would I agree to an on-the-record interview about the trial? His soft but intent eyes blazed into mine with all the purpose of the righteous few. An interview, formal or otherwise, was out of the question, I assured him, but I told him I had no reservations about his access to my material in the defense files, documents that I may have generated, evidence he was eager to get his grasping hands on. I told him, as did most of the other attorneys on the defense team, that I could not speak directly to the trial itself, since that would be a violation of client-attorney privilege. He gazed at me and just smiled and shrugged his shoulders, as if he knew something I did not, as if time's trap had long since been sprung. When we shook hands, he looked around my chambers, taking it all in as if for a final time, perhaps sensing, as is a historian's wont, the precariousness of all human honors.

It was that conversation that had set off a nagging sense of buried dread during Cordelia's performance as Clara. There was something about Weinstein's scholarly demeanor that unnerved me, something in his eager pie-eyed face, kestrel-brown eyes, and absolute conviction that the truth must and could be ferreted out—that giant conspiracy against man and God! There was the same whiff of fanaticism in Drosselmeyer's glinty lust for my young daughter. The very thing that jogged loose a memory of an incident I had totally forgotten about.

On the opening day of the second Hiss trial, when I was just getting my sea legs for the upcoming contest, I was approached before the court session had begun by George Altmann, the artist, who, I vaguely remembered, had held an important position in the Federal Art Project. (I had seen an Altmann portrait study of a child in the Hisses' Volta Place Georgetown residence.) More recently, he had worked as a court reporter for the *Herald Tribune*, covering the first Hiss trial. I had been struck by his illustrations in the papers and how vividly they brought to life the various characters in the proceedings. I believe he cornered me on the courthouse steps, perhaps on an inside stairwell. Pressed by a scrum of family and friends and reporters, I was standing there when he suddenly pushed through and introduced himself and whispered something close to my ear, which I didn't quite hear. I got the sense he was a little overwrought; his dark eyes were blurry and reddened beneath a French beret, his hands shook, his goatee was gray and uneven, and there was a distinct smell of cheap whiskey on his breath. As we parted, he thrust a manila envelope inscribed with my name into my hands, and stared me hard in the eye, as if to seal some kind of bargain. Then, as he turned, he grabbed my arm for a last moment, holding me in his troubled stare. "For your eyes only," he hissed through compressed lips. Then he gave me an icy smile. "For Priscilla Hiss, a token of my esteem." I thought it all pretty damn queer, but I was so overwhelmed with the crisis at hand—opening day of the trial—that I distractedly stuffed the envelope in my briefcase and thought no more about it.

Only many days later, when I again discovered the envelope stuck in the side pocket of my briefcase, did I bother to examine its contents. There were nine sketches, each beautifully executed with exquisite nuance and detail. Much better than the kind of dashed-off caricatures

Altmann provided in his court reportage. I immediately recognized the first two portraits of Alger and Priscilla Hiss, both faces looking younger by at least ten years: attentive, even pensive, as if they might be listening to a compelling speaker—an ornithology lecture was my first thought. Some of the other faces were vaguely familiar, but I couldn't immediately place them. At any rate, the trial was under way and I was panicked with my responsibilities, and so I hastily concluded that these drawings were simply tokens of appreciation to me from Altmann, portrait studies of people in the Hisses' circle, people he thought I knew or might have some connection to. Without any more ado, I stuck the sketches back in the envelope and deep-sixed it in the defense files, perhaps thinking that at a later date, at the end of the trial, I might retrieve them as souvenirs. I promptly forgot all about them. And there they remained for over fifteen years.

But then came Weinstein's supercilious scrutiny, his certainty. It got me thinking: Did he blame me? Had I missed something? Would he bring up the Chambers-Blinger fiasco? He was clearly a Hiss partisan. Would I be thrust back into the spotlight just when Cordelia was blooming—she, of course, had no memory of the trial, and so remained immune to its venomous spawn. As I racked my brain, I remembered the Altmann sketches and began to wonder about them. Why had he given them to me in the first place and in such a clandestine manner? Did he really mean them as a personal gift? And why would a great artist, renowned in the twenties and thirties, be reduced to doing court sketches for the newspapers? What had happened to his stellar career? An alcoholic, a desperate man? Or did it go deeper? Had he handed me evidence of some sort that he thought useful to the defense team to have in its possession? That prompted me to get one of my clerks to do a little checking into George Altmann. The first thing he came up with were newspaper accounts of Altmann's untimely death in Woodstock on Christmas Eve, 1949, during the trial's holiday break, just weeks after he'd handed me those nine sketches. The newspaper clippings seemed to range from speculation about a bizarre accident to the suggestion of suicide, but nothing in the way of foul play. The tenor of the reporting further jogged my memory, and I recalled having heard about Altmann's death sometime after the holidays, in early January 1950, upon resumption of the trial. His absence among the press reporters had been noted. Perhaps one of my associates on the defense team had mentioned it? But I didn't remember being particularly perturbed—we were too busy to think about anything except the next day of testimony.

But the fact that Altmann had died on Christmas Eve—Drosselmeyer's lusty glint knotted my stomach—spooked me. I am hardly a superstitious man, but the anxious face of George Altmann began to preoccupy me. My sleep suffered. Had I made an error of judgment? Had I overlooked the obvious?

And suddenly the idea of an eager-beaver young historian, even if he had gone to Yale, getting his hands on those sketches gave me fits. As an appeals court judge who had adjudicated many appeals based on new evidence, or withheld evidence, or tampered evidence, I was only too aware how illegally handled evidence or sloppy defense preparation could get a case reversed. Then it occurred to me where my real jeopardy lay: If the material Altmann had turned over to me proved to be evidence relating to the trial, either favoring the defense or the prosecution, and we had technically still been in the discovery phase, then I had been duty-bound, legally bound, to share it with the prosecution. And if those nine sketches did indeed prove to be evidence, perhaps critical evidence, and Allen Weinstein got his grubby hands on them, he might well accuse me of illegally withholding evidence from the prosecution during the trial, a charge of improper conduct that could ruin my reputation. And worse, if the withheld evidence proved to somehow favor Hiss, it might even result in overturning his conviction.

It was risky, even foolhardy, given my position as a federal judge, but I managed to phone up one of my old partners at the firm where the defense files were archived and request permission to check over a few of my old papers for a law journal article I was planning to write. With his go-ahead, I went to the office archives and, after about an hour digging, located the envelope—untouched and unmarked by the firm archivist but with my name printed big as life on it in Altmann's hand. I simply sneaked it out in my briefcase. It was only then, after laying the nine sketches out on my desk and studying the faces for hours, and having one of my clerks do some digging in the newspaper archives, that I figured out who they were—except for one. Besides Alger and Priscilla Hiss, there were seven others: Laurence Duggan had been at State with Hiss in the thirties and forties; Noel Field had also been at State with Hiss in the thirties; Harry Dexter White had been an assistant secretary of the Treasury, working directly with Henry Morgenthau; Lauchlin Currie had been a White House aide to Roosevelt during the war; Marvin Smith had been at the Justice Department and a friend of Hiss's going back to his early Washington years; and, finally, William Remington, whom I recognized as having been on the War Production Board with me during the war. The face in the ninth sketch, a stocky man with a jowly, abstracted stare, I could never place. Of the seven, White had died of a heart attack at his summer home in Fitzwilliam, New Hampshire, in 1948 (newspaper commentators, years later, speculated on suicide and even foul play), while Duggan, Smith, and Remington had all died violent deaths, Duggan and Smith from falls under ambiguous circumstances before they could testify at the trial, and Remington, a convicted spy, bludgeoned to death four years after the trial, while serving time in prison with Hiss. Currie and Field had, for all intents and purposes, fled the country before the trial and so were unavailable to testify. Of the seven, the one who worried me the most was Marvin Smith, who fell to his death down a stairwell at the Justice Department in 1948, same year as Duggan died in a fall from his office's sixteenth-story window. Smith figured directly in the Hiss trial, since he had signed the auto-transfer document that Hiss used to turn over his Ford roadster to a member of the Communist Party: If Smith had been alive and able to testify to that effect, Alger Hiss would have been in even deeper jeopardy than he already was on that count.

After much pondering, and it didn't take an art historian to figure it out, all the sketches seemed to come from the same sitting or gathering, possibly a Communist cell or study group, probably in Washington in the late thirties. Certainly, Alger and Priscilla looked about ten years younger than at the time of the trial. Presumably, George Altmann must have been a member of the same Communist cell while working for the Federal Art Project. I had one of my clerks research the newspaper-clipping files for more information, and he came up with a number of sinister articles from the forties and fifties speculating along precisely these same lines: a suspicious pattern of foul play that, one way or another, connected many of the ambiguous deaths surrounding the Hiss trial. They were all witnesses who had never testified. Potentially witnesses that I had a vague memory of having seen on a long list of possible prosecution witnesses: a list on which many of the names had been crossed off. Had George Altmann been on the witness list? I couldn't remember.

I was left with a feeling of brooding unease.

What George Altmann had handed me was either damning evidence of a possible conspiracy or nothing useful at all. If Altmann had been willing to testify about the circumstances surrounding the sketches, much less anything he might know connecting his subjects to a larger conspiracy, that might have been an entirely different matter. The sketches would have been admissible only if he'd been willing—or been alive!—to testify about them. And the fact that Altmann had handed them to me (voluntarily given up possession), a member of the defense team for Alger Hiss, but without any explicit explanation, seemed to indicate, at the very least, a certain ambivalence on his part. I suspect he didn't want to be called as a witness: What Communist or former Communist ever did? Had he given me the sketches to tip me off to the truth as he knew it? Or to prevent the government prosecutors from possibly subpoenaing him and the sketches, which they would certainly have done if they'd known of their existence? Had he divested himself of this physical evidence as a means of protecting himself, or protecting Alger Hiss? Should I have informed Alger or the defense team about the sketches? Had I failed—an oversight—to do my duty? Were the sketches a kind of insurance that Altmann had withheld for over ten years? Not unlike, it struck me, the famous Pumpkin Papers, the secret State Department documents with Alger Hiss's handwriting on them, which Whittaker Chambers had hidden and withheld as insurance against the Soviets' fingering him for retribution when he broke with the GRU. Was that what Altmann had slipped into my hands on the fly? An insurance policy . . . which I failed to deliver on . . . that resulted in his death on Christmas Eve in '49?

And what had prompted him to hand me the damn things, of all people on the defense team, in the first place? A man I'd never met.

As I sat in my chambers late at night drinking cup after cup of coffee in the winter of 1969—Annie had already departed for Hermitage to spend her last months after all her chemo treatments had failed to stop the spread of her uterine cancer—I felt bewitched by unseen sinister forces beyond my control, or even knowledge. While Alger Hiss hitched his wagon to the growing antiwar movement to overturn his conviction in the court of public opinion, while Allen Weinstein scoured the FBI and defense files to establish Hiss's innocence.

After Annie's death, as Cordelia and I floundered on the home front to find our way, as Alice and Martha struggled in their own lives to regain some semblance of a life without Annie's commanding presence,

I removed the sketches from the locked files in my office and put them in my briefcase to take up to Hermitage over a July weekend in 1969. My thought was to burn them, to be rid of any and all memories of that damn trial and the fiend who had plagued our lives. Even on her deathbed at Hermitage, a hospital bed moved down to the great room, where she could gaze up at the ship's keel ceiling, Annie refused to forgive me for my role in the trial, still convinced that my infidelity to the truth had resulted in the death of our son, a sin that I refused to either admit or seek forgiveness for.

So, after dinner with Cordelia, on a warm July night, I made an excuse to build a roaring fire in the great room, where I sat in my chair, preparing to burn the envelop, as if by doing so all the ugly connections to the trial might perish, as well. I remember sitting and staring into the crackling flames, turning to the carved solemn faces of the two Gothic angels who preside at the family hearth—"your bitter angels," Annie used to jeeringly call them, since she regularly disparaged their presence. I found I just couldn't do it, unburden myself of the evidence, such as it was, or, more's the case, a record of professional failure and disgrace and private pain. First, I decided simply to stick the envelope behind my bookshelves and let it gather dust for eternity—at least my eternity. But when I woke the next morning, I heard Cordelia playing Annie's Steinway. I was deeply moved and appreciative of her courage to do something that could only have proved heartrending, to let the ship's keel ceiling once again echo the heavens with Annie's spirit, even in imperfect form.

And when I saw her shining face framed by her golden hair across the breakfast table, the solution just popped into my head. I asked Cordelia to do me a favor: Would she drive across the Catskills to Woodstock and return some sketches by George Altmann to his son? As part of my clerks' research, they had turned up the name and address of Altmann's son, James Altmann. I had even once contemplated getting in touch with this James Altmann to see if he might shed light on the nine sketches, if they might have been recorded in Altmann's inventory. "Woodstock?" she asked. "Bob Dylan's Woodstock?" I had no idea to whom she was referring. I nodded with a smile, searching her skeptical face for hints of Annie's lingering grace. Perhaps it had something to do with my fastidious nature, a criticism often voiced by Annie, especially in legal matters: the thing on which I always prided myself. Didn't I have a responsibility to return George Altmann's artwork to his rightful heir, who, morally, legally, or even as a matter of artistic legacy was best placed to decide on the disposition of those sketches—whatever that might be? Perhaps, I was simply relieving my conscience. Of what—then and even now—I am unsure. By keeping the sketches out of the clutches of Weinstein, perhaps I had fostered an alternate history, one in which George Altmann never handed me that envelope, in which Alger Hiss was found not guilty, in which the brutal deaths or exile of at least six of those depicted in the sketches represented not a dark conspiracy against our country, but some random coincidences, and thus deserving to be buried by the sands of time.

Or was I saving George Altmann from the diligent Weinstein? The artist's name, unlike mine—infamous and ridiculed—never appears in the historian's magisterial tome on the trial, *Perjury*. Weinstein, to give him his due, had let the evidence be his guide, and so confirmed the conviction on two counts of perjury of his erstwhile hero, Alger Hiss.

And so I added a sweetener to hasten Cordelia on her way. I slid my car keys across the breakfast table. I told her she could drive my pride and joy, my red Mercedes coupe to Woodstock. And so I handed her the nine sketches, sealed in a new envelope with the name and address of James Altmann printed on the front, the very contaminant that I'd hoped would protect her from the disaster and heartbreak of the past. And so I got the alternative history that, perhaps, I richly deserved. And a grandson, who, given his name and the passage of time and his extraordinary intelligence, might yet prove my saving grace: a scientist, no less, conversant with the heavens—as if born under the sway of our magnificent ship's keel ceiling—Annie's star-dusted grandchild and heir, the right man at the right time to ponder the unseen world that rises and sets all around us, and the shadowy turnings where I went astray. And so save Hermitage and the family honor.

12

Back to the Garden

HE EASED ONTO the off-ramp of the thruway, threading the E-ZPass lane, taking the turn for Route 375 and Woodstock, and so weaving down the chilly darkness that, under normal circumstances, he could drive in his sleep.

George shook his head and cracked his window for some fresh air.

"Cold," she said.

"Just for a few minutes. We're almost there. And I'm sorry you had to go through all that—and now, probably more from where that came from. As they say, no good deed—or offer—goes unpunished."

"I told you, George, it's really okay. I don't mind being hijacked. I wouldn't be here otherwise. Actually, I enjoyed myself. That business about your grandfather and Alger Hiss, and George Altmann—a sketch artist covering the trial . . . well, kinda cool family history, don't you think?"

"Oh my God, surely not an acquired taste."

"How come you didn't mention any of that in your catalog essay?"

He took a deep breath of the loamy pine-scented air whistling by his ear and sighed, shaking his head.

She eyed him intently. "Want me to drive?"

"I'm okay," he said, and he raised his window a tad.

"George, my parents, when they disappeared, I had nothing. Or almost nothing. I mean, I was stuck living with my aunt, who not only hated my mother, but who was an evangelical crazy to boot. I'm not telling you a sob story or feeling sorry for myself . . . but you have no idea how lucky you are."

He waved his hand to indicate the road and the vague lights of houses they were passing.

"Welcome to my home . . . back to the garden."

"I have to fess up: Never having been to Woodstock, my offer of an art-handling gig did not come without ulterior motives . . . a little curiosity, too, to see this place: Dylan, right—and a real old-time artists' colony?"

"Ah, my groovy hometown."

"You say that with such disdain."

"Sorry, the wine and my aunt, always a bummer."

"She couldn't have been sweeter to me—Stan, too. Though she did seem to have a thing about Mama Annie." At mention of the name, the fingers of her right hand leapt to her chin, her nose, as if exploring for some defect. "It was really quite touching how they both insisted on my keeping Cecily's blue cardigan and jeans."

"I think they enjoyed seeing her stuff on you."

"Did I tell you that the cardigan was handmade in Italy—Gucci from Saks? It must have cost a fortune."

George smiled. "Oh, they loved spoiling Cecily."

She ran her hands lovingly over the soft arms of the cardigan. "Funny, in Cecily's room, in the house, there's not a photograph of her or Billy—the family. At least none that I could see."

He raised an eyebrow at this. "You don't miss much. I guess it's an artist's thing—huh?"

"Hmm . . ." She held up a wooden hair-pick comb. "Look what I just found in the pocket."

"Cecily must have forgotten it."

"But it's for an Afro."

He smiled to himself. "See the lights through there?" He pointed to a driveway off to the left. "That was Bob Dylan's second home after he left Hi Lo Ha at Byrdcliffe, after he got overwhelmed by the influx of hippies."

"Very cool."

"Lots of action, according to my aging-hippie mom. She knows all the mythic scuttlebutt. You see"—he nodded, an uneven grimace on his face—"her ex-husband was an electrician, technician, carpenter, and soundman; he was pals with all the early greats: Dylan, Tim Hardin, Van Morrison, Hendrix, Joplin, the Band—the whole bunch. He was their main man, touring roadie for years . . . the guy who cleaned up their messes, so to speak, the one on intimate terms with their drug dealers."

"The Band—really? My dad's favorite." She patted his thigh. "How nice for you, coming home."

The giddy pleasure in her voice only deepened his growing dread.

—

Jimmy, "Jimbo" to his cronies, long-limbed, long dirty-blond-haired corralled by a sweaty red bandanna, long, tapering chin with a half dimple, wiry, muscled arms and gravel-voiced, meticulous and careful about anything having to do with his work, electrical or mechanical—a master carpenter, yet utterly carefree—"cruelly careless of others' feelings," accused Cordelia—around people while under the influence or not. Nicknamed "Live Wire" by his various touring crews for his boasted conquests and dire warnings during electrical storms. To his young son, he had been warm and charming and often charismatic, full of stories of magical moments onstage, of monster hits first performed before a live audience ("I was there, buster, I was there—and the pussy was on fire!")—of critical tweaks he'd contributed during recording sessions (his proudest acknowledged in the liner notes of *Music from Big Pink*, 1968). In the industry, he was liked, even loved for his readiness to help talents far larger than his, to get the best out of recording sessions or concerts, to save a star's ass by turning off a mike when the guy was too stoned to get through the lyrics, or too deaf or inebriated to tune his guitar. His claim to enduring fame: He was the tech guy who, along with Jock Roberts and Joel Rosenman, had first walked Max Yasgur's pasture in its pristine state and conceived the layout for the concert, placing the stage at the base of a hill, a natural amphitheater, along Filippini Pond, and, under enormous pressure, assembled the team to design and build the concert stage in record time.

That alone kept him in the running in the fame game, that and the fact that no one got electrocuted. And so Jimbo found himself in a glorified limbo, both embraced and dismissed by that magic circle of genius in which he'd played a part and yet not. As was his role in his son's life, a fleeting presence until George was thirteen, being constantly on the road, on tour, but his vivid personality making up for it in the weeks and months on "home leave" back in Woodstock, when he'd take young George around to local recording or jam sessions and teach him the soundboards, basic wiring, and carpentry, and how to fix almost anything, from cars to electronics to broken furnaces. But the fights with his wife, fueled by drugs and booze and jealousy, could also be terrifying, sometimes lasting days and nights without end. Many were the long, lonely uphill trudges from the school bus stop to home, age eight or nine, only to find his parents still passed out from the night before.

Jimmy and Cordelia lived their passions full throttle, for each other, for their crowd, both abetting Jimmy's jealousy and resentment as they cleaved close to the inner sanctum, basking under the golden tantalizing face of fame and genius as the seventies turned into the eighties. Jimbo might have been embraced for having the knack to bring out the best in the talent—to know exactly the sound they were after—but Cordelia was the more musically gifted, and, worse, the more lusted after by the troupes of musicians always filtering in and out of town. If Jimbo slept with every unclaimed groupie on the road who dropped her panties—so his wife screamed right in front of young George on more than one occasion—she did worse, in Jimmy's eyes, because her affairs were in Woodstock, in the garden, and, adding insult to injury, though never spoken or admitted, sleeping with his employers, the "boys": "my friends—my fucking best friends." Even the kingpin, manager Albert Grossman, had his smarmy eyes on Cordelia, if not to bed her, to somehow harness her star quality, even if just as a dancer-singer backup for one of his groups. Worse still, Cordelia literally inspired a handful of singer-songwriters to memorialize those rumored infidelities: their golden-haired lady, their blue-eyed darlin', their mountain meadow dancer, their evening angel. All this allowed Cordelia to touch the beating heart of that ring of fire that Jimbo had first introduced her to and considered his preserve. Cordelia, his wife, the one thing of dazzling beauty to call his own that the talent didn't have—and wanted.

But what really pissed off Jimbo: Cordelia, that radiant flower child, never seemed to be trying to score; she was just there—hanging out, stopping by, pitching in, delivering drugs—and with enough natural talent that in a crisis, or on a drug-addled whim, she could even fill in on keyboard (Annie's musical gift lingering like a conjured spell through the miasma of cigarette smoke, dope, and booze), and well enough that only the pros would know the difference. She could even sing a pitch-perfect imitation of Joni Mitchell if called upon. And that's what did it, the last straw: her artist's citation on an album's liner notes for singing two vocals and playing keyboard on one track in 1982. Jimmy just disappeared after that infamous Band tour of Japan in 1983, never to return to Woodstock. Not a phone call or letter to his thirteen-year-old son, as if he'd dropped off the face of the planet, which, of course, he hadn't, but simply remained permanently on tour, basing himself first in L.A. and later in Seattle with an aging backup singer from the Blackhearts.

If Jimmy Altmann had simply disappeared from his son's life, that might have been a blessing of sorts, but he didn't; he was still the main roadie for the top bands and musicians, many of whose kids went to Woodstock High with George. So sightings of a drunken Jimbo on the road sifted and trickled into the local rumor mill and turned up in the guise of off-color jokes and snarky, cruel innuendo, and plain vanilla dirty sneers on the faces of kids he passed every fucking day in the halls, especially those in the in-crowd, who held him in utmost disdain, hooting at his ineptitude in the gym and on the playing field and scrawling insults on his locker. Even now, George had sickening memories of the piss yellow hallways of Woodstock High, echoing with catcalls and bleak laugher, his name, Altmann, grunted out in rapid succession. These obscenities were often coupled with the names of obscure over-the-hill has-beens, women who, in some circuitous fashion, were rumored to have bedded his father during some pathetic gig in some far-flung shithole. The overheard whispers were the worst, leaving to his imagination Jimbo's latest run-in with the cops for drunk driving or bar altercations.

It didn't help that his talents in math and science put him far ahead of the others in his class, that his mind was always elsewhere (the comfort of a billion light-years), or the fact that he garnered constant praise from the faculty, who pointed him out as the model for scoring an Ivy ticket. Even his record number of AP classes in math and science won him no friends, certainly no girlfriends—not in a school where musical and artistic talent was the coveted ticket to popularity and prestige, where genius and fame was the currency of the realm, where even the most indispensable techies were the lowest on the greasy totem pole of the music industry. Nor did it help that his mother had boyfriends of her own, some famous, some not so famous. A beautiful, not to mention talented, mother who's sleeping her way around town—inspiring songs!—touches plenty of third rails: that glinting spark of fear and hate flicking dangerously in the wary glances of passing sons and daughters.

George's happiest day was graduation day.

Princeton astrophysics had been his escape into a well-ordered universe.

—

"Ever heard of Joseph-Louis Lagrange?" George asked Wendy.

"Who?"

"A French mathematician who worked out the points in space in the rotating Earth-Moon system, where the gravity of the Earth and Moon and the centrifugal forces of the rotating system come into balance. These places are called Lagrangian points and there are five of them. They're good places to park satellites, even a space station—the ultimate parking place—you might say, the ultimate betwixt and between."

"Stranded, cast adrift," she offered. "Lost in space—I get you."

"In high school, if your parents weren't artists or musicians, you were zilch. And physics geeks were less than zilch."

At this, she smiled. "Okay, try being an English lit and studio geek in high school—in a less than tony suburb of Houston. Where the cheerleaders ran the place for their football-player boyfriends."

"Ah . . ."

"So, that why we're not listening to any tunes?"

"Check the glove compartment."

She pulled out some old cassettes and CDs and nodded approvingly.

"Funny, like I said, my dad was really into the Band. But then, he was a Texan, first, last, and forever."

"Canadians, you know, except Levon Helm, who was from Arkansas. I went to school with his daughter, Amy. But her mother had enough sense to put her into a fancy high school in New York. Mom hung with all those guys." He rolled his eyes. "Go ahead, be my guest—ask her about *the boys*. She'll tell you how she filled in on keyboard in jam sessions—how all the *boys* wanted her. Jesus, they even wrote songs about her."

"No . . ."

"She'll be thrilled—trust me."

—

The moonlight only intensified as they resumed climbing on the twisting mountain road, attended by the scent of wood smoke and sere leaves crushed to a slick mash, while ahead, caught in the high beams, lurid vertical columns of teal blue lichen scribbled hieroglyphs on the oaken palisades. George pointed out matter-of-factly the driveways of the famous and once famous and now long forgotten, once household names from the glory days of the late sixties and seventies. He turned abruptly at a hidden drive where, emerging from behind a scrim of trees, a tiny white farmhouse, windows aglow, shimmered on a gentle rise in the ambient moonlight, like a scene out of a child's bedtime story. The Tahoe bounced in the rutted gravel road and George grimaced at each annoying jolt, drawing Wendy's attention to the ruined fieldstone walls fading off through the trees, and the pasture below and the remnants of a woodlot, which gave way to a view of the town and valley.

"Welcome to Alice's rural slum."

"Love it." She laughed, as if enchanted.

"It's about fifteen-odd acres, including the barn and a couple of sheds." Getting out of the Tahoe, he motioned toward the large red barn slightly downhill from where they stood, its cracked and peeling façade a mauve-pink color in the moonlight, looking like a ghostly hulk cast adrift, lapped by overgrown meadow grass.

"Nice view," she said, stretching her legs, gazing over the valley, where strings of distant streetlights blazed wearily in the distance.

"Like I said, the paintings are stored in the barn, Altmann's studio."

"Jesus!" she exclaimed with a shiver, squinting as she threw her backpack over her shoulder. "Is there any kind of climate control?"

"No, it's really terrible, like a sieve. We run space heaters in the winter—fire hazard, of course—to keep the air above freezing, but that's about it."

She pressed her palms together, as if genuinely distressed. "Thank God you're going to save them."

"Well, the good news, since the Trade Center attack, is that at least she can sell this dump now, when she's ready. Plenty of offers from the local real estate mafia trolling for some rich Upper West Sider looking to escape the city, touch the magic of Guston or the myth of Dylan." He shook his head. "She didn't even bother to get the lawn guy in to mow the meadow this year."

Wendy touched his shoulder, a calming touch, spreading her free arm. "But George, it's all about place—this place that inspired the art. I can smell it." She gestured to the night sky and the blush of faint starlight. "And *you*, who never said boo about that Princeton astrophysics degree."

"Ah," he said with a sarcastic shrug, "all those twinkling little beauties with their pasts to tell . . . *what you are.* Except our vision is occluded by dwarf galaxies, runaway stars, heated gas clouds, ultra-high-energy particles, much less dark matter—a distorting lens on all

our best efforts. Like all that lawyerly rigmarole over dinner tonight—
what's to believe?"

With a flushed-cheek sincerity, she said defiantly, "The work,
George, the paintings."

Out of habit, he checked Cordelia's late-model Toyota Camry, his
lips twisted in concentration as he bent to examine the tread on the
tires. With a grunt, he motioned for Wendy to follow him up the path
of bluestone slabs, their irregular borders hemmed with a good four-
inch growth of crabgrass and battered dandelions. He couldn't resist
pulling up handfuls of the intruders and tossing them aside.

The white clapboard farmhouse presided on a slight rise over the
upper part of what had originally been the farmyard, nestling in the
shadow of one gargantuan oak and outriders of firs, where a grove of
ancient apple trees stood, lush and fruit-laden. A veranda with a white
railing and porch swing was illuminated by lights from the windows.
Hummingbird feeders dangled like ruby earrings from under the
eaves. Mounting the squeaking wooden stairs, they both turned to the
two-seater porch swing, where it drifted in a slight breeze, as if just
abandoned by fleeing lovers startled at their arrival. George knocked
sharply to announce himself, pulled open the screen door for Wendy,
then pushed in the battered green front door and ushered his guest
inside. They walked straight into a living room of bare plywood walls,
chock-a-block with nondescript carved fruitwood furniture, much of
it antique or secondhand, all repainted in soft creams and pastel blues
(reminding George for a moment of Annie's decorative scheme in
the master bedroom at Hermitage). Dirty shag rugs covered the pine
floorboards. In a cozy corner, near an ancient woodstove, a medley of
scavenged easy chairs and a worn sofa congregated, all covered in cotton quilts of various nondescript patterns. Against the inside wall that
connected with the kitchen stood a spotless Yamaha upright (the "Jap
piano," a wedding present from the Judge). Half a dozen unframed
Altmann canvases hung on the walls, interspersed with a few concert
posters of the Band and Paul Butterfield and other Woodstock-based
groups of yore, all signed to Cordelia by various band members. In pride
of place over the ratty sofa was a metal-framed New York City Ballet
poster advertising *The Nutcracker*, the winter season of 1968–1969. In the
bottom corners of the poster were scores of congratulatory inscriptions
from company members, including a big swirling signature in silver ink
of George Balanchine.

George poked around, as if apprehensive of any alterations, running a hand over the piled antique packing cases, varnished to a rich bronze patina, containing his mother's library, mostly well-worn Penguin classics with black spines, then moving on to her worktable by the staircase, piled with plastic utility boxes containing gemstones and metalwork hardware for her jewelry business. Sidling up to the Yamaha and sounding middle C, he looked at Wendy with a hint of supercilious pleasure.

"In tune," he proclaimed, sniffing the air, as if only just detecting the telltale odor of baking bread.

Seemingly summoned by the dull echo of the note, Cordelia hurried in from the kitchen while drying her hands on a dish towel, making a beeline for Wendy to give her a big hug and kiss, as if they were long-time pals.

"Wow, aren't you something!" she exclaimed, admiring the blue cardigan and tight jeans. "Love the sweater, dear."

"Alice lent it to me. Her daughter's."

"The prodigal Cecily, who just divorced her famous surgeon of a husband: 'pride of the race.' So I heard from Alice this morning, among other things." She turned and hugged George. "Well, you don't look any worse for wear after surviving both the Judge and Alice in twenty-four hours."

"Battered and bruised." George cocked an eyebrow at Wendy.

"Good job, Georgie"—she gave him another kiss—"with the Judge, I mean." She looked at Wendy as she passed a hand through her faded blond hair, a bemused smile playing on her sensuous full lips. "I think Allie already had her Armani funeral outfit picked out."

"Alice's a hoot," said Wendy. "Stan, too."

At this, Cordelia smiled benignly. "Well, that'll be a first. So, I just talked to the Judge this evening and he sounded peppy as hell. Felicity said she hasn't seen him so engaged in years. And something about a condo in Florida—what was that about?"

George looked at Wendy apologetically. "Mom, I think it's a little late to bore Wendy with any more about the Judge. She got an earful over the dinner table."

Cordelia, sporting a gray THE BARN CONCERTS sweatshirt and jeans, threw up her hands and clapped, eyes raised. "Hallelujah, Lord. I wouldn't wish *our* crazy family on my worst enemy."

"A judge and an artist," said Wendy, perhaps a little giddy with exhaustion. "How cool is that for grandfathers?"

Cordelia, bemused, gave Wendy another appreciative look, as if not quite sure what to make of such unbridled enthusiasm in the younger woman, her gaze lingering on the muscled peaks of Wendy's shoulders and long legs, then on her wide blue eyes, still full of high-voltage curiosity. She was almost as tall as George, who stood beside her, slouching. Cordelia slapped her son playfully on his butt and caressed Wendy's shoulder.

"Stand up straight, George; you've got a live one on your hands."

"Like I said," he replied, "battered and bruised."

"At Daddy's retirement dinner from the Second Circuit, I sat at his right arm on the dais—his only daughter who showed—and listened to a baker's dozen of his clerks and fellow judges shower him with accolades and affection." She shrugged. "I had tears in my eyes . . . Who woulda thought?"

Wendy had turned her attention to an Altmann canvas. "Wow, it's like I've come to the source." She walked over to examine the surface of a small oil hanging on the wall between two six-over-six sashed windows. Granite outcroppings in an overgrown meadow. She ran her fingertips across the impasto. "What a hand, what a feel for mass and line, the way he carves and sculpts with the paint. Look, he's even got sand or gravel embedded in the pigment."

Mother and son looked on, appearing slightly nonplussed, as if this near stranger had barged into their lives to inject some long-lost youthful enthusiasm.

"My first Altmann collector!" exclaimed George, going with her energy and placing a deft kiss on his client's cheek.

"Needs cleaning—no?" asked Wendy.

Cordelia laughed, observing the two. "I'm still reeling, George. How you did it, I don't know. These things have been a curse since I married Jim. He couldn't give them away, I couldn't sell them, and yet we felt we couldn't just dispose of them."

"Oh my God," said Wendy, "that's just so scary . . ."

"Mom, Wendy just paid a lot of money for two Altmanns. A little respect, please."

Cordelia sat down in her easy chair, next to a side table with an ancient cassette player and dog-eared Penguin classic, Jane Austen's *Persuasion*.

"Sorry, I've got to get off my feet. I was restocking books all day at the Golden Notebook—my mother's revenge." She picked up the Jane Austen and nodded at Wendy. "You mentioned our Jane at dinner the other night and so I thought I'd reread it again."

George wrinkled his nose and glanced, a little embarrassed, at the ashtray on her side table, where a half-smoked joint lay tilted into a smudge of ash.

"Jesus, Mom, I thought you'd given up the pot, at least smoking this shit—it's the last thing your lungs need, much less your brain."

"If you knew how many stupid tourists I had to deal with today—'Can you tell me where is Woodstock? . . . The mus-s-s-ic please.'—it just helps me relax. Medicinal, don't you know. And you don't need to be so judgmental, George, with your mother. Hah"—she clapped, glancing at Wendy—"I sound just like Annie."

"Annie?" echoed Wendy, then caught herself. "Of course, your talented mother, who played Carnegie Hall."

Cordelia's eyes flickered unsteadily—something in Wendy's proprietary tone. George took a seat on the sofa and reached over to where Cordelia kept a pile of party tapes of her favorite music, labels beautifully printed in a feminine hand listing the names of the artists and titles.

"It's chilly in here," said George, looking through some of the cassettes. "Do you have the furnace on?"

"I just turned it on before you arrived—first time this fall. I think there are logs for the woodstove out by the barn if you want to bring some in."

"Did you have it serviced, like I told you?"

"I guess I forgot. It seems to be working."

"Since we almost sold out the show, maybe now you can take a pass on the dope in exchange for some good old pinot noir."

"What, and get buzzed like you? How much did *you* have to drink at dinner, Mr. G.?" Cordelia sighed, casting a pointed look at her son.

"Whatever it took to keep a step ahead of the law. Your big sister must have put back at least two bottles on her own."

"There were no alcoholics in our family, as far as I know. And God knows I tried to give Jim, my alcoholic ex-husband"—she turned to Wendy with an exasperated look—"the benefit of the doubt, what with his difficult upbringing. I mean, it can't have been easy being dragged out by your mother at midnight on Christmas Eve to go find your father's frozen body in the Sawkill."

George looked up from where he was inventorying Cordelia's playlist on the inside cover of a cassette.

"And George Altmann, by all accounts, had his own drinking problem."

"I can't tell you how many times I was ready to walk away from the whole kit and caboodle—burn the barn down for the insurance . . ."

"Oh my God!" exclaimed Wendy.

"That's another thing," said George. "I've got to come up with an appraisal and get everything under the gallery insurance coverage."

"You were a dancer," said Wendy, as if eager to change the subject, pointing to Balanchine's signature and fulsome words of praise.

"Can you believe this frumpy, rheumatic old lady once danced light as a feather?" She cackled and batted eyes at her distracted son across from her. "Bet you can't."

"Rumor has it," offered George, looking up, "according to Alice, you were the main attraction around these parts in the early seventies."

"Well . . ." She paused, as if unsure whether she felt indignation or secret pleasure. "That's all the damned legacy I'll ever have." She smiled gamely at Wendy, muttering with an upturned twist of her top lip, "Once, with Mr. B., it was just me and Suzanne."

"Which one of these songs was it you always used to hum?" asked George.

"Song?"

"I know it's none of my business," interjected Wendy as she returned to another Altmann canvas of airy clouds over a green valley, abstract horizontals of soft-edged color, with undertones of purple and burgundy burning through. "The suicide thing, I mean." She pressed a nervous finger to her lips. "But the works in the show from 1949"—she pointed to the canvas—"this place, these paintings . . . well, it's the work of an artist at the peak of his powers. There's no darkness, no despair—just sheer wonder at God's creation."

"Hallelujah," cried Cordelia at this sudden outpouring of emotion. "That's just what we need around here, some old-time religion."

"Sorry, I'm such an idiot." Wendy waved a hand in front of her face, as if overheated. "But there's something about actually being in a place where a great artist worked."

"Wendy," said George, without taking his eye off a particularly long playlist, "is actually an artist herself, Mom—and a very good one. Who woulda thought—huh?" Whether he was consciously echoing his mother's expression of minutes before was unclear.

"Ah," said Cordelia, eyeing the young woman as if something had suddenly come clear in her mind. "Takes one to know one. Believe me, you hang out with musicians . . . dancers enough; I know all the signs."

"I spoke out of turn," said Wendy, apologizing.

"Not at all," replied Cordelia, turning to her son. "Your father always liked to call it a suicide when he wanted to excuse his own fuckups. Or when I made excuses for him to Martha or Alice." She frowned, a searching expression tightening the tiny crow's-feet merging into the laxity of her upper cheeks. "How did he put it? 'There's just no fucking way you slip off Sawkill Bridge.'"

"Did he really say that?" asked George, bending closer to his mother, as if to better evaluate her credibility. "I guess I just wasn't paying much attention—the years, I mean, before you two split up."

"Didn't I read in your essay, George, that the coroner ruled it an accident?" asked Wendy, as if trying to break the tension, or possibly be helpful.

"Spit it out, Georgie," said Cordelia, staring back at her son. "What's bothering you?"

"Play us your favorite cassette, Mom. Or something on the *Ya-ma-ha*," he said, mimicking the Judge's sneering intonation.

"What cassette?"

George stacked the cassettes back on the side table.

"As if anybody in this fucking town could care less."

"A prophet is not without honor . . ." offered Wendy, as if looking for a way to bring the conversation around.

"You performed a miracle, Georgie, ditch water into wine. One minute we couldn't give them away"—she snapped her fingers and smiled—"and suddenly they're treasures, along with this beautiful and talented woman you just brought home to me."

"*Hallelujah!*" exclaimed George in imitation. "Even I can smoke to that." He picked up the joint and waved it around. "To art and commerce."

"It's such a fucked-up business," said Wendy, going over and snuggling in with George, as if relieved to finally join mother and son. "The great ones do it because they have to do it and don't care about the money. But you have to care about the money—besides making a living—because the money is the only objective validation of artistic worth in the eyes of the art market, even the museum curators."

George put a comforting arm around Wendy. "Welcome to the art circus, baby, the celebrity freak show, the fame game, the brass ring of ambition." He turned to Cordelia with a knowing smile, as if to the world's expert. "You should have seen her today, Mom, walking on air—above it all—a goddess on a wire."

"You know," said Wendy, blushing as she placed her head against George's shoulder like a little girl grateful for the show of affection, "after last year, after the two planes, the twin towers, after everything changed . . . I kept wondering if things could ever get back to the way they were. Know what I mean . . . kinda like this place?"

"You're joking," said George.

"Ah," said Cordelia, bleary eyes intrigued with something in the demeanor of her young guest, of unbridled ambition requiring unconditional affirmation. "Your mountain goddess is a romantic, too, just like poor Annie, who always wanted the world to play by her golden rules and wouldn't take no for an answer. But the great ones always do—God knows this town is littered with their roadkill." She tossed a Bic lighter to George. "Light us up, baby love."

13

Dark Matters

GEORGE WOKE SLOWLY and then came to rapidly, as if rising from the bottom of a murky lake, only to lunge to the surface and surge into a brilliant sky. He blinked in the moonlight still streaming through his window, chagrined to find himself back in his boyhood room, alone, older—by minutes or years, he wasn't quite sure—lying back on his bed with a chunk of the Judge's manuscript still clutched in his hand. He looked at his watch and realized about three hours had passed since he'd dozed off. Switching off the ancient flying saucer Tensor reading lamp on his bedside table, he closed his eyes in hopes of a return to dreamless oblivion. The dope clearly helped. But he remained wide awake, his heart pounding. Not quite an anxiety attack, but his brain was seething with doubts about a past that once, though not exactly happy, had seemed benignly predictable in its odd and often jarring unpleasantness. He opened his eyes again to the lunar landscape of his youthful obsessions framing the frosted window—bookshelves and walls chock-a-block with childhood memorabilia. One of many reasons he'd carefully escorted Wendy past his bedroom to the upstairs guest room . . . a thought that had him tentatively fingering the roll of fat at his hip and waist, just above the hard-on in his jeans.

In truth, he felt intimidated by Wendy; there was something a little off-putting about the ease with which she ingratiated herself with his harebrained family, and her wild enthusiasm for the artist, his namesake—and not a little freaky to find his home ground transformed through her eyes into a shrine to a creative power that made a mockery of his childhood obsessions. He winced at his *Star Wars* posters and collectibles. How many times had he told his mother to just throw out all his junk? Which had resulted in her clamping onto it even harder. An incurable pack rat (an instinct that had probably saved the Altmann paintings after Jimbo deserted her), with her own archive of memorabilia from Albert Grossman's Bearsville Studios, not to mention her scrapbook dwelling on that muddy, crazy long-ago mythic weekend of sex, drugs, and rock and roll. Not to mention her nude photographs (bane of his high school days . . . "Wow, dude, look at that full bush") enshrined first in old issues of *Life* and now iconic imagery increasingly populating every corner of the Internet.

He sat up on the side of the bed, gathering in the stray pages of the Judge's memoir, wondering, in the harsh glare of moonlight, if some part of him, too, hadn't been sucked into the ether, thrown out on the darkened stage of the night under some huge spot . . . still searching for his lines . . . his faltering mojo. Or in this case—he weighed the pages of the Judge's memoir—a randomized algorithm with an open-ended function that was driving him crazy.

Alice was right: In the memoir, the Judge had indeed lied about the receipt of the nine sketches from George Altmann, claiming to have been given them before the trial began, and so—if true—putting him legally in a much more problematic situation, as he'd readily admitted over dinner. George tapped the typescript. And that meeting with Allen Weinstein in his chambers on Foley Square in 1968, as if some mythic nemesis had appeared this time out of the ether with a sarcastic glinty smile in his inquisitive eyes, a sticky-fingered Drosselmeyer, first to ferret out the sketches, now to sink Alger Hiss for good, and in so doing irreparably damage the Judge's reputation.

At the foot of his double bed, on a card-table desk in front of his single window, his laptop screen saver beckoned: star charts fading in and out, as if the Milky Way had detected his wakefulness, or been the cause of it, summoning his return like a forsaken lover. Beyond the screen, beyond the grid of twelve frosted panes, the backlit woodlot glowed eerily, scene of so many childhood reveries—fractal geometries of a huge and rare survivor, a first-growth oak cartwheeling its Kali-like arms into the night sky. In his research for the Altmann catalog, he'd come upon a rare sketch pad (the absence of more sketches in Altmann's artist files had puzzled him) that the artist had devoted to that lonesome survivor, drawing the oak from every angle and in every kind of lighting, as if fascinated with the gesticulating life force of those titanic arms embracing the sky.

He went to his desk, switched on a lamp, and replaced the Judge's pages beneath the copy of Whittaker Chambers's *Witness* (re-creating the first moment he'd come upon the volume in the Judge's office), staring again at the cover and into that morose baggy-eyed, world-weary face in the shadow of a crumpled fedora. Just flipping through the pages that the Judge—and Annie!—had underlined and annotated, it was clear that both husband and wife had been drawn to many of the same stories and recollections, but seemingly for different reasons, responding to different sensibilities in the author, or to Chambers's dire warnings about Soviet penetration by agents of influence of the highest offices in the land, agents, who once in place, dared not break from the underground apparatus.

Taking up the book, the pages fell open at the following:

> It seemed to me that the deserters from Communism whom the party had killed had nearly all made one mistake. They had shared in advance with other Communists their doubts, fears and plans to break. Out of friendship, or pity, or loneliness, they had tried to move those others to break with them. Their comrades had then betrayed them. I resolved to say nothing to anyone. Yet, like the others who had broken before me, I found that I could not leave these people whom I had known intimately for years . . . without trying to tell them something . . . I also worked around the subject with Alger Hiss . . . Hiss thought my attitude was the usual subaltern's grudge against his superior . . . Later I ventured into the much more perilous field of Communist politics, criticizing the Russian purges and especially the character of Stalin. For the first time, I saw Alger glance at me out of the side of his eye. "Yes, Stalin plays for keeps, doesn't he?" he said. I had not heard the expression used before except in marbles. I thought that it was a neat summing up. I also thought that I had gone too far, and stopped.

Here and in other passages underlined in Annie's pencil, she seemed to be singling out sections that proved Chambers's claims in court of a friendship with Alger and Priscilla, when he'd served as a clandestine courier, picking up, copying, and returning top-secret papers. He had sported a slight Russian accent (from having been around so many Soviet intelligence agents), which only confirmed his bona fides in Alger Hiss's mind. While the Judge tended to note the darker side as seen through Chambers's eyes, underlining in blue three times "Stalin plays for keeps, doesn't he?" Often Annie wrote in an exacting clear hand in the margin, as if in a note to her husband: "Yes, of course Chambers was telling the truth. The vividness and specific details, the emotional candor confirm his veracity beyond question! Oh, Edward, hung by your own petard, your integrity corrupted by your own willed falsehoods."

To which the Judge had penned many years later in a paraphrase of the author: "No revolutionary can hope to change history without taking on the crimes of history."

Annie had clearly read the book first; after all, it had been given to her and inscribed by the author in 1954, and her underlining and commentary in pencil was sometimes responded to repeatedly in the Judge's hand, in bold blue ink, presumably many years later, and, certainly given the retrospective tone of his responses, sometime after his wife's death. The marginalia he appended to hers was mostly in agreement or pleading professional allowances, as if still contending issues in the trial, or pleading extenuating circumstances, often verging on pleas for her forgiveness. Again and again the Judge singled out passages in which Chambers described in chilling clinical terms the threat he felt himself under after his break with the GRU apparatus (carrying a gun and fleeing to Florida with his family for a time), and the parts, all the more ironic, describing his friendship with Alger and Priscilla Hiss, as if the Judge found that relationship (the very thing he'd tried to disprove in the trial!) between the two couples, Chambers and his wife, Esther, and the Hisses, deeply moving, poignantly so, noting in his own commentary how it revealed a bond of loyalty and love between the couples that stirred feelings of envy in himself—"a capacity for fellowship": the depths of a comradeship about which he'd had no inkling, either personally or professionally. "LOVE," he wrote in caps in the margin about the couples' vacation sojourn in a country cottage, "beyond mere affection or Party discipline. They were pals, friends, confidants about their children. My God, I had no idea Priscilla, much less Alger, had such depths of humanity to them—or was I blinded by my own lack of compassion?"

"And yet," he wrote in another marginal comment, "the moment he broke he was as good as dead."

The Judge rarely commented on Chambers's style, unlike Annie, who relished certain felicitous phrases, not to mention the moving stories of his childhood and the anguish he felt breaking with the Soviet underground and finally betraying Hiss, Harry Dexter White, and many others in his GRU apparatus to the FBI. Of course, it was in the Judge's nature to single out the bald and convincing facts, although clearly moved by the sincerity of Chambers's confession of self-doubt and remorse about the damage caused by the spying—his betrayal of onetime comrades, even when couched in expressions of commitment to the betterment of the world. A painful contradiction captured often movingly in Chambers's sensuous and soulful language.

Strangely, even on a quick thumbing of the pages, the section of the book that seemed to draw the most scrutiny in terms of marginal commentary from his grandparents was a section describing a trip Chambers took from Washington to Fitzwilliam, New Hampshire, to the summer home of Harry Dexter White, an adviser to Henry Morgenthau, the secretary of the Treasury, to retrieve a paper on the reform of Soviet monetary policy on orders from Moscow Central. Alger and Priscilla Hiss had in a moment of reckless whimsy determined to join their spy handler for the road trip, Priscilla insisting that they take her favorite Route 202, the most scenic, since it avoided cities and wound through the countryside. It was a route they had taken often before when driving through Pennsylvania together. "So," wrote Annie in the margin, "it was the three of them on that trip. I'm sure Priscilla managed to wrangle Chambers into this disaster. When I think about little Teddy, something just breaks in me, the already broken thing, again and again and again!" "Yes," responded the Judge in carefully printed blue ink, as if compelled to alleviate his dead wife's distress, "a disaster for them, for us, and, yes, poor Teddy. Even if Chambers failed dismally to prove the trip ever even happened in the trial. And thank God for that!"

George's finger hovered on the Judge's words. He was perplexed, sensing both hurt and relief.

"Why Teddy—little Teddy?" he murmured.

He then slowly closed and caressed the cover of the book, for the first time in his life finding himself moved by the wounded feelings of the one man he'd always revered as a pillar of probity and self-confidence. He sensed, too, in the distant echo of Hiss's offhand comment about Stalin to his friend and handler, a kind of free-floating threat, a hint of evil, of lurking fanaticism even at the distance of sixty years or more, of which he'd been, until that moment, blithely unmindful. An amorphous evil, to which the sensible and soothing voice of his grandmother, allied with the courageous witness of Chambers, seemed to offer an antidote, invoking a higher power of human decency and compassion and moral courage. In her spare, insightful commentary, Annie, a woman always more legendary than real to him, for the first time came across as a living, breathing figure in her gentle, albeit sometimes sharp, verbal jousting with her husband as both responded to yet a third voice, a voice of wisdom and searing insight, that of Whittaker Chambers. This colloquy between three wounded, like-minded souls as they contested with the enigma of Alger Hiss now floated back to George across space and time from—of all things—the heavily underlined and annotated pages of a book. And in this oddest of odd relationships between reader, authors, and their subject, he detected something infinitely sad, if not lethal, something unsaid and unsayable between his grandparents and the author, a verbal dance, literally at the margins, around some inexpressible truth or lie that no one dared to put into so many words. Not between themselves, not in the fullness of time, not in their lifetimes, only in whispers and hints between the lines—if that. Now bequeathed to him to decipher. George again thumbed the well-worn ink-stained pages of Chambers's memoir, sensing the harrowing stake his grandparents—bookish souls to their fingertips—had in this tale of trial and witness and confession, which even now thwarted their love, despite the fact that death had long ago parted them.

But the strangeness didn't stop there: Annie's voice, especially in its more righteous, robust tones and aggrieved anger, championing Chambers's story—defending his humanity, highlighting the creative probity of a literary soul mate—reminded him in some uncanny way of the brash self-confidence of Wendy: always defending the correctness of her instincts, of her first impressions, her artist's insights. As she had upon their arrival in Woodstock, her cheeks flushed with indignation at his disparagement of his home, his family, all the while extolling the primacy of art (well, what artist wouldn't) over the mundane preoccupations of family quarrels and simmering resentments. So much like Annie, who preferred to be guided by her feelings rather than legal abstractions based on dubious evidence to the contrary. Just as Wendy, indignant and full of herself, felt compelled to champion George Altmann's art over the half-baked conclusions in his catalog essay, as Annie had the goodness and veracity of Whittaker Chambers in his memoir against the lies of Alger Hiss. Writ further in Wendy's unshakable conviction that Altmann had been drawn to life and light, not to the darkness of alcoholism, depression, and suicide. A darkness not unlike what Chambers had described in *Witness*: a brother's early suicide, his own attempted suicide, the ever-present threat of Stalin's henchmen, only to find half the nation turned against him as he testified against Alger Hiss.

George felt a cold shiver pass through him as he instinctively reached for the Altmann sketches in the manila envelope at his elbow.

"Nine sketches," George mumbled, feeling a little shaky as he gazed over at the manila envelope at his elbow: how, out of the past whirlwind of controversy and bitter hatred, the art had survived—tangible proof of guilt, perhaps the antidote to the venom that had spread through the bloodstream of the Dimock clan decade after decade, a poison that threatened, if not the family's demise, certainly that of Hermitage. He'd even detected as much in that stray tear in his aunt Alice's eye over dinner.

And how long before Alice called up Felicity and found out that he'd lied about leaving the sketches where he'd found them?

Oh Lord, won't you buy me a Mercedes Benz?

George scowled at Cordelia's stoned rendition on the Yamaha just hours before of Joplin's plea (recorded just days before her death, so his mother blithely noted), wondering if her penchant for the song had anything to do with that fateful drive to Woodstock in the Judge's ruby red Merc coupe to return these very same nine sketches to the man who would become her husband and his father.

And now, he in turn had become the means, returning them yet again where they'd once been dismissed by Jimmy Altmann on the same day he'd bedded the messenger, if not in the Merc then amid the tomato plants, no less, behind the barn. A thing he'd more than once shamelessly—"tomato-head George"—alluded to in the hearing of his young son.

The astrophysicist in him was drawn to the vague sense of recurring patterns, even the possibility of unseen laws at work, as perverse on the human scale as the cosmic: the tantalizing, even comforting, prospect that a diligent meticulous working of details might present a solution.

This brought to mind Jimbo's boasting growl, his hearty, if not inebriated, laugh, his always ironic commentary on his own set of foolproof first principles—mostly lame excuses, which more often than not caused young George to wither with shame, as if his father was possessed to kick start his maturity, so they could be more like pals than father and son, where the real pay dirt was to be found: a souped-up sex life of his own.

"Georgie porgy, you know what my job is in life: sex, man, sex. It's in the music; it's what the concert scene is all about. Trust me. I'm the guy who gets it all set up, the lights and mikes and the arena; I weave the spell so the big guns can get up there and strut their stuff, and so the chicks can bask in this wave of throbbing sound—the vibes, man, those dancing vibes, the rhythm like a thing alive humming through their bodies, lighting up their sweet oozing pussies—lighting their fire. I make pussy happen out there for the boys and girls. I am the bringer of life . . ."

Such embarrassing drunken riffs caused George to flinch, enough to almost allow himself a hopeful take on Alice's cruelty, bringing into focus yet another alternate reality, as if parallel universes were his fate du jour. And a need to reground himself in the familiar: the vestigial artifacts of his own fucked-up youth, much of it carefully stored on the cinder-block and two-by-eight shelving, crammed with his discarded science fiction novels, high school and college physics textbooks, and assorted science projects. There, cobwebbed against the ceiling, sat his trophies from Woodstock High for math and physics club, chess club, *Star Wars* club. At eye level on a broad shelf was parked his precious collection of *Star Wars* memorabilia, trading cards, various busted-up lightsabers, and Lego spaceships, including his favorites, the *Millennium Falcon*, *Jedi Interceptor*, and *Imperial Star Destroyer*, like some intergalactic demolition derby in miniature. Detritus of a misspent youth carefully concealed in his Princeton days, when furtive chatter in the halls of the Astrophysics Department about *Star Wars*–obsessed childhoods was a guilty pleasure only indulged out of the hearing of their professors.

Pinned to the few remaining spaces on the pale blue plywood walls were a couple of *Star Wars* posters featuring a buxom Princess Leia, along with his chess tournament ribbons arranged in a pinwheel by Cordelia, a Princeton class of 1992 pennant—also Cordelia's addition—and, pride of place, a signed poster of Carl Sagan. Cordelia, he now discovered, had also added his framed Princeton diploma in astrophysics and certificates in math, computer science, and engineering physics. Perhaps, in his mother's mind, major-league bragging rights (he was reminded of the Judge's power wall at Hermitage) to her son's academic achievements at least offered her status talking points when dealing with her tony regulars at the bookstore, now that her glory days hanging tight with Albert Grossman's legendary acts were long past. In fact, she was a survivor, a revenant, with Grossman long dead, along with many of his legendary clients—Janis and Jimi heading up the tragic list.

When feeling down or a little high, as when she'd staggered off to bed that night, she couldn't resist waxing philosophical: "Well, I may be divorced and keeping company mostly with vibrators now, but I had a hell of a better ride, with wonderful men, whose voices and music will last the ages, than my older sisters, whose sex lives have been on the scrap heap from the get-go."

Dimock pride. A thought that now gave him more than a little pause. How much of that Princeton astrophysics Ph.D. had been about satisfying the Judge, proving himself, bettering the competition? A purity of ambition frozen out in the vastness of space-time: a grand love affair that had turned into a dead hand clutching his heart.

George shivered, realizing how cold it was. He went over to the radiator and found it lukewarm. He'd checked the boiler before turning in; the burner was crudded up and the heat exchanger had a slow leak. He wondered if he could manage the maintenance himself (Jimmy could have) in the morning or if he needed to get in the HVAC guy, when he'd probably be told the boiler needed replacing.

Outside, beyond his frosted window, the full moon seemed a dead-weight on the sprawling branches of their Methuselah white oak, as if some sort of terrestrial-cosmic tug-of-war hung in the balance. He stared at the bloated bronze-and-lemony sphere with a wisp of a cirrus cloud jostling its upper curve. The oak branches, twisted upward in a succession of thirty-degree angles, undulating as if alive to the tidal pull of the moon, while one of the thickest branches, having strayed into the dead center of the fiery sphere of brightness, seemed almost dissolved, transformed into a translucent vein, or like a pale umbilical cord, nourishing the curled form of some fetal sky god.

He sighed and blew on his hands. A new boiler would be expensive.

He tapped at his laptop. At least the Wi-Fi signal was strong—small blessings. Time to add his data to the digital ether. He created a spreadsheet, plugged in his phone, and uploaded the photos of the Altmann sketches, arranging them just as he'd found them on the Judge's corkboard, then the newspaper clippings, and the names and data found on the note cards. With these digital forensics accomplished, an approximation of a holograph of how the Judge's logical mind organized evidence, he added an additional line equation with Alger Hiss's name on the left and George Altmann's name on the right, pondering the best algorithmic equation to bring coherence to their separate fates, an equation that would necessarily include at least the other eight names of those depicted in the sketches and one Edward Dimock, if human fates could be so quantified.

He clicked on the image of Alger Hiss to enlarge his thumbnail photo: debonair, cool, and efficient, with a ruthless—so it now seemed to him—piercing stare. If Hiss—he took a deep breath, trying to bring to bear as much pure logic as he dared—was a spy, as detailed by Chambers, perhaps a very important spy, then it followed that his confederates in the sketches—four—well, maybe three—who suffered violent deaths, two who fled abroad, one convicted of spying, one yet unidentified—were either spies as well, or, at the very least, must have known about Hiss's spying. If George Altmann had indeed come within the gravitational field of that conspiratorial body (knew more than was good for him), his life, too, might have been put in peril, enough of a threat to require elimination . . . which an ambiguous fall (like that of Laurence Duggan and Marvin Smith) from the Sawkill Bridge would have tidily accomplished. The Judge's soul-searching agony over how best to interpret the nine sketches certainly made that a reasonable assumption. It would be just like him to lay out the facts and test first his and then his grandson's gumption and intelligence to see if he could find his way to the right answer where his mentor had failed. This strategy resembled so much of the Judge's interaction with George's cousins, even his grown children, as if life was but one long parlor game, with the Judge forever employing the Socratic method around the dinner table, or pointing out clues on hikes to plant morphology or birdsong as a way of fostering critical thinking.

At this, he typed into the Google search bar: 3415 Volta Place, Washington D.C. A local realtor's page showed a recent listing for the property on a maple-lined street in tony Georgetown. The red brick home was tiny, narrow, three stories high, almost cute, lacking anything of a sinister aspect.

George closed his eyes, exhausted as much by memory as present prospects. Why bother? What did it matter? Alice was right; she was always right, in her bitchy way. The stain on the Judge's reputation was indelible.

And any hope of justice—he stared at the faces of the people on his screen, all of whom were dead—had long been precluded. Even

the afterlife of these possible crimes—the devastated lives of the victims' families—had most likely faded into oblivion. Well, he thought,
nodding, almost. Rationally speaking, he assured himself, all that really
mattered, the one pathetic residue of space-time, of the myriad particle interactions that constituted the world, were, as Wendy insisted,
Altmann's paintings—"things," and perhaps the life and reputation that
went into their creation. "That at least represents some kind of bedrock
truth—right, George?" he asked himself aloud, requiring the company of
his own voice. "Now that the works have been so brilliantly monetized,
packaged as the wounded genius of a celebrated master—he survives!
George Altmann beats the odds. He's the one winner in all this."

George pumped his fist, then shook his head, frowning.

"And Hermitage?"

As if the saving of Hermitage and the Judge's reputation were one
and the same.

He was a scientist, damn, it. And conspiracy theories went totally
against his grain because they always stressed correlation over cause
and effect. And even though the Judge had been there, in the cockpit
of history, he seemed as incredulous and uncertain about his own narrative as anyone—if the memoir was to be taken at face value.

Or if Alice and Martha, not to mention his own mother, were to be
believed, the Judge cared only about himself.

"Doubt." Of all the Judge wrote, the evidence he presented, the quaver in his voice the night before, that was the most compelling thing:
doubt. And so unlike him.

Doubt, uncertainty, curiosity—the ticket to every scientific advance
in human history.

"Keep it simple, George," he scolded himself.

The only certainty, the only logic he could count on was this: If just
one or more of those cases of ambiguous death or disappearance could
be proved to have been deliberate orchestrations by the KGB, the probability of George Altmann's murder rose dramatically.

And with that proof, the necessity of reinterpreting Altmann's late
paintings.

"George, that's the one thing you owe the world."

Already he could sense Wendy holding his feet to the fire; she would
insist on a revised catalog essay that spoke not just to the truth about
Altmann's death but also to the glory of the life force that had gone
into the late work.

He looked up a moment at his reflection in the window, where his troubled moonlit eyes stared back at the not unappealing fantasy of a mysterious rock star for a father, something the teenager who had once inhabited this room might well have reveled in, and the soaring stature (how cool to be the love child of a celebrity rocker!) it would have given to his shitty high school years. He smiled sardonically at such a pathetic notion, at his ghostly face in the window above his laptop screen: dirty-blond hair in cowlicks, puffy dark-ringed eyes, overweight body, hardly rock star material, much less a biographer or editor of note, much less a gallerist or astrophysicist . . . just another empty vessel to be filled with all the improbabilities—Heisenberg's phantom uncertainties conjured out of space-time, from before he was born . . . before any of them were born.

"What a pitiful joke you are, George."

He rested his palm on the volume of *Witness*, feeling again the tug of his grandparents' contest for the truth within its pages, the thing that had torn apart their marriage.

With that, with one click of his mouse, he reached into the ether of the past in the guise of Google search: eight names in the nine sketches.

Saturday, March 17, 1951, Drew Pearson on the Washington Merry-Go-Round: **Duggan-Field link may be clue to seven unsolved disappearances or deaths following revelations in Alger Hiss case; whereabouts of Noel Field is No. 1 American mystery in Europe.**

Frankfurt. The No. 1 American mystery of Europe continues to be the sudden and unsolved disappearance of four Americans in the Noel Field case after Field was named by Whittaker Chambers as a member of the communist cell in the U.S. State Department. This case is now being linked for the first time with another unsolved mystery in the United States—the strange death of Laurence Duggan, found in a snowbank 16 floors below his New York office. Duggan also was named in the State Department investigation, though cleared by the Justice Department.

The amazing thing is that a total of seven people, including Harry Dexter White and Marvin Smith, have now died mysteriously or disappeared even more mysteriously following revelations in the Alger Hiss case . . .

Heart pumping furiously, George read the rest of the article, uncertain if he was glad or disappointed to find that this thing—more abstract than real—had legs, that it wasn't just the Judge's obsession. He pulled up his spreadsheet and added in the new data.

Harry Dexter White: "Later it was reported that the real cause of his death was an overdose of digitalis, not heart failure . . . suicide or foul play rumored . . . buried hastily by a brother who was a member of the Communist Party"; "Walter Marvin Smith, Justice Department attorney found at the base of the Justice Department staircase where he had fallen, been pushed, or jumped on October 20, 1948 . . . wife insists: not a suicide; Smith was the only eyewitness to the transfer of the Hiss automobile to a Communist organizer"; "Strange death of State Department official Laurence Duggan. Falls sixteen stories with one galosh on, one off."

And then there was William Remington, convicted by a jury in 1953 of lying about turning over secret papers to Elizabeth Bentley and sentenced to prison, where he was murdered by two inmates, one of whom used a piece of brick concealed in a sock to bludgeon him. Remington died two days later of his injuries, just days before Alger Hiss was released from the same Lewisburg prison. The motive for the murder remained unclear, although the two inmates claimed they were anti-Communists. The two young murderers were sentenced to life for their crime.

From the *Washington Daily News*: "William W. Remington now joins the odiferous list of young Communist punks who wormed their way upward in the Government under the New Deal. He was sentenced to five years in prison, and he should serve every minute of it. In Russia, he would have been shot without trial."

The venom of that judgment, much less the fate of Remington, sent a chill down George's spine.

Two highly improbable and unresolved deaths by falling. Surely, if such things had happened, fifty years later, something . . . someone would have turned up to tell the tale, or the truth been ferreted out by the ubiquitous Google.

"By now," he muttered, furiously typing away in the Google search bar, as if persistence alone could wring answers out of the past.

As he pursued the subject, he found pages and pages of Google results, newspaper accounts of the day, many on conservative sites spelling out the evils of Hiss and his fellow conspirators, while left-wing sites dismissed the same charges as conspiracy theories cooked up by the lunatic fringe abetted by Nixon and Hoover. Even the *New*

York Times, in its obituary of Hiss from six years before, described the charges against him of spying as unproven, circumstantial, and highly controversial. More than a little flavor of that opinion had flowed across the dinner table at Alice and Stan's.

And yet, captured in this same gravitational field was the possibility of a series of diabolical crimes—utterly unresolved—now with implications for the death of his grandfather Altmann. This crime began to take on a real shape in his mind as he glimpsed more and more screaming headlines from newspapers of the period.

He reflected on a false narrative, to which he himself had contributed and perpetuated in his Altmann catalog essay. A potential error that Wendy, to give her credit, going purely by intuitive insight, had rejected out of hand without benefit of concrete knowledge of the circumstances: a clairvoyance that was in itself not a little troubling.

Now annoyed at his carelessness and confusion—his paralyzing indecisiveness—he clicked around on the Internet, scanning more newspaper stories on the figures in the Altmann sketches. In every case, the one consistent factor was ambiguity and inconclusive evidence, with the possible exception of Noel Field, fellow State Department colleague of Alger Hiss, who had so mysteriously disappeared before 1950, and who, according to recently released files out of Hungary, had confessed to the Hungarian secret police in the fifties that, yes indeed, he'd known Hiss was a fellow spy, and so had fled behind the Iron Curtain for fear of being arrested by the FBI.

George checked the citation on Field: Allen Weinstein's *The Haunted Wood*.

"That's it," he almost shouted out, seeing his cell phone on the night before held up to the ship's keel ceiling in the great room at Hermitage while the flames danced in the fireplace: the connection that had made all the difference.

"Allen Weinstein, archivist of the United States of America," he read out loud, pondering each word.

He thought of Alice's dismissive snort at the mention of Weinstein; and the almost paranoid description in the Judge's memoir when he heard that the young Yale scholar had been blessed by the Hiss forces to write the definitive book on the trial. How extraordinary, this scholar, the Judge's onetime nemesis . . . how Weinstein's latest book had preserved the old man's life with the final proof of Hiss's guilt. To fight a final battle for redemption.

And yet the Judge either had trouble remembering who Weinstein was at dinner or couldn't bring himself to admit it was the same author, or he fully recognized the significance of Weinstein's new book coming twenty years after *Perjury*, proving not just the two charges of perjury from the thirties but also that Hiss had done even more damage as a spy during the much more crucial period of Yalta in 1945, when Stalin enslaved half of Europe. Had an inkling of that far graver offense prompted the Judge's illegal raid on the defense files in 1968 to remove the Altmann sketches? Had he and Weinstein, irony of ironies, been on the same journey for decades?

And like a guilty reflex, he felt again the presence of Wendy Bradley, as she had grabbed his arm two nights before on Twenty-third Street: *George . . . if it's not in the art, it's not there. Trust me, I know about these things.*

"Who the fuck is Wendy Bradley?" he spouted with indignation.

He picked up his phone, weighing it in his hand, nodding with guilt at his betrayal of her trust as he connected the phone again to his laptop and downloaded the photo he'd surreptitiously shot that afternoon, when he'd momentarily switched from her phone. He then deleted the jpg from his phone.

He stared at the enlarged photo on his screen, where she clung upside down on the overhang of the boulder, grasping an angle of a rocky ledge with her outstretched right arm, another grip at eye level with her left hand, her left leg bent to a hold waist-high, her right dangling in air, every muscle and sinew in her body stretched, her rib cage a tight concavity, with only the lovely curve of her left breast absent tension. Her ponytail dangling to the line of the indent of her bra strap, her taut skin iridescent with the approaching sunset.

Not a little annoyed at the stirring in his crotch, he typed her name into Google.

Top hit was her studio site. Obviously she got good search optimization and had lots of followers. "Wow . . ." The paintings were gorgeous, full of thick creamy impasto depicting the sheer sides of granite cliffs, out of which a woman's figure, more abstract than realistic, emerged like a shadowy spirit from the rock face, reminiscent of Michelangelo's half-completed sculptures emerging from the marble, still immured, specters longing to be fully born. The texture and faults in the stone merged seamlessly with the skin tones. "Fuck, she really can paint." Pearlstein with a tad more fluidity and a model posed to exhibit strength and agility, not languid disinterest. Flipping through the site, he could tell she definitely had her shit together: a signature style, a feminist angle, a conceptualist handle, and commercial to boot—erotic and wild and dreamy—just plain stunning artistry.

Yale undergrad, summa cum laude in art history and philosophy, and MFA—both in European literature and applied arts. George R. Bunker Award in recognition of an outstanding student in painting/printmaking.

"Fucking brass ring."

Her profile on the climbing school site listed all her professional accomplishments and teaching qualifications. She taught everything from Rock Climbing 101 and 102 to Top Rope Setup and Glacier Skills & Crevasse Rescue.

"Holy shit . . ." There they were, harrowing photos of her Everest climb in 1996, the deadliest season in history, when twelve climbers had died trying to reach the summit. He recalled her oddly dispassionate tale at dinner, how her party had just managed to avoid the blizzard that caught the party ahead of them, killing eight, including two legendary veterans of the mountain. At twenty, she'd been one of the youngest women—the youngest American woman—to reach the summit of Everest. How had she put it? "Sometimes patience, meticulous evaluation of risk, and keeping the testosterone on simmer make all the difference."

He could find nothing about her childhood or high school years, nothing from before Yale. No mention of her parents on her Facebook page, or her "crazy" aunt and uncle, who had taken her in after her parents died. As if her life had only begun with Yale, like one of her figures, emerging from Jonathan Edwards College fully formed.

So he tried: *Bradleys, accident, deaths . . .*

Houston Post, September 26, 1989:
Bradleys Killed on Mount Wake, Alaska
Husband and Wife Climbing Team Fell to Their Deaths
The internationally renowned husband and wife climbing team of John and Sarah Bradley were killed yesterday climbing Mount Wake in Ruth Gorge, Alaska. Rangers and rescue crews found their bodies nearby at the bottom of a gully. Initial reports indicate that Sarah Bradley had fallen first in a rappelling accident, and that her husband had subsequently slipped or fallen in an attempt to reach or recover her body. An investigation is under way. The Bradley husband and wife team had climbed five of the seven summits, including Everest,

Aconcagua, Kilimanjaro, and Mont Blanc. They were preparing for
an assault on Mount McKinley next spring. The Bradleys are sur-
vived by Wendy Bradley, their thirteen-year-old daughter, at their
home in Houston.

"Thirteen . . ." noted George, as if that bad-luck number represented
some bizarre correlation of loss in their lives.

Not a little numbed, he read through the dozens of articles and
glowing tributes to the Bradleys: rock stars of the climbing fraternity.

At a sudden knock on his door, he hurriedly closed his laptop.

"You're still up. Were you talking to yourself?" Wendy stepped
unprompted into his room and shut the door rather decisively behind
her. She was wearing her spandex climbing tights and fleece vest. "Did
anyone ever tell you your guest room is fucking freezing? I woke up a
Popsicle. I could see my breath in there." She lay back on his bed and
pulled the comforter up around her.

"I think the boiler's shot; it's cold in here, as well."

"Not as cold."

"Why don't I go down to the sofa? You take my bed."

"Don't be a baby; there's plenty of room. And I'm not going to fuck
you. Besides, I've got my fusion leggings on, polyester and spandex, and
even if you were hung like an iron horse, you couldn't penetrate these."

She pulled the crazy quilt more firmly around her, giving him a
friendly, if defiant, smile.

"Steam-powered, I don't think so."

"I think the dope gave me bad dreams."

"No wonder, after a day like this," he said only half-jokingly.

"I really like your mom; she's nothing like your aunt."

"The family flower child."

"Like"—she gazed around his room, taking it all in—"so long ago."

"You think? Sometime it feels, around here, like I was born yesterday."

She eyed him with a compelling earnestness.

"I'm not a kid, George, not one of your millennial crybabies. You
can't be more than—what, five or six years older? Hardly a seducer of
babes in the woods."

"Oh, I was well trained by Princeton HR to keep my hands *off* the
students."

"I'm not trying to sleep my way into a gallery show, George. I have
collectors; I have a following; I have a life."

"I hadn't gotten to your life—or your lack of representation yet."
He lied with a straight face, trying to repress the guilt in his voice. He
pushed a lock of ruffled hair off his brow, smoothing down a cowlick,
and gestured gamely. "And you said it yourself, the other night at
the opening: You didn't like what I wrote about George Altmann's
suicide."

"That what's got you hot and bothered—sleepless in the garden?"
Her eyes went to his shelves as she continued her inventory. "All I know
is what the art tells me, and it doesn't tell me that—no way José."

"So, I have a consensus problem, or perhaps a parallel universe
problem. If George Altmann didn't slip or fall or have an accident—
which, the more I think about it, seems highly unlikely—and didn't
kill himself, then the alternative presents a whole host of unresolved, if
not unresolvable, issues." He tightened his jaw. "Kind of like the dark
matter problem, how an invisible force, a particle—if that's what it
is—interacts or doesn't with the strong and weak nuclear force, electro-
magnetism or just plain vanilla gravity, giving it a six hundred percent
boost. Unless it's in a class of forces we know nothing about, a parallel
universe nudging ours around the edges."

"You're losing me, George. Come on, just spit it out for me."

He went to his bureau and pulled out a Woodstock High sweatshirt
and handed it to her. She gave it a sniff and put it on.

"Come, sit here next to me."

He pulled up his spreadsheet of the Altmann sketches and all the
other information he'd gathered, and spent half an hour clueing her in.

Well into his download, he sensed her stiffening, her stare riveted
and eyes more attentive, as if moved by a deep sense of injustice in
response to his rather tepid rendition of the circumstantial evidence
as he knew it. He found it more than a little eerie that as he spoke,
named the names, her fingers reached out time and again to the cover
of Whittaker Chambers's *Witness*, lifting the flap slightly, as if compelled to take a sounding within. And when she finally spoke, her tone
of voice was no-nonsense, decisive, as if she were now back on Everest,
deciding whether to wait for clearing weather or to go.

"So," she said, resting her palm fully on the copy of *Witness*, as if
taking an oath or trying to sum it up for the jury, "George Altmann
might have been a witness to Hiss's spying, or at least might have been
able to confirm his membership in a Communist cell, which would
have destroyed Hiss's credibility during the trial."

"Well"—a sheepish crinkle appeared on his cheeks—"it sure wouldn't have helped his case."

"I don't really get your algorithms," and she nodded at his computer screen.

"Don't worry about that, just a way of trying to conceptualize the thing."

"Where," she demanded, "*are* the original sketches?"

He got them out for her and switched on his desk lamp.

"My God, how that man could draw, what a supple hand—gorgeous." She shivered and blew on her fingers as she handed the sketches back one by one. "They're detailed studies, you know, part of an ensemble."

"Meaning what?"

"I can tell better tomorrow in the daylight: part of a larger work."

"You think?"

"Same ambient lighting, same style, same paper . . . same feel for the physiognomy of his subjects."

"I never saw anything quite like these until yesterday, his early work."

"Does it bother you that your grandfather might have been a Communist?"

He was surprised at the sober tone of her voice.

"Only that—until yesterday I'm not sure I thought about communism one way or another. I missed it, at least in so far as it explains his work, what happened to him."

"So, you're suggesting Altmann, an ex-Communist, might have been killed, executed, to keep him quiet? That's what Stalin's henchmen specialized in—ever read *Darkness at Noon*, by Arthur Koestler?"

"Well . . ." This forthright precocity quite staggered him, as if her superior education allowed her access to insights, if not conclusions, that, at best, he, as a scientist, might only tentatively sound. "No. I don't know what to think, except it seems more and more a possibility— especially *if* your instincts are right."

She looked into his troubled eyes and gently, even kindly, pushed a lock of hair off the crease in his brow.

"Oh, right—definitely not the work of a depressed alcoholic." Her eyes now strayed to his *Star Wars* memorabilia, as if needing some comic relief, perhaps intrigued by the design of his Lego spaceships, or intent on lowering the tension. "So, George, this changes a *lot* of things."

"You can say that again." He handed her the sketch of the Judge at the defense desk, given him by Alice hours before. "It kinda messes with the deck chairs in my little corner of the universe."

"Handsome guy"—she held the sketch under the lamp admiringly—"like Gregory Peck. Master of your universe—huh."

"Alice gave it to me tonight. When Altmann worked as a court reporter."

"Ah." She smiled, getting up and going to his shelves. "A long time ago in a galaxy far, far away . . ." She began fingering the Lego spaceships. "Like what you're struggling with, does it really matter if we *just* know about it—the truth, about exactly what happened?"

He pondered this for a moment. "It doesn't matter in the sense that it may not change the past, but it distorts the present, in that we're living a lie, a false consensus reality. And then, of course, I'll need to revise the catalog essay."

"Let's call it a false consciousness." She smiled. "I was a European lit major, part of the jargon. What you mean to say," she said, correcting him again, "you, your family didn't even know Altmann was a Communist?"

"Pathetic, isn't it? I thought I'd been pretty diligent. I went through his archives in the barn but found nothing about anything like that. I didn't pay much attention to the mural work of the thirties—his figurative stuff. Don't much care for it, can't sell it."

"So"—she lay a comforting hand on his shoulder—"if we're living a lie and we find out it's a lie . . . that really does change the past, which is the only present we can ever know. Since memory, time, *is* our present. The Proust thing, *n'est-ce pas?*"

He pondered yet another hole in his education for a moment, admitting, "Not my thing, Proust. Not unless you establish a consensus of opinion, at least in this universe."

"You keep saying that. Are you saying there is more than one universe?"

"Well, there are, worst luck—probably multiple universes, not necessarily parallel, perhaps an infinite number—most likely, in fact, where everything as we know it is replicated down to the last proton, quark, and charm."

"Are you fucking with my mind, old boy?" Now she was almost girlish, flippant, flirtatious.

"Particle physics—weird: You don't wanna know, young lady."

"You mean, like us here in this"—she picked up the Lego *Millennium*

Falcon and took it for a quick spin—"this *kid's* room of yours . . . replicated beyond the moon and stars?"

"Most likely."

"Are they not having sex like us, too?"

"Maybe, hog wild."

"With benefits, no doubt. Except I don't believe it. I only believe in
what I can do and touch." She flew the *Millennium Falcon* in front of
his nose to demonstrate. "And climb and see and paint and occasionally
fuck. At least that's what my course on Martin Heidegger taught me,
among other things. And a single lifetime in which to experience that:
being in the world. Alive, I guess."

He watched as she neatly brought the *Falcon* to a safe landing in its
place on the shelf.

"I'm not talking metaphysics; I'm only interested in evidence that
can be quantified: refuted if wrong, reproduced if right."

"So, if *your* Alger Hiss *is* a spy—maybe a mighty big spy, the chances
they wanted to silence a potential witness like George Altmann only
improves."

"Or the reverse: If George Altmann was murdered, then Alger Hiss
was probably a pretty damn big spy."

"Right here and now"—she placed a hand on his shoulder, squeezing, as if feeling the need to indulge the playful girlish flirtatious thing
and lower the performance pressure—"in this universe, the one where
we're talking and not having sex."

"The possibilities, of course, are really infinite . . . that in at least one
universe, that is exactly what happened: The Soviet KGB brutally murdered my grandfather—if he was my grandfather—on a bridge over
the Sawkill"—he motioned to the moonlit window—"less than a mile
from here."

"What was that—did I miss something?"

"Forget it."

Her hand on his shoulder gripped harder, as if to physically overpower him with a sudden change of tack.

"They did or they didn't, right here and now, and everything you *are*
depends on that reality, the outcome of that reality. And those amazing
fucking paintings."

He stared into her compressed forceful gaze, her moonlit eyes, the
righteous register of her voice, as if coming from somewhere outside
them.

"You . . ." He shook his head and let it go. "Sometimes the endless possibilities kind of get to me." He shrugged. "Just like it freaks me out that we're living in an infinite universe, a multiverse, at least two or maybe more."

"Oh that." She laughed now with a kind of repressed hysteria, as if it had all been a joke. "George, admit it, you're telling me this shit just to seduce me. Get this young girl all confused, hot and bothered." She licked her lips lasciviously. "But I only believe in the here and now."

"Listen, I'm with you . . . really, but if the data doesn't support it . . . and I'm afraid the data all points to infinite expansion, which means exactly what it implies: infinite possibilities, from the big bang on out."

"But you can't prove that—even I know that, because we can't—you said as much—fucking see it or touch it."

"But," he protested, "if the data supports the theory, you have to deal with the implications of the theory."

She turned to the *Star Wars* poster of Princess Leia, again reprising the larky teenager in heat. "What would your Princess titty-fuck Carrie Fisher have to say about infinite expansion?"

"Sad, to think, well, there might be clones of her, so to speak, somewhere else in the multiverse she—like you said—could never see or even—traveling the speed of light—reach, since everything already had a fourteen-billion-light-year head start."

"Sorry, George, it just doesn't make intuitive sense. Everything has limits. Maybe things can be infinitely big, but not infinitely small—there has to be a limit, someplace. And even *your* big bang"—a flicker of doubt in her smile, with a hip check to his shoulder—"how does something so small get so big, so fast, much less go on forever?"

He turned in his chair, nodding to himself, and gestured to the shimmering silhouette of the white oak and its cyclopean embrace of the moon-glutted sky.

"It starts out like the proverbial acorn, a subatomic speck of inflating material, which keeps doubling itself forever, gathering energy, parts splitting off to form noninflating big bang universes like ours, while others go on to create other big bangs, and embark on their own inflations to create even more universes, some slowing to create random galaxies based on quantum fluctuations, while other produce more big bangs and so on ad infinitum."

She clapped her hands and giggled, tossing her head from side to side with a goofy smile.

"I love it when you talk dirty to me." Her smile turned into perplexity. "But even your lovely oak tapers off at the sky, and knows it limits."

"Think of it like a repeating fractal, stretching out into space, reaching out to those stars beyond the moon, entangling those stars to produce more suns and planets and solar systems and Milky Ways, feeding off star dust to create more and more and more."

"Stop." She put a finger to his lips. "I prefer to stick with the oak tree, right where it is in your backyard. I can climb it, paint it, feel its shade in the summer and admire its leaves in the fall, when it feeds acorns to the squirrels."

She reached her hands to his neck again and began massaging, until his shoulders loosened and his breathing eased.

"But the good news," he went on, closing his eyes, "is that everything in our universe is fine-tuned to support the existence of life, just the right balance between dark matter and dark energy to produce galaxy formation." He sighed. "Same with the electromagnetic force and the weak nuclear force."

"So Princess Leia can find her Han Solo."

"Yes, so maybe we're not entirely alone."

"Ah," she purred. She yawned, gave him a final pat, and crept over to the bed, pulling the comforter around her. "You've exhausted me, Jedi, truly, and we didn't even do it." She patted the space beside her. "You'll see I'm a good Princess Leia, diligent and loyal and virginal to a fault."

He lay down beside her, when his phone buzzed with an incoming text.

"Who's texting you at four in the morning? Not my competition, I hope."

He held up his phone, reading the text.

"A client. A middle-aged woman, a wife, a mother, a widow, who can't seem to find just the right spot for a painting her husband bought her just before he died. She's trying the bedroom again, so she can wake up, when she can sleep, and have it greet her every morning."

"Kiss me, Han, and go to sleep."

14
The Red Merc

GEORGE FOUND HIS mother in the kitchen, making his favorite breakfast, scrambled eggs and bacon and cinnamon French toast. The whole-wheat bread had been freshly baked the night before; the milk and eggs came from a local farm. "All organic—don't know about the cinnamon, though." Her shoulder-length brassy hair swayed as she sang along to some vintage Van Morrison on an ancient cassette player in the corner of the warped pea green Formica countertop. Sunlight poured in the windows over the tin-bottomed sink.

"Long night, huh?" she crooned in her sultry, breathy, singsongy voice. She was still wearing her BARN CONCERTS sweatshirt, now matched with sea blue yoga pants with chartreuse piping. Pausing Van, she shot him a sly smile, which he remembered only too well from childhood. She was letting him know he'd been caught out (you could hear everything in the house), but that she wasn't exactly disapproving, and might, if the outcome suited her, be more than a little supportive.

"It's not what you think." He dropped a wrench and an oily rag by the sink. "And how is Van, by the way?"

"Van—Jesus, I haven't laid eyes on him in over twenty years. He lives out on the coast now—long way from 'Brown Eyed Girl.' Which he hated." She sighed. "Your gorgeous girlfriend is off jogging. She grabbed a cup of coffee and a quick chat and flew out the door. Said not to wait on breakfast for her." She looked her son up and down in his jeans and Princeton Astrophysics Department sweatshirt. "Well, tiger"—Cordelia placed her hands on her hips: proud mom—"I haven't seen you wearing that in a while."

"First thing"—he poured himself a cup of coffee—"that came to hand in my bureau for crawling around in the cellar." He brushed cobwebs off his shoulder.

"She's incredibly fit, not like some people I know."

"She earns her living being fit, among other things."

"Once upon a time, I was, too, in my City Ballet days."

She stood back from the stove, raised her right hand over her head as if pulling a string attached to the back of her neck, assuming first position and a blue-eyed coolness that hinted at her onetime star power onstage.

"You still look great, Mom."

"Precisely the compliment I was fishing for. I can't afford Botox anyway." She pulled down two plates from the cupboard. "Notice I even lit a fire in the woodstove this morning for you lovebirds."

"Listen, I got the boiler going again, but I think we need to get in the HVAC guy to check the system for the winter. The boiler may be on its last legs."

"Well, at least *you* had somebody to keep you warm last night."

"We didn't sleep together—we did but we didn't. She almost froze to death in the guest room."

"Ah . . . how much will it cost?"

He came over to the stove to warm his grease-stained hands, and reached into his back pocket and kissed his mother.

"Here's a check for ten thousand dollars—your half of the Altmann sales so far. More, later, when the other checks clear."

"You don't need to do that."

"Of course I do. They're your paintings. That's the deal we agreed to."

"Let's hope your father feels that way."

He jerked back as if burned.

"What the fuck does he have to do with it? You haven't heard from him, have you?"

"He's been writing again. There's a letter for you, over there on the counter by the sink."

He went over and picked up the envelope where it leaned against a potted basil plant. He examined the handwriting, the postmark.

"Seattle?" He stuffed it in his back pocket. "Do you suppose he could have seen the announcement for the show?"

"I think I mentioned it in a letter; he was asking about you."

"Oh, fuck . . ."

"I think he's struggling. Being a road manager ain't a young man's game. He must be sixty . . . or is it sixty-one?"

"Just as long as he stays in Seattle."

"It rains a lot. He says he's been off the sauce for nine months, regular AA attendance."

"It was a year the last time."

She gave a slight wince at the harsh edge in her son's voice, shrugged, and swept a hand though her unruly hair as she set the plate of eggs, bacon, and French toast on the compact round kitchen table of red laminate. George rocked the table on its chrome-plated tubular steel legs and reached down to try to adjust one of the levelers that hadn't functioned for thirty years.

"Oh, give it up, George." She held up a leaf-shaped bottle of maple syrup. "Pretty neat, huh? Dan Garmich is tapping the trees on his place, did I tell you? We sell half his production in the bookshop now—that'll tell you something about the reading public today, or what's left over from Amazon."

"So, how's Levon?" He gave one of the legs a last kick, looked at his hands, and went to the sink.

She eyed her son with a bemused frown.

"Hanging in there. After the throat cancer, it's hard to believe he'll ever get his voice back; but hey, he's still with us, and there's always the drums and mandolin. Talk about talent to burn—*The Right Stuff*— huh—although I don't think he and Robbie ever made up. Did I tell you Amy has her own band now? She's so striking with those big blue-gray eyes and sultry voice. Goes to show, talent does run in families. I always thought you two would make a great pair."

"Levon still pissed they never included their set in the film?" He dried his hands and took his seat.

"Y'all check out the deluxe edition on DVD: The Band, Credence Clearwater Revival, Tim Hardin. They've now included their sets. Pity, though"—she frowned, a hint of a hoarse Arkansan accent creeping into her voice—"with Tim gone, and Rick dying like that three years ago, and Richard before him."

A shadow crossed her face and for a moment her shoulders slumped.

"Just stay away from the booze, George; it creeps up on you." Cordelia went to the window and stared out, clearing her throat. "Cocaine almost did us all in."

"Not bad," he piped up with an instinctive note of optimistic counterpoint while shoveling in the French toast and checking e-mails on his phone. "Another sale yesterday, the large cloudscape." He glanced up to catch an unguarded moment, his mother's distant stare into her garden, where the sunlight caught her face at a stark angle, showing the lines and sagging jowls, her reflection in the glass. Her age was beginning to show, even for a Dimock with strong cheekbones and her mother's fierce eyes. "Here," he called to her, "take a look at these Altmann sketches." He shoved the envelope across the table. "Tell me what you think."

She came over and slid out the sketches and began to go through them, a smile of vague recognition playing across her face.

"Where did these come from?"

"The Judge had them posted on a corkboard in his office. Ever see them there?"

She shook her head. "After Mom died, after I married Jim and you came along, I don't know that I ever saw much of his office at Hermitage, kind of kept to himself: Achilles brooding in his tent."

"But familiar—right?"

"Sure, they're the ones he bribed me to return to Jim. That's how I met your father in the first place."

George looked up and cocked his head.

"So, you *did* return them to James Altmann?"

Her eyes narrowed defensively. "To *your* father."

"Then how come I found them pinned to a corkboard in the Judge's office?"

"Because Jim didn't want them, couldn't have cared less about them."

George rolled his eyes. "Sounds just like him."

"He's still your father, George."

"What did the Judge do when you took the sketches back?"

"Do? He had the cops out looking for me and the Merc—last thing on his mind." She shot out her elbows on her hips, eyes scrunched. "What's with you anyway?"

"Did he know who these people were? Do you?"

"When I drove up here in Daddy's Merc, polished like Dorothy's ruby slippers, when Jim came over, he could barely see me for the wheels I was driving."

"Did he even bother to look at them?"

"A glance or two and he just tossed the envelope back on the passenger seat."

George pushed the sketch of Alger Hiss across the table.

"Familiar?"

"I guess."

"It's Alger Hiss, Mom. How can you not know that?"

"Okay, yeah, sure, now that you mention the name."

"So the Judge never even explained what it was you were returning to James Altmann?"

"Jim—your father."

"Fucking Jim."

"Listen, I don't know what's gotten into you, but it was a very difficult time that summer after Annie died."

"Difficult?"

"Daddy and I couldn't bring ourselves to go up to Hermitage that summer, not until the Judge's vacation in August." Cordelia pushed the sketch of Alger Hiss back across the table and cupped her hands over her face for a moment, then examined her palms. "Hermitage was so much Annie's . . . Her stuff, her spirit was everywhere. In some strange way she had loved Hermitage almost more than her music, more than Daddy, more than any of us, as if her better self came alive there. She always said she played better at Hermitage than in her best recitals. As a little kid, if I woke up early to her playing in the great room, I'd creep over to a corner of the banister and peek down, and there she'd be, stark naked, eyes closed, playing, practicing pieces that Mr. B. was setting to choreography, torso swaying, boobs, too, as if imitating the dancers in rehearsal. Not a little creepy—seeing your mom like that—for a little girl. She always complained how if she had been able to take a little of Hermitage with her on tour, how it might have been different back in the thirties and forties, when her concert career was at its height. Of course, that's how Alice and Martha remember her, full of self-criticism, doubt, frustrated, pushing herself even harder than she pushed them. The Dimock curse . . ." She looked uneasily at her son, as if perplexed by a jarring sense of disjunction, of two discordant images vying in someone she once loved. "But she was happy with me," she quickly assured her son. "She loved Mr. B. and her work, helping to make dances. She was especially loyal to those she admired."

George grew very still, intent on her mercurial expressions, as if hearing a faint echo of his grandmother's words penciled into the margins, defending Whittaker Chambers.

Mother and son stared at each other as if both a little lost, searching for a common wavelength.

"She seemed so angry at the Judge," he now prompted, "about the trial, among other things."

"That's why it was so terrible, when the cancer hit Annie out of the blue: She was on top of the world with her career, working with Mr. B., and even she and Daddy were getting along better than they had in years. Whatever it was between them, she seemed to be repairing the damage . . . in her way. For the first time, as Daddy put it, she was content, serene. I think that's why Daddy was so devastated in the end, the suddenness of how she was taken. Why he left it to me to deal with her stuff; he couldn't bring himself to touch her clothes in the closets or even move her books from the inglenook in the great room. It was like she'd finally found peace and might still walk in at any moment and catch us in the act of willfully desecrating the place, the space where she breathed her inspiration—you know, the great room, the ship's keel ceiling, where she'd insisted on putting her hospital bed, so in her last weeks she could just stare up at the ceiling illuminated by firelight and the Tiffany lamps, as if intent on making it forever hers. Even when I played her Steinway, it just got us all spooked. The acoustics, the way the sound floats and reverberates from the ceiling, it's quite magical, but it's always her sound—and not—and always will be." Cordelia shook her head, perplexed. "Know what I mean?"

"I wouldn't dare try to play now—not for the old man."

"Daddy and I were both really quite depressed, miserable. Daddy spent a lot of time alone in his office, or pulling out books from their bedroom shelves, reading passages they had read together, as if in search of God knows what in the way of consolation. He felt abandoned. Daddy and I were closer in the months after she died than we were before or have been since. That's how that stupid kerfuffle happened, when he insisted I accompany him on that dumb speaking engagement . . . the Ritz-Carlton in Boston." She shrugged painfully. "We kept each other afloat."

"So, he never told you why he was having you return the sketches?"

"Just that they belonged to the family"—she shook her head, as if annoyed at her son for gnawing this particular bone—"like it was some kind of legal thing, some kind of obligation to be gotten out of the way. You know how he is about punctiliously executing stuff to the letter. Frankly, I wouldn't have done it if he hadn't bribed me with the 280 SL; he never let me drive it." She laughed. "That was his biggest mistake—letting me drive the Merc. By the time I found Jimmy's house, stopping to ask folks directions—not Dylan, sadly—I thought I was one hot babe."

"You were the perfect accessory."

Cordelia frowned, but with an amused twinkle in her eye.

"We were crazy—Jimbo and I—about each other, George. I know that's hard—embarrassing—for you to believe."

George stared at his mother and carefully wiped his mouth. "You haven't lost your touch with the French toast. Take a look." He spread the sketches across the table. "This is Priscilla Hiss and the rest of the gang. Probably a Communist study group from the thirties. Probably George Altmann, my namesake, was a member of the Communist Party. Probably hung out with these people. Does that surprise you? Did Jimmy Altmann ever mention anything about his father's being a Communist?"

"Jesus, what's with this *Jimmy Altmann* business?"

"George Altmann handed these sketches to the Judge at the beginning of the Hiss trial."

"Okay, so . . ." Cordelia got up and went to the stove, dipping more bread into the batter, waiting for the pan to heat again. She turned back to George. "Listen, I've certainly heard Alice and Martha go on about the Hiss trial over the years, but it never seemed to have anything much to do with me. I never heard Annie or the Judge mention it—not to me. It was all part of that world before Teddy died, before I came along, when they had different lives."

"And Jimmy Altmann—"

"Jim"—she snorted in irritation—"hated his father. He had to grow up in the shadow of that gruesome accident—imagine at age eight being hauled out of bed in the middle of the night on Christmas Eve in the biting cold and dragged through the snow to find your father lying in a frozen creek with his head bashed in. Around here, from what I gathered from Jim, nobody but nobody liked George Altmann for beans. Jim spent his life trying to live down that unsavory inheritance."

"So why the fuck did he saddle me with the name?"

"That was my idea"—Cordelia threw back her head with an impetuous smile, waving her outspread fingers in mock horror—"to get back at Daddy. Would you have preferred to be called Edward or Jimmy?"

"Well, I guess that went over big-time with the Judge, along with Jimmy's kidnapping his daughter, the statutory rape of a seventeen-year-old, and grand auto theft."

Cordelia smiled with almost giddy nostalgia at the mention of that still-delicious scandal, and in perfect imitation of the Judge's nasal vowels upon news of their wedding: "*And another damn Commie Jew in the family.*"

"'Commie Jew?'"

"Yes, I thought it was just an all-purpose slur. Let me guess: Alice's been filling your head with shit again."

"She did mention she'd handled your divorce for you and some of the counterclaims filed by James Altmann in the proceedings."

"Proceedings. We couldn't even find him to serve the divorce papers."

"You are divorced, right?"

"Alice got a court order convicting him of desertion and failure to pay child support and back taxes. It was all rather complicated."

"So, you're not legally divorced. What is the status of the house, the barn—the paintings?"

"Desertion of wife and child—yes, we're divorced. And the property is legally mine; I pay the taxes. Alice saw to that."

"An estate, artwork, can be a different matter."

George stood, anxiously narrowing his eyes as he carried his plate to the sink—a look that Cordelia immediately confronted.

"Wachu been fixin' ta do . . . britches not tight enough?"

"The paintings," he replied, bridling at her slangy Arkansas accent, "properly handled and marketed, could be worth millions. There's got to be well over nine hundred out there in the barn."

"So, spit it out: Did Alice tell you something different?"

George rinsed his plate and carefully placed it in the draining rack. Then he took a studied breath and punched the play button on the cassette player, letting Van Morrison's plaintive love song "Someone Like You" fill the kitchen. His chin quivered, as if the music touched on something of his difficult adolescent years.

"She mentioned that Jimmy Altmann had questioned the paternity of yours truly."

"So, that's what's got your knickers in a twist. Damn her, up to her old lawyer tricks. Well, that's just bullshit. Listen, I'm not proud of any of this. Jim and I accused each other of just about every sin under the sun in our drinking days. God knows how many bastards he sired on the road. Women were wild about him; he had hands . . ."

"Fuck—enough!" he screamed.

"Alice is like the Judge—she works you over big-time when she wants something."

"Clearly, Jimmy believed it enough that he could just walk away from his only kid and never even bother to write or call."

"George, your father is a weak man, a disappointed man; he's a frustrated wannabe who came of age around geniuses, first his father, then the likes of Dylan. We both were surrounded by people like that. Annie was the real thing, too—and her expectations. And Balanchine, my God, was another. But Woodstock, Jesus, George, we lived and breathed the music. And you've got to hand it to Jimmy; he survived his father's suicide, his mother's adoration of her lost husband. And to her dying day she, slowly losing her mind, forced Jim to keep the banner of the great artist alive by keeping the barn repaired—'that fucking mausoleum,' as he called it, to a defunct genius whom nobody liked and whose work nobody wanted. Somehow he kept this place going after his mother died, working odd jobs—no chance for college. He taught himself everything; he was a talented carpenter, electrician, and soundman. Even his bass playing wasn't bad. He worked for everybody around here, all of Albert Grossman's groups, from the Band to Dylan, Jimi Hendrix, Joplin, Peter Yarrow, the Muldaurs, Paul Butterfield—you name 'em . . ."

"Van Morrison?"

"Yes, Van"—she flipped the French toast in the pan—"but he had terrible teeth. So don't go there, if that's where you're trying to go. I was never attracted to him, except for his music." She went to the window again and stared out at the barn for a moment, smiling as she caught site of a young woman jogging in from the road. "Listen, we all messed around back then; wives, girlfriends, sex, and cocaine were the air we breathed, the crazy mix that fueled the flames. Like I said, I'm not proud. Jim and I knew the score, and there's a price for everything."

"So, you were hardly hijacked?"

"When I first met him that morning driving Daddy's 280 SL—oh my, with his long hair blowing in the breeze, his eyes dazzling, like a rock 'n' roll Adonis to a seventeen-year-old who'd been cooped up in an all-girls school and ballet class with gay guys for years. He didn't lay a hand on me, not at first; he just folded me into his latest gig, building the stage on Yasgur's farm, putting in all the electrical systems. He was planning to build his own recording studio and ended up building Albert's. Anyway—yes, he hijacked me and the Merc and took me for the joyride of my life. I got recruited as his assistant and gofer. I helped him build the stage, George. I got to hang out backstage and help set up all the groups, get them on and off the stage. I was there, George, at the center of the universe . . . witness to something that changed the world, forever. And yes, I believe that—that love can change the world—that sex for a woman should be a gift and not an obligation."

She shook her head, as if her enthusiasm contained as much pain as not, pulling a shaking hand through her hair, honey-lit in the light from the window.

"I never told you this, but growing up, well . . . there was this—this nuclear winter between Daddy and Annie. My childhood was happy, but between them it was like a kind of ice age: no warmth, no sexual chemistry. They barely touched hands. Slept in different bedrooms. A child just accommodates—see. And believe it or not, Jim showed me something alive and good—even if he ended up showing it to a lot of other women along the way. And you're not my 'Woodstock love child,' as you once described it; that child ended up a miscarriage three months later. Nor are you the result of a 'random sex act,' also your words—see, I remember everything you say. Jim and I, in the early days, were absolutely crazy and devotedly in love, when we thought that all the world needed was love and the musical genius to make it all happen. And all we wanted was to be a part of it . . ."

As the next song began, they both fell silent, listening . . . *searching a long time . . . someone exactly like you.*

Tears welled in Cordelia's eyes and she turned to the window as she hastily wiped them away. "He hated that they loved me, that I got to play a few gigs, that they gave me credit—a fucking one line of liner credits when Richard was down with the flu."

She returned to the stove and flipped the French toast onto a plate, carefully cutting and arranging the pieces, sprinkling cinnamon, adding a sprig of mint. She placed the plate on the table, just so, even straightened the cutlery. Then she went to her son, grasping his arm and bringing her face close.

"Listen, I like Wendy, I really do, but be careful. She—I don't know—reminds me a little of Annie—not just—well—women, too, in the business. I've known plenty. Women who recognize their own talents and deficits—who will do whatever it takes to make up that deficit, whether it means working themselves to death to master an impossible perfection—it's a female thing, trust me—or breeding with some man who they think can produce the child who will have it all, some guy who can take their talents to the next level, enough to make it bigtime, be numbered among the immortals. It's an instinct as deep as time itself. We're such goddamn fools to believe we can heal the universe."

"Mom, really . . ."

"My God, she thinks Anne Elliot is Austen's greatest heroine."

"What?"

"Oh, I'm there, too—it's scary, but Anne is—well, she has this almost preternatural acuteness of perception about others as well as herself. Her willfulness. Like our Annie . . ."

"Well, hi everybody." Wendy sashayed into the kitchen, face sweaty, hair pinned up, and went over and kissed George and Cordelia on the cheek. "Oh my God, French toast. I'm so starved."

"Okay," said George, not a little perplexed by the chemistry between the two women, "I'm going to call the HVAC guy right now. And run your Camry down to the Jiffy Lube for an oil change and winter checkup. Wendy, I'll meet you in the barn in about an hour and we can get to work packing and loading."

15
Romance

How eloquent could Anne Elliot have been,—how elo-
quent, at least, were her wishes on the side of early warm
attachment, and a cheerful confidence in futurity, against
that over-anxious caution which seems to insult exertion
and distrust Providence! She had been forced into prudence
in her youth, she learned romance as she grew older—the
natural sequel of an unnatural beginning.

—Jane Austen, *Persuasion*

"OH MY GOD, aren't you cute."

Wendy sat at the breakfast table, still sweating from her jog, fork suspended over a plate of beautifully arranged obtuse triangles of French toast while Cordelia turned the pages of her album.

"I thought I was a forest fairy. And there's the Judge again, fly-fishing on the Neversink. I was his 'Cordy Bird.' That's Annie, my mother, playing the Steinway at Hermitage; we called it 'Mr. Carnegie's piano,' since she'd played it in a recital there in the thirties. That's how I grew up, like I simply woke up to the sound of her playing . . . A curse, I suppose, since I never had the technique, not like Alice."

"She's so . . . stately, transcendent."

"Do you think?

"And the room . . ."

"Yes, Hermitage, yes—I guess George hasn't taken you there yet—it's fiercely guarded by an ogre." Cordelia laughed and touched Wendy's hand to let her know she was only half kidding. "I'm sure Alice told you awful things. But the Judge's bark is far worse than his bite. Long

as you stay on his good side. His weakness"—she gave a throaty guffaw—"beautiful strong women, so you're perfectly safe." Cordelia
offered her patented sarcastic upper-lip twist and turned for a moment
to the kitchen window, where a commotion was under way on the bird
feeder as a flock of red-winged blackbirds elbowed out the competition.
She pouted as she realized her pale blue hydrangeas had seemingly
turned brown overnight. "Yes, Hermitage is pretty special, the magic
of the woods, or at least a girl's childhood in the woods suspended
between music and birdsong."

Wendy voraciously dug into the French toast, murmuring as she
reached to turn a page. "I had five years of piano lessons before I escaped
my nutty aunt for Yale."

Cordelia cocked her head with a flicker of interest.

"There you are again," said Wendy, "fishing."

"I must have been fourteen or fifteen—my boobs are sure all in—a
couple of years before my mother got sick. Annie never liked fishing—
delicate hands—so I took it upon myself to keep Daddy company. There,
that's the pause; he'd always tell me a proper cast is all about the pause.
You see, the thing is, in our family, you had to prove yourself useful for
something—that was the cross you had to bear." Wendy glanced up to
the older woman's face, as if suddenly catching something of a mysterious forlorn beauty there. "Even if they liked to pretend otherwise
with me. My older sisters, Alice and Martha, got the full treatment:
Their Annie always seems quite different from mine. I was the baby, the
afterthought, the changeling late to the game, pretty damn lonesome.
There were other kids around, but they were off-limits, especially the
boys across the lake. Annie saw to that. My parents doted on me, but
the more they avoided making demands, the more I figured I had to
prove myself in their eyes."

Wendy pointed to a photo of a young Cordelia seated at a huge
Steinway, feet barely reaching the pedals.

"There's your Annie, again," said Wendy, now with a knowing
intonation.

Cordelia glanced at Wendy, a tinge of unease or vague apprehension
sparking in her eyes. "I had to beg her to give me piano lessons; she
resisted to the end—a will of iron. She refused to criticize my playing,
like I could do no wrong."

"How lucky for you, to have such"—she paused, searching, an electric intensity in her voice—"strength at your elbow. My father was like

that; to watch him tie knots was like watching an artist at work. Gosh, what a beautiful room, that beamed ceiling—what's that . . ."

Cordelia hurriedly turned the page, changing the subject. "Oh, there's Teddy. Teddy, well"—she sighed—"was our rower—the brother I never knew. Teddy rowed at Yale, Olympic-caliber; he died in the Korean War, before I was born. He haunted Hermitage, at least for me, the big brother I never had. Annie barely mentioned his name, but she didn't have to. On the rare occasions when Alice and Martha came to visit, I'd hear them whispering about Teddy between themselves, out of hearing—sore subject—of Annie or the Judge. Martha was the worst; she seemed to slink off by herself and head for the boathouse, as if always in search of something that really wasn't there. It was a little creepy, let me tell you; it was as if I were an imposter, or a too-delicate substitute, the kid who needed to be spared memories that weren't any of her business. And then the women around the lake, even walking with their kids, would sometimes stop by the piazza and chat me up, not to talk so much, but just to gaze at me, my face, as if reminded . . . the longing in their eyes . . ."

"Wow, that's you in ballet class. Who's the guy standing next to you at the bar?"

"Mr. B. Look how young and handsome he was. I was sixteen."

"George Balanchine?"

"My secret lover—my idol, along with every other girl at SAB."

"You slept together?"

"No way. He only slept with his wives and principals. I guess it was Suzanne Farrell back then. But he sure felt me up plenty at the bar, giving corrections. I had my first orgasm at the barre."

"No way."

"Pretty damn close. Just the feel of his hand on my inner thigh."

"What a great body. That's so awesome you danced with the City Ballet."

"I was in the chorus for *Theme and Variations*. I did Clara in *The Nutcracker*. And here I am with Agnes de Mille rehearsing *Rodeo*."

"No way—I love the cowgirl getup."

"Agnes—Miss de Mille was such an inspiration, an inspiration for women of my generation. She had a place just up the road from Hermitage, Merriewold. Unfortunately, my tendonitis kept flaring up. Then Mom got uterine cancer."

"How sad for you."

"You don't want to know. As one of her oncology nurses said to me at seventeen, 'Enjoy your tits and female bits while you can, because that's where God will strike you down.'"

"What a terrible thing to say."

"I get my dried-up uterus sonogrammed every year."

"Oh, wow—this is so cool—what, backstage at Woodstock?"

"That's my ex, Jim, building the stage and doing the electrical work. And there we are doing a sound check."

"Wow, handsome guy."

"And some. As Jim always liked to brag, when the groupies couldn't get a band member, the girls were always just as eager to fuck him and get the inside scuttlebutt in the bargain. Jim knew his way around women, there's no denying that. He spoiled me for any other man. Only thing he liked more than women and music were fast cars, which is how we ended up together."

"Is that you? Oh, Cordelia, you're spectacular! How absolutely daring of you going full commando, and around all those people."

"The full bush, before Brazilians came along. Don't mention it to George; this is all a huge embarrassment to him. This photo was featured in *Life*. As they say, an iconic image."

"Well, you are his mother," said Wendy, summoning a degree of dignity in her voice that gave Cordelia pause.

"Yes, well, it didn't help him much in high school: the naked hippie mom."

"Oh, there you are again. You obviously attracted the photographers."

"George thinks we just lost our minds. That it was all sex and drugs and rock and roll. What he doesn't understand is that it goes way beyond the music. When the world was fixated on violence and war, nuclear winter—when violence was glorified in the streets by many, like my damn sister, Alice—don't get me going on that subject—to force social change . . . well, we were about a whole new relationship to the Earth. Our peace was not just about Vietnam but also about returning to a saner and sustaining relationship to the planet—and one another. Everything we called for is writ large today: a cleaner planet, zero carbon initiatives, hybrid cars, wind and solar, recycling, local produce, organic farming—a community of caring people: *We* did that. It's not just about more and better orgasms; it's about giving back to the Earth and drawing strength from it and one another."

"Hey, what's not to like about more and better orgasms."

"Don't mention it to George, but women's sexual rights is where all other issues of inequality begin. When women are truly on the same playing field, sexually, everything else falls into place."

"Yes . . ." Wendy gave Cordelia a high five. "Oh my God, there you are with baby George—isn't he cute!"

"First time back at Hermitage since I returned the Judge's Mercedes, a little worse for wear. It wasn't until George was three or four that we were accepted back."

"You're not serious?"

"The Judge hated Jim at first. He did everything—even tried to pay him off—to prevent us from marrying. Jim was blue-collar and lived in what my father considered the 'squalor of a rural slum.'" Cordelia popped her eyebrows to indicate the kitchen and house. "Alice says it was because he was Jewish, not that he really cared. But George saved me. Once the Judge got to know George, how intelligent he was, things were okay. And he grew even fonder of George once Jim was out of the picture; the only thing the Judge likes more than being right is getting to pick up the pieces and do things his way. Of course, he predicted our breakup from the start and was mightily pleased with himself. 'Good sex will only get you so far,' as he put it."

Cordelia rolled her eyes.

"Who are the other kids?"

"The cousins trooping down to the Neversink aqueduct. My sisters' kids, all older than George. Five cousins in all."

"Right, right, I met Karen and Erich at the opening. Which one's Cecily?"

"The gorgeous one," said Cordelia, pointing. Wendy bent eagerly to the photo.

"Oh . . ."

"The cousins—'that unkempt rabble'—spent most of their summers at Hermitage, having swimming and tennis lessons, going fishing, hiking, reading, and birding, getting indoctrinated into family lore—*and* Mr. Carnegie, of course—piano lessons."

"Hmm," murmured Wendy with just the vaguest notion of a proprietary tone of advice, "sounds like they needed Annie around."

Cordelia chortled, a hint of unease in the flicker of her lashes.

"During the week, they'd hike to Handytown, an easy few miles before dinner. When the Judge arrived on weekends, or in August, they took the longer hike down the abandoned railroad tracks to the old

Neversink abutments for a picnic and fly-fishing—when the Judge," she added, cackling, "had eve-r-y-body's attention."

"Two walks, two ways," suggested Wendy with a quixotic smile. "Your Swann's Way and Guermantes Way."

Cordelia shot an edgy glance at the younger woman.

"Christ, you even sometimes sound like Annie—she was so into Proust." Her voice rose with jokey, if uneasy, sarcasm. "I'll stick with Jane Austen."

"And Captain Wentworth." Wendy squeezed Cordelia's shoulder affectionately. "Comes from being a European lit major in college, along with the art history—and five years cooped up in Galena Park."

"Galena Park?"

"A suburb of Houston—as my mother always said of her sister, 'Well, she would marry the po' side of town.' You might say I read and sketched my way out of town."

Wendy bent closer to the album, hair in a wild pinwheel where it was pinned above the long tendons in her neck. Her eager face was aglow from her jog, now flushed a soft pink from caffeine and sugar.

"Your rabble, they're so much bigger than George with his cute baby fat."

"The Judge's rabble," she said, correcting Wendy. "I think George suffered from so many years of being the runt of the litter over all those summers, when good table manners, intelligent conversation, and proper social skills were touted as the keys to the kingdom—and landing your browns. Books, too, of course, at least two a week over the summer. Oh my God, the book reports." She raised a suffering palm to her forehead. "We Dimocks are a bookish clan. As Annie always said—I think quoting Proust—'a book compresses into a few hours a lifetime of experience, sets free in us all the love and misfortunes, the joys and sorrows in this world.'" A dramatic sigh and knowing maternal smile. "Thank God George survived to find his own way."

"Oh, there could be worse things." Wendy laughed, leaning in close to Cordelia, as if to impart a confidence, attempting to draw the older woman yet tighter within the snug orbit of her youthful zeal. "Galena Park . . . trapped?"

"Oh, aren't we all in our way. I do blame myself for keeping George trapped here when he could have gone away to school on the Judge's nickel. All I had to do was finish my missed semester at Brearley to take up my place at Radcliffe—my mother's, Annie's last admonition to me on her deathbed—if my tendonitis didn't get better."

Wendy hugged Cordelia, rubbing her back.

"You were lucky to have your Annie; and I keep telling George how lucky he is to have a mom *like you*."

Cordelia bent and kissed Wendy's flushed cheek

"The Judge saw something in him . . . that made all the difference."

"Oh"—Wendy laughed, pointing again to the album—"isn't that the cutest thing, waving his lightsaber around on the beach!"

As if summoned by the women's forensic lovefest, George strode officiously into the kitchen.

"A new boiler," he announced. "I'll put it on my credit card and take it out of the show profits."

16

In the Eye of Nature

Is it that by its indefiniteness it shadows forth the heart-
less voids and immensities of the universe, and thus stabs
us from behind with the thought of annihilation, when
beholding the white depths of the Milky Way? Or is it, that
in essence whiteness is not so much a color as the visible
absence of color, and at the same time the concrete of all
colors; it is for these reasons that there is such a dumb blank-
ness, full of meaning, in a wide landscape of snows—a
colorless, all–color atheism from which we shrink?

—Herman Melville, *Moby-Dick*

WENDY BRADLEY PANTHERED the squeaking floorboards of
Altmann's barn studio like something caged, ravenous, cheeks flushed,
inspecting every rack and worktable with promiscuous abandon. She
rifled through drawers of studies. Picked over trays of rolled-up zinc
tubes, analyzing the color organization of his palettes—"Naples yellow,
viridian, alizarin—and yes, yes, yes, zinc white, lots of zinc white—
that's where he gets his translucency, his colorless atheism—hah!" With
her thumbnail, she scraped at the crusted daubs of faded oil paint as if
scratching an old wound. Lovingly, she inventoried the mouse-gnawed
brushes adhered to the bottoms of rusted cans with torn or faded labels,
stirring up scents of age-encrusted linseed oil and turpentine, as if
energized by the aromatic essence of addled time, something of its still
warm embers, remnants of a fervent devotion that might yet be blown
back to life. Above, the clouds suddenly parting, glints of sunlight pen-
etrated the spiderwebbed skylight, revealing floating filigrees of dust

218

and bat droppings. Radiant lemony light now filled the barn, impelling her cantering fingertips to invade the racks lined with varnish-darkened canvases—a swipe of a spit-moistened fingertip like a surgeon's scalpel to part the dusky flesh, to probe the open incision, where the faint whisper of original inspiration now revealed itself, so allowing the sunlight to sink into the glazes, deep into the translucent colors, exposing the true mark of the paint stroke, the syntax of brushwork . . . the artist's fingerprints as telltale as a writer's words on a page.

———

George found all her carryings-on both captivating and off-putting, and possibly threatening (his mother's ambivalent warning much on his mind). For once inside the sanctum, she had no qualms about playing the art expert to his devotee of the scientific method, and, consumed with seemingly boundless energy and expertise, impugning his inadequate stewardship at every turn. Nevertheless, he left her to it, beginning his prosaic inventory as he combed the racks for replacements for the sold works.

As he did so, he chattered away, less to explain away his own failures than to preclude the anticipated criticisms of his wholly inadequate Altmann essay.

"It's not that I'm incurious or an idiot. I mean, after dipping into Chambers, I get the Communist thing, even the underground spying thing—how Altmann, an artist, might have gotten caught up in the politics of the day." He continued to talk as she rummaged around in cluttered cabinets, not a little desperate to align the assumptions he'd once proudly made in the catalog essay with the new data. He could imagine George and Mattie Altmann leaving New York City in 1930 and buying the old farm with their savings from the prosperous twenties, figuring they could live more cheaply here than in Greenwich Village after the Depression blew the bottom out of the art market. Altmann could still take the bus back into the city and his teaching job at the Art Students League. But even that was a dying proposition, as fewer and fewer students could afford the fees. Even the League's summer classes in Woodstock had a drastically reduced attendance. Devastating for a man once revered, snapped up by big-time collectors, as even his portrait commissions dried up. "They were starving, literally—and just to get enough wood to heat the stove in winter exhausted their resources. So, I guess the communism thing had its appeal." Altmann survived on a few commissions and winning two major competitions, one in Albany, one in Cleveland. He was president of the Woodstock Artists Association for much of the early thirties. A leader, admired by his colleagues.

What had saved him, financially, was a connection to the powers that be in Washington, someone who knew somebody, leading to his hiring by the Federal Art Project in 1936 to run the mural program. A regular check and a good one. He moved down to Washington, leaving his wife to take care of the farm. Between 1936 and 1939, he was back in the thick of the art establishment, a power player, an important administrator able to dispense mural commissions to his fellow artists. Then it all changed. At the end of the summer of 1939, with the war in Europe, he up and resigned from the FAP and moved back to Woodstock. Where, seemingly overnight, he became a pariah. He was scorned by his dealers; artists cut him dead in the street. He was dropped from membership in the Woodstock Artists Association. For ten years, until his death on Christmas Eve 1949, he was an outcast in the fraternity, at least to most. There may have been a few friends, a few fellow modernists in the Woodstock artists' colony, a few drinking buddies who stood by him. His style completely changed. He gave up his figurative work for abstract landscapes. Jarring, daring, expressive abstractions that nobody would show, that no award competitions would accept, and that his old clients and dealers rejected out of hand, even during the more prosperous postwar years. As his failures mounted, his drinking increased. He became more irascible and disliked by his neighbors as he was forced to take court-reporting jobs in New York when the money from the Washington years ran out.

Wendy interrupted his musing when she found him working in the racks, pulling out and inspecting canvas after canvas.

"Take a look." She handed over a couple of dusty volumes.

He examined a cheap thirties edition of Marx's *Das Kapital*, and a more expensive leather-bound edition of the works of William Wordsworth.

"Where'd you find these?"

"Tucked behind a shelf of old junk, brick-a-brac, pots and vases for still life setups. There's more, poetry mostly, Emerson's essays, Thoreau, Frost, artists' biographies, the Pennells' Whistler biography, and Titian. My God, he's got a first edition of Rockwell Kent's illustrated *Moby-Dick*, signed by Rockwell to 'Comrade Altmann'! And like your copy of *Witness*, he's underlined the hell out of the pages."

He began flipping through the pages of Marx, chagrined at the extensive underlining.

"Pretty stupid, how I missed this."

"Hell, I've read Marx—big deal. Look at the Wordsworth, though, look at the poems he's read and commented on: 'The Old Cumberland Beggar,' 'The Ruined Cottage,' and 'Michael.' All early works, when the poet was still inspired by the French Revolution. These are Wordsworth's most moving poems, heartrending, about the collapse of old families and lives, the ruin of a beloved homestead, full of wonderfully controlled pathos and a feeling for—well, human dignity and human suffering."

He glanced up from the foxed and mildewed pages of the Wordsworth, noting the accusatory tone in her voice, like a veiled indictment as she pointed to an underlined passage and read it:

> And let him, where and when he will sit down
> Beneath the trees, or on a grassy bank
> Of highway side, and with the little birds
> Share his chance-gathered meal; and, finally,
> As in the eye of Nature he has lived,
> So in the eye of Nature let him die!

She looked up, with tears verging. "An old beggar, an outcast, living on the edges of a rural community . . . living and dying in the eye of Nature." She shook her head. "These are poems of hope, or, worse maybe, the terrible delusion of hope that keeps one going, even in the worst of times. Maybe, what do you think, even more dangerous than despair?"

"Hope," he echoed, "like his years as a Communist?"

"No," she scolded, "the hope of creation, of leaving something behind." She wiped a tear. "How could you have missed this?"

He gestured apathetically at the canvases he'd selected. "People buy the paintings."

"These are his fucking books, along with the others back there, what he drew on for strength and inspiration. His humanity, damn it, the stuff that went into his art. And it's not just me being artsy-fartsy: your kind of evidence. You think genius just appears like freshly fallen snow? He didn't just give up on social realism and Party propaganda, his deep feelings for humanity and for social justice; those feelings were translated into something more powerful in his late landscapes, a more abstract essence, in which color and form and symbol speak to the soul." She gestured to the canvases he'd pulled from the racks. "See: He ditched narrative for feeling, for the pathos of ambiguity and mystery, for light and atmosphere—a whole unseen dimension. Don't you feel that pathos, the melancholy of his whites and off-whites—how their transparency mirrors the viewer's humanity!"

"Calm down, will you? I don't need another fucking lecture out of you. You sound like Stan with all your highfalutin *pathos*."

"It's like you looking through your telescopes—or whatever—and missing an entire constellation."

"Fuck you."

She waved a hand, fanning her flushed face. "I know, it's none of my damn business." Her eyes teared up again and she turned away to return the books to the cabinet.

"It's okay," he murmured, hearing his adviser's admonition to the young grad student: "A scientist's job is to be relentlessly self-critical."

"I fucked up."

She turned on her heels, clutching the book to her chest.

"It's all here, George. Wasn't that what you were saying about Whittaker Chambers last night, that he was first and foremost a writer—a truth-teller—so when he broke with the Party, and the Soviets and his whole world turned on him, he had to fight his way back into the light; his book, his autobiography, his witness was the work of art that came out of his personal struggle, his hope for a better world. Like Altmann, can't you feel the struggle in every brushstroke?"

"*Witness* was Chambers's way of regaining his lost years, the years that, in the trial, were dismissed, as if they'd never been, as if some part of him had never been, his friendship with Alger and Priscilla Hiss, among other things."

"Who turned on him just like everybody in the art world turned on George Altmann."

At this notion of correlation, his brows knit in consternation, as if he'd been indicted for professional incompetence, and, worse, a failure of imagination. Another thing added to her growing list.

"I saw the books, but it just never occurred to me."

She looked at him kindly now, apologetically. "It's okay; you were focused on the art, as you should have. But the context matters, as well. Artists are only human; they drink from the same well."

"Yes, yes . . . but the good news," he replied hopefully: "At least the information was not lost—it's never lost, not really."

At this plea in bar, she broke into a smile and came to him with a tender, almost motherly gesture, caressing his cheek.

"There is one more thing: Did you check his collection of recordings?"

"I suppose."

She went over to the corner and the antique Victrola in a mahogany cabinet and retrieved a recording from a large collection beneath.

"No way." He stared, baffled, at the 78 rpm recording of fourteen Mozart sonatas by Annie Davenport. The album showed a young woman with long blond hair in a black gown seated at the piano, fingers poised above the keys. A diamond brooch, a stave of six notes, glittered below the right strap of her gown. "It's a 1936 recording, when she was near the height of her fame before the war. The Judge liked to play this and others when we were kids."

"Coincidence, do you think?"

"What else. She was a rising star—like you."

"Oh, but she's gorgeous. Look, there's a price label from the Carnegie Hall Record Shop on Fifty-seventh Street, right across the street from where he taught at the Art Students League."

"Rare," he said, pointing out the hand-lettered note on the price label. "Five bucks was a lot of money for a record back then. He must have bought it sometime later in the forties, after the war, when her recording career had faded."

"You know," she said, sighing as she touched the downturned face on the cover of the album, "what scares me, George? It's the indeterminacy, the fragility of, well, life's enterprise . . . know what I mean? Like the barn could've burned down; you could've gone on in astrophysics . . . The mold and mildew and cold—like one minute those towers were there—and then they weren't. Sometimes it still feels like we're perpetually on the edge of the abyss."

"You, of all people!" He shook his head disparagingly. "It's the randomness of the damn thing; that's what gets me. I mean, just look at us—here . . . how crazy. How the fuck—sorry—did you come along?"

She smiled contritely as if, for once, chagrinned by her impetuosity. "Like Lucretius—do you know the passage, George? *Incerto tempore . . . incertisque loci.*" A look of diffident sorrow fluttered on her moist lips. "At an uncertain time, at an uncertain place. Or as Meredith put it, 'We have it only when we are half earth:/ Little avails that coinage to the old!'"

He nodded glumly at a mind (fucking Yale!) more facile than his. "Thanks, that sure makes me feel like a washed-up one-trick geek."

"George"—she took his hand and ran a fingertip over his palm—
"all you need to know is that when an artist touches a loaded brush to
canvas, that is the act of creation, when meaning enters the world—
structure out of chaos, right? That's the moment when past, present, and
future become infused with our humanity. Surely you've spent enough
of your adult life witnessing the thing—out there . . ." Her voice fell
off and then recovered itself in a hoarse whisper. "That moment, that
ecstatic dance in nowhere land."

So saying, she took his left hand in hers, placed her left on his shoulder, as if to embark on a waltz, staring intently into his eyes and then
breaking off with a giggle.

He smiled, pondering. "The interaction, or reaction, in which nature
entices the world into being . . . and so gives it meaning."

"That's what your grandfather was doing—see, you're closer to the
truth than you realize." She turned in a gentle spiral with her head
thrown back. "This is your lost world, your parallel universe—not something billions of light-years away. I can feel it—you were born to save
this. The art is what saves us from all the bad stuff that happens, that
trumps evil with good, the truth to stand up to the lies—that makes
hope a reality, not a soul-destroying illusion, as Wordsworth feared."

He laughed uneasily at both the deep mystery and the comfort of
her words.

"You're doing the right thing, George."

"Well, how about you help me first to find something to sell before
my little corner of the universe goes broke."

With this, George once again began a more methodical inventory among the racks for replacements, using the calculator on his cell
phone to tally up the sizes of the sold paintings that required replacing,
trying to factor in the style and subject matter so as to keep the hanging mix about the same, wondering how quickly he could get frames
made for the new ones, if his restorer could do a rush job. He selected a
dozen possibilities, leaned the canvases against the wall, and called out
to Wendy to get an opinion.

At first, he got no answer. Then, from across the studio, her voice
startled him. "He's still here, you know, George." She was somewhere in the clutter of artist files, clearing her throat from all the
dust, coughing, her taut voice echoing from the mote-swimming rafters. She appeared and triumphantly handed him a small canvas. It
was a self-portrait: a long beetle-browed face with deep-set eyes sunk

within wine-dark rings, and a scattering of dark hair drifting out from beneath a beret and falling to the collar of a paint-smeared artist's smock. "That little mustache is like Thomas Hart Benton's; and the rugged boxer's nose . . ." She laughed, a playful fist tapping the tip of his not dissimilar nose. "It's dated 1928—when he was not much older than you. Look at the confidence brimming in his eyes, the debonair cockiness of his first success, the handsome artist returned from Paris and the Beaux-Arts, with prizes on his belt, a man about town . . . who has no idea what's about to befall him or the country." She eyed him with the impatience of a schoolmarm coaxing a reluctant student. "This, too, needs to be cleaned, and included in the catalog: the artist as a young man."

"Yes, ma'am."

"And there are nudes back there that will put some lead in your Johnson. They even get me turned on. He liked women. Do you suppose his wife posed, or did he sweet-talk some of his students into posing? What chick doesn't want to be immortalized? Jesus, I'd have loved to have been painted by him; he knew his way around a woman's body like he knew his way around the contours of a rock formation. You gotta include one of the nudes in the new catalog, George, to show the world that he'd mastered the academic tradition and then transformed it into a tool to express the living landscape."

She handed him the self-portrait and assumed a pose, thrusting her chest forward, arms back in support, quickly brushing off the cobwebs and mouse droppings on her jeans. Then she grabbed the canvas from him and brought it up to her nose. "Genius smells like this, you know. I can feel his presence in the space, his beret pulled over one ear at a sexy angle, his neatly trimmed mustache; I can see how he organized it so everything was in easy reach, how he loved the northern light coming through the skylight, which, by midmorning, had a certain silky quality that caught fire when he brushed on the wet pigment, when it steamed off his model's body."

"Keep it; it's yours," he said, hoping to put an end to her pestering.

"Really?"

"My numero uno client—you deserve it."

"Don't get carried away by your success with the show."

George looked up from the calculator on his cell phone, not amused.

"Success? I'm just trying to move the merch, cash in before the next rent increase. *And* pay for the new boiler."

"George, you can't leave the paintings here. It must have been near freezing last night; I could practically see my breath when we walked in."

"I'll get the space heaters fired up."

"You can't depend on your mother to do all that. She's a lovely woman, but she can't remember to get her car serviced. You need to move everything to a climate-controlled storage facility. The craquelure on some of the canvases is really bad; some have been chewed on the tacking edge."

"Expensive. Maybe if we put in some foil-backed insulation."

"He'd expect you to protect his legacy."

"Who?"

"George Altmann. You're his namesake—that's what he'd want his grandson to do, make sure his legacy is safe . . ."

George looked at her now with fed-up exhaustion: "Did anyone ever tell you you're relentless?"

She bounced a flattened palm off her forehead. "I know, I know, it sounds crazy. But I know how it was with him; I know how he walked in here every morning with his mug of coffee—like the old white porcelain ones on the top shelf in the kitchen; how he took his time walking along the path though the garden, past the hydrangeas in summer, the lilacs in the spring, stopping to smell them, savoring the texture as he gazed off over the valley, getting the feel of the world into his fingertips."

"Enough already."

"In another universe—your favorite subject, George—he'd have eluded his killers and continued working for another twenty years, changing the course of American art history. He'd be as famous as Rothko. Maybe he is, somewhere, and we don't know it."

"Okay, okay . . ."

"I jogged over the bridge this morning."

"And?"

"It's different when you're in the actual place—places have spirits, you know, other dimensions."

"Okay, so while we're into quantum weirdness here, why don't you come over and give me your thoughts on these canvases."

"I'm sorry."

"No you're not. I've still got some old Ritalin if it helps."

"I underpaid, you know. You should raise prices—slowly, but raise them." She went over to the canvases he'd picked out. "So, what's the total count on the late works?"

"If you include the watercolors and pastels, well over a thousand pieces."

"You don't want to undervalue them. You need to think about placing the work with museums, big-name collectors . . . developing Altmann's market." She swiped at her jeans, dusting herself off. "I'll take these two, at the original price; you pay for the cleaning and I'll buy and pick out the frames."

"Where do you get off, Wendy—just where?"

"On the condition you move the rest of the estate to a proper art-storage facility." She smiled as if to make light of the thing. "To protect my investment."

"You don't like my choice of frames?"

"I just prefer my taste."

"I'll give you an option to buy—how the fuck do you have the money to buy them anyway?"

"None of your business."

"You're just a little scary, Wendy—you know?"

"Where are the sketches, George, the ones you were showing me last night?"

"You really want to go there—again?"

"You've got me intrigued . . . It's an artist thing, like I said: You can't separate the life from the art."

He went to his backpack and removed the manila envelope and handed it to her. She took out the sketches and began to arrange them on the floor, where they were illuminated by the skylight. She continued to arrange and rearrange them, stepping back and viewing them from various angles.

"They're definitely an ensemble. Look at the grouping now. See how they work as an ensemble? All the faces interrelate in a semicircle, an interlocking composition. While the artist, Altmann, is situated not quite at the center exactly, but just off to the side, near the speaker the others are listening to, the person who's leading the discussion." She stood very still, as if having found just the precise spot, nodding thoughtfully. "So, where's his early stuff from the thirties—this period?"

George pointed to the far corner of the barn, near a wood-burning stove, its pipe stack elbowing a right angle into the beamed ceiling.

"I've got a feeling that a lot of his work from the thirties went missing, or he may have simply disposed of it—not that there were many easel paintings from that period, mostly preliminary studies for murals. I think my mother mentioned that Jim, her husband, remembered that he burned a bunch of things in a barrel sometime before he died. For that matter, I couldn't find much in the way of studies for the late work."

She began going through the racks and artist flat files, pulling out drawings, examining them.

"Except for *your* sketches"—she eyed his raised eyebrows—"he didn't burn those."

"So it would seem."

"No artist's inventory of the work from the thirties?"

"Yes, but nothing referencing the sketches."

"You're going have to interview your father, you know. Or if you're not up to it, I can do it for you."

"I'll bet you can."

"Did you ever go through this stuff?" she asked with almost maternal disdain, motioning to a large flat file in the corner and raising an eyebrow, as if to say, Like the books.

"I poked around. There're things in there from his student days, when he studied at the Beaux-Arts in Paris, and from his years teaching at the Art Students League in the twenties. A lot of figure studies and drawings for mural commissions."

She knelt to the bottom drawers of the flat file and dug though more drawings. From another drawer she pulled out a large folded sheet, struggling for a glimpse of the composition without having to bother unfolding the whole thing. She grunted and brought it over to where the sketches were laid out in the sunlight. She opened out the sheet, fully three feet by six, a detailed rendering of a mural project.

"Ha!" she exclaimed.

"Holy shit . . ."

"Look, all nine figures: six seated around the table, one standing on the left, two standing behind on the right. Looks like tempura and ink, watercolor for these larger spaces."

George knelt beside her and flattened the heavy woven paper, trying to decipher the imagery: a Sunday lunch, a farm family gathering around an oval table covered with a checkered cloth and set out with loaded serving dishes, a large turkey. The composition had the look of a stage set: a schematic proscenium, a pitched roof of red clapboard to suggest a farmhouse, while behind the figures was a sashed window with yellow curtains parted to reveal a field of corn. To the side of the window was a tall cupboard displaying crockery, a pair of oval mirrors, a coatrack, and a framed drawing of a child.

"What the hell is it?" asked George.

Wendy pointed to some writing in block capitals on the bottom of the sheet, squinting to read the faint lettering in pencil: "Society Fed and Freed Through Justice—Justice Department, 1938."

"It's grotesque—a parody, don't you think?"

"Pretty hokey stuff. A farm family, in the Midwest, I suppose, sitting down to a humble meal: bread, vegetables, fruit—fruit of the land; there's even a dog."

"Well, we know he ran the mural division of the Federal Art Project from 1936 to the summer of 1939, but I don't recall that he ever executed a mural himself during that period."

"Something he thought best forgotten." Wendy picked up a couple of the sketches and rearranged them to align with the mural study. "The sketches are much more detailed, but the faces in the study are certainly recognizable. Here's your Alger and Priscilla Hiss—still the power couple. The paterfamilias seated at the center, while the others surround him attentively, like disciples—sons, perhaps, or hired hands by the look of the overalls and boots, and the one here on the left serving coffee looks like he's wearing a chef's outfit, and the two behind the table on the right, in their Sunday best; and this lone doggy in the business suit—maybe the local banker arriving to foreclose or whatnot."

"Our anonymous . . . visitor."

Suddenly, they both looked into each other's faces, both going for their phones, madly punching in text on Google. She was quicker on the draw. She held her phone up to his face.

"It's really there, on the sixth-floor landing of the Justice Department: *Society Fed and Freed Through Justice,* by George Altmann."

George squinted at the small screen, shaking his head.

"This is so beyond quantum weirdness . . . Hiss's whole crew, study group, Communist cell, underground spy ring—whatever—emblazoned right there on the Justice Department wall . . . disguised as a kind of Grant Wood farm fantasy." George looked from the screen back to the mock-up, beyond incredulous. "I mean, people would have recognized them, don't you think?"

"I wonder how recognizable they'd have been in the mural, on a wall high up, wearing all that farm getup, the hats and stuff." She picked up the sketches of Alger and Priscilla Hiss to compare them with the mock-up. "She's almost ridiculous in the gingham dress with cameo brooch and lace collar. But what a handsome couple. There's more than a hint of admiration in Altmann's rendering, certainly for Priscilla. Look at her keen, attentive eyes and the conviction in the angle of the cheekbones and the certainty in her mouth. The sketch has a certain emotional quality—yes?" She then held up the sketch of Alger Hiss to the skylight. "And his rock-solid jaw and the intensity—wait . . . there's an inscription in pencil on the back of the sheet, like it's almost been rubbed out."

"Three four one five Volta Place, September 7, 1937. Their house in Washington, Georgetown."

"So, he was there, George. Altmann, like your Whittaker Chambers, must have been in their home."

"Along with the whole gang"—he picked up the sketches one by one—"Harry Dexter White, Treasury Department, died fifteen months before the trial, supposedly from an overdose of digitalis; Laurence Duggan, State Department officer, unaccountably fell sixteen floors to his death about a year before the trial; Walter Marvin Smith, Justice Department lawyer, fell down six flights of stairs . . ."

"And our mystery man, our banker"—Wendy pointed again to the figure standing behind by the door—"who has either just arrived or is just leaving, hanging up or retrieving his coat."

"Did Chambers know about this—this huge breach of security in his apparatus? Obviously Hoover's FBI and the government prosecutors in the trial didn't know. Could the Hisses or anyone on the defense have known? It would have been like a sword of Damocles hanging over their collective heads."

Wendy turned on her heels and went over to pick up the Altmann self-portrait, holding it up to the light, as if consulting those youthful, masterful eyes, purple-ringed, deep-socketed. She seemed intent on reading something in that face, some confidence as yet unimparted. And then she turned to George with a half-knowing smile. "Like his little joke, a whoopee cushion left in his wake when he escaped Washington—the truth, hiding in plain sight."

"But without the sketches . . ."

"George, like I said, I jogged into town and back this morning, over the Sawkill Creek Bridge, the route you told me he walked most days. It was rebuilt in 1936. Unless something has drastically changed in the last sixty-odd years, there's really no way he could have accidentally fallen to his death. He either hopped the railing and threw himself down onto the rocks or he was thrown headfirst over the railing."

He looked into her fevered, flushed face, electric, impassioned.

"Jesus!" he exclaimed, as if something in her flighty convictions had finally sparked the imaginative leap in his methodical mind. "He probably had no idea—right; until sometime in 1948, when he sees a newspaper headline that Alger Hiss is going to be tried for what amounts to espionage. And it's like, Holy shit, those ratbags I immortalized on the walls of Justice are going to be recognized. What the fuck did I do with those sketches, the ones from Volta Place—what I figured was just some stupid Communist study group jabbering about the latest Party scuttlebutt—same kind of trash we mulled over in my old Greenwich Village days."

At this spontaneous voicing of a dead man's thoughts, she looked up from the portrait, wide-eyed, curious, as if not quite believing her ears: the appearance of this shade before them.

"George, as you said, three of his subjects were already dead: White, Duggan, and Smith?"

George stared blankly up at the skylight.

"What do you do? Lie low, hide the sketches like Chambers hid Hiss's top-secret papers—the evidence, the insurance in case they come after you, your wife and son?"

She put a comforting hand on his shoulder. "You go to someone on the Hiss team, your grandfather Edward Dimock, and hand over the incriminating evidence and hope you've sufficiently fed the wolves."

"Lots of luck, with your mural as big as life on the top landing of the Justice Department stairwell where Marvin Smith fell to his death."

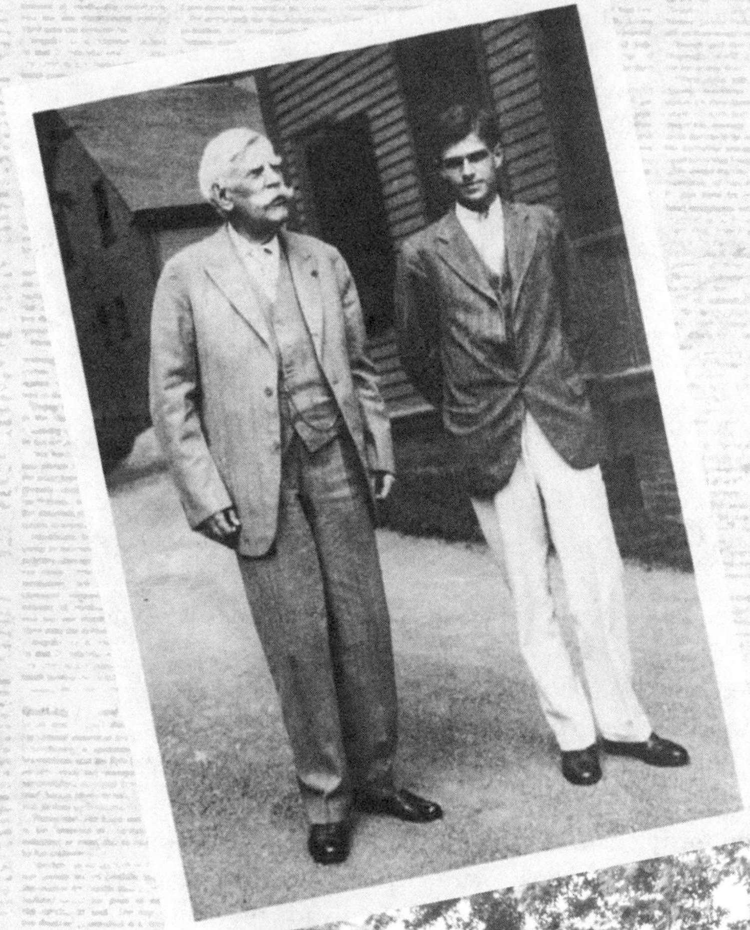

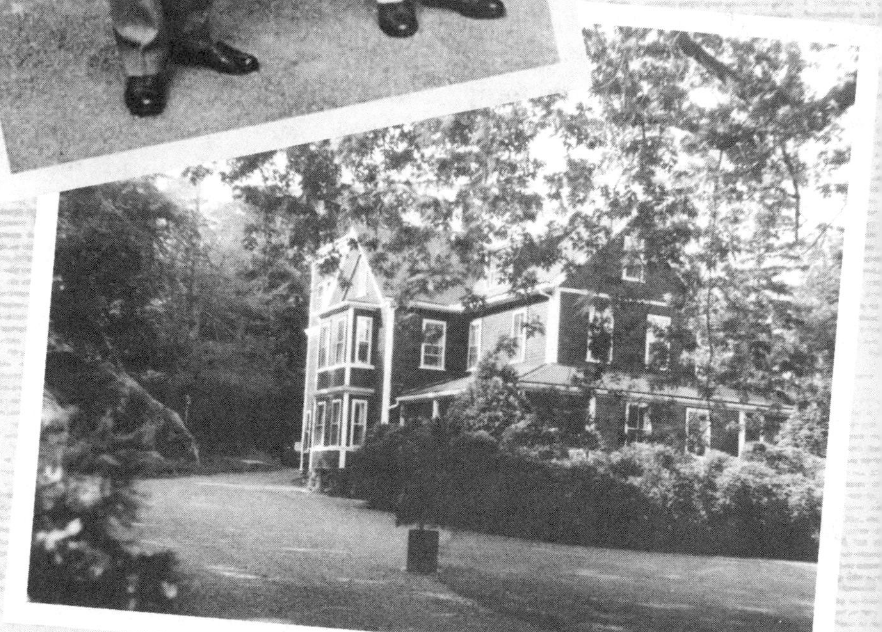

17

A Life in the Law and Out:
Memory's Foibles

When we are born, we cry that we are come
To this great stage of fools.

—William Shakespeare, *King Lear*

AT A CERTAIN age, one is invariably confronted with the what ifs in life, the chain of events that led to one thing as opposed to another, the specter of an alternate history. A thing quite different, I believe, from regrets: the result of mistakes and poor judgment, conscious and—how I abhor the word—*unconscious* errors. The trouble with memory, the mental process of disinterring the past from the present, is that it is never the past as it really was, but only the past one has now layered with the memories that came after, the future that is forever one's past, which distorts the pristine circumstance of that distant place and time. I realized this profoundly when I first tried to understand the role of Alger Hiss in my life—specifically, how I ever met him in the first place. It's not as if I knew all the members of my Harvard Law class, much less the vast majority of those ahead of me. And now, especially now in the process of writing, I discover, time and time again, to my dismay how much I'm forever barred from obtaining the clarity of vision that I came to treasure in both my professional and personal dealings. How that adulterating lens slips into place, a feeling not unlike foreknowledge of what was yet to come, and so clouding the picture irrecoverably.

And none more so than in the case of Alger Hiss.

So, when I embarked on this, the most painful part of my memoir, dealing directly with Hiss and the trial, I found myself staring blankly out my office window at the lake, peering through a nave of arching white pine boughs dappled with purple light, desperate to remember the first moment I'd laid eyes on Alger. Only then, suddenly bewildered, did I find myself transported back to the last place I'd ever expected to find myself with a young Alger Hiss. For it was not at the law school in one of our constitutional law classes, as I had always assumed, but sometime earlier, in, of all places, Harvard's Memorial Hall, with its spacious bowing oaken beams and stained-glass windows so designed to approximate for the sojourner a place of peace and repose when honoring the fallen. A meeting of such casual happenstance that it had entirely slipped my mind until that moment looking out through the stately pines to the lake. A discovery so shocking that I hastened to secure the thing like an ornithologist finding the flashing colors of some rare species caught in his collection net. A species of memory that maddeningly blurs before my eyes the harder I gaze, undergoing one metamorphosis after another as I reach to the keys of my typewriter in hopes of pinning it in place. For no sooner had this once-lost moment begun to take on substance and shape on my page than it generated more doubt than certainty, more heat than light, like a tumbleweed in escape, root and stem accreting and releasing, scattering willy-nilly yet more seeds of suspicion across my pages.

How to explain lost time?

Perhaps it was this hallowed stage itself that proved to be the culprit, for I had returned so many times to Memorial Hall over the years, the family associations growing and deepening with each visit, to the point that the individual moments began to blend and take on a more proprietary character, infused with charm and nostalgia, which, at least in my heart, preferred Alger's abeyance.

I had always been told by my father, Dr. Dimock, who was a friend and classmate of Oliver Wendell Holmes, that I must be sure to visit Memorial Hall when I was accepted into the law school. (For some reason, I had never attended Harvard reunions with my father, perhaps because he found it too difficult after my older brother, Jack, had been killed in 1918 on the Western Front in France—he also had a memorial along with those from his class who died in the First World War.) And so on my first day in Cambridge, I dutifully paid my respects to the Harvard boys who'd made the ultimate sacrifice in the Civil War. Half a score had been close to my father and his classmate Justice Holmes (Dr. Dimock had saved Holmes's life after he was shot at the battle of Antietam, along with many under the gallant William Francis Bartlett, himself wounded three times during the war, who rose from the ranks to become the youngest Union general in the war.) But my father's greatest sorrow was reserved for his classmate Richard Davenport (my wife Annie's grandfather), who was killed while fighting next to Holmes in the Cornfield at Antietam. Further hallowing Memorial Hall as the sanctum sanctorum of my most patriotic memories.

It was an early afternoon of the fall of 1927. I'd just settled my accommodations. I remember walking through Harvard Yard and admiring the mighty elms that grew there, only just tarnished by the Dutch elm disease that would soon take its terrible toll. (On my last reunion, just ten remained.) Memorial Hall, that Victorian Gothic extravagance of curving wooded beams and exotic, to my eye, hanging chandeliers, has an arched ceiling like an upside-down ship's hull, reminding me not a little of our own ship's keel ceiling at Hermitage. I walked the length and back, enjoying the splendid light in the stained-glass windows raining splinters of transparent color everywhere, in some cases opening glowing portals in the dark paneled walls lined with portraits and marble busts of these heroes of the Civil War, who now gazed peacefully out on eternity.

I lingered before Davenport's memorial (trying to recall anecdotes about this talented young man told me by my father), absorbing the inscription, when I noticed another figure moving in my direction, reading the memorial plaques of great deeds in battles of a mere sixty years before. Upon reaching where I stood, he turned to me casually and spoke in an earnest voice.

"Nothing we can ever do with our lives will approach the sacrifice they made to free the Negro slaves."

This sentiment so exactly echoing my own mood prompted a conviviality, if not candor on my part, that otherwise would not have been broached to a stranger.

"So young," I think I finally replied, turning and looking this stranger over. "Still boys, really, younger than we are. How did the moral fervor that so moved them in the cause of human freedom get so lost in our careless generation?"

This sudden heartfelt exchange served as our introduction, and Alger Hiss held out his hand to me as a second-year student at the law school. My first impression—and I struggle mightily, as I write, to keep it solid—was his aura of distinction, of an impeccable politeness, with perhaps a slight fastidiousness in his dress. He went on to tell me that he regularly visited Memorial Hall to remind himself of how much still needed to be done in the struggle for justice, especially for Negro rights. We were only too aware, painfully aware, that the lynching of Negroes was still a regular occurrence in the South. Alger, standing in the glittering prismatic glow that fell upon the portraits and busts from the stained-glass windows, was imposing in his light gray summer suit and green striped tie, looking fit and tanned, his dark eyes and compact features—betrayed only by protuberant ears—bespeaking a relaxed confidence and, dare I say it, an otherworldly grace. We chatted amiably for a few minutes more about the law school, as students belonging to the same august institution might do, and it occurred to me later that he'd made a fine job indeed of his cross-examination of a total stranger. I believe he soon got out of me my father's connection to Justice Oliver Wendell Holmes, how they had been Harvard classmates and Dr. Dimock had treated Holmes when he was shot in the neck at Antietam. For poor Richard Davenport, whose portrait was the immediate object of our gaze, he could do nothing. Alger eagerly pressed me for more anecdotes, to which I probably responded with avidity, so many were the stories gotten from my father about the medical corps. Especially the sad fate of Davenport, a man of extraordinary artistic sensibility and so unsuited for soldiering, a creative soul sadly snuffed out at Antietam. Again and again, Alger plied me for more about Holmes, and I must have surely let it out that I aspired to clerk for the justice upon graduation from the law school, especially given the family connection, not to mention the honor of working for such a legendary figure.

I remember the keenness of Alger's stare as he listened, ears flapping, soaking up every detail as if to file it away for future reference. Two years later, Alger preceded me by one year in that clerkship with Holmes, a clerkship that would provide Holmes and me with much in the way of intriguing conversation when my turn came the following year.

Had I put the idea of Holmes into Alger's head? Or was it just circumstance? Felix Frankfurter had recommended us both. Again, in retrospect, I realize that though I knew nothing of Alger Hiss on that warm fall afternoon in Memorial Hall, he may well have known something about me—not that he let on for an instant. What I did not know then, and only found out about much later, was that he was courting

Priscilla Fansler, an early flame of mine from freshman days at Yale. Priscilla and I had spent many weekends together and had developed an intimacy, certainly a physical intimacy, at least twice at Hermitage. We loved to hike and bird-watch. She was intelligent, a great student of languages at Bryn Mawr, full of life and ideas and very much in rebellion against her Main Line Philadelphia family. On the one hand, she respected my background and aspirations in the law; on the other, there was a wildness in her, a radicalism that caused her to react against people like me in a rather factious way, which could be most trying and even irritating at times. Hers was a spirit that thrived on controversy, if not risky adventures, and she was prone to snap decisions, which resulted in an ill-advised early marriage and child. I kept a flame for her—we wrote, stayed in touch—but at a wary distance. Priscilla was never a great beauty—pert, lithesome, witty—but always full of zest and unrequited yearnings that made her an electric presence and caring creature at her best. Enough, that the Alger Hiss in Memorial Hall, unbeknownst to me, was head over heels in love with her, wooing her madly, in fact, even as she had already attached herself to yet another, with more complications to come, into which—a damnable business—I would soon be dragged. I assume, though she later never admitted as much, Priscilla must have told her admirer all about me, now that we were at the law school together, most likely touting my foibles and strengths—as she was wont to do to my face with promiscuous abandon—or even my eligibility as the kind of man who could properly take care of her, and so sparking Alger's curiosity, if not his competitive instincts, to see what had been and might still be on offer.

In this light, as I write looking out over lake, I see another Alger beside me, his rapt face examining me—a potential rival!—from head to toe, a man very much interested in everything about my family, my New England roots, even though we had been in New York City for two generations. To which, Alger responded in kind, in obliging tones, given our seemingly sympathetic outpourings, that a sad scarcity of New England's old moral fervor reached drowsy Baltimore—"festering below the Mason-Dixon line"—from where he, so he bemoaned, hailed. Funny, how that phrase has stayed with me. I think I might have observed that Maryland had been a slave state and had to be forcibly tied to the Union by the imposition of Federal troops. I remember him smiling at this as he made it clear that his family was not "that old Baltimore," but a Baltimore of ancient ladies and gas lamps, as he put it with a hint of derision. His father, a successful businessman, had relocated there as a boy. However he explained himself, I came away with the distinct impression (an impression that lingered until only very recently) that he'd come from wealth, breeding, and culti- vation—literature and art were high on his list—bird-watching, too (which forged an immediate tie)—things we valued in our crowd, what detractors might describe as noblesse oblige; and like many of us pro- gressive spirits coming out of the frivolous high-flying twenties, we both seemed intent on doing good, not just making money. I think I found Alger attractive in his lofty idealism, the easy camaraderie of the moment, even though we were never to become intimates at the law school. My sense, from talking to others, is that Alger was never inti- mate—respected, certainly—with anyone in the law school, including those of us of a reformist bent along the lines of Woodrow Wilson.

And yet that first memory of Alger continues to flicker and alter like the soft sunlight thought the stained-glass windows of Memorial Hall. Was he there to inspect and size up a man whom Priscilla had once loved, a man—knowing her only too well—whom she'd most likely taunted him with as the kind of establishment figure she ought to marry? Was he picking up pointers? Getting the lay of the land? And what did he find in me—if anything worth his while? I some- times feel the way my grandson describes the contradictions on the quantum level, where one can never be quite sure of anything, where electrons jump around as soon as you dare lay eyes on them. But more to the point, I know now that Alger was lying to me then, or, if not exactly lying, skirting the truth ever so brilliantly. Perhaps, even then, weaving and blending bits of truth and half-truths in a brilliant cloak of invisibility.

In fact, as I now know, his father had not been a successful busi- nessman, but had committed suicide when Alger was a young boy. There had been little money in the family, and Alger had attended Johns Hopkins on scholarship and lived at home. In 1926, his older brother, Bosley, after a youth of promiscuity and drink, had, sadly, died, an invalid, of Bright's disease. In 1929, before his graduation, his sis- ter Mary Ann would drink a bottle of Lysol, brought on by emotional distress from an abusive marriage, and die horribly. Later that year, I would, through the good offices of my father, arrange for Priscilla to have an abortion due to a jilted love affair with a married man, whose own wife got pregnant, thus causing him to decide against a divorce and a second marriage—for both of them—to Priscilla, leaving the coast clear for Alger to step in, pick up the pieces, and grab his prize right in the midst (breaking the rules of his contract) of his tenure as Holmes's clerk.

Which begs the question regarding that first meeting: Was I staring at the face of my Iago, who was already seeking out my strengths and weaknesses to further his own secret nefarious ends? Surely Iago's famous words—"I am not what I am"—suit the circumstances, and not only then, but later during the trial, where my last-minute desperate recruitment seems now more the culmination of many years of sizing up his accomplice for just such an eventuality, which would prove, if not my downfall, the near destruction of my reputation and marriage. Was my first meeting just a test run for the dissembling to come, this Iago who seems a born inventor of lives, an experimenter willing to take on one mode after another to achieve his dastardly ends? Should I hold tight my Proteus in these pages before he undergoes yet another transformation? Or dare I imbue him and his lady with an aura of tragic sadness, ferret out a humanity in those deep blue trustworthy eyes sheltering from the shame of family skeletons and tragic failures, a humanity, if parts of Whittaker Chambers's *Witness* are to be believed, that runs much deeper than mine? What brother did I ever nurse back to health? Much less suffer not one but two family suicides? Or should I settle for a brilliant Houdini, perhaps? An Olivier with superpowers of self-control and self-fashioning, so allowing him to effortlessly walk the halls of power in hopes of fomenting its doom. Did he even then, before the Depression laid the country low, secretly despise the very upper-crust milieu he sought entrance to? Did he have any idea what he was brewing up in his soul to spring upon the world twenty years later? Was it all planned from the start, or did he simply slip into the camp of Mephistopheles in an unguarded moment, perhaps when he first heard the siren call of Priscilla Fansler's socialist fantasies—how many I endured on our walks to Handytown!—and so fashioned the necessary secret life that would keep his beloved fascinated and loyal?

Was Priscilla perhaps a secret sharer to our colloquy in Memorial Hall? In how many asides and letters has she hinted as much? Coy lady. Was poor Alger already in love with her, a woman who had spurned him not once—two years before—but twice? Who married first one imbecile and then almost married another two-timing lecher, before finally marrying Alger after the abortion I arranged and paid for. Does that image of an upright puritan from gaslit Baltimore untouched by vice glow all the stronger, knowing that, as Priscilla told me during a walk in Riverside Park before her sad death, Alger was a virgin on their wedding night? Priscilla, who may well have taught him a thing or two about subterfuge and untrammeled desires, the very thing that poor Bosley's libertine lifestyle exemplified and which, at least on that day of our first meeting, must have weighed on his soul, given the presence of that pantheon of heroes.

But the thing I ponder most—repressing anything in the way of sexual jealousy—as I examine his young face in the aura of those gallant souls who had given their lives for the Union and to free the bondmen: Was I so blind as to miss the rapacious cruelty of a man who might do anything for his cause? The iron discipline? Whittaker Chambers certainly thought he saw it years later, in 1938, when he defected and tried to get his comrade Alger to do the same. Saw enough in Alger's hardened stare that he immediately purchased a gun and fled with his family to Florida. Of course, in 1927 in the peaceful aura of Memorial Hall, reports of Stalin's extermination by famine of millions of kulaks still awaited us two years into the future, and the rapacious Red purges would have been a thing as yet undreamed of by me, by Alger—by any of us. Did his later knowledge of such atrocities, instead of repelling him, only harden him to the necessity of history's butcher's bill? And so steel him deeper into himself? For any birder knows that the quiet, the stillness, the perfect camouflage is the inbred advantage of the greatest raptors, how the Cooper's hawk so stealthily deceives the victim's wary eye. In the human species, no less a ruthlessness has been employed to justify the noblest of ends.

And so I think I prefer to keep my Alger safe in Memorial Hall, as yet untouched by what was to come, and what he was to become, and what I have become (wisdom gained in the crucible of deceit), in hopes that it all might be untrue, that all might have gone a different way—if he had met a different woman, if Roosevelt had taken more immediate action to save the banks and the Depression had been ameliorated, if a thousand fools, or a hundred thousand, had not been taken in by their fantastic misguided cravings as the Depression unleashed chaos on the land in the guise of arrogance, deceit, and resentment.

And that Alger Hiss may still be truly innocent, as his *New York Times* obituary hopefully states, giving him the benefit of the doubt.

But perhaps I am no less a fool—or just an old fool—to believe that such alternative narratives are possible, that anything might have been different—that I could have made a difference if I'd seen into the heart of such a deadly charmer. And so I must embrace that young man in the fading light of Memorial Hall for who he was while we were still young: a young idealist, like myself, in hopes of making the world his oyster. That life made fools of us both. Not that I relish the role of being one of Lenin's useful idiots, whose minions, as Chambers suggested, were groomed to be coddled as fellow travelers, harmless do-gooders who had no idea of the devil they were consorting with. Or as my fellow Groton alumnus Dean Acheson told me a few weeks before the trial, when I asked him if he had any doubts about Alger's bona fides—he'd turned on me with a snarl, as if I'd tweaked his flowing mustache, much less his amour propre: "If he was a Soviet agent, it was the greatest con job in history. Or perhaps I've been living on another planet all this time, same as you. If true, none of us is safe—none of us. And you, dear Edward, better make damn sure it's not true; otherwise, the New Deal and everything we hold sacred is fucked—and worse. He was at Yalta, too, at Franklin's right arm, and let me tell you—just between us—the old boy was more dead than alive. If Alger was a Soviet spy then every agreement at Yalta falls into disrepute."

Yet I'm no longer so sure of anything, for finally, after years of putting it off, I've now read Whittaker Chambers's book (Annie's copy, alas) twice, if not three times, over, where he reveals a hidden world to Annie's scrupulous—dare I say unforgiving—eye, and Alger as our underground man, someone who would do Dostoyevsky proud, combining the revolutionary guile of Stavrogin (there twice noted in Annie's hand) with the nihilism of Shagalov. And yet withal, Chambers still writes so convincingly, and out of such sympathetic love for his subject—speaking of Priscilla Hiss so tenderly that it has on occasion brought tears to my eyes, and scorn in Annie's hand—that the author's flawed genius shines all the more brightly for his essential integrity and humanity—and that of his comrades! So much so that he was loath to lay his hand upon his old friend. An author trying to redeem his own life—as do I, by bearing witness, while seeking to give meaning to the evil that has metastasized during our lifetimes. If the truth will make us free, Chambers will have it out, at least in his God-ordained universe. As will I now—still lacking the final definitive proof, either confession or documented evidence—even as I find myself coming around more and more to Chambers's final pronouncement on his antagonist: the truth I struggle to come to terms with in the heart of that young eager man standing before me in Memorial Hall on a sunlit afternoon in 1927: "No other Communist but Alger Hiss understood so quietly, or accepted with so little fuss or question the fact that the revolutionist cannot change the course of history without taking upon himself the crimes of history."

Like the great horned owl: By the time you hear him coming the talons will have drawn first blood.

18
Crime Scene: George Altmann

The most merciful thing in the world, I think, is the inability of the human mind to correlate all its contents. We live on a placid island of ignorance in the midst of black seas of infinity, and it was not meant that we should voyage far. The sciences, each straining in its own direction, have hitherto harmed us little; but some day the piecing together of dissociated knowledge will open up such terrifying vistas of reality, and of our frightful position therein, that we shall either go mad from the revelation or flee from the light into the peace and safety of a new dark age.

—H. P. Lovecraft

BY MIDAFTERNOON THE temperature had reached the high sixties, as if summer were intent on a valiant comeback, a hope heralded in the thrumming gurgle of the Sawkill weaving its way beneath their feet. A comforting thought to this odd couple, especially after a depressing hour digging out the police report on George Altmann's death in nearby Kingston (yet another overlooked bit of evidence), conjuring visions of ice and snow and mayhem. They walked the road that crossed the Sawkill Bridge, she with inbred physical prowess, he with careful, even plodding, steps, walking it time and again, across and back, weaving from railing to railing, stopping to look down into the rocky creek, repeatedly grasping the guardrail, as if needing to acknowledge its persistent separation of the elements, measuring distances in their minds. Then they would return again and again to the documents he was carrying in a folder, reading and rereading, taking out the Xerox copies of the black and white photos, inspecting one and then another and another and going back to the first. He grimaced at the close-ups of the damage to the temple, the matted blood-frozen hair, the split lip below the tiny mustache, but she seemed almost indifferent to the horror. "Sorry, I've seen worse."

Finally, after half an hour of prowling the access points to the bridge—a single steel-beamed structure painted Kelly green on the underside—they came together at the midpoint, as if some unspoken conclusion had crystalized, gripping the wood railing and staring downstream to take final bearings for the journey that beckoned.

Along the curving banks, the maple leaves had turned a shocking blood red in places, buckshot victims of midnight frost, splashing the darker greens of pine and hemlock like cowering and disoriented witnesses at a crime scene. Downstream, a light breeze whispered in racing runes on the gleaming surface, while below, jostling wavelets corralled the larger granite boulders, slipping with a nasal hiss by the flat, sharp-edged fins of bluestone. The muddy bottom was speckled with gray and tan pebbles shining through congeries of drowned leaves, ghostly reminders of ancient vintage. Just by the bridge, two massive oaks leaned out, seeming to mock the watchers at the railing, mimicking their vague sense of longing and loss where the overhanging boughs listened attentively, posted to some immemorial duty until their dun leaves, too, would become numbered with the fallen.

"It's so deceiving, don't you think?" she asked. "Nature is so good about all this, covering up violence and death. The vultures and crows, the wolves and coyotes strip the flesh, and bacteria take care of any remaining soft matter, while the waters sweep away the bones, so no one believes it can happen to them."

"What a lovely picture you paint." He tapped the file impatiently on the railing. "My mother always said that the most devastating thing for the family was that he died in the place where he found the most consolation and peace, standing here, listening to the stream after a long day's work in his studio, on the way to or from town."

"What's with you and your father that you didn't, at the very least, talk to him about all this? I mean, at least a phone call—you owed the essay at least that much."

He scowled at her insistent hammering. "You don't want to know—trust me."

She knew enough now to know when to change the subject.

"He'd been drinking in town?"

He opened the folder and looked again at the coroner's report.

"Blood alcohol high, but not that high."

She continued, as if something had caught her eye in a glittering pool of aquamarine as the clouds shifted and the light tumbled like thrown dice. "Except on places like Everest, in the killing zone, where the bodies lie preserved, unrecovered and unrecoverable. 'Green Boots,' they call one, passed by anyone on the northeast route, like a fucking landmark. As if to make sure you're properly clued in: Don't get into trouble now, motherfucker, because all anybody cares about now is getting to the summit and back alive."

He put his finger on the number on the page, as if he hadn't heard a word. "Not enough to make him falling-down drunk; I mean, he made it this far from the tavern."

She removed her wraparound sunglasses and squinted.

"But enough to lower your guard, to be less aware of your surroundings—that's always trouble."

"It was Christmas Eve, in the middle of nowhere: a place he loved, that nurtured his soul."

"How poetic, how perfect." She slipped the sunglasses into the pocket of her fleece vest. "Why do you always call him 'Jim'? After everything, your father obviously thought enough of his father to name you after him."

At this, he seemed to bristle, closing the file and again beginning to ponder the array of rocky pools in immediate proximity to the railing where they stood.

"Another one of my mother's goofy ideas, to get back at the Judge."

As if this annoyed her somehow, she scrambled up on the guardrail and adroitly stood on the weathered two-by-four handrail.

"What the fuck are you doing?" He reached out to the spandex length of her calf, but she ignored him and began to walk the length of the railing, as if on a Sunday stroll in her climbing boots.

"I can get a better feel of distances from here," she proclaimed, returning to where he stood. "And it's only about a ten- or eleven-foot drop. I'd have a hard time spraining an ankle, unless I hit an uneven rock and broke a leg."

"Will you get down? You're giving me the creeps."

"Relax, George—you, Luke Skywalker, so cute—didn't you walk on the wild side as a kid? It just helps me think."

"The stream was frozen with an inch of ice. The road had ice on it, according to the police report, so I suppose he could have slipped—somehow."

She glared with a dismissive frown.

"You're about the same height, George. Look where the railing comes up above your—are those love handles, George? Where's your center of gravity? Even if it happened as the report speculated—Altmann slipped on the ice, staggered into the railing, and flipped over—it'd be near impossible. And if he did, he would have fallen straight over the side, into the pool below, the ice below. The rocks are a good fifteen feet farther out. If I hurled myself"—and she bent her legs as if to spring—"I couldn't reach that far—or maybe just."

"So maybe he fell on the ice, staggered up a couple of steps, and fell forward again headfirst onto the rocks. Enough to be knocked out until the cold killed him."

"Give me the goddamn coroner's photo." She held out her hand.

"How can you stand to look at that thing?"

"Oh—what's left of a body that's fallen fifteen hundred feet into scree—you don't wanna know."

He opened the file and handed up the photo.

"No, I don't."

"Jesus," she said, grimacing, "how did the coroner describe the head injury?"

"Trauma to right temple, lacerations to scalp . . ."

A flock of goldfinches, lemon drops against the green, scattered out from the nearest trees along the stream bank. They both turned for a moment, a little amazed.

"Trauma, my ass; his skull has been bashed in. Terminal velocity, that's what it would take to inflict that much damage. Or someone braining you with a rock."

He looked away and shook his head.

"What's the matter?" she asked.

"Forget it."

"George—you okay? Sorry, baby."

"No nature, no vultures and coyotes and streams, to wash it all away."

A dark look flashed across her face. "Why do you think I try to get out of the city as much as I do?"

He looked down at the other photos.

"I guess when they photographed the scene, his body had been moved to the stream bank by Jim and his mother. I think she left him with the body while she drove into town to get the police and ambulance." Holding up a photo showing an ice-encrusted rock and bloodstains, he pointed. "It could be any of those or none of those. There've been floods in the last sixty years. How do we know the rocks weren't closer, that things haven't been disturbed since then?"

She jumped down from the railing and handed him back the photo.

"Okay, just stand there a moment; let yourself go limp, like you're a bit drunk."

"I don't get drunk very often."

"Do your best. Now look away from me."

As he turned his head, she ran at him, hooked her hands under his left armpit, and jerked up, lifting him an instant so that he staggered and dropped the folder.

"What the fuck . . ."

"I'm pretty strong," she panted. "I might have been able to surprise you and push you over, but not hurl you over. It would take two."

He looked at her as if he didn't quite recognize her, rubbing his upper arm as he went to recover the scattered pages. Taking a deep breath, he reshuffled the pages in the folder once more, pointing to a typed document.

"Bruises on the upper left and right arms, consistent with a fall."

"It would have taken two strong men, from the right and left, to heave him into space that distance."

He closed his eyes, as if to collect his thoughts.

"And finish him off with a rock."

"Yes"—she nodded—"about ten pounds."

"'Any fool can commit a murder,'" he said with a significant look, as if reciting from memory, "'but it takes an artist to commit a good natural death.'"

"An artist?"

"Whittaker Chambers. The Judge underlined the sentence in his copy of *Witness.*" He smiled at her with almost wicked pleasure. "Perhaps you qualify."

"I'm just trying to help, George."

"Laurence Duggan fell sixteen stories into a snowbank on Forty-fifth Street just days after Hiss was indicted by a grand jury. Marvin Smith fell six flights of stairs at the Justice Department two months after a House committee had questioned him on Hiss's transfer of his Ford roadster to a Communist operative . . . all a little over a year before whatever happened here."

"So, they'd had plenty of practice."

He began rubbing his arm again, scissoring his jaw, perplexed.

"And yet Altmann covered both the first and second trials; he was there every day, in sight of Alger and Priscilla Hiss, their defense team, sketching the proceedings for the *Herald Tribune*."

"What's the expression—'hold your enemies closer'?"

"Did he know they were enemies; did they know they were enemies?"

"Priscilla was there. What you want to bet he sketched her every day."

"Why . . ."

"Because he liked her, because she's a woman, because she'd keep him safe. Men are fools, trust me."

He gave her a long skeptical look, never quite sure when she was serious.

"Even handing over the sketches—his insurance—to Edward Dimock wasn't enough to keep him safe."

"Okay, he trusted her—Annie, believe me; I've seen it happen."

With this assurance, she turned and began walking away. He remained staring for a while longer.

"Jesus, do you suppose he screamed—had time to scream?"

She kept walking, as if she hadn't heard, then stopped and turned, staring at the road. "You scream . . ."

He followed along after her. Then she went to the railing once again, maybe a last look, or something had caught her eye.

"You know, it's kind of like those little crosses with fake flowers and a name by the side of highway, where somebody died in a crash, put there by a member of the family who wants to believe the place of the accident is hallowed by what happened." The shadows along the bank had grown longer and deeper, the treetops lording over the stream. "I guess we like to believe that, except when you see it for real . . . passing those frozen bodies on Everest: It's damn creepy and you wonder why anyone with half a brain would want to put themselves through such hell."

"Hmm." He turned back to the railing as well, keeping at a safe distance, as if wary of the lengthening shadows. "I'm a coward at heart. I thrive on predictability. I love patterns, constants, like the speed of light, Newton's gravitational constant, even the Planck constant—an acquired taste, since it makes for its own uncertainties. That's our problem, isn't it"—his chin rose in concentration—"how to measure cause and effect? How to sift out what is and what isn't a variable, so that a simple correlation, no matter how tempting, isn't mistaken for a cause."

She seemed not be listening or, more likely, was talking past him, which was how they more or less communicated.

"Ambition's boxes a foolish little girl thought needed checking, but no more." She made a face of regretful idiocy as they turned off the bridge. "I'll be with you in a moment; I've got to pee."

He walked back to the Tahoe, his mind now returning to the underlined passages in blue of the night before, describing a dismaying if not hellish pit of despair and horror: how terror had been the accepted instrument of Stalin's policy, secrecy the existential foundation of the underground, how any deserter from this clandestine cabal posed an immediate threat and so had to be swiftly eliminated.

Terror, he thought, seeing again the black smoke and flame belching from the silver skin of the north tower.

When he turned back from the Tahoe after stowing his backpack, he saw her bent over the W-beam guardrail at the approach to the bridge, vomiting.

19

Sugar High

WHEN SHE RETURNED to the car, he handed her a cappuccino and tapped the wax-paper bag in his outstretched hand as if it might contain a dangerous reptile.

"Not quite Starbucks," he said, "but the frosted whole-grain doughnuts will still fly you to the moon on a sugar high."

"The Sinatra version, I hope."

"Is it possible you're more retro than I am?"

"No, worse; I live in a time warp of the mornings my father drove me to school on his way to work. We always listened to his tapes on the way to the mountains. I'm really thirteen, you see, a case of arrested adolescent development."

He seemed to ponder this, absorbing the thought and prompting his subsequent observation.

"You were . . . close?"

"My alpha and omega—yes."

"So, family, well, if you look carefully"—and he pointed, bringing his extended arm close to her cheek—"you can just make out an almost invisible line, there and there, bisecting the valley, once the route of the D & H Canal, following the ridge of the Shawangunks. See those gaps, barely a faint scribble among the trees and fields, headed for the Roebling aqueduct at High Falls and then Rondout and the Hudson and the sea beyond."

"Funny, all the years climbing." She squinted and shrugged. "Now that you mention it, I believe Cordelia showed me something about the canal in her album—the Neversink, wasn't it?"

"Oh, you really did get the full Cook's tour."

"Your grandfather's place, Hermitage—wow. Lucky you, to spend your summers there as a kid."

"Oh, there was a price . . . but perhaps I got off easy."

"Is his memoir part of that price?"

"You don't miss much."

She took his arm. "George, if I, like Odysseus, had ten minutes in the underworld with my father . . ."

He put his arm around her and squeezed.

"The D & H, now that you put it that way, is a way station in the Judge's underworld."

"So, dear Cicero, show me."

Back in the Tahoe, which was packed with bubble-wrapped canvases, George took a mile detour up 209 and pulled off onto a grassy verge, pondering a moment the advisability of leaving the Tahoe with its precious cargo, and then led her along a vague path through some farmer's fields and down into a shallow copse where, out of nowhere, two parallel walls of rough-hewn granite rose from the leafy earth, quickly ascending to a height of about fifteen feet. Sturdy beech saplings clamored in what had once been the narrow confines of a canal basin, spindly branches elbowing high above against the dusk, like prison yard inmates reaching for the last gleams of sunlight.

"This is, if I remember rightly, lock twenty-one, lifting the D & H on the way to the High Falls aqueduct about a half mile ahead. Not as elegant as the Neversink aqueduct in our neck of the woods—that's, by the way, a matter of faith in my grandfather's mind—but still a nifty piece of engineering in its day, along with these locks, especially when you think how all this rock had to be cut, transported, and fitted by hand. Ah, you see, here"—he reached to a rusted length of iron protruding from the face of the wall—"a stay bolt; this would have held the planking in place along the sides of the lock."

"You're really into this," she said, wolfing down her second doughnut.

"Oh, let's just say there's a vague comfort in man-made artifacts, even hundred-year-old ruins, compared to staring into the eternal abyss of space, when even fourteen billion years doesn't amount to a can of beans."

"Hill of beans."

He gestured behind them. "A mere forty miles by coal barge to the Neversink aqueduct and Hermitage, where perfection reigns."

"So, am I down for a visit to your Shangri-la?"

"An intrepid female like you." He put his hands on his hips and threw his head back. "'You boys and girls think you'd prefer a little

chaos around here rather than *my* rules—do whatever the hell suits you
like a bunch of wide-eyed anarchists—laze away the summer. Is that
it? Well, a good dose of overnight camping might be just the thing, a
couple of days in the bush so you can spend some quality time with the
skeeters and snappers, the timber rattlers and black bears, under a leaky
canvas and a cold damp rain.'"

She laughed, enjoyment at his antics flooding her face, so much so
that for a brief moment he was tempted to go and kiss her sugary lips,
but just as quickly put the temptation aside.

"George, from what I can figure, your father and the Judge—I suppose Alice, as well—are some of the last people alive to still remember
George Altmann." She grabbed hold of the cut stone and lifted herself
onto the wall. "Your last chance."

"For what?"

"Justice," she replied, and began to scramble up the sheer wall as if
it were a jungle gym.

"Don't you ever get scared?" He positioned himself below her, anxiously looking up.

"Fear of falling, you mean?" She swung herself upward and laughed.
"George, first you identify your fear, classify what is really bothering you;
then you eliminate the probabilities of any physical danger, and that way
you limit the fear that can affect your performance. When alpine climbing, as long as I could safely down-climb, I never felt any fear."

Ninety seconds later, maybe less, she had summited and raised her
arms in triumph.

He picked up the wax-paper bag, contemplated the remaining
doughnut, and then grabbed it, muttering to himself, "Sugar high."

As he waited for her to circle around and make her way back down
to the desultory remnants of the canal bed, he slipped out the letter
from his back pocket that he'd picked up that morning in the kitchen.

Dear George,
Well, what to say, except I'm between tours. Actually, I haven't managed to find another touring gig in quite some time, and I'm holed up
here in Seattle and it's raining like shit, and I'm getting tired of being
on the road with a bunch of kids, which is one of the reasons I'm writing you. Tour managing is a younger man's game. In truth, I'm writing
you because I'm sorry that I haven't written in so long—so long that
I can't even remember the last time I did write to you.

And I'm sorry. I'm sorry I walked out on your life twenty years ago. Your mother may have deserved it, but you didn't—whatever the case. And even if there are still many unresolved issues between me and Cordelia, none of it was your fault, and you deserved better from me. Age puts things in perspective. After my last tour managing Crosby, Stills, Nash & Young—they're not getting any younger, either—and listening to their "Teach Your Children Well" night after fucking night, well, it began to get to me, that bit about being on the road and having a code to live by. And damned if I lived by any code in regards to you, besides teaching you a thing or two about fixing leaks and changing spark plugs and such like.

Age does something to you, George, besides just blowing out your knees and back and rotting your teeth. It fills you with regrets. And I have way more than my fair share. There's no going back; I know that. There's no forgiving for what's done, for the twenty years that have separated us. The truth, what bothers me most, is the realization that what I did to you was just about as bad as what my father did to me. And at about the same age. Leaving us—me and mother, that is—the way he did, without a word, without a reason, and leaving us to deal with the goddamn mess he left behind. He made me hate myself, feel that somehow I might have been responsible, or might have done something to save him, like being a better son—or appreciating his art—and so maybe he wouldn't have done the terrible thing he did. That question still fills my dreams. It made me hateful of my mother, my life, even the place I grew up in and the people who cared about me. That I might have managed a repeat of that with you now gives me bad dreams, as well.

God knows how much shit I left you to deal with. For years I justified it in terms of your mother's infidelity. And when you ended up going to Princeton, I figured that maybe whatever I did had been for the best—that I hadn't fucked you up so much after all. But the thing weighs on me, and even though I know I can never make it right, I feel like I should give it a try, or at least make it clear that I don't blame you for anything that went south between me and your mother. And I take responsibility for my own fucked-up actions. That's part of what we try to do at my AA meetings, admit our weaknesses and our fucked-upness and take responsibility for who we are and for those who matter to us.

Anyway, I wanted you to know as much, and that if I can take away any of the pain I caused you, I'd like to at least talk it over. As I wrote your mother, I'm sober almost a year and intend to remain so.

I've spoken to Levon about maybe helping out at the Barn, and so I'll try to get my sorry ass back to Woodstock within the month—a long drive in my beat-up Chevy. I don't quite know how I'll work things out with your mother, but I owe her the chance.

Truthfully, I'm tired and I miss fucking Woodstock. And I miss the old boys in the Band, even though Rick and Richard are so sadly gone, and Robbie's now a big shot in L.A., and Levon has been fighting cancer. How the Grim Reaper takes the best. But Levon sounded kindly on the phone, reminiscing about the early days at Big Pink when I helped the fellows set up the recording studio in the basement. Oh, those were the days—those were the days, with Bob—they really were. So, there it is.

Thanks for hearing me out,
James Altmann

20

Twin Beams

IT WAS PAST dusk as they approached the GW Bridge, blue lights spangling the darkening sky, the wounded city looming up from the river. George was prompted to put the Band's 2000 remastered version of their 1968 album in the CD player, as if to insulate them further. "James Altmann—for what it's worth—is on the liner notes: assistant studio engineer." This pained acknowledgment turned out to be a conversation stopper, as Levon Helm's good ol' boy drawl of a voice filled the Tahoe, and tears welled in Wendy's eyes, so much so that she kept her face firmly turned to the Hudson, aglitter with the moonlit shadows of fuel barges herded by toy tugs, the great artery pouring itself from the heart of the land, as it had over a century before when the same river had floated thousands of coal barges on their last leg south to tidewater. Not unlike, it might be argued, the Tahoe, too, carrying a precious cargo out of the Woodstock hills: energy, aesthetic and otherwise, to inveigle the fickle desires of the urban multitudes.

Wendy, who'd momentarily been distracted, suddenly turned from the river, all abuzz. "I hate to say it, George, but the truth, if it—I know, I know—turns out to be the truth, could be a terrific marketing tool in terms of moving Altmann quickly into museum collections. Just think of it: an American artist murdered by the KGB at the height of his powers. It will galvanize Altmann's rediscovery. How he stood up to Stalin and the claptrap of social realism for a revolutionary abstraction, free of European bullshit, free of the dead hand of history and the pathologies of a monstrous century. What do you think—the real deal, an authentic American genius?"

At this, all he could do was whistle under his breath, for his eyes, too, had caught sight of the twin beams reaching out of the glow of a thousand arc lamps into the empty night.

He parked at the loading dock for his building on the corner of Twenty-second and Eleventh Avenue. While she stood guard, he got the night watchman to unlock the loading bay's door and the freight elevator. Carefully, lovingly, they carried the dozen bubble-wrapped canvases like sleeping children, one by one, into the freight elevator and leaned them carefully against the back wall, which was hung with grimy quilted moving pads. (He flinched inwardly at adolescent memories of how he'd once flung the canvases around the old studio barn to save them from a sudden leak.) Then, on the twelfth floor, they each carried a canvas down the silent corridors, past dark glassy rectangles with vaguely stenciled names and hours, until reaching the dead-end entrance to his gallery, Dark Matter. Zero random foot traffic, zero street visibility, relentless rent increases.

This crushing realization was momentarily replaced by the mirage of a more glittering future: a storefront window down the block on Twenty-second Street, not far from the likes of heavy hitters David Zwirner and Gagosian—all denizens of the celebrity fueled Art Basel fair franchise. As he unlocked his door, he conjured yet further guilty visions of Miami Basel, of Altmanns hanging in his booth with Gustons and Rothkos, modern masters, contemporaries of Altmann, acclaimed by the glitterati circus, where power collectors hungrily opened their checkbooks at the mere dropping of a name or the glimpse of an iconic signature style. Jolted by a sudden beeping, he hurried into the darkened gallery to disarm the alarm system as Wendy followed behind with a canvas. As he switched on the gallery lights, the Altmann exhibition, canvas after canvas, surged to life around them . . . miraculous, a confirmation of their most fervent desires.

She touched his arm as she put down her bubble-wrapped canvas. "Wow, water into wine. Better than sex—huh?"

He smiled. "I wouldn't know."

For a few minutes, he walked the gallery, bathing his eyes anew, fresh, discerning eyes, freed of past associations. His attention was jacked and juiced by the multitude of red dots discretely placed over the prices on the 3M title stickers affixed to the off-white walls.

"He's . . . as good as we think?" he said to Wendy, who now stood in front of one of her purchases with a lost expression.

"Better, George. Even better than I remember from opening night—if such a thing is possible. The silence, with just us, and now that I have a sense of where and how the synergy—the alchemy—happened." She touched his arm. "See, the truth does matter, like I can feel the poetry of Wordsworth and Emerson and Melville's zinc white; I can read it in every brushstroke."

"Oh my God, the others."

They rushed back to the freight elevators for the remaining canvases.

Carefully unwrapping the replacement works, they leaned them against the walls beneath their sold brethren. Switching some, standing back, switching again, they conferred about frames, about cleaning and varnishes.

"Wow," she noted, "what a difference once cleaned, night and day."

"I feel a little guilty, about replacing them so soon, just to extract more money while the going's good. I should at least leave the show intact until the end of the month, when my next exhibition is scheduled."

"Well, just keep them in the back room and let people know there's more where these came from."

"Maybe, except it's always easier to sell what's hanging, especially when so many have been sold."

At this, she smiled knowingly. "How much do you need the money?"

"I barely break even. Last year, as you might expect, was a disaster." He went over to a side table stacked with a pile of Altmann catalogs and held up a copy. "And now I have to deal with an essay that may not only be perpetuating a lie but, as you keep pointing out, fails in so many ways to do Altmann justice. And once enough of these get out, once this becomes the common wisdom about Altmann, it will be harder and harder to change it. And the worst part, if I try to be truthful with myself, is that I probably grabbed the suicide narrative and ran with it because it seemed, at the time, like a great romantic notion that might sell paintings, and, candidly, I really didn't give a shit in the beginning—I really didn't believe, not until they started coming back from the restorer, cleaned up. It was just a desperate gamble, a bunch of hype to keep the gallery afloat. The profit margin would be good, just restoration and framing costs, no commissions, no splitting sales with artists—like you."

He shrugged, as if to make light of his confession. "And reprinting a second edition will cost over forty thousand."

She placed a steadying hand on his shoulder.

"I can help with his books; I'll go through them and write you a separate essay, if that helps—from an artist's perspective."

He looked at her skeptically, warily, falling silent, as if she'd taken it too far.

"Look around you, George. These are bearers of joy and beauty and meaning—right? And you do what you have to do so the art can make its way in the world. We all have to market ourselves, and it sucks. Now that I've glimpsed his world, Altmann's world, I know he couldn't have killed himself." She tossed back her hair and gave him a mocking look, something brittle and cold in the crinkle at the corner of her eyes, a glint verging on scorn—perhaps at her own admission—as she held a spread palm against the impasto of one of her purchases, pressing the canvas lightly to feel its surface tension, palpitant, electric, as if pledging her troth. "Would you really rather be back in Princeton staring at billion-year-old worlds—now burned to cinders?"

Her words (how cunningly she read him, he thought), though a comfort of sorts, also saddened him, as even her encouragement only conjured tedious visions of commerce and transactions: how the sold works would soon be bubble-wrapped and handed over to professional art handlers to be boxed in cardboard or crated, some to be hand-delivered to apartments all over town, to be marched past doormen up to spiffy condos—as opposed to co-ops—of the young and upcoming collectors who increasingly swarmed the more upscale, name-brand galleries. He found his assistant's updated sales list left on the desk in his office, and began to go over the names and addresses, looking for a pattern, a confirmation that his modest marketing campaign had really produced such stellar results. Something, anything, to defray the dark cynicism that always seemed to lurk in the back of his mind, a thing abetted, much as he might deny it, by the way his aunts, Alice and Martha, had heaped snarky remarks on the buyers at his Altmann opening. The Judge's cutting "wheeler-dealer." A client list that now included one Wendy Bradley of Park Slope, Brooklyn.

"A steal, do you think," he said with a hint of malice, handing Wendy the list, "when you consider what twenty-somethings out of the Yale School of Art are getting in their first shows?"

At this, she handed back the clipboard without comment and walked to his artists' racks, pulling out a few canvases with a bemused, if not judgmental, cant of her head.

"Which one of these is the artist that poor man picked for his wife's birthday?"

"You're looking at her. She's scheduled again next month, after the Altmann closes. Her first show since nine-eleven. It was the only thing that got her painting again; for almost ten months, she couldn't pick up a brush. Her studio's in Brooklyn Heights; the twin towers were, like, on her fucking doorstep."

"Competent, if a little run-of-the-mill, but just plain ol' vanilla seems to go far these days—huh?"

She replaced the lush still life of purple irises with the merest hint of disdain and went to his ceiling-to-floor office window overlooking Eleventh Avenue.

"*The Wall Street Journal*'s review comes out next week," he said, holding up a Post-it note from JJ, his assistant. She didn't turn or respond.

Instead, she tapped the window, her head rising, as if intent on inspecting her vague reflection in the rain-spotted plate glass, when, in fact, she was echoing the ascent of the twin beams from the cavernous space fifty blocks to the south.

"Fuckers," she said, barely audible, pressing herself close to the glass and lowering her gaze as if to fully gauge the twelve-story drop below.

21

Underground Queen

HE DROVE HER home in near silence, windows open to the welcoming sounds of a city in recovery, the jarring of steel plates, the wail of police sirens whiplashing the heads of nervous pedestrians, another bridge (Roebling's masterpiece thirty years on from the Neversink aqueduct), another river, another island. Her Brooklyn studio loft was on the edge of Park Slope, overlooking Green-Wood Cemetery. When he parked and got out, the quiet of her neighborhood was again a comfort.

He helped her with her crash pads and offered to carry them up to her studio.

"I can carry them; you don't have to come up."

"I'll just get your stuff in the front door. We don't have to call it an official studio visit."

She shrugged, resigned. "Whatever."

They ascended three flights of narrow stairs in what had once been a brick factory building, intriguing remnants of a cement company's name in big scarified letters under the eaves, perhaps, once upon a time, a thriving concern, the notion struck him, when the D & H Canal had been at its height. Entering her studio, she switched on the lights, grabbed the crash pads from his arms, and did her best to quickly stow her bulging backpack and harness of flex cams, carabiners, and Camalots in a curtained storage area crammed with ropes and other climbing gear. She was clearly frantic, if not embarrassed, and in a matter of seconds he knew why. The loft, with its fourteen-foot ceiling, was huge, spectacularly huge, running along Twentieth Street, with a long series of wide plate-glass windows overlooking the cemetery. "Full of stony stares morning, noon, and night," she quipped. As if such an extravagance of light and space were not enough, there were even skylights and more track lighting than in most galleries.

The exposed brick walls had been lushly repointed, the new Sheetrock walls of the built-out bedroom, bathroom, and kitchen were painted a neutral off-white, the old pine flooring planed and polished and buffed to a rosy yellow-ocher glow. Everything had been laid out for efficiency and ease of access, all with a love of exposed raw materials, like a perfectly ruled ledger.

The strip of north-facing windows ran the entire length of the studio—"my Tombstone view," as she called it—like airy arms encompassing four massive easels in a semicircle, each bearing a large canvas, all in various stages of completion, an arrangement, so he noted, allowing simultaneous scrutiny and comparison. Oak worktables provided ballast to the ensemble, displaying regimented tubes of color arranged like assault groups of toy soldiers. Each worktable was festooned with canvas brush holders hung like saddlebags on their flanks, where bristles long and short, flat and rounded daubed the air. Drying paintings were stacked against floor-to-ceiling vertical racks, at least, by his quick count, fifteen canvases in progress, along with the four on the easels. She was clearly a workhorse. Toward the back were pull-down screens for projecting digital images. In a corner was a large horizontal file drawer neatly labeled: SKETCHBOOKS, PHOTOS, LANDSCAPE STUDIES, NUDE STUDIES, ROCK FORMATIONS, YALE, PRIZE SUBMISSIONS, AWARDS SUBMISSIONS. Ambition to burn. Neatly arranged on the top were colorful boxes of pastels and colored pencils, bottles of ink, pens, pencils, and Winsor & Newton charcoal sticks.

"Sorry, it's kind of a mess."

He laughed.

He'd never witnessed—and he'd been in over a hundred studios—such a spotless and obsessively laid-out work area. The track lighting—he went to the ranks of light switches, trying out the dimmers on the spots and floods—alone must have cost a small fortune. Ceiling fans were evenly spaced between the AC ducts. Not to mention the deep zinc sinks in the work area, and a kitchenette with a brand-new double-doored sub-zero fridge and a Viking stovetop with a cavernous hooded exhaust fan. He knew fifty-year-old successful artists who had been showing with Zwirner or Boone for years who couldn't have afforded such an extravagance, who still worked out of cold-water shoe boxes.

"So, you were just kidding about not having a gallery?"

"A few well-received group shows, no gallery . . . I'm picky about representation."

"Online sales, private sales?"

"A few, when I think something's ready—if it makes sense, if the buyer's right."

"Pricing?"

"Make me an offer and I'll tell you if you're close. The finished work is in those racks by the slide projector."

"Okay, okay . . ." He began to poke around her work area, not even asking permission, now that he'd caught her in at least one whopper—about exactly what and how big, he wasn't sure, but enough that it gave him carte blanche to ferret out the thing . . . the flaws in her story.

He began with the finished or nearly finished canvases, placing them on easels, working the dimmers to get the optimal lighting levels. He was intent on faultfinding, if the work failed to stand up to the images he'd glimpsed online: sloppy technical skills, inept drawing, one-dimensional use of color; derivative, striving to shock, overreaching for the new-new thing, the trending, politically correct theme.

Mightily impressed, he tried to be casual, to calm her nerves as she wandered abashed and seemingly helpless while he rummaged her life. Perhaps anxious, she flipped on the sound system for some Fleetwood Mac and Stevie Nicks.

He nodded at her choice of music, seeing in his mind that thirteen-year-old in her dad's Range Rover on the way to school in a tony Houston suburb. That slightly unnerving time warp they both seemed to inhabit, which was now leading him deeper, toward the black hole of her life.

But her creations quickly reclaimed his full attention, calmed his apprehensions. Her color was sensuous, and she displayed a love for textured surfaces full of lush impasto. They were tensile, tough, invoking symbolic form and natural abstraction.

And then it hit him, as his mind patiently established the connection between the creator and the creation: the alchemy she had managed to achieve—the vertical granite and horizontal limestone outcroppings in both tight and blurred focus, stressing the hard-edged stress cracks and fissures in the rock, and, too, the embedded layers of schist scribbled with moss or lichen; all this living, breathing, earthy dermis transformed into a womb embracing its human counterpart: curves of human flesh, extended arms, clinging legs, back and torso tensed, muscle and sinew bulging in the desperate attempt to emerge, birthed from the Earth and there pictured clinging against mother Gaia on an invisible umbilical cord while ascending the sky. He felt only exhilaration in the imagery, not danger. Only the softness of her firm breasts remained unaffected by gravity, full of longing—the erect nipples—for the human touch. This interplay, if not melding, of flesh and stone was realized with transparent washes of paint, much of it mesmerizing in its complexity, in the intermingling of flesh tones and soft-edged sedimentary forms: flesh and stone equally transparent and yet equally solid.

He picked up a tube of zinc white on her worktable. "Jesus Christ, Wendy, how long have you known about Altmann's work?"

She grimaced, as if he'd caught her out.

"Is that all you have to say?"

"No, no . . . it's just . . ."

"Last week in the *Times*. At the opening."

"How long have you been working on these?"

"Some for years, some for months."

"Is this all freehand, or are you painting from photographs?"

"Don't you see, George, what an eye he had?" This came out as the first admission of guilt since they'd arrived at her studio. "There were no photographs, from what I could tell, in his studio—anywhere. No sketches either. But he must've done it from sketches, or freehand, out of his head. It's why those damn nine sketches of yours are so freaky— where are the others? Ingres couldn't have done it better."

She gamely demonstrated her methods, setting up two slide carousels to simultaneously project images on a pull-down screen of a rock face, some close up, some more distant, along with nudes of herself climbing or lying on an outcropping; adjusting the depth of focus, color saturation, playing with the layered images until she had some approximation of the composition she was seeking.

"Then I slide a primed canvas in front of the screen and make more adjustments to the projected images; then I go at the canvas with charcoal to rough out the lines and volumes and find the most compelling interaction of shapes; then I go into the volumes with color washes until I've built up some approximation of overall tonality; then I'm on my own. I put the canvas I've started away for a week or two and come back to it fresh and see what I can find."

"You don't need to make excuses—not to me. It's just, like you say, a little freaky is all."

"It was weird, George, being in his studio: I felt like I'd been there before, in another life, another time. I knew the space as if it were my own. Even as he'd gone way beyond the figure, as if the figure was finally superfluous for him—only the need to approach nearer the essence." Her shoulders sagged, as if dragged down by an invisible weight. "Like I—my physical self—don't exist . . ."

He looked at her uneasily, feeling the struggle, the perplexity in her voice, and so tried to bring the conversation back to practicalities by assuming a curatorial pose. He pointed to the canvases on the four large easels.

"So, tell me, what, exactly, are you exploring in the imagery?"

"The feeling of rock and the struggle of flesh to withstand the pull of gravity in the extreme . . . like being born, I guess."

"What, in extremis, are you trying to achieve?"

"Flesh and stone transmuted into color, a quality of impasto, a texture of surface that appeals to the sense of touch, a dream of life high and free and infused with dirt and clean air. The freedom of the hills close to the sky." She tossed back her hair with an expression of violated innocence. "Like the better part of my damn childhood."

"What turns you on, artistically?"

"The rubbed-in tones of Degas. Whistler's pastels of Venice, especially his muted tonalities of sky and cracked plaster walls and the reflected damp light off a shadowed canal."

"Do you like Pearlstein?"

"He's too indoorsy, too much a painter of studio flesh under artificial light."

"Do you prefer landscapes or nudes?"

"I'm trying to capture that Proustian dialogue of the subjective flesh interacting with the unseen—the invisible soul inherent in nature."

"Oh, sorry I asked." He couldn't resist a sarcastic eye roll. "Anyway, pure abstraction has been done to death, don't you think? You've carved out your own niche"—he couldn't help smiling—"so to speak. The work is distinctive, attractive, a signature style all your own."

She turned, as if his praise (the commercial viability), true or false, wounded her, causing her to retreat to one of the spacious industrial windows embedded in aluminum casements overlooking the panoply of marble monuments across the street—some vast, even palatial, some mere tottering slabs, all with a livid nacreous glow bathed in the halation of city lights and backlit by a rising moon: fantastic architectonic geometries of death stretching almost as far as the eye could see.

"Ninth-month midnight," she offered, by way of contrition, or possibly explanation.

"Midnight?"

"Whitman . . . But we are all of the earth, the dark womb, the alpha and omega." She gestured to the beyond, to the Elysian Fields—all that had once been—where willows spilled their now-spent leaves, the Greek and Gothic tombs and spiky monuments to families long fled Earth's grasp. "I like the struggle of the human figure, grappling with the natural world, as I said, the flowers and trees, born out of it, reaching to the sky, always reaching . . ."

"Well then, would you call them self-portraits? I mean, you, your nudes, are so chameleon-like, blending with their backgrounds, born and reborn . . ." He smiled haltingly, as if trying to respect her sensitivities, her vision, his praise gravitating to artistic merit rather than monetary worth.

"Hardly. Just flesh and bone pushed to the limits of physical endurance." She threw back her head as if a little frustrated at where the interrogation was going, and so retreated once again, two windows down, as if giving herself more breathing room. "What is this inquisition all about, George?" He maintained his ground, staring intently at her muscular shoulders, the tendons rising into her neck, her hair bunched with an elastic band, then to where her face was reflected in the glass, a transparent specter overseeing her domain, high cheekbones and the delicate upturned tip of her nose transposed upon the litter of crosses, urns, grieving angels, and funerary statues of every faith known to humanity, family mausoleums with massive columns erupting like Hades' portals from grassy hillsides, built-to-last memorials for clans who had once served the city and were no more. "What," she went on, placing a palm against the glass as if in solidarity or to caress her still-girlish features, "do they care?"

"I care," he interjected lustily, "how Dark Matter might market you."

"Ah!" She laughed like a child who'd caught an adult fibbing. "I don't need marketing, George. Only that the work speaks to the likes of you."

"Wendy, your stuff is fucking gorgeous. I mean, pretty damn erotic, at least some of it—actually, a lot of it. Do you care if guys get turned on?"

"Women, too, hopefully—totally. And yes"—a flush returned to her cheeks—"my colors and forms should have a certain quality of sensuous release. I want people to touch, to feel the life in the paint—yes, turned on." She laughed uneasily, as if at some private joke. "To rise from the dead."

"Your work is good"—his eyes widened with glee—"more than good. But you don't need to hear this from me—you *know* . . ."

George took a step toward where she stood, now drawn by the image in the glass, like a faded photograph, but as he did, the angle caused her to fade, her image replaced by the sky above the necropolis, to the north and west of the moon, where the Pleiades dimly reigned, mere hundreds of stars, an open cluster of youngsters, like kindergarteners excitedly showing off their stuff to proud parents. The thought brought him up short.

"Ah," she moaned, "not in a league with George Altmann. I worry that the photographs end up being a little gimmicky, confining, substitutes for the real thing, for real talent, which is visionary, not, God forbid, photorealism. Her voice rose now, as if to reclaim a faltering dignity. "Not that I can't draw when I need to."

She turned away from the stygian landscape of tombs and phallic obelisks, walking briskly past him to one of her recent canvases, eyeing it critically.

"Not to worry," he called after her, a little dumbfounded that she felt the need to compete with the dead, as well. "You're still young—plenty of time to run."

"It's not easy, George, to hold on to your feelings and not go mad with so much shit happening in the world. To resist buying into the fearmongering. To flinch at every Boeing on final approach to La Guardia."

"Is fear a feeling, do you suppose, or a response? You strike me as absolutely fearless."

"Hah, that's my camouflage. 'Chameleon,' you said."

"You're . . ." And he moved to her side, reaching a hand to the canvas at her elbow. "You're the rare talent, the genuine article. I wish I could say the same."

"Oh, George, you just live too much in your head. Your space-time is just what indigenous people felt about their place on the land, when time was one with their quotidian lives, at one with the rhythmic cycles, their holy places aligned with the sun or the North Star, the breeze that rustled the leaves, the spirit moving across the face of the waters—how the Greeks described it, *pneuma*." She placed her outspread palm next to his on the canvas, pressing as if on the billow of a sail. "See . . . it's alive—that's how my father always described it after an ascent—the living presence where you set your feet on the ridgeline to stare out upon the horizon. That's the feeling—the spirit—I'm after in my painting, when I'm in the zone. But this last year . . . it's been so fucking hard." As if exasperated with her attempt to explain herself, she retreated to the window once more and for a moment bowed her forehead to the plate glass, resigned. Not unlike, so it struck him momentarily, one of the sorrowing angels in the gray distance. He moved slowly to stand beside her, where he could feel her bodily warmth against the cold night air radiating from where her breath congealed on the pane, as if her spirit, too, yearned to join the chorus of the charnel wastelands beyond. Something in him wished to offer comfort as much as to contradict her: a need to plead his case one last time.

"All our suspects are dead and gone, Wendy, even those deaths, like the Judge, marked in limbo."

"No, they're not." Her eyes were an electric blue as she found his. "I came to that conclusion the morning after the Altmann opening, standing here with my cup of coffee, watching the mist rising over the graves. They're just like us—staring back at us, wondering, What was it all about? We owe them that much, George. We owe it to George Altmann and all the others . . . the truth. Without meaning, just *being* is pointless."

Her blazing certainty sent a chill through him.

"But what chance do we have without data, witnesses, *facts*? I still cling to that, maybe more than ever. My faith in the scientific method—'my fat head,' as you call it . . . doubt. Not all of us can be fucking artists, you know."

"There are facts and there are *facts*." She lifted her eyes once more to the marble halls and inky-hollow porticoes, as if to scrutinize those endless but invisible lists of carved and inscribed names and dates that populated her vision. "Oh, they left more of a mark on the world than just this"—and she waved from where they were standing by the window to her stony canvases—"in the underground—you see, where they always find their way back into other people's lives, especially the children's, George. Trust me, I know, I know they're calling out to us, George, like your grandfather's paintings called out during your childhood, like your grandfather's memoir does now, to give their lives and struggles meaning, to give them rest, to give us rest, to allow us to go on. We owe it"—and she reached for his hand—"to their children, or their children's children if nothing else."

He turned, not a little bewildered, but gave way and, smiling, as if in thanks, laid a gentle hand on her shoulder.

"You ask too much of life."

"Or not enough."

"Funny, you kind of remind me of him, the Judge—or his alter ego, on our hikes as kids, standing in this abandoned homestead deep in the woods—Handytown, we call it. We'd linger there to listen for the hermit thrush and help him repair the bluestone walls. And when we complained and asked why bother, he'd hold up an admonishing finger, smile sweetly, and tell us to listen, *listen*. He'd whisper as a breeze played in the lilacs by the crumbled cellar hole, 'They're still here, waiting to tell their stories . . . our blood offering.'"

22

Playing for Keeps

THE ANONYMITY OF the city was now a relief. Driving alone through the empty light-swarming streets was a relief. Getting away from Wendy Bradley was a huge relief. Finding a parking space like a mirage near the door of his apartment on Fourteenth Street east of Third Avenue was a rare blessing. Even his gingko trees, just beginning to turn golden, provided a friendly welcome for a weary time traveler retreating from the stony ranks of Green-Wood Cemetery and their presiding queen of the underground.

Why should he feel guilty? He already had three women artists in his stable. Women sold. Women, young women, were good for business. She'd be good for his program.

And he did not sleep with his artists. So far, so good.

Under less charged circumstances, he would have offered her a contract then and there.

He paused on the steps of his stoop, surveying the ranks of gingkoes.

She was *so* fucking intimidating: the sheer predatory energy. Reminding him of when he was twelve, when first bitten by the *Star Wars* bug; even when he was twenty and nearing his undergraduate degree in astrophysics, when he lived like a caffeinated maniac while getting his hands on the latest research data from the Hubble telescope, when his curiosity drove him like a demon. Until the vastness crept up on him during his graduate years, when the sheer size of the numbers began to weigh, and the thing, the wonder, began to drain away into the infinity of the night sky and somehow turn to dread.

He stared up into the amber-green underlit canopy of gingkoes stirring in the cooling breeze, breathing in their pungent odor as the females began to bear fruit . . . maidenhead trees in whose shade dinosaurs had once tread.

"Time, man, just give it time . . . pneuma . . ." He opened the door.

To his amazement, he found an Amazon package leaning against his mailbox, as if fate, in the form of a missive out of space-time, had tapped his shoulder. *The Haunted Wood*, by Allen Weinstein, along with his previous book on the Hiss trials from twenty years before, *Perjury*, ordered just twenty-four hours ago while staring out at that harvest moon from his boyhood window. Mounting the rickety wooden stairs to his apartment, he stared at the silver-gray-and-sepia cover of *The Haunted Wood*, split-screen images of Pennsylvania Avenue and Red Square, vintage photos of Washington and Moscow. With the Berlin Wall down now for thirteen years, that improbable Cold War confrontation had seemed, even a year earlier, only a relic of some archaic age. No longer, not after 9/11, and the prospect of yet another dark age of revolutionary violence as American forces in Kuwait prepared for the invasion of Iraq, as the fight continued in Afghanistan.

The chaos and clutter of his tiny one-room efficiency initially offered a comforting retreat when looking up from the disquieting cover of *The Haunted Wood*, but then quickly struck him as a complete embarrassment—that he might have brought her here—any woman, for that matter—to his slummy man cave. "Thank God . . ." His curiosity to see her place had trumped any other option. A pea green plaid sofa bed, secondhand chairs and tables, and laminated particleboard shelves containing remnants of his physics and cosmology textbooks, journals, art history texts from his intro courses, Dark Matter catalogs. Two walls were hung with strip-framed canvases by his gallery artists—the only distinctive, vaguely inviting touch. Utilitarian was how he justified his savings on rent, the place where he slept when he wasn't at Dark Matter. No better than the five or six dorm rooms he'd occupied at Princeton. Even Cordelia was a better housekeeper. He scrounged a couple of Coronas from the door of the refrigerator and dropped down in a creaking brown vinyl La-Z-Boy (scavenged off the street) across from his single window, offering a view of the upper boughs of the gingkoes, their paisley patterns softly illuminated by the streetlights, a pleasing spiral galaxy of lunar moths.

He put *Perjury* aside for the moment and pondered *The Haunted Wood* in his lap, flipping the pages, first reading the chapter headings and then checking the index for the eight names in the Altmann sketches—the subjects of Altmann's Justice Department mural! All were there: Alger Hiss, Priscilla Hiss, Henry Dexter White, Lauchlin Currie, Noel

Field, Laurence Duggan, Marvin Smith, and William Remington. No mention of Edward Dimock or George Altmann, as if their fates had long ago been consigned to the dustbin of history. No sign, either, in the many photographs, of a match for the unidentified subject of the ninth sketch, the mystery man in suit and tie, hanging up or removing his coat in the mural. Weinstein, with the benefit of over fifty years and a boatload of new data, deployed a plenitude of biographical detail compared to the more intimate, literary pages of Chambers's *Witness* (expanding Chambers's personal account of the Soviet underground in the late 1930s with mind-boggling insights into the vast penetration that occurred during the war and later). Chambers had close dealings only with Alger and Priscilla Hiss and Harry Dexter White (and a few others), the most prominent members of his GRU apparatus. Leafing through Weinstein's pages, returning again and again to the section of black-and-white photographs, George found himself drawn to the potential victims in the Altmann group: especially Duggan, White, and Smith, as if their shared fate offered the best hope of confirming Altmann's fate. Remington, convicted of spying, had been murdered in 1954 (four years after the Hiss trial) by two convicted felons in Lewisburg Federal Penitentiary. Of the four victims in the sketches, given the time frame and circumstances, it was Remington who was the least likely to have been murdered by order of the Soviets. Although, as Weinstein pointed out, Remington had not only admitted passing information to Elizabeth Bentley but had offered the FBI over fifty names of people he accused of either being Communists or fellow travelers. He had been brutally bludgeoned to death on November 24, 1954, just three days before the release of Alger Hiss from the very same prison. "About as clear a warning to Alger Hiss to keep his mouth shut after his release from Lewisburg Federal Penitentiary as one can imagine."

Nevertheless, he settled on the three—White, Duggan, and Smith— the stark, blurry newsprint monochromes of their faces (reminding him, oddly, of indistinct gallery clusters at the edge of the visible universe)—as the crucial keys to the fate of George Altmann. And then there was the book itself: If it hadn't popped up on top of his Google search at the very moment he'd been seated across from the Judge— phone held up to the cosmic narrative of the ship's keel ceiling—things might well have gone a different way.

He saw the author seated hungrily across from the Judge in his chambers. The glinty-eyed smile. Weinstein, the Judge's nemesis, who had indeed mocked his sleazy cross-examination of Chambers in *Perjury*. The diligent historian who'd prompted the Judge to lie and steal the Altmann sketches from the defense files. Who'd gone on, in effect, to save the Judge's life—or pretty damn close. As bizarre a digital lifesaver as might be imagined, as if he'd simply plucked a fact or two out of that vast blue event horizon, a glittering nugget—Order of the Red Star—that changed everything. But that, of course, if the history of science was any guide, was precisely how paradigms shifted and new consensus realities came into being. What seemed serendipitous in the moment was only the slow accumulation of often unseen forces, random fluctuations of particles resulting in new information, new clusters of significant matter, an evolution and winnowing out of the unfit, precipitating a watershed of new data, and so finally altering perception or what amounted to the common wisdom. Memes of change now delivered at the speed of light over the Internet, or slightly slower by Amazon's one-day delivery in New York City.

By tomorrow, the Judge, too, would have his own copies of Weinstein's books. What would that fiercely critical intelligence now find in Weinstein's pages? Hazy fragments of his life transforming before his weary bloodshot eyes? Or confirmation of his worst fears? Exposing his errors of judgment . . . his lies? (His receipt of the Altmann sketches, for starters.) A man who would never lie . . . Or as the Judge had once put it to him: "The trick, George, is never to lie to yourself. Lying to others is hurtful, damaging; sometimes a white lie is acceptable to save the feelings of another. But lying to yourself is emasculating, soul-destroying; it leads to hell, to the concentration camp and the Gulag."

When he looked up again from Weinstein's book to the ghostly gingkoes beyond his window, two hours had passed.

His skepticism was slowly being ground down, or at least rechanneled. They were coming to life for him—especially Laurence Duggan and Harry Dexter White, not so much poor Marvin Smith, who remained a lowly Justice Department attorney, a shadow of a shadow, who seemed to have no afterlife to speak of, either in Weinstein or on Google. Deaths: violent, suspect, ambiguous, unresolved . . . a category likeness to George Altmann's. How the apparatus moves swiftly to deal with deserters.

The tall, dapper, intellectual, and forever anxious Laurence Duggan, head of the State Department's Latin American division and pal of Alger Hiss, had fallen sixteen stories to his death on West Forty-fifth

Street just days before Christmas 1948 (yet another correlation that
caused George to take a deep breath: almost a year to the day of
Altmann's death on Christmas Eve 1949); a Phillips Exeter/Harvard
man, pedigreed, married to an ebullient, ambitious, beautiful blond
woman, and scion of a distinguished family; president, like his father
before him, of the Institute of International Education, from whose
office he'd fallen. By 1948, mostly out of the spy game, as the FBI
closed in, he was terrified of being exposed, and so vulnerable, and so a
threat to talk, to testify: so expendable.

And Harry Dexter White, assistant to the Treasury secretary:
bespectacled round face, brilliant, flighty, mercurial, often careless—
terrified, too, as the Hiss case heated up (resigning abruptly from his
post as first U.S. director of the IMF, an organization he'd been instrumental in creating at the Bretton Woods Conference), of exposure in
the days before his miserable death from an overdose (self-inflicted or
no) of digitalis at his Fitzwilliam, New Hampshire, country home. He
could be supremely self-confident, but when faced with exposure, he
became a quivering, nervous wreck who would surely have collapsed
under intense questioning from government prosecutors in the Hiss
trial. Never a member of the Communist Party, so never under its discipline, but a deft spy who had surrounded himself with a coven of spies
at Treasury, a nest of spies reaching into the White House and State
Department and as far afield as China.

George found his heart racing, his mind's eye returning to the Sawkill
Bridge on Christmas Eve of 1949 . . . again and again: two figures emerging from the shadows on either end of the bridge and coming toward the
slightly tipsy artist huddled against the cold at the center rail.

He began to grasp that Soviet espionage had gone way beyond anything Whittaker Chambers had described from his limited firsthand
experience in the years before he broke with the underground apparatus in 1938. (Weinstein's research from decrypted Soviet cables and
KGB files was impressive.) The real revelation in *Haunted Wood*, though
still tentative, often only hinted at, was how deeply the Soviet spy ring
had influenced American foreign policy during the war and after, how
those invisible hands had succeeded in not just stealing secrets but in
steering so many crucial and fateful decisions that benefited Stalin.
Invisible, even now, with the possible exception of the headline-grab-
bing trial and execution of the Rosenbergs for enabling a network of
Stalin's agents to steal the atom bomb secrets.

The early explosion of a Soviet nuclear bomb—years earlier than the best experts had judged possible—was a fact, verifiable, as was the stealing of secret technology to facilitate that outcome, but influence, the chain of decision making, the human element behind the creation of the postwar world were harder to pin down, beginning with the mis-calculations that led to Pearl Harbor, then the Morgenthau Plan, to the division of Poland, to the forced return—most to their deaths—of millions of Soviet refugees, the Sakhalin Islands to Stalin, along with extra voting rights in the U.N. . . . Mao's triumph . . . the Korean War . . .

Weinstein's account cast a shadow over such issues, even as he deftly tried to stick to the hard facts: There had been over five hundred Soviet agents throughout the government, military, and defense industries. Secrets by the thousands had literally been airlifted back to the Soviet Union as part of the Lend-Lease program orchestrated by Harry Hopkins, White House adviser to FDR. Nevertheless, in George's mind, the Altmann group, as he began to regard them, were clearly at the power center: between Harry Dexter White at Treasury, Laurence Duggan at State, Laughlin Currie in the White House, per-haps spearheaded by Alger Hiss at State, these men had clearly been critical decision makers in Washington, able to do enormous damage, something Whittaker Chambers had darkly hinted at but without the means of proof. Presumably, as Chambers had described the process in the late thirties, Priscilla Hiss had continued in these later years to abet her husband by typing copies of secret State Department documents, to be passed on to their GRU handler and Moscow Center, this while her husband was a guiding hand in postwar policy making.

Lauchlin Currie, Canadian-born economist, tall, acerbic, brilliant, Harvard-trained, close to Harry Dexter White, spent the war years in the innermost circles of the White House, and had been privy to many major decisions shaping the postwar years, working hand in glove with Hiss and White. As the FBI closed in in the late forties, Currie escaped to Colombia, marrying a Colombian and giving up his U.S. passport, never to return. Weinstein's account of Currie's role within the Roosevelt administration was balanced and nuanced, leaving it to the reader's imagination what an agent of Stalin's in such a position of power might have been capable of. For one, assuring that Alger Hiss accompanied FDR to Yalta.

While Noel Field, though clearly spying in the thirties, was out of the picture by the war years and after. On orders from his KGB handlers, Field had left the State Department before the war for a position in Geneva to aid Jewish Communist and antifascist refugees, but so placed to be of potential use to the KGB during the crucial years leading up to war and later—a role that largely never materialized. Nevertheless, Field had intimate knowledge of Hiss's spying during the thirties and possibly later, something Weinstein had laid out in detail from Hungarian intelligence files released after 1989. Fearing kidnapping by the FBI and a forced return to the United States to testify in the Hiss trial, Field fled behind the Iron Curtain to Czechoslovakia, where he was arrested and handed over to the Hungarian secret police, then held incommunicado for years, along with his wife, jailed and tortured, and used as a convenient pawn in Stalin's show trials to destroy Czech and Hungarian Communists who'd fallen afoul of their master. Noel Field and his wife remained loyal to the end, never leaving Eastern Europe. Field died in Hungary in 1970.

Of all the Altmann group members, George felt a certain pang of sympathy for Justice Department attorney Marvin Smith, who fell six flights to his death. Like George Altmann, Smith looked more than ever to be an unlucky bystander—perhaps a onetime Communist but no spy, an innocent victim of the GRU for having signed the transfer document on Hiss's used Ford roadster (a transaction that loomed large in Hiss's conviction). Weinstein made only passing mention of Smith's violent death, a mere footnote quoting his wife, Inez, who had protested to the authorities that her husband could not have committed suicide, that his untimely death had to have been some freak accident. "Marvin would never have left me and our daughter, Jeanne, like that; he clung to us like crazy during the week before he died, like he never wanted to leave home for work in the morning." And in those brief sentiments from a bereaved wife, George caught something of the haunted face of Wendy Bradley reflected in her studio window . . . the children, the endless lifetimes of uncertainty.

White had two daughters, Joan and Ruth. Duggan had one daughter, Stephanie, and three sons, Laurence, Robert, and Christopher. Smith had one daughter, Jeanne.

George Altmann had one son, James Altmann, "Jimmy," "Jimbo." *And* a grandson. At this, and locking stares with George in her studio, Wendy had insisted they revisit the sites of the deaths of Duggan, Smith, and White.

"Forty-fifth Street, the Justice Department, and White's farm in Fitzwilliam, New Hampshire. Places have spirits, you know; they may hold their secrets deep but something always remains."

At first, he'd wondered if she wasn't a little unhinged, but now he detected a curious itch in himself to see this thing through. He was intrigued as well by the passage in *Witness* describing the journey of Chambers and the Hisses to Fitzwilliam, New Hampshire, and White's summer place, which had so attracted the comments of both Annie and the Judge. And the blue underlined sentence where Chambers told how deeply troubled he was by Duggan's fatal fall from his New York office window during the Hiss case, a State Department officer, a spy he'd never met but had often heard the Hisses discussing. Helen, Duggan's wife, had been a beautiful blond, a live wire by all accounts, and eager, too, to do her bit for the Party. Clearly, reading *Witness* had heightened if not confirmed some deep-seated suspicions the Judge had long harbored about the fate of Altmann's subjects.

It was the ninth figure in the Altmann group that somehow gave George chills. The man with the lean, hardened face in the sketch, dressed in a business suit in the mural, in the act of coming or going, hanging or unhanging a coat and slouch hat, leaving or staying, as if his lack of identity only added to the indeterminacy of his belonging to the Volta Place group. Perhaps only a bit player like Marvin Smith, mused George, who only wanted to remain offstage, in the wings, out of harm's way . . . an invisible among invisibles, as if the greater the invisibility, the more portentous the threat, a threat directly proportionate to the phantom's ability to blend in, chameleon-like, to his surroundings, and so lose himself to history.

With Hiss, the exemplar.

Leafing through the pages, George sensed a reluctance on Weinstein's part to spell out the full implications of his scholarship. A man who was born into left-wing circles, where a careless word against the party line made you a pariah, a target, he preferred to let the facts speak for themselves as to the catastrophic harm that might have been done to the country by Stalin's secret agents. Much was left to the footnotes, plenty of dark implications for future scholars to mine. He appeared to be a man very much aware that he must scrupulously maintain a scholarly probity and distance, and not jump to unfounded conclusions. George found this a comfort—the methodology he respected, the comfort therein—even as his dread grew page by page, as every new revelation pointed up the growing necessity for the KGB to protect Hiss—their boy, their bearer of the Order of the Red Star—from exposure, along with the damage inflicted to the benefit of Soviet interests . . . and so the cold-blooded professionalism of those two figures moving in from the shadows along Sawkill Bridge on their Christmas Eve mission . . .

George found himself flipping back time and again to the grainy photos of the Soviet operatives, some passport photos of young and handsome KGB agents in their heyday, others simple snapshots of when they had gathered with Weinstein for late-night drinking sessions in their Moscow apartments only years before, old, grizzled, disheveled men in ill-fitting clothes blowing off steam about their glory days.

If Alger Hiss had indeed been the key player, the linchpin between State, Treasury, and the White House in the giveaway at Yalta, the Soviets would have done everything in their power to protect him, to destroy the weaklings, the waverers, to sideline any loyal but potentially damaging witnesses, to do whatever necessary to conceal the conspiracy at the heart of the American government: the mole, the flickering shadow who presided invisibly in the dazzling reflection of his prestige and patriotic ardor, right at the very pinnacle of the establishment ranks—*Harvard Law Review*, assistant to an assistant secretary at State, president of the Carnegie Endowment for International Peace, the man who sat at Roosevelt's right hand at Yalta, whose wife lunched with Eleanor Roosevelt.

George felt a cold pressure in his chest as he recalled the folder of Priscilla Hiss's letters in the Judge's file cabinet, some quoted in the memoir . . . almost as if daring his grandson—or anyone, for that matter—to take them at more than face value. The Judge's college sweetheart and lover, a woman who had turned to him to get herself out of scrapes, to get her husband out of an all-time scrape, but who, in the end, had remained loyal to her lights, silent, even as her husband dumped her for another woman, a younger energetic woman who, along with their son, would champion his cause for redemption.

Another son, another child, Tony Hiss, who would spend a lifetime defending all the contradictions of his father's controversial life.

George couldn't help feeling sorry for Priscilla Hiss, a woman whose vital energy had drawn to her lovers of many stripes: Edward Dimock, Alger Hiss, even George Altmann, if his sketch of her was any proof. Even Whittaker Chambers and his wife had found in Priscilla a sensitive soul, committed to doing good even if for the worst of causes.

Again and again, George found his mind returning to the cork-board in the Judge's office, that bizarre contraption of sketches, note cards, grainy photos, fragile clippings, and red stick pins. The old man, too, had been struggling to grapple with Weinstein's phantoms, trying to visualize their linkages, that neural network of human beings, now reduced to finely limned portrait heads seated in a circle, tantalizingly camouflaged in the Justice Department mural.

"Weinstein," George said aloud to himself, as if to savor the sound of that name, that scholarly persona on the back jacket flap, whose large intelligent eyes stared out at him from behind wire-rimmed glasses (as they had once done at the Judge). And now he was enthroned behind a broad desk in his office at the National Archives. Again he flipped the pages at the back of the book, buttressed, too, by thousands of footnotes from KGB files, deciphered Soviet cables, and interviews with octogenarian Russian intelligence officers still bursting with rheumatic pride at their penetration of the Roosevelt administration. He weighed the book in his hands, the substance, the weight of scholarship, a welcome ballast in stormy seas. A potential ally.

Once again his fingers flipped to the photos of seedy-looking spies and even seedier Soviet operatives from the forties; and later photos from 1996, where the balding, bespectacled author and scholar sat with the ancient revenants in the KGB's retirement home in Moscow (those lucky few who had survived the purges and the Gulag), discussing old times, how they had literally run rings around the inexperienced FBI. He looked at the photos of the white-haired ex-KGB agents sitting with Weinstein, glasses of vodka clutched in shaking fingers, cigarettes dangling from lips. George bent closer to the glossy black-and-whites, peering through the smoky haze. Had any of them ordered the hit on George Altmann, a pesky flea to be crushed out of existence? Or had any known of the order, or suspected such?

He rubbed at his tired eyes, watching where the gingkoes ominously stirred.

Then he reached into his backpack and extracted the Judge's typescript, bringing the pages to his nose, smelling the yellowed paper, the scent of mold and dust and pine . . . and time . . . scent of betrayal. Was its value, now, as a historical document composed when all—or at least most—of the facts hung fire, when the thing was still in doubt? Perhaps its main value was the doubt, it occurred to him, in the ache of an unrequited curiosity, or perhaps a whiff of self-justification, if not betrayal and guilt, that floated up from the pages and made the account so compelling: how a traitor at the very heart of the establishment had, so effortlessly, betrayed not just one man but his country and his class. And, too, like Chambers's *Witness*, it contained firsthand accounts of Alger Hiss as yet untainted by the certainty of his perfidy, a young idealistic man, head bowed in supplication to the young Harvard heroes in Memorial Hall, outraged at the treatment of Negroes in the South, the Alger Hiss who had blithely and proudly walked the corridors of power, going about his espionage, as if above suspicion, aghast and incensed that anyone would have the gall to doubt his bona fides, attested to by the best and brightest America had to offer. Even after his conviction, half the country, for almost half a century, still believed him! George just shook his head at the wonder of it: that alternative life, that parallel universe, where there remained such a deep need for the public Alger Hiss to remain forever untarnished and respected, loved, even revered as one of the finest America had to offer.

How had one man orchestrated such a thing?

And with that question hanging fire, George drew closer to the agony, now a shared agony—how the Judge had struggled with his Iago: how such opposites could coexist in one man? Such menace with humanity? And, as through a glass darkly, George began to sense in the Judge's pages a plea, not so much to history, but to his family, especially his wife, Annie, his conscience, and to the man who had brought them together, Oliver Wendell Holmes.

He looked up, as if his heart had skipped a beat, only to see the Judge and Annie lying there in the August darkness as she offered him one chance, one last chance in a thousand, given her age, the miracle that had given Cordelia and her son life, a loveless coupling that, so he now realized for the first time, had been presided over by Alger Hiss.

Why else, how else, would the Judge have included such a private moment, such a devastating moment in a public record?

Except to inveigle his progeny? Or to lay claim to that progeny?

That flicker of doubt brought George close to exhaustion, he found the e-mail address for the office of the director of the National Archives and sent the e-mail he knew he was bound to write. Evidence, yes, he had evidence; he had gold that any scholar worth his salt would kill for.

Allen Weinstein had been an adviser to Boris Yeltsin, and with his contacts in the old-boy KGB network had unparalleled access to any number of faltering if self-serving memories. Something, of course, no ex-agent would want to admit to but which, in veiled terms, might possibly be confirmed or denied: that such an execution, an artful death, might well have been arranged. He turned to the back flap and again examined the photo of the author: widow's peak, glasses agleam, intent laser-focused eyes, scholarly dishevelment. This man had also written the definitive account of the Hiss-Chambers trial, *Perjury*, a task he had initially taken on with the blessing of Hiss himself, when Weinstein had believed wholeheartedly in Hiss's innocence, until the facts led him elsewhere. Upholding a conviction for lying about events that had taken place over ten years before the trial, in the late thirties. When the real damage . . .

"Never lie to yourself . . . live in truth."

He heard the Judge's voice in his own, and yet how strange that always such admonitions had been attributed to his wife, Annie, as if it was she he looked to, to whose sovereign love and grace he bowed . . . for absolution.

A man who had lost faith in his own probity.

George took out the Altmann courtroom sketch that had been secreted in Alice's copy of Weinstein's *Perjury*. He held it up to the light, admiring both the hand of the artist and the subject, the young Judge seated at the defense table in December of 1949, that lovely jaw and dimple set for combat, the burning righteousness ablaze in the eyes, a lock of dark hair like an accent above the compressed brows, a man then at the first peak of his power and prestige, not unlike his client on trial for perjury. The sketch, like a mystical palimpsest combining the essence of both men, the artist and the lawyer, and the vague consanguinity of the beholder's bloodline.

The man who would become the Judge, still bathed and fortified in Annie's love, before their word crumbled in guilt and blame.

"I am a Jedi, like my father before me."

George shouted this youthful idiocy a few more times, using various voices and characters to break the silence, the echo chamber of his brain, to force a smile, to put himself in touch with some earlier version of himself, when the Judge was still a vigorous and utterly intimidating figure of righteous authority, of a world—a more ordered past invulnerable to lies and creeping chaos. Like a young, naïve Luke Skywalker who, having gone in pursuit of one truth, instead found another, a truth much more dangerous to one's peace of mind, if not sanity.

Frustrated, exhausted, he grabbed his last Corona and opened his window for some fresh air. He was met with the not so fresh stink of the gingkoes. Every fall, for a few weeks, the female trees bore fruit coated in butyric acid. Dropping onto the sidewalk and street, crushed under vehicle and foot traffic, the fruit gave off an odor of rot, and worse, as if someone had vomited on the pavement. It didn't seem as bad this year as in the past; perhaps the chilly night had something to do with it. In the distance he could hear the gathering storm as the trash trucks prepared to assault Fourteenth Street, counterpoint to the more distant hum of traffic on Third Avenue. He was struck by a sensation he couldn't quite decipher: of displacement and unease, reminiscent again of his grad student days as he obsessively pored over the first data from the Hubble telescope, looking for telltale patterns, for something overlooked or never seen before by the eyes of man.

"Priscilla Hiss. What would Weinstein do for those letters?"

———

Minutes later, standing in front of his bathroom mirror, waiting for the hot water in his shower, he stared at himself, at his shock of sandy hair, the slate blue eyes reddened at the corners, weary, anxious . . . befuddled. He scowled at the more than perceptible sag of his gut, his unshaven genitals—when was the last time he'd even had sex? He could have been a full professor. Donald Spier, his doctoral adviser, had dangled as much: "George: best facilities to do the research, first access to new data, financial security—well, decent money—harnessing your passion to curiosity, access to the best grad students—what more could any scientist want out of life?" Instead, here he was, in his early thirties, trying desperately to keep afloat a second-rate gallery by promoting the art and life of a dead white male artist—in theory, his own bloodline— by way of Jimmy Altmann, who, frankly, made him sick.

He opened his bathroom cabinet, looking for some shaving cream and a new razor, only to be met with a skirmish line of expired prescriptions: Xanax, Klonopin, Ambien, Zoloft—the usual suspects, antidepressants prescribed by his aunt Martha. Even Martha, who had gone to seed, had counseled him after his Princeton breakdown to go to the gym regularly and exercise to reduce anxiety. He'd given up his gym membership at the Princeton Club for economy's sake. Penny wise, pound foolish. He closed the cabinet door and turned his mind to the nude photo of Wendy now secreted on his laptop, and the lush, sensuous paintings. Smiling, he stepped into the shower at full mast.

"Soap-a-dope."

Later, lying in bed waiting for sleep, he picked up a pad and wrote out an equation, and then another, settling for one of his favorites, Einstein's field equation:

$$R_{\mu\nu} - \frac{1}{2} R g_{\mu\nu} + \Lambda g_{\mu\nu} = \frac{8\pi G}{c^4} T_{\mu\nu}$$

How elegant, how simple, how intellectually and emotionally appealing. And yet even Einstein had realized his mistake, his misbegotten hope for a static universe, instead of a chaotic, expanding, dynamic—where shit happens—universe—accelerating forever. Even Einstein preferred a universe where God did not play dice. Even Einstein . . .

He sighed, somewhat resigned, as his cell lit up. For the next few minutes, he and Wendy texted back and forth.

Can't sleep.

Not to worry, our spiral Milky Way not scheduled to impact Andromeda for ten billion years.

I miss you!

You miss George Altmann.

Him, too. I can't wait to get my paintings.
Except I can't sleep with them.

Order on Amazon: Weinstein, The Haunted Wood, and Whittaker Chambers, Witness. Read. Then we need to confer.

Okay, but conference must be scheduled at my gym, Chelsea Piers. How about starting tomorrow after work? Bring workout stuff. I'll send you a link for the proper climbing boots you need to buy. Get in

*training for the long haul. And you'll bring a Xerox
of the memoir—right?*

As discussed.

*Did you really like
the work?*

☺

*Did you keep the nude
photo of me, you sly dog?*

I deleted it from my phone.

Liar.

I never lie.

*Shall I send you another
in real time?*

Don't tempt me.

23
A Life in the Law and Out:
Clerkship with Oliver Wendell Holmes

PERHAPS THE MOST perplexing aspect of my relationship with Alger Hiss was how it affected not just my relationship with my wife, Annie, but with Oliver Wendell Holmes; or more precisely, how Alger's dealings with Holmes has retroactively tarnished, if not distorted, my most cherished memories of the man who changed my life more profoundly than any other. The man who introduced me to my helpmeet, the love of my life: a wife of impossible standards. For much to my chagrin, Alger had preceded me by one year in that cherished clerkship with Holmes. A fact, of no great moment at the time, but which begins to waver and alter as I reflect, as I find myself plagued by doubt: if that Alger was already the Alger who would later be put on trial for treason, or the earlier, more innocent version I had first met in Memorial Hall—and only now reclaimed. A meeting so innocuous, so unmemorable in its way, that I'd entirely put it out of my mind. As was the case with Alger's designs on Holmes, which slipped by me at the time like a sail over the horizon. Posing the question, was the invisibility, the process of change, the malleability of human nature—in other words, Alger's perfidy—a singular and extraordinary event, or did it have more to do with how the country changed in those years, and how that alteration in climate, that rising fog of distemper, if you will, allowed Alger to shift and reshape himself and so effortlessly hide behind that pasteboard mask, remolding his features so successfully that his invisible cloak of deception became the very symbol and innocuous byword of his treacherous trade—and our generation? But even the stealthiest of hunters leaves footprints in the blowing whiteness, the same snowy wastes that dazzle as I struggle with decrepit memory, blinking, squinting, as I only now espy that circuitous trail of deceit from my crow's nest above the lake's icy pallor.

—

Washington in October of 1930 was a sad and scared town. And I call it a town because, to me, it seemed like a village compared to New York. Quaint, slow, southern, damp and humid, shell-shocked by the Depression. Things would not change until the election of Franklin Roosevelt in 1932 and then the arrival of his hordes of New Dealers the following year, with Alger and Priscilla Hiss on their heels soon after. That dark, rainy fall when I arrived to clerk for Justice Holmes, the Hoover administration was desperately trying to dig out from an economic mud slide. The White House and Treasury were searching for ways to save the banks upon which the lifeblood of the economy depended. I had had a good secure job offer coming out of Harvard Law with Parker-Stewart in New York, which was doing a bumper business in bankruptcies and salvaging companies with reorganizations. But a recommendation from Felix Frankfurter to serve as secretary to Holmes was not something to be lightly turned down. Holmes had been my god since boyhood, when my father had regaled me with stories of his exploits in the Civil War and then the courts. The justice had been a Harvard classmate and close friend of Dr. Dimock, who had attended the wounded Holmes after the battle of Antietam. I am particularly proud of the fact that the position was offered me without the connection to my father being a factor, although Holmes must have certainly registered my name when Frankfurter made the recommendation. I did have one reservation, or perhaps incentive: Alger Hiss had served as secretary the year before me, something I suppose I vaguely resented while finding myself not a little intrigued. No question Alger was more than capable, but I never got over the feeling that, somehow, Alger had hoodwinked me—that I had put the idea of clerking for Holmes in Alger's head even as the specifics of our first meeting in Memorial Hall the fall of 1927 had been conflated with editorial meetings of the *Law Review* and such. In effect, he had smiled and chatted me up while courting Priscilla Fansler and stolen my birthright—or that, I fear, is how it had first seemed to me then.

In fact, it had already gone well beyond that. I knew all about Alger's clerkship with Holmes from Priscilla, whom he'd married while still on the job. Priscilla had boasted of their ruse to me—of all people, how she had forced Alger's hand on the marriage date. It was clearly stipulated in the job description that Holmes wanted his secretaries to be unmarried

because the position required prodigious hours and the full attention of
the clerk to his duties. But once Priscilla had her abortion and broke
with the cad who had gotten her pregnant, she wouldn't wait, and Alger
rightly feared she'd walk out on him—"strike three," as she put it to me in
a rare moment of candor—if he didn't give in on the precipitous date. A
woman with a young child from her first failed marriage has no time to
waste. So Alger only told Holmes the day before they were to be married,
thus confronting "the old badger" with a fait accompli in the middle of
Alger's clerkship, when he'd be hard to replace on short notice. Of course,
both to Holmes and to me, Alger pretended not to have known—or
forgotten—about the bachelor provision in the terms of employment.
Alger and Priscilla laughed about it for years to come, mocking the
antediluvian Holmes at parties, even after his death. But Holmes never
forgot, not so much because of the deception and excuses, but because of
his deep affection for Alger, even admiration, which made the betrayal
all the more perplexing—especially to such an astute judge of his own
character and others, who harrowed the souls of those closest to him.
On these touchy issues, I remained mum, never revealing to Holmes
Priscilla's confidences, or the complete truth of their deception—dare I
say, precisely the kind of deception that would later become the very core
of their marriage alliance.

When I arrived at Holmes's residence on 1720 Eye Street that
October, I was conducted upstairs to his book-cluttered study, where he
did all his research and writing. The old lion glowered in his den, by then
in his late eighties and ailing. A prostate operation had left him enfeebled;
he had a hacking cough and asthma—as had his father, the great aphorist and poet Dr. Holmes (yet another tie to my father, who had studied
under Holmes senior at Harvard Medical School). Sadly, his beloved
wife, Fanny, had died the year before after falling in the tub and breaking
a hip. His mind was all there, razor-sharp, witty, acerbic, and up-to-date,
but his capacity for work was not what it had been, although his ability
to turn out decisions—or turn a phrase, dissents or opinions—was rapid
as ever: laconic and crystal clear in logic and expression. His judgments
were always convincing, no matter where one stood on the issue. When
I sat down that first day before his expansive mahogany desk and he
peered at me through thick spectacles, with his white walrus mustache
and even whiter windblown hair, I felt I was being scrutinized by a
living legend, an embodiment of granite-ribbed New England. Here
was a man, now a bit fleshy and heavy, who had been wounded three

times in the war against slavery, who had discussed philosophy with Emerson sixty years before, whose father had been an eminent physician and man of letters, who had planted his battle flag in defense of the Constitution and the Bill of Rights—our foremost champion of free speech. A freedom fighter writ in the bone. And what were the first words out of his mouth?

"Edward, I presume you are not married, nor intend to get married within the next year."

"No sir. There was a woman quite a ways back, but no more."

He surveyed my face, my body—perhaps a trait from his physician father—for telltale deformities or ticks.

"*Law Review*, handsome position on offer with Parker-Stewart, as the British like to say . . . no woman waiting in the wings?"

"No woman who will have me, at least for a year."

(Of course, I knew exactly what this inquisition was all about.)

"I'm not suggesting celibacy, mind you. Serve me well and I will provide you with an excellent woman next summer at Beverly Farms. The least I can do for your beloved father." He flicked his screech owl-like tufted eyebrows with a twinkle in his rheumy eyes. "Now, tell me about your father. I owe him my life you know. Without his intervention at a dressing station just thirty miles north of here—well, we wouldn't be having this conversation."

(Only later did I realize that this reference was to the battle of Ball's Bluff on the banks of the Potomac, not Antietam. It turned out that my father had run across his classmate in a battlefield medical station not once but twice, saving his life in both instances. A coincidence that further bonded us, as if destiny had anointed my eager brow.)

"And we wouldn't have your marvelous dissent in *Abrams v. United States.*"

"Ah, I see the progressive forces have overrun even the most stalwart bastions of the Harvard Law School . . . and so the world crumbles. Fortunately, I've got everything in railroad bonds. As you will soon see when we make an excursion down to Riggs for a little clipping ceremony."

I proceeded to dutifully quote a key passage of *Abrams v. United States.*

"'But when men have realized that time has upset many fighting faiths, they may come to believe even more than they believe the very foundations of their own conduct that the ultimate good desired is better reached by the free trade in ideas—that the best test of truth is the power of the thought to get itself accepted in the competition of the market, and that truth is the only ground upon which their wishes safely can be carried out. That at any rate is the theory of our Constitution. It is an experiment, as all life is an experiment. Every year, if not every day, we have to wager our salvation upon some prophecy based upon imperfect knowledge. While that experiment is part of our system I think that we should be eternally vigilant against attempts to check the expression of opinions that we loathe and believe to be fraught with death, unless they so imminently threaten immediate interference with the lawful and pressing purposes of the law that an immediate check is required to save the country.'"

Holmes looked at me and smiled; I think he was chagrined by my youthful ardor.

"I see you are much in the progressive camp of your predecessor, Mr. Hiss."

"Ah, I think that depends, sir, to the degree he would agree to let the experiment run its course in safety, much less if the marketplace of ideas was to be left unhindered as the sole arbiter of our liberty."

"Are you implying he is a socialist?"

"Perhaps no more than most in the younger set today, after the crash."

"And you, Mr. Dimock?"

"I believe in evolution within the boundaries of the Constitution while defending it at all costs . . . if and when it comes to that."

"Does the country need saving now?"

"I think we need to remain vigilant. I think Alger and Priscilla contemplate a return to Washington and government, along with most of the smartest Harvard men I know."

"So, you have taken this position as bodyguard?"

"It is my honor and privilege to do so."

I cringe now at the catty, if not unkind, nature of my retort, perhaps due to jealousy more than any real concern about Alger's patriotism at that early date. Of the two, it was Priscilla who wore her socialism on her sleeve. And yet, the irony does not escape me: Twenty-four years later, Congress passed the Communist Control Act of 1954, which outlawed the Communist Party and banned avowed Communists from serving in certain influential capacities. This along with various loyalty oaths were the direct outcome of my failure to defend Alger Hiss in 1950. These anti-Communist provisions I would have to grapple with as a judge, with Justice Holmes's opinions always on my mind. To this day, I wonder how Holmes would have ruled, if, indeed, he would have found the Communist menace a clear and present danger, as in his marvelous 1919 dissent. And whether, even then, in 1930, I had detected something dangerous in Alger's nature, or, for that matter, Priscilla's, even as we shared so many of the same hopes for our country.

———

Over that year, Holmes and I became close. In some respects, he was the father I might have wished for, and I was the sort of son who might have given him some satisfaction in terms of progeny following in his footsteps as a jurist. (He and Fanny had been childless, something of a mystery, since everyone in his circle knew he was a ladies' man.) Nothing was ever said along these lines, but the affection was surely there as I helped him with the mundane necessities of reviewing *certiorari* petitions and correspondence. I summarized briefs for him, mostly verbally, not that he didn't check my work thoroughly to make sure I'd gotten things right. Of course, I knew only too well that Alger was a hard act to follow. Not that Holmes made direct comparisons, but I thought I could detect at times a querulous look in his eye, his voice, as if harking back to the way my predecessor had done things. Alger was always on his mind.

During that dark year of the Hoover administration, I occasionally returned to Boston to see friends and would run into Alger and Priscilla. He had a well-paying position at Choate, Hall & Stewart, but seemed intent on returning to Washington as soon as possible. He seemed excited at the prospect: how they were going to change the world, turn the country around, and solve the unemployment problem while addressing Negro rights. Or as I remember his words: "Destroy the decrepit social structures of mismanagement and greed." He was doing pro bono work for something called the International Juridical Association, specializing in agricultural issues and defending the rights of farmers. My sense was that Priscilla was more eager than even he to "do something—anything—to change this rotten country." I'd never seen her so excited; her cheeks were flushed with agitation when we chatted rapid-fire about future prospects in Washington. We barely mentioned Holmes, except in ironic asides, as if my work for the justice was more of an embarrassment than an accolade. I detected a subtle shift in Alger's tone, from his once high regard to a not so subtle rejection of Holmes's ancient prejudices, which favored the wealthy and capitalism's slave drivers. (Not that in later years he wouldn't often boast of his time with Holmes to polish up his bona fides.) The implication being that he and Priscilla were the team of the future, forging a new tomorrow. But the subtext was that I had lost out, both in the race for her hand and the future's brass ring.

"Does he have you read to him in the evenings?" Alger once asked me as I headed for the train back to Washington. "It took some doing on my part, you know, to talk him into it, in hopes I might be able to slip in some more progressive viewpoints."

———

I find myself struggling as I look back to identify the inflection point, as Washington began swelling with bright exquisitely educated young people intent on throwing over the old order and saving the country from more Hoovervilles. Was it just Alger and Priscilla or the times that swept us along like a flash flood? I was certainly with them in spirit. Who at a young age is not moved by such energy and idealism and commitment to overthrow a moribund and unjust system? One could feel that energy, like the sex drive, like a good binge. And Washington was so compact in those days, at least for a while longer, before the New Deal, before the war turned it into a company town, that we all breathed the same heavenly elixir of youthful hope. Everything was in walking distance from our outpost on Seventeenth and Eye Street: the Supreme Court, still in the Capitol Building just off the rotunda, the White House and Treasury and the old State Department building—cheek by jowl, all within a ten-minute walk. One knew or met nearly everyone of interest either over lunch or at evening receptions and dinners. And yet I found myself uneasy and eager to leave Washington, eager for my summer sojourn with Holmes at Beverly Farms. There was something slightly frivolous and careless about the new people; for all their enthusiasm, they harbored a disdain for the limitations on government power provided in the Constitution—a power they sought, instead, for themselves.

Something Holmes, too, seemed to increasingly recognize as our year together drew to a close, when he took moments from our work to reflect.

"You know, Edward, the Constitution enshrines the separation of church and state, and yet these new people, if I didn't know better, want to turn the state into their church: They want to rule *for* the people. What do you think?"

"Something like heaven—their heaven at least—on earth."

"What kind of heaven would that be, do you suppose?"

"I suppose the sort Mr. Stalin has got going over in Russia."

"Well, sir, we had our revolution, too, and then we wrote the rules to govern ourselves, and a Bill of Rights to boot. Tell me, sonny, of all the rights enshrined in those first ten amendments to the Constitution, what was the paramount concern of that founding generation?"

"Freedom of speech, I suppose, or protection against unreasonable searches."

"I can recite them to you, and clearly my memory is better than yours. It was the right to a trial by a jury of their peers, or to be indicted only by a grand jury. The reason, sonny boy . . . because, first and foremost, they didn't want a despotic king or his government officials having control over their lives, their property and livelihoods. They knew of what they wrote, and Stalin's heaven would be a hell on earth for any true American soul."

"It would certainly take a fair amount of wrecking to get us there."

"Will they, the new people, wreck us, Mr. Dimock?"

Although I feared that might come to pass, I couldn't yet answer that question.

—

Then in June of 1931, with the Supreme Court's adjournment, we moved operations to Holmes's summer residence in Beverly Farms, Massachusetts. Those glorious summer days serving Holmes never leave me, even if I was nurtured—my primal love—on the woods and lakes of the Catskills. It had been a busy year and the four-month court adjournment proved no less busy in many respects, especially as the logistics of moving paperwork between the post office and the house was very time-consuming. Most of my day was spent processing *certiorari* petitions from the lower courts. I would often read them to Holmes or provide outline reviews for him to evaluate and then return the petitions to the post office for mailing to Washington. But with the warm days, the blue of the sea and the smell of the earth, Holmes, especially toward evening, became more expansive and philosophical. That was the time reserved for my reading to him from books of history and literature on his porch. He joked, often inquiring if I was in the mood to "improve my mind" or if I would rather have at a murder mystery. As much as I missed Hermitage that summer, I was charmed by the intellectual beehive within the walls of those steep-pitched gabled roofs and brick chimneys set amid a scattering of pines and granite outcroppings. And always there was the scent of brine and sea wrack wafting in on the evening breeze, that and the ripeness of wisteria and honeysuckle and hydrangea. And the fusty closeness of an overstuffed Victorian interior, of dark mahogany backbreakers and curio cabinets packed tight with books, law journals, and the professional mementos of life in the law, and days soldiering with comrades in the Twentieth Massachusetts. His walls and desk were layered with sepia photos of Grand Army reunions, of rigid young men in blue uniforms, long dead on the battlefields of the South. And the signed volumes of Emerson, Longfellow, Hawthorne, Thoreau, Prescott, and Motley, and, of course, those of his father, Oliver Wendell Holmes Sr. A feast for mind and soul. Between the man and his home, one felt in privileged proximity to the wellsprings of what had once made our nation great, the strength we drew upon from the white heat of revolution, and the comfort of home fires around which the glorious past might take wing. What a mind and heart that feeble frame still contained, what a noble brow, beneath which his steely gray eyes watched you with infinite curiosity—still watch, as I realize, to my horror, as I write: I am now the same age as he was then.

"You read well, Edward. I can hear your father's voice and intonation, a New England nasal cadence, which is pleasant to my ear. A damn sight better on the ear than the stentorian phrasing of your former colleague, Mr. Hiss. Do you still keep up with our Mr. Hiss?"

I was surprised, and not that the question came up so directly. Even though I'd heard relatively little about my competitor, I'd detected a level of curiosity about Alger than went beyond purely professional matters.

"I believe they are planning to move down to Washington in the future."

"You know, he married, quite abruptly, in the middle of his term of employment with me."

"It seemed quite sudden."

"Did you know the girl?"

"Priscilla? Yes, sir, I knew her."

"Ah, you must know something I don't—how delicious."

"Something?"

"Was she pregnant, a condition that precipitated the hasty nuptials?"

"She already had a child by a first marriage."

"Yes . . ."

"And there had been a second pregnancy, but not Alger's child."

"Another child?"

"No."

"Oh my goodness, not yours?"

"If it was, the outcome might have been very different."

"Oh, this gets more delightful by the moment—if you don't mind my pressing you for the facts."

"I knew Priscilla years ago, when I was at Yale, and still living with Dr. Dimock in New York. He had a duplex on Fifth Avenue."

"Tell me about her—my rival for Alger's duty and attention."

"Very attractive, red hair, slim, a lot of nervous energy, intelligence like the snap of a whip, literary and academic, with a strong social conscience."

"Did you want to marry her?"

"I doubt she would have had me."

"What, with your background and good breeding? You'll make a fortune in the law if you go that route. Certainly the right kind of husband for a woman with a child to support."

"That was just it; there was a bit of a romantic brazenness in her, of careless desires for the infinitely good and improbable."

"You mean even for an idealist like yourself?"

"My father always taught me to look for the practical solution."

"I remember only too well how we both got caught up in the bloody results of the impractical, the abolitionist cause."

"Some say he was the best surgeon of his generation."

"Well, he, thanks to the abolitionists, got the experience of a lifetime compressed into a few years. To my benefit, mind you. They didn't expect me to live, but he failed to follow the orders of the attending surgeon."

(This again was at Ball's Bluff where Holmes had been set aside in the medical clearing station with the hopeless cases, and my father, recognizing his friend, had treated his chest wound, whereupon he had made a miraculous recovery.)

Beyond the porch where we sat, the sunset was amber and bronze in the highest boughs of the surrounding pines, the air redolent of the shore at low tide and smoke from his pipe.

"But tell me more about this Priscilla—you like 'em strong-willed and romantic, heh?"

"I had the impression, wrongly, that her first marriage and divorce, and son, had tempered her romantic enthusiasms. Not enough to prevent her from falling again for the wrong man, a married man, who reneged on his promises to her when his own wife became pregnant. She seemed sometimes desperate, and then with the slump, she may have been more eager for permanent support."

"So, gallant Alger steps in on the spur of the moment to save the lady in distress."

"I believe it was far from the first time that he'd offered."

"How well did you know him at Harvard Law?"

It was then that I realized that Alger had been an invisible intermediary between us since I'd first come on board—that he'd probably sat in my very chair only the summer before; it was all in the tone of the justice's inquiry, like that of a jilted lover. Something had moved him about Alger and it bothered him.

"I knew him—barely. A year ahead of me on the *Law Review*. We shared classes at a distance, nothing more."

"Did you find our Alger, well, sympathetic in such an academic setting?"

"I think of him as more of an art and literary man—a bird-watcher, an interest we shared in those halcyon days during the boom after the war. I don't think anyone at the law school, even in his class, knew him intimately, but all had the utmost respect for his intelligence, industriousness, and dedication to the law. The progressive spirit, so to speak, saw much of its fervor reflected in Alger's humanity. On the *Law Review*, I thought he displayed a razor-sharp intellect and a compassion for the subjects of the cases in question. I was impressed with that: his genuine desire to improve the common lot. That was something I think we shared, something I admired in my father. My father did a lot of pro bono doctoring, spending many days in the summer attending to the poor boatmen on the Delaware and Hudson canal, their wives and children. He was scandalized by the low wages, how the company exploited their labor. No matter how much he complained to his cronies at the Harvard Club, the company would do nothing—of course, it was soon out of business anyway."

"So you and Alger are both do-gooders."

"That the law might shape our better instincts, build a flyway for our better angels."

"All the way to hell and back: saving your souls while saving the world."

The cynicism and even despair in his voice shook me.

"Sir, did not Alger want to save you, as well?"

"I was already saved, not once, but twice. Your father saw to that. But those of us who have passed through hell's door and back will never be the same. And Alger always struck me as a special case. Perhaps I neglected to mention it, but the reading"—he waved his hand toward where I sat with open book in my lap, a gesture of intimacy—"the private reading, unofficial and off the books, so to speak—and filling in my Black Book for me, that was all Alger's idea. After Fanny died, I was truly down on my luck in that regard. She had the loveliest mellifluous voice. No one else would do with my tired eyes. Alger was very sneaky about it, the way he got me around to his plan of having him read to me. He went behind my back, you see, mentioned it to a friend of mine, the English ambassador, and had him come by and tell me how much he enjoyed having his assistant read to him in the evening—to save his eyes after a long day."

"Hardly a federal offense."

"Ah, but you see, it was the son who read to the ambassador, not an aide or assistant. Reading aloud is a very private and intimate affair."

"Well, I, for one, am delighted to do it, that I can be of service. I consider it an honor."

"Well, you're off the hook, since you did not employ a ruse to turn this old dog to new tricks."

"Alger likes to help people; it's a very generous disposition. Hard to hold anything against a man like that."

"A con is still a con, even if one employs affection for a good end."

"He knows a thing or two about endearment."

"Even if he took Priscilla away from you?"

"I think it was more riding to her rescue at an opportune moment."

"And marrying in the middle of his term of employment—when he knew damn well what was expected. All part of his plan to have me thoroughly buttered up so that I wouldn't fire him on the spot. Any other, I would have thrown out on his ear, but, in truth, he had thoroughly worked his way into my affections, even if his reading voice was not as good as yours or Fanny's. There is an iron discipline in our Alger." Holmes let out a geyser of smoke and waited for it to clear the space between us. "His helpful kindness and amiability has barbs set."

"Priscilla once told me she considered Alger's family a shabby mess, run-down Baltimore, gentility gone to seed."

"Goodness, I thought . . . And yet she married him?"

"This was years ago. I think Alger admitted much to her that he kept from others. She told me his father, a grocer, had killed himself when Alger was two. His married sister, Mary, killed herself by drinking a bottle of Lysol when we were at Harvard Law. And his brother, Bosley, died of some disease—Bright's disease, I think Priscilla told me."

"She told you so much? Good Lord, that is much to confide, much less for any man to bear. I had no idea—no idea at all."

"She said he was really a saint."

"A martyr, taking her on and her child—as you said, saving them."

"And, I fear, I'm no saint."

Holmes's face went into eclipse for a moment as he turned to the fading light through the pines, his lips pinched below his flowing white whiskers, his gaze showing hints of troubled doubt, if not credulous wonder.

"He thoroughly charmed me with his good graces, probity, and airs of fine breeding, as my father would have called it. One doesn't quite know whether to be admiring or a little frightened of the disciplined will required to maintain the illusion of such—how to describe it?—an untroubled soul."

"Enough to have finally overcome any lingering doubts in Priscilla."

"Poor you. Was it desperation, do you think, or did they offer each other—what?—your romantic dream, a secret alliance, between the sheets or otherwise."

"Perhaps a kind of compassion for the world of which I'm not capable."

"Sonny, the world needs competency, not compassion. Men like your father who could save lives—not take them . . . for some absurd cause."

"To end slavery?"

"Certitude leads only to violence; the cause that fires a man's soul can just as easily be turned to disaster and the crucifixion of the unbelievers."

"Surely, sir, you do not regret the abolitionist cause for which you fought and came so close to paying the ultimate price?"

"I saw my best friends quite literally disintegrate before my eyes, hideously so. It leaves a raw distaste for do-gooders of all kinds. Spenser had it about right: Life is a battle"—he gestured between us, as if signifying the intimacy of a professional camaraderie—"and it is our job to keep the contestants from wrecking everything. They who seek great changes are despots at heart. I don't care to boss my neighbors and to require them to want something different from what they do—even when, as frequently is the case, I think their wishes more or less suicidal. If I learned anything from Mr. Emerson, it was an innate skepticism: a thing that might keep more men alive if it was universally applied. A little bit of doubt and skepticism goes a long way."

"As you have upheld the First Amendment rights of numerous socialist organizations, unions, anarchists, groups who opposed the last war, who would change everything if given the chance. And who knows, bomb throwers among them!"

"It's their right to spout poppycock, to seek advantage for their people—it is just human nature to pursue one's advantage as we ride the wave of change. Experiment away, better that than killing millions for your cause. Look at you: strong, fit, idealistic, and as competent as any law clerk I've had the pleasure to have work for me—almost as much as our Mr. Hiss." He smiled and shot his brows. "His determination to have his way with an old man like me was quite breathtaking. In the race of life, he will go far."

"He *and* Priscilla . . ."

"Be glad you are not yet weighed down with responsibilities. A wife is one thing, a child, but another man's child is quite something else. You are lucky to have been born between wars. The world of my youth, when our hearts were touched with fire, is now a desolate place to which I can never return, where Emerson and my father were the firebrands to my spirit. I recommended Emerson to our Mr. Hiss, but he never took me up on it. I even had him reread some of Emerson's finest essays to me, and I could hear it in his voice that the transcendentalist spirit had no place in his heart."

"Shabby Baltimore."

"Ah, so you *are* jealous of our Alger?"

"I think I marvel at his determination to tame or be tamed."

"Aha . . ." He laughed heartily. "Remember, competency is plenty enough to get you through. With all the idealism, commitment, and artistic prowess of our generation, we still couldn't prevent a terrible war—Wilson's stupid war. Another, in effect, civil war in which civilization sought to destroy itself. I think all our present troubles were stirred to life out of that witch's brew of bloodlust."

"My father despised Wilson. The war hastened his disillusionment. Frustrated that he could take the healer's art only so far, that cancer so utterly defeated all his best efforts. They turned him down in 1917 to go to France with a surgical team. Too old, they told him; said that he would do more good teaching young surgeons at Memorial Hospital in New York. In his last years, he has sat alone in his Palm Beach bungalow, brooding in his tent, a guest at all the millionaires' homes and on their yachts, the men whose children he brought into the world. 'War profiteers,' as he calls them, some, the older ones, who made their first money in the Civil War, and their sons in the Great War."

"Surely, *you*, his son, have been some consolation."

"Do you think the law can heal, can bring about social justice?"

"It was not intended for that. The law, justice, administered fairly, is our only buttress against chaos. The courts are there to allow the various competing social interests a clearly demarcated field on which to fight it out. No more, no less."

"Well, it looks like Alger and those of like mind are about to bring the fight to the whole country, gloves off, hand-to-hand. In our last conversation, Alger seemed frustrated by his law firm, the inability of law to change anything, the 'deadweight of habit and ingrained greed.'"

"So you do keep up?"

"With Priscilla on occasion. She likes to scout the probabilities of life, the options."

"Perhaps your Priscilla will build him a happy home. Children—his own—might change him."

"Let us hope so, for both their sakes."

"And for your sake"—he paused as he relit his pipe—"I have a promise to keep—a reward. I've taken the trouble to invite a wonderful young woman to dinner, a distant cousin about your age, lovely as she is talented. She has performed on the piano with the Boston Symphony and will play for us tonight. Her name is Annie Davenport; her grandfather died beside me at Antietam."

"The Colonel Richard Davenport in Memorial Hall?"

Holmes smiled at me like an old libertine deep in his cups as he put his pipe to his lips.

"One and the same."

And yet throughout our conversation, as if engaged in some silent conspiracy against my mentor, I could not take my mind off Priscilla's last letter to me of a little over a year before when Alger sat where I sat, which still resided inside my jacket pocket.

1458 RIVERSIDE DRIVE
THE EASTERWOOD
July 11, 1930

Dear Edward:

Of all the people in the world to whom I even remotely fantasized about being required—by society's stipulations, of course, and good upbringing—to send a thank-you note for a wedding gift, it was never you. Quite the opposite. Perhaps, and I certainly hope it is the case, you never dreamed of being on the receiving end of this note—and late as ever! But here you are with my note in hand—how crazy life turns all our expectations upside down! Of course, I didn't invite you to my first wedding, for obvious reasons. Chagrined, I am, as well, because you were so right and I was so wrong. But I refuse to hate you—or entirely love you, because you are forever right. My strong right arm when I get myself in deep water. Though not this time, my sweet Edward—third time lucky. And smack dab in the middle of this terrible slump, which has so turned all our lives upside down and filled the streets with the homeless and unemployed.

Except your luck, of course—nothing ever seems to affect you, who would land on your feet even if an earthquake should fell all the skyscrapers of Wall Street. And so, if proof be required, you send a ten-piece silver serving set from Tiffany that must have cost more than our entire—oh so simple and humble—wedding reception! How could you, Edward, be so generous, so goddamn ridiculously thoughtful, when people are starving—yes, in front of the soup kitchens where I serve the destitute? My mother couldn't even afford something like this, much less give it as a wedding present. Even having such a beautiful thing—and yes, yes, it is truly beautiful, and Danish modern, Jensen, no less—around our humble apartment—a travesty in our Quaker simplicity. Surely you see, how impossible—what would our friends think to see us displaying such bourgeois status symbols? But I love it, Edward, because it speaks to me of you and your damned optimism, that all will be fine if we only keep our noses to the grindstone and our wits about us. Alger just laughs at my distress and says that we should secretly sell it and give the money to those who need it. That is the proper Quaker thing to do.

But I will not sell it, and every so often when you come to visit, or when I am alone for tea, or on my own for dinner, I will take it out of hiding, polish it up, and indulge myself in fantasies of more queenly times, and think of you—always you.

Thank you, my dearest, my prince-ever-charming. Your kindness—or should it be forgiveness?—moves me deeply in these dark days. Stuck as I am in New York while Alger wastes his career at the beck and call of that doddering archaism of the old order, the right-righteous Justice Holmes, from whose presence I am forever banned. Alger assures me he's got the uproar over our marriage smoothed over and, as he puts it, now has the old man reading out of his hand in Beverly Farms.

Love,
Pross

Suicide or Accident Incredible in Death of Laurence Du...

...vershoe Offers M...
e Neither...

Spy Probe Figure Dies i... ...lunge

...Falls 16 Floors ...rk

...ambers Denies ...e Ever Accused ...tm of Spying.

...k... (AP) Whit... ...ers said Tuesday ...ceived any state... ...ers from Lau... ...ho plunged to ...night ...mer high... ...ment offi... ...t in testi... ...ese un... ...mittee ...n Red ...hat ...'s

SPY CASE FIGURE PLUNGES TO DEATH

Charged With Aid For Reds

Laurence Duggan, Formerly in State Dept., Was Named in Quiz

WASHINGTON — (AP) — Rep Mundt (R., S.D.) said today he hopes the house un-American activities committee will change its methods to insure fairer hearings for future witnesses and accused persons.

The acting chairman told reporters that for the next ten days committee members will concentrate on a report to the new congress. He said the report also will contain recommendations for altering procedure at committee hearings.

Although the group plans no further public meetings this year, it scheduled a closed-door session tomorrow with Francis B. Sayre.

Duggan had been named before the house un-American activities committee as one of six government officials who allegedly passed secret documents to ex-Communist Whittaker Chambers.

U. S. district attorneys in charge of the grand jury investigation declined to reveal if the jury had planned to subpoena Duggan. But in Washington, Acting Chairman Karl E. Mundt of the house un-American activities committee said he was "sure that without doubt the grand jury in New York would have wanted Duggan as a witness."

The body of Duggan, a former advisor to ex-Secretary of State Cordell Hull, was found in a snowbank outside his office building on West 45th street at 7 p.m. yesterday.

Detectives said he apparently decided to go out the window while putting on his overshoes, preparing to go home for the night. Duggan was wearing neither his coat nor hat. One overshoe was on. The other was found in his office.

...on the 16th floor ...time.

Caption
Last Rites for Victim of Plunge

Friend of Hiss

Alger Hiss, former state department official now under indictment for perjury for denying he delivered government secrets to Chambers, said he was shocked at the death of "one of my very good friends."

"He was a victim of persecution," Hiss said. He refused to elaborate.

Rep. Mundt said that the testimony naming Duggan was given the committee during a closed session Dec. 8. He said Isaac Don Levine, editor of the anti-Communist magazine Plain Talk, testified ...Chambers had named Duggan ...his six sources of infor-... — Assistant Secre-... ...rle.

The Rev. Edwin Broderick of St. Patrick's Cathedral is shown, upper photo, giving the last rites to Laurence Duggan, 43, director of the Institute of International Education and a former state department official, after he plunged to his death from the 16th floor office on West 45th street in New York City late yesterday. The house un-American activities committee planned to question Duggan in connection with the current spy probe.

...gan Plunge...

NEW YORK. — (AP) — Whittaker Chambers today said he never had received any state department papers from Laurence Duggan who plunged to death last night.

Chambers told newsmen in reference to testimony before the house un-American activities committee that Duggan's name was among six he mentioned. "I did not mention all these people as having turned over those papers. I did not name Mr Duggan as passing over papers to me.

NEW YORK— UP)—Laurence Duggan, 43, former state department aide who plunged to his death from his 16 story office window last n... was reported today to ... had information of va... the federal grand j... vestigating espionage.

...roken line traces path of fall of Laurence Duggan, forme... ...ment official who died Monday night in a plung... ...e in a West Forty-fifth street buil... ...to the sidewalk...

Cops Press Probe of Duggan's Deat...

WHERE DUGGAN PLUNGED TO DEATH Interior of the office at 2 W. 45th St., Manhattan, from which Laurence Duggan plunged 16 stories from window at left.

When Duggan's body was found in a snowbank under his office window at 5th and 45th St., he was wearing one overshoe and was hatless and coatless. The other overshoe and his hat and coat were found in his office. Detectives said it was apparent he had been preparing to go home.

Funeral services were scheduled tomorrow noon.

24

Crime Scene: Laurence Duggan

"RELAX, GEORGE, THEY'RE cool. We're just two eager-beaver scholars doing our thing."

She was wearing a long woolen plaid skirt past the knee and a white
blouse, her hair in a tight chignon, showing to advantage the sumptuous play of her long neck tendons as she cast her glances here, there,
and everywhere. He wore a rumpled suit and tie, as close an approximation to the role as he could manage.

Wendy smiled at the four twenty-something employees at their
workstations. She was intrigued with the new concept of a high-end
Internet dating site, specializing in graduates from top universities. In
the waiting area, she'd patiently filled out one of the online forms for
kicks, peppering George with pointed comments and questions about
what he considered relevant for compatibility, checking off, tongue in
cheek, where they missed the mark. He had come to appreciate her
humor, a teasing verging on the outrageous, always confrontational,
while elbowing obstacles to intimacy rather than delicately navi-
gating them. She'd grinned in triumph—"Almost a perfect match,
amigo!"—holding up the form, then going on to force him to admit
that algorithms, no matter how refined, failed to elucidate matters of
the human heart.

———

The large office had been stripped back to brick walls and concrete
floors, leaving much of the building's mechanical systems visible,
painted in restful, if bright, colors, giving the pipes, ductwork, and
exposed lighting fixtures a decorative flair. A modern space scrupulously scoured of the past. The team, most of them in their twenties,
sat at their monitors, appearing totally disinterested in the doings of

the couple by the center window overlooking Forty-fifth Street. They were clearly preoccupied with sorting the intimate lives and fantasies of thousands.

"Do you think these are original windows, or have they been replaced?" He began a forensic examination of the center window, fingering the sash chain. "Solid brass. Looks original but could have been replaced. The casing has been repainted—who knows how many times, certainly since 1910, when it was built."

She pulled out the tape measure from her Prada handbag and began measuring from the concrete floor.

"Thirty-three inches exactly, as in the police report, the newspaper articles from 1948."

"And an eight-inch wind deflector," added George, lifting the window slightly to inspect the exterior casing, finding screw holes that had long been sealed. "Here they are. The wind deflector would have almost come up to my waist, and I'm the same height as Laurence Duggan." He peered down from the window of 2 West 45th Street, all sixteen floors, to where the traffic was backed up like a Dinky Toy parking lot.

"How could his wife have called it an accident? Even if you wanted to climb out, much less throw yourself out, it would take some doing. And it was cold, even for December, below freezing. The window would hardly have been just standing wide open."

"Well, the insurance company must have thought it possible, since they paid off for an accident." George unslung his backpack and got out their growing file of photocopied pages from old newspapers, much of it gleaned from Google. He nodded as he read. "'Helen, his wife, rejected the idea of suicide outright. The insurance investigators confirmed that minutes before he fell, he'd called his wife to say he was catching the seven-thirty p.m. train home. There was a birthday party for his father, Dr. Stephen Duggan, director emeritus of the Institute of International Education.'" He looked at Wendy with a pained grimace as he added his own commentary, eyeing the snack table and coffee dispenser where Duggan's desk would once have been. "So, he was following in dad's footsteps, head of the IIE, a man Laurence adored. They were making plans for Christmas with their four children."

She snorted, something she could barely control. "Jesus: Stephanie, Laurence, Robert, and Christopher . . ." This pronouncement now took on the tone of a litany, if not an obsession. "Seems like the Christmas season really brought out the bloodlust in those KGB hyenas."

He turned a pained squint from her flushed face and returned to the UP story of October 24, 1949, a little under a year after Duggan's death, with the second Hiss trial set to start in November, seeing in his mind the tall, gangly, square-jawed, hollow-eyed Duggan standing by the window. "His wife, Helen, also noted he'd recently had back surgery but hadn't been wearing his brace that day—she called it a 'corset.' There was snow and ice." He raised a finger, modulating to a higher-pitched voice, as if listening to someone far off: "'It was bad underfoot. I asked him to wear my corset. He laughed. When he started to lean over to put on his galoshes, I told him to bend his knee and lift up his foot instead of bending over.' Mrs. Duggan had paused and looked out of her window, according to the interviewer. 'We were married sixteen years. Never once did he come into a room without saying, "My gosh, it's stuffy in here," and then, swish, up would go a window.'"

For a few moments, the introduction of a woman's voice cast a silent shadow between them.

"See, she's trying to explain why Duggan had the window thrown open. Probably wanted the insurance money—or worse."

"Worse? That's pretty damn cynical of you."

"Bad back," she said. "Can you imagine someone with a bad back heaving himself up on the sill and over the wind deflector?" She banged the metal casing of the window for emphasis, and one of the young men with earbuds across the room turned with a distracted glance from the intimate details he was plundering on his screen. She smiled fetchingly. "Weird, isn't it . . . *they* have no idea; even their boss, the founder of the company, has no idea." She glanced, dismayed, around at the raw brick and exposed mechanicals. "Squeaky-clean . . ."

"Owner of the building, the rental agent . . . hardly likely to pass on that kind of nostalgic memorabilia to a new tenant." George flipped a page. "Even if they cared." He raised his hand as if to further dramatize his tale. "Christmas shoppers passing by on Forty-fifth Street noticed something odd: Duggan, whose body was lying in a snowbank, was wearing a single rubber overshoe on his right foot. The left overshoe was still in his private office, along with his hat, overcoat, briefcase with Christmas cards for mailing, and an airline ticket for a flight to Washington the following day. On his desk was a draft of his annual report on the IIE, with references to a *sick world* and a *world of gloom.*'"

"But it was Christmas—George, the four kids . . ."

"Stephanie, Laurence, Robert, and . . ." He bent closer to the page.

"Christopher." She closed her eyes, reaching for a deep breath, and then stared into his. "Surely, you, or at least your father, can imagine what those kids must have gone through—the agony of uncertainty and loss. Not knowing what happened or why." She gripped his arm. "You wrote back to your father, right?"

"He doesn't have an e-mail."

"Just write him, damn it—just do it, for the scholarship, the catalog. We need his witness."

"Still think"—he gestured dismissively to the bare brick walls—"that places have spirits, that something remains?"

"Us . . ." she murmured.

George saw the ache in her eyes and looked back to his notes, flipping pages as if fast-forwarding through time. "To her dying day, Helen Duggan rejected the possibility of suicide."

"Well, of course, she would, because she had to have known the truth: She'd offered her services, according to Chambers, enthusiastic to do her bit for the good cause. But, of course, she couldn't share *that* with her children." Her voice rose with caustic fury. "Even when the truth would have alleviated the grief and awful doubt for them! Like you— don't you feel relieved, knowing the truth about George Altmann?"

"We're not quite there yet."

"Aren't we?"

"I got the appointment with Weinstein for next week."

George stared as her agitated face calmed, her expression reflective, giving him respite to return to the pages in hand. "Detectives investigating circumstances around Duggan's death noted that the window from which he fell had a wind deflector that came to the height of a man's waist; it was not cracked or broken, as might have been the case in the event of foul play. But, on the other hand, they noted it would have been difficult to have fallen over such an obstacle accidentally. A priest walking down Forty-fifth Street heard Duggan scream out as he fell. Suicides, according to the experts, do not scream as they fall."

She turned from him abruptly, her face contorted in a look of horror. He touched a hand to her shoulder in a calming gesture.

"Yes," she hissed, "accident victims fucking do scream." She grabbed his arm as if to steady herself, and brought her lips close to his, uttering in a near whisper. "And yes, it would take two strong men to heave him out. And any wife who didn't tell her children the truth doesn't deserve to call herself a mother."

"Duggan," he offered, as if pleading for her understanding, "wasn't as disciplined or determined as Hiss, according to Weinstein's book. Stalin's purges freaked him out. He was anxious about being exposed." Again he checked his notes. "Code name 'Nineteen' in the Venona decrypts of Soviet cables, the KGB's most productive source of secret intelligence within the State Department when Duggan was chief of the Latin American Division in the late thirties." He gave her a knowing look. "The Soviet's golden boy until Alger Hiss assumed that role after 1939."

"And we're certain, right, that Duggan could have fingered Hiss, if he sang to the FBI, or if he'd been called to testify in the trial?"

George flipped through the file and handed her the photocopied page from Weinstein's *Haunted Wood*:

> Duggan was tall, slim, scholarly, passionate about Marxism, and class secretary for his Harvard class of 1927. According to illegal station chief, Boris Bazarov, in a 1936 cable to Moscow Center, Alger Hiss tried to recruit Duggan for his GRU (Soviet military) apparatus in 1936, but Duggan let it be known that he preferred direct contact with his existing Soviet handler; "19 [Duggan] further reported that overall his line of action is completely clear to him and that the only thing that induces him to stay in a job he despises in the department, having to wear a dinner jacket for 2 weeks at a time when attending a reception every evening (with nearly 20 countries in his division), is the notion of being useful to our cause. He reports that he is not quite firm in the saddle yet and does not yet have access to everything. Many envy his extraordinary career, a career highly unusual for one of his age (he is 32-33), but after several months will be able to consolidate his position. It is true that he is widely known as a liberal and a typical New Dealer and that his family is known for its liberalism. But that is not a problem. To be on the safe side, he asked that we meet with him once a month and would very much like our man to make shorthand notes of the meetings. He is unable to give us documents for now, but later, apparently, he will manage it."

Although greatly concerned about Stalin's purges in the late thirties, Duggan continued to pass reams of sensitive information and top-secret documents to his Soviet handlers. In 1939, after the signing of the Nazi-Soviet pact, Whittaker Chambers went to Adolf Berle, then head of security in the State Department, and outed Duggan as a Soviet spy, along with six others, including Alger Hiss. Berle, a near-genius, the youngest graduate of Harvard Law School, did next to nothing. His report to Roosevelt on the security situation elicited a harsh profanity from the President. Undersecretary of State, Sumner Welles, who had been Duggan's sponsor and protector internally at State, did take notice of Berle's list of security concerns, removing Duggan from his sensitive post as head of State's South American Division, and promoting him to a position where he could do less harm, thus ending his days of high productivity for the KGB. While Alger Hiss' career and productivity as an agent of influence, nevertheless, began a steep rise during the War years.

She shook the page after reading it again. "Yes, yes, do you suppose his children are aware of this, the new scholarship, the new evidence—if their mother never told them? They'd have to be, what, in their sixties?"

"The KGB thought she was a lot bolder and even more dedicated than her husband." He searched for the place he had underlined. "'His wife, Helen Boyd Duggan, was a beautiful, tall blond, well read, reserved, athletic, and independent. According to Duggan's KGB officer, Helen was disappointed with her own lack of success and eager to *do something real.*'" George scanned down a few more lines. "'Her husband does not have much influence over her. She could be exceedingly useful, if we could succeed in recruiting her.'"

Wendy shook her head, as if trying to get her emotions in check.

"There, she fucking kept it from the children. If you were one of his children, how would you rather remember your father—as an idealistic KGB spy murdered by Stalin's thugs, or as a patriotic American who inexplicably, accidentally killed himself and ended up a twisted wreck in a snowbank with one galosh on and one off?"

George flipped a page back. "The first pedestrians on the scene said he was still alive . . . for a few minutes."

"Enough . . ." She held up a hand and backed away.

"The speculation at the time was that he'd been persecuted by the House Committee on Un-American Affairs, that Chambers had named him as a spy, first to an assistant secretary at State, Adolf Berle, then later to the FBI. Even Alger Hiss implied Duggan had been unjustly accused and so hounded to his death."

"So, for the kids, the possibility of suicide must have hung over them all their childhood . . . for fucking ever."

"Calm down," he said, noticing the office workers turning to look at her.

"I'm okay, really."

"Listen, they could blame the Red-baiters . . . a victim of persecution."

"A victim—right!—like George Altmann, I suppose."

George was almost immune to this preoccupation by now, and he shuffled his notes systematically, glancing around the office, smiling gamely for any employees who might have been distracted from the love lives on their screens.

"Wendy, it's hardly the same. Duggan was clearly overwrought. He knew he'd been fingered by Chambers in 1939 and so reassigned to a less sensitive job by his patron, Undersecretary of State Sumner Welles, and again after the war, when he came under suspicion after Elizabeth Bentley included him in her list of agents she gave to the FBI. He was paranoid about both the FBI and the KGB, that if there were so many traitors in the purged ranks of the KGB, his name would leak out—as it did. He must have suspected it was coming—that something was coming."

"And George Altmann didn't? You don't think he'd have handed those sketches to your grandfather if he wasn't worried as hell about retribution from the Hiss forces? And the Justice Department mural: His last laugh had turned into his sword of Damocles, as it did for Walter Marvin Smith."

George looked at her glumly, not a little shaken. He turned to the window as if to collect his thoughts, fingering the sash lock. Across the street was a huge steel and glass building of very recent vintage, rank upon rank upon rank of shimmering panels mirroring the slim neoclassical contour of 2 West 45th Street . . . and a window on the sixteenth floor, which had once been the office of the president of the IIE, where now another face stared out onto the glassy-eyed canyon below.

He turned quickly, businesslike, and tapped the file and rattled off the timeline:

"Twelve days before his sixteen-story plunge, Duggan's name had been mentioned in HUAC hearings as a possible Soviet agent. Ten days before he fell, the FBI interviewed Duggan and asked him about his association with Soviet handler Hede Massing; he claimed that he had rejected all her attempts to recruit him. Five days before"—he glanced out the window, distracted by a sudden spasm of honking traffic below—"Alger Hiss had been indicted on the two counts of perjury by a grand jury. That same day, a Soviet KGB officer, Sergey Striganov, who had met with Duggan in his office in July, called again to try to set up another appointment: Duggan refused. Within an hour after his death, three New York detectives scoured his office and found nothing amiss and no suicide note. There were no signs of a struggle. The window of Duggan's office was wide open and snow on the ledge had been partly brushed away. There had been no one else in the office area at the time except for a cleaning lady, who reported that she hadn't seen anyone else."

She took the file from his hands and leafed through until she located the underlined passage in the photocopied page from Weinstein's book, reading in a soft, quivering voice. "'Sumner Welles, ex-Undersecretary of State, Duggan's patron and friend, who had removed Duggan from his job as head of the Latin American Division in 1939 when Berle told him of Chambers's accusation, immediately rejected the possibility of suicide and called it foul play, insisting on a full investigation into the death of his onetime protégé.'"

George stepped away, as if physically assaulted by her accusatory tone, moving again to the wide-open window and the grind of traffic below, his gaze lifting from the gritty street to the looking-glass phantasmagoria beetling the sky across the street, like some teetering fun-house mirror, some tower of Babel, reflecting a million points of light, mocking his stare, and in its blinding dazzle thwarting any hopes of a single answer or neat algorithm to solve the tragic dilemma he faced. So, from the lofty heights of his concrete and steel aerie, a return to basics, Occam's razor, the simplest answer—Newton's second law: Force equals mass times acceleration; or more to the point for one Laurence Duggan: Acceleration is directly proportional to force and inversely proportional to mass. "Witnesses," he repeated slowly, as if to staunch the rising nausea, "said he was still alive after he hit the snowbank." For a moment more he watched the fleeing figures hurrying home in the approaching autumn dusk, and then slowly closed the window, needing to make an end of it.

"So," he pondered, wary now of her sometimes trying presence, "the people who should have known, would have known—knew."

"Of course, they knew," she replied impatiently. "Alger Hiss knew. Chambers knew. Jesus, George Altmann *knew*—he'd sketched them all at Volta Place, left his little joke on the walls of the Justice Department—that he could be next!" Her quivering chin sank to her chest for a moment as she paused to regain her equilibrium. And then in a softer more reserved tone, she added, "And your grandfather, the Judge, knew, or surely suspected—right, George? Right? Why else return those sketches to your father if he didn't feel some responsibility, some guilt? A lesser man would have simply burned them, like he suggested in his memoir. He was hedging his bets, as he still is—with you, baby."

He looked at her with glittering eyes, more thoughtful than shocked, a hint of comfort in his now-firm lips and chin.

"Well, now that you mention it, why not ask him that yourself—why not—on the way to Washington next week." He shoved his file back into his backpack. "I think you're just the elixir the old man needs."

He [Duggan] received me cordially, was attentive, gave me a detailed account of the institute's work, showed me his office, and having done this, led me to the door. I detained him with a question, and we talked for another 10-15 minutes, but then I had to leave because Duggan, having led me the elevator, let me know unequivocally that it was time for me to go. He had not wished to talk about anything other than the institute and had tried the whole time to take an official tone. I got the impression . . . that he was constantly on his guard, anticipating that I would ask some unexpected question.

—Sergey Striganov, KGB operative,
reporting to Moscow Center on his
July 1948 meeting with Duggan

25

A Life in the Law and Out:
Martha and the Theory of Unconscious Motivation

OF ALL MY children, I fear Martha was most affected in the long run by the Hiss trial, in the sense that I had the poor judgment to actually discuss aspects of our defense strategy with her in the years to come. Another strike against me from Annie's perspective. Alice pretty much dismissed the whole business as a foolish waste of everybody's time and a distraction from the underlying "pathologies" of the system. While at the time of the trial, poor Teddy reacted badly to the criticism of me from his classmates, and so took it upon himself to prove himself the patriot, for which he required no proof. But for Martha, the iron somehow struck deeper. She took my disastrous failure—bringing on two psychiatric witnesses for the defense—a strategy insisted upon by Priscilla and Alger Hiss—as a personal insult and a stain on her reputation.

"Father, if you only knew how many times in the middle of some session, one of my patients has popped up—the thing hanging fire sometimes for months, or even years—and asked, 'Was it really your father who brought those psychiatrists into the Hiss trial, the debacle that sent poor Alger to jail?'"

But an enigma is an enigma, and Martha remains the most splendidly enigmatic of our girls. Even though raised in a bookish family, she always stood out as the quiet one, the studious one, our grand intellectual—"an instinctive intellectual to her toes," Annie liked to say. She was at once acutely observant of others and blind to her own charmless quirks and utterly absorbed in her world of texts and ideas, distant and aloof yet equally ready to jump in to ameliorate family quarrels—ultimately landing the accolade of "celebrity psychiatrist"—*New York* magazine, 1983. A role she always assumed as her birthright. She was the go-between, ready to coax truces between her siblings Alice and

Teddy, even between Annie and me. For Cordelia, she was the older, wiser sister and confidante on all matters dysfunctional. Our curly-haired, faun-eyed brunette could be remote and uncommunicative for days and weeks on end, and then just as suddenly enter the family fray with a torrent of revelations, as if she'd discovered the holy grail, the magic elixir that would solve all that ails the human condition—if not Freud, then Dostoyevsky, Nietzsche, or Virginia Woolf. Herr Freud captivated her teenage years, only later to be brutally jettisoned for a pantheon of animist gleanings from Jung, and later still, Anna Freud and Martha's celebrity lodestars, Karen Horney and close pal and confidante Margaret Mead. Over the years, all her heroes were at one time or another enlisted to ameliorate our family quarrels and various upsets: if only we had the gumption to reveal our inner selves to one another, learn to examine our dreams and "truthfully" probe our unconscious will to power.

Besides books, Martha was besotted by her dreams. How many mornings at breakfast did she arrive in the kitchen, agog, twitching with excitement, to regale us with yet another of her vivid fantasies of the night before. Of course, she was, too, a little wary, lest her darkest nightmare recitations reflect badly on us, our malign influence as parents, or, worse, become the fodder for Teddy's scorn and teasing. Annie's dismissive retorts—"What does our sulky dreamer have for us this morning?"—only confirmed her worst suspicions about her mother's abusive upbringing. She sought the most frightful disinterments of the psyche, the most elaborate mental constructs, to explain every defect in human nature—including her own insecurities, which she lovingly shared on our hikes. She believed in the unconscious, repression, and universal archetypes the way people in my father's day believed in the Holy Trinity. She was a scholar of the first rank, winning all the prizes at Chapin and later at Radcliffe in the classics and psychology.

As an adolescent, Martha read Greek in the bathtub, Latin on the john, and Freud and Adler under the covers. She was an indoor plant, happiest curled up with our guardian angels by the fire, reading *To the Lighthouse* or *Moses and Monotheism*. Only Teddy could draw her outside, cajole her to accompany us birding, or hiking to the Neversink, or, best of all, accompanying him while fishing on the lake, and later serving as cox in his single scull. He was the only one who could make her laugh, even as he laughed her out of court when she began to explain his daredevil antics by reference to Freud's death drive, or *Todestrieb*, in

Beyond the Pleasure Principle. When Teddy would tease timber rattlers or balance on one foot on the precipice of the D & H abutments to scare Martha, he'd refer to his high jinks as "jiving on Toad Street," to everyone's amusement but Martha's. Teddy turned her theories inside out and loved nothing better than making fun of Martha with lewd jokes about penis envy, offering to lend her his equipment if she felt so insecure about her lack. She, in turn, attacked him for his lame-brain girlfriends who, so she said, were only interested in ministering to his needs, which Teddy then explained was his way of escaping Toad Street. Her sexual jealousy of his girlfriends was proverbial. Sex always seemed a little impossible to her; she always said the act was too beast-like, too much the response of the reptilian brain. Though quite lovely as a teenager, she seemed to shrink before the fiery beauty and sexual exploits of her elder sister, Alice. She never had a real boyfriend, even at Radcliffe, where she had many of the male professors in the psychology department wrapped around her little finger.

Annie thought she scared men off with her analytical mind and disgust with her own body. "She overthinks everything," Annie would tell me, "as if fearful of anything that smacks of a sincere feeling, lest it grab her like the creature from the black lagoon." Her refusal to care about her dress, attend tea dances, or participate in the barest essentials of social chitchat, drove her mother crazy. She even refused to attend debutante parties for her Chapin pals, much less have her own. Annie was convinced her self-absorbed frame of mind hampered her piano studies. I remember Annie's exasperated high-pitched voice ringing down the corridors of our apartment, or in the great room at Hermitage: "Stop thinking about the music, damn it. And I don't care if you've got your damned period, either. You don't have to analyze the phrasing, Miss Freud; just let it move you, let it flow—feel for once in your stupid life."

Of course, Martha spent her college years analyzing her fraught relationship with her mother, attributing her problems with "boys" to Annie's repressed frustrations and unrequited longings for deep affection, which, no doubt, I was at least partially responsible for. Annie's troubles, according to Martha, always went back to some repressed feelings in her "puritanical childhood"—the dark ages of toilet training or unhealthy attachments to an alcoholic father, which, of course, only endless therapy could uncover and redeem. I never heard so many tortured tergiversations of the mind as when Martha returned from Radcliffe with the latest revelations of Karen Horney or Margaret

Mead, whom she met in her Columbia Med School years, and who had proclaimed the battle for women's rights won, so Martha assured me. She lunched with Margaret often and wrote joint papers with her on how we are all shaped by culture and how our sex roles are simply learned behavior, and could just as easily be unlearned as women made their escape from under the thumb of the ruling patriarchy. If we could just get more people to undergo psychotherapy, so she assured me, the country might be weaned from a complacent yielding to prejudice.

In some ways, Martha was hit hardest by Teddy's death. We all grieved, but we all made our accommodations in our different ways. Alice, always the competitor, assumed Teddy's mantle to master the law and save the downtrodden. Annie had another child and another career and another love in Balanchine's ballets. I became a federal judge and threw myself into a workload that left little time for grief, much less anything else. And Martha? As Annie explained it to me, drawing on her love of Proust and George Elliot, Martha internalized her grief and made her lost Teddy the cynosure of every therapeutic theory she ever devised for her patients.

"I swear, that daffy daughter of mine finds a little of her forbidden love for Teddy in every patient she treats. Who knows, maybe she actually helps people that way. What do I know; I'm just her repressed mother."

Even years after Teddy's death, Martha kept insisting that Annie and I submit to psychoanalysis, slipping her colleagues' business cards under the door of our apartment. Never a dinner or holiday gathering passed without the subject rising like Marley's ghost. At her wit's end with her mother, who simply sailed over her preoccupations, Martha became more and more determined to address my inner demons.

"Which demons are those, dear?"

"Your need to dominate. You never remove your judge's robes. You inflict your views on everyone else, like you did with Teddy."

"And what views are those?"

"That you know better than anybody; that the law is the be-all and end-all; that your rules are all that matter; that good order will save us from the unchecked chaos of our souls."

"Those aren't views, only facts. Though I don't see myself in the business of saving souls."

"Your prejudices against anyone who doesn't think like you, unless, of course, they went to Yale or Harvard Law. That's how you got into such a mess with the Hiss trial."

"Is that so . . ."

"I'm just trying to help you understand your unconscious motivations."

"And that has something do with Alger Hiss?"

"Why you never talk about your mother."

"She died when I was eight. I barely remember her. It does make me sad, though, I must confess."

"With psychoanalysis, maybe just a year or two, you'd start to remember what she *did* to you. Mother, too, of course, would benefit, but I've long ago given up on her. When was the last time you two even spoke to each other?"

"Did to me? She died, poor woman, of breast cancer. Leaving her husband, the greatest specialist on gynecological cancers in America, feeling moribund and helpless. I think it almost broke him."

"You see, you never told me that. Clearly your grief, if not for Teddy, or the mother you barely knew, played a part in your taking pity on Priscilla Hiss and screwing up your defense of Alger Hiss."

"Who told you such a thing?"

"That's the opinion of half my patients: They all think Priscilla is a stinker—especially now."

"Now?"

"Since he got out of jail ten years ago, she refuses to enlist in his crusade to clear himself."

"Poor Priscilla. It never ends."

"And let me tell you it interferes in my professional capacity to remain both aloof and empathetic. I've even had journalists pretend to be patients to see if they couldn't get something out of me—about you—the Hisses!"

"Perish the thought."

"Don't be so sarcastic. I'm a healer. I just want everyone to be, well, happier."

"Well, Jefferson would certainly approve."

"Not so rigid, more empathetic, more forgiving of others. You and Mother, for instance."

"Perhaps we should reenlist Dr. Binger for Annie? Is he still around, that charlatan who almost destroyed my career—the man you, darling, once considered the cat's meow? But all the Bingers in the world, and all the happiness on the planet won't bring back Teddy, Martha. Nothing will. I know Theodore can be taxing, but aren't your children some consolation? He'd be their uncle. When I have Karen and Erich with me at Hermitage, I bring up Teddy all the time; I encourage them to walk in his shoes, to get to know all the things he loved. I give them his childhood books to read. That's all we can do."

———

It is an oddity that the only two men who consistently stood up to Martha were her brother and her Polish husband, Theodore, whom she first met after receiving a Guggenheim grant to study postwar trauma on children in Poland. Theo—as she decided to call him, so as not to remind her of her brother—was a Polish Jew and had barely survived the war, during which he had fought the Nazis as a member of the partisan resistance. He was a Communist intellectual and up-and-coming sociologist. For every one of Martha's convoluted ideas or pitiful explanations of the human condition, Theo could come up with a dozen counterexamples based on Durkheim, Max Weber, or Marx, whom he quoted, not without a sneer and pained grimace, to her with complete textual authority—the patriarchal spirit incarnate! It made for a talkative, if fraught, marriage. How she married the one man who could so devastate her intellectually is beyond me. Unless he provided some haunting echo of her lost brother.

Theo, older by about ten years, clearly married her as a way to escape the Iron Curtain. But he did manage to get her pregnant, twice, before tending his harem of mistresses full-time, first at Hunter College and then at Columbia, where he taught sociology and rose to full professor. As far as I could ever make out, they always slept in separate bedrooms. Theo's "airheads," as Martha referred to them, were mostly pretty and impressionable grad students who found their professor's European accent and old-world charm irresistible. Martha even admitted to me—her lack of inhibition in personal matters as she grew older is simply staggering—that the only way Theo finally got her pregnant was by using a pornographic magazine for the first conception, and having one of his mistresses on hand, so to speak, for the second. Of course, she acknowledged, and excused, all Theo's infidelities and his deficiencies as both husband and father as being due to the trauma of the war years, along with the loss of his parents—his father, a doctor, his mother, a nurse, both shipped off to Auschwitz. And, I believe, though he rarely mentioned it, a brother, an officer in the Polish army killed by the Soviets in 1939.

For the most part, Martha and I got along pretty well during her childhood and adolescence. Her animus was largely directed at Annie, who pushed her piano studies to the limit of the poor child's endurance. The Hiss trial changed all that. I made the cardinal error of agreeing to bring in two psychiatrists—Carl A. Binger and James Murray—to testify for the defense against Chambers. I should have held my ground; I should have threatened to resign; I should have walked away from the biggest mistake of my life. But Alger and Priscilla (I'm haunted by her pleas) were dead set on having them as expert witnesses, and so I bowed to their foolhardy judgment.

26

A Life in the Law and Out:
No More Where He Came From

THREE THINGS CLARIFIED for me when I joined Hiss's defense team: Alger was fully in charge, his lawyers were close to despair, and there seemed to be what I can only describe as a bizarre division of labor: an insider group of legal gunslingers fed by a shady coven of investigators, and a more public group of esteemed trial attorneys. The two groups rarely met or discussed matters. The insiders moved in the shadows and shared only what they thought we needed to know, we who faced the judge and jury and the public. Alger set this guarded tone; he gave the marching orders.

At first, I was pleased to be colleagues with so many top Harvard Law men, and not a little amazed at the level of financial resources available for investigation and research. Where the money for Alger's defense fund came from, I never knew. The first trial had been a near-run thing, a hung jury, though lead counsel, Lloyd Stryker, had managed brilliantly in many respects to mislead and distract the jury from the critical facts that wouldn't go away—namely, the top-secret State Department papers copied on the Hisses' Woodstock typewriter, which Whittaker Chambers had hidden away and then sprung on the Hiss defense team. Stryker, with all his bluff and theatrical flourish, had clearly been playing for a hung jury from the first because he felt that was the best he was likely to get. But such a defense by misdirection could hardly be replicated in the second trial. The world had changed: Stalin's minions were on the march.

The amiable southerner out of Boston, Claude Cross, our lead counsel for Hiss in the second trial, had only one good option: stress the truthfulness and upstanding trustworthiness of Alger, and the bad character of the ex-Communist Whittaker Chambers. This was a formidable challenge by any stretch. By late 1949, China had gone Communist, the Soviets had the atom bomb, Eastern Europe was firmly under the thumb of vicious Communist regimes—all satellites of Moscow—and more American Communists or KGB spies, so it seemed almost every day, were either admitting their guilt or exposing others.

Pressure from HUAC investigators and the FBI, and growing paranoia in certain circles, had seemingly resulted in a rash of mysterious disappearances and deaths of potential witnesses for the prosecution, notably those of Laurence Duggan, Harry Dexter White, and Marvin Smith, the first of many more to come as the fifties unfolded. As the trial date approached in November of 1949, we had no idea how many more Communists might be dug out from their holes by Hoover's myrmidons, while McCarthy waited in the wings to start slinging even more mud. No matter how well we groomed the jury pool, the growing fear of Soviet infiltration of American institutions would be staring at us every day from the jury box. But our real problem was Whittaker Chambers and the secret documents he had produced out of nowhere, a pumpkin patch no less. In the voir dire, only one out of sixty potential jurors expressed concern about believing the testimony of an ex-Communist like Chambers. If Chambers were to be believed, then the secret State Department papers (copied on their Woodstock, so confirmed by FBI forensics experts) with Hiss's name on them, which Chambers had turned over to the government, would be viewed as credible evidence— damning evidence. The Woodstock was irrefutable: We had to discredit Chambers. Alger made that absolutely clear, and he was right.

To complicate our task, we had a senior and very experienced judge, Henry Goddard, a dyed-in-the-wool Republican and stickler for the rules of evidence. I knew well from previous experience that Goddard would give great latitude to both sides for the introduction of witnesses. Good news/bad news: We would get to present our friendly psychiatrists to opine on Chambers's history of deceit and malice; while the prosecution would, in contrast to the first trial, most likely be allowed to have Hede Massing testify, along with other Communists, ex-agents, and assorted fellow travelers—all potentially prejudicial to our case. Infamously known as the "Redhead," Massing was an admitted KGB agent, who claimed Alger had been a spy connected to the so-called Ware Group, run by Chambers for Soviet military intelligence. Of course, it was solely her word against Alger's. And, as we would soon find, to our dismay, the prosecution, with all the resources of the FBI at its disposal, would turn up even more damning evidence to convince a jury that Chambers and Hiss, as well as their wives, had had a four-year long, quite intimate friendship. These intimations of a friendship, as more evidence trickled in, perplexed me greatly.

In fact, they chagrined me to my toes, as I caught fascinating glimpses of Priscilla Hiss provided by Chambers and his wife—facets of Priscilla that had entirely escaped me over the years—glimpses of an invisible counterlife, one that, nevertheless, rang absolutely true in my mind. In *Witness*, Chambers poignantly described in detail his friendship with Priscilla. According to Chambers, Priscilla found in his wife, Lise, as she was known to the Hisses, someone she could talk to, open up to about her child from her first marriage, and all the joys and tribulations of motherhood, which the two women shared. It was, by this account, a relationship between two couples that was fun-loving, spirited, carefree, and literate. This friendship, which was unusual, if not frowned upon, in the clandestine world they inhabited, was based almost entirely on character and not mind, as Chambers described it, since Alger, so he found, was a little stuffy and not taken by ideas, except those of Lenin and Marx. These parts of *Witness* Annie found entirely convincing, and they only added to the grudge she held against me for my treatment of Chambers. Faced with such moving and transparent testimony by our witness, I realized that Alger was testing more than my personal loyalty to him, or the Harvard team. He was testing my fealty to Priscilla. And he was holding something back, perhaps protecting her.

In the defense's files, I discovered affidavits that Priscilla Hiss had been a member of the Socialist Party. We assumed the prosecution had the same information. And it was also clear that she was a competent, if not expert, typist. Alger couldn't type worth a damn—something I knew well from my time with Oliver Wendell Holmes, when I was told how often a typist had to be gotten in for my predecessor during the summer session in Beverly Farms. Since the crux of the defense's case was that Whittaker Chambers was perpetuating a forgery by typewriter to ruin Alger Hiss—for God knows what reason—this information about Priscilla, should it become established by the prosecution, would be very damaging to our case. This was one of the crucial reasons why the defense, long before I had been brought on, had gone to such incredible lengths to run down the Hisses' lost Woodstock typewriter before the government got their hands on it. A pyrrhic victory, so it turned out, which only strengthened the prosecution's case when experts determined that the secret documents in question had indeed been typed on the Hisses' Woodstock.

Clearly, the only real hope we had was to keep Priscilla out of the limelight and focus all our resources on calling into doubt the government's case, which meant utterly destroying the credibility of Whittaker Chambers. That's what Alger Hiss had brought me on to do—destroy Chambers by deploying our famous psychiatrists, Binger and Murray. And make sure the jury saw Chambers as a pervert and pathological liar. Not just a liar but a warped sexual deviant and crazed psychotic with an irrational hatred of Alger Hiss. When I sat down with Alger, he could not have been more clear or confident that Chambers was a nutcase. We had Chambers's own deposition in the Baltimore libel case, and all the detailed transcripts of his testimony in the first trial, so plenty of details about his checkered life, occasional homosexual liaisons, and days in the Communist underground, as well as his years of his interactions with Alger and Priscilla! All either Alger or Priscilla would admit to was that they'd known a journalist, who called himself George Crosley, for brief periods in 1936 but not after January 1937 or anytime during 1938, when the secret State Department papers came into Whittaker Chambers's hands. Only under enormous pressure did Alger finally admit that Chambers might indeed be this phantom George Crosley—not "Carl," as he'd actually been known to them in the underground. Thus the government's charges of perjury for transmitting those same secret documents after 1937.

I protested mightily to Alger that not only did I have no expertise in such psychosexual matters but, due in no small part to my daughter Martha, I was no fan of Mr. Freud, whom I considered just above a humbug. Alger only smiled.

"Edward, that is precisely why the jury will believe you, because you are not an enthusiast. Not like Pross."

"But Alger, where do these allegations about homosexual encounters and assorted vices come from?"

"They come in every day."

"But from where? Do we have names, dates—witnesses?"

"They come across Harold's desk; he has his networks out there, his contacts among the kind of people Chambers spent his time with."

"Communists?"

"Literary types, artistic types, and a few Communists slithering out of the gutter."

"This you have in all good conscience from your lawyer, Harold Rosenwald?"

"You doubt him? Harold was editor of the *Law Review* at Harvard. He gets to the bottom of things; he gets tips from all and sundry."

"But in court, under cross-examination, these things—tips—will not hold up unless there is direct testimony and evidence. Otherwise, it's hearsay. And even then, well, even with a disreputable character like Chambers, it will be hard to prove these so-called pathological disturbances, as Binger puts it: 'pathological predispositions which are frequently found in the psychopathic personality.'"

"Binger is a brilliant practitioner . . ." Alger leaned across the table, as if to impart a very personal observation. "Priscilla thinks very highly of him; she's read all his books."

"I have to tell you, Priscilla or no, I find a lot of it, well, unintelligible, and not exactly convincing. And if I find it convoluted and lacking logic, what will the jury think? I don't believe a jury has ever been presented with such a psychiatric defense before."

"They'll believe you, Edward. You're old New York, Groton and Yale and Harvard Law, son of a famous surgeon, bedrock of society. Your work with the WPB was praised by Roosevelt and Truman. And your wife is a famous concert pianist from impeccable New England stock, DAR—yes. We're depending on you; Priscilla is confident that you are the right man at the right time and place to make the case." He leaned forward again, his eyes glittering. "Psychoanalysis *is* the future, Edward."

"Alger, forgive me, but as a member of your team, I must ask you: Is there something about Chambers, an aspect of your relationship with the man, that you haven't informed us about? I ask because you seem so convinced that our experts, Binger and Murray, can elicit confession of such monstrous allegations—the man was a top editor at *Time* magazine for nine years!—which, on the face of things, seem barely credible."

"They are the experts; I have absolute confidence in their abilities to convince a jury."

"Do you and Priscilla know Binger personally?"

"We've met him."

"Alger, again, forgive me, but I must ask: Do you believe these things about Whittaker Chambers because he broke with the Communist

underground, or because he, well, your Mr. Crosley, ended his relationship with you—what shall we say?—on bad terms?"

"Don't be ridiculous, Edward. You've read all the transcripts, all my
depositions. I stand by every word: I only knew him as George Crosley,
and it was barely a passing acquaintance." Alger stared at me directly
with all the sincerity he could muster, as if daring my doubt. "It's the
total weight of the evidence against Chambers, you see, the broad
picture, that the jury needs to absorb. And then ask themselves the
single question: Who is lying—me or Chambers? Look at the character witnesses lined up to support me: the finest public servants of our
generation. Look at my record, Edward, you of all people."

———

I have often thought about that "you of all people," and the note of
shame attached. Was it because Alger assumed Pross had kept me up
to speed on his great successes: a man who had sat next to Roosevelt
at Yalta, praised by Truman, an architect of the United Nations, not to
mention fidelity to Harvard, the law, the country?

I soon realized that Alger was prepared to go for broke: no more
hung juries—innocent or guilty, nothing halfway. I gently suggested
to Alger that we should stop our insistent portrayal of him as the fair-
haired boy, a paragon of virtue, knight in shining armor—just a little
too perfect.

"Alger," I said, "no jury can believe in such perfection; it's a stage prop.
They will be more inclined to believe you with a few flaws, with some
sympathetic stories from your past of family difficulties. Perhaps you and
Mr. Chambers—your George Crosley—found, well, some convivial subjects, sympathetic subjects: You, too, had a brother who died."

Alger looked at me with the ferocity of a cornered cougar, causing
me to feel that if I so much as moved a muscle in that direction, I
would feel his bite on my jugular. Perhaps Pross's babbling to me in
the early days took him by surprise. I realized then that nobody else on
the defense team had the foggiest idea about his troubled youth, family
tragedies, nuggets dropped from Priscilla's fingertips to me when she'd
first spurned his matrimonial overtures in the late twenties. I realized
then that his shining image he presented to the world was the one
thing that kept him going, kept him alive: It was all of a piece. Whether
out of pride or shameful habit, he'd conjured an image as the golden
boy of the New Deal: We were going to march into battle with our

knight in shining armor strutting the boards, all flags flying—and flags of his choosing.

—

Alger bristled. "Listen, until this imposter George Crosley—Chambers— whatever he chooses to call himself—appeared out of thin air, testified against me to try to ruin my life and reputation, repeating and elaborating his lies, I had almost totally forgotten our brief interaction."

I remember staring into Alger's compressed face, his protruding ears, those slightly far apart pale blue eyes watching me with a rigidity and intensity I'd never known. I was going to bring up the *Time* magazine connection again, where Chambers had spent the past nine years as an able and respected editor, but decided against it.

"And are you safe—well, in regards to your colleagues in the State Department? No accusations there . . . you know, from the likes of, say, a Laurence Duggan?"

"I knew him only in passing. God knows how Nixon and Hoover must have harassed and threatened him."

"You think it was suicide?"

"What else? Poor man . . . probably been caught with a copy of the *Daily Worker* or something equally innocuous. A nervous Nellie, I hear told."

"But four children. One can only imagine the weight—poor dears— for the rest of their lives."

Alger's forthright expression barely altered.

"Four . . . yes."

"And this fellow Harry Dexter White, an assistant secretary at Treasury, testified before the House Committee on Un-American Activities, like you, and dies of a sudden heart attack only days later?"

"Terrible. A brilliant man, a patriot—to be treated like that. I only knew him in official interactions, and, oh yes, we met in San Francisco during the talks on the formation of the United Nations. Something of a toady to his boss Morgenthau."

"Daughters, I believe he had lovely daughters."

"Ah, daughters."

"And this man Marvin Smith, in the Justice Department, a friend of yours? I mean, his name *is* on the transfer document for your old Ford."

Alger stared through me with what I can only describe as an impenetrable look of invincible conviction.

"Sad . . ." He shrugged, as if mystified. "There will be no more where he came from."

With that, he rose abruptly from his seat, our conversation at an end. I was going to ask him how well he'd known Smith's wife, Inez, and their daughter, Jeanne.

—

So I studied like a demon to get myself up to speed, reading up on Freud. I needed to get an outside opinion about Dr. Binger and our backup psychiatrist, Dr. James Murray, who taught at Harvard Medical School. It would be tricky if it came out that I had gone to any local people in the psychiatric community and made inquiries. So I caught the train up to Cambridge and visited a colleague now on the faculty there. We had a nice lunch on Brattle Street, and then I walked back through the Yard to Memorial Hall, where I could pay my respects to Annie's grandfather Richard Davenport. It was then, staring up at the portrait and memorial plaque to that handsome, brave, and talented soul, that I, oddly, found myself returned to my days in Holmes's employ, to his study in Beverly Farms, when I had first seen a photo of Richard Davenport's face, a mere bit of silver on copper. Memory of that moment, of Holmes's description—his tear-stained eyes and quivering jaw—of his friend's bloody death in the Cornfield at Antietam, jolted me and affected me quite profoundly. And oddly, it may have been that strong emotion—the family association through Holmes and Annie—that so firmly blocked out my first memory of Alger Hiss standing beside me in the very spot I now stood, his eyes shining with an inner radiance, when we had seemed part of a brotherhood of youthful aspirants—when we identified with freedom's noble cause etched in the faces of those young men in blue.

It was then, walking the echoing floor of Memorial Hall, that I thought about my conversation an hour before with my Harvard colleague. I had gone over the gist of the evidence we had on Chambers's rather irregular lifestyle, his underground days living in the shadows, even his literary output, which, though not to my taste, seemed quite competent. I made no mention of Chambers's most recent decade as a writer and senior editor at *Time* magazine, the thing I hadn't pushed with Alger, since it so ill-fitted the scenario that he and the members of the defense team were trying to put forth as the common wisdom.

"Oh," my friend exclaimed, "Carl Binger has one of the most insightful minds in the field! And Dr. Murray is greatly respected.

He's designed the most impressive psychological assessment tests in the profession."

"And what do you think about this psychopathic personality disorder business?" I asked him.

"Something of a catchall—a wastebasket classification, but nonetheless a perfectly useful analytic tool to evaluate a warped psyche."

"What would convince you, if you were a layman, on a jury, say, that someone was a pathological liar?"

"The accumulation of lies over time, a pattern of deceit that asserts itself time and time again: a pattern of behavior. And by the look of your Mr. Chambers, what I read in the papers about the first trial, his life is one long string of perjuries." He looked at me with raised eyebrows. "But you've mentioned little about his mother. I suspect she was overly protective, interfering, overbearing—that's always a recipe for disaster. All these different rolls he's played: poet, spy, translator, religious convert—all desperate masks for the approval of a careless mother."

"Would a man's writings, say his short stories or poetry—he wrote quite a bit in his Columbia days—offer insights along those lines into, well, such negative patterns as you describe?"

"Oh, more than anything. Literary works in particular touch on the unconscious and offer profound insights—especially into defects in the formation of conscience. A psychopath reveals himself in both words and deeds, frequently acting impulsively or in a destructive manner. Freud was very clear on this point; literature, from Shakespeare and Dante to Milton and Dostoyevsky, sheds profound light on both characters and their authors. It's why Freud was so convinced that Shakespeare was the seventeenth earl of Oxford. The biography of de Vere perfectly explains so many of Shakespeare's characters—uncanny, really."

"Insights enough to explain the malicious framing of a friend, even a mere or passing acquaintance?"

"So many great authors write out of revenge, to settle a score, to crush an ideological opponent. Especially someone who might have once been a close friend, or, worse, a competitor, either for love or glory, where there was an erotic attachment, anything that harkens back to a feeling of rejection on the part of a demanding mother."

"Well, I understand how you might believe that, academically speaking, but what about a jury?"

"Edward, you know better than I that a jury will believe anything an expert tells them, once it's all been properly explained. Everything we are goes back to how we've been brought up. Problems almost always turn out to be the result of early childhood trauma—neglect, sexual abuse, playing on weakness and fears, the withdrawal of love—that bring on crippling pathologies later in life."

His remarks reminded me of something Martha had recently said about Annie: "Just look at Mother. She's still in love with her alcoholic father, who treated her so badly, who never gave her the kind of love and support she so desperately needed. Take her infatuation with Proust, who was so attached to his mother and grandmother—precisely what she lacked in her childhood. That's why she's so rigid and hard on us, so unyielding and demanding. Her music is her way of escape."

I looked up at the young face of Richard Davenport in his memorial portrait, those kind translucent eyes, an artist's eyes, a poet's expressive mouth, something, surely, of my beloved Annie in the long tapering fingers draped over the pommel of his sword.

Annie's father barely knew his father, whom he lost at six . . . just tales of a brilliant, unrealized life. How does any child live up to a hero's early death?

"I'm not ascribing fault or blame; she just needs to admit to herself the source of her pain," Martha had said.

"You really think she's so hard? I always thought I was the disciplinarian."

"She's got you so trained to her tyranny that you can't tell the difference."

Again, I gazed up at the handsome portrait by William Morris Hunt of Annie's grandfather in his vivid dark blue uniform with its gleaming brass buttons. And nearby was the luminous marble bust by Daniel Chester French of William Francis Bartlett, just touched with a ray of rose-tinted light from the arched windows above.

By all accounts, Richard Davenport was a very talented young man, a poet and musician, who, nevertheless, when the bugle sounded, took up the abolitionist cause, even if soldiering was uncongenial to his essential nature. At least that is what Holmes had told me. A man not cut out for battle, not like General Bartlett, a born leader and intrepid soldier. Fearless. A friend, as well, of Dr. Dimock, who respected Davenport all the more for his gumption: "Courage for the courageous is one thing; bravery in those for whom soldiering is not a calling is bravery of the highest order."

Again I was reminded of something Martha had said to me recently: "Oh, Father, all men think they are cut out for battle. That is why you always gave in to Teddy, always handing him guns and knives for Christmas and his birthday; you two positively revel in violence. Even your beloved brown trout, you know, feel something when so cruelly hooked on the end of your line."

I realized that Martha couldn't care a fig about her great-grandfather Davenport—or her grandfather Dimock—much less any of those other sterling souls staring down from on high in Memorial Hall. Their cause, their deaths, their sacrifices were complete abstractions to someone like Martha. And their war was just another example of the reptilian brain at its worst, producing the aggressive behavior of little boys who'd never grown up, who'd never been properly potty-trained, or nurtured in the love of their fellow men. There were no great intellectuals or philosophers or literary men on the walls of Memorial Hall—all the men pictured had died too young to come into their own and become what they might have become. What a loss to our country! And Holmes might have been among them had it not been for Dr. Dimock, who saved his life when the other doctors had given him up for dead. Richard Davenport, whose blood Martha carried, remained a cipher to her. And sadder still, I remember thinking, with Holmes long gone, how there was no one left with a living memory of that exceptional fellow and his kind. Except, perhaps, something of him remained in our darling Teddy (alone of our offspring), who had taken it upon himself earlier in the fall, when Yale played Harvard at Cambridge, to visit his great-grandfather in Memorial Hall, and write me a long letter of appreciation about his bloodline.

That sad memory, I recognize in retrospect, of my darling boy standing there in Memorial Hall, perhaps wrapped in his Yale scarf for game day, his face lit up in the play of light from the stained-glass windows above, formed yet another bastion in memory's defense, leaving my first meeting with Alger Hiss deep in the stygian shades, where it properly belonged.

If only my memory hadn't failed me, if only I'd had the eyes to pierce the invisible veil and so illuminate the demonic presence at my elbow. Something that, surely after my pretrial interview with Alger, might have suggested an Ahab in thrall to his creature: "Leap! leap up, and lick the sky! I leap with thee; I burn with thee; would fain be welded with thee; defyingly I worship thee!"

A man indeed who could fill his ship with able and willing hands all in pursuit of a goal that was, in the end, but an odyssey of omnipotent madness and perhaps unbegotten horror.

—

I had hoped in the weeks leading up to the trial that I might at least be given the opportunity to meet privately with Priscilla. We hadn't written or seen each other since the war, when I spent three years in Washington working for the War Production Board. I was not a little desperate to get her perspective on things: how much in agreement she was about the path down which we were proceeding. Once upon a time, Alger wouldn't have made a move without her approval. Now, it became quickly clear, a meeting wasn't in the cards. I was told we had her testimony in the can and she would rigidly stick to it. Others on the defense team whispered their doubts, some wondering if it was really Priscilla who had somehow gotten her hands on those secret documents, that she had typed the Woodstock copies, that she was the secret Soviet agent and not Alger, and that he was gallantly protecting his wife. I have to admit that the thought crossed my mind, as well. Of the two, in their early days, she had certainly been the impulsive one, the hot-blooded socialist who might fly off the handle and do something crazy and harebrained. Even Chambers had testified that she was a card-carrying member of the Socialist Party. Alger was too smart, too careful to leave a trail that might tarnish his establishment bona fides.

Observing them in the courtroom over the long days of the trial, I could detect no conjugal warmth, much less passion; rather, they sat as perhaps a brother and sister might sit in face of a forbidding ordeal of parental disapproval. At recesses, they stood by themselves, smoking; at day's end, Alger grasped Pross's arm and led her gently, if firmly, to the exit. Only occasionally did our eyes meet, and only for a split second, when I thought I detected a deep abyss of pain. This seemed all the worse, since I felt powerless to relieve it. Pross seemed to float through the courtroom in a somnolent trance, her movements often stiff and unconscious, as if her mind were somewhere far distant. I wondered if she ever thought of our bird-watching days in Riverside Park. Twenty years before, I'd been quite convinced that Pross had caught her man; now I found, as the trial unfolded to its catastrophic end, that it was Alger who had her—and us—in a taloned grip. If not that of the devil himself, it was certainly the grip of a protean, fire-breathing Ahab, with his foot placed firmly on the neck of all earthly love. Despite this, I was determined to defend her husband against all odds.

———

And so for all the world to marvel, I put it to our Dr. Binger, who sat with a supercilious smirk on the stand, listing all the damaging facts about Whittaker Chambers, about sixty minutes' worth, and then popped the question.

"Doctor, as a psychiatrist, do you have an opinion within the bounds of reasonable certainty as to the mental condition of Whittaker Chambers?"

"I think Mr. Chambers is suffering from a condition known as psychopathic personality, which is a disorder of character, of which the outstanding features are behavior of what we call an amoral or an asocial and delinquent nature: a recognized mental disease."

Under questioning, Dr. Binger went on to note these symptoms: withholding of truths, as itemized in Chambers's many perjuries; stealing; insensitivity to the feelings of others; role playing; bizarre behavior; unstable attachments; panhandling; abnormal emotionality; paranoid thinking; and false accusations.

My heart sank as I encouraged Carl Binger to reel off these inanities, knowing the prosecution's formidable Thomas Murphy would make mincemeat of his testimony the moment I turned over the witness. Chambers had been a KGB underground agent. Of course he had lied. He readily confessed as much. Even the thickest juror understood that was simply his job, ipso facto, stretching the truth. As when Chambers had lied in his passport application to travel to England on a mission to set up a Communist apparatus in London. Lying, as Chambers cheerfully acknowledged, was the mother's milk of the Communist underground—the secret life that required role playing, subterfuge, unstable attachments, and a host of more or less unsavory behaviors. Behaviors that Chambers had come to reject in order to save, as he put it, his soul. And these were precisely the tactics that Alger Hiss had embraced—admitting nothing, lying about everything—if he was indeed following the modus of a master spy, as Chambers had meticulously detailed. Surely the jury didn't miss the irony!

Under prosecutor Murphy's relentless pounding, Binger was forced to admit he'd never even interviewed Chambers and had derived his distasteful laundry list of character defects from the Baltimore deposition and the subject's early writings, mostly taken out of context. But where Binger really hoisted us by our own petard was when he started analyzing Chambers's courtroom demeanor as he'd observed it since the opening of the trial, noting that the witness had "apparently had very little relationship with the inquirer" and often looked off or up at the ceiling, as if searching for thoughts previously uttered. Dr. Binger made much of Chambers's conditional responses: "It must have been," or "It would have been," or "It should have been" . . . what to make of that!

Thomas Murphy's cross-examination of our witness became the high point of the trial, first when he pointed out that the very notion of a psychopathic personality had recently come into disrepute among the psychiatric community as a useless term, certainly not useful for research—an accusation that Dr. Binger unhesitatingly agreed with. The smiles on the jurors' faces were enough to know we were doomed.

When confronted by Murphy that lying on official documents had been in the very nature of Chambers's KGB work, Dr. Binger again agreed to the internal contradictions of his testimony.

"Well, I am not attempting to pass on the nature of his lies. I am stating that he has told many lies, that repeated lying is one of the indications of psychopathic personality."

"Can't we agree," asked Murphy, "that lies are not, ipso facto, evidence of a psychopathic personality?"

"Yes, lies by themselves are not evidence."

Murphy, referring back to Dr. Binger's testimony about Chambers's habitual use of phrases such as "must have been," "should have been," "would have been," pointed out to the doctor that they'd combed through the testimony of Chambers and only come up with ten such usages, whereas, going through Alger Hiss's testimony, they had found 158 such usages.

"Now, do you form any conclusions, Doctor, by the use of the phrases?"

"No."

Murphy then reminded Binger of his count of the times that Chambers had looked up or away from his questioner, and confronted him with the count of his own demeanor over the previous day: "We made a count this morning of the number of times you looked at the ceiling, and during the first ten minutes, you looked at the ceiling nineteen times; the next fifteen minutes, twenty times; the next fifteen minutes, ten times; and the following ten minutes, ten times. That is a total of fifty-nine times, and I was wondering,

Doctor, whether that could be considered symptomatic of psycho-pathic personality?"

Shifting uneasily in his seat, as if to accommodate a silent fart, our good doctor gave Murphy an insipid and pained smile.

"Not alone."

Over my strong objections, and the only time I ever saw Alger close to panic, we decided to go forward with our backup psychiatrist, whom we had thoroughly prepared. This was our Harvard man, Dr. James Murray. We hoped to try to staunch the blood already spilled by Dr. Binger. And, if anything, Murray proved a greater disaster with his hasty evaluation of only selected writings of Chambers. Worse, he clearly displayed a mind already made up when he agreed to testify, and then put the jury to sleep.

Through it all, from farce to disaster, Alger showed remarkable for-titude—only the slightest hints of outward concern. While all agreed that poor Priscilla was close to a nervous breakdown, as her once cher-ished beliefs in the psychiatric profession, much less the infallibility of her husband and his cause turned to ash. And a husband, though con-victed, though incarcerated, still returned fire for fire, as if convinced that drawing righteous outrage from the revolutionary ideologies of the age—of all ages, I suppose—would, in the end, redound to, if not guarantee, his apotheosis.

In this, I sometimes wonder if I don't catch glimpses of a Joseph Smith or John Brown, even as I settle on the figure of Ahab to atone for my benighted trust.

27
Quid Pro Quo

"WELL," SAID MARTHA, opening the door of her apartment, first a crack, then wider, in a jokey approximation of a nervous shut-in. "If it isn't my favorite nephew and his sidekick in crime." She gave George a girlish frown, flung the door wide, and kissed them both, holding Wendy's hand in a lingering handshake as she took in her sporty attire. "Lovely to see you again, dear."

"Crime?" asked George, sniffing the air, which was laden with the aroma of a Polish borscht curdling in the musty confines of a pre-war Upper West Side dowdiness, a half century of clutter, of mildewed books and ratty carpets and drooping potted palms.

"You've got Alice—if the receiver had teeth, it would have gnawed my ear to the bone by now—all in a tizzy about the Judge's memoir and something about sketches you removed from the Judge's office." Martha flipped bangs of reddish brown hair off her unplucked scrolling eyebrows ("Daddy's," always noted Alice), as if needing to better examine her nephew's face. "And what's this crazy business about Alger Hiss?"

"Oh . . . definitely a crime," said George.

Wendy held out a bottle of wine tied with a red ribbon.

"Happy anniversary, Ms. Dimock. It's really kind of you to include me."

"Call me Martha, dear."

"Yes, happy anniversary," added George, surveying the narrow entrance hallway hung with his aunt's trophy wall of "patients, ex-patients, should-be patients, and brilliant colleagues." Signed and profusely inscribed photographs by the likes of Margaret Mead, Gloria Steinem, Betty Friedan, and Bella Abzug, the latter having pride of place by a mahogany coatrack with epically baroque brass hanging hooks.

"Oh my dear"—Martha slipped a hand in one of Wendy's jumpsuit pockets like a sly Artful Dodger—"you're our bright young shining star; Theo has been dying to meet you ever since I mentioned seeing you at George's opening. Just make sure Theo keeps his paws out of your pouches, and a good slap in the face is always a good bet." Martha reached to adjust a framed pencil sketch of Karen Horney, and sniffed. "Smell that *barszcz*—he's been retreating to his roots recently. Wendy, since you're the main attraction, why don't you go through to the kitchen and introduce yourself, and he can open the wine for you. He just gave me, at enormous expense, no doubt, one of those fancy-schmancy corkscrews shaped like a rabbit"—she flashed her brown eyes and popped her heavily lipsticked mouth, yellow teeth stained red—"and he's just dying to screw away. Karen and Erich and the kids are in the living room watching the play-offs."

"Ah, what inning?" asked George, relieved, then made a move to follow Wendy toward the sound of the TV.

"No, you stay here a moment." Martha squinted, putting on her reading glasses, which had been hanging by a cord on the front of her matronly dress, better to scrutinize her ex-patient. "How are you, Georgie? You haven't made an appointment or called me in over two years."

"I'm fine, really."

"No recurrence, no anxiety attacks? You haven't renewed any prescriptions, as far as I can tell."

"Just a year ago, after the World Trade Center, I took some Klonopin for a few days."

"Jesus—you and half the city. I can't believe you were down there—that you had to see that."

"I'm okay, really."

"Even if it doubled my business." She shook her curls, face to heaven, as if scolding the hallway ceiling of cracked and peeling paint—the very thought of such an affront to insular Gotham. "Are you serious about this Wendy?"

"Hanging out."

"Sleeping together?"

"Hard to say."

"That's great news. I mean a young man . . . you look good." She reached to his waist and squeezed. "Are you working out? You've lost weight, or is it just the good sex?"

Martha's scrutiny deepened as she slipped the glasses back to her broad bosom. Her brown hair was tinged with discreet red highlights after a recent visit to her colorist, while her finely lined face showed patches of misapplied makeup.

"So, what's all this about the Judge's memoir that you won't share with Alice? You will share it with me, won't you? We both have professional reputations at stake."

"Of course I will. And I don't know why she should be so o o on the warpath. It's a little complicated. He designated me, legally, as his executor and the editor of his memoir, before it goes to Norton. That was a few weeks ago, when he was still planning to starve himself. Now he's contemplating making some changes. In fact, he just phoned and asked me up to Hermitage tomorrow to discuss the changes."

"Changes? At this point—what's there to change?"

"There's this book called *The Haunted Wood*, by Allen Weinstein, about the KGB penetration of the U.S. government in the Stalin era. It pretty much settles the case that Alger Hiss was a Soviet spy. Well, the Judge has now read the book—or Felicity has read it to him—and I guess he may want to make some adjustments in the memoir, which he stopped working on about five years ago."

"You've read the memoir?"

"Yes, along with the Weinstein book, and his previous book, *Perjury*—on the Hiss trial, among other things."

"Some of my older patients—in this neighborhood—have been quite troubled by that book—and the earlier one. They don't believe a word of it, of course, and, needless to say, they don't like Weinstein. The nicest thing they have to say is that he was a Bush nominee for something or other—'*Eh, Weinstein, what do you expect from such a stinker.*'" She grimaced at her unprofessional, perhaps unbecoming mimic of a Yiddish accent. "Most think he's a traitor."

"A traitor to what?"

"Hiss, of course. Hiss expected Weinstein to write a book exonerating him; that was the deal they had, according to Priscilla. As I recall, Hiss gave Weinstein complete access to the defense files. Weinstein makes the case for Alger's getting screwed by the government."

"*Alger?* You knew Hiss?"

"Mostly in his last years, in the seventies and eighties, when he was touring college campuses to rehabilitate his reputation. Priscilla"—she raised a finger to her lips—"as I think I mentioned, was my patient in the years after Alger dumped her, before she died. But that's just between us."

"You don't seem particularly bothered by the whole thing."

"He mistreated her." She frowned and sighed. "I'm not interested in politics, Georgie; I'm interested in *you*—and the human soul, the human condition. Politics is a distraction and waste of time and energy. All my patients are Bush haters; that's all they want to talk about. They blame him for their troubles; they bore me to tears. And the Hiss trial was a farce, such a distraction, bringing on the whole McCarthy fiasco." Her eyes deepened in a squint. "Even *if* my practice was born out of that mayhem in the late fifties. The victims of Red-baiting, people whose lives were turned upside down by the witch hunt."

"I don't get it: Are you saying it was a witch hunt without witches?"

"I'm telling you it was a distraction from what really mattered. It produced a fever of paranoia that destroyed lives. And, I should add, your grandfather, the Judge, made a fool out of himself in his failed defense of Hiss, besides damaging our profession."

"Ah, yes, Drs. Binger and Murray."

Martha took his arm firmly and stared gently into his eyes. "Speaking of whom, does the Judge have much to say about all that, about his family?"

"Oh, it's very personal, very poignant, a side of him I, of course, had no idea about."

"He talks about us, his daughters?"

"Yes, movingly—really. Like he's trying to figure it all out, where he might have let people down, where he might have done better. But the Hiss trial clearly preoccupies him, as if it were a turning point or a path not taken. That's why the Weinstein book seems to have taken him by storm."

"Pshaw"—she blew out her lips—"a man who messed with his own daughter, his granddaughters."

George bowed his head at this now slightly tarnished accusation that had first rocked his adolescence and then lingered like a faint rattle in the woodpile.

"Let's not go there . . ."

"It was *his* idea, you know, to use two highly respected psychiatrists, top men in their field, to refute the testimony of that horrible overweight fellow with the sallow face, Chambers, the accuser of Hiss. Highly unprofessional—to enlist psychiatrists in a political squabble. We're humanitarians first and foremost: Our role is to help people better understand themselves and help them heal."

"The Judge readily admits his poor judgment in agreeing to have Binger and Murray take part in the trial."

"Oh"—her eyes lit up—"James, James Murray. I heard later that the girls at Radcliffe fawned all over that wonderful man, had orgasms, squirming in their seats, during his lectures." She patted his cheek. "I've made you blush."

"Nothing my unfiltered aunt Martha says makes me blush anymore, not after the women today." George turned to inspect a faded black-framed photo of a middle-aged Margaret Mead seated before an RCA microphone, hands outstretched in mid-sentence. "But my sense from the memoir is that the Judge felt, well, coerced into employing those two expert witnesses, Binger and Murray, to prove Chambers had a *psychopathic personality*."

Again, Martha placed a hand on her nephew's arm, as if the usage of trade terminology was not quite to be countenanced by a one-time patient.

"Don't be ridiculous, George. Unlike Alice, I don't like to speak ill of my father. But there's no more charitable way to put it: He's very free with the facts and he's first and foremost a brilliant lawyer, and like most brilliant lawyers, he will wrap you up with his arguments, like a python its prey, and squeeze you, gently at first, harder later, until you find the air has been ejected from your lungs and your soul engulfed."

"I didn't know there was, well, such a death struggle."

"It was foolhardy of him to enlist psychiatric experts, much less throw around technical terms in front of, as the kids put it today, a clueless jury. And then employ gross exaggerations and manipulations of subjective opinions. And in a trial that was less about evidence and more a political circus. Chambers was clearly a disturbed individual with a mother fixation, a God fixation; he had probably been in love with Hiss at some point and they had an ideological squabble or falling-out—trust me, I have it from the horse's mouth."

She raised her eyebrows in a knowing look. George tilted his head with a dubious squint. Martha bent close to his ear.

"She—did I tell you already?—was a patient of mine for many years after Alger dumped her for another woman." George was about to speak, when she pressed a finger to her lips. "That's confidential, you understand. Just between us. Not that some kind of discreet—he needn't know—quid pro quo might not be arranged with regard to the memoir."

George nodded—brows pressed in tight under his now neatly barbered blond hair—his expression one of skepticism.

"So . . . you don't think it matters, the outcome, whether Hiss was guilty or innocent?"

"What matters is that the Judge confesses to his abuse of your mother, and to fooling around with my daughter *and* my sister's."

Before George could protest, Martha froze him with a look of sly knowingness. "Priscilla, poor thing, was bewitched by that man's book, *Witness*. Which she considered a pack of lies. And yet there were parts that seemed to touch her profoundly, how it was possible for such a wicked man to also catch so much of her and Alger's essential goodness and simplicity. My God, she could quote from it almost verbatim: their organic reaction to the life around them, a profound suspicion of the pursuit of pleasure as an end in itself, a distrust of materialism and its easy notions of success and gain, a love of labor—their Quaker thing, I suppose. And so into birds, just like Daddy. This disturbed her greatly, and her son—Alger not so much, as if two completely different worlds lurked within the pages of that 'awful thing,' so she called it." Martha raised her head as if to survey the gallery of her patients and admirers and laid a heavy hand, forefinger smeared with lipstick, on her nephew's shoulder. "I think the real question is, Why do *you* even care?"

"Good question."

She threw up her hands. "How many old Reds have I baby-sat on my couch, certainly in the early years: disillusioned, bitter, betrayed, holding grudges against the world and one another, so tied up in knots that they were unable to move on from the Party idolatry of their youth. They simply can't understand that the only way the world is changed for the better is by healing one person at a time. From which flows healthy social change, equal rights—equality, which flows from the bottom up, from a small group of committed citizens, as Margaret always put it, and not from the mouths of politicians."

George followed her loving gaze to the photo of Margaret Mead, smiling to himself as he then took in the signed photographs of Gene McCarthy and George McGovern, and three New York City mayors.

"Politicians?"

"The most miserable narcissists and megalomaniacs—unhappy people."

"You don't think it matters that Hiss was stealing secrets?"

"Secrets—who cares if he was or wasn't? We were on the same side against the Nazis. Most Communists I knew were leaders in the crusade for civil rights and workers' rights. Even the Judge was a progressive in the early days. He believed firmly in equality before the law."

From down the hall came the roar of a crowd on the TV, his cousins cheering.

"Sounds like a Yanks homer," he said expectantly, edging away.

"Tell me, George, does he talk about—in the memoir, Annie . . . and Teddy?"

"Yes, it's quite personal, almost confessional—surprisingly so—in some respects."

At the mention of "confessional," her eyes lit up. "Ah, as a man, perhaps you have a hard time understanding these things, George: the predatory ways of powerful narcissistic men." She squeezed his arm, the merest hint of alarm at the corners of her eyes. "You know, you really *must* let me see it."

"Of course I will. I asked him on the phone when I could share it with the family, and he said he just wants to consult about the Weinstein book, if he needs to make any changes. Then there's his editor at Norton."

"How can that stinker Weinstein matter a damn to his memoir?" She threw up her hands. "What's done is done."

"Well," he said with a knowing smile as he turned away, "I've got an appointment with the stinker next week in Washington. He's now the director of the National Archives."

"Ah, the *Bush* appointment."

———

"Georgie!" His older first cousin, Karen, moved to embrace him as he entered the living room. The television, glaring out like a sally port from battlements of mahogany-shelved books, blared the Yankees play-off game. Her flowing dark hair fell over the padded shoulders of her somewhat dated print dress as she reached to enfold him in her arms, squeezing him close, so that her breasts nestled tight against his lower rib cage, then adding a playful erotic wiggle for welcome. "Still my little boy, my darling space boy, my little Luke." She laughed, exuding something of her mother's hothouse intelligence, then pulled away abruptly, as if caught out by Wendy, who was walking in with a tray full of wine-glasses from the kitchen. "Aha, Georgie's Princess Leia." Karen giggled, making a face at her teenage son, Max, who had turned in his seat at his mother's antics, and took the tray from Wendy, while giving the younger woman a quick once-over: compact boobs, hair in a chignon, cheekbones to die for, and the full-length orange jumpsuit, perfectly tailored down to the elaborate array of pockets on the sleeves and thighs, and two with perfectly positioned brass snaps at the breasts. "Wow, and how's it going, Wonder Woman?" She gave Wendy a hug and a kiss. "I was kinda hoping you were going to wear that knockout Gucci number from the opening."

"Do you like it?" Wendy bent to Karen's ear, adjusting an Hermès scarf around her neck. "A bitch to pee."

"Such a Princeton thing."

"Well"—Wendy shrugged as she took a glass for herself and one for George from the tray—"when in Tigertown . . ."

Erich, tall and lanky like his father, with Slavic features, had been watching the play-off game on the ancient RCA, seated next to Karen's son, Max. He got up and shook hands with the new arrivals. Then Erich's thirteen-year-old daughter, Nancy, earbuds firmly implanted, came over from a far corner, where she'd been doing homework. Fair-haired Nancy was tall like her dad, thin, graceful, with a narrow tapering nose and large eyes. She politely greeted her cousin and Wendy, only to beat a quick and diligent retreat back to her chair and homework.

"Hey, bro," Erich said, high-fiving his cousin, "good to see you back in standard George attire"—he eyed the torn jeans and Chelsea Piers sweatshirt—"after your opening. You had me worried for a while at your gallery that you'd gone to the moneyed dark side in that slick getup. Have you lost weight, George?"

"Workin' out, man, thanks to Wendy."

Erich gave Wendy a lingering smile of appreciation.

"Lucky boy. I couldn't take my eyes off Wendy at the opening; little did I know you were going to join us for dinner. I was trying to get up the nerve to go over and chat you up."

"Wasn't it a fabulous show!" said Wendy. "You should go see it again before it closes."

"Sold out," added George, "almost twice over. Hey, what's the score?"

"Max," said Karen, "come say high to your cousin George and Wendy. She's a mountain climber—she's climbed Mount Everest."

"Hey, Max," said George, high-fiving the fourteen-year-old with long, stringy hair, "how's it going with the Angels?"

"Third inning," said Max, shaking Wendy's hand, barely able to look her in the eye. "Four to three, Yanks. Rodriguez just homered with one on."

"Way to go, Alex." George punched Erich's arm, now distracted by activity at the bird feeder hanging by the side of the window. "Wow, wood thrush on a feeder, on Riverside Drive—you don't see that very often."

"Mom puts dried blueberries and raisins in her mix," said Erich. "She picks up a few migrating pairs who are looking for fruit and berries."

"Very cool."

George went over to the window overlooking Riverside Park and the Hudson River beyond. Edging closer to the glass, he gazed down the fifteen stories to the curving street, the sidewalk draped in brassy maples, blots of more vivid orange and yellow against the snaking procession of parked cars. An involuntary shiver leapt up his spine as his gaze returned to the busy feeder. "They must be resting in the park," he announced to no one in particular. Wendy came over and touched her glass to his. He put his arm around her and squeezed. "Headed south . . . smart fellows. They know it's going to be a cold winter." He was peculiarly aware that his usage, "smart fellows," was an echo of how the Judge would have described the thrush. "I'll show you this spot tomorrow, Handytown, where in June and July the hermit thrush"—he smiled to himself—"*sing like a choir of angels*."

As if on cue, the mottled radiator at their feet began to spit and hiss.

"Pretty creepy, your aunt Martha living on the sixteenth floor," she said, gazing down, measuring distances.

"When did that occur to you?"

"The moment you pushed the button in the elevator."

"Same here. Except we're safe; there's no thirteenth floor. So it's only fifteen stories."

"Of course, all the difference in the world."

"Duggan," he offered for no particular reason at all, "was class secretary for his Harvard class of 1927."

"Yup, just a hop, skip, and a jump from his office, the Harvard Club, a block away."

For a minute, they distracted themselves with more of the same dark humor, which had crept into their interchanges, especially the analysis of calamitous scenes when juxtaposed with those of calm and normalcy— the razor's edge contiguity; the precariousness, which the well-ordered playground in Riverside Park brought to mind, where mothers, dark-skinned nannies, and maybe a few fathers were beginning the last roundup, dragging reluctant, tired children home in the onrushing dusk, trailing tricycles and plastic bats and dogs describing leashed half arcs. Back to safe apartments as the days shortened, the shadows lengthened, and night drew its cloak of uncertainty in tighter embrace.

George again turned his gaze to the bird feeder, where a goldfinch was spilling seed. On sudden impulse, he opened the window and reached out to the bird feeder, a heavy metal and Plexiglas cylinder with wooden perches.

"Look at the bracket holding this thing; it's practically pulled free from the brick—the damn thing is hanging by a thread." With that, George grabbed the feeder and lifted it off its hook and into the apartment, spilling seeds everywhere.

"Careful!" exclaimed Wendy, who had slid her hand into the belt of his jeans.

"Hey, Erich, tell your mom that she's got to get the bracket for the bird feeder fixed?" He reached out the window again and wiggled the bracket. It came loose in his hand. "Jesus, that feeder could have fallen to the street and killed someone."

Erich got up from the couch and inspected the scattered birdseed on the Oriental as George handed him the bracket with the two rusted anchor screws. Bits of friable mortar still clung to the threads.

"That feeder has been there ever since I was a kid. I'll tell Mom to get the super to stick it up again."

"Does the building allow you to hang shit like this out the windows? I'm sure there's a city code about hanging bird feeders. It's a danger to public safety, and the birdseed that gets dropped attracts pigeons and rats."

"Oh relax, Lukie; you're always such an alarmist. You had to have yanked out the stupid motherfucker. And the damn super will charge two hundred bucks just to screw it in again."

Wendy smiled politely.

"Where does your mom keep the broom and dustpan?"

———

Theo, tall, dapper, white hair swept back from a prepossessing brow, golden tan gilding his wide cheekbones, held up his wineglass at the head of the table in a toast to his wife. With a professorial tenor voice, he graciously acknowledged their four decades of connubial bliss, much of his suave Eastern European intonation still evident, all delivered with the smooth undertones of a fulsome intellect.

"And after everything . . . what more can I add except congratulations for her endurance, and, need one admit it, my humble apologies to my dear wife for having had to put up with my *cheatin'* ways all these many fulfilling years."

"Productive years—just look around you." Martha raised her glass to her husband's. "And, you could have been *so* much worse, Theo."

"How's that possible?" asked Karen.

"He didn't get any of them pregnant—as far as I know," said Martha.

"Cool it, you two," scolded Erich, indicating that the kids were within earshot.

"The borscht is great, Dad," said Karen. "At least you never kept any of them barefoot and pregnant in the kitchen."

"Forever sixty—that's my motto," proclaimed Theo, holding his glass aloft.

"The Pill, and abortion rights, equal pay for women—we have you and your generation to thank for that, Mom," said Karen, with a nod at her niece.

Max looked up from his phone, caught his cousin's eye, and pressed a choking hand to his throat. Nancy stuck out her tongue.

"Come on, you two," said Erich.

"The borscht is one of your better efforts, dear."

"Borscht sure beats divorce," said Nancy with a wicked smile, shaking back her long auburn hair as she looked around, producing a momentary silence.

"It's really Jewish, you know," said Theo. "All of the finest Polish cuisine is Jewish. And oh, by the way, Harvard University Press has just picked up my thirty-years-out-of-print *Sociological Underpinnings of the Nazi Party*."

Wendy raised her glass. "I'm so honored to be here on this occasion. I mean, I don't mean to gush, but all those people, the photographs out in the hall—I can't believe you knew all those famous people, Martha."

"Thank you, dear," said Martha, eyeing her family with a wide-eyed crease of pain, as if to say, *My family who couldn't care less?* "Some were patients; the rest should have been—but that's confidential, you understand."

"Rich, too," said Theo, "to afford your fees, dear."

"Ah, the moneyed rich and powerful—how I wish I had a few more of those," said Karen. "Twice a week—huh, Mom, some for five, even ten years. What an income stream in those halcyon days. Unfortunately, psychotherapy, analysis for the good of your soul, has gone out of fashion. You have to prove abuse now—or shoot up a 7-Eleven—to even claim therapy on your health insurance."

"Put you and Erich through college—with a little help from Theo."

"Us poor downtrodden academics," said Theo, sighing.

"You were a star, Dad," said Karen, "on the playing field and off. All the beautiful baby-sitters of my childhood testified as much."

"They were darn cute, that's for sure," added Erich.

Theo held up his soupspoon. "A man's religion is his supper."

"I could never quite figure out which religion we are," said Nancy. "Now Mom suddenly wants me to go to Shabbat services on Friday evenings."

"Since when?" asked Erich, not a little taken aback.

"We're humanists," replied Martha to her granddaughter, raising her eyebrows at Theo.

"In times of stress," said Theo, "people return to the shelter of order and tradition. Now Nancy," he went on in a more convivial vein, "since we're on the subject of religious experiences, did you know Wendy, right here"—he patted Wendy's hand where she sat to his right—"actually climbed Mount Everest?"

"Yeah, Mom told me," interjected Max, returning to his phone.

Nancy scowled at Max, "Oh, just the highest mountain in the world." She turned to Wendy, who was seated next to her. "Wow, that's so way cool. Were you ever afraid of falling?"

"Not of falling. Just about having the stamina to keep going when there is very little oxygen to breathe. And not getting hit by a sudden storm at altitude."

"How high were you?" asked Max.

"About the cruising altitude of a seven forty-seven."

"You must be proud," said Karen. "I mean, how many women have managed that?"

"Twenty-nine thousand and twenty-nine feet," said Max, holding up his phone.

"Put it away, Max," said Karen.

"No," said Wendy, "I was a fool—the youngest American woman."

"Really," said Martha.

"It's a male fantasy thing, a check mark on a to-do list. Climbing should be about the skill and beauty of the climb, not taking terrible risks and grinding your lungs to icy pulp."

"Well said," and Martha saluted with her glass. "At Wendy's age, we were throwing that little bearded shit Sigmund Freud off his mountain."

"Ah, the defenestration of Vienna—out goes our little Viennese fascist," said Theo, "and in comes your pal Timmy Leary and his crowd of druggies. Do you remember, Martha, when you and Alice got that cover profile in *New York* magazine, 'Feminist Radicals for Gender Equality'? The Dimock sisters take on Freud, racism, and sexism in America."

"When was that, exactly, dear? And how did Alice get mixed up in all that—the feminist-Freudian part?"

"Sometime in the early seventies, the Black Panthers, wasn't it?"

"I could never quite see how sleeping with one's clients in prison was going to move the needle on racism. Much less almost getting herself killed in the process. I think Wendy is a much better role model for young women today. How many women in our day ever aspired to climb Everest?"

"I'm really a rock climber"—Wendy threw back her head, intently alert to the drift of the conversation—"a granite hugger."

"Nancy's science project this year is about the possibilities of life in outer space," announced Erich, proud dad. "Hey, George, since you're our family spaceman, you should give Nancy some pointers."

"What do you think are the chances of life in the universe, Cousin George?" asked Nancy.

George smiled at Nancy. "Well, statistically, given an infinite or almost infinite number of stars with goldilocks planets within just the right orbits and propitious chemical makeups, life should be abundant in the universe. On the other hand, we're not entirely certain how life evolved on Earth, if it happened once or many times, if it was an extreme fluke of circumstances or quite an ordinary occurrence given the right conditions. Knowing that probability would give us a much better idea about the chances of life out there."

"The rarity, you mean?" asked Nancy. "I'd like to think it was rare, at least that would make us feel a little special."

"Well," George began, pondering her question, "life is about electrons and protons, about information, if you will, and if information is unconstrained, it would be hard for us to predict what life would look like on other planets, even given the same laws of physics. Not to mention four extinctions that we know about. So what we think of as life might indeed be rare and very different from the kind of life in other galaxy clusters. Trouble is, our window for communication is so slender, the century or two when we might have the technology to send or receive a signal before we blow ourselves to smithereens."

"Such a happy thought—after, you know . . ." noted Martha with a scowl.

"Thank you, Luke baby," said Erich. "Nancy, I think you should get your cousin George to advise you on your science project for the winter term."

"Yes," Martha put in. "You should really go back to teaching."

"God, I love your getup," said Karen to Wendy.

"Me, too," said Nancy, looking admiringly at Wendy. "Do mountain climbers get to wear stuff like that?"

"The jumpsuit?" Wendy laughed, holding out her arms and tapping the pockets. "This is just something a designer-artist friend cooked up: *pocketLady.com*. That's the brand. Soon to make a splash on the Internet."

"In my fourth-grade class," noted Erich, "it's already the frigging cell phone thing." He turned a jaundiced eye on Max's phone. "Connected and yet disconnected. All the kids are texting or messaging twenty-four/seven but lack all the deeper interpersonal skills. I keep trying to limit the texting thing with Nancy—not that her mother could care."

"Mom likes being able to text me at all times, especially after—you know—last year."

"One thing for sure," said Theo, "we never did—what do they call it now?—helicoptering. And we certainly never tried to polish your social-climbing skills."

George piped up: "Wendy is actually a fabulous artist. In fact, you're the first to know that she's signed with Dark Matter for her first one-woman show this winter."

Karen frowned. "Jesus—really, what sort of things do you do?"

"Mostly landscapes with figures, or figures with landscapes —depending."

"Oh my," exclaimed Martha, "I feel for you young lady! Talk about a tough field for a woman. How many great women artists have I treated, who were thwarted at every turn. Forgive me, but such a narcissistic and yet vulnerable group. Who was that one, Theo, I treated for so many years—the alcoholic woman, you know?"

"Agnes Martin," said Karen.

"Agnes—oh, yes, Agnes . . . she was always so broke, so enraptured with Rothko, always trying to outdo the boys. She could only pay me with paintings."

"You have some Agnes Martins?" asked Wendy, not a little astonished.

"Three or four at least. Two in the office, one in the hallway, and a few in my bedroom."

"Remember that funny thing she wrote, Mom?" said Karen, as if testing her mother.

"Did she write something?"

"The gray one in the bedroom: 'To Martha, who saved me more than once from my demons.'"

"Ah, that lovely geometric abstraction." Martha drained her glass and gazed fondly at Wendy. "And where did you study art, dear?"

Erich looked perturbed. "See, that's such a status thing you're bringing up, Mom."

"I'm just interested, and I think City College worked just fine for you, Erich. By the way, how's the long-in-coming dissertation on the cotton trade between Genoa and Sardinia in the twelfth century?"

"Venice and Sicily," said Erich.

"Well, it looks like it's still between you and George in the Judge's sweepstakes to see who's going to get the first Ph.D. in your generation."

"Oh, leave it be," said Karen. "Next you'll be on to who got the Dimock nose."

"Why don't we all think about spending Thanksgiving at Hermitage," suggested George.

"The kids hated it," Martha said dismissively.

"That's really not fair," said Karen. "I loved my summers at Hermitage when we were kids."

"Oh, really," said Martha. "Since when? All I ever heard out of you and Erich were complaints about how you had been so regimented—'the Dimock concentration camp,' I believe you called it."

"The piano lessons were a bit much," said Erich. "Although that Romanian at Juilliard that came up was quite something—Caterina. She sunbathed in the nude on the beach."

"*You* saw her, too?" said George with a nostalgic smile.

"Remember," exclaimed Karen, turning to Erich down the table, "when Mom came up that summer with the Rorschach tests for the cousins! We used to compete to see who could find the most salacious imagery."

"Mating bats," said Erich with a snicker.

"Copulating clowns," added Karen, giving him a sneaky smile.

"George," said Martha, "you were always the most interesting in terms of testing, you saw things in the Rorschach that no one else saw."

"Nebulae," proclaimed George, delighted (how much they shared and how different), "exploding planets and black holes."

Karen waved her hands and laughed. "For Christ's sake, nobody believes in that mumbo jumbo anymore. The Brits don't even trust the test—they've practically banned the ink blots for giving false and misleading results. People keep fooling with the coding guidelines for scoring and it still gives inconsistent results."

George nodded at Karen with a knowing smile. "The Judge doesn't care anymore about the boathouse. Besides, I think it's about time for Nancy and Max to see Hermitage and spend time with the Judge. He's not going to be around much longer."

"Don't go there, George," said Martha. "Pandora's box."

"I really do miss Hermitage," said Karen.

"Oh my God," said Martha. "You and Cecily blew up the whole house of cards."

"Brought down," said Erich.

"Yup, almost burned down the boathouse," said Karen, casting a deliciously wicked look at her son, Max, who sat listening intently to the adults.

Theo cleared his throat. "Martha, I think you blew things way out of proportion with your old man. And, it's time to bring on my main course, my *bigos* stew with pork and mushrooms. Max, why don't you hop to it."

"*My dirty little Jew,*" said Martha, imitating a growling male voice as she glared down the table at Theo.

Theo raised his glass in salute and smiled.

"Dear, you have no idea what real anti-Semitism looks like. Your father is a pussycat compared to the real thing."

"Funny," said Karen, "I was dreaming about Hermitage only the other night, that I was back there with Cecily and we were getting up to no good."

"No good?" asked Max, arriving with the *bigos*.

"Whenever I'm in Riverside Park and smell the white pines, I think about Hermitage," said Erich, smiling at George. "How say you, Luke the Cruddyback Kid?"

"Thanksgiving at Hermitage," said George, smiling at Nancy and Max. "What about it, guys?"

28

Handytown (Annie's Way)

How could I be expected to believe in a common origin uniting two names which had entered my consciousness, one through the low and shameful gate of experience, the other by the golden gate of imagination.

—Proust

GEORGE AND WENDY walked slowly, hand in hand, along the winding woodland path, shadowed far above by the white pines resting their weary shoulders on the swirl of gray tethering a late-October sky. Along their way, the second-growth hemlocks, snug and warm (survivors of the bark peelers over a century before) were already hunkered down for winter; they reached out delicate fingers to the sojourners, as if curious to touch their colored fleeces of hot pink and pumpkin orange (bow hunting season was upon them), hers a North Face, his a Patagonia, perhaps a little in awe of these travelers from realms of pinnacled peaks and barren shores. The circuitous unmarked path through deep woods, seemingly leading nowhere, was mimicked above in the random streaks and curlicues of sailing cirrus clouds reflecting brassy glints of a faltering western sun. The stealth of their footfall on damp pine needles and moldy leaf litter was less that of hunters, or even birders, than of explorers of the unseen, or at least that is how it felt to her after a brief introduction to timeless Hermitage before their walk, invoked at each obscure turning, which seemed to reveal only summer's melancholy ruin in the spindly cinnamon-mottled ferns and tottering gray thistle and the bear-mauled stumps sporting carillons of nodding mushrooms. She felt this loss as an ache in her breast, sharpened by the sudden staccato tattoo of a pileated woodpecker, like a warning shot, bringing them up short. They turned to the encroaching mauve blush interlineated between the stark ranks in all directions: nothing. She gripped his hand—a woman more comfortable at height with a vista and her downclimb secured—as they continued along the invisible path to nowhere.

She sighed to herself with relief as the claustrophobic wood finally spilled into an old clearing set off and crisscrossed by lichen-stained and moss-mortared bluestone walls. Even the sky seemed to lighten, falling on the scattering of black birch, dogwoods, and the ruins of an ancient apple orchard like an airy veil. Meadow grasses still tall and green garnished the less shady spots of the twenty or so acres, presided over by sun-bleached mullein and dour milkweed, flanked here and there by barberry bushes flecked with points of shimmering crimson. Rabbits scampered at their approach.

"Welcome to Handytown," he announced with a reverent whisper.

"Fly Gap," she replied.

"Fly Gap?"

"A ghost town I used to visit with my father in the Texas Hill Country."

She crisscrossed her arms and rubbed her shoulders, as if needing some assurance of her physical presence, then sat on a firm section of wall, marveling at how well the bluestone ramparts had survived almost two hundred years as he went on to describe Handytown in a voice oddly unlike his own. In every direction the walls ran plumb line–straight, as if asserting some immemorial instinct to order, a painstaking project of generations to thwart the unruliness of wild nature by the imposition of man-made artifacts, to tame something of the rough-and-tumble randomness of the trees and rocky earth—more rocks and roots than earth. The perfection of these walls benefited from help of more recent vintage, as he demonstrated by lifting a few recalcitrant "fellows" and, with a slap and a grunt, merging the stones with their brothers in the most glaring gaps.

He smiled with the joy of reminiscence. "The Judge can identify the different hands of the wall builders, a signature style, you see, like that of any artist. He used to tell us, I think quoting Thoreau, that you can read the stories of the old farmers in the scribble of their walls. But the most beautiful walls are along the Neversink hike, where the old Mount Hope and Lumberland Turnpike merges with the railway bed of the Port Jervis & Monticello."

He took her hand and pulled her up and led her through the knee-high grasses, waylaid for moments at patches of sagging sweet fern, still perfuming the air, until reaching the luminous center of the clearing, where two huge lilac bushes, shorn for the winter, stood like disheveled guardians before the rock-ribbed ruins of a cellar hole. She fingered the few heart-shaped leaves hanging by a thread and eyed the bent trunk of a silver birch, a sylvan jack-in-the-box that sprang supple and tall from the brambles at the bottom of the cellar hole. The peeling white bark, notched with dark blottings, shimmered mysteriously in the fading light, only to fountain into a blur of milky iridescence and pale saffron against the russet-gray woods. She smiled wistfully at the loveliness of the moment and brought her nose close to a cluster of withered lilac blossoms, in forlorn hope of spring's long-ago scent.

"The silence," she said, sighing.

"Yes," he replied, and waved her on, "you'd almost think we were alone. The Judge sprinkled Annie's ashes here, by himself, alone; not even my mother was with him. We don't even know where—he never spoke about it."

At the backside of the clearing, on a slight incline at the forest's edge thick with blueberry bushes, seven great upright slabs of bluestone rose from the forest floor, as high as their heads, each with crudely fashioned arched crowns, like a row of blind Venetian Gothic windows. Nowhere could she detect lettering or dates or names incised, chiseled, or even crudely scratched into the lichen-mottled faces. Something about the anonymity of these mute grave markers made her hesitant to draw too near, lest a careless touch cause one to topple.

"Hardly your Green-Wood Cemetery," he noted, half in jest. "First citizens of Sullivan County come into the country after the Revolution." He slapped the ragged edge of the central monolith and tidied up a few creepers along the base. "Which stone is for the patriarch, David Handy, even the Judge could never determine. When his father, Dr. Dimock, first discovered Handytown, he told his son he could just manage to identify their garden and cornfield, their meadow and pasture. But as kids, we could never really figure out what was what; the Judge liked to think he could."

He collected some brittle miscellanies of Queen Anne's lace and lay a bouquet before the central grave marker, his eyes distant, as if filling with memories not his own, only to turn quickly to catch the flutter of a falling leaf, the alarmed chatter of a red squirrel, and the sudden flutter of a shadow, followed by the death swoop of a red-tailed hawk taking their measure before disappearing deeper into the forest.

"Why did they come *here*?"

In answer, he gestured for her to follow, leading her to the far side of the clearing, where a hidden spring nestled among the mossy roots of a sprawling first-growth oak (spared by the Handys to shelter their water supply). Tucked among the roots was a blue enamel cup of indeterminate vintage, more chipped than not. He knelt, brushed away a few floating leaves, and ceremoniously dipped the cup into the clear, still water so as not to disturb her mirrored image, now revealed at his side, upon which he gazed momentarily, distracted by the distorting angle of vision—this seeming stranger. His eyes lingered on her face for a few more seconds as he tried to decipher her mood or perhaps question the wisdom of encouraging this beautiful but possibly dangerous outsider to participate in a sacramental rite dear to him and his family. He glanced down at himself in turn, as if to clarify his reticence, that it might not be some other who handed up the blue enamel cup. Her fingers were cold where they touched his. She closed her eyes as she drank, savoring the taste as if of the very essence of suspended time.

"So sweet, so pure . . ." She shivered, handing back the cup. "I thought Hermitage—the ship's keel ceiling—was a work of art, but this—this is, well . . ." She shrugged, as if helpless to express her feelings. "*Your* Handytown, I guess." She gestured to the tall white pine surrounding the perimeter of the clearing. "Like gods staring down."

"As a kid, I was always in awe, like believing in ghosts. The people who had lived here and were no more. How the Judge treated the place with such reverence. The hike to the Neversink abutments was always more exciting: the fishing, scavenging for spikes in the old railway ties, hanging out with the cousins, and the sun always seemed to be shining. While the walk to Handytown was different, reverential, rainy, peaceful, late in the day or when time was short, when the right mood struck."

"Hah, your Swann's Way."

"What?"

"Nothing."

Something in him bridled and he turned back to the mirrored surface of the spring as if to better catch some hint of betrayal in her reflected face. Often attracted to her musings, he was discomfited by the way she so guilelessly appropriated the stories of others—the living or dead, real or imagined—as if to make them her own.

He nodded in reply, perhaps in refutation. "The Neversink was for sport; Handytown was our religion." With this, he held up his cup in mock salute, drank, and bent for a refill before again handing it back to her.

"Like I said: fountain of youth. Or would that amount to truth serum?"

"Plenty of memories along the Neversink. And if you hadn't read that stuff about Proust in the memoir, in the part where Annie lay dying in the great room, staring up at the ship's keel ceiling . . ."

He shook his head, aware of the critical tenor of his voice, and leery of accusing her of further deceit.

"Yes," she said with a hint of guilt as she fingered the cup, "that, too. Trust me: It's a little creepy, like some part of me is losing my mind—or perhaps your family is a mind-altering drug—too many mushrooms." She laughed, as if to make light of the whole thing, but nervously shook back her hair as her eyes deepened with a contemplative expression. She breathed deeply before again venturing another sip. "See—I have a photographic memory: a curse or a blessing. And even when I'm not trying, whole pages of poetry just stick in my brain. Paintings in museums. The bodies of women in the street. Images I want to translate into paint. But sometimes it gets to be too much—the voices, I mean." Glancing shyly into his curious eyes, she laughed again, giddy, like an impetuous child caught in the act. She struck a comical pose, holding out the cup, as if mimicking some marble goddess by a Renaissance garden pool, or perhaps the figure of Aquarius on the ship's keel ceiling that had caught her fancy an hour before, and tipped out a thin glittering liquid stream to cloak their reflections among the floating leaves. "It's just a little disturbing— don't you think?" she said, sighing, "the silence, the longing in this place . . ." She bent and replaced the cup exactly where he'd retrieved it, nestled among the roots. "Such sweet sadness."

Somewhat confounded by her antics, he countered with the facts as they'd been conveyed to him. "The hardships of the first settlers are almost unimaginable. Once a year, David Handy would cart his load of cedar shingles to Newark for the supplies that would last him and his family the rest of the year. These were fields here once, cornfields, the Handy family's fields. Imagine the isolation. And the growing season so short, the way the Catskills gets such a head start on fall and winter . . . cold tonight, too."

"I can hear the Judge in you."

"You might want to contain your admiration until we've actually had a chance to discuss things with his highness after his nap, the god of all he surveys."

"He can't be that bad, George, not the part of him that enters your voice every time you talk about this place, and when he writes about Annie."

"Brainwashed, huh."

"The better part, maybe?" She spread some ChapStick on her lips. "And the memoir—it's like I've seen what he's describing, especially when his writing is inspired by books or maybe your Renaissance ceiling; then his prose takes flight and becomes so full of feeling. You should encourage him along those lines—the legal stuff pales in comparison to when he writes about his family—Annie and Teddy, and, of course, Hiss and Holmes. Like Chambers in *Witness*: The best parts are about his life and family, reflections on people in his spy network, his farm in Maryland. It's those passages where it rises above biography to literature." He gave her a disgruntled look. She took a deep breath, calming herself, staring up into the darkening sky, where a pale quarter moon hovered, as if at anchor off one of the topmost boughs of pine. "My God, that ceiling's incredible; I can't get it out of my mind—you see, that's the problem: Things stay with me." And she pointed to her head. "I mean, I had no idea. I've seen the ceiling in black-and-white reproductions in textbooks on Italian art history, but its location was always given as 'unknown.' I assumed it was somewhere in the Veneto. And then, walking into Hermitage, there it was! This thing, this image that had existed in my mind's eye—and it's *there*." She shook her head in a kind of consternation. "Like something of me is there."

"Well, it may not be *there* much longer. Yale may be angling to take it on, maybe lock, stock, and barrel."

"No, no way." She frowned in horror.

"He's going slowly broke: taxes and upkeep."

"It belongs right where it is," she stated with proprietary indignation.

This spurred some need in him to confront her, as it always did when she insisted on the world accommodating her.

"Oh, our Giordano Bruno has been there for only a little over a hundred years—what's the difference if it moves on once again? Hell, in an infinite universe, it arrived less than a second ago."

She scolded him playfully. "Your mind games are not helpful to your cause. It's your birthright. It's in the memoir. Remember how much Annie loved it, how her playing made it come alive?"

He looked at her with an uneasy half-smile, puzzled how her indignation triggered in him a feeling of safety, while her more outlandish desires reminded him of his loss of the same. He gently took her arm. "It's cloudy today. Wait till the sun is shining in the west over the lake; then the ship's keel ceiling truly comes alive. It will really blow your mind." She turned in his grip and kissed him, lingering to transfer the balm to his lips. "Remember"—and he placed a finger over her mouth—"not a word from you about the memoir; that's just between us."

She smiled enigmatically. "Yes, sir. Just between you and the Judge."

He looked up through the overhanging boughs, where in the fading light the sky was beginning to shed stars, recalling something. "There was a time, when I was really young, when I thought the stars and planets up there in the ceiling really *were* the stars and planets, and the figures were real people, and what was outside in the night sky—the dark, scary night sky was only a poor approximation of the pale blue cosmos under our roof. Later, I sometimes spent hours daydreaming there while waiting my turn to practice, or for our once-a-week recitals. Or reading Carl Sagan." He ran his fingers over the collar of the blue cardigan she wore beneath her fleece, of which she'd become increasingly fond since their dinner at Aunt Alice's. "Let me tell you, when my cousin Cecily played, the music—the acoustics of that ceiling were something else—talk about heaven."

They began to walk again, heading back before the light died. Passing the ancient orchard, where the battered hulks of apple trees, rigging shredded, were crumbling to earth, she paused, angling over to one still standing tall and largely intact.

"Don't bother," he said. "Long ago, the Judge and Teddy tried pruning a few, lopping off downward-growing branches that were dead or diseased, or suckers growing at the base, but they were already too far gone."

She pointed into the topmost branches of the one old tree that still retained a few of its boughs.

"Look, an apple."

"I'll be damned."

She grabbed a branch and scrambled up to where she could reach it. "Here," she said, dropping the apple into his waiting hands and climbing down.

The apple was of good size, a pale yellow-green peppered with swirls of scarlet and crimson around the stem, no wormholes. Some of the scarlet patches seemed to rise to the surface, brighten, and then fade to obscurity, like tiny clouds on a miniature Jupiter. He looked up at her, not a little incredulous, even skeptical, as if she'd just plucked the thing out of thin air, perhaps a magician's trick concealed in the pocket of her fleece, another sleight of hand, like her prodigies of memory.

"Dare I?" he asked, looking to her for guidance.

"Let's not go there; you're hardly the type, although you've never really told me what happened to your astrophysics gig—what you saw out there, or didn't."

There was a wicked but affectionate glint in her eye, and he found himself clutching the apple to his chest.

"Well," he said, looking over the clearing, squinting now in the pale evening light, a hint of sorrow or loss in his tone. "Think of Handytown. It's spring, you see, and there are wildflowers everywhere. And you're a bee and you think, Cool, all these wildflowers to visit, each with some nectar, perhaps even a nice little story to tell. And you start out on your journey and suddenly the surrounding trees disappear, like a stage set flying up and away, and all you can see is more flowers stretching as far as the eye can see in every direction, way beyond the horizon, farther than you'll ever be able to fly, or even think about flying, so far that you'd never make it back to the hive anyway, so weighed down with nectar. You see: too many damn stories and not enough time to tell in a thousand life-times." He looked down at the apple, weighing it in his hand, admiring its beauty and then handing it to her. "When you stare long enough into deep space, that's the kind of feeling you get—*infinity*."

She placed a hand on his shoulder and then gave him a brief hug.

"We'll take the apple back for your grandfather, a gift from the distant Hesperides. I always loved the name Erythea—huh, Jason."

"Yes," he said, oddly beguiled at such a notion. "We'll quarter it, for the three of us and Felicity."

"It's almost dark," she said.

"I can find my way back blindfolded." He smiled at the hint of panic in her voice and took a last look around, then glanced at her down-turned face as she contemplated the fading swirls of color around the stem of the apple. He was moved by a sudden wistfulness. "Oh, but this is bare bones. Wait till spring, wait until the maples and oaks return, and the marsh marigolds and purple loosestrife and lilacs—and the mountain laurel—oh, the white and pink of the laurel . . . and the hermit thrush. Their song, here of all places, will break your heart."

She squeezed his hand in hers, wanting to hurry him now, her voice a yelp of pleasure. "Ah, yes, your hawthorns—I just knew it."

As they reached the path into the woods, she turned back one last time, a troubled look compressing her brows.

"Déjà vu," she murmured.

"What's that?"

"Like I've been here before."

"You've just read about it."

"Yes, that must be it. He and Annie used to walk here. And Priscilla Hiss mentions it in her letters."

"Yes, that's all," and he took her hand, urging her forward.

"You see," she said, her hand tightening in his, "you have to forget to remember."

—

George drew three of the four Stickley chairs a tad closer together in a cozy arc around the roaring fire, placing the Judge between them, with the medieval angels—as ever eerily aswoon—providing a jury of two for the gathering. The great room and the ship's keel ceiling bloomed to life as George pulled the chain switches on the four Tiffany lamps (three bulbs each, twelve chains, a ritual illumination). At the Judge's elbow, a blush of purple wisteria, indigo grapes, and drifting butterflies shimmered on his wineglass.

At first, Wendy couldn't take her eyes off the bejeweled lamps, bewitched like a child witnessing a magic-lantern show. Then she began wandering with her wineglass from dinner, craning her neck at the serial illumination of the ship's keel ceiling, squinting where the blue overhead depths, at each snap of a chain, revealed more mythic and astrological figures in the beam work, where the portrait head of Giordano Bruno presided: a disenchanted sun god pondering his reduced circumstances from the underside of the central crossbeam. Leaving off, she drifted over, as she had that afternoon, to the Steinway grand and reconnoitered the silver-framed photos of the pianist, each frame polished to an electric sheen in the penumbral backwater away from the fire. This votive altar to Hestia cast yet another spell over the young supplicant, where the candles still flicker, where the incense still smolders in silent memory of a radiant talent . . . urging impetuous youth to flee herself, perhaps to assume her true self, tempted like Prometheus to steal what the gods had left for the pickings.

—

"I wonder if Florida—Siesta Key, I think you said—would be anything like Beverly Farms in the summer." The Judge had settled himself in his favorite chair after making his way on his walker with Felicity's help from the dining room. "You see, that summer near the sea I spent with Justice Holmes never leaves me."

"Where you met your wife, Annie," Wendy said with unchecked exuberance, only to pause mid-thought, as if caught off balance. She stood warming herself by the mantel like a ballet dancer, head back, bust out, a tight chignon showing off her jaw and flushed cheeks. She'd been examining the stopped Louis XVI clock, the graceful blue-and-white Chinese vases; now she was fingering the carved Whitman inscription in the bluestone as her intrigued gaze traveled upward, where the famous figure of Phaeton in his flaming death spiral through space had again riveted her attention.

The Judge looked at her sharply, a hint of pain at the corner of his weary eyes.

"How do you know that? Did I mention it over dinner?"

"I told her, Judge," said George.

She stood balanced with an outstretched arm on the bluestone mantel, her face suddenly etched with emotion.

"No, sir, I read it in your memoir."

"Oh my God," groaned George.

The Judge looked sharply at his grandson, betrayed.

"Sir," pleaded Wendy, "forgive me—us—but it's wonderful, especially the parts about Annie. I'm sorry if it wasn't meant for my eyes, but I was deeply moved by what you wrote about your wife."

"Judge," said George, fumbling for an excuse, an apology, "I had to share it with Wendy, a second pair of eyes—call it 'editorial eyes.' I'm too close; she has distance. She sees things I don't. I'm too logical, and, after all, she has a degree in literature from Yale—so you guys have an institutional loyalty." He tried to smile. "Something you've always put much store in."

The Judge bowed his head, hair disheveled, pondering. "George, our understanding was that only you were to read it and give me your thoughts for revision."

Wendy went to the old man and laid her hand on his where it lay trembling on the wooden armrest of the Stickley chair. "It's my fault. I talked George into it. I can't lie about this"—she cast a panicked look at George, biting her lower lip—"only, only the writing is beautiful, really more literary than historical; I can feel the books that passed through you and became part of your memories, especially your memories of Annie."

"Well, your praise is cold comfort." He shot her a piercing look but did not remove his hand from hers. "My intention was to set the record straight, for my family at least. I felt I owned them that much, to do justice to the Hiss disaster."

"And what a disaster—now we know," said an alarmed George. "Disaster of all-time disasters."

The Judge winced. "That bad, George?"

"No," said Wendy, almost pleading, patting his hand and backing away. "Your Annie comes through beautifully, inspiring—really."

"Well," said the Judge, his face brightening, the firelight sparking in his baggy eyes, "Annie was certainly a great reader. And she filled this room with music like the sweet breath of the gods." His eyes rose to the beamed space above, glittering with points of gold and silver against a spectral blue vibration, more oceanic than celestial. "But tell me, I'm curious, what did I write about her that you find so moving?" He looked anxiously at George and then to where Wendy's hand had again found his. "It's been five years, I think—isn't that right, George? I only remember in the vaguest terms what I managed to get in there."

"You did read the new Weinstein book I sent you?" asked George, as if to stick to the subject.

"My eyes, you know, but Felicity read me much of it, I believe. A little hard to follow. Felicity's not the best reader. Of course, it's all Greek to her."

"He was guilty, Hiss, as hell—and then some."

The Judge looked troubled, as if George's certainty, his forcefulness, was more than he was ready to allow for. He turned again to Wendy, the more sympathetic presence, whose stare was now drawn to the ship's keel ceiling, seeking out more and more of the astrological and mythological figures, as if the patterns were beginning to come to life for her, as if falling under their spell.

"Tell me, my dear, tell me about Annie."

She seemed startled, distracted, wobbling on her long heels for a moment as she went again to the mantel and steadied herself on the carved bluestone to warm her goose-bumped legs.

"Sorry, I'm just a little overwhelmed." She took a deep breath. With a wan smile, a quiver in her cheek, her eyes tearing up, she fingered the Whitman inscription. "I mean, between these lines and our walk to Handytown."

She laughed as she recited the lines carved into the bluestone mantle, as if disbelieving her eyes, her voice, her feelings, even where she was.

> In the door-yard fronting an old farm-house near the
> white-wash'd palings,
> Stand the lilac-bush tall-growing, with heart-shaped leaves
> of rich green,
> With many a pointed blossom, rising, delicate, with the
> perfume strong I love,
> With every leaf a miracle—and from this bush in the
> door-yard,
> With delicate-color'd blossoms, and heart-shaped leaves of
> rich green,
> A sprig, with its flower, I break.

She paused, as if listening to the faint echo of her rich cadences above the crackle of the fire.

"Sorry, I could go on—not to show off or anything."

The Judge nodded with appreciation.

"Your generation, someone who knows Whitman much less can recite him, how strange—heh, George?"

"That's what I meant by a second pair of eyes," he replied, now with a hint of pride, if not relief.

"I studied with Harold—Harold Bloom at Yale. He insisted we put stuff to memory, for 'mental hygiene,' he called it, to fill our souls. Whitman was his guide, his source: 'the poet of our climate,' he always said—a shape-shifter to mirror all our innermost and hidden yearnings." She made a face of abject helplessness. "Things just stick in my head—a curse or a blessing."

"Dr. Dimock had those lines inscribed there when Hermitage was built because he had met the man, the poet, when he was a doctor in the hospitals in Washington. Whitman served as a nurse. He had no idea the man was a poet, but he was moved by his humanity, the comfort he offered to the wounded, dressing their hideous wounds, writing their letters. Only later did he discover, in a letter from Holmes, who the poet was, that very same male nurse. And the connection, of course, the memorial to Lincoln."

"Ah, your Justice Holmes, and his house in Beverly Farms, where you met your Annie, when she first played for you."

"Go on . . ."

She began slowly, haltingly, carefully reciting the things she remembered. She described their first meeting and later how they had walked on the beach in the light of the full moon.

"Oh, yes, I remember now. She wore yellow shoes."

And she went on to describe their honeymoon in Venice.

"Where your Teddy was conceived," she whispered in a lowered voice, embarrassed but with a hint of wonderment. She continued, but more circumspectly now, casting side glances at George, as if requiring his assurance, editing, skirting later scenes of their marriage—that of Cordelia's conception weighing on her mind, like a sharp object she feared to touch.

The Judge smiled, a joy rising in his tired eyes as she paused, not quite daring to take it any further.

"And I love your blue cardigan, by the way." He smiled, now with a teasing air, like a younger man. "Annie would've quite approved." He touched a finger to his nose, sliding his palm across his sunken cheek as if not quite certain of his mortality, and then smiled, perhaps relieved, his teeth gone yellow-gray. "Yes, Annie and I were a team, a good team in our early years. It's a tragedy that she never lived to see her grandchildren as adults."

"Well," said George, warming to the subject, "now you have great-grandchildren, Nancy and Max. And I think I've got everybody convinced to spend Thanksgiving at Hermitage. How would that suit you, Judge? High time you met them."

This seemed to break the momentary spell.

"Alice—never. Martha, don't count on it. Cordelia, my lovely Cordelia, now"—he winked at George—"that would, as always, be a treat." He cocked his head. "And will Wendy dare join us?"

Wendy leaned forward, a little breathless and unsure, as if her narration had left her displaced, a little lost. And with a sure motion, as if needing to fully unburden herself, she reached behind her head and pulled the bobby pins from her chignon and let her blond hair fall across her broad shoulders, where the tresses were highlighted in the firelight. And in a throaty voice, as if coming from outside herself, she replied, "Judge, how could I not. And I must admit, the rest—the memoir, I mean—is also compelling in its own way. I mean your Alger Hiss, your Ahab—shall we call it a mystery, or perhaps a morality tale?—is like something out of John le Carré, or maybe Graham Greene."

"*Edward*—please, young lady," and he raised a hand as if to disguise the hint of delight that danced in his heavy-lidded eyes. "What do you think, George, with your wonderful brain for things scientific, is it still a mystery, do we keep it a flawed mystery, or do we make changes according to the dictates of Mr. Weinstein's evidence? Will it suffer improvement?" The Judge, perhaps having digested the effects of his dinner and wine, seemed more agile of thought, now pondering the surprisingly exotic pleasures of their conversation, the presence of this remarkable young woman, glancing again and again into her intent face, her long hair translucent on one side with amber and ruby from the Tiffany lamp shade nearest her chair. Then he returned his gaze to the flames, reaching his large trembling hands forward as if needing to warm them or find some purchase on the subject that had lain tantalizingly beyond reach over dinner. "Is this to be the denouement of our evening, you two? Of my life—thirty years on the bench and it all comes down to that damn trial?" And again he spread his hands wide. "A nice ring—though I was never partial to Greene's *The Third Man*—a mystery title. Need something catchier for my memoir. I'm sure my publisher would agree. Who today wants to read effusions on the law? Even now, after hearing from Mr. Weinstein . . . we seem to have more of a mystery than ever."

"How he got away with it?" offered George. "Why people believed in him?"

"Why he did it?" replied the Judge, correcting him. "Motive is always the crux of any criminal investigation. Luckily for us," and he waved, perhaps indicating the glowering Steinway grand in the corner and the empty piano seat, "human mysteries fade like birdsong in August, but places remain to inveigle us with their memories. A man who would both betray his country and his class." He adjusted himself, his herringbone jacket, his Century Club bow tie, as if once again presiding at his bench. "Now, you see," he continued, his voice quickening, as if Wendy's reminders had touched his bleak heart, "there weren't as many lovely tall pines as we have here at Hermitage, but the North Shore sported some fine old pastures and evocative scrub oaks—*Quercus ilicifolia*—and 'my cedars of Lebanon,' as Holmes called them, and shapely granite outcroppings. Around the porch where we sat, when I read to Justice Holmes . . . the honeysuckle and woodbine flowed as if from out of a dream, and roses galore. I do rather yearn for the sound of the sea and the smell of brine infused with the scent of roses, along with the nasal drone of Holmes's voice as he sought to give me guidance and direction. Imagine, such a bloodline through his aphorist father to Longfellow, Prescott, and Hawthorne. Oliver had a scientific and logical mind, rather like yours, George, a Darwinian to his fingertips, which is why I always thought science would be just the thing for you." He turned to his right, where Wendy sat in her short dress with her long-muscled legs crossed and displayed to good advantage. "What do you think, my dear, should he have stuck with astrophysics?"

"He'd be a great teacher; he explains things so even I can understand them. Well, maybe not so much dark matter and parallel universes. But a more literary mode has its value in revealing the truth, as it did for your Whittaker Chambers—why his book will live on."

"Speaking of which, I couldn't help noticing—how to describe it?— the sparring between you and Annie in the margins of *Witness*. It's quite something, that dialogue between you two, quite moving in its way."

The Judge shot him a glance, not of alarm so much as repressed, perhaps guilty pleasure.

"Yes, I only found her copy after she died, hidden behind her books in our bedroom."

"Why hidden?"

He shrugged. "She liked Chambers and clearly admired his writing, his Quaker simplicity, his truth-telling, and felt I'd treated him badly, which I freely admit in the memoir. It pains me how she kept her copy to herself, as if a secret talisman, a personal accounting of all my failings, in the trial, our marriage, if not my culpability in Teddy's death."

"I couldn't help noticing how you both seemed drawn to the section where Chambers and the Hisses make that road trip to Fitzwilliam, New Hampshire, to pick up a paper Harry Dexter White had written on Soviet monetary policy."

At this, the Judge smiled wanly, his eyes lifting and glittering fiercely in the firelight, like a man who is contemplating a lie but is, nevertheless, feeling better for it.

"That was the weakest part of Chambers's testimony; we made mincemeat out of his account of that trip to Fitzwilliam. The prosecution could not come up with a shred of evidence that it had ever happened."

"Obviously, Annie thought otherwise."

"But she—her loyalty, you see—would." He sighed. "After the trial, I was damaged goods in her eyes, never fully forgiven."

George seemed annoyed, as if thinking back to Aunt Martha's image of that stealthy python, Aunt Alice's warnings about his grandfather's lawyerly brilliance at misdirection. "So what happened to your Harvard colleagues on the defense team that so many went to the dark side: true believers in Stalin's tyranny?"

The Judge's eyes deepened, perplexed. "They lost faith in their country and their essential selves, thus leaving themselves prey to the siren song of foreign intrigues and poisonous ideas. The Depression damaged and distorted many of the best minds. Good faith and fair play and the generous hopefulness of the past turned to spite and callous disregard of their birthright."

"Listen," said George with a hint of impatience, "we're driving straight down to Washington from Hermitage in the morning. We've got an appointment with Allen Weinstein at the National Archives day after tomorrow. If there's anything you'd like us to ask him, from your perspective, after reading his book, now's the time."

"It certainly clarified a lot of things for me—even with Felicity's reading. Not like his first book on the trial, where he took me to task for my rough treatment of Chambers."

George nodded. "So you did read his first book, *Perjury*, on the trial? A gift from Aunt Alice perhaps?"

"Oh, I must have dipped into it, since I feel a guilty ache at its mention. I believe I tossed it in the fire."

"Surely you had to do what you had to," she said in an agreeable tone. "I mean, after he confronted you in your chambers, demanding an interview."

"Did he now? I'd forgotten. Oh yes, he made much of our Yale connection, as if old college ties might stay his knife—eh?"

"Martha's Upper West Side crowd hate his guts, especially now that their *stinker* has been appointed director of the National Archives," said George.

The Judge smiled softly. "I believe Weinstein became a pariah among his own kind with that book, *Perjury*, something of a sensation among a certain set."

"What *kind* is that?" George demanded.

"Jewish left-wing intellectuals, ex-Communists—it took guts to go up against his own crowd, *and* Alger Hiss."

"Are you," Wendy asked hesitantly, searching for the right words, "relieved, happy, that Alger Hiss turned out to be just what your jury convicted him of being?"

The Judge pondered this, his fingers pulling at an earlobe. "I'm more concerned that my memoir makes me out to have been a gullible fool . . . or worse."

She said with an overwrought eagerness that seemed to spring from some pent-up emotion, "But at least no one can blame you any longer for having failed to defend an innocent man."

The Judge smiled at this, turning to search her intent face as if for clues to her tone. "Kind of you, young lady, but that is not how the score is kept in my line of work: Our job is to get the client *off*. Win at any cost. Or, as my favorite Yankee, Yogi Berra, put it, 'We made too many wrong mistakes.'"

"And call me Wendy," she said with a girlish flounce, crossing and uncrossing her legs.

George shot her a look: Enough already. "I'll leave you with a copy of the memoir. You let me know what changes you'd like to make."

"But how . . . can I get through it all? My eyes give out so quickly. And I can hardly ask Felicity to read it over to me—God knows what ideas she'd get in her head. She was close to Annie, you know. Besides, she'd blab all about it to Alice and Martha—and your mother. Alice already had her looking around for something in my study."

George blew out his lips in exasperation: "The sketches . . ."

"What sketches?" asked the Judge in all perplexity.

George pushed on: "But I'll have to show the memoir to Alice and Martha—*and* Mom, at some point."

"Not until I tell you so," said the Judge suddenly, as if alert to danger. "And if I pop off in the meantime, you take it straight to my editor at Norton without consultation of any kind with my daughters. Including your good mother. Is that understood?" He glanced at Wendy, who gazed upward, as if deep in thought. "It's one thing to have a sympathetic outside perspective, certainly on the quality of the writing, but I can't have those who bear a grudge twisting my words."

Wendy's attention flickered back from the far reaches above.

"Oh, Edward, for the most part you seem pretty fair to your children, more than fair—there's a lot of love in there. More than I ever got from my mother, let me tell you."

George's eyes flashed to attention at this admission.

"As I said, boys and girls, I don't really remember what's in there—I mean precisely what's in there. I'm not sure I'm up to it . . . changes."

"It strikes me," George said, "that you and the rest of the defense team—like you said—were just trying to do your job, what you had to do, even if you had poor cards to play."

"Don't butter me up, George. No need. The worst of it is how Alger, if such a thing is possible, has become even more invisible to me—post-Weinstein, so to say . . . Every moment, every memory of him takes on added dimensions." He gestured to the mantel, where the blue-and-white ginger jars and stopped clock were bathed in vague chiaroscuro. "Every utterance on his part traffics in double meanings, as if he is both more alive to me than ever, and constantly undergoing metamorphosis before my eyes, with my life—what's left of it—transforming in the wake. It seems the very air we breathed back then was infused, as it were, with some kind of intangible hypnotic mist"—his hands rose as if in benediction, only to drop again to his khaki thighs— "the cloak he wrapped himself in and so remains hidden, barely casting a shadow, still weaving his invisible spell . . . still covering his tracks."

George's eyes widened: "Like in Memorial Hall . . ."

"Memorial Hall?"

"Where you first met him."

"Did I?"

"During the trial," Wendy asked, redirecting the conversation, "did you ever detect some faltering on Hiss's part, a lack of confidence?"

His eyebrows pinched and rose. "Don't you see the dilemma of time, of evidence: What once I saw as panic over a wrongful indictment now seems like panic at being exposed as a spy—and maybe worse."

"Worse?" asked George, rising to put another log on the fire.

"At that moment, the charge was perjury, about timing and transactions—lying, essentially. Events from over ten years before and secret documents, which, in the light of a catastrophic war of recent memory and an impending Cold War of mutual annihilation, seemed like chicken feed, almost inconsequential in the scheme of things."

"Small potatoes," echoed George with a dismissive frown. "So you and your pals figured, Why throw the baby out with the bathwater?"

"You know, I believe what convinced me was that in the grand jury hearing he could have just admitted that, yes, he'd passed a few innocuous State Department papers to a man he'd known as Carl, thinking he was a journalist for some socialist newspaper or the like, trying to be helpful. And that would have been that. The statute of limitations had already run out. He couldn't have been indicted for spying. And he could have then brazened out the reputational harm and probably gone on much as before. But he did nothing of the sort; in fact, he brazened it out to the end. Guilty men don't act that way."

"Unless," said George, "he had no choice. You implied as much in the memoir."

"Did I?" He closed his eyes, strain showing in the crumpled furrows on his forehead. "The thing that impressed me was the magnitude of his support, the prodigious amount of research—the brain trust he assembled—provided by his multitude of handlers." He leaned back in the red leather Stickley chair, as if taxed by the continued effort.

George shot a look at Wendy. "You mean that they might have been willing to kill to protect him?"

Silence . . . broken by the sharp snap of long-seasoned oak logs. The Judge simply nodded and closed his eyes, sighing to himself for long moments. Then he looked at his grandson, seemingly annoyed.

"I almost wish you'd never bothered me with the Weinstein book. At a certain age, all one really wants is a little certainty and to put one's regrets away in a drawer and throw away the key."

"Listen, twenty-twenty hindsight is always easy," Wendy offered, looking at George, as if hoping to soften the edges of the thing broached.

"Thank you, dear. I can only blame myself for what I knew and saw, not suspicions without substance. Your Weinstein had all the facts, all the evidence we never saw: the prosecution's files, the FBI's, much less those Venona decrypts of Soviet cable traffic and KGB archives—mother lode, I suppose. What amazes me is that the government, the FBI, had all the evidence from the Soviet decrypts and they never even used it against us in the trial."

"That's not entirely accurate," said George. "The information from the Soviet decrypts came after your trial. They didn't even use it against the Rosenbergs and others. There were too many national security issues at risk. They couldn't introduce evidence that would give away the fact that they'd broken the Soviets' code."

Wendy leaned forward, reaching to the arm of his chair, carefully examining his face. "But surely you had your doubts—you must've had your doubts about Alger Hiss. There was a pattern of deception going back, as you wrote, to his time with your mentor, Justice Holmes."

"What about Holmes?"

"That Hiss had lied to him about marrying Priscilla."

The Judge nodded to himself. "Yes, yes, but a pattern of deception in little things does not a traitor make. And he was one of us, damn it, our tribe. Even Chambers—and now, by golly, we know his book is more than true—loved him so much that he tried to avoid accusing him of espionage. It was Hiss's own team, long before I was hired, that forced Chambers's hand on revealing the secret State Department documents he had hidden, which resulted in his indictment in the first place."

"I've read it now, *Witness*," she said. "The humanity of Chambers . . . well, it touches one, the way he held back from destroying those who would have destroyed him. In your copy, Annie's copy, she notes that time and time again."

The Judge looked at her with a troubled gaze. "I never read *Witness* when it was first published—what, two years after the trial? I thought it fictionalized trash from a delusional mind and burned the copy Alice so cruelly gave me for Christmas."

George sat up ramrod straight, reaching to his backpack for Annie's copy. "Chambers wrote an inscription for her."

"Yes, yes, that was quite a shock." His gaze lengthened. "I gave it a thorough read, as well. In its pages, I was chagrined to discover— all the places where my dead wife had underlined during the years before, when our marriage was on the rocks—a side of Alger and Priscilla I'd never known. Lives couched in his beautiful prose and philosophical . . . sensibility—is that the right word? Or perhaps literary"—he looked to Wendy—"as you suggested. I felt foolish, incurious, a dunderhead. What Annie had silently held against me— the death of our boy—over all the last years of our marriage. And just a few years ago, while trying to finish my memoir, I read it yet again . . . finding my own annotations next to those of Annie, and it was as if I'd passed through the looking glass, seeing my life and my times from yet another angle, her angle, her grief . . . and disappointment in me. And although Chambers's politics and religious mania, his Manichean worldview, is not to my taste, one can't but respect, as you say, the inner humanity, if not the truth of his confession—his 'witness,' as he calls it. Inspirational, even."

Wendy couldn't suppress a smile, but it was a smile of kindness.

"There's a certain similarity between Chambers's memoir and yours: You were both dealing with the same man, the same diabolical liar, who, in a sense, distorted your life—stole something of your soul. It's Chambers's style and tone that brings out both Hiss's humanity and diabolical nature to such poignant effect. Like your Ahab, your Iago in the memoir."

George sprang up, as if uneasy or even fed up with this train of thought.

"Speaking of patterns, I can't get your corkboard, your rogues' gallery out of my mind. What bothers you most: whether you were simply fooled or . . . Hiss's possible victims?"

At this, the Judge's upright figure seemed to go slack, his breathing slowing as he peered directly into the fire, flicking a glance at the guardian angels, the stopped Louis XVI clock on the mantel. First there was a dutiful nodding as he brushed back tufts of white hair that had strayed over an eye; then he began squinting, as if the fleeting shadows were now gaining substance in his mind. "Without Weinstein's evidence, even lacking direct evidence of something heinous—if that's where this is going—those of us on the defense team, the outward-facing defenders to the judge, jury, and public, were kept in the dark about the machinations of the innermost circle. What struck my colleagues at the time—and I struggle even to remember their names, much less their faces—I think it is fair to say, was the exorbitant lengths to which Hiss's Praetorian Guard was willing to go, the prodigious amount of cash expended, the dark recesses plumbed . . . the silence of potential witnesses for the government. And yes, things of which Chambers caught unsettling glimpses in his pages. Even now, when I awake in the middle of the night, it is Chambers's voice I hear. What I first considered his dire imaginings. And worse, how badly I treated the man on the witness stand. Not a day went by over thirty years on the federal bench that I didn't feel like a failure because of that—something I would never have allowed to happen in my court."

"Rest assured," she offered, her eyes lowering from where she'd been exploring the depths of the ceiling, "you more than made expiation for sins real or imagined in your memoir."

"The prodigies"—George raised his impatient voice—"or the patterns: the falls and disappearances and witnesses who never showed?"

The Judge raised a finger and rather grandly pointed it at George's breast. "There—that's what you should ask Weinstein; get his opinion. Or take Chambers's word over mine."

"Chambers?" said George, again riffling the pages of Annie's dog-eared copy.

The Judge laughed at his grandson's consternation and turned a twinkling eye on Wendy.

"The model for my memoir, you said. Well, why not." He waved to the book in George's hand. "Didn't I underline something toward the end? If not me, certainly Annie . . . something touching on our thoroughness."

George flipped the ragged pages and found the heavily underlined passage: "My investigators worked almost wholly to locate witnesses who could corroborate my story about Hiss. Nearly always, they found that Hiss's investigators had been there first and that possible witnesses had sometimes suffered strange black-outs of recollection.'" George held the page up to read the Judge's scribbled note in the margin: "'Or worse!'"

Wendy, as if drifting back from her own thoughts, suddenly weighed in.

"But you were *there*, Judge." The agitation in her voice attracted the stare of the two men. "On the defense team: Didn't it even come up, the disappearing witnesses? Surely, between your colleagues, there must have been some—what?—raised eyebrows, whispers, questions?"

"And what, exactly, would we have questioned? Remind me."

She leaned in from her chair. "In your memoir, you make only passing mention of Laurence Duggan, who fell sixteen stories to his death; or Marvin Smith, who fell six flights to his death; or Harry Dexter White, who died suddenly of a heart attack; or Lauchlin Currie and Noel Field, who both fled overseas and so were unavailable as witnesses for the prosecution. All numbered among Altmann's subjects, pinned on your office wall with their names, details, and newspaper clippings with alarming headlines."

"I brought it up with Hiss—didn't I? I asked him point-blank. Isn't that in my memoir?"

"Yes, sir, so you wrote," replied George.

"Yes, you mentioned Duggan, White, and Smith," she confirmed. "And to your eternal credit, you even asked after their children."

At this praise, the Judge gave a tentative, tepid smile.

"He blamed their deaths on the times, on the furies of the Red-baiters. Don't you see, without the full enormity of the facts, it made perfect sense; nobody could believe anything else. As Chambers wrote, we lived in a certain fragrance of opinion, of attitude, as invisible, if you will, as it was all-encompassing. Even twenty years later, when I pulled the sketches from the defense file and saw those faces again, I was shocked, as if I'd unearthed a grave, the undefiled, intact bodies of the dead and missing staring at me. That's how alive they seemed to me. Perhaps it was the skill of the artist to have so vividly kept them alive, but for me, in that moment, it was as if the dead hand of the past had reached out and tapped my guilty shoulder. Perhaps I hoped by returning them to your father, their bloodless shades would, once more, fade away into that anodyne fog of which we spoke."

"You never met any of the others in the sketches besides Alger and Priscilla?" asked George.

"Oh, I met Duggan and White and Currie occasionally during the war, when I worked in Washington for the War Production Board.

Sometimes in business meetings, but mostly at social gatherings. But I had no direct professional dealings with any of them—chain of command, so to speak. Nothing in the way of personal ties that would have rendered their fate consequential in my heart."

"Noel Field?" she asked, checking off the name on her pad.

"Never."

"Marvin Smith?"

"Never."

"What about Remington?"

"Don't I mention him in the memoir?"

"Only in passing," said George.

"Not much to say, really. William was on the War Production Board with me. A lovely man, eager, hardworking; silver-blond hair and brilliant blue eyes, attractive as he was competent."

George and Wendy glanced at each other as she scribbled on her pad.

"So you did know him quite well, then?" She glanced up from her pad.

"Well?" His eyebrows arched, his brow beetling. "How well do we really know anyone—eh? Outside of staff meetings, a few briefings, perhaps a cup of coffee on occasion, I rarely saw him. He was assistant to the director, my boss, Don Nelson. William was a Dartmouth graduate, I believe—capable, very capable."

"What did you first think when you found his portrait among the Altmann sketches, with Hiss and the others who'd been accused of spying?"

"I don't remember, exactly."

"You didn't think, Wow, the assistant to the director might have been a spy?"

"Remember, at that moment, during the trial, there were only accusations flying around, no proof. No one had accused William of anything at that point."

"And later in the early fifties," she said, continuing to take notes, "when he was put on trial, when his first wife turned on him and testified to his spying? It must have been quite a shock."

"I was a judge by then, a busy man."

"And then when he was murdered in Lewisburg prison in 1954, just a few days before Hiss's release?"

"Strangely, not until later, when I retrieved the sketches from the defense files, did that really hit home. The sketch, I suppose, captures the spirit of that young eager beaver as I remembered him. Neatly barbered blond hair, handsome, open face, quick intelligence. A man who should have gone far. A terrible fate—awful. Of course, he would have had access to a lot of confidential information on our war-making capacity, something the Soviets were always eager to know about—to get their hands on a bigger piece of the pie, so to speak."

She looked up at the Judge, his eyes a watery gray in the firelight, and then at George as she continued. "And you had no idea?"

"Disheartening, to put it mildly—what more can I say?"

She scribbled on her pad, adding a florid question mark. "It wouldn't have looked good if Weinstein had found those sketches, considering you and Remington worked closely together."

"Hardly close. Remington was about the last thing on my mind; otherwise, I would have gone into more detail in the memoir."

"Yet another ambiguous death."

"I believe his murderers were common criminals."

"And Altmann's weren't?" she said with a hint of indignation.

George shot her a warning look and picked up the thread.

"So, their names never came up among the defense team—as people, witnesses to worry about?"

"Duggan and White and Smith were already dead, don't forget, long before I even came on the team."

"What about Marvin Smith, the Justice Department attorney involved in the transfer of Hiss's Model A Ford to a Communist Party member?"

"Hiss's cavalier dismissal of that man, a friend of his in Justice, gave me pause."

"Hiss got out of his chair and ended your conversation," she said with a distant look, as if she was picturing the moment in her mind.

"Who?"

"In your memoir, Hiss walks away when you bring up the subject of Marvin Smith."

At this, the Judge smiled, more in relief than recollection.

"If Marvin Smith had been there to testify that he, as notary public, had signed off on Hiss's deed of transfer for his Ford, it might well have meant the case right there."

"Could Hiss or his confederates . . . the KGB have been responsible?" she asked.

"I don't think even Chambers could quite believe such a monstrosity on the part of Alger, and Chambers knew him better than any of us . . . a side I never saw."

"Ha!" exclaimed George, exasperated at his grandfather's perplexity. "He believed it enough to carry a gun, like yours—that Smith & Wesson snub-nose you kept in your bedside drawer for years—just in case . . . the snappers, the timber rattlers . . ." George shrugged.

"It's still there," affirmed the Judge. "You never know."

"Damn right. And just like you, Chambers couldn't have known everything at stake; he'd been out of the underground over ten years by the time of the trial."

Staring up at the ceiling as if a little spellbound by the play of the spheres, Wendy sighed softly. "That's the beauty of his writing, his intimations of those glimpses into the dark side of a soul he'd once loved."

"Yes, yes," the Judge responded eagerly, as if she'd offered him a way out, a way through. "I was a new boy, and my elders only reluctantly shared their history or doubts. We lived in a bubble on the defense team. I had my responsibilities: how to best destroy the creditability of Whittaker Chambers. I only saw part of the picture. Alger had his own lawyer, Harold Rosenwald, who handled the investigators. Harold had been close to Alger since Harvard Law School. Harold was there from day one, when HUAC first interrogated Hiss. Harold was the mastermind. We took our orders from Harold and our lead counsel, Claude Cross . . . and Alger."

Wendy looked at George with a faint smile, as if to say, Some things he remembers like yesterday! "Yes, you wrote as much: The dirt on Chambers came by way of Harold Rosenwald." She halted a tiny sketch of the Judge and began again to take notes. Her cell phone voice recorder had been on for some time.

"Harold had his creatures out everywhere, like nothing I've seen before or since."

"'Creatures'?" she prompted. "I don't recall you using that expression in the memoir."

"*Investigators* is the polite term, those trolling Chambers's Communist past. Occasionally, I'd catch glimpses of them loitering in the office. Seedy, flabby-faced, bad complexions, sour-eyed fellows in ill-fitting cheap suits. One felt a little dirty in their presence. They never spoke around us, as if they'd gone mute; spoke only to Harold, I guess."

"There," she murmured, "you've just updated your memoir. That scene adds so much to the verisimilitude; it touches the senses, your sensations—the kind of detail that gives Chambers's *Witness* such power, enduring power."

"What was it with Harvard in your day?" asked George, assuming a more jocular tone, as if trying to lighten things up a bit while keeping the memories rolling. "All of you on the defense team were Harvard Law; and most of the KGB spies in Altmann's sketches went to Harvard, except Priscilla Hiss. And Marvin Smith."

"It's not a little disheartening." The Judge shook his head. "I'm only glad Justice Holmes never lived to see the like. His Harvard roots were generations deep."

"What the hell was in the Harvard water?"

"'Disinterested, dedicated public service': That's how Alger once described it, and Felix Frankfurter, our guiding light, exemplified it. Social activism, but hardly socialism, much less communism. Most of our classmates were Republicans, hard-right conservatives. And Frankfurter recommended both me and Alger to Holmes."

"Your Harvard loyalties, trumped—or obscured . . . that comforting fog you were mentioning: How could you have worked cheek by jowl— the way Chambers described so many of his contemporaries—and not have realized that you were being used, manipulated?"

"So," Wendy asked with a sudden intensity and directness that had lain dormant for a few minutes, "why did George Altmann go to *you* with the sketches?"

The Judge turned to the young woman, abashed. "Surely I mentioned that in my memoir?"

George immediately jumped in. "You wrote quite explicitly that he gave them to you before the trial—right? In the morning, before the gavel fell to open the trial. You were concerned that if Weinstein discovered them in the defense files, you might be in jeopardy for concealing evidence from the prosecution in the discovery process."

"Goodness, I must have been in a confessional mood five years back, since, quite obviously, nothing about all that sheds a good light on me professionally."

"Why a confession?" she followed. "You were only doing your job."

The Judge nodded, squinting, his gaze straying from the young woman to the upturned ecstatic face of the angel seemingly watching over her shoulder from the hearth.

"A lawyer having an envelope thrust into his hands on the steps of a courthouse from a near stranger before the start of a major trial— well, alarm bells should ring. He should, as soon as he has some privacy, examine the contents to see what bearing it might have on the case at hand."

"And you did what?" she asked.

"I believe . . ." He closed his eyes in concentration, brow clenched. "I believe I shuffled them into my briefcase and promptly forgot all about them—what with everything on my mind. Only later, after adjournment, perhaps in my office, perhaps at home later that day, did I pause to examine the sketches. And I remember . . . I remember thinking, well, how beautiful they were, especially the first one, on top, the one of Priscilla. Not the tense, terrified Priscilla seated at the trial, but the Priscilla I remembered from years before: full of intelligence and empathy and passion for life—birds and plants . . . things alive. I wanted to hold on to that, to that sketch, that work of art that persevered my memory of her in better days. And so I think I just stuck the envelope in the defense files the following morning, thinking I'd deal with it later, and promptly forgot all about the thing in the chaos of the following weeks."

Wendy looked up from the yellow pad where she'd been busily writing.

"Lovely, lovely, you're doing beautifully. This flushes out your feelings; this makes sense—the human dimension."

George bristled at the lovefest and stood abruptly.

"But years later, when you caught wind of Weinstein's interest, you went back into the defense files and disinterred the sketches. Clearly, they had meant something more to you by then."

"Yes, I was angry, I suppose. Because, as I said, the reappearance of those faces came with a pang of conscience, of creeping guilt, that I'd been reckless, that I probably should have been more thoughtful about the disposition of those sketches."

"You're absolutely sure Altmann gave you the sketches before the trial opened?"

"Isn't that what I wrote in my memoir?"

"Yes," said Wendy, "you wrote exactly that."

"Why"—George now took a step away from the fire, where he'd just landed a log, casually leaning a hand on the head of the wooden angel nearest the Judge—"would he have given the sketches to you, and not, say, Harold Rosenwald, Hiss's confidant, fixer—whatever—or to Edward McLean, who along with Rosenwald directed the investigative work on the defense?"

"Whose 'creatures,'" she said, "must have already been nipping at George Altmann's heels, enough to prompt him to cough up the sketches in the first place."

George turned to Wendy's impassioned eyes, as did the Judge, who then looked at George with a nervous twinkle in his eyes.

"George, this young lady has a mind like a steel trap."

"Judge, she went to fucking Yale—like Teddy. This bulldog climbed Everest. She's fearless. Like I said, another pair of sympathetic eyes on *your* defense team."

This little ironic twist in George's voice seemed to deflate the Judge's mood for a few moments; his hands became still in his lap.

"Perhaps," the Judge finally said, smiling wanly, "he thought me a more *sympathetic* figure. It would be nice to think so."

George went back to his chair and pulled a piece of paper from a file and handed it to the Judge, who inspected the dashed-off drawing of a handsome young man with dark-rimmed glasses and an imposing chin and dimple, brows shot forward in fierce concentration.

"Where did this come from?" asked the Judge.

"George Altmann gave it to Alice as a souvenir on the opening day of the trial. At the *end* of the day, when the trial adjourned and your family gathered around to congratulate you. Seems like George Altmann was bestowing souvenirs right and left that day. Oh, and she had it stuck away in her copy of Weinstein's *Perjury*—nice touch, don't you think?"

"Well, I'll be." He handed the sketch to Wendy. "Not a bad rendering—what do you think?—of a man in his prime."

"Handsome, with all the convictions of his upbringing and class, integrity to spare. No wonder Altmann handed the sketches to you as opposed to Hiss or Rosenwald. He knew he could depend on you."

The Judge examined her face, waiting. "*And?*"

"Yet, the odd thing is, George Altmann, one of the greatest artists of his day, died only weeks later in a tragic accident and so disappeared from the record, literally, until a month ago, thanks to your grandson. You, according to your memoir, never came across the name of George Altmann in your trial preparation. There's nothing in Chambers's or Weinstein's books." She leaned across and placed her hand on his arm, gazing deep into his troubled red-rimmed eyes. "Except, of course, he was right about you . . . In the end, you saved him." She looked across at George. "Right, George?"

The Judge drew back into his chair, as if visibly shaken by this veiled accusation. Then, with a hard edge to his voice that had remained hidden until this moment, he replied, "Jews, Communists, ex-Communists, onetime left-wing intellectuals like Chambers and Weinstein—and like Altmann—they have a nose for conspiracy, for those for 'em and agin 'em."

The Judge smiled at George with a faint hint of malice, prompting his grandson to come around and sit on the armrest of Wendy's chair and take her hand.

"Who," he added, "might know when the dogs are on the scent, or when an offering to the gods is required for survival, a gift, a show of fealty that might get him off the hook?"

"A fine balance," and the Judge raised a quivering flattened palm. "Just read Chambers: Even staring into the abyss, he could barely bring himself to lower the boom on Hiss and the others for espionage, those, as he put it, with whom he'd 'broken bread.'"

In a voice just above a whisper, Wendy said, "He had, finally, to give up on the human instinct for love and loyalty."

George squeezed Wendy's hand as if for strength. "Altmann, like Chambers, came to you, caught between the Scylla of prosecution by the government and the Charybdis of retaliation from the KGB. Both took the precaution of holding something back: Altmann the sketches, and Chambers his life preserver—the Pumpkin Papers—just in case."

The Judge inspected George's face, as if noticing something for the first time in his profile: the cheeks now leaner, the rugged nose and soft mouth, highlighted by the flames, cowlicks touched with sparks of gold.

"You're—you've lost weight, George. You, his grandson, you carry his blood—what do your instincts tell you?"

"He had evidence and he was a witness to Hiss's being a member of a Communist cell in Washington in the thirties. Three of those members were already dead, two were in virtual exile and hiding, and another, Remington, would foolishly confess to being a spy and end up in Lewisburg prison, where he, too, would be murdered. And as you wrote in your memoir, Altmann knew Priscilla and Alger Hiss personally. You saw a sketch of his in their home, in Volta Place, after Holmes's funeral."

"Did I? My God, I'd forgotten that."

"I hope," said George, "not a selective memory."

"You," the Judge replied, a hint of indignation in his voice, "can trust what I wrote five years ago was to the best of my recollection."

"Altmann went to their home on Volta Place not just once, but at least twice. You had it from Priscilla Hiss."

"Yes, of course . . . I wrote as much. I've tried to be perfectly open, truthful."

"And then there remains our anonymous man, our ninth man. Shall we, for fiction's sake"—George made a facetious face at Wendy—"call him the *Ninth Man*?"

"All this was irrelevant to my one task at the trial. No surprises out of left field that might do our case harm."

"Altmann"—George's voice almost broke with emotion—"must have thought the sketches would be safe with you—that he'd be safe. As you've said, the sketches without his testimony, or his testimony without the sketches, would've amounted to hearsay. So he left the sketches in your hands."

The Judge leaned far forward in his seat.

"Are you—the two of you—accusing me? Are you telling me George Altmann was murdered and I'm in some way responsible?"

Wendy leaned around George and again placed a sympathetic hand on the arm of the Judge's chair. "We're almost certain he was murdered."

George added, "Judge, just a few weeks ago, in this very place, you hinted as much to me. And now, frankly, after Weinstein's book, it beggars belief that it could have been an accident"—he glanced at Wendy—"or suicide."

The Judge sat back, his face pale and troubled.

"Your father, Jim, in the brief occasions when the subject came up, suggested that suicide was the most likely scenario."

George shot back, "He fucking would—to excuse all his own sorry fuckups. Sorry, sorry." George raised a palm in surrender. "So, you did press him on the death of his father?"

"Only in passing. He was, worse luck, my son-in-law, after all."

"Suicide was the most likely explanation, given that an accident was so unlikely and foul play not suspected. Not to mention that no one, at least in Woodstock, seems to have even realized he was once a member of the Communist Party. Much less that he'd been in possession of evidence that would have been utterly compelling to the prosecution in the Hiss trial."

"*Not* without his testimony," echoed the Judge.

Wendy looked at George and pulled out a photo from her backpack and handed it to the Judge, who examined it in his lap for almost a minute, perplexed.

"I don't follow what this is all about."

"It's a mural in the Justice Department by George Altmann. If you look carefully, you can see he's used the nine figures in the sketches as character studies for the subjects around the farmer's table."

"It's like a cartoon . . . This is bizarre, fantastic."

"An inside joke, perhaps Altmann's parting shot, a sarcastic memorialization of his Party days. Like Chambers in 1939 at the signing of the Nazi-Soviet pact, he was probably horrified at how things had come to pass, what he'd gotten himself into."

"Well," offered the Judge, "that's very much to his credit. It was 1939, as you say, that separated the fanatics from the sturdy souls who recognized their errors. Those with integrity. Forgive me, but your father, Jimmy Altmann, is not such a man. He is a person of the most uncertain views and even less determination to do something useful with his life. I objected vociferously to your mother's marrying the man, and was hardly surprised by his desertion of her and you. *You*, George, given everything, are something of a miracle, at least in my book."

Wendy reached over and patted the Judge's hand, then got up and put another log on the fire. She turned back with a curious smile.

"And you never showed the sketches to Hiss or Rosenwald?" she asked.

"Of course not. I'll stick by what I wrote in my memoir: the truth as I then knew it."

"Nevertheless," said George, not a little dismayed at the pose he found himself adopting, "on or about the date that Weinstein obtained permission from Alger Hiss to have full access to the defense files, when he filed Freedom of Information petitions for access to the FBI and Justice Department files—sometime in the late sixties—you, according to your memoir, chose that moment to surreptitiously remove the Altmann sketches from the defense files."

"There you have it, children," said the Judge facetiously, now seeming to relish the moment. "The old boy—eh?—covering his lily white ass, his reputation. And I think one of the first questions you should ask the formidable Mr. Weinstein is how much difference would the existence or nonexistence—or rather, the submission of those sketches as evidence for the prosecution—have made to the eventual outcome of the case? I, for one, would be fascinated to know."

Wendy smiled. "Will it get you off the hook of history?"

"Probably not, my dear. But my conscience regarding an oversight might be soothed."

She picked up the copy of *Witness* and presented it to the Judge, as if in court to swear in a witness, smiling as she whispered above the crackling flames. "Strange, that Whittaker Chambers never mentions your name—not once in over eight hundred pages: nothing about the man who unleashed the worst garbage the psychiatric community could muster against his character."

The Judge took the book, fingers exploring the dark, jowly face beneath the brim of a fedora on the cover.

"A Quaker, a Christian . . ." Blinking rapidly, him gaze deepened as he nodded. "Not a day goes by that I don't see his sad, sleepless eyes in the witness box. The man who wrote that his whole life, its peculiarities, strengths, and weaknesses, had been lived to make him witness to the good and evil he had done. How did he put it? To have evaded that responsibility would have amounted to the destruction of his own soul. My God, that we all should live by such convictions."

"*Your* false choice between the god of communism and his Quaker God?"

"Yes, a false choice, a false dichotomy. Something that Emerson long ago on these shores felt able to dispense with. Here, George, grab my copy of Emerson's essays on the shelf right here." George knelt and pulled out the well-used leather-bound volume. "Which Alger Hiss and Whittaker Chambers—in their different ways— sought to redeploy . . . if resurrection is to be our gold standard." The Judge took the volume from his grandson and flipped the pages, the one with the marked passage practically opening itself beneath his fingers. "But your race, so to speak," he continued, "is between man and eternity—your department—eh, George? Or as Emerson put it, as it was first put to me my by mentor, Justice Holmes, as I read the following to him: 'Life only avails, not the having lived. Power ceases in the instant of repose; it resides in the moment of transition from a past to a new state, in the shooting of the gulf, in the darting of an aim. This one fact the world hates; that the soul *becomes*; for that for ever degrades the past, turns all riches to poverty, all reputation to a shame, confounds the saint with the rogue, shoves Jesus and Judas equally aside.'"

The Judge's calm, mellifluous cadences brought about some long moments of thoughtful silence, as if family history, or some standard of decency and healthy regard for the eternal, had been called forth, prompting Wendy to spring from her seat and warm her raw, blistered hands by the fire for a moment before turning to the two men with a near-ecstatic expression as she recited from memory:

"'In the hour of vision, there is nothing that can be called gratitude, nor properly joy. The soul raised over passion beholds identity and eternal causation, perceives the self-existence of Truth and Right, and calms itself with knowing that all things go well. Vast spaces of nature, the Atlantic Ocean, the South Sea,—long intervals of time, years, centuries,—are of no account. This which I think and feel underlay every former stage of life and circumstances, as it does underlie my present, and what is called life, and what is called death.'"

There followed the silence of the crackling flames abiding, as the Judge followed with his finger on his page, rereading the passage again.

"How did I do?" she finally asked.

George laughed. "Beware, she had a photographic memory."

The Judge eyed her as he might an esteemed colleague who had just opted to support his opinion. "Funny, the things you remember," said the Judge finally, closing the book. "When you find yourself, after all, only a minor character in the play of life."

Wendy bowed slightly, as if leaving the stage, her eyes smoldering softly as she moved off toward the shadows, face tilted to the play of the cosmos in the spaces above.

"Nothing can bring you peace but yourself," she echoed from beyond the circle of light.

"So," said George, taking a long brass poker to the fire, nodding into the hungry flames. "Alger Hiss, even after his conviction and jail time, throughout the sixties and seventies, when he fought to retrieve his reputation in the courts, when you were rising on the bench, on the verge of a Supreme Court nomination . . . he was only trying to keep going, stay alive—he had no choice but to seek *resurrection*—in this moment or the next, especially if he still believed the forces of history were marching in tandem—what?—with the likes of Ho Chi Minh, Mao, Pol Pot, Castro . . ."

"Holmes told me, and with some pleasure, I believe, that, after his marriage to Priscilla, he had tried to get Alger to read Emerson to him, to see if the Sage of Concord sat well with the voice of his young intern."

"And?"

"Alger lost his energy, Holmes noted to me; his heart was never in it. I suspect Alger believed, as Holmes put it, in the collective force, the voice of the mob, not the democracy of one."

The Judge handed George the copy of Emerson's *Essays*, open to the frontispiece, which was signed to him by Oliver Wendell Holmes.

"Ah, a Harvard man besotted by your siren song of foreign tyrannies. But not, it seems, his faith in his self-creation."

"Ah yes, the artwork of his own hand. After all, he decided on a reputational defense—all that was really left to him . . . to any of us."

"And that you, needless to say, were the right man at the right time to make that possible."

With that, they both turned to a voice out of the shadows in the far corner.

"But why would Chambers have signed a copy of *Witness* to Annie . . . of all people?"

To this, the men had no immediate reply, their eyes drawn to the translucent shadows beyond the reach of the fire, where the Tiffany lamps branded the Steinway's glimmering flanks with halations of bruised rose, touched in places with airy blue arabesques, as if mirroring some skylarking spirit loosed from above. A seated figure now presided, her long blond hair atremble with hints of azure and mauve, falling to an invisible keyboard . . . and silent no longer . . . vibrating floor and ceiling . . . soundings love-laden and deep and possibly fathomless.

Chopin's Etude No. 3 began drifting over the great room.

Key Witness In Red Trial Killed In Plunge

WASHINGTON, Oct. 21 (UP) —Authorities today were investigating the justice department death plunge of a key witness in the Hiss-Chambers congressional hearing.

A preliminary report was expected later in the day on the death of W. Marvin Smith, 53, a specialist in criminal law on the staff of the department's solicitor general.

Smith's day after circular sylvania justice d fice work been pac of his of before th eral Phil in recent ed despor Smith House u committe was rev a docum of a 192 one Will his sign Hiss wor the justi when the

The prominen tween H ment Chambei named war Co Washingt Hiss t had "th he gave Washing said His car ove ganizatio At the

Smith, Figure in Alger Hiss Case, Plunges to Death

WASHINGTON ities Thursday investigated the justice department death plunge of a key witness in the Hiss-Chambers congressional he The body of W. M 53, a special: on the

man said that in re seemed

Smith was called house un-American act committee Aug. 24 aft revealed to have notari ument transferring the 1929 Ford from Alger Hi William Rosen. H identified his signa he and Hiss worke office at the justice in 1936 when the t d.

auto transaction f tly in the dispute ss and Whittaker C 'd the house group he Ford when he g the use of his Wa ment. Chambers sa on turning the c ommunist organiza

WITNESS IN SPY CASE ENDS LIFE

Had Notarized Transfer of Car from Hiss.

Washington—(AP) Authoritiestoday were investigating the justice department death plunge ofa key witness in the Hiss-Chambers congressional hearing.

A preliminary report was expected on the death of W. MarvinSmith, 53, a specialist in criminallaw on the staff of the department's solicitor general.

Smith's body was found yesterday afternoon at the base of a circular staircase near the Pennsylvania avenue entrance to thejustice department building. Office workers reported that he hadbeen pacing the corridor in frontof his office for nearly two hoursbefore the plunge. Solicitor General Philip B. Pearlman said tha-tin recent days Smith "had seemedde-spondent."

Smith was called before a house un-American activities subcommittee on Aug. 24 after he wasrevealed to have notarized a document transfer-ring the title of a1929 Ford from Alger Hiss to oneWilliam Rosen. He iden-tified hissignature and said he and Hissworked in the same office at the justice department in 1936 whenthe transfer occurred.

y Dies in Story Plunge

placed in suggest characteristic pos ctangular table drap d red-checked tab

ck-a-block—horn reit—dining room en slanted downw ewer's space to sumptuous harves l ears of corn, a ples, sheaves of g ittle out of place the idea of good a golden rack of l two crystal deca e mural carried th

U.S. Atto. Dies in Plu. wn Stairwell

INGTON, Oct. 20 (AP) , Smith, 53-year-old jus- ment attorney, was when he plunged -story stairwell of ment Building. said Smith had pressed during

ber of the ral Phillip on that

etown as a De

Widow Rejects Suicide Verdict

WASHINGTON, Dec. 2. (A))— The widow of W. Marvin Smith, justice department employe who died in a five-story plunge two months ago, expressed belief today was not suicide and

Key Witness In Hiss Case Dies in Plunge

Washington — (AP) Authorities today were investigating the justice department death plunge of a key witness in the Hiss-Chambers con-gressional hearing.

A preliminary report

un-American tee on Aug. vealed to h ment transfe 1929 Ford fr William Ros signature an worked in th justice depar the tra

Identi The auto prominently i Hiss, a form official, and of Time maga as a leader of

29
Crime Scene: Marvin Smith

All that matters is what did people who worked closely and intimately with me think of me . . . They saw my every gesture, my every movement, my every facial expression. They heard the tones in which I spoke, the words I uttered, the words spoken by others in my presence. They knew my every act relating to official business, both in public and in executive conference.

—Alger Hiss, testimony in court

I was at the Hisses' when Alger drove the Ford away. I was still there when he came back after having turned it over to the party. He was very pleased with himself. I never asked him any further details about the transaction. I would have been shocked if I had known that he had asked a colleague in the Department of Justice (the late W. Marvin Smith) to notarize the transfer of title.

—Whittaker Chambers, *Testimony HUAC*

Probe Death Plunge of Key Spy Witness
WASHINGTON, Oct. 21, 1948 (UP)—Authorities today investigated the death plunge of a key witness in the Hiss-Chambers Congressional hearing.

A preliminary report was expected later in the day on the death of W. Marvin Smith, 53, a specialist in criminal law on the staff of the Department of Justice's Solicitor General.

Smith's body was found yesterday afternoon at the base of a staircase near the entrance to the Justice Department Building. Office workers reported that he had been pacing the corridor in front of his office for nearly two hours before the plunge. Solicitor General Philip B. Pearlman said that in recent days Smith "has seemed despondent."

Smith was called before a House Un-American Activities subcommittee on Aug. 23 after he was revealed to have notarized a document transferring the title of a 1929 Ford from Alger Hiss to one William Rosen. He identified his signature and said he and Hiss worked in the same office at the Justice Department in 1936 when the transfer occurred.

The automobile transaction figured prominently in the dispute between Hiss, a former State Department official, and Whittaker Chambers of Time *magazine, who named him as a leader of a pre-war Communist underground in Washington.*

U.S. Worker's Widow Holds to Accident Belief

WASHINGTON, Dec 23, 1948 (AP)—The widow of W. Marvin Smith, Justice Department employee who died in a five-story plunge two months ago, expressed belief that his death was simply an accident.

She said she feels certain that it was not a suicide and was not connected in any way with his appearance as a minor witness in Congressional spy hearings.

Smith's death has been recalled in some newspaper accounts of the death of Laurence Duggan in New York this week.

On Oct. 20, Smith hurtled to his death down a circular stair well in the Justice Department. The coroner's verdict was suicide.

Mrs. Smith was never reconciled to the suicide verdict. She said that there is something unexplained about her husband's death. "I have to believe he was murdered."

She said: "As for my husband's death, I know he did not kill himself. But how do I explain that to my young daughter, Jeanne? She is devastated; she wanders the house like a lost spirit. It's all I can do to get her to eat."

———

George and Wendy stood on the fifth-floor landing of the southwest corner staircase in the Justice Department, holding tight to the
railing, and stared down the five spiraling flights to the lobby floor,
where, embedded in the slabs of white marble (she called it nacreous
off-white), a jet black omega symbol echoed the banister's sinuous
Art Deco descent. Target of their pained gaze. Impact point. Ground
zero for one W. Marvin Smith. Behind them on a curving wall was
a sprawling mural depicting a Midwest—think Grant Wood—farm
family gathered at a sumptuous Thanksgiving repast. They had just
discovered, to their consternation, thirteen figures were seated and
standing—not the nine in the sketches, nor the nine in the preliminary study found in Altmann's barn studio, nor the nine in what turned
out to be a poor quality close-up of the mural found on the Internet,
which, it turned out, showed only the central ensemble—figures from
central casting in various rustic rural getups, if not comical outfits.
All were placed in suggestive or perhaps characteristic poses around
a rectangular table draped with a vivid red-checked tablecloth. The
chock-a-block—horn of plenty conceit—dining room table had been
slanted downward into the viewer's space to dramatize the sumptuous
harvest of just-ripened ears of corn, a bowl of green apples, sheaves
of grain (looking a little out of place but essential to the idea of good
and plenty), and a golden rack of lamb, along with two crystal decant-
ers of wine. The mural carried the jejune, if not hilarious, title *Society
Fed and Freed Through Justice.*

"Of course there was something unexplained about her husband's
death!" Wendy suddenly exclaimed, as if all the frustration of the last
weeks had suddenly caught up with her. She turned from the stairwell,
looking again at the wall mural.

"It's okay," he said, trying to calm her as he struggled to return the
photocopied clippings to his file. He glanced back down the long corridor, where dark-suited men and dark-skirted women scurried from
offices, where the Federal Protective Service armed guard, who had
accompanied them from the Pennsylvania Avenue entrance, loitered,
keeping a vague eye out. "Remember, we're art historians, researching the
art and life of George Altmann. Everybody here still seems so jumpy."

"All the accounts in the newspapers," she said, following his gaze
and waiting a beat, "talk about Smith pacing up and down in the hallway in the hours before he fell—'agitated,' they wrote, as if waiting for
something, for someone. And of course he would have been agitated;

who wouldn't be if you had this fucking mural hanging over your head? It must have seemed like the sword of Damocles, larger than life, depicting him along with Alger Hiss, Laurence Duggan, and Harry Dexter White—all of whom had recently been named by Chambers and Bentley in their testimony before HUAC and were being actively investigated by the FBI. What the fuck, two months before, W. Marvin Smith himself had testified to HUAC that it was his signature on the transfer deed of Hiss's Ford. You'd be pacing the halls, too, if you heard that train whistle headed your way."

"What do you think of the mural?" George asked in a studied voice, having learned how best to calm her. "Artistically speaking—besides the Doppler effect."

She drew a hand across her face, took a deep breath, flicked a strand of hair behind an ear, smiled at the guard, who was leaning against a marble column down the corridor, and refocused.

"It's crap, a total inanity, George, and George Altmann knew it. It's a conceit: Christ and the twelve apostles! You can almost feel his dripping sarcasm and distaste for the treacly propaganda. Like he was getting back at them *and* the government for hiring him to produce something so insulting to his artistic integrity. Even the faces are more generalized than in the sketches, as if synthesized to fit some heroic social-realist template. Look," and she pointed, "the extra four figures must have been stuck in at the eleventh hour. See how they're crammed around the central nine, painted over what was already finished—see the pentimenti showing through?"

"Faces definitely not as recognizable as in the sketches," he said. "I mean, he could hardly have the U.S. Justice Department pay to have"—he pointed to the added figures on the right and left—"Stalin, Lenin . . . and Trotsky hanging on their walls. A baker's dozen."

"If we didn't know what we know—without the sketches . . . no, I don't think we'd recognize anybody, not with the straw hats and muddy overalls and cowboys shirts. Like those smart Harvard boys— jaws strengthened, cheeks heightened—are kinda slumming with the real folks, incognito, in plain sight. Turns out your grandfather was quite the practical joker—like I said from the start, it's a visual whoopee cushion." She turned back to the stairwell, grabbing hold of the railing, as if to return to the unpleasantness at hand. "What's so weirdly eerie, the design and detailing of the metal work in the staircase is really quite beautiful." She shook her head, her hair loose and falling over her reddened cheeks. "In a kind of fluid Art Deco way. Aluminum"—she tapped the railing with her knuckles, noting the lotus leaf design in the metalwork—"and the marble slabs everywhere—kind of like the Miracoli in Venice—rather cold, even if the veining is quite spectacular. Which makes this whole mess only that much more horrific."

He looked at a note in his file. "Marvin Smith landed on the marble floor of the lobby, sustaining a broken neck, crushed skull, bruises and lacerations, bleeding badly."

"*Headfirst*, George, just like your grandfather. He had to have been—only way—thrown down headfirst. That's why he wouldn't have been able to grab on anywhere and save himself."

"Unlike with Duggan, terminal velocity wouldn't have been reached."

"You're the physicist. Even with Duggan, it would have taken—what?—at least fifteen seconds, or fifteen hundred feet. They both required," she said icily, "a helping hand or two."

"Somehow being indoors," he said, "a staircase . . . the intimacy of the thing makes it that much more . . . grotesque—a desecration, I guess."

She pulled out her tape measure and measured from the floor to the top of the railing. "Fifty inches. You, me, anyone near six feet couldn't just accidentally flip over this. Accidents like that just don't happen. People grab banisters, even on the way down."

Again, he consulted his notes.

"Nobody heard a scream."

"He couldn't have even caught his breath, it would've been so fast."

"Even if he knew they were coming . . . something was coming."

"Whaddya wanna bet his wife had no idea he'd been a Communist or fellow traveler back in thirties." She said this with an angry jut of her jaw toward the mural behind them, at the hired hand in dungarees. "And this down the hall from his office, just waiting for someone to come along and recognize him along with the others under investigation. My God, Smith must have endured months of Altmann up on a scaffold painting the thing."

He reached an arm around her waist, holding her close for long seconds, feeling her breathing as his imagination tracked hers.

"Do you suppose Smith and Altmann recognized each other? Did Smith cower in his office? His blood pressure pounding in his ears as he caught wind of what was being painted." He sighed into the collar of her cashmere sweater. "I can't believe I dragged you into this."

"Nobody drags me into anything, baby." With that, she smiled at the guard, who had been watching them, waved, and turned again to the mural that dominated the stairwell, gesturing in a sweeping motion from left to right and back. "It's just, I can't get his daughter, Jeanne, out of my mind."

"That really bothers you, doesn't it?"

"I've fucking been there."

He stroked her face, pulled a strand of hair off the shoulder of her gray sweater.

"What I can't figure is what the Judge is holding back."

"How much, you mean. Alice has no reason to lie about the timing of when Altmann handed him the sketches—right?"

"Not that I can think of."

"Or it could just be faulty memory. I couldn't escape the feeling night before last, how he inhabits a different country from the one we do, presided over by that marvelous ceiling, bewitched and bewitching—us . . . Or maybe I'm going a little crazy, stargazing, I guess, spellbound. It creeps me out, a little like falling in love with your professor's genius."

"Not like your Harold Bloom, I hope?"

"Different . . . the woman he loved—Annie; that magical ceiling is filled with the spirit of her love, or its creator's love, which is, I guess, one and the same. Know what I mean, when something beautiful catches you unaware and you feel this joy of rediscovery, the thing missing in your life?" She spun on her heels. "Making this"—she glared at the mural with a furious look of disdain—"a total travesty."

He couldn't help smiling at her agitation, how her blue eyes grew wide and lustrous beneath her creased brows, that erotic flush of perplexity that he found so essential to her nature.

"Ah, just when you think *you've* got his number—well, he sure couldn't take his eyes off your legs." He patted her rump, where her elegant fawn-colored leather trousers clung tight. "But I think it's more of a game of wits for him. He enjoys knowing something you don't, being a little wiser, offering you a chance to surprise him, to outwit him. That's why he sorta likes me, or the astrophysics boy-wonder thing, because I know stuff he can't quite get his head around—it intrigues him, as if human nature isn't enough of a mystery. He's curious . . . as bird-watchers tend to be. And talk about curious, the thing he said just before he went off to bed: how he and Alger Hiss always ended up talking about birding during breaks in the trial, sightings, behavior, how that made him always want to believe the best about his client."

"Yeah, I got that in my notes, as well. Like he said, he prefers winning, at least not coming out a fool in the history books."

"Oh, I think it's more than just winning. The only thing better than winning or even being right all the time is living up to your exemplary standards. *Although*, he does take enormous pleasure in being right."

"Like George Altmann, making fools of your enemies." She laughed uneasily, pointing to the corner of the off-kilter dinner table, where, slightly removed from the rest, one George Altmann, or a caricature of George Altmann, sat with pencil poised over a pad, red beret slipped to one side of a wide forehead, revealing a missing ear, a cropped red beard contouring a narrow chin. "Disguised as van Gogh, no less." She reached to his face for a moment, her fingers examining his chin. "To make sure history knew how he'd sat in with the disciples and captured their earnest idiocies for all eternity."

"Didn't one of them have their ear cut off when Christ was arrested?"

"Malchus, a slave."

"Servant of the high priest."

"Saint Peter cut off his ear, defending Jesus."

"Fra Angelico, right, somewhere?"

And so they continued for another few minutes in a conversational feedback loop, two minds probing each other as they probed the past. Like an old couple, they had fallen into the habit of finishing each other's sentences, enjoying the comfort to be found there.

"Altmann just couldn't resist the temptation of turning it into a Last Supper," he went on. "Notice Alger Hiss's longer hair, his soulful eyes, and how Priscilla, her head slightly inclined to the left, echoes the face of Leonardo's John the Evangelist, as if she's swooning over her savior."

She seemed to ponder this proposition for a moment, waiting for the thing to clarify in her mind.

"In Leonardo's original, John looked more like a woman than a man, a young Mona Lisa, except here with a cameo brooch and gingham dress—creeps me out."

"Except"—and George pointed to a handsome youth in jeans and a cowhide jacket, a red bandanna tied around his neck, seated to the right of Duggan and White—"W. Marvin Smith, whose office was just about where our security detail is standing, knew he was no savior . . . and had no taste for martyrdom."

"I'd sure as hell be pacing the landing, too, right here where I can see down both corridors, and what's marching up the stairs or appearing out of the elevator."

"Do you suppose Hiss knew about the mural?" he asked. "Would his old pal W. Marvin Smith have told him about *your* travesty?"

"You mean what had first been a spiteful joke, or premonition of things to come, that by 1948 Hiss, the faltering big kahuna, faced the possibility of an indictment and trial? Of course Smith told him—his longtime friend Alger. And Alger probably told his consigliere, Harold Rosenwald, and his KGB enforcers."

"The Judge seemed genuinely clueless about the mural."

She grabbed his arm. "That's how they played it—right? The public-facing team operated on a need-to-know basis, as long as Altmann could be kept out of the picture."

His gaze lifted to his grandfather's mural with renewed acuity. "Look at how he placed Alger and Priscilla, the aura, the power couple, god and goddess surrounded by their adoring minions, as if he was just a little enthralled, or maybe he did have a premonition . . . call it a prediction, a theory—even a hope that he might bring them down."

"Gods of deception."

"Ah . . ."

She couldn't repress a sarcastic laugh. "And avenge himself, as he did by adding those four figures in a rush after the Molotov-Ribbentrop Pact of August 1939."

"We know from the Judge's memoir that when he visited the Hisses after the funeral for Oliver Wendell Holmes in 1935, there was an Altmann sketch of Priscilla's son by her first marriage hanging on the living room wall at Volta Place."

"Priscilla had studied with Altmann at the Art Students League in the early thirties." She now eyed him intently, her words carefully deployed, as if needing to align their thoughts in perfect tandem. "But by late 1949, and the beginning of the second trial, by the time Smith, Duggan, and White had already been martyred, Altmann must have known he was under threat. Why else would he have handed those sketches to the Judge? You don't think when he waited—pacing—on the Sawkill Bridge on Christmas Eve, it wasn't on his mind?"

"I can't figure if the Judge knows more than he's letting on, or has just forgotten. Like how he happened to find Annie's signed and inscribed copy of *Witness* only after she died."

She pointed again to the mural, as if needing to further demonstrate their bona fides to the security guard, who'd begun glancing more frequently at his watch.

"What was it about Hiss? How could he have had such power over the minds of colleagues and friends while remaining invisible? Something even Chambers struggled to resolve in *Witness*: a mirror to every soul who gazed upon his righteous face. Altmann caught something of that even in the fucking mural, don't you think? The charisma, the aura—a man with a thousand faces . . . and none."

"Who would do whatever it took to survive."

"Hiss"—she eyed him, squeezing his hand—"or the Judge? To protect something more precious still."

George nodded to the security guard, who was holding up his wrist, pointing to his watch.

"Our time is up. Did you get enough photos?"

"Wait," she said, pointing again. "Look at them. Doesn't it creep you out, all those content and well-fed people still innocent of the fate awaiting them?"

George took her arm to steady himself, to steady her. He couldn't quite put it into words, even as he attempted to: the equation trying to write itself in his mind.

"Sixty light-years, you see, isn't so distant, in the scheme of things. There are potentially habitable planets in the Milky Way, only sixty light-years away."

"You mean," she said, her voice quickening, "if they're seeing us now, our light that is—the world that was—they could be watching George Altmann finishing his mural in 1938?"

"For them, he's still painting; for them, he's still a master of figurative art."

"So what would they think?" She took his arm, moving closer. "Laurence Duggan, a lowly cook pouring coffee, a bit servile, but he certainly looks better fed, weightier, less hollow-eyed than in the photographs of him from the time he took a dive out the window on Forty-fifth Street. Before his back or his conscience or the KGB gave up on him."

"Coffee," he intoned. "He was director of the Latin American Division at State—involved with our economic policy in South American countries, the world's major coffee producers."

"Aha!" She nodded eagerly at the narrative conceit, a return to Yale seminar days with Harold Bloom. "And Harry Dexter White—the pencil behind his ear, and Lauchlin Currie, the slide rule in the pocket of his overalls. Young Harvard economists all, eager New Dealers; young and virile farmhands in muddy boots, raring to get back to the fields and the next Five-Year Plan. Make Stalin proud."

"Our stargazers might be a little confused by your—what?— literary explication when they checked in ten years later . . . what fate had in store."

"What do you suppose they would make of the man in the well-tailored business suit, hanging up his coat or taking it down? He looks particularly lean and agile and very hungry—a man in a hurry. I don't like the look of him. I doubt our friends sixty light-years away would like him, either, but at least they'd know if he was coming or going."

"Funny," said George, "did you notice? He's the only one wearing a business suit, a bit out of character. He looks rather out of place, our *ninth* man, our . . . Judas?"

"Maybe he's the local banker come to foreclose on their farm?"

"And Priscilla Hiss . . . still young and full of herself. Not the anxiety-ridden wreck from the trial who would be ditched by Alger and end up a neurotic, wasted, lonely woman on Martha's couch."

"You almost sound . . . if not *sad*, George, then at least a little sorry for her."

"Reading her letters coming down in the car . . ." He shrugged. "I suppose it could all have been different."

"Hey, she could have been your grandmother!"

"God forbid!" He laughed.

"You know, George, the Judge doesn't need to be sixty-light years away. He still sees them—what, some seventy years ago, like what he wrote about visiting Alger and Priscilla at their home on Volta Place in 1935 after Holmes's funeral. Before the war, in the midst of the Depression, still full of their fervent hopes of world revolution. There's a part of him that remains back there—don't you think? Innocent, like the rest of this crowd on the wall, innocent of their sad fate. Look into their eyes, George, their dreaming eyes—Altmann got those right. Even they couldn't have guessed what time would bring them, where they'd end up and the treachery that would mark their end. They could never—like Chambers wrote—believe such a thing about themselves . . . why the Judge finds it so hard to remember. These are *his* people . . . the sfumato . . . yes?"

"Sfumato?"

"That mesmerizing—'anodyne,' he called it—mist . . . that invisible force field—*your* dark matter."

"Dark *energy*," he corrected.

She moved closer, squinting, her face aglow with wonder as she pointed.

"The *pedimenti*, George, the ghostly figures, done in such a hurry, on the fly. It wasn't just his little joke; he was trying to disguise the thing, the central ensemble, maybe to protect himself. Unlike our stargazers from afar, he couldn't anticipate what fate had in mind for him, what a break would mean. That even the best insurance wasn't enough against such merciless gods."

30

Lost in a Haunted Wood

THEY HAD TO wait fifteen minutes beyond their appointed hour in the antechamber of Allen Weinstein's office before his assistant ushered them through leather-padded doors patterned with brass nail heads and into the sprawling inner sanctum, where the nation's archivist awaited them behind a broad mahogany desk, peering skeptically over his metal-rimmed reading glasses from a document in his hands. He removed his glasses, revealing tired gray eyes and a thin no-nonsense face beneath a high lined forehead, where wisps of white hair were neatly combed. He surveyed the supplicants with an enigmatic half-smile, rose and rigidly held out his hand to shake, as if compelled to an official greeting, while waving them to two seats catty-corner to his almost empty desk, a gleaming expanse reflecting an elongated green-shaded reading lamp. This was in stark contrast to the orderly, if cluttered, office crammed from floor to ceiling with battlements of heavy bookshelves and strategically situated side tables flanked by comfortable leather chairs, where stacks of recently arrived scholarly tomes teetered.

George took his seat and tried to absorb the scattering of official imprimaturs during an ice-breaking chitchat: the draped American flag in the corner beside the tall metal casement window overlooking Constitution Avenue; the official seal of the National Archives—a splayed eagle and the words *Littera, Scripta, Manet*; carved panels depicting the great historians: Thucydides, Herodotus, Parkman, et al.; and a modest power wall in an alcove behind their host with honorary degrees and photographs of the scholar and soon-to-be national archivist shaking hands with Reagan and Bush senior, William Buckley, a swearing-in with Bush junior. The niceties done, George got up from his Windsor chair and walked around the desk to Weinstein's side.

"May I?" he asked.

"By all means," Weinstein said, crisp, businesslike, succinct. "That's what you're here for."

George proceeded to lay out the nine sketches in a semicircle across the desk facing Allen Weinstein, in the configuration Wendy had carefully determined matched the original grouping of the sitters at Volta Place. Weinstein, perhaps bemused or impatient, waited until George was done before putting on his reading glasses, first giving the group a quick scan, then going one by one by one, bending closer and back and even closer to some that drew his attention, or where particular details required closer scrutiny. George returned to his seat, all the while watching Weinstein's face intently. The archivist maintained his skeptical scholarly composure for a good three or four minutes, with only the merest flicker of doubt or alarm flashing in his narrowed gray-brown eyes, brows pinching once, twice, a third time, at something—George thought it was their ninth man—before reassuming a more remote pose. He nodded, more to himself than to his visitors, now touching individual sheets, lifting up a delicate edge with a fingertip, finally picking up one and holding it gingerly up to his desk lamp for inspection, perhaps searching for watermarks.

Wendy bent forward in her chair as if a tad impatient with the performance and swept an authoritative hand across the polished mahogany where the nine sketches were now arranged in a line like large tarot cards.

"I'm pretty sure that's the configuration in which they were seated, given the way the light falls and the direction of their gazes. It seems like a group portrait—all at one sitting; I estimate about two hours to execute nine drawings with that level of detailing."

"Their eyes turned to Alger Hiss, you mean," offered Weinstein, with just a hint of a pleased smile curling the corner of his pinched lips.

"Yes," she said, "in the Hisses' Volta Place living room. You can find the address and date faintly annotated in pencil on the back of the sketch of Alger Hiss."

Weinstein immediately picked up the Hiss sketch and held the verso up to his reading lamp, squinting, nodding.

"I don't suppose you've had a paper expert, a conservator, check the age of the paper?"

"Why?" asked George. "We know the provenance, the artist's hand."

Weinstein smiled uneasily, something approximating a world-weary but wise avuncular expression.

"Young man, in a court of law, or worse, an academic forum, the first issue of business would be whether these were faked, either period fakes, say around the time of the trial, or even more recently. During the Hiss trial, the defense spent untold dollars and time trying to prove the secret State Department papers turned over by Chambers and copied on the Hiss typewriter were fakes. Even ten years ago, these sketches would have been potential dynamite in certain circles—now, alas, fading on the horizon. And yes, even now, in one case"—he eyed the sketch on the far right—"explosive."

"We can leave them with you—with the National Archives," said George. "Let your people have at them and then you're welcome to retain them, for safekeeping, for the record."

"Generous, thank you. As the ninth archivist of the United States"— his eyes danced as if in mockery of such an officious title—"I accept your gift on behalf of the National Archives and the American people." He patted the flag pin on the lapel of his worn pinstripe suit. "My assistant can assist you with a gift form on the way out. And I must say, never in a million years did I imagine that the grandson of Edward Dimock would show up on my doorstep with such offerings to the nation." He shot his eyebrows with an ironic smile. "Much less on this particular doorstep . . . with a cast of characters I have lived with for almost half a century—but here"—he squinted, thin lips poised, as if at a loss for words—"something very immediate, something very alive, so unlike the newspaper clippings and mug shots. Clearly your artist, Mr. Altmann, was very talented. I feel in a quandary that I never knew him or his work."

"That will change," noted George with a hint of pride.

"So," said Wendy, "you're really *not* questioning the authenticity?"

"No, given the source, but I wouldn't go about spouting this new evidence, so to speak, without the forensic expert's full sign-off. I can run them by the FBI lab people—that should do it."

"You mentioned my grandfather, Judge Dimock. He writes in his memoir that you went to his chambers on Foley Square and asked if you could interview him on the record for your first book?"

Weinstein's face lighted up with the pleasure of recall.

"My God, I was intimidated! I couldn't quite believe that I had the chutzpah to barge in like that, but I was hoping that on the spur of the moment he might feel in a more candid mood. All the others on the defense team had turned me down."

"Client-attorney privilege?"

"They had been on the losing team and I was going to try to sec-ond-guess them, where they had failed."

Leaning forward, Wendy said, "He was intimidated by you; thought you were out to make him look worse than he already felt for beating up on Chambers."

"I was wondering just what he was most concerned about hiding."

"Hiding?"

"If he'd been a member of the Communist Party at some point, a faithful friend and colleague of Alger Hiss—a fellow traveler. One could never quite tell about the defense team: the dupes and the faithful. Of course, their briefs and memos were preserved in the defense files. A few whispers from colleagues about the inner workings. But I did hear, in a roundabout way, from your—is it your mother or aunts?"

"Alice and Martha Dimock—my aunts."

Weinstein turned to his computer screen on a side table and tapped in the names and examined the search results.

"Yes, Alice Dimock, who in a *California Law Review* article critiqued my *Perjury*, basically giving the book a handsome review but trashing her father and the defense team for 'concocting' a reputational defense of Alger Hiss, while neglecting to attack the institutional biases of the government and FBI, and so failing to undermine the prosecution's case by delegitimizing the system that sought Hiss's unjustified conviction." He clicked his mouse. "Your other aunt"—Weinstein punched a few keys and squinted—"in the journal *Psychological Science* of 1979, referencing *Perjury*, attacked the defense, and specifically Edward Dimock, for the 'unprofessional' strategy of using two psychiatrists to assault the character of the prosecution's star witness, Whittaker Chambers. A case of criminal abuse that 'only made the conviction of Hiss more, not less, likely.'"

"That sounds about right," said George with a sheepish shrug.

Wendy caught George's eye. "That not the way the Judge tells it in his memoir."

"Memoir?" asked Weinstein, his eyebrows again shooting high over the steel frames of his glasses.

"Unpublished," said George. "A work in progress."

"He must be . . ."

"Ninety-five. And his memory is beginning to fail him."

"Sorry to hear that, but he"—Weinstein paused, brows flexing at the calculation—"must be the last remaining member of the defense team. And no one left from the prosecution. By God, they're all gone." Allen Weinstein sat back, as if a little overwhelmed by this discovery, lips pressed down in bereavement: the playwright facing an empty stage, his dramatis personae having, one after another, bowed out. "When did he write the memoir?"

"He finished, or, rather, petered out, about five years ago."

"He's now read your latest book," she said, looking at George. "To say the least, it's filled his tattered sails."

"A life saver," said George. "Although, with some doubts put to rest, others seem now to have claimed him . . . his imagination inflamed, if that's the right word. He's been a little anxious of late about how he comes out, all things considered."

"And for you, Mr. Weinstein," asked Wendy, who had been studying his face closely, as if eager to put pencil to sketch pad, noting the spark of interest in his eyes at the mention of "memoir," his gaze straying again and again to the sketches, especially the last on the far right, but carefully, like a poker player fearing the give-away tell, "how does the existence of the sketches change things for *you*?"

"Well," he said looking at Wendy, eyes aglitter, "a remarkable and absolutely unique documentation of a Washington Communist Party cell or Soviet spy ring circa 1936. The first documentation I know of confirming, or at least implying, that these nine people knew one another as Communist Party members. Only William Remington"— and he turned one of the sketches on the desk toward his guests—"ever admitted as much, much less spying for the Soviets—and went to prison. Frankly, what beggars the imagination—why I'm more than a little nonplussed—is a man like Alger Hiss even allowing such a thing: the recording of their likenesses at such a meeting. Against every rule of tradecraft, as Chambers would surely have warned them. Of course, as we now know, with the transfer of his old Ford roadster— his undoing—to a Communist operative, Hiss could be impetuous at times. And this was 1936; they were all—well, wet behind the ears." He smiled, touching the sketches here and there with a strange fondness. "Neophytes . . . babes in the woods."

"Ah," said George, "your title."

"Auden . . . 'Lost in a haunted wood/Children afraid of the night/ Who have never been happy or good.'"

"Feast of the gods," she said in a sibilant throwaway tone.

"Gods . . ." Weinstein replied. "Oh yes, of course."

"In the memoir," she said, "speaking of the unhappy, Altmann's relationship, so it seems, was with Priscilla Hiss, who may have been, well, behind the idea."

"Ah, the memoir," said Weinstein turning his wan gaze to George, "you wouldn't have a copy to spare?"

Wendy interrupted before George could answer. "So, you don't know about the mural in the Justice Department?"

"Mural?"

"Here, I'll e-mail you a photo." She got out her phone and sent the photo.

A moment later, Weinstein was staring wide-eyed at his computer screen.

"This is almost impossible to believe."

Wendy got up and stood beside his chair, pointing out the figures in George Altmann's mural, analyzing the composition.

"So, you knew nothing about this?" asked George.

"First I've heard of it—my God, it's just down Constitution Avenue."

George went on. "You're the leading scholar in the Hiss-Chambers affair, and if *this* got by you, along with George Altmann, who appears in none of your books, then it's probably accurate to assume that no one knew, except, perhaps, W. Marvin Smith."

"Who you figure clued in Alger Hiss," noted Wendy with an ominous tone.

"Smith . . ." mused Weinstein.

As if frustrated by the cautious pace of conversation, she motioned to the enlarged photograph on the monitor that Weinstein was still minutely examining.

"Of course, the thing is more like a cartoon, a caricature, a bizarre homage to Leonardo, and unless you were specifically looking for these people . . . only Priscilla Hiss really looks like herself."

"Good Lord," said Weinstein, "he's included Lenin, Stalin, and Trotsky."

"Clearly an inside joke," said George, "or a sneer and snub as he resigned from the Federal Art Project in the fall of 1939 and headed home to Woodstock."

"By adding the four figures—and it looks like a rush job, a last-minute adjustment—he's, in a sense, disguising the original conception, inspiration, I suppose."

"I don't quite know whether to laugh or cry," said Weinstein, shaking his head in wonder. "The Nazi-Soviet pact was always the final straw for the sane ones."

"W. Marvin Smith had to have known," echoed George, again prompting Weinstein.

Weinstein looked at George with a kind of inbred reluctance to jump to conclusions, turning his attention to the sketch of the mild-mannered Smith, pondering it, then to his monitor, enlarging the painted version of the eager, still-young lawyerly face in the guise of a hired hand.

"Yes," said Weinstein, nodding, now tapping rapidly at his keyboard. "I have all my research notes digitized." He shot a glance out his window at the sudden wail of an ambulance siren on Constitution Avenue. "It's extraordinary, when you think about it . . . over twenty years ago now, when I was on Bill Buckley's *Firing Line* with the publication of *Perjury*, after I'd interviewed thousands of people involved in the Hiss case, read tens of thousands of pages of FBI files and trial notes and transcripts to write the book, and Bill asked me, with his typical insouciance, about my 'herculean' labors, if I expected that more evidence about the case would appear over time from participants. I didn't hesitate. I nodded yes—of course. I fully expected that as the years went by, as the old Communists neared the end, there would be memoirs and perhaps recollections about the good old days in the Party, filling in the gaps in the record, offering details and color about the halcyon years when the Party and the New Deal were on the march. And you know what—" He jabbed a few more times at his keyboard—"nothing. It's as if a veil of silence descended, as if all those lives just evaporated into"—he glanced at George—"a black hole. The only thing that changed was the Venona decrypts and access to the Soviet intelligence files after 1989—the two years of access that Random House bribed a bunch of retired KGB officers to obtain in 1993. That's it—and now these sketches—and I guess this crazy mural. For the most part, our dramatis personae took their memories to their graves." Weinstein tapped in some more search terms. "Sad, don't you think, for our history, for our understanding of the past, that for so many of them—what, shame, guilt, fear, regrets?"—he shrugged—"the grand illusion took such a terrible toll."

"Dark matter," offered George.

"Dark matter?" questioned Weinstein.

"An astrophysics term for an invisible adjunct to gravity that, nevertheless, seems essential to the formation of the universe as we know it. In human terms, as I discussed with my grandfather, a kind of veil of desire, of fervent expectations that shapes the expectation of an era. Within families, as well, I guess . . . that certain something that holds the whole shebang together while putting everyone at odds."

"Curious," pronounced Allen Weinstein, smiling, not unimpressed by this explanation.

"Talk about a haunted wood," said Wendy flippantly, now retreating back to her chair.

"Ah, here it is—I knew *George Altmann* rang a bell. Looks like your grandfather did indeed have an FBI file—a copy in the prosecution files—as a suspected member of the Communist Party—you can easily request that, you know. Running the mural projects for the Federal Art Project would have prompted an FBI security check, even in the thirties, when security was almost nonexistent. Clearly, whatever affiliations they turned up were not enough to bar him from the job, since most artists at that time were socialists or Communists. But here's something: Priscilla Hiss had studied with Altmann briefly at the Art Students League in the early 1930s, and she had subsequently recommended him for the mural position to Holger Cahill—friend of the Hisses—who ran the Federal Art Project." Weinstein again raised an exclamatory digit. "So, there's Altmann's connection to the Hisses, why he might have been invited to sketch the comrades, probably at a social gathering, a cell meeting where they discussed the latest news, gossip, and doctrines put abroad in the *Daily Worker*—that kind of thing." Weinstein swiveled in his chair back to the sketches, as if in renewed admiration for their creator, and then returned to his keyboard. "As an artist, working in the Federal Art Project, he can hardly have been in the information-gathering business—certainly nothing of much interest to any GRU or KGB apparatus."

"Except," said George, "as a witness against the likes of Alger Hiss. Dangerous: a man who had broken with the Party in 1939."

Weinstein, cheeks flushed, nodded, tapping away at his keyboard.

"Hah, he's in my notes from the prosecution files. Altmann was on a list of potential prosecution witnesses with suspected ties to Party circles that included Priscilla and Alger Hiss. They probably got his name from the same FBI security file on the FAP position. Never called as a witness in the first trial because his testimony was deemed weak or irrelevant to the main thrust of the prosecution's case. But on November 12, 1949, a few weeks before the beginning of the second trial, he *was* interviewed by the FBI . . . admitted to having been a member of the Communist Party in the thirties, but abandoned all ties after the August 1939 Nazi-Soviet Pact. Admitted to knowing Priscilla Hiss when she was a student at the Art Students League in the early thirties, and, occasionally, socially in Washington. On one occasion, it seems, he did a pencil portrait of her son. He claimed that the only Communists he knew had been in New York in the thirties. When asked for names, he refused, calling it 'ancient history I'd rather forget.'"

"So, he refused to name either Alger or Priscilla Hiss, or the others in the sketches."

"So it would seem."

"Was he off the hook with the FBI?"

"Partially, a half sinner . . . not naming names. But a traitor to the Party: You were never supposed to divulge a Party affiliation—period."

"Could he have been called as a witness in the second trial?"

Weinstein moved his chair back from his monitor and gestured to the screen and the facsimile of the government's typescript witness list. "There's a check mark by his name and penciled in following the check mark is 'FBI,' meaning he'd been interviewed."

"The sketches, then, would have, at the very least, constituted evidence that he'd lied to the FBI—about not knowing members of the Communist Party in Washington."

Weinstein raised an open horizontal palm, thumb wavering up and down: "A judgment call . . . he didn't lie; he just refused to name names: and who's to say the subjects in the sketches were Communists, much less spies—could've been a cocktail party, for all George Altmann—as a witness for the prosecution—knew. The defense, Edward Dimock, would have described it as 'circumstantial,' not much better than hearsay. But it would certainly have had an impact on the jury."

George leaned forward, intent to impart the heart of the matter. "Mr. Weinstein, what if I told you that George Altmann gave the sketches on your desk to my grandfather, Edward Dimock, on the first day of the second trial?"

"Gave them to Edward Dimock? I thought you told me you discovered these in the artist's estate?"

"Well . . ." George grimaced at his inexactitude and with a jut of his eyebrows offered an explanation, relating what the Judge had told him, and the version of the story in the memoir. "That's just between us—agreed?"

Weinstein nodded, listened attentively, his intelligent eyes moving from one face to the other, blinking rapidly as the new information was processed, then staring into space for a few long moments after George had fallen silent.

"I believe your grandfather's words to me when I sat in his office and he glared at me across his desk were, 'I don't give a tinker's damn about the Hiss case anymore.'"

"Clearly," said Wendy, looking at George for confirmation, "he didn't want you to find the sketches in the defense files."

Weinstein offered a significant look at both of his visitors. "What he did, removing them on the sly, constitutes file tampering: a criminal offense. For a federal appeals court judge, he was jeopardizing . . . everything."

"He, the Judge, wanted to know what you would have made of them, the sketches, if you had discovered them."

Weinstein pondered this. "I don't know. Without context, without explanation who they were by—without Edward Dimock's help— or any knowledge of George Altmann—what could I have made of them?" He looked significantly at George. "Which makes his memoir prima facie evidence." And again his glance lingered on the right flank of the lineup on his desk. "Perhaps I was unduly harsh in my implied criticism of his treatment of Whittaker Chambers, in his use of the so-called psychiatric defense against Chambers."

"No apologies." George waved a dismissive hand. "I don't think he'd fault you for a moment. I think it was much on his mind in writing the memoir; he makes no excuses, cuts himself no slack. He considers it a terrible blunder—a moral lapse—an unforgivable lack of judgment on his part."

"I always found it strange that Chambers never mentioned his name in *Witness*, the man who really treated him very badly in the trial."

"Odd, too," said Wendy, her voice rising, "when he could simply have taken them home and burned them."

"Why," said George, "his intention remains to have the memoir published only after his death."

"I see," said Weinstein with a touch of disappointment.

"What does it tell you," asked Wendy, "about George Altmann's predicament, that he chose to hand these sketches over to Edward Dimock, when he, too, could have simply burned them—the evidence?"

Weinstein didn't hesitate.

"The mural. As you've been hinting: W. Marvin Smith, dead the year before. Clearly, George Altmann feared for his safety. He was safe from government prosecution as long as he didn't lie under oath to the FBI, as long as he didn't hide or destroy evidence, as long as any such evidence was no longer in his hands." He gestured with an open palm to the sketches. "A signal to the defense that he was not a threat, even if he were to be put on the stand."

"The mural would have been hard to destroy—the evidence," said Wendy.

"With his admission to the FBI under oath," said Weinstein, "if the prosecution had put him on the stand and asked him—under oath—if he was in possession of anything to connect Hiss to the Communist Party, or for that matter Soviet intelligence . . . he could legally reply in the negative." Again, he raised a flattened palm in a balancing motion. "If, as you have described it in your grandfather's memoir, the defense came into possession of potentially incriminating information about their client before the start of the trial, when the discovery process was still binding, the defense would have been legally bound to share that information with the prosecution."

"So, Altmann was signaling to Edward Dimock that he was not going to cooperate with the prosecution if he was called to testify?"

"That is a reasonable assumption . . . proof, as well, that he had willingly given up evidence in his possession."

"And Edward Dimock, if you'd come upon those sketches?"

"Would have come under scrutiny for having withheld evidence during discovery. Or even if the discovery period might have technically passed, he could be accused, in retrospect, of withholding evidence gathered before the start of the trial. A sitting federal judge"—Weinstein shrugged—"I fear, in the game as it was then being played back in the seventies, I might well have been compelled to make inquiries of Judge Dimock, inquiries that might, at the very least, have resulted in—at my insistence—a candid interview for my book *Perjury*."

"Playing for keeps," suggested George with a sour smile.

"Young man—in scholarly circles, in those days, you have no idea."

There was a long pause while the three seemed to ponder the branching paths before them. An interlude in which Weinstein couldn't seem to resist repeated looks at the sketches—two now facing away, seven still facing him—across the gleaming surface of his desk.

"Mr. Weinstein," said Wendy.

"Call me Allen, please." He smiled, gesturing as if to indicate that the trappings of his huge office should not disturb the intimacy of their confab, then winked. "I'm still, at heart, a refugee of the sixties."

"Have the deaths and disappearances around the Hiss trial ever given you much pause? I'm thinking of the deaths by falling of Laurence Duggan and Marvin Smith; the sudden death from a heart attack of Harry Dexter White; the murder of William Remington in Lewisburg prison, and the flight of Lauchlin Currie and Noel Field overseas and so beyond the reach of subpoenas to testify. That's six of the nine in Altmann's sketches, leaving only Alger and Priscilla Hiss, and the unidentified figure, which seems to have so caught your fancy."

Weinstein smiled at his young and coolly forthright inquisitor, the smile of an admirer of quick intelligence or a good sparring partner. He removed his glasses to rub his eyes, then put them back on as he bent forward and picked up the sketch on the far right.

"Harry Hopkins, you mean?"

"Harry who?" asked George.

"Harry Hopkins," and Weinstein turned the sketch 180 degrees for their examination of the thin-faced, lantern-jawed figure. "Personal adviser to Roosevelt. His right-hand man and most trusted confidant." He eyed them both intently for long seconds, as if to make sure the seriousness of the thing had fully sunk in.

"Shit," said George. "Even the Judge, Edward Dimock, couldn't identify him."

Weinstein tapped the sketch. "A younger, 1930s version," he said, squinting, "as distinct from the White House adviser, who was sickly and gaunt and hollow-eyed by the later war years."

Wendy shot forward in her seat. "Did you recognize him in the mural, the man in a suit by the coatrack, hanging up his hat? It's not clear whether he is coming or going."

"I did indeed, but only because I recognized him in the sketch and was looking for him. He's the lit stick of dynamite"—he adjusted the sketch—"you have just landed on my desk."

"He was unwell during the war?"

"Stomach cancer, I believe. He died of medical complications in 1946."

"So, it's a big deal if there's proof he was a member of a Communist cell in the 1930s?" asked Wendy.

Weinstein winced. "Hardly proof. He might simply have been stopping by that afternoon, a fellow traveler among friends. And who's to say Altmann didn't just throw Harry Hopkins into the mix for the hell of it?"

"You seem to wax hot and cold on this," said George.

"My friends, you're young, so you have no idea of the political blood spilled in defense of Alger Hiss. I have members of my family, childhood friends, who still will not speak to me. And in this case, we're dealing with your country's history, with people's reputations. With a beloved president." He pointed to a far corner of his office, where a stately portrait of FDR hung. "In a court of law or under scrutiny of peer review by historians, this piece of paper with the likeness of a young Harry Hopkins would be dismissed, and the person or persons behind it questioned harshly—if not vilified." Weinstein looked intently at Wendy. "You said you were an artist. Who's to say you didn't just concoct this sketch of Harry Hopkins in the style of George Altmann."

"That's crazy," said George.

"Of course it is," said Weinstein, "but the story of Alger Hiss is crazily impossible. And we are dealing not only with ghosts who haunt—not just the history and mythology of our country but also the ideological touchstones of our politics. People who care deeply, passionately about a narrative that gives them wings to fly." He waved to the American flag behind him. "That is my job, my role—and that is crazy enough. There are legions of folks, perfectly reasonable people on most subjects, who consider me an illegitimate apostate in this position. That I have sold out my birthright. I once thought Alger Hiss was a god, until the facts—surprising, unyielding, brutal facts—led me elsewhere. Memories are long in this great land of ours, very long."

"Politics," she said. "It's all a little beyond me."

"Once upon a time," said George, as if to break the silence that had fallen, "I was an astrophysicist . . . Doubt is our mother's milk. I admire your care and scrupulous attention to the interpretation of data."

Weinstein nodded in acknowledgment, looking first to George and then to the eager-eyed woman seated on his right. "If Harry Hopkins is to be accused of being a card-carrying Communist, or, worse, part of a wartime Soviet Washington apparatus, the proof has to be pretty ironclad for any historian to go near it. And let me tell you, we have the testimony of Hiss's Soviet handler, Askmerkov, to his KGB students in Moscow that he had personally run Harry Hopkins as a spy. This was related to me in London by one of those protégés who had defected to the British." Weinstein paused, as if concerned he was giving more away than intended. "Still, hearsay, in a court of law. Harry Hopkins literally slept in the White House; he lived in the White House during the later war years. Nobody was closer to Franklin Roosevelt."

"So," said George, "even though Altmann dutifully turned over what evidence he had, there was always the chance . . ."

"If George Altmann, among other things, had convincingly testified in a court of law in 1949 that he had witnessed Harry Hopkins at a Communist Party meeting in Washington in the late thirties, along with these others, that would have had sweeping implications."

"So, where do *you* stand?" Wendy pointedly asked.

"Probably no single figure in the Roosevelt administration did more to promote cooperation between the Soviet Union and America before, during, and right after the war than Harry Hopkins. As part of Lend-Lease, Hopkins saw to it that the Soviet Union got everything—and more—they required in terms of war matériel and supplies of every description: from bombers and tanks, to radios and electronics, to rubber and bullets and butter. There were credible reports that under official Lend-Lease, not only was secret atomic technology shared but uranium was supplied to the Soviets. Hopkins's loyalty to Roosevelt was absolute. His enthusiasm for Stalin was boundless. More than once, that we know of, he tipped off the Soviet ambassador about FBI wiretaps and security investigation of Soviet assets. Hopkins—with Lauchlin Currie's input—Secretary of State Edward Stettinius, translator Charles Bohlen, and Alger Hiss ran much of Yalta for Roosevelt, who was then ailing and losing his grip on affairs. But as an historian, I would still, even now, want to handle this"—and he tapped the sketch of Hopkins—"very gingerly. Hopkins was a patriot who may have just got carried away by hopes Stalin would prove a dependable ally."

"So, this thing is bigger than just Hiss's guilt or innocence?"

Weinstein sat back, as if a little exhausted. "We're only just beginning to see, as if through a glass darkly, a world we barely knew existed, a past that is not past."

"And the others who died," said Wendy, now pressing the issue, "Duggan, Smith, and White?"

"Before 1989, before the Venona decrypts and access to the Soviet intelligence files, I dismissed the rumors that swirled around those deaths—and many other odd or simply tragic suicides—as just that: rumors . . . coincidences. The pattern of unexplained deaths and disappearances was certainly remarked upon at the time by many right-wing journalists—those at the *Chicago Tribune* in particular—but there was as yet no conclusive evidence that these upstanding public servants, sons of Harvard, had been Soviet agents." Weinstein now began turning the other sketches outward with the drama of a blackjack dealer. "And with regard to Laurence Duggan, Marvin Smith, and Harry Dexter White . . . nothing concrete has ever been turned up proving murder. So saying, the Soviets made a specialty, an art form, really, of ambiguous deaths. That way, Moscow Center both avoided blame and spread fear and uncertainty. Confusion and disinformation were key to their modus operandi."

"But now," said Wendy, "you've spent years in Moscow; you've interviewed and spoken to ex-KGB guys who would actually know the truth."

"Truth!" He sat back in his swivel chair, as if exhausted at the mere thought. "They don't know where the truth lies; it's buried with the millions executed in cold blood in Lubyanka, in the frozen tundra of the Gulag. The men I talked to were proud survivors of a system that devoured its most loyal sons. They were . . . well, let's just say that nothing, *nothing*, surprises me anymore. Or perhaps more to the point, I used to think it was just about espionage, the stealing of documents, information, technology, atom bomb secrets, but after reading their faces—ten vodkas to the wind—I now realize the endgame was much more: It was all about influence. The Soviets under Stalin came close to controlling our foreign policy and directing it to their advantage. And what's more, they knew it—and bragged about it."

"Bragged?"

"Researching *Haunted Wood*, I spent a lot of time in Russia, after the *fall*, so to speak, of the Soviet Union. For two or three years, '92, '93, under Yeltsin, we had access to the KGB security files, at least to a degree, and a chance to interview many of the aging intelligence operatives from the Stalin era, heroes of their trade. Many I sat down with over vodka for interviews. Old men with gray hair and blurry vision and thick glasses who had once strode the earth like gods—or that is how their wistful tones about intelligence operations in the thirties and forties made one feel: masters of deception. It was all they could do to contain themselves, to drop hints around the edges about their successes. One told me how their intelligence operation in the United States had enjoyed greater success than anywhere else, even during the early days of the Weimar Republic. Another one—he could barely repress his glee, just rattled off some broad statistics . . ." Weinstein tapped at his computer keyboard and peered at his screen. "This is from an interview that came out just after *Haunted Wood* had gone to press. 'The increase in volume of information to Moscow Center from its Washington agents in State, Treasury, and the White House rose fantastically during the war years, from fifty-nine reels of microfilm in 1942, to 211 in 1943, to 600 in 1944, and by 1945 it had risen to 1,896. So much was coming in that they were hard-pressed to photograph it all in Washington, and process the information in Moscow.'" He turned from the screen. "Stalin knew everything; every move we made was communicated in real time, and everything contemplated was communicated far in advance, so that they knew all the cards in our hand before we had even decided which ones to play. Most especially at Yalta."

This confession of incredulity swept over his interlocutors, and George found his gaze going to the curtained window and the sprawling city beyond and the huge FBI building they had passed, a metropolis crawling now with added security seemingly on every corner.

"How's it possible?" he heard himself ask.

Weinstein, as if perfectly interpreting his incredulous gaze, smiled.

"Small town. Some called it a small sleepy southern town. The FBI was overextended and most of their agents were farm boys, or the like, from Dubuque, who had no idea what they were up against. They were awkward, dressed badly, frightened easily. They were used to going up against common criminals from blue-collar backgrounds, not sophisticated Harvard-educated spies who considered themselves members of an elite secret club on the cusp of changing the world. Stalin's intelligence agents had been at the game long before this; they were world-class conspirators and con men by nature and breeding, with experience going up against the Gestapo and the most brutal forces of repression. They faced death or the Gulag if they failed, or even if there was the perception—the whiff— of failure, or disloyalty. They were survivors; they were cold-blooded killers." He shook his head. "And yet, to read Whittaker Chambers, they were awkward and crude and out of their depth, like Chambers himself, and yet they carried the aura—Chambers's pseudo-Russian accent—of a glittering dream, as blood thirsty as it was compelling."

"And Duggan, Smith, and White—" Wendy began, but Weinstein cut her off.

"And George Altmann, I presume . . ." Weinstein looked from one to the other with a fixed stare. "Why you are here, where this is going: Was George Altmann murdered by the KGB?"

Wendy and George glanced at each other like slightly guilty children caught in an obvious subterfuge.

"Something," George said, nodding, "along those lines. We're almost certain that it couldn't have been an accident and highly unlikely it was suicide."

"Generally speaking, Soviet intelligence—special tasks they called it—eliminated traitors—that is, operatives and agents who worked directly for them, who either broke from the Party or the KGB, certainly those who told or might tell what they knew to enemies of the Soviet Union, who threatened other agents or the security of the apparatus. If an example needed to be made."

"Like Whittaker Chambers?"

"Like Chambers, Ignace Reiss, Walter Krivitsky, and many others. But people who spied for them, not under the discipline of the Party or the apparatus, so to speak, as long as they kept their heads down and their mouths shut, were not in much danger of being executed if they broke, or refused to continue spying, stopped turning over intelligence."

"Like Chambers . . ." she asked.

"Only by the skin of his teeth. He was smart, he knew the ropes, knew what he had to do. He let it be known that he'd hidden away critical documents that could blow up his GRU networks should he or members of his family be killed. Nor did he go to the FBI and name names of members of his Washington apparatus—not until later, not until 1939 and the Nazi-Soviet pact, when he gave the names of Alger Hiss, White, Duggan, and Lauchlin Currie to Adolf Berle, an assistant secretary at the State Department. At the time he broke, he immediately went into hiding, first in Florida with his family, and later on a rural farm near Baltimore."

She said, "He also bought a gun. And it's pretty clear from *Witness* that they would've killed him if they could have."

Weinstein looked at Wendy, cocking his head with admiration.

"You've read *Witness*?"

"We both have," said George. "And interestingly enough, the Judge has read it three times and his copy is heavily annotated."

Weinstein turned with a look of unalloyed curiosity at George, immediately returning to Wendy, as if to cover his tracks.

"Amazing, in this day and age. I could never get my students at Smith to read it, so I assigned them about twenty pages—all they could handle." Weinstein removed his glasses again and rubbed his eyes. "Amazing, time, you know . . . what was once a confession along the lines of Saint Augustine, a religious, even a spiritual, odyssey of the soul—although some would still dismiss it as right-wing propaganda—has, at least in my view, become the best detailed insider account of Stalin's attempted subversion of our country that exists."

"A survivor's manual," she offered. "But essentially a work of literature—which sets it apart, which gives it enduring power."

"Yes." Weinstein gazed at the young woman with a hint of awe, as if sensing some repressed indefinable power in her graceful demeanor. "I'm sure he'd insist on the soul's journey to God, but yes, the GRU would probably have dispatched him even earlier, before he defected, when he was ordered back to Moscow during the purges—a dead man walking, should he have followed the orders from Moscow Center."

"So, in theory," she continued, "your civilians—Duggan, Smith, White, and George Altmann—should have been left alone, especially since they had bowed out quietly and weren't threatening to spill the beans."

"There are exceptions, of course, situations that might require special handling."

"You mean threatening Alger Hiss . . . or what Hiss was protecting?"

Weinstein picked up the sketch of a bespectacled Lauchlin Currie. "White House aide working hand in glove with Harry Hopkins, a facilitator for Hopkins and FDR and Alger Hiss. Fled to Colombia before the trial." He placed the Currie sketch facing outward now with the others, then picked up the sketch of Noel Field and flipped it outward, too. "Held incommunicado behind the Iron Curtain in a Hungarian prison during the trial and for years after. Hopkins, of course, was dead by then. While Alger Hiss remained unperturbed, formidable, and in control, and in control of Priscilla, even if she was cracking under the pressure." He flipped the sketches of Duggan, Smith, and White, pondering, as if searching for the most apt expression, the precise word. "Undependable . . . running scared."

George stood, suddenly agitated.

"George Altmann was a pipsqueak," he said, raising his voice, "an artist, hardly political, and he'd turned over these damn sketches to Edward Dimock."

"He panicked." Weinstein sighed and shook his head. "If Edward Dimock had shared the sketches with the defense team, with Hiss—well. A man who panics, who is running scared, is undependable, not to be trusted to hold his tongue under interrogation. And he'd already squealed to the FBI once."

"Bastards!" she exclaimed, reaching out to George.

"He never shared the sketches with his colleagues on the defense team, so he confirms in his memoir."

"Still," Weinstein continued, a hint of doubt flickering in his eyes, "to have ordered execution squads to eliminate the three men—four— in question—possibly Remington later—systematically so on orders from Moscow Center, the rationale would have had to have been larger than the guilt or innocence of Hiss. The level of Stalin's paranoia may have been extreme but the world Hiss, White, Hopkins, and Currie had helped bring into being at Yalta would have had to have been under immediate threat to trigger— what shall we call it?—such *drastic* action."

Wendy stood now as well and reached to the sketch of Harry Dexter White, noting his oval face, shiny hairless forehead, and rimless glasses; even in repose, there was a certain rigidity and fiery intolerant cast to his features.

"But . . . the very people who had, what, given them what they wanted?"

"White had already done his worst; he was finished, a sick man, but possibly close to breaking. Maybe his heart attack saved them the trouble."

She pointed to the sketch of Laurence Duggan.

"Long since served his purpose, not just a useless asset but a security risk should he break and spill the beans on the others. Even his brother mentioned he had a weak stomach and had been ordered to drink milk to try to settle it."

"And Smith?"

"A minor bit player, but if he'd testified on the transfer of Hiss's Ford—well . . . Or, as you point out, knowing about the mural just doors down from his office may have been the clincher on his doom."

George nodded intently. "Why suddenly . . . so certain?"

Weinstein sighed, a look of wonderment on his face as he again pondered the sketches, as if they were specters rising before him. Slowly, deliberately, he turned to the last of them: husband and wife.

"So alive," he murmured, more to himself than to George. "And how odd for you, both grandfathers involved in the Hiss trial."

"Not by happenstance. Edward Dimock tried to return the sketches to the artist's son, by way of his daughter, who became my mother."

George adjusted the sketches of Alger and Priscilla Hiss, aligning them with the others. "But you didn't answer my question."

Weinstein smiled and sat back in his seat, waving them to their chairs. He picked up his phone to call his assistant and cancel his next appointment. He motioned to the far corners of his spacious office, as if attempting to embrace both time and space. "The world as we think we know it, the comforts of memory, the past that is never the past—or as Faulkner put, 'It's not even past.'"

"But doubt," prompted George, "as you suggested, a scholar's strong right arm."

"As a scholar . . . well, it was this feeling I got sitting with those ancient intelligence officers, as I told you, legendary colonels of the KGB and GRU. I expected, after the fall of the Berlin Wall and the breakup of the Soviet Union, to find shattered and disillusioned doddering men who had seen their life's work come to nothing. But instead—albeit they were broke, for sure, and wanted the money for their cooperation from Random House—I found men who had to fight to hold back all that they knew, whose glinting eyes and garrulous lips fairly drooled with pearls of information, hints, feints of recollection, teasing me with allusions, dropping names like Harry Hopkins and Henry Morgenthau as if they had been mere puppets dancing at their fingertips. How many times I watched"—Weinstein paused to hold out his hands in front of him, his fingers prancing like a marionettier—"their rheumatoid shaking hands, veined and sun-damaged, their fingers moving in a show of exquisite skill . . . It was always 'Ah, my good friend Weinstein, if you only knew—if you only knew.' The diplomatic bags were always full to bursting, they claimed. And they would make swimming motions with their flattened palms, as if seeing those packed C-47s take off, heading for Siberia and then Moscow Center. They bragged about flying trunks of information out on the Dakotas from our air bases in Great Falls and Fairbanks. They would never divulge the whole story—they were still KGB to the bone—just enough to drive you crazy with anticipation of the next dollop of honey. Fragments, names, places, events—see if you were quick enough to pick up on the context, if you might provide them with something in return. A good intelligence man never gives anything away for free. Except when he's had enough vodka to loosen his tongue and his pride gets the better of him."

"Could you get out of them whether certain people had been murdered by a hit squad?" Wendy asked, still agitated.

"Never. Even if they'd known about it, they would never have admitted to anything so distasteful. They might brag about the liquidation of an enemy, but not the liquidation of an innocent witness. It would offend their delicate consciences—that terror was ever resorted to: Stalin's mother's milk."

"What about records?" she asked.

"Probably verbal communications; anything put to paper would have been destroyed to protect reputations. Better to employ the apparatus to destroy a man's reputation the way Edward Dimock did Chambers's. The ad hominem smear was second nature, a totalitarian tactic refined to the purity of an art form: to tar and feather Chambers with insanity, homosexuality, and God knows what perversions of body and spirit they could cook up in that witches' brew of a pathological personality."

George stirred uneasily in his chair.

"Like I said, he makes it clear in his memoir, he's not proud of that tactic. In a way, the memoir is a kind of an apologia,"—he glanced at Wendy, a silent admission that the word had obviously been hers first—"for—what?—a failure of nerve, failure of character, failure to live up to his impossibly high standards."

"He wouldn't be the first. The apparatus corrupted everything it touched," said Weinstein darkly.

"What are you suggesting?"

"If you could provide me with a copy of his memoir, I might be more specific—more helpful to your finding what you want. That memoir, you said . . . written five years ago—so already an historical document, before the new . . ."

"You're not suggesting—you said 'corrupted.'"

"You see, that was one of the things that fascinated me when I went through the defense files: It was quite clear that much of the dirt that was dug up on Chambers had to have come from Communist Party or even KGB sources." Weinstein again raised an inquiring finger. "Which poses the interesting paradox, all these lawyers from white-shoe firms, Harvard men of the establishment, like Edward Dimock: Where did they think the dirt was coming from and provided by whom? And where did the funds come from, tens of thousands of dollars, for the two trials and then the appeals?"

"You mean," said George, "how did Edward Dimock resolve that paradox . . . of the Soviets and Harvard Law pulling on the same oar?"

"You've had the advantage of reading his memoir." Weinstein looked at them both knowingly. "You tell me. How much did he suspect?"

George looked intently into Weinstein's ironic, if not sardonic, eyes, not a little spellbound.

"You mean," he asked, "when the experience, the moment of the thing, turns into mere data . . . photons from a distant star? When the scientists, the academics, take over the ruins of our past lives."

"Ah, you mentioned you were once an astrophysicist." The national archivist leaned forward with a glittering, intent stare. "Why, it must be a little like playing God to look out at all those lost worlds, all that lost time, and grapple with the big picture—which only *you* can see, for the first time, a picture that rightly seen—or I suppose analyzed—changes the very nature of reality."

George nodded, as if transfixed at the turn of inquiry. "He, the Judge, in his memoir, struggles, as if the radiance of Hiss's smiling face, the light of such integrity, still obscures the truth, like a cloud of cosmic dust and gas, rendering even a relatively close galaxy near invisible."

At this, Wendy laughed out loud. Then suddenly she leaned forward, tossing her head, her blond hair ashimmer, giving in to her instinct for casual flirtation, as if her force of personality was more than enough to navigate that invisible field of gravitation that hovered so tantalizingly before them.

"Once an astrophysicist"—and she raised her eyebrows at George— "always an astrophysicist." Again she smiled fetchingly, an ingénue in bloom. "But the memoir is less about facts; it is way more nuanced than that. It's really more a literary work, like Chambers's *Witness*: what's between the lines. The Judge's impressions of people and things and moments are far more revealing—the life of the spirit. Love, too, I suppose. Did George mention that his stargazing includes letters from Priscilla Hiss to Edward Dimock?"

George made a face, something between dismissive and disgruntled (that she'd played his ace card), while Weinstein seemed to freeze with anticipation in his swivel chair, as if struggling to preserve his savoir faire.

"Letters," echoed Weinstein, as if making light of the whole thing, "imagine such archaic methods of communication in our disposable e-mail age."

George, retrieving his poker face, waved a hand as if to dispel a silly rumor or change the subject.

"Alger Hiss must have been thrilled with all your research."

"He was a very angry man when my editor at Alfred Knopf told him in my presence that I'd changed my mind about his innocence in *Perjury*. Never spoke to me again. And strange to say, I think he even expected the Soviets to cover his ass after 1989, to officially absolve him of ever having been a GRU agent. They did, halfheartedly. And in the brief window when we had access to the KGB files, they never confirmed he'd been an agent, but the proof slipped out anyway—that, along with the Venona decrypts. I often wonder in his last days if Alger was bitter about that, that Moscow hadn't done more to protect him. Or more to the point, protect his—White's, Currie's, and Hopkins's—achievements, which some might argue included the enslavement of much of Eastern Europe and China."

Weinstein carefully slid the sketches of Alger Hiss and the others, so accused, forward across his desk: four horsemen of the apocalypse.

"Achievements?"

"I tell you what—I have a proposition for you. Let me help you on your journey, for it will long outlast mine. And surely Edward Dimock's, as well, as your grandfather nears the end of his."

Weinstein rose from his chair, went to a nearby bookshelf, slid out a thick volume, and carefully placed it on the desk.

"My personal copy of *Witness*, a first edition. When I first read it, I considered Chambers the devil incarnate, a stooge in the employ of Nixon and the FBI, a Manchurian candidate of the right wing. Now, whatever one thinks of Chambers's politics, his religious faith, his chronicle has turned out to be an intimate, fascinating *story*"—a nod of acknowledgment to the young woman seated before him—"of a certain time and place in our history, a milieu of the underground that has largely escaped recording elsewhere. Irreplaceable. And yet"—he raised a cautionary finger—"there are two glaring anomalies. As I noted to you, Chambers failed to mention Edward Dimock in *Witness*, who had treated him so badly in the trial. Why such an oversight—even for a Quaker? He didn't spare others who had tried to harm him. Years ago, when I was researching *Perjury*, I turned up an old friend of Chambers, an ex-Communist who is named anonymously in *Witness*, who confirmed almost everything about Chambers's narrative. But even he couldn't explain the omission of Edward Dimock. And even later, in the years before his death, there is no record from the lips of any of Chambers's friends—and I asked this of Bill Buckley—who ever heard him say a bad word about Edward Dimock."

Weinstein flipped the pages to a section heavily underlined and annotated.

"And the second glaring anomaly, the tale of Chambers's trip with Alger and Priscilla Hiss to Harry Dexter White's summer home in Fitzwilliam, New Hampshire. Chambers included details of the trip in *Witness*, even though those precise details about the trip were disparaged by the defense in the trial, and all my subsequent research was unable to confirm any part of the story—about this road trip on Route 202—through Pennsylvania and north to White's Fitzwilliam, New Hampshire, summer home. Except—except that Alger and Priscilla Hiss were indeed absent for five days, not the four claimed by Chambers, which he testified to under oath and later wrote about in *Witness*. I have a written affidavit from the Hisses' baby-sitter that they were away for five days at the end of August 1937. In *Witness*, Chambers could easily have left out this road trip, or at least corrected the time line by including the extra day—the fifth day . . . what delayed them and how they spent those twenty-four hours. Something, more details, specifics that might have nailed down the veracity of the thing. Especially since the trip serves no essential purpose—no reason for Chambers to have included it, except another confirmation that he and Alger had been together after 1936 per the second perjury count. Yet he stuck to the damn thing in *Witness*, like a dog to its bone, and in interviews before his death: this oddity, this anomalous need on his part to record—*memorialize* may not be too strong a word—a four-day automobile journey from Volta Place to Fitzwilliam, New Hampshire, to retrieve a useless paper on monetary reform in the Soviet Union from Harry Dexter White . . . when, if it happened, we know it lasted five days. Something is missing."

"Time," Wendy said. "Memory."

"The Judge's copy of *Witness* belonged to his wife, Annie; it was signed to her by Whittaker Chambers," said George with a pained look.

"Oh my God!" she exclaimed, rising from her seat quickly and going to the office window. She closed her eyes a moment and took a deep breath. "George, the Judge's—no, Annie's copy of *Witness*, the part about the trip to Fitzwilliam, Annie underlined it and wrote in the margin, 'She stoops to conquer—and how!'"

Weinstein drifted back in his chair, his eyes tightening with intense concentration or even apprehension. "The name of the Goldsmith play they attended by the Peterborough Players on the night of August 10,

1937—testified to by Chambers in the trial—the only night the play was presented, according to the FBI investigation."

"One missing day you said," murmured George, as if something in his mind had locked up and just as quickly slipped free. "Just a hurried perusal of Annie's copy and the section on the trip to Fitzwilliam draws the eye for both her and the Judge's comments in the margin."

"Comments?"

"She seemed intent, well, on rubbing it in, that it was obvious, at least to her, that Alger and Priscilla Hiss and Chambers had been together on that road trip in August of 1937. While he scoffs, something to the effect of there not being a scrap of evidence."

Weinstein became uncharacteristically still, as if frozen by some realization. He opened his mouth as if to speak, blinked rapidly, and then seemed to think better of the thought as he quickly swiveled around in his chair, needing to change tack.

"Well"—a convivial if not carefree tone—"I suggest you drive it, Volta Place to White's country home in Fitzwilliam, New Hampshire. It's still there. Lovely part of the world. I've made the trip. Stick to old meandering Route 202 all the way, fifty miles an hour tops, beautiful landscapes. It's two days up, two days back."

"Priscilla Hiss," intoned Wendy in a dreamy voice, staring blankly, as if seeing the very page in *Witness*. "She loved that countryside."

"She wrote about it in her letters?" asked Weinstein.

"No," said George, glaring at Wendy.

"So"—Weinstein lifted his eyebrows and leaned forward—"here is my proposal. You provide me with a copy of Edward Dimock's memoir and Priscilla Hiss's letters—with my word of honor that I will not publish a word from them or about them without your specific approval, or until after your grandfather's death—or until Norton publishes, if that is a concern. In turn, I will e-mail you with my thoughts and observations on the memoir, and respond likewise to your queries. And I will provide you with something more." He bent down to a file drawer and extracted two documents, one thick, one just a few pages, and slid them across his desk. "How's your Russian?"

"Nonexistent."

"I'll have my assistant make a copy of both of these and an English translation of the Pavlov material, with the understanding that as part of our agreement you show them to no one else until such time that I've had a chance to get them into print myself, which, given the time constraints of this job, and other more delicate complications—in my official capacity—I may not get to in the foreseeable future. The first here, is part of a memoir of a KGB officer who had—what shall we call it?—*very* direct dealings with Harry Dexter White; we agreed I'd edit his pages, and Random House has paid him a king's ransom, if he lives long enough to enjoy it. The Pavlov memoir will put the White farmhouse in Fitzwilliam and his death into troubling perspective—believe me. The second consists of a rough draft and notes of a book I'm planning to write on Yalta, relying upon, among other things, Secretary of State Edward Stettinius's diary stored in the archives of the University of Virginia, detailing the help provided him by Alger Hiss during the run-up to Yalta, during the conference itself, and its aftermath. You see, as I contemplated a new updated and revised edition of *Perjury*, I was suddenly struck by an omission, an absence staring me in the face, call it the ghost in the courtroom of the second Hiss trial: Yalta. The entire focus of the trial was on Hiss's perjury concerning events from the late thirties, while the disastrous ramifications of Yalta, which in 1950 were just becoming glaringly apparent, had been almost entirely overlooked."

George looked at Wendy where she stood staring blankly by the window, as if seeing something in her mind, and then hesitantly reached out to the two documents, one a typescript, the other copies of diary pages.

"Disastrous, you said."

"If it had been confirmed that Stalin had a spy in FDR's inner circle at Yalta, confirmed in 1950, it would have shattered whatever legitimacy Yalta had in the postwar world. And Hiss would have been on trial for treason, for his life, for crimes against God and humanity."

George flinched. "Your condemnation of Edward Dimock in *Perjury* for his 'cruel, smarmy, and unprofessional defamation' of Whittaker Chambers was only slightly less vehement."

"His crime, if you will, was against the system of justice he was sworn to uphold. Obviously, he was willing to cut corners with Chambers, hiding these nine Altmann sketches from the prosecution to benefit Hiss, and then stealing them from the defense files to thwart my endeavor to get at the truth. A sitting federal appeals judge." Weinstein turned his palms out, pale white, the life lines strong in their conviction. "Perhaps I let him off easy."

"As did Chambers!" Wendy exclaimed, drawing the men's gazes where she stood in the sunlight, just beyond where the American flag was draped on its brass eagle-topped pole. She tapped on the glass, as if sending a signal or catching sight of something of interest. Then she turned, blinking in the wan autumnal light, a tall, forthright figure of a determined woman. "Facts are facts. Any fair exchange, for the *between the lines*, the tone, the sensations—the artworks, so to speak—should include something of like value. As the Judge described it in his memoir: the haze, the atmosphere, the high-pressure system that hung over that trial—what, exactly, is or was at stake?"

Weinstein drifted back in his chair, nodding, as if struck by the firmness of her voice, perhaps the fairness of her observation.

"You ask for the gift of the gods (I was young, just a twenty-three-year-old scholar at Yale rooting for Alger Hiss)"—and he smiled gently to himself, a look of world-weary nostalgia—"now that they're all gone . . . or almost." His eyebrows dipped and rose as he removed his glasses and rubbed his eyes. "Your alma mater," he suggested to George, who was leafing through a file, "not far off Route 202. A professor of physics, Donald Spier—who dropped the dime on Klaus Fuchs, must be emeritus and some. I spoke to him on the phone for *Haunted Wood*, but he wasn't very forthcoming. He worked at Los Alamos as a young physicist. Got caught up in the FBI investigation into the Rosenbergs, roped in to explain the technical matters at stake, knew all the dramatis personae. The execution of the Rosenbergs left him a little disillusioned with the aid he'd provided to the FBI and Army Intelligence. Of course, Hiroshima can't have helped his disposition any. Perhaps he'd have a word with you"—his admiring gaze returned to where Wendy watched from her post by the window—"the two of you." He squinted in the brightness while cleaning the lenses of his glasses with a checkered dishtowel produced, like a conjurer's sleight of hand, from his side pocket. "A little light and shade on your hunt, for your—what?—atmosphere of the mind, zeitgeist, that elusive pneuma that kept even my garrulous ex-KGB octogenarians awake at night, guardians of a tottering treasure house. An anxiety they were less than chatty about: losing agents and access, much less having them executed. A desperate FBI hunt against the clock to uncover that same treasure—and well under way by the second Hiss trial." He took a deep breath and smiled as if to dispel the hint of dreaminess in his eyes. "After all, *time* for you astrophysicists is your stock-and-trade."

"Donald was my doctoral adviser."

"Yes, I know." He blinked and replaced his glasses. "It was the first thing that came up when I checked your bona fides after your first e-mail. My first thought: Edward Dimock and Donald Spier—what a coincidence." Weinstein pressed his palms together, his fingers intertwining. "Well, so we have our quid pro quo." And again he turned an inquiring face to the woman by the window, her eyes now turned to his, sparked with a brilliant sky blue.

From where George sat, reeling with the new uncertainties, she seemed bathed in a veil of intense sunlight, a sibylline glow, as if she herself had been the invisible thing all along.

31

A Life in the Law and Out:
Funeral of Oliver Wendell Homes

STRUGGLING WITH THE Alger Hiss matter has had the odd effect of, in some mystifying way, condensing memory, or perhaps sharpening it. As if the struggle, in retrospect, to re-create certain moments in the past results in both crystalizing those same dynamic moments while weeding out the less vigorous growths, a kind of mental triage on the battlefield of one's life. Bringing to mind something Annie mentioned once to me after returning home from a rehearsal of a new work of Balanchine's. She seemed in rare spirits, aglow, hugging Cordelia every moment while preparing dinner. And then she turned to me at the dinner table, her face lit up like a klieg light. "Edward, do you know that piece that used to bedevil me, the Brahms piano quartet, that I'd only practice at Hermitage because the inner voices of the piano part used to throw me, that I couldn't get them to properly harmonize? Well, this afternoon at rehearsal with Mr. B., for his new ballet using the Schoenberg orchestration, I was playing the piece and suddenly those inner voices, as I watched a pair of dancers, a boy and girl, learning the steps, sang out perfectly, spiraling out in perfect counterpoint one instant and intersecting in lush harmony the next. Oh, I was in absolute ecstasy, because, you see, I was reminded of those long, frustrating afternoons of years ago under the ship's keel ceiling, and suddenly it came out right, as other dancers joined the first two, as if the figures in the ceiling had come alive to me, and in their intricate spiraling steps had shown me the way back to the inner soul of the music. It was as if some part of my past—those thirty measures or so—had been given back to me as a gift. I guess real genius is like that, Mr. B.'s steps, that is, showing me the way—you might say discovering or rediscovering the truth. But how glorious, like some Venice moment of long ago when I played the Scuola Grande di San Rocco!"

I wish I could reproduce the smile on her face, the happiness in
her voice, for in them were memories of the best years of our marriage, the thirties, when the children were young, when Annie's career
was still thriving, when I was making money despite the Depression,
or because of it. Years, oddly enough, I associate with my first meeting
with Alger and Priscilla Hiss in Washington, during the sad occasion of Oliver Wendell Holmes's funeral in March 1935. A meeting
I have plumbed like a forensic pathologist for clues as to what was to
come. I have been back to Washington many times since. I lived there
for almost a year while clerking for Holmes, for three years when
on the War Production Board, and commuting by train for countless meetings over the postwar years, and yet that single day stands
out, overshadowing and diminishing all the other Washingtons of
memory, as if it has hardened into a kind of keystone, a rainy portal
through which I am bound to gaze in search of the protean nature
of the Hisses. For though I would see them socially on occasion
during the war, they never again invited me to their home. Perhaps
this intensity of remembrance is because it was precisely the period
that Alger and Priscilla, if one is to take Chambers's *Witness* at face
value, were beginning their clandestine work, setting up their networks, getting their feet wet, turning over secret documents to their
handler, Chambers, whom they knew only as Carl, inveigled, like
impressionable schoolchildren, by his Russian accent.

Or is it because that day is forever alloyed with such a profound
sadness for the loss of my mentor and friend, now, too, annotated by
Chambers's narrative of the Hisses' Washington days at Volta Place,
which seems to color my gaze of these two different Hisses, the ones
I thought I knew and those bosom friends of Chambers. The tint is
gray and misty as my pair of Hisses sometimes clash, sometimes blend,
but mostly merge in an ambiguous fog of untethered impressions. For
I find myself yearning not for the accused spy and his accomplice,
but for those lovers of nature—birders, filled, if Chambers is to be
believed, with a deeply humanitarian spirit and friendship for him and
his wife, Esther. As long as Carl was Carl with his peculiar Russian
accent. And so, as I peer through a glass darkly, I find my memories
reflecting back at me in ways that leave me more and more baffled, if
not a little uncomfortable and perplexed: an unfinished soul wandering in the wasteland.

—

Just the smell of rain, or a soggy street, the rattle of a train, and I find myself returned to that cold March day in Washington, where I'd gone to pay my last respects to Oliver, my mentor and friend, who introduced me to his godchild Annie, my beloved young wife, who would have joined me if not still indisposed back in New York, awaiting the birth of our third child, Martha. I was fully expecting that Alger and Priscilla would be no-shows, given Priscilla's catty remarks about Holmes after their wedding. Perhaps the Depression, too, colors my memories on my soggy walk from Union Station, even if Washington was in churning ferment compared to the soup lines in New York. The place, even on a rainy day, seemed to bustle with fresh progressive faces eager to put their shoulder to the wheel of the New Deal and a quick recovery. When I met up with my colleagues at the new Supreme Court building, all of whom who had clerked for Holmes, Alger was nowhere to be found. He's just taken up a new job at State, noted someone with a skeptical raising of his eyebrows. "He has his eyes on bigger things. Why not a larger stage when America has only breadlines," said another of my cynical colleagues, wiping raindrops off his glasses. Such sarcastic comments surprise me, in retrospect. Were these accurate reflections of Alger's persona at that time? A general view? I was one of the youngest in that crowd, the next to last of his clerks; some had been ahead of him at Harvard Law, while some were old Washington hands. Was I far from being alone in detecting a more radical bent? Nevertheless, well within the bounds of the progressive politics we had been pursuing since Wilson's presidency. We talked among ourselves as the funeral procession got under way, all of us successful eager beavers, recalling to one another how Holmes had made the legal system a living, breathing thing for our generation, how the common law, come alive in Holmes's opinions and descents, had served as a model for a more flexible and evolving code of justice, inclusive of both stalwarts and dissenters.

So, we band of brothers, disciples of the great man, climbed into two Packard limousines we'd reserved in the funeral cortege, two in a line that stretched for blocks, which would take us to Arlington Cemetery. Holmes's flag-draped casket on an open caisson was drawn by six liver-colored horses, with an honor guard of four soldiers on horseback and a company of foot soldiers marching behind. A solemn horse company led the way. Eleanor Roosevelt, looking chilled and dour in her mink fur, was there; her husband was awaiting the cortege at the cemetery. It was a long, slow last journey for Oliver—as he had asked me to call him after my marriage to Annie—through the gray streets of Washington, where he had labored for almost thirty years, while the outskirts of Arlington Cemetery were, if anything, bleaker still, with barren maples and plane trees riding the undulating grassy rises that would, all too soon, be packed with more dead from World War II and Korea. It is in Arlington where Teddy now resides alongside his Marine Corps comrades. My sweet Teddy (a sorrow, of course, only adding to my impressions of that day, swirling back through time), still in New York, safe and warm in our new apartment overlooking the park on Fifth Avenue; waiting for spring and a return to Hermitage and the lake and the forest creatures he would grow to love so dearly. Never did I imagine I was rehearsing a similar miserable visit to Arlington Cemetery some fifteen years later. And yet they, too, have become one in my mind.

I was troubled, as well, that Holmes had forsaken his Massachusetts forebears in Cambridge and Boston, and most of all, Beverly Farms, where I felt I had known him best, from whose soil he had drawn such strength and character. Where he and his father had been intimates of Emerson. But it was only fitting that he should be laid to rest on a national stage, next to his comrades who had fought to rid the nation of slavery's abomination. We young men in the Packard, mostly Harvard Law alumni, like our mentor and friend, repeated his stories to us over that long, damp journey—such as how as a young wounded soldier he had seen Lincoln standing on the ramparts of Fort Stevens when Jubal Early attacked Washington. Many of us had tears in our eyes as we spoke openly of our feelings and memories, laughing knowingly at familiar anecdotes rendered in his New England nasal twang, sure we were witnessing the falling away of a generation, and a man the likes of whom we'd never see again.

Later, at a dinner at the Hay-Adams Hotel, Alger arrived as if he'd just stepped out of his office, impeccably dressed in a pinstriped gray suit, looking as handsome and vital and engaged as ever. And a lot dryer than the rest of us, who had stood in the rain at the grave site as the Marine Corps guard blasted away at the lowering cloud cover. He shook hands all around, introducing himself where necessary, and then took a seat next to me and apologized for missing the funeral— due to a crisis at State. Perhaps I was pleased that he joined me, since there were plenty of other prospects there: judges, legislators, men with big reputations in top firms. Did he feel more comfortable with me—once he had ascertained that Annie was not with me? Only now do I catch the boatload of pride—that Priscilla had chosen him over me?—in his voice as the evening wore on. We exchanged news about each other's careers, mine defending corporations in New York from confiscatory taxation—bullying by the NRA, his a stint on the Nye Commission, looking into profiteering in the last war—ancient history he described it, for he had just finished a few months at the Justice Department before being lured away by an offer at the State Department working for Wilson's son-in-law, Francis Sayre. "Less money but more important work. I fear a reduced budget that doesn't bring a smile to Priscilla's face." He listened politely to much of the fond conversation about Holmes around the table and gamely raised his glass to his old boss with the others, but I had the sense his heart wasn't in it. He mentioned that his stepson, the child from Priscilla's first marriage, Timothy, had been sick and he and Priscilla had been up the previous few nights tending the boy. While we listened attentively, surrounded by inebriated smiles and laughter, he often asked me to identify faces with which he was unfamiliar, inquiring about where they worked, taking special note if in government jobs. I realize now he had no real interest in those who, like me, were down from New York or Boston, who worked in private practice or corporate law. Was he out talent-spotting for potential recruits?

Suddenly, he sprang up as if a whistle had blown, and took my arm, insisting I return with him for a nightcap with Priscilla.

"She would be disappointed, Edward, if she didn't see you."

I was in no doubt that the summons had come from Priscilla.

"What do you have there?" he asked, his eye always sharp for the telling detail.

I held up an old leather-bound copy of Emerson's essays, signed to me by Oliver, which had been bestowed upon me before dinner by Holmes's last secretary.

A look of disdainful satisfaction flickered in Alger's eyes as he said, "It took some doing to talk him around to allow me to read to him. But it was the least I could do."

There, in my mind's eyes, a flicker of the ruthless and the humanitarian, almost indistinguishable.

It had stopped raining when we left the Hay-Adams, and so we decided to walk to their home on Volta Place in Georgetown. A chance to walk off the rich meal and fine wine we had consumed, or so he had suggested at the time. But as I look back on that brisk two-mile stroll up Pennsylvania Avenue, past the Treasury Department, the White House, and the State Department, all nestled cheek-by-jowl, where he pointed out to me the window of his office in that battleship gray Victorian monstrosity, I sense that he wished to get across an idea about himself, that he wanted me to realize how close to the seat of national power he had drawn, not so much a question of bragging rights or titles—certainly not money, but an insinuation about relative value in terms of one's life trajectory: pulling the levers that really made a difference. Just in case I might believe his legal skills were being wasted on foreign affairs, as a number of his *Law Review* colleagues, proud of their Harvard degrees, had suggested to him over dinner.

I remember we touched on the international situation and the rise of Hitler, and he put in a few good words for Stalin's latest Five-Year Plan. Who among us in those days was not a little impressed by the godlike prospect of one man simply decreeing a more vibrant economy? Roosevelt and Hopkins had been at it for two years, even though the results were mixed at best, with more of the like to come. But even these conversations are not uncontaminated by time and the reflections of Whittaker Chambers. For when I bear down on memory, when I struggle to see Alger as he was then on the damp sidewalk of Pennsylvania Avenue, his arms spread wide so that the White House was encompassed by his left, with Treasury just beyond, and the State Department grasped in his right, I vaguely recall something he said, a calculation he'd made—an offhand remark, to the effect that in the realm of foreign policy, it required only the correlation of about five or six voices in the executive branch to get, as I think he put it, "the freight train rolling off the siding and down the main line." I believe that is accurate; I believe he told me as much, though, at the time, it slipped into the ether for lack of context.

It was a boast, and so I dismissed it as a husband's insecurity over bringing home his wife's ex-lover.

My recollection of their tiny home on Volta Place is more certain, and I try to keep the picture clear and uncontaminated by the overlay of what followed. But I find it harder and harder to keep Chambers from their door, for his scenes are often as heartrending as they are terrifying, while his language seems to touch on truths far deeper than I've been able to plumb. I had an almost immediate sense of a hermetic life enclosed in those walls: simple, charming, tastefully furnished rooms with few knickknacks. There was no bourgeois redundancy or extravagance of any kind, nothing to impress except the necessary books on politics, art, literature, psychology—the usual suspects: Freud, Adler, and Jung—and, of course, plentiful volumes on birds. It was a place conducive to clarity of mind and spirit, not unlike a monk's cell, with the possible exception of their compact parlor toward the rear, which looked out upon an intimate garden patio, thus connecting them to nature. Here, around a tiny Chinese coffee table inlaid with flying cranes and balanced on delicately carved legs, was set a semicircle of various chairs, a motley collection of Windsors and various antique fruitwood cousins of a Shaker style, mostly straight-backed, some with ragged cushions on the seats, others with cane bottoms, seating fit for a Friends congregation, looking not a little as if such a meeting might just have broken up. Upon entering, Priscilla fell on me and greeted me warmly, seeming to be greatly relieved that her son, Timothy, was better and "finally" fast asleep, and so we'd have some uninterrupted time together. "Adult conversation, like the old days!" she exclaimed, looking longingly at the array of chairs. I thought, she was almost giddy at the prospect, as if I might have brought a bunch of fellow lawyers in tow. I was glad to see that the trials of motherhood had not extinguished her feisty spirit nor caused her to retreat from her fervent opinions on art and politics.

"Oh," she shot back as I kidded her on the duties of being a diplomat's wife, "I save Alger from himself, whenever he gets too stuffy. Fortunately, we don't have to circulate in diplomatic circles—not like some of our friends who must dress up in penguin garb most nights of the week." And she looked at me forthrightly, a sarcastic twinkle in her blue eyes. "We don't have time for such things. Alger's work keeps him late, and often as not he brings work home with him."

Did she really express this in so many words? I believe she did, even as Chambers's gloss on such a comment brings a twitch of unease to my lips.

"We do have a small garden in the back," said Alger almost apologetically as I examined their spartan surroundings, pulling down some well-thumbed Lenin from a shelf. "And the bird feeders bring in a cavalcade of customers. Not quite the same as Glen Echo, just up the road, but a surprising variety, without my needing binoculars to observe them."

"Riverside Park in the spring," I offered, "if spring ever comes. Although I take my son and daughter birding in Central Park these days, when we're not in the Catskills."

She offered me a drink, but I demurred after such a long day and all the wine consumed at dinner. I asked for a cup of tea, which brought on a storm of hilarity on Priscilla's part as she began rummaging in a hall closet, triumphantly producing the Jensen silver tea service: my wedding present.

"Goodness," she exclaimed, "it needs polishing!" She looked at Alger like a naughty schoolgirl caught with something she shouldn't have. "You can blame my scrupulous husband, who feels we mustn't be presumptuous around our less well-off friends during this awful Depression."

I protested with a tease: "What, a diplomatic corps full of Princeton, Harvard, and Yale men—hardly! I think it fits perfectly with your duty to represent your country, especially if you should go overseas to Moscow where a silver service will most surely be appreciated by the comrades."

Alger took in stride my lighthearted digs.

"Pross loves your wedding gift, as do I, but given the times, I can't see asking the maid to spend the time to keep it polished. And for certain guests . . . well, it just wouldn't do."

"Until better times, then," I suggested, moving from the books on their shelves to the simple Picasso and Matisse prints on the wall, and two framed drawings, one of an infant, the other a fetching sketch of Priscilla, underneath the staircase leading to the floor above.

"Aren't they wonderful," said Priscilla, "the drawings, I mean—our boy Timothy goes without saying. George Altmann, you know, he may be tapped to run the WPA mural project."

"That's Pross's doing," said Alger proudly; "she's recommended him for the position to Holger Cahill, not that Holger will require much convincing."

"I spent a few months studying with Altmann at the Art Students League back in the dark ages, when he did the sketches," she said. "He's really a genius, you know. Alger and I have so much enjoyed his company and his take on things artistic back in Gotham. If he has the time, we're going to have him do an oil portrait of Timothy."

She looked at Alger a little sheepishly and I replaced the drawing of Priscilla on the wall. I couldn't help wondering, though of course I didn't ask, why they hadn't had children of their own.

"He's got your wonderful upturned nose, Pros, and your fiery eyes."

"God forbid," said Alger.

"Perhaps your George Altmann can do a portrait of Holmes for the Harvard Law School, even if it's just a copy from a photograph.

Somebody was just saying tonight that the commission for the portrait was never completed due to his final illness."

"I'm sure Altmann has better things to do," said Priscilla. "Much more important things." And she looked knowingly at Alger.

Alger grinned. "Pros isn't much of a fan of Holmes, after the hard time he gave me about marrying in the middle of my clerkship."

"The old dinosaur," said Priscilla.

"It *was*, after all, specified in the contract," I replied.

"Oh, Edward, always the letter of the law," she said.

"I was unmarried at the time," said Alger, "and expected to remain so until the end of my tenure."

"Surely a damsel in distress trumps the niggling requirements of a Stepin Fetchit for that horrible old man."

When I raised my eyes to object, Alger cut me off.

"He did vote to sustain the conviction of Eugene Debs under the Sedition Act, when he clearly understood that a few words at a socialist rally were unlikely to affect the army's ability to recruit soldiers."

"I think we all agree the law was poorly drafted and is too sweeping in its powers and implications. On the other hand, as written, Debs was clearly beyond the pale in calling for the obstruction of the war effort—and he knew it."

"Debs was too timid for his own good," said Priscilla. "He was a reformer like Roosevelt, and the time for timid reform is long past."

I noticed Alger signal to her to be more circumspect.

"Yes," I said, "Holmes had his blind spots, like all of us, but he was a man of ironclad integrity and scrupulous when it came to the truth."

"His truth," snorted Priscilla, "his convenient truth—guardian of the system that keeps men like him and his minions in control."

"Alger," I replied, knowing I would irritate Priscilla, "you have to admit he was always willing to give an ear to a controversial point of view; in fact, he believed strongly that the strength of civilization was precisely in its capacity to allow, if not foster, the clash of opinions in the safety of the judicial system. Where the two sides could blow off steam without doing structural damage."

"Just to give enough latitude," said Priscilla indignantly, "enough bend in the system so as to keep the exploiters in power."

"We hear," said Alger, as if to redirect the conversation to less controversial subjects, "that the old roué played matchmaker with you and Annie."

"Oh, Annie was the granddaughter of a great friend of his youth, Richard Davenport, who was killed at Antietam."

I remember distinctly that the name Richard Davenport had been broached by me, and yet I'll be damned if it conjured our first meeting in Memorial Hall, for neither one of us referred to it further. Another phantom, perhaps to go along with my brief, if intense, sojourns with Priscilla in our college days.

"Did you never meet Annie at Beverly Farms?" I asked.

"Never."

"Holmes had known her since she was a child. During the summers at Beverly Farms, she would come once a week to play the piano for him and Fanny. Surely—"

"Never met her. Must have been my day off."

Of course, he was then married to Priscilla during the summer break with Holmes, and returned to New York many weekends to be with his wife. Another thing that Priscilla held against Holmes: She was never invited to the inner sanctum of Beverly Farms.

"As you know, he was lonely after Fanny died, and Annie was a special comfort to him. She had a striking likeness to her grandfather—Holmes couldn't take his eyes off her while she played. When she'd leave, he'd turn to me with tears in his eyes and describe her delicate brow and deep-set eyes, and a voice, as he put it, 'like poetry read aloud.'"

"Oh, Edward," said Priscilla, "you make a girl positively jealous. I bet she has all the Beacon Hill virtues: social grace, a lovely voice, a transcendentalist disposition, and someone told me she plays the piano like Clara Schumann."

By Priscilla's sarcastic tone, I took it as gospel that such virtues were anathema to the modern woman.

"Well, she was a student at the New England Conservatory. When she was nineteen, she was asked to substitute on short notice for an incommoded French pianist to play the Mozart D Minor Concerto with the BSO in Symphony Hall. But since moving to New York, and with Alice and Teddy to take care of, she complains bitterly about the lack of practice time. But fortunately for me, she insists on getting me out of the office for a concert or two every week at Carnegie Hall."

"Well, I only get to practice on the typewriter nowadays," said Priscilla. "We don't have room for a piano. Maybe when Timothy is older." And she gave Alger a curiously hurt look that I couldn't quite make out but which, in retrospect, I know was due to a sore subject between them: committing to having their own child.

I remember looking out the window at the tiny lamplit street in Georgetown, the bare branches of the maples like spun webs against the dark. Their living room seemed barely able to contain the force of their personalities, especially compared to the hustle and bustle of their apartment in New York of years before.

"Front-row seats at the symphony, I expect," said Alger a few moment later, coming in with the tea things, "for a corporate lawyer on the way up."

"Oh, desperate work, Alger, bankruptcies, restructuring, buyouts—trying to hold the pieces together."

"Union busting," said Priscilla, "whatever it takes to keep the workingman down."

I noticed Alger shoot another warning look at Priscilla.

"The Roosevelt administration throws rocks at the businessman, but if the businessman can't find a way to make a profit, there will be no wages to be paid in the first place, high or low."

I was, of course, even then, fully aware of Priscilla's membership in the Socialist Party; she had once taken me to a meeting on Riverside Drive. Fifteen years later, during the second trial, all of us on the legal team suspected that Alger was just trying to cover up for Priscilla, that *she* was the true Communist.

"Edward," said Alger, "you should try your hand at government work, get your hands dirty, get in the thick of it and see if we can't find ways to stimulate production, build more roads and ports, make our agricultural system more efficient, rationalize industry—that kind of thing."

"Oh, he doesn't want to do *that* kind of thing, Alger," said Priscilla, laughing; "that doesn't buy front-row seats at Carnegie Hall."

"Did you say 'rationalize' or 'nationalize'? Not a Five-Year Plan along the lines of Mr. Stalin's?"

"Edward, you should think about it; I'm sure I could get you a position in the Treasury Department or even at State. They need smart fellows like you to work on trade negotiations and the like. Washington is now the world stage, where everything is happening, where issues from around the world first touch on our shores. I always thought you were one for the thick of it."

"Not after my year clerking with Oliver—a year of Washington backbiting was enough for one lifetime. As old Holmes used to say, I'd be a disaster at politics because I'd shoot my big mouth off too much. He also said I'd never make it as a judge because I couldn't stand living in poverty."

Alger shrugged at this, as if I'd somehow missed the point.

"He was loaded," said Priscilla. "Alger used to go down to Riggs and clip his bonds for him."

"Railroad bonds," I said. "I wish my father had been as smart; he's lost almost everything in the market."

Alger sat forward in his chair, as if to make a serious point.

"Holmes, like so many of his breed, was always happy to tinker with the system just enough to prevent its extinction. He always thought the clash of the capitalists and workers could be finessed by elegant rulings, that a little delicate surgery here and there will save the patient, when, in fact, the agony is just prolonged. The Supreme Court doesn't even have the common sense and decency to let Roosevelt at least try doctoring around the edges, not that blocking New Deal reforms will make a whit of difference one way or another."

"Goodness, Alger, I never took you for such a pessimist. Didn't Oliver ever bend your ear about his hero, Chief Justice John Marshall, who had to so carefully navigate his way through the thicket of Federalist and Republican struggles in the early days of the republic, when Jefferson and the Republicans were all for France and the Revolution, for states' rights, which for the southern states meant preventing the federal government from meddling with their peculiar institution of slavery? And yet Marshall, a Virginian to the bone—and a Federalist—fought and finagled over thirty years with his opinions to keep the Constitution intact, establish the primacy of the federal government in law, *and* the separation of powers, with the Supreme Court as a coequal branch."

"Marshall was a slaveholder," retorted Alger acidly. "And in *Cherokee Nation v. Georgia*, he upheld the right of Georgia and that madman, President Jackson, to force an entire peoples to abandon their native soil and relocate across the Mississippi, with thousands dying in the forced march. A crime against humanity."

"They were all slaveholders, and Washington was the only one to free his slaves upon his death. But my point, Oliver's point, was that John Marshall, by his dexterous opinions, balancing the exigencies of the day against the ultimate aim of preserving the union, managed to preserve and strengthen the Constitution and so maintain the forum, the umpired playing field of the Supreme Court, allowing opposing economic and political forces to find accommodation and compromise."

"And the Civil War?" asked Priscilla.

"A failure of compromise—my God, how Oliver went on about that—but it was Marshall's work—yes, a slaveholder—that allowed the mechanism of the Constitution to evolve and endure, that made Lincoln's terrible duty possible, and so by force of arms put an end to the abomination of the bondsman."

Alger laughed. "An end? The South still holds the Negro in bondage. Why, in this very town, in this great nation's capital, the Negro is still separate and degraded, unequal and persecuted, thanks to your Marshall—or Holmes."

"A policy of segregation instituted by Wilson and upheld by your hero, Roosevelt. And by the by, Marshall reversed himself on *Cherokee Nation* in the *Worcester* ruling, unanimously ruling that the Cherokees had all the rights of a sovereign nation, not that it prevented your madman Jackson from his nefarious policy."

Alger rolled his eyes. "Roosevelt's a pompous fraud, a rich and spoiled brat playing at politics."

Priscilla placed a gentle restraining hand on her husband's arm.

"Can't you see what's happening in Europe, Edward?" Priscilla straightened her shoulders and leaned toward me as if now in tight tandem with her husband. "Hitler and Mussolini, those fascist bastards, are taking over everything. They're persecuting Jews and Communists and union leaders—anybody who disagrees with their policies."

"Well, some accuse Roosevelt of acting like a dictator right here. He sometimes seems to be taking a page out of Stalin's Five-Year Plan."

"Eleanor won't let that happen," said Priscilla scathingly. "That ugly bitch seems to have her fingers in everything, as if stirring up all the do-gooders in American can save the people from the plutocrats."

"A little unkind of you, Priscilla," I said, sipping my tea. "She was at the funeral today; she looked miserable, you know, standing in the rain with the rest of us. Did I ever tell you, Alger, my father brought many of their children into the world, and Teddy Roosevelt's, too? My God, the Goulds and Rockefellers, the Carnegies and Morgans—he made a hell of a living off your plutocrats, Priscilla. He brought their offspring into the world and tried to save their wives from various insidious cancers—failing more than he'd like to admit. A few years back, as I held his feeble hands, once strong and agile, wielding a quicksilver scalpel, he looked at me and shook his head. 'We are born between piss and shit, and we die in our own piss and shit. I battled cancer all my life and it spared me, only to leave me dying slowly now of kidney failure. Thank God you took up the law like Holmes and so you may have a legacy to leave behind.'"

At this intimate confession produced by too much wine and exhaustion, both husband and wife fell silent, as if embarrassed for me.

"In corporate law, I don't think so," said Alger pointedly but politely.

"Enough to make a living for the moment," I replied. "As I mentioned, my father has lost almost everything in the market. His apartment in New York won't sell and his small home in Palm Beach is worth nothing. And I have his home in the Catskills to maintain."

"Ah," said Priscilla, "Hermitage, if I remember."

Alger shot a not very happy face at his wife.

"We heard your wife had gobs of money," said Alger.

"Her family, yes. A lot of Boston real estate. Nothing much has come her way at this time, and with the Depression—well, who knows?"

"Perhaps you should read more widely," said Alger. "Marx is a very subtle and logical thinker; his insights are broad and magnificent on the inevitable logic of history, the iron laws that shape our destiny. I think Stalin has it about right."

"Surplus value, isn't it? But when the government gets to suck up all the ill-gotten gains, what is left for businesses to grow, and who gets to decide how it's spent?"

"The workers, of course," said Priscilla. "The proletariat does the work, so they should benefit."

"Have you been there, to Moscow, to observe the workers' paradise?"

"We haven't had the pleasure," said Alger, giving a wave at their bookshelves, which were filled with the latest volumes on politics and psychology, "but the reports are most promising in the *New York Times*. And what comes across my desk at State from our ambassador in Moscow is even more so."

"My father hated many of his patients—or their husbands, mostly for their shortsightedness and lack of concern for their workers. Near our place in the Catskills there's an old canal, the Delaware and Hudson, now defunct. As a young doctor, he used to treat the boatmen and their families, gratis, over the summers. The working conditions and pay were abominable. At the Harvard Club, savoring the best Bordeaux, he pleaded with the owners to improve things for the boatmen, but to no avail. The railroads had them by the throat and were slowly strangling their business. But he did manage to prevail on your plutocrats to support his pet projects, Memorial Hospital for one, the American Cancer Society for another. They gave him millions, as the Rockefellers did for their research institute. 'To assuage their sullied consciences,' as my father puts it; 'even the rich can't take it with them.'"

Alger looked at me impatiently but with a curious intensity. "It doesn't make up for the ruination of workers' lives and the continued exploitation of the poor. The condition of the Negro in the South is beyond condemnation."

"You should tell it to your Mr. Roosevelt, who failed to support the federal antilynching legislation for fear of a southern backlash against his New Deal."

"Roosevelt," sneered Alger, "is a feckless dabbling amateur, forever covering his wheelchair-bound ass."

"Playing with his stamp collection," sniffed Priscilla.

I looked sharply at Priscilla, in hopes of moving us away from this unpleasant subject. Her fair face and prim demeanor disguising a molten core, reminding me of all our talks of years before, our bird-watching in Riverside Park, things we had once shared and which she now shared only with Alger.

"It seems to me that once"—I smiled at Priscilla as if I, perhaps unkindly, was echoing something out of those youthful years—"Mr. Freud was to be our savior, his magnificent insights to be the elixir of our sick souls. Sex wasn't it, or the unconscious: If we relieve ourselves of all our repressions and allow our true sexual urges their full expression, all our sins will be put to flight?"

This reminder of our past, that it was I, after all, who had paid for her abortion by the best gynecologist in New York (an esteemed colleague of my father's, which caused much uproar without explanation on my part), seemed to fluster Alger. Talk of sex or things libidinous always made him uneasy.

"Well, I guess that settles it, then. If we all have enough sex, the world will propagate itself splendidly without our intervention." And he looked fiercely at Priscilla.

She laughed and raised her cup as if in a salute.

"I'm all for that. Didn't Freud suggest that to chase away our inner demons we must kill our fathers and rape our mothers and so relieve civilization of its discontents?"

"Ah," I said, "your uncle Stalin seems to have that much well in hand in the Ukraine."

Alger stood, as if fed up with the drift. "Freud clearly has his uses, if only to kick over civilization's pretenses for a more disciplined model that allows the full pursuit of our mind's capacity, to the benefit of all, and to a cause larger than oneself."

I followed suit, standing to make my departure. "Well, saving the industrial base of our country may—someday—have its uses, Alger."

Priscilla kissed me on the cheek and patted my hand as if to say, Always a good loser.

Alger got in a last shot on the way to the door. "You lack the tragic sense of history, Edward. There's no saving the dead, even if Lazarus could roll away that stone." He bowed to me curtly. "You'll find plenty of taxis one block down on Wisconsin Avenue."

Alger's Ford roadster was parked smack-dab by his front door; it would have taken him ten minutes to drive me to my hotel.

—

When I close my eyes to ripples of a summer breeze over the lake, and concentrate on the name Volta Place, what do I see? Two white-sashed windows starkly focused on the dripping sidewalk maples; and two at the rear framing bird feeders in an enclosed backyard—curtained by teary bamboo; and that not uncozy parlor with a semicircle of odd chairs, silent personages turning their backs on what would be the scant daylight filtering through that screen of bamboo, as if to focus, these phantom guests, on an interior world of books and galvanic ideas—invisible firebrands to their revolutionary soul, as Chambers would have us believe. And yet, too, something he admired: a humble sparseness of sensibility, a Quaker asperity—the kind of thing Chambers noted so wistfully in *Witness*. And yet I cannot but detect through the mist of time an engine of relentless desire, a desire to rule, as the gods once ruled the ancients by stacking the deck with ruthless appeals to jealousy and grievance. How proud and driven to succeed that remarkable couple seems to me now.

Was I being tested, my mettle assayed, my fictile qualities prodded and massaged by delicate hands? Granted a glimpse of a charmed circle? Of a wisdom to lift the soul above the profit grubbing of Wall Street? The Olympian heights of a more just society? Such tasty morsels of revolutionary and even romantic platitudes seemed harmless enough. Freely available to all in our circle of that day and time.

I had always prided myself on being the smartest person in the room—even at *Law Review*—and yet this Zeus and his Hera, his amanuensis at her typewriter, had let me know in no uncertain terms that their sensibilities, carapaced in a ruthless faith, trumped all.

Was I tempted to take up their cause? Surely. For good intentions always appeal to our better natures, burnishing the sterling image we most treasure of ourselves. Actions, as my father always insisted, speak louder than words: how you live your life. But I suspect I was at best a provisional convert, a lost soul to be kept in limbo for the day when I might prove useful.

Of one thing I am certain, through the war years, the three years I was in Washington on the War Production Board, when I had an apartment at the Wardman Park, they never once invited me back to Volta Place (though we ran into each other at various social gatherings). Nor did they even deign to reply to my few invitations to join us at our apartment when Annie—who, I think, intimidated Priscilla—was down for a weekend from New York, or when she played a concert at Constitution Hall. I even dropped off two tickets at Volta Place, giving them to the Hisses' maid. Never a word.

They were too busy.

32
Volta Place

IT WAS EARLY evening when I reached the Hisses' house, probably between six and seven o'clock. They were then living on Volta Place in Georgetown, in a house whose narrow end faced the street. It was, in fact, flush with the sidewalk. I went in through the little gate, at the right side of the house. A colored maid, probably Claudia Catlett, who was a witness for Hiss at his trials, came to the door. She said that neither Mr. nor Mrs. Hiss was at home. I left. But as I stood for a moment in indecision on the sidewalk, Priscilla Hiss drove up. She headed in to the curb on slant to park. The headlights swept the sidewalk and I stepped into the beam so that Priscilla could see me clearly and would not be frightened by a loitering figure.

Her greeting was pleasant but not effusive, and I decided at once that Alger Hiss had been warned of my break . . . I had to go to the bathroom. Priscilla followed me upstairs. The bathroom was at the front of the house, facing the street. Directly to the right of the bathroom door, there was a bedroom door. A telephone was on a little table near the door. As I went into the bathroom, Priscilla went into the bedroom. I closed the bathroom door and thought: "This situation is tight." Before I washed my hands, I opened the bathroom door halfway. Priscilla was speaking in a very low voice into the telephone. I walked directly up to her. She hung up. We went downstairs in silence.

At that nerve-tingling moment, Alger Hiss came home. We were in the living room and he saw me the moment he came into the house. He was surprised, of course, and his surprise showed in his eyes. But he smiled pleasantly, said: "How do you do," and made me the little bow with his head and shoulders that he sometimes made when he was being restrained. It was both whimsical and grave . . . some question was asked which I answered in the faintly foreign tone that I had always used in the underground. The reaction was electric: "You don't have to put on any longer. We have been told who you are." To understand what was meant, it is necessary for me to explain that Alger Hiss, like everybody else in the Washington underground, supposed that I was some kind of European.

The angry answer at the dinner table meant that two facts were known: I was an American; I had broken with the Communist Party. Alger, who was sitting at the head of the table, to my right, tried to dispel the awkwardness. He said something to this effect: "It is a pity that you broke. I am told that you were about to be given a very important post. Perhaps if you went to the party and made your peace, it could still be arranged." I thought: "Alger has been told to say that to me." The "important post" was perhaps Bykov's old project of the sleeper apparatus now doing service as bait. I smiled and said that I did not think I would go to the party.

I began a long recital of the political mistakes and crimes of the Communist Party. This gigantic ulcer of corruption and deceit had burst, I said, in the great Russian purge when Stalin had consolidated his power by massacring thousands of the best men and minds in the Communist Party on lying charges.

I may have spoken for five or ten minutes. I spoke in political terms because no others would have made the slightest impression on my host. I spoke with feeling, and sometimes with slow anger as the monstrous picture built up. Sometimes Alger said a few objecting words, soberly and a little sorrowfully. Then I begged him to break with the Communist Party.

Suddenly, there was another angry flare-up: "What you have been saying is just mental masturbation."

I was shocked by the rawness of the anger revealed and deeply hurt. We drifted from the dining room into the living room, most unhappy people. Again, I asked Alger if he would break with the Communist Party. He shook his head without answering. There was no more to say. I asked for my hat and coat. Alger walked to the door with me. He opened the door and I stepped out . . . We looked at each other steadily for a moment, believing that we were seeing each other for the last time and knowing that between us lay, meaningless to most of mankind but final for us, a molten torrent—the revolution and the Communist Party. When we turned to walk in different directions from that torrent, it would be as men whom history left no choice but to be enemies.

As we hesitated, tears came into Alger Hiss's eyes—the only time I ever saw him so moved. He has denied this publicly and derisively. He does himself an injustice—by the tone rather than by the denial, which has its practical purpose in the pattern of his whole denial. He should not regret those few tears, for as long as men are human, and remember our story, they will plead for his humanity.

—Whittaker Chambers, *Witness*

It was a little disturbing to find a parking spot—on a cobblestone street chock-a-block with parked cars—right in front of 3415 Volta Place, almost as if the space had been vacated as a special dispensation for these seekers after time's more intractable mysteries. The Tahoe fit with room to spare. George looked at Wendy and she at him, and both nervously shrugged as they took in the tiny home in this quiet maple-lined residential quarter of fashionable Georgetown. Just a ten-minute drive from the National Archives. Easy walking distance from the State Department, Treasury, and White House in the old days, the thirties and forties, for the nine subjects in the Altmann sketches, to their offices, to seats of power and influence. A chilly thought that only added to the chill of an early November in Washington, and the warmth—safe, familiar—of the Tahoe's interior. For a long time they just sat there, near comatose, as if sealed in a time machine, listening to Van Morrison (indulging childhood nostalgia, their parents' as much as theirs), staring at the narrow redbrick town house: miniature, like a dollhouse, with three floors and a pair of white-sashed windows staring back at them: solemn, opaque, unsettling. The red bricks in the sidewalk, an antique herringbone pattern, undulated eerily like miniature waves, or disturbed gravitational fields, upended in places by subterranean roots. The evenly spaced maples, the older and larger at least, witnesses to the very events now deeply embedded in their imagination. And those ungainly oldsters, some tattered and bare in places, with broken boughs, having already sloughed plenitudes of yellow-orange leaves, seemed yet another disconcerting reminder of their race against time, the always tenuous hold of memory among the living. The leaf-strewn street like some threadbare runner on eternity urging them on.

There was, too, Weinstein's fascination with the Judge, the hint of near-panicked bereavement in his voice at the possible imminent loss of that last remaining human link to the trial, which had made his scholarly reputation ("By God, they're all gone"). And there was also the image of that still handsome and vigorous man in his judicial robes who gazed imperiously across his desk at the impudent scholar come uninvited to his chambers, who aspired to upset the conviction of Alger Hiss, who even wondered if the honorable Edward E. Dimock might have once been a member of the Party, or fellow traveler, given his alliance with the Hiss defense team, and so sympathetic to his plea for insider information to destroy the government's case. This amplifying their own sense of having been swept up by the Judge's bifurcated voice, that of the memoir and that echoing from the ship's keel ceiling, now converging with yet more invisible currents (Annie's annotation to Chambers: "She stoops to conquer—and how!"), in turn generating further entanglements through space and time, not unlike a Medusa's head, where the blood of one slain serpent only birthed others.

—

"What's the matter?" Wendy finally asked, lowering her window a tad to breathe the sere leafy air, breaking the spell, as she turned her head once more to the tiny house.

"To quote the Judge's favorite wisecrack: 'Déjà vu all over again.'"

She nodded with a concealed smile. "Tell me about it."

He sighed. "So, who's telling the truth?"

"I'll take that of a scholar, whose only skin in the game is a reputation for accuracy and fairness . . . and, well, the truth. And now you've even got your doctoral adviser to turn to, for another perspective."

"Spier? I'm not going there—no way."

"Why, because he's disappointed in you for not finishing your Ph.D.?"

"Because he was one of the most brilliant minds I've ever known. I respect him too much."

"So?"

"I'm not going to waste his time on something he'd probably rather forget. At a Christmas party, after a few drinks, he once told me how Hiroshima and Nagasaki haunted his dreams for years. As a young postgrad he worked on the Manhattan Project."

She seemed perplexed at this, gazing at another squadron of floating leaves.

"Somehow I never quite connected Hiss with all that."

"That's what I mean."

"Well, frankly, I'm a little aghast you went for Weinstein's deal." She fingered the two files she still held in her lap. "A few pages, a chapter from some random Russian agent's memoir in *Russian*. And Weinstein's first draft and notes on a book about Yalta. Hardly a fair trade for original artwork?"

"The Judge does mention Yalta in the memoir—right?"

"You want the page number? Briefly, just a passing conversation with Hiss."

"Listen," he said, giving a guilty sigh, "Weinstein's career was made— irony of ironies—substantiating the conviction of Alger Hiss. Why else do you think he got appointed as head of the National Archives? And *The Haunted Wood* is just icing on his cake. The Republicans—heroes to the neoconservatives—love a lefty turncoat who's seen the light. The worst is . . . I feel totally disloyal about all this. First there was you"— he smiled gamely and tapped her shoulder with his fist—"and at least now I have an excuse for Aunt Alice: I turned over the sketches to the National Archives."

"From what I can make out, you're the only one in the family who can even stand the Judge, much less is loyal to him."

"And you—Weinstein?"

"Trust but verify," she replied with a fetching smile. "The Judge will never know, George."

"That's not . . . I was going to say 'That's not how he raised me,' but that would be an absurdity." He looked at her, taking in the tension in her face, the slight squint at the corner of her eyes, as if hungrily examining the cracks and fissures in the brickwork of 3415 Volta Place for handholds, perhaps a second-story job. "The old guy trusts me. He was the only one who ever believed in me. And I put his most intimate judgments about his family *and* himself into the hands of a man who disparaged him professionally, who's been hungry for his secrets for at least thirty years. And if the subject comes up, I can't lie to him."

"You were going to lie about me."

"I was going to get him used to the idea. And *you* certainly charmed your way out of that."

"Talk about intimate, it's not a little bizarre that the Judge included the circumstances of Cordelia's conception in the memoir. I mean, why?"

To this, his gaze turning inward, he could only shake his head.

"Listen," she said, placing her hand on his, "if the Judge is really on the up-and-up about getting to the bottom of things . . . he needs help—maybe all the help he can get—remembering. He just needs a little prompting—he's a lawyer, after all, like you say: data, facts, evidence, corroboration, his stock-in-trade. He needs your help."

"Well, we let Weinstein's assistant photocopy the memoir and letters, a memoir somewhat dated, lacking, like you say, the critical evidence that would have resolved—how many questions, anomalies, doubts? Just think about it, five years ago, when he still had all his faculties, if he'd had the new facts in Weinstein's book, how it might have changed his perspective, the memoir he would've written."

"Well, he's got 'em now." Her voice soared in pitch. "Listen, he's such a big Emerson fan, and Emerson was all about the dynamic of the moment, the transition from one state to the next, evolution—right?—past to future, metamorphosis—analogizing—he gets it. Besides, this is more about what happens to Hermitage when he's gone. And now he's got you, to edit things—reinstate his sovereignty, his mastery—do him proud—just the way you two see fit."

"If you'd only known him when." He waved dismissively. "He's gone downhill. And it won't save Hermitage."

"But that's kinda the point that Weinstein made to you: You've got a period piece, a document that freezes in time how the world looked—reality, at least to him—how . . . well, *intangible* it was. There's value in that. In the same way, *Witness*, now that we know more of the underlying facts, has a certain rare flavor, a poignant truth-telling that only time and the evidence could bestow upon it, turning what might have been just a self-justifying memoir, a political or religious screed, into a work of art."

"God only knows," he said somewhat facetiously.

"Like Proust struggled at the end to complete his sprawling novel. How, sick and bedridden, he rushed to try to pull all the years and memories back from oblivion and give them order and significance by translating them into a unified vision, the landscape of his youth, his *Swann's Way* and *Guermantes Way*."

"Ah, cribbing Annie in the Judge's memoir again."

"You don't think her music, her books made a difference to her? You don't think the ten years of your life spent staring into space, searching for lost time, didn't change you? Isn't that what the fuck we're doing?"

"Jesus, you and Marcel! Enough already. Sometimes I think you prefer his fictional childhood to your own."

At this, she seemed to bridle, falling silent, nodding off kilter, as if shaken by a blow, only to turn away with an intent stare at the white door of 3415 Volta Place, branded with three wrought-iron straps in the shape of spear points.

"A world"—she reached to a falling leaf outside the window—"more infinite—as memory is infinite—than your juvenile warp-driven *Star Wars* bullshit."

"*Star Trek*—and so why the fuck go and mention the Priscilla Hiss letters?"

"You had a bite; I just wanted to make sure the hook was in deep. Besides, the letters support the veracity—the insider account—of the memoir. That should be a comfort . . . of sorts."

"That she'd been to Hermitage?"

"That she'd been to Hermitage . . . before Alger." She gave him a significant look. "Your old guy obviously had the hots for Priscilla—big-time, once upon a time. Something that clearly didn't escape Annie."

They remained silent for almost a minute, until he picked up the thread.

"Weinstein will certainly catch any inaccuracies or self-serving details about the trial."

"Listen, any lies . . . well"—she waved a hand like a magic wand—"then you can just fix them in the final editing, whitewash the published memoir. You'll be the Judge's savior."

"I wouldn't do that," he said indignantly.

"Wouldn't you? Then why worry . . . if the truth doesn't matter?"

"And the trip from Volta Place to Fitzwilliam, New Hampshire—what do you make of that?"

She turned again to the window. "It mattered to Weinstein; it mattered enough to Annie. I suppose I can cancel my classes at the Gunks this weekend. We can stop by Hermitage on the way back and debrief the Judge."

"I was supposed to help JJ pack up and ship out the Altmann show and hang the new exhibition. But hell: a missing day from over sixty years ago."

"A whole day." She laughed and snapped her fingers. "Well, let's get started." She opened the door and turned to him, flipping a strand of hair behind her ear. "See, we're time travelers, George, you and I. Warp-speeding it, except in this case we don't need wormholes—and, better yet, we can just change *everything* . . . and ultimately . . . who *you* are." She smiled with an enigmatic squint. "And even who *we* are . . . or will be. Even Einstein couldn't manage such a cool trick, *n'est-ce pas, mon cheri?*"

"I dare you to knock."

"Remember, *Luke*," she teased, as if now needing to spur them on, "something of you is a part of this place: both George Altmann and Edward Dimock. Call them our tenth and eleventh men, for fiction's sake—and you'll make it twelve at this feast for the gods."

"And Whittaker Chambers."

"Chamber . . . yes, Chambers, a baker's dozen, of course."

"Leaving you as our artist—our creator of worlds."

Standing on the sidewalk, she glanced again at the house, her eyes traveling up and down its brick façade as her carriage shifted on her narrow hips, eager for the ascent. He closed his door and drew close to her but did not touch her, as if it might break the mood, as if some force field lay invisibly about her.

"What you don't get about Proust—not in your standard model, places had souls for him—souls/beings/presences—invisible, like dark matter . . . and only detectable through the imagination catalyzed by memory. Can you say as much about your galaxies, your stars? Or perhaps you've forgotten." Her slashing shoulders went silent. "Whether the steeple of Saint-Hilaire, or his beloved pink and white hawthorns, or even a random stand of three trees glimpsed at sunset. The past for him lay hidden somewhere outside the realm of time or intellect—or your Hubble telescope—contained in the essence of a place or object: the taste of a madeleine, the tinkle of a spoon, the texture of a napkin—set free in the sensation of a fugitive moment. When an involuntary memory catches us unaware. That's what we're about: We're always—don't you think?—in search of those places and things, of which we have no real inkling, hoping against hope that we may stumble upon them before we die and so hear their voice in ours. As an artist, if that's to be my role in this mess—that's what I hope to find . . . and, if I'm lucky, recognize it when I do." With this, her voice calmed, as if confessing all she dared. "Every ridgeline invokes a different mystery, every horizon, daring you on to your death while living at peak experience—that's why I climb, why I paint. That's what I learned from *my* father."

———

And in this light, the picture began to assemble itself in their minds, first from the sketches, the mural, the Judge's memoir, Chambers's *Witness*, and finally the place itself hidden behind the white door with the three wrought-iron straps on that September afternoon in 1937. Or that is how it felt when a woman's face peered out at Wendy from the darkness, coalescing in retrospect as they later drove north on Route 202, as the far-flung details filtered back through the intervening years to create a picture in their mind's eye.

According to the *Evening Star* of that Tuesday, September (courtesy of the Google gods), it was only seventy degrees, cool for that time of year after the typically malarial heat of a Washington summer, as yet without benefit of air-conditioning. Of course, Harry Hopkins and Laughlin Currie were not yet in the White House; Hopkins was head of the WPA—a herculean job, though of no particular interest to the Soviets—at an office far down Pennsylvania Avenue and so may have taken a cab on his own, arriving late at the meeting (a memory of which Altmann may have included in his mural, where a tardy Hopkins hangs up his suit jacket); while Lauchlin Currie, a close friend of Harry Dexter White, was then working with White at Treasury, and so may have walked with or shared a cab with his comrade as they shared office gossip about their boss, Henry Morgenthau, who would become their cat's paw, when White served as an assistant secretary during the war and Currie was an economic adviser at the White House. Two of the Volta circle were rising stars at State: Alger Hiss and Laurence Duggan, and so may have taken the opportunity to stroll down Pennsylvania Avenue from the old State Department building, that gray "Victorian horror cheek-by-jowl to the White House," although they may well have taken the obvious precaution of traveling separately, even if State Department security was notoriously slack in those prewar years. At the time, the FBI was woefully understaffed and undertrained, more preoccupied with potential German and Japanese spies than lurking NKVD agents, who had proliferated tenfold when the Roosevelt administration, after a sixteen-year hiatus, recognized the Soviet Union in 1933.

Of those two at State, Duggan was the star in the NKVD pantheon, something that probably rankled Alger Hiss, which was hinted at in Altmann's depiction of a thin-featured, patrician-looking face, bespectacled, scholarly, a hard mouth evoking a man of fiercely held opinions. If Duggan looked confident, he had reason to be. He was the golden boy, protégé of Undersecretary of State Sumner Welles; Duggan was the State Department jockey on whom Moscow Center had placed its bets—the NKVD, not the GRU (Soviet military intelligence), which ran Hiss and White by way of Chambers—and they were pushing him to

broaden his access to information beyond his present position as head of
the Latin American Division: Stalin wanted intelligence on European
and Eastern European developments, as well as developments in Asia.

Like the FBI, Uncle Joe was most worried about the Nazis and
Japanese, the threat of a two-front war. But at this moment, on this
lovely fall day, Duggan was still riding high, although within a year
of the Volta Place meeting, he would start to get jittery, nervous,
paranoid—even as his beautiful, blond, athletic wife, Helen Boyd
Duggan, yearned, as well, to offer her services to the Soviets; he constantly complained to his NKVD contacts that the relentless purges
of high-ranking "traitorous" Soviet officials in Moscow (800,000 were
shot between 1937 and 1938) had made him vulnerable to detection by
the FBI. He was right, but for the wrong reasons. It was Chambers who
would defect, who, after the Nazi-Soviet pact of 1939, would expose
Duggan, along with Hiss and White, to Adolf Berle, State Department
security director. Berle's intervention caused Duggan to be discretely
removed from his job, only to be saved by being given a promotion by
his mentor and friend, Undersecretary of State Sumner Welles, who
placed him in a job where he no longer had access to important military information. And so a terrified Duggan, although he continued to
provide information, would ultimately prove a great disappointment to
his NKVD handlers, while Alger Hiss and Harry Dexter White, seemingly untouched by Chambers's betrayal, working in tandem, surged
ahead to become Stalin's go-to minions at State and Treasury.

The pitifully obscure Marvin Smith, a onetime colleague of Alger
Hiss's at the Justice Department, probably arrived on his own; the new
Justice Department building, where he would meet his death eleven
years later, sprawled in his own blood on an inlay of black marble (an
omega symbol of all things), was then just two years old.

And poor handsome William Remington, blond, blue-eyed, the
youngest at the meeting, would be betrayed to a grand jury by his
ex-wife, Ann Moos Remington (also a Communist), who testified her
husband was a Communist and had paid dues to Elizabeth Bentley. He
was convicted of perjury and spying, and subsequently brutally bludgeoned to death in Lewisburg prison in 1954. Remington must have
been in town on business, since he had recently been employed by the
Tennessee Valley Authority. During the war, he would work for the
War Production Board, at which time he passed documents on aircraft
production and synthetic fuel technology to Bentley, his KGB handler.

Remington was the only member of the Volta Place cell whose wife turned on him, who voluntarily confessed and provided the FBI with names and information—and paid the price.

Their hostess, Priscilla Hiss, though not employed by the government, and with a young child to worry about from a disastrous first marriage, must have avidly welcomed the familiar faces at her front door, and, as the only woman, might have relished the attention of the men absent their wives. She surely held her own doctrinally, even if she resisted spelling out her contributions to the underground: tediously typing copies of the secret documents Alger brought home night after night from the State Department, so they could be returned the following morning to his office safe, making sure they'd be ready for Whittaker Chambers. Chambers came by once a week to pick up the copied documents, in addition to one set of originals from that day, to be photographed either in labs set up for the purpose in Washington or Baltimore, at which point the copies were destroyed and the one set of originals returned to Alger first thing in the morning for return to his office safe.

For the moment, it was not entirely clear—no matter how hard George and Wendy struggled to visualize the thing—how George Altmann came to be at the Volta Place meeting (a point that would only be clarified weeks later after the return of Jimmy Altmann to Woodstock). They speculated endlessly about this. Had Altmann been there earlier in the afternoon, sketching an older Timothy—for the oil portrait she'd mentioned to Edward Dimock—and had somehow simply lingered on, a fellow Communist among Communists, even if the others had long gone far beyond the legal bounds of Party affiliation? Why hadn't Alger Hiss nipped such a dangerous plan in the bud? Wouldn't he have been aghast to arrive from the office and discover George Altmann still there with the others, finding that Priscilla had orchestrated such a foolhardy episode? Alger had been warned often enough by Whittaker Chambers for much lesser compromises of security to realize such a breach jeopardized the apparatus by, in effect, making a record of the cell meeting, witnessed by one who, though sympathetic, was not and never would be a Soviet agent. A foolhardy breach of the most basic tradecraft. The very fact that these spies from different networks, both NKVD and GRU, were meeting as a group was in itself a horrendous breach of tradecraft.

But they were all still young and eager and thrilled with their clandestine work—invulnerable. An American independent streak that their Soviet handlers complained about endlessly in cable communications with Moscow Center.

As George and Wendy, invited in by the housekeeper, wandered the interior of Volta Place, they settled on an answer that turned out to be remarkably close to the truth: Alger Hiss had been presented with a fait accompli by his over-enthusiastic wife and was forced to concede the issue, at least at the start. Possibly it was just a lovely day and Alger's animal spirits were up, and the good conversation lubricated by a passable chardonnay, and ambition ran high among these independent-minded Americans (which always frustrated their paranoid and disciplined Soviet handlers); and they might well have been flattered to have a famous artist among them, recording their earnest and purposeful likenesses—if not for posterity, then as souvenirs of the occasion. But how could they have possibly guessed the final disposition of the sketches in the National Archives? And this after being used as studies for a mural in the new Justice Department building, where their likenesses would be on display for decades to come, long after they were forgotten, a kind of Keystone-Cops immortality, even though disguised as rural farming folk. And yet—who knows—this was a fate they might well have preferred to that of fickle time's pronouncement on them as traitors, filled as they must have been on this fine afternoon at Volta Place with such splendid plans to remake the world, blessed, too, by lovely weather and Priscilla's gracious, enchanting smile, something of which was retained in the Justice Department mural, where she presides like a Victorian queen bee, her coronal of bobbed hair set off by the window behind, filled with a lush, almost diaphanous blue sky and rolling green pastures from sea to shining sea.

And Altmann, like any artist, as Wendy pointed out, tended to hoard studies. "Material is material; who knows when something might come in handy, or inspire something entirely different?" she said.

As Wendy stared out the back window of the tiny parlor, she added, "I'll bet he started with Priscilla Hiss, since her face is the most finished in the mural, so very—those electric eyes—like her, and then the thing sort of took on a life of its own, what with the other sketches near at hand."

The Hispanic housekeeper led them from room to room downstairs and then upstairs, after Wendy had chatted her up in perfect Spanish and given a detailed description of how her grandparents had once lived in the house. He and Wendy now pondered what Altmann could have been thinking for the two hours or so that he sat sketching this group, presumably taking in the discussion of latest events in Europe, or the application of Marxist theory to the moribund American economy, the progress or failure of the New Deal to bring them closer to the revolutionary conditions that would make the takeover of the American government possible. Did it go beyond theory? Did they exchange success stories, tradecraft? Brag? Were his ears buzzing? Did these Harvard brain trusters really believe in the ultimate success of their revolution?

For Altmann, from a lowly Jewish family of Eastern European origins, the Volta circle might well have seemed like a Harvard reunion, since five of them—White, Duggan, Alger, Field, and Currie—had attended Harvard as either undergraduate or graduate students. Did George Altmann feel like an imposter, having no college degree? Altmann had left high school in the Bronx to study full time at the Art Students League, and then had won a scholarship to the Beaux-Arts in Paris in 1926, where he had exhibited at the Salon of 1928. He may not have been a Harvard man, but in the art world of the day he was already a star, certainly in Communist Party circles, where his proletarian background placed him among the workers' elite. Critics, most of them Marxist art historians, had described him as one of the greatest figurative artists working in America. Being from a blue-collar background and a New York member of the CP probably gave Altmann additional cache among the Volta Place circle. So maybe he felt right at home in that narrow sitting room overlooking the back patio and garden, which, on that late afternoon in September, must have been flooded with western sunlight, filtering through the rustling bamboo in the garden and casting a lovely golden light over his subjects' faces, perfectly highlighting their quick intelligence and fervent eyes, as they listened to and discussed the latest editorials in the *Daily Worker*, or mulled over more arcane literary subjects in *The New Masses*, articles and stories once written and edited by none other than the likes of Whittaker Chambers in his early days as a Marxist propagandist.

"One thing for sure," Weinstein had said to them as they turned to leave, "Altmann's subjects are full of ambition—just look at their eyes and those intent faces—ambition to burn."

Perhaps Altmann felt right at home in such a circle of ambitious individuals. To a man—and one woman—that Volta circle was, according to cable reports from their Soviet handlers, "frantic with ambition." They fawned and competed for attention—anything to

serve their Soviet masters—giddy with the romance of their venture, enraptured by the faux-Russian tone of Chambers's voice, which
touched on some faraway siren call of revolutionary ardor: an ardor
further fueled by their sense of secrecy and elitism, of a double life, a
secret life, a double consciousness, like Russian dolls nestled one inside
the other, shielding the molten white core behind a docile bureaucratic
exterior, belying the tattered veil of bourgeois values they were so eager
to throw off. As Chambers noted drily again and again, they were
impatient with the government they officially served, which frustrat-
ingly bent only very slowly—or not at all—to those ardent desires, led
by a president, as Chambers wrote—not with a little amazement—
they hated with a passion because of his half measures, echoing the
Bolsheviks' hatred for the meandering milquetoast Mensheviks, hopelessly moderate half-assed revolutionaries.

Of the ten at 3415 Volta Place that September evening in 1937,
including the artist, George Altmann, five would die in middle age
from accident, suicide, heart attack, and stomach cancer—or murder—
within fifteen years, while two escaped to permanent exile to avoid the
FBI and testifying at the Hiss trial.

Of the exiles, Noel Field, like Laurence Duggan, for an all too brief
shining moment at Volta Place, had been the great white hope of Soviet
intelligence, a former State Department employee and an eager and
willing government insider, contested over by the NKVD, which owned
him, and the GRU and Alger Hiss, who wanted him. Even in Altmann's
sketch, Field's narrow face, sensitive mouth, dark, brooding eyes spoke of
a keen yet simple-minded innocence that would prove his downfall. In
the spring of 1936, the NKVD had encouraged Field to take a position
with the League of Nations in Geneva, where they believed he'd prove
more useful as war approached in Europe. Try as he might, Field found
that his position in Geneva provided little in the way of intelligence useful to those in Moscow, even as he worked tirelessly in the antifascist
cause and later, during the war, as director of the American Unitarian
Universalist Service Committee's relief operation in Marseilles.

For all his good work, he got too close to agents Stalin considered
enemies, and in 1949, months before the second Hiss trial, Field was
kidnapped by Hungarian agents under orders from Stalin and smuggled out of Czechoslovakia and then on to Budapest, where he was
held in prison for years, mercilessly tortured for confessions to buttress accusations against victims of Stalin's wrath in the show trials

of the early fifties. His wife, Herta, who was also later arrested, was convinced that American agents had kidnapped him to return him to the States to testify against Hiss. Confined in a Budapest prison from 1949 to 1954, he confessed, to no avail, countless times that he was not an American spy, but a Soviet spy, and so identified Hiss as a friend and fellow spy, information that would only emerge out of Hungary after 1989, when Allen Weinstein assiduously gathered it from the Hungarian secret police files and meticulously deployed these facts in his book *The Haunted Wood*. Noel Field died in Budapest in 1970, an unrepentant Communist to the end. Speaking of his years of imprisonment and torture, he stated, "My accusers essentially have the same convictions that I do, they hate the same things and the same people I hate—the conscious enemies of socialism, the fascists, the renegades, the traitors. Given their belief in my guilt, I cannot blame them. I cannot but approve their detestation. That is the real horror of it all."

All that remained of such unextinguished fervor now resided in the glassy eyes of a narrow face in a sketch in the National Archives, and in a vague approximation of the same on the walls of the Justice Department in the shadowed features beneath the brim of a farmer's straw hat.

"My God," Wendy said suddenly, just out of the hearing of the housekeeper, "do you think that during all those years in a Hungarian prison, after the days and nights of torture, Noel Field ever looked back to this place, the happy hours seated with his pals, the bamboo swaying beyond the window, when they thought the world was their oyster? Talk about light-years away . . ."

He motioned for her to keep quiet as the housekeeper waved them on to the bedroom.

The other exiled member of the Volta circle, Lauchlin Currie, became a special adviser to Roosevelt in 1939, second only to Harry Hopkins as a White House enabler of Soviet influence at the highest reaches of the American government. At Volta Place in 1937, Altmann sketched Currie with a long, scholarly face, gentle hooked nose, and deep-set, wide-apart eyes. The soft-spoken Currie, Canadian by birth, had little to offer his handlers at this time. He was a lowly Treasury official with his pal White, and the ongoing Depression took precedence over issues of military affairs, even as Hitler stirred fears and Japan became more belligerent in Manchuria. But Currie would not disappoint. In 1939, as a senior economic adviser to Franklin Roosevelt, a post he would retain until the president's death, in 1945, and that would give him access to the most vital U.S. secrets and strategic policy in real time, Currie became a critical agent of influence for Moscow Center.

He would use his position to intervene to protect and keep his fellow spies in positions of access government-wide—with at least seven agents in Treasury alone, when Treasury, during the war under White and Morgenthau, became, along with State, central to postwar planning. In June of 1944, Currie provided the KGB with the critical information that, contrary to stated policy, Roosevelt was willing to accede to Stalin's demand that Russia be allowed to keep the eastern part of Poland, illegally taken under provisions of the Nazi-Soviet pact of 1939; and, in addition, Roosevelt would be willing to put pressure on the Polish government in exile to that end. To further this precooked outcome, Currie would see to it that Alger Hiss accompanied Roosevelt and Harry Hopkins to Yalta, where an enlarged Poland, its boundaries extended westward, would be virtually handed over to Stalin, along with an agreement for the return of millions of Russian nationals to their almost certain execution. With Roosevelt's death, Currie would leave the White House; later, he would come under intense scrutiny from the FBI after his role as a Soviet spy was divulged by Chambers and Elizabeth Bentley during the Alger Hiss investigation. Most likely warned by his Soviet handlers or threatened by Hiss and his protectors, Currie subsequently left the United States to work as an economist in Colombia, married a Colombian woman, and let his U.S. passport lapse. He never returned to the States, denying he was a Soviet agent to the end.

"So," Wendy continued, staring out at the curtain of bamboo rising against the back fence of the patio, "of the ten who were in this room on that day, including George Altmann, we know for a fact that one was murdered in prison, three fell violently to their deaths, one died of a sudden heart attack from an overdose of digitalis, one died of stomach cancer, one fled behind the Iron Curtain, and one hightailed it south of the border, while only the remaining two—Alger and Priscilla Hiss—pretty much lived out their lives. Eighty percent attrition . . . how statistically does that compute, say, for the general population? You're the astrophysicist; what do your stargazing probabilities tell you?"

"A statistician would tell you that if the events you're analyzing are causational and internally coherent, you first eliminate the causal factors. Thus you remove the Hisses, Alger and Priscilla, which leaves you with a hundred percent attrition. So no one in the Volta Place cell escaped unscathed, with the possible exception of Harry Hopkins—even the KGB couldn't produce a diagnosis of stomach cancer."

"Volta Place cell . . . huh? Like a virus, a plague."

To this, he only gave her a fed-up pout and continued to poke around, not unpleased at the thwarting of her Proustian sensibilities, and her most ardent intuitions. The interior of 3415 Volta Place yielded no clues, no answers . . . no essences whatsoever. It had been completely redone, gutted, in fact, and rebuilt from the studs to the rafters, with only the original pine floorboards on the first floor remaining. Even the onetime Quaker simplicity of the Hisses' era of occupancy had been obliterated with a mixture of South American baroque-modern, full of heavy couches and padded armchairs—"a Botero fleshiness," as she termed it—with decorative items in brilliant tropical colors, which the housekeeper proudly showed off, extolling the most excellent taste of her employer, a military attaché at the Brazilian embassy. They spent some time in the parlor at the back, staring out a modern picture window and sliding patio door to the intimate garden, where the November light still filtered through a screen of bamboo that reached high above a back fence of rusted chain link.

The bamboo endured.

Perjury Prisoner William Remington Killed In Attack

Former Government Employee Dies In U.S. Prison Hospital

LEWISBURG, Pa. (AP)—William W. Remington, former government aide serving a three-year term for perjury, died today at the federal penitentiary here from injuries suffered in an attack at the prison.

Remington's death was announced by Acting Warden Fred T. Wilkinson. He suffered head injuries Monday when hit on the head with a sock-covered brick in his dormitory squad room.

Wilkinson said the identity of Remington's assailant "is fairly well established" but did not disclose whether it was another convict, nor give the reason for the attack.

STATEMENT ISSUED

Wilkinson issued this statement:

"Inmate William Walter Remington died in the institution hospital at 7:31 a.m. today, Nov. 24, 1954. On Tuesday afternoon an operation was performed by an outside surgical consultant and the institution medical officer.

"The investigation by the Federal Bureau of Investigation and prison officials is continuing and all information will be presented to the U.S. Attorney."

William Remington Dies After Beating in Prison

Lewisburg, Pa., Nov. 24 (AP)—William W. Remington, former government aide serving a three-year term for perjury, died today at the federal penitentiary here from injuries suffered in an attack at the prison.

Remington's death was announced by Acting Warden Fred T. Wilkinson. Remington suffered head injuries Monday when hit on the head with a stocking covered brick in this dormitory squad room.

Wilkinson said the identity of Remington's assailant "is fairly well established" but did not disclose whether it was another convict, nor give the reason for the attack.

Remington, 34, a former U.S. Commerce Department official, was sentenced to serve three years for falsifying that he had never been associated with Red organizations.

Wilkinson issued this statement:

"Inmate William Walter Remington died in the institution hospital at 7:38

Cabe special agent in charge of the Philadelphia FBI office, declined comment on Remington's death. He said a statement would be issued "when we have made an arrest."

Wilkinson reported that Remington was found by his quarters officer in a dazed condition on the low his third floor dormitory quarters. He said that part of the prison was occupied by a small number of prisoners, consisting of n for the day, and

the attack, suf of the face and able fractured

N. J., where n aunt. Mrs. ton said the ble shock" to

of the family urary mak ts.

's second where in

emington not on, not ud, he ondi

three res)")

Red Perjurer Killed With Brick in Pen

Head Surgery Fails
William Remington

WILLIAM W. REMINGTON
... brick in sock fatal

LEWISBURG, PA. AP—William W. Remington, former government aide serving a three-year term for perjury, died today at the federal penitentiary here fro injuries suffered in an attack at the prison.

Remington's death was announced by Acting Warden Fred T. Wilkinson. He suffered head injuries Monday when hit on the head with a sock-covered brick in his dormitory squad room.

Wilkinson said the identity of Remington's assailant "is fairly well established" but did not disclose whether it was another convict, nor give the reason for the attack.

Wilkinson issued this statement:

"Inmate William Walter Remington died in the institution hospital at 7:31 a.m. today, Nov. 24, 1954. On Tuesday afternoon an

RELATED STORY PAGE 5-B

operation was performed by an outside surgical consultant and the institution medical officer.

"The investigation by the Federal Bureau of Investigation and prison officials is continuing and all information will be presented to the U.S. Attorney."

Remington was confined in the same prison as Alger Hiss, former top State Department official, who has served 3½ years for perjury. Hiss is scheduled to be released on parole Saturday.

Remington was sentenced to three years on a charge that he lied when he denied giving anyone secret classified information.

He was sentenced on Feb. 4, 1953 and started serving the sentence April 15, 1953.

Convicted Perjurer Remington Dies Following Prison Attack

Ex-Government Aide Fatally Injured By Blow On Head

LEWISBURG, Pa., Nov. 24.—(AP)—William W. Remington, former government aide serving a three-year term for perjury, died today at the federal penitentiary here from injuries suffered in an attack at the prison.

Remington's death was announced by acting Warden Fred Wilkinson. He suffered head injuries Monday when hit on the head with a stocking-covered brick in his dormitory squad room.

Wilkinson said the identity of Remington's assailant "is fairly well established; but did not disclose whether it was another convict, nor give the reason for the attack.

Remington, 37, a former U.S. Commerce Department official, was sentenced to serve three years for falsifying that he had never been associated with Red organizations.

...

REMINGTON was confined in the same prison as former top Star...

not be The Wilkinson said that Remington's father, F. C. Remington, in Remington said the identit well established; but did not a convict, nor give the reason fo attack.

asked that Remi viet spy ring courier, confessed to the knew a young Communist party when he was a student at Dartmouth college

Elizabeth Bentley, material to

Prison Blow Kills Remington

LEWISBURG, Pa. (AP)—William W. Remington, former government aide serving a three year term for perjury, died today at the Federal Penitentiary here of injuries suffered in an attack at the prison.

Remington's death was announced by Acting Warden Fred T. Wilkerson. He suffered head injuries Monday when hot on the head with a stocking-covered brick in his doritory squad room.

Wilkinson said the identity of Remington's assailant "is fairly well established," but did not disclose wether it was another convict, nor give the reason for the attack.

Remington, 35, a former U.S. Commerce Department official,

institution medical offic

"The investigation by eral Bureau of Investiga prison officials is conti all information will be to the U.S. Attorney.

Remington was confir same prison as Alger mer Remington was tothree years on a ch he lied in denying he Wilkinson reported that gton was found by his officer in a dazed condi second floor stairway below his third floor quarters. He said that p prison was occupied by number of prisoners, of night workers in forth by janitors

33
Crime Scene: William Remington

ON THE FOLLOWING day, as George and Wendy made their way on Route 202, just north of Wilmington, they took some comfort that the road, though widened in places, remained virtually the same as it had in the 1930s, as did the passing landscapes of farmers' fields, and the names of cities and towns, however much these places had changed in the interim. Weinstein had traced on a map the exact route Whittaker Chambers and the Hisses had driven in August 1937 to Harry Dexter White's summer home in Fitzwilliam, New Hampshire, to pick up the document he'd authored on the reform of the Soviet monetary system. Moscow Center had ordered its immediate dispatch, much to the chagrin of Chambers.

After tracing the route, an odd look had appeared on Weinstein's face as he again fingered the sketches of Alger Hiss, Harry Dexter White, Lauchlin Currie, and Harry Hopkins.

"Out of the hundreds, if not thousands, of Soviet agents throughout the government, war industries, the media and entertainment industry, these are the four—with the possible exception of the atom bomb spies, the Rosenbergs, Fuchs, Greenglass, and Gold—who really mattered. And Altmann was there . . . in their halcyon days." He had smiled uneasily at this hint of nostalgia, as if struggling with a persistent knot of sarcasm, this man who had begun as one thing and ended up another, a man given to precision when confronted with imprecision, one still finding himself in a losing battle with slippery facts. "And another thing, Hiss and White were in Chambers's GRU, the Soviet military apparatus; Currie, Duggan, Field, and Remington were in another apparatus, NKVD or KGB as we know it today. In theory, members of different apparatuses weren't supposed to know one another, much less mix or discuss underground business. And yet these brash careless

Americans obviously couldn't give a damn about tradecraft, and the Altmann sketches are the first concrete proof I've seen to that effect." He'd shrugged, as if almost amused, as he sent them on their way.

Now George slowed and merged into the right lane.

"Hard to keep it to fifty miles an hour, which is what you figure they averaged in 1937."

"Depends if Priscilla was driving or not." To this observation, he had no good reply, but he could sense, as usual, that she was getting wound up about something. "Did you get the feeling that White, besides Hiss, Currie, and Hopkins, of course, was the one who really perplexes Weinstein? I mean, why else would he have suggested this crazy trip?"

He looked at her with raised eyebrows. "Perplexes? Unnerves him, I'd say. Chambers perplexes him. The Judge perplexes him. Did you notice how he kept coming back to that day he met him in his Foley Square office, when he suspected the Judge might have once been a Communist or fellow traveler—that he was hiding something?"

"Well, now we all know he was—the sketches."

"Well, at least that factoid shook him up—not quite what his memory might have led him to expect." He smiled to himself. "Brother, do I know the breed: Scholars are scholars—guys who've worked over the same field for thirty years—their life's work, their identity. And they're never satisfied until they've turned over every damn rock, fitted every piece of the puzzle, until the evidence fits their theory. But the problem is always the same: You've got to have a theory to go after the evidence, but if you fall in love with the theory, it will distort the evidence you find."

"Is that why you quit astrophysics—that nagging Heisenberg thing, that uncertainty principle?"

He switched on the windshield wipers as a cold hard rain began to filter down from a line of dark clouds.

"A burned-out case."

"Speaking of which," she said with a hint of agitation in her voice, twisting a lock of hair around her forefinger, "know what I found most scary? What he had to say about the others, especially those British spies, the Cambridge five: Maclean, Burgess—"

"Kim Philby."

"Yes, Philby. How they were all racked with doubt and anxiety, alcoholics, as their nerves frayed over the years, as they feared discovery, to be revealed as betrayers to their class and country. How only Alger Hiss never broke, never wavered, never drank, as if lying and subterfuge came as naturally as breathing—how did he put it?—as if passed on in his mother's milk. A man incapable of guilt or shame."

"As the Judge would say, 'a rare bird.'"

"The others: White, certainly Duggan and Noel Field and Remington—all lost their nerve. Remington confessed to passing information to Elizabeth Bentley, then gave names of fellow Communists to the FBI, then recanted his confession, then his Communist wife turned on him and he ended up convicted for perjury in 1953, like Hiss, ending up in Lewisburg Penitentiary." She looked up from the map in her lap, as if the thing had been staring her in the face all along. "My God, we're only about half an hour south of Lewisburg."

The Daily Item *(Sunbury, Pennsylvania), March 3, 1954*
Priscilla Hiss's trip to Lewisburg is a slow, tedious affair, requiring several changes in trains and modes of transportation. She must come to Scranton by train and change there for a railroad line to West Milton. There she meets a bus which carries her to Lewisburg and the trip to the penitentiary is by taxi cab.

A surprise to everyone within Penitentiary walls is the fact that Hiss does not acknowledge or carry on conversation with several of his former friends and acquaintances, including Harry Gold, William W. Remington, and David Greenglass, brother of Mrs. Julius Rosenberg who was executed as a spy. All see each other, know each other and say hello . . . nothing more.

Wife and Son Meet Hiss at Gates on His Release from Lewisburg Prison—Proclaims His Innocence, Saying Charges Against Him Were Untrue—Ignores All Questions Concerning Remington
LEWISBURG, PA. (AP) Nov. 27, 1954—Alger Hiss, convicted of lying when he denied giving government secrets to a Communist spy ring, was released today. He immediately proclaimed he was innocent, asserting the charges against him were "untrue."

Hiss, wearing a hat and well-worn gray topcoat brought to the penitentiary by his wife, told newsmen at the prison gate:

"I shall renew my efforts to dispel the deception that has been foisted on the American people."

"I am very glad to use this chance," he said, "the first I have had in nearly four years, to reassert my complete innocence from the charges that were brought against me by Whittaker Chambers."

Chambers, formerly a senior editor of Time *magazine now living in retirement on a farm in Westminster, Md., accused Hiss of being a member of a Communist Party group; Chambers accused Hiss also of turning over secret State Department documents.*

The telephone at the Chambers farm rang, unanswered, today, but a newsman managed to gain entrance and obtain a short statement— typed personally by Chambers on a scrap of letter paper. It said:

"The saddest single fact about the Hiss case is that nobody can change the facts as they are known. Neither Alger Hiss nor I, however much we might wish to do so, can change these facts.

"They are there forever. That is the inherent tragedy of this case."

Hiss, appearing somewhat haggard but smiling with his son at his side, said he hoped to tell the story behind his conviction and "to dispel the doubts" about his position.

Hiss ignored all questions concerning the slaying of William W. Remington in the prison earlier this week. Remington, like Hiss, was convicted of perjury in connection with congressional queries about communism.

However, Hiss and Remington were never linked together in the same Washington Communist associations.

The Scrantonian, *November 28, 1954*

Hiss spoke off the cuff . . . for nearly two minutes without interruption . . . The lines about his lean jaw tightened and harshness crept into his voice as he mentioned Chambers's name.

"For nearly four years I have had no opportunity to answer the fantastic invention that politicians and members of the press have been free to invent about me. I have to wait in silence while in my absence a myth has been developed. I hope that the return of the man will help to dispel the myth."

As he shouldered his way past reporter and photographers, he said that he and the other prisoners were "revolted and horrified" by the death of William W. Remington in the Lewisburg Penitentiary.

Three fellow convicts are accused by the FBI of beating Remington over the head with a brick wrapped in a sock.

Whenever George reread these clippings, his stomach knotted and an image flashed in his mind of his mother, seventeen-year-old Cordelia, driving the Judge's red Merc to Woodstock.

———

They stood by the Tahoe alongside the road and gazed out over the dried husks of a cornfield and, beyond this, to some fall-shorn wood-lots, trunks darkened by the recent rain, that gave way to a low hill of plowed fields and mowed meadows where the imposing redbrick complex of Lewisburg Penitentiary sprawled upon the green brow of the hill. The rain had passed, replaced by a chilly breeze sending legions of mottled gray stratus clouds marching to the east. They had driven as far as the front gate, spending some time looking up at the looming entrance with its strangely elegant Italianate brick arcades, until a security guard asked them what their business was. Now from a safer distance, they could observe how the precise ensemble of buildings that made up the complex were all of a distinctive red brick, some, bizarrely, sporting Venetian Gothic-style windows, all over-shadowed by a massive, tall central tower, also of the same red brick, looking oddly like a crenelated Renaissance watch tower transposed from Siena or Bologna. Only the surrounding walls were of plain white stone capped with glinting razor wire, dripping with raindrops.

"I'm glad we made the detour," she said. "Seeing this place puts Hiss's forty-four months into perspective."

"You think?"

"How miserable it must have been, how scary. After all, Remington was murdered there in his cell by three fellow inmates only days before Hiss was released." She handed him some more photocopied newspa-per clippings from a thick portable file folder they'd been using over the previous weeks to store research material. "I mean, it could've been him with his skull smashed in."

"Whaddya think? Payback for Remington's having confessed to the FBI, for squealing about fellow Communists—or a going-away warn-ing shot over Hiss's bow, not to do the same?"

"Everything had changed by the time he got out. It was the height of the Red Scare. Just a year before, in June, the Rosenbergs had been executed. How weird they stuck the atomic spies David Greenglass and Harry Gold in there as well with Hiss and Remington."

"You almost sound sorry for Hiss—their own, but oh so silent, Volta Place circle."

She gestured toward the massive brick tower, its western façade a rich dark crimson red from the line of showers.

"I can't help thinking how awful it must have been for Priscilla and their thirteen-year-old son, Tony, to have had to make the trip from New York to this gloomy place once a month. Remember, your aunt Martha telling us at dinner how upsetting it was for Priscilla to make that long journey. They were allowed four hours, which they split between two days. How to explain such a thing to her kid, who was crazy about his dad. Martha said she always admired how diligently Alger Hiss wrote letters to his son, to stay in touch, to relate things about his life in prison in a way a thirteen-year-old could understand— how he came to be locked up. Remember what she said, how in his letters Hiss liked to describe the view from his prison window, the weather, the landscape, the changing seasons, the birds. He could've been looking out to where we are now, seeing that same cornfield, that copse of trees . . . so close"—she shrugged, as if a little mystified by the conjunction of time and space—"so far."

"Let's get going," he said, reaching into the back seat to return the clippings to the file folder; "it's a long trip, and this detour won't make it any shorter."

"You don't think they made detours back in August 1937 on that road trip?"

"Detours?" he asked, her sympathetic tone now grating on him. "Maybe that's what Weinstein has in mind. But just remember: It was Hiss who forced Chambers's hand to reveal the stolen State Department documents in the first place. If Hiss had done nothing, just let the accusations be, he'd have avoided the damn trial; he'd have avoided this . . ."

She gave him that slightly dismayed look that he'd come to know so well, a look that was less about dismay and more about looking for the next handhold, a crack, a fissure, a crossing point on the traverse, taking on the thing that might remain obscure or ambiguous in his mind but that was becoming crystal clear in hers.

"And where would you be?" She handed him the last of the clippings on Remington. "He spent three years during the war working for the

War Production Board; the Judge had to have known him better than his memoir lets on."

He swept a hand toward the prison, barely hiding the irritation in his voice.

"So, send him a postcard from historic Lewisburg. Maybe it will jog his memory."

FBI Cite 3rd Prisoner in Killing
Supplies Motive in Remington Case
LEWISBURG, PA (AP) Nov. 26, 1954—The FBI today charged a third inmate at Lewisburg Federal Penitentiary today with the murder of William W. Remington, former government economist convicted of perjury, and in so doing provided the first clue to the motive for the slaying.

Norman H. McCabe, special agent in charge of the Philadelphia FBI office, announced that Lewis Cagle Jr., 17, of Chattanooga, Tenn., has been charged with the murder of Remington on Monday.

McCabe said Cagle admitted in a statement "that he along with McCoy and Parker, planned to ransack Remington's room on Nov. 22 and the assault took place while they were in his (Remington's) room." Cagle, according to the FBI, admitted that Remington was killed when he surprised the three defendants ransacking his cell.

A spokesman for the prison said an investigation was continuing along other lines, but that officials in the prison were not in a position yet to discuss what other motive might be involved.

"There was nothing in Remington's room of any value," the spokesman said. "Only cigarettes, a few candy bars and personal items. Absolutely no money."

The other two prisoners referred to were George Junior McCoy, 34, of Grundy, Va., and Robert Carl Parker, 21, of Washington, D.C., who were charged with participating in the beating administered to Remington with a part of a red brick wrapped in a stocking.

The robbery motive announcement halted rumors that Remington's death may have had a connection with Communism. There had been speculation that the fatal beating may have resulted from prisoner resentment over publicity accompanying the scheduled release of Alger Hiss tomorrow. Hiss, like Remington, was jailed for perjury in connection with congressional investigations of Communism. Both had been honor prisoners at the penitentiary.

Remington was found in a dazed condition, blood pouring from wounds on the head and face on a second floor stairway below his room. He had been beaten with a piece of a brick encased in prison-issue sock and had lost much blood. He died in the prison hospital on Wednesday, two days after the beating.

Lives Quietly in New York
Remington's Wife Known Only by Maiden Name

NEW YORK (AP) Nov. 24—The New York Post *quotes the wife of William W. Remington as saying he was attacked in prison by "a couple of hoodlums who got all worked up by all the publicity about Communists."*

. . . Mrs. Remington who married the slain former government employee between his first and second trials, lives under her maiden name with a blond 18-month-old son.

The Post *said Mrs. Remington, an ex-Washington newspaper-woman, consented to the interview only on condition her maiden name and the name of her child not be disclosed.*

Only a few neighbors and close friends know her identity, she said. She has an income from free-lance writing.

Talking with reporter Arthur Massalo after the beating of her husband, but prior to his death, Mrs. Remington, a slight, soft-spoken woman in her late 20s wore blue jeans, a sweater and loafers.

"The warden said Bill was an honor prisoner, sharing a dormitory with three other honor inmates," she related.

"Bill had been working the midnight-to-8-am shift as an attendant in the prison hospital.

"My husband thought he was getting along well with the other inmates. But there are strange people in penitentiaries and apparently outside, too."

She said she had not received permission to visit her husband after the beating.

"He's dying," she said at that time," and I can't do a thing to help him."

Remington is also survived by two children by his former wife. They are Bruce, 12, and Galeyn, 10.

Wilkes-Barre Times Leader, 25th November, 1954
. . . Prison officials said Remington was slugged early Monday morning while sleeping and that he apparently tried to reach the hospital below his room when he collapsed.

FBI Investigating Death of William Remington
LEWISBURG, PA (AP) Nov. 25—The New York Journal American *quoted Mrs. Remington as saying:*
"They killed him. They killed him because they thought he was a Communist. Oh my God, my God! No matter what they thought he never was a Communist."

For half an hour, Wendy remained sullen, quiet, brooding, but as soon as they again reached Route 202, headed east, her spirits seemed to pick up.

"Do you think in Priscilla's wildest dreams on that road trip in August 1937 she could've imagined her husband behind bars, that the man driving, Chambers, would, within two years, betray them, then write a book about them—testify about that very same trip to Fitzwilliam that both would deny ever happened?"

He glanced at her agitated face as she tapped her knees with calloused fingers, noting how these flashing mercurial emotions came on like sudden rain showers out of nowhere.

"What I don't get is why she and her husband insisted on joining Chambers in the first place. And why did Chambers agree to the two of them accompanying him on official underground business, breaching the most basic protocols of tradecraft—that agents be kept in the dark about each other? Chambers should have known better."

She let out a sudden whoop of pleasure and began dancing around in her seat, flinging her arms about like an excited child, as if to erase her recent melancholy ruminations.

This was hardly the first of such eruptions, but for the first time he began to wonder if she had a screw loose. It was as if some kind of transfusion had taken place: the way she channeled the girlish, even reckless, exuberance of a young Priscilla Hiss. The same careless exuberance Priscilla must have used to overpower the caution of her husband and Chambers's reticence, winning them over to the delights of a road trip through country she'd loved since childhood.

"It's the places don't you see, the names—she'd known them since she was a kid driving with her dad. Pennsylvania names—don't you just love them: West Goshen, Malvern, Paoli, Gwynedd . . . how the hell do you pronounce that?"

"She was a *Bryn Mawr* girl," he offered, her presence now seeming part of the same high-pressure system that had barreled through after the rain. Then responding to her earlier question about going to visit White, he added, "And of course they knew White—even if Chambers didn't know they knew him—a Volta Place regular."

"Doylestown and Lahaska and New Hope—oh, I love it. And the countryside is so beautiful." She stared longingly at a straggling tree line of gnarled white ash and sugar maples, like an awkward border of cinnamon-yellow stitching between two mismatched pieces in a quilt, a stubble of cornstalks in the foreground, straight furrows of plowed-under dirt beyond. "These farms and rolling hills can't really have changed that much in sixty-five years—you think? Didn't you like road trips as a kid?"

"My—Jimmy Altmann spent his life on the road."

"As a kid, my dad and I used to drive for hours to Enchanted Rock on the Big Sandy Creek, where Dad taught me to climb. Pink granite dome—a big beautiful pregnant mother of a thing, all four hundred and twenty-five feet of her. A geologist and chemical engineer—you see, he knew the country like the back of his hand. After taping up my scrapes and bruises, Dad would quiz me on my homework for hours there and back to Houston. We'd stop for dinner at his favorite restaurant in Austin, Barley Swine—ever had barbecued butternut squash?"

"Can't say that I have."

"To die for, at thirteen."

He heard the fluty quiver in her voice and knew not to pursue the subject directly.

"It was August, high summer. It would have been greener. Maybe they spent that missing day birding—that might have delayed them. Don't you think? Funny, for such an outdoors girl, you never got into birding."

"Not in the genes, I guess, the critter thing. God knows, we ran over enough rattlers on Texas Seventy-one—ugh! Horses, that's another matter. Mom was a horsewoman, Olympic-caliber, before she started climbing after marrying my Dad. I had my first orgasms at eight while learning to canter on an English saddle; the instructor called it polishing the saddle, keeping your pelvic bone in contact and not your tailbone."

———

Half an hour later they had reached the Delaware River.

"We need to take the bridge through New Hope to Lambertville; this part of 202, the toll bridge, has got to be brand-new, certainly since 1937."

"Hey, we're just a few miles from Princeton—a little detour for Professor Spier?"

"What I can't figure is why Chambers simply didn't have White send him the damn paper on Soviet monetary policy."

"Orders are orders . . . I guess. Hey, want to give me a tour of Tigertown over lunch—huh, Cool Hand Luke? The Astrophysics Department—that would be mighty cool: your stargazing days. Surely, in those days, your Epsilon Reticuli days, even Chambers and the Hisses must have stopped for lunch. And, hey, maybe Dr. Donald Spier can join us, like Weinstein suggested?"

"You're the most relentless, if not half-crazy, human being I've ever met."

"Lucky you never met my mother."

He handed her his phone.

"Dr. Spier's office number should still be on my contacts. Here's the deal: one shot, one call. If he's in and can see us now, we stop. If not, the subject is never broached again."

POWER OF UNIVERSE LOOSED AT JAPAN BY ATOMIC BOMB

Our Missle Has 20,000-Ton TNT Strength

SECRET ATOM BOMBS TO WIPE OUT JAPAN

LOOSE NEW TERROR BOMB

ATOMIC BOMB LOOSED AGAINST JAPANESE

U. S. Bares Use of Most Terrible Weapon

Deadly Atomic Bomb Hits Japan In Vast Sweep Of U.S. Planes

Revolutionary Weapon Enters Pacific Battle

Japanese Report Great Destruction And Huge Death Toll In Hiroshima

34

Now I am become Death, the destroyer of worlds

I find it unfair that you should be fighting the common enemy alone. If I can do anything to help you, you can count on me.

—Julius Rosenberg (Liberal) to his KGB handler,
Venona decrypt, fall of 1942

Intelligence on Liberal's wife. Surname that of her husband. Christian name Ethel 29 years old. Married 5 years. Finished middle school. A fellow countryman in 1938. Sufficiently well-developed politically. She knows about her husband's work and role of Meter and Nil. In view of her delicate health does not work.

—Venona decrypt (decrypted fully in July 1948)
of cable sent on November 27, 1944, from the
New York Station to Moscow Center

THE MOMENT WENDY made the call—in the soothing expectation of her voice, the insistent but carefree tone—George felt as if he'd slipped one gravitational field (Priscilla Hiss) for another. She was a woman used to having her way, of making her way, of making things happen. She was effortlessly relentless, going by pure unaffected instinct. And even though that constant pressure might be discomfiting at times, it was also a relief, to let oneself drift under the spell of such a temperament, the serenity of pure muscle memory. Her presence allowed him breathing room, as if surrounded by a warm current into which one might slip at the merest whim and see where it might take you: places where his mind was as yet unequipped to go. Like a narcotic, he sometimes mused, a sugar high with benefits.

——

Donald Spier was encamped in his office in the Astrophysics Department, seated at the same old battered desk he'd had since arriving at Princeton in 1947. Always a disaster zone, it was spilling over with battlements of journals and computer printouts. It could just as easily have been five years before, except he had definitely aged, nearing eighty, his mind all there, but without the same fight and energy. His wife of forty years had died the year before and George was devastated that such news had not reached him, that he could have been so out of touch—a letter from the department to his home in Woodstock remained unopened—with the man who had inspired him since he was a teenager.

"Well, George, of course, I was hoping against hope that your call"—Professor Spier smiled knowingly at Wendy—"represented a sudden conversion experience, Paul on the way to Damascus, and a need to return to the fold."

The old man had a long, sun-bleached face, gray hair to his shoulders, and bleary eyes that had witnessed the explosion of the first atomic bomb at Alamogordo, New Mexico, along with thousands of similar events in the farthest reaches of the universe.

"Oh, I've been working on him," said Wendy with an adoring smile. "I mean, half the time I don't get what he's talking about—the dark matter thing, the quantum weirdness thing. But he's wasting a lot of brainpower on running his gallery—great for me of course, but hey, he could do it in his sleep."

Days or even hours before, George would have rejected such talk out of hand. Now he just smiled, bathed in the paternal approval that had once meant the world to him. An office that had once seemed more like home than home.

"Ah," purred Professor Spier, half-amused, not a little hopeful, his pale, thin face again crinkling in a smile that shored up the lose skin at his cheeks and jawline. "Yes, dark matter and dark energy and the like—unsettling. Why we need him back." He glanced again at Wendy, sensing an ally. "With the upgrades at CERN coming online in the next few years, we should have some marvelous new data to work with—for young minds." His eyebrows reared above his metal-framed glasses, his pale gray eyes magnified, sparked with the dusky light of the millions of worlds he'd gazed upon for over fifty years. He was wearing the same nondescript jacket, white shirt with frayed collar, and thin hexagon-patterned tie that George had known him to wear year in and year out. "My mind, I fear, is pretty much exhausted. A young man's game, George. Plenty of good years left. You could leave the gallery for your dotage at fifty."

Wendy reached out like a proud mother and patted George's hand. "It's just the issue around his grandfather's memoir and the Hiss trial that's got him flummoxed right now."

"As I told your Mr. Weinstein, I got caught up—for my sins—in the Rosenberg investigation. I was barely conscious of the Alger Hiss fiasco at the time."

George, sheepish, felt a bit jittery in the familiar surroundings of a previous life, his eyes drawn again and again to the all so familiar photos from the Hubble telescope that adorned Donald Spier's office walls.

"My maternal grandfather, Edward Dimock, is struggling—he's ninety-five and on his last legs—with his role, his legacy, in the Hiss trial. The memoir dropped in my lap to edit. And even with the new conclusive evidence on Hiss's guilt, he feels somehow blinded, as if there was something happening, kind of like—you might say—spooky entanglement at a distance, something granular, a quantum field of forces beyond his reckoning that bore on the trial in ways he finds troubling. An ambiguity that for a legal mind like his is disconcerting, if only for the sheer invisibility of the thing. You see, he always raised me to be a stickler about facts, evidence to support your argument—a curiosity about how things work, how things happen—a confidence that cause and effect matter: matter and motion. That the larger patterns will be borne out in the details—that life is not a crapshoot. Not unlike you, Dr. Spier—or, dare I say, Einstein."

"Don't, please, George—Jesus, after all these years." He laughed, as if amused by an old joke, an age-old problem they'd knocked around since he could remember. "It's always the same—eh?—young man: that we can't measure both the position and momentum—stuck with a half-truth in favor of a statistical prediction, and a future we can, at best, feel our way toward. Yes"—he gestured at the document piles on his desk, the backs of his white hands showing raised blue veins—"I've returned to the Einstein camp these days. Perhaps it's an age thing: that there is a brass-bottom measurable reality out there."

"Yes," Wendy quickly noted, concerned where things were headed. "More—what we're looking for—kind of a feeling for the zeitgeist of the times that might have impinged on the case."

Donald Spier smiled gently, acknowledging her concern, and then nodded with a curious tilt of his head at his onetime advisee.

"In all our years, George, you never mentioned your grandfather, much less your father. Your brilliance was, well, sui generis—not to embarrass you or butter you up. Of course, it's all in your dissertation, the high-energy windows in the spectrum, the gamma ray bursts of high energy—mysterious, tantalizing little devils. Hopefully, the space-borne gamma ray telescopes in the offing will provide us with the data to prove your thesis." He jutted his wiry jaw toward his crammed book-shelf. "Maybe only a little updating will be required, and resubmission, and then your orals will be a triumphant breeze. You know, I still turn to your dissertation—not just for the substance, mind you, but for the youthful intrepidity of your theories, which reminds me so much of my early days—dare I say, my Los Alamos days . . . worst luck, when I was just finishing my postdoc at Chicago."

Well aware of the delicate subject, George said, "Still, you must have been thrilled to have been picked for the Manhattan Project—working with Oppenheimer and Fermi."

"Honored." He smiled, his lower lip drooping to one side. "I was a lot younger than you, George. It was a privilege to work with that caliber of scientists, to do fundamental research into fission energy, even if camped out in the middle of nowhere. To help the war effort and not be drafted. I was so filled with intellectual curiosity that the fact we were building a plutonium bomb that could wipe out an entire city never entered my head until we actually tested the damn thing. Then it got very real. Not a day goes by that I don't stare at some photograph of a distant star cluster and find myself reminded that we brought something of the energy of those distant suns to bear on Mother Earth. Perhaps a crime against humanity, stealing the power of the gods. And after Nagasaki—that was the plutonium bomb I worked on," he added, nodding at Wendy as if in explanation—"I swore I'd never go near the government or atomic research again." He gestured around at his office. "I wanted to get as far away from the government or politics as possible."

George nodded sympathetically. "And yet they came back to you?"

"They bamboozled me is what. Barged though my door right here in Princeton, the FBI did, first threatening, then cajoling, then practically pleading for my help. Their lead investigator, a guy named Bob Lamphere—smart, intense fellow, a cop with a law degree, cagey as hell, on a mission—wanted to know, and in a hurry, about a lot of my colleagues at Los Alamos. Personal stuff. Politics. I figured out pretty quickly that they were looking for someone who had spilled the beans. Which I found, as I told Bob at the time, almost laughable, considering the level of security, the isolation we worked under. But he seemed pretty sure of himself, and pretty damn desperate—unsettlingly so. Like maybe I, too, was on their list of suspected traitors. Once he decided I was safe, Bob began to look to me for technical advice about the development of the bombs and who was involved with which processes, the critical breakthroughs and so on."

"When was this?" asked George.

"Late 1947 into 1948 and 1949. I kind of got to like Bob. I was impressed by how much an FBI man already knew about people I knew, people I respected, friends. It was a little bizarre, let me tell you—talk about a quantum field from out of the past in which the goal posts kept moving, a bunch of unstable particles—human beings if you will, a snapshot in time, in which I was being asked to predict where certain people might have turned up, what information they might have communicated, and the probabilities of how it might correspond with a future, our then present, which was less of a mystery and more a probable nightmare."

George cocked his head. "You mean identifying the atomic spies, Harry Gold and David Greenglass, who helped convict his sister and brother-in-law, Ethel and Julius Rosenberg?"

"We were just there, at Lewisburg," murmured Wendy, as if unsettled by one more coincidence. She turned to the windows, gazing at the spires of Princeton's Gothic campus.

"Never knew them, of course," said Spier, following her stare for a moment. "Lamphere, he was quite a fellow, square-jawed, a straight shooter about the crisis they faced. Bob got me down to Washington, to FBI headquarters, put a hand on my shoulder, looked me in the eye, and asked me to sign a document swearing me to secrecy. I wasn't happy; it was a little like Los Alamos all over again, and the stakes—at least for me—were a lot higher, but I did it for Bob because I could see he was taking a chance on me—God knows, they were desperate enough. He then drove me to an army intelligence center in Arlington, a place that had once been a school for girls. There I met their decryption expert, Meredith Gardner, both a linguist and mathematician. Brilliant fellow—genius, spoke at least a dozen languages fluently, taught himself Yiddish when he was eight—the kind of brain that feeds on its own accumulations of knowledge. I identified with Meredith, the struggle with the near-infinite permutations in the decryption process; they called it 'Venona.'

"When I met him on my first day in D.C., he'd been working for at least a couple of years on the Soviet cables that had been collected from the war years. You see, they had been collecting the things from Western Union and the like during the war, but without being able to read them. Then with the Cold War, the intelligence boys made a huge effort to break the code and decipher them. Progress had been painfully slow and frustrating until they got Meredith on the case, and by 1948 Meredith had broken enough cables that they began to suspect that the Manhattan Project had been infiltrated by Soviet spies and critical information conveyed to Moscow. Meredith showed me one of his decrypted cables from June 15, 1944, in which the New York KGB guy informed Moscow that he'd received from an individual with the code name Rest the third part of Report SN-12 Efferent Fluctuation in a Stream—the gaseous diffusion method for producing plutonium. I couldn't believe what I was seeing; it took me back four years to that hot summer in Los Alamos, to that incredible moment when all our hard work had finally paid off. Bob and Meredith could see it in my eyes; I guess I must have looked like I'd seen a ghost, a ghost of a ghost. 'How bad?' asked Bob. 'If they had the full report, they had everything they needed to produce a plutonium bomb, like the bomb we dropped on Nagasaki.' Meredith showed me another deciphered cable. He said the Soviets called the project they were trying to infiltrate 'Enormoz.'"

"How did you feel?" asked George. "To find all your work, well, stolen—betrayed by colleagues you had trusted."

"Fortunately, not my colleagues. It was the strangeness of the thing, seated in the dark room at a table with only Bob and Meredith, and a few scraps of paper, words pulled out of the ether from four years before and only now coming to light—in Russian, of course: words, repeated patterns, code names, fragments of lost time, details on the wind, but details that raised the hair on the back of my neck. Bob, in particular, was sweating with nervous exhaustion—his career was on the line. Meredith was like a dog with a bone, gnawing out letter after letter after letter. I remember coming up with an analogue, not unlike what I was doing every day, staring into the past, gathering data on events millions of light-years in the past—a supernova perhaps, except in this case, it was more like detecting an asteroid that had broken free of its orbit in the Kuiper Belt. Perhaps only boulder size, or perhaps a mile wide, but a ghost against the blackness, invisible, lost to view, but you knew the damn thing was out there because it was no longer in its old orbit, and might well be on a collision course with Earth."

George looked at his adviser with a sullen squint. "The Soviets had the technical data on how to build a plutonium bomb and you guys were wondering when it was going to explode."

"It was like living the nightmare of Heisenberg's uncertainty principle. We—Bob and Meredith and I—were staring at the scanty bits of evidence, trying to make out the telltale patterns, and yet no matter what we did, our observations seemed to come up short, as if the data were distorted, dancing before our eyes, refusing our predictions, thwarting a usable—Bob's word was *actionable*—outcome, denied access to the present moment and what we feared was coming. Meredith and his team labored eighteen hours a day, working against the clock we knew was ticking to identify the traitor in our midst and the couriers who transmitted the stolen documents to Moscow."

"Gold and Greenglass . . ." murmured Wendy, her eyes withdrawn as if seeing the picture being painted in her mind.

"They had me down to Arlington every few weeks, where Meredith shared newly deciphered cables with me, even those only partly deciphered, to see if anything popped out. Code names, details about people I might have known, fleeting references to places and things. I had this ridiculously naïve idea that science was above politics, the result of my Midwestern background, which I shared with both Bob and Meredith. I racked my brains, but I couldn't draw any connection between the code names in the cables and the snippets of information about them—presumably colleagues I might have known. The worst part, I began having nightmares, plagued with doubt, starting to believe the worst about people I'd worked with for years."

Donald Spier slumped back in his chair, removing his glasses to rub his tired, bleary eyes. And as he did so, George glimpsed in the old man's face something he'd never expected to see, something he'd never quite imagined in all the years he'd worked under his adviser: a young man about the same age as he was, confronted with a paradox: the thing he'd loved turned to bile in his heart. For a moment, stunned, he turned to the office windows, to the flickering yellow in the fall trees of the campus, the Gothic crenellations of Firestone Library, students jostling their way to classes: happy memories of that younger self when curiosity ruled his life, when he hung out to all hours, avidly pouring over the latest data from the Hubble telescope. Returning his gaze again to Spier, who was still fumbling with his glasses, he grasped like second sight how a young man's thirst for knowledge, the spell of curiosity might indeed be weaponized, translated into the crown jewels—contested over—murdered over—without hesitation or remorse. Tears welled in his eyes as he resisted the impulse to rise from his seat and embrace the old man he was to become. Wendy reached a steadying hand to his.

"Having your work hijacked is one thing," said George barely above a murmur, "but finding out people you worked with, whom you respected . . ."

Spier, his face lifting at the tenor of his onetime student's voice, fumbled to replace his glasses and attempted a wan smile as he returned George's stare, brows pinched, as if now aware of something he hadn't noticed before—sparking yet more memories. He nodded with all the vigor of a younger man.

"Yes, yes, it was hellish. That little room, that table strewn with half-decoded messages, coffee cups and Coke bottles—just the three of us—and I was expected to cast my memory like a net into that cryptic sea of words and come up with a real name, a flesh and blood person, our Judas. We drank coffee, Meredith consumed endless Cokes, and Bob smoked like a fiend. And all the while I searched down and down into memories then four years old and fading, changing each time I accessed them. Bob was always pacing, going nuts; he had half a dozen surveillance teams out following possible suspects, phone taps—you name it. Most were based on the flimsiest of clues. We knew we were in a race against time—against the KGB, which must have gotten wind that the FBI was after its agents and informers. Bob had to assume the agents in the Venona decrypts were still active, still passing on secrets.

"I remember Bob turning to me, his blue eyes wide with desperation. 'How long would it take them to build the bomb if they had all this information in '44?' he asked. I could only shrug, thinking of the millions of dollars and tens of thousands of man-hours on the part of the most brilliant minds of our generation, the hundreds of blind alleys and sudden breakthroughs it took to find the right techniques to produce enough plutonium, the engineering challenges to produce a chain reaction. I think I had tears in my eyes when I answered, whether out of guilt or sense of betrayal or perhaps fear. 'Four years ago: any day now, anytime.'"

"When was this, still 1948?" George asked.

"Oh, the leaves were down, so it must have been the fall of 1948. They had me down to Washington and Arlington Hall at least once a month by then—maybe a dozen times, right through 1949. During that period, Meredith decrypted more and more cables describing materials being transmitted from Operation Enormoz." Spier shook his head in disgust. "By the time Meredith was done, years later, we realized it was worse than we'd even imagined. In 1944–1945, KGB agents Alexander Feklisov and Anatoly Yatskov, who handled Rosenberg's network out of New York, delivered about three thousand pages of stolen technical documents to Moscow Center. These were turned over to the Soviets' Special Committee, known as Laboratory Number 2—precisely what they needed to construct a Soviet A-bomb. My estimate in 1948 turned out to be off by less than a year: We detected their first atomic test in September of 1949. It shocked the bejesus out of Bob, the White House, the military— everybody was in a panic. Bob and Meredith had to redouble their efforts; the FBI and army intelligence were given untold millions in funding to find the traitors before they could do any more damage. Even on the outside, in the corridors of Arlington Hall, in Bob's office at FBI headquarters, I could feel the frenzy, the fear."

"My God!" exclaimed Wendy, who had been quiet and pensive for many minutes. "September 1949 was the run-up to the second Hiss trial."

Donald Spier looked into her face, the hint of alarm in her flashing eyes. "Ah, your atmosphere . . . the frenzy—hardly zeitgeist, I think."

"When did you nail down the data, the clues to Greenglass, Gold, the Rosenbergs?"

"Oh, they came later—nothing of my doing—it was the Los Alamos traitor, he came first. I believe it was early 1949, when Meredith broke a cable in which Rest—code name for the spy who had passed on the paper on the gaseous diffusion process—was described as part of a British contingent of scientists brought over in 1943 to help on the Manhattan Project; and later a note to Moscow by his handler that he had a sister in Chicago he'd visited over Christmas. 'Did you ever hear about a British physicist at Los Alamos who had a sister in Chicago?' Bob asked me. I thought and thought, and the vaguest of vague memories percolated up, sometime near the end of my tenure at Los Alamos, a Christmas party and one of the British scientists, Klaus Fuchs, asking me about Chicago, where I'd done my postdoc studies at the university. He wanted to know what he should see in Chicago when he visited his sister for Christmas. I knew Fuchs more by reputation than from a close working relationship. But I always thought of him as German— his accent, not British, and something about his being a Quaker, about how Quakers celebrate Christmas. 'The Art Institute,' I told him. 'Not to be missed.' Bob just closed his eyes and shook his head, and then he nodded to Meredith. Bob had believed it was the head of the British contingent, Rudolf Peierls. But that turned out to be wrong. They had Gestapo files on Fuchs; he had been a rabid Communist and had escaped from Germany to England by the skin of his teeth. Bob looked at me with tears of frustration, if not fear. 'The son of a bitch is now back in England and he's still working in the most top-secret nuclear research lab in the UK.' That broke it. From there, they worked their way back to Gold, Greenglass, and ultimately the Rosenbergs—Julius actually passed on the secret material to his Soviet handlers in New York."

"So the Hiss trial must've meant almost nothing to you—to the FBI?"

Donald Spier shrugged. "I was oblivious, of course. For Bob and the FBI boys, the national security crisis was about Fuchs and closing down the Rosenbergs. For Soviet intelligence, it was about doing everything to save their networks, to protect their people, to preserve access to secrets. The stakes were huge, what with the development of the hydrogen bomb in the offing. I don't know what was worse, that the genie we'd conjured had been stolen, or that the bottle was now also in the hands of another power—namely, Stalin, who would have had no compunction about using such a weapon to his advantage. They had Fuchs in their sights, but his enablers were still out there, possibly still turning over more information from sources as yet unrevealed. Meanwhile, the KGB was trying to protect them or get them out of the country and safely behind the Iron Curtain. There was a behind-the-scenes race going on between the FBI and the KGB, one to uncover and capture the spies and their enablers, the other to keep them in play, to keep the technology flowing, or get their people out of the country and safe from arrest."

George glanced at Wendy, barely disguising the frustration in his voice. "And on January 21, 1950, Alger Hiss was convicted of perjury, for passing State Department secrets to Whittaker Chambers—from the late 1930s."

Donald Spier noted the tone of his former student's voice and shrugged. "I believe it was sometime in January 1950 that Fuchs finally confessed to British intelligence. It took another few years for Bob to run down the Rosenbergs and the others. By then—thank God—I'd exhausted my usefulness. I was only glad that it hadn't been my immediate colleagues, other Americans. And that none of the information I provided helped in the Rosenberg case. Not that they didn't deserve to be convicted and go to jail. But execution, I don't know. Certainly not Ethel, not a woman with two kids. It shook Bob and Meredith up, as well; Bob did everything in his power to prevent their execution. He went to Hoover and pleaded his case. Hoover had the sentencing judge, Irving Kaufman, explicitly inform Julius and Ethel that if they cooperated with the FBI, that if they revealed the names of their recruits and other information, the death sentences would be rescinded and they'd only do jail time. But they wouldn't budge; they wouldn't admit anything, not a word. They had FBI agents with pen and pads outside their cells on death row, pleading with them to save themselves, to just give up the basic facts about their spy networks and who their Soviet handlers were. But to no avail. As Bob put it to me years later, when I visited him while attending a conference in Washington, 'Julius and Ethel were either the most iron-willed ideologues of all time, taking orders from their handlers to fall on their swords for the cause of world revolution, or their handlers had let them know in no uncertain terms that they and their children would be killed if they talked.' Bob gazed right through me when he told me this, with genuine sorrow, I believe, and shook his head in despair: 'I'm not sure which option would have taken more courage.'

"I remember Bob's bitter laugh when he said, 'All Moscow would have needed to do was own up that the Rosenbergs had assisted in the great battle against fascism during the war; that would have been enough of a signal to Julius and Ethel that they could freely confess.' And it wasn't as if the KGB didn't try to get their people out. Bob tracked down one guy in Mexico City and got him extradited and sentenced. Greenglass and his wife were given money and orders to flee to

Mexico, but his nerves failed him; his wife was ailing. But those KGB operatives had their own necks on the line: They told agents, 'If you are caught, you don't open your mouth under any circumstances.' That was the discipline. As Bob put it, 'Confession was not part of the deal.'"

Wendy turned from the window and attempted a smile for their host.

"We were just in Lewisburg three hours ago, where Alger Hiss was imprisoned, along with Harry Gold, David Greenglass, and William Remington."

Donald Spier cocked his head as if trying to recall a vague memory.

"Remington . . . Remington. Bob's FBI boys investigated that man's murder; I remember him talking about it years later. Bob was with the CIA by then. We were having dinner at an Italian restaurant in D.C., the Roma, on Connecticut Avenue. Bob told me they could never get to the bottom of the Remington case. Three punks with no motive that made sense. Bob wondered if it might be payback for the execution of the Rosenbergs, or a warning to the others in Lewisburg to keep their mouths shut. As Bob put it, 'The KGB has a long memory; they never forget.'"

New Jersey Rites Held for Remington

RIDGEWOOD, N.J. (AP) Nov. 27, 1954—William W. Remington today received the last rites of the Episcopal Church in simple funeral services in the small stucco house of worship of his boyhood.

Fifty persons, including his widow and mother, attended the 12-minute service for the 37-year-old convicted perjurer in St. Elizabeth's Church, three blocks from the home of his parents. He was described as brilliant, top man in his class at Dartmouth, always full of youthful enthusiasm—that sadly got away from him.

Six policemen stood guard outside the church because according to patrolman Nick Lembo, anonymous phone calls of a threatening nature had been made to the funeral home and the rector of the church.

There were no untoward incidents, however.

Seated in the first pew of the nearly-full church were Remington's second wife, Mrs. James Remington; his mother, Mrs. Frederick C. Remington . . . Lembo said Remington's 78-year-old father was too grief-stricken to attend.

The widow, dressed in a gray alpaca coat and black hat, wept quietly during the brief service.

35
Lunch at the Old Ebbitt Grill

So I called White from a drug or cigar store near the Treasury. White was not surprised that I should tell him over the telephone where to meet me, though I would never have done this in the old days. He said he would be right down. He was delighted to see me. "Back on a little trip to inspect the posts?" he asked cheerily. White, I concluded, had not been told about my break.

We started walking. I set the course and he came along just as in the past. We went to a candy and soda shop, sat down at the back and ordered coffee. White, with whom my relations had never been particularly friendly, was never so communicative. He talked, as usual, about "the Secretary" (Henry Morgenthau), about George Silverman, but not about the apparatus. I did not ask him about it. But at some point, he asked me: "Are you coming back to Washington to work?" I answered to this effect though I no longer remember the exact words: "No, I am not coming back to Washington to work. I am not here 'to inspect the posts.' The fact is that I have broken with the Communist Party and I am here to break you away from the apparatus. If you do not break, I will denounce you."

Harry White was a nervous man. At first he merely bent over his coffee and said nothing. Then he tried the "you don't really mean that" rejoinder. I left him in no doubt that I meant that. I do not remember the rest of the conversation. I doubt that we said much more. I remember only that we were both embarrassed and that that made me stiff and probably grim . . . I never saw him again. For some time, I thought that I had surely frightened White out of the underground. Certainly the flow of documents from the Treasury must have dried up temporarily. But, according

to Elizabeth Bentley, White was active again in her apparatus a
few years later.

—Whittaker Chambers, *Witness*
(Harry Dexter White meeting, 1938)

IT IS MAY 13, 1941, nearly two years after Stalin signed the Nazi-Soviet alliance, dividing up Poland and allowing the Soviets a free hand in Finland and the Baltics, when Vitalii Pavlov arrives in Washington fresh from Moscow. Germany has conquered most of Europe and is mopping up resistance in Yugoslavia and Greece, while the majority of Nazi forces are assembled and poised on the eastern borders of Poland and Hungary for Operation Barbarossa, the invasion of Russia, which will take place a month later, on June 21. In Washington, Pavlov, the new legal Soviet agent of the NKVD, makes a call from a pay phone on the street to Harry Dexter White in the Treasury Department to arrange an important lunch meeting at the Old Ebbitt Grill. Four years before, Whittaker Chambers thought White had heeded his warning to quit the Washington apparatus run by Soviet military intelligence, the GRU. White did nothing of the sort. A year later, the NKVD took over White from the GRU and integrated White into its fast-expanding Washington apparatus. White, nervous as ever, reluctantly agrees to the meeting. Pavlov is young, blond, and handsome, and barely speaks passable English; he has barely finished training as an NKVD agent; Stalin, after eliminating most of his experienced NKVD operatives, is now scraping the bottom of the barrel for agents to handle the hundreds of spies in place throughout the U.S. government. Stalin finds it hard to believe Hitler will attack anytime soon, notwithstanding detailed Soviet intelligence about the massive Nazi buildup on Russia's western flank. The NKVD knows better and fears, above all things, a two-front war and a Japanese attack on the Soviet Union's exposed eastern flank in Asia. The NKVD has been grooming White (along with agents in Japan and China) for years in anticipation of this eventuality. When Whittaker Chambers ran White from 1933 to 1937, he provided top-level secret intelligence on U.S. relations with Japan and China, a White specialty, and prime focus of the Treasury Department, which handles relations with Japan on such crucial matters as trade, raw material embargoes, and immigration policy—not to mention military and financial support to the Nationalists fighting both the Japanese and Mao's Communist guerillas.

Vitalii Pavlov takes a table at the Old Ebbitt Grill and places a copy of *The New Yorker* by his plate, as described in his phone call to White. It's a warm day, even for May in Washington, and air-conditioning has yet to find its way to this famous Washington watering hole, and so Pavlov finds himself sweating profusely, knowing that much more than just his career is on the line. He is relieved that he seems to be the only blond patron—how he'd described himself to White—during the busy luncheon hour. When Harry Dexter White walks in, Pavlov identifies him immediately from the description provided by his predecessor, Iskhac Akhmerov, (known as "Bill" to White) White's previous GRU handler (post Chambers), now in Moscow, facing an uncertain fate. White is of medium height, a bit overweight, with a mustache not unlike that of Hitler (a man White already holds in pathological contempt) and wearing metal-framed round glasses. Although nearing fifty, White has an almost childlike face, ruddy cheeks, and a sometimes timid manner that makes him look slightly younger. He wears an impeccable charcoal gray suit and spiffy tie. Pavlov and White exchange pleasantries as they search for common ground and a safe point of departure for this important conversation.

Pavlov, only twenty-seven and very much in awe of the highly placed White, apologizes for his broken English and tells two quick lies in succession. He says he's just come back from China, where he's spent too many years, where he had recently spoken to White's old friend "Bill" (Akhmerov), who is temporarily stationed in China. Pavlov has never been to China and Akhmerov is confined to Moscow; under suspicion as a traitor, he faces possible execution if this operation does not pan out as hoped.

—

"Bill has told me a little bit about you," Pavlov says. "He asked me for a favor, which I willingly granted. He emphasized that I should try to be very genuine and that it was impossible to postpone the message until he returns home and can meet you."

"When is Bill coming to the USA?" asks White.

"Bill wants to come back as soon as possible, no later than the end of this year (if he hasn't been executed by then). He is trying to figure out the American and Japanese attitudes. The expansion of Japan into

Asia has him constantly alert. This is why he asked me to meet you, only if you don't object, to get acquainted with the idea that he's most involved with right now."

"I had a good impression of Bill when I met him a couple of years ago. He's obviously a very wise person. I'll be glad to listen to you."

"I must apologize again for my lack of English knowledge," says Pavlov, dipping into his coat pocket and producing a folded piece of paper, which he then passes across the table to White, who unfolds it and begins reading. Pavlov watches intently and notes the look of astonishment and apprehension in White's eyes.

White then looks up. "I'm amazed at the concurrence of my own ideas with what Bill thinks, according to this." White a little breathless, his perspiring face a bit pale, tries to tuck the note into his breast pocket but is stopped when Pavlov sticks out his hand and indicates he wants the note returned.

"I'm going to China in a couple of days, and Bill wishes to know your opinion. In fact, he is so worried whether he is going to see a management of the USA of the Japanese threat, and whether something will be done to bridle the Asian aggressor."

With just a touch of a nervous stutter, White replies, "You can tell Bill from me, I'm very grateful for the ideas that correspond to my own about that specific region . . . I've already started to think about what is possible and what is necessary to undertake . . . and I believe with the support or a well-informed expert, I can undertake necessary efforts in the necessary direction . . . Did you understand everything I just said?"

"You are grateful of ideas that correspond with your own about that specific region . . . You have already started to think about what is possible and what is necessary to undertake . . . and you believe with the help of a well-informed expert, you can undertake necessary efforts in the necessary direction."

White nodded his head in appreciation: "Karasho," he said in Russian with an American accent, "your memorization is very good . . . Let me pay for lunch . . . I ordered it."

—Operation Snow: Half a Century at
KGB Foreign Intelligence by Vitalii Pavlov

—

The note passed by Pavlov to White contained an outline of the critical points of Operation Snow (White), a Soviet plan to influence U.S. foreign policy with the intended effect of redirecting hostile Japanese military moves away from Soviet territory and forces in the Far East, and so thwarting a feared northern thrust into Manchuria and the Soviet maritime territory bordering the China Sea. The hope was to encourage a southern Japanese strategy, to prompt military expansion southward by attacking and capturing territories in the Philippines and Dutch Indonesia, and so secure the critical oil and raw materials already scarce due to the pressure of U.S. sanctions and embargoes.

A few days after his meeting with Pavlov, White would compose a long memo recommending in the strongest terms a reconfiguring of U.S. diplomacy toward Japan in such a way as to incrementally bring about this end, on the one hand offering relief from embargoes while also requiring Japanese withdrawal from China and other strategic concessions to U.S. power in the Pacific that would be totally unacceptable to the Japanese military. Although this first memo would have little immediate effect in the month or so before the German invasion of the Soviet Union in spring 1941, White would produce yet another memo soon after, calling for a dramatic hardening of U.S. opposition to Japanese aggression in China, while threatening more sanctions of critical supplies of oil, rubber, and steel. Enlisting the fervent support of Treasury Secretary Morgenthau, White and his Treasury associates, many of them either members of the Communist Party or Soviet spies and agents of influence, would begin the process of ratcheting up U.S. pressure on Japan in a more forthright and aggressive manner. In this they were abetted by Soviet spy Lauchlin Currie in the White House, right hand to FDR's closest adviser on foreign policy, Harry Hopkins, and Alger Hiss at State, who would help lay the groundwork for a shift in American diplomacy in Asia with his State Department bosses. By late 1941, the cumulative pressure on U.S. foreign policy exerted by White, Morgenthau, Currie, Hopkins, and Alger Hiss—and the rash actions of Dean Acheson (unilaterally toughening sanctions)—would result in further oil sanctions and a State Department stance hostile to what the Japanese considered their vital interests. This, despite the pleadings of top U.S. naval brass that the navy was unprepared for a war against Japan in the Pacific, especially given that war against Germany in the Atlantic theater seemed imminent. After numerous attempts at meetings to head off a confrontation with the United States, the

Japanese government under Emperor Hirohito then agreed to abandon a northern thrust into Manchuria and the Soviet Union for a southern strategy in the Pacific to secure the raw materials upon which Japan's survival depended, a decision that precipitated the long-planned surprise attack on Pearl Harbor. And so, at a crucial moment, when the Soviet Union was reeling under a Nazi invasion in the West, Operation Snow (embraced and championed by White) proved a lifesaver for Stalin and the Soviet Union, preventing the catastrophic eventuality of fighting a two-front war with both Germany and Japan.

Ex-Official,
Spy Inquiry
Figure, Dies

FITZWILLIAM, N. H., (AP)—He and Harry H. re also the only ones who had never been mbers of the Americ nist Party.

'hite preferred his ro ider, independent fellow traveler, a frie of the Soviet Unic ingly made a speci ing what was best ns in Moscow, ot subject to Party Which always annoye er,

ttaker Chambers rced to indulge W us breaches of securi he only knew as Carl s prickly independel mann perfectly captur spectacled cherubic fa d-mannered mustache ial (White's secretar surv colleagues often im about the brush which resembled While in the Justice nt mural, finished a White's face is thin alized'

CAREER ENDS—H
White, former Treasury
cused in spy inquiry, suc

Figure In S
Inquiry Die

FITZWILLIAM, N. H.,
—(AP)—Harry Dexter
who had gathered at
Place that day in Septe
1937 five later died sud
unexpectedly, in middle
of those five, only Harry D
White was the victim of
attack—natural causes,
sort.

Charges Recalled
He and Harry Hopkins w
so the only ones of the
ho had never been form
mbers of the Americ
nmunist Party. White pl
ed his role as an outside
ependent operator, fello
eler, a friend and ally of th
t Union who seemingl
a specialty of decidin
was best for his patrons
cow. And so he was not
to Party discipline.
always annoyed his
Whittaker Chambers
as forced to indulge
frivolous breaches of
whom he only knew
was this prickly in
ce that Altmann
aptured in the be
cherubic face of a
ered mustached
(White's secretary
y colleagues often
about the brush
hich resembled
e in the Justice
ural, finished a
te's face is thin
ealized, if not
leological cer
nothing of the
nercurial tem
ed by Cham
ny meetings.
e deceiving:

WHERE HARRY DEXTER WHITE DIED—White's
Summer home at Fitzwilliam, N. H.
days after testif

White, Quizzed in Spy Probe, Dies Suddenly

Boston, Aug. 17 (A.P.)—Harry Dexter White, 56 former Assistant Secretary of the Treasury, accused of Soviet espionage activity during the current spy hearings in Washington, died unexpectedly at his Fitzwilliam, N. H., summer home late yesterday, it was disclosed today.

The economist, who helped draw up the Bretton Woods monetary agreement and had a hand in drafting the

Harry Dexter White
Dies Suddenly

so-called "Morganthau plan" for postwar Germany, succumbed after a heart seizure.

It was a recurrence of a disorder which he said was troubling him when he testified before the House Un-American Activities Committee last week.

Wife With Him.

At the hearings, White denied he had been a member of "an elite Red underground group" and that he supplied information to a Soviet espionage network. He returned from Washington Friday.

He suffered the fatal heart seizure at 5:45 P. M. yesterday. His wife and a local physician were with him during his last hours.

His body was brought to Boston to await funeral services and private burial. Rabbi Irving Mandell of Temple Israel will conduct services Thursday.

A Harvard graduate, White went to work fot the Treasury in 1934 and rose rapidly. He bacame director of the monetary research division in 1934 and was appoointed Assistant Secretary under Secretary Henry Morgenthau Jr., Jan. 3, 1945.

In denying charges at the committee hearing Friday, White said he was reco vering from a heart seizure and asked for a 10-minute recess after each hour of testimony. White demanded and was granted permission to deny the charges against him under oath.

He termed the accusations "unqualifiedly false" and added:

"The principles under whihc I live make it impossible for me to do a disloyal act to the United States."

He had been doubly accused.

Miss Elizabeth T. Bentley said White was one of 30 wartime Government officials who fed information to a Soviet spy ring for which she was courier.

"Going Places."

Magazine editor Whittaker Chambers, a former Communist, said White was a "fellow traveler" and that he belonged to an underground group set up by foreign agents among persons "who appeared to be going places" in the Government.

After the hearing White stopped at New York en route to Fitzwilliam and consulted a physician, who said ther was evidence in the hearing had weakened him and advised him to rest. White wnet to bed immediatly upon reaching his Summer home.

A native of Boston, White was a World War I veteran.

arry Whit
ies Under
Red' Cloud

FZWILLIAM, N.H.—(A and Harry Hopkins the only ones of the had never been fo nbers of the Amer nmunist Party. White red his role as an outs ependent operator, f veler, a friend and ally c viet Union who seem ade a specialty of dec at was best for his pat Moscow. And so he wa bject to Party disci hite's secretary and Trea olleagues often kidded bout the brush must hich resembled Hitler).

• • •

MISS BENTLEY had tes hat White through his Treasury position had h Communist agents by pu certain Government empl toward key positions they could gain secret mation.

White had been a depart ment, monetary expert for a dozen years.

He went to Washington in

36
Crime Scene: Harry Dexter White

The distinction between past, present, and future is only a stubbornly persistent illusion.

—Albert Einstein, 1955

You know I live in a remarkable country, Allen, we can predict the future and understand the present perfectly, but the past . . . the past keeps changing every day.

—remark made to Allen Weinstein
in Moscow by a Soviet historian

OUT OF THE ten, including George Altmann, who had gathered at Volta Place that day in September 1937, five later died suddenly, unexpectedly, in middle age; of those five, only Harry Dexter White was the victim of heart attack—natural causes, of a sort. He and Harry Hopkins were also the only ones of the ten who had never been formal members of the American Communist Party. White preferred his role as an outsider, independent operator, fellow traveler, a friend and ally of the Soviet Union who seemingly made a specialty of deciding what was best for his patrons in Moscow. And so he was not subject to Party discipline. Which always annoyed his handler, Whittaker Chambers (who was forced to indulge White's frivolous breaches of security), whom he only knew as Carl. It was this prickly independence that Altmann perfectly captured in the bespectacled cherubic face of a mild-mannered mustached intellectual (White's secretary and

Treasury colleagues often kidded him about the brush mustache, which resembled Hitler's). While in the Justice Department mural, finished a year later, White's face is thinner, harder, idealized, if not aglow with ideological certainty. There is nothing of the fragile ego and mercurial temperament detected by Chambers in their many meetings. But looks could be deceiving: White had a venomous temper and an overweening ambition, matched only by his faith that economic policy—the great lever and skyhook of civilization for any Marxist economist—could be used to shape a more just and equal world.

Sitting in that charmed circle at Volta Place, as an economic adviser at the Treasury under Henry Morgenthau, he knew that he and Harry Hopkins were the highest-ranking members of the government in the Volta Place group. Even if Alger Hiss and his feisty wife ruled the roost of dues-paying Communists at Volta Place on that fine September afternoon, White seemed to savor his independence and access to power. He was biding his time, slowly but surely packing the Treasury Department with his GRU acolytes, while the true levers of power hovered at his fingertips in the person of his boss, Treasury Secretary Morgenthau, a fellow Jew and Hyde Park crony of Roosevelt. Morgenthau, paradoxically or not, was the weakest, least experienced member of FDR's cabinet, and yet he had the greatest sway over the president, with the possible exception of Harry Hopkins.

No one bathed in that sumptuous bamboo-filtered sunlight at Volta Place could have predicted that this Harvard Ph.D. by way of Stanford, from poor Eastern European Jewish roots, a brilliant economist, would eventually rise to the exalted position of assistant secretary at Treasury, while being served by a cabal of Soviet spies on his staff, allowing him to champion Operation Snow, and later go on to formulate the Breton Woods Agreement on international monetary policy, and later still plans for the IMF and World Bank. Henry Morgenthau, barely a second-rate intellect, had no idea—no clue, even as in the years to come he became increasingly reliant on White's every recommendation, rubber-stamping his policy papers (many with the backing of Lauchlin Currie and Harry Hopkins in the White House, Hiss at State, and at least seven other NKVD-GRU spies in the Treasury Department). It was White who first aligned, then guided the Treasury to near-sycophantic support of the interests of the Soviet Union from 1939 to 1946, all the while promoting Mao and the Chinese Communists over Chiang Kai-shek and the Nationalists. In many respects, he outgunned Alger Hiss's subterfuges at Yalta.

Not even Whittaker Chambers, who ran White like he ran Alger Hiss for Soviet military intelligence, ever grasped the full extent of damage to American interests caused by White and his confederates—the most damning, the most terrible proof of which was now contained in the file Weinstein had handed George, an excerpt from the as yet unpublished memoir of White's NKVD handler, Vitalii Pavlov (who had replaced Iskhak Akhmerov in 1939, who'd replaced Chambers in 1937). As Chambers noted in *Witness*, perhaps he had just been looking for White's motives in all the wrong places; and so he, too, missed the tragic train wreck of disaster from Pearl Harbor to the Morgenthau Plan, from the abandonment of Poland at Yalta and the monstrosity of human suffering that became Operation Keelhaul, to the three-billion-dollar cash giveaway to the Soviets in postwar Germany, and, last but not least, Mao's ultimate triumph.

When, the night after meeting with Donald Spier, George and Wendy read the translation of the Pavlov excerpt detailing White's meeting with his new handler in May of 1941 at the Old Ebbitt Grill, their conception of that gathering at Volta Place began to shift once more, like a grainy home movie out of the thirties run backward, in which White's face, as he sat next to his comrade and fellow Harvard economist and Treasury colleague Lauchlin Currie, took on a different cast of light, darker, insidious, not quite that pleasant afternoon at Volta Place of just days before.

They then began to see a harder intensity in the eyes and in the sallow round face of the man wearing a western-style bandanna in the mural, a Harry Dexter White seeming more petulant, proud, pushy, and perhaps skittish, depending on how well his boss, Secretary of the Treasury Henry Morgenthau, had been treating him that day or that week. White might have thought he was the smartest man in the room, but he knew that his power to influence was directly tied to the gullibility of Morgenthau (gentleman farmer and neighbor of their boss Franklin Roosevelt), who sometimes bridled when his in-house puppet master pulled the strings too abruptly. Like the others seated around him, White was besotted with Stalin and the latest Five-Year Plan, albeit he, like everyone else in that charmed circle, had never been to the Soviet Union.

When White returned to his summer home in Fitzwilliam, New Hampshire, eleven years later, a dying man after downing a bottle of digitalis on the train from Boston, barely staggering onto the platform of the tiny Fitzwilliam station—he had been hounded in the previous weeks, first by the FBI and then by the NKVD—he may well have thought back to that pleasant afternoon at Volta Place, seated in the catbird seat, and wondered how it had all come to this: how a Soviet asset of immeasurable worth at the highest pinnacle of the American government, who had conspired to further the ends of Moscow Center at every turning, could have been abandoned at the end. Lying in bed for two days in his idyllic summer home with Mount Monadnock a stalwart presence beyond the window, he might at least have taken some comfort at how coolly he'd played his hand back in May of 1941 at his first lunch meeting with Vitalii Pavlov across the street from Treasury at the Old Ebbitt Grill. How he'd put to memory the orders from Stalin to encourage an ill-prepared United States to risk war with Japan as if the plan had simply reflected his own thinking. And then calmly paid for lunch.

Ever the lone wolf, when dying painfully of heart failure in his bed at his summer home in Fitzwilliam, New Hampshire, White must have taken solace that he'd served his untutored masters well, including his triumphant organizing of the Breton Woods Conference in 1944 at the Mount Washington Hotel, also in his beloved New Hampshire. And how, even as the FBI closed in, he'd brazened it out to the end, managing at the eleventh hour to still obtain Truman's appointment as the first director of the IMF in the spring of 1946, although he resigned a year later, with no warning or explanation to anyone. He'd withstood criticism, lashing out in petulant indignation to the press and later to HUAC: How dare ex-spies and Communists like Whittaker Chambers or the "Red Queen," Elizabeth Bentley, accuse a man of his exalted stature, stellar reputation, and accomplishments of common-as-dishwater spying? (This plea, a reputational defense, was not unlike that used by Alger Hiss in his two trials.) And so, just three days before his death, he topped off his public career with a grandstanding display of patriotic rhetoric for the press in a HUAC hearing in August 1948. With brave, patriotic words, he delivered a ringing endorsement of liberal democracy and the American way, a speech that all would remember, and so left a stirring impression, a self-righteous clarion call recalled by many for decades, confirming that his sudden death just three days later was that of a righteous soul hounded to his grave by false accusations of treason, laid low by lies from smarmy creatures like Chambers and Elizabeth Bentley, ex-Communists, who, in turn, released McCarthy and the Red-baiters from their fetid dens.

When confronted by then Congressman Richard Nixon with a photo of Whittaker Chambers later in this histrionic public hearing, White suddenly realized that his accuser was, in fact, his old GRU handler from the thirties, from Volta Place days, the man he'd only known as Carl, who had traveled all the way to his summer home in Fitzwilliam for his brilliant paper on reform of Soviet monetary policy. This was the man who'd warned him on the street outside the Treasury building in 1939 that if he didn't break with the GRU apparatus he, Carl, with the Russian accent so beloved of Alger Hiss, would be forced to expose him. At that terrible instant, Nixon's face screwed up in an inscrutable grin: White—probably fingering the bottle of digitalis he carried in his vest pocket—knew he was done for.

He would be dead three days later: sudden, mysterious, tragic. Returning from Washington and the HUAC investigation the following day to his summer home in Fitzwilliam, New Hampshire, White either died by his own hand—racked by nervous anxiety and exhaustion—by overdosing himself with digitalis or by the intervention of a Soviet hit team that might have forced his shaking hand. According to the attending doctor, who did a cardiogram, White's heart was in bad shape and showed all the signs of a severe heart condition. The local doctor was unaware of the circumstances of White's return, the anxiety and fear of exposure that had marked his last days and months. So neither this doctor nor his colleague who wrote the death certificate bothered with a coroner's examination or a toxicology report. White's brother-in-law, a member of the Communist underground, arranged for the body to be spirited across the state line to Massachusetts in the middle of the night (where cremation did not have to be included in the instructions of the deceased's will), where it was cremated, and his ashes buried.

Harry White, Quizzed in Probe of Spy Ring, Dies Suddenly
FITZWILLIAM, N.H. (AP) Aug. 17, 1948—Harry Dexter White, 56, former assistant secretary of the U.S. Treasury, who this past week denied he was a member of an "elite" group in the Communist apparatus in Washington, died yesterday at his summer home.

A heart attack, suffered Saturday, only a few hours after his return from Washington, caused his death, Dr. George S. Emerson said.

White testified before the House Un-American Activities Committee that the accusations of Mr. Whittaker Chambers and Miss Elizabeth T. Bentley were "unqualifiedly false."

Miss Bentley had testified July 31 that through White's high Treasury position he had helped Communist agents by pushing certain government employees toward key positions where they would have access to secret information.

Hiss arrived a bit perturbed . . . He was upset for two reasons, he said. He had to contact a friend at the Harvard Club, with whom he had a 6 p.m. appointment, and he had just learned of the sudden death by heart attack of his friend Harry Dexter White, former Assistant Secretary of the Treasury, whom we had questioned four days earlier on the charges of Chambers and Elizabeth Bentley that he had been a part of the stated Red conspiracy.

"I would like the record to show," Hiss said, after being placed under oath, "that on my way downtown I learned from the press of the death of Harry White, which came as a great shock to me. I am not sure that I feel in the best possible mood for testimony."

—Robert Stripling, chief investigator, House Committee on Un-American Activities, August, 17, 1948

"Chambers is an enemy of the republic, a blasphemer of Christ, a disbeliever in God, with no respect either for matrimony or motherhood . . . he believes in nothing . . . and as to the intimacies between the Hisses and Chamberses—incredible! Take just one instance, the visit to Harry Dexter White's summer home. They motor four hundred miles from Washington to Fitzwilliam, New Hampshire, so they can sit in the car while Whittaker Chambers goes down and talks to a dead man, a man now dead, and they cannot refute him, and then go to see 'She Stoops to Conquer.' If a man ever stooped to conquer, Chambers has."

—Lloyd Paul Stryker, lead attorney for the defense in the first Hiss trial, in his closing argument before the jury, July 6, 1949

They spent some time walking—"casing the joint," Wendy said, and laughed not very convincingly—the rutted gravel and dirt farm road bordered by woods thickened with clotted patches of glaucous rhododendrons. They were both reeling from the implications of the Pavlov excerpt they'd read in their motel room the night before.

The road served as an entrance drive to what had, once upon a time, been the Whites' summer residence. George left the Tahoe parked on the state road, concerned about trespassing in *Live Free or Die* New Hampshire. They were trying to elucidate the images of Whittaker Chambers and Alger and Priscilla Hiss arriving at Harry Dexter White's summer home in Fitzwilliam, New Hampshire, in August 1937 as described in *Witness*, and further detailed in Chambers's testimony, both in discovery and at the trial (fortified with transcripts and other telling details provided them by Allen Weinstein). If they hadn't been so nervous, they might have even enjoyed the upright pitch pine and tightly clustered dun-leafed oaks, with the near-shorn maples forming the understory of most brilliant color, enlivened by fan-shaped slivers of silver birch.

Emerging from the shadowy woodlot, the dirt and gravel road continued in a semicircle to a modest red farmhouse on a rise set amid rolling green lawns bordered by more distant overgrown pastures and frost-shorn cornfields. The house looked to be all of one floor—perhaps also having a room or two in the attic—with a single brick chimney, all of it conforming to the black-and-white photo in the pages of a *Life* magazine article of November 23, 1953, which Weinstein had provided. Except now, two young girls—one blond, one dark-haired—in jeans and down vests played on a rope swing hung from the massive bough of an oak off to the side of what looked to be a newer two-car garage addition. The trunk of the oak, as in the *Life* photograph, was still girdled with a band of rusted metal. It was chilly, though a warming trend was in the offing, and the girls' breath was just visible. Brooding gray clouds overhead were touched by chinks of brassy sunlight on their underbellies. Blood orange maple leaves covered the grass in blowing, shifting shoals, lapping crescents of taller unmowed grass beyond the lawn, where stone walls corralled even more leaves in slanting piles like shingle against a breakwater. In the middle distance, more crumbled fieldstone walls bobbed across untended pastures choked with high-bush blueberry, thus the name Blueberry Hill. Wendy cast longing looks toward the horizon, where a mottled olive-gray Mount Monadnock presided like royalty over the North Country. Closer at hand, to the rear of the house, was a duck pond—just as Chambers had described it—flat and gunmetal gray, verging on icy stillness, but still animated, at least to an artist's eye, by a red Adirondack chair strategically angled on its grassy slope to take in the rugged Monadnock.

"I hope you aren't planning for me to go knock on their front door," she said. "Just in case the Whites are *still* in."

"I thought you were really into all this—places, what with all your Proustian sensibility. What do we call it: the White house, or home? A little off, I mean the political association, the color . . ." He shrugged. checking the *Life* photo from 1953 showing white clapboard and continuing in a jocular tone. "The usage conjures ambiguous meanings . . . for a *red* house."

"What would you prefer? Let's stick to Blueberry Hill, like out of a kid's book. Besides, you're our expert stargazer. What reports from Epsilon Reticuli?"

"I think knocking on the door would make us look ridiculous, morbid even. After all, this is our fourth—what do we call it?—crime scene. Sites of suspicious deaths, suicides, murders. What do your literary antennae tell you?"

"Lewisburg makes five," she said, correcting him. "What do you find most disturbing about Remington's murder?"

"The perfection of its ambiguity—doubts, if not fear, instilled in both traitors and pursuers alike—the FBI and CIA. The long memory . . . bet it even scares you."

"Do you think the Judge is lying about Remington, too, since they both spent three years working on the War Production Board?"

"You'll get your chance to wheedle that out of him tomorrow. It was a big organization; their paths didn't necessarily have to cross."

She turned on him with a crinkle of pain in the compressed corners of her eyes. "The thing that really bothers me is Remington's funeral service, when his first wife and two children were a no-show. That's monstrous, that a mother would deliberately leave such an empty void in her two children's lives."

"His first wife was an ex-Communist—hell, she sold him out to the FBI, testified in court he'd paid dues and turned over papers to Elizabeth Bentley. She'd hardly be welcome—if she wasn't already in hiding."

With those succinct data points to soothe her agitated mind, he watched her closely as she gathered her windblown hair, rubber band at the ready, then returned to the Harry Dexter White file in his hand. "Looks like they've added a two-car garage and screened-in porch with a view of the pond and Monadnock. No longer just a bucolic summer residence. That's a late-model Silverado in the garage. These folks look to be locals, year-rounders. Probably armed to the teeth."

He handed her the photocopied pages from *Life* magazine of November 1953: a stark photo from a very low angle, grass unmowed, showing the Whites' Fitzwilliam summer home as a brooding presence against a threatening sky, with two silhouetted oaks, one looming like a Halloween prop in the foreground, the other a broad-shouldered presence wildly gesticulating against impinging lowering clouds.

"Well," she offered, "the *Life* photographer sure thought the shoot required an ominous tone, and he didn't even know about Pavlov and Pearl Harbor. Charles Addams couldn't have done better. Looks like they've lost one of the oaks—there, see the stump?"

"So . . . we know that Harry Dexter White died of a heart attack in that house, in his bed, in August 1948, a few days after he arrived home on the train from Washington."

"Two days. And he had two daughters. Just like those two cute little girls," she said, stretching out her arms. "Except those two are about the age they would have been when Chambers showed up ten years before, in August of 1937, with Alger and Priscilla in tow. Not yet bratty teenagers."

"Were you a bratty teenager?"

"I was idolatrous . . . I was thirteen going on eighteen . . . innocent as a rose," she sang halfheartedly.

"Sorry, I didn't mean . . ."

"I know you didn't. How could you."

"How did *you* find out?" He dropped his distressed gaze to the leaf-strewn grass.

Ponytail completed, she gave a dismissive flounce of her shoulders.

"How terrible for the girls." Her voice took on a searching ache. "It's August, you're at your idyllic summer place, where you've been going since childhood, since you could remember—warm and safe—and your father arrives home suddenly from the railroad station more dead than alive."

"Careful," he said. She had taken a few steps forward, as if something in the scene of childhood dreams had drawn her attention. "This is still August 1937, last time I checked, and we don't want anybody thinking we might be planning to kidnap the girls." He looked back toward the road where it emerged from the copse. "We're also trespassing."

"Look at you, already feeling guilty—you, the cosmic voyeur. Sticking to your science, like your good professor told you. That you'd come around and see the light."

He looked down at his file and shuffled pages.

"Like Allen said, how could you be in a car for two days, driving north on Route 202. . . friends, belonging to the same Communist apparatus, and never speak the name of another member of the same underground apparatus—the man who is the object of your journey? Who had been in your house at Volta Place, clearly a pal of Alger Hiss, whose death he clearly found upsetting. Chambers never explains it."

"It's *Allen* now, is it?"

"He just e-mailed me apologizing for the rough translation of the excerpt from Vitalii Pavlov's memoir."

"Like the salivating dog."

"Who met White for lunch at the Old Ebbitt Grill in May 1941."

"*Allen . . .*" she sniffed, exchanging incredulous looks.

"What do you want me to call him, Dr. Weinstein?"

"E-mail him, ask him if he knows anything about the KGB guy who handled Julius Rosenberg, and when they knew their 'Mr. Liberal' was in trouble—when that Bob Lamphere had his quarry in his sights." She stuck her hands in the back pockets of her jeans. "The Hisses were probably bird-watching. They probably stopped along the way to do a little bird-watching—that's why it took them the extra day on the return trip that's got your Allen so hot and bothered."

"Somehow, I can't see Alger and Priscilla just hanging back at the car along the side of the road, as Chambers testified in court, while he waltzed up the drive to pick up the manuscript from White. Their pal from Volta Place—just cooling their heels back in the car. Twenty minutes, Chambers testified he spent with White, who was playing with his two little girls."

"Here's the thing: Chambers never knew about the Volta Place group, that these Harvard guys had their own gig going on the side, out of sight of their Russian handlers. What a nightmare. If Moscow Center had caught wind, they'd have flipped out. Alger and Priscilla must've known enough to play along and lie low."

Her intuitive certainty seemed to flummox him, and he fell silent, reviewing the notes.

She pointed. "Don't you feel sorry for his two daughters . . . Joan and Ruth? I mean, for the rest of their lives . . . Dad accused of being a spy—and, of course, they could never believe it."

"Let's stick with August 1937 and the little girls, when such disasters lay in the future."

"When they believed in their father, Daddy, absolutely . . . Daddy's girls," she continued, just a hint of wistfulness in her voice. "Barbecued butternut squash."

"Would it be different for boys, do you suppose?" He shuffled pages while he mused. "Okay, and later, after he died, after he was accused?"

"Daughters are loyal; they'd stick by him to the end of time."

"A heart attack is different."

"Not if it's an overdose." She looked longingly, squinting, tilting her head as if trying to make out something she'd overlooked before . . . the stuffed animals cradled in the arms of the girls. "And they'd never forget this place, the two sisters—how could they?" She continued staring at the two little girls, where they were whispering endearments to their pets, giggling as they pushed the swing seat back and forth between them. He could tell she was only barely resisting the temptation to go speak to them. The girls, the one with long blond hair, the other with shorter auburn hair and bangs, remained absorbed in their game of seating some stuffed animals on the swing seat, oblivious of the two strangers standing by the fieldstone wall at the entrance of the drive to their home. Oblivious of danger . . . of fickle time. "It's probably just the way the White girls always remembered it. I bet they came back here, stayed as long as they could; some part of them never left Fitzwilliam. People are that way, you know. Like you and Hermitage."

He handed her an article from the *North Adams Transcript* of August 30, 1955.

"The state attorney general had the place searched in 1953 and certain contents handed over to the HUAC subcommittee, including a Russian songbook translated into English . . . 'Lenin Our Leader' was one of the songs."

"So the wife and girls were still here seven years later. That had to be pretty traumatic to have your summer home searched. Like you, rifling the Judge's office."

He bridled at this, making a face, then took a seat on the stone wall.

"Hardly the same." He gave the back of her knees a playful shove, her legs buckling. "Like you, Priscilla wouldn't have been able to resist. She'd be sitting right here with Alger, or he'd be standing a little behind, in the shadows of the trees, their little joke on Chambers. Smiling to themselves as they watched him go up to the front door and knock—their Volta Place pal, big shot at Treasury. Tradecraft be damned. Perhaps they secretly, like us, watched White playing with his two little girls. Chambers wrote how they longed for children of their own."

"That's it—how sweet—you just answered Dr. Weinstein's question: Chambers was really just trying to save himself, like we are."

"Like us?"

"Don't you think?" Sitting, she fingered his cheek, his chin, as if recognizing something in his expression. "Right . . . we just want to make sure we really exist, that it's all not an illusion—life is a dream— get it?" She waved to the horizon. "Think about it: Alger and Priscilla were right here, watching, and yet they testified in court that it never happened, that they never drove all the way here on Route 202, and Chambers never picked up White's report on reform of Soviet monetary policy. Worse, they were not only trying to defend themselves but also to erase Chambers by erasing his memory—and creating an alternate reality, a parallel reality that would change everything—for those two little girls, too . . . if their father had never been a spy. They were trying to protect those two little girls from what was to come, the accusations about their father. And that's why Chambers was forced to include the trip in his testimony and book: defend his existence in this world, even when it meant a cruel shadow would haunt those two little girls for the rest of their lives. And White's wife, Ann Terry White, who wrote children's books, of all things. You see, if you pull one brick out, the edifice of time crumbles—everything becomes suspect."

"But the daughters would have rejected Chambers's version of the world because it contradicted the way they remembered it. They'd want to preserve their *own* existence, where their father remained a hero and dutiful public servant of the New Deal. The man they knew and loved." He reached to some strands of blond hair that had escaped her red rubber band and were blowing across her wide forehead.

"Well, men are like that: It doesn't matter to you, not really. You prefer all your data points, your Hubble view of the heavens, so aloof from people's lives."

"Okay," he muttered, and checked the *Life* magazine article again.

"Even White's neighbors didn't think much of him. The local farmers described a man who wanted his privacy at all costs. Another farmer had always grazed his cows on part of the land and, after White bought the place, he wrote a letter asking permission to continue doing it; White wrote back, saying he hated cows. There was a spectacular blueberry patch on his land; that, too, was off-limits to the locals."

"But his daughters, wherever they are, whatever their age, will never believe any of that, not that Chambers was here to pick up that academic paper, not that their father gave away secrets or did terrible things. I feel for them, if they're still alive—sensing the tides turning against them, stealing their childhood, the rumors and doubts creeping up on them—like you, like your dark matter . . . always threatening the way things are."

"Dark energy," he said, correcting her. "The forces of chaos and change are always on the move, even as that keeps things in equilibrium as the expansion of the universe accelerates." He nodded toward the playing girls. "No one—nothing escapes."

"'In nature every moment is new,'" she recited in a voice full of longing; "'the past is always swallowed and forgotten; the coming only is sacred. Nothing is secure but life, transition, the energizing spirit . . .'"

"Emerson?"

"The Judge had it underlined in his copy, or maybe it was Oliver Wendell Holmes."

She bowed her head, as if giving a blessing for the gifts at hand. For a while, they looked on in silence, watching as the two girls pushed the swing in tandem and began counting aloud as they gently rode their stuffed animals on the back of the breeze, the same breeze that stirred the blond girl's long hair, as it stirred the longer grass and ruffled the threadbare blueberry bushes beyond.

"What," he asked, as if going over and over the thing in his mind, "was he thinking as he lay dying in his bed in that house, after, just days before, denying everything he'd believed in before HUAC, to the acclaim of the press. That, or remembering an August day when Chambers had driven all the way from Washington just to retrieve a paper he'd done on reforming the Soviet monetary system? When he'd come to the door and found Carl standing there, Mercury sent all the way—well, presumably on Stalin's orders."

"From Mount Olympus." She nodded, squinting. "He'd be remembering his young daughters on that day, playing on the swing in the summer sunshine."

"Always the dutiful daughter."

He handed her a page from the file, the underlined excerpt from Allen Weinstein's book.

The death certificate, already filled out, was presented to White's doctor, George Emerson, by two unknown men while he was attending a difficult birth many miles away from his deceased patient. He signed, thinking the men were with a mortuary; they were never seen again, never identified. An order for his immediate cremation was signed by his brother-in-law, a Dr. Wolfson, a New Jersey orthodontist and known Communist. New Hampshire law requires that for a cremation to be done the request must be in the deceased's will, so the body was transported across the state line to Boston where the cremation took place.

"Two men?" she said, her hands sliding over the granite boulder, cold to the touch, working a jagged edge.

"Two men . . ." he reiterated, pulling out a copy of a story in the *Boston Globe* of November 15, 1953. "William Blodgett, town clerk told the reporter: 'They got that body out of town purty fast. A driver and assistant from the Boston funeral parlor got me up at midnight to sign the permit to remove the body. He wanted to take it to Boston that night.'" George shrugged. "He'd passed his sell-by date."

"Two young women—terrified out of their minds as their father died in agony before their eyes."

"Nixon," he countered, "always claimed that when they showed White the photographs of Whittaker Chambers at the hearing, the committee could see it in his eyes, the changed expression on his face, 'bugged out'—because he recognized the man in the photos, the man he'd only known as Carl. His tone, his body language changed after that, even as he put up a spirited defense of all the Communists on his team in the Treasury Department."

She turned and took his cold hands and squeezed them between hers, as if frightened about how easily they seemed to be slipping between worlds.

"He'd be remembering how Carl, all those years before, almost to the day, walked up"—she squinted—"the line of paving stones to his screen door on orders from Moscow Center to get his plan for the reform of the Soviet monetary system. You see, he was watching his girls, could still smell the mowed grass, the sweet fern in the meadow, the sound of laughter as his girls in the blueberry patch filled their tin pails hanging by strings around their necks. Perhaps the girls had been playing on the swing, perhaps, like us, Chambers and the Hisses watched them, and smiled, and maybe Priscilla decided it was time to have their own child."

"In space-time . . ."

"Be damned! George, dear Luke, those little girls couldn't care less. They'll never even know or care about the strange man who died in their house in a past inconceivable to their young hearts. As long as they don't believe in ghosts."

"Space-time doesn't exist within space and time—space and time exist within it."

"Stop, before I get a headache. Look," she said, pointing to smoke coming out of the chimney. "Somebody's started a fire in the wood-stove. And soon they'll come out and tell the two little girls to come inside for lunch, for soup and peanut butter and jelly sandwiches, and warm themselves." She sighed. "Whoever they are, I hope they will have a long and happy life . . . and get into the colleges of their choice."

They stood and began to walk back toward where the Tahoe was parked. He took a final glance at the *Boston Globe* article.

"Seems the house was broken into sometime in October 1952, mat-tresses stolen—one full size, three smaller ones, along with a maple chest of drawers with blankets in it, a trunkful of clothes. The local sheriff, Frank W. Walter, told the reporter it wasn't the FBI because they'd have alerted him."

"So the KGB wasn't taking any chances that something might have been left behind."

"Two days up and two days return on the back roads, on Route 202. And yet"—he checked again the notes that Allen Weinstein had given him—"the affidavit from the Hisses' baby-sitter attests they were away for five days."

"They lingered . . . they lingered," and she looked longingly at Mount Monadnock.

His phone buzzed and he got it out and squinted.

"Allen didn't waste any time getting into the memoir." He held out the phone to her as he summarized the e-mail. "He wants me to ask the Judge if he—or Annie—ever met Chambers before or after the trial, or only when he cross-examined Chambers in the witness box. He's wondering if the Judge ever felt under threat from his client, Alger Hiss."

"E-mail him back that you want to know everything he's got on the Rosenbergs' KGB handler—the guy—what's his name—Professor Spier told us about. And while you're at it, see if he's got any more thoughts on Remington's murder in Lewisburg prison."

Again, they turned to go, and again, he turned back to the idyllic scene, the farmhouse, the trickle of smoke against the fall-shorn landscape. The two girls gathering up their stuffed animals at another call from the house.

"What?" she said.

"Of course, you're right."

I write on behalf of my sister, Ruth Levita of Stanford, Conn., and myself to protest Sam Tanenhaus's review of Daniel P. Moynihan's "Secrecy: The American Experience" (Oct 4). In that review our father, Harry Dexter White, is once again vilified as a "Soviet agent." . . . But neither these considerations nor White's own vigorous and eloquent denial of the accusation against him can sway countless uncritical thinkers. In the 50 years since White's death, the slow alchemy of time has done its work: by dint of constant repetition, the unsubstantiated accusations have been miraculously transmuted into firm historical fact.

Those who would defend White's reputation are faced with the notoriously difficult task of proving a negative. Nevertheless, as the daughters of a brilliant economist who served his country loyally and with distinction, my sister and I remain confident that, in the words of Coventry Patmore, "The truth is great, and shall prevail, / When none cares whether it prevail or not."

—Joan (White) Pinkham, Amherst, Mass.
November 22, 1998, *New York Times*

I write to protest that in Benn Steil's April 9 Op-Ed article, "Banker, Tailor, Soldier, Spy," old allegations of espionage against my father, Harry Dexter White, are once again repeated as fact.

In support of his statement that White was guilty of spying for the Soviet Union in the 1940s, Mr. Steil cites a handwritten memo that my father allegedly gave to Whittaker Chambers, a self-confessed Soviet spy. Mr. Steil then declares that White's guilt was firmly established by Soviet intelligence cables published in the late 1990s.

The content and provenance of all these documents have been studied in depth by serious scholars and have been found to raise as many questions as they answer. However they are interpreted, it can by no means be said that they establish my father's guilt. It should be remembered that White himself vigorously and eloquently denied the accusations against him . . .

—Joan (White) Pinkham, Amherst, Mass.
April 16, 2012, *New York Times*

First Atomic Spy Trial Nears Jury

Atom Spies Tell Jury Story That Rivals Fiction

NEW YORK, March 22 — AP — ... KGB and GRU immediately ... most of what Sasha described ... "political" networks, cut off ... with many of their spies, ... withdrew their legal and illegal ... until other arrests ... or the spy fever ...

SPY SUSPECT CITES RIGHTS

Rosenberg Charges Revenge Motive

NEW YORK, March 22. (U.P.)— Julius Rosenberg, on trial for his life as an accused atom spy, refused seven times today to answer ...

WITNESS TELLS SPY SUSPECTS' BID FOR SECRETS

Accuses Ex-Friends in Espionage Trial

New York ...

Spy Defendant Asked Secrets, Witness Testifies

Said W...

ROSENBERGS DIE
Pair Executed for Atom Spying

Supreme Court and Eisenhower Reject Couple's Last Pleas

OSSINING, N.Y., June 19 — Atom Spies Julius and Ethel Rosenberg died in Sing Sing Prison's electric chair shortly before sundown today. The executions followed quickly after the Supreme Court set aside a stay of execution granted Wednesday by Justice William O. Douglas and President Eisenhower's refusal to grant them clemency.

SING SING PRISON, N.Y., June 19 (℗) Atom Spies Julius and Ethel Rosenberg were ordered electrocuted late today betraying their country's secrets to Russia and threatening the lives of millions bringing the world closer to an atomic

The Justice Department set the time for doomed couple's death in Sing Sing Prison electric chair after a day of suspense in the U.S. Supreme Court denied their final appeal and President Eisenhower again refused executive clemency.

Warden Wilfred Denno announced the first the and wife espionage team would be put to death gray-walled prison's death chamber "before which comes at 8:30 p.m. (5:30 PDT) today at

Later he said the first execution would come EDT, with the second a few minutes later.

END OF TRAIL—Summons to death in electric chair came swiftly for Atom Spies Ethel and Julius Rosenberg after stay was revoked and clemency was refused.

GUILTY AS ATOMIC SPIES

Federal Jury Convicts Electrical Engineer, His Wife and a Radar Expert of Giving Secrets to During World W...

py Defendant Asked Secrets, Witness Testifies

Said We Must Keep Reds Supplied Even Though War Is Over

NEW YORK, (AP)—One of the ... defendants in the nation's ... trial was accused ... 1945 there ...

New York Police Break Up Hysterical Rosenberg Rally

Supreme Court Again Gets Rosenberg Plea

Washington (AP) Justice ... son today turned ... supreme ...

37
Bitter Tears

ALLEN WEINSTEIN'S E-MAIL was just the beginning for George, the beginning of a cycle of slowly accumulating data, research and more research, leavened by heart-wrenching speculation that began as a trickle, increased upon his and Weinstein's further sleuthing around the publication of the Judge's memoir, and then precipitously fell off as Russian sources clammed up, as Putin clamped down on his old intelligence agency, and by natural attrition as all those who had once been active in the American Communist Party or Soviet and American intelligence circles in the 1940s and 1950s passed from the scene. And with them, the divisive Hiss versus Chambers controversy, which had so riveted and divided the country for over fifty years.

After George's impromptu meeting with Donald Spier, Allen Weinstein had managed to contact Rosenberg's KGB handler, Alexander Feklisoy, or, as Weinstein had written in an e-mail, "Sasha" to his comrades, who had been delighted to memorialize their glory days in his rather breezy free-with-the-facts memoir of the war years, when he ran Julius Rosenberg and later Klaus Fuchs in England. Weinstein had described an overseas call, when he had caught Sasha in a rather chatty mood, probably after a late-afternoon lunch washed down with plenty of vodka. Sasha had offered up some color on the subject that he had neglected to broach before. His florid memory reached back to when Elizabeth Bentley, an American spy runner, defected in 1945, and gave the FBI eighty names in her network—including those of Alger Hiss, Harry Dexter White, and Laurence Duggan (all confirmed as early as 1939 by Whittaker Chambers to the FBI). The KGB and GRU immediately froze most of what Sasha described as their "political" networks, cut off contacts with many of their spies, and withdrew their legal and illegal handlers until either arrests were made or the spy fever died down, and the coast was clear again to resume political work. "Amazingly"—Sasha's word—only Alger Hiss was ever actually indicted in the immediate postwar years, and that for spying activities back in the "dark ages"—again Sasha's words—before the war. But, so Sasha noted, the "scientific and technical" networks, which he was largely responsible for in the United States, and which he ran out of the Soviet consulate in New York, continued their work during this period much as before. These technical spies were simply too important because they were handling the critical material surrounding the continued development of the atomic bomb, a network spearheaded by the Rosenbergs. Although not as productive as during the war years, the scientific networks were still transmitting critical data on new technologies to Moscow Center. Sasha was committed to protecting "his boys" both past and present, along with what remained of the political networks, not so much because they still retained value—years after Yalta and the Iron Curtain—but because any arrests, interrogations, or trials of Soviet agents might impact the still-ongoing spying on atomic research facilities, prompting the FBI to investigations further afield. (Weinstein noted that what brought suspicion on Alger Hiss within the State Department in 1945, precipitating an FBI investigation and interview of Hiss, forcing his decision to quit the State Department for the Carnegie Endowment, was precisely because he'd asked for access to documents on the atomic bomb program, an area not covered by his political responsibilities.)

It was the "Bentley betrayal" that caused Moscow Center to remove Sasha from the New York station in early 1947 for reassignment to England, where, under diplomatic cover, he would take over as handler for Klaus Fuchs ("Rest" in the Venona decrypts), who had returned to the Cavendish labs in the UK. While back in Moscow in May or June of 1947, on home leave before the start of his UK posting, Sasha found himself summoned to a meeting with an icy-faced Lieutenant-General Sergei Romanovich Savchenko, the head of Soviet intelligence, and Leonid Kvasnikov, once his New York boss, then head of the KGB's Tenth Directorate for Scientific and Technical Intelligence. They made it clear to Sasha that there was no room for mistakes—their instruction couched as a dire warning. Sasha paused on the phone line to Weinstein as he tried to recall their exact words. "An arrest in the United States would be in and of itself a serious setback; any kind of problem could be potentially disastrous for Soviet scientific research." Although Sasha didn't reference the Hiss indictment and trial per se—he was, after all, KGB, not GRU, and focused on scientific and technical matters, not political—his tone made it clear that the Soviets, during this crucial period in the early years of the Cold War, were prepared to do everything in their power to protect their most important assets: access to game-changing nuclear technology. By implication, Hiss (even with his usefulness then past) was one of theirs, and his fate crucial to sustaining ongoing Soviet penetration of U.S. nuclear secrets. As Sasha put it to Weinstein with a long sigh, "When dominos are lined up, the first one to fall down draws all the others with it."

As Weinstein had pointed out, when Hiss fell, his conviction both energized and hastened the unraveling of the Rosenbergs (if not the conviction of William Remington) and scores of other Soviet assets in the scientific and technical arena, at the very moment when the Soviets were desperate to steal the next-generation technology for building a hydrogen bomb.

Hadn't the Judge told him as much, or at least intimated as much, when describing that baffling disturbance, the nervousness and anxiety, the emotionally charged paranoia among his colleagues on the defense team, what he referred to as a "palpable change in atmospheric pressure"? Surely this was the result of orders from Moscow Center to protect Hiss at any cost, lest his falling domino precipitate the loss of the Soviet's scientific assets, as well.

And worse, Moscow knew precisely why their scientific assets were in danger. In the months before the second Hiss trial, the slow, painstaking decryption of the Venona cables that would ultimately spell the Rosenbergs' doom had been revealed to Soviet intelligence by longtime Soviet spy Donald Maclean (code name "Homer" in the Venona decrypts), then operating out of the British embassy in Washington. Maclean tipped off Moscow that the Americans had broken the Soviet wartime cables and were on to Klaus Fuchs, which meant that the Rosenbergs weren't far behind. (Maclean, Guy Burgess, and Kim Philby, in their turn, were all ultimately confirmed as spies by the Venona decrypts, while Alger Hiss would only be detected by a meticulous dissection of the Venona files in the years to come. Unlike Hiss, who maintained his ironclad equanimity to the end, the British spies all folded under the pressure of disclosure, Maclean, Burgess, and Philby ultimately escaping capture and dying early of alcoholism during their

Moscow exile.) The pressure on Soviet intelligence to save their people mounted daily in the run-up to the second Hiss trial.

Then came the testing of the first Soviet atomic bomb in August of 1949, just months before the opening of the second Hiss trial, only adding to the fervor as American intelligence went into overdrive to ferret out the traitors in their midst. The KGB was under extraordinary pressure not just to protect their scientific/technical spies but, if necessary, get them out of the country and behind the Iron Curtain. If Hiss were convicted, the KGB knew—and they were proved correct—that the publicity would turn public opinion against the Soviet Union for a generation, ratcheting up even more scrutiny on their spy networks. A shift in public sentiment that McCarthy quickly took advantage of, resulting in the conviction of William Remington and others, while casting a long shadow over the likes of Lauchlin Currie, Harry Dexter White, and Laurence Duggan.

Alger Hiss, whether he knew it or not, had his finger in the dike, even as he escaped detection by the Venona decrypts until years after the trial.

According to Weinstein, Sasha, when speaking of the Rosenbergs, had said, "We did everything within our powers—everything. I wept bitter tears—very bitter tears—for my dear comrades."

Weinstein had little sympathy for Sasha's crocodile tears: The Rosenbergs were much more valuable to the Soviets dead than alive. They died with their secrets, their deaths made for worldwide propaganda to stir the hearts of the faithful, and Soviet scientists could claim that they managed to build the bomb on their own, without having to steal secrets. While the Rosenbergs became martyrs to the American Left. Only four years after their execution, the Soviets launched *Sputnik* in 1957, seemingly confirming their prowess in science and technology over the moribund West.

And what of William Remington's murder? George found himself haunted by his and Wendy's visit to the redbrick stockades of Lewisburg prison, the cold rainy day, the crenelated tower streaked with damp, the barren fall landscape upon which Alger Hiss had gazed and described in poetic letters to his wife and son. Remington was a man the Judge had clearly admired, of whom, in fact, he'd been very fond, even if reluctant to admit as much. Remington's demise was yet another case of an ambiguous death that refused closure, one that left his wife and children abandoned to a life in limbo and doubt. Was this

retribution for his betrayal of his Communist comrades to the FBI—
the one unpardonable sin? Weinstein had no doubts who was behind
it. Just the changing accounts as to his killers' motives were a giveaway:
anti-Communists out to settle a score, thieves out to steal Remington's
meager possessions when they were surprised by his return to his cell
and so silenced him. In other accounts, the killers found Remington
sound asleep and simply bludgeoned him because of their hatred of
Communists and outrage at the imminent release of Alger Hiss. The
newspaper stories and the official records all disagreed, as did the
admissions of the murderers as they constantly changed their stories.
Of course, there was nothing to steal, as Weinstein had noted in his
e-mail. These lowlifes were car thieves. Weinstein postulated they were
promised a substantial sum of money upon their release, probably by a
KGB cutout posing as an anti-Communist crusader. That Remington
was a convicted traitor only made the prospect more alluring.

In all the vast literature on the Hiss case and his subsequent life,
not a word about Remington's murder had come up. Strangely, in
Hiss's brief memoir written in 1988, he gave the murder of Remington
less than a paragraph, placing it a few weeks before his release from
Lewisburg prison, when, in fact, it was just three days. He described
how the prison authorities wanted to then segregate him from the
general prison population for his safety, in case Remington's murder
had been politically motivated. Hiss, by his account, refused, and settled on having a prison guard shadow him for his remaining days in
Lewisburg. In passing, Hiss noted that Remington had seemingly
found it prudent to keep his distance from his more infamous fellow
inmate during the months they served together. George couldn't help
wondering if Alger Hiss had remembered that few days as three weeks
out of lingering fear from that period, that the Remington murder had
really been a warning to him should he ever be tempted to change his
story or admit his guilt. Or if his wife should do so. Often George
found himself tempted to give Hiss the benefit of the doubt: Perhaps
it was guilt that Hiss might have felt, that turned three days into three
weeks in his faltering memory, as macular degeneration set in and the
light began to fade, as he thought back to that lovely summer day when
Remington was a guest at Volta Place and their hearts were young and
life stretched forward with infinite possibilities. Sad, really, a tragedy,
a good man who panicked and broke and betrayed the Party and his
apparatus to the FBI and so paid the price. ("Stalin plays for keeps.")

A fair-haired young man who refused to speak to Alger Hiss in prison out of fear or resentment or even awe that Hiss, his onetime host, had never wavered, never broken, never admitted anything. And so, George decided, Remington's tragic death had remained buried in some dark quiet corner of Hiss's soul, and perhaps in the Judge's, as well.

Pondering all these imponderables, George found himself sometimes buoyed on hopes that in some small measure the Judge's memoir, faithfully edited, might provide closure for Remington's children, and all the others.

—

It was late afternoon on the piazza of Hermitage. The day was oddly warm for November, so the Judge had grabbed the opportunity to convene outside. They sat in a cozy huddle of creaking pea green wicker chairs, George and Wendy in their unzipped parkas, the Judge swaddled in a red-checked wool coat with black buttons, and sporting an ancient Bulldog blue-and-white moth-eaten wool hat with earflaps pulled down and tied under his chin. In his gloved hands he cradled a pair of Nikon binoculars and every now and then glassed the lake through the trees. He was relishing the afternoon, the reprieve, and the fall leaves and migrating bird life as much as, if not more than, the conversation.

"Well, you seem to have become quite the fans of Mr. Weinstein," he said, with the binoculars held tight to his eyes, then lowering them with a glance to a nearby bird feeder, where white-breasted nuthatches scrambled for seeds, shuttling back and forth to the trunk of a nearby oak.

His grandson looked to his partner in crime as if for moral support.

"Seems your reservations about his first book, *Perjury*, were well founded. He remembers like it was yesterday meeting in your chambers and he sends his warm regards. Turns out he was as suspicious of you as you were of him."

"He was pretty damn hard on me in that book—wasn't he?"

"He was."

"How hard?"

"Damn hard . . ." George made a face at Wendy. "At least he didn't accuse you of being a Communist or fellow traveler in thrall to your client."

"Wouldn't have been the first. In the fifties, I was called a Commie-lover to my face more times than I care to remember." He placed the binoculars on a side table and gestured to the bird feeder. "Hardy birds, those nuthatches. Hang about all winter. If you watch closely, one will grab a sunflower seed from the feeder, fly to the trunk of a tree, hand it over to its mate, who will either hide it in a fissure in the bark or crack it open, while the other makes a return run to the feeder."

"Weinstein came down hard, too, on Binger and what's his name, the Harvard shrink, for using that psychopathic personality disorder stuff against Chambers."

"Didn't I"—asked the Judge squinting, his blue-gray eyes watering—"cover all that in my memoir, George?"

"What was the name of that Harvard psychiatrist? The one Alger Hiss encouraged you to hire, or so you wrote."

"Priscilla, too," Wendy offered. "Who seemed greatly enamored of psychiatrists. You visited with them at Volta Place. Bookshelves full of Freud and such."

"Hmm . . . I suppose. I seem to forget as much as I remember these days."

"Neuroplasticity," said George. "You're as good as ever, but storage space for information has its limits, even on the Planck scale. That's what makes your memoir such a precious historical document—and why it's important that we get it right."

At this, Wendy rolled her eyes, leaned forward, and offered an encouraging smile.

"Why wouldn't you talk to Dr. Weinstein back in the late sixties when he first got permission from Hiss to access the defense files, when he asked to interview you for *Perjury*?"

"So, that came up, too, did it?" The Judge glared at his interlocutors as if now onto them. "I suppose I was too damned busy, young lady: a federal judge on a short list for the next Supreme Court opening. Why in God's name would I want to dredge it all up again? And I knew he'd either find reason to blame me for not dismantling Chambers's story adequately enough to get Hiss off or he'd end up blaming me for using distasteful methods to try to destroy Chambers. Either way, I'd come off the loser. Did I not? In the early going, in case you don't know, your pal Weinstein was very much a lefty, a supporter of Hiss and out for blood."

Felicity pushed open the front door to the veranda with a tray of steaming mugs of cocoa and placed them on side tables at their elbows.

"What time shall we say for dinner?" Felicity asked.

"How about eight?" said George. "That way, Wendy and I can get in a quick walk and a shower. It was a long drive from Fitzwilliam."

"Take her to Handytown during my nap," said the Judge, "and bring me a report."

"Will do," replied George.

"What about grilling steaks outside?" asked the Judge. "Can we still get away with that, or is it too cold?"

"For you, Judge, we can make it happen," said Felicity with a loyal salute as she retreated indoors.

"If you get the coals going," called George after her, "I'll do the steaks."

They hoisted their steaming mugs and sipped, staring out where the lake glittered beyond the trees, dotted with the gliding shapes of Canada geese and ducks.

George replaced his mug on the table and took a deep breath.

"Judge, I have to tell you, Dr. Weinstein was absolutely blown away by the sketches."

"Sketches?"

"Altmann's sketches of Alger and Priscilla Hiss and the others in the Volta Place spy ring. The sketches you buried in the defense files."

For a moment, the old man looked blankly around.

"Did I?"

"So you wrote in the memoir."

"Of course . . . that crew." He turned back to the lake. "Don't know why those Canada geese hang around these parts, such easy prey for the foxes and coyotes. They were never here in such numbers back in the old days."

"Snappers," said George, wincing. "And prima facie evidence of a conspiracy by Soviet intelligence to subvert the U.S. government."

The Judge nodded, more to himself than to his company. "*Branta canadensis* . . . Did he really go that far?"

"We had to explain," Wendy offered, "how you came by the sketches."

"And what did you tell him?" His eyes twinkled with pleasure, as if in sudden appreciation of the tag team he faced. His voice steadied: "*Young lady?*"

"Wendy . . ."

"We told him," said George, "precisely what you wrote in your memoir."

"So"—there was a hint of irritation in the Judge's flickering cheek muscle—"he knows about the memoir, does he—*now?*"

"Only that you stuck the sketches, with little, if no, premeditation, in the defense files and pretty much forgot about them for twenty years."

"That's right, I did—didn't . . . I."

"The sketches," she said, pausing, fingering her mug thoughtfully. "Dr. Weinstein examined all of them closely. He noted that if the sketches had fallen into the hands of the prosecution, they might have had quite an impact, added an entirely new dimension to the government's case in the trial."

"Ah, said the spider to the fly." The Judge grinned, raising a leather-gloved finger, as if beginning to relish the conversation, nodding slowly. "Then I did the right thing; I did my job."

George laughed, the change in the Judge's demeanor infectious.

"He was amazed that you, a sitting federal judge, would risk removing the sketches illegally from the defense files."

"Well, you certainly were discreet, weren't you?"

"Dr. Weinstein has promised us his total discretion."

"*Weinstein*! So he couldn't get his sticky academic fingers on the things."

"He's running them by an FBI lab to make sure they're genuine. Which reminds me, I'm supposed to get him a sample of Altmann's handwriting."

George glanced at Wendy, like a copilot going down his preflight checklist.

"You *gave* him the sketches?" The Judge sat up, alert, annoyed.

"To the National Archives," his grandson replied, smiling. "They'll be there, along with your beloved Constitution, for safekeeping. And we kept copies, of course."

"Well . . ."

"For what it's worth," said George, "Dr. Weinstein mentioned that others on the defense team, your colleagues Edward McLean and William Marbury, kept detailed records of their participation, much of it expressing deep skepticism about Hiss's veracity."

"Did they really?" The Judge made a face of intense displeasure. "So who's the bigger fool, McLean and Marbury for having deposited their doubts in the files, or Alger Hiss for allowing Weinstein to stick his nose in them in the first place?"

Wendy looked over the top of her mug with raised eyebrows. "Clearly, you had your doubts, as well; why else deep-six the sketches in the defense files? And then remove them illegally? You were tampering with evidence, with the historical record."

The Judge laughed with pleasure.

"George, you've got a live one. Pretty damn frisky for an artist," continued the Judge, his slate blue eyes coming alive and gleaming beneath the wool liner of his cap. "And I told you: Call me Edward—no ceremony need be maintained, not anymore. I've been out of chambers for decades." He smiled archly at his interrogators. "And yet now, so it seems, my property resides in the National Archives . . . snug as a bug in a rug."

"You're the *man*," said George. "The last witness standing who participated in the trial. Weinstein waxed almost nostalgically."

The Judge laughed to himself, bemused, gently rocking forward and back. He raised another finger. "An artifact of history."

"Sorry, Edward," she said, "but it's important for George to get the details right—the truth. Among other things, so he can make sure your memoir is accurate in all particulars. You don't want a man like Dr. Weinstein picking it apart for faults after it's published. The *New York Times* would be sure to have him review it."

She smiled at George, as if hoping to be helpful.

"*Ars longa, vita brevis*," said George, as if trying unsuccessfully to make light of the whole affair. "I suppose I should really be thanking you. If you'd just destroyed them, burned them like you burned Dr. Weinstein's *Perjury*, I wouldn't be here."

"Well now," the Judge said, grinning, "there *you* are."

"And the Justice Department mural is there, too—big as life, presiding over the staircase where Marvin Smith fell to his death." She bent a canted face toward the old man, looking into his eyes. "Damn creepy, it was, too."

"Judge," said George, lingering with his cocoa, "did you ever feel—I dunno—under threat in any way during the trial . . . or after?"

"Other than my reputation, you mean. Is that what you're—or is it Weinstein?—after?"

George shrank back in his seat, a little crestfallen, guilty.

"Did you follow the Rosenberg trial? You were a judge by then, correct?" asked Wendy.

"As much as anybody; I read the papers."

"Did you agree with the judge's sentencing, the death penalty?"

"Not for Ethel. It seemed much of the evidence against them was circumstantial, gathered from witnesses trying to save themselves."

"It's in Weinstein's book: The decrypted Soviet cables confirm their guilt, although they were never introduced into the trial because of security concerns. But one thing's for sure: The KGB were intent on doing everything possible to protect Hiss, because his conviction would energize the investigation to identify the Rosenbergs, one way or another."

The Judge nodded. "The weight, the number of investigators, the barrels of money—the frenzy."

"The atmosphere of—"

George cut her off. "The subjects of the sketches—George Altmann and two others—died violent deaths within a year of the trial—Altmann during the second trial—and a fourth, William Remington, was murdered in Lewisburg prison just days before Hiss was released in 1954." George paused for a reaction but, getting none, continued. "Noel Field, a potential witness against Hiss, was held in a Budapest prison cell at the time of the trial, tortured by Stalin's agents, not only admitting he was a Soviet spy but testifying Hiss was one, as well. Lauchlin Currie fled to Colombia. I mean, these people weren't fooling around."

"Are you suggesting that Alger Hiss threatened me, coerced me in some manner?" The Judge smiled deliciously. "Or—how shall I put it?—a sympathetic fellow traveler or worse? Is that the best your Weinstein could come up with?"

"It crossed his mind when he met with you in your office."

This brought the conversation to a halt as the Judge's gaze drifted off toward the lake, where the late-fall sun was sheltering in the topmost boughs of the white pine, a warming slant of lemony glow finding its way to where they sat, easing a liquid radiance across the shellacked floorboards, a gentle lapping where their shoes were placed. The old man seemed to be drawing sustenance from the sentinel pines presiding like old friends over his faltering estate.

"Edward," Wendy said forcefully, "Dr. Weinstein told us that George Altmann was on the prosecution's list of potential witnesses."

The Judge seemed to start in his seat, his Adam's apple rising in the vee of his checked shirt.

"George, is that in the memoir?"

"No, it's not. It's not even in Weinstein's first book, *Perjury*. He dug it out while we were with him from some FBI files. George Altmann's name was on a preliminary witness list for the prosecution, when he was interviewed by the FBI because of a connection with Priscilla Hiss going back to when he was teaching at the Art Students League in the twenties. But for whatever reason, they did not bother to put him on the official trial witness list for the prosecution, which would have had to have been shared with the defense—right?"

The Judge sat forward abruptly, looking Wendy soberly in the eye. "Then I did not know—thank God for that!"

"If you had," she asked, "would that have changed your reaction to receiving the envelope with the sketches?"

"Of course it would." He shot a fierce look at George. "That fact must be included in the memoir, every detail."

"Yes, sir. Evidence he placed in your hands before the opening of the trial."

"Because," Wendy interjected, her voice rising in exasperation as the Judge's attention seemed to drift off again, "what he put into your hands—didn't Alice mention something about being there, George?— was obviously evidence that would have made him a star witness for the prosecution—with the Justice Department mural as big as life to support his testimony. Talk about proof!"

She flopped back in her seat, fanning her face.

"Sorry, sorry . . ." she huffed out.

George looked on sullenly.

The Judge smiled uneasily at her show of emotion but, clearly intrigued, replied in an authoritative voice.

"If a prosecution witness or a potential witness had sought out a member of the defense team to impart pertinent information or physical evidence outside the hearing—before the official start of the trial—as was the case here, and defense counsel had entertained that overture in full knowledge that the person was a witness for the prosecution, and then did not inform the judge, that would constitute grounds for a mistrial. A judge could penalize or even call for the disbarment of a lawyer who had acted so underhandedly, negligently, especially if he'd instigated or encouraged such an undertaking."

Wendy looked up, holding his eyes. "And yet you accepted the sketches before the trial and hid them—call it what you like."

"Yes," said the Judge with a stern nod at the young woman and his grandson. "I am guilty of negligence, of a kind . . . what any defense lawyer worth his salt would have done. When in doubt, whether of harm or benefit to the client, act as if it were simply out of your hands." He rubbed his gloves together as if washing said hands of the thing.

"So to speak," added George.

"So to speak."

"And yet when you learned Dr. Weinstein had been granted access to the defense files—that lefty supporter of Hiss—you beat him to the punch and surreptitiously removed the sketches. At least that's what you wrote." She nodded for effect and drained the last of her cocoa. "And then later gave them to Cordelia to return to George Altmann's son."

"How did I describe my meeting with Allen Weinstein in my memoir?"

George looked at Wendy and replied.

"That he more or less barged into your chambers unannounced. A lefty historian in cahoots with Hiss to prove the government wrong, the defense team inept, and so get his conviction quashed. Prompting you, so it seems, to take matters into your own hands."

The Judge seemed to ponder this, his brow furrowing, then his chapped lips elided into a cynical smile at the young woman.

"Well, bully for me—good for doing it, and good for admitting it. And now you've brought the thing full circle: You've put the sketches into the hands of the government, of my nemesis, and so the full truth will out."

"And exactly what truth is that?" asked George.

"Oh, some feeling, some sentiment that perhaps those sketches were fated to be placed into my hands—there"—he flashed a glittering smile at the attentive face of the young woman now bent to his—"call it a romantic gesture. Although, God knows why he picked me of all people on the defense team."

Eagerly, Wendy leaned in even farther. "Ah, your infatuation with Priscilla Hiss."

He shot her a wry look and turned to his grandson.

"And just for the record, when I tried to return the sketches to your father by way of Cordelia, I retained—yes—the sketch of Priscilla . . . for a memento. In fact, if I search my conscience, the fact that I didn't destroy the sketches in the first place—or the second, for that matter, probably had more to do with that sketch of Priscilla, which, when I opened the envelope Altmann gave me, was on top. Hers was the first face I saw, in all her youthful beauty and intensity of spirit."

"The romantic gesture," said George a touch acidly.

Wendy reached a reassuring hand to George's and said to the Judge, "The sketch elicited memories, feelings—how sentimental, how wonderful."

The Judge laughed. "Oh, how my daughters would frown at such a thing. Sorry, George, that my scruples or my lack of such ended up sticking you with the father you have."

"No, no!" Wendy suddenly erupted with a kind of concealed rapture. "It's wonderful. That's all got to go in the memoir. It's not just new evidence but also a telling portrayal of the feelings that motivated your actions."

At this, George scowled, bristled. "Did you ever have Priscilla . . . here?" He pursed his lips, as if pained but determined to bring up this delicate matter. "After Yale days and all that."

The Judge's stare deepened as he looked toward the lake, and then he turned to warmly engage his accuser. "At your age"—he shot his eyebrows knowingly at Wendy—"right here, right in the chair you're sitting in. Full of pep, energy, and allure. I was a youngblood still at Yale."

"Surely . . ." She paused and then seemed to pick up a previous thread. "When Cordelia returned the rejected sketches to you, at some point, it must have grown on you, nudged your conscience, occurred to you that the sketches had a direct bearing on the trial of the century. When Dr. Weinstein's book came out in the late seventies, confirming the perjury conviction, setting off a firestorm of controversy and recrimination. Why else would you have posted them, the suspects, on your office corkboard?"

"That has quite the ring: 'trial of the century.' My God, young lady—Wendy, you remind me of Annie in some ways . . . same eager, self-righteous aggressiveness."

"Sir," said George protectively, "that's hardly fair."

"I meant it as a compliment. You think artists are immune from ambition and willful self-promotion—not the great ones, even if your Chopin leaves much to be desired."

At this, she laughed and sprang up and kissed the Judge on the cheek and rubbed his shoulder.

"I'm honored. I only had lessons for five years. And at least you didn't describe me as full of pep and allure."

"I always felt that Altmann brought out Priscilla's quality of mind, her toughness, her flinty disposition . . . her essential, if flawed, humanity. And, as I recall, I think I just began with Priscilla's sketch on my office wall, and . . . over time, the others took their place there as well as I began sifting through the material for my memoir. I suppose you could say it turned into my *rogue's* gallery."

Wendy returned to her chair, and her eyes lit up, as if energized by the direction the conversation was taking. "And you saw her, occasionally, in later years, after she divorced Alger Hiss?"

"We corresponded *occasionally* after the trial. A few desultory walks in Riverside Park when he was in Lewisburg and later. A sad, broken woman. I will never forgive Alger for that."

"And?" asked George, as if unsure where to insert the next shovel blade.

The Judge waved dismissively. "When Alger started enlisting his relationship with Justice Holmes in his campaign for exoneration—to have his conviction overturned. When he accused the judicial system for his woes. When in interview after interview he went on and on about how close he'd been to Holmes, how much he respected him as a mentor and paragon of judicial probity. When I knew different. When Alger pushed his fucking luck too far."

"Turning up like a bad penny," she suggested. "Something my father always said about unsafe climbers."

George bent forward, as if to change the drift by imparting a confidence. "You might be interested to know that Dr. Weinstein was immediately able to identify your mystery man in the ninth sketch." From a file in his lap, George handed the Judge a photocopy of one of the sketches.

"Do you have to keep calling him Dr.?" He examined the photo of a middle-aged man, a certain look of diffidence in his polite stare. "Sounds like my Jewish proctologist."

"It's a young Harry Hopkins."

"Harry who?"

"Hopkins—Harry Hopkins. A younger Harry Hopkins," George said. "When he was in better health, when he ran the WPA in the thirties. Mr. Weinstein had no doubt."

The Judge stared pointedly, his gaze then drifting off to the topmost boughs of the white pine, touched with shimmering gold by the lowering sun.

"Hopkins was Roosevelt's right hand . . . a Communist?"

"Weinstein said he promoted pro-Soviet initiatives throughout the war."

The Judge shook his head, incredulous. "You can say that again. There were times when he overruled us on the War Production Board, insisting on providing matériel to the Soviets that was already in short supply when it came to our own forces." He turned to the lake, water-reflected light playing softly in his blue eyes. "Well, I'll be damned . . . He always looked a little like death warmed over when I knew him."

"Edward," asked Wendy in a cool, confident voice, as if mention of Annie had assured her place, "do you recall the story in Chambers's book—it was a contentious point in the trial—about their trip, their drive northeast on Route 202—Chambers and Alger and Priscilla Hiss—to Harry Dexter White's summer home in Fitzwilliam, New Hampshire?"

The Judge gave them both sharp looks.

"We made mincemeat of Chambers over that confabulation—did we not?"

"Yes, you did. The prosecution couldn't come up with a scintilla of evidence to support his story. And yet he stuck to it like a dog with a bone."

"So that's what this business about Fitzwilliam is all about—what, exactly, is it you two are up to?"

George weighed in: "According to Weinstein, the trip from Washington in the thirties would have taken four days, two days to drive up and two days to get back, as Chambers described it in *Witness*; only they were gone five days, at least according to the Hisses' baby-sitter."

"If I remember, Alger dismissed the whole thing as delusional—never happened."

"And yet," Wendy noted, "in your copy of *Witness*, in Annie's copy—she's underlined Chambers's description of their road trip to Fitzwilliam, and written in the margin 'That conniving bitch!'"

"Goodness—hardly sounds like Annie. Well . . ."

George eased forward in his seat. "She blames Priscilla for insisting on accompanying Chambers and then, oddly, mentions Teddy, almost as if blaming Priscilla for what happened to Teddy. And you wrote in the margin how it was a disaster for Teddy as well."

The Judge blinked rapidly, his gaze drawing inward. "She always blamed me—one way or another—for Teddy. What more can I say?"

George shrugged at Wendy and continued, "In 1948, White died there of a heart attack, an overdose of digitalis, after being accused of being a spy."

"White . . ." The Judge sat back, as if suddenly unsure of himself. "Pain in the neck, wise guy, from what I remember. Treasury forever poking its nose into things it had no business doing. Scrappy fellow, a terrier pulling Morgenthau's leash. Unpleasant in the pushy way of a powerful bureaucrat. Both White and Morgenthau were Jewish, so they had every incentive to conspire to beggar Germany after the war—the Morgenthau Plan—you know. Turn the Reich into a farmyard. Our military had a fit, because once that got out, the Germans fought harder than ever to save themselves."

Wendy raised her eyebrows at George before saying, "Another witness you didn't need to worry about." Her voice was now husky, soft, almost distant.

George gave her a look of knowing dismay, his lips pressed tight in a restrained grimace. "Judge," he went on, "did *you* ever meet Chambers outside the witness box? Before the trial or after?"

Perhaps the Judge hadn't quite heard, because his stare had returned to the comforting presence of the tallest pines. Then he gave a shrug, almost of resignation, and a knowing smile.

"Now I remember the young Mr. Weinstein striding into my chambers, sans appointment, a man on a mission, wearing a Yale tie for my benefit, I suppose. What else did he want you to get out of me?"

George replied, "If you had some connection with Chambers before or after the trial."

"If I had, don't you think I'd have written as much in the memoir?"

"And yet," Wendy said, giving George a significant look, "you said you read *Witness* not once, not twice, but three times—your wife's *inscribed* copy."

"Did I tell you that?"

"You left the copy for me on top of your typescript of the memoir," said George.

She leaned in now, modulating her voice as if in imitation of a woman she'd never known. "Did you or Annie ever meet Whittaker Chambers outside of court—before or after the trial?"

"Whittaker Chambers," he pronounced the syllables slowly and distinctly, "hardly ran in our circles, or we—God forbid—in his. Nevertheless, there is much to admire—and more so now—in the excellence of the writing. After all, he was a senior editor at *Time* magazine. Surely, if he had met me, he would have written about it in his memoir—eh?" The Judge leaned toward his interlocutors. "You two have become quite the prosecutorial team—or is it, dare I ask, editorial team? Just what do you intend to make of me?" He smiled wickedly. "Perhaps, I should have put the thing in the hands of Alice; wouldn't we have had a time of it then!"

Wendy leaned forward in her chair, as if defending her ground.

"Besides art, I studied French literature—a lot of Proust at Yale, the workings of memory, the nature of time . . . alas, not space-time." She laughed, patting George's knee. "Edward, you have an artistic touch— not to be wasted. The more of the real you, the more of your feelings and sensibilities we get into the memoir, the more it will ring true."

"Ah . . ." The Judge nodded at the flattery and turned with a kind of serene pleasure, glancing to the lake where a sudden squawking of geese was to be heard. "My wife, Annie, loved Proust, but I struggled. She had me read *Swann's Way* to her when she was dying. Perhaps as a punishment for what she considered my sins."

"Oh, no!" exclaimed Wendy. "It was her parting gift to you, a way of returning to your childhood sensibilities and associations, your mother's kindness and unconditional love." She turned to George with a hint of wildness in her eyes. "Don't you think, George, that the sections on Annie are some of your grandfather's finest, most evocative writing in the memoir?"

The Judge raised an admonishing finger. "She was certainly enamored of Chambers, why she never forgave me. But don't let Chambers get to you with his theological mumbo-jumbo. He makes a false dichotomy: It's not either God or Marx—or Freud, too, I suppose; Jesus or Stalin. That's the kind of engaging self-serving nonsense that the Right likes to indulge in for all their many sins. Liberals and humanists and nonbelievers are not ipso facto on the side of the Communist devil. Rational man does not inevitably lead to the Lubyanka execution chambers, no more so than the man of faith inevitably leads to the rack of the Inquisition."

"Edward," she said, as if with the renewed earnestness of an artist entranced with a certain cast of light, "I think it has more to do with a loss of faith, a loss of identity—the thing Hiss was trying to steal from Chambers by, in a way, putting Chambers on trial for framing a false reality—and so denying him . . ." She swept a hand through her hair in frustration and leaned forward, her voice smoldering, verging on the flirtatious as she struggled to explain. "Those precious spots of time. And you . . . you hold, if not our destiny, at least George's in your hand. The last witness . . . to an era fraught with broken faith."

The Judge waved dismissively to George as if she, a petitioner before his court, had finally overstepped her bounds or gotten in over her head.

"Go fetch Stephen for Wendy, George. Have you told her the story?"

George patted her knee, leaped up, and went inside, then quickly returned with a framed, gold-matted, black-and-white portrait photo and put it into her hands.

"Recognize the author?" the Judge asked.

"Can't say that I do," she replied, shaking her head at the long, rather sour, thin face of a young man with unruly hair, his eyes tight and lusterless.

"Stephen Crane, my girl. Perhaps not in Proust's league but beloved by me and my father and Justice Holmes. Holmes was always amazed how well Crane got the feel of the battlefield, the utter confusion, the loneliness and insignificance felt by the individual soldier. Well, Crane wrote *The Red Badge of Courage* right up the road here. His father and brother were members of the original Hermitage syndicate. Stephen knew my father, Dr. Dimock, and spent many an afternoon on this very veranda picking his brains about the sights and sounds of southern battlefields, where my father had saved lives treating the wounded. And when I was a small boy, I remember hearing how the newly famous Stephen rode up on his bay mare, hitched the horse on the railing, and gabbed with my father—perhaps sitting in your chair. My father said that before you knew it, the young author had tears in his eyes. If he said it once, he let it out a bushel of times: He was terrified he'd never write anything as good again as *The Red Badge of Courage.* He was a famous man that day when he rode over here, after years of struggle. And you know what he wanted to talk to my father about? How troubled he was; he feared he had only one great book in him. And he was right, of course. He drove himself mercilessly; he traveled far and wide, injuring his health, but everything that followed was a disappointment."

She'd been holding the framed photo, staring intently.

"He died young," she said, just above a hush. "Tuberculosis, wasn't it?"

The Judge went on: "People tended to confide in my father, people do with a doctor. Stephen was a sensitive soul, gathering the memories of others and weaving them into a literary spell. A nice trick"—he gave a knowing smile—"if you can do it. He, too, captured an era, as you put it, of a faith crumbled in the nightmare of the Civil War."

"Wait, wait!" she exclaimed, and pulled out her phone, switching on the voice recorder. "Do you mind? We need to get this in the memoir."

"There's a kind of sardonic irony in his pages that I rather enjoy. Not unlike the ironic voice of my mentor, Justice Holmes, whose father, Dr. Holmes, keenly observed the withering away of the hard-boiled puritanism of his youth, and in his old age the failure of the Unitarian faith in the aftermath of the Civil War, while Oliver subsequently was forced to endure the onslaught of Marx and Freud—economic man and sexual man, and with the Great War, as he called it, the recrudescence of Nietzsche's will to power, Robespierre's terror to the imposition of revolutionary virtue—totalitarian man. And now I suppose we're presented with a new faith, terrorism for the sake of terror. Well, thank the Lord I won't be around to see how you deal with this newest monster of human depravity. I fear I must keep to my faith in the law and Emerson's poetic moment and leave the rest up to you two."

George, restless now at hearing the old stories, the old blather, removed one more photocopy and handed it to the Judge.

"Recognize him?"

The Judge stared long and hard, his eyes touched with a certain melancholy that had not been there before.

"William Remington, isn't it? Haven't we touched on him already? I believe he worked on our staff at the War Production Board. We called him Bill. Lovely blond hair and the softest blue eyes I ever knew in a man. Smart as a whip—a Dartmouth man, if memory serves."

George slumped back in his seat, as if now fed up beyond words.

Wendy reached for the Judge's knee and gave it a gentle pat.

"You barely mention him in your memoir."

"Why would I? He was one of a dozen young economists on the staff. What was there to write about?"

"Jesus, Judge!" George sprang up, trying to calm himself. "Remington was convicted of perjury—spying, of passing aircraft-production figures from your office to Elizabeth Bentley. And he's in the Altmann sketches—in your possession."

"So, so, I'll include anything more I can remember in the memoir if you think it's so important. I couldn't care less."

"But surely his conviction for perjury—and then brutal murder in prison—must have affected you more than just a passing reference would indicate," accused George.

The Judge waved a gloved hand. "Oh sit down, George."

"We were just at Lewisburg prison the other day," she explained. "It was horrible how he was murdered by a group of inmates. Maybe the KGB was behind it."

The Judge nodded, eyes closed, as if trying to be helpful. "Yes, yes, I remember something now, like an osprey grabbing a fish too large and being swept down to his doom . . . how tragic, poor boy. He was so young, a narrow, beseeching face, always attentive, quick of mind and spirit, eager to please, and such lovely blue eyes. I'm trying to put a face to his wife, but I'm afraid I can't." He opened his own blue eyes and sighed. "Did I ever tell you, George, about the purple-throated hummingbird?"

"Probably, yes, but I've forgotten."

"Well, the purple-throated hummingbird has a wonderful trick up his sleeve: He has learned to imitate the sound of a bee. And do you know why?" He paused in delicious expectation as his listeners glanced anxiously at each other. "Because the only creature the tiny humming-bird is deathly afraid of is the bee: A single sting can kill him. And so the purple-throated hummingbird prospers mightily—buzzing away— as he harvests nectar, with none of his colleagues to say him nay."

"You felt sorry for him, then?" prompted Wendy. "That golden boy on the staff?"

"It's hard." The Judge sighed, tiring. "You see, there were people over the years, people I didn't know—total strangers—who would come up to me on an occasion and pat my shoulder and whisper in my ear their admiration for my client, as if they knew something I didn't, as if I were really one of them. People, many in the highest offices in the land, I can tell you. Even if Hiss had admitted his guilt on the courthouse steps, they would still have needed to believe."

George stared blankly at his grandfather. "During your trial, did you have any inkling, any sense, that the FBI were hot on the trail of the Rosenbergs, Gold, and Greengrass? That your ill-dressed goons, Harold Rosenwald's investigators, were agitated, concerned, nervous?"

"Haven't we covered all this? Wasn't that all later?"

She spoke now in a near whisper. "Your atmosphere—the mist of uncertainty, the terrible ambiguity."

The Judge waved her off, as if now exhausted by the whole thing, needing his nap.

And yet she persevered, now more a rumination to herself. "As were the Hisses, so spellbound by their Carl with that authentic Russian accent—a belief, a faith even deeper than time because rooted in your will to power; or is it, do you suppose, the romantic imagination? But then, you never met *their* Carl . . . except in the pages of *Witness*. Too bad, really, since he and Alger Hiss were such great bird lovers. Do you remember how Chambers wrote about a ground robin on a fence post, with Hiss at his side, and Hiss asked him, 'Do you know what he says?'

Chambers didn't know the old country translation of the robin's song. 'Listen,' Hiss said: 'Sweet bird, sing!' According to Chambers, it didn't seem silly to him, for Alger was completely captivated by the bird's song. As he wrote, 'I have no more vivid recollection of Alger Hiss.'"

For a long moment, the Judge stared into the young woman's face, as if mesmerized by this feat of mimicry, or perhaps the echoing blueness of her wide eyes mirroring his.

"Ah, yes, his one true human quality, that love of birds, as he'd related it to Chambers about having seen his first prothonotary warbler at Glen Echo, when he and Priscilla would rise at dawn on Sundays and ramble along the banks of the Potomac. The very thing—his enthusiasm—that gave him away when he first mentioned that sighting while testifying before HUAC. A golden ray of light that took his breath away, confirming to the committee that Chambers had indeed been telling the truth." He made a move to rise from his chair but halted for a moment longer as he cast a sharp look tinged with sarcasm at Wendy. "Annie could imitate the song of the hermit thrush on the piano, uncanny, really. She loved nothing more than escaping to Handytown, or into her books, or to Venice if she could, or up here alone under the ship's keel ceiling—places where her inspiration took flight, whether mourning for Teddy or the fame that eluded her, or my sins, real or imagined."

South Korean Capital Of Seoul Falls to Reds After Sneak Invasion

Truman Charges Red North Koreans With Unprovoked Attack

Communist North Ko Invades South; Kills 4,0 Takes Towns, Declares W

Paris Cabinet Falls; New Elections Loom

Industry Pool Plan Periled

Sen C.

Seoul Prepares Appe To M'Arthur for Ai

KOREA

MANCHURIA

SEA OF JAPAN

THE 38TH PARALLEL

EDS INVADING KOREA

U.S. Will Hold Russia Responsible

REDS STRIKE—Map shows

ED CAPTURE OF SEOUL LOOMS

38

Dead Drop

THEY LAY ON George's childhood bed, exhausted.

A mind, a man, fading before their eyes; in moments quick and elusive as the devil, in others lost and wandering—haunted: full of more questions than answers, of doubts rather than certainties—lies and loss and intrigue all apiece. The last of a breed. The last of a world entire.

"I can't press him anymore; I just can't do it."

"Yes," she agreed.

"Like I'm persecuting him for something I can't even name."

"What can we do to save him—Hermitage?" She laid a hand on his. "George, the ship's keel ceiling is entrancing beyond my wildest dreams. I can't get it out of my mind." Her voice was quivering with repressed desire. "It holds a thousand secrets, the obscure or even not so obscure artists who contributed to it. It's a wonder—a whole world in jeopardy."

"Sorry, this world is problematic enough." He was preoccupied with e-mails on his laptop. Problems with hanging his next show at Dark Matter.

"As Tennyson wrote."

"No, spare me."

"'Or that the past will always win / A glory from its being far; / And orb into the perfect star / We saw not, when we moved therein?'"

"Not now."

"It's like we've become part of a story written long ago in a book only discovered yesterday."

"Enough already."

"We've got to find a way."

He clicked on his most recent e-mail from Allen Weinstein, pausing a moment before responding to her. "If we registered most of the land under 480a for tax purposes, and begin lumbering it in parcels, selling a few acres of hardwoods every year, that might generate a little cash and relieve some of the tax burden. But, of course, he doesn't want to cut the trees. You heard him; he says they talk to each other and he's not of a mind to disturb their conversation."

"Of course they talk, the mother trees to their young." She sighed. "And Altmann's paintings are potentially worth millions; we have to get them into a climate-controlled storage facility."

He'd begun reading. Across the room, the leaded-glass windows, cracked a few inches to draw in the mild night air, shimmered with moonlight off the lake, the tall pine a silver-onyx, like velvet ribbons hung on the sky. There was the barest breath of a breeze, a soft whisper calling out to her.

She got up from the bed in her bra and panties, a sultry heat in her padded step as she went prospecting again among the shelves: a young man's life, redolent of crusted sweat and well-oiled baseball mitts, a Spalding tennis racket in an ash-wood press held by rusted wing nuts, tins of cruddy lures, moldy nature guides from which slipped dried leaves and splayed colorless petals, all redolent of some musky animal scent, perhaps aftershave tinctured with the lingering astringency of silver polish. She reached up to the glittering rowing trophies on the top shelf—mirroring her inquisitive eyes—and fingered the ribbons and medals, bringing her fingertips to her nose as if that might be the talismanic source: the charisma of a great athlete. Then a shelf of handsome Conrad first editions, inscribed offerings for birthdays and Christmas from proud parents.

Reaching the bottom shelf, she examined a shoe box containing piles of rusted iron railroad spikes. She picked them up, sniffed them—creosote?—and dropped them clanking back, wiping off her stained fingers on her white cotton panties. She pulled out a few Groton textbooks with broken spines, and then a Yale yearbook, turning the yellowed pages containing the monochrome faces of the class of 1953. Brought up short, she walked the yearbook over to where he lay absorbed and pulled off a strand of blond hair clinging to the left shoulder of his fleece. She shivered, as if possessed by a sudden specter as she pointed out the many inscriptions of love and fellowship, and one in a bold hand under his freshman photo. She read the latter aloud: "'Voted most likely to become chief justice of the Supreme Court.'" As if frightened by her own voice, she glanced, unnerved, to the Yale banner of the class of 1953 on the wall above the bed.

"He was already dead when his class yearbook came out. And yet his classmates not only included him but still predicted his triumph in life."

He waved her off, still engrossed in the e-mail.

Chastened, she slipped the yearbook back into its place, letting her fingers flow across more artifacts until she struck upon a child's album of bird feathers. She took it down and leafed through the thick, brittle pages, reading the labored block letters of an eight-year-old: BALD EAGLE, RED-TAILED HAWK, GRAY OWL . . . She drew out one of the largest feathers, admiring its mottled russets and gray-blacks, first brushing it softly against her cheek, her nose, then across the curve of her breasts, eyes pinching shut for seconds, as if further indulging the sensuous touch that might yet release the absent thing in full.

Replacing the feather, she moved to the paneled wall nearest the bureau and a photograph of Teddy Dimock in his khaki uniform—suntanned face and brilliant smile—standing with his comrades by a military truck, their rucksacks stacked for transport. The photo was labeled in a flowing woman's hand, a mother's hand: Camp Lejeune, February 1950.

"Here," he finally said, handing over his laptop. "You obviously need to read this."

George went to the window and stared up at the sky, hoping to find some comfort in the familiar constellations blinking out their messages from worlds and times long before even Homo sapiens roamed the earth. He could almost hear Weinstein's voice when he read his e-mail now, in this case the sympathetic tone of a father of sons, who had been so moved by the fate of Teddy Dimock in the Judge's memoir that he felt compelled to share the story of one William Weisband: a story that certainly reflected on the Hiss trial but more sadly on a father who had lost his beloved son in Korea.

William Weisband was a low-level KGB courier in the thirties. Born to Russian parents in Alexandria, Egypt, trained in the Comintern's Lenin School, Weisband proved to be a talented linguist who spoke perfect Russian and unaccented English. In the mid-thirties, he worked as a courier between New York and agents in Washington, presumably crossing paths with Whittaker Chambers and possibly members of the Volta Place cell. He was later transferred by the Soviets to California to gather technical information from West Coast war industries, and served honorably with army intelligence during the war, though always staying in touch with his Soviet handlers. By 1946, Weisband was working for the military at Arlington Hall, the nerve center for the U.S. Army's Signals Intelligence Service (SIS), the best in the world at the time. This was the very same building where in 1946 Meredith Gardner would make his breakthrough decipherment of the Venona cable traffic, gradually uncovering the penetration of the Manhattan Project and the spying of Klaus Fuchs and the Rosenbergs, and ultimately Hiss himself. In 1946, the National Security Agency, as it would later be called, managed another singular triumph by breaking the Soviet radio codes (distinct from Soviet wartime cable traffic, the Venona decrypts), thus allowing almost complete access to Soviet military logistics traffic in real time. This meant that American commanders and the president could monitor Soviet military capabilities and dispositions and detect when Stalin was bluffing and when he wasn't.

In the early years of the Cold War, this was a precious, invaluable resource of firsthand, near-real-time intelligence. Because of the defection in 1945 of Elizabeth Bentley, who gave up the core of the existing Soviet political spy networks to the FBI, including most of the agents in the Volta Place sketches, along with those confirmed by Whittaker Chambers both in 1939 and later, the Soviets were forced to pull back their operatives for fear of disclosure and arrest, and closed down most of their political networks. Leaving their long-serving agent William Weisband, now burrowed deep in the NSA at Arlington Hall, in the dark and out of touch with his KGB handlers. But in 1948, right as the Hiss-Chambers confrontation was becoming front-page news, as the hunt for the atom bomb spies began in earnest, the KGB began reactivating all their networks in the United States, selectively at first, and very carefully. Help in the form of new KGB agents, both legal and not, now became available for their iced agents, including protecting the likes of Alger Hiss, who was under enormous pressure to confess.

William Weisband, working in the bowels of Arlington Hall, monitoring Soviet radio traffic, was soon contacted and reactivated by a new handler, Yuri Bruslov, in February 1948. "Zhora," Weisband's code name in the Venona decrypts, then proceeded, over the next year, to hand over reams of secret documents to the Soviets, verifying in detail the extent to which the SIS had broken the Soviet military codes. He stuffed secret documents under his shirt on his lunch hour and after work, and left them in dead drops for his Soviet handler, or passed them through the window of a waiting automobile in a brush pass.

The result was devastating. Suddenly, in late 1948, over a period of a few months, every one of the Soviet military cipher networks that the NSC had broken "went dark." The Soviet Union instituted a much more secure cipher system for radio communications. The American military was left deaf and blind. As 1948 turned into 1949 and Hiss was headed for indictment and trial, the once-cold networks were reactivated, upgraded, and put at the disposal of Hiss's KGB support team, with orders to protect all existing assets at any cost. But of more catastrophic import, as 1949 turned into 1950, as the second Hiss trial came to a climax, Stalin approved plans for a North Korean invasion of South Korea, something he would have done only with the acquisition and successful testing of an atom bomb in late 1949. The North Korean military was totally dependent on massive transfers of Soviet arms and logistical help, which included weapons, aircraft, artillery, tanks, trucks, fuel, and ammunition. An enormous buildup that American intelligence completely missed because of the loss of all radio intelligence and access to Soviet logistics communication. All thanks to William Weisband.

If the U.S. government had known about the buildup and the imminent attack, it could well have prevented the outbreak of the Korean War by way of diplomatic warnings and an immediate infusion of military assistance to South Korea. Nor did it help that Alger Hiss's great friend and longtime supporter Dean Acheson, then secretary of state, had neglected to include South Korea within the perimeter of the American security zone in Asia during a well-publicized speech, thus leaving the impression, certainly in Stalin's mind, that the United States had no interest in standing up to a possible North Korean invasion of the South. If the FBI had managed to break Hiss or White or Duggan in the mid-forties—or Currie or Field, for that matter—the name of William Weisband would mostly likely have come out and his spying been cut short, thus sparing the lives of the 35,000 American boys killed in Korea, including one Teddy Dimock.

—

Wendy looked up at him with tears in her eyes. But George was now distracted by a text message on his phone.

Your father just drove in from the coast—sober but with a terrible toothache.

39

Bad People

GEORGE BACKED THE U-Haul truck up to the barn door and got out, waving Wendy, driving the Tahoe, to a nearby parking spot on the grass. The Tahoe was crammed with sheets of cardboard, rolls of bubble wrap, and packing tape. Not a little put out, he walked up the dirt path from the barn toward the house, where a battered blue-and-silver Ford F-250 pickup truck was parked. His mother's Toyota was nowhere in sight. The Ford was rusted around the wheel housings, right-side mirror askew, door dented, rear bumper hanging at an angle. Even the seaweed green Washington state license plates were banged up and rusted. The tailgate was collaged with faded bumper stickers, those promoting Kiss, Pink Floyd, the Band, and Van Morrison being the most legible. He glanced in the window of the cab at the sheepskin coverings on the front seats, matted flat and stained to a pewter-tinged off-yellow. Passenger seat and floor were layered with Burger King wrappers, plastic water bottles, and unfolded road maps harboring nests of coffee-stained Styrofoam cups. He ran a hand over the right front tire, the tread nearly smooth to the touch. The inspection sticker on the left front windshield had expired two months before.

He glanced at Wendy, who stood down the hill, watching developments. He gave her a thumbs-down, as if to say, Some things never change, and marched up to the front door of the house. Knocking loudly, he announced himself, waited impatiently, yelled again, and then returned to the barn to begin unloading the packing material from the Tahoe.

"Maybe Mom's sneaked him out somewhere. Sunday's her day off, and she knew we were coming." He shot a glance at the Ford pickup. "Coast is clear."

Wendy had been staring off at the view, where, beyond a thinning tree line on the downward slope, the rooftops of Woodstock patterned the valley, and beyond to the distant autumn-shorn hills streaked with veins of cinnamon and crimson: a view she already cherished, as if once belonging to another of her kind.

She gestured to where an aluminum ladder leaned up against the roof of the barn. A half-empty box of gray shingles, a plastic bucket of sealant, and roofing tools lay to the side. A large area of recent repair was clearly visible on the roof.

"He's not wasting any time," she said, "getting back into the swing of things."

"Fuck," he spat. "We should have done this a week ago, instead of taking that stupid trip to Fitzwilliam."

"What's gotten into you?" She squeezed his arm, barely able to contain her excitement as he slid back the barn door and the age-old scents filtered out into the warm November afternoon. "Look, this is good—a man around the house to fix stuff, that's just what Cordelia needs."

"Whose fucking side are you on?"

"It's not a matter of sides. You're off the hook."

George looked at her as if she'd lost her mind. "He's fixing the leak in the roof."

"So, that's good."

"You're such an idiot."

She swung her right palm at his face but pulled her hand back at the last instant, then turned on her heels and walked away toward the house.

"You're not an idiot," he called out. "Come on, let's get the paintings packed."

She remained sitting on the porch swing, not watching him unload the packing materials, swigging a bottle of water. After about ten minutes, she walked slowly back, plugged in her earbuds, and silently began helping. They didn't exchange a word for almost an hour. As they pulled the canvases from the racks for wrapping, her fingers kept straying to the swirls of impasto, and she was unable to resist carrying a canvas to a patch of sunlight from the overhead skylight, licking her lips as she communed with her alter ego, rubbing her thighs in something approaching a yearning for sexual release.

"Aren't you at least curious?" she asked, as if the situation had finally gotten the better of her.

"About what?"

"About Jimmy Altmann—Jesus, George, he's your blood." And she held up a small canvas landscape shimmering with repressed light in the mauve-green blurs of cedars from an oblique angle on a hillside. "He's a link—he knew the artist—maybe the last man alive who really knows anything about him."

He paused a moment, sweating, breathing deeply, the tape gun poised in midair. "Alice is meeting with me and my mother sometime tomorrow to offer us legal advice. According to my aunt, my mother never got the divorce finalized because they could never track down Jimmy Altmann on the road and serve him with the papers. Like I told you, there's a paternity issue to boot. So they published the petition for divorce through the courts, put notices in newspapers and such, still without a response from her husband. So, my mother, legally speaking, was abandoned by her husband, with back taxes owing on the house and not a cent of alimony or child support. Thanks to Alice, and the Judge, who paid the back taxes, she did get the house and land transferred legally to her name." He shot her a worried glance as he continued to tape down the bubble wrap. "But the status of the contents of the barn—the estate, according to Alice—is problematic. The artwork might still be considered his personal property."

"You sold out your show twice over," she protested, as if a little panicked. "Properly marketed, a new catalog and essay—a great American artist murdered by the KGB—museum acquisitions . . . your legacy, and Hermitage . . . millions."

"By the way," he said matter-of-factly, "your check for the fourth painting didn't clear, according to JJ."

She closed her eyes, mortified.

"Sorry, I don't keep that kind of money in my checking account. I sold stock last week. The check will clear when JJ redeposits it."

"Stocks, huh?"

She stuck out her tongue and turned away.

He snorted. "Get wrapping. I've been having anxiety attacks about him stacking the paintings in that disaster of a pickup truck and heading for the hills."

"George . . ." She eyed him with a fierce no-nonsense crinkle of her eyes. "You're too emotionally—understandably so—close to this whole business with your father."

"You have no idea," he said with a scowl. "And even when he was here, he wasn't here. His old girlfriends—like a pregnant seventeen-year-old—from the road were always turning up, looking for him."

"Poor little Georgie." She chucked her shoulders as if throwing off a burden. "Listen, baby, Jimmy Altmann was there on the night

George Altmann died—even if he was only eight years old. Let me talk to him about his father and what happened. I'll record it on my phone, a formal interview, everything he remembers."

He waved it off. "You're more than a fucking force of nature—tooth and claw, survival of the fittest—the way you barge into people's lives and try to take over. You're a fucking vampire—you fucking deserve each other. And he's *not* my father."

"Whatever"—she blinked back tears—"he's a witness—a witness! Don't you get it, you immature shit. You owe it to the memoir, even if he's not your old man."

"Jesus, you arrived at Sheila's opening dressed to kill, sashaying around like it was an Armani runway, while she was cowering, full of dread about her show and the Cantor Fitzgerald widow who'd been waiting a year to meet her."

"I helped her. I hugged her and gave her moral support."

"You upstaged her."

"I tried to sell her stuff."

"Which you obviously thought was second-rate. You're so damned competitive."

"What's good is good . . . I can't help that."

"Half the time you were going on about George Altmann."

"Fuck, they're your clients—that's what they wanted to talk about."

"I distinctly heard you—so slyly segueing to your own stuff—and your show."

They turned to the sound of the sliding barn door.

Cordelia and Jimmy Altmann walked into the barn. They stood transfixed at the scene of packing, at the thirty or so paintings already bubble-wrapped and leaning up against the wall for transfer to the U-Haul truck. Cordelia made a wacky face and did a little tap-dance number, arms outspread, as if to say, We're here. George and Wendy stood like deer caught in headlights at a long table, a rough oblong of plywood laid across two sawhorses, tape guns in hand. George mockingly stood to attention and saluted.

"Well," said Cordelia, "you two didn't waste any time."

George looked from his mother to the tall, rather haggard figure sporting a prominent gray handlebar mustache and wearing a plaid tan-and-black wool jacket. The man, now in his sixties, who was his father, at least on his birth certificate, stepped forward and hitched up the belt of his worn blue jeans.

"Rumor has it, a long, cold winter's in store. We got a late start with the rental truck; we were hoping to get the packing done today," continued George in a sheepish tone. "But it looks like we'll still be at it by morning."

Jimmy Altmann, his long gray hair swept back behind his gold beringed ears, took another couple of tentative steps, his cowboy boots beneath the ragged cuffs of his jeans resounding on the warped floorboards. He fingered his stubbled jaw with the look of a man who had just awakened from a dream. His mouth was strangely slack, skin worn from decades of sun exposure, deeply lined, with dark bags under his bleary, bloodshot eyes. Those eyes seemed to deepen with memory—or the need to hold on to what was left of memory—as he silently bypassed the couple to inventory the racks of canvases, the worktables. Moving with a pronounced limp in his right leg, he began handling the paint-encrusted easels in the shadowed corners. Then, the thing assayed in part or whole, he strode over to George and held out his hand in a formal greeting.

"Hello, George. You've grown some."

They shook hands. George did his best to avoid eye contact.

"I'm not sure I would have recognized you," said George.

"Not sure I'd recognize myself," said Jimmy Altmann, passing a hand over his compact brow to brush back a lank of grizzled hair, his crooked, arthritic fingers then going to his whiskered jaw. "At least not here." He shrugged. "I'm Jimmy," he said to Wendy, reaching out to take her hand, lingering there to stare appreciatively into her curious eyes.

"Nice to finally meet you," she said. Beads of perspiration lined her brow; she had the uneasy but intent look of someone who has recognized a face, or thinks she should recognize a face: the Altmann crinkle along the bridge of the nose.

"Ain't she a beaut," sang out Cordelia, her GOLDEN NOTEBOOK sweatshirt swelling out magnificently across her chest, bracketed by a pink down vest. "Wendy paints even better than she climbs mountains." And Cordelia went over and put a protective arm around her, as if claiming this willowy protégée for herself. Her ears, dangling a best-seller from her jewelry line, gave off a melodic tinkle, flashing silver points of lapis lazuli.

"Jim's a bit woozy," she went on, giving George a quick kiss. "We just got out of dental surgery in Kingston." She shot a disapproving frown at the man again wandering the barn like a lost soul. "George, your father just arrived with three severely infected teeth—God knows how he endured the pain cross-country—and no health insurance, much less dental coverage. And since it's a Sunday, we had to go to the emergency room. So we just spent the day and four thousand dollars—charged to my Visa card—on dental surgery. He's still full of Novocain, and got a life lesson that oral hygiene has its benefits."

"The teeth only started really bothering me in Kansas City," noted Jimmy, inspecting the rusted piping from the woodstove where it rose to the rafters.

Cordelia gave a hoot of displeasure, if not disgust. "You need to be more health-conscious. Wendy drags George here"—she grabbed her son's upper arm and gave it an admiring squeeze—"into the gym three days a week. She teaches rock climbing, among her many talents."

"Rocks for Jocks," mused George.

Jimmy sauntered back around, eyeing Wendy, and she him, with an uneasy, if wistful, smile. "Damned if you don't remind me more than a little of Cordelia," he proclaimed, a drooping lower lip valiantly forming the words, "when she first arrived in Woodstock. She was the belle of the ball around these parts. Even Levon fell for her, and the other boys could barely keep their mitts off. Robbie always said he had you"—he kept his eyes fastened on Wendy—"in mind for his early love songs—remember, Cordy?"

Slapping his shoulder, Cordelia said, "Jeest, Jim, don't spout crap like that around the kids. That's the last thing she or George wants to hear." She sighed. "Did I mention, Levon and Robbie still aren't talking, even after Levon's cancer surgery?"

"Robbie!" Jimmy arched his thick rectangles of eyebrows, a dark coffee color in contrast to the mustache and hair, and gave a knowing look. "Got himself the rights to the boys' songs—always an eye on the main chance."

"Far out," purred Wendy, who, as if goaded by some instinct to mimic the lurking specter of past lives, raised her arms above her head and threw her head back in an ecstatic approximation of Cordelia's famous pose in *Life*.

This extemporaneous act—near madness, in George's mind—resulted in his version of a reality check. "Actually, as a wild and crazy artist, not to mention collector, she's a great fan of your father, George Altmann. In fact, she owns three—soon to be four—of his paintings, *and*," he added, raising a finger in a sarcastic gesture, "she's desperate to interview you about him."

"Interview me?" Jimmy Altmann shrank back as if physically assaulted, then casually moseyed over, his limp more pronounced, to the bubble-wrapped canvases, as if to inventory what was about to walk out the door. "I've been interviewed about the Band, of course, about Dylan, Janis, Van, Richie, Jimi—you name 'em—but not . . . in a million years, George Altmann." He gave George a curious, somewhat supercilious look. "*The* George Altmann—ha-ha."

"Oh," George assured him, "she just waves her wand and drops a boatload of fairy dust and you're off to Never Never Land."

"Pixie dust." Jimmy smiled. "Weren't those the days, huh, Cordy?"

"Like I told you, George runs a gallery now. He just finished a very successful George Altmann show in New York." Cordelia, noticing something off in George's expression, smoothly added, "And he's written a splendid catalog—haven't you, George?"

"Is that why you're wrapping up all the canvases?" asked Jim. "Are they headed for New York?"

"They're headed for a climate-controlled art-storage facility in Brooklyn," said George firmly. He pointed to the canvas lying flat before him. "The cold, the freezing temperature, the damp, the mice pee and poop—none of that is good for the preservation of the paint surface. There's already a lot of craquelure going on, and not a little lifting of pigment, and some are more than a little fragile."

Jim smiled painfully and wiped spittle from his drooping lower lip, then resumed his slow, rambling circuit, as in search of some fugitive reminder of the past.

"My father couldn't sell anything in the last decade of his life, once he gave up his early figurative style. Stone broke by the time I came along, and resented the world—all this—for not allowing him a living." Jimmy tilted his head to one side and pulled at the right tip of his mustache, as if reviewing some long-standing injustice. "After he died, my mother couldn't get anyone to work with the estate—and God knows, Cordelia and I gave it a try a few times." He winced at George and Wendy. "If just to get the barn cleaned out."

"You referred to it as a bunch of crap," said Cordelia. "A fire hazard."

At this, he again retreated to the ancient cast-iron stove in the corner, rapping his knuckles on the rusted iron.

"I remember coming in here in the dead of winter when Dad was working. My mother would send me over from the house to let him know that dinner was ready. He had no idea of time; he was oblivious of everything . . . didn't even own a watch. I always thought that was odd. He'd have the woodstove blazing away, his hands in gray woolen gloves with the tips of the fingers cut out, and often he'd lay his palette on the stovetop for a few minutes to get the oils to loosen up for him. Two or three kerosene lanterns were always blazing away. I could see his breath. Then he'd go back to the canvas and attack it—I always thought, being a kid, he looked like a swordsman attacking his foe. The surface of the canvas would sing out at his strokes."

"Oh," said Wendy, following his every move with a rapt gaze, "do you remember—I've been dying to know—if he drew directly on the canvas before applying pigment, or did he work from notes and begin with pigment? I can't detect much in the way of underdrawing."

Jimmy Altmann sidled away, almost reluctantly, from the woodstove, as if it still provided needed heat, and moved into a square of fading sunlight from the skylight, a creeping saffron oblong floating across the floorboards. He stared up—the loose skin at his neck tightening, his gray hair almost a youthful blond—into the cobwebby rafters, perhaps in search of the young boy he'd once been.

"He was always drawing, scribbling away. He took a sketch pad with him when he walked into town—'keeping his hand in,' he called it. He'd sketch his bar mates, total strangers, trees—he loved tree patterns. Pages from his sketchbook were pinned all over the walls." Jimmy went to the wall where the easels were stacked and peered at the two-by-four supports, pressing a fingertip to the surface. "Pinholes. As a kid, I kinda thought the place was haunted with his sketched faces, with his skeletal trees, with the drawings of cliffs and boulders he used to bring back with him when he went out on fieldtrips. I could never make sense of them. Most were just intersecting shapes, with a few color notes. Then he'd turn the sketches into"—he paused, trying to remember—"'po-chade' he called them—from Henri, he liked to say, little oil sketches on wood that he'd prop on the windowsills around the house to dry. In the evening, with a book of poetry open on his lap, he'd look up and catch sight of those drying pochades, and a little smile would creep across his face as he contemplated the work before him for the next day. He kept this old Victrola busy as well"—he eased over and caressed the mahogany cabinet—"and he played various Mozart piano sonatas and quartets, depending on the mood of the picture. He always said his pictures were in four-part harmony. 'Today I'm painting the cello line,' he'd say. And the next day it would be first violin. He liked to layer the pigments, you see, sometimes one right over the other or side by side or letting the one beneath 'burn through,' as he put it, so the whole thing hung together for him."

Wendy scampered over and pulled out the Mozart recording by Annie Dimock from the record rack and handed the album to Jimmy.

"Do you remember this recording?" she asked. "Did he ever mention Annie Dimock or her playing?"

"Well, I'll be damned," he exclaimed. "Don't remember this." He held out the album cover to Cordelia. "Not a word about her, the artist, that I remember. But I suppose I must've heard the record playing."

Cordelia intently examined the cover, the striking image of her mother seated at the piano, fingers poised, a diamond brooch glinting on her black gown.

"My God, has this been here the whole time"—she shot a look at Jimmy, at George and Wendy—"and we never knew about it?"

"Forgot to mention it," said George. "Wendy turned it up a few weeks ago."

Jimmy gave a helpless shrug as he shook his head in wonder. "How he loved Mozart."

Cordelia, now clutching the album to her chest with a lost look, exclaimed, "I'll be damned, Jim, that's the first time I've ever heard you talk about him like that!"

George squinted warily at Wendy, who listened, lips slightly agape, eyes sparked with what he could only describe as a hungry look.

Jimmy Altmann looked at the others in all innocence, as if he'd been caught in an indiscretion, and shrugged.

"You know what," he continued, "at a certain point, the little kid you once were becomes a different person. Not you exactly, but different."

"I always thought you despised him," said Cordelia, again staring at the photo of her mother, as if to detect something of herself in the fiery eyes beneath concentrated brows.

"Despise . . . despise"—his voice was searching, distant, then rising with indignation—"what people said about him after he died . . . the suicide—you don't wanna know. People who were once his friends and admirers—motherfuckers. Never heard the end of it in school." He picked up a palette and worked an ancient daub of blue with his thumbnail. "How mother clung to all this." He gestured to the four walls of the barn. "She revered him. Her identity had been formed around his early fame in New York art circles, his big-shot days in

Washington. She could never really accept his death, that his genius might not survive. Her loyalty weighed on me, how she never wanted anything to change in here, like it was a fucking shrine to his memory or something. Even if nobody around here gave a fuck—the way they turned on him." Jimmy flashed a look at George and then nodded at Cordelia. "It wouldn't take much, you know, to weatherproof the barn some, and get some more heaters and humidifiers in to keep the temperature and humidity regulated."

"The leaks," interjected George, "the ice. A power outage and the temperature falls below freezing."

"You could always hook up a generator."

"Twenty thousand bucks for starters," said George.

"Cordelia said you sold out the show."

"Did you know George Altmann, your father"—Wendy paused for a moment, as if coming out of a daze, hesitant—"was a member of the Communist Party?"

She and Jim Altmann locked eyes for a moment, as they had previously. He took her in fully, his careworn baggy eyes moving up from the scuffed climbing boots to the elegant close-fitting Nike warm-up suit in navy blue, where, below the swoosh in white, were the words Yale Women's Crew.

"Sure, I guess so."

"What?" said Cordelia. "You never said anything to me about that."

Jimmy Altmann shrugged. "I mean, years ago, after my mother died and I was cleaning out her things, I came across a bunch of his letters to her when he was working in Washington. Seems he hung out with a bunch of Reds—'bad people' was how my mother referred to them after he died. And plenty more around here—Woodstock . . . crawling with Commies, she always said. But what do I know. By the time I was a teenager—after the McCarthy business and all—if there were any left, they all seemed to have gone to ground."

"Letters," said George.

"Letters?" echoed Wendy.

"Sure, in a biscuit tin under a broken floorboard with some of my mother's stuff in the attic. Or that's where I found them after she died. But that was over forty years ago."

40

Mother Russia

WASHINGTON, D.C.
June 3, 1937

Dear Mattie,

How I miss you and the cool pine breezes of Woodstock. The heat and humidity in Washington this summer are almost as unbearable as the pitiless art world politics of the FAP. But what can I expect as an artist turned supervisor who has sold his soul for a steady income—the first in my life! And let me tell you, administering the mural section for Holger Cahill will make me no friends and plenty of enemies. Cahill and Audrey McMahon, the gal who heads the New York section, let me take all the heat while they pontificate above the fray. I thought the pitched battles in New York—Christ, I don't miss the John Reed Club!—and the Artists Union were pretty rough going, but that was child's play compared to what goes on in the hallowed halls of bureaucracy. And there is more belt tightening, which will hit the New York artists hardest, since they already split the lion's share of the moola. My brother comrades accuse me of humiliating them, impoverishing them by insisting on the means test. No choice, I plead: It's the law. I have allotted to myself one mural in the program for the new Justice Department building—one measly mural—and I get phone calls and letters, dead cats through the window, condemning me for taking bread out of the mouths of needy comrades. And worse, if I try to maintain a level of quality in the program, much less patiently explain that portraits of Lenin and bloodsucking bankers will not be acceptable in a U.S. government building or post office, I am condemned as a lackey of the capitalist class—only interested in lining the pockets of the bourgeoisie! Me, once the darling of *The New Masses*. The aggravation is endless.

Now that I've escaped my bloodthirsty dealer—poor Melvin, who hasn't made a sale in years—and have embraced the New Deal like the Second Coming, I find myself lacking inspiration of any kind. Truth be told, my revolutionary convictions are taking something of a beating— don't let on to the boys in the Woodstock Artists Association! To be honest with you, I don't see how the mural projects can legitimately be said to raise the revolutionary consciousness of the masses, much less give expression to the class struggle. Even more depressing, most of the artists who apply aren't even third-rate; they don't have the most basic drafting skills. And they're always the ones who delight in telling me that formal modernist devices are just an evasion of what they call "reality," and even the mildly talented condemn my criteria of excellence as symptomatic of bourgeois degeneracy. Enough!

The thirty pieces of silver I can lay aside each year should give us three years of living expenses in Woodstock!

Write to me, dearest. Are the raspberries ripe behind the barn? How are your tomatoes this summer? How I long to get back to my studio . . . And you!

Love, George

WASHINGTON, D.C.
July 7, 1937

Dear Mattie,
A cool spell for July even as the battles around the Justice Department mural project heats up. I have claimed a space for myself on the sixth floor, a triptych separated by two fluted pilasters. An odd configuration, both compositionally and thematically, that I plan to make the best of by alluding to Renaissance masters, perhaps a little Leonardo's *Last Supper* with some Pisanello—the Princess of Trebizond in Verona— and Durer's studies of horses and various animals, etc., on the side panels. Something to make the damn thing interesting. Or perhaps something of my favorite painter, Giovanni Bellini—ah, that Venetian light and atmosphere—*sfumato*, they call it. Why not his *Feast of the Gods* in the Widener collection? Apostles, saints, gods—who now, do you suppose, are the elect among us? The ridiculous working title imposed by the powers that be, Holger Cahill, is *Society Fed and Freed*

Through Justice. How the hell to embody such bullshit into scenes of a prosperous Midwestern farm family at Thanksgiving dinner?

And even the P gives me a hard time for not being sufficiently doctrinaire, for making concessions to nationalistic themes—fascist themes, so I was informed by one comrade the other night after a few drinks. What the hell do they expect—New Deal or Old Deal, this is still the same U.S. government Deal!

Can't wait for my August vacation—counting the days!

WASHINGTON, D.C.
September 30, 1937

Dear Mattie,

Sorry for not having written in such a long time; just keeping up with paperwork takes up most of my days. A few weeks back, I was invited by Priscilla Hiss—you met her at the League many years ago—to her home in Georgetown to sketch her for an oil portrait as a birthday present for her husband, Alger. (You recall I did a likeness of her and her son some years back in our New York days.) She is quite the swell upper-class gal, but without the usual airs of superiority. I suppose I should thank her for the FAP job—she's a friend of Holger's! Priscilla had no real talent when I first taught her at the Art Students League, but she is very intelligent and quick to anger at injustices real or imagined. Her husband, Alger, is now a big shot in the State Department, a smart-ass Harvard lawyer. Their house is tiny, like a slice of Swiss cheese, even by Georgetown standards, even smaller than our farmhouse in Woodstock. But they are quite the artsy couple and are up on the latest fashions in art and books and Dr. Freud and regular readers of the *Daily Worker*. Reproductions of Picasso and Matisse hang on their living room walls. And I must admit, it is flattering for me to be among people who appreciate me as an artist, and as a comrade; they are much more respectful of my position in the FAP than our crowd in New York and Woodstock.

As I sketched Priscilla, she responded to my complaints about the FAP by showering me with questions about the mural program. What did I think the best way for the artist to depict the will to struggle? What to say to that? She even questioned if an overemphasis on the misery and suffering of the workers—she specifically mentioned

Cikovsky and Soyer—could possibly uplift the masses and inspire them to the "barricades." I wanted to tell her that she romanticizes the situation too much, but feared to disillusion her. Besides, it is always nice being lionized for keeping the revolutionary fires burning—and in such fervent and pleasant company.

Priscilla sat for me in her kitchen, barely room for a stove and sink, where the light from the backyard provided adequate illumination. As I drew her and we chatted, she stared out the window, distracted by two bird feeders hung in front of a scrim of bamboo. This produced the most delightful dreamy expressions on my subject's face, illuminating her blue eyes as various "friends" came to feed. The goldfinches and scarlet tanagers put a rose madder glow in her cheeks. She bemoaned the fact that she and her husband had so little time anymore for excursions up the C & O Canal, where, so she told me, they'd seen a prothonotary warbler—"the yellow—the yellow," she exclaimed, "would take your breath away." Oh, she was attractive all right with her blood up, but not to worry, too much steel and gristle for my taste.

She was mightily pleased with the drawings of her and we agreed it was a fine starting point for a full portrait. Priscilla insisted on paying me something upfront, even though I told her it was fine to wait until we started on the oil. "Anyway, I'm on the government dole now," I said. At this, she smiled and shook her head politely and handed me twenty dollars. I was about to leave—it was then late afternoon—when she held me back, as if overcome with a sudden inspiration. "No, why don't you stay—can you stay for a couple of hours?" Her eyes blazed—an impetuous, forceful woman. She told me they were having a meeting of like-minded men of goodwill, New Dealers, who were determined to make fundamental changes, as I was at the FAP. She thought I should meet them, that they would be honored to hear my thoughts as a great artist on the best way of moving forward. "I'm an artist, not a politician," I protested. She only winked at me and held my arm tight. "You will be our shining star."

Minutes later, her husband, Alger, arrived, a very compact, cool, and competent individual, neatly tailored and with a commanding self-confident air about him. She introduced us and informed Alger that she invited me to join "the group," as she called it. It was instantly clear that he was not happy at this diktat from his wife—at the "sudden addition," and he eased her away into the kitchen, where an intense discussion ensued between them. I was made uneasy at this state of affairs and thought I might just slip away and save them further embarrassment. But as I was about to go, Priscilla returned with a triumphant smile—the cat had swallowed the canary—and presented me with a glass of wine and a cracker with cheese. "It is decided," she said, "you will be our guest of honor, since you are relatively new to Washington, a resident in good standing." She raised her eyebrows knowingly and looked around, as if to make sure we were not to be overheard. "Since you are clearly behind on your dues to our Washington chapter, I insist you pay in kind." She tapped the sketchbook under my arm. "And while you're at it," she whispered in my ear, "get something good of Alger, and I will include it in my birthday present to him. We'll never convince him to pose otherwise. I will take care of everything."

Then they began to arrive, men in suits, carrying briefcases and the *Evening Star*, all eager beavers in their thirties or forties, all very educated, mostly Harvard men, working in the State Department and Treasury, one in Justice, no less. And to my surprise, Harry Hopkins, Holger's boss, and so my ultimate taskmaster, who heads the WPA. Hopkins had never heard of me, of course; he oversees thousands and distributes millions of dollars. If Roosevelt is Zeus, Hopkins is surely Apollo, dispenser of light and reason, and in the case of the WPA, moola—lots and lots of moola. All bow to his largesse. A State Department colleague of Mr. Hiss, Laurence Duggan, a tall, stately diplomat type with a long nose and intense eyes, did know my work from New York days past. He recalled with admiration an opening at Marvin's gallery ten years ago. Seems his father, who runs some kind of educational institute in the city, took him to the opening. Knew a lot about South American artists—Orozco and such—and wanted my opinion on the Diego Rivera murals at Rockefeller Center. How nice to still be remembered as a rising star. What a dream those days now seem. Priscilla introduced me to all her arriving guests—a Noel somebody, and a man named Remington, a distant cousin of the artist—filling their ears with praise of my work and, judging by her tone, giving assurances that I was a safe and trustworthy foot soldier in the cause.

She directed me to a chair closest to the windows in their intimate parlor, facing the others, then brought in extra chairs from the kitchen to fill out the ensemble and carefully arranged the seats to face me and the garden windows. I could tell from his disgruntled glances that Alger was not pleased with this arrangement but was too distracted by welcoming conversations with his confederates to make further complaint. And so, following the chatelaine's orders, I slipped open my sketch pad and began to take their likenesses, first Alger's and then the others.

What a lot of intelligent talk, what a lot of theory was tossed around that evening, stuff that stretched my poor brain to exhaustion as I tried to capture their various characters. Editorials in the *Daily Worker* were discussed, analyzed, and argued over ad nauseam. Everybody had ideas about how best to implement new policies that might radically change the country. I realized soon enough that some of these guys were truly big shots, movers and shakers, passionate about their plans—full of heated emotion as they argued politely but forcefully among themselves. Meanwhile, I tried to capture that determined brainpower with my pencil. Then the discussion moved to the international scene and developments in Spain and Germany, and, of course, in Mother Russia. The group relished reports of the leaps and bounds of worker prosperity—that Dnieper dam project seemed to be on everyone's lips, especially the Remington fellow, who had worked with the TVA and who praised it mightily, gushing like a car salesman. Stalin's latest Five-Year Plan was another cause for a salute with raised wineglasses.

Alger Hiss, his eyes like klieg lights beneath his dark brows, led much of the discussion, like some college professor weaving a spell among eager students. Except when economic theory was their focus—then this excited round-faced guy with thick glasses from Treasury, Harry White (later he came up to me and asked if I might be interested in illustrating a children's book his wife writes—the chutzpah of the guy!), took the floor, abetted by his sidekick, Lauchlin Currie—I think at the Federal Reserve, with a face like an undertaker and morose eyes, a Canadian accent. These two demon numbers guys threw figures around like circus acrobats tossing Indian clubs. All Greek to me. Harry Hopkins seemed more amused than enlightened by the gab session, and often caught my eye and winked, as if to say, I need to be outta here; I got better things to do. He excused himself early, grabbed his hat, and rushed out the door. Whenever there was a lull in the talk, Priscilla got out another bottle of chilled wine, refilling our glasses, while encouraging me to express my opinions—from a worker's point of view, from an artist's point of view— as if I qualified as a common laborer, since I worked with my hands.

I tried to weigh in as best I could on how art might be used as a visionary weapon in the class struggle. Sounds good, doesn't it: visionary weapon! I went on about how art was the expression of the life force, a way of visualizing our solidarity as human beings, of the need for justice for the Negro race, and rights for women. Priscilla's eyes—let me tell you—lit up at those words. But I warned, too, that intellectuals and artists can overthink things. How even artists must be careful not to indulge in highfalutin abstractions, but draw our inspiration from ordinary lives, and not let our art become the plaything of the aristocrats, status symbols to be manipulated by the Fricks, Carnegies, and Rockefellers—as if their good works excuse their bloody repression of strikers. I explained how the capitalist economy exploits the artist by isolating him from his fellow men, commodifying his production, and then quarantining him like a monk in his cell, so that he pines away and suffers in mute isolation. How art for art's sake, once the beau ideal of fat cats on Wall Street, is now a pitiful and discarded idea. Oh, Mattie, how they lapped it all up! I told them we must seek solidarity with the downtrodden, with the life of the streets, and so form a community of like-minded believers in the communal uplift of art. I think they actually liked the line I took. I almost convinced myself.

When the meeting broke up on that lovely fall evening, with streaks of sunset still visible on the undersides of passing clouds, I was prepared to hand out my sketches to the group as they made their way to leave. But no, that was not Priscilla's plan. She raised her arms to quiet things, clapped once, twice, got people's attention, and then announced, "Friends, I asked George Altmann here this evening to favor us with his artistry and his superb insights on the future of art and artists in America, and on both counts he has proved a magnificent addition to our brother—and sister—hood. He has agreed to make his sketches available to you all in his studio for a fee of five dollars, when he will, perhaps, polish up his renderings and mat them for you. At which point you—like me—might want to consider a sketch of your spouse, or even a full-blown portrait from one of America's finest artists while he still remains in Washington . . . as we all know, still something of a cultural backwater. Just give me a call and I will point you in the direction of Mr. Altmann's studio door."

Priscilla seemed mighty proud of her little coup—as proud as I was stunned by the sheer gall of her commercial audacity. So much so that I could barely get a word out, only to say good-bye to my sitters, who all, to a man, assured me they would be in touch to pick up the finished product. And that Harry White insisted on arranging a meeting with his children's author of a wife.

Now, almost a month later, not one call, not a peep from Priscilla about picking up her sketch of Mr. Hiss, much less a sitting for her full portrait. Like the whole business never happened. Not surprising, since Alger Hiss was the only one not to shake my hand as I departed from Volta Place.

WASHINGTON, D.C.
October 12, 1938

Dear Mattie,

The dedication ceremony for the Justice Department building murals went off without a hitch. Many dignitaries put in an appearance, including her majesty, Eleanor R., standing in for her husband, who had better things to do. And who could blame him. The mural program got a fair amount of attention from the press and critics, who bent over backward to be encouraging. Just between us, many of the murals are stinkers, with poor compositions and bad renderings. The subject matter is pretty insipid as well, plain vanilla and mostly uncontroversial—stuff that the bureaucrats can't object to. Considering all the bitching and screaming I've had to put up with over the last two years, I consider myself lucky to be done, my manhood intact, and still employed. Holger just went to Eleanor R. a few weeks ago and got Jake Baker fired because Jake wanted to give the regional offices more autonomy. I keep my mouth shut and my head down.

As a work of art, I consider my mural far superior to the others, although nothing I could ever care about deeply. I can take some pride and satisfaction in the craftsmanship, the vivid brushwork and formal composition, but a thing conveying little true emotion, much less inspiration. The format and the political constraints simply don't lend themselves to anything but pedestrian conceptions. I think my faces good, expressive of the individuals in my Volta Place sketches, but, of course, mythologized for effect. Not that any one of those Einsteins could care less. Even after I phoned Priscilla Hiss—who was cool but pleasant on the phone—clueing her in on my little tribute to her hospitality of last year, and then sent them an official invitation for the unveiling, neither she nor that bupkes husband of hers, nor any of those other big-shot mavens, bothered to show up. You would think they might be excited, or at least intrigued, to find themselves memorialized in the halls of the Justice Department. Not that I will ever be invited back to Volta Place.

Bigger comrades to fry is my guess. But at least I think I got Priscilla's shikse essence, her steely compassion, her electric mind, to go along with the husband's prickly self-confidence and goyish hauteur. So there you have it: my Mary Magdalene and her infallible Savior, surrounded by gods and demigods of our New Deal age. But I must admit I'm partial to the background landscape, which, though stylized to fit the composition, does convey the feel of our Woodstock hills and fields in the late afternoon, when the atmosphere is rich with green and mauve, alive with sensual tree shapes, invoking, at least for me, the smells of sweet fern and pine needles after rain. Yes, I do believe there may be some truth and feeling there, surviving the gornisht politics.

So, my dear Mattie, I count my silver shekels, my blood money, and calculate just how much we have in the bank, how much time it will buy, precious time back in Woodstock with you and my studio, where I belong. Doing something good, if not useful, with my life, my talent. Maybe enough for children—what do you think about that? Blood money for a chance at a new life—new art, wouldn't that be a scream?

WASHINGTON, D.C.
August 28, 1939

Dear Mattie,
I don't know if you've seen the news—I know a gal can be so isolated in Woodstock, but it is in all the newspapers that Stalin has signed a nonaggression pact with Hitler. Rumors of war are on everyone's lips. I can't believe it is true, such a betrayal of everything we believe in. And now worse is coming, the P is officially condoning such treachery, not just excusing it but supporting it as a glorious alliance against the capitalist degenerates. Such hypocrisy and double-dealing sicken me. Washington gornisht bureaucrats sicken me. I was able to sneak into the Justice Department last night, claiming I had a few corrections to make in my mural, and spent a few choice hours touching up my masterpiece, adding some cloven-hoofed clowns, adjusting my cast of gods and demigods to better reflect the poisonous treachery of our Dorian Grays.

I'll take the Friday-morning train to New York and the afternoon bus to Woodstock. A final escape to your loving arms and sanity. We have much to talk about and lost time to make up for. Fire up the violin. And time for poetry—imagine that!

NEW YORK
June 5, 1947

Dear Mattie,

After finishing up with the court session yesterday—an early adjournment—I made the rounds again of the galleries with some of my new
landscapes. I couldn't even get the boss men to look at the work—all with
the same dismissive face: not taking on any more new artists. "New?" I
said. "I've been in the business since the twenties." They couldn't care or
they've been warned off—running scared. I've been blacklisted by the P
for sure. Persona non grata. Those weak-kneed Stalin-whipped pussies.

I tried the Art Students League again to see if I could get my old job
back teaching figure painting, or even a new job teaching principles of
abstraction and composition. No luck—blackballed there, as well. I ran
into my old pal, Raphael Soyer, still teaching his rather tame figure class,
as he has for over twenty years. I asked him what the story was, to give
me the lowdown, and he just looked at me despairingly, guilty as hell,
and shrugged.

"They don't take to turncoats" was the best he could come up with.
"Keep your head down, George; these are not happy times—the furies
are loose in the land."

Raphael is just finishing up a gorgeous portrait of a lady playing the
piano on a concert stage. The best thing I've even seen him paint, dazzling the way he captures his subject's fiery spirit, her physical dexterity at
the keys. I complimented him (once I could paint circles around him and
he knows it) and told him he's made much progress in the last ten years,
since we taught together at the League. He thanked me for the praise
and said this pianist brought out the best in him, inspired him both when
he watched her in concert at Carnegie Hall and later when she posed in
the studio. Seems she chattered on about Mozart and books and politics
and charmed his pants off. "I practically fell in love with her," he said.
"Yes," I said, "and I can see why." I asked for her name. Annie Davenport
Dimock, he told me. "Oh, I've heard of her, of course." "Yes," Raphael
said, "you can still find her records from before the war." Her husband is a
big-shot lawyer and he commissioned the portrait for her birthday—five
hundred bucks! I couldn't take my eyes off this Annie by Raphael, like a
fiery angel, like a picture of womanhood from the old days, when women
stood up for the important things—like the suffragettes, for equality, for
Negro rights. So I went right out to the record store across the street

from Carnegie Hall and, wonder of wonders, they had one of her—now rare, they inform me—recordings from the thirties: *Annie Davenport Dimock Plays Fourteen Mozart Sonatas*. A present for you, my love. Let us see this weekend—I'll take the 6:15 bus—if Raphael's angel lives up to her billing.

Your loving George

41

The Earth Alive

THEY DECIDED ON the front porch, with its view of the barn and overgrown meadow, beyond which the town's window mosaics—an off-kilter arrangement of ivory, beige, and eggshell whites—nestled beneath starlight and the incipient blush of the moon on the far hills. Here the artist and his wife, George and Mattie, so Jimmy told her, had once liked to sit upon warm summer evenings to "view the heavens, while she played violin and he read her *his* Wordsworth." Jimmy insisted Wendy take the wicker swing seat, while he pulled up an old Windsor chair, one spindle broken and hanging loose. Drawing on over thirty years as a lighting technician, he made sure the glow from the living room window fell in a soft blaze on the left side of her face, highlighting her cheekbones and tapering nose and just-washed hair—a lush brassy sheen—where she sat in businesslike mode with her phone carefully set on a footstool between them and a notepad at the ready.

"Facts—huh?" he said. "Okay, I can take it—if you can. Fire away. Thirty years on tour, I've seen worse than what was lying on the ice of Sawkill Creek."

She switched on her phone's voice recorder.

"Surely not . . . your own father?" She glanced in the window, watching as George and Cordelia washed up dinner plates in the kitchen, where a tinny cassette player rocking out some bluesy Janis Joplin sat on the counter.

"Great musicians, slowly drinking away their genius, cooking their brains on cocaine . . ." His knowing eyes closed and he pulled at his handlebar mustache. "A guy we all loved, along with a million fans . . . three in the morning, hanging by his belt from a shower curtain rod that barely took his weight."

"Let's not go there."

"Agreed." Jimmy leaned forward, squinting. "You remind me so much of Cordy when she was eighteen. But then"—his lower lip pressed into his upper for emphasis—"George was always closer to his mom."

"We won't go there, either."

"I got you. I still don't see how this is going to change anything—no way was it an accident."

"That depends." She seemed to bristle and stared off a moment to where the crescent edge of a full moon was birthing, a somber lavender blush bathing the ragged horizon. "You said earlier that your mother got you out of bed on Christmas Eve? Why would she do that, drag her little boy out into the cold night?"

"Because my father was two hours late getting home. He may have been a drinker, but he stuck to his schedule—always ready for work the next morning, even Christmas morning."

"But given the weather and you were—what?—seven or eight, safe and sound in bed."

This he pondered mightily, his long calloused fingers drumming the worn knees of his Levi's as his gaze drew in tight to the withered mead-owsweet populating the field off to the right of the barn, breathing in the scents harbored on the stillness.

"She did seem to dither a bit—and, yes, I was eight, now that you mention it. First she woke me, and then she told me to go back to sleep, and then later, suddenly, she was bundling me into my winter coat and hustling me out the door."

She followed his gaze to the meadow, where ghostly fieldstone walls were rising from the depths, scaly with moonlight. "Surely it would have been better to have just left you safe and sound."

"She didn't want to leave me, that's for sure . . . as if she suspected some kind of lurking danger in the house."

"As if she was expecting something—someone?"

"He was two hours late. I guess she just didn't want to leave me alone."

"Did he often stay out late or get falling-down drunk?"

"He was a drinker, but not a violent one, not an angry one . . . mea-sured, just enough to ease the pain and frustration of a stalled career. That was my understanding, looking back at that eight-year-old boy."

"What did your mother tell you, exactly?"

"She seemed frightened. She assumed he'd had one drink too many and had either passed out in the bar or, worse, fallen on the icy road, since nobody had brought him home."

"Had that happened before, somebody brought him home?"

"Yes, yes, I suppose it had." He withdrew his gaze from the meadow reluctantly, eyeing her pad, and pulled pensively at the ring in his ear. "Of course, my head was a little fuzzy with sleep. I remember the Christmas tree was lit downstairs; even the presents were there. He hadn't grown up with Christmas trees, but he was happy to go with my mother's tradition—Norwegian, she was. It was cold, snowing—not bitter, bitter cold, but in the twenties, plenty cold enough to freeze to death. So we took the old Ford coupe down the icy road, slipping and sliding on the downhill grades, and on into town, barely creeping along the road he walked almost every day, fishtailing, looking around for any signs. My mother's eyes weren't good—maybe that's why she took me with her. Driving, especially at night, scared her. I remember rubbing off the frost on the side window as the snow kept falling. When we first crossed the Sawkill Bridge, I saw nothing. And in town—I guess it was about one by then—we found no sign of him or anybody else. Shit, it was Christmas Eve. The two bars he frequented were long closed and dark.

"And so we made our way back, going slower and slower, skidding, terrified, peering into the snowy dark. There were at least two inches of snow on the ground. Then I saw something as we passed back across the bridge, since I was in the shotgun seat . . . an area of snow disturbed on the downstream railing. My mother stopped the car at the very center of the bridge over the Sawkill. I jumped out—the snow was deeper on the bridge—and found footsteps leading up to and away from the midpoint of the railing, where there was a long gap in the ridgeline of snow, where someone must have been standing, since the snow was scuffed up a lot on the asphalt. I screamed. Mother had a flashlight with her. There was a half-moon behind the clouds and the snow glowed a kinda milky gray. Mother shined her flashlight down into the frozen creek. I saw him first—my eyes were way better—splayed out on the ice below the bridge."

"Right below the bridge, like he'd just slipped and flipped over?"

"No . . . not exactly, more a ways out, where there were jagged rocks sticking up above the ice. Just a white figure lying facedown out there, arms spread, half-covered in snow. My mother wailed something awful. We couldn't tell it was him exactly, not in the dark, but we both knew the wool coat he wore. Mother left the headlights on and we rushed across the bridge and down to the bank, slipping and sliding on our butts, and made our way out to him where he lay on the ice. The ice was pretty solid and there were footsteps in the snow going out to where he was, as if he might have just wandered out there, slipped and fallen."

"There were footsteps out on the ice leading to the body?"

"Barely, the snow was covering them fast."

"More than one pair of footsteps? Or just his? Like maybe he'd walked out on the ice and slipped and hit his head?"

"Why would he do that?"

"You tell me. One pair or two?"

"I think it was more than one, but I wasn't exactly thinking clearly and it was dark, even with the flashlight. Of course, after we got to him, there was a whole bunch."

"How awful for you."

"My mother threw herself on him, clutching at his coat, brushing off the snow as if to save him, and finally got him turned over. His face was terribly smashed in from the fall, coated in frozen blood, his lips hanging loose, eyes a frozen stare. She was sobbing, trying to hide his face from me by keeping the flashlight turned away. But it was horrible. I threw up on the ice. His body was still warm—or at least she said so, because she was suddenly desperate to drag him back to the safety of the bank. We both did. I had one arm, she the other. But we couldn't get him up that steep bank, a deadweight, too damn slippery. And the snow kept falling, harder than ever."

"You said you saw footsteps on the bridge, too, right?"

"Sure. There were footsteps on the bridge, coming from both sides. I suppose my father's, when he walked into town and then when he returned."

"Had it been snowing earlier, when he started out?"

"No, no, just flurries."

"Just a single pair of prints, from the direction of his home?"

"Why do you keep asking?"

"Didn't the police ask?"

He eyed her now and then let his gaze drift back to the meadow.

"Hard to tell in the falling snow . . . but maybe more than one pair. You see, my father liked to pause in that place on the bridge and stare down the Sawkill; he made sketches there of the rock patterns and the leaves on the bottom. He often talked about how he loved the translucent quality of the water passing over rocks, the muted shapes"—he paused as if something in the very words struck him—"and tones."

"But it was snowing, you said, so the set of prints in the snow when he first crossed the bridge on the way to town, if there had been prints, would've probably been covered by the time you and your mother got there."

"Well, I suppose."

"So what you saw, the footprints, could have been a lot more recent—could have been someone else's?"

"Where you going with this? Anybody could have walked across that bridge that night."

"Christmas Eve, in that weather? How likely is that?"

"Well, I don't know."

"So those footprints could have been more recent, could have been someone else's?"

"I'm not deaf—not yet." Again he pulled at the gold ring in his ear-lobe. "What are you trying to get me to say?"

"And what about the footprints in the snow on the ice, leading out to where his body lay—how did they get there?"

"Jesus Christ, who knows? He'd been there for at least an hour—much as anybody could figure, when the police checked with his bar buddies. Could have been anybody."

"Anybody! And they'd just have just left him there like that?"

"Little lady, the world's a fucked-up place."

"What did the police have to say about the footprints?"

"By the time they got there—my mother left me with him while she drove back into town, and don't think that hasn't fucked with my head over all these years!—they were tramping all over the place and the snow had deepened, so I doubt there was much left to bother any-one's mind about. My mother was hysterical and we were both frozen stiff. I couldn't talk for my chattering teeth. The police did what they could, I suppose, but there must've been six inches of snow by then. And later, I think everybody was just as happy to call it some kind of freak accident, so as not to saddle us with a suicide, which was what everybody, at least behind our backs, said it had to be."

"Wait a second. The police photographs show a figure sprawled on the ice."

"Whoa—girl, you two have really been digging into this mess, huh?"

She nodded sympathetically but with a repressed anger glittering in the pale blue irises of her eyes. With an added breath or two for ballast, she continued with the no-nonsense voice she employed with her students.

"You tell me . . . the difference between an accidental overdose and hanging yourself on a curtain rod."

At this, Jimmy winced and blinked, his gaze escaping to the distant hills and the rising moon, closing his eyes so that his squared-off eyebrows billowed out, drawn tight above the tilt of his nose.

"I think they had one of the deputies pose in the spot where we'd found him for that photograph. I think my mother led them out to the spot by the rocks."

"So the photo of the body sprawled by the rocks isn't even your father?"

"I guess not. I mean, nobody was going to drag a frozen body back out there—I mean, Christ! Anyway, by that time I was huddling in the back of the sheriff's car, half-frozen and scared witless."

"And so, what do you think?"

"All I know: It wasn't an accident."

She shot back, "Why?"

Her tone, her abruptness, seemed to break something in him, as if through the confusion of a disrupted life he had caught a glimpse of something: a fable, a story, a perspective once lost to the man that eight-year-old had grown up to be.

"He always drew such strength, such energy from the earth—rivers, streams, veins of rock fascinated him—the earth alive—know what I mean? Hard to believe . . . not there, not in a place he loved to the bottom of his heart."

She looked up from her notepad, pen poised, as if she'd been interrupted by the voice of a different person.

"And your mother?"

"No way. Mom was always convinced he'd been done in by his enemies—somehow, God knows!"

"Enemies?"

"People who shunned him and his art. The 'haters,' she called them, out to ruin him and his career. Haters who, when we were at his funeral, ransacked the house and turned his studio upside down."

She scribbled furiously on her pad even as she continued in an even tone. "During the funeral, someone was searching the house and studio?"

"A mess, like you wouldn't believe. 'Just to spite a dead man' was how she put it."

"But maybe looking for something?"

"Like what?"

"Those letters to your mother."

He shook his head in dismay, running a hand though his long hair. "God only knows; I only found them in the attic because a floorboard up there broke when I was cleaning out stuff. There was a bunch of old magazines there as well, glowing reviews of his shows from the twenties in *The New Masses*. She was always secretive as hell about their early days."

"You think it could've been people from around here, Woodstock?"

"Hah, three of his drinking buddies turned up at the funeral, and none of them was an artist. What does that tell you about the rumor mill, the whispers behind our backs in the village: how a man could have so much contempt for his family to do such a thing, to leave a wife broke, a son fatherless on Christmas Eve? In the end, it got easier to accept the common wisdom—right . . . son of a suicide. Even if deep down I thought I knew better—but not enough to explain it any better."

"Tough on you." She sighed, as if struggling to maintain a professional distance, examining his crumpled posture in the old Windsor chair. "The children always get the worst of it." For an instant, their eyes met in recognition. Then, as if alarmed by what he saw, he turned to the light of the living room window, where Cordelia was seated at the piano with her son.

"The worst part," he said, casting a wary side glance at his interlocutor, "like my AA sponsor says, is how that sense of betrayal becomes an excuse for all your own failings: when you're tempted just to give up, when the booze is just the easiest way out. Something in school nobody ever let me forget, not even later with Levon and Rich and the boys, who had their own drinking problems. They see that false bottom in you and with it that lack of respect no matter how well you do your job."

She slumped back in the porch swing, as if the interchange had exhausted her, still nodding gamely while she continued taking notes. For almost a minute they sat in silence as Cordelia's playing of a Mozart sonata sweetened the night air.

"Being an artist," she began, searching for the right words, "is a tough life, full of self-doubt, indecision, anxiety—even the best lose heart, drink, do drugs, get depressed."

The light from the window lit his haggard cheeks. "That's the thing I could never get Cordelia to understand—she with the charmed life and talent to spare, the woman every guy in my crowd fell for. She never dealt with the dark side, like when I got stuck with the job of clearing out the Malibu digs of one of the guys, the Shangri-La studio—before your time. He'd managed to stash two thousand empty bottles of Grand Marnier. Took me an entire day to clear out that shit—can you imagine!"

She just shook her head and nervously twirled a strand of hair around a forefinger. He turned to the window, listening now to Cordelia's Mozart.

"How about that," he said with a curious smile, "never heard her play Mozart before, never."

"Could your dad have been depressed, could a sudden bout of despair have turned into an act of desperation—even on Christmas Eve, in a place he loved?"

"Now you even sound like Cordelia, blaming me for George's depression in high school, and at Princeton, too, so she likes to tell me. If not for what I did, then a genetic disposition. Wanna bet that's her sister talking. Or my therapist—how her face lit up when she got that out of me. Only got me more anxious, that maybe I'd end up like him: a suicide. God, how that weighed on me . . . how many long nights on the road, stuck in a shitty motel room with a chick who was pissed off I wasn't actually a member of the band. And the worst is, you start adjusting your memories to justify the fuckup you've become."

"You make up stories," she offered.

"No excuses—that's the best thing about AA."

"Being sober must help."

He laughed for the first time, perhaps not a little entranced by the Mozart sonata. Facile . . . soft, delicate, an echoing call and response, transporting.

"You know, being here with you, I can almost picture them on evenings in the summer after dinner. He'd read her a little Wordsworth. She'd perform a little on her violin; she was pretty good—in the violin section of the Metropolitan Opera when they first met. You see, Carnegie Hall was right across the street from the Art Students League. He loved her playing him the Bach violin suites or the second movement of Mozart's fifth violin concerto, and she'd sing the orchestral accompaniment. Funny, I'd totally forgotten that. I gave up the violin after he died."

At this, she looked up from her notes, eyes rekindled, ablaze.

"The Wordsworth volume in the barn, with all the underlining?"

"You don't miss a trick."

"The poet's sympathy for the poor and downtrodden, for those who endured by faith and even false hopes, or languishing attachments to the land. So even after he broke with the Party, those sympathies remained, even after he gave up on political narrative in his art for a more abstract narrative, a more universal narrative about the wonders of nature."

He smiled in a way she hadn't seen before, inwardly, tentatively. "Well, they'd play a few hands of whist, too. I'd hear them from my bedroom window—George's room. I'd hear them laughing because my mother always won, or so she said."

"She, of course, knew about his Party affiliations; perhaps she was a member, too, as you say, in their early days. By all accounts, anyone who broke with the Party might pay a price."

"'Enemies . . . bad people, hacks, second-raters,' as she always called them. 'Out to get your father.' Right to the end of her life, she was skittish as hell. A noise in the night, headlights in the drive, and she'd look at me all spooked."

"They played for keeps."

"Listen, all this political stuff—his years in Washington; I mean, hardly a reason to kill someone—right? A pain in the ass . . . but a gentle spirit like that." He sat forward to be closer to the young woman, as if drawn by his own unaccustomed use of the words *gentle spirit*.

"And, as you said, he kept working harder than ever."

"Like he'd gotten hold of a vein of gold—'gold and lapis lazuli,' he called it, his pictures of the Shawangunks. 'My Eros in the stone, my Persephone rising from the earth.'"

"Yes . . ." she whispered, responding to the wonder in his eyes, urging him on.

He laughed and gave the porch swing a push with the pointed toe of his boot, letting the chains on the rusted eye loops sing in accompaniment to the Mozart.

"Their laughter was such a comfort to me as a child, out here in the moonlight. When my mother played her violin for him. Their best years—the war years, strange to say—before he had to get jobs as a court reporter for the newspapers in New York. Whenever there was a big trial, he was the man they called. He'd take the bus to Kingston and then into the city. Enough to put food on the table and buy art supplies. He'd spend the week in New York and return on Friday night and go right back to his studio. He'd applied for his old job at the Art Students League, but they would have nothing to do with him anymore. 'Old hat . . . *old hat*,' I remember him complaining to mother—'*me, old hat!*' Where once he'd been a rising star, where students flocked to his classes, now nobody wanted him. As my mother put it to me after his death: They hated him for ditching all those 'hacks and second-raters for an art that would last the ages.' I guess—the letters—he made a lot of enemies in Washington. Disgruntled artists and the like he didn't favor for FPA jobs."

She moved closer, glancing at the audio gauge on her phone.

"Enemies . . ." she intoned darkly, and reached out a hand to his, pressing lightly. "Jimmy, you're a witness, maybe the last to your father's talent. What do you remember best about him?"

His gaze, his bloodshot, tired eyes, returned to the distant welcoming hills.

"Jesus, he used to wear me out with all his walking. Hours we'd hike over the hills and through the woods, while he stopped to sketch, when a thing caught his eye: a dead oak, an outcropping of stone on the forest floor, or a shaft of sunlight through the canopy that caught a carpet of moss, so that the greens ran riot. It fascinated me how much he saw, how these things came alive under his pencil, as if it were all a kind of conversation going on. He'd give me a lot of these sketches for my room when I was a little kid, especially the critters. He'd write a name in perfect block letters: barn owl, scarlet tanager, swallow, or goldfinch. That's how I learned to read, learning my birds, my wildflowers, sounding out the names or, later, epigraphs from his poets, syllable by syllable, stringing the letters together so that the sounds merged seamlessly with the image."

"He made up stories for you." She leaned in close. "He never gave up hope."

"That's right"—he searched her searing eyes—"damn right."

In the silence, as Cordelia paused between pieces, she managed to recall the line for which she'd been searching.

"'Oh, Sir! the good die first, / And they whose hearts are dry as summer dust Burn to the socket.'"

"What's that?"

"Your Wordsworth, who saw everywhere signs of endurance in the lay of the land."

His eyes glimmered with a dull luster as Cordelia began again.

"It was as if the landscape were filled with lives visible only to him, that he felt somehow bound to share with the world. Like they were part of your family—know what I mean? Sheltering in the woods and among the old fieldstone walls." He paused, as if only now waking from the dream spread around them. "Golly, I'd almost forgotten, how much he was fascinated with those old walls, as if they, too, spoke that secret language of the earth, the stones scribbled across the meadows by the first farmers, each stone piled one upon the other, one syllable after another, all their lost stories rambling away." He glanced at her, as if surprised by the thing uncovered in his own voice. "Light, he used to say, the *quality* of light was the hardest thing to capture, where it reveals the underworld as it rises from the earth to meet the sky . . . oh, you know, trees—trees jabbering to one another—and outcroppings and such born into the sunlit world. Yes, the way he saw such things, even in the bleakest midwinter: They were *so* alive."

Her stare was fixed on his tearing weariness, her eyes luminous, as if reflecting his memories, absorbing his rich dusky voice, now so full of yearning.

"Oh," she mimicked, as if to disguise something in herself while reaching out to him, less the daring of lovers than that of a daughter to a father. "He was so meticulous, the way he had everything ordered in his studio. I can almost feel his routine, the rhythms of life that went into creating those wonderful canvases."

"Yes." He nodded, smiling fully into her brimming sea-stained eyes. "He had beautiful hands, you know, strong but delicate. He did everything just so; he carved his pencil points just so; he had me help stretch his canvases just so, just the right tension, just the right primer and shade of off-white. He showed me how to cut wood, how to split wood to burn in the iron stove to heat his studio. And . . ." He paused, as if listening to the last hum of crickets, the sere scene of sweet fern in the night meadow, returning his gaze to his long, arthritic fingers interlaced upon his bent knees. "I always loved working with my hands, even if my violin lessons didn't come to much." He spread his fingers and held his hands out before him, a prayerful oblation before the meadow altar. "Witness, you said . . . the way he'd pause at his easel when I interrupted him, look me up and down, lifting his white eyebrows in that sly way he had, as if to share a secret, and tell me to go over to the old phonograph and wind it up and start the record over again. Then, standing with his brush, he would conduct for a moment, listening intently, and tell me to come over and hold his brush while he moved it across his canvas—to get the 'rhythm of the paint,' he called it—and how this color or that color aligned itself with the treble or bass, the melody or the harmony. 'Do you feel the music?' he would ask. 'Do you feel the lime green here, as it swings into motion, as it reaches to this fern green, how the texture of a stroke transforms the color, fern into shamrock or sweet basil. See how color is only color according to what sets it up, surrounds it, the undertones coming through, like the silence between the notes that sets them free—like people, maybe?'"

She reached across the divide between them to his knee, entranced by his recollections.

"Like George's music of the spheres."

"Oh, you're a sly one."

She patted his knee with the merest spark of guilt in her flashing smile.

"Tell me something: When Cordelia arrived with those sketches that day, in her father's red Mercedes, when you slid them out of the envelope, what did you think?"

"I only had eyes for her—and the Merc; otherwise, I would have simply burned the damn things—and good riddance—right, if those letters are to be believed."

42

Free Energy

SHE TOSSED THE phone on the bed.

"That's where the digital recorder ran out."

"You're a fucking piece of work—you know it. The way you had him eating out of your hand."

"How sweet of you, George." She shook her head, her eyes pleading, as if deeply disappointed in him. "But that's not it—not at all."

George, propped against the brass headboard, glared at her where she sat at the foot of his bed in her T-shirt, combing her hair, staring out the window at the gargantuan white oak, now nearly denuded, sinewy arms silhouetted against the pale darkness. A biscuit tin of folded letters on his lap was illuminated in the glow of a Tensor lamp shaped like a flying saucer on the bedside table.

"I just can't believe . . ." His voice faltered. "You just snapped your fingers and got all that out of him."

"What, exactly?"

"Spilling his guts like that—you're quite the . . . I don't what *you* are—a budgerigar."

"What?"

"Like the Judge was telling us at dinner: how the budgerigar perfectly imitates or fills in the song of its mate."

"Just what *am* I, George?" She turned and glared, as if fighting back tears. She pointed her hairbrush at him. "And what does that make you, exactly? He's . . . a man, a husband, a father . . . finding his way home."

"Budgerigar . . ."

"And a real art historian would be gaga over this." Her voice shifted into a higher register as she reached for her phone. "It's gold, baby, such a firsthand account of Altmann's working methods, his inspiration. It will make your namesake come alive in your essay."

"*Your* essay—*your* memoir," he said icily. "Obviously, I'm no fucking art historian."

"Then who exactly are you, George Dimock Altmann?" She gestured around at the outermost halation of the bedside lamp: a child's fantasy of *Star Wars* posters, fleets of Lego starships and the collection of lightsabers. "Or is it poor Luke," she said, cocking her head—"still searching for your badass father?"

"The guy's an asshole. I'm just as happy not to have anything to do with him."

She gave a dismissive shrug, not a little incredulous. "What's wrong with you? It's all coming together." She indicated the biscuit tin of letters. "This fucking house was ransacked during the funeral—and the barn. That clinches it, in my book. Your dad told me that Mattie had hidden the tin of letters and other Party stuff way under the floorboards in the attic: a fluke he literally stumbled upon them when a board snapped. No way this doesn't become part of the Judge's memoir: He—you—can't escape this now. You fucking own it—or it owns you—whatever."

His eyes, hurt, resentful, lost, burned into hers.

"Listen." She sighed, nodding contritely, as was her wont, brushing her hair with slow, measured strokes, as if signaling a return to a more even keel. "Jim's been in AA now for two years." She held up her flattened palm to his face, as if to say, I know, I know. "That's what they do: They open up about themselves, confess, stop making excuses . . . a new lease on life."

"And why not, with a beautiful sympathetic young woman holding his hand."

"Why so disparaging, George? Like he's such a bad person, like I'm just a manipulating bitch—a budgerigar." She forced a smile. "How come I never saw this mean streak in you before?"

"Why do you think my mother finally ditched him?"

"He said something about Cordelia always sleeping around with his best friends—Levon somebody. How it drove him crazy: the band boys always wanting her, if they weren't writing songs about her."

"She has more talent in her little finger . . ." He lowered his face and rubbed his brow. "But it's true, he and Levon go way back . . . to the Big Pink basement tapes, and Woodstock—the festival, that is. When there's so much talent, charisma, and ambition to burn, the kids and lovers take what they can get. You don't think that fucks with your mind?"

He tossed the tin of George Altmann letters onto the bedside table and turned to her with an intent stare.

She eyed the letters. "What?"

"You read them?"

"Spit it out."

"He had no idea they were spies, working for the KGB. He figured they were fellow Party comrades—big shots, Harvard boys playing at revolution. He had no inkling what he was witnessing that day at Volta Place."

She studied his expression, fingering the bristles of her hairbrush, as if trying to read him before he could read himself. "Until Hiss was indicted. Then like a lightning bolt out of the blue, his past caught up with him."

He smiled icily: the budgerigar vibe.

"And . . ." He laughed, as if to give her a split second to beat him to the punch. "Altmann gets hired by the *Tribune* to cover the first trial—imagine that: watching Alger and Priscilla squirming in the dock. Then it must have occurred to him: Three of the Volta Place spies are dead, two in hiding . . ."

"He was . . ."

"In deep shit."

"And he was pissed," she said indignantly. "Five bucks a sketch . . . and nobody showed."

"Alger Hiss obviously put a stop to that."

"Budgerigar . . ." She went on with a half-smile.

She stared around, perhaps with a hint of guilt, a tad disconcerted, not displeased, like a magician at the reveal.

"Anyway," he said with a look of mild wonder, "not to worry: Nothing remains the same once it's been observed, neither the observer nor the observed."

At this, she rolled her eyes and worked her shoulders up and down, relieving tension. Then, adjusting her gray Chelsea Piers T-shirt, she began brushing her hair again.

He watched her intently: the immemorial female ritual. The penumbral ring from the lamp barely illuminated her torso and head, leaving the rest of his room—like the murky desires of adolescence itself—in shadowy darkness.

She announced to no one in particular, "I told him nothing about our suspicions. I wanted him to come to his own conclusions."

"The Judge would be proud of you."

Her eyes widened in a fierce predatory expression.

"If it was my father . . . who came back . . ."

"Don't go there."

"Where do you want me to go, George?" She held up her calloused palms. "I'm shaking, George, because I feel so angry, and . . . so-o-o in touch with him—the artist, what went into those paintings. What just happened on the porch was such a beautiful gift, and you're too fucked-up to see it or care."

"So New Agey. That's your criteria for forgiveness, Lazarus's curtain call?"

"He's your flesh and blood."

"Not according to him, not according to Alice, who filed the divorce papers."

At this, she got up and went to the window, her taut muscled frame barely concealed by the T-shirt and panties, now fading into momentary eclipse, softening to shadows under his gaze as her hands went to the side jambs, as she began leaning forward and back, as if drawn to the embrace of the huge oak beyond.

"I'll take Cordelia's word—a mother knows."

"Right," he said with a sarcastic frown. "Alice is picking up her daughter, Cecily—who walked out on her husband—at Kennedy tomorrow morning on the red-eye from San Francisco. So we've rescheduled for the afternoon to get all the legal issues sorted out." He squinted at her in the semidarkness, sensing her desire to escape, to climb the damn oak tree if given half a chance. "What a fucked-up family—huh, every which way."

She reached to the wall of Sheetrock next to the window, exploring with her fingertips, turning on the desk lamp to better light the area, squinting as she brought her face close, murmuring first to herself and then to him.

"Pinholes—thumbtacks, lots of them, under the paint."

"What?" he said in a tired, distracted voice, as if she were some stray spirit wandered in from the night.

"This was your father's room, when he was a boy. On Christmas Eve—"

"Enough."

"He burned the sketches—Jim did." She switched off the desk lamp and turned to him on the bed. "After my audio ran out, that's what he told me. After the funeral, when they found the house turned upside down, all the sketches pulled down and torn, the ones in the barn, too. He burned them. No reminders."

"Amazing those goons didn't just burn down the barn, and finish the job."

She winced and turned again to the moonlit oak, her hips unconsciously undulating, as if yearning to shimmy up into the muscular arms of a lover.

"Well, now we know . . . now we know why there are no other sketches." She remained at her vigil, giving a shrug of resignation or maybe relief. "At least you got the heating fixed. It's almost toasty in here." She slipped off her T-shirt and pressed herself against the window, her breasts against the glass, as if still intent on fathoming any remaining subterfuges of a November night. The light from the flying saucer lamp fell across her shoulders in a muted blue mist, delineating the black spandex bra strap against the white of her back as she breathed deeply, the dentil curve of her spine arcing into the flat indent above her coccyx, slipping discreetly beneath the broad waistband of her Under Armour panties. He lay there, admiring the seamless molding of her buttocks and the barely visible, if equally delicious, wedges of her hamstrings.

"You see," he said, gesturing vaguely, as if to include the congery of reaching branches that continued to absorb her gaze, "the quantum world turns certainties into possibilities, or at best probabilities, but there's no knowing for sure, no definitive outcomes—not for sure . . . not for anybody."

She stepped back from the window, perhaps to better catch her pensive reflection in the glass. "You can't mean that a fall from the Sawkill Bridge or the World Trade Center doesn't change the world as we know it? Or do you mean how do we find a way to live with those uncertainties?"

"Believe it or not, I thought the art gig might provide—I dunno—a little certainty."

"Oh . . ." She waved a giddy hand toward the scrap heap of Lego starships. "You deluded little boy: George, you ask too damn much of life, or maybe not enough. But then, maybe I rather love you that way."

"We can't all be celebrity artists and just make it up as we go along."

"God forbid. Why do you think I climb?" She raised her face to her luminous reflection. "Otherwise, I'd go insane with doubt and fear. There's no escaping, baby." She turned from the window and stepped forward as if into the welcoming ambient light, hands on her hips. "That's what was really going on the other night with Jean, your— why do you always call her your Cantor Fitzgerald widow?—client, at Sheila's opening. You're terrified to say her name. Why can't you call her *Jean*, George?"

"Yes, Jean, and—no thanks to you—when she bought another of Sheila's still lifes, she told me that she was going to hang the two together, the one that *he* loved best with the one *she* loved best."

"What's wrong with a little solace?"

"That's not what I had planned on selling."

She crossed her arms across her breasts, as if needing to steady herself, take a stand.

"That's the market, George. We do make it up as we go along—not just what's out there but all the crazy stuff inside that connects with what's out there. You don't think I'm *not* selling sex, on some level? I get it; I'm not proud. What's on the canvas is only a projection of our brains, what our brains want us to see. That's what Cézanne tried to do: show us what we cannot see, which is how we see." She sat down on the bed with sudden assurance, confronting him where he lay sprawled with a skeptical pout. "What Jean sees in *her* still life is as much a part of her as what Sheila—in her way—managed to get down on canvas. You don't think that connection is important? If not, I'm just wasting my fucking life."

"*In her way*," he mimicked.

"Okay, she's a fucking master of contemporary still life painting. And I hope my work gives you a hard-on."

He stared fixedly at her posed womanly shape, bemused.

"Oxymoron, isn't it: still life."

"The French got it right: *nature morte*."

"Why not market your stuff as sex lifes?"

"Whatever it takes, amigo. To feel something. Hey, maybe a hundred years from now some fourteen-year-old is going to see one of my paintings in his parents' bedroom and stroke off to my twenty-something body. How's that for outlasting space and time?"

"If it's really so alive," he pondered, half-intrigued, "it's energy— free energy. And if your art—call it *information*—communicates such a response, why shouldn't the universe, too, be in the mix, at least reflected on the quantum level—in every one of your itsy-bitsy, teeny-weeny brushstrokes, as well? I mean, particles, waves—strings—whatever the fuck—have to draw free energy from their quantum fields, which

fill everything, all space and time . . . like us, especially you, my complex Cheshire Catwoman, appearing here, there, and everywhere until
entropy catches even you by the tail."

She laughed, half out of relief, half delighted at his quantum riffing.

"Budgerigar," she said, and growled menacingly, baring her teeth.
"At least you're feeling something, George Dimock Altmann: the
change—don't you?—out of the past? The echo of the depth charge in
your balls. Your bending, curving space-time thing. There's no getting
away from it, George—for any of us."

"Complexity demands more dense flows of free energy, which
makes it all the harder to keep your shit together, degrading into heat
energy—your hotness gone up in smoke."

She put a finger to his lips.

"That's what I do, baby." She took a deep breath, running her hand
down his shoulder to the new muscles across his chest. "I'm that good,
you know—but you do know, right?"

His eyes glittered as he watched where her breasts rose with emotion above the spandex.

"I'm a simple guy, and physicists, especially theoretical physicists,
like simplicity, like to reduce complicated things to one simple law.
Like why have four force fields, four fundamental forces: when maybe
gravity mixed with dark matter—sprinkled with a little of *your* hotness,
can unify them all?"

"Oh dear." She shifted off one bra strap, then the other.

"You're my unified theory—my one and only."

"I love it when you talk dirty to me, baby—such a turn-on." She
wiggled her hips suggestively.

"You're it, baby."

"One cunt fits all."

"Mass converts into energy, and energy into mass . . . and so nothing
really dies. As long as we keep fucking—keep the free energy coming—forever, huh?"

She stood and went to him, placing his hands on her hips. The
lamplight was like a fevered flush on her skin. "Oh, I think Proust or
Virginia Woolf already beat you to the punch on that score—how she
put it: '. . . we are the words; we are the music; we are the thing itself.'"
She took a deep breath. "Do you *want*—while we're on the subject—
children, George? Or just fucking for fucking's sake?"

He tried a weak smile and shrugged as she turned up this card for
the first time.

"What . . . just another change of free energy into heat energy."

"Genes, right? Isn't that what you're telling me?" And she pressed his hands into her flesh. "Keeping the Judge's gig afloat."

"And if he's not my father? And if George Altmann wasn't murdered?"

"What did you say about information? That it's all about the interchange of information—language, stories—that's what makes us who we are: by controlling the information flow around us, right?" She stepped back, bending, stretching muscles in her legs, as if warming up for the main event. "Then you—I have been served notice by the universe and there's no turning back."

"You mean my pussy-whipped self," and he reached to stroke her left breast. "But the thing is, it goes deeper than that: Force fields allow for distant objects to have an interaction, quantum entanglement—don't you know—even at distance . . . responding"—and he withdrew his caress—"without even physically touching each other."

At which, she removed her bra and began touching herself, rubbing her nipples until they stood out as hard points.

"Umm . . . I don't know about the *without touching* part."

"Time, mass, speed, distance, they all intertwine within these fields, at least in the universe we think we know."

"Oh, that's so hot—don't stop." She went on in a mocking, larky, sultry and laughing voice, slipping her fingers into her crotch. "How about the universe in which you get a hard-on without even touching me, just looking at my paintings, exchanging invisible particles—photons, isn't it? What kind of energy field is that George—the one that gets you hard?"

"You mean the one that trumps gravity."

She nodded in the direction of the *Star Wars* poster of Princess Leia. "You're so my Jabba the Hutt—because that huge Jabba cock really gets me off."

"I didn't even know he had a cock, much less a mega cock."

"That's the point: It's all in the imagination, your entanglement thing."

There was a sound, creaking, footsteps on the floor above.

He glanced up and frowned. "I still can't believe he's sleeping up there in the guest room."

"Cool it—your Mom is handling things just fine."

"There's always been too much sex in this house—growing up, that is."

"Maybe it really is your unified force field, George." She slipped a finger in his mouth. "Does taste count?" She examined him from stem to stern: his leaner, meaner body. "Tell me you're not getting hard."

He kissed her fingers. "I'm not getting hard."

She stood, shot her hip, and slipped off her panties. Then she strad-dled his thighs, hovering and gyrating, barely touching, a cosmic lap dance, as she gathered up her hair in two hands and held it bunched above her ears.

"Carrie knows best. She's so into that Altmann nose and eyebrows, the dimple—even if it does look better on your father."

"Hadn't you heard? I take after the Judge."

"I like mongrel breeds."

"Jabba cock and all?"

"Balls deep, baby," and she reached to the crotch of his shorts.

"It's too creepy—here."

"Learner girlfriends," she asked in Yodaese, "you had not?"

"Zero."

"My coy master. I need the information, their stories—tell me what they looked like. Tell me what they sounded like. Tell me what they liked. Tell me how they smelled. Tell me how they liked to come."

"It's a little too creepy with all my stuff around."

"Your lightsaber doesn't think so. Let's see if we can get Princess Leia turned on. I think she likes my tits."

She stuck out her tongue at her shadowy rival and then began kissing, sucking, tonguing, only pausing in her ministrations to make suggestive faces at her hovering sister.

"I never realized you were so into the voyeur thing, or is it the ménage à trois thing?"

"Carrie is just too cute with those side cinnamon buns." She slid him down her throat and held him deep, working her tongue all the while. "You come," she gasped, sticking her tongue out at a nonplussed Carrie Fisher, "from two Aquarians—those guys practically invented sixties sex."

"I can't believe how you're taken in by my mom's bullshit."

She moved to his lips, running her tongue into his mouth.

"How do my tits hold up to Sheila's?"

"What's with you?"

"So where's your porn stash? No old copies of *Penthouse* to share?"

"So, what's *your* porn profile?"

"Finger painting, you mean. I like to watch girl-on-girl stuff, rollick-ing lesbos licking vadges and such like."

"No kidding."

"Don't get any ideas. I'm not really *all* that bi; I just like the anatomy, the tenderness, the proficiency, the real orgasms. Sometimes I watch while I'm painting, for inspiration, to get the creative juices flowing."

"What a relief: not mountaineers with muscles for brains."

"Baby, I may climb with those guys, but they prefer watching themselves having sex to watching me."

"Run that by me again?"

"My mother, too, was such a sixties kinda girl; she was liberated before the word was even invented."

With that, she straddled his face, thrusting her hairless pudenda against his lips.

"Oh baby, right there, keep flicking my clit—yes." She deftly spread herself for his tongue. "We're sixties castoffs, baby. Now, don't try to talk with your mouth full."

After her first orgasm, she got up and returned to the window, as if requiring a refresher of the lunar night, while working out a cramp in her thigh. Then she went over to his shelf of Lego space-ships, touching them fondly.

"I love your little boy's room; it's such a turn-on. It's still so *you*, full of first loves, first passions—talk about your free energy. After thirteen," she said, sighing to herself, "I never really had my own kid's room again . . . just a lot of rooms, first in my uncle's house, and, after he proved problematic, in my grandmother's house, and she was already half-gaga, and a strict Pentecostal to boot—worse than my aunt. Like I was Alice down the rabbit hole, sinking back in time." She reached for something on a high shelf. "Oh my God!" she exclaimed, running her fingers along the ribbed handle, caressing the crossbar, laughing wildly when it switched on and unleashed to full length.

She turned off the bedside lamp and held up the lightsaber with a whoop of triumph. The blade glowed with a silver-blue iridescence as she swung it over her head, bathing her corded torso in a flickering, cool neon shimmer, disjointed, like a silent film, before sound, before words, a pure emanation of free energy seeking to create something where there had once been only randomness.

Then she straddled his crotch, sliding the shaft of crystal blue between her bobbing breasts, running her tongue over the tip, then lowering it to her crotch like a witch riding a moonbeam.

"God, if it only vibrated," she moaned.

"The Force be with you."

"Do you mind . . ." She bent to kiss him, her tongue jousting with his. "You know how much Jedi knights love reverse cowgirl? Besides, it just drives me crazy. Jabba hits all the right spots."

"Go for it. I love nothing better than staring at your asshole."

She maneuvered deftly in the saddle, keeping him safe inside, and began riding him while swinging the lightsaber in her right hand and massaging herself with her left. The bed creaked; the brass railing banged the wall like a struggling victim.

"Keep it quiet," he hissed. "You can hear everything in this house."

"By the way, I forgot to pick up my prescription last week, Jedi. Just thought I should mention it, the quantum uncertainty thing—a little random sex . . . *n'est-ce pas?*"

She handed him the lightsaber.

"A little swordplay around my rear end might save the day."

43
Uncertainty Principle

A SCREECH OF tires in the driveway. George and Wendy looked up from their worktable.

"Ah," said George, turning to the open barn door, "the Wicked Witch of the West has arrived."

Alice scrambled out of the green Audi station wagon like a sleek pointer from a dog transport cage, long nose held high, eyeing the squalor, moral or otherwise, visible to her penetrating gaze in the chipped paint and broken porch railing, the unmowed meadow, much less Jimmy's crumbling Ford pickup, making mental notes to be deployed by the prosecution. She smoothed the legs of her pantsuit and made a grab for her pocketbook and phone, then slammed the door and stomped up the stairs to the front porch. "Cordelia," she yelled, leaving the front door ajar.

A few moments later, another woman emerged from the passenger side—earbuds, light brown hair in cornrows, leather pants and unzipped down vest. She stood by the car as if a little lost, looking around, then down at her phone with a hint of annoyance.

George, smiling for the first time that day, turned to Wendy. "CeCe—Cecily, Alice's daughter. It's been over twenty years since she got run out of Dodge by the Judge."

"She doesn't look too happy."

George led Wendy over to make the introduction. Cecily looked up from her phone, extracted the earbuds, and smiled, her light coffee-colored skin radiant in the fall light beneath an array of darker cornrows, delicate long lips poised expectantly, then a grin of delighted sarcasm.

"Well, if it isn't Georgie," she said. "My oh my—my little pudgy Cruddyback Jedi, what's happened to you—boy?" She embraced her first cousin and grabbed his upper arm. "Muscles, too." She turned and greeted Wendy. "And I've heard a lot about you, girl—the Hillary of the mountains, the O'Keeffe of the brush." Cecily lingered, bathing the younger woman in an admiring scrutiny, holding her right forearm for long moments, then nodding at George. "So, are you two an item?"

George put a protective arm around Wendy. "*What you see is what you get.*"

This echoed Flip Wilson punch line from their childhood banter brought a smile of recognition to Cecily's lips. She sidled over and hip-checked George with a playful guffaw.

"Oh honey: *The devil made me do it . . .*"

George turned to Wendy, beaming.

"Cecily was my favorite cousin—the only one who didn't give me constant shit."

"You were my honey-haired homeboy. I was the general and you the buck private in the Judge's boot camp at Hermitage."

"You and Karen, two pyromaniac sex fiends—man, did you guys heat up the place for us boys."

Cecily laughed and eyed Wendy again from head to toe.

"Is he still smart as shit?" She gave George another hip check. "My little man, my brother Skywaker, was the only cuz I could sit with by the lake on a quiet August night and, even as a kid, he could regale me with stories about the stars—deep shit, the deepest." She sighed and laughed. "What a smart little cracker you were—always wide-eyed with wonder at the heavens."

"We had fun, didn't we?"

"Like—you and me—the whole fucked-up world didn't exist."

"Has it really been—what, twenty-one years . . . since the Judge threw you out for almost burning down the boathouse?"

"Oh my God . . ." Cecily shot a bemused look at Wendy, who stood becalmed, with an air of wonder akin to loss. "Our Fourth of July bombshell, when Karen smuggled in all those illegal fireworks from across the river in Matamoras. I'll bet the Judge never got over it, either. But that's what we do in this crazy family." She winked at Wendy. "Especially us uppity niggers, we burn shit down—or haven't you heard?"

"That's an awful word to use," said Wendy, now examining Cecily's face, the elegant Dimock nose and blue eyes set off by a satiny mocha complexion, taking in the sleek leather pants, maroon halter top beneath a ripped down vest with bedraggled lift tickets still hanging from the zipper. "Besides, you don't look very black."

Cecily laughed. "It's okay, girl, don't get all upset and politically correct on me. It's not necessary; I'm cool. Obviously, your boyfriend here hasn't clued you in on the dark sheep of the family." She eyed George with something between mockery and feigned pain.

"I just hadn't gotten that far, CeCe—can I still call you C. C. Rider?"

"Can I still call you the Cruddyback Kid?"

"No," said Wendy, getting a handle on their banter. "He prefers just plain *Sky*."

"What's this gallerist thing I've been hearing about? You were supposed to be the gifted one, the Judge's great white hope, the Yale Ph.D.—only success in our generation . . . our Jedi astrophysicist."

"Oh, all I've got left is to defend my dissertation—someday."

"Soon," interjected Wendy with a possessive nudge.

Cecily, bemused, gave Wendy a significant look. "The Judge puts a lot of store in those sheepskins."

"So," said George, "I heard you'd settled down—married, right, to some rich and famous doctor, a Stanford surgeon? Alice said you were headed for med school."

"Well, sawbones is now my brilliant ex. As for med school, I was or will be—maybe NYU *this* time. But for now I'm just a run-of-the-mill Oreo, a nurse practitioner in transition."

"That's cool," said Wendy.

"NYU? You were always such a West Coast girl—wasn't that what you told me as a kid? How you needed to get back to San Fran—your Bay Area roots?"

"Things change. My divorce just came through."

"Sorry," said George.

"It's okay, Sky—I'm still in the land of the living. And I'm still young—maybe not as young as your youngster here, but young enough to still do damage." She eyed him with a seductive twinkle in her lustrous pale blue eyes.

He giggled shyly. "It's so great to see you—really. You were the life of the party; summers at Hermitage were never the same without you." He laughed out loud as he segued into a half-remembered nostalgic shtick they had once shared. "*Under the stars with Geraldine!*"

"*Your angel of mercy—Killer.*"

"Killer, I love it!" Wendy laughed.

"How is the old honky Judge? I hear the old redneck is on his last legs."

"He's hanging in there. In fact, there're plans afoot to have Thanksgiving at Hermitage."

"You gotta be shittin' me. Mother Alice won't go near that *evil* man—so she says."

"Martha, Karen and Erich, and their kids are in."

"Then count me in, too, brother cuz."

"So, how come you're shotgunning it to our rural slum with Aunt Alice?"

Cecily looked around, frowning. "Why do you think we're early, straight from the airport? That drive from Kennedy was bad enough. How about I come stay with you in the city until I get a place of my own?"

"You're welcome to stay at my place," said Wendy with impulsive enthusiasm. "I've got a guest room." They both looked at Wendy with bemusement. "Besides," she added, shrugging, "I need to return your sweater."

From inside the house, a Mozart etude drifted out over the warm fall afternoon. And, as if summoned by the call, a moment later, Cordelia screeched to a halt in her Toyota on the gravel drive.

———

Dinner around the kitchen table came off with remarkable civility. Alice, on her best behavior with her daughter, Cecily, in the mix, was all sweetness and light after having huddled with Cordelia in the kitchen for much of the afternoon. Despite the more than ten-year difference in their ages, Cecily and Wendy had fallen into each other's arms like nostalgic sorority sisters, teaming up to help Cordelia produce a fabulous meal of roast chicken with lemon and rosemary served with marinated and grilled vegetables—last of the season from the kitchen garden: squash, carrots, heirloom potatoes, and mashed turnips with cream. Alice had contributed the wine, a six-pack of Napa Valley pinot noir that was consumed with relish by those gathered around the table, with the exception of Jimmy, who pointedly drank ginger ale. Prompted by Wendy, he nevertheless did his best to entertain everyone, especially the younger generation, with extravagant and daring tales of life on the road with Woodstock's own, the Band, and a host of legendary acts.

"When Jim busted the microphone in New Orleans, we called it quits. Six months later, Jim was dead in that bathtub in his Paris hotel."

"That poor son of a gun," said Cecily, cradling her wineglass. "How those Dionysian eyes and leather hips could stir the pussy juices. I often wonder if they'd brought him into my ER if I could've saved him."

"How come the Band never made it into the Woodstock film?" asked Wendy.

Jimmy glanced at Cordelia with a raised eyebrow.

"Their manager, Albert Grossman, never agreed to Jock Roberts's contract. Not that we didn't keep the film rolling."

"And you left Robbie's mike on," added Cordelia in a good-humored dig.

"Yeah, well, I was the one who dragged their car out of that mud pit with a tractor and got 'em on the road home."

"My dad was there," announced Wendy. "Drove down from MIT. He and his chemical engineering pals. They brought a tent and provisions and boasted they stayed dry as five knuckle bones in a fist."

Cordelia smiled mischievously across the table. "My, my, don't you hold your cards close, young lady!" She turned to Jim. "If they'd only included Tim's 'If I Were a Carpenter' on the twenty-fifth anniversary director's cut." Her face flickered with sadness. "Poor Tim." She sighed, her eyes tearing up. "'Oh, Sir! the good die first' . . . well, there you go." Her eyes met Wendy's in a knowing glance.

———

After dinner, "my girls," as Cordelia now referred to Wendy and Cecily, took turns with the cleanup, while Cordelia played a few licks on the Yamaha upright in the living room, much to Alice's growing annoyance.

"Christ sakes, Cordy, I know you can't afford a decent piano, but can't you at least keep the damn thing tuned, even playing that shit?"

"I did have it tuned last year. The summer humidity always spoils it."

Later, the sisters—Alice leaning on a slightly more sober Cordelia—were standing in the living room with their wineglasses as Cecily took over the piano.

"Annie would have just insisted she stop playing, that it was a sacrilege to murder Chopin that way," said Alice. She went over to where George stood admiring his cousin's playing. "No, it's E sharp at the end of that phrase."

Cecily, who, among the cousins, had been the best pianist of her generation, immediately stopped, stood, and walked past her mother without a word and went back to help Wendy in the kitchen. Alice sat down and without even glancing at the music, her long fingers a blur, began to play Chopin's Etude No. 6, first as if to demonstrate her daughter's error, then burning up the keys with dazzling technical flourishes, as if she could simply overpower any off-key notes by force of will.

Cordelia, a tad tipsy and gushing, clapped, with tears in her eyes.

"Oh, if you kids had ever heard our mother, Annie, play. Allie, you always had her talent, right down to her expressive eyebrows and the way her body moved on the piano bench when she played."

Alice lowered her face into her hands and shook her head. "Cordelia, you never knew the real Annie, who couldn't give a fuck about her three—sorry, her four children. Touring half the year, teaching the other, she was too preoccupied to care. As long as we practiced and preserved all the social graces and did our bit for the Junior League, she was satisfied."

"Oh, Alice, you weren't there in her last years, when she'd given up all that for City Ballet. She was sweet and encouraging and so helpful to the dancers. Mr. B. was half in love with her, too. Later, she just retreated into her books, especially after she got sick."

"Do give up on the 'Oh, Alice' bit, Cordy; you sound like a southern belle out of *Gone With the Wind*. And the only person she was retreating from was Daddy, who was too damn preoccupied with his court and mistresses—and *you*. I mean, what a farcical name for a daughter in this day and age—out of some English country novel of Mom's, I suppose."

Cordelia bristled. "Why the cruel streak, Alice—at this point?"

"Loyal Cordelia. Amazing how you stick by the old buzzard after everything."

"He's family; he's the only father we've got, the only grandfather the kids have left."

Alice looked around the tiny, spare living room, barely able to contain her disdain. Jim sat in a corner with the local paper as if nothing were amiss, while George, Wendy, and Cecily were still in the kitchen, finishing up and talking among themselves.

"Right, do you remember the day you two announced you were going to get married, and he insisted that I fly in from Berkeley to come here and talk you out of it? And you asked us to come by for dinner. So Daddy picked me up at the airport and drove me here. He wanted a witness; he wanted my opinion, or so he said. I can see it now: Daddy walked in past the trash in the driveway, almost tripped on the snow chains lying around, knocked and opened the door, and you weren't here, nor was Jim, and there was some guy totally stoned out of his mind sleeping on the sofa. The place reeked of weed and BO, and dog shit and worse. There was dog shit under the sofa, covered in cobwebs and dirt balls. There were empty bottles everywhere. And then you sauntered in wearing your hippie dress, bandanna around your head like something out of central casting for Cheech & Chong, and a disheveled Jim with the fly of his jeans open and carrying two cold pizzas and a six-pack of Bud. And the fucker on the sofa with hair like a rat's nest finally woke up, looked around in a daze, and puked on the floor. That was Daddy's introduction to your little love nest and your husband to be, the guy who'd kidnapped his daughter for two weeks in his stolen Mercedes."

Jim shrugged off Alice's accusatory stare as if he hadn't heard the litany of complaints, which, considering his poor hearing, was probably just as well.

"That was Levon, most likely; he'd just gotten back from a tour of the West Coast and his girlfriend had locked him out of his house."

"His child's mother, no less," added Cordelia with a wry frown.

Alice turned a withering stare on her sister. "Do you remember the conversation we had with you? How Daddy warned you about the consequences of marriage to such a man of—what was Daddy's expression?—'irregular habits of mind and carelessness about the well-being and safety of others.' Much less an eighth-grade education."

"The irony is," said Cordelia, wide-eyeing it in Jim's direction, "professionally speaking, he's meticulously competent and a stickler for safety. You don't get in the electrician's union in New York State otherwise."

Jim put his newspaper down and raised his hands in an act of surrender. "I was a fool; I hated school—and actually, it was tenth grade, when my mother got sick and lost her job. Kids made jokes about my father killing himself." He shrugged and put a hand to his temple and popped his thumb. "My father had been the most obsessively meticulous human being on earth, everything in its place and a place for everything. He ran the house like his studio and expected my mother to do the same. I ran my recording sessions the same."

Alice scowled. "So what happened to you along the road to Nowheresville?" She held up a palm. "No, don't answer. So, why don't we get down to the unfortunate business of figuring out just what the fuck Jim is doing here and just how long he intends hanging around." Alice grabbed a bottle of wine and refilled her glass. "Christ, I almost sound like the Judge."

Cordelia seemed to visibly pale and, steadying herself on the arm of a ratty armchair, lowered herself into it, as if withdrawing from the fray, an ingrained habit when her older sister went on the warpath.

Jimmy Altmann pulled himself up and sat forward as if to better hear the pronouncement on his fate in the guise of his onetime sister-in-law; his eyes were a little glazed and unsteady, dark-ringed, even if he was the only sober one in the room. He glanced up and saw George now standing in the passage from the kitchen.

"This is my home," said Jim. "I was born and grew up here."

"Dare I remind you," said Alice, "you walked out on your wife some nineteen years ago without so much as a good-bye."

"I did say good-bye; I just didn't come home back from that Japan tour."

"For two decades, you never paid a red cent to your wife or provided any kind of child support. Your whereabouts remained unknown for such a length of time that Cordelia gave up—against my advice—even trying to have you served with divorce papers."

Cordelia stuck up her hand like a child in middle school. "We did try, Alice—three times, if you remember, and the documents were returned because of no forwarding address."

"Touring—here today, gone tomorrow—is a crazy business," said Jim. "The scene just kinda overwhelmed me."

"Bullshit," said Alice. "You left her with three years' back taxes to pay on the house and property. If her father, Judge Dimock, hadn't paid those taxes, plus interest and penalties, she would have been thrown out of this 'rural slum'—the Judge's words—and been left on the street. But you probably couldn't have given a damn."

"I didn't figure much of anything. I was an alcoholic; I was—"

"Don't give me the AA boilerplate." Alice got unsteadily to her feet and began pacing. "So, in case you haven't been informed, the divorce was finalized and we got three court-approved decrees of abandon-ment: wife and child abandonment *and* property abandonment. Which means you long ago lost custody or rights to see your child, so to speak." Alice glanced at George, who now sat intently on the piano bench, holding Wendy's hand. "In addition, the deed to this property, the house and land and everything on it, has been legally conveyed to Cordelia. Those legal fees were also absorbed by the Judge, with some relish, I might add. So in effect, you are now trespassing."

"That's a little harsh, Alice."

Alice raised her meticulously plucked and dyed eyebrows at her sister. "And, by the way, the amount Daddy paid to bail you out after Jim gave you the heave-ho is supposed to come out of your share in his will." She turned toward George with an inquisitive squint. "Has anybody laid eyes on his most recent will?"

Jim interrupted, staring into his palms as he spoke. "The paintings were bequeathed to me by my mother in her will. Her last wish was that I get recognition for my father's genius."

"Aha," proclaimed Alice, as if she'd caught out the defendant. "Then you can try to sue for their recovery, but I doubt any court in the land will give you the time of day. Not least because for the last nineteen years Cordelia has been slaving away peddling postcards and jewelry to tourists to pay the property taxes and upkeep. And given the hefty legal fees involved, you don't have a snowball's chance in hell of recovery. No judge is going to look favorably upon the appeal from a husband and so-called father who walked out on his wife and her son and left said wife and child to face financial ruin."

"It wasn't quite that bad, Alice. I mean we did have a house and community, a place to make a new start." Cordelia made a face. "And if Daddy hadn't come up with the money, I guess we could've moved back into the apartment in New York, or gone to Hermitage."

"Jesus, Cordelia, you may be a masochist when it comes to men, but don't be so wishy-washy."

"I have written my wife—"

"She's no longer your wife."

"I've written both Cordelia and George. I make no excuses for my behavior, none whatsoever. All I'm asking is to spend some time in the place that was once my home, the place that belonged to my parents . . . just a chance to get reacquainted with my family. Especially now."

"*Now*—what does that mean?"

"Nothing really." He glanced at George, eyes blinking rapidly. "Well, actually, now that so much has changed."

"The way to do that—sober doesn't count—is to get a place of your own and a job somewhere nearby, if that's what you're really up to, and ask Cordelia and George to meet you on neutral ground. Not just show up out of the blue and expect everybody to welcome you in like some lost soldier of fortune."

"I didn't say no when Jim returned," said Cordelia. "I just was surprised. And his teeth were hurting him so much, I told him go lie down in the upstairs guest room."

Alice bit her lip in a silent scolding of her witness for the prosecution.

"Yes, and you paid, too, for the dental procedures. Cordy, you're a saint or a fool or just a plain-vanilla masochist."

"I think the first step," said George, "is a legal settlement that takes care of any outstanding property rights. Once that is addressed and confirmed, other matters can be addressed without pressure or misunderstandings."

"Well put, George," said Alice with an approving nod at her nephew. "And, as a matter of fact, I've taken the bull by the horns and drawn up a legal document touching on those very issues." She handed Jim a manila envelope out of her handbag. "This a formal renunciation of any and all claims on the property—house, barn, land—*and* its contents."

"So this is an ambush," said Jim, vaguely sweeping his hand at the Altmann canvases hanging on the living room walls.

"If it had been an ambush, Jimmy boy, I would have walked in here with a court order and the local sheriff and had you escorted from the premises, along with a restraining order that restricted your presence to within five hundred yards of this property. And then we'd see about filing for years of back child support. So consider yourself getting off easy."

"Is this what you want, Cordelia?" Jim asked.

Cordelia shook her head, lost, overwhelmed. "Jim, it's all a little abrupt . . . We all need time."

Alice continued: "You're a lucky man, Jim Altmann. Cordelia is the least vindictive woman in the world. I mean, you're the man who fell for the gorgeous rich girl driving her daddy's red Mercedes coupe. Who made her queen bee at Woodstock—immortalized in *Life* and *Look*." Alice turned on Cordelia, eyes flaring. "You don't think Daddy saw those photographs—a sitting federal judge?" Alice nodded and turned back to Jim. "My sweet younger sister called up her big-shot Daddy, who called me up—not Martha, mind you—and who had *me* fly back from Berkeley yet again, this time to take care of yet another mess, a divorce and financial catastrophe. And this time we found her all alone with a thirteen-year-old son in tears because his father hadn't come home for eight months. Cordelia, selling preserves on the streets of Woodstock—and, *oh yes*, with a cocaine habit to boot."

"Jesus, Alice," said Cordelia, her head drooping, "don't you ever know when to quit?"

"My sweet young sister, our flower child, who survived Daddy's depredations with such insouciant aplomb, only to be taken in on the rebound by this once-upon-a-time guru techie of infamous Woodstock fame. First it was Daddy's seduction at the Ritz-Carlton in Boston; then it was your drug-addled boozer Jimmy here, who—correct me if I'm wrong—when in town, brought his women home to *your* bed while you were working in that pothead shop on Tinker Street. Until your son was dropped off by the school bus one fine day and found the man he thought was his father and a strange woman stark naked and passed out on the floor, surrounded by drug paraphernalia. At least you testified as much before a county judge during divorce proceedings."

"I never said Jim wasn't his father—because he is his father."

"Not what you told me, baby sister."

"I was just pissed. I was justifying myself to you."

"She'd been having an affair with Levon for years, not to mention the other boys," said Jim, catching Cordelia's eye.

"I was only filling in on keyboard for Garth or Richard when they were indisposed," pleaded Cordelia.

"And if it wasn't Levon, it could have been half a dozen others." Jimmy threw back his head in frustration. "They bragged about it on tour. And, worse, wrote her into their fucking lyrics."

Alice just shook her head at this pathetic excuse from the defendant and went over to her sister and spoke softly. "The saddest part, I don't think you've got a conniving or malicious bone in your body. If not innocent, exactly, you certainly lack common sense, never mind the most basic feminine wiles. Daddy's little angel . . . where did you come from, Cordy?" She cocked her head in wonder. "Couldn't have been from Annie—not her style, none of her steel; and from everything Martha and I could make out, she wouldn't let Daddy touch her after Teddy was killed. They had separate bedrooms on opposite ends of the apartment. And why the hell do you think Daddy offered Jim here fifty thousand dollars *not* to marry you?"

Cordelia glanced in disbelief at Jim, who returned her dismay with a broad smile.

"And come to think of it, why pay the back taxes and legal fees and child support for George and keep you in this dump, when, like you said, he could have pretty much forced you back with him on Fifth

Avenue, put George in Collegiate, or even his beloved Groton. He certainly talked about it enough when he picked me up at the airport and
drove us up here." A curious look came over Alice's face and she sidled
over to George and studied his face for a moment. "You know, I think
that had been his intention all along, to reclaim you and your mother.
How did he put it in the car on the way? 'Why, she could take Annie's
old room and he could have Teddy's.' Hah, Annie's old room—can you
believe it! And then something happened as we stood here, Cordy, with
little George sulking and confused at your side." She continued examining the subjects before her. "Did he see something in George that—I
don't know—put him off? Perhaps the Altmann nose—a hint of Jewish
blood? Or was it because you, Cordy, defiantly refused to ask for help
that he changed his mind? Or he feared something in himself? Do
you remember how he suddenly walked around this pigpen, nodding
to himself, hit a key on the out-of-tune 'Jap piano,' flinched, and then
spun around as if everything was decided and ordered me to draw up
the papers, complete the legal niceties, and he'd, in effect, buy this place
for you and keep you here? Why'd he do that, Cordelia? Why didn't he
take you home? Annie, if she'd been alive, would've had you and your
son back in a flash, if only to shame you and reform you." She tottered
over to the New York City Ballet poster and pressed a fingertip to the
scribbled name with a large *B* executed with a flourish. "My God, I saw
you dance at Lincoln Center once. You were stupendous; you could
have been the toast of the town." Her gray-green eyes touched with a
hint of wonder, if not nostalgia, she turned again to her little sister. "But
not Daddy. And you know why—and why he insisted I do all the legal
work? Because he was guilty about something, whether he'd let Annie
down, or molested you at the Ritz-Carlton, or because having you back
with those notorious nude photos at Woodstock would have proved
problematic when he was still on a short list for the Supreme Court.
Or maybe it was as simple as the fact he didn't want you and George
hanging about messing up his love life in the city with his mistress du
jour." She went and tapped George on the shoulder. "What does he
have to say about *that* in his memoir, George—why he abandoned *you*
to all this shit? No, don't answer. Because you don't need to answer. I
already know."

Cordelia gave her sister a petulant shove. "Just stop bullying, Alice.
You and Martha"—she shook her head vehemently—"made more out
of the Ritz-Carlton thing than it deserved."

"Tell that to Karen."

"Hey, Karen *and* me," said Cecily, piping up from the kitchen door, giving Wendy a quick squeeze and going over to her mother. "Don't I get some blame—or maybe credit, even if Karen did most of the flirting?" She stuck her tongue out at her mother. "You're always hounding everybody, throwing your weight around. Why don't you just leave these good people in peace?"

"*Me?*" she said, glaring at her daughter. "When you just walked out on the most brilliant, accomplished, and highly regarded surgeon on the planet—without even bothering to at least breed with him—a man who's a credit to his race."

"Oh my God! Another of your black saviors, huh? Is that it? Talk about fucking guilt."

Alice raised her hands as if in surrender.

"That's it," she yelled. "I've got better things to do than once again provide free legal help every time someone in this family fucks up her life. No more wasting my time on a bunch of aging hippies with your moronic banter about the good old days when you were going to save the world with peace and love, as if only the music and drugs could make it all better. The younger generation might lap up your good-times shit, but it's not going to change anything in this fucked-up racist country." Alice gave Cecily, who had now retreated to where Wendy sat with George, an icy look. "And now we're going to have another war in Iraq cooked up by the Bushes, another war to get everybody distracted from the continuing inequality and greed in this country. While fattening the pockets of Halliburton and the oil companies, manna from heaven for the arms dealers."

"Did you know that your nephew was almost killed on nine-eleven?" scolded Cordelia.

"Well, not exactly," said George with a hapless shrug, slipping a hand around Wendy's arm.

"Look at those three," said Alice, waving at George, Wendy, and Cecily as she began to gather up her papers. "Just like all my students, timid lemmings. They have no idea what made their world." She assumed a more dignified pose. "The real story was always in the streets, organizing communities, demanding minority rights, fighting in the courts to free the innocent and oppressed, and electing leaders on the side of the people. Demand equal rights—not handouts for the special interests and big business. And now we have a brain-dead generation of kids who have no idea how the world really works. My students are clueless. They make pilgrimages to Woodstock for some of that sixties vibe, peace and love and sex, sex, sex. They watch porn on their laptops during my lectures."

Cecily raised her right fist in a black-power salute. "Mother, blow it out your ass and let these people take care of their own shit. You stuck me with one hell of a fucked-up story—more than enough for a lifetime."

Alice eyes blazed out at her daughter.

"At least I saved something of your father—little you care. Even if he managed to get himself killed, and almost get me killed."

"And Billy killed, too, I suppose." Cecily spun away from her momentarily stunned mother and stalked off to the kitchen.

George stood, eyebrows knotted, clutching Wendy, who looked on, uncharacteristically speechless.

"Come on, Cecily," yelled her mother, "we're outta here."

"You've had too much to drink," said Cordelia. "Maybe George can drive you home."

"Listen," said George, "if everybody will just calm down a minute. I told the Judge we'd all try to make it for Thanksgiving at Hermitage. Can we agree to that? Martha, Karen and Erich, Nancy and Max are all on board."

"No damn way," said Alice. "If that old fascist thinks he's going to get one last chance to do mind-fucks on his offspring, he's got another think coming." She spun around and almost tripped, catching herself, going face-to-face with George. "Here's the deal: You send me a copy of the memoir and Stan and I will consider Thanksgiving. It's about time we got our stories straight, since the old man has obviously got you hog-tied."

"Oh, Alice," said Cordelia, "Daddy's ninety-five. He hasn't got much more time left. Can't we forgive and forget?"

Cecily came hurrying back and put her arms in solidarity around George and Wendy.

"I don't mind seeing the old guy—and he's the only goddamn grandfather I've ever had—even if he still blames me for trying to burn down his boathouse. I have a hankering for Hermitage right now; I still dream about those woods and lakes. In some ways, those were the happiest times of my life, hanging with the cousins there"—she cocked her head at her mother—"without you."

Alice grabbed her keys and turned for a final volley.

"Oh, that was another emergency flight—from a conference in Santa Fe to pick you up that summer when his highness kicked you out." She pointed a finger at George. "The memoir or else."

44

A Life in the Law and Out: Yalta

I OFTEN FOUND it odd that Alger put so much store by his connections with such luminaries as Dean Acheson, Francis Sayre, Felix Frankfurter, Oliver Wendell Holmes, and John Foster Dulles, especially as character witnesses—when, during the war years, when I was on the War Production Board, I regularly heard a much more exalted list of names dropped from Priscilla's lips at social gatherings, including both Eleanor and Franklin Roosevelt, Harry Hopkins, Laughlin Currie, Henry Morgenthau (and Harry Dexter White at Treasury), Cordell Hull at State, Henry Stimson at War, and others in the top echelons of government. None of these names, central to the planning and signing of the Yalta agreement (much less the development of the atomic bomb), was broached in my pretrial discussions with Alger, nor were they mentioned except in passing to HUAC or the FBI. Alger was clearly playing down his role at Yalta. I, perhaps naïvely, thought by playing up his role at Yalta, it would help the credibility of our case: such great confidence in and enormous responsibility entrusted to my client Alger Hiss! Yet time and time again he insisted to me that his role was minimal, mostly administrative in nature, while emphasizing that the accomplishment he was most proud of was his role in the formation of the United Nations to promote world peace. When I pressed him on Yalta, based on my understanding from conversations with Priscilla in various social settings during and immediately after the war—she boasted gleefully about his illustrious associations, saying that he had pretty much been the president's right-hand man—I was laughed off. Alger reacted as if he was a little fed up with Priscilla's boasting: He'd been nothing more than a "glorified clerk" keeping track of briefing papers for Stettinius—secretary of state, "in way over his head"—and Franklin, who "half the time couldn't even remember what time of day it was."

"Well," I proposed, "Franklin and Hopkins are dead, but Currie, Harriman, and Bohlen are still with us—why not at least invoke their names, play up their confidence in you; and why not Eleanor and Currie and Bohlen as character witnesses? Let's tout your role at Yalta to the sky, since that will surely resonate with the jury. Any juror worth his salt will be impressed to know that you sat in with Roosevelt at Yalta, with Churchill and Stalin!" To this suggestion, an alarmed Alger was unequivocal and dismissive: "Franklin was a rank amateur who presumed on his charm rather than marshaling the details of the business at hand." Alger further demurred: He would not presume on the time of the former First Lady, and besides, he barely knew Lauchlin Currie, who was now out of the country in Colombia. "Bogotá," he mentioned offhandedly, as if the place was, thankfully, on the dark side of the moon. Again, Alger insisted he'd played a very minor role at Yalta and had only been included at the last moment for his expertise on the "bureaucratic mechanics" of organizing the United Nations.

When I persisted along these lines, noting that Alger was, after all, one of only four immediate political advisers to the president— along with Stettinius, Hopkins, and Bohlen—Alger turned on me with sudden fury, eyes glittering: a fox, who, spying the succulent bait in a leg-hold trap, disdains the deadly prize with a circuitous detour. With another dismissive wave, he lowered his voice and with a knowing smile couched in an offhand remark informed me, "The dirty little secret, Edward, Yalta was a joke from start to finish. The Soviet NKVD had Roosevelt's headquarters bugged from top to bottom; there was not a discussion that we had privately among the American delegation—or, I dare say, with our allies—that did not end up in a hand-delivered report to Stalin at breakfast the following morning. He knew every-thing, all Roosevelt's stupidities and inanities and misplaced confidence in his charm and ability to play honest broker between Churchill and Stalin. So, forget about Yalta; never mention the word *Yalta* in the trial. I just so happened to catch Stettinius's eye and he took me along to Yalta to hold his hand—a neophyte secretary of state way out of his depth—since I knew my way around the technicalities of the staff work. Edward, the issue is Chambers and those fake papers he says I gave him back in 1938. That's the thing, the only thing that matters. Your job is to destroy Chambers's credibility, and with his credibility gone, his lying testimony goes up in smoke."

I think, at the time, I was quite taken in by Alger's sincerity—perhaps seeing it as modesty on his part, the way he played down his Yalta role, which, on the face of it, only made sense, given his position as a career staffer. Now, almost fifty years on, I'm not so sure. How was he so knowledgeable, if not blithely sanguine about the bugging? Alger Hiss, was, if he was anything, a brilliant lawyer and understood the looming implications of Yalta as well as anyone in the foreign policy establishment in the late forties, of which he, as president of the Carnegie Endowment, was a premier member. He was also one of us; we shared the same background and values as all those who voluntarily took up his defense. And so his word—his judgment—even his confident tone, mimicking our own, became our lodestar. And I have to keep reminding myself—when I have second thoughts—that this was late 1949, before the full implications of Yalta were fully realized, so I tell myself; and yet we had a pretty good idea of Stalin's perfidy in the Soviet's proxy takeover of Czechoslovakia and Poland. And so among members of the defense team, I think we simply closed ranks, kept our doubts to ourselves, and justified our focus on the indictable offenses with the admonition: Alger's got enough problems with what happened in 1938, so why bring up the subject of Yalta and the postwar situation and get blamed for that, as well? Legally, strategically, he was right: The focus had to be Chambers and the so-called Pumpkin Papers stolen from the State Department in 1938 (copied on the Hisses' Woodstock typewriter), and doing whatever necessary to protect Alger's good name and bona fides.

But I did make one last feeble foray into more recent events—how could I not, since only that August we had found out the Soviets had exploded their own atom bomb—by in the most offhand manner, simple curiosity, so to speak, broaching the question if Alger, while at State, had had any inkling of the Manhattan Project, since he circulated at such high levels, and had, in fact, been separated from the State Department for requesting materials on atomic energy development, far beyond his bailiwick of expertise. He just laughed at me as if I were the village idiot. "Edward, for mercy's sake, I was a terrible student at Johns Hopkins in math and science—no head for figures—why Pross balances our checkbook; I wouldn't have known the difference between a proton and an electron to save my life. I was as shocked as everyone else by what happened at Hiroshima and Nagasaki. My God man, you were a top dog on the War Production Board—didn't you have an inkling?"

And that was how the subject was left: A great lawyer never answers a question he doesn't want asked.

45
Yalta Redux

*I think it is accurate and not an immodest statement to say
that I did to some extent, yes.*

—Alger Hiss's response to a question during the
1948 HUAC hearings about whether he had
"drafted or participated in the drafting" of parts
of the Yalta agreement

*In the persons of Alger Hiss and Harry Dexter White, the
Soviet Military Intelligence sat close to the heart of the
United States Government. It was not yet in the Cabinet
room, but it was not far outside the door. In the years following my break with the Communist Party, the apparatus
became much more formidable. Then Hiss became Director
of the State Department's Office of Special Political Affairs
and White became an Assistant Secretary of the Treasury.
In a situation with few parallels in history, the agents of
an enemy power were in a position to do much more than
purloin documents. They were in a position to influence the
nation's chief enemy, and not only on exceptional occasions,
like Yalta (where Hiss's role, while presumably important,
is still ill-defined) or through the Morgenthau Plan for
the destruction of Germany (which is generally credited to
White), but in what must have been the staggering sum of
day-to-day decisions. That power to influence policy had
always been the ultimate purpose of the Communist Party's*

> *infiltration. It was much more dangerous, and, as events have proved, much more difficult to detect, than espionage, which besides it is trivial, though the two go hand in hand.*

—Whittaker Chambers

OF ALL THE subjects in the Judge's memoir, the section on Yalta, though short, ultimately proved the most disturbing and the most controversial, for its implications reached the furthest. In George's continuing correspondence by e-mail and phone with Weinstein, the subject of Yalta came up repeatedly. Perhaps it was because Weinstein was so perplexed at how both he and Edward Dimock had failed to grasp the full implications of Hiss's role at Yalta during the trial. And how guilelessly Hiss had finessed his participation at Yalta not only to Dimock and his defense team but also to the prosecution, the public at large, and in the many interviews the young scholar did with Hiss for his definitive book on the trial, *Perjury*. Never at any time, not even many years later in his 1988 memoir, where Hiss discussed his time at Yalta, did he mention publicly the Soviet tapping of the Livadia Palace. Only to his defense lawyer, Edward Dimock, did he mention this.

And only after Hiss's death was the tapping conclusively revealed by Stalin's translator, Valentin Berezhkov, during a conference on Stalin at the University of California at Riverside in 1998. It was then that Berezhkov blithely informed a roomful of stunned academics that Stalin had been presented each morning with a complete transcript of every-thing said by members of the American delegation, including Roosevelt, in their private quarters. Roosevelt had been warned about this situation of compromised security, but he had cavalierly dismissed it, either out of hubris or due to severe depression, or perhaps he was so overconfi-dent that he didn't care. For an hour and a half each morning, Sergo Beria, part of the Soviet eavesdropping team, briefed Stalin on the haul of intercepted conversations from the previous day. Stalin, so it was later reported, was less interested in the content than the tone of the bugged conversation, the intonation of the participants, if arguments were stated with conviction or without enthusiasm. It was the personal profiles of the members of the American delegation that Stalin relished, calculating that insights into the players' weaknesses offered him the surest path to getting most of what he wanted.

"You sure your grandfather didn't get wind of that 1998 conference when Berezhkov spilled the beans?" asked Weinstein on a phone call.

"No way. Besides, the memoir lay untouched for five years; there's no way he climbed those stairs and added the stuff on the tapping of Livadia Palace."

Weinstein was clearly puzzled, if not skeptical, at the brazenness of Hiss's revelation to his defense lawyer. What had prompted the canny Hiss to run the great risk of sharing such a secret with his defense lawyer years before? A desperate, even crazy, risk—all to convince Dimock to take the job? How could he have calculated that Dimock would sit on such a revelation for years—that he wouldn't grasp the sinister implications of what had been tossed off as a careless aside? Unless his trust in Dimock went beyond that of a hired gunslinger to damage Chambers's testimony? And why hire Dimock in the first place, a man whose background was in corporate law and not criminal defense law?

George's discussions with Weinstein led to his trying to picture the scene of the American delegation gathered in the Livadia Palace, where once the czar and his family had summered, where Alger Hiss worked diligently with his colleagues and his president, while behind the scenes daily betraying them and his country. This was a president whom for decades after, and in his 1988 memoir, Hiss claimed to so admire. How could two such people inhabit the same body?

For Hiss's betrayal went even further than his knowledge of the Soviet bugging of the Livadia Palace, only one of the Yalta venues occupied by the American and British delegations. Prompted by the Judge's Yalta revelation, Weinstein had again called on a favorite source in Moscow, "Dimitri," to confirm Valentin Berezhkov's story on Soviet tapping, telling him—coming at it from a different direction so as to allay his suspicions as to his real object—that the Stettinius diary in the archives of the University of Virginia had revealed a secretary of state often mystified and perplexed at the way Stalin seemed to anticipate and deftly manipulate each new political issue under discussion from one day to the next. (When Weinstein had researched the Stettinius papers for answers to the secretary of state's perplexity, he discovered copious notes advising Stettinius's biographer to inquire of Alger Hiss on matters that the former secretary of state was unsure about, including the precise language of the secret protocols confirming the Polish boundary settlements and other issues concerning the return of refugees.) Apparently, Roosevelt had specifically asked for Hiss to remain behind an extra day at Yalta to complete the drafting of both the Polish agreements and another secret codicil to the Yalta agreement requiring the Allies to return all Soviet citizens, refugees, or prisoners of war who remained behind in the western sectors of Europe. This was the infamous agreement known as Operation Keelhaul, which resulted in the return of two million souls to either slavery or death, an agreement kept secret from the American people for fifty years.

How was Uncle Joe so well prepared? Weinstein mused to Dimitri. How effortlessly he played Churchill off against Roosevelt, or subtly enlisted Roosevelt as an anti-imperialist to get what he wanted out of Churchill on Poland, Romania, Yugoslavia, and from Roosevelt territorial concessions in the Far East. Once returned to the subject of those glorious Yalta days, Dimitri had admitted something he'd never mentioned in previous conversations: During Yalta, he'd been a translator for General Mikhail Abramovich Milstein, who, so he now let on, had been one of Hiss's control officers from 1935 to 1938, when he had served as vice consul at the Soviet consulate in New York. Dimitri proceeded to tell Weinstein that at Yalta, General Milstein—"Who needs microphones?"—got a daily private briefing from Alger Hiss on the American negotiating posture and, in return, received instructions from his Soviet handler—all to the end of facilitating an agreement to further the ultimate goals of the Soviet Union. Weinstein described Dimitri's faltering voice suddenly energized on the staticky overseas line; the "old buzzard" told him that Stalin had been particularly intent on the Polish land grab and the ceding of the South Sakhalin and the southern group of the Kuriles to the Soviet Union, along with most of Manchuria, a quid pro quo for a Soviet declaration of war on Japan. Concessions, included in a secret protocol, that an ailing Roosevelt and his generals were eager to agree to if it meant the saving of possibly hundreds of thousands of American lives.

George found himself trying to weigh in his mind if Hiss's betrayal at Yalta had substantially changed the outcome of the settlements, enough that the Soviets would have done almost anything not just to save their master spy from conviction but also, perhaps more important, to distract attention from his spying at Yalta, which if definitively revealed in 1950 would have severely crippled both ongoing Soviet espionage and relations with the Western powers, as well as compromising planned aggression in Korea and elsewhere. Yet another motivation for the brutal dispatch of any and all who might pose a threat to Hiss.

How Hiss had ended up at Yalta in the first place was a question that Weinstein pondered endlessly. Clearly, Hiss's supporters in the White House, Lauchlin Currie, Harry Hopkins, and others, had thought it crucial to have Hiss at Yalta, Weinstein suggested. They must have convinced FDR to take along this relatively low-level State Department officer, whose expertise had mostly to do with the agreements for the creation of the U.N., a subject and project dear to the heart of Franklin Roosevelt. In his 1988 memoir, Hiss attributed his selection as a matter of chance when Roosevelt rejected Stettinius's selection of James Dunn, then in charge of European affairs at State, and the natural choice for the Yalta job. But Dunn was a conservative, as Hiss duly noted with some relish, and so out of favor with Roosevelt, who preferred his own left-leaning advisers. Hiss considered the veteran and more experienced State Department hands as out of step with the reformist zeal of the New Deal, including his contemporary, George Kennan.

From the perspective of forty years, Hiss had duly noted in his memoir Stalin's monstrous crimes against his people, but he had also written that at Yalta the wily dictator struck him as considerate and well mannered, appearing to be genuinely conciliatory on most issues. "It is interesting to speculate as to the reason for Stalin's flexibility and agreeableness at Yalta. It seems to me unlikely that this mood . . . simply masked intransigence. After all, it was we, not Stalin, who came bearing requests," Hiss wrote.

"Bearing requests . . ."

George found this phrase more than a little troubling.

Perhaps Poland had been a foregone conclusion even without Hiss's treachery, even if Roosevelt and Churchill had been tougher in negotiations, insisting on strict guarantees that a fully representative Polish government would be established with free elections monitored by outside observers. But the fact that the American delegation was bugged, with Alger Hiss delivering an update on evolving American strategies each morning, meant that Stalin knew everything about the weakness and rifts among his opponents and how best to exploit them. The Soviet dictator had been a master at alternating bullying with gracious and deft politicking, playing off Roosevelt against Churchill to make sure his brutal takeover of Poland—a Poland greatly enlarged to the west—succeeded, and without firm democratic protocols or interference from Allied observers. Then again, as Weinstein pointed out to George, it was not only Alger Hiss but also Stalin's spies, including the Cambridge Five, who had thoroughly infiltrated the Allied governments, often getting diplomatic documents to Stalin before even Western leaders had a chance to read them. Roosevelt never fully realized the implacable enemy he was up against, an imperial conqueror who used his revolutionary politics as a means to further the grip of the Soviet Union on captive nations. Roosevelt's gravest vulnerability, which Alger Hiss and other American spies in the White House, State, and Treasury exploited to the full, was his penchant to bypass career diplomats and experts and pursue his diplomatic ends on his own terms, relying on a few trusted advisers, many influenced and guided by Stalin's spies. This, and his over-reliance on his instincts and charm left him vulnerable to Stalin, who knew Roosevelt's gambler's instinct as well as he knew the president's cards before they were even played.

George found himself often returning to Whittaker Chambers's words whenever something truly puzzled him about Yalta, who'd written so incisively on Stalin's temper, of a mind drawn to a strategy of multiple deceptions, "which confuse the victim with the illusion of power, and soften them up with the illusion of hope, only to plunge them deeper into despair when the illusion fades, the trap is sprung, and the victims grasp with horror, as they hurtle into space . . ."

Had such illusions of power and hope, the deft manipulation of Stalin's agents, so softened up an exhausted Roosevelt that he was willing to forgo his democratic principles? So much so that he and Churchill agreed to redraw international borders and forcibly resettle millions of people without consulting the nations affected. Under unremitting pressure from Stalin, FDR and Churchill agreed to the return of millions of Soviet prisoners and refugees, which would result in their almost certain death. Nor did Roosevelt object to the partition of the Balkans into spheres of influence—concocted months before in Moscow by Churchill and Stalin—between Great Britain and Russia, nor granting Stalin a de facto sphere of influence in Asia. The end result was Stalin's domination and brutal repression of Eastern Europe and territorial gains in Asia.

Toward the end of the conference, Roosevelt was increasingly exhausted and sometimes disoriented, urging a conclusion once his fundamental goals had been met of a Soviet entry into the war against Japan, and Soviet agreement around the formation of the U.N. The compromises he made to achieve this were done without the support of the old State Department hands, leaving Alger Hiss and other Soviet agents back in Washington to tip the scales in favor of Moscow Center. Interestingly, at Yalta, it was Hiss and other State Department officials who objected to Stalin's request that the Soviet Union be given three votes in the General Assembly, by including Belarus and the Ukraine as original voting members. One country, one vote had been the guiding principle on the formation of the U.N. first worked out at the Dumbarton Oaks Conference in 1944. But Stalin complained that Britain could count on all its commonwealth nations to vote on its side. In the end, Roosevelt overruled Hiss, Stettinius, and his State Department and agreed to Stalin's demand: The principle of one country, one vote was abridged, but the practical effects were negligible, since the real power ultimately remained with the Security Council controlled by the great powers. Of course, Hiss, whatever his real stance on the matter, had been keeping Stalin abreast of the U.S. negotiating position every morning through Milstein, so Stalin knew that an exhausted Roosevelt was wavering on the issue and that his demand for more votes was in the bag.

Several years later, Charles Bohlen, the translator for Roosevelt at Yalta, testified that Alger Hiss had few if any substantive conversations with the president, only with Secretary of State Stettinius, and mostly about U.N. matters. But Bohlen may have forgotten or been unaware that Roosevelt nominated Hiss to brief his American military advisers on the political issues that were near and dear to his heart, clearly finding in Hiss a sympathetic ally, an ally who then passed on these military discussions to Milstein, his Soviet handler. Such insights into American strategies and internal squabbles allowed Stalin to anticipate day by day, moment by moment, exactly what he could push for and get and what he could trade away on matters of no importance to him. The real reason Stalin may have appeared so conciliatory to observers at the conference, acquiescing to the Allies "bearing requests," was that much of what he wanted had long been precooked. The real damage had been done over all the previous years, with secrets delivered and policies tailored and aligned with the interests of the Soviet Union by agents of influence.

Kim Philby, Donald Maclean, and Guy Burgess may have leaked more secrets to Stalin, but Alger Hiss, Harry Dexter White, and Lauchlin Currie as agents of influence at the highest reaches of the U.S. government did far more damage. And only Alger Hiss brazened it out to his death.

George found it hard to shake off these countless imponderables. As Alger Hiss sat in the dock during his trial, did he assuage his nerves by taking pride in his part in the Soviet successes at Yalta, which by 1950 were disturbingly apparent? Did he see the Iron Curtain as a triumph, with more to come? Did he still take heart in advancing the revolutionary cause? Did he feel the pressure from his Soviet handlers to remain stalwart and unflinching, to keep the focus away from Yalta and on those obscure, useless State Department documents from another era, produced by that smarmy turncoat, Whittaker Chambers? Did Stalin follow the trial in the Kremlin, putting out the word that Hiss and his secret life must be protected at all costs lest the FBI turn with renewed vigor to rounding up his atomic spies?

These questions in George's mind were, and remained, as impenetrable as the nature of dark matter.

It was uncanny, if not a little spooky, how often the faces he'd pored over in old grainy black-and-white photographs taken at Yalta took on a life of their own in George's imagination, sometimes in dreams, sometimes while just staring up at the night sky. He would picture these faces around a large table covered by a white tablecloth in the Livadia Palace: Alger Hiss looking dapper, intent, conscientious, seated just to the left and behind Roosevelt and Stettinius; the president's face drawn and drained, eyes sunken, dark-ringed, mouth slightly agape; and across the huge table, Stalin in his general's uniform, his mustached face thrust forward, hair swept back, Georgian nose beaklike, eyes sharp, glittering, and intent, predatory; and Churchill's balding round head, his body overweight and bowed down, the prime minister chewing his cigar, keenly observant, blustering, garrulous, aggressive; and the other Americans who knew Hiss well: Charles Bohlen, Roosevelt's trusted translator and Russian expert; Ambassador Harriman, agile, canny, who knew Stalin's crimes better than anyone in the U.S. delegation; and Harry Hopkins, pale and sickly (confined to his bed during most of the Yalta summit), the president's closest adviser and confidant; and the president's military advisers, King, Marshall, and Leahy, men of proven worth and integrity with the lives of hundreds of thousands of their soldiers depending on a good outcome at Yalta. All supporters of a beloved, if failing, president. Patriots. And yet each and every day Hiss had unflinchingly gone to his Soviet handler, Mikhail Milstein, and given away the most closely guarded secrets of his president and his country, all the while circulating among his colleagues without a hint of unease. Unflinching betrayal. It is one thing to sit in an office and sneak out top-secret documents to one's Soviet handlers, another to be in the thick of a world-changing moment, a war-ending conference, a negotiation affecting the fate of millions, surrounded by your brave countrymen and allies who have been in a fight for survival for over four years, who are all pulling on the same oar to create a lasting peace—and to betray them, each and every one, every day and every hour, as you share the most personal confidences, sharing meals and toasts, sharing bedrooms, standing in interminable bathroom lines each morning.

And this betrayal was celebrated at the American delegation's first stop after Yalta, in a secret meeting in Moscow, where, in a rushed ceremony, Alger Hiss was taken aside from his colleagues, when the chief of Soviet intelligence bestowed on him the Order of the Red Star for his services to the Soviet Union. It was the one and only day in his entire life that Hiss set foot in the Soviet Union.

What kind of man is capable of such a thing, and capable of keeping the deception up for decades, never letting up, never letting go, never admitting anything?

The answer to which George detected in the soft steady tones of one Whittaker Chambers, who offered hints when recalling a strange if unlikely savagery in Alger Hiss from the thirties, whether about his boyhood growing up in Baltimore or his President, Franklin Roosevelt. "Hiss's contempt for Franklin Roosevelt as a dabbler in revolution who understood neither revolution nor history was profound. It was the common view of Roosevelt among Communists, which I shared with the rest. But Alger expressed it not only in political terms. He startled me, and deeply shocked my wife, by the obvious pleasure he took in the most simple and brutal references to the President's physical condition as a symbol of the middle-class breakdown."

A pleasure that allowed for betrayal under circumstances of the most intimate working conditions.

With Chambers, there had been a bond of affection, even love of a kind, between spy and spymaster, agent and handler who shared a grand faith, a grand conspiracy to change history. Chambers's affectionate reflections floated back to George like a familiar refrain: Hiss's "kindness and unvarying mildness, a deep considerateness and gracious patience that seemed proof against any of the ordinary exasperations of work and fatigue or the annoyances of family or personal relations."

A man who "talked constantly about birds with an enthusiasm that he showed for little else." Perhaps, in the end, it simply came down to a shared political faith in the future of communism, a feeling that he was part of something bigger, a secret community of believers in which he would be revered and cherished, as history proved him right. There was never a question of blackmail, or money, or gain, no obvious motivation of revenge or resentment against his Harvard peers, or even an underlying virulent hatred of the upper class (a resentment that had motivated the British spies Philby, Maclean, Burgess, and Blunt), many of whom he'd broken bread with most of his life, much less an inferiority complex that might have bolstered a craving for power or influence, or even fueled a sense of superiority, which belonging to a secret cabal often infers. Certainly not after 1950, when communism had proved itself a dangerous and corrupt monstrosity, or after Stalin's death in 1953, or Khrushchev's devastating speech of 1956 enumerating Stalin's bloody crimes, or the millions dying of starvation during Mao's Great Leap Forward, or Pol Pot's slaughtered millions.

Or was conscience, as Chambers pointedly noted, never the issue for a dedicated Communist, who saw his government as the illegitimate machine of a class he was committed to overthrowing, and, if necessary, by violence? When betrayal was a moral act driven by a faith that even reveres betrayal—sons against fathers, husbands against wives—when championing the cause of the future hopes of mankind. "No other Communist but Alger Hiss understood so quietly, or accepted with so little fuss or question the fact that the revolutionist cannot change the course of history without taking upon himself the crimes of history."

Or perhaps the inverse ratio of Hiss's faith finally kicked in as the fifties turned into the sixties and seventies, as the body counts in China and Cambodia mounted year by year, as the Soviet tanks rolled into Prague: as good a reason as any for Alger Hiss to never admit anything, to cover his tracks, to endlessly seek vindication, to proclaim his innocence while boldly supporting Ho Chi Minh against American imperialism. Hiss's purported innocence was believed in by half the country, and usually by the best educated and informed, as if each half existed in a different world. Not unlike, it often occurred to George, the strange disjuncture between classical physics, where events occur in a predictable pattern, and the underlying quantum world of particle physics, which behaves in a way very different, a discordant and random way that our human senses cannot comprehend, which baffles and disconcerts the rational mind, if not outright contradicting many of the agreed-upon laws of the standard model. A model perhaps of how two competing or even different stories can coexist simultaneously in the same mind, as different times can coexist simultaneously in space-time, all part of the same universe where the world as we think we know it fails to reflect or accommodate the underlying—or perhaps hidden—reality—or unreality—that sustains it.

Did Alger Hiss and his comrades at Volta Place inhabit such an invisible parallel universe, based on revolutionary laws of morality and conscience that went against everything considered decent and humane, necessary, at least in their minds, to bring into existence a new and higher way of being by resolving the dialectic of history? A precarious consciousness based on a faulty theory, which in practice proved disastrous. A disaster, which when it became apparent to most, simply caused that revolutionary consciousness to evaporate, along with those who survived, who disappeared as if they had never been, taking that parallel secret world they had once embraced to their graves. A universe, or call it a story, a narrative once inhabited by one Alger Hiss, who either never wavered in a misbegotten faith or simply disappeared into some part of his original self when time and space proved that faith a road to hell. Who became, finally, a ghost even to himself.

46

Gunks

GEORGE LOOKED UP at the blue rope line stretched tautly above him, as if hanging from the sky, or at least where it disappeared into the sky beyond the cliff face, and then back down to where Wendy stood holding the belay, giving him just enough slack. She was guiding him up the rock face, shouting suggested handholds and where to place his feet on the thin ledges and fissures in the sandstone.

"Move to your left about a foot and grab with your right hand and swing out and up."

"What happens if I mess up the footing?"

"Why do you keep asking that? Just do exactly what I tell you. You can see where I placed the anchors. This is easier than Chelsea Piers—child's play. Embrace your fucking fear—that's the point, and don't forget the view. Are you looking out at the valley and all those gorgeous patterns of ruddy orange against the russets and grays?"

He looked out over the Rondout Valley, where the trees were mostly bare except for the stalwart oaks clutching modest clusters of tarnished leaves, as if to hide their ravaged and naked bodies. He wanted to see if he could detect the line of the D & H Canal where it once ran down the center of the valley, but prolonged gazing, much less keeping steady, was too unnerving. Below, she had shrunk to a doll-size figure, orange helmet, feet spread, both gloved hands gripping the belay. He grabbed the nearest angle of cold sandstone, examining the striations for a few seconds, vaguely appreciating the millions of years he'd traversed in the last few minutes.

"Fall splendor," he muttered loudly, pulling himself up, "is past its peak and won't amount to a damn if I mess up and kill myself."

"You can't fall. Not with me holding you. I know this pitch like the

610

back of my hand—well, almost as well, but as well as I know every vein of your lightsaber."

"Well, that's cold comfort, even if the real estate is limited." He steadied himself and made the grab with his chalked fingers. "What if the rope breaks? Just kidding."

"Go for it, George," she called. "You're plenty ready, you're more than strong enough, and if you slip, you won't fall more than a foot, and you just redo the move until you get it right. Just like we did a hundred times on the climbing wall at Chelsea Piers."

"Something about real rock—it's damn cold by the way—that gives me the creeps."

"If you need to cheat, grab any of the anchor bolts; they're solid as bullets, and so is the sandstone—millions of years solid."

"Okay, *there*," he shouted, shifting his weight. "Now what?"

"Just repeat, just follow. This is a cinch. I've taken fifteen-year-old girls up here."

"Everything is a cinch until an accident happens."

He was sweating even in the cool forty-degree afternoon.

"Keep going." She gave the rope a tug to remind him he was attached on his harness. "Do you think for one moment I would even put you in a position where I'd lose the best toy boy ever?"

"Ever lose a student?"

"Don't fuck with me, George, or I'll climb up there and kick your fat ass to the top."

"Okay, here goes." He reached with his extended leg and got purchase and swung himself up the extra inches.

"Good, now grab hold over there to your right and swing up a little more."

"Don't you ever worry about dying?"

"We're all going to die, George. At least you'll get to die with this ascent and view off your bucket list. Now look at the goddamn view. Enjoy the clean air, the fall foliage, the thrill of your body's getting into shape and overcoming gravity. You're a fucking eagle up there, George—sort of. Surviving the fear is the tonic for whatever ails you."

"I thought feathers were only for angels."

"You don't qualify for the duty—yet. Keep going, or I'm just going to have to drag you up on the rope."

"You're not strong enough."

"Wanna bet?"

She pulled hard on the rope and for a moment he dangled like a broken puppet in thin air.

47

A Life in the Law and Out: Our Bunce Moon

AS I APPROACH ninety, struggling to finish and polish my memoir, I find myself, paradoxically, relying more and more for guidance on my mentor, Oliver Wendell Holmes, and not a little chagrined that I'm now about the same age as he was when I knew him best—as if advancing age should provide us answers when, in fact, it only shakes lose more questions. My preoccupation is partly out of concern that I have not adequately served his great spirit, both professionally and personally, nor fleshed out the agile quality of his mind in these pages. And partly, too, because of the recent death of Alger Hiss at ninety-two last November, 1996, who served as clerk to Oliver the year before me. I take no satisfaction in having outlived Alger and I hope his final years were good to him. But I do find it distressing that both publicly and within the circle of his family and admirers he touted to the skies his relationship with Justice Holmes, even serving as editor on a condensed version of the Holmes-Laski letters. I would never begrudge him nostalgic feelings for Holmes, not now, but I do find it galling that he enlisted the good justice to burnish his image as a great patriot and all-American champion of the New Deal, both during the trial and in later years when trying to overturn his conviction. When I know their relationship was anything but smooth. All I can offer are my own memories and reflections on Holmes, the man who bestowed upon me the love of my life, my wife, Annie.

Indeed, my heart seems drawn to the true north of our one summer at Beverly Farms, when we had known each other for almost a year, when we had the luxury of more leisure to reflect on life and history than afforded by our busy official duties in Washington. Day after day—can it really be more than sixty years after his death?—I find my gaze drifting from my typewriter, from the decades of opinions and dissents stacked at my elbow, to the windows thrown wide, where the loamy scents of high summer are wafted to me on the afternoon breeze, listening for the song of the hermit thrush, for those sighing liquid melodies—longing queries from heaven's gate—filtered from the boughs of white pine bannering our lake: Oliver, sir . . . Oliver, sir . . . Oliver, sir, what would you have done if Alger Hiss had asked you as a young lawyer to defend him? And would you have trusted Alger's word over a onetime Communist agent whose autobiography now rests at my elbow, whose languorous, world-weary eyes watch me from the cover, piercing my guilty conscience, whose testimony seems to gain more and more weight in my mind as the years go by, whose insights into your Alger and mine ring increasingly true, as do his judgments on our life and times?

And what of my cruel and—worse—unprofessional treatment of Chambers on the witness stand: a vicious means to a misbegotten end? And if, indeed, Alger really was a spy, along with so many of his bright-eyed comrades—dare I say, some of the best Harvard men of their generation—what then? Oliver: What had happened to the country you so loved and served so loyally that its best could stoop to such treachery? And what, sir, of the destructive forces that have since riven our land and done such damage to my own family? What would be your thoughts, you, who, as a young man, watched in horror as so many brilliant and brave—yes, Harvard boys—lost their lives on southern battlefields in the cause of extirpating the evil of slavery from our land, only to have it linger like a hundred-year miasma to our very own day. Along with its kin offshoot, a form of slavery in malevolent disguise, a different kind of enslavement perhaps—the Gulag and concentration camps—but equally virulent in terms of the moral and physical degradation inflicted on millions, along with the systematic elimination of its political enemies.

I take some comfort that you never had to witness the insidious spread of this virulent plague's poison across much of the continent of Europe, only to reach our shores and spread its tentacles to the very heart of our governing institutions. And what if "our" Alger, as you often referred to him both in terms of endearment and bafflement, turns out to be guilty of far more than just perjury? What would have been your final judgment on our generation for allowing such a disaster to befall us? A sin of commission or omission? That so many of our best justified or turned a blind eye to—or even silently condoned—such a malicious horror in our midst? Perhaps the new century will consign our benighted generation to well-deserved eclipse.

Oliver, sir: It is with such questions poised on my lips that I find my mind rising to the sky and speeding over lake and forest, over rolling hill and dale—admiring the patterns of stone walls as an eagle riding the thermals, past peaceful white-steepled towns and careworn cities, my faulty-fading memory gravitating back to the eternal sea and shore of that long-ago summer, where my memory, again gathering depth, finds its soul mate waiting in your rough-as-granite New England voice as it would greet me each morning at breakfast to go over the day's missives from Washington, my hours directed in service to your skeptical, irascible tone of practical common sense, a Solon, who, paradoxically, with world-weary sagacity in the twinkle of your aged eyes would almost always advocate caution in your rulings, giving due deference to doubt and intellectual humility, which I, too, have tried to follow in all my opinions and dissents. What astonishes me is how almost seventy years ago, in the summer of 1931, enthroned in your high-back wicker rocker on the veranda overlooking your garden and the sliver of blue sea beyond, where I read to you everything from detective stories to poetry and history, Oliver, sir, you had already detected the spreading rot. Was it that—it now occurs to me—which inspired you to provide me with an anchor and helpmeet and so allow me to enter the public arena, for which I had, then, so little taste, much less calling?

"Edward, a man in public life needs a strong right arm, and, as the Athenian hoplite knew only too well, an equally solid shield on your right flank."

Of course, Oliver, sir, you were referring to Annie, but I now wonder if that observation, that lingering sense of betrayal in your tone, was not prompted by Alger's sudden marriage—and breaking faith—of just the year before? Perhaps an admonition—how did you put it?—"that when like enthusiasms marry in a blind rush, there is no break on the downward slope of folly."

Just hearing your friendly voice in my inner ear, I'm inundated with the smells of your lush summer garden—fountains of gay hollyhocks and nodding sunflowers, azure chrysanthemums and satiny purple day-lilies—a raiment tapestry of vivid color, a perennial font of perfume forever imbued in my mind's eye with the briny scent of a northeast breeze. Dare I admit that your aged stentorian voice now reminds me almost too much of my own temptation, my irascible bête noire—"to badger innocent youth"—as a way of honing the opinions of an antediluvian has-been. I believe it was you who warned, "An old man's garden

requires constant weeding, Edward, lest the long rearward view be lost
for the brambles." I like to believe that your stories have become second nature to me now, that something of the spirit of Emerson and
the caustic Oliver Wendell Holmes Sr., has come to inhabit my mind,
along with your beloved anecdotes from Marshall, Blackstone, and
Shakespeare; if not your habit of dispensing epistolary gems of hard-
won wisdom as casual asides tossed into the laps of the young. What
you liked to call "our higher purposes, our ultimate calling," as if such
ideals were the most natural of guideposts to good habit and firm character. Isn't that the role of the aged in the lives of the young: clear-eyed
windows onto the past? Something so thoroughly instilled in your goddaughter, Annie, that for her it was pure instinct.

"For a New Yorker, your reading of Emerson is quite evocative,
Edward, even for one who has heard many of those same phrases from
the lips of their author."

"If," I replied, and I closed his well-thumbed and underlined volume
of Emerson's essays (signed and inscribed to his father by the Sage of
Concord), more than a little in awe of the very notion, "only because I
unconsciously imitate your cadences, sir, if not your style, after so many
dictated letters."

"But your mind is your own, Edward. I appreciate your candor and
your reasoned take on the affairs of men—a rare thing in the younger
generation."

"Not so rare among the scientifically minded of my peers. And from
my father, Dr. Dimock, who, I fear, has become disillusioned with the
limits of medical science, if not the evaporation of his stock portfolio
recommended by his wealthy patients."

"One feels for these people, Edward, who lost everything in the
crash. No one has been left unscathed. And economic hard times
poisons the body politic, turning one interest against the other." He
pulled at his long, flowing white mustache, staring off over the garden, where sunset's purple shadows lengthened among a cornucopia
of pinwheeling petals. "Fortunately, I lacked the moneymaking instinct
and so kept all my inheritance and Fanny's money in dull-as-dishwater
municipal bonds."

"My father lost almost everything in 1929. His Fifth Avenue duplex
isn't selling, and even his bungalow in Palm Beach—where he broods
on his disappointments—is worth nothing. Our place in the Catskills,
his pride and joy, is a tightening noose around my neck. He put most

of his family money into the thing, including an Italian Renaissance ceiling that Stanford White talked him into. I feel enormous pressure to preserve this family legacy."

"Ah, your Hermitage." He winked reassuringly. "Well, by this time next year, you'll be rolling in cash, now that you have those offers from—what, six or seven Wall Street firms?"

"Clearly, you disapprove."

"A man needs to keep a roof over his head. I have been luckier than most with my father's legacy, my dear Fanny's, too, I dare say . . . enough to allow me the luxury of public service, and the company of great books and the occasional etching or two."

"Your name, of course, well . . . the clerkship carries much weight."

"Oh, I've always been useless to the moneymen, but a lad like you, with your background in New York society and the accolade of ranking at the top of your law school class, you're just the ticket."

"Yes, staving off bankruptcies or concluding bankruptcies or reorganizations. Hardly the stuff to make a reputation in the law."

"Saving the economy, saving the productive heart of the nation, has its uses. Without that, without jobs, we will surely go down to ruination as the socialists grow in strength and numbers, and add yet more straitjackets to the economy. In a land of scarcity, doctrines of class and racial envy and resentment grow apace."

"You think we're headed for Bolshevism?"

"I've had close friends, Harold Laski for one, who, long before this present disaster, had advocated near as much. Your predecessor, our Alger, was much enamored of Harold's writings. They are all steeped in the same European radical thinkers, theoreticians who abstract the human condition and turn it into models to have their way with the world."

"To listen to many just out of the law school, especially Alger, Wilson was not radical enough. Even Franklin Roosevelt is now dismissed by his onetime supporters as a party hack, a second-rate intellect in the service of preserving the ruling class. They seem to want to overthrow the whole rotten mess."

"Our Alger, really? He struck me as more circumspect, at least in his opinions around me. And something of a stickler for the letter of the law."

"Perhaps it is just talk. A stickler for the iron law of wages, perhaps—or is that his wife, quite the socialist?"

"Ah, your long-lost love, Priscilla."

"Oh, she first needed finding for that to be the case. She tried marrying money and that ended up a disaster. And again, an affair with another married man, another disaster. So now she's married—most admirable—humanitarian aspirations . . . who knows quite of what sort. Alger keeps his cards close to his chest, as you know."

Oliver nodded with that wry, sometimes enigmatic smile of his.

"Pretending he knew nothing of the stipulation that my clerks remain unmarried for the duration. Then a fait accompli." He smiled searchingly. "Young feller, you, too, seem drawn to strong, smart women."

"I can't imagine a marriage without the spark of spirited discourse."

Again, the smile, now more pensive, perhaps wistful.

"Fanny loved those chrysanthemums in the late summer—nothing made her happier. A woman of simple tastes, really. We never discussed the law."

"Yes, there is abiding comfort in the procession of seasonal blooms, especially wildflowers in abandoned pastures—something of a specialty of our place in the Catskills. Beauty that couldn't care less about a devastated banking system and breadlines."

"Nature—the perennial recrudescence, as Emerson knew, was our saving grace. His words, his example, saved my sanity more than once: that incessant struggle between freedom and fate. That character *is* fate, the thing you were born to be, from which there is no turning back." He nodded to where I held Emerson's *Essays* in my lap, as if struck by a particularly resonant memory. "For a long while, I thought the catastrophe of the Civil War would change our country forever—and not necessarily for the better. Half the nation devastated and poisoned with race hatred, the other goaded into pursuit of unheard-of riches. What has surprised me was the eagerness, within one generation, among the brightest, most accomplished minds, to enter once again into the slaughter pen that was the Western Front. It was all theory for them—who had never known the cruelty of battle—a chance to use the military to reorganize and rationalize the country along the lines of their book-conjured fantasies. Any of us who actually experienced the devastation of war would have been much more reluctant, especially given the Maxim gun. Concentrated rifle fire was terrible enough. Now, I begin to wonder if the Great War was more of a catastrophe than simply the hecatombs of casualties. It has spawned a fanatic faith in man's worst delusions."

"My father has never gotten over my brother's death in 1918; he was shot down just weeks before the Armistice."

"Forgive me, I forgot you had told me. How terrible for you."

"He was the intrepid one, the star athlete—fearless; I fear he has left me a careful plodding coward."

"Not all are meant for soldiering, like my foolishly brave Richard Davenport."

"I thought you were something of a supporter of Woodrow Wilson, delusions and all?"

"God forbid, young man. Certainly not getting us into that mess, a mess we should have stayed well out of. It has unleashed the furies of hatred and murderous abstraction on the European mind, a pathology that now has made its way to our shores in the book bags of every professor and intellectual who ever studied in Europe, fans of Bismarck, the lure of Prussian efficiency."

"Wilson, I suppose, a Princeton academic."

"A theoretician to the core—an intellectual mountebank. Do you know what one of his first orders of business was upon reaching the White House? Woodrow imposed segregation in the federal government, separate offices and changing rooms and bathroom facilities for Negroes. He, and in the name of the progressive cause, gave in to the worst instincts of the white race, presumably due to his Virginia upbringing or to satisfy the southern roots of his party. An absolute disgrace, but indicative of a certain mentality his dollar-a-year men brought to the operations of government. The imposition from the top down of distasteful policies and laws, resulting in a forceful alteration of the nation's relations between its citizens and government, and the creation of a subservient plebian class, ordered, if not taught, to serve the god of the greater good. And during the war, my Lord, they insinuated police spies everywhere to crush even the whisper of opposition. The Sedition Act was a monstrosity of dictatorial control."

"Well, Hoover's certainly made a mess of it. I suppose, if this economic situation continues, if Roosevelt steamrolls the judiciary as well, if you dare lift your pen to block them—as you say, for the greater good, who knows what may be the outcome."

"And let me tell you, Teddy Roosevelt was no innocent when it came to trying to put pressure on the Court. Never forgave me for my dissent in his Northern Securities Case to use the Sherman Anti-Trust Act against Morgan. And Wilson's minions certainly turned the screws on the Court to preserve their Sedition Act."

"My father used to sail on Morgan's yacht to Europe in the summer. They always liked to have a doctor on board in case of medical emergency. He never liked them much but saw it as an opportunity to obtain funding for his Memorial Hospital, cancer research, you see, and the American Cancer Society."

"There—you should be proud." He nodded and chuckled. "Teddy always resented Morgan and his cronies for their money. But bigness, in itself, is not a crime as long as it is not in restraint of trade or competition."

"How did you put it? 'Free competition is worth more to society than its costs.'"

Oliver pulled himself up in his rocker and nodded with a cautious frown.

"Oh dear, did I say that? Sounds about right, but I have no memory of having said it. How pathetic when we forget not just history but our own history, as well."

"Having helped you draft your most recent opinions, I can tell you, you haven't forgotten much; and your felicity of style remains undiminished. And Teddy's appointment of you to the Court was one of his most inspired decisions. Nor should he have expected you to simply rubber-stamp his wishes, especially when misplaced."

"Careful with the flattery, sonny—you remind me of our Alger after he thought he'd put one over on me: marrying suddenly on the sly. Besides, it does an old man little good and leads the young to sycophancy and feeblemindedness. And I felt sorry for Teddy—how, in the end, he was hoisted by his own warmongering petard, losing one son and having two others badly wounded. He fanatically believed—after a few minor skirmishes in Cuba—in the efficacy of war. Wars to shape the world, to strengthen the nation, so that the fittest survive . . . the nation, I suppose, united in some misbegotten allegiance to the martial spirit."

"But surely, *your* war was worth the sacrifice?"

"It never need have been fought. It was a failure of compromise—the true American genius, what, as jurists, we are pledged to foster."

"Dr. Dimock has always said he learned more of his trade in his first year in the medical clearing stations than during a lifetime in his New York surgery."

"As well, indeed, I know."

"Father, a man of science, pursed medical research in women's cancers at Memorial Hospital, developing new surgical techniques, new medical instruments, many named after him. Yet he remains frustrated that the survival rates for his patients—including his wife—for most cancers have not improved in his lifetime. Somehow, those frustrations have come between us; he always did tend to leave his bedside manner at the hospital."

At this turn to such melancholy themes (perhaps thoughts of his own wife, Fanny), I remember Holmes's gaze drifted off to his garden, where the shimmering shadows expanded and merged and the air was charged with a soft misty light, a crystalline glow in the high cirrus clouds against the blue, a light that remains fixed in my imagination as belonging to that place and time, that old man and his garden, redolent of the enduring earth and eternal sea.

"And so you, like me—both of us the sons of doctors—took up the law, the tried-and-true, eh, my lad. Even as experimentation is now all the rage, science our new savior. I suppose the reins of history have shifted from the hands of the theologian and priest to a new class of secular saviors. Something Marshall caught a glimpse of when he served as a delegate to France after the Revolutionary War: enforced equality by guillotine, which inoculated him against the French disease. A similar transformation devoutly to be wished for—no doubt, in the impatient minds of today's young. Do you think our Alger susceptible to such—what Lincoln Steffens referred to as the 'Russian-Italian method'?"

"Stalin more likely than Mussolini. That Mussolini certainly has his supporters in the pages of the *New Republic*, especially in the present crisis. I suppose it all comes out of Nietzschean authenticity, a kind of egomaniacal progressive utopianism—going right back to Thomas More. Or your John Marshall's aversion to equality by guillotine."

"Well, hard not to see something of Mr. Darwin at play—or Spenser, I suppose—almost everywhere on the world stage today. Perhaps Marat by a different name—eh? Although our Alger seemed strangely enamored of that mountebank Dr. Freud. Tried reading him to me a few times, but his abstractions of the human mind just gave me heartburn."

"Oh, Freud is tops in Alger and Priscilla's circle, along with Cézanne, Monet, and van Gogh, framed reproductions of which they received as wedding presents for their walls."

"You've been to their place?"

"A small apartment in Boston. But he's looking to return to Washington soon if Roosevelt is elected."

"Oh dear, do you suppose our dear Alger wants to put his shoulder to the wheel of another administration like Wilson's—moving ahead by trial and error, pruning out the weaklings, bullying the Court to have its way?"

"Thank God, you stood up against Wilson, in the end, with your great dissent on the Sedition Act. Preserving the First Amendment."

"The law is the only thing left to us, Edward, and the Constitution."

"Your wonderful, 'clear and present danger.'"

"Sonny, I learned at your age, that I was not God—no man is. And that at best, we, as judges, are merely referees in the eternal struggle of competing social forces and self-serving claims by every interest group under the sun. Our certainties today may become tomorrow's laughingstock. We are a rough-and-tumble democracy and so our role is simply to provide the ground rules for bare-fisted economic competition. So we arbitrate. And so our laws evolve—and we with them, and with time's blessing and benediction—good laws comprehend the raw experience of things, not some abstract visionary straitjacket of logic. You, I fear, have your job cut out for you."

"Where is such wisdom to be found except"—I tapped the Emerson in my lap—"as you say, in the pages of time and history."

At this, Holmes smiled sweetly, his face bathed in the waning translucency streaming through the garden and flooding the veranda where we sat. I recall an expansive gesture he made, as if to include space with time and history, from sea to shining sea. A gleam of contentment lit up his brown eyes beneath his exorbitant white brows.

"Life is a roar of bargain and battle, but in the very heart of it there rises a mystic spiritual tone that gives meaning to the whole. It transmutes the dull details into romance. It reminds us that our only but wholly adequate significance is as part of the unimaginable whole. It suggests that even while living, we are living to ends outside ourselves."

"Hardly scientific, sir? Your—what?—romantic Emersonian dream."

At this, he smiled, as if caught out by his candor.

"We, my dear Edward, are just glorified storytellers. For even the law comes out of our deepest desires, whether the hope for justice or security or predictability—or Jefferson's—that great hypocrite— pursuit of happiness. The law is the witness and external deposit of our moral life. Its story is the story of the moral development of the race . . . the very things that tend to make good citizens and good men. And—I dare say—good women." He held up a finger as if in admonishment of his prolixity—or at the sound of a taxi coming up the drive. "Which is why I have invited a certain lovely young lady to both entertain us and join us for dinner tonight. Someone, I suspect, very unlike your Priscilla—the Helen to my undeclared Trojan War with our Alger. A woman who has no political axes to grind—at least not in my hearing."

And that is how I came to first meet Annie, my future wife.

Oliver, even in old age, remained a handsome, debonair figure, a ladies' man at heart, a flirt, and, as he readily admitted to me, a man with his own history of romantic exploits. He once confessed as I read to him out of Fielding that years before he'd been in love with some Englishwoman, a beauty of "aristocratic mien," was the expression he used—a love "for the most part from afar," but an affair that, so he assured me, never diminished his loving but childless marriage to Fanny Holmes, who had died only two years before after a fall in her bathtub.

Clearly, he'd had Annie in mind for many months as he eyed me with that gentle, if mischievous, stare: a partner, if not an air brake on the downward slope of folly.

"A man should not marry for money, of course, but a man who aspires to the service of his country *and* the law can be best served by a mate who allows him the freedom of action to pursue higher goals, and refrains from prodding him to second-guess himself breakfast, lunch, and dinner. There is more to life, Edward, than fifty thousand a year as a corporate lawyer. Success is one thing; real happiness, in service to your country, another."

There had been plenty of high-spirited young women coming through Washington in those days, and many of a most determined progressive sensibility, which the justice found quite disheartening, even as they fawned over him with admiration, for he always remained the darling among progressives, who idealized his flexibility and tolerance of spirit, and stinging dissents. It soon became apparent why the match he had schemed up had had to wait until the summer recess, when we decamped to his summer home in Beverly Farms.

"Her name is Annie Davenport, my goddaughter, a Boston girl who has kindly taken a break from her busy concert schedule to come by and play for us before dinner."

Annie Davenport was a professional musician and granddaughter of Holmes's closest friend at Harvard, Richard Davenport, "an artist, a scholar, a poet—a font of infinite sensibilities and imaginative insights." They had joined up together in the Twentieth Massachusetts, and Davenport had been lying next to Holmes at Antietam when "his head was blown apart like a rotten pumpkin by a *minié* ball through the temple."

At this, his face darkened and he closed his eyes to the sunset halation glistening on the hollyhocks.

"Annie gets her musical gifts from Richard. His poems and songs are still recited and sung at Harvard reunions. His talents were many and his spirit profound. I lost many friends in the war, but Richard's loss struck me hard because he was not meant to be a soldier. He joined up because of me and my Harvard brethren, like Francis Bartlett, whom he idolized. He was married as well to a strikingly beautiful and intelligent woman. Francis and I, no matter how hard we tried, failed to talk him out of it. You see, Richard was in touch with our better angels, with our higher beings, as Emerson would have put it. As a student, I listened to him play the piano for hours. Often, he had me around to his parents' home on Beacon Hill and showed me La Farges, Hunts, and Innesses before those artists were household names, and spoke of faraway Europe, where he'd spent much time as a child and later studied. It was his descriptions of Venice that always remained most vivid in my mind, and later inspired me to take Fanny there on our honeymoon, where we read his poetry to each other as we drifted like swans on the lagoon."

As I have already noted in these pages, it is only within the last year that I have recalled my first meeting with Alger Hiss in front of the Davenport portrait in Harvard's Memorial Hall. Even Holmes's mention of General William Francis Bartlett, whose noble white marble bust by Daniel Chester French resides nearby, did not awaken the memory as we sat admiring the sunset over the garden, as if only the Alger Hiss of later infamy could unleash that recollection by providing it with another context—an ulterior motive on Alger's part; or that Annie's embodiment of that memory—the recrudescence of Richard Davenport's sweet face and luminous eyes in William Morris Hunt's portrait—somehow, as Holmes first introduced us, rendered Alger an imposter in our circle, an outsider erased from that scene in Memorial Hall, who, even with protective coloration, deserved banishment. Nevertheless, an omen, a trick of memory, which haunts me profoundly.

As if time, as my brilliant astrophysicist grandson likes to remind me, is merely a fluid and mercurial stream of photons radiating every which way, more chimera than real, each moment open to interpretation, depending on one's vantage point or proximity in an expanding ever-changing universe. "A parallax view," he called it. Yet another paradox, as if life as we know it is not uncertain enough. For if I hadn't planted the idea of a clerkship with Oliver Wendell Holmes in Alger's mind on that forgotten day, if he hadn't tried to pull a fast one on Holmes by breaking his employment contract and marrying Priscilla, I doubt Holmes would have been so keenly sensitive on the subject of his clerks remaining single during their tenure, and so dramatically warning me off any thoughts of repeating Alger's trespass, then, perhaps in unconscious recompense, playing matchmaker with the perfect helpmeet he felt I required. The polar opposite of poor Priscilla, at least in terms of the possibly jaundiced description he'd squeezed out of me.

But perhaps the greater irony in these hard-won recollections is the realization of Oliver's deep affections for Alger's humanity and kindness, which stirred some uneasiness in his heart that he could not fathom, even an apprehension verging on alarm, or as he had put it to me, quoting his favorite source, "'Lilies that fester smell far worse than weeds.'" Dare I say, prompting my own convenient memory lapse as Alger had sought to insinuate himself into our ranks by so deftly drawing about him that cloak of familiarity and institutional loyalty. Prompting the greatest enigma of all: Did he change? Did marriage change him? Was there a public and private Hiss—a secret Hiss? Or even a third Hiss—and Priscilla, now forever residing in the pages of Whittaker Chambers's *Witness*? As if, in the end, we are all mere stories on a page.

—

Or it may simply be that the memory eluded me on that sultry August afternoon, because no sooner had Oliver spoken the words than "little" Annie Davenport arrived in the local taxi from her parents' place in Gloucester, a town nearby. Holmes tightened his bow tie and adjusted the collar of his serge suit and struggled up from his rocking chair on the veranda to introduce me, receiving a heartfelt hug in return from the statuesque Annie, who was almost as tall as Holmes! At nearly six feet, she was thin as a rail, and had a Brahmin bearing, a porcelain white brow and blue eyes and reddish blond hair up in a bob, with tresses falling to her ruddy cheeks. Her prominent chin was touched with drops of perspiration in the heat of that summer day. She wore a blue chiffon dress, just below the knee, and sensible yellow walking shoes, laced, not strapped, as she always insisted. When she spoke, her large, expressive hands came alive, descriptive of her feelings moment to moment as a sculptor molding an air figure. Holmes had known Annie since she was a tiny girl; he'd stayed close to Richard Davenport's widow, who had been pregnant with Annie's father when Richard was killed at Antietam. After a brief tour of Holmes's regimental memorabilia, and photos of young Richard in his crisply tailored uniform, Annie sat down at the piano (the tuner had come the week before; it was I who picked him up and delivered him back to the station) and played an impromptu concert for us.

I sat mesmerized as she composed herself, sweeping any loose strands of hair back from her face, massaging her neck for a moment as if to get more mobility, even slipping the straps of her dress—daringly, I thought—inches off her shoulder to allow her arms free reign, her fingers poised over the keys like a hummingbird over a flower. She closed her eyes for a moment, as if to pass from the present into another realm, and so attain a higher state of consciousness—that demeanor of intense concentration I would come to know so well. And then she began, her flexing chin and nose hovering above the keyboard as her agile fingers became a blur, as every tendon and muscle in her torso became focused on bringing the music to life. Her playing was magnificent, inspired, transporting—and rightly so for a star student at the New England Conservatory. The raw energy of her playing on that sultry evening caused her to perspire heavily, and between pieces she gamely pleaded for a dish towel to dry her face, fingers, and arms.

She was only twenty-four and had already performed two Mozart piano concertos at Boston's Symphony Hall. If I was justly impressed, Holmes was rendered teary-eyed, trembling, as if something of the spirit of the music had taken him over. He would later tell me that her delicate cheekbones and shining eyes, her passionate interpretation of Mozart, Liszt, Brahms, her ecstatic expression as her head canted left and right were exactly like her grandfather's features and expressions—she was his spitting image. "Even skipping a generation, she's got all Richard's musical talent and her grandmother's flinty poetry of speaking. If that isn't a case of evolution preserving the best traits of a family, I don't know what is."

At dinner, I found Annie's erudition and opinions on many subjects to be remarkably attuned to her godfather's, whom she referred to as "Uncle Ollie": brittle, sharp, irony-honed to a razor's edge on everything from the banking crisis and stock market crash to a recent performance by Horowitz at Symphony Hall. She'd been an art history and literature major at Radcliffe while pursuing her piano studies at the Conservatory. I was dazzled, of course, and Holmes often raised an eyebrow in my direction as he brilliantly flirted—risqué jokes I would never have dared—with Annie over our meal, winking at me as if to congratulate himself on his latest protégée—and of many years making, whom he was now putting through her paces for my delight.

Later, when Holmes went off to bed, Annie delayed the local cab company that was scheduled to pick her up for the return to her parents' summer home in Gloucester. She said she wanted to see a bit more of her godfather's memorabilia and photographs hanging on the walls, "without Uncle Ollie pontificating about their sacrifice." So we went around to the daguerreotypes of Richard Davenport, commemorating his enlistment in the Twentieth Massachusetts. He had such a sensitive long nose and deep-set eyes, and was posed in a brass-buttoned blue uniform, with a pistol in his belt. In Holmes's will, these photos were to go to Annie, and they now hang prominently in Hermitage, along with others of an even younger Richard in a gondola in Venice with his adoring mother—a minor New England poet. Annie's favorite was of her grandfather in white tie and tails, conducting the Harvard Glee Club. She would reach out her curious fingers and touch these objects, as if to feel or intuit some essence that lingered behind the glass, these mementos of a long-lost past, of which she was a living, breathing revenant. At such moments, her face became meditative, as if some invisible energy was translated from her fingertips, or some desire of hers manifested, in turn, by the mere proximity of these objects. Or perhaps she was reanimating them, as she did Mozart on the piano, with her own longing—some fugitive spirit forever hovering in the penumbral radiance of these artifacts of time and memory, which only she, a feral necromancer, could release. Often, she would pick something up: a program from a commemoration ceremony, a spyglass, a brass button embossed with the insignia U.S., turn it this way and that, bring it to her nose, and inhale deeply as she closed her eyes.

"Do you read, Proust, Edward?"

I admitted to this glaring gap in my education.

"Perhaps it is an acquired taste," she suggested breathlessly. "You see, Proust wrote out of some desperation to preserve his past, the people and places of his beloved childhood in Combray. Yes, people, places—even waterlilies on the Vivonne, and, of course, his beloved steeples and the scent and color of hawthorns, the cast of afternoon light or the sound of a garden bell or a constellation of three trees along the roadside that spoke to him, were so alive to him—whispering to his inner ear—that he yearned to tell their stories. And we, the same, I suppose—all that is left of them. When Uncle Ollie is gone—like my grandmother, now two years gone—he will be the last man to have known Richard Davenport, to bequeath his living memory. All we will have is their stories—oh, and I suppose their things. But things are still things, as opposed to art . . . which instills things with a living spirit." At this, she motioned me over to a painting of Venice by the artist William Gedney Bunce, who, so she told me, as a young Connecticut cavalry officer from Hartford, had been wounded in the leg and so survived to study art in Europe and go on to become one of the greatest artists of his day, collected by Queen Victoria and his rich patrons in Hartford, Boston, and New York.

"But nobody remembers him now—sad, don't you think?"

We stood in front of this long horizontal painting in an elaborate gilded Barbizon frame, a composition as simple as it was compelling of lagoon and overarching sky, two strips of hovering luminosity meeting at an indistinct horizon. And the more we stood looking, the more the shimmering oranges and brassy golds with slashing strokes of searing yellow seemed to waver and pulse before our eyes. Barely a note of the city could be detected, except for a ghostly campanile to the far right and a few diaphanous sail geometries nosing the invisible longitudinal of sea and sky. Looming at the sky's apogee was the mysterious presence of a still-slumbering moon, casting a pearl-bright iridescence over this oceanic quietude.

"I never even realized it was Venice."

"It's Bunce's interpretation of the spirit of Venice, or more properly, the spirit of the artist in thrall to the dance and play of light at sunset, and this translated to pure expression of color and paint stokes. The painter's soul—don't you think?—revealed on canvas. Nothing so trivial as a tourist *veduta*. It is sheer feeling that has transcended mere technical mastery—dare I say time itself . . . the eternal."

We stood a while longer, transfixed.

"Goodness, Annie, you make me feel as if I have not yet lived. Not that I don't know and admire Cézanne and van Gogh, but this is something of a different order altogether."

She merely sighed, more attentive to her own preoccupations. "It always saddens me that I barely remember the stories of Venice from my father, who, not yet even born at the time of Antietam, never really knew his father, but was raised on anecdotes from the lips of his mother—and Ollie. Mother couldn't care less—not her clan—and grandmother loved to hear herself talk but failed to systematically record her memories, thinking her poetry an adequate substitute."

"The Memorial Hall portrait of Richard Davenport is very fine," I offered.

"Monuments." She shrugged, with a despairing lowering of her quivering chin, reaching a moment to the canvas as if in supplication. "My father suffered under the genius of his martyred father, never feeling he amounted to anything, even as he made a fortune in the property market, drinking himself into an early grave. That is quite a dispiriting family legacy to be saddled with, Edward. Or do I call you Ed, or Eddy?"

This confidence she imparted quite staggered me.

"Edward is fine."

"Edward, they are still lynching Negroes in the South; those people celebrate in the presence of their lynched victims; they dance and booze up in glee to gruesome death." She pulled herself to full height and eyed me intently. "Well, I like to believe that my grandfather died for *something* better than that."

I was quite taken aback by her forceful tone, her connection to her past—hardly the aloof aesthete of Holmes's description.

"My father, who was a surgeon in New York, has had his disappointments as well. He saved Holmes after the Battle of Antietam and honed his surgical skills on the wounded. He made his career treating the wives of the wealthy, delivering their children and treating their complaints and diseases. (I remember how she looked sharply at me, for I had avoided the word *cancer*, as if not to injure her sensibilities, or tempt sad Fortuna; and so I switched tack.) He spent many of his summer weekends treating the sick and injured boatmen along the Delaware and Hudson Canal, which once ran near our place in the foothills of the Catskills. He did much good in the world, but somehow it never seemed enough. It was he who recommended I avoid medicine for the law."

"Uncle Ollie says you have the finest legal mind of any of his clerks in the last thirty years."

I was stunned at this, since I held myself in low esteem in the eyes of my mentor, overshadowed by a proficient and caring Alger the year before. Secretly, I was relieved, if not pleased, perhaps emboldened.

"Well, he is clearly besotted with *your* talent."

"Oh, but I am absolutely hopeless. The only thing I know how to do well is play the piano. An unforgiving taskmaster that sometimes frightens the daylights out of me. Nor can I compose or write books—just a vessel for others' genius."

Strangely, on that confessed note of doubt, I believe our marriage pact was conceived and then later sealed that night. Without a word, she went back to the phone in the pantry and delayed the taxi once again.

—

We walked the beach in deep conversation for some hours, staring out at the hovering moon, which silhouetted a series of abandoned pilings of a ruined jetty, lonely sentries lined up on the beach and continuing their formation in lockstep over the smooth bay, there to bear silent witness to our "Bunce moon," as we began to call it that night and did so ever after, a conversation piece in our marriage, a touchstone to that silvery orange orb hovering over the vast lagoon in "Ollie's Bunce," which came to us as a wedding present, and later resided in Annie's studio at Juilliard. "Oh, those rotten pilings remind me of *pali*, so the Venetians call them, that mark the shipping channels—hitching posts"—she laughed—"for their sleek black steeds. Oh, and there on the horizon could just as well be the campanile of San Marco or San Giorgio, or even that of Torcello under the stars." I was enchanted how her voice leaped in joy at the melodious Italian names (she spoke Italian and French perfectly), how her hands stirred and undulated at the mere mention of such places—the skilled tool-making hands of our prehistoric ancestors—as if ever on the verge of taking on a life of their own. Annie had been to Venice many times as a little girl with her grandmother—a formidable society lady, who, like a religious pilgrim, revisited the sites where she and her lost "genius" husband had been happiest—and later as a touring pianist.

With a sigh, she said, "Alas, the acoustics of La Fenice always left something to be desired for a solo pianist—oh, lovely for opera and the voice, but the elliptical design and crowded surfaces of plasterwork tend to dampen the clarity for purely instrumental works. But the Scuola Grande di San Rocco, the sonorous clarity there suits piano and small ensembles perfectly, the sound is utterly divine; I thought I would never recover from the experience. I still hear it in my head, you see, whenever I play. And surely Vivaldi and Scarlatti had the acoustics of Santa Maria della Pietà in mind when they composed, as did Mozart, of course, the concert halls of Vienna. Mozart drives me wild as I try to get his delicate, echoing sonorities to sing, how something seemingly so simple can be so damnably treacherous, to ease up the inner voices so they ring clear as a bell. I hear him laughing at me sometimes, right in the middle of a piece, as if delighted at the skirmishing counterpoint of the voices, which used to defeat me more times than not."

"Speaking of voices, we have an original sixteenth-century Renaissance timbered ship's keel ceiling at our country place in the Catskills. From Padua, it seems, full of quite wonderful astrological figures and intricate geometrical designs. My older brother, you see, played the violin; he always said the sonorities in the living room, under the ship's keel ceiling, were divine. As a boy, I used to lie in bed in the morning, and listen to him play, the whole house alive with the sonorities."

She touched my arm. "You're fibbing, of course."

"No, really, Stanford White stole it, I suppose, from some falling-down palazzo near Padua and nearly bankrupted my father. I get letters from scholars asking to view the thing."

She rose on her toes and her glittering eyes feasted on mine, and then she laughed and turned away, as if my earnest tones alarmed her.

At Radcliffe, Annie had graduated Phi Beta Kappa, summa cum laude in art history and English literature, and knew all her Bellinis and Tintorettos, her Titians and Veroneses, and so, as we walked the beach that night, staring out at the star-speckled sky mirrored in the sea, I often found myself floundering in her conversational wake but buoyed by thoughts of our wonderful ship's keel ceiling—now come alive overhead. "My grandmother bought Uncle Ollie's Bunce (a former Union cavalry officer, you see) for him back in the 1870s as a wedding present when he married Fanny, and to honor his friendship with her dead husband. We have three Bunces in the dining room at home. My grandmother was convinced that Bunce had been influenced by Bellini and Titian in his uses of transparent glazes to achieve that mysterious atmospheric effect, what the Italians call *sfumato*, a feel for the quality of space itself, which not only encloses the world upon which we gaze but draws us in—inward to ourselves. Light, color—sound, don't you see, Edward, the music of the spheres as the ancients understood it, the stories of the gods, brings us as close to a transcendent state of being as we can hope to know in this life."

Again her hands reached out in supplication to the moon-besotted horizon, as if in a plea to her demanding gods, and then she touched my shoulder, as if needing to wake me.

"Am I boring you?"

"I grew up on a Catskill lake, very unlike the sea. A body of water compact with stillness and silence, surrounded by tall pines, full of bird life, especially the hermit thrush, whose song, as my father once described it, is like choiring angels on high. And that ship's keel ceiling, well, I believe its theme *is* the music of the spheres."

Again, she gave me a sharp, quick glance and girlish laugh. "I assume you mean its iconography. Are you trying to seduce me, Edward?"

"I'm afraid my upbringing was much more prosaic than yours. I was raised as a trout fisherman (in the shadow of my older brother who was lost in the war), a birder, and, at least as a child, a collector of wildflowers. That was the scientist in my father, his passion for the identification of wildflowers, when he wasn't repairing old stone walls. He always said he could tell the time of the season to within a week by the appearance of a wildflower."

"Who—your lost brother—played the violin . . . how sad for you."

"Oh, to see him cast his line . . . like a conductor to the four winds."

"Perhaps, being a city girl, I have missed out."

"Oh, I doubt that."

"Then you will have to teach me."

As we walked on the sand that evening, I found Annie's mind to be capacious and eager for new knowledge, and yet profoundly conservative in spirit, if anything, more so than her godfather, Justice Holmes. She revered the past like any good Boston Brahmin, but not necessarily her Puritan ancestors, and certainly not the society of wealthy mill owners, investment bankers, and property speculators in which she grew up. Rather, Annie, for lack of a better word, was a romantic, drawn to the wonders of the past preserved in music and books—and pictures, for which she had a keen eye. She had talked her mother into buying many modern masters, including Monet and Degas, promised gifts to Yale and on extended loan there. That was the only past that truly mattered to her: the art that lived on and transcended time and space. And yet, sadly, she remained convinced throughout our marriage that this obsession—the emotional energy that infused her musicianship—represented a fatal character flaw, a kind of moral jeopardy or laxity: a neglect of the present and her duties to her fellow men. She feared the fate of the aloof dilettante and so practiced her music like a demon, as if only her technical accomplishments might assuage her guilt about her lack of fellow feeling, notwithstanding her later exorbitant contributions to various charities. As we strolled, this bedeviling guilt came up again and again, preying on her conscience, to the point that I wondered if she might be slightly unstable, something, too, I had once detected in the overwrought Priscilla Fansler at about the same age. Again and again, she probed my responses, which tended to be couched in logical, if not legal, argument as I struggled to address her conundrum: how to justify our private passions and professional achievements when set against our responsibility to leave the world a better place than we had found it. Something, I suspect, that had hung heavy over her father, who had made much money in Boston real estate, but had felt a singular failure in the eyes of those who had known and revered his father before him, elders who had cast a disapproving eye on his prosaic youth, when he showed none of the promise that they so longed to detect in deference to their aging memories.

"Well," I replied finally, not a little exhausted, "a man who builds a factory that employs a workforce of ten thousand and then uses the proceeds to endow museums and concert halls surely does God's work. As much as a musician who fills Symphony Hall and touches the hearts of thousands with the profundity of Mozart. Life, or the living of it, whether rich or poor, is nourished and offered solace by the artist, who requires at least a modicum of prosperity and security to thrive . . . to produce the art, without which there can be no real life at all. In science, I believe it would be described as a symbiotic relationship. After all, we can't be all things to all people, but must do our best with our God-given talents and trust that others will do the same, and so, by pulling at different oars, keep the ship moving steadily forward. If that is not the promise of America, that all shall have equal opportunity to follow their dreams—to the benefit of all—then I don't know what more we're all about, exactly. Do you?"

At this, she stopped her wandering along the shore, looked down at her hands for some moments, and then simply reached out to me and took my hand for the first time that night. And she held it tight, startling me with her strength.

"Shall we?" she asked, and motioned to the low, gentle surf, glistening with a bluish purple haze. We kicked off our shoes, I rolling up my cuffs, she hiking her dress, and we walked toward the water, toward the horizon, where the moon dipped to the shimmer of its ivory reflection, a pale, flickering, weightless, and inviting presence merging with the trembling blur of the horizon.

"The eternal sea," she murmured, and proceeded to recite to me Matthew Arnold with a distinctly Italian flare, which at that moment seemed touched with a transcendentalist rapture. "My grandfather recited poetry to his wife as they stole across the lagoon in their gondola, Wordsworth mostly, but some Keats and, of course, that lecherous young Byron." At this she laughed like a schoolgirl getting caught telling a naughty joke. We continued to stand in silence, watching the setting moon, feeling the lapping waves, which came up to our knees, indeed, seemed to connect us to some dreamlike Elysium.

"Do you know Frost? We can't just live in the past."

"Frost?"

"A poet—you will know of him, I promise." And she recited the words that have haunted me ever since.

> *My object in living is to unite / My avocation and my vocation / As my two eyes make one in sight./ Only where love and need are one, / And the work is play for mortal stakes, / Is the deed ever really done / For heaven and the future's sakes.*

And then she turned to me, as if frustrated at my reticence, and reached down a hand and splashed me with a yelp of joy. As I recovered my balance, she grabbed my arm and kissed me with as much passion as she would ever again in all our married life. For a proper Boston girl, she had absolutely no inhibitions, or even practical precautions.

Later, when we walked back in our bare feet, damp and sandy to our briny souls, like creatures conceived of the tides, she kept breaking out in wild laughter as if at some private joke, so loud that I feared we'd wake the neighborhood, if not my employer.

"Perhaps, according to your calculations," she continued between giggles, making a rowing motion, "you can take up the slack for all that's lacking in me?" Then she tugged with both hands at my arm, as if impatient for my reply.

"That shoe is on the other foot. I have nothing of your talent, except in its appreciation."

"Uncle Ollie thinks you will be appointed to the Supreme Court one day."

At this, I had laughed gamely, whether in fear of a trap or bitter delight, I can't say, but loudly enough that she felt compelled to place her hand over my lips. And failing to have any Wordsworth or Matthew Arnold at my fingertips, I spouted the first thing that came to mind from the writings of our benefactor.

"'An intellect great enough to win the prize needs other food besides success. The remoter'"—and I gestured to the waning arc of the pale moon just slipping past the horizon, the sea a translucent star-studded membrane radiating ripples to the sky—"'and more general aspects of the law are those which give it universal interest. It is through them that you not only become a great master in your calling, but connect your subject with the universe and catch an echo of the infinite, a glimpse of its unfathomable process, a hint of the universal law.'"

"Ah," she exclaimed, "perhaps, Edward, you are more of a transcendentalist than you give yourself credit for!"

"No, I stole it from Ollie." I laughed. "Perhaps your Robert Frost would approve, or perhaps I should have followed in my father's footsteps. Science is the future, the theories of Einstein, his general relativity, which, as far as I can understand, means we are all connected by the same force of gravity, each one of us exerting our pull on one another, whether we happen to cotton to our fellows or not."

At this, she grabbed my hands in hers, swinging us around in a circle like some child's game of ring around the rosie, faster and faster, holding tighter and tighter, until we both became dizzy and fell into each other's arms to keep from collapsing.

"And perhaps," I puffed out, "since it is too late to call you a taxi, I had better run you home in the Ford before I get the sack from your godfather."

She only smiled.

"And a pocket full of posies."

———

In September 1932, safely out of the employ of Justice Holmes and so honoring his dictum regarding unmarried clerks in his employ, we were married in Boston's First Unitarian Church. At the Union Club reception afterward, Holmes, with a wicked glint in his eyes above his imposing bristle of thick whiskers, took me aside and admitted that long ago he'd been in love with Richard Davenport's wife, the "first Annie," whom my Annie had been named after: "The mirror image and perfectly evolved for speed." He laughed heartily and put his massive hand on my shoulder. "So, my dear Edward, although I gladly did you a big favor introducing you to your future wife, I did it for myself as well, to retain a glimpse of the Annie that was your bride's grandmother, and to see that something of Richard's talent is passed down to your children. As for you, you will have a pedigreed helpmeet to guide you through the rough patches of life, to help keep your eye on the bright uplands in these benighted days—just as long as you can hang on to her. She is a no-nonsense girl touched by starlight. And, oh yes, in case you haven't discovered, the Davenports own prime real estate all over Boston. Independent means gives a man latitude to do important and useful work in the nation's vineyard. Let me know when to put in a good word when there is an appellate court opening. But don't hesitate too long; my days are surely numbered. Since Antietam, borrowed time."

I squeezed his bowed shoulder, that rock of ages. "I will do you one better, you old lawgiver, my dear Solon. How about my pledge to name my firstborn son Teddy, after your great benefactor."

"Not Oliver, young feller?"

"No, you are sui generis, dear sir. Besides, I don't want to be calling my boy's name all over the house, echoing in the rafters, and have you suddenly appear."

He smiled and took my arm and bent close. "I was hoping to see Alger and his bride at these festivities."

"They were invited, but Priscilla in a nice note claimed that work in New York keeps our Alger from attending."

"Pity, I'm always interested in laying my ancient eyes on that pretty woman."

And so we parted for the last time. Annie saw him during his last days but was too close to giving birth to Alice to travel from New York to his funeral.

For all his kindnesses toward me, and perhaps misplaced confidence in my abilities, I still believe that Annie was Holmes's handpicked answer to any second thoughts or lingering feelings I dared harbor for Priscilla, the woman, the siren, who had waylaid his Alger.

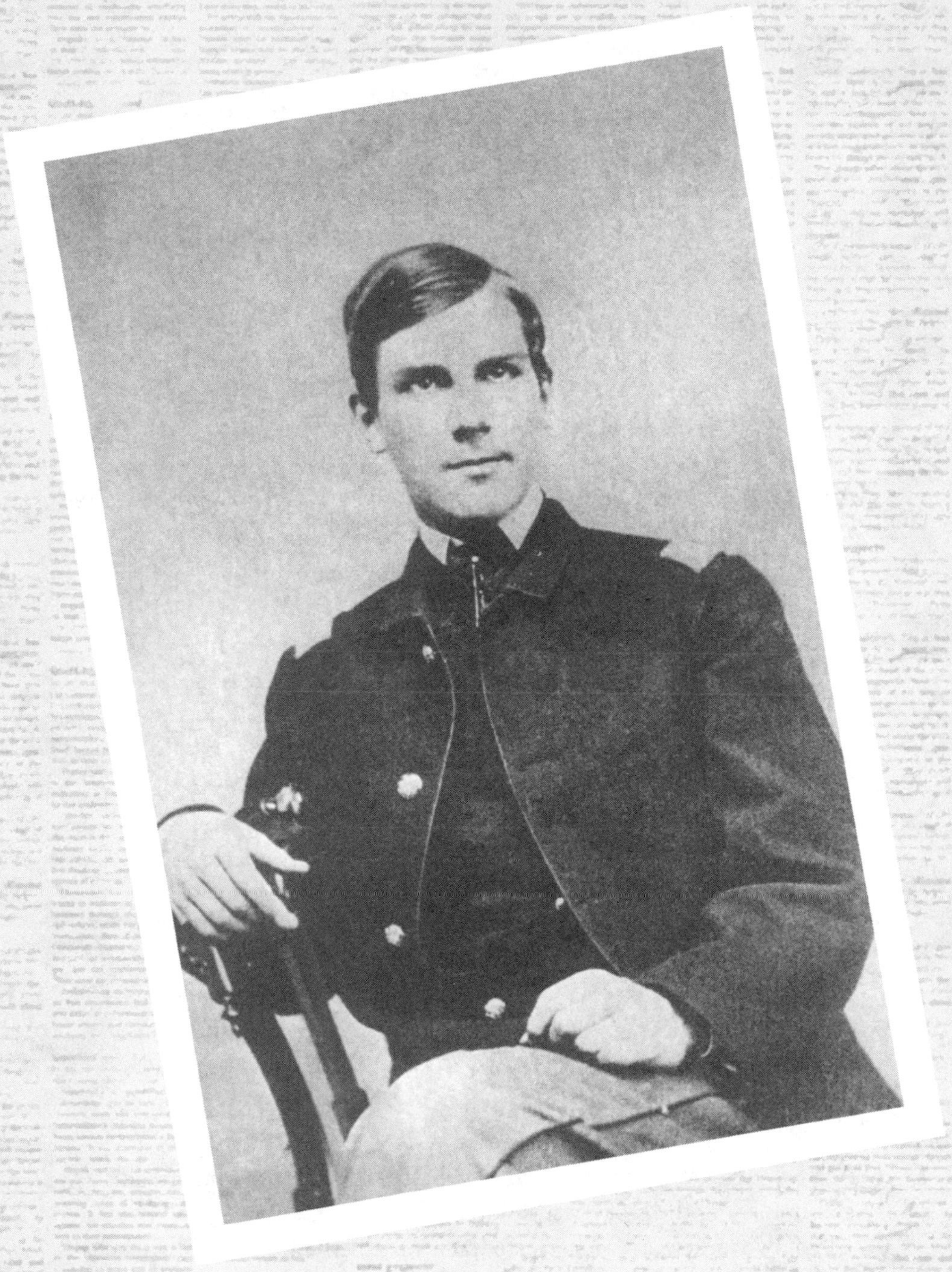

48

Random Fluctuations

The bird's song was lengthy and repeated more than once. A small group gathered, watching and listening silently. When the (rose-breasted) grosbeak finished, no one spoke as we went on to our workplaces. I was refreshed; my senses sharpened as if by a great aesthetic experience. I cannot think of another time when my spirits were so lifted that I was oblivious to my grim, oppressive surroundings.

—Alger Hiss, recollections from his
time in Lewisburg prison

The first sight through glasses of a resplendent wild bird is breath-taking. The colors are so brilliant and alive, the bird itself so self-contained and, as Mommy puts it, "competent." You see the bird whole, as a fellow person-ality—the way his (or her) "friends and relations" do (at least that is the way it seems)!

—Alger Hiss, in a letter to his
son from Lewisburg prison

GEORGE AND WENDY blew into Felicity's kitchen at midday and began unloading the groceries.

"I got two turkeys, as you suggested, at—no expense spared—Citarella, one to feed the table, the second to feed the aftermath of the bloodbath."

"Since when did you become such a cynic?" asked Felicity with her sidelong smile as she began a quick examination of the turkeys, smiling as Wendy brought in yet more bags of groceries. "And the chestnuts?"

"All the way from Italy via Zabar's," she chimed, holding up a jar of preserved chestnuts and singing out, "*Castagne, sì, molto bene.*"

"Big birds," said Felicity, with a skeptical look at her oven, scissoring her jaw. "If they fit, it'll be by a hair."

"Never refer to me as an item; I'm a bird . . . *ucello grande.*" Wendy laughed, neck stretched high, hands on hips, elbows flapping. "Tin foil on top, my aunt always said, will keep the phoenix from ashing." She caressed the older woman's elbow. "Did all the stuff for the kids come?"

"And how," noted Felicity with a conspiratorial air between women. "I left the gear in their rooms for you to deal with."

"Speaking of big birds," said George, "how is he?"

"Still eating, not too spry, a little fuzzier in the head. I got the doctor in last week to check his vitals, and he says congestive heart failure."

"Meaning what?" asked George with a frown.

"Could die tonight or five years from now. I mean, whaddya want, he's ninety-five."

"Well, that must've been a comfort. Did the doctor tell him that, sword of Damocles?"

"Sword?"

"Of Damocles: an expression of precarious fate."

She scowled. "Judge insisted on *the* 'verdict' and took it in stride. Except for the changes."

"Changes?"

"Revised his will once again," she said, with another conspiratorial squint at Wendy. "And then got the caretaker to help me shift some stuff around in the bedrooms—changes. And you two got a promotion."

Wendy looked at George. "Promotion?"

"You've been moved to the master bedroom."

"Graham's Dock, the Judge's old room?" asked George, horrified.

"Erich's Nancy is going into *your* old room, Cuddebackville—first of his great-grandkids. And Karen's Max is going in poor Billy's old room, plenty of boy stuff, see, still in there. You know"—she made a motion of washing her hands—"Alice never touched it. Not that he'd let on, but the Judge is pleased as punch to see something of his great-grandkids at Hermitage."

"Oh shit," said George, "Graham's Dock, that's just what we need." And he made an exasperated face at Wendy. "Strap on the body armor; it's going to be sniper alley, a real turkey shoot all Thanksgiving."

"Oh, you'll survive," said Felicity. "He even had a new mattress—ten in all—delivered last week for you two, among other things." She smiled meaningfully. "Not that I approve of this sleeping-around stuff."

"Have you heard from Alice?"

"Yes, she's fuming like a clogged chimney, but I've got her old room all prepared for her and Stan."

"Cecily," said Wendy, "called to say she's going to take the bus to Woodstock to catch a ride with Cordelia."

"Oh," said George, trying to gauge the tone. "She could've just taken the train to Port Jervis and we could've picked her up. I wonder if that makes it more or less probable that Alice and Stan will show."

"More," said Wendy, turning for the door and the rest of the groceries. "Mothers and daughters—trust me."

George raised an eyebrow at Felicity once Wendy was out of hearing and began helping to unpack the groceries.

"How's he really doing?"

"Slipping. Hard for him," she went on in a flat voice, "once the birds leave. He gets real lonely. Like he says, 'It's just me and the nuthatches.' Most everybody he ever knew is dead and buried. Just as well—he's in no shape to attend funerals."

"Keep your fingers crossed he doesn't change his mind about Florida. Lots of birds."

"Can you believe the weather? Supposed to be in the seventies tomorrow."

"Global warming." He glanced out to where Wendy was struggling with some bags. "By golly"—and he grinned at Felicity, hearing the Judge's phrasing in his own—"maybe we can all do the Neversink on Friday—wouldn't the kids get a kick out of that."

"George," said Felicity, white-hair helmet tilted, eyeing him with a scolding look of distaste, "that was the most disgusting magazine in the bottom drawer of your bedside table. What if Nancy had found that thing?"

———

Wendy stopped in the great room as George parked the Tahoe in a clearing behind the garage to make space for the other arrivals. She turned and turned, canting her face upward to the ship's keel ceiling, revealed in all its splendor by the saturating light through threadbare trees of a late-November's early afternoon. George was so right about the fall light. She saw that now, things she hadn't seen before emerging from beneath the milky varnish, shadowy and delicate figures peering down out of the blue geometries, enmeshed in the elaborate filigrees. She felt in her bones the ceiling's intimate vastness, a cosmos conceived to comprise a human scale, if not the secret longings of the imagination. Again she located her favorites: a heavy-breasted Venus rising in a sinuous dance from her planetary seraglio; a hugely muscled Phaeton tumbling from his sun chariot, his three powerful piebald steeds pinwheeling in free fall; and poor pathetic Icarus plunging head over heels past the horrified face of his bearded father, leaving only a contrail of burning feathers (*yes*, she thought, the Judge's elder brother). Such reflections prompted by this symphonic array of sensual joys and their attendant disasters brought sudden tears to her eyes, as if deeply touched by the enduring legacy of such ancient themes, mirroring, at least in her mind's eye, the self-inflicted disasters of a faltering clan, if not that of her own.

Her reverie interrupted by the sound of George's return, she briefly reviewed the silver-framed photos on the Steinway grand, touching the face of a young twentysomething Annie seated at the piano in Boston's Symphony Hall, as if in a whispered pledge of solidarity.

—

For a few moments longer they remained marooned in the doorway of Graham's Dock, perhaps hypnotized by the lake-reflected sunlight illuminating the swath of leaded glass in the central bay window, which, in turn, seemed to ignite the white-paneled walls and the cream and off-white furniture, as every surface—swarmed by dust mites—came vibrantly alive while distilling some unearthly stillness: time—pine scented, fallow, undisturbed, compassed in silence.

"Geronimo," George finally barked and dashed in, only to throw himself headlong on the king-size bed. There, he remained, facedown, spread-eagle, unmoving.

"Wow, Felicity wasn't kidding," said Wendy as she began a forensic exploration of the dressers, the changing table, opening the now mostly empty bureau drawers and closets. "Oh George, all her clothes are gone, her brushes are gone, a whole two bookshelves replaced with your books." She began to itemize more of the missing articles: "The photographs of Annie and Teddy and your aunts. And the portrait of Annie by Raphael Soyer—damn . . . all gone." She turned to George as if distraught and not a little troubled to find him still a spent, uncaring figure dropped out of space. "What's the matter?" she asked, opening another closet. "Hah, this is filled with your old stuff." She opened another bureau drawer and pulled out a Princeton T-shirt and held it up to her nose. "Freshly laundered, too. Oh my God, your stroke mag— she must have found it!"

At this, he turned over on his back like a petulant child and scowled.

"Felicity stole it. Thing is, I'd gotten kinda used to Teddy's room."

"Bad habits," she replied not unsympathetically. "But I'll miss her, too, your *Penthouse* honey with the huge muff."

He blinked and rubbed his eyes, as if waking, gazing around, needing to absorb the alterations in small doses, to carefully record the data points as they arrived on his internal spectrometer. Then he stood, swayed as if off balance, finding his sea legs.

"I guess—well, I never knew her—Annie," he offered. "So . . . he's clearing the decks."

"Oh, but we did—we did, in the memoir, George." She shook her head with girlish wonder. "I really did, and I've even grown sort of fond of her—like how she'd be as a mother." She stopped suddenly and looked at him contritely. "Sorry, I'm being ridiculous—pushy, as you always accuse me of being—*and* it's none of my damn business anyway."

She returned to the empty wall where weeks before the Raphael Soyer portrait of Annie had hung, just able to detect the rectangular space in the paint, a warmer creamy white than the sunstruck surround of the wall. She turned to him, wide-eyed, as if the bare wall had jogged loose a lurking recollection.

"The portrait of Annie, in Altmann's letter to his wife, which he so admired in Soyer's studio: George, do you suppose that's why he gave the sketches to the Judge? Remember what Alice said about how after the first day of the trial he tried to hand the charcoal sketch of the Judge to Annie, and when she refused him, he gave it to Alice. And then he put the envelope with the Volta Place sketches into the Judge's hands, spoke something in his ear, and quickly walked away."

George drew up beside her, running his finger along the edges of this pale shadow of a shadow, as if by limning this oblong halo, something of the lingering presence of the portrait might yet reveal itself. In turn, summoning within himself the voice of his aunt and that of his grandfather Altmann in the letter, and the photo of Annie Davenport on the record cover discovered in the barn, until their voices and the images merged convincingly in his mind.

"Yes," he murmured, "she, or her music or the painting, could, I guess, have impelled him to do such a thing."

"He . . . he believed in the integrity of the creator," she offered. "That her husband had to be a good man married to such a talented woman, an artist like himself, whose recording of Mozart's sonatas found their way into his paintings."

He stood a little dumbstruck, staring at the empty space, fingering the nail hole in the white paneling.

"Is it possible that it could be as simple as that—a tortured soul inspired by the playing of a woman he didn't know, a thing so arbitrary, so random a happenstance? If he hadn't been looking for a job, if he hadn't seen the portrait, if Soyer had had it covered up or put away or had already delivered the commission . . ."

"You're the astrophysicist, the brainiac—master of quantum probabilities; expert on how whole worlds come into being."

"Random fluctuations," he muttered almost in despair with a wave of his hand. "You don't suppose the Judge has an inkling, do you, even if we never mentioned Annie's recording of the Mozart sonatas in Altmann's studio?"

"Don't look at me: I never mentioned it. And you never confronted him with Alice's memory of Altmann handing over the sketches at the end of the first day of the trial."

"I can't bring her into it. And we've pressed him on the timing, and he sticks to what he has in the memoir." He turned from the wall and eyed her sharply. "You don't suppose he suspects something?"

"Because he got rid of the portrait? That we're holding something back?"

"Aren't we? Aren't we as suspicious of him, like everybody else— afraid that we've been seduced by his charm?"

He was about to go on, when he caught sight of something over her shoulder in the far corner of the room. She followed him as he walked over to the painting in an ornate gilded frame, now caught in a beam of sunlight from the lowering sun, a narrow horizontal composition depicting an expanse of glittering water at sunset, overhung by an even vaster sky streaked with orange and amber and chrome yellow pigment; the paint marks, arrayed with slashing abandonment, like a Hubble rendering of cosmic energies, reflected light from sky to lagoon and back, a picture of molten energy congealed in perfect stillness. And emerging from beneath this scrim of sumptuous color, the palest of pale moons, a stage moon waiting in the wings. She reached to the impasto, letting a finger ride the radiating ridges, then to the artist's name in small black letters in the right-hand corner, as if reading braille.

"No," she purred as if in reply, or perhaps relief, "he's just substituted *their* Bunce."

"From the memoir," he echoed, mesmerized for a few moments by the play of her fingers over the impasto. "From Oliver Wendell Holmes's Beverly Farms living room."

She reached behind the frame and lifted it gently from the wall, peering behind, feeling underneath with her fingers.

"He's had it cleaned and relined—recently, too, a new foam-board backing." She bent close to the pigments, touching the canvas surface with outstretched fingertips, and then stepped back to see the whole. "And a good professional job, beva glue lining. It's more spectacular than anything I ever imagined. I'd never even heard of William Gedney Bunce—barely warrants a mention on Google. Who woulda thought it?"

He retreated to the wide bay windows. "Where's it been all this time? That's what I'd like to know." He tapped a pane, as if distracted by a fetching lenticular swirl in the antique glass or contemplating the different view of the lake from his old room. "I don't remember it from his apartment in New York, but then I was just a kid."

"It was in her Juilliard studio, their wedding present from Justice Holmes."

He nodded to her with a hint of iciness, how she seemed to have put entire pages of the Judge's memoir to mind with her prodigious memory. "You don't miss a trick," he said drily.

"No, no." She shook her head as if momentarily panicked, her voice quickening as it rose. "It's because of you he's done all of this. And you're the one who's got to tell him . . . about Sawkill Bridge, about Yalta, and William Weisband—and the rest. It's got to go in the memoir—don't you see? And Annie is the key to the whole thing."

He just shook his head, as if now immune to her outbursts.

"What did Mom always say?" He examined her overwrought face as if for clues, then turned to the sight of some glittering objects in a nearby alcove, nodding to himself as he answered his own question. "'Hermitage was *always* Annie's.'"

She withdrew from his scrutiny to the bookshelves, relieved to find the remaining shelves still filled with Annie's favorite novels, including *A la recherche du temps perdu*, in the original French Pléiade editions. Meanwhile, he veered to the alcove, with its inviting white wicker chair, where more new arrivals had taken up residence, these behind glass in antique gold frames, smoky images of figures in beaked gondolas, and one in particular, a silver-on-copper portrait of a strikingly beautiful young man in brass-buttoned Union blue gone to dark sepia, hand on a holstered pistol . . . a bloodline transfusion.

"Or like Alice always says, a brilliant lawyer—like Alger Hiss, huh—manipulates the truth in so many ways, you can never figure out where the real lies are buried."

49

The Defense Rests

"AH, THERE YOU are. Cocktails are served," the Judge proclaimed as they came around to the fire. "How's Handytown deep into fall?"

Wendy bent and kissed his white-whiskered cheek and George followed with a vigorous handshake.

"Strangely warm," said George, taking a sip from his waiting wineglass. "And not even a red squirrel to chatter over the Handy graves."

"Did you replace a stone?"

"Two or three . . ."

"'What they had already written for want of parchment' . . . Thoreau, I believe."

Wendy, dressed in tight jeans and an open pink fleece, her cheeks flushed, gazed up at the ship's keel ceiling as if captivated anew, murmuring, "So soulful, the russets and purple-grays and the old bluestone walls hedged with barberry, alizarin red—haunting, the human things that linger . . ." And she gestured broadly to the tantalizing figures above, so much changed from the afternoon light of just hours before, now a pale blue mist sparked by firelight, in which the larger cosmic geometries seemed to burn through the beam work, like delicate interlacings of silver and gold inlay.

"Speaking of parchment, Wendy has a present for you," said George, feeling compelled to do almost anything to delay a reckoning he secretly dreaded.

"For me?" asked the Judge, adjusting his Century Club bow tie, smoothing the dun-colored lapels on his herringbone jacket.

"Now?" she asked, still distracted.

George went to warm himself by the fire. "An early Christmas present, before Florida, before the gators arrive." He glanced up at the Louis XVI enamel clock, tempted to give the minute hand a nudge, even if the key had long gone missing, and then to the weird sisters, guardians of the hearth, tail feathers drawn tight like Batman's cap, surely rigged for escape velocity. "While we still have time." He fingered the apostrophe eyes in the ecstatic upturned face, the familiar wormholes in the cheeks, possibly for good luck.

"Florida?" queried the Judge, not quite getting the drift.

Wendy returned with the bubble-wrapped eighteen-by-twenty canvas, unwrapped it, and leaned the painting against the Delft tiles of the fireplace, adjusting its angle slightly so that the illumination from the Judge's reading lamp produced a rich glow in the pigment. The Judge dropped his volume of Emerson's *Essays* to the floor as he leaned far forward, looking out over the top of his steel-rimmed glasses. He motioned them to bring the painting closer and Wendy held it up for him at eye level, where the light of his reading lamp fell to best advantage.

"My Lord, is that a woman clinging to the rock face, a nude woman?"

"It's a self-portrait," said George, not without a hint of pride in his voice. "It's what Wendy does, stone nudes."

"Lucky you." The Judge winked at George.

"For now at least," she said somewhat apologetically.

"Is she climbing, or just hanging on for dear life?"

"Oh, a little of both, I guess."

"It's lovely, dear," said the Judge, now concentrating, "truly lovely, and unusual, I must say. I don't think I've ever seen anything quite like it, the way the limbs of the body merge in and out of the sedimentary layers in the rock formation. A living, breathing fossil—heh. Seems to me you're on a par with Georgia O'Keeffe, how the layers of limestone swirl and undulate as if in counterpoint to her straining limbs—a compositional tour de force. But I do believe your brushwork is more secure than Georgia's, your transitions more subtle perhaps—don't you think so, George? The thing is both sensuous and visually complex."

Wendy, shaking with emotion, biting her lips, wiped a tear from her eye. "Thank you," she said, and she bent again and kissed the Judge on the cheek. "Your kind words mean a lot, or do I have Annie to thank for developing your artistic sensibilities?"

"Annie?" He seemed taken aback, as if hardly recognizing the name, much less the reference. Then he smiled broadly in the direction of the Steinway's shimmering ebony flanks in the corner. "Oh my, I shouldn't tell you this, but she would come down at the break of dawn, disrobe, and play the Steinway in her birthday suit. A terrific thing for a young husband to see and hear. And when she returned to bed, well, she shot the lights out, did my Annie."

She resisted the urge to grab her notebook, which she'd left at the ready on the side table by her chair. "I'm not sure it's a fair exchange for hanging your Bunce in our—George's bedroom."

The Judge's heavily bagged eyes tightened while he pondered yet another name, his face then brightening, as if recognizing the thing in Wendy's rapt gaze. "Ah, Annie's Bunce."

"Some of the best parts of your memoir are about Annie," she gushed, "where it really comes to life, not that your discussion of the law, your most important opinions, and your calling on the bench aren't compelling, as well."

He smiled enigmatically. "You mean about Alger Hiss?" Then turning to George, he said, "Will you hang it in my bedroom—across from my bed, next to the sketch of that virile young man at the defense table—he would surely admire such a fetching nymph . . . or"—he gave a knowing squint—"lovely Scylla! Then it will be there to lure me from my bed, just like the old days."

"We'll get it framed for you next week," said George. "Simple gold strip frame with a warm red ground, no ornamentation, but two-inch width, enough to give it presence and impact."

"A pick-me-up," said the Judge. "I could use some female energy these days."

George laughed. "What, Felicity not enough girl power for you?"

"Annie must have been a handful," Wendy commented, grabbing her wineglass. "Hard on herself, hard on you, the kids."

George cautioned her with a fiery glance as they took their seats on either side of the Judge's chair.

"And I guess I should thank you," said George, "for Graham's Dock. But I'll pay for that in spades tomorrow."

"I don't think Teddy, dear Teddy, would mind. He'd want his room to go to younger folk like Max or Nancy, to whom I've had only the pleasure of writing. Felicity argued that Billy's old room was more up-to-date for a boy." A fragile wistfulness came over him as he pondered this delicate imponderable. "Did I do Teddy justice in the memoir? Poor boy, he never had a chance to really live an adult life, not with going directly into the Marine Corps from Yale." His face darkened. "I'm not one to believe that military service represents an advanced level of maturity or manliness, that mastering the art of killing somehow qualifies one as an intrepid adult. The Second Amendment opinions I've written requiring licenses to carry concealed handguns produced more threatening mail than all the rest combined."

"You did him more than justice," assured George, "though it's hard to understand why he would have reacted so badly to your defense of Hiss—given he was headed for a career in law—the name of the game: what defense lawyers do."

The Judge gazed up at the ceiling, where a scene of Glaucus and Scylla appeared in the penumbral glow of the four Tiffany table lamps, the handsomely muscled nude Glaucus, a fisherman replete with a fish's tail, appearing out of the star-flecked waves to claim the fair, equally nude siren Scylla from behind, his hands clamped below one small breast and the other, fingers spread wide, clamped over her pubic area, in a pose of possession, but a ravishment welcomed in the sea nymph's elated face and upraised arms.

The Judge grimaced. "Sad, all those young men swarming to the colors again. Now godforsaken Afghanistan, and soon Iraq, if that madman in the White House has his way . . . damn mess. Hopefully, if it comes to war, the generals will get us in and out quickly—unlike the Vietnam disaster." He turned to George with a starchy stare, running a finger inside the collar of his button-down shirt. "Maybe it was just as well your mother turned out to be a girl—not cannon fodder for Vietnam . . . But you're too old now—right?—for the draft anyway?"

"They gave up on the draft, Judge, years ago. All volunteer military now. Not that Teddy was drafted, still safely in the bosom of Yale."

"These religious ideologues, these false prophets of absolutism are the bane of existence, of tolerance and doubt, exactly as Justice Holmes always warned me. As soon as one coven of bastards is dispatched to history's dustbin, another pops up."

"Comte's positivism," suggested Wendy, with a light touch to the arm of her host's chair. "Robespierre's violence."

"What was that, dear?" asked the Judge. His face brightened as another thought came to mind. "Every day, to and from my courthouse in Foley Square, climbing the subway stairs at Chambers Street, I'd see those twin towers capturing the first and last light of day in the distance . . . beacons, wonders of physics—right, George?—and human ingenuity. Something permanent, heh, when in my trade all we have is the burden of proof sustained by the preponderance of evidence, or beyond a reasonable doubt when a defendant's life and liberty are on the line."

George, in his ratty sweater and fleece, his ancient grass- and blueberry-stained jeans, stretched his hiking boots out toward the flames. The logs in the fire popped suddenly and the stack careened forward. George shot up and grabbed the tongs to reset the burning wood, throwing on an extra log for good measure.

Wendy picked up the conversation, as if intrigued by an offhand thought. "The same Foley Square—the federal court building where the Hiss trial took place?"

The Judge smiled at another of life's little ironies. "You'd almost think I'd never escaped."

George got up and went to retrieve his backpack from where he'd left it in the corner.

"We've got something more for you"—he held up some papers, handing them off to the Judge—"which I thought you'd like to see before dinner, before the family arrives tomorrow."

The Judge fingered the pages, putting on his reading glasses, squinting, trying to make out the writing.

"Even with my glasses, it's hard for me to read type this size."

"It's okay," said Wendy. "George can give you the gist."

"We got these from Allen Weinstein. Long and short, Harry Dexter White spent the early forties through the end of the war working directly under the command of the Soviet Union, from the run-up to Pearl Harbor—you don't want to know—to the Morgenthau Plan to turn Germany into a farmyard, to the final giveaways in Poland and the postwar settlements in Europe and even the loss of China to the Communists. The whole time, working hand in glove with Alger Hiss, he was acting directly on behalf of Soviet interests. It looks like Alger Hiss, along with Harry Hopkins and Lauchlin Currie in the White House, White at Treasury, did much to formulate the policies pursued at Yalta, agreements pretty much along the lines ordered by Stalin: Soviet acquisitions in eastern Poland, the coerced return of Russian refugees, ruinous reparations out of Germany—you name it. Pretty damning evidence that Hiss, instead of being a mere functionary at Yalta, as he portrayed himself in your trial, was, in fact, a critical part of the Soviets' Washington apparatus, manipulating government policy to promote Stalin's designs. In fact, sitting at Roosevelt's right hand at Yalta, Hiss reported each morning to his Soviet handler on all overnight discussions by the U.S. delegation. So it's pretty clear that your client, Alger Hiss, was protecting a lot more than his indictment for perjury relating to stolen documents from the late thirties. If his role as a spy at Yalta had been revealed, the legitimacy of Stalin's land grabs in Eastern Europe and the Far East would have been further undermined. He had the whole weight of the KGB behind him . . . doing whatever it took to shield him from conviction, including the elimination of witnesses who threatened him, who might have revealed his critical role in solidifying and expanding Soviet hegemony in Europe—a conviction that would, and did, galvanize the desperate search for the Rosenbergs, which was ongoing at the same time your trial was under way."

"Witnesses including George Altmann," said Wendy. "The facts are nearly conclusive that he was murdered by a KGB hit squad on Christmas Eve of 1949."

"My God." The Judge lowered his face into the papers clutched in his trembling hands. "Facts, or just conjecture?"

"All circumstantial evidence," replied George. "But enough that it becomes almost impossible to believe otherwise. I mean, the pattern of unexplained deaths . . . the indisposed witnesses—the stakes on the table."

"Do you suppose Alger or Priscilla knew?"

"You're sure you never showed the sketches to Hiss or anyone else on the defense?" asked George.

"I'll stick by what I wrote in the memoir."

"Because it was over Christmas and the New Year's holidays"— George stared intently into the dazed eyes of his grandfather—"the papers barely reported on the untimely death of Altmann in Woodstock, an artist whose best years were behind him, a forgotten man."

"Well," the Judge winced, "Alger always held his cards close."

"And yet," Wendy broke in, "Hiss opened up to you about something that he never mentioned to anyone else during the rest of his life. It's a crucial piece of evidence in your memoir."

The Judge looked to them both, waiting, curious, possibly anxious.

"Well . . . out with it."

"Do you remember what you wrote about Hiss saying that the Livadia Palace had been bugged?" asked George.

"Did I?"

"You did. Hiss said it in an offhand way as if it might somehow diminish his role at Yalta."

"I had no idea. Or I guess I forgot."

"The extensive bugging was only revealed for certain by an ex-Soviet agent a couple of years ago."

"So I was right that I heard it from Alger?"

George looked at Wendy with a smile of vague relief and nodded.

"But there's something else," said Wendy, trying to repress the hint of panic in her voice.

"No . . ." said George.

"He needs to know, George." She reached out a hand to the old man's shoulder. "Hiss was part of the Washington apparatus that tipped off the Soviets that their military communication codes had been broken by U.S. Army intelligence in the run-up to the Korean War."

George grimaced at now being forced to go fully into the painful subject. "This resulted in the Soviets changing their military codes in the year before the outbreak of the Korean War, and so left the United States completely blind to the buildup of military forces along the thirty-eighth parallel. And a war that might well have been prevented—if the United States had been forewarned—except for a KGB mole at the heart of U.S. Army intelligence, one William Weisband, not a comrade per se of Hiss's but they were certainly pulling on the same oar. Sorry, Judge, but there you have it—pretty much the worst of it."

They sat in silence for a good minute, the Judge staring blankly into the fire.

He finally nodded. "And I defended the son of a bitch."

"You and all your colleagues on the defense team," said George, as if trying to soften the blow.

"You couldn't have known," Wendy said. "Even Chambers—although he suspected—had no idea. And I suppose his—Chambers's—'all the best people' never had the foggiest, either. Even Weinstein, when he wrote *Perjury* in the seventies, didn't know the half of it, not with any certainty, not until very recently, and even now, only after his latest book . . . how deep the damage ran."

The Judge looked up from the papers, blinking back tears, a slight trembling in his sallow, drooping cheeks.

"Perhaps I should take heart that at least I'm in good company with all the *other* gullible fools, or that I'm only guilty of credulity, as opposed to professional misconduct."

"So why remove the Altmann sketches from the defense files?" she asked. "Take that risk, even with Allen Weinstein lurking in the wings, as you wrote. For that matter, why keep it in the memoir at all—who's to know when or how they were given to you?"

The Judge smiled weakly, perplexed. "A bad feeling . . . the thing had me by the short hairs. You don't think lawyers and judges aren't obsessed with such missed clues? And if I have one duty remaining to me, it is to the record."

"Enough of a violation—file tampering," added George, "if discovered, to have lost your judgeship?"

"Let's leave it at a bad conscience; that multipurpose excuse pretty much covers it, don't you think?"

The Judge stared off glumly, his unshaven chin trembling.

"Judge"—George took a deep breath and flicked a glance at Wendy—"your exchange with Hiss about Yalta in the memoir—that you suggested it might prove a positive point in his favor—that he then dismissed the idea out of hand—adds mightily to the historical record."

"Thank God I did something right; I have no memory of that at all."

"Of course, maybe that was the real Hiss strategy all along: misdirection, to keep the spotlight off his role at Yalta. Betting that if worse came to worst, he'd be convicted for perjury about an obscure crime in the thirties, while avoiding conviction for espionage at Yalta and the uproar and damage to Soviet policy that would have then resulted. Brilliant—when you think about it."

Wendy bent forward in her chair. "And you kept Priscilla safely out of it, even when she had to have typed all those top-secret papers."

"That was the least I could do—prevent her from ending up like another Ethel Rosenberg."

"She's certainly grateful to you in her letters."

"You noticed I made no attempt to hide those."

"Still, it's odd her mention of Handytown—twice," noted George.

"Surely I told you. When we were in college, when I was at Yale and she at Bryn Mawr . . ."

"The porch swing," Wendy suggested lightly, gesturing upward to where the gods frolicked. "I mean, you can hardly be blamed for lingering affections; it's only human."

A flicker of relief or consternation played across the old man's weary face.

"If only Annie had been as forgiving as you, dear." He sighed. "But of course, she was right, she was always right, and now, I guess, more right than she even knew."

Wendy reached decisively to his hand, pressing it on the armrest. "I think you need to get more about Annie in the memoir—right or not—so that her children and grandchildren have a better sense of"— she paused, as if searching for the right term, glancing up to the ship's keel ceiling, where it glowed and flickered a luminous blue-gold—"who they are."

"Yes, yes, I can certainly take that under advisement. And what about the revisions, George? Wasn't that the whole point of the exercise, that we were going to make revisions in the memoir? Don't we now need to make changes according to the new evidence? I mean . . . I'm not suggesting I make excuses for what I did or didn't do, only . . . in light of these new facts, the whole truth . . ." He gave a pitiful sigh. "Except I'm not sure how—for me—it changes much."

"Well," said George, with a searching glance at Wendy, "we can do anything you want."

At this, a hopeful look on the Judge's face changed to one of apprehension. "But in all candor, I don't remember most of what I wrote—not in detail, not in the nuances, and the devil is certainly in the details."

"Like when George Altmann handed you those sketches after the end of the first day of the trial."

"If that's what I wrote . . ."

The Judge stared off, his face rising to the ship's keel ceiling, his stare deepening in a half squint.

George looked at Wendy with raised eyebrows, but she silently shook her head.

"We'll help you," she said, "get things exactly the way you want them—Emerson and Annie and even Proust if need be, won't we, George? A best-seller from the only member of Hiss's defense team to give the inside story."

Again, a hint of relief as the shoulders of the herringbone jacket gave way slightly and the Judge's stare retreated from the infinite. "I'm not suggesting we put things in a better light; I'd never do that."

"Tell you what," said George. "Between now and Christmas, when we drive down to Florida, you can look over your memoir as much or as little as you like, whatever you're comfortable with. And on the drive—it will take at least three days, but I figured you might enjoy a road trip instead of just flying—we can even read parts of it to you and you can make suggestions for revision. And once we're down in Siesta Key, at your condo on the beach, you'll have even more of a chance to reflect—a change of scenery, distance, and all that—on changes."

"Florida?"

"Remember, you agreed to spend the winter in Siesta Key. We've rented a condo, with a piano even, and the bird life, much less the women, will be spectacular. Felicity is thrilled at the prospect."

Wendy's voice rose as she pursued this happier direction. "And Annie—think about how much she loved the beach. It'll take you right back to some of your happiest memories in Beverly Farms, right? I found those reminiscences some of your most evocative writing in the memoir. More stuff like that maybe—and Venice days, why not."

The Judge turned to Wendy, as if drawn to her enthusiasm, her kindly tone.

"You and George would have liked Annie." His eyes twinkled as he examined her face. "And Annie would have loved you, Wendy. You know, one of the things she loved about her days—her second career, she called it—with Balanchine and his dancers was helping out the young ballerinas with their musicality, teaching them how to really listen to the music. I was not a little overwhelmed at her funeral how literally hundreds of young women turned up—her 'girls,' as Balanchine referred to them—who came to pay their respects, all with tears in their eyes. I think the turnout rather overwhelmed Alice and Martha, and even poor Cordelia, who had been part of all that, to witness such an outpouring of love."

Wendy grabbed her notebook. "Oh my God, none of that's in your memoir!"

George, watching, still amazed at the spell this enchantress wove, added his two bits.

"And maybe you'll recall more about those chats with Priscilla during the war, when she bragged about all the big shots they knew, and later walking in Riverside Park, discussing your defense of her husband—to go along with your descriptions of the river and gardens and the migrating bird life."

George's slightly supercilious tone seemed to intrigue the Judge, his heavy-lidded blue-gray eyes popping wide with firelight.

"Priscilla," he finally said as his gaze drifted upward again, "was always somewhat wistful about the war, as if it had been a heady time for them . . . before her life became one of trial and regret. 'If only Eleanor and Franklin had been around and willing'"—his voice rose in imitation, a faint quaver of a Main Line accent, sounding the r's—"'Hopkins and Stettinius and White—they could have put in a good word for Alger with that jury of yours and all this foolishness would have been long over and done with.'"

His imitation of a dead woman's voice, as if filtering out of the vast-ness of the blue haze above (another story, another mortal tumbled from the imperium), left them reeling, unsteady—a voice they had never heard, except as an approximation in the memoir, in the Priscilla Hiss letters.

Wendy looked over at George, as if now in a slight panic herself.

"Anyway," she exclaimed nervously, her voice rising, "Florida will be just the thing for you, to get away from the cold, a chance to step back . . . your summer at Beverly Farms, walking on the beach with Annie—your *Bunce* moon!"

The Judge now eyed her intently, his face softening, his lips curling in an appreciative smile touched with a hint of malice or possibly delight.

"By the way, I've taken your thoughts on board, Wendy, about the intended gifts of Annie's to Yale. You know, they invited Annie and me to the opening of the Louis Kahn building in . . . let's see, must have been 1953, two years after I took up my appointment to the Second Circuit." He smiled. "Who would've guessed it, that my defense of Hiss punched the ticket for my promotion?"

"What gifts?" asked George.

"Of course," he went on, as if once again presiding at his bench, "Annie would be mad as hell. But then again, she'd have traded her firstborn for another shot at Carnegie Hall after her bad review in the *Times*. Artists never forget, you see . . . even a perceived slight. Try liv-ing with *that* if you dare."

Wendy pulled herself forward in fierce sympathy. "Good for her—fuck the critics." She flopped back in her chair and closed her eyes, as if exhausted by it all.

The Judge gazed at her, beaming.

"Annie did that, after a long practice session, when she was pleased with how it had gone. A fine performance would always put her in a good mood. Playing here at her favorite piano under the ship's keel ceiling would put her in a rare and splendid mood, when she felt she'd sounded the depths of some piece to its shimmering soul. Made the rafters sing. That got her through, got us though, until Teddy died, after which she could never find that peace again, never, you see, quite find her way back—even with Cordelia . . . here." And he gestured to the blue infinity of Giordano Bruno's star-studded galaxy, as if embrac-ing the playground of the jealous gods, the treacherous undercurrents and unchartered snags of the human condition. "And she could never forgive me for my treatment of Chambers. She, as was her wont, saw Teddy's death . . . well, as God's, or at least Providence's, verdict on me . . . and, I guess, hers, as well."

George now bent forward, eyes tightly focused.

"What gets me: How did she come by that signed copy of his book in the first place? And why was she so fixated on that trip to Fitzwilliam, New Hampshire?"

As Felicity called them for dinner, the Judge said with a troubled smile, "She always loved repentant sinners. Don't we all?"

50
A Life in the Law and Out: Annie's Way

OCTOBER 16, 1949

My dearest Edward:

Of course, I shouldn't be writing you (I've been forbidden to communicate with anyone on the defense team outside official channels)—but you know that. I simply—"lack of control," you always termed it!—couldn't help myself. Just to thank you for taking on Alger's case after the nauseating obscenity of the first trial. I knew you would stand by him—and me, even after all of Chambers's beastly lies—that man once known to us as George Crosley, whom we barely knew—a life we never knew—a phantom haunting our nonexistent past: You can't imagine how weird and terrifying! It's as if some alternate existence, some unseen universe, has claimed one, of which you have no knowledge or memory. As if we had married in some other life and now suddenly find ourselves in a world totally inscrutable to ourselves—who we really are! Fact and fiction so intricately bound as to leave us befuddled—lost to each other. Not that I haven't imagined such a thing—with you, I mean, another life. Surely such a thing has at least entered your mind over the years? On our walks in Riverside Park?

I assured Alger, even with <u>our</u> ups and downs, our "history," as you once called it, you were the best choice to lead his character defense. People believe you: Your word is your pledge. The Dimock name carries weight in New York. And for that, I owe you more than I can say. You have always been there for me—from when we first met at that Yale dance, to that squeaky porch swing at Hermitage, to our birding consultations in Riverside Park, to the stupidities of my first marriage, and saving me from even worse when you arranged everything with your father's colleague. And what did I do to thank you? Marry Alger, despite your sensible entreaties to give it more thought. Even as I thoroughly disliked his dowdy Baltimore family with all their nasty provincial snobbisms and underlying pathologies. Me, a Bryn Mawr girl! But I have gotten past all that, Edward. The "best people" bore me—not you, my dearest—with all their careless self-serving noblesse oblige. Alger helped me to see past that, to get in touch with the essentials of our common humanity. Not that Alger doesn't have his faults and foibles—like all of us. My Lord, how stubborn he can be, and foolish, too, to entangle himself in this travesty. Nonetheless, his commitment to social justice is absolute. He is a fine and loving father as well, first to his stepson, Timmy, and now to our young Tony. (Poor child, this whole awful business is so distressing and bewildering that we had to hide him away at our Vermont place in Peacham during the first trial, and now plan for him to go to rich friends on Fifth Avenue for the upcoming horror show.) That, believe it or not, is what you two have most in common: the love of your children, which I once witnessed with great pleasure, as if it were only the other day. Only a man of unyielding faith could have taken me on after my early mishaps. Or conceived the U.N. to promote world peace. Or been appointed president of the Carnegie Endowment for World Peace. And how does Fate repay: this disaster, this imposter, this Chambers of Horrors, this rotten pudgy creature who has crawled out of the sewer to try to destroy all the good Alger has done for the world.

What is the expression? No good deed goes unpunished.

Or is it Fate paying me back? Did I brag too much to you in the past? Did I let the perfect peace of Handytown go to my head?

I can just see your face as you read these words, nodding judiciously and saying to yourself calmly—oh how calmly: Surely they were due for a fall. I cringe at how I must have carried on at some of those wartime receptions, when I hung on to your arm with one too many gin and tonics to the wind. For bragging to your Annie, if only to assure her that I had no more interest in you. But I was so proud of Alger, how, against all the odds, he had risen in the ranks, how everyone in the State Department depended on him, how word of his mastery had reached the highest levels in the White House. (Where are those defenders now? I ask myself.) If I was full of myself, if I still thought I needed to prove something to you—forgive me. Regrets and second thoughts are crippling as one ages. And, you have to admit, you were always a bit dismissive, if not skeptical, of my enthusiasm for Alger, or as you told me once: "Be careful where you place your bets—win, place, or show for beginners."

Thank you for not taking my faults out on Alger. You are a good person, even if you wear your Groton, Yale, and Harvard Law pedigree on your sleeve. As Alger wears his Harvard credentials like a lifesaver, or is it a noose around his neck? The same with our Justice Holmes, as if that clock can be turned back with the flick of the hour hand! It sometimes seems half Alger's law school class is on the defense team. But you are my shining star and comforting right hand, in such good company with your fellow Groton alumnus Acheson, not to mention Frankfurter and Dulles, and the rest of the old crowd—those who have not yet died off, who have rallied to the cause. You may still be part of the world that made you—aren't we all?—but I think underneath, in your soul, even if you don't share our Quaker faith, you—Annie as well—are touched by the Inner Light, and are at one with us, until such time when we can build, together, a better world.

Again, thank you for your hard-pressed loyalty.

Love,
Pross

As I near the completion of my memoir, it seems as if I have passed some obscure point of no return—or lack the energy for further revision, and I find that I'm drawn more and more to the personal (the siren song of highways and byways, of lives imperfectly lived), and so struggle increasingly with family reminiscences—the what-might-have-beens, as if some balance has shifted, as if my professional life fades in importance, or will simply take care of itself in the course of things, my opinions and dissents finding their way into the fabric of settled law—or not. Although disappointed in failing to obtain the often-promised Supreme Court nomination, I feel that I faithfully fulfilled my duty on the Second Circuit for forty years. And I like to think that my work on the War Production Board also contributed a modicum to victory over fascism.

Perhaps this instinct to nostalgia—is it suffering or pleasure? I wonder—is more and more prompted by the early-morning mists rising into the upraised arms of the white pines, like shifting shoals of memory, revealing those stalwart and prayerful worshippers in patches of airy green, where the ripe brown cones hang like carillons from the uppermost branches, waiting for a stiff breeze to sound their changes, as Annie once filled the beam work of the ship's keel ceiling with her pensive song.

I am still a firm believer that what matters is a man's character in the conduct of his professional affairs, while his background, his family life, with all its possible prejudices and foibles, should little affect his judgment. But this facile demarcation is a fool's fixation. Annie's unquiet memory on this score still haunts me like a constant refrain from almost every quarter of the compass.

"Edward, your effectiveness as a lawyer and now a judge has always been in inverse proportion to your success as a husband and father."

"Of course you took the job because of Priscilla; win or lose, you come out smelling like roses: With Alger out of the way or back in the saddle, you get another chance with her, or at least her undying loyalty."

"Surprised at Teddy—surprised? Why do you suppose he was the only one in the family not to stick around to the closing gavel of the trial's first day to congratulate their famous papa? Headed out of that courtroom at lunch break, he was as good as headed for Korea."

Perhaps I feel guilty—wounds and all—for not keeping her memory more alive after all the unhappiness and bitterness of our final years. Even as she still sits in judgment over my life, as if hastening me along into the shadows, as do her confidantes—Ariadne languishing on her far shore and Terpsichore dancing among the stars—watchfully staring down at me every evening in the great room. Annie, who cruelly gave up on the young man she had once loved, that handpicked starry-eyed young lawyer so dear to her and her godfather. Oliver, my mentor and, yes, friend, who, so it sometimes seems, deliberately set her watch over me, so that her condemnation is equally his. Annie was a stern taskmaster by even her own account. My one consolation: She was a woman never satisfied with any performance—not her own (not even her early recordings and rave reviews), and certainly not her children's. Annie condemned herself as much as me for being selfish with our careers, for not being better parents—although, God knows, she doted unconditionally on Cordelia. To this day, I feel her jaundiced eye—turning her head from the piano to the echoing shadows above, listening as if for a reply to the fading notes—if not for my failure to be a more loving father and so keeping our son safe, then certainly for my treatment of Whittaker Chambers. So, maybe, at the last, it is a defense brief I am writing, perhaps a justification of memory's deceptions—deploying the same kind of excruciating self-flagellation for sins real and imagined that Chambers did in his memoir. The very sins—not to be outdone by even Saint Augustine—I once used against him on the witness stand.

Or perhaps—a more charitable reading of my quest?—mine is a search for the Inner Light of the Quaker, the truth and justice of the Unitarian conscience, or even the forgiveness of Chambers's omnipotent God. But I think I prefer Lincoln's notion: the redemption of our better angels. And yet such otherworldly faiths have all led to disasters both public and private for their advocates. The fate of my dear Priscilla is but one example.

And so I stick by the Constitution and the common law, the great balancer of all our diverse interests and desires, and so let my personal failings fall where they may. And, of necessity, to Emerson, who saw poetry in the landscape and its creatures, the journey's end in every step along the road. Who wrote, "to live the greatest number of good hours . . . is wisdom." Who extolled life's capacity for self-renewal: "I am Defeated all the time; yet to Victory I am born."

—

This truth of the eternal present I owe to Annie, and, in turn, Annie's truth to my daughters, lest their mother, and the grandmother of their children—now grandsons and granddaughters—hardens into a figure-head of a strict obedience, less a living, breathing, loving presence in their lives than the caricature of a fierce schoolmarm who crippled their self-esteem with impossible demands.

Alas, turning again to the mists over the lake, I find my abilities to recite chapter and verse, as once I could from the bench, sorely diminished; there are only glimpses, glimmering moments burning through, impressions, feelings, sensations, much as how she saw and lived her life, often—as she advised me—through the pages of her beloved Proust.

Moments that repeated themselves, some ad infinitum: slamming the piano cover in the great room and throwing herself into the chair across from mine by the fire.

"Drat, drat, drat . . ."

"Don't be so hard on yourself."

"I can't feel the damn thing; I can't get the voices to ring clear."

"You make impossible demands, dear."

"No more than you, Edward. No more, no less. A waste of life's gifts is the unforgivable sin, why Proust was desperate to complete his opus before his early death. That and the gift of children are the greatest gifts—don't you think, Edward? Gifted children: not a thing to be wasted. Oh you have your mighty law, your opinions to leave behind—this"—and she swept a feeble hand toward the ship's keel ceiling as if to an echo—"but what do I have except for my children?"

"Yes, at least you have Cordelia . . . and me."

She grimaced and closed her eyes.

"If only I were a composer and had something . . . God knows I've tried, but the thing, the gift, the genius to glimpse the unseen— the inspiration eludes me. Like the Vinteuil sonata, the little phrase. Sometimes I can almost hear it . . . as if it's at my fingertips."

And so she saw her cancer diagnosis as her just deserts. A divine retribution for her failures, if not mine. As if love were never enough.

———

During her last weeks, she insisted that we set up a hospital bed for her in the great room, thereby abandoning the bed we had shared and the view of the lake we savored like paradise, the room where three of her children had been conceived, for the room with the Delft fireplace ("my audience of sixty-eight little Indians," she called the figures depicted on the tiles), for a view of the ship's keel ceiling, a view of an immeasurable yet comprehensible vastness, a vision that changed by the minutes and hours according to the play of winter sunlight off the snow, where her "best self," as she described it, had once played, bringing to life the very fabric of her beloved Hermitage. So we stoked up the fireplace until our tutelary angels were like roasted chestnuts to the touch, kept the furnace blasting, and on the coldest days ran space heaters. We got in a Barbadian male nurse to help her around and Felicity to manage the house. I got up just on weekends until a damnably long trial was finally finished, and only then did she suffer me to read to her again, as I had during our first years, a carryover from my days reading to her godfa- ther, Justice Holmes.

———

"Perhaps, if you make it to the Supreme Court, you will write a book someday, Edward, about *you* certainly—but possibly about me and the children, as well. And as much as you despise him, Proust—well, he might offer you some guidance, even some insights into yourself, as he has for me, one artist to another. Does that count you out? I think not. Isn't a judge but an artist to try men's souls? But I'll take it easy on you and you may start off with the Combray section, which is all about his childhood, and then we'll see, depending on how long I last. I'd love to get at least as far as Balbec—Balbec by the sea. You'd like that, too, since you so revere your Beverly Farms days with Uncle Ollie and all the pretty girls on the beach. And then we can skip to Venice—remember Venice, Edward?—we made our son there—and then, if I make it that far, to the grand finale at the prince de Guermantes's party, where the ailing older Proust discovers the true nature of time and memory from the sensation of an uneven paving stone. Remember the baptistery of San Marco? We spent an hour there on our honeymoon. But don't worry about his literary abstractions, which I know you hate almost as much as Freud (you and Martha); listen for his landscape poetry, how suffering transforms us and leads to enlightenment. And don't call him a mommy's boy or a homosexual; that's not the point. The point is not so much the nature of memory as it is the way the accumulation of memories about people and places in our lives offers us insights into the journey. He's the poet of suffering, Edward, that through suffer-ing—so that maybe this vile business of dying can help us both—there comes insights, even enlightenment." She glanced over hopefully at me, and then back to the ship's keel ceiling, her face like a mask, a sarcas-tic shrunken grimace, and motioned to the morphine drip. The cruel winter light, reflected off the snowbound landscape, like something out of Dante's Ninth Circle, drove splinters of crystal into the blue above. "And where I've underlined, those are important bits; see if you can read those—if you dare—with some feeling.

"Ah, the little Vinteuil phrase from the sonata, that always moved me greatly, how Swann discovers that this haunting theme—this soul-ful fragment that becomes the leitmotif of his passion for Odette—was actually composed by a retired piano teacher he knew from Combray, a shy, retiring, put-upon composer with a disrespectful daughter—even worse than Alice—whom he'd dismissed as a provincial second-rate musician. How often I think about that Vinteuil phrase when I come upon something ravishing in an obscure piece by Brahms, say, where, in its second movement, the andante, there lies concealed some passage of infinite and subtle beauty that only a near-perfect performance can elucidate, as if tempting you to make it your own discovery, that only with the most accurate and sensitive voicing one might give it a new birth from the keys. A kind of first love, I suppose, something pure and untroubled—incorruptible.

"Now, here's the thing, something even you might be able to appreciate: the two ways, Swann's Way, or the Méséglise Way, and the Guermantes Way, or Vivonne Way. You see, Proust treats these two paths, two hikes—the hikes to Handytown and the Neversink, *n'est-ce pas?*—like symphonic compositions encompassing his Combray childhood, the people and places, the smells and sights of the pink hawthorns adjoining Swann's park, and the twin steeples of Martinville, and the flowering lilies along the glittering waterway of the Vivonne, flowing past the precincts of old nobility, the tattered remnants of the Guermantes family of old Combray. The first, Swann's Way, is shorter and good for days of threatening weather or failing light—familiar?— while the Guermantes Way is longer, perfect for endless summer days and fine weather. Well, without getting into all the particulars, and how these two ways finally merge in the last volume, *Time Regained*, you, of all people, with your nose for history, should be able to appreciate how his Swann's Way—Handytown—embodies the same sense of a family's history, the reverence for place and youth, sweet memories, order, the past or time ever present—ah, there's your Emerson, no less!; while the Guermantes Way—the Neversink hike—describes the movement out into the wider world of the social order and the deep past, and so transcends the present moment for the future, lifting our gaze, you might say, toward the infinite horizon. So now keep reading and see if such associations—perhaps, for you, the song of the hermit thrush at Handytown and the smell of lilacs in the spring, and the sound of rushing water on the Neversink and the gleam of a leaping brownie on your line—don't remind you of your own youthful journeys. That is, remember, feel again, come alive again, and find something of your youthful passionate self in these pages, and not just the 'mental masturbation' in your words, of an oversensitive aesthete. How he put, somewhere far down the line: The true paradises are the paradises we have lost."

Sometimes, she would have me reread passages she had long ago underlined or noted with marginal comments, immediately recognizing them, anticipating before I'd even turned the page, wondering out loud to herself—and to me—if the words had lost some of their power, if the words had the same meaning for her at that sad moment as they had once had in her salad days, or perhaps if the epiphany had proved true or accurate and had indeed forecast the fate that life had in store for her. These were moments, this dialogue with Proust, when I felt I had entered into the deepest intimacies of her past: her fears, her insecurities, her neglected loveless girlhood: the alcoholic father she barely knew and never talked about.

"Read on, where I've marked."

"The whole art of living is to make use of the individuals through whom we suffer simply as steps enabling us to obtain access to their divine form and thus joyfully to people our lives with divinities."

"There," she said, laughing, "you have it: my epitaph."

"God forbid."

"Oh dear, oh dear . . ." And she motioned once again to the morphine drip. "And of course, what you can never admit is that Uncle Ollie was reading Proust in his eighties and finding much consolation for his long-ago lonely youth in his beloved Pittsfield—the granite outcroppings and filipendula bushes. Like you, Edward, loneliness, don't you think? A boy overshadowed by an older brother of tremendous promise who died young in the war. Why do you never talk about Jack and your father's grief? You really are a very lonely man, Edward, living on half rations of love. Sorry, but there we are."

Does that explain the last eighteen years of our marriage: how she transformed grief over Teddy into a new appropriation of her nature, her talent, her very life? A life that required a different path, journeying away from her husband (her own bedroom, her own studio at Juilliard), doting on Cordelia ("my soul survivor"), while immersing herself in a new career, or should I say, in the genius of George Balanchine? Music no longer an end in itself, but translated into dance, into an approximation of her beloved ship's keel ceiling, where the music of the spheres underwent one metamorphosis after another, transformed on stage every night into the tall, sleek, vital young goddesses of Balanchine's creation—and her Guermantes Way?

We only made it as far as Balbec, alas, only dipping our toes in Venice and *Time Regained*.

At the end, she'd raised a finger off the blanket and smiled with a faint whisper: "Teddy, my only love." Which was followed by her last words: "Hold the line . . ." Spoken not to her shipwrecked husband, but to that blue cosmos above and a son emerging godlike from the sea to embrace the nymph of his desires (a mother's worst fear), that dangerous siren call that led him to his fate shivering in a trench on a frozen hillside in Korea.

———

Every now and then, when I get up in the morning from our bed in Graham's Dock, I will gaze over at the Raphael Soyer portrait of

Annie and smile, wondering, What if we'd gotten beyond the beach and grand hotel at Balbec and those lovely carriage rides with Mme. de Villeparisis (whose debauched youth and freewheeling spirit Annie so admired)? And sometimes I'll wander over to her shelf and flip through her underlined pages in Proust's final volume, *Time Regained*, and peruse a few of her marked passages, ever hopeful that something will turn up—an insight, an answer from the beyond left unsaid, an overlooked clue to her fate and perhaps mine, if not for inspiration to conclude my memoir.

And there it was—her epitaph at last—underlined twice over:

> *But art, if it means awareness of our own life, means also awareness of the lives of other people—for style for the writer, no less than color for the painter, is a question not of technique but of vision: it is the revelation, which by direct and conscious methods would be impossible, of the qualitative difference, the uniqueness of the fashion in which the world appears to each one of us, a difference which, if there were not art, would remain forever the secret of every individual. Through art alone are we able to emerge from ourselves, to know what another person sees of a universe which is not the same as our own and of which, without art, the landscapes would remain as unknown to us as those that may exist on the moon. Thanks to art, instead of seeing one world only, our own, we see that world multiply itself and we have at our disposal as many worlds as there are original artists, worlds more different from the other than those which revolve in infinite space, worlds which, centuries after the extinction of the fire from which their light first emanated, whether it is called Rembrandt or Vermeer, send us still each one its special radiance.*

In the margin, she appended this: God be Praised!

Those words enchanted me. I remember looking up from her underlined page to the window overlooking the lake, and beyond to the path to Handytown, and the path down the Neversink, but seeing still further afield, to the place where our two ways met and merged, her Proust with my Emerson, who wrote, "Art is the path of the creator to his work." Who found in all poetic forms a path into the self, "another world or nest of worlds; for, the metamorphosis once seen, we divine that it does not stop."

—

So, in that encomium to the eternal present, to the creative force of the moment—the artistry of our desires—I found the inspiration to go on, to return us to Venice, where Teddy, the lodestar of the first half of our marriage, was conceived on our honeymoon. It is an image that never leaves me: Annie's ecstatic, sweat-streaming face looking down at me, silhouetted by the light from the balcony of our room at the Danieli (where Proust had stayed), her brassy gold hair wet upon her brow, blue eyes burning, she still panting, the soft whisper of the waves and the shimmer of the canal-reflected light on the stuccoed ceiling of inter-twined dolphins.

"I felt him pass into me, Edward, like a ray of spring sunlight. It will be a boy."

She was hardly a virgin on our wedding night; we had been taking precautions, though without due diligence.

"Not on the crossing to Southampton?" I offered.

She shook her head and smiled serenely.

"I had it all planned out." And she kissed me oh so tenderly. "It had to be here—thanks to you, my perfect lover."

She slipped off me and carefully lay on her back for many hours with *The Captive*, Proust's fifth volume, partly set in Venice, exclaiming at familiar names: "Ah, the Bellinis—do you suppose the one in the Frari or San Zaccaria? . . . Oh, yes, the enchanting Carpaccios and Albertine's silly jacket . . . you see, dear, everything he encountered here in Venice, reminded him of home, of previous lovers, even his child-hood in Combray, as if his past were only transposed into a different and far richer key in every passing moment."

Hints, I suppose, of our coming life, when parts of her simply drifted away, out of touch, beyond recall for us mere mortals in her wake, as she said: transposed to another key, an itinerary of perfection unobtainable, of desires unfilled and unfillable, with an exquisite sensibility chained to her standards and hers alone.

Later, walking on the Riva to the municipal gardens, as we did every day, the issue of names was hotly debated.

"Not Richard?" I inquired, thinking to memorialize her grandfather Richard Davenport's love of Venice.

"That name ruined my father. No child should be saddled with undo expectations or the thwarted desires of their parents."

"God forbid."

"Like Proust wrote of desire: It is like a chord, and take one fundamental note away, even if we can barely hear it . . . the thing withers and dies."

"Well, I considered Oliver, of course, but as you noted . . . expectations, certainly on our part, if not the child's."

"And you don't care about . . . Edward?"

"Not a jot, perish the thought. Dimock is plenty. Half my father's deliveries were the second or third so-and-so, and he thought the whole business the height of presumption and egotism—talk about undue baggage on a child."

"I thought about musicians, composers, of course, but again, I feel, unfair."

"A good American name, I think. Do you want a pianist to follow in your footsteps?"

"Oh God, no . . . not unless he has the talent, of course. If only I had the strength, much less the size of a man's hand."

"Well, there's always Theodore—the Oyster Bay branch. Ted and Teddy have a nice ring to them. And, of course, we have him to thank for Oliver's appointment."

"I think Ollie might be pleased, though not the Rough Rider."

"Nor the trustbuster, but certainly the outdoorsman, a champion of preserving the wilderness. You know he's in the guest book at Hermitage, twice as a guest of Dr. Dimock, who attended his first wife and mother in extremis—terrible thing. Can you imagine? And his sons were ahead of me at Groton—champions all."

"Didn't he encourage his sons to enlist in the Great War? I remember Ollie talking about that."

"Quentin, shot down over France, was the youngest son, a scholar beloved at Groton, a live wire, perhaps recklessly self-confident. An inspiration to his fellows."

"You'd never encourage any son of ours to enlist?"

"Not in war as pointless as the last."

"Never, I hope."

"Word of honor."

"Then I won't even suggest Marcel."

She said nothing more on the subject as we stood in the Giardini, filling our lungs with the sea air while watching the sunset shimmer upon the lagoon. We were discussing the concert we were planning to attend that evening at La Fenice, when suddenly she stood to attention, a goshawk catching movement, raising a flattened palm like a salute above her intent eyes.

"Look, with the campanile just there, and those sails there—why, it's our Bunce sunset. And the pale moon, as Proust liked to say, hovering in the wings like an actress waiting to come onstage. We'll tell our little boy all about it, that he arrived on a last ray of sunshine over the lagoon, like a young god—Apollo, I think—yes, Apollo."

"God of music, well . . ."

I remember the amber sunlight swimming in her hair; and kissing her deeply, thinking nothing could ever take away that magical moment of desire unbound.

———

Annie doted on Teddy, as any mother would her first male child. But she was no less impatient with him than later with the girls. And yet Teddy seemed to know almost instinctively—a giggle, a smile, a hug, an insouciant remark—how to tame an overbearing mother. And later, to hear his sisters tell it, seduce half the young women around the lake. Teddy was raised on music, beginning with piano at age six—diligent, at least to start, with enormous physical ability but without the "spark," or focus, according to Annie. And so she switched horses—"lest I be driven crazy"—to Alice, pitting her against Teddy in the race for praise, if not affection, with Martha a distant, if conscientious, third. Teddy worked just hard enough to keep up with Alice and then threw in the towel when he went off to Groton, though he played at school concerts. With the demands of her career, Annie's interest in her brood rarely went beyond the children's piano practice. She breast-fed for a couple of weeks, put them on the bottle, and turned them over to the nanny. Nor could she wait to get Teddy and the girls past their children's books, which she found excruciatingly boring. She pushed them to graduate to Conrad and Hawthorne, Melville and Jack London—*Call of the Wild* was always a bedtime favorite. Fortunately, she spared them Proust, all except Alice, who as the anointed one on the piano, gravitated to Proust on her own, partly to curry favor with her mother, partly as one-upmanship over Teddy. Alice and Proust—something, to this day, I find inexplicable.

Strangely, for a Boston girl, who was raised summering on the North Shore, or playing concerts in Europe and Venice, Annie took almost immediately to Hermitage and our Catskill fastness. Perhaps it had something to do with unpleasant memories of her alcoholic father and their place in Gloucester ("my unhappy Balbec"), but I think it was the quiet she cherished, our forest stillness, and, yes, the acoustics in the great room, where she loved to practice, often staring up in wonder at the ship's keel ceiling, a place she always said allowed her to get closer to the music than anywhere else, especially her beloved Mozart. "There's something magical about the ceiling and the paneled walls—Stanford White, womanizer that he was, at least got something right—how the configuration of the crossbeams, or the ancient varnish, both dampens and enhances certain sonorities. Of course"—she always smiled when she said this—"having a captive audience of the gods—and my little Indians—is always an inspiration." She often complained that if she could only bring Hermitage on tour, along with her favorite Steinway, she'd be the next Alicia de Larrocha.

———

Fear.

I often thought Annie fearless. Who would drive up to Hermitage in the dead of winter for weeks at a time by herself so she could practice in peace and quiet, working up new repertoire as she prepared for a concert. Who could take the stage before thousands and barely bat an eyelash. And yet, that most serene of presences frightened her: "The lake, Edward, the water so dark and somehow forbidding, really quite terrifying. Children just sink and disappear from view. Not to mention the snapping turtles, the water snakes, and God knows what else that lurks down there." And so she always kept an eye out, even seated on the piazza in her favorite wicker chair with her long, elegant nose in a book, glancing up as she snapped a page, her gaze lingering on the boathouse where the children were having their swimming lessons. And yet the lake claimed them one by one, first Teddy, who always knew how to prey upon her fears by submerging himself until she panicked, only to spring to the surface like a laughing jack-in-the-box as he splashed her; and then Alice and Martha, and even loyal Cordelia went their own way, until Annie, too, slipped under the darkness, leaving only me to follow.

A darkness which is simply the past to which we are all fated, out of which the snappers appear, as Herr Drosselmeyer appeared to me out of a darkened stage, as Alger Hiss from the shadows of Memorial Hall: specters of a past that is never past.

Which is only to say that even in a sometimes-trying marriage, beset with tragedy, we were a happy family, in our way, for a time, until Alger Hiss summoned me to his aid.

—

Annie was dead set against me joining Alger's defense team for the second trial.

"Are you crazy? The man's guilty as hell, even if he was at Harvard Law with you. Even if he clerked for Ollie. Your mutual admiration society shouldn't blind you to a bad apple. Can't do you or your career any good to get caught up in this circus!"

Annie barely knew Alger and Priscilla, only from a few receptions during the war years, when she'd travel down to Washington for a visit. But at one of those receptions, Priscilla, in her catty way, had let on that we had once been lovers. Which resulted in a ruined weekend of torturous explanations and a cold shoulder for months.

"And she's even worse—crackbrained, you know, and foul-mouthed and pushy—way too intense and sure of herself—like a woman who's come to Jesus and lost her mind. And smug to boot. The way she brags and drops names—enough to make one sick. And you know, it was she who insisted on a quick marriage and pulling a fast one on Uncle Ollie."

When I tried to share with her the challenges of the trial, that our democratic ideals of fairness were coming under attack by the far right, Annie had no patience.

"Alger Hiss is simply too good to be true. If he just once mentioned a few defects of character or mistakes, he would be a much more believable witness. And why are they getting you to do the dirty work on that man Chambers? I find him utterly believable and sympathetic—don't you? A man who confessed to his errors and made a new life for himself as an editor at *Time*—that's something to be admired, in my book. And speaking of books, have you even read his book reviews? They're full of brilliant and sensitive insights and wisdom. I'd rather trust a man so widely and intelligently read, who writes so persuasively about literature, than a self-satisfied bureaucrat kingpin preening about his connections to the powerful."

That was the Puritan conscience—admitting one's sins—in Annie.

But then, Annie was a woman who disliked Franklin Roosevelt and his New Deal minions, a man, in her mother's Boston circles, who was considered a frivolous lightweight with barely a second-rate mind (even if Ollie had qualified that with a "first-rate temperament")—and worse, someone careless in both his public and private life. *Careless* was a term of dark condemnation in Annie's family, as it was to Justice Holmes. Annie admired Eleanor Roosevelt's public-spiritedness but thought her enthusiasms ran roughshod over her judgment about people who manipulated her.

"That Priscilla of yours just went on and on about her lofty highness, Eleanor of Hyde Park. She's a name-dropper, Edward, always talking about how she and Alger run around with all the top dogs in the White House, all the pedigreed pooches."

Nevertheless, Annie did her best to remain supportive over those long winter months between 1949 and 1950 as the trial unfolded. She faithfully attended the opening day with the girls and Teddy (who put in a perfunctory appearance) and then read the accounts in the papers, shaking her head and chuckling to herself as more and more of the evidence turned against Alger, when even his early supporters began to waver.

"Where's her Eleanor now? I wonder." She put down the paper with the front-page photograph of Alger leading Priscilla down the steps of the federal courthouse on Foley Square. "Alger—look at the smirk on his face—will have to be a Houdini to get out of this fix. Surely I'm not telling you anything you don't already know. Your lovely Priscilla looks like a deer caught in the headlights. And who wears white gloves anymore? And that hat, like a sailor's cap—awful! What the hell did you ever see in her? And what if he does turn out to be a spy? How is that going to help your career? I just hope that wicked man doesn't sink your chances for an appeals court judgeship, which is what Uncle Ollie always wanted for you."

When Alger was convicted, she neither rubbed it in nor tried to console me. Her silent, self-satisfied, quixotic smile was enough, as if a rival had been put up against a wall and ceremoniously shot. All she wanted was to reclaim the life we'd once had outside the klieg lights of "your trial of the century," as the pundits termed it. But that cruel winter of 1950 seemed to pile up one disaster upon another. In short order came the Korean War, following on from the shock of the Soviets' testing of a nuclear bomb and the Red takeover of China. One could almost feel the ground shifting in the country as all Stalin's enthusiasts went to ground, and paranoia about Soviet depredations began to stalk the land. From skepticism about the existence of any Soviet spying whatsoever, overnight, Americans found spies hiding under every bed in the land. A sinking feeling made all the more terrible for those of us on the defense team, when Alger fired us all for a new team to take on the appeals process. We slunk back to our firms, never talking about the trial among us, nor to the press or others, as far as I know. And for good reason: I think we were all a little spooked when it was discovered during the trial that over his last years at the State Department Alger had been scurrying around, trying to lay his hands on anything and everything to do with the U.S. nuclear bomb development program. That and the subsequent discovery and conviction of the Rosenbergs made us persona non grata in many of the watering holes we'd once frequented. I got dirty looks whenever I darkened the doors of the Century, or the Yale or Harvard clubs. I remember in the early fifties sitting alone in the Harvard Club dining room under the founder's portrait of Dr. Dimock, with Teddy Roosevelt's full-length portrait across the way, and not a single greeting would come my way all evening. That would change in time, but it was a long dry spell.

———

It was Teddy's housemaster at Stiles College who phoned to tell us that Teddy had left a month before the spring term ended his freshman year and enlisted in the Marine Corps. The shock to Annie, who always thought Teddy confided everything to her, was extreme. "How could my son not tell his mother?" We knew that one day in the future the draft might be a possibility upon graduation—although acceptance at Harvard Law School might delay things—or even the CIA, where many of his friends ended up, but hardly the Marine Corps. But instead of this eventuality, with the onset of the Korean War, determined to expedite things, he joined the Marine Corps as a private. When we finally got hold of him on a long-distance line at Camp Lejeune, we found him immovable in his purpose and happier than he'd been for months.

"It's the real world down here. Infantry training—well, it's like I've been preparing myself for this all my life at Hermitage."

That left Annie speechless. She was beside herself, as was I, even if I didn't let on, even as I felt an unacknowledged surge of pride in my son's decision, especially as I endured the ongoing beatings and ostracism that followed from the Hiss trial. Longtime clients refused my services. Only the eager, confident tone of Teddy's voice over the long-distance line, the happy yelp in his voice, offered succor during those dark months.

Annie took a flight down to Raleigh and a taxi to Jacksonville, North Carolina, and Teddy managed to get a pass out of Lejeune for dinner. She came back a changed woman.

"He's ashamed of you, Edward. Ashamed because you defended that traitor Alger Hiss. That's all he heard at Yale over the last six months, that a Groton and Yale Skull and Bones man had enlisted in the cause to defend a Communist spy and traitor. You let him down, Edward, and now he has to go out and prove himself a killer. And an officer—they've promoted him to first lieutenant."

"That's ridiculous and you know it."

"He'd never tell you to your face. And even now I can see right through you: how proud you are of him."

"I'll always be proud of him."

"Right, just like your idol Theodore Roosevelt, who drove his sons to be soldiers—another dead in France, one wounded in the South Pacific. Men!"

"Don't be absurd."

"You promised me, Edward. And you lied about that, too."

—

Several months after Teddy's funeral, I got a call from a weary President Truman in the White House, not to console me for the loss of my son—I don't think it even registered—but to let me know that my name had been put forward for a vacancy on the Second Circuit, where for ten years I would have the honor to serve under one of the greatest jurists of his generation, Learned Hand.

During the confirmation process in the Senate, the fact that I'd lost a son in Korea whitewashed any lingering questions about my role in the defense of Alger Hiss, and I squeaked by.

In Annie's mind, I had sold my soul for Holmes's brass ring.

We slept together only one more time in the remaining eighteen years of our marriage, as if the lake had claimed us too, before our time.

51

Never Really Leave Us

CORDELIA EASED HER battered Toyota up to the front entrance of Hermitage, saw there was no one to greet on the front piazza, and skirted around to the back, where she found George's Tahoe tucked behind the garage and Felicity's nondescript Honda parked in front. She got out with Jim and Cecily, both holding grocery bags. There they remained rooted where they stood by the open doors, as if cautious about leaving the safety of the car, or, more likely, absorbed in memories of the last time each had been at Hermitage. Although Cordelia had been there within the past six months, she was buoyed by mostly happy memories of Thanksgivings past, including Annie's last, that bittersweet fall of 1968, after a spring and summer of assassinations and riots, when her mother had already been diagnosed but still seemed to be rallying. Cecily's last Thanksgiving had been at seventeen, with Billy, her beloved brother, and all the cousins packed in a clamoring gaggle around the dining room table, the Judge gaveling for order, when Hermitage (this realization almost sank her on the spot) had been the only real home she'd ever loved. Jim couldn't remember his last Thanksgiving, period, only a vague memory of silver candelabra decorated with trout (how was that possible?) and of Cordelia in a beautiful red satin dress with her hair all done up and George as a little boy dressed in a dark suit and a borrowed tie of the Judge's and feeling like a fifth wheel.

So, different outposts of Time, same patriarch, and a near-illusory splendor—smoke evaporating from a redbrick chimney into the clear sky—teetering on the brink.

Cecily was the first to be fully lifted off her moorings by the tides of memory, dropping her bags to the damp, leafy earth with a little whoop of pleasure while spinning around like a giddy two-year-old, arms outstretched as if to fully absorb the lichen- and pine-scented air under the Argos-eyed presence of bay windows glittering with a dull diamonded luminescence amid the gray clapboard shingles.

"Oh my Lord—ambrosia of the celestial gods!" Cecily exclaimed. "And the boathouse, Aunt Cordy, the boathouse is still there. They fixed it." She paused and listened to the silence of the woods, now absent summer birdcalls. "Excuse me, folks"—she wiped a tear from her eye— "but I have to go down to make sure the patient is really alive and kicking—or at least . . . this patient."

"Jeest," said Jim, working his bearded jaw as he watched her go, shaking her head as if to some silent rap lyric, "I'm not sure I can do this thing."

"You'd think she was still crazy sixteen," said Cordelia, ignoring Jim, "and in heat, not a divorced woman pushing forty." She smiled, a little wide-eyed herself. "And still beautiful. Don't you love it—not a line, not a sag—her olive skin!" She reached into the trunk and took out more grocery bags and lined them up neatly next to those of her niece. "Wendy sure does—worst luck."

"Huh?"

"Oh, nothing; they're just shacked up together is all—model and muse, according to George. What a waste, not even managing a kid with that black paragon of a Stanford surgeon of a husband of hers. Even Alice was crazy about him—*kiss of death*," she added under her breath.

Jim grimaced as he worked his bad leg. "You always thought kids were the fix for what ails a marriage."

"You say the most ridiculous things. Kids fix the world we can't fix. I can't imagine a life without George; he's the one good thing we managed."

"You managed."

She scowled. "The only thing worse than being ridiculous is feeling sorry for yourself. Here, take the groceries in to Felicity and then carry our bags up to my room."

"You're not leaving me alone with your old man?"

"He can barely bark anymore. He can barely move anymore, and his memory is going. Hey, maybe he's forgotten all about you, Jim. Think of that: a stranger, a clean slate, a new start. Which would be a sad day for him, since he was so delighted with himself when you walked out on me and George, because you proved him right, in spades . . ." She laughed with the raw wonder at the possibility of such a renewal, as if casting such an incantation over Hermitage. She placed a steadying hand on Jim's shoulder, a slap on his blue-jeaned butt. "Ward Cleaver—what a huge disappointment."

"Who?"

"I forget you grew up without a TV."

"And all this time I thought he hated me because my father was a Jew and, as we now know, a Commie to boot."

Cordelia turned from the shadow-streaked façade of Hermitage, her brows furrowing, as if something had occurred to her.

"Actually, to hear George talk about it, he figures the Judge was already pretty apprehensive about you from the get-go, guilty about your father, that is, whoever gave the orders. Why send me to deliver those sketches in the first place? Why else bring along Alice—if not for moral support—when he arrived at Woodstock to save me from your cradle-snatching clutches?" Her eyes flickered with amused dismay at the strangeness of it all, easing into a hint of chagrin as she caught sight of the garage, where the Judge's red Mercedes coupe was parked under a tarpaulin.

"Sure as hell didn't endear myself when I refused to take those damn sketches back—like I'd pissed on his shoe."

"Evidence, at the very least, of a guilty conscience . . . in such a man . . ." She deliberated a moment more and shrugged, as if whatever mongrel thought she'd unearthed was trumped by delight at the red coupe, on whose hood her palm now rested. "Listen, I don't give a damn; what's done is done. But it's not the old man we need to worry about; it's Alice and Martha." She raised her unblinking eyes to the bristle of his mustache. "Now, you stand up for George—your brilliant son—hear. This memoir thing has got my sisters in a tizzy. We need to stand by him"—she bent even closer to his ear—"do you hear? He's our whole world—and the new furnace, thank God—not your dusty liner notes nor mine. Did you bring the results of your DNA test with you?"

He slapped his back pocket.

"I thought Alice wasn't coming?"

"What—with Cecily here, and a chance to stir up trouble and get her paws on George and the memoir? Alice *and* Stan will come." She opened her arms and breathed deeply, as if to dispense any lurking bad karma, turning her head to the sun-drenched sky and shaking back her curls of gray-streaked blond hair. "I'm off for a walk to Handytown, by myself—clear my head. Just get the stuff out of the car and stop worrying. Felicity was concerned about space problems, so I told her just to put us in the same room—like old times. So that will certainly be remarked upon. Bye."

"You're leaving me by myself to go in there?" He began to gather up the shopping bags.

"Felicity will be your bodyguard." She pulled open the top snaps on her fleece. "I wonder where George and Wendy got to. Must be out walking. Nice how it's warmed up a bit." She made a face at his apprehensive frown. "Oh, all right, here, give me some of those. Why don't you come with me? Your limp seems better, and you could use the exercise."

Bags in hand, he stopped by the garage and glanced at the tan tarp covering the Mercedes coupe, a look of mild curiosity merging into one of fond recognition. He turned back to Cordelia with a broad smile as he caressed the hood.

"Do you suppose this baby could use a tune-up?"

———

Cecily stood absorbing the musty interior of the boathouse, which had once served as her bolt-hole, where she had hidden from the Judge and her cousins and brother, Billy, when the latter had pestered her beyond endurance. It was where she'd brought her books to read, mostly nature guides, sitting on a dock and identifying wildflowers while cooling her feet in the water. She was so relieved not to find a ruin, almost as if nothing had happened except for faint burn marks in the paneling behind the boat racks, which held cobwebbed canoes, kayaks, and, on the top rack, a one-man shell—a sleek blond beauty designed for speed. She ran a hand along the shiny hull, dragging a trail of dust along the rich blood-orange teakwood, a fixture of her childhood: "Teddy's shell." Strictly off-limits to the cousins. Battered and cracked oars and paddles remained at attention, regimented in peg cradles on the wall, the more antique inscribed with a *D* on the blade. Some latent curiosity stoked by equally vague but enticing memories impelled her to rummage through the lockers storing life jackets and tackle boxes, digging through the mess of reels and tangled lines to discover near the bottom a scarred rosewood tackle box with brass fasteners, inscribed in gold letters with the name Teddy. Her eyes widened, as if the name had just echoed on the wind, or been conjured at her fingertips by the sensation of the arrow-like hull, and so she eagerly pried open the fasteners. There, beautifully organized on two shelves of teakwood compartments, she found a collection of ancient lures. Never much of a fisherman, she nevertheless found the colorful creatures spellbinding: tiny toy fish with toy eyes and toy scales and serious, if rusty, hooks. A single oblong blue box was tucked away in the bottom corner. It was labeled FLIPPER: CHANGE THE ACTION BY FLIPPING THE TAIL. "Flipper," she said, smiling and thinking of dolphins. She opened one end of the cardboard box, which seemed suspiciously light. There, safely concealed within, was a thin foil packet. "No way." She slid out the square packet with the pale blue helmeted head of a Trojan warrior. Feeling the soft rubber ring safely sealed within, she couldn't resist bringing the packet to her nose and breathing deeply, as if of the immemorial male desire secreted within, but with it a hint of sadness, too, that her celebrity husband had not trusted her enough to stay on the Pill. She sighed, glancing around, as if guilty of some desecration (a word the Judge used regularly for infractions real or imagined), then carefully replaced the packet and tucked the blue box back in the corner of the tackle box. In so doing, she managed to prick herself on a hook.

"Oh my"—she sucked the bead of blood off her finger—"if that boy still hasn't got a sting in his tail."

Bemused, giddy with pleasure, she tiptoed around the bat and swallow droppings, trying to identify the scorch marks left on the beadboard paneling, just below where squared-off sections of more recent repairs had been made. She and Karen had tried using bailing cans, but the fire had outdistanced their efforts. Spreading her palms on the paneling, she laid her ear against the wall, as if listening for a heartbeat.

"Sorry, boathouse, we really weren't planning to burn you down. The fireworks were only a special celebration for Billy's birthday—that's all it was."

A bumped paddle fell from its peg cradle and clattered to the floor. Startled, she turned to the vivid memory of the seventy-four-year-old Judge charging down the rutted, root-strewn path to the boathouse, falling, picking himself up, and hurtling into the flames to carry out the one-man shell to safety just minutes before the Sparrow Bush fire department arrived.

Cecily slid back the door to the docks sheltering under the steep overhanging roof supported by four knotty pillars. Spying a broom, she swept the floorboards of barn swallow and bat shit, desiccated moths, and brittle dragonfly exoskeletons. The smell of cool lake water staunched an ache in her, and so, finishing her sweeping, she let herself down to the weathered two-by-fours of the deck, first lying back, luxuriating in the warmth, her pulse slowing, then sitting up and reaching out with the toe of her right running shoe, tapping out a Morse code on the placid surface to the distant pine-studded shore. There was an autumnal sparseness she had yet to get used to. She watched as each ripple spread on tiny feet, tiny arcs of liquid light in pleasing regimented tea green array. The repeated patterns comforted her, the same way studying wildflower guides and later biology in high school and organic chemistry in college had comforted her: the certainty of tree patterns, the way things mimic and interact and connect. She remembered how she and little Georgie would sit on the dock at night and he'd tell her everything about the sky and she'd tell him everything about the flora and fauna of the woods, and it all seemed to connect, as if the same free energy coursed through all things. Cecily, a born naturalist, in the Judge's opinion, had won every prize and contest going, sadly upstaging her brother, Billy, in the Judge's eyes.

"Oh, Billy . . . how I miss you, baby." She glanced up to the overhead beam swarming with jittery crystal apertures of reflected light. "Where are you, my brother?"

In the hint of a breeze through the trees, she almost thought she could make out her brother's voice in all its goofy, daring, unhinged, and embarrassingly candid Stan-like strangeness (a born stand-up comedian). Even now she could hear Billy and the other boys conniving in the great room around the Monopoly board, shouting across the lake in a canoe as they held up a fish, screaming as they ambushed the girls along the trails, squabbling on the float at the beach, competing for attention, preening in their wet bathing suits the moment some random girl from across the lake came down for a swim. When she and Karen had learned stealth early, flirting later, secreting themselves to overhear conversations and so play on the boys' weaknesses, their vulnerability, their furtive need to impress when not jerking off in the craziest damn places. And so her and Karen's power grew summer by summer, as if in perfect sync with their boobs filling out, as the older boys around the lake began infiltrating the circle of cousins, elbowing Billy and Erich aside (little Georgie looking on perplexed from the sidelines), hanging out, smoking dope. Dealing drugs was Billy's way of holding his own in the competition for bragging rights among the cousins. And getting laid by the older girls.

With sudden clairvoyance, she felt anew that sexual power, first to dominate the boys, then to ease her way out from under the Judge's tyranny. All it took was carelessly going without a bra in a tight T-shirt or wearing a skimpy two-piece back from the beach to Hermitage . . . anything to disconcert the old man as he emerged from his office lair in the late afternoon for his walk or swim, to check in on the progress his grandchildren had made in tennis or piano, or book reports . . . "Oh my God, the book reports," she laughed aloud now. The Judge would read their reports before dinner and then discuss their summer reading assignments around the table. "Facts, not fiction," he'd say, raising an exacting finger; "concrete examples, not random anecdotes. Civilized discourse, boys and girls, requires the acquisition of both the manners and intellectual acuity of scholars and gentlemen—that means you two as well, Cecily and Karen."

She remembered the way the Judge had eyed her, curiosity mixed with a kind of sarcastic irony. Did he know about her father? Did she feel the need to be better than everyone else because of being a half-breed? Not that it had helped her marriage any.

"'Civilizing the barbarian hordes,'" she repeated, recalling the Judge's response when queried by neighbors at his annual cocktail party on the veranda. Then he'd explain, "I have only the brief summer months to undo all the damage their negligent parents inflict over the rest of the year."

Billy always got the worst of it.

"Don't answer a question with a smart-alecky question, Billy," he'd say. "Besides a lack of respect, it reveals a feeble mind. Again, I asked, what are the three cardinal foundations of the American way of life? The answer . . . again: private property, due process—that's where I come in—and enlightened but limited government, per our Constitution of checks and balances. Everything, dare I say, that your mother, Billy—*and* Cecily—seeks to disrupt in court proceeding by way of obfuscation and distraction. Alice may think she has the tactical advantage by putting the system on trial, but the strategic advantage remains firmly with the government, *and* the people by virtue of the law, and ultimately the jury and ballot box."

She paused in her tapping, listening again for fall's sweet, if oppressive, silence, bending forward to catch her reflection in the water, a diaphanous face shadowing the leafy bottom and abandoned sunfish nests, those exotic features, not quite black, not quite white, not quite anything except for the elegant nose (Alice's, but a tad shorter) and wide, sensuous lips, eyes electric and "dark as sin"—so described by her ex: attractive to all but now attached to none. She wondered how many of the boys around the lake even remembered her, still fantasized about her—the two or three . . . or four—maybe five—she'd jerked off while they fondled her magnificent tits. The golden-haired summer boys, so she thought of them—her lake boys, who liked to sidle up to her around the campfire on the island in the middle of the lake and steal a kiss, a feel, pretend to keep her warm—anything to make her cousins jealous, especially Karen, who competed madly for male attention. Oh the wonder of those adolescent-kindled desires harbored by boys who cared less for her exoticism, her brains, her professional-caliber piano playing than for her physical prowess, her laugh, maybe her edgy repartee, and occasionally her kindnesses to her favorite white boys, her oh-so-privileged white boys, scorned by Alice on principle and so never mentioned, boys who wrote to her from fancy prep schools, and later Princeton and Yale, boys she might have dated but dared not, boys she might have loved and even married, if nothing else but to get back at her mother. Oh the wonder of such teenage desires, which had nothing to do with politics and everything to do with the thrill of the human touch, sweaty fingers in her crotch and eager lips and rock-hard cocks . . . and yet those desires had totally failed to engender happiness, much less children of her own, to repopulate the lake and woods with her own kind . . .

Again, the fall silence, the brittle blur of blueberry and barberry bushes both oppressed her and fascinated her: the ganglia-nebulae of nature laid bare, hardwired dormancy in preparation for the spring and new buds and boatloads of berries. Did her lake boys all have children of their own now, lily white beauties, like her cousins' children, Karen's Max and Erich's Nancy?

She blinked back tears. Were there new children now to return to the lake in July and August and pick the blueberries, the ever so sweet and tender tiny low-bush blueberries that grew in such abundance along the shore that you could just slip under in a canoe and shake loose handfuls?

"Oh, I thought you must be with someone," said Wendy, coming through the boathouse out onto the twin docks. "Cordelia said you might be here." She sat down next to Cecily and casually kissed her on the lips, the two lingering in the kiss, friendly, knowing. "George and I just got back from Handytown."

"Oh . . . Handytown . . ." Cecily echoed in reply, as if somewhat abashed to hear the familiar name from someone not out of her lake past. "Handytown, how are those lonely old bones under their blue-stone slabs?"

"Still lonely." Wendy pulled bits of withered ferns from her laces. "Especially now that the hermit thrush are gone—that's George's take."

"He seems pretty gone on you," said Cecily, flicking a glance at Wendy and holding her eyes.

"And me on him," she replied, and caressed Cecily's thigh.

Cecily flinched, not at the touch so much as at the materializing of desire out of her daydreams of moments before.

"You're not playing with him, girl? He got beat up enough as a kid."

"But I can share my heart, just a little, can't I?"

Wendy swirled her hair around her hand and lifted it behind her shoulder.

"You young women." Cecily shook her head in a kind of wounded wonder. "Sex is like a sixth sense—I dunno how you quite manage it. What about George?"

"Oh, he's still a little in love with you from childhood; I connect him to that. Call it an artist's prerogative: she and her muse."

"'World enough and time . . .'" Cecily frowned and shook her head in disbelief. "Lord forgive me, but I wish I had hair like that." Wendy dropped the strand she'd been playing with and stroked Cecily's dark arc of kinky hair. The younger woman's touch releasing her innermost thoughts, she said, "You know, I just had this terrible realization: how much I love this place, like my heart is buried five fathoms deep here. Isn't that awful. How hurt can have a half-life that sort of decays into love—how can that be? And how much I miss my brother, Billy, who was cooler than cool, and so damned funny."

"Ah, you're just ahead of the game, when suffering turns into its opposite. It takes time and distance, the fermentation of memory for the love to come through. The Proust thing, you see: True paradises are the paradises we have lost."

"Mother Alice gave me a copy when I was seventeen for my French AP, and I didn't make it through the first page."

Wendy laughed and splashed with her feet.

"You guys—your problem is, you don't realize how lucky you are." She leaned way back, so that her hair fell to the deck and her face was bathed in the warming saffron light creeping under the overhang of the roof.

Cecily followed suit, where more and more whorls of diamond-amber had appeared in the beam work above, the abandoned swallow nests like knotty imperfections in antique glass.

"This place is *so* not Berkeley. It's everything—that's the crazy part—I'm not supposed to be."

"Don't be ridiculous, Cecily. You're like George; you overthink everything. All that really matters is that it's your family, your heritage, your memory incarnate—and it's unspoiled and perfect. You guys are so politically correct about stuff. The things that really matter just are, because *they are*."

"Humpf—whatever gets your motor running. Girl, you were never stuck on the plantation when the Judge ran it like a reform school for rich kids."

"Looks like you've survived the abuse just fine." Wendy reached to Cecily's chin and turned her face to her watching eyes. "You're so damn beautiful, I'd love to do some nude sketches of you lying on the rough wooden decking—see, how the curly knots in the wood match your skin tones? But you know that: Your skin tones drive me wild."

Cecily laughed with a dismissive rolling of her eyes.

"Don't even breathe such a thing—not here! Truth is, Billy and I could really only be brother and sister in this place, not like the odd couple we were at home, at New Paltz High. And having that old man beat up on us cousins made us like a little band of brothers. So we could spend the summers bitching about *his* rules as opposed to bitching about one another and our fucked-up lives."

"Have you seen the Judge yet?" She looked at her watch. "I guess it's his nap time."

"It's been over twenty years since he kicked me and Karen—and then everybody else—out. I'm not sure I can handle it; even in his seventies he was such a virile, incredibly handsome man. We could never live up to his impossible standards. And yet, as much as we didn't dare admit it, we always craved his approval in the worst way."

"Her standards . . ." Wendy nodded thoughtfully. "I think his wife, Annie, treated him rather cruelly—talk about standards you could never live up to."

"Annie? Who the fuck are you to offer such an opinion? You don't know anything about her. She died when I was a little girl, when we still lived in Berkeley."

"Sorry, it's not my place to criticize. I get it. But sometimes I feel like I know her, and I admire her as much as I fear her." She tapped the toe of her shoe, for a moment dissolving their reflections. "I feel for the Judge, for the unfairness of his loss."

"No wonder Mother Alice is so on the warpath about George—and you, it seems—messing with the Judge's memoir. First thing out of her mouth when she picked me up at Kennedy."

In a dreamy voice, staring at their reflections, Wendy said, "Unfair of Annie to blame him for the Alger Hiss mess, what happened to Teddy."

"Teddy?" Cecily intoned, looking at the tip of her finger, where a tiny crimson drop of blood appeared. "What I always heard from Aunt Martha and Mother Alice was that he spent the last decade of their marriage fooling around with other women, younger women, his law clerks."

"You hurt yourself." Wendy grabbed the finger and sucked it clean in a twinkling of an eye.

"Gosh!" exclaimed Cecily, as if not quite believing what had happened.

"Blood sisters," Wendy said, and she squeezed her hand.

"Teddy . . . well, that Alger Hiss thing, way before my time." Her expression darkened, as if she were perplexed, once-invisible moments in time beginning to connect in unexpected ways. "But coming here summers it was always Teddy this and Teddy that; how to cast a line, how to play the piano, how to hit a backhand, how to fit a stone at Handytown—all the birdcalls you didn't yet know. You could see that golden boy in the Judge's glittering eyes, sizing you up." She frowned, her stare deepening over the lake, as if she were struggling to catch sight of that fleeting presence, perhaps a broad backed rower sprinting across a ribbon of sunlit water.

"You see, the Judge writes so movingly about Annie in his memoir; she really comes alive."

"Mother Alice offered me two thousand bucks if I could manage to swipe a copy from George."

"No—"

"She—how you think I ended up in your apartment? Five minutes after she picked me up at the airport, she was right back to manipulating one thing or another. No way could I stay with them. She figures George is in cahoots with the old guy, always been his favorite. And *your* Annie, let me tell you, like Teddy, was the benchmark of perfection in the Judge's telling. Table manners—oh my God." She squinted in the lowering sunlight. "I mean, I never knew her, but looking back and all, it's like her eyes were everywhere, watching us: the photographs hanging around every corner on the walls, even on her Steinway—Annie's 'torture machine,' we called it. He—get this—even had a place laid for her at the end of the dining room table, as if at any moment she might just show up!"

Cecily held out her hands as if impelled to inspect her long, supple fingers and polished nails. Wendy mirrored the gesture and then reached over and placed her raw and calloused palm against the older woman's, as if comparing reach, the disgrace of her broken dirty fingernails. They giggled like half-frightened schoolgirls when their fingers intertwined.

"Annie was like the fairy godmother we never had. Not that it ever stopped Mother Alice from bitching about Annie almost as much as she does about the Judge. Especially now that he seems to have taken such a shine to you and George—George, our little space boy, the master's great white hope—me, too, I guess, for a time, to see who was going to land that Ph.D. brass ring." She sighed, wetting her lips. "But then, my mother is an equal-opportunity activist. The way she fawned over Louis, my ex, thoroughly creeped him out."

Wendy reached to Cecily's face again, cradling it for a moment, locking stares.

"I'm just a pair of alien eyes on the outside looking in, but you . . . you've got her nose and cheekbones—Annie's. I can see it in the portrait by Raphael Soyer that used to hang in Graham's Dock."

Cecily blinked at Wendy, as if the conversation were getting increasingly odd, perhaps baffling, as if this preternaturally talented young woman had touched some third rail—yet a source of heat lightning not to be dismissed lightly.

Cecily tried laughing it off, more in bafflement than pleasure. "You're lucky, *stranger*, not to be faced with measuring yourself against Father Time, the sixteen-year-old Oreo who was supposed to rock the world."

"You rock my world."

"Your world don't count—sorry, sister Wendy. The only world that counts around here is the Judge's world. And I won Annie's piano prize, damn it, and the Stanford scholarship, and every other stupid blue ribbon, including a wealthy, talented, charismatic world-class surgeon—a black man to boot, and I still ended up with the booby prize. And," she added, sighing, "I miss my Billy like crazy, like something of him will always be hanging out here, and stupid me is just too blind to find him."

At this outpouring, Wendy seemed slightly taken aback, as if whatever healing magic she possessed or thought she possessed had its limitations.

"The dead, you know"—she paused, pondering, gesturing to their twin specters mirrored in the water—"never really leave us, even though life tries to dispossess them." She motioned shoreward, where Hermitage's windows caught orange glints of waning light. "The rooms fill up and their places are taken by others, whose feelings are drawn from the same wells—inspirations, I suppose. But you see, there's never enough love to go around and the dead always get short shrift. We pretend it doesn't matter, that they don't care, but they do. They're always dying while we're still living, and then die all over again when we do. We're their subjects. We can't leave them to languish even if we wanted to."

Cecily watched her fellow shadow merge in and out of the submerged leaf litter, a thousand-yard stare couched in the younger woman's wide-eyed squint.

"Whooee, that's what comes from living over a fucking graveyard. You say the damnedest things, girl. Sorry, but I'm glad I got my own place, starting next week."

"You didn't tell me."

"You knew I was looking for something in the city near NYU med school."

"Listen, I know I tend to get carried away. But this place has a spooky beauty and serenity about it that kinda gets under your skin."

"*You*"—Cecily laughed—"are spooky."

"I know how you feel about Billy."

"No, you don't—you don't," she scolded.

"Okay, I don't."

"You see, I went to visit him, oh, eight years ago, when he was in rehab in a flossy clinic in Sausalito. Mother Alice paid the full freight. Billy took after Stan, wanted to be an actor, make movies, do stand-up comedy. But he couldn't take the rejection. And when I spoke to his therapist, she kept asking me about this place, about Hermitage. And I asked her why, and she told me that Billy kept bringing it up in their sessions: the only place he'd ever felt happy, that felt like home. 'Summoned by da Judge,' that's how she repeated Billy's words to me— see, he revered Flip Wilson. Billy, of course, just dismissed it when I mentioned it . . . embarrassed, like he'd let down the side. And Billy was the most badass of any of us, going to Monticello to score drugs for us cousins, the original juvenile delinquent. When Karen and I almost burned down the boathouse, the Judge immediately blamed Billy, because that little idiot used to stash his drugs here, in the boathouse, under the seat of the rowing shell—the holy of holies, of all places! When the therapist's report got back to Alice, she just flipped out, and a week later Billy found himself flown back east and relocated to a halfway house for abusers in fucking Poughkeepsie . . . counselors but no therapists. Mother Alice hates shrinks. Three months later, he OD'd in a Walmart bathroom."

Wendy pulled her legs under her. "Oh, Cecily, I'm so sorry."

"I could've kept him with us . . . but my husband didn't want white druggie trash around the house. He thought Flip Wilson a disgrace to the black race."

Wendy reached to her shoulder, about to speak, but the older woman called a halt with a flattened palm.

"Billy was one funny dude. He kept us tied up in stitches. My lily-white half-brother could do this perfect imitation of Flip Wilson, every routine." She smiled to herself. "*Summers wid da Judge*. He played it at comedy clubs all over the Bay Area, everything but actually doing blackface—his way of keeping those happy memories alive. Staying close, I suspect, to me even as we never talked about the obvious."

They sat in silence for a minute, watching the shadow play of the great pines, the ruddy oaks holding out before contributing to the muddy morgue at their feet.

"Does the Judge know about you and your husband?"

"My ex? Who knows what the Judge knows—he be Mr. Omniscience incarnate. Or what Felicity got out of someone. As Mother Alice says, that man always keeps his cards so close to his chest that he can check his heartbeat to the second. As a child, I felt like he saw right through me, more of me than I cared to know about myself."

"In his memoir, he doesn't let on about your father, but he knows." Wendy paused as if she might have stepped over some line and shrugged. "Nothing that can't be adjusted."

"You can be one pushy little bitch—know it! Just whose world exactly you fixin' to adjust? Sorry, but your necromancy and artistic license don't give you carte blanche to mess with everybody's life. Especially here, Hermitage. Not that there ever seemed to be any secrets . . . for long."

Wendy stared off, chastened. "Any man—wait till he sees the paintings—would be crazy to ditch you."

"Like I told you, I ditched him."

Cecily turned to Wendy and gave a playful yank to the remnants of a French braid she'd given up on that morning.

"Listen, girl, my life's my own damn fault." She shook her head, gesturing to the overgrowth nearest the boathouse. "And in July and August, those blueberry bushes are so full, you'll want to mate with them. We had to shoo the squirrels and waxwings away. Karen and I would be sent down to pick for Felicity. Never the boys—never the boys."

"Did you . . . just fall out of love?"

"Louis—hell, I thought I was madly in love, but maybe I was just in love with the perfect solution. A professor at Stanford medical school, both a surgeon and a leading geneticist in the field—what's not to love?" She chucked her chin. "Louis's doing the most cutting-edge stuff in what they call 'precision health,' catching stuff before it goes bad. So, we were the perfect showcase couple: I was his good nurse-practitioner wife (I never finished med school) working in the ghetto, a black doctor's wife who looks and acts white, who takes care of *his* people, whom he no longer wants to bother with because he's out saving the world and hanging out on *Oprah*. And it pays better. Black women resent me for having nabbed the ideal brother, and black men think my ex is so fucking smart to have gotten some white-looking pussy without the penalty of actually marrying a white woman, and whites don't know what the fuck to make of me. Just like you."

"I don't care about any of that—just you."

"Listen, sister, I really like you and I'm happy for you and George. You just make damn sure you look out after him the way I used to do in the summers—my main lake boy."

"George is . . . well, hard to read sometimes. Like with everything on his mind—his dad and grandfather and stuff—and on the way up here yesterday in the car he was beating up on himself for failing to provide Nancy with a better answer to her question about life in the universe a few weeks back. Not encouraging enough, as if he'd failed her."

Cecily laughed and slapped her knee.

"That's my George all right, always a worrier. But I like people who are just so damn into their own business that the bullshit rolls off their backs. I actually liked that about Louis, too, at least in the beginning."

"I guess there're all kinds of bullshit."

"Not that you've told me a damn thing about your folks, except as close as I can figure it, you had a great mom and dad you can at least hold close forever."

"I'm sorry"—Wendy shook her head with sudden vehemence—"I'd take even Alice on a bad day over my mother."

"Well, as they say, be careful what you wish for, 'cause once she gets her hands on your and George's situation—the full treatment—you may care to revise such a stupid remark."

"And yet you came back."

"Why do you think I've been hanging out in your apartment? She's one complicated bitch. I don't even know where to start. She's this righteous angel in the cause of social justice; she's the wicked witch of the judicial system with charisma to burn, and yet she's so full of nameless demons that she even scares the shit out of her admirers. That, and she had no time for Billy—Stan, neither."

"Really? He seems like an okay guy."

Cecily smiled and gave the ailing French braid another shake.

"Poor Stan, talented Stan, blacklisted Stan—blacklisted, don't you love it." She nodded in disbelief to herself. "Really a perfect father, a loving father, a good man, until I smelled a rat. Until it was pointed out to me one fine day in junior high that my skin color was just a bit mocha and my hair a tad nappy. And then people began looking at me a little strange, not hostile, actually, but with a note of respect and even admiration. The black brothers and sisters treated me like an exotic pet, cool but maybe dangerous, since I was always top in my class. And then there was Mother Alice's old Bay Area crowd, who'd blow through town, spend a night—fugitives, most likely, with haunted eyes and twitchy cheeks. They used to stare at me wide-eyed and caress my head and say the nicest things, like they were a little in awe, like I was some fairy princess with secret powers. When I finally got clued in that something wasn't quite on the up-and-up, and went to mother hen, she tried to brush it aside, like I was seeing ghosts, but it was ghosts all the way down. One day when I just wouldn't quit bothering her, she took me into her office and pulled down a book from her special shelf of authors and friends—the usual suspects: Saul Alinsky, Huey Newton, Bobby Seale—a book of poems and letters: *Soledad Brother: The Prison Letters of George Jackson.*

"She handed me Jackson's book and told me to read it; led me to the door of her office and closed it behind me. I took it to my bedroom and lay down and stared at the photo on the cover of a beautiful black man with an unkempt Afro, toothy smile, and long nose, almost angelic with his heavy-lidded eyes beneath the elegant curve of his eyebrows. The letters were filled with rage and bitterness about the plight of the black man—this was the sixties, you understand—especially black prisoners, and how America and the system oppressed all blacks, and how there was going to be an uprising, a black prisoner revolt that was going to sweep the nation. How the brothers would start a revolution to overthrow the government along the lines of Castro's Cuba. I'd never encountered such rage in the pages of a book. I was maybe thirteen by then, and we'd left the Bay Area years before, when I was a little kid—only a vague, somehow scary memory for me. The world of anger and hatred in the book was nothing like the world of New Paltz and the rural university community where we were living after we left California. Blacks were kinda cool, a special breed apart, respected for their authenticity. The black athletes in high school, and especially those on the NYU campus, were kings; they got all the white pussy they wanted.

"I kept the book under my pillow, staring at the photo of George Jackson—dreaming about him, reading and rereading his words, trying to imagine him, to feel him—the thrill of his presence underneath my pillow. I wasn't a compete fool. I knew my mother was testing me, like she always challenged us by trying to shock, by confronting us with the evils of America, making you viscerally react. Like you were in the witness box and she wanted to see what you were really made of. Of course, I was secretly thrilled, to think I might be the daughter of such a powerful man, a black hero, a prison poet—so much cooler than Stan, with his one Academy-nominated film. But some of the pieces didn't fit. Like where I was conceived. Like why we moved from Berkeley—in such a big hurry. George Jackson had been in jail since 1961, and he died in a prison yard shoot-out ten years later.

"When I finally confronted her, marched into her study with the book clutched against my chest, she just looked up from her typewriter, got up, took the book from my hand, and eyed me closely 'Do we reshelf the book, or not?' she asked. I couldn't get a word in. She went on, telling me in so many words, 'All I need to know from you is this: Do you really want to be his daughter or not? Life will never be the same for you.' She handed the book back to me. 'So, you can either go put that book back on the shelf and go do your homework or you can join the fight.' Instead, I handed her the book and the next day went to the library—this was pre-Google—and hunted through the periodical index until I managed to dig up most of the story on George Jackson. Turns out Alice had been his lawyer, working to spring him from jail on appeal of his robbery conviction. I also found out she'd been Huey

Newton's defense lawyer—and his lover, and had gotten him off from a murder-one charge. She'd been famous in that radical world of the sixties in Berkeley. But the violence—the crazy violence: It just left me trembling. In 1970, George Jackson's seventeen-year-old brother, Jonathan Jackson, in a mad attempt to get his brother released, had stormed a Marin County courtroom, pulled out a shotgun, kidnapping the judge and some jurors, and tried to escape along with three prisoners on trial. The attempted kidnapping ended up with Jackson and the judge dead, along with two of the prisoners in a shoot-out with police. This precipitated another surge of horrific violence at Soledad, where George Jackson was a prisoner.

"For months, I lived in agony with those awful images bottled up inside me and just avoiding my mother, barely talking. I couldn't sleep, much less collect my thoughts. I couldn't go to Stan; I felt I was betraying him. My schoolwork started to slip. I found myself crying all the time, slipping between anger and depression. Even when Stan figured out what was going on, he wouldn't get involved, telling me it was between me and my mother. My once-loving father became cold and distant, as if I'd done something unforgivable—crossed that invisible line. George Jackson, if he was my father, had been a cold-blooded murderer. He'd bragged of killing a dozen men in prison even before those he slaughtered like pigs on the day he died. At the dinner table, I'd watch Mother Alice, trying to detect what she was thinking, what she'd felt for this man on the cover of the book with those half-lidded eyes, whose words formed some part of me, but without the anger and injustice that had prompted them. Just stirring, sometimes beautiful words: a way of being. I couldn't even talk to Billy—now a stranger, a half-brother—about it. If anything, he was envious of my mysterious father. Finally, I marched into her office, and she just got up from her desk, walked over and locked the door, and sat me down like a lawyer with a client.

"'So, what's your decision? Do you want George Jackson to be your father or not? It's your choice—that is your right, to go with the flow or infiltrate the system and take the power from the inside—power is all that matters. I'll refile the birth certificate.'

"'I thought you told me I had no fucking right, no choice.'

"'Of course you have a choice. And it's your right to keep Stan's name, or my name, or change it to Jackson, or do whatever the hell you please. But if you do choose Jackson, you'll never be able to return to the gorgeous little princess you once were. Not in this fucked-up country.'

"That's how she went on, eyes blazing, examining every pore in my face as if to determine whether I was really hers or some changeling. I realized in that moment that whatever she'd felt for George Jackson was something off the chart, nothing gentle or nostalgic, but radio-active, lightning in the night, like a cattle prod on your clit, a fixation rooted so deep, she couldn't even give it a name. As she went on, her face became bathed in something like orgasmic sweat. I only wanted to head for the hills."

Cecily kicked out at the surface of the lake, obliterating their reflections.

"I told her the obvious thing: He couldn't be my father because he'd been in jail when I was born. She just smiled at me, like I wasn't tough or canny enough to be Jackson's child, and waved me away.

"'Oh,' she said, 'back in those days, anything was possible, if you wanted it bad enough.'

"And so we left it like that, for years, until I was an undergraduate at Stanford. I did some snooping around, located people who'd known her in the Bay Area, talked to people at her old law firm, even a retired guard at San Quentin. Somehow, someway, during visiting hours, as his lawyer, she'd managed to fuck George Jackson in the visiting room of the penitentiary. In fact, they'd been caught in the act, and the guards had dragged her out of the visiting area with her long skirt bunched up and her panties hanging off one ankle. This gross infraction resulted in her being banned for eight months from visiting her client. Everyone said she was devastated, beside herself with indignation, like a caged animal. One of her colleagues had to take over George Jackson's case. In 1969, Jackson was transferred from San Quentin to Soledad. And in August 1971, Jackson met with his lawyer; minutes after the lawyer left, George Jackson, now back in his cell, miraculously produced a gun out of an Afro wig he'd been wearing and took his guards hostage. The confrontation ended with three guards and two white prisoners dead, drowned in their own blood, their throats cut with a razor embedded in the handle of a toothbrush. George Jackson then rushed out into the prison yard, pistol blazing. They had sharpshooters stationed in the guard towers: one bullet shattered his shin, the second hit his fourth rib and ricocheted upward, going into his jaw and blowing off the top of his head."

Cecily closed her eyes and gripped the edge of the dock, swaying back and forth.

"When I was in my first year of med school, in anatomy class, I couldn't help reenacting that forensics report in my head and the mess that bullet had made to the smiling face on the cover of his book of prison letters. When I worked in ERs, every time they brought in a black gunshot victim, I thought about George Jackson. It got me more and more depressed . . . and that's when Louis came along, smiling Louis—my doctor, who picked up the pieces and shoved the square pegs into perfectly round holes."

Cecily fell silent and tapped her foot on the surface of the lake, sending ripples fleeing for cover. Wendy reached for her hand.

"You should tell the Judge *your* story; in fact, it should go in his memoir. In a strange way, it connects to his past, to his father, Dr. Dimock, who treated the wounded in the Civil War, to Oliver Wendell Holmes, and to your other great-grandfather, who died at Antietam to free the slaves."

"Little girl, you're a piece of work. Let me tell you something: Among Mother Alice's old crowd, I'm somebody's ghost: the love child of some black activist, or maybe, just maybe, the love child of the great martyr himself. I'm part of her mysterious karma, her black power past, her legendary Black Panther lovers. Not that it didn't almost get her killed. There were some among the radical brothers who thought she'd betrayed George Jackson all those years before, that it had been her idea to sneak in the gun that would get him killed. They wanted revenge for his murder. The Panthers sent a killer after her to settle up. The day after she got wind of that shit, she and Stan, Billy, and yours truly were on a plane to New York."

"The Judge alludes to those years in his memoir—not so much about you as about how Alice's carrying-on screwed up his chances of a Supreme Court nomination."

"Oh my God—so that's it, why she's so on the warpath."

"Actually, I think it's got more to do with the Alger Hiss trial. She doesn't want him to escape the onus of having failed to defend an innocent man, or, for that matter, escape by ending up on the right side of history after all, given that we now know Hiss was guilty."

"She's used to being the queen bee, top dog—she pulls Stan's leash and he comes to heel. Her own legacy is her be-all and end-all."

Cecily went silent, her gaze going past her phantom lover for a moment . . . the distant shore, the tiny wooded island off to the south where the cousins camped out, where midnight rendezvous were things of salacious legend. A huge moss-green-backed shadow passed between their reflections and the leaf-entombed bottom.

"Ugh," muttered Wendy.

Cecily collapsed back onto the dock and spread her arms and closed her eyes for a minute, barely seeming to breathe, and then, slowly opening her eyes again, she gazed upward, as if to regain something of the interrupted peace of minutes before.

"You still here, or am I just dreaming?"

"Just dreaming."

"I always thought the fire was just his excuse to get rid of the ugly duckling, the cowbird in his nest."

"Just last night he was bragging about your piano playing—how you were the only one among his grandchildren who had the 'spark.' On your way to being a doctor, like his father."

Cecily laughed. "I just figured if I married a black doctor it might get me closer to the thing. I thought working in an inner-city clinic might get me closer to it. But to be honest, I'm not sure what that thing is. You can't save the world; you can't even save your people if you can't save yourself; and you can't save yourself if you're always full of anger and longing for what doesn't really exist."

Cecily sat up, and Wendy leaned her head into Cecily's shoulder.

"Just like George," said Wendy, taking her hand. "You both abstract things; that's why he's never sure what's real and what's not."

"Your George is a deep dude, same as when he was a little boy—when he was my little lake boy. He'd come down here lugging his big fat fancy telescope—Judge bought it for him on his eighth birthday—and set it up on the edge of the dock so he could stay up all night looking at the stars. We'd find him here in the morning, curled up in his sleeping bag, cutest thing you ever did see. I think you're good for him. At least you put some serious muscle on him—*hmm, looking good.*"

"He's running scared, like all of us. I think nine-eleven really freaked him out."

"Yeah, Cordelia was telling me about that on the way up. She loves you, by the way, thinks you put some backbone in our stargazer."

"I'm trying to be strong for him—but what do I know; I'm just a kid pretending . . . to him . . . to you."

"You—I've never seen—talk about muscle—on a girl, or chutzpah, for that matter, among other things. You, the conqueror of Everest."

"I keep climbing so as not to go crazy, to stay outside of my head. And I need to stay in touch with the climbing community. It's a very exclusive and small group, the really best ones."

Cecily put an arm around Wendy and drew her tight.

"I hear you."

"So many in my parents' generation are dead. Accidents, falls, two lost climbing Everest the same summer I was on the mountain. But over time, hanging out, I picked up bits and pieces of climbing scuttlebutt about my parents, about my mother. She was fearless, reckless; she wanted to be the best woman climber in the world. She was competitive with my father, who had all the physical gifts and nerves of steel but kept his day job as a geologist and oil industry executive. He loved the outdoors and respected the danger—which he passed on to me as a kid. She always had something to prove. I was told they complemented each other. He liked her ambition, indulged it but also kept her in check, most of the time. I remember overhearing one guy say, 'It turned him on in the sack—both of them.' They pushed each other; it was part of the charge, the attraction. But my mother could be careless, and that drove my father nuts. He'd lecture her about safety protocols and she'd go off in a huff. People told me, 'She always wanted to lead, to be the rope gun.' She was charismatic. So was he, but much more low-key. She thought she lived a charmed life. As a girl, she was a champion horsewoman, Olympic-caliber; she'd be thrown on a jump and never so much as suffer a bruise. Indestructible. One woman climber in their circle told me what she always used to say to her girlfriends, 'Men are like horses: To ride them, you have to dominate them.' I heard more than once that nobody else would climb with her. He made it possible for her—financially and otherwise—to do her thing: records, first-woman ascents—the brass rings of the fraternity."

"How old was she?"

"Thirty-four—and getting older."

"And she had you, in the bag."

"He wanted more. But she didn't want to waste the year and some it would take for another pregnancy."

"Oh, don't tell me that—not that . . . the race with time and mortality."

"With herself." Wendy lifted her face to Cecily's. "They were descending from a difficult climb. Downclimbing is always harder, more dangerous than ascending. You're tired, your adrenaline is low, and it's anticlimactic, especially if your ascent was unsuccessful. They had given up on the summit because of bad weather coming in. She had wanted to go on, but he vetoed her. She was pissed. It was a steep step and their thirty-meter rope was just long enough to get them down to where their belay was set under an overhang. The plan was that my mother would rap down on the single strand, putting in a couple of pieces at a traverse, and then my father would follow. He had pointed out that the rope, eight point five millimeters, was slippery in her Reverso. When he later explained this on his satellite phone, he noted that he had suggested putting a knot in the end of the rope, but she had shrugged it off and gone ahead. He said she rappelled to the traverse, then disappeared out of sight. A few minutes later, he heard a scream and the sound of falling and a thud. That's when he got on the satellite phone and reported in. He was nervous, exhausted, distraught. She had the whole rack, most of their rope, so it wasn't easy for him to rappel down safely. He had to downclimb, and it was tough and slow, cold and draining. The light was fading. At the point where her rope would have ended, he found a marginal nut. He then downclimbed to the top of the step, then made a thirty-meter rappel to reach a shallow gully. There he found an impact mark near a tongue of rock at the bottom of the step. It was getting dark. He phoned in his progress, estimating that she'd fallen thirty meters down a rock fall of sixty to seventy degrees to the step, then flipped and gone over the side of the cliff another thirty-five meters of free fall, then he figured about three hundred meters tumbling down into the gully. They told him to stay put, to bed down for the night, and that they'd send a rescue team to him at first light. But he refused; he said she might still be alive and he was going to get her. That was his last communication. The next morning, they found his body a hundred feet from hers. It hadn't been a particularly difficult descent, but he'd been exhausted and overwrought and it was dark. He'd simply slipped."

Cecily put a hand on her shoulder and then pulled her into an embrace.

"And me going on about all my pointless bullshit."

"All for lack of a knot, for a knot that even some of the most experienced climbers prefer to dispense with because it catches in crevices and has to be untied and tied again—time-consuming. And she hated waiting for anything. Even at the checkout in Walmart, she'd send me ahead to get in line so she wouldn't have to wait."

"So, you've been gathering stories."

"For years, I watched their faces, some of the greatest climbers of their generation, seeing the awe and admiration in their eyes, the boner they still had for this larger-than-life Amazon, who could drink men under the table, even as they secretly saw her as the killer of their beloved buddy. Her competitiveness and carelessness and his dogged loyalty killed them. His faith that his love for her would get her through—although he never allowed her to take me climbing. And I feel her spirit in me every day and don't know where to hide: whether to love her or hate her—for taking away the father I adored. And that in-betweenness is the worst thing: It leaves me feeling lost, with the tank half-empty. I guess my work, my painting is a way of trying to keep her spirit alive, or keep her safe, or where she can do the least harm . . . somewhere beyond time."

They had been staring down at their reflections in the lake, their shadows on the murky bottom, when a cry pierced the silence and their faces rose to the distant island, where, in the blue sky above, two bald eagles with talons locked were cartwheeling through space.

52
Third Man

Those were among the most enjoyable and rewarding hours I have ever spent. His responsiveness was often more enriching than whatever text was at hand. I learned as much, if not more, from him about history, government, and literature than from most of the professors who taught me. But I have learned more from him as a human being. Pain and disappointment never seemed to dominate his life. Rather, what I saw was excitement about a new book, passion about the events of the day, and pleasure—easily and warmly expressed—in friendship. The fineness of his daily contacts is what conveyed his breadth, depth, and reach.

—comment by one of Alger Hiss's readers
when he was in his nineties and
suffering from macular degeneration

MARTHA MOTIONED FROM the backseat of the Saab. "I still don't see why you couldn't have talked Max into coming—it's Thanksgiving, for heaven's sake."

"Well, he sure loved Ouest last year," said Karen, jutting her delicate jaw forward where her hands gripped the steering wheel. "Maybe we shoulda just stuck with that."

"The turkey was a bit dry," her mother reminded her, gazing out the window at the glitter of sunlight on the Hudson. "Even Theodore could have done better, but we know how much your father reveres Thanksgiving."

Theo looked up from the *New York Times* in the shotgun seat—"I'm not into Turkey Day, as the kids say; the Pilgrims were an intolerant, self-satisfied bunch of religious zealots."

"You never talk to him, Dad," complained Karen, impatient with the backup on the West Side Highway. "If you had encouraged him a little, maybe he would have come, instead of hanging out with his zaftig girl-friend's family *all* Thanksgiving."

"Jennifer, she's nice," said Nancy from the backseat, not looking up from her phone. "She has the coolest Gucci backpack."

"At fourteen—his girlfriend?" said Martha, patting back her unruly head of brown hair, gray at the roots. "You're leaving them together at her place to shack up all weekend?" She shrugged. "Better, I suppose, than his being with his skirt-chasing father."

"They hand out—for the asking—condoms from the school nurse." Karen looked from the mirror and turned abruptly into the left lane. "Besides, she relaxes him; Max isn't so anxious when he's around her. When he isn't around his father."

"Why so anxious?"

"Christ, Mom, you've been shrinking Upper West Siders for forty years—those Karloff twins in his class, father—you know . . ." She gestured to the southbound lane.

"Oh, that . . ." Martha, squinting, turned to the window as if she'd missed something, her eyes lingering on a fuel barge headed to tidewater on the Hudson. "Our generation was so much simpler; we just wanted to get in touch with ourselves, our real selves, to feel better about ourselves."

"Mom, I hate to tell you: Nobody cares about their goddamn real selves anymore, much less our unconscious drives . . . just so they're not around when the next attack hits or a dirty bomb goes off in the city." Karen abruptly switched lanes again, to an angry honk from a huge black Mercedes sedan behind. "The only self that matters now," she said, glancing in the rearview mirror and slapping her left blinker, "is your one and only—ugh, or at least the one that can best survive the competition."

"Take it easy, sis," scolded Erich from the back.

"You think it was a bed of roses—for women? We fought like hell for women's rights—maybe not like Alice, but we fought. That's why I always worked on coping mechanisms with my patients. It worked pretty well with you—you never seemed to have any problems with self-esteem."

"What fucking self-esteem?"

"Hey," said Erich, "pipe down, Karen, and concentrate on the driving."

"You sure Alice's going to even turn up?" asked Theodore.

"She called this morning, enlisting me."

"For what?"

"To get George to cough up the Judge's memoir before he white-washes the record."

"Pray tell, how's he going to manage—what record?—such a thing?"

"Search me, but she's got it in her head that with all this business about Alger Hiss being proved a spy, the Judge is going to try to weasel out of his part in the whole fiasco. Much less his infidelities and other unmentionable crimes."

This produced a hiatus of embarrassed fretful silence.

"Who's Alger Hiss?" asked Nancy, looking up for a moment and then going back to her phone.

"The person I feel sorry for is poor Priscilla and her son, Tony, what they had to go through. I feel awful I could never help her."

"Do you suppose there's something to this Hiss *really* being guilty business?" asked Theo, glancing in the side mirror and pressing back a wisp of white hair.

"Sssh," said Martha in a stage whisper, a finger to her lips, "we're still in the neighborhood. Alice says George is in cahoots with Allen Weinstein—you know, the man who wrote the famous book about the trial. Well, now she's read his latest book, too."

"Oh that, yes. I never did like Hiss much, a little too self-satisfied and smug, above it all. Wasn't he right there at Yalta with FDR when those big shots gave Poland away to Stalin's killers?"

"You never told me you felt that way."

"You never asked about your hero. Seems to me you once praised him for teaching other inmates in prison to read and such like."

"Hardly my hero. I'm the one who's always criticized Daddy about using psychiatrists, much less Freud, to go after Chambers. And I blame Alger for Priscilla. A few years after he got out of prison, he dumped her for another woman, a big fan who just fawned all over him, telling him everything he wanted to hear. Married her after Priscilla died. Poor Priscilla, she never got over it: the accusations, the trial, the prison, then the separation, when she couldn't keep playing the martyr's wife. Worse, she was racked by anxiety and guilt about the effect of the disaster on her son Tony."

"Mom," said Karen, "should you be telling us this stuff?"

"Oh my dear, they're both long gone now. I only wish I could have helped her more."

"Quite a trick that Hiss managed," said Theo, "enlisting the ruling class to defend him, in effect, defending their sworn enemies, the ravagers of the wealthy and the bourgeoisie." He nodded to himself. "Now there's an idea for an interesting article: 'The Social and Symbiotic Dynamic When the Establishment and the Champions of the Proletariat Join Ranks in a Common Cause.' Catchy, don't you think, Erich? Maybe you should get your nose out of the sixteenth century for something more modern—a hot topic for a journal article."

"How can it possibly matter?" Erich, now sporting a new goatee, shrugged. "Talk about ancient history. Hardly my field."

"Speaking of which," continued Theo, "how's that Ph.D. dissertation of yours—what was it, sixteenth-century Sicilian wheat trade?"

"Venetian high-end luxury trade in the thirteenth century. And teaching fourth graders American history all week leaves me with zero time and energy. But I've applied for a research grant to work in the Venice archives year after next."

"So there you go," said Martha reaching forward to tap Theo's shoulder. "Now that George is out of the running."

"Maybe," said Karen, eyeing her mother, brother, and niece in the backseat in the rearview mirror, "I should have mentioned to Max about the D & H Canal and the Neversink aqueduct; he's kinda interested in history and engineering stuff."

"Yeah," echoed Erich to his daughter, "maybe we can hike down to the Roebling aqueduct on the Neversink, Nance, same guy who built the Brooklyn Bridge. Pretty cool stuff, huh, Karen?"

"Ah, the famous Dr. Dimock," noted Theo, "famed for bringing all those million-dollar babies into the world. Talk about the filthy rich, all those Astors, Vanderbilts, Rockefellers, and baby Goulds."

"Hah, I got a Rockefeller grant to study childhood trauma in Poland—where I met you, Theo, my love."

"Hey, Nance, your great-great-grandfather founded Memorial Hospital and the American Cancer Society."

"Poor Priscilla," continued Martha, shaking her head at her vague reflection in the window, "she told me that during the trials they had to hide poor little Tony away, for fear he'd be overwhelmed by all the hatred and publicity. First they sent him to their summer home in Vermont, and then during the second trial, Daddy's trial, they had him hidden away in the apartment of some wealthy family on Fifth Avenue. She felt terrible about it—imagine having your father tried for treason when you're eight or nine and only being able to read about it in the papers, feeling helpless to defend him. Priscilla said he had nightmares and terrible feelings of abandonment and disloyalty. She was beside herself, kept blaming herself. She was always bemoaning the situation when talking to me: 'How did we come to this, from Alger hobnobbing it with Roosevelt and Truman?'"

"I don't get it," said Karen. "Seems to me, once upon a time, we were supposed to be proud of the Judge for trying to save Alger Hiss. I remember in third grade at Dalton parents coming up to me, people I didn't know, and embracing me, thanking me for my grandfather's noble defense of Alger Hiss."

"Actually," said Erich, "my memory is that you, Mom, and Aunt Alice always blamed the Judge for failing to get a not-guilty verdict. Or maybe that's what the Judge used to tell us around the dinner table at Hermitage—'Still in the doghouse, you see, for Mr. Hiss'—when you guys never showed up in the summers."

For a moment, silence reigned as Martha seemed to ponder this echo of her father's voice in her son's. Then a look of bewilderment came over her face as this conundrum rankled. Finally, turning to Theo, she said, "Which is it, Theo—font of all wisdom?"

"Seems to me your old man—*now*—loses every which way: damned if he did, damned if he didn't. As long as he did his job. In my book, if Hiss sold out Poland, they should have put him behind bars and thrown away the key. Those fucking Reds shot my brother at Katyn."

"Theo, really, for God's sake, don't ever say something like that around our friends, or my patients—what's left of them. You'll get us lynched."

"And whatever your crazy sister is up to, I can guarantee it's about *her*—whatever's in the old man's memoir—probably about Cecily. She ever tell you who the father was?"

"We don't talk about it."

"God knows what he's got about *you* in there."

A hint of alarm sparked in his wife's eyes.

"It was always Cecily's delicious secret," said Karen. "But I'm not sure she even knew, at least not when we were kids."

Erich smiled. "She once told me her real dad was Jimi Hendrix."

"She told every guy who ever came on to her a different name," said his sister, rocking her head in a jazzy riff.

Nancy looked up from her phone. "Why does my great-grandfather live up in the woods all by himself? Max thinks it's pretty creepy."

"You're not scared, are you, Nancy?" asked Martha, a tad distracted. Her granddaughter was seated between her and her father in the backseat. Nancy was texting.

"Of course she's not," said Erich. "Bin Laden doesn't even know where Hermitage is."

Nancy gave her dad a goofy look at the stupid joke. "All my friends got brand-new cell phones last year."

Erich patted her knee. "Yours works fine. Think of it as a kind of sleep-away camp, except without all the other kids—well, maybe those who come up for Thanksgiving with their folks. And it's a big old house by the lake where your great-grandfather hangs out. It's pretty spectacular, actually."

"Is Mom going to be there?"

"We actually invited Mom, but she politely declined; she's in San Francisco with your other grandmother."

"So why haven't I met him before? He just sends Christmas presents and birthday cards with checks."

"He's a busy man."

"Well, maybe if I had a boyfriend, I could sleep over, too, like Max."

"Plenty of time for boyfriends," said Erich. "Besides, this is Thanksgiving, when families have a chance to get together. Your great-grandpa, once upon a time, was an important man—a famous judge."

She looked from face to face, as if half aware of the earlier conversation. "Did he do something wrong?"

Karen smiled lasciviously and shimmied her shoulders, barely resisting making a wisecrack.

"Theo," said Martha, catching her daughter's vibe and quickly returning to a previous subject, "you have no idea how torturous it was for Priscilla and her son to have her husband in jail for four years, to see him once a month for a few hours, for her son to grow up under such a preposterous situation where half the country and all their many friends thought Alger was a hero and the other half thought he was a traitor. What was the boy supposed to think—that his father was two different people, that there were two different worlds? And always wondering which one was the real one—which of his memories were real. Imagine trying to grow into maturity living with such a . . . such a crazy house of mirrors."

"But surely," protested Theo, "if she knew the truth, she could've just told the kid and put him out of his misery."

"Typical. How cruel of you. How could she? With half the country and all their friends revering her paragon of a husband."

"And never to you?" asked Karen. "I mean, the whole basis of a doctor-patient relationship is one of getting to the truth. An adult client lies to me and they're out the door."

"Whatever the case, she was locked into their reality, and it tore her apart because after he got out of prison she'd couldn't keep playing the dutiful role of noble wife any longer. She wanted them to go hide in some little town and teach high school kids. But for Alger, loyalty was everything."

"Or else," cried Theo, raising a fist. "I don't have to tell you—or have you forgotten—what it was like in the fifties in Poland, my dear. You saved my bacon by marrying your brilliant professor."

"Blueberry pancakes and bacon every Sunday for breakfast!" exclaimed Erich. "Remember, sis—Felicity's breakfasts? We picked blueberries by the boathouse."

"I found my thrill . . ." crooned Karen.

"How come I've never picked blueberries?" asked Nancy.

"On Blueberry Hill . . ."

Martha suddenly brought her hand to her mouth as if to stifle a cry. "The Zabar's bag of cocktail goodies."

"I packed it in the trunk," said Theo, engrossed again in his paper.

"So if Great-grandpa is ninety-five," said Nancy, "it must be a pretty healthy life up there in the woods, right?"

"He eats lots of blueberries," said Erich with a smile. "Remember, Karen, tramping through the blueberry patch, getting eaten alive by mosquitoes?"

"Vows you made . . ."

"Enough, sis, already."

"Since when?" said Karen. "You and Billy barely ever picked. Felicity always sent me and Cecily—and space boy, little Georgie—down to the boathouse to pick from the canoe. She always said the sweetest berries came from the bushes that dipped their toes in the lake."

"Billy boy—how I'm gonna miss him." Erich sighed. "I never laughed so much in my life. He had a thing for you, too."

"You think? . . ." And Karen waved it off with a half-smile. "Aunt Cordelia says there are bears now."

"Bears?" said Nancy. "*Blueberries for Sal* . . . Great-grandpa sent me that book for my birthday once."

"Really?" asked Erich. "Did I know that?"

"He was a good father, you see," said Martha in a dreamy voice. "Wrote to Priscilla and his son three times a week. And yes, helped his fellow prisoners learn to read. But of course Priscilla had to get a job, something with Doubleday, working downstairs in the basement in the packing department—out of sight. And so their son was a latchkey kid, coming home to an empty house after Dalton. The child was frightened, lonely."

Nancy looked up. "Where am I going to stay?"

Everyone looked around inquiringly.

Coming to, Martha replied, "Felicity is putting Nancy in Cuddebackville."

"George's old room?" said Erich.

"Cuddebackville?" asked Nancy.

"Lucky you," said Erich, giving her knee an excited squeeze. "It's full of cool books and fishing gear and stuff."

"Teddy's old room," said Martha, eyes blinking, as if trying to focus on something as the Hudson inched by. "It's a wonderful room, dear. Felicity had to get a whole crew in to change the rooms around—fumigate the place most likely . . . *boys*."

"Where's Luke Skywalker going?" asked Erich.

"And his jailbait Wonder Woman," added Karen with a dismissive toss of her head.

Nancy looked up, noting her aunt's tone. "Wendy, she's so incredibly cool. She promised to give me climbing lessons at Chelsea Piers."

"No way," said Erich.

"Oh, it's perfectly safe," said Karen. "You were always such a scaredy-cat, Erich. You never wanted to swim because of the snappers."

"Remember when crazy Billy put a snapper in the Judge's Mercedes coupe and it ate the leather out of the seat?"

"Snappers?" asked Nancy.

"Think ninja turtles," said Karen, cracking a smile. "Billy, oh Billy . . ." she sang out, distracted. "Remember how Billy boy used to stash his drugs in that old one-man shell in the boathouse?"

"Teddy's!" exclaimed Martha, as if thoroughly disconcerted, distracted by the glitter off the river, or perhaps some aqueous epiphany that was only now coming into view, her eyes tearing up. "Oh dear, my poor Teddy. And that's what did it, you know: For some reason, he absolutely believed that man Chambers, no matter how much I tried to explain his pathological lying."

"There, you just contradicted yourself," said Theo with a hint of triumphant sarcasm.

"Chambers?" asked Nancy.

"You see, I remember Priscilla like it was yesterday, lying back on my couch, her face drawn, eyes sunken with worry, voice a faint tremor. She told me a story of when she and their son would visit Lewisburg prison once a month to visit Alger. They used to stay overnight at the Lewisburg Inn. And on one of those visits her son Tony had somehow gotten hold of these back issues of the *Saturday Evening Post*. Well, the *Post* was serializing Chambers's book. And unbeknownst to her, Tony began reading the stories about his father being a spy from the pen of Whittaker Chambers. Now you see, the time about which Chambers wrote was the thirties, before Tony was even born. But here's the thing—the devastating thing that drove her son—and Priscilla—nearly crazy: Half of what Chambers wrote was absolutely spot-on about his father—the spitting image of the Alger they knew; and then suddenly, in a split second, another Alger would appear on the page, saying and doing things that Tony knew to be absolutely nothing like his father. And yet, here were these two identical figures in black and white: the man he knew and this imposter sometimes inhabiting the same sentence—with millions of readers reading about this fraudulent interloper! 'Well,' cried Priscilla, looking at me with those haunted eyes, 'what was I supposed to do? What could I say? How to explain this monster who savaged Roosevelt and his physical condition, who described the president as a symbol of the middle-class breakdown? Stalin playing for keeps? I was beside myself. What was my little Tony to make of this creature of Chambers's warped mind, who now lives so vividly in the minds of millions? My confused little boy finally settled on thinking of this other Alger as a kind of fantasy, a third Alger to go along with the public Alger and the family Alger. Like the Third Man, I suppose, a phantom figure living in the shadows, invisible, skulking like some sinister Orson Welles fugitive, whom both Tony and I are fated to meet each and every day we walk down the street in the eyes of complete strangers.'"

This outburst, this vivid wail of hurt and protest out of the past, seemed to exhaust Martha, and she slumped against the window. The others were silent, not quite sure what to make of this dead woman's voice in that of their mother, wife, and grandmother.

A 767 heading for La Guardia passed low upriver, dipping its wings and revving its engines as it made a sharp right turn. All faces in the car swiveled skyward, flinching, heads shaking.

Karen pounded the wheel impatiently. "It's the Cross Bronx that always jams things up."

Nancy turned to her grandmother. "That's a sad story, Grandma."

Theo folded his paper in his lap. "Your grandmother and mother just love to listen to other people's stories, and your dad loves stories out of history, while I love stories about how people interact in groups on large scales. When you think about it, we're all about stories of one kind or another."

"What's my story?" asked Nancy.

"Hey," said Erich brightly to Nancy, "your cousin Cecily is going to be there."

"A goddess on the piano," chimed in Theo with a delighted smile, an appreciative flicker of bushy eyebrows.

"Oh my God, CeCe!" exclaimed Karen, smiling for the first time that day. "I can't wait."

"C. C. Rider," crooned Erich, "*what you have done now?* . . . She was absolutely on fire when we were kids."

"Won all the Judge's stupid prizes," remarked Karen, now with a hint of disdain.

"And all mine," said Erich with a distant smile.

"Have I met her?" asked Nancy.

"Only when you were very little," said Erich.

"Yes, well," said Martha, wiping a tear, "Alice certainly had Annie's spark." She shook her head, casually examining her hands. "That's one genetic marker that's somehow went defunct in this family."

"Nancy practices every day," said her proud father

Nancy looked up from her phone. "But I'd rather be an astrophysicist like cousin George."

"Good idea," said her father. "She's such a math whiz, you know."

"Cousin George promised to take me to the new planetarium before Christmas."

"Hmm," said Martha with a sigh, "I must have forgotten to ask Felicity where they're putting George and the mountaineer. Either that or she told me and I forgot. By the way, that Wendy thought my Agnes Martins were spectacular examples, some of her very best. So, at least I think I helped Agnes."

53
Shooting the Gulf

🖂

To the astronomer, the earth is a moveable observatory,
enabling him to change his place in the universe . . . as
if this planet were a living eye sailing through space to
watch them . . .

—Emerson

ALICE MARCHED INTO the living room, with Stan, hunched over with their bags, bringing up the rear. They found Felicity on her knees, bent to the fireplace as she set up the logs for a fire.

"Where is everybody?" demanded Alice. "Where's his royal highness?"

Dusting her hands, Felicity pulled herself up from the threadbare cushion she'd been kneeling on. Alice gave her an air kiss on the cheek.

"He just went down for his nap. The others have all gone out for a walk around the lake with George. Handytown, if there's enough light left."

"Did Cecily come with Cordelia? I've been trying to call people all afternoon and I get no answer."

"Cell phone service is spotty at best. Cecily arrived early with Cordelia and Jim."

"She brought *Jim* along?" asked Alice, incredulous, eyes rising now to where the ship's keel ceiling had come alive—gold highlights shimmering against a vibrant sea blue—in the afternoon light.

"Older but wiser, perhaps," said Felicity, now further dusting her hands on her gingham apron.

"They're not in the same room, are they?"

Felicity shrugged. "Space problem—I just do what I'm told."

"Little slut," grumped Alice, her gaze still under the spell of the ceiling above. "After all the time I spent on nailing down the property agreement."

"Really," said Stan, flopping into the Judge's armchair and picking up a book on the floor by his feet. "Pipe down." He leaned back. "My God, I'd forgotten how spectacular this ceiling was. Just look at the lush colors and intricate designs—almost cinematic, don't you think, in their diaphanous complexity: scene flowing into scene, story into story. And in this light . . . transporting."

Felicity picked up the cushion and began moving off. "Martha and Theodore arrived about two hours ago with Karen, Erich, and Nancy. We're packed to the rafters." Felicity smiled sympathetically at Alice's distracted face, where the thin autumnal glow from the bay window highlighted her short auburn hair touched with wisps of gray. "That Nancy is a pistol, ran around this place like she was on a scavenger hunt. I never heard so many questions; the poor Judge was exhausted."

"And Cecily?"

"I believe off with Wendy in a canoe to explore the island. Seems those two have become great pals. My, Cecily has bloomed into a handsome woman."

Alice, distracted, said, "Divorced woman—and he is a wonderful doctor . . . The island, huh?"

"I never had the pleasure," said Felicity with wide, knowing eyes. "I'm sure the Judge would have liked to meet him."

Alice scowled and began to wander the great room like a lost soul, staring upward, peaking around rafters at various mythological and astrological figures, as if in search of something, her voice uncertain, subdued.

"Did you tell the Judge about the divorce? Dropping out of med school was bad enough."

"Not a word," said Felicity, a finger to her lips, then turned back, dusting the gong by the entrance to the dining room. "But Wendy did mention something about Cecily applying to NYU med school for the spring."

"Oh," said Alice, with a hopeful smile. "Did you hear that, Stan? She's thinking of NYU for med school. Maybe she'll stick it out this time."

Stan was still gazing up at the ceiling, transfixed. "East Coast, huh," he said with a quick smile. "Well, that'll be the berries."

"So," said Felicity, heading for the kitchen, "Cecily is in Ellenville, just like old times, right next to you and Mr. Stanley in Brown Haven."

"And Billy's old room? Were you able . . ." Her voice faltered, her eyes tearing up.

"Yes," assured Felicity with a sympathetic smile. "Hardly touched anything. A new mattress, some new outdoor gear and equipment and clothes that Wendy provided—boys' stuff, you know. And I had to get rid of the girlie magazines in the top of the closet."

"Oh, so . . ." Alice's narrow face darkened with indecisiveness, then, going over to one of the carved angels by the fireplace, she placed a hand on its upturned brow, where a jagged fissure ran deep, like a martyr's stigmata. Tapping a finger, she lifted her gaze once again to the ceiling, canting her head as if to better make out one of the figures under the glare of the varnish. "Well," she said, looking at Stan, who now had the leather-bound book open in his lap, "boys will be boys."

"For some reason, Karen's Max has been delayed, so for the moment Spring Glen remains unoccupied, if you want have a peek in there," said Felicity.

"No, no bother." She shook her head decisively.

At this demurral, Felicity smiled serenely. "Honey"—she rapped the gong with a knuckle, sending a sweet, sad note reverberating through the great room as the two women's glances met fully, the hushed undertones registering in Alice's milky gray-green eyes with a dull longing—"I've been there. Time heals."

As Felicity headed back for the kitchen Alice began a slow, deliberate inventory of the artifacts of her childhood—the gold-matted daguerreotype of Stephen Crane, photos of the Neversink aqueduct, the Tiffany lamps—her eyes straying again and again upward in a kind of controlled rapture of memory, as if needing to decode anew the figures in the ceiling—her favorites, the associations—with their poignant reminders of girlhood and adolescence. Almost reluctantly, she gravitated to the Steinway grand in the corner with the silver-framed publicity photos of Annie, where a well-used edition of Chopin Etudes lay tellingly open on the music stand.

"What do you think, Stan?" she asked her husband, who now sat absorbed, turning the pages of a book in his lap, reading glasses hanging off the crook of his nose. "If we're right next door, maybe Cecily will think we're cramping her style."

"What style is that, dear?" said Stan. "She didn't seem to mind when she was a kid."

"But we were hardly ever here when she was a kid . . . or Billy, either." She sniffed.

"Are you okay, dear?"

"Of course I am. I mean, we could stay in Graham's Dock, I suppose; the Judge hasn't been there in years."

"Didn't Felicity say something over the phone about George and Wendy being in there, since Nancy's in Cuddebackville? You weren't pleased."

She nodded, having forgotten, gazing tentatively toward the central staircase. "Don't suppose George has got a copy of the memoir here with him?"

"Relax, dear, stop obsessing," said Stan. "This is absolutely the most remarkable book, essays by Ralph Waldo Emerson. And get this, it's inscribed by Emerson to Dr. Holmes, and then from Oliver Wendell Holmes to Edward Dimock. Isn't that something! Imagine, from the hands of Emerson, to Holmes senior—poet and aphorist—to his son, the great justice, and here to your father. The *time*, Alice, just think of it." He waved toward the ship's keel ceiling and then the Whitman quote chiseled into the bluestone mantelpiece. "When giants wrote our literature: Mark Twain and Henry Adams and Henry James, Thoreau, Hawthorne, and Melville."

"I didn't think you cared about such things, old books and ancient authors and the like—much less Proust. Hardly the stuff of your Hollywood milieu."

"Maybe that's been my problem. How did old Ben Hecht put it? 'An outhouse on the Parnassus' . . . I guess something to sink your teeth into." Stan gestured to the tessellated glittering blue. "It's like something I saw once as a teenager in Ravenna: all those crazy stories high on the arches, like a kind of cosmic comic strip. Do you suppose that's where I got the bug?"

"I thought it was the lure of the casting couch—so you always liked to say."

"I feel, I feel, I don't know what I feel exactly, but maybe a little like I've let the important things get by me. Not that I didn't consider myself an educated man. But the business, you know, during the Depression, was all about escaping—politics, too, of course—and not so much about our life and times. Not like Tennessee and Elia, when I lost my best years. What I wouldn't give to have done *Splendor in the Grass*."

"Anyway"—Alice was examining her mother's fingerings in the Chopin score—"I wouldn't be caught dead staying in Graham's Dock, where Annie was so ill."

"Maybe there's something to George's Alger Hiss thing. What a film that would make: *The Greatest Spy Story Never Told*."

"Don't go there." She flipped a page of the score, scowling. "I'm the only one who understands how the Judge's mind works—not just DNA but also the legal training. He's using George, cultivating George to hedge his bets for the long term, for his legacy. Felicity read him the new Allen Weinstein book, pretty much confirming Hiss's guilt. So he doesn't want to be left in the dustbin of history as a bigger incompetent than he already looks. Trust me: It's one thing to defend a guiltless man and fail, another to defend someone as guilty as hell and fail and not even know he was guilty. I always knew the difference. Who's the bigger chump? The one not to have seen through his client's lies and been taken in by the swindle, or, worse, a willing dupe? But he's too good, too respectable, too self-righteous— his stellar self-image—to lie straight out in his memoir; he'll either conveniently forget or misremember and let honest, gullible George fill in the blanks—whatever it takes to make out that he'd had it all figured from the get-go and was really out to put Hiss away the whole time. Either that or he's hiding something—but what? Why else keep little George in that rural slum around Altmann's paintings—pay for his gallerist gig—if not another hedge on his legacy. Another sly move to observe all the legalities and yet put himself on the side of truth and justice. That's how he wants it to come out. Watch him work the angles over this weekend. Jesus, can you believe George just turned over those Altmann sketches of Hiss and his crew to the government."

Stan nodded to where his finger had come to rest on the page. "You should know, angles. And there's still a journal article for you in it."

"For forty years he's been staring over my shoulder."

"Alice, dear, let the young have their day."

"Well, now my daughter has teamed up with your Catwoman. God knows what those two are cooking up—I mean, the island."

"The island?"

"Oh, nothing."

Stan, his thin, debonair face creased with the barest hint of a smirk, raised his right hand in surrender, or a call for silence, reading from the open book in his lap: 'Life only avails, not the having lived. Power ceases in the instant of repose; it resides in the moment of transition from a past to a new state, in the shooting of the gulf, in the darting to an aim.'"

"Oh yes, he read that—along with Conrad—to us as kids, with me, Teddy, and Martha sitting around the fire. It was always such an ordeal of indoctrination."

"Why make such a fuss? They made you what you are—mostly for the best." He blew his wife a kiss. "We must make way for the young— youngbloods, not old fools." Stan waved magisterially to the ceiling, the spare sunlight filling his eyes. "Forget about your old man; he's only one part of you. You go back to all the others. What about that great-grandfather of yours on Annie's side, who died at Antietam, an abolitionist, a poet, a musician—right, baby? The Judge was always wanting you to see his memorial at Harvard, right? Who was that guy?"

"Richard Davenport."

"There you go, Mr. Davenport. Now what would he make of Cecily, do you think? Our beautiful daughter: reconciling the races with such a radiant and talented human being. I know it doesn't make up for dear Billy, but it's something. Let's be proud of her—of both of them."

Alice reached a shaking hand to the keyboard and sounded a note, which rang clear and pure in the blue spaces above.

"See those figures up there, to the right of your left shoulder? Glaucus possessing the sea goddess Scylla, before Circe turned her into a monster. Well, it's one of the more beautifully painted figure ensembles. And the face of Glaucus—blond, blue-eyed, gorgeous cheekbones—a fisherman, a god, with prophetic powers—he is a dead ringer for my brother, Teddy. Everybody in the family said so; it became our little inside joke. Well, the thing went right to Teddy's head. He was already a great fisherman, and a ladies' man. And that image of possession—the naked Glaucus rising up out of the sea to grab the nude Scylla—became Teddy's obsession as a teenager. I mean, not that all the girls around the lake didn't want him anyway— spoiled brat. Well, the island was where we always went to make out at night, our petting park. We'd canoe out there and meet up with some boy or drink or party. But not Teddy; he always swam out stark naked for his assignations, and the poor girl would find herself sitting there under a pine by the grassy shore in the moonlight, and out of the lake would come Teddy, swaggering, maybe with a bottle of wine in his hand—probably hard already, like some satyr—and just plonk himself down beside the aghast girl like it was nothing. Oh, he'd laugh about it—how the girls couldn't keep their eyes off him, how they felt the need to show their stuff, too—he was infamous. The girls would titter about it. But it didn't stop them, didn't stop him—God's gift, our Glaucus. Even after he was killed, so Cordelia used to tell us when she was a kid up here in the summers, women would sometimes just stop by on a walk around the lake, go up and touch the railing of the piazza with a kind of wistful expression on their faces, some with kids in hand. Their lost Glaucus . . ."

"And you and the island?"

"I wasn't in Teddy's league, but I did okay." She gave a half-smile, shrugged, and sounded another note, closing her eyes, lips pursed with emotion.

"Play."

"Annie, when we were kids here in the summer, on Sunday mornings, we could hear her cries from Graham's Dock, sometimes for hours."

"Ah . . ."

"You don't think there's anything going on between Cecily and Catwoman?"

"Don't be ridiculous. She's an artist—artists are artists. Let's go up; I need a nap."

"It doesn't bother you that the Judge—and Teddy was a chip off the old block—messed with her and Karen, and probably Cordelia?"

"Cordelia always laughed off that business. Talk about a chip off the old block: You were the best lover a man could ever have." He rose stiffly from his chair and tried out a lascivious leer on his white-whiskered face. "Come along, old girl."

She shook her head, her eyes filling with tears.

"I can't, I just can't. I'll have to peek into Billy's room and it will unhinge me."

"Come, we'll go together."

54
Unfettered Desires

GEORGE SAT IN the white wicker rocker and pulled off his hiking boots to examine the beginning of a blister on his heel. At the sound of voices—a conversation on the piazza—he got up and looked out the bay window at the lake. There, through the surface glitter, he spied the old green canoe with two women seemingly on the return trip from the island. So that's where they'd gone. They were taking their time, paddles poised, drifting, luxuriating in the lowering sunlight. The woman he longed to love, and the woman on whom he'd had a childhood crush that lingered to this moment, as if the longing and lingering had merged into one. As had time past and present.

Turning from the intoxicating lake glitter to the sibilant white of the bedroom, he found himself overcome by an ardent yearning, as if he'd slipped back into some approximation of a quantum existence: granular, indeterminate, wholly relational, as if those two women could be any two women, and desire ubiquitous, timeless, where everything, *every thing*, every presence existed only in relation to another random act, whether of love or subterfuge, and so precluding past or future—exacting, at best, a shimmering phantom residue, perhaps a fading memory of places, of canoers, of lovers and rooms, of presences forever evading his touch, and so outdistancing his chance at love.

He breathed deeply, laved by these specters of unfettered desires, as if longing to hold on to the luxurious moment when a sunlit room could so deftly share its secrets with the human heart: moldering books, sunstruck photographs, a painted moon under varnish, even the enduring hint of a man's cologne—that invisible yet how real photon-haunted spectrum of other people's habitual lives, lingering like that canoe on the lake, nudging the unknowable to come, while buoyed on an equally indistinct past. Dreamers begetting dreams, the very thing, that childlike indulgence of the here and now that notions of an infinite universe—staring at galaxy clusters millions of light-years away—had so cruelly demolished in his soul. Vast distances, killing distances, distances so glutted with the flickering, faltering, failing, fleeting light of the infinite that only a heartless madman would even try to fathom its extent.

He flopped back into the rocker, closing his eyes for a few moments in dubious retreat from his nagging fears, only to spy upon opening his eyes a discarded pair of blue panties under the bed, which he hastened to retrieve, bunching them to his nose as if to re-anchor himself in the sensuous reality of her sex. He stood again by the window, where the canoe had barely made any progress, paddles shipped, figures turned one to the other, heads bent eagerly forward: an intense conversation, no doubt. Nothing surprised him anymore about Wendy: her deft navigation of his family, drawing out stories while withholding her own, her artist eyes reading you like a fucking book, hammering in her anchors when confronted, belaying her way into confidences, while tying her knots, locking carabiners as she worked the nearest traverse to reach her goal—whatever that was! He held the panties to his nose once again, as if they were the only sure down payment on eternity.

———

"Oh, there you are. We must've just missed you guys at Handytown," sang out Cordelia, waltzing through the door in her hiking boots. "I was just about to go down and help Felicity with dinner before she gets the Judge up from his nap." She made a goofy, perplexed face as she eyed the subtle alterations to the room. "Congrats to you," she said with raised eyebrows, "the anointed one—*and* Wendy."

"Hardly." He slipped the panties into the back pocket of his jeans.

"Hey, you deserve it. You stuck by the old buzzard. Loyalty is worth something, even in this fucked-up family. Not that you won't pay in spades."

"You sure Aunt Alice's coming?"

"She and Stan are already here, according to Felicity." She glanced out the window, nodding with a knowing look. "Why, those two are getting on like a boathouse afire." She giggled. "So how do you like being king of the castle?"

"I don't, not a bit. I prefer where I was. You should be here."

She flapped her arms comically, like an escaping white swan.

"No way José. And not Alice or Martha, either. Too many unpleasant memories, too close to the dirty nest for comfort." She retreated to the bed for a moment, smoothing the white cotton bedspread, testing the new mattress, fingering the sky-blue top sheet with its cream-colored wavy trim. "Whoa, what a thread count!" She smiled in recognition. "I shouldn't tell you this, but this was Annie's favorite color. She insisted on us using the same sheets for her hospital bed near the end, when we moved her down to the great room. Kept me up here at Hermitage for over six months . . . looking after her. Not for the faint of heart—no, not at all. She had a stoic streak, a New England thing, I guess, the way she contested with mortality, like she contested with everyone and everything. Probably—God only knows—where Alice got her bloody-minded streak."

"You're hardly a pushover, Mom."

"Alice and Martha will tell you I got off easy, after Teddy died, that Annie was a changed person, easier to get along with, more caring. Well, they weren't around much to lap up such maternal blessing as came my way, certainly not in the last year of her illness, or all the years Daddy was cheating on her right and left, when he and Annie didn't speak for months on end, when I was enlisted to relay messages. Not that she ever complained. They slept in separate bedrooms in our New York apartment, because, as he claimed, he didn't want to disturb her when he got home late from the courthouse or some function. But we all knew he was off screwing his girlfriends."

She bounced on the mattress and gave him a knowing smile.

"I'm glad you and Wendy are sexually compatible. It does matter, you know."

"Jesus, Mom."

She went again to the window, now watching carefully, while talking as if to her reflection.

"Why would anyone come up here in January to die in this damn cold and isolation? Why so suddenly, when she knew Daddy was judging a hugely important trial he couldn't get away from except on weekends? So I'd have to play the dutiful daughter and give up half my senior year and a critical six months at the School of American Ballet. Mr. B. was furious. Alice was doing her wild and crazy thing in Berkeley and Martha had her desperate patients. So I got to read to her about Marcel and his snotty friends in French, while she corrected my pronunciation every other sentence, until my French was almost as perfect as hers. If I complained about Daddy's not being able to get up because of a snowstorm, she'd just laugh it off. 'Well, now he'll have his Priscilla to himself, with Alger out of the picture.' Can you imagine having to listen to such shit from your parents?"

"She, Priscilla Hiss, wouldn't have him. Not as a lover."

"Oh, aren't you a font of information. No wonder Alice wants to get her hands on the infamous memoir. We're all supposed to work on you, you know."

He smiled icily. "I sold my soul for Graham's Dock, it looks like."

"I'll bet none of his sexual indiscretions, shall we say, are in there."

"It's deeply confessional."

"I doubt he caught much of Annie. She was always a riddle, wrapped in a mystery, inside an enigma—or was that Russia?" She laughed good-naturedly and turned again to the room, as if on the hunt for something that wasn't there. "When I asked Annie why she wanted to put herself through a winter up here, she just smiled in her distant, stoic way.

"'Preparation is all'—can you beat it!" She laughed, more a laugh of utter disbelief than one of mirth. "'With the exception of Teddy, all of you were conceived in this bed,' she told me with a certain hint of sarcastic pride, of determination against the odds, before we moved her down to the hospital bed under the ship's keel ceiling. 'In the heat of July or August, when we actually had time for each other—where else would I want to die?'" Cordelia shook her head. "At seventeen, still a dutiful virgin—that really bummed me out."

George stood rooted, not a little mesmerized, hands in his pockets, intently listening.

"And Teddy was conceived in Venice."

"Where'd you hear that?"

"The Judge's memoir."

She raised her eyebrows in a skeptical, if not wary, expression.

"There you go, probably full of more wishful thinking than anything else. Ah, well . . . Annie told me—this was right before she died—that she'd gotten pregnant before they married, not during the honeymoon in Venice."

George's stare deepened.

"They were married a month later in Boston. She liked to call Teddy her 'Venetian Apollo,' and she'd point up to the ship's keel ceiling, where that handsome dude hung out with his Venus, you know, the chick with the great boobs and golden hair, whom I always fancied as a kid—we all had our favorites. Alice and Martha thought Glaucus was a dead ringer for Teddy. Near the end, as if in a dream, a morphine dream, staring into the blue, she'd go on and on about Venice, when she'd played La Fenice, something about the acoustics, and someplace else she loved."

"The Scuola Grande di San Rocco."

"Well . . ." Cordelia turned a bemused look her son's way, as to an echo, and as she did, her eye was caught by an apparition that propelled her across the room to the William Gedney Bunce painting of Venice, now bathed in soft, luminous rays from the lowering sun. She smiled, eyes touched with nostalgia.

"How about that! . . . This was in her studio at Juilliard. Even Mr. B. admired it. Haven't seen it for years. Goodness, it's really quite striking"—her outstretched fingers made hovering shadows on the canvas—"I don't remember the colors being so vivid, and the sky—such a whirlwind of brushstrokes—wow."

"He had it cleaned."

"Oh, did he now—just for you!" Now steeped in skeptical curiosity, she began poking around the bookshelves. "Looks like he left you her French editions of Proust; I'm sure you're thrilled. Well, just in case this has all gone to your head, he's had everybody's room turned upside down. Photos from my childhood and ballet, all her Trollope and Jane Austin, and when I opened my bureau drawer, I found all"— her breath caught and she tried to blink back sudden tears—"all her favorite Hermès scarves carefully wrapped in blue tissue, the ones I'd loved as a little girl, with musical instruments and dancers and birds. Oh God, and they still smelled of her Chanel No. 5."

She wiped away her copious tears, clearly unnerved.

"Wendy reads French, totally into Proust."

"Ha!" she exclaimed. "George, you're finally seeing his modus operandi, the way he builds his case, covers his ass, brief by brief by brief."

"Mom, I think he's trying . . . really."

"Of course he is—he's dying."

She returned to the window and pressed a longing palm against the panes, tracing the leaded latticework with a finger, as if to ground herself in the familiar.

"You see, the year she got sick, 1968, was a horrible year, with the King and Kennedy assassinations and all the riots and cities on fire, and I think in her mind it was like her cancer was just a part of that hatred and calamitous breakdown, the shots echoing, smoke, police sirens, which she watched on TV in horror from her hospital bed, and later when she started the chemo. As if her perfect world of music and beautifully trained and perfectly behaved dancers was being destroyed, within and without. That's why she came back here that January, to escape all that, to lie there in the great room with her books and stare up at the ceiling, which had provided her some of her happiest moments at the piano—that perfect little universe hovering up there in the blue. I'd see her eyes rise as I read to her, as the sunlight altered, and new figures would appear beneath the varnish, as she'd try to make out the intricate geometries—so perfect, so orderly. Sometimes she'd have the male nurse, a lovely man from Barbados with a happy laugh and mellifluous voice, change the position of her hospital bed so she could see some different part of the ceiling when the light reached it. And she'd explain to him about the gods and goddesses, as if they were close friends and confidantes of hers. Funny, she never minded at all being helped—carried—by him—Cyrus was his name—to the bathroom, being bathed by a black man, got on like the Queen of Sheba with her consort—*Cyrus the Great*—like one of her deathless gods come to earth. So that's how she wanted it, to get back to her perfect, unchanging world, her perfect planet Mozart under the stars—while the rest of the world was falling apart—to the end."

George came over and put an arm around his mother as she wiped away tears.

"Why wouldn't she forgive him for Teddy?"

"Forgive, forgive . . . maybe she just wasn't capable. Not that Daddy didn't long for her forgiveness. When his damn trial was over, he came up full-time in the early spring, that lovely, final, perfect spring. Just in time for the return of the birds. I remember the sound of his voice reading to her, Proust in the Moncrieff translation, which I thought was a bit cruel of her, since in no way was he partial to Marcel. But I think it was good for them, as good an ending as they could make, his voice like a liturgy, like some ritual confession or atonement out of their past. And to give the devil his due, he was genuinely devastated by her death. For weeks he wandered Hermitage like a lost little boy, taking long walks to Handytown, sitting in her chair on the veranda for hours at a time, as if to welcome in her stead the return of the birds, one by one, sometimes sounding a note on the Steinway. For the most part, he left it up to me to sort out her things here and in New York, to give orders to Felicity, instructing her what to give away to the Junior League shop, what to keep. And it was that August that he managed to sweet-talk me into driving his Mercedes coupe to Woodstock—just weeks before that name became synonymous with our age, the messiness and disorder and wildness that Annie so abhorred. Returning those stupid sketches to Jim as if they were just another part of her effects to be dealt with and discarded."

"Maybe it *was* his way of atonement. Discarding the evidence that might have saved George Altmann's life."

"Well, it bought me the life I ended up with—the un-Annie life she would've abhorred but which, at that moment, after that long winter of her death, seemed like such a liberation, a second chance at childhood, at sex, at life. I'm sorry. I know you think it's all bullshit, but there it is."

"Evidence he could have just as easily burned and nobody would have been the wiser. What kind of man does that?"

"Evidence? . . . Sawkill Bridge, you mean. You don't wanna know how all that has blown Jim's mind. He's like a mongrel pup around the house, like nothing is quite real to him, not as he remembers it." She smiled indifferently, pushing back her blond bangs. "All of a sudden, he's proud as punch about his dad, feeling better about himself."

"Maybe the Judge has got more of a conscience than you and your sisters give him credit for. Because he suspected something that he couldn't quite believe—or prove, enough that he wanted to tempt fate, to tempt the world with the truth, even an invisible truth. The thing that had destroyed his life, his marriage."

"Well, Alice and Martha think he's using you as an ally to assuage his guilty conscience. They blame him for Annie, for all the years running around with other women, a powerful man, an important man, in line for a Supreme Court nomination—a man who craved the approval, if not love, of women, the kind of adulation his wife would never give him, Annie, who treated him no better than a country lawyer—or at least that's Martha's take. Sad, I guess, how little love was lost between them."

Cordelia sighed, a faraway look entering her blue eyes as she tousled her son's hair.

He gave a hapless shrug, as if trying to feel his way out of the labyrinthine memories that had him in thrall. "You know, after Teddy died, she refused to sleep with him again."

"Oh!" She stood back and eyed him, incredulous. "Well . . . did he tell you that, too?"

"He wrote as much in his memoir." He stared into his mother's blue eyes as if with fearsome recognition of something in himself, perplexed, searching for the right words. "Well, once, a one-shot deal—once after Teddy died."

"Once! Well, thank God for small miracles." She laughed uneasily, reaching to her son's hand in solidarity. "That memoir is going to be the end of this family. Maybe I need to find you some body armor or a bodyguard—or is that what you've got Wendy for?" Not a little shattered by this intimate nugget of family lore, she wandered unsteadily on her feet for a moment until drifting to the sanctuary of the bed, where she sat, a claimant on the past. "I never heard that from him, or from her—never a peep about such a thing . . . and she opened up to me completely in her last days, or so I thought. Maybe not about her own lovers."

"Hers?"

"Well . . . who really knows?" A tremulous distant expression entered her eyes. "Just before she died, she took my hand and squeezed it, squeezed it hard, and looked into my eyes with a fierce tearful squint. 'You almost killed me seventeen years ago giving birth, but then dancers are used to dancing on their graves.'" She waved a hand as if to make light of the sudden memory. "Like I said, an enigma."

"Nevertheless," he said with a puzzled shrug, "a strange thing to include in a memoir, and in such detail."

At this, Cordelia patted the bed with both hands, sighed, and stood and went to the window as if needing some fresh air. "The sorority sisters are back from their cruise to the island—oh my." She turned to her son, brows flexed in a worried look. "Don't let that girl break your heart."

"Heart? What's to break?"

"Oh honey, you're the coolest catch—look how much weight you've lost!—any girl could have. Even if she's a little scary at times."

"Tell me about it."

"Talk to Cecily; she's been around the block. She's a great judge of character."

"Speaking of old loves," he said with a sigh. "You never heard anything between them while growing up about Alger or Priscilla Hiss, or Whittaker Chambers?"

"I never knew they existed until I was in high school, when some total stranger might come up to me and shake my hand and tell me what a great man my father was for defending Alger Hiss. When I unloaded that at home, all I'd get was a vague smile: 'Oh, a long time ago, Cordy.' Only at the end did stuff slither out, like when I was reading to her from Proust and she'd make some crack about how Marcel's ridiculous pining over Gilberte—or was it Albertine, or maybe Swann over Odette?—how ridiculous men were. 'Like your father and Priscilla Hiss, ready to sacrifice his soul to protect her,'" she'd say.

Cordelia winced, as if she'd touched some exposed nerve, then paced over to the simple country bureau, painted an off-white, with pale blue knobs, where she straightened Wendy's brush, her wallet and cell phone. She glanced at herself in the equally simple white-framed mirror and made a goofy face. "The old scoundrel relocated Annie's silver-backed brushes to the bureau in my room. That's why I stopped by just now—changes in the cages." She laughed to herself and turned again to her son by the window. "Same with Alice and Martha—he's trying to give them back their mother. Annie tried not to show it, but she was horrified at Alice's part in that disorder and chaos of 1968. Always dismissive of Martha's interminable psychobabble. Well, she loved me and I damn well performed—her beautiful little trick pony—whatever it took to please her *and* Balanchine. Luckily, she didn't live long enough to see my ballet career collapse, or have to deal with Jim. But there's not a day—*What would Annie think about that*!—I don't feel like I let her down."

Distracted, George was watching where Wendy and Cecily were walking up the winding path from the boathouse.

"You didn't really bring *him* along, did you?"

She came back to his side, following his gaze.

"He's better, honey—really. He's trying his best."

"Mom, we may still have to take legal action against Jim. Hermitage, Thanksgiving, this is hardly the place and time to have him around."

"Jim has the results of his paternity test with him. How about you? Just a swab on the inside of your cheek. That will settle it for both of you, so I don't have to waste any more time or energy on the subject."

"You're not sleeping in the same room are you—if you know what I mean?"

"Yes, I know what you mean. And yes, but we're not sleeping together—yet, if you know what I mean."

"*Yet?*"

"We're no longer spring chickens, George. And nothing's perfect. None of us is. I made mistakes. Your father made mistakes. And we've both suffered. Wake up. Learn from our fuckups. And he hasn't touched a drop since he's been back."

"Alice e-mailed me to say that I shouldn't say boo about the paintings—give him ideas."

"That's how lawyers think. Alice expects—and finds—the worst in everybody. And anyway, she's just trying to get you to cough up the memoir."

"But you did sleep with Levon? I mean, the kids always gave me funny looks in school."

"Listen, the reason Jim never came back from that Band tour of Japan was because Levon—bigmouth Levon, when he was drunk or high or fucking some groupie, bragged in Jim's hearing that he'd bagged me years before and gotten me pregnant. Believe it or not, once upon a time, all the boys wanted me."

"Had he—Levon?"

"Yes, we'd slept together, but he didn't get me pregnant. I *was* pregnant—that's what I told him at the time."

"Jesus fucking Christ, it was all over high school, how Jim, a lowly techie, a roadie, couldn't keep his own wife from playing around."

"Woodstock's a goddamn rumor mill. For what it's worth, I was very discriminating with my cheating, unlike your father, who only got the leftovers. I can't deny I was drawn to men with talent and charisma."

"Like Levon?"

"Hell, like Balanchine, like Annie was. Yes, like Levon, a drummer, an actor, a singer and songwriter who changed the world with music. And now he has throat cancer, the poor dear, so let's leave it at that."

"Alice advised against the test until he signs the property agreement. The test result will be admissible in court. If he can prove you cheated on him and I'm not his son, he has a good case on the property settlement—and the paintings, which are now worth a lot more than the property."

Cordelia backed away from her son with her lips twisted up in near incomprehension.

"You're almost worse than she is. Since when did *you* become so cold and calculating about money? Is that Alice's lawyering, or what your Wendy—one pretty damn pushy broad—thinks?"

"Money—me into money—commerce! How fucking bourgeois."

From below came the sound of the piano in the great room, Chopin, the music seeming to reverberate right out of the floor, faint but almost crystal clear. Mother and son were frozen in place, listening, the stress of the conversation draining from their faces, until they just stared at each other in a suspension of disbelief.

"My God," Cordelia finally managed to say, "she's good."

"Alice?"

"No, she and Stan are napping in their room."

"Of course, it's Cecily; she must have kept it up over all these years." George smiled, listening, relaxing, gravitating to the window, where the sun was caressing the limbs of the white pines across the lake. "Know what some of my happiest memories are? Down at the boathouse, at night, with my first telescope. The one the Judge gave me for my eighth or ninth birthday. I spent nights exploring the stars, the galaxies, until I fell asleep, with all the sounds of the universe like a lullaby: the screech owls, the flutter of bats, the bullfrogs, the lapping water against the pilings. Me and a chorus of critters all alone with the stars." He moved across the room to the big walk-in closet. "It used to be in my closet in Cuddebackville—Nancy's room now."

"Teddy's room, where Annie slept when I was growing up."

"How about that!"

She turned with a smile to her son's excited voice from the closet.

"Well, thank the Lord for Nancy. At least people might behave themselves."

55
Gratitude

ALICE OPENED THE window of her room and took a few deep breaths of the late-afternoon air, as if needing to settle her mind. For a minute, she watched the two women drifting in the green canoe—an image calling up adolescent memories—and then returned to her bureau, whose drawers were piled high with old books and magazines from her son's room, including a few T-shirts that Felicity had neatly arranged in a bottom drawer. Going through her son's things, she kept brushing back her stringy hair from a fretful brow, chucking her bony shoulders as if trying to relax them.

"Besides the *Mad* magazines, there's all these books on Flip Wilson—that black comedian; books on jokes and comedy and how to do stand-up; *Manchild in the Promised Land*, by Claude Brown; even the writings of Frederick Douglass. He never read this stuff at home—I had no idea."

"Flip who?" asked Stan, lying back on the bed, trying to nap.

"A black comedian—a book on sketches from his TV show, even a biography, *Flip: The Inside Story of TV's First Black Superstar.*"

"Obviously, he was trying to get closer to Cecily."

"Did he ever talk to you about such things?"

"You were the one to tell."

Alice sighed, arranging the books again, holding one of the T-shirts, emblazoned with the words THE DEVIL MADE ME DO IT, up to her nose.

"The rest of his stuff is in boxes in the basement, marked with his name."

She wandered over to the painting of Annie seated at the piano, hands poised above the keyboard, blond hair a flurry of brushstrokes, from under which an intent, soulful face stared into painterly spaces of ocher and gray: regal nose, quivering parted lips, eyebrows the merest swerves of flickering pigment, half-lidded, ecstatic eyes.

"I can't believe he parked the Raphael Soyer portrait in my room. I suppose that's my booby prize for being gazumped out of Graham's Dock by George and his girl wonder."

"It's a beautiful painting," said Stan, eyes closed. "Raphael Soyer was quite something in his day, I believe. But then, weren't we all?"

"After all I've done for George and Cordelia, trying to extract her from that dreadful marriage, and now what does she do but bring shit-for-brains Jim to Hermitage—for Thanksgiving no less. Well, that's gratitude for you."

"Relax, my love. Why would we want to rattle around in that glaring greenhouse? You once told me how you always tiptoed past your parents' room for fear of drawing your mother's ire over some real or imagined trespass."

She blinked rapidly, registering something.

"They read to each other—we dared not interrupt them there—when we were kids . . . one of my first memories, especially Sunday mornings."

"Well," he said, raising his eyebrows, "you certainly had nothing nice to say about her high-society friends in our receiving line, or the musicians—her colleagues—who all asked after you and how your piano was going." His long, arthritic fingers rose and fell across his chest. "And anyway, who wants to fuck around in their parents' bed—not that that would be an issue *now*."

Alice turned and glared at her husband.

"It's the principle of the thing; it's the biggest room, with the best view of the lake." She waved at the portrait. "And this is all about the Judge, *mutatis mutandis*, manipulating our lives."

"What's left to manipulate? Besides, it's a beautiful painting of a very talented woman who happens to be your mother—so by rights it should go to you."

"Like the memoir, just another swipe at me."

"Hey, maybe there really is a screenplay in this Hiss business. He was always such a pompous ass, bragging about his connections—and what a shitload of trouble he stirred up for the rest of us."

Distracted, Alice scowled and went back to the window, pondering.

"Oh, she wasn't really so bad, not like Martha always makes out. Actually, as a girl, I revered her as a musician. I mean, seeing your mother—a woman—play Carnegie Hall was a pretty big damn deal, Stan."

"You coulda fooled me." He yawned again and rubbed his eyes. "Every time you sit down at the piano, I feel you're tilting with ghosts."

Her face darkened with displeasure.

"And look at all the talent Cecily inherited," he added.

At mention of her daughter, a half-smile appeared on Alice's face as she opened the window farther, a breeze stirring her hair.

"I had one of my students in my criminal law class do an Internet check on your Catwoman."

"No."

"What do you want? After all, my daughter is shacking up with her in the city. Anyway, her dad was a huge Exxon exec in Houston, MIT chemical engineer, geologist, world-class climber; he'd climbed Everest and bunch of those other highest peaks. Her mother came from nothing, or next to nothing; grew up in a blue-collar suburb of Houston but somehow crawled her way up, first as a champion rodeo rider and horsewoman, then climbing with her husband—out to beat the world. But then they died in that climbing accident when Wendy was thirteen. There's nothing about Wendy—no guardians, relatives, street addresses— until she shows up at Yale on full scholarship from some crappy public school in a run-down 'burb of Houston. Then she's shooting the lights out, winning all the academic prizes, the painting competitions; once she graduates, she's approached by all the top galleries but turns them all down. Everything checked out. And she really did climb Everest in 1996, that ill-fated season when all those people died. And here's the thing: Her team of climbers completely escaped. Wanna know why? She managed to talk her team leader out of trying the final ascent during a break in the bad weather. Somehow this twenty-something girl challenged the authority and experience of their guide, a veteran of Everest. So her team waited, while the others got caught in the freak storm that killed something like twelve people, including at least two legendary climbers who'd conquered Everest a dozen times between them. Later, when her team made the ascent, it was a breeze. The team, even the Sherpas, were in awe of her equanimity and poise and strength, as if she had some preternatural powers of prophecy—staying out of that storm, you see. They called her the 'ice maiden': determined, distant, uncomplaining, set on her own agenda, unphased by the accidents and deaths. She just soldiered on under conditions that tested men with years more experience. Except, *except*, she had this thing about stopping on the route, the last day of the ascent, through what they call the killing zone, when they'd pass frozen bodies from previous ill-fated expeditions. And get this: She insisted on kneeling by each and every one of these frozen bodies—some just days old, placing her hand on the corpse as if saying a prayer. It spooked her team, because nobody stops; everybody prefers to pretend the dead aren't there so as not to be unnerved by the dangers of that final leg to the summit. But she stopped; she kept her eyes out for the bodies nearly immured in the ice and snow, as if driven to pay her respects. Everybody on the team remarked on it. They were in awe—someone so young—but they loved her; she was their luck."

"My God, what a story. Do you think she'd share it with me?"

Alice was watching intently out the window. "I think all this secrecy about the memoir comes from her; she's got Cecily and George in thrall, if not the Judge. It's a little creepy, don't you think? Notice how she's always listening, always observing?"

"Hey, she's an artist. And I'll bet she's got a great story in her. Why don't you write that down for me. That's great material; I might be able to put it to use. I'm looking forward to talking to her again."

"I'll bet." She went to the mirror over the dresser and gathered back her graying hair, examining the slackness in her jaw, the wrinkles around her gray-green eyes. "For Christ's sake." She held up a cloisonné tray of vintage hairpins and tortoiseshell barrettes, gasping with pleasure as she handled the familiar objects. Then she picked up a small calfskin jewelry case with a Tiffany monogram and opened it slowly. "Oh my God . . . oh my God." She almost stumbled as she drifted to the bedside to show her husband the gleaming diamond brooch in the design of a musical phrase. "Annie's. She wore it on her black concert gown for performances." Alice glanced, as if for confirmation, at the portrait and the silvery glints of light depicted in bold impasto below the right strap. "She always had me pin it—her Vinteuil phrase—on her gown . . . for luck."

"There you go. See, your father is trying to make nice. Take it as a blessing."

She walked over to the window and held up the brooch to the lemony orange slant of light on the horizon, turning it this way and that, the six-note staff transformed into glowing rubies, her hand trembling slightly. "I could give it to Cecily."

"There you go. She always liked fine things—unlike her mother."

"It must be worth a small fortune." She carefully returned it to the Tiffany case. "How typical of him, just leaving shit around for you to find, as opposed to just handing it over."

"I think it's a nice touch, not making a big deal, not asking for your gratitude."

She slipped the case into the bureau drawer and, as she did, caught sight of something else. She withdrew a sheaf of music manuscript paper, four pages, which she intently examined.

"What is it?" her husband asked.

"It's in Annie's hand, the beginning of a composition: *Homage to Vinteuil, the Little Sonata—for George.*"

"George?"

"Balanchine, you figure. Something she was working on, maybe for a ballet. It's mostly a bunch of phrases with bits of development here and there—unfinished."

She cocked her ear, chin quivering, as if hearing the music in her head. "Her one regret . . ." She sighed as she carefully stowed the sheets.

"And who's this Vinteuil fellow?"

"Oh, just a character out of Proust, a piano teacher, a composer who wrote a sonata, in which was embedded a little phrase that Swann identified with his lost love for Odette, where he found consolation, a cure, of sorts, for the jealousy that destroyed their love."

"You read Proust?"

She turned to the window and the encroaching azure-purple sifted by the highest of the white pines, squinting as if to catch some glimpse—surprised by herself—of something she'd forgotten.

"I . . . I revered Proust. At fifteen, sixteen, I read him through, then again, and again later at Vassar. The part where Swann contemplates the Vinteuil phrase, the little phrase, so inspired me that I decided to become the greatest woman pianist of my generation. Teddy had his Conrad, Martha her Freud, and I had my Proust—the profoundest of them all."

Her husband laughed, incredulous. "You—Proust! I couldn't get through a single page of the guy. Who woulda thought it."

Then she turned suddenly to the Soyer portrait, as if sensing she was being watched. She walked across the room and reached a shaking hand to her mother's face, murmuring, "What does it all matter? It means nothing."

"What was that, dear?"

She glanced back to her husband. "Swann was inspired by the phrase to empathize with the composer's sorrow, his regret and loss . . . a dead wife, a disrespectful daughter. The little phrase illuminated the darkness of his soul, his dreams—how did Proust put it? 'We shall perish, but we have as hostages these divine captives who will follow and share our fate. And death in their company is somehow less bitter, less inglorious, perhaps even less probable.'"

"Lovely, dear, lovely—how you remember that."

Again she reached to her mother's face.

"After Teddy died, it was like they no longer had time for each other."

"Ain't that the truth."

Alice winced.

"We had time, didn't we, Stan?"

"For a time . . ." Stan picked up a thick book on his bedside table and examined the cover, uttering a mild grunt of surprise. "What are you going to do when you don't have your old man to scrap with anymore? You've already worn this one out." He smiled gamely and finger-combed wisps of white hair off his temple and snapped on the bedside lamp to better read the text on the back of the book.

"She never got over me refusing her that church wedding, but I did it for you, not to insult your people."

"My people! The Pope himself couldn't insult my crowd of secular nonobservant know-nothings. Those *hilonim* would have been thrilled to attend a Unitarian service on Park Avenue, instead of up here in the buggy woods. All their poor relations spent their summers in bungalow colonies down the road in Monticello; the better off—like my folks—stayed at the Concord or Grossinger's. For them, our wedding was totally downscale."

"She never forgave me for that, either."

"What—for marrying me, you mean?"

Stan watched where she now stood in front of a framed black-and-white photo of a first-prize ceremony, where her younger self stared back in serene triumph . . . long, shapely legs, skilled fingers cradling a silver trophy, a pretty, if narrow, high-cheekboned face full of graceful joy in her smiling lips and resplendent eyes.

"Can you blame her, Allie? You had such a talent for the piano."

"Piano wasn't going to change anything."

He shot his eyebrows. "Ah, but Cecily did."

"Oh, please, let's not go there again."

"I don't care, Allie; it's who you are. My heart leapt when she arrived a few weeks ago. I've loved her as my own since day one; you know that, but love, so it seems, is never enough for you."

"I saved something of him—that was enough. I knew he was doomed."

"And speaking of screenplays, look at this, Kazan's autobiography, and—holy smokes—it's signed to me from Elia!" He held the frontispiece closer to the light. "'For Stan, the man with a golden pen in the golden age of cinema, Elia.' What the hell? How did this get here?"

"I told you that Wendy had your number." With that, she returned to her vigil by the window for a moment. "They're back."

"She can have it any day. See, your old man is still looking for love," Stan said, smiling as he looked up from the book.

"In all the wrong places," she sang, and then came over and slapped his stocking feet playfully. "I had my first boy in this bed—if you don't mind my saying. It smelled of him for years."

"A treasure."

"He really was a boy, seventeen—a rainy night on the island, so we sneaked into the house—and he came all over the sheets before he could even get it in. Sneaking around—so terrified of Annie—getting those sheets washed before anybody found out."

"How exciting, to *be* that boy."

"You were my famous director, my piece of the Hollywood Ten."

"Worst luck."

"You stood up for your principles against HUAC; you refused to be bullied, to give them names. I was thrilled by your courage."

"And I got one year in Danbury, and a career going nowhere. You know," he said wistfully, "if your father had only managed to get Hiss off on that perjury charge, it all might have turned out differently; the Supreme Court might have taken our appeal. The whole thing fell apart after the Hiss conviction, not that the Korean War helped. The smart guys like Kazan, Gene Kelly, and Danny Kaye just reneged on the whole thing and got away scot-free."

"Was Danny Kaye—the Court Jester, Hans Christian Andersen—a Communist?"

"A Jew and a Communist, or maybe a lapsed Commie, like me."

"You *were* a member, weren't you?"

"I dropped my membership—stopped paying dues in 1939 with the Nazi-Soviet pact."

"You never told me that."

"I felt bad, like I'd let the side down. But like Kazan, I was sick of their bullying and bullshit. Even if HUAC was a bunch of fascists."

"So you weren't actually a member?"

"Not in good standing."

"Why didn't you just tell them?"

"I had friends. You had to give them names to get off the hook. My friends were more important."

"I'm sorry, but the secrecy thing was idiotic. Why not just admit you wanted to overthrow the government and have done with it?"

"Like your pals in Chicago, the Weathermen, the Black Panthers—where did that get anybody?"

"We got the voting rights act and desegregation."

"Lee Harvey Oswald and LBJ got you that." He waved her over. "I'm tired, Alice. I need a nap; you need a nap. Lie down with me and pretend we were once lovers."

She lay down, looking up at the play of light from the bedside lamp on the beadboard ceiling, as she had often done as a child.

"But you really were a Communist, once upon a time . . ."

"You had to be an idiot not to see the stupidities and sectarianism, what a murderous bastard Stalin was, how 'message discipline,' as they call it today, turned into bad clichés and even worse screenplays. Trumbo and Kazan, the good writers, knew the truth; some just came to admit it sooner rather than later. Or as John Ford always advised: When there is conflict between the truth and the myth, print the myth."

"Myths to live by," she said dreamily.

"I keep hoping I have one last screenplay in me—maybe your tale about George's girl."

From below in the great room came the sound of Chopin.

"Oh . . . listen."

"One of your sisters?"

"They stink." She propped herself up on an elbow. "It's Cecily—listen, she's good. She's been practicing and she didn't even tell me."

"She's all the best of you."

"I miss Billy, Stan, I really do."

"I know you do. So do I." He squeezed her hand. "Shush, listen to our daughter. Isn't she wonderful?"

"Do you think Billy was happy here?"

"He was."

"It's the D-flat Nocturne . . . Yes, I'll bet she's using Annie's fingerings."

"Just listen."

"I was always hoping that Billy and Cecily would, you know, wake up someday and stop seeing us as parents and instead see who we really are. I wanted them to understand what we stood for—how much we sacrificed, just how much we put on the line."

"Kids have to live their own lives. Now shush."

She squeezed his hand.

"You took a stand."

"I'd still trade it for one decent picture, one Academy Award . . . That would be the berries—just one great screenplay."

"What more can you ask of life than to be on the right side of history?"

"Every now and then you sound like a real Commie."

"You old Reds were idiots. You got to take the system from the inside. Even Lenin had that much figured out."

"Shush, listen to our daughter."

56
Good to Go

The use of symbols has a certain power of emancipation and exhilaration for all men. We seem to be touched by a wand, which makes us dance and run around happily, like children. We are like persons who come out of a cave or cellar into the open air. This is the effect on us of tropes, fables, oracles, and all poetic forms. Poets are thus liberating gods. Men have really got a new sense, and found within their world, another world, or nest of worlds; for, the metamorphosis once seen, we divine that it does not stop.

—Emerson

THE JUDGE'S PALE eyelids flickered as the music began to weave its spell, tapping into some timeless pool of his dreaming mind—or was it, he began to wonder, simply another fay melody drifting free of Giordano Bruno's infinite reaches, time's fugitive exile, remote, tantalizing, enchanting, fleeing that perfect imperium sheltering some of his happiest childhood memories? He blinked again, trying to focus, still not quite sure where he was.

"Chopin," he whispered to himself, and again, as if the naming were a lifeline. The D-flat Nocturne . . . Annie's favorite . . . her concert encore . . .

"Hah, I'm still here," he murmured. And he began a deliberate count of the twenty-eight lozenge-shaped panes of leaded glass beyond the foot of his bed, animated with swallow gray light and mauve pine shadows.

Morning?

How many mornings in the early days, the old days had he woken to her playing in the great room, the notes incantatory flames rising as if from some vast star-cradled nursery? When he'd creep to the banister and catch sight of her naked figure, like a goddess descended to earth. Her face and shoulders dipping and rising, from side to side to side to side, a fleshy gentle current, her long, slim, powerful fingers rippling like freshets along the Neversink. Then later coming to him . . . a fiery Aphrodite to consummate her pleasures.

My God, they're all here! he thought.

He'd have to pull himself together and make sure he said only the right things; candor had always been his downfall. He smiled through his various aches and pains and the uncomfortably full diaper, letting his senses contract to the purity of the sound, the phrasing, that telltale phrasing as it drifted from the great room, as if the ship's keel ceiling was crowding on sail, billowing to life, allowing his beloved Hermitage to journey once more—perhaps one last time.

Lordy, she's good, almost perfect, a dead ringer for how Annie played it.

Had Alice actually showed up?

There had been a year when she was eighteen, her first year at Vassar, when she could play it almost as well as her mother . . . Yes, yes—there in the lingering arpeggio on the repeated phrase—exactly right. Perfect. He blinked rapidly at the wonder of the thing, catching sight of a liquid glitter through his bedroom window, a vein of gold in the underbelly of a stray cloud . . . Annie's blond hair flowing as she dipped and rose and dipped again, strands just brushing the keys. He smiled at the sensation of that cascade of golden filigree pouring across his face as she mounted him—light's embodiment, how once he thought it one of her few affectations, how she wore her hair down only in concert performances and lovemaking . . . and in the great room, under the ship's keel ceiling, with the windows thrown wide to the piney breezes of summer.

How happy she'd been in those precious moments of perfection, like time stopped on angels' wings.

Pleased, she'd glance up at her naked counterpart, languishing Ariadne abandoned on her Naxian shore, and nod. Not unlike, it occurred to him, when anchored knee-deep in the Neversink after a perfect singing cast, he'd hear that exiled naiad's murmuring call (or was it Teddy's Scylla?) whispering past his hip waders, ecstatic, senseless, immune to time's hurrying call.

He found his fingers tapping out the rhythm on the patchwork
comforter over his decrepit body, tempted to just throw back the cover
and spring up and make a mad dash for Handytown before cocktails
and dinner. But there, confronting him, was the reality of the twin brass
knobs—tarnished, dented—of the antique bedstead (in what was once
the cook's bedroom) framing his pathetic power wall of presidents,
and, worse, the ruthless mirror above the monstrosity of a mahogany
bureau that Annie had banished from Graham's Dock after their marriage, where, hard by in a glimmer of sunlight, a few faded photographs
of Annie hung: Annie posed in the Giardini on their honeymoon;
performing at Wigmore Hall; arm around Uncle Ollie at the their
wedding—a pathetic residue, hope on half rations.

But thank God for Nancy!

He smiled, seeing the lithesome dark-haired beauty again bound into
the great room only hours before, Annie's great-granddaughter—imagine
living to see such a thing! Such a splendid chestnut-haired child, those
sparkling, intelligent eyes lighting up the place, and her delicate nose and
that little curious laugh as she set out to explore the great room with all
its photographs, a million questions trailing in her wake, exhausting him
after only half an hour. "Who are these people? Are these donkeys—how
cute!—on the towpath? Those little boys in the straw hats are barefoot,
ouch! And what about this old bridge—but it doesn't look like a bridge?
Is this the thing, the aqueduct that Roebling built? Wow, we were just
talking about it in the car coming up."

Oh, Annie, oh, Annie . . .

And yet even with this whirlwind of a grandchild dashing around,
Martha seemed a little slow on the uptake, a little lost in her reveries.
And schoolteacher Erich not a little dumbfounded by how his daughter's curiosity was fired up to such fever pitch—smart as the devil,
surely Groton material. Erich had something of Annie's height and
bearing, but still weighed down by adolescent insecurities: tentative,
sour, cynical, withdrawn. Having an academic lothario for a father!
And yet he'd somehow managed to produce such a lovely quick-witted
daughter, with a little help from her lawyer mother, the pleasure of
whose acquaintance had not been afforded.

Martha had definitely lost a step or two . . . bemused and obtuse,
just as happy to withdraw to a corner—as she had as a child—to clini-
cally observe the human race, the commotion around Nancy, to analyze
everyone's behavior from on high, or sniffing around the bookshelves

to see what other people were reading, as she had as an adolescent . . . nothing of her mother's wit and charm and exuberance and sheer zest for life. Afraid of men, afraid of sex—of passion, which she diagnosed as an ailment peculiar to the male of the species, a threat to her dignity, a thing first to be endured and then treated as a chronic condition. And yet, maybe, something of Annie's spark had managed to soldier through, somehow outflanking that gangly theory-soaked Pole, Theodore, so stuffed to the gills with academic malarkey, and, worse, that nonsense about Shakespeare being Francis Bacon. But, who knows, maybe Theodore's contribution of brainpower to Karen and Erich, Nancy and Max was worth something in the race of life. Nothing short of a miracle that something of Annie had so magnificently survived all that dilution in little Nancy.

What did I write about Martha in the memoir?

He couldn't quite remember but now hoped he'd been kind. She really did care about helping people in her own misbegotten way. Had he noted her regard for Binger and Murray, those idiot shrinks he'd put on the stand to do their demolition job on Chambers? If he had, maybe he should tell George to take it out—truth be damned: no need to leave behind hard feelings in a family. He pondered this for a moment more: the one thing—the truth—he had always prided himself on, as had Annie. What else had he left out?

And with this, his sympathies drifted to poor Karen, abandoned by her darling Max, occasionally showing moments of Annie's sly wit, her sexual allure, at least as a teenager, if always a trifle lost, a little sad, fumbling for something missing or never found. Troubled by the neglect of boys at the lake and later by that philandering (Cordelia's description) husband of hers, and now perplexed by her son, Max (spoiled rotten by his father, according to Cordelia), who had been waylaid by some girlfriend and her rich Riverside Drive cliff-dwelling family. Karen, desperate to put a good face on things—suggesting that Max might still show up—was clearly upset that Nancy was getting all the attention, not helped by Martha's excuses and clinical diagnoses, echoing her daughter's concerns about anxiety issues after the Trade Center attack. Pity about Max . . . nothing some fresh air and long hikes and a little fishing couldn't cure.

He closed his eyes for a moment to better concentrate his waning energy as the piano playing began again.

Ah, the C Minor Nocturne, that lush, pensive rumination, with a brittleness in the opening treble voice like the pacing of an insomniac . . .

until singing out above those stirring chordal progressions—how every tendon and muscle in Annie's neck sprang to electric life, her brow furrowed as if beset by labor pains, mist of golden hair caressing the ivories . . . Oh, Annie. He opened his eyes, as if infused with sudden urgency. Could it be Martha? No, hopelessly lacking in physical skills, which was why she always attached herself so desperately to Teddy, as if to absorb his effortless prowess and serene equanimity—godlike, really—something, of course, that would be utterly inexplicable to Freud's benighted epigone.

My God, she took it hard, almost as hard as Annie. Teddy's death left her stranded—strange—while it launched Alice.

Transported by the music (numbing his own ache at Teddy's loss), he found himself pondering again his memoir, concerned he hadn't done right by his daughters, that too much candor might be hurtful, that keeping the family together and saving Hermitage were the only things that really mattered.

Wendy—George's Wendy—could she have been practicing over the last few weeks? My Lord, what a scary talent—but then so was Annie's.

His eyes searched the nearer wall, where a pair of new arrivals hovered on the beadboard paneling: a black-and-white sketch of a handsome young lawyer bent forward with a hard, attentive stare, concentrated on testimony, evaluating his opponents for the merest chink of vulnerability. As much a portrait of George Altmann: his secret sharer, at the height of his powers, the man he had so cruelly betrayed . . .

"I did what I had to do," he muttered, wincing at such an unconvincing boilerplate excuse. "Any defense lawyer worth his salt would have done the same."

Again his mind returned to the memoir, a blur of pages, and with it a nagging sense of guilt. Why should he feel any guilt? At least he knew he hadn't lied, because his conscience would never allow it. But had he left something out of the story? Yes, yes, he should have returned those sketches personally to Jim Altmann instead of bribing a reluctant Cordelia with the Red Mercedes. But he'd handled the evidence exactly as the law prescribed . . . hadn't he? No requirement he share it with the prosecution.

He closed his eyes, as if prompted by some impulse to contrition, a yearning for grace, which the music might hasten into reach.

Wendy!

He glanced at the now-framed canvas (cheek by jowl with the Altmann court sketch), resplendent in all its soft, lush earthy colors—a work for a young lion—a sensuous nude of an intrepid woman clinging to a rock face, every muscle and tendon stretched to breaking point, leaving only the firm softness of those girlish breasts—oh, for all the world like Annie's. Oh the miracle of it.

Some vague stirring in his loins—a nothing, as the fading notes in the penultimate phrase were nothing . . . nothing but the memory of something.

Yes, there was something in that girl's eyes, same as he'd seen in Annie's eyes when she'd looked across from the piano at him, or from her chair by the fire: an artist whose eyes saw right through you, and, what's worse, who knew something you didn't know and wasn't going to share it with you. Just as she'd hidden that copy of Chambers's book behind the other books on her bookshelf, just like he'd hidden the Altmann sketches behind his: a fellowship of mutual deceit, as he'd described it in his memoir. How well they had perfected that little game of loving deceit, the pretense of not wanting to hurt the other while keeping the critical evidence under wraps, to be doled out in silent guilty stares.

Love? All artists care about is leaving something of their spirit behind.

Ah, yes, dear . . . the E-flat Major . . . yes, yes, yes. He remembered the way Annie had caressed the keys, wrist and hand like a lover's caress—outstretched pinkie hovering, hovering, only to rejoin the other fingers as her whole body gave in to the tidal current, eyes deep but focused, wearing that black thin-strapped gown that dipped to the upper curve of her breasts, the way she held her left hand to her breast as the right rippled up the keyboard on the final passage, as if to her very heart, caressing her beating heart.

He sighed, tears staining his withered cheeks, as he saw again her electric blue eyes looking up from the keyboard across the great room, piercing him to the quick.

Just *when* exactly did you hear of the death of George Altmann, the court sketch artist, dear?

It was as if her voice had emerged from the phrasing of the treble line.

Didn't I put that in the memoir? Didn't they ask me—George and Wendy? They should've asked me. Any good prosecutor—one of the first questions to be asked. Perhaps I misjudged those two. Alice would know instantly that was key.

Edward, come now, I was in the courtroom. All the court reporters knew, remarked upon after his sad death on Christmas Eve; he was one of them. The *Tribune* had to get a new sketch artist in to cover the rest of the trial. Surely you must have known as soon as the trial resumed after Christmas?

The truth: It was as if he'd always known the truth . . . but hardly an answer for a jury, or convincing enough to be set down in a memoir. How do you explain a certain menacing squint in the eyes of your client, or, more to the point, the death-mask stares of his henchmen behind the scenes?

A bemused smile, a hint of relief as Mozart's Sonata No. 16 in C Major echoed through the walls. He remembered how young Cordelia had nearly mastered it before turning to ballet. Dear Cordelia, Annie's Hail Mary, the most beloved, the faithful daughter who was there when Annie's spirit flickered out, so cruelly before her time, like a gust of wind a candle. But even Cordelia never quite had the touch, not like this, not like Alice, not the articulation infused with such breathing, palpitating life. For ballet, she'd had it in spades, until that unfortunate nagging injury, then seduced and ruined by that ne'er-do-well alcoholic husband, Jim—how could she have brought him along—for Thanksgiving, for Christ's sake!

Once again, Annie's voice interrupted his ruminations.

Clearly, dear, you knew during the trial about that ghastly death of George Altmann, knew enough to keep those sketches under wraps. Enough to later try to make feeble amends—and using our Cordelia for such a distasteful purpose and so leading her to that nemesis of a husband.

But it produced George, he pleaded, our best hope.

He wiped his tears and brought his hands together on the quilt, intertwining his fingers as if in prayer or to test their remaining strength. Always the great mystery that Alice, of all people, had the gift, had Teddy's physical mastery, and yet could find no reward or meaning in her talent, much less solace in the music, as if unable to embrace its spirit or allow it to soothe her inner demons, her unbridled rage at the injustices of this world. As if, unknowingly, she'd inherited the fiery abolitionist fervor of her great-grandfather, a man she cared not a whit about, not even enough to warrant a visit to his memorial at Harvard, even as those same righteous demons rode her back, demons self-conjured and quenchless in their bloodlust, driven to the creation of one child, Cecily, and the sad neglect of another, Billy, named after another great artist, Billy Wilder. So he had it from Stan.

Poor Billy, talk about a sad case, always overshadowed by that larger-than-life cowbird sibling sneaked into the nest. Billy, likable in his way, a free spirit, always amusing, never taking himself seriously, except to ingratiate himself with the other cousins. Self-deprecating to a fault—antithesis of his mother—and always uncomfortable, like a stand-up comic who had forgotten his punch line. Finding Billy's drug stash in Teddy's shell was no small thing—a scandal that could have ended a career if the press had ever gotten hold of it—standing there like an old fool with a plastic bag full of cocaine in hand, while the police arrived with the fire department, and later accompanying the fire inspector to examine the illegal fireworks. Talk about a close call, with cousins Karen and Cecily first denying their pyromaniacal idiocy, until Cecily finally confessed, taking all the blame on herself.

Little Cecily, my diligent cowbird changeling, who, even with a mocha complexion and brown hair, still looked more like Annie than her own mother . . . along with her talent—oh yes, the spark, a soul survival against all the genetic odds. And so proud of her beauty, her brains, her musicianship, how she turned every male eye. What do you suppose Richard Davenport would have made of such a spectacular mixed-race great-great-granddaughter?

He smiled to himself, shaking his head against the pillow at the sheer audacity of the thing, Alice's folly, even if it might well have kept him off the Supreme Court.

Oh . . . yes, that last repeated phrase, radiant, lingering, "a universal splendor," Annie had called it. What was it she always quoted? "Glory in the flower . . . We will grieve not, rather find strength in what remains behind" . . . that primal sympathy.

Which brought to mind Annie's advice—or had it been Proust's advice?—uttered almost in her last breath, to seek out those lost bastions of involuntary memory that had the power to endure time's wastage, and so pass them on to the generations to come, as his father had done with him in his gruff Victorian cadences as he'd followed along as a little boy on the trail to Handytown, or on longer expeditions down the Bush Kill to the Neversink, filling his steps with stories of people and places gone by, tales of the early settlers, tales gotten from the canal men in the last days of the D & H Canal, and how he pointed out where the Roebling aqueduct had once been etched against the sky like some Piranesian wonder of the first machine age, enough that he could almost imagine the thing, before turning to the real business of the day, those dimpled pools on the translucent face of the Neversink, where a young boy might cast his line—singing in the air, singing above the voice of the river, and so merging into eternity.

And he saw his father's hands, big, dexterous, skillful hands, a surgeon's touch as he demonstrated the tying of a fly. Or a long finger to his lips as he pointed skyward to the song of the hermit thrush. Hands that gripped the fallen bluestones at Handytown to return them to their place in a fallen wall.

And he heard his father's voice once more, or perhaps it was Justice Holmes's, the two blending much in his mind in the last years: how human conflict was less in our nature than our bloody-minded ideas, whether rivalries of clan, class, religious or ideological, which ran roughshod over the essential bonds between husband and wife, mothers and daughters, fathers and sons—that self-inflicted wound to quash the human need for love. Without love . . . a life, indeed, of half rations. Thus a judge's duty, to provide a space for free and open discourse, for justice, for grace, for spacious time to heal, for that scarcest of scarce resource—that most sacred duty: love.

"Love . . ." Had there been a scarcity of love, a drought at Hermitage that had blighted the generations?

Had he so neglected—means to the detriment of ends—that duty as a father . . . and husband?

Even a judge should not recuse himself from love . . . even if we are the bulwark, the *cordon sanitaire*, the oasis of order and sanity surrounded by chaos, that prepares the ground and so gives love the space to bloom.

That's why he'd left his memoir in George's hands—and now Wendy's—because George, in his abject loneliness, confronted by what he described as an expanding and indifferent universe, would know what best to do. Would search out the truth he'd left out or forgotten or neglected. Surely, with Teddy's brains and conscience, even lacking his intrepid physical courage, George was the one to do the right thing by way of his uncaring universe . . . as did the marsh marigolds and lady's slippers and lilacs left in its wake. As did a talented artist as brave as she was canny, willing to sacrifice Mssrs. Monet and Degas for the sake of love.

A universe, or perhaps in its old-fashioned guise, fate, that had called for the sacrifice of a son and the love of a wife . . . all to the end of saving their lives, if not their souls.

Or, as that rather harried, if not exhausted, voice over the long-distance line from the White House had put it, congratulating him on the Senate vote approving his nomination: "The right man at the right time in the right job to hold the line and protect FDR's hard-won gains from that madman McCarthy. The father of a decorated soldier. He, Teddy Dimock, would be most proud."

—

"Yes, Felicity, come in."

The door opened and Cecily entered with a cup of steaming milky tea, her head tilted impishly left and then right, tiptoeing around in a spirited, playful manner, flashing a broad smile beneath her elegant nose and laughing eyes.

"No, it's me, your long-lost granddaughter and firebrand, come to bring you your tea and get you up for cocktails. Felicity is struggling with dinner, even with Cordelia's help."

"My changeling," he said, collecting his wits from the far-flung outposts of memory.

"Your what?" she asked, her eyes taking in the spare bedroom, hung with a scattering of signed photographs and letters of appreciation from at least five presidents—as much as she could make out on a first pass. "Dark in here. Why don't I turn on a light."

"It was you, playing . . ."

"Why, of course it was—who else. Have you forgotten that I won the Annie prize to be the first cousin to master the Chopin Etudes? That ten thousand dollars sure did me a world of good."

She brought the tea over to the bedside table and helped him sit up, plumping the pillows against the brass bed railing.

"You don't need to do all that," he said shyly, a hint of wonder in his bleary eyes at his granddaughter's efficient ministrations.

"Oh, I'm used to it, Judge. I may have dropped out of med school, but I'm still a fully licensed nurse practitioner. That means I can do practically anything a doctor can do, most of it better, and a lot of stuff a doctor won't deign to do. So look on me as a twofer." She put a pillow behind his head, smoothing down a cowlick of white hair. "So, how're you feeling?"

"I'm fine." He looked into her kind eyes, at the high, lovely coffee-complected brow, the long, curly dark hair with blond streaking falling in bunches to her shoulders. "I could swear it was Annie playing."

She laughed. "It was . . . I was cheating, I was using all her finger-ings. That Romanian bitch on wheels you had up from Juilliard didn't like Annie's fingerings for beans, but I always used them just to piss her off."

"I must have been away in the city. If you'd only told me . . ."

"I wanted that prize in the worst way."

"Competitive—huh, like Annie." He sipped his tea, savoring the infu-sion of warmth. "How long has it been, Cecily? You were still a girl."

"More than twenty years, since I was seventeen—going on thirty—when I almost burned down the boathouse and you kicked me out."

"I'd never kick you out," he protested with a faint smile. "Karen, perhaps, but never you."

"Well, you sure weren't exactly happy. And then when Alice and Martha got wind of you feeling up my—and Karen's—boobs, well, that was kinda the straw that broke the camel's back."

"I did nothing of the sort," he said indignantly. "It was Alice and Martha, feeding off each other, making up stories, just like when they were girls."

"Oh yes you did, at the beach, because Karen and I were having a contest to see who could grow and show the biggest, best tits and get you—and the boys—to fetch a feel. You were our grand prize."

She took his hand in hers and placed a finger on the underside of his wrist, looking at her watch as she took his pulse.

"You wouldn't be half a man if you didn't at least try."

"Well, if I did, I apologize." He was staring intently at her hands. "You do have beautiful hands, though."

"Oh, no need for flattery, I'm cool. Now, why don't I take your blood pressure." She reached for the pressure cuff hanging on the paneled wall by the bed.

"No need for that."

"I'm a nurse, remember. That's my job, to make sure your ticker keeps ticking, and if you need another feel of my boobs to keep it ticking, that's way cool, too." She glanced at the painting on the wall by the bed and smiled wickedly. "But maybe you're already good to go in that department."

57

Tormented By Destiny

THEY LAY IN each other's arms, snuggling under the down comforter, watching the moonlight laving the shadows on the ceiling.

"I think I drank too much wine," she said.

"He really pulled out all the stops tonight, what a charm offensive. The Bordeaux, that Saint-Emilion, was quite something."

"It's warm, don't you think?" she said, and she flipped back the comforter.

"Even warmer tomorrow. Maybe warm enough to hike down to the Neversink aqueduct on Friday. Nancy was sure excited at the idea."

She reached to his crotch and began with gentle persuasion.

"How 'bout another round?"

"I think you exhausted Jabba last night. I mean, you only came five times."

"Six . . . you fell asleep."

"Must be all that clean air, the mountain lion thing or are you . . . You are scary, you know."

"It energizes me, or relaxes me, depending." She raised herself on one elbow to see him better. "What's bothering you? The show not selling as well as you hoped?"

"I told my mom about that strange passage in the memoir where Annie gives him that one chance to get her pregnant. I think it kinda threw her for a loop."

"Well, it would. It gives me the creeps, such cruelty."

"And he lied about Annie conceiving Teddy in Venice. Annie told her she was pregnant before they got married."

"Another lie—what?—to preserve the proprieties, to preserve Annie's fantasies."

He reached a hand to her breast, marveling at the whiteness of her skin as the moonlight filtered in just above the highest boughs, her pale, erect nipples casting tiny shadows. He noticed a stack of old books on her beside table.

"You've already been at her books, I see."

"Oh, Annie's you mean. Yes, she annotated her French volumes of Proust in French—can you believe it? It's really quite magical for me, the original . . . her French fingerings." She kissed him tenderly. "How you doing?"

"Sorry, a little weird with everyone here. I mean, at the table tonight, you could just cut the resentment with a knife, about our room—something. I keep waiting for someone to barge in and demand we leave."

"I barred the door."

"Actually, I was amazed how well everyone behaved at cocktails and dinner. You'd think we were a regular family."

She laughed. "Thank God for Nancy. The adults acting like adults. But you have to admit the Judge was wonderful, so incredibly solicitous of everyone."

He kissed her lips. "Cecily has him wrapped around her pinkie—almost as much as you do."

"Oh, she gets the charm prize all right. But you know what I really love about her? It's all real and genuine. Love for people just flows from her—just like her playing after dinner. Even Alice behaved like a lamb." Wendy moved to kiss him deeply. "Chip off the ole block"—she giggled—"prison block."

"So," he asked hopefully, "that's what you guys were talking about in the canoe, on the island?"

"Eagles."

"Eagles?"

"The Judge—remember?—touched lightly on it in his memoir."

"Yeah, right—that's the point. How did it stack up against what she had to say? I mean, had to be a little freaky."

"Oh," she demurred, "we were just indulging in a lot of silly girl talk."

"Cecily never said boo—at least not to me—when we were kids . . . part of her allure."

"She's mine now—*my* mysterious muse. Those penetrating eyes—don't you think? Wait till you see my most recent work. Her skin tones are simply ravishing, like clover honey in sunlight against the rock formations. We'll give her a starring role at Dark Matter next season—a twofer."

He kissed her tentatively. "You two are quite the . . . what?"

She laughed. "Oh, but Nancy—she's the real pocket rocket. Wow, that girl doesn't miss a trick. Those wide fawn-colored eyes were taking everything in at the table tonight."

"I promised I'd take her down to the boathouse tomorrow, if the conditions are good and I can fire up my old telescope."

"Sorry, I've been distracting you." And she began again with her ministrations.

"No, it's just the memoir thing—it's got me tied up in knots, the way Alice keeps prodding me on the subject."

"I thought she was rather subdued and behaving herself. While Stan was—in the most avuncular way—pumping me with questions about climbing Everest."

"Pregnant," he mused, staring at the far wall, "under their Bunce moon."

She seemed to flinch at his words, her palm moving up to her solar plexus.

Then she laughed. "Wow, when Annie wanted something . . ."

"Oh, just another white lie, another anomaly in the data."

"Not for her it wasn't." She rested her hand on his heart. "She loved Venice. I'm sure they concocted the story for propriety's sake. Surely we can allow him a little poetic license in his memoir."

"The poetry, maybe."

"Gosh, George, people *need* stories, little myths to live by—we all do."

"Fine, but where does it all stop? Where do the little white lies become big fat self-serving lies? I don't like being used. My mother found that part in his memoir about Annie refusing to sleep with him after Teddy's death—except for that once—almost impossible to believe. As she put it, 'A woman who played the piano with so much passion couldn't just leave it in on the concert stage.'"

"Let Cordelia deal with it—it's her life."

"And how."

"He's depending on us—on you, baby"—she kissed him, lingering with her tongue between his lips—"to do the right thing."

"And just what part of the right thing is that? The grandson part, or the astrophysicist part—God forbid the Weinstein part?"

She pitched her voice higher, changing gears. "Well, now we know where the Raphael Soyer portrait got to."

"Funny, Aunt Alice seemed almost pleased."

"You know, we've got to include Altmann's letter about seeing Annie's portrait in Soyer's studio, too. He was obviously a little in love with it, if not Annie's playing. Do you suppose . . ."

Her voice fell away, as if even she was exhausted by the imponderables. For minutes they remained quiet, staring at the moonlit white of the ceiling, the oscillating shadows and pine-sifted apertures.

When she spoke again, it was as if out of a dream.

"I spent almost an hour with Nancy explaining the mythology of the ship's keel ceiling. She couldn't get enough of it. They've taught her almost nothing in school. And as I was explaining the gods and goddesses, the stories, it occurred to me that it's really a kind of elaborate mnemonic system, a way of remembering the night sky by peopling it with stories."

"Giordano Bruno wrote a book for King Henry III, *On the Shadows of Ideas*, elaborating on his mnemonic devices."

"No way . . ."

He gestured to the play of light and shadow: "That's the thing," he said, sighing. "It's like there are two systems at odds: his stories about the law, his life and family, and the disaster of the Hiss trial. And whenever those two systems collide or overlap, the data distorts—the observations fail to account."

"Then take it from Annie: the two ways, to Handytown—Annie's Way—and the Neversink. After all, he remembered enough—cared enough to include her thoughts."

She bent to kiss him but could tell his mind was elsewhere.

"It's this unsettling gap, this interaction between two quantum fields—how things really are and how we perceive them. Is it a problem of perception, or poor data, or the failure of language? Or he just lies or forgets—even as his words leave shadows. It messes with my mind."

"Yes, *your* mind, George. Like, *in* your mind. What was it Chambers wrote—how he no longer saw men and women as good or evil, kind or cruel . . ." She paused, seeing the text in her mind's eye. "But as individual beings, tormented by destiny—terribly so because each was enclosed beyond the power to change in the ordeal of his individuality." She shook her head and sighed. "So let the damn stories find their own way; they always do." She pulled herself up on her knees. "Maybe I could sit on your face."

"I don't like being lied to and I don't like being made a patsy."

She nibbled his ear.

"George, just leave stuff out that doesn't quite measure up. That way, he's off the hook, you're off the hook: What you don't know can't hurt you. That's why he's depending on you. It's not a fucking theory for an academic journal; it's a pathway forward."

She flung a knee across his thighs, straddling him, playfully but forcefully holding his shoulders to the mattress with her hands. Then she swept her eyes across the room as if to encompass the moonlight and those nagging luminous shadows, and where the Bunce, translucent with pale fire, seemed like yet another window—a portal onto yet another dimension.

"All that matters is saving this—and Nancy—this moment, which is the only future we've got."

He looked into her impassioned eyes. "What more have you got cooked up? Spit it out."

"It's all about preserving the world. Why else did Proust write, and Chambers give witness, and Altmann paint—and the fucking memoir. That's all any of us can do . . . Just look into Nancy's enchanted face."

And in her moon-glutted eyes, he could see again the firelight in the great room after dinner, while Cecily played the complete Chopin Etudes, and the Tiffany lamps gave out a bucolic glow, and Nancy, laughing hysterically with all the wine she'd drunk, stood at the Judge's knee as he paged through his birding guides and sang out his famous repertoire of near-perfect birdcalls. While, from on high, the deathless gods stared down in amusement at all such human folly, joining the laughter as they blessed this rare mortal gathering on the cusp of their airy shores.

His reverie was shattered by the buzz of his cell and an incoming e-mail.

"Leave it," she snapped.

Hello again, George:

I've been thinking over our previous exchanges—about your revised catalog essay—and realized that I haven't been entirely candid about my original response to your magnificent George Altmann show in the *Times*. My reaction to the works and your informative catalog was entirely genuine, as I've reiterated to you, but it was also prompted by a vague memory of the artist when I was going through my father's letters, diaries, and reviews from the thirties and forties, when he was chief critic for the *Times*. I had been struck by his highly favorable reviews of George Altmann's figurative—shall we call it social realism?—work of the thirties. But found myself troubled and intrigued by his abrupt change to a scalding attack on Altmann's move to abstraction beginning in the forties and continuing right up to his death in 1949. Why the change of heart? My father was such a progressive critic, who loved European abstraction, who wrote some of the most perceptive reviews on Kandinsky as far back as the twenties. How was it he hadn't responded to Altmann's abstract landscapes of the forties? Abstractions so far ahead of their time, an avatar to so much of what de Kooning and Rothko and Guston would achieve a decade later? Why had he turned on Altmann so viciously? I wondered if it had something to do with America's cultural cringe in those prewar decades and later, when we bowed at the altar of Picasso and Matisse, when we thought our own artists second-rate.

So, a week ago, I returned to my father's archives and dug out a tattered bunch of pocket calendars, which also occasionally served as notebooks for impromptu interviews or jotted reflections on studio visits. I found the following notation for July 14, 1940: "Received a phone call from B. this morning informing me that George Altmann had defected from the P and was considered a potential snitch and saboteur, and therefore was to be banned from all NYCP functions—his art dismissed." And this from February 3, 1945: "Instructed that Altmann's latest elitist and bourgeois reactionary offerings are to be either ignored or criticized for their failure to celebrate the revolutionary values of the workers. Any gallery that handled his reactionary work is to be boycotted."

My father never mentioned or admitted that he'd been a member of the Communist Party, which may explain why he was then dropped from the *Times* in the late fifties, during the McCarthy era. If his disparagement of George Altmann's late abstraction was due to directives from Party officials, as I fear is the case, then he, indeed, deserved to be fired. Something he was bitter about for the rest of his life but grievances he never aired publicly against the *Times*. For me, personally, this discovery is both disturbing and yet clarifying (right word?). Sadness about my father's moral cowardice in the face of genius, and relief that at least it wasn't his aesthetic judgment that was at fault. And, I suppose, some redemptive relief that now, following in his footsteps as art critic for the *Times*, at least my aesthetic instincts were right in recognizing greatness when I happened upon it. Although, truth be told, not without a tip-off from a fabulous young woman artist out of Yale, who I now see is offi-cially on your roster with a show scheduled for the spring! Congrats to her and to you for recognizing her blazing talent!

For your eyes only: I have whispered in the ear of the head curators at MoMA and the Whitney. You can expect to hear from them.

I would be happy to make the material in my father's diary available to you for your planned revised and enlarged essay for the Altmann cat-alog. It is crucial, in my opinion, that the historical truth about George Altmann's pathbreaking art and career be accurate in every detail, even if a shameful reflection on my father, whom I adored.

Best, Judith
P.S. Happy Thanksgiving

58
Lost Souls

OCTOBER 23, 1952

Dearest Edward:

Forgive me for not writing sooner. With Alger now in prison and our son, Tony, fully on my hands under these dreadful circumstances, it is all I can do to keep my sanity.

But my complaints are nothing compared to your loss of Teddy. When I got the news, I was sunk in despair. This worthless, stupid, unnecessary war, and now with China in it, as well. Where will it stop?

I know how much you doted on your beautiful boy. I remember him so vividly, decked out like a little Indian, his album of bird feathers—so alive to his tiny world of rods and reels and birding guides that our presence barely flickered in his thinking. As a mother of sons, I will remember him like that, as a golden-haired Hawkeye guiding us safely, and keep a tiny piece of him safe with me forever.

We expect the FBI has the phones tapped and the incoming mail opened. I'm followed everywhere, but I should be able to drop this in a postbox undetected. My life has been reduced to near nothing, while Alger's is reduced to invisibility, though his letters to me and Tony are touching and filled with perceptive ruminations on his incarceration, his fellow inmates, and quite lovely renditions on nature and the seasons as glimpsed from his prison window. Tony and I are allowed to visit at Lewisburg prison once a month for four hours (a ten-hour trip by train and taxi), so we split it up into two-hour segments over two days and spend one night at an inn in Lewisburg. The prison visiting room is quite pleasant and we are allowed to hold hands and hug, but for a young boy, the whole thing is so incomprehensible, when he is surrounded by friends in New York who not only revere his father but are incredulous that such an injustice could happen to such a good man. If an adult can barely comprehend the circumstances of such a travesty, how can the simple nature of a child?

One would think that at an oasis like the Lewisburg Inn a child would be safe from the madness, and yet even there the *Saturday Evening Post* found my son in the guise of that fraudster Chambers. How to explain such fabrications to a sensitive child. It is as if he is forced to contend with at least two different fathers—the one he loves and Chambers's sinister doppelgänger—imagine! As a mother, it is pure hell. Surely, as a father you can understand our duty to provide a happy and stable upbringing for children, not a three-ring circus of uncertainty and hatred. It is sheer agony trying to shield him and provide him with a healthy and normal childhood.

But who am I to complain when your Annie has lost so much more.

How fate makes sad fools of us all. So I trot along, bit in mouth, still wearing Alger's silks, my bounded duty. I now have a job downstairs in the packing room at Doubleday—out of sight, where I won't upset the customers. Worried sick that I'm not there when Tony gets home from school. The way things are going with the popularity of Chambers's book, I wouldn't blame you if you turned on Alger, on us—no, I wouldn't blame you at all.

Again, my condolences for your loss. I weep for your and Annie's lost child.

Love,
Pross
P.S. And congratulations on the appeals court.
Not that I ever had any doubts.

Karen hesitated before the door of her parents' room, concerned, trying to decide on the appropriate demeanor: dour, chatty, or nostalgic—her preferred mood of the moment. There was no response to her knock, so she carefully eased open the door into the near darkness and stale closeness of a room left unaired for ages. Spotting her mother lying with a book by her bedside lamp, she assumed an upbeat demeanor, waving her arms with the pent-up excitement of a child brimming with things to tell. Jabbering on but getting no response, she pulled up a chair to the side of the bed. Martha blinked and turned her head on the pillow, her disheveled brown hair showing a good inch of gray at the roots (very unlike her mother to go so long between colorings), her face slack, cheeks sunken, her eyes expressing confusion.

"I must've nodded off."

Karen, a little panicked at how her mother seemed to age before her eyes, said, "You went up early. Weren't you enjoying Cecily's playing?"

"I needed to find something."

"Well, Nancy *was* exhausting," she huffed, glancing around in the semidarkness. "Why, you and Dad haven't even unpacked."

Karen turned on another lamp and got the two small roller suitcases and unzipped them on the bed, carrying things to the bureau by the window. "You need some air in here," she said, cracking the moonlit windows. "The air is delicious." As she did, she glanced here and there, as if perturbed by the piles of dog-eared paperbacks that had been stacked on the floor by the bookshelves. Many lay with spines up, pages splayed like nesting doves.

"Looking for something?" asked Karen, nodding toward the book piles.

"It's nothing."

"What's the matter, Mom? You barely opened your mouth at dinner."

"Oh, I'm just losing my mind."

"You're just tired after sitting in traffic all morning—I'm tired."

"No, I mean it . . . memory overload—as if Hermitage just tumbled in on me. I didn't realize how long it's been, and yet there are moments when it seems like yesterday. Like when I'd looked up from my plate and saw Teddy making faces at me from across the table, where he always sat—where George was sitting."

"It happens to all of us. I kept thinking—talk about making faces—how much I miss Billy. How Max, the little idiot, should be here. And that Wendy had Billy's old room all ready and waiting, loaded up with all kinds of goodies: fishing gear and camping stuff and outdoor wear like you wouldn't believe."

"Yes, I feel for Alice and Stan—can't be easy." Martha sat up on the bed to watch her daughter unpack, swinging her feet to the floor. "I was going through all my college books this afternoon—I guess they all got left here during my grad school years and I never bothered to collect them."

"Yeah." Her daughter smiled, a hint of happiness in her full lips. "Same here when I walked into my room. What a reader I was as a kid." She sighed, again inspecting the book piles. "Were you looking for something?"

"Well, yes and no. I don't know if it's here; in fact, I'm not even sure if it exists."

"What's that, Mom?"

"Oh nothing, just a letter Teddy wrote me from Korea."

"Shall I put Dad's stuff below or above your drawers?"

"We haven't shared a room in donkey's years."

"Everybody's got new mattresses. Just my luck."

"But your father—" Martha jounced, testing the mattress.

"It'll be fine; he's been yacking it up with Uncle Stan, like old pals, and now he's noting down all Dr. Dimock's books in the shelves of the great room—'literary snapshot of a bygone era,' he calls it. Something for a paper he's doing on how popular books shape social norms."

"Yes, old friends," murmured her mother, gazing fondly in the direction of her book piles. "That divinely handsome Jung. Sorting through, I was reminded of the joy and intellectual insights I first found in those pages, that smarty-pants girl holed up on the piazza or in the boathouse, nose in a book. Except, what, exactly, got me so excited?"

Karen, trying to liven things, picked up a book from the nearest pile.

"*Hola, amigo,* Karen Horney—my namesake: *The Neurotic Personality of Our Time,* 1937, first edition. That's me all right!" Karen flipped the underlined pages. "Wow, and she signed it to you—1955. You must've just finished up at Radcliffe."

Martha smiled for the first time at the familiar name. "Maybe my first year at med school. I remember Karen being so cross at Daddy for using Freud like a—what did she call it . . . 'cudgel,' yes—against that terrible man in the Hiss trial."

"As we well know," her daughter sang out to soften the sarcasm, "Ms. Horney was no fan of Herr Freud. Imagine being stuck with that name today."

"Then I worked with Margaret for some years—didn't I?"

Karen looked on intently, her mother's eyes vacant, perplexed.

"*Coming of Age in Samoa,* you know, has been discredited." Karen put the last of her mother's things away in the dresser and began on her father's bag. "Any mother with a son knows better—hell, even God knows better!"

"It's all such a muddle, you see . . . and coming back . . ." Martha sighed, a lost expression on her face. "This place seems so . . . well, fluid, so mixed up. Do you suppose seeing my father after so long—oh, how he's aged—has prompted a regression to that disgruntled lonely child I once was? Ridiculous, I know, but when you knocked on the door just now, I thought it might be Annie come to tell me to turn off my light before I ruined my eyes."

Karen turned with a pair of sneakers in hand.

"You lonely?"

"Annie called me a snooty wallflower just because I refused to be introduced into society at the annual debutante ball."

"Annie disparaged Freud when you were a teenager, right?" Karen shook her head comically. "Maybe she was more of a proto-feminist than you realized. I bet Annie and Karen Horney would have just loved lighting a funeral pyre for Dr. Freud."

This thought seemed to catch Martha off guard, for her lips tightened and her pale cheeks flattened.

"Annie, too, was furious how Daddy had enlisted Freud to go after that awful man, Chambers. And"—Martha raised an admonishing finger—"she accused me, of all people, of putting him up to it."

Karen shook her head, bemused, if not a little incredulous.

"Well, now we hand out Cymbalta and Zoloft like bubble gum at Halloween. Ritalin, too, for the hyperactive kids in your life. Half my women patients wonder if Viagra can help them, too."

"I know you're disappointed about Max."

"Listen, Mom, you've helped hundreds, if not thousands."

"I can't remember a lot of their names."

"Oh my God!" Karen had just opened the top bureau drawer. She held up an oblong black leather case with a brass clasp and took it over to her mother. Sitting down, she held the case under the lamp, revealing a gold-embossed marine emblem stamped into the leather. She struggled with the recalcitrant clasp. Three medals glittered against the black felt. Her hands shaking, Martha took the case, while fumbling with her reading glasses.

"For God's sake . . ."

"Teddy's?" asked Karen.

"Yes, yes, of course. Hateful, aren't they?"

"Oh, Mom."

Tears streamed from her mother's eyes.

"The old bastard."

Karen went to the bureau for some Kleenex, returning with a framed faded color snapshot that had been hanging on the nearby wall. When her mother had dried her eyes, she handed her the photo of a tall athletic figure, blond hair blowing, arm raised, waders knee-deep in the Neversink, the glint of a line caught by the shutter in a singing loop above the flowing water.

Karen said in a consoling tone, "This used to hang in the Judge's office, by his desk. He's left these things here for you, Mom."

Martha looked from her daughter to the medals to the photo, as if baffled.

"Have you seen your father?"

"I told you, Dad's still downstairs messing around. He never goes to bed until late."

"You know what I always liked about your father?" She pressed the leather case against her breasts. "His equanimity: Nothing ever bothered him. The Judge could make some scorching anti-Semitic remark and he'd just laugh it off."

"Shall I get him for you?"

"Nancy seemed happy, didn't she?"

"Nancy's fine; they took her off the clozapine a few months ago. She feels safe here—the way she's opened up, being out of the city. Even if she's been going through withdrawal symptoms all day with her phone off the grid. God knows what Max is getting up to right now—hell, let someone else's parents launder the sheets and towels."

Martha held the photo of Teddy on the Neversink up to the bed-side lamp, squinting, turning it this way and that to relieve the glare on the glass.

"Did I ever tell you that Max reminds me of my brother in some ways, even with his dark hair? How the girls loved Teddy. We all did. Annie was the worst; she always spoiled him, indulged him—her God's gift. Till he believed it, too; till he thought he could do no wrong. '*My little bookworm*' . . ." She grinned like an embarrassed schoolgirl at the recitation of a naughty couplet.

Karen pushed back two strands of tangled hair that had strayed over her mother's eyes. "I couldn't believe how Erich was sucking up to the Judge tonight. I guess he recognizes a good thing when he sees it."

"Nancy does seem quite taken with Hermitage." Martha raised a knowing eyebrow at her daughter. "Enough, well, maybe, to keep her close to her own family, if you know what I mean. And Max, too."

Karen, a hint of relief at this confirmation of her own calculation, took the framed photo and rehung it. She nodded appreciatively.

"I have to tell you, I'm feeling pretty stupid that we made such a stink about—you know . . ."

"Oh," gushed Martha, rising to the bait, "it wasn't just you and Cecily. After he became a judge—such a celebrity in his circles—he had women falling over him. His fawning law clerks in their short miniskirts were the worst. Celebrity, power—let me tell you, goes right to the male libido, like crack cocaine. But Cordelia—unforgivable."

"Cecily and I . . . well, it was really just a game, a competition; I envied her boobs—still do. Did you see how she and the Judge were thick as thieves tonight?"

"Listen, the old goat molested his own daughter—so you two got off easy."

"Aunt Cordelia just laughs that business off now."

"She didn't when I had her in therapy. She was in tears. Imagine waking up with a hangover in your father's bed at the Ritz-Carlton smelling of sex, to put it non-clinically. The trauma explains everything, how she went off the deep end at Woodstock, became a sexaholic—just sex, sex, sex with every man who took her fancy. Revolting against every standard Annie ever set for her."

"Not enough to keep George away from Hermitage all those summers," said Karen indignantly.

"Speaking of Cordelia," said Martha, as if now coming back to life, "she asked me the oddest things before cocktails tonight. She wanted to know if Annie had stopped sleeping with Daddy after Teddy died."

"Uh-huh."

"If maybe she'd been so traumatized that she lost her sex drive, or something to that effect."

"Well, you *are* something of the world's expert on faltering libidos."

Martha's face darkened at her daughter's default sarcasm.

"What to say to that? I mean, one's parents' sex life is taboo."

"Well, clearly they had some kind of sex life—Cordelia, for instance."

"That's what I told her. But she seemed more interested in exactly when—when, well, they drifted apart, separate bedrooms and all that. Probably not helped by his obsession with Priscilla Hiss."

Karen rolled her eyes as she stuck the two bags in the closet, now thoroughly tired of the subject. "I feel like a fool not getting Maxie up here before—away from all the goddamn money and status-seeking bullshit."

"Imagine going from the pinnacle of the Washington establishment, socializing with Eleanor and Franklin at the White House, to being broke and sick and ending your days in the Village Nursing Home. I felt powerless to talk her through her trauma, to get at the cause of her depression—poor girl, dying nearly alone—what, fifteen years ago now—while her son and husband were still out trumpeting his innocence. I think she died of a broken heart, literally. Sometimes it seemed she just came to me to reminisce about the Judge, who, deep down, she felt saw the good in her."

"Well, some people you just can't help. I hope you didn't gossip about him to her; that would have been totally inappropriate."

"Strange, I do have a vague memory of her being here at Hermitage when I was a child. I was reminded of it somehow when we drove up this afternoon and Nancy leaped out of the car and dashed up the stairs of the piazza." Martha squinted, an inward gaze. "And occasionally Priscilla would mention Hermitage in an offhand, dreamy way during our sessions, as if maybe hoping I'd engage with her on the subject, or might offer her tidbits about Daddy, her first love from Yale days—fat chance."

Not a little fed up, Karen whipped out her cell phone and held it up hopefully to the moonlight through the window.

"That's what I need, a first love." For a moment, she caught sight of her reflection in the geometry of lozenges, tossing back a stray strand of hair, raising her chin to better examine the full lips and adequate, if filled-out, cheekbones of the flirtatious teenager of years before.

"This time, dear, find yourself a fellow who likes fly-fishing."

"Maybe I should try bribing Maxie. I mean, Nancy is so excited about her room, just filled with all kinds of outdoor gear and fancy tennis and swimming outfits. Like she's hit the L.L. Bean jackpot." She shook her head at her recalcitrant phone, grumbling.

"Try the Judge's phone in the morning."

"Ah," she exclaimed, "he won't know it's me calling!"

She stuck out her tongue and smiled hopefully at her reflection.

"I hope they left Teddy's Yale banner and trophies alone."

"Nancy? Are you kidding? Now there's a Groton banner hanging above her bed—and in Maxie's room, too!"

Karen spun on her heels, a swagger in her step as she returned to her mother's side and placed a conspiratorial hand on her shoulder. With the other, she pointed out where, on the highest bookshelves, like the transmigration of weary souls, a freshly polished collection of rowing trophies now glittered, basking in the moonlight.

59
Pieces of Time

🖳

"DAD, HOW COME you don't like Hermitage?"

"Who says I don't, honey?" Erich opened the window in Teddy's old room and tapped on a pane as if to ascertain its soundness, then turned his sheepish angular face to his somewhat tipsy daughter's inquisitive stare. "In fact, I was really, really happy here at just about the same age you are now. But then I was lucky: I had Karen and Cecily and Billy and George."

"Then how come I'm here for the first time when Great-grandpa has been here like forever?"

Nancy had been trying on various fishing and hiking outfits and was clomping around her room in brand-new Merrell hiking boots, trying to break them in for the next day. Erich found the room transformed from how he remembered it when he and Billy would sneak in to mess with George's stuff or short-sheet his bed. Partly it was the smell of plastic packaging material, nail polish, various perfumes (each had to be tried on), and the walls and shelves banished of dated school and college photos and musty books, except for a well-worn Jack London anthology, a beat-up album of bird feathers, and, oddly, the vintage collection of American first editions of Joseph Conrad novels (which remained steadfastly in pride of place), many with their original dust jackets preserved under Mylar sleeves. Erich found himself drawn to the Conrad for reasons he now struggled to explain.

"Oh, it's just one of those things. Your mom and I were always so busy—going to see her folks in the Hamptons and everything. She's, you know, such a beach person."

"I think Mom would like it here, even if it isn't exactly her East Hampton scene."

"Do you think? Certainly a lot less social life—at least until the summer." He smiled, a hint of nostalgia evident in his expression. "Unless you like bears."

"Even if cell phones don't work." She stopped pacing for a moment, whipped out her cell phone for a quick check, and turned to the black-and-crimson Groton banner now in residence over her bed. She struck a pose of indecision, giddy and giggling, swishing her shoulder-length hair back, first right, then left. "Like half my class is now thinking about going away to school."

She went over to the bureau, where the perfume bottles were arranged like chic crystal chess pieces, and examined her face in the mirror, pulling back her hair and securing it with an antique silver barrette engraved *Carnegie Hall, 1947*, which had come stowed in a blue Tiffany pouch. She met her father's stare in the mirror. He secretly noted with a hint of sadness her mother's fair skin and upturned nose, and now with her hair back hints of a grown-up independence that snapped in her intelligent eyes. Turning with the quick and easy smile of a model on a runway, she thrust her hands deep into the pockets of her webbed fishing vest, spreading it wide to better show off her brilliant orange hiking pants with zippered pockets on the thighs.

She hiccuped and frowned goofily. "Not as many zippers as Wendy's jumpsuit, but pretty cool." She flicked an array of zippers up and down to demonstrate. "I'm going to wear it when Cousin George takes me down to the boathouse tomorrow night with his telescope."

"Amazing how Wendy managed to get everything perfectly your size."

She went to the window and leaned out into the moonlight, squinting at the luminous ivory furrows across the lake, the bewitching vigil of the white pine where the uppermost branches embraced the pale night.

"I mean, it's a little spooky here with all the old photos and the living room with that ceiling that is just the most beautiful thing I've ever seen with all those naked goddesses—wow. And the forest—I mean everywhere you look—like, like, you know that part in *The Lion, the Witch and the Wardrobe* where they step through the wardrobe and suddenly the clothes turn into tree branches and they come out into Narnia in winter." She followed the zigzag path down to the boathouse, where the moon shadows harbored patches of sheerest white. "And I guess Mom was right after all to make me take piano lessons."

Erich, with a lanky awkwardness, thoughtfully fingered his goatee and then pulled back a corner of the flowered bedspread to reveal equally new sheets and pillowcases decorated with wild birds. "No lions." He smiled. And there by the bedside table, like a solitary revenant of all that had once been, was a framed photo of Teddy standing on a dock in his letter sweater. The white sweater was emblazoned with a black *G*. In one hand he held a long sculling oar. Next to him was his coach, whose face was in shadow under a slouch hat.

"So handsome!" said Nancy coming over. "And the sweater is so cool. And look at those muscles in his legs."

"When I was a kid," he said, nodding, slightly high himself, "Teddy was like one of those gods in the ceiling—to hear the Judge go on: how good he was at everything, how much he loved fishing and birding and rowing."

"What happened to him?"

"He died in the Korean War."

"When was that?"

Erich went over to bookshelves and began a nostalgic inspection of the collection of Conrad. "For all the money your mom and I pay for Calhoun, you should know a little more about American history."

"Maybe we haven't gotten as far as the Korean War."

Her father began slipping out volumes of Conrad, examining the covers, feeling the spines, flipping the underlined pages. "This was Teddy's collection of books by Joseph Conrad. And you see, when we were even younger than you, we'd gather around the fire in the great room before bed and the Judge would read to us from these novels while we gazed up at that ship's keel ceiling—such a sea of stars—just like you tonight by the fire with your great-grandfather." He paused, his chin quivering, blinking rapidly. "And I barely remember the stories, but I remember the places . . . the sea, the sound of the wind and waves, the silver moonlight, sailing over plains of darkness like the smoothest obsidian . . . sunsets, too, I suppose; and, I don't know, maybe it kind of got into my blood: ships, cargo ships plying their trade from one exotic port of call to another, and the creaking of ropes and the chatter of different languages and the smells of brine and spices from the East." He attempted an indifferent smile, but his bewilderment was such that his lips quivered into a half frown.

Nancy touched her father's hand.

"I'm the only one in my class who even knows where Sicily is."

"You see, when I first saw it, Segesta, that is, an ancient town that goes back before even the Greeks in the northwest corner of Sicily,

I fell in love. There's a beautiful Doric temple there, the most splendidly preserved temple in the ancient world, even if it was never quite finished. It lies in a valley, and in the summer . . . well, these rows of perfectly aligned old columns, weathered by time and war, a temple gazed upon by the Greeks and Romans and Carthaginians and Vandals and Normans and Germans and French and Aragonese . . . well, it's still there, sailing along after thousands of years, lapped by meadows of millions of colorful wildflowers—oh, the scents of oleander and hibiscus, laurel and lemon groves—and all under this brilliant blue sky. I guess I was quite taken with it—quite haunted by the feeling of all that had gone on there but was no more. That's what historians do . . . well, we try to fill in the pieces of time that have crumbled away."

A little wide-eyed with embarrassment at this near confession, Nancy turned from her father's face to her bed and ran a hand over the plaid wool blanket folded neatly at the foot.

"Wow . . . and Teddy slept here. You sure his ghost isn't around? Don't ghosts return to places they love?"

"I'm not sure about ghosts, but I have a feeling that if he were still around, he'd be very happy to know you're hanging out in his old room."

Erich went over and sat down next to his daughter on the bed, and shared with her an illustrated edition of Conrad's *Youth*, the dust jacket protected under Mylar. Beneath the title in faded burgundy lettering was a grid pattern of waves, a design which, upon closer inspection, turned out to be stylized leaping fish.

"Look, you see, it's got his name in it." And he read, "'For our darling Teddy, Mother and Father, Christmas 1945.'"

"Wow, that was a long time ago. Way before I was born."

"Me, too." He continued, reading a passage from the book: "'I remember my youth and the feeling that will never come back to me any more—the feeling that I could last for ever, could outlast the sea, the earth, and all men . . .'"

"Really . . . Dad?"

He wiped a tear. "Someday you may come back to this very room, your room, and pick up this book—which kinda belongs to you now—and you'll feel . . . well, something like that, even if you don't right now."

He handed her the book and she held it to her chest.

"Maybe if I read some of his books, well, maybe he'd—his ghost would, like, be appeased."

"You'll be a secret sharer." He smiled wistfully, returning to the shelf to pull out the tooled leather-bound album of bird feathers, flipping slowly through the pages labeled in a child's hand as he mused. "I think I remember your great-grandpa saying something about how Teddy liked traveling in his mind and was all set to join the navy after Yale, or maybe it was law school. That when he fished the Neversink, he used to dream about how the same water rushing past his waders would make it to the Delaware and into the sea and the far ends of the earth, a wave lapping on a palm-studded beach in Hawaii. And that's the feeling that got me hooked—the connections, I mean: how trading voyages in olden days in the Mediterranean provided the glue to hold civilization together. The Venetians were remarkable; they built a fabulous city on trade, mostly transporting luxury goods from the Levant to the West, to the rest of Europe. But they also needed to trade with Sicily; they needed Sicilian grain and raw materials to feed their people, kind of like what your great-grandpa was saying to you when we arrived today about the D & H Canal transporting coal from the Pennsylvania coal fields to New York City, where we live. Sorry, I know I'm sounding like a teacher."

She smiled at her father, intrigued, unexpectedly pleased, still holding the Conrad tight.

"Can we go visit that old canal?"

"Why not, sure."

"I mean"—she slipped out of the fishing vest and began folding it carefully—"it's not really the same without Max here."

"Hey, maybe you can help—Karen had a great idea: We'll try him in the morning on the Judge's phone. Maybe you can tell him about all your cool new stuff and how much fun you're having."

"How come you never told me the stories Great-grandpa told us at dinner tonight?"

"Didn't I?"

"I guess he still misses Teddy," she said, placing the Conrad on her bedside table and touching the photograph, as if drawn to a talisman.

"But now he's got you, his great-granddaughter—now that's *really* something special . . . four generations of Dimocks."

"Can I bring my friends here in the summer? My boyfriend even?"

"You have a boyfriend?"

"Everybody has boyfriends . . . certainly by next summer. And then Max can bring Jennifer and we'll have a party."

"Hey, why not a book party. When we were kids here in the summer, it felt like it was timeless, all the time in the world to read, like what they say about Venice—timeless, as Segesta was for me."

His daughter was leafing through a magazine.

"Did you pick that up from downstairs—the *Groton School Quarterly*?"

"It was on the bureau with the other stuff. It looks like a really cool place. The kids seem supersmart and like they're enjoying themselves. *And* they have a girls' rowing team."

"Well, there you go."

60

A Life in the Law and Out:
Without a Price

AS I DRAW to the end of my memoir—or my memoir draws to the end of me—frankly, I'm not sure which—I feel I must offer some kind of summary, or perhaps a closing argument, even if, as I fear, the thing itself may remain unfinished, the jury hung, a plea in abeyance. The reality is, I struggle. It is a struggle with age and time, infirmity and energy, or its lack. Just a few weeks past, I fell on the stairs on the way down from my office and landed in the hospital, bruised and battered, for almost a week. My doctor says that at ninety most mortals find their stair-climbing days are long over, and since I have no aspirations to join the deathless gods who grace our ship's keel ceiling, I must bow to the inevitable. I could relocate my office to the first floor and an annex of the great room, but I wonder if such proximity would be tempting our household gods and nature. My office, with its capacious view of my long-lamenting pines, where my boon companions, the bald eagles and red-tailed hawks, drift in ravening patrol over the lake, has served my purposes for sixty years and I doubt that without my time-stocked aerie (eight file cabinets strong) I should find either the inspiration or peace of mind to further pick through the bone piles of memory. So here it is: my final draft, a summation—a conclusion still hanging in the balance, waiting for the right pair of eyes to give it wings.

———

Two people have fundamentally shaped my life. From the proceeding pages surely the weary reader would suspect that Oliver Wendell Holmes would be one of them. Yes, in a sense, certainly as a jurist, but not quite so much as a man. When my wife Annie died, twenty-eight years ago, I realized that something in me had died with her. Our relationship had languished toward the end; it never really recovered from Teddy's death. Nevertheless, we had soldiered on and, together, raised another wonderful child, Cordelia, if not quite in his memory, certainly in his spirit—and a free spirit at that. If Holmes had championed free speech and the free exchange of ideas as antidote to our murderous natures, Annie taught me the power of love—the incarnation of love in the expression of felt life, both the challenges and practical responsibilities of love—a kindness to one another that insists on the rules of reciprocal behavior—the golden rule—as the foundation for a more human and more humane world. Hers was the very human face of Holmes's abstractions—stirring abstractions, but still abstractions.

—

Our true spiritual life was to be found at Hermitage, in our woodland hikes and the flickering life and song of the birds, while in the evenings, with the fire roaring, in contemplation of books, with the infinite majesty of the ship's keel ceiling our crowning glory. In a very real sense, Annie made Hermitage hers: from her loins the progeny to populate it and the creative spark, the music, to animate its spirit, a spirit to soar beyond the mere earthbound pursuits—fisherman, naturalist, jurist, and antiquarian—of her husband.

But not without a price. If I have learned one thing, it is that every gift comes with a price, every talent with a sting in its tail. If Annie had to put up with a lot from me, and certainly from our children, she was not easy to get close to or know intimately, an intimacy she saved for her music and legion of admirers, of whom, I suspect, I had only an inkling. As an artist, she inhabited a far country of her own, a place attuned—truly—to the music of the spheres. I can never look up at the ship's keel ceiling and not think of her, or more to the point, the vast regions of her soul that remained forever beyond my reckoning.

Who was it who wrote, "How well can we know anybody?"

Strangely, one point of intersection in those vast interstellar spaces was Joseph Conrad's tales of the sea—the one author we shared unreservedly, especially his descriptions of long voyages and exotic locales, places of quiet and serenity, of tranquil sunsets beyond the reach of the telegraph or mail steamer. A simpler time, perhaps, a counterpoint to Annie's Proustian inner life, or to her vain search for artistic perfection. Or perhaps because we agreed on reading Conrad to Teddy and the girls in the great room, stories our son seemed to relish like the elixir of the gods, while the girls as they grew older drifted away to their own favorites. That tradition of reading by the fire, in the company of our odd yet homely medieval angels, continued over many summers with my grandchildren: a spur to their imagination if not their bonds to a world larger than life.

But the sting remained, that torturous Catherine's wheel of self-doubt counterbalanced by suppressed pride in the perfectibility of the world—enough to drive her husband and children wild with frustrated inadequacies. For if you—those closest to her, her progeny—could not live up to her performance standards, or share in her creative drive, you were somehow lost in her eyes, even as she pledged otherwise when Cordelia miraculously appeared. Something surely passed down from her abolitionist grandfather, Richard Davenport, and branded deep by surviving her alcoholic father, who, when he didn't beat her, often inexplicably abandoned her during his worst binges.

For Richard Davenport, a sensitive poet and musician who nevertheless volunteered for battle, was much more of a committed abolitionist than Holmes, and that abolitionist faith in unfettered freedom—without mechanism of compromise or amelioration—somehow came through to Annie like an express train out of a tunnel: the absolute necessity of freedom for the liberation of all human souls, along with the concomitant recognition of the responsibilities that freedom demanded: to make the best of oneself. "Good Lord, deliver us," so Holmes exclaimed to me once after a visit by Annie, his whiskers bristling. Holmes, who had witnessed the body counts—as had my father—considered such absolutes the height of folly, if not madness. But that absolutism burned white-hot in Annie's veins, standing out on her pale forehead when she performed Beethoven. (A white heat, dare I admit it, that also attracted me to a young girl at Bryn Mawr, Priscilla Fansler.) That same incandescence of spirit that infused her playing both awed and sometimes scared her children, except for Teddy, who sailed serenely on with a following wind of his own. Or, perhaps in Alice's case, it hardened her, causing her to embark on a fanatical crusade to eliminate our nation's original sin in a single generation. And it did not fail to leave its mark on Martha, who dived headfirst into the turbid depths of the human psyche in preference to the crystalline injunctions of "Annie's rules."

Annie's cancer, coming in the spring of 1968, seemed a demonical counterpart to the tragedy of that *annus horribilis*—an especially

destructive force for a woman who required peace and order to fully
realize her gifts. A great supporter of Martin Luther King Jr., she
was crushed by his assassination and the rioting and civil unrest that
followed, which equally inflamed her eldest daughter. She looked at
the television hour after hour from her hospital bed in her weakened,
painful state with utter disillusion as all her hopes seemed to crumble
before her. While I, from my bench, found myself turned into a reactionary by the crackpot Left, where once I had been something of a
star in progressive circles. Holding the line, Holmes's and Annie's line,
on civility and compromise to the benefit of the greater good, I found
myself pilloried by members of my own family as a rigid mastodon
of the establishment. The rigged system, as it was scornfully described
in the sixties, of which I was a prime exemplar, came under repeated
attacks from all my children in their various guises as avatars of the
future millennium. Something, dare I say, I'm glad Annie never lived
to see, even as I tried to uphold some of "Annie's rules," as my children
and their children came to describe her tyranny.

And so it was during these trying times, two months after Annie's
death, in that simmering July heat of 1969 at Hermitage, that the
second most important person came into my life, or I should I say
back into my life, since we had first faced each other as adversaries in
court, although, sadly, he had died some years before Annie, before I
might have tried to make amends. While struggling to sort out her
effects, I came upon a book she had carefully hidden behind other
books in her bedroom library at Hermitage. It was a well-thumbed
first edition of Whittaker Chambers's *Witness*. Signed and inscribed
to her by the author! I stood shaking with amazement, seeing that
signature on the frontispiece and an inscription of endearment. That
she had surreptitiously read and reread this book—personalized by
the author—while not whispering a word to me, deeply shocked and
saddened me. I felt betrayed, our trust grossly violated. If not a secret
or admired lover exactly, a man I had loathed. I had resisted reading Chambers's memoir from the first moment it was published to
both acclaim and infamy in the early fifties. I had no desire to stir
up or rehash painfully memories of my professional lapses, especially
about the man I had so cruelly sought to destroy in the witness box.
Something, I realized the moment I laid my hands on that secreted
volume, Annie had never forgiven me for—finding both consolation
and confirmation of my perfidy within its heavily marked-up pages.

I was unmanned with disillusion and feelings of bitter rejection. My first instinct was to destroy her copy, but my curiosity got the better of me, and I found myself drawn to explore its pages through her eyes (her extensive underlining and annotations), only to discover sides of Annie's spectral self that I had been oblivious of, even though it was a side of her that had been front and center all along.

Worse, I discovered our mutual subterfuge—one of many—for I, too, had hidden something: the Altmann sketches stolen (there is no other word) from the defense files, which I'd hidden behind my books in my office at Hermitage. That we had both chosen similar hiding places, cheek by jowl with the books we honored, in the one retreat we believed beyond the reach of the world's corruption, told me something: We both wanted our deceits to be unmasked and shared. This realization prompted me to take her copy of *Witness* and place it beside the sketches on my desk, the author's cover photo—that melancholy, world-weary face—joining the pencil portraits, so I assumed, of many of the same agents he had once named and tried to break from the Soviet underground. First I placed the sketches of Alger and Priscilla Hiss—whom Chambers had clearly loved—on either side of the volume. The others I arranged in two rows beneath. Those ten faces stared back at me, not unlike the faces in a jury box examining the soul of the accused. It was in that moment of grief that my own failings and white lies and suspicions came tumbling in on me. Or as Annie had put it just before she died, "my lack of imagination," which obscured insights into unimaginable crimes.

So, just weeks after scattering Annie's ashes at Handytown, I began to plow through Chambers's autobiography. Although I was first put off by his decidedly Manichean vision of a Christian God in valorous opposition to the devil's communism, I soon became enthralled with his days in the GRU underground and the vivid description of his friendship with Alger and Priscilla Hiss. I discovered in his pages not just the genuineness of that friendship—the very reality of which we sought to destroy in the trial—but a friendship that often verged on love, and a bond of far greater depth and profundity than anything I had ever enjoyed in my life, much less with Alger and Priscilla Hiss, whom I had known off and on for nearly forty years. I realized, to my chagrin, that my relationship with Alger, and even more with Priscilla, had itself been a subterfuge, an insubstantial cardboard caricature of true friendship, or much worse. Something that Annie's fervent underlining with her blue fountain pen literally underscored. But this revelation only set the stage for something even more terrifying.

When Chambers broke with the Soviet spy network, he went to Alger Hiss (and Harry Dexter White, as well) to try to break them from the iron grip of the Stalinist underground. He described to them in brutal detail the bankruptcy and terror of Stalin's totalitarian regime. He pleaded with them. He threatened that he would be forced to expose them if they did not break. Chambers's description of Alger Hiss's dismissal of his plea sent shivers down my spine, as it had the author's. Chambers knew in that moment, something confirmed many times over in the years to follow, that in a mere twinkling of an eye—his confession, his break—his onetime friend had become his mortal enemy, and would have no compunction about killing him, his wife and children, or anyone else who might threaten the espionage apparatus or his Soviet masters. Or in Alger Hiss's steely retort: "Stalin plays for keeps."

This revelation alone, that love and affection could be so instantly transmuted into such vicious hatred by the mere withdrawal of that shared ideological faith—once the bonding agent of that same love and affection—transforming it into an otherness that required the heretic's extermination from the earth, shattered my complacency. It was in that moment, sitting on the veranda in Annie's favorite chair, turning her underlined pages of *Witness*, that I understood my diabolical role in the Hiss trial: I, with my reputation for probity and high-mindedness, had been selected to undermine the truth of Chambers's testimony precisely so as to allow the killers to remain on the loose and so go about their bloody work with impunity. And not a few of those victims were surely depicted in Altmann's sketches.

How devastating that Annie's commentary in the margins of *Witness* had finally opened my eyes—as if she had been preparing her case precisely for me: her legacy, along with Proust, and even Conrad, in whose book *Lord Jim* she had underlined the following passage: "Hang ideas! They are tramps, vagabonds, knocking at the backdoor of your mind, each taking a little of your substance, each carrying away some crumb of that belief in a few simple notions you must cling to if you want to live decently and would like to die easy!"

How like Annie, I thought, how like Holmes! That in life we failed at those few simple notions—those simple truths bestowed generation after generation, our deepest longings writ down on the pages of time. As Chambers had seen fit to do in the years left to him, witnessing his failings and faults, a confession that portrayed a gentle soul of great spiritual depth and sweetness, whose suffering offered profound insights into the human condition. A man who loved his wife and children and the land he farmed, who in life was sought out by troubled colleagues at *Time* magazine for confession and consolation. Moments of time, epiphanies, singled out repeatedly in Annie's underlining: "Moreover, it is only the sins of the spirit that really appall me. The sins of the flesh affect me chiefly as unseemly and embarrassing, like the lapses of children, and for the same reason, because they betray the terrible immaturity of the spirit, at whatever age they occur."

With this realization—dare I call it conversion?—how I had so misread the spirit-seeking character of this good man, and my Annie—a thousand points of memory suddenly began blinking red as the ground shifted, and continues to shift to this very day, so prompting me to the writing of this memoir. For my own sake above all others. And so, if I am to be truthful, I embarked on a memoir in Chambers's confessional mode, which, perhaps by its very nature, resists completion. At least without all the facts of the case. Facts, evidence—or is it contrition?—that have outlasted Chambers and those eager young faces in George Altmann's sketches, as they may well outlast me.

In those last days of a warm July in the Year of our Lord 1969, I found myself returning again and again to the sketches laid out on my desk, searching those familiar and unfamiliar faces for answers. How little I knew any of them, including poor William Remington, brutally murdered in prison, who worked on my staff at the War Production Board, and of whom I have only the barest memory of an honest and good face, a smile over lunch, an eager worker. I shuffle my jury around like tarot cards, as if some different configuration might reveal their various fates—my fate. Of these souls in limbo, only Priscilla, now long gone as well, holds a lasting purchase on my heart, her face and eyes aglow with a subdued radiance (as if both the artist and I saw something of our better selves in her fierce grasp at life).

How many times was I tempted to burn the other sketches? But Priscilla held me back.

Then it came to me in a flash of searing insight: Like Chambers, who held back and then hid some of Hiss's purloined top-secret papers as a form of insurance, I had, unwittingly, done the same. During the trial, it was more instinct than premeditation—a vagrant, uneasy snatch at self-preservation—that led me to bury the evidence. All I knew was that a sense of creeping guilt stayed my hand to condemn these prisoners of fate to the flames, along with a growing premonition that by sending these shadowy figures back out into the world, shadows of shadows returned to the healing daylight—some cosmic clock turned back—these guilty exiles and their descendants might find some consolation if not closure at last. Some peace of mind. And for myself as well, since I am soon to join them.

And so I concocted the absurd plan to have Cordelia return the artist's sketches to their source, or as close to that source as was then humanly possible. I kept only the sketch of Priscilla, as if by so doing, she might escape the opprobrium man or God had in store for us all.

And even though the sketches were returned to me like bad pennies only weeks later, they had quickly and succinctly done their worst: I had lost a daughter and gained a grandson, a brilliant boy, to whom I may have unknowingly bequeathed the very sins I had hoped to scatter like seeds on the wind.

Facing a jury without a final verdict.

———

They are all long gone now and I am surely not far behind. If I have been granted a reprieve to ponder our joint fate, whether for sins of commission or omission, certainly in Annie's eyes, it is to make amends for a failure to love unconditionally—as she failed, as all men who walk this earth are bound to fail. It is Chambers's faith in kindness and decency that sustains me at each faltering dusk, as the winters grow longer, as the return of the hermit thrush lengthens year to year. As I now put my work aside for good or ill.

Not an evening passes that she doesn't rise from her piano and place an admonishing hand on my shoulder: . . . the truth, dear—not in your law books, nor my Proust or Mozart, nor even in your beloved birdsong or the distant but chilly stars overhead, but in ourselves.

Or as she underlined Chambers's sad lament: "I came to feel that the problem of evil was the central problem of human life, and that it took as many forms as there were men and women."

But *in finis*, I still turn for consolation to my Emerson: "I am Defeated all the time; yet to Victory I am born."

61

Somebody Exactly Like You

33 HOUSTON STREET
June 23, 1969

Dear Edward,

I am still grieving from our last conversation in Riverside Park. I had no idea that Annie had been so sick. How unbearably sad for you and the children, even with all the strains in your marriage—something I guess we share. But I find comfort, as I hope you do, in images of you scattering her ashes at Handytown, as you described it to me. What a perfect place of grace and repose for her spirit to rest.

I was touched as well by your kind words that you are sustained by something of the love you felt for me in the old days—"when," as you put it, "life had a sweetness of possibilities, when we talked into the night about art and literature—and yes, politics!" I am glad that something of that love remains, as it does for me, although I'm a tad skeptical, given that you clearly still believe I am or was a Communist. Even as you so loyally—or disloyally (I wonder which?)—defended Alger. (Never once have I detected an iota of disappointment in your voice over the outcome of the trial!) Perhaps professionally crestfallen, if not disdainful, when Alger so abruptly dismissed you and the others on the defense team for the appeal.

I must admit that I was not a little put off and hurt about how you kept bringing up the subject of George Altmann, as if the thing, now, after all these years, suddenly, inexplicably, weighs on your mind. So what if he handed you sketches of Alger and me? As I told you, I studied for a few months with Altmann at the Art Students League in the early thirties, and then put in a good word about him to Holger Cahill for a job at the FAP. Altmann did a pencil sketch of me and Timothy when we were in New York, a birthday present for Alger, sketches you admired when you visited us during Holmes's funeral. The artist was over to Volta Place once, maybe twice—I can't remember—to do a sketch of me and Alger for a portrait that never came off. Alger was too busy to sit, and so he may have sketched me, but never Alger—never busy Alger. As far as I remember, he never delivered that finished sketch of me. So perhaps that is what he gave you—or is there more? You can be so infuriatingly cagey sometimes. I hope the sketch is a good one—you said it was a fine and glowing study—and will keep my memory alive in you of those hopeful years of the New Deal. Especially now as Alger has cast me aside for another woman, a more stalwart—or deluded—helpmeet who will assist him in his dream of redemption, that endless campaign that I can no longer sustain.

At least your Annie stood by you to the end, through your tragic loss of Teddy, and presented you with yet another wonderful daughter.

Now with me out of the way, divorce or no, Alger can pursue his dream of overturning his conviction. He is more and more in the news again as a new generation takes up his cause. All I ever wanted was to disappear, maybe change our names, live a small life in obscurity, perhaps teaching school. But no, Alger insisted on clearing his name, mounting appeal after appeal, now throwing himself back in the spotlight in campus speaking engagements, using the antiwar movement to galvanize his quest, all the while condemning the dark forces of repression arrayed against his acquittal—which would include you and the defense team for failing him in the first place.

Did I mention in Riverside that Alger, as part of his quest, has agreed for a young Sancho Panza, a Yale scholar, Allen Weinstein, to write a book about his case? It seems that Alger is very much captivated by Weinstein's enthusiasm and so has given this young bulldog his blessing and complete access to the defense files. Weinstein has already filed Freedom of Information requests to open the relevant FBI files. Oh, what a Pandora's box will be found therein. What do you think, Edward? Will this Dr. Weinstein turn up the damning proof that it must have been me who was the Soviet spy, typing up all the stolen documents that I somehow got my hands on without Alger's knowledge, maybe slipping them out of his briefcase on the sly? Isn't that what you and the rest of the defense team speculated about—that Alger was only protecting me? Even now! (Is that why you were peppering me as we walked with questions about those George Altmann sketches—hinting at the artist's "sinister death" during the trial?) Good and great and forever stalwart Alger protecting his demented, traitorous wife. Well, now team Alger & Weinstein will have their chance to lay me low, sacrifice the wife for the good of the country and Alger's final redemption, if not apotheosis.

Oh, how wicked of me to go on like this with your recent loss of Annie. For I am so sorry about Annie, truly I am—she was the best part of you. So wonderfully dignified and above the battle of life. And dare I admit it? Yes, I went to some of her concerts when we moved back to New York in 1947—I believe her last performance at Carnegie Hall— and I was moved beyond words. Do you not think I'm tempted at her cruel and untimely demise to embrace your grand life living on Fifth Avenue instead of the hovel of my dingy Village apartment? The very thing, the glittering prizes you offered me all those years ago at Harvard Law. Grabbing onto the gilded coattails of the federal bench, the very system that condemned Alger. But our loss resulted in your gain: You stuck up for Alger, along with his great and good Harvard crowd, and they rewarded you in spades. How is it you—always hedging your bets— come out smelling like roses?

I'm not unfeeling, Edward; I feel your loss in the touch of your hand, your Annie and Teddy—he'd be in his mid-thirties by now—even as we're saddled with yet another worthless imperialist crusade in Vietnam. And you, my sad love, hating everything about the Vietnam War while you still have to defend the Korean War and Teddy's sacrifice, at least to yourself. Yet another subject that would tear us apart in the end. And I could never replace her, Edward, never.

The damn trial, my dearest old friend, has frozen us in time. That's why I never agreed to divorce Alger, even if it would have made things easier for him. We are forever condemned to walk this earth as public figures—history has us in its toils, much to my chagrin, and we shall be chained to each other in this life as well as the next.

I can just hear your reply to me, as you told me on our favorite bench by the flower garden—oh, those glorious spring blooms, the riotous color and heavenly scents of the tea roses—that the past is the past: that all people fundamentally want the same thing for their children and their children's children, no matter what we once believed. Easy for you to say, since the world you have embraced has triumphed and you with it. All I see is the rottenness, a hall of grotesque mirrors, and the sham world we must endure. For me, it is all a mirage, a bad dream, a prison cell where spring never arrives, the hermit thrush refuse their song, where nothing is as it should be. Whatever happened to that circle of fervent, hopeful faces? I ask myself. I can feel your hands on my arms as you shake me, like a child, as if to waken me from that bad dream to the hope of those spring blossoms, the gold-finch in the lilac, cradled in your strong embrace, telling me again and again that it doesn't matter if something of our lost love might still be blown back into life. And what if that were true, and what if I never was a Communist? A socialist, yes. Then the system you so esteem and uphold has done Alger and me a grave injustice, has hollowed us out—and our marriage, our boys, exiled our children to perpetual infamy and an agony of self-doubts, and left me, at the last, a refugee, a ghost in a life that is no longer my own. At least I now have a job with Harcourt copyediting the words of others—a small consolation for a small life.

Could you love a ghost, a failed spirit? I think not, Edward. You are a strong, resourceful man—even after the loss of Teddy and Annie. You power through your caseloads and wave your opinions to the eager crowd. And with three healthy and successful children—three daughters, no less—carrying Annie's righteous fervor, each stronger than the one before. Alice, your firebrand for civil rights, and Martha's reputation for saving troubled souls flying higher than ever over West End Avenue. Seeing Cordelia dance at Lincoln Center last Christmas with you filled me with a joy unknown in years: the daughter that in another life might have been mine. I was so envious of her youth and beauty and how she has translated your strength of mind and Annie's sensitivity of spirit into something ethereal and transcendent. Lucky father! Annie will live in her. You need a whole woman who can absorb your love and energy and give you something alive in return—not a stillborn faith.

I will miss you. I will never forget you. And the better world that might have been, that one day might still be.

Remember me as your George Altmann sketched me: full of hope and passion—and yes, promise.

Love,
Pross

Cordelia stared up at the moonlit sash-shadowed ceiling of her child-hood room, drifting in and out of sleep, uncertain where dreams and memories spilled one into the other. She was troubled yet exhilarated. She clutched a Hermès scarf, bringing it to her face every time she woke to again drink in the happy elixir of Annie's perfume—a scent that oddly caused a quickening in her crotch, an urgency for male possession, the very thing that had always sparked her most creative drives, even as it filled her with guilt and self-loathing: love and desire and a reproachful heart alloyed as one.

"Oh my God," she whispered under her breath so as not to wake Jim, pressing the scarf against her mouth to further mask her dismay. A "one-shot miracle"?

For the rest of that afternoon and evening, after her son's bombshell, she had wandered Hermitage like a lost soul, barely opening her mouth except to Martha at cocktails, nearly silent at dinner. Then, in a near trance, she had searched the glittering depths of the ship's keel ceiling illuminated by the Tiffany lamps for the thing that now possessed her, as if the lustful gods who had once so tantalized her girlhood and adolescence might yet provide, if not an answer, the dispensation for which she now yearned more than ever. And with Cecily's playing of Chopin, so like Annie's, the soft reverberation of the notes from the far reaches of that happy cosmos seemed to further reveal untapped memories of her mother's secret—and yes, unfaithful life, the carnal doings of those celestial beings a telltale tip-off, not unlike the fervent yet gentle ministrations of their earthly counterparts: Balanchine, for one, in his prime. Along with the tender but firm touch of at least two other ballet masters, who had showered her adolescent self with extra attention, while constantly hanging around Annie at rehearsals like lost dogs, always sidling up to the piano bench to casually caress her shoulder, massage her neck, planting an affectionate kiss on a flushed cheek in thanks for her working overtime.

She pulled the scarf away from her face, as if now mildly shocked at such casual intimacies, gazing upward, squinting through a milky haze of star dust, envisioning what had once seemed only the playful flirtations of careening bodies, intimacies indulged on the fly like second nature in the ballet world. And yet . . . the sultry half-parted lips of her mother at a caress to the nape of her neck, her head bent to a sweaty armpit, holding hands during a rehearsal. Memories now so vivid, so obvious, they gave renewed license to her own history of guilty pleasures. All gifts of the moon's enchantment. She felt her heart throbbing madly, as if sprouting new wings, sprouting seeds buried a thousand kisses deep—even if her son's report of a loveless and cruel conception proved to be true.

Fixated on the elongated ghostly sashes, she found that this alternate life of romantic subterfuge only grew more deliciously in her dream-intoxicated mind, vindicating a lifetime of erotic yearnings that had once seemed, at best, a lascivious balm to her parents' cold and passionless marriage. The world as she'd known it. She buried her face again in the perfumed silk, bringing instantly to mind an adoring sparkle in her mother's blue eyes while dining at Café Fiorello, near Lincoln Center, as she flirted with a virile ex-dancer and régisseur of the City Ballet: frosty pink nails lovingly exploring the dimple in his unshaven chin, a girlish laugh, a quiver on her gleaming lower lip, hands entwined across the linen tablecloth.

A moan escaped her and she reached to her crotch as if to quiet the pangs of a near-extinct youth, only to begin a slow, joyous searching motion to coax the thing free once more, as Balanchine's hand near her groin as he corrected her position had once coaxed the same thing to life, as had her first kiss—shared with another girl in the changing room of the School of American Ballet—as had a passionate kiss with that handsome young lawyer on a banquette at the Ritz-Carlton, and, somewhat later, an assignation with Jim in the tall grass behind the barn, his calloused fingers and then his tongue eliciting her first orgasm, waking her fully from a seventeen-year slumber and an addiction to her own body.

"For somebody exactly like you . . ." she sang softly to herself.

A performer at heart: her mother's child at the last.

She brought her fingers to her face to smell her own sex and laughed out loud.

"Oh, was that you?" he whispered, and reached out to find her hand.

"Sorry," she said, "just drifting off."

"You're sweating."

"It's so weirdly warm."

"I never expected to be in this bed again."

"You shouldn't be, even if George was made here."

"Oh . . . yeah, I'd forgotten about that."

"That? It was the only *that* for us in a whole year of one of your endless tours."

"Well, that's good karma then, for the bed, for us."

"Don't get your hopes up. It's a new bed. Even with the DNA test, George and Alice won't be as easy on you as I am."

"So, who's calling the shots?"

"What shots?"

"Well, I thought your old man was quite the charmer tonight. He seemed to have most of his wits about him. He didn't insult me once."

"Oh, give him a half a chance. He's just buttering everyone up for whatever he's got up his sleeve for tomorrow."

"Kinda cool, George getting upgraded to the master suite."

"At what price? I'm sure the Judge did it just to get a reaction and see how well he handles it. Survival of the fittest."

"Do I detect just the slightest tone of maternal pride?"

"And joy . . ."

"So, what's up with you—can't sleep?"

"I'm trying to remember something my mother told me, after my first night onstage at Lincoln Center. She said something like 'The moment you were born, I knew; the following month, still nursing, I took up the offer to be Balanchine's rehearsal pianist and get off the concert treadmill.'"

"Well, how 'bout that."

"I was just going through some of Annie's archive before bed, which, miracle of miracles, found its way onto my shelves over there by the window. God knows where he had that stashed away. Well, some of the earliest ballet programs, new ballets premiered, signed by Balanchine and the dancers, the conductor, go back at least a year before I was born, within a year of Teddy's death."

"So . . ."

"Forget it."

"Well, someone's got to take over the master suite at some point—right? Run this place? Who gets all the moola, anyway?"

"We're not exactly sure there is any moola—or very much anyway—left. I just hope George can hang on to Wendy. Hey, what's that?"

"What?"

"I thought I heard shouts and a slammed door coming from Graham's Dock."

"Oh, it's probably nothing. Just the young fry enjoying themselves. Why do you think it's the door of Graham's Dock?"

"Are you kidding! As a kid, how many times did I hear Annie slam that door at night on the way to Teddy's room to bed down?"

"A little weird, her dead son's room."

"Talk about weird—something too good to be true—about Wendy. I'm not sure—hear those footsteps?—I like whatever is going on between her and Cecily, either."

"Haunted house, huh?" He laughed. "I think she's quite the operator. I've seen hundreds like her in the business, überfemales, rock stars who know exactly what they want and how to get there. They pick their way over men, pick their brains, and then discard them like used tampons."

"That's a disgusting thing to say. I was just wondering if I'm not a bit like her—like my mother."

"Oh really—female ambition—perfection, let me tell you: the right mixes, balances, fades, to get just the right sound or just the right lighting to cover up that pimple on the left cheek . . . and then you're a nobody, and not a mention on the album credits."

"George needs someone to buck him up—the thing he didn't get from his father—to focus his talents and give him confidence. His Princeton adviser told me he's got a world-class mind. I hope they're in that big ole bed right now making babies, or at least practicing like crazy."

"You were great in bed—a natural."

"Don't go there. I have a slutty reputation in this family that I can never live down."

"You were hardly a virgin."

"But I was, I really was."

"You never told me *that*—you were a quick fucking learner. You coulda started a brush fire that night."

"I've got enough problems for having let myself be seduced by my father."

"No way!"

"Oh, you don't wanna know."

"You're not serious. You never mentioned that."

She stared up at the ceiling, where the aqueous pools of pewter light still swam against the lines of tongue-and-grove paneling, if in a lower, more muted key, as if now lowering her back to earth gently.

"In the year my mother was sick, before she died—and after—the Judge was absolutely devastated. For a man so assured of himself, with all his affairs, he was oddly dependent on her for so much . . . approval, I guess, like all of us. 'To light his way,' he liked to say. Well, if what George told me is true, if what the Judge wrote is true, it certainly wasn't the sex he missed."

"*George*? I don't get you."

"I told you: You've got to get those hearing aids. George is supposed to edit the Judge's memoir—*if* he survives Alice and all her machinations. According to George, it's as much a confession as a totting up of all his accomplishments."

"About you, fooling around with you?"

"Are you kidding? That's the point; it's selective, self-serving—that's his modus operandi."

"Fooling around with his daughter?"

"Listen, it was June, after Annie died, my senior year at Brearley. I couldn't graduate until I'd made up courses I'd missed over the winter, before Radcliffe would officially take me. I was also madly trying to get back in shape for City Ballet, for a place in the main company for the fall season—pro forma, so all Annie's pals—or lovers!—assured me. That's how I got injured, you know.

"Her *lovers?*"

"Just joking . . ." She winced and sighed. "If you'd seen the faces at her funeral." She brought her scarf to her face for a moment, breathing deeply. "Both Dad and I were—it was like we were stranded on a desert island up here with each other, without her there to tell us what to do. I had no one to bitch to about the workload, or complain to about the other girls trying to steal the limelight. We were still little girls, exploited, manipulated, played off one against the other. I was a favorite and hated for it. Worst of all, I didn't have Mom to tell me which option to take: Radcliffe or City Ballet. The Judge and I were all that was left of the team. I knew he needed me—proud father. So, even with everything else I had to do, I agreed to accompany him on one of his speaking junkets; he was politicking like mad for an upcoming Supreme Court vacancy. It was his first function after Annie's death. We were in Boston at the Ritz-Carlton, where he was going to be awarded a medal by the Massachusetts Bar Association, an annual event in memory of Oliver Wendell Holmes. So there I was, hanging on the hero's arm at the reception as his friends and admirers and ex-interns came up to him to offer their condolences for Annie's passing. That was tough, really tough—all those eyes looking for Annie in me. And I could tell some of those young women interns still had more than a passing interest in the old bulldog.

"I dutifully took my place besides him on the dais, where Annie had always dutifully sat. By the late sixties, much to his chagrin, he'd become the establishment rock star. And, of course, I was bored and feeling increasingly rebellious as the evening wore on, needing a little excitement—a contradiction of terms at a lawyers' convention. Needless to say, I managed to get myself pretty damn drunk on the kir royales being passed around. I flirted with some of the younger guys, all recent Harvard Law grads and delighted to let me know it. One guy in particular took a shine to me. I was supposed to be on my best behavior, as the great man's daughter, as representative of the Dimock name. But Paul—I think that was his name—was a real hunk, smart, made his way up from Southie, played football at Harvard. Even without the booze, he was wildly attractive.

"Near the end of the evening, the Judge caught me kissing Paul on a banquette in the hotel bar. Paul had his hand up my dress and I was actually getting turned on—talk about great hands—in a way I'd never known; I was close to having an orgasm and practically swooning. Without a word, Daddy just grabbed my arm and walked me out of the bar and to the elevator. I was so drunk, he practically had to carry me. I was terrified of being sick. He ended up taking me to his room, not mine—it was closer, a suite. My room was a long way down at the other end of the hotel. He dumped me on his bed and I passed out. Then he left me and returned to the reception, where his friends and supporters were waiting for him—he was lobbying to keep that top spot on the short list for the Supreme Court.

"The next morning, I woke up with a huge hangover. And there was Daddy, curled up in bed right beside me. I didn't know what had happened. All I remembered was that good-looking Paul in the bar, and how turned on I'd felt, and how wet I was. I was totally embarrassed to find my father there, me there—let me tell you, to find myself almost naked, wearing just my bra, in his bed, full of all these sexual urges and worse. When I went to the bathroom to pee, I was really messy, but I was probably just ovulating. My dress and panties were in a heap by the bathtub."

"Are you telling me your father, the old monster, raped his daughter?"

"No, I'm not telling you that, Jim—you never fucking listen. I'm telling you how I probably fucked up. Years later, when you were on the road and George was a troubled kid, I hit a bad patch where I fell into a depression."

"You never told me that."

"You were never fucking around, Jim."

"I get it . . . I'm sorry."

"I let Martha get her claws in me. I'd take the bus into the city for therapy sessions a couple of times a week. She was convinced that all my troubles came from some early trauma. So we plowed through the years and up popped the night at the Ritz-Carlton in Boston and, hey, presto-chango-alakazam—*incest*! Oh, wasn't Martha just bubbling over with excitement, like she'd stumbled on the Holy Grail. She latched onto that event or nonevent and drilled down on it until I didn't know which way was up. And, of course, that explained *everything*: my unconstrained promiscuous sex life, and why one man would never satisfy me, and, don't forget, my exhibitionist excesses at Woodstock! Oh my God, how she went on. The depression, too, was payback for my sins—Daddy's sins, maybe even Annie's if you can twist this thing enough ways . . ."

"You okay?"

"It's exhausting, just thinking about it. And my therapy sessions happened that summer—with George safely away at Hermitage—of the infamous fire in the boathouse and the various fibs, half-truths, or pure bullshit from Cecily and Karen that the Judge had molested them at the beach. Inappropriate groping was what it amounted to, at worst, from what I could ever make out. Well, Martha got ahold of that, too, and that's what really set my sisters on the warpath. They accused the Judge to his face of raping his own daughter—me—and a long-standing pattern of depredations against his granddaughters, attributing everybody's unhappiness and problems—including Annie's cancer—to his rapacious womanizing. Anybody had a problem with her life—look no further than Daddy. Of course, he went ballistic and threatened to cut everybody off and banned our children from Hermitage."

"Wow, I guess I really missed out on the fireworks."

"You missed nothing. All I knew was that your son had the happiest summers of his life at Hermitage. This place was the only point of stability in his whole shitty life at Woodstock. He was struggling with depression, as well. So I went crawling back to the Judge and pleaded with him that it had been a misunderstanding and that I wasn't blaming him for anything. By abasing myself, I got back those teenage summers at Hermitage for our son: time to hang out with his grandfather. While pissing off everyone else in the family. But this place has been the one thing he could count on. It got him through the torments of high school, it got him through lack of preparation for Princeton physics, *and* it helped him survive *you*."

"How you always like to dump it on my back. I wouldn't put it past you to have cooked up that whole little story about the Judge fucking with you, using it to blow up the Judge with your sisters and their kids, just so you'd have this place all to yourself and George. You and that Wendy."

"You're such an asshole, Jim." She pulled her hand away and turned on her side. "What a terrible thing to say. I don't think I've ever heard you talk about a woman you hadn't fucked or disparaged, usually in that order."

"You don't think using the paternity thing against me wasn't manipulative?"

"You brought it on yourself. Listening to bigmouth Levon. Hoisted by your own petard!"

"My what?"

"Big words for a big mouth."

"So, he didn't really molest you—right?"

"Oh, who knows? I was always a little in love with Daddy. God knows he spoiled me; both he and Annie did. Did I have feelings for him? Sure. But I probably came to at some point in his hotel room and needed to pee and took off my dress and panties in the bathroom. I think the Judge just came back from the reception, too tired and too drunk to do much of anything but get into bed and go to sleep. Maybe we cuddled in the night, or maybe I dreamed I was cuddling with that Southie guy in the bar. I mean, what daughter isn't a little in love with her father? He was a virile and strong man. Even my mother still wanted him—or wanted him to want her, to punish him for God knows what. We were all competing for his favor, his love. What daughters don't?"

He took her hand again and brought it to his face, kissing her fingers.

"I can smell your cunt, just like when you were eighteen."

"Seventeen. You wish . . . I wish."

"I can try to make it up to you. I know it's not much, but I can try." Jim sighed. "It's so strange being back in Woodstock, being home, when it's not exactly my home anymore. And not what you think I mean. But after everything George and Wendy have been going on about—about my father . . . well, nothing is quite the same. I mean, I find I can't hate him anymore. And with the hate gone, well . . . pity, I guess, even respect—you know, around the edges. Once I hated the paintings; now . . ."

"They're filled with love."

"Hmm, a famous and talented artist for a father . . . who woulda thought . . . and maybe he even loved me."

"What a waste, how you took it out on everybody—your poor mother."

"But we had some good times, didn't we?"

"We did."

"Tell me one thing: Did Van write that song about you?"

"He did."

"Did you sleep with him?"

"No, bad teeth."

"I only wish I coulda written that damn song for you."

62

With Music Sweet as Love

RUBBING HER EYES, Karen entered the kitchen and found her aunt Cordelia already busily preparing the turkeys.

"You're up early, Aunt Cordy," said Karen, who was dressed in a beige sweatsuit and Nike running shoes. She sniffed the air for brewing coffee as she did a few stretches.

"What a huge motherfucker of a turkey," said Cordelia, laughing whimsically. "George really outdid himself. This baby only just fits in the oven."

"You certainly seem in a good mood for so early."

"Do I? Well, I guess I just *love* cooking," and she smiled conspiratorially, giving a sensual wiggle of the hips as she flashed her TURKEY emblazoned sweater. Her cheeks were flushed, and there was a glimmer of lapis lazuli at her earlobes.

"Well, I got woken up a bunch of times by all the commotion in Cecily's room last night. You know how the bedroom walls are paper-thin."

"Oh, like what?" Cordelia asked, a hint of displeasure in her voice.

"Mostly screams of laughter . . . God knows what else."

"A party—you didn't check it out?"

"Are you kidding—me, a divorced woman!" she cackled. "CeCe's a wild one. Erich had such a crush on her as a kid. Too bad they're first cousins."

Karen went to the open kitchen window above the copper-bottomed sinks and breathed deeply of the warm fall air, her voice resonant, almost hopeful. "Could almost be late summer . . . well, sort of." She sighed, turning an intent gaze on her aunt as she flicked back with her wrist a lock of reddish blond hair from her pale forehead.

"I'd never met Jim before; he was always like some remote romantic figure hanging out with rock stars, to hear George tell it when we were kids."

Cordelia appeared slightly crestfallen. "Well, there you go—*good* for George." She gave Karen an uneasy glance. "Loyalty, just what this family needs a little more of," she added in a sarcastic tone. "Jim is Jim. Go ask him about any of the great groups of sixties and seventies—he'll talk your ear off." With a knowing purse of the lips, she continued basting the turkey with olive oil and spices, then nodded with a resigned pout. "At least, through all the bullshit he helped me make George. So, what's with yours—your ex?"

"Roger? Never see him. Max gives me reports when he goes to visit his new family in Boston. His stepmother is ten years younger than I am. Now they have a year-old baby and a three-year-old girl. He always told me he hated children, but it looks like he only hated having children with me."

"In case you haven't noticed, men never know what the hell they want, *unless* it happens to be you. Thank God for vibrators; otherwise, we'd be a captive nation."

Karen winced, continuing as she went to get herself a cup of coffee. "Of course, Max's dad has now started an e-mail campaign: thinks New York is unhealthy for his son, after nine-eleven. As if Boston is a bastion of safety. I don't think I could endure another custody battle."

"Listen, it totally fucked with George's head, being there—"

"Where is George, by the way?"

"I think he's off with Erich and Nancy to Handytown to pay their respects to Annie—tradition, add a stone to a wall."

"Nice." Karen grimaced. "Well, can't complain. Business—anxiety meds and the like—has never been so good. At least it looks like Wendy's got George well in hand; he hangs on her every word. The Judge, too."

"Oh, I think Cecily takes the charm prize. Right—the two of you, the jailbait thing . . . *dans le temps*."

Karen looked up from where she was pouring milk into her coffee and glanced at her reflection in the kitchen window, her gaze going to the cars parked beyond, covered in leaves, and beyond this a corner of the lake glittering with silky purple-gray light.

"We were stupid teenagers."

"Join the club." Cordelia glanced up from the turkey with narrowed eyes. "Did you know Alice threatened to press charges?"

"No!"

"Anything, heh, to keep the old man off the Supreme Court."

"How stupid, the games we played."

"We play for keeps in this family, in case you haven't noticed. That's what I like about Wendy—seems like she can give as good as she gets."

Cordelia looked at her niece askance, prompting.

Karen shrugged. "I could've almost sworn I heard Wendy's voice in there last night."

"Cecily's been using her apartment. Posing for her paintings. George says she's now found her own place in town, nearer NYU."

"Rumor has it Wendy hung a nude of herself in the Judge's bedroom."

"A gift from George; he's representing her."

"Well, maybe she could talk to Max; she's got everybody else eating out of her hand. Might break his addiction to what's on offer." Karen sucked in her cheeks for emphasis. "Here, let me help with the stuffing. Maybe I'd make a good sous-chef, a dicer and chopper, instead of a shill for big pharma."

"Dear, you'll wish you never offered, because I've got six large onions that need to go in the stuffing, and for the giblet gravy." Cordelia picked up the rubbery neck and wagged it at Karen with a leer.

Karen grimaced and began chopping, concentrating ferociously.

"At least we didn't sleep with him."

Cordelia cackled.

"Forgive me for saying this, Karen, but my older and wiser sister is prone to extreme exaggeration once she gets a diagnosis in her head."

Karen chopped rapidly, tears streaming.

"So, how did *you* sleep last night?"

"Try a little perspective on being fifty, your boobs dragging and living alone—try shoveling out four feet of snow last year, just to get to your car."

"You're so refreshing, so up-front, so uninhibited—so unfiltered . . . always acting out. The perfect great-aunt for pussy-whipped Max."

Cordelia looked up and smiled as Martha and Alice entered the kitchen, holding up her oily hands—coated in herbs—in surrender.

"If this bird was a he, he'd have come by now."

"You're crying, dear," said Martha, going over and kissing her daughter and then Cordelia. "Happy Thanksgiving. Where's Felicity?"

"Oh, she's getting the Judge bathed and armored up. So I volunteered to entice Big Bird into the oven."

"Thank God for Felicity," said Alice. "Can you imagine if one of us was stuck with that job, how humiliating it would be?"

"For you or Daddy?" Cordelia mugged at her elder sister. "We wouldn't have the strength to move him around anyway."

"Felicity lifts weights; I've seen them," said Karen, wiping at her eyes with a dish towel. "She told me she's getting in shape for Florida—Siesta Key, she said."

"Since when?" said Martha, hair disheveled, looking a little lost. "She can't leave Daddy."

Cordelia pirouetted with a flourish. "Daddy has a rental condo in Siesta Key from Christmas through April. We're all invited for winter getaways."

Alice scowled. "George put him up to that—or you?"

"I don't know how he survived winters up here. I barely did when I took care of Mom the winter before she died."

"Ah, Annie's love child," snorted Alice, going over to the coffeemaker. "So, he's got the bucks to rent a condo. Which reminds me: Has anyone seen his will recently? And what's the old bugger going to do, dear Cordy, with this place anyway? And where's George got to? We have business to discuss."

"How should I know," said Cordelia indignantly.

"Off to Handytown," said Karen. "With Erich and Nancy, to do the stone thing."

"Oh come on, Cordy, you and George have been thick as thieves, nosing up on the inside track for years."

"That's hardly fair, Alice," said Martha. "Cordy's suffered terribly at his hands—unforgivably."

Cordelia glared. "Drop it, will you? I was just embarrassed is all."

This seemed to go right by Martha as she examined her smallish hands, looking for her wedding band and engagement ring, which she'd left on her bedside table; then she turned with a quivering smile to her elder sister.

"You know, Alice, I thought it was quite touching of you last night when you left it to Cecily to play that Chopin after dinner . . . like old times. You know, she holds herself just like Annie did—a little spooky, what with the glittering ship's keel ceiling all lit by the lamps and the firelight. I was sure I'd be dreaming about her last night, but, oddly, I don't think I did. Instead, I had a dream about Teddy down by the old railroad right-of-way, and the tracks were still there. He was trying to find spikes in the rotted ties, except the spikes were—"

"No more dreams, Martha, please," said Alice. "Actually, I thought Cecily played a lot better than I ever did. Of course, she's had time on her hands recently."

"I was struggling, see . . . struggling to get the spike out of the tie, and Teddy was hopping around like a gorilla, making fun of—"

"Enough of Teddy's monkeyshines," snapped Alice, pausing to wrap a rubber band around her long hair, her claret-colored kimono falling open. "I thought you were going to tell me it turned out to be a silver stake to be driven through Dracula's heart." She retied the sash with a hint of amusement. "Remember how Mother used to love those Bela Lugosi movies? I think it was her one weakness in life, vampires." She giggled as she leaned her head to the side, pretending to swoon and expose a succulent expanse of neck. "Speaking of which, who barged into Cecily's room in the middle of the night?"

Cordelia cackled and bared her teeth. "I vant to drink your blood . . ."

Martha turned from the open refrigerator with a yogurt in hand. "Remember how Annie forbade us to snack between meals, or even open the icebox?"

"Annie's rules, including no sneaking around to one another's rooms at night," replied Alice.

"That," announced Martha, "was just in case Teddy tried to sneak a girl into his room on a rainy night."

Alice flicked her eyebrows and feigned a swagger, as if to say, Not the only one. Then her voice turned soft, oddly forgiving. "Ah, your bad-boy Teddy. Remember how he'd sneak down to the kitchen and get us all ice cream and we'd devour it in his room? And next morning, Annie would confront us and he'd smile and lie straight to her face, and it was like she was turned to stone; she'd just walk away."

"Teddy could slither out of anything," added Martha.

"Well," said Cordelia, scooping up Karen's pile of chopped onions and transferring it to a mixing bowl. "She did just the opposite with me. She was always encouraging me to eat, anytime, anywhere—I guess there was a lot of anorexia going around SAB."

Alice glared at Cordelia, then said, "I could swear it was another woman's voice I heard in Cecily's room last night—George's vampire, who's now *hanging* on the Judge's bedroom wall."

"Such a talented painter, don't you think?"

"Actually," said Karen, "I assumed it was Cecily and Erich."

"Some people have such a talent for raising the dead," mused Alice, swishing her kimono like a cape and going to the window, as if listening for something just out of hearing. "I mean, besides corrupting my daughter, her laughter even reminds me of Annie. It wasn't as if I was even tempted to check up on Cecily; I'd never do that. But it spooked me. I kept waking up, as if someone had knocked on my door. I called out for them to come in. But nothing. And then it would happen again, and I realized it might just have been a knock against the wall from the room next door, or even Billy's old room, on the other side of ours. Of course, Stan was dead asleep. And the moonlight was streaming in, illuminating Annie's portrait on the wall—you know the one—like she's in a swoon of ecstasy at the piano. And then I'll be damned if I didn't hear the piano from downstairs, distant but clear, some little bit of Mozart, halting, a child's thing. It must've been one in the morning. So I grabbed my toothbrush, like I was off to the bathroom, and peered over the banister, and there in the faint glow of a Tiffany lamp is lonely little Nancy trying her best to play Annie's Steinway. It brought tears to my eyes—poor girl. And that's when I heard this voice behind me in the dark: *Good girl, now go and brush your teeth and get right back into bed*. I spun around, but of course there was nothing, just a beam of moonlight from my open door. But it was just the tone of voice Annie used when she sent me up from the breakfast table to comb my hair. Scared me . . . really."

Cordelia, having paused for a moment, returned to stirring the ingredients for the dressing. "Felicity has Mom's idiosyncrasies down to a tee." She tapped her spoon, as if summoning everyone's attention. "From the way she sets the table to the recipes for meals. Crystal finger bowls and doilies—she set them out first thing this morning. Talk about a little spooky."

"Do you remember when she found *Lady Chatterley's Lover* under your mattress?" asked Martha, pondering her sister's uncharacteristically lost stare out the window, as if needing to call her back. "Marched downstairs and threw it into the fire in the great room."

"I'm sure it exploded into brimstone!" Alice's eyes lit up, recharged as she raised a lecturing finger, reciting, "'A woman has to live her life, or live to repent never having lived it.'"

"'I don't want a woman as couldna shit nor piss,'" rejoined Martha, as if suddenly in the spirit of the thing.

"That's so gross," complained Karen.

"Remember, Alice, when Mother caught wind of that strip-poker game on the island when we were camping out with the gang? And she sent Daddy to investigate."

"I was desperately trying to lose," said Alice, smiling, "even if the Dalton twins both had their eyes on your Carol Doda boobs."

"Do you think!" exclaimed Martha with a twinkle of nostalgia in her baggy eyes. "Weren't Daisy Wright and Teddy there—the summer before he went to Yale?"

"Teddy and Daisy grabbed a canoe and intercepted Daddy halfway to the island in his rowboat and sweet-talked him all the way back to Hermitage. They pretended they'd forgotten to bring marshmallows or something, and they kept telling him what a great time everyone was having singing around the campfire. Teddy and Daisy sat him down in the kitchen over beers, and she charmed him so completely that he entirely forgot the whole thing."

Cordelia and Karen looked on, a little abashed.

"Roger Dalton had quite the cock," Alice mused airily. "Bent to the left like an elbow."

"Alice, no."

"Yes, our last real summer here, before Teddy went off to Yale and early crew practice. I had such a thing for Roger." Her voice rose with the thrill of near escapes and escapades. "Annie made me wash my own bedsheets for that whole wonderful summer."

"Good God, you two . . ." said Cordelia, "no wonder I could never get any around this place as a teenager—you'd used them all up." She smiled pensively. "As a kid, I remember that woman, Daisy Wright, stopping on walks around the lake with her son. She always wore blue sundresses and a straw hat, hardly hiking gear. She'd just waltz up to the piazza to say hello. Nothing more—just said, 'Hello, how are you . . . lovely weather' with a wistful look, a smile as she leaned on the snubbing post by the steps, and then went on her way again with her blond boy."

"Oh Daisy had a thing for Teddy all right," noted Alice.

"She was such a bitch," said Martha.

"Oh, don't be such a poor sport, just because Teddy took her out canoodling."

"Poor thing," said Cordelia. "I don't think she ever married, or if she did, it must have ended pretty quick."

"Oh," chimed in Karen, "Daisy's son, Benjamin, was a dreamboat—the strong, silent type with long blond hair and gorgeous blue eyes. We girls couldn't keep our eyes off him when he showed up at the swimming beach with his kids—you know, the older married guy everyone had a crush on."

Cordelia said with a furtive smile, "Kind of a straight arrow for my tastes. Benjamin went to Annapolis. Besides"—she shrugged—"with Annie watching me like a hawk . . ."

"You know," said Alice, "I decided I'd never have children with Stan, just to spite her for refusing to fly out to the hospital in Berkeley when I gave birth to Cecily." She sighed wistfully. "Then, one night, I was about to go put in my diaphragm and somehow it struck me it was the kind of prudent thing that Annie would insist upon. So I told myself, Fuck it. And that's how I got pregnant with Billy. As the kids say, go figure."

"Oh," purred Karen. "I *loved* Billy. He was my favorite cousin, so funny and sexy—if we hadn't been cousins . . . well, we *really* liked each other."

With a pained look and blinking rapidly, Alice turned from where she'd been standing by the window and hurried over and gathered Karen in her arms.

Cordelia raised her arms as if in a blessing. "Oh, ladies, old, and getting older, and still so young . . ." She went and put her arms around Alice and Karen in a three-way hug, motioning Martha to join them. "But we'll never really grow old here; we'll just haunt the place, like Annie, with our younger selves, maybe our better selves. What do you think, Martha—what would Karen Horney have to say for female solidarity?"

Martha looked up from a yogurt she'd been pecking at with a spoon, as if unable to decide what to do with it, then went over and joined the circle.

"Who remembers the last time we joined hands?" asked Cordelia.

"After Daddy scattered Annie's ashes at dawn, at Handytown, all alone," said Alice, "then dragged us there and insisted we each recite a verse of Shelley's 'To a Skylark.'"

"And he took the last verse," said Martha. "What was it again . . . 'harmonious madness.'"

"Was I there?" asked Karen.

"You were such a cute little girl," said her mother.

"'Hail to thee, blithe Spirit!'" sang out Cordelia. "I went first."

Alice, her voice aquiver, began reciting: "'Like a high-born maiden / In a palace-tower, / Soothing her love-laden/ Soul in secret hour / With music sweet as love, which overflows her bower . . .'"

"'Thou lovest: but ne'er knew love's sad satiety,'" warbled Martha. "My God, how Daddy laid it on, as if such a thing were possible."

"Oh," said Cordelia, wiping a tear, "at Handytown anything was possible as little girls—free of hate and pride and fear."

"Or the island." Alice laughed, as if to make light of such an outbreak of sentimentality. "Talk about unsatiated love, all those boys' inept, fumbling fingers."

"My childhood may not have been as exciting"—After Martha took a couple of steps and placed a hand on her daughter's shoulder—"but I was perfectly happy here, with my books and coxing for Teddy."

Alice laughed. "Teddy had it all. All those little cunts just spilling over for him. It drove me crazy how easily it all came to him. You remember how he loved to make fun of me on the piano, how I couldn't hit more than an octave, how he'd breeze over the most difficult passages—and fart? Yes, stand up from the piano seat, bow and *fart*, laughing in my face as he disappeared down to the boathouse."

"Because you always had to compete with him," said Martha, the four women now linking hands. "He knew exactly how to get your goat."

"Well, I got the last laugh, beat him at the Judge's own game, the only game in town that really mattered: the law—because it's the lawmen, in the end, who get to make the rules, or break them, whenever and however they see fit."

"Not Annie's rules." Cordelia laughed.

"I found a letter from Teddy this morning in my organic chemistry textbook," murmured Martha to her daughter, but no one seemed to take notice.

"And where is my darling Cecily?" asked Alice.

Karen grinned into her aunts' faces: "She and Wendy hogged the shower this morning early and then took off in the canoe headed for the island. Some last goldenrod for the table setting."

Alice took Cordelia's arm in a gentle but firm squeeze. "Well, you can tell your brilliant son he'd better have the balls to keep his beautiful witch to himself; seducing my daughter is not in the cards."

At this, Felicity walked in, holding up a yellow legal pad, and sang out to the gathering, "The seating chart!"

63

The Element of Fire Is Quite Put Out

THE TABLE SETTING was indeed breathtaking to behold for those who had never experienced the full Dimock panoply, and even for those who had only vague memories of glory days past. Felicity had more than outdone herself. "In memoriam, for Annie," she announced as she rang the gong at the entrance to the dining room. Although Annie had only bothered going whole hog on special family occasions or when called upon to advance her husband's career.

The heirloom Lenox blue-and-white china, the Federal pattern with a broad border of cobalt blue and just a touch of unostentatious gold leaf edging now graced the long rosewood table. Handblown Venetian glass goblets of a sinuous pale sea blue touched with turquoise, acquired on the Judge's wedding trip directly from the factory showroom on Murano, anchored the upper right edge of the Burano lace mats, matching the aquamarine diadems on the base of the crystal finger bowls, tinting—"spellbinding," noted Stan with a cinematographer's eye—the lustral water a bluebird hue. The family silver service, consisting of discretely ornamented platters and cutlery, engraved with a restrained *D* trailing a stylized bird's tail, went back five generations to a Salem sea captain, who had lost three fortunes and secured four. "Echoing the blue tints of the ship's keel ceiling was Annie's idea," said the Judge, presiding. The six silver candelabra with their pedestals of leaping trout stood at rigid attention, polished to a sheen of stately, if somewhat baroque, exuberance. The rosewood Sheridan table—"Annie's addition, five generations in her family, under which a young Richard Davenport had once stretched his long legs—your great-great-great-grandfather, Nancy," commented the Judge—now extended, with the added inserts, the length of the chestnut-paneled dining room, the slightly undulating surface magically alive with spates of sapphire and lemony gold flame, here and there giving off russet glimmers from the banks of windows overlooking the lake. Ornamental miniature pumpkins and squash and even sprays of tattered goldenrod (Wendy's and Cecily's contribution) added to the autumnal effect, which Nancy (in homage to Handytown) had carefully arranged, as if around a secreted woodland pool from which phantom trout sprang after flickering fireflies.

The one anomaly in the scene that drew more than a few curious glances was a large flat package wrapped in brown paper, leaning into a corner nearest the fireplace.

Nancy could barely contain herself. She'd insisted on wearing her new hiking boots and Orvis fly-fishing vest over her Donna Karan fire red twist-front silk dress (provided by her mother, youngest female partner at Skadden Arps). She constantly circled the table as she inspected her handiwork, the place cards, gold-edged and embossed with a forest green *Hermitage*. Each was lovingly inscribed with a diner's name in a fluid "Hummingbird" calligraphy, which, so she had assured the Judge, was both elegant and stylish. Nancy wore her hair in a tight chignon, like Wendy, into which she'd proudly stuck a dusky gray-black bald eagle's feather pilfered from Teddy's album in her room: a touch of the Indian brave.

The only problematic placement had been who would get to sit at the head opposite the Judge: "Annie's place." It had been Annie's place as long as anyone could remember. Only Alice, Martha, Cordelia, and the Judge, of course, remembered Annie's days reigning opposite her husband. In the beginning, or what seemed like the beginning to Alice and Martha, it had just been the three of them, the two sisters seated across from Teddy, under the watchful gaze of their parents. Teddy seemed to have spent every moment of every meal making faces at his siblings (anything to get Martha to crack a smile) and telling outrageous tall tales about his latest woodland adventures, or elaborate fibs, all to flush out a response of horror or laugher from the women. That era, the days of charming Teddy, ended for Alice and Martha with the Hiss trial.

Later, it was just Cordelia seated by herself with the Judge and Annie, (occasionally with friends up from the city or from around the lake), with the seasonal appearance of Alice or Martha at Hermitage for special occasions.

Then came the era of the cousins' summer visits, with Annie then gone, even though her place in the family retained its distinct

aura, singled out constantly by the Judge with a wave of his hand—
"What would Annie say to that?"—as he enforced table manners
and explained matters of etiquette in the same precise terms he presented preliminary instructions to his juries. These were the halcyon
summers of Karen and Erich, Billy and Cecily, and George, little
George, Cruddyback George, aka Luke Skywalker, whom nobody
wanted to sit next to, at least not in the early years. So seats were
assigned by Felicity to prevent squabbling; and if a parent—wonder
of wonders—should show up over those distant summers, the Judge
would graciously wave his hand and say, "Dear, why don't you take
Annie's place tonight. She would be so pleased." Less an honor than
a reminder that no one could come close to taking Annie's place, a
point demonstrated by every correction of the children's bad table
manners, and the absence of her crackling insights on life and politics,
music and literature that had once ignited table conversation.

And then the final era (unless the present proved to be the avatar of
one to come), that sad, desultory period beginning some fifteen years
before, George's high school and college years, when he ate mostly
alone with the Judge, when Cordelia occasionally put in an appearance
if she could get away from the bookstore (Woodstock aswarm with
tourists in high summer season), seated across the table from her son,
while Annie's place remained conspicuously vacant. "Nice to have a
break from just us two boys, right, George? Your son, Cordelia, edu-
cates me on astrophysics while I explain some of the finer points of how
a judge must adjudicate in court. Dare I say, the dynamics of an expanding universe and the mercurial dynamics of a courtroom—a family,
too, I suppose—have much in common. Isn't that right, George . . .
change, adaptation, the dying out of stars? Dear me, what a melancholy
fate when our sun, too, burns itself out—is it a red dwarf or white
giant?—and turns into a black hole and gobbles us all up, well . . . damn
shame . . . damn shame. And yet we labor on in our vineyard, eh."

The night before, in the hubbub of arrivals, Alice has simply appropriated Annie's place, but now the seating plan "from above" dictated
differently. Cordelia was given Annie's place, with George at her right,
Wendy on her left, and Jim next to her in a kind of uncertain, yet-to-
be-determined limbo. Alice—three Bloody Marys to the wind—was
seated on the Judge's right, with Martha on his left, the two sisters
paired with each other's husbands, while their children and Nancy
filled in the rest of the table. Cordelia was hardly thrilled with the

arrangement, already reeling from the remark in the kitchen that morning about "nosing the inside track"—nor was George, dressed in his one
gallery-opening suit, who seemed definitely out of sorts and avoiding
eye contact with Wendy across the table. She was dressed in a stunning
sky blue low-cut Gucci dress, with a peasant "country" fringe worn off
the shoulder, which daringly showed off the strappy muscles in her
back and upper arms, and the firm cleavage of her breasts. (Word of her
nude self-portrait in the Judge's bedroom had spread like wildfire, as
had the observation that George and Wendy hadn't exchanged a word
all morning.) Noted Alice to Stan, "She matches the table setting, too."

The Judge now presided at the head with much of his regal bearing still intact, if a little fragile, a stoic air even with his chin sagging
and his arthritic fingers somewhat swollen, hunched over and shaky,
with the brass buttons on his blue blazer beaming like miniature suns,
buoying his blue-and-white Bulldog bow tie. While his family, at least
at first, seemed aloof, dreamy, as if enchanted by memories of their
own eras, of Annie's rules, which in a way had provided the comfort of
certainty and habit. If anything, he seemed more bemused than proud
to find himself back at the head of his table—"still in existence," as he
had mumbled to Felicity when she woke him that morning, perhaps
remembering eras even longer ago, unplumbed by the rest, when he
and Annie retained sole sovereignty as a newly married couple in the
depths of the Depression, or even before Annie, when it had just been
him and his older brother, Jack (John, brilliant and gifted John, who
died in the Lafayette Flying Corps in 1918, just days before the armistice), and Dr. Dimock, and his imposing, if overweight, wife, Elsie,
the mother he barely remembered, who had once sat in Annie's place
(although a different table, which had been moved to the apartment in
New York to make way for Annie's Sheridan) . . . a woman of enormous character and grace, a society doyen who had helped her husband
round up funding for Memorial Hospital and the American Cancer
Society . . . gone almost without trace, without the barest anecdote in
her wake, except for a scattering of faded snapshots, as if she had never
existed, not unlike, so it had always seemed to a younger George, the
time before the big bang . . . quite unimaginable.

What did linger, jointly, communally, in the splendid formality
of the atmosphere, was a sense that meals in the dining room—"the
chestnut room"—had always been a proving ground for gentle-
manly (and gentlewomanly) behavior, and intelligent sparring, rules

of conduct and debate scrupulously enforced by the Judge—"What would Annie think of buttering up your entire roll like that!"—along with the art of civilized conversation, which he led by example, praising well-thought-out and logical arguments when they were packed with convincing and concrete detail, while disparaging sloppy thinking based on clichés and "untethered generalizations." Invariably, in eras past, the Judge either picked fights on certain topics or tried to divide the table into warring camps, not unlike the way he ran confrontations in his courtroom, a habit or giddy pleasure that went back to his earliest days on the Groton debate team, and again with the Yale debating society—he'd been president in 1926–1927—as a means of practicing the art of thrust and parry in preparation for the main event, the "active business of life," as it had once been described to him by Endicott Peabody at Groton. This aura of the arena still retained a kind of hovering, if lax, energy, a vestigial note of anxiety and competitiveness—to assert and prevail.

This gentle elbowing for attention was somewhat checked by the addition of Martha's granddaughter, thirteen-year-old Nancy, whose excited presence encouraged the adults to be on their best parental behavior and so uphold the pleasing fictions of family tradition. A tradition that received a surprising last-minute boost when Wendy scampered ahead of the party after Felicity rang the gong, and placed a shiny cellophane-packaged CD in the center of each plate. The cover of the CD, actually a boxed set of three CDs, showed a cropped version of the Raphael Soyer painting of Annie now in Alice's room, just the pianist's bent face, golden hair, and hands upon the keys: *The Complete Recordings of Annie Davenport Dimock, 1933 to 1939.* The effect on the gathering was one of stunned silence, followed by exclamations, with the Judge holding the CD in his arthritic hands, shaking, tears streaming, and then just staring at Wendy in wonderment.

Pulling himself together, the Judge now sat up straight and announced, "My father never said grace, I have never said grace, but Annie had her Unitarian grace, and so here it is, folks:

> For food in a world where many walk in hunger,
> For faith where many walk in fear
> For friends in a world where many walk alone
> We give you thanks, O God
> Amen."

If George thought he'd dodged the limelight in the immediate prox-imity of Annie's place—avoiding Wendy's piercing scrutiny—Felicity's flourishing presentation of the turkey, which got walked around the table on a huge silver platter, not once but twice, as if engaging in a contest of musical chairs, only to be presented to him with an exultant cry of "Happy Thanksgiving," instantly disabused him of that hope. The gorgeous honey-colored beast seemed to draw all the latent snarky attention in the room—given the chance to evaluate George's carving prowess, while he was required to gently ask each diner's preference.

Erich was designated sommelier and carefully poured the Judge's best Bordeaux, a Saint-Emilion Grand Cru, Château Pavie, 1978, still dusty from his cave deep beneath the central staircase. Only Jim, in wrinkled herringbone jacket and string tie, would forgo the libation with a discreet palm over his glass, while the others savored the trans-formation of their goblets into a rich, deliciously plummy tint.

"I want to drink a toast"—the Judge raised his glass—"to Thanksgivings past and present and thank you all for coming and put-ting up with an old man, much less with memories of many years, some better than others—especially you, Nancy, whose youth and beauty and intelligence, I think all would agree, is the star attraction in our family firmament. I only regret that Annie is not here to see you, to play for you, to take you birding and introduce you to the sights and sounds of the birds come spring . . ." He blinked rapidly. "Ah, the heavenly notes of the hermit thrush at Handytown, where I, too, am to be scattered. But perhaps when spring comes again"—his chapped lips quivered as he tried to catch the eyes of his family—"someone at this table will introduce you properly to our birds." He lifted his glass higher. "As Robert Frost put it—what was the poem, Cordelia?"

"'Never Again Would Birds' Song Be the Same.'"

"Yes, yes . . . 'the daylong voice of Eve / Had added to their own an oversound'"—he nodded pensively—"I really believe they missed her playing. So, to Annie"—and he held up the CD with a nod down the table—"and Wendy, our wonder worker, thank you from the bottom of my heart."

Everyone at the table raised their glasses as one.

"But I also wanted to toast to others who are no longer with us and drink to their memories. The first is my mentor, Oliver Wendell Holmes, a great man and defender of the First Amendment, who, not unimportantly, introduced me to my wife, Annie Davenport.

Without Oliver and Annie, none of you would be sitting here today."
They drank again, and the Judge, beaming, his sallow, fleshy cheeks
touched with broken red capillaries, continued once more, consulting
a yellow legal pad at his elbow. "Annie was the love of my life, my
strong right hand, my compass, and I think it is fair to say that she
made you—Alice, Martha, and Cordelia—what you are in spite of
yourselves. You all have Annie's gumption and determination—and
talent, even if you choose to navigate by different stars. And the next
generation: Karen, Erich, Cecily, and George, you, too, have benefited
from her blood—genes, as you would have it today. I see something of
her in all of you, perhaps a mystery to yourselves but which surfaces
at times in the most remarkable ways." He nodded now at Cecily, his
white eyebrows shooting above his tortoiseshell reading glasses. "And,
of course"—and he raised his glass a tad higher and looked directly
at Nancy, perhaps transfixed for a moment by the bald eagle feather,
a primary with a fringe of white at its base, and she beamed in blissful expectancy—"you, Nancy, especially you, the newest to our flock,
who, in the flicker of your eyes and your shy laugh and your quick,
inquiring mind, remind me so much of your grandmother Annie.
She would be so proud of you, dear. But don't wear the feather"—he
laughed—"in the city; you'd be liable to be arrested. And do keep
trying with the Mozart."

"Great-grandmother," Alice interjected, serving the Judge from a
silver dish of sweet potatoes.

"I stand corrected, counsel."

"There's a lovely portrait of Annie in my room," said Alice with
a wry smile, inclining her chin for a moment toward her left breast,
where a dazzling diamond brooch, a stave of six notes, burned like a
beacon; "come in and see it later, Nancy. Oh, and besides being a great
concert pianist, she was a rehearsal pianist and performer for George
Balanchine and a bunch of City Ballet choreographers who were
devoted to her—*absolutely* . . . devoted. Isn't that right, Cordy?"

Cordelia, her shoulders swathed in an antique Hermès scarf decorated with ballet motifs, grinned right back at Alice (who had been
huddled with Martha much of the morning) and the Judge with a
serene smile and held up her wineglass in salute.

"Right on, soul sister."

"That's Annie's piano in the great room," noted the Judge to Nancy,
the previous exchange going unheeded. "She made it sing, as it still

sings under the talented hands of her children and"—he nodded at Cecily—"her grandchildren."

Martha's Theodore raised his hand in supplication. "May I take this opportunity to acknowledge my humble contribution to the Dimock gene pool?" He rose unsteadily, dressed in a beautifully tailored Italian suit and rumpled nondescript tie scavenged from the back of the closet in his room after he realized he'd forgotten to bring his own. "Though Polish Jews, I think we added some smarts to the line—perhaps not street smarts—why the benighted Poles were happy to see us dispersed to the wind." He gestured to the roaring fire with a sorrowful expression: dispersing smoke witnessed by world-weary eyes. "But for such illustrious goyim"—he grinned at Stan, with whom he'd hung out on the piazza most of that morning—"a scholarly seriousness with a dollop of chutzpah and good Polish borscht, I hope. Whatever the case, I love you, Karen and Erich and Nancy."

"And Max," Karen reminded him.

"And Max, of course."

"I heartily welcome the transfusion, Theo. Some of my most esteemed colleagues are Jewish—a proud race, and rightly so." The Judge held up his glass. "It was Felix Frankfurter who recommended me to Holmes, and later for the Second Circuit."

"Oh my God, spare us," groaned Alice. "At least you never got to rule on Holmes's opinion in *Buck v. Bell*, and that Virginia eugenics case for forced sterilization."

The Judge glared. "The opinion still stands as a block to unlimited rights to abortion under the Constitution. You should be pleased."

"Cool it, dear," said Stan.

"And what about our dear George Altmann," piped up Theo, "seated so silently over there? Surely Altmann is a Jewish name—something over all the years I believe we've never touched on, your Jewish roots."

"My father was Jewish," offered Jim. "My mother Norwegian."

"So that makes George one-quarter Jewish, enough to be sent to the camps—eh, Stan?"

"But surely the source of the creative spark in our young George," replied Stan, beaming.

"My Mom's Jewish," piped up Nancy.

"Yes, that makes you the winner in our little genetic sweepstakes," said her grandfather. "You, dear, are three-quarters Jewish and so by definition the smartest of all the Dimock offspring."

"Certainly the most inquisitive, with the possible exception of George," said the Judge.

"My God!" exclaimed Alice. "Really, you two."

"Ah," proclaimed Stan, "why I named our Billy after the great Billy Wilder, an Austrian Jew run out of Germany by the Nazis and the greatest director of our generation. And so that by rights gets Billy up to at least three-quarters, which explains his extraordinary creative powers as a comedian. Right, Cecily?"

"Tell it like it is, Dad," said Cecily with a broad smile. "And I thought I was the family polyglot black sheep."

"Ah," continued Theodore with a sweep of his hand, "we Jews have made you all what you are: a single omnipotent God—a damned jealous one at that, demanding constant sacrifice and absolute belief and fervent worship. And of special import for young George, linear time—eh, George? As opposed to the Philistines'—Greeks, didn't you tell me once, Erich?—belief in recurring cyclical time. Haven't we been right, hasn't your field of astrophysics proved us smarty-pants Jews to be correct in predicting that time has a beginning, a middle, and presumably an end, that history is unique? Your big bang and such like?"

Theodore stared imperiously down the table at his nephew.

"Infinity . . ." said George, faltering for a moment, "would certainly seem to be linear, even without an end, unless time ultimately enfolds upon itself, spiraling around like the ouroboros in the ship's keel ceiling swallowing its tail. In which case, if you believe some proponents of quantum gravity, our big bang was just one in a series of big bangs that keep repeating forever in an endless series of beginnings, middles, and ends. So like Einstein's intuition of a finite universe without boundaries."

"Like a great screenplay," offered Stan.

"Einstein," chortled Theo, "another Jewish genius who changed the world."

"Sounds good to me," said Cordelia, patting her son's arm while beaming, as if pressing some silent secret to her heart.

The Judge, seeming somewhat bewildered, raised his hand to halt the conversation.

"And there is one more," continued the Judge, moving on, "missing from our family fellowship, my son Teddy, and brother to Alice, Martha, and Cordelia. Teddy lit up our summers at Hermitage like no one else; he embraced the land and its traditions, fishing and hunting and hiking down to the Neversink, where he liked to cast his line by the abutments of the old Roebling aqueduct for the D & H." For a moment the Judge seemed to lose his train of thought, glancing at his legal pad. "Oh . . . yes, Teddy . . . I like to think that Teddy died not just for his country on some godforsaken speck of frozen hilltop in Korea but also for the cause of freedom. Or as Justice Holmes would put it, for freedom of thought and expression in all its most wonderful human forms. Teddy was what Dr. Holmes, Oliver's poet raconteur father, called a 'white-pine Yankee,' of softer grain, no longer needing to wrestle with angels and devils"—a pointed eye at Alice on his left—"a traditionalist happy to embrace his New England faith in the individual soul"—a wink at Martha—"the passion for justice, the potential in human nature and delight in the woods, the love of life and its ultimate goodness—writ in airy banners across the sky." Bloodred wine sloshed over his fingers at his mimicry of those airy banners. "So, I propose a toast to Teddy, and to the American boys poised to go into Iraq in defense of our country and the values for which we stand."

"Christ," exclaimed Alice, reaching for the wine after having already drained her second glass, "Teddy didn't die for his coun-try—he died for a misbegotten anti-Communist crusade cooked up by Truman, who managed to hoodwink the U.N. It was a farce and waste—just like this bullshit of invading Iraq, which will only end up another disaster like Vietnam."

The Judge closed his eyes for a moment, as if to regather steam.

"You might want to consult on that, Alice, with the North Korean people, or at least those living in freedom in the South—the starving millions, and millions more dead and enslaved—and ask them how much of a waste was Teddy's sacrifice."

She refilled her glass and raised it high. "I will drink to Teddy, not another imperialist crusade."

"Teddy thought your trial of Alger Hiss was a complete sham," announced Martha out of left field and with uncharacteristic conviction.

The Judge fell silent, nodding, not pleased.

"Annie and I were taken utterly by surprise when he enlisted." He raised his eyes, seeking out the subdued George. "Isn't that right, George, isn't that what I wrote in my memoir?"

"Oh my God—the infamous secret memoir!" exclaimed Alice.

"Yes"—George nodded—"you wrote as much."

Alice exchanged a knowing look with Martha. "Teddy was ashamed—and his Yale buddies only made it worse. If you hadn't tried to defend Hiss, and worse, destroy the prosecution's star witness in such an underhanded way, he'd still be here today."

"What's *Hiss*?" asked Nancy, curious.

The Judge didn't seem to hear, his blue eyes drifting to the windows.

Alice drank deep. "Aren't you forgetting somebody, Daddy?"

"Have I left someone out?"

"Billy, Daddy, my Billy, our Billy." She reached across the table, where Stan watched hollow-eyed, dressed in a tuxedo he'd hastily retrieved from the back of his closet without bothering to check what he'd actually packed.

"Yes," said Stan, straightening his black tie like a character out of a thirties B movie.

The Judge's face hardened as he fumbled to put his glasses back on and consult his notes.

"Of course there's Billy. You interrupted me; I hadn't gotten to Billy yet."

"It doesn't matter. You always made him feel so damned inadequate. You undermined me with my own children."

"Oh shut up, Mom," said Cecily, who was dressed in a gray-striped Armani dress borrowed from Wendy. "Of all of us, Billy loved this place most; he was always right behind the Judge on our hikes, taking it all in, making jokes, keeping us in stitches. *This* was the one place he felt safe, where he could relax and be himself."

"Thank you, Cecily," said the Judge. "Billy, if memory serves, was the one in your generation who got Annie's physical dexterity. Correct me if I'm wrong, Alice dear, but I believe he played piano duets in the great room with you."

"Me?"

Cecily smiled sweetly and raised her glass.

"He played them with *me*, Judge . . . he the white keys"—she giggled—"me the black." She spread her fingers wide. "Oh, how that boy had a reach. If only his demons had found peace in his playing . . ." Cecily beamed. "And don't forget who won the 'Annie prize' for mastering all the Chopin Etudes."

The Judge raised his glass. "To Billy . . . we all miss you, son."

"This is so fucking ridiculous," said Alice, wiping tears.

"Aunt Alice," said Erich, indicating Nancy at his elbow, "please."

"He had a better reach than Daniel Barenboim, ten inches at least. Just like Teddy—the reach Mom dreamed about, and drove herself crazy because Teddy refused to practice." She eyed her sister across the table. "Do you remember, he'd come in to dinner from rowing on the lake and Mom would reach to his hands at the dinner table—to check if he'd washed them before dinner—taking them in hers, cradling those huge strong hands disfigured with calluses and blisters, and she'd just weep right there in front of us all."

"He played—brought down the house—at Yale," said Martha, suddenly perking up. "He wrote me all about it. They nicknamed him 'Rubenstein.'"

At this, a shadow of dismay passed fleetingly over the Judge's face: a bit of news from his old school that had somehow escaped him.

"To Billy, my brother," said Cecily standing and raising her glass. "I love him and miss him. I celebrate him, just like we"—and she motioned to the cousins, Karen, Erich, and George—"were going to do on his birthday with a little fireworks display off the boathouse."

The cousins all laughed.

Karen drained her glass. "And truth be told, I was more than a little in love with Billy, with his stringy blond hair and broken nose—so there. Smoking dope with Billy and drowning our adolescent angst: When we were high with Billy, we were absolutely fearless."

"We were buddies," said Erich, glancing around at his cousins. "Chilling with Billy around a campfire was awesome."

"You smoked dope, Aunt Karen?" asked Nancy.

"Your aunt was just kidding," said Erich with a guffaw.

"She was a total pothead," said Cecily, laughing.

The Judge smiled faintly. "Then just what was it I found under the seat of Teddy's shell, all wrapped up tight in plastic?"

"Oh, that was cocaine," replied Cecily. "Billy was so *the Man*; all the kids down the lake were getting their fixes from him."

This put a momentary damper on conversation as all but Jim sipped from their glasses, while the cousins exchanged nervous glances.

The Judge, thankfully, flipped a page in his legal pad. "Well, now that we've got that little affair settled after twenty years, I thought we might get down to some family business. Just in case no one has noticed, I'm not getting any younger, as they say, and I've made provisions for the future of Hermitage, among other things. It does my heart good to have you all back here under one roof after—what shall we call it: a hiatus, perhaps a dark age?—and with some expectation that the family, especially with me fading from the picture, might actually, after all, want to keep up Hermitage. I like to think of this place and the land and its lore as a rallying point for all that's best in our family. Annie certainly thought so, and her family had a pile at Gloucester, let me tell you, that made this place look like a tourist rooming house." He raised a shaky finger. "And a sacred duty to keep alive the memories of those souls who once worked and loved this land, just as we now replace a stone for Annie."

The Judge stared around, as if to make sure he had everybody's attention, and then turned again to the legal pad at his elbow.

"And Annie, you see, still has much to do with the future of Hermitage—that is, if you all agree." The Judge paused, enjoying the expectant faces. "I'm sure there has been much speculation about my finances, which are now stretched thin due to the usual issues of age and infirmity and the ruinous taxes of New York State, which have doubled in the last decade alone. Upkeep, well, it's a historic house, now on the National Register of Historic Places. The ship's keel ceiling alone is a national treasure—a world treasure that any number of museums would grab at, and pay a king's ransom, but Hermitage would never be the same without it. Fortunately, a young lady seated at our table"—and he motioned with his glass to Wendy—"came up with a spectacular solution, which I fear my addled legal mind had entirely overlooked. Wendy here suggested that I look into the deed of promised gift from Annie to the Yale Art Museum of the Monet lily pads and Degas ballet dancers, which came down in Annie's family, and which have been on view there for over three decades, enjoyed by thousands of students and visitors. My lawyer writes that the deed of gift is actually in both our names and only becomes effective on my death. So while I survive, the gift can be rescinded. So, thanks to Wendy, my lawyer has notified Yale that I intend to welch on the gift of the Degas dancers, which will now be put up for auction at Sotheby's in the spring. The proceeds, invested, will fund the endowment of the family trust to maintain Hermitage. Sufficiently so that the house and land, upkeep, and all taxes and maintenance should be more than adequately covered in perpetuity. The instrument of trust requires the formation of a board of trustees, which is set out as follows. I remain the sole trustee until my death. At which point, the head trusteeship will go to George—the armed gentleman who so competently carved our turkey"—with a furrowed brow, he looked at George and Cordelia, seated at the head in Annie's place—"along with Cecily and Erich. The board is so constituted as to represent the three families: Alice's, Martha's, and Cordelia's. The three members of the board will have a majority vote on all matters pertaining to maintenance and usage and the expenditure of funds for capital expenses. Included in the trust is a scholarship fund that will pay full tuition for any member of the three families who requires financial assistance for boarding school, college, or graduate studies."

"How come I'm not on the board?" asked Karen.

"There can only be three board members—three families. Martha is the only one of you with two surviving children. It's something you can adjust between yourselves. Perhaps you can take Erich's place if he wants to decline the board position or move off at some later date."

"You did it because he has Nancy here," said Karen. "You always preferred girls, damn it."

"Dear, you just contradicted yourself."

"It's okay, Karen," said Erich. "We'll trade off."

"Forgive me," said the Judge, "but I haven't had the pleasure of meeting Max."

"Where is Max?" asked Martha suddenly. "I haven't seen him all day."

"Mom," said Karen, laying a hand on her mother's, "you know he couldn't make it."

Martha looked around the table at the expectant faces, and then at her husband. "Ah, the siren girlfriend."

"It doesn't mean he's any less interested in Hermitage than Nancy," said Karen.

"Well," said the Judge, "that may turn out to be the case, but for—what?—fourteen years or so he hasn't been given the opportunity to make that determination, much less learn the ropes, get some dirt between his toes, a little fishing and camping perhaps . . . customs of the country."

"So he's being punished; I'm being punished."

"We'll trade off," said Erich again soothingly.

Wendy raised her hand as if in class. "Let me talk to Max when you can get him on the landline. I think once he hears about the goodies waiting for him in his room, he might feel tempted to check it out."

"How 'bout right now, then?" said Karen to her brother.

"Give it a few years," said Erich, "till things settle."

"Hold it—hold on," said Alice, raising a flattened palm. "This is totally out of order. Why are you proposing skipping a generation? It should be me, Martha, and Cordy."

"You three would be at loggerheads," responded the Judge. "And then when one of you passed on, there'd be a mismatch of generations on the board. Best to start afresh, with a clean slate. You three don't want to be saddled with all this anyway . . ." And he waved a weary hand.

"This sucks," said Karen, pouting.

"Karen," said the Judge, "it's purely a practical matter, as I just explained. Max will be eligible for all scholarship help in terms of his educational aspirations, as will Nancy, and George's and Cecily's children one day. Why, Nancy has already expressed interest in Groton, and I've assured her that if she has good grades and can get in, all her tuition and expenses will be covered by the trust."

"What?" Erich shook his head, looking at his daughter.

Nancy sat up straight and beamed. "I think it looks like a really cool place, Dad. Lots of my friends are now going away to boarding school."

Martha raised her hand. "Teddy loved Groton and his friends there didn't seem so bad when they came here over vacations. Remember, Alice—and at his funeral, ten of his classmates and the headmaster came, and each one was kinder than the next in offering their condolences."

"Oh boy," sang out Alice, "the trap was set and you gullible idiots walked right into it with eyes wide shut."

Wendy pulled back her chair, shot a disappointed glance at George, and stood, causing the commotion to settle.

"I'd like to propose a toast." She held her glass at her waist until she had everyone's attention. "But before I do, I'd like to propose something to our host: Judge, Monet churned out hundreds of lily pad paintings, and the market, especially in terms of Japanese buyers, and even Chinese, is very strong right now. The Degas is much more important and rare and quite unique among the artist's work on that subject. Hate to have that disappear into a private collection in Asia and never be seen again. Might I suggest you sell the Monet instead, which will do plenty well at Sotheby's, and leave the Degas with the Yale Art Museum. And while doing so, change the gift dedication, something to this effect: 'Given by Edward Dimock in memory of his loving wife, Annie Davenport, and in honor of his daughter Cordelia, a dancer with New York City Ballet.'"

The silence was such that the cracking flames of the fire sounded a conflagration.

Cordelia burst into tears. Alice rolled her eyes, her chin sinking to her chest.

The Judge, wiping at his eyes, tapped a soupspoon: "I leave it to the new board: I vote aye. What say you Erich, Cecily, and George?"

"Love it, sister Wendy," proclaimed Cecily, while the others answered in the affirmative.

"Now," continued Wendy, "as an interloper at this gathering"—she cast another bemused look across the table at George, who refused to meet her eye—"and, yes, this is still part of my toast, I want to make a presentation in honor of our host and my friend." She went to the corner of the dining room where the mysterious brown paper package awaited, having been dropped off by an art-handling service the day before. She stripped the paper from the framed canvas and hefted it in two hands and turned it toward the diners, walking it slowly to the head of the table, where the Judge watched expectantly. "Judge, this is a gift from George and me, one of George Altmann's most spectacular paintings of the Shawangunks, even though highly abstracted. This"—she lifted it higher for all to gaze upon—"was painted only a few miles as the crow flies from Hermitage, overlooking the route of the Delaware and Hudson Canal. There seems to be a perfect place to hang it by Annie's Steinway in the great room, across from the Inness, under the ship's keel ceiling. A painting—and we've got a letter from the artist to his wife telling how much he admired the portrait of Annie in Raphel Soyer's studio and immediately went out and bought one of her recordings—that may well have been inspired by her playing. Imagine—*imagine*! If you spend a while studying the paint handling and colors and absorbing this wonderful depiction of the stratified rock layers, the clinging lichen, the filigree of cracks and fissures and fossils, the hints of plant life and erosion by wind and rain—well, you might get the feeling of all those millions of years passing, and the endurance of our world as we know it. That's how it speaks to me anyway, to the infinite geometries and forces and energies of our splendid universe—right, George?" she said, casting another glance at George, who refused to weigh in—"captured by a master artist, whom I feel perfectly complements the lost painter or painters of your ship's keel ceiling: a tiny fragment of our world created out of the infinitudes of the cosmos. Two artists, two visions of the terrestrial and cosmic, living hundreds of years apart but sharing the same soul of beauty—or what Emerson described as—right, Judge?—'another world or nest of worlds: for the metamorphosis once seen, we divine that it does not stop.'"

She went and leaned the painting in the window bay and walked back to her place to recover her wineglass, which she held at eye level, inspecting for a moment the glimmer of turbid damask and crimson, as might an alchemist of old.

"So, I want to propose a toast to the Judge, who, if he hadn't preserved the Altmann sketches and had the courage to first try to return them to Jim Altmann"—she nodded at the perplexed, bewhiskered face next to her—"and then turn them over to Jim's son, George, so that they might serve as evidence to at least one terrible crime—none of us would be here today, either. Those Altmann sketches now reside in the National Archives, a testament, a witness, to a time and place and a journey your family and other families—your children and their children and other children—and the country have endured and maybe even emerged into the light of justice a better people. Judge, thank you for your convictions and your dedication to see that justice is finally done."

She raised her glass, and all around the table, even though slightly mystified by the whole thing, joined her.

"Judge, I love you."

Alice looked around as if totally flummoxed.

"This is crazy, what a three-ring circus—what do these sketches have to do with anything?"

The Judge, wiping tears, said, "Thank you, dear. On behalf of the family and Hermitage, I accept your gift . . ." Slightly stupefied, he gazed over at the painting by the bay window. "I had no idea—I had only George's splendid catalog—how beautiful in real life his work could be; it's more spectacular than words can express. And yes, I think I catch your drift about the ship's keel ceiling—the kindred spirits."

Stan, intercepting his wife's incredulous outburst, waved his glass high.

"I second the motion. And Judge, I admire your ruling for the ruling class, especially since there are so few WASPs left—a dying breed—don't you agree, Theo? You know, it's a real problem for casting these days for theater classics: How do you teach the notion of *savoir faire*, *noblesse oblige* in acting class, the nonchalance of a privileged class, when there are no good role models left—scattered like ashes to the wind? Where's the next Cary Grant or Jimmy Stewart, or even Gregory Peck, for that matter?"

"Would Bing Crosby make the cut, do you think?" asked the Judge. "Though, from a relatively humble background, I believe."

"Der Bingle . . . well."

"*High Society.*" The Judge cracked a sly grin. "Grace Kelly, wasn't she a dream doll, like Annie, same cool, impossible beauty."

"There is no society like high society," echoed Theo with a touch of glee as he raised his glass in imitation of a swell. "I'm sure Veblen would agree with you wholeheartedly, especially this lovely display of conspicuous consumption."

"Listen to you two." Alice, clearly upset, took another sip of her wine. "This is the man who defended Alger Hiss—a Soviet spy, if your minions down the table are right—a man, a paragon of the Harvard establishment doing Stalin's bidding. Teddy was ashamed—right, Martha?—that's the bottom line."

"I'm with you on this, Judge," interjected Theodore, seated next to Alice, a hand going to pat her arm. "Stalin was a piece of shit; he killed my eldest brother at Katyn, a loyal Polish officer *and* a Jew."

"But Theo," pleaded Martha from across the table, "you were a member of the Communist Party in Kraków when I first met you; I thought that was terribly romantic at the time."

Theodore scowled, chagrined. "Anybody who was anybody or who aspired to be somebody in those days had to be a member of the Party."

The Judge, having been preoccupied with the dazzling blue tonalities in the painting, turned back to his eldest daughter. "Have you ever graced Harvard's Memorial Hall with your presence, Alice, where your great-grandfather Richard Davenport is memorialized? The man"—the Judge tapped the rosewood table with his knuckles—"who put his feet under this very table. Believe it or not, he'd probably be proud of you and Cecily for fighting the good fight."

"And you, instead of confronting the government, the system, Nixon and Hoover, you were obviously playing some elaborate con game, hedging your bets, playing up to the Truman administration while defending Hiss, keeping your options open on both the Left and Right to grab your brass ring whatever the outcome of the trial. A good defense lawyer would have decimated the system and so confounded the jury that they couldn't convict."

"Dear Alice," the Judge replied, leaning forward, as if relieved that the battle had been properly joined, "may I remind you who wrote the majority opinion nullifying the Seventh Circuit Court of Appeals ruling, which got off all your pals, including Kunstler and the Chicago Seven, or was it Eight? I ruled the Chicago judge had been biased on the jury selection. But there is no doubt that under the law they were guilty of crossing state lines with the intent of inciting a riot. That is the system at work, and I might suggest, bending over backward to preserve freedom of expression even when the violent overthrow of the government was *exactly* the intent of those people."

"Don't be so damned smug," said Alice.

"Let's lighten it up," pleaded Erich.

"Well," said Cecily, raising her glass, "this half-breed nigger is in on the Judge's offer, especially since I just got into NYU medical school starting in January. And I'll trade Claude over a student loan any day."

Alice looked at her daughter, not a little pleased. "Third time lucky, well . . ."

Karen moaned. "Maybe I just wasn't beautiful enough or smart enough like Cecily—maybe my table manners sucked."

Martha reached a hand to her daughter. "Karen, you were a luminous and sensitive teenager—the best daughter a woman could want."

"Oh Karen, stop feeling sorry for yourself," said Cordelia, now beaming. "You're still gorgeous, and Max is as handsome and smart as they come."

"Yes, indeed," said Martha. "And now you don't have to take you know whose money for Max's tuition—if he tries to break the custody agreement."

"Why is this Hiss guy always coming up?" asked Nancy, obviously intrigued by all the delicious gossip flying around.

Alice smiled, enjoying the free-for-all, her métier. "Clue in your granddaughter, Martha, about Priscilla Hiss."

"What the hell is this all about?" The Judge sat back, shaking his head. "What witches' brew are you two concocting this time around?"

"You didn't know Priscilla Hiss was a patient of Martha's for years?"

"But Alice," said Martha, "I can't reveal anything Priscilla said in analysis; it's privileged, just like with your clients."

"You didn't feel that way yesterday in the car," said Karen.

"I had no idea," murmured the Judge with a plaintive look.

"Oh, Priscilla, yes . . ." said Martha, smiling at the hum of attention. "I have this image of her lying there—must have been when I still had my couch—with her hair pulled tight behind her head, just a few wisps of gray sticking out. She had the most beautiful gray eyes, and that purring Bryn Mawr tone in her voice. I don't think I've ever known a patient so tied up in knots. Poor thing, not a moment's peace."

"My God!" The Judge sighed. "What did she have to say?"

Wendy and George leaned forward.

"She was slowly losing her mind," said Martha a tad vaguely. "She got things mixed up a lot, what with all the stress and anger . . . a heart condition." Martha continued sipping her wine. "I think she always had something of a crush on you, Daddy. You know how it is: the life you might have had with another man—I hear it all the time."

The Judge frowned, eyes drifting off, drained. "It's all in my memoir. We were lovers in the twenties, before Harvard Law, long before I married your mother, long before her second marriage to Alger Hiss."

"Who is Alger Hiss?" asked Nancy insistently, now a little annoyed at being ignored.

"Alger Hiss was a Russian spy," said Erich to his daughter. "Remember, we talked about this in the car yesterday. Your great-grandfather defended Hiss in a famous trial."

Martha's head was shaking, as if something wasn't quite clarifying and the wine not helping. "Priscilla always called you her 'shining knight,' the man her Quaker parents would have preferred for her to marry. I remember her laughing about it, saying how her parents looked down on Alger Hiss as coming from a second-rate family out of second-rate dowdy Baltimore."

"Ah," said Alice with a worldly toss of her head, "the kiss of death: the man your parents want you to marry. Not like you Stan, the Commie Jew they couldn't abide—and I mean that as a compliment."

Martha reached to her father's arm with a gentle pat. "I remember Priscilla always telling me about your discretion, Daddy, about how much she appreciated that in you—that you never pushed her to disclose more than she was willing to tell."

The Judge bent forward toward his daughter. "How was she, dear, in those last years? I never saw anything of her after . . . well . . ."

"A sick woman. She always told me"—Martha paused, as if to carefully measure her words—"she was convinced you knew all her secrets."

"Secrets?" echoed the Judge with lowered eyes.

"She always kept coming back to 1953, something about 1953 and the *New York Times*."

"Well," offered the Judge, "Alger was still in jail; it had to be a hard time for her family."

"Oh it had nothing to do with Alger, because whatever it was still weighed on her mind twenty years later—like yesterday. As if it had been a shock to her system, something she never got over."

"In the *New York Times?*"

"Yes, 1953."

Stan sighed and shook his head. "That was the year when Stalin died, when Khrushchev gave that damning speech before the Politburo condemning the terrible crimes of Stalin, chapter and verse. It utterly devastated any of us who had ever been in the Party or were still in it. Yes, a shock. How many I knew sneaked off into the shadows and never raised their heads again. A whole world, a way of life, a belief—a faith transformed into the stink of the slaughterhouse."

"And good riddance," added Theo.

"She just wanted to be free," said Martha. "Poor lady."

Theodore held up his wineglass to Martha and Stan and the Judge.

"The dead no longer have the convenience of confession, only those they leave behind." He put a finger to the back of his neck, pointed at an upward angle. "And here's where they placed the bullet for my brother."

"Alger Hiss was a liar and murderer," said Jim, his hoarse voice barely above a hush as he looked around the table, his lips pressed in a grimace.

"I had a patient once," continued Martha with a vacant stare at the nearest candle flame, "a handsome lady, a great pal of Alger's before he died. Twice a week she'd travel out to East Hampton or somewhere to read him the *New York Times*. You see, he suffered from macular degeneration and required readers. She said he was such a gentleman, such the perfect ladies' man. You would've thought she was almost in love with him the way she went on about his excitement at a new book, his passion for events of the day."

The Judge smiled gently at Nancy, who had been trying to follow the discussion. "We hoped he wasn't capable of those things. In fact, a whole generation hoped he wasn't. We wanted to believe that he couldn't be." For a moment, his voice caught in his throat at the sight of the bald eagle feather standing up bold as brass in Nancy's chignon—a moment of doubt, of vague panic which then passed as quickly as it had come. "Well, it turned out he was lying to everyone. It was a very sad moment in American history when we woke up to the evil in our midst."

Stan stared into his glass: "We wanted peace and justice and workers' rights. Civil rights for blacks. We wanted an end to segregation in the South. To beat fascism. I think we just got hijacked by the wrong people along the way."

"You old Reds," slurred Alice, blowing a kiss to her husband across the table, "with all your secrecy and skullduggery—such pathetic losers, lovable in your earnest naïveté, but pathetic. When the real action was always in the streets."

George held up his hand as if to bring the conversation to a halt or begin things anew.

"Seconds, white meat or dark matter?"

He sliced deep, expertly curling back the white flesh. He was saddened by the fact that he hadn't the guts to keep up his end of things, when he knew the Judge expected him to take the lead (still the snotnosed kid). He'd been totally caught off guard by Wendy's gift of the Altmann painting (not to mention the deal with the Monet), one of the two she'd bought on opening night, just as he was devastated by the e-mail from the *Times* reviewer of the night before, which enraged him, sending Wendy fleeing, for all he knew, into the arms of Cecily. He'd never screamed at anybody like that in his life. And he knew everybody knew (just like when he was a kid) that he couldn't even look her in the eye to express the sense of betrayal he felt, the way she ran rings around him, like a chess master always three or four moves ahead. But how to hate such a dynamo of free energy (dealing with her own demons), much less love someone you could never truly trust because you couldn't trust yourself?

As he handed off plates, he found himself filled with both love and dread at the swirl of conversation, what was being created or re-created around the dining room table, which in his mind's eye sometimes took on the guise of a spinning gaseous cloud of hydrogen, helium, oxygen, carbon, and nitrogen atoms, slowly cooling, spiraling and coalescing into this odd little solar system, as gravity and fusion began the process of forming a new generation of planets around a dying sun. Was it the money that now jump-started the free flow of energy to provide structure, coherence, and direction—information, "Annie's rules"? Or the memories, or the love, or the place, or that so elusive truth about the past? He didn't know, but he realized he had to try to say something. The Judge expected it of him. And he could feel the disappointment in Wendy's tender perplexity—after she had boldly taken the precarious step of presenting the Altmann painting, while whitewashing the implications of the sketches—that he hadn't taken up her rope line. And he recognized in that moment that the Altmann painting, as with the Judge's memoir, were artifacts of time and memory, less repositories of reputations, of talent or fact, as vessels of infinite sensibility, writs of love and passion by whose stars they were fated to navigate.

He had to do it, for Nancy's sake, if no other.

So he raised his glass for silence, his carving duties finally done. "The universe may not care about us, but we do. We are the only way the universe can rightly know its cold, dark heart. The essence of which is change: all the time, everywhere and absolutely. Leaving us only with the lifeboat of this planet, which was George Altmann's genius to see, leaving us to man the oars on a sea of infinite expansion . . ."

He raised his glass again. "Here's to you Nancy, the youngest of our kind at Hermitage. We come here for the peace and quiet because we are surrounded by chaos everywhere—and I mean everywhere, way beyond the tragedy of the past year alone. This is our habitable zone, or Goldilocks equilibrium." He gestured to the table of leaping trout and the lines of perplexed, if intrigued, faces.

"How fragile this is. If we don't insist on some kind of order—a moral order, a legal order, even a standard model order—a place of our heart's contentment where love can find a safe harbor, the universe certainly won't do it for us—the universe doesn't care. For the universe, we're just another random two ten-thousandths of a percent quantum fluctuation amplified by gravity to become who we are, much less the probably hundreds, possibly infinite number of near copies. Only what we *do* and how much we *love* gives any meaning whatsoever.

"And all I can know for sure is who loves me and whom I love"— he caught the eye of his mother and then all the others—"and what I care about and what others care about, even if we have different ideas about how to get there. I know I loved and miss Billy, who shared with me my first peek at a *Playboy* centerfold. And Erich—yes, you, brother, who first got me high. And Karen, who first told me about the facts of life in quite explicit detail when we watched a bunch of wood ducks humping by the boathouse. And Cecily, whom I had a terrible crush on, and who indulged my puppy love and never took advantage. Mom, who never gave up on me no matter how much weird stuff I was into. And Jim, well, I guess it's been a journey for both of us. And even though I never knew Annie—and never had the touch, I hear her spirit everywhere, some better played than others—and yes, the birds surely picked up a note or two. I have suffered before the Judge's bench as much as any of you, but I'd rather face his sentencing at the end of time than any other. And even though I endured as an inmate in Cuddebackville, Teddy's lair, an entire lifetime, so it often seems, reminded at every turning of how I'd never live up to all those stupid rowing trophies and ribbons, I wouldn't change it for the world. Toss the trophies, Nancy"—George smiled fondly at his cousin—"and only do the Groton thing if you feel deep in your heart you will find loyal friends and joy in learning there. Curiosity is the only thing that matters, that leads you beyond the constraints of your own life into forbidding and fascinating passions. And tonight, we'll look at some stars together from the boathouse and you'll see where the real action is at Hermitage."

He closed his eyes and nodded, sighing to himself.

"And yes, I miss Teddy, even if I never knew him, because he loved this place and his love somehow endured and entered the landscape in every birdcall and breath of wind over the lake . . . yes, in every dip of the oar. Call it superposition if you like—and no, I won't go there, not here, not now. And I miss my other grandfather as well, even if I never knew him . . . until recently, and now with something of his luminous genius a part of all this—to George Altmann." He paused for an instant as he lowered his glass, catching Wendy's rapt stare; he was running out of steam even as he wondered if he should say more about the sketches, about the spy William Weisman, who had tipped off his KGB handlers that army intelligence had broken the Soviet military codes, so blinding the White House and allowing Stalin's orchestration of the Communist attack on South Korea (which a warning from Truman might well have prevented), or the Rosenbergs' treasonous gift of the atom bomb to Stalin years earlier than the Soviets could have developed it on their own, a bomb without which Stalin would never have dared sign off on the attack of South Korea . . . where Teddy was to die on a lonely hilltop overlooking the Chosin Reservoir. But this would have to wait for the memoir, even if Wendy—and he knew she would try—might insist on adding daubs of her own sensibility, her feeling for imaginative reinvention, as had been Annie's wont . . . as if the dead might yet be raised. Besides, he was now aware of the Judge's expectant stare and consoling smile. Why burden his heavy pack with more? He'd said enough, said his piece, confirmed moments later when the Judge took up his glass in reply and motioned to Nancy.

"You see, Nancy, your cousin George always liked to talk about the paradox of the present, where the past and future collide indeterminately, a zone—right, George?—of heated friction"—and he gestured broadly, glancing to the horizon over the lake, where the tree line met the sky—"often incomprehensible to us mortals, a limbo in which we struggle. But not here, not at Hermitage, at Handytown. You are safe and on firm ground here, in the bosom of your family. Where we can, in our most generous moments, live out our lives as best we can as seekers after the truth—and beauty. That is what a judge tries to make possible, why I cling to the law, to our system of justice based on common-law tradition—flawed as it may be, which in its way encompasses George's dynamic meeting point between past and future: a forum—as here at our festive table, a quiet, ordered space, where tales about the past with all its flawed humanity and conjectures about future motivations clash and jostle and find reso- lution of a kind. The crucible, in a larger sense, beyond our borders, where the destiny of men and women are decided, where fate hangs in the balance, weighed by a jury of one's peers, who are charged with deciphering those same invisible acts, the stories that constitute the past, which so often confound us. Leaving us to seek out the truth, in hopes that justice might be served, in effect creating the future, like George's clouds of cosmic gas and dust and whatnot that form new stars and solar systems."

The Judge grinned with the pleasure of his métier, as if young again and trying to catch the eyes of his jury, especially the happy eyes of the faithful daughter seated at the far end of the table in Annie's place.

"You see, Nancy, we are never truly alone. As Edmund Burke, a great thinker, put it, we the living, our world, is an association between the dead, the living, and the unborn. Less a contract than a trusteeship of a shared inheritance, a continuous chain of giving and receiving, so that the good we inherit is a gift not to be wasted, but safeguarded and passed on to those who come after us. Not unlike a family—what do you think?—even the best of families, bedeviled by conflicting loyalties and discordant memories but in the end held together by the bonds of place and shared, if sometimes trying and discordant, memories. The past is never the past, but only eternally reborn in each passing moment. Emerson put it better than I ever can. Why I miss Annie, my wife, Nancy, your great-grandmother, who in her playing of Mozart came as close to perfection in the passing moments we inhabit—so uniting past, present, and future—as we are likely to achieve as flawed human beings. And yet, she, her story, is *here*—still with us." And he held up his set of CDs emblazoned with the euphoric face from the Soyer portrait. "So, my dear girl, don't let the world scare you; yours is just one more story to be cherished."

The Judge smiled sweetly, tears streaming down his flaccid cheeks, as if either perplexed or moved by his own words, or more likely assured of his jury's verdict, and raised his glass to Nancy's radiant smile.

64
Infinity in the Palm of Your Hand

GEORGE AND NANCY sat on camp stools at the end of the boathouse dock, well clear of the sloping roof. The night sky encompassed them with a deep translucency the like of which she had never witnessed before, even as the far pine-serried horizon blotted the milky haze of a robust moon, and so for a few minutes more cloaked its full brilliance.

While they took turns bending to the eyepiece of his old and battered Meade Polaris reflecting telescope, she remained uncharacteristically silent, as if possessed by nagging doubts over the luncheon conversation. Often she just gazed out longingly at the lake, where, reflected on its calm face, distant pinpoints of light were herded into eternity. He in turn felt adrift, reeling from his fight the night before with Wendy, only adding heartbreak to the accumulating unknowns that had yet to find resolution.

"Okay, you're looking at Orion, the hunter. I think I remember the Judge telling me that was Teddy's favorite constellation."

"Oh, right, the jacked god with the humongous sword and shield on the ship's keel ceiling—that cool kilt he wore above the knee."

Nancy, new Nikon binoculars dangling from her neck, was wearing a shocking orange wool hat (caution for would-be hunters) and layers of outdoor gear, as if fitted out for a polar expedition. Her half-broken-in hiking boots dangled great loops of lace.

"Rigel, at the bottom right in Orion, is the brightest star. While Betelgeuse at the upper left is the next brightest. Rigel is a blue-white supergiant and Betelgeuse a red supergiant—and it's not even the Fourth of July."

He smiled at his lame joke.

"Did you say Beetlejuice?" she finally got out, still distracted.

"I believe that is the reference." He tapped fondly the telescope's metal housing, less out of chagrin at the image quality, than at the comforting compactness of the Milky Way after a decade working with the vast imagery from the Hubble telescope. "Well, you see, telescopes are like time machines. This is how we can gaze back at stars and galaxies through cosmic time, and so discover how they evolved and so where we are . . . well"—he shrugged—"headed—in the universe of things."

"Cousin George," she began, turning her worried eyes to his with a questioning pout, a vague tremor of panic, "just how many galaxies can we see? It seems awfully humongous out there."

He laughed. "This is kindergarten," and he tapped the telescope again. "Like you training those binoculars on a bald eagle across the lake."

"How many?" she demanded.

"Maybe one hundred billion at least in the observable universe—a lot more than what you're seeing right now."

"Galaxies?" She looked pleadingly at George and then back to the comfort of the lake. "That's an awful lot . . . that's awfully big."

"You don't wanna know," he said, repressing the sense of awe in his voice.

"Have you taken Wendy down here to look at stars?"

"Why do you ask?"

"Oh, just because how she describes things makes me feel better, like how she explained the ship's keep ceiling to me last night." Nancy shrugged, her lips compressed in a plaintive pout. "Maybe we should just stick with *our* planets and stars, our Milky Way—right?"

"Well, maybe we can do better," he said, noting the ache in her voice. "Look around you. What's the most obvious thing?"

"Where?"

"Here and now."

"The lake, you mean?

"Well, okay, the lake—water . . . maybe Hermitage."

"And us . . . and Wendy?"

"Yes, after all, in this tiny corner of the universe the molecules have become so complex that they've achieved consciousness, enough to paint paintings and write books and, if you like, see our reflection in the stars. So, I think we qualify as intelligent life."

She smiled, possibly a little relieved.

"To tell stories, like the Judge said."

"Stories, too."

"Was Giordano Bruno right? So that they really burned him alive."

"Oh, about many things. But perhaps you should consult William Blake, one of Wendy's favorites. 'To see a world in a grain of sand and a heaven in a wild flower / Hold infinity in the palm of your hand and eternity in an hour . . .'"

She smiled, fingering her binoculars. "How this is so beautiful; I never knew night could be so beautiful, like all this time I've had my eyes shut."

"The crucial thing is that water"—he paused as if listening to a last cricket or two in the spindly blueberry bushes along the shore, or a tailfin splash, something—"at least for most of the year, isn't ice, and doesn't evaporate as steam in the summer, not yet anyway. We live in the habitable zone, a planet, our Hermitage, with a long-lived sun. Close your eyes, take a deep breath."

"Smells like pine and this old dock and the lake and my new stuff."

"And . . ."

"You want me to say oxygen."

"See, smart cousin of mine—like I said, intelligent life. Sure you're not too hot?"

"Yeah, I was wondering about that: whether we're really all alone in the universe or not."

He cocked his ear to a distant rhythmic sound. "Of course, the problem with intelligent life is that the same technology that might allow a woman like you—the Jodie Foster thing—to communicate over millions of light-years of space, requires the same level of technology that might very well allow us to blow up our advanced civilization, which makes the window for finding out about one another over many hundreds of thousands of years a very small one, indeed, maybe as little as a few hundred years. So, we're really threading the cosmic needle, here—big time."

She seemed to ponder this, nodding.

"Blowing things up, like the World Trade Center towers?"

"No, hopefully, those monsters are the least of our problems. People have survived the atom bomb, the two world wars, then Korea and Vietnam, so we're doing okay."

"So even if there are aliens out there, the chances we get to communicate with them—hang out—is pretty slim?"

"Well," he replied, smiling, "just look at us." He moved his stool close to the edge of the dock and leaned over, encouraging her to do the same, so their heads appeared reflected in the lake, two airy sojourners, their way pricked out by starlight. "You see, very few exoplanets have stars like our sun, maybe only eight percent. Stars that don't exhaust their fuel too quickly, stars that live longer but whose luminosity might be too low, which means our exoplanet has to hug too close, and so is tidally locked, like our moon, into an ellipsoidal-shaped orbit—a Hermitage, you see, without tides—without seasons. Not a nice place to hang out, no, not at all."

She unzipped her new coat and tossed it aside, luxuriating in a cool breeze that had sprung up.

"That was a little weird at lunch, what the Judge was saying about there being no present."

He laughed. "The Judge tends to twist things I tell him—or make analogies—so he can understand them better. The present exists all right, like time exists, except there isn't really a single *kind* of time. You see, it's more like an event, something passing, contingent on many factors, like place and speed and different rhythms." He paused, listening. "Maybe it's better to think of the present—or present time—as an event that is always changing, not something . . . well, so permanent. Not *being* so much as *becoming*."

"Becoming, like you and Wendy?"

He had to laugh. "You like her, huh?"

"She's so unbelievable cool." Nancy held up her wrist to his nose. "Smell—what do you think?"

"Nice."

"She said it was Annie's favorite."

He pondered this and sighed. "Here, put your hand over your chest. What do you feel?"

She pressed her hand into her camouflage tunic.

"My heart."

"So, your heartbeat . . . you're becoming."

"Like the earth, like Hermitage?"

"Seasons, cycles, change . . ." His voice trailed off as he squinted over the lake, again hearing a familiar sound.

She took a serious breath as she followed his curious gaze. "So, not too hot, not too cold, enough atmosphere and normal orbits."

"Water, lots of water, where Mars and Venus missed out."

"So with everything, would the aliens be more like us or that nasty, drooling monster Ripley fought?"

"Ah, so how did you like Sigourney Weaver?"

"She kicked ass—like Wendy."

He laughed. "Well, just wait till you get to meet the bats and barn swallows in the spring. And the blueberries in July . . ."

The dock groaned as he reached to make another adjustment to the telescope.

"Do you believe . . . in ghosts?" she asked, biting her lip, as if worried it might be a stupid question.

"No—and you?"

"I didn't, but being here, the way people talk about my great-uncle Teddy, and Annie . . . there's a kind of feeling." She shrugged. "In the air."

"She's in all of us, like star dust." He patted her shoulder and pointed. "Hey, a shooting star—go ahead and make a wish."

They gazed at the arc of fading light splinters. And as they did, the sound came again, a faint echoing splash, now a long silver shadow seeming to nose free of the shadows on the lake, a line moving in quick rhythmic pulses across the water. And again that whisperlike cadence beating out time, as if summoning the moon to light its way, a buttermilk moon now just cresting the treetops and, in turn, revealing the glow of a sleek racing hull and the heartbeat of drumming oars.

"What's that?" exclaimed Nancy, grabbing his arm.

"A rower, sculling," he answered calmly, as if this was the thing he'd been half-expecting all along.

"Oh my God!" she exclaimed, pulling off her wool hat.

"Ahoy," shouted George, switching on a flashlight and waving it.

The rower shipped oars a moment, then dipped his left and adjusted course, slowing, gliding toward the boathouse. In less than a minute, a young man in a single shell nosed to within an oar's length of the dock where they were seated. He was tall, even seated, his bare arms ropy with muscles.

"Hello, folks," he said, greeting them with a quick salute. He was perhaps sixteen or seventeen, with blondish hair and broad shoulders and flashing moonlit eyes in a lean square face.

"Happy Thanksgiving," said George.

"Happy Thanksgiving," echoed Nancy.

"You guys, too." The shell drifted around, an oar blade touching the dock. "I'm Benjamin Wright Jr. We're neighbors down the lake."

"Of course—sure, Ben—I'm George Dimock Altmann, and this is my cousin Nancy, the Judge's great-granddaughter. I remember you from the beach when you were a kid."

"Oh, yeah—you were at Princeton, right?"

"Yup."

"Well, it's incredibly warm, huh? I'm trying to work off Thanksgiving lunch," said Ben. "And stay in shape for the spring season. My grandma stuffed us all to the brim."

"Where do you row?" asked Nancy.

"Groton first eight."

She took a deep breath, sitting up straight as she swept hair behind her ears. "How cool—do you like it there?"

"If you don't mind the work. I'm better at rowing than studying."

"I'm thinking of applying for next year, the third form."

"Cool, the girls are supersmart." He grinned, swiping at his sweating brow with his upper arms. "You guys looking at the stars?" He pointed an oar blade at the telescope. "Nothing I love more than rowing at night and looking at the stars, even if I don't know enough of their names. Grandma Daisy quizzes me all the time. And my dad's in the navy, so he knows his stars like the back of his hand."

"How is your dad?" asked George.

"He's captain of a destroyer deployed to the Gulf. Tough on Mom." Ben bent toward the dock, squinting as if to better read their faces. "Grandma Daisy is worried too, but she's a real trooper."

"Better captain on a destroyer than a marine going into Iraq," assured George.

"Amen to that, sir."

"My cousin George is a Princeton astrophysicist, so any time you want to come by to bone up on astronomy, he's the best."

"Man, how cool is that." Ben smiled at Nancy. "Are you here in the summers, at the beach? I don't think I remember you."

"Oh I will be, for sure."

"That's good, 'cause everybody around the lake has been wondering what ever happened to all the Dimocks."

"We're back!" Nancy laughed, holding up her hand.

"Nice to meet you." And Ben raised his oar as if to shake her hand. She held the wet blade, her grip tightening, then letting go. "See you next summer. Or if you do an admissions visit to Groton, just ask for me. I'm a student tour guide. I'm sure Judge Dimock has our telephone number. My grandma Daisy tells stories about him all the time."

"He's ninety-five and still going strong," said Nancy, not without a hint of pride.

"Totally cool. Grandma will be thrilled to know he's okay. Well, I'd better be on my way."

"Take it easy, Ben," said George, returning the salute and pushing off on the oar blade.

"Have a great semester," said Nancy, waving. "And good luck to your boat."

"And your dad and his crew—Godspeed," added George.

They silently watched where the moonlight settled on Ben's pumping back and shoulders, a dark shirt and white *G*, his sleek shell gathering speed, a diminishing silhouette fading to shadowy points of light, and then to almost nothing, the barest echo.

"Oh my God," said Nancy, and raised her hands to her face. "*Have a great semester*—what a stupid thing to say."

"That was a little weird," George said finally, more to himself than to Nancy. Somewhat spooked, he began feverishly to make adjustments to the telescope and returned to his lecturing tone as he motioned to the eyepiece. "Have a gander at Andromeda."

Reluctantly, she lowered her binoculars and bent to the rubber eyepiece of the telescope.

"Andromeda," she said with a hint of longing in her voice. "Wendy pointed her out: the goddess with the great body chained to a rock or something."

"Our closest galactic neighbor in the Milky Way," noted George, trying to recover his comfortable lecturing voice, even as he realized that the blazing moon had caused many stars to evaporate from view, transforming the sky into a cloche dome over the lake. "Sadly, our Andromeda is a relatively old lady with only a few new stars being born out of the interstellar medium. You can't quite see them with this old telescope—not now with the moon—but those faint disks of gas and dust eventually form into stars and planets."

"So Andromeda is saved by Perseus so she can have babies"—she gave her teacher a sly smile and giggled—"like you and Wendy?"

"I wouldn't go *that* far!" He laughed uneasily, pondering the lake as if still not quite believing in Ben Wright. "In the real world, you see, gravity births stars and also disperses the elements of dead and dying stars, enriching the interstellar medium with heavier elements, heavier than hydrogen and helium, like iron and oxygen, carbon and nitrogen, the stuff that goes into planet Nancy." He gave her shoulder a friendly shove. "Everything we see, touch, feel, our bodies, came out of the thermonuclear processing of stars."

She sighed. "Ben was pretty gorgeous."

He looked at Nancy fondly, unable to suppress a chuckle of wonder at the unalloyed love welling up from the vastness. "Like his dad, who, if memory serves, is a pretty no-nonsense kind of guy."

She again adjusted her chestnut hair, now even more lustrous in the moonlight. "All this makes me feel a little lost, pretty insignificant."

"Remember, smart girl—because your three-pound brain can grasp all this, or, better still, make you fall in love with the beauty of the cosmos—*you* become the center of the universe, kind of like, well, like you're looking into a mirror."

She smiled, a little skeptical, then bent over again to stare down at the polished surface of the lake, canting her face from side to side, as if not quite sure what to make of the young woman there.

"So, how far did you say the Andromeda Galaxy is from Earth?"

"Two and a half million light-years away."

"Yikes." She laughed, reaching with the toe of her boot to splash her reflection, giddy with daring.

"The distances can be a little daunting, I know. Our Milky Way is one hundred thousand light-years across and one thousand light-years on the vertical."

"So thin?

"Like a humongous pancake with an air bubble at the center. Most of the action takes place in the spiral arms. Hermitage, actually, occupies a pretty obscure backwater. One day, maybe you can travel to the southern hemisphere, to a mountaintop in the Andes, in Chile, where you'll really be able see the center of the Milky Way in all its splendor." He nodded to himself with a hint of nostalgia. "You'll never forget it."

She giggled and held out her arms as if to an invisible lover. "I think my three-pound brain prefers this. I mean, it's hard enough to get to know people right next door." Her voice quivered for a moment, and there was a forlorn expression in her eyes as they turned to his.

"It's a bit of a paradox: You'd think the brightest stars would be the closest to the Earth, but they're not; the stars we see best tend to be of the highest luminosity and are very far away," George told her.

"Yeah, tell me about it. Like *Many Moons*, you know, when the court jester asks the sad princess how far away the moon is, and she tells him it's no bigger than her thumb and it hangs in the branches of the tree outside her bedroom window. And so he promises to climb the tree and get it for her. Then he makes a pretend moon out of gold and the next night comes to her bedroom and tells her he climbed that tree and plucked it down just for her, and he hangs it around her neck like a charm, so that she gets better."

"Ah, yes . . . explaining that the night sky simply grows a new moon." He chuckled. "Who read you that?"

"Mom did in my favorite chair in my bedroom in our old apartment—Mom's apartment. She even gave me a star chart to go over my desk, along with Dad's maps of the Mediterranean and Venice. When I was little, he gave me a really cool reproduction of a sixteenth-century map of Venice, a bird's-eye view that shows every house and palace in the city. Before bed, he'd point them all out, one by one, going down the Grand Canal. My favorites were the Ca' d'Oro and the Palazzo Dario. He could tell the history of each and every one. He's promised to take me to Venice someday."

"How cool, the way your dad is so into Venice."

"Yeah, but hanging out now every other week at Grandma Martha's isn't much fun. She's getting a little strange."

"About *your* sad princess—there's nothing wrong with pretending, at least about some things."

She bridled and sat up straight. "That won't get me into Groton. So how do we know the *real* distance to the stars?"

"Well, in principle it's quite straightforward. We use the inverse-square law that relates brightness and a star's luminosity. That allows a calculation of the distance . . . well, if we know the intrinsic luminosity—a little tricky, especially when there's a lot of cosmic dust, which tends to obscure things."

"Luminosity?" she asked, bending to the eyepiece.

"Compared to the sun, our sun; there's a scale, see. And we can tell luminosity—the amount of light energy a star emits—by the star's color, blue being the hottest and red not so hot, on a scale established many years ago, what we call the 'main sequence,' describing a sweet spot for star lifetimes. Anyway, the important thing is, every star tells a fascinating story, like the Judge said about your story."

She laughed and shoved him. "*We?*" she asked, pointedly.

"Oh, you know, the astrophysics community."

"Wendy says you're the smartest guy on her planet."

"Hardly. I'm more like your sad princess and would prefer the moon hanging in the branches of that tall white pine down the lake, where I could climb high and pluck it down whenever the spirit moved me."

"*She* wouldn't have gotten into Groton, either."

65
Children of Light

WHEN GEORGE RETURNED from the boathouse to Graham's Dock, he found Annie's French Pléiade edition of *Swann's Way* lying on the bed with two letters in their envelopes half-concealed within its pages. And a missive from Wendy on three Post-it notes was attached to the tan cover.

Dear George,
Well, Annie almost managed to outdo her husband in terms of concealing the critical evidence. I guess she figured he'd never go near her French editions of Proust, even though he must have plowed through her shelves to discover that hidden volume of Witness. I can't help wondering why she hid the letters in the first place—Priscilla's is written to both of them—instead of sharing them or destroying them, and just who she thought might someday discover them—if not the Judge, certainly no one likely to realize their import. Or perhaps she wasn't hiding them as much as simply keeping them safely hidden inside the book she most treasured in life—for her children—for you—until she figured out what to do, before life ran out on her. Or, dare I speculate, in a divorce proceeding the letters would have served as evidence of her husband's lying, even as Priscilla, by writing to both husband and wife, was clearly renouncing any lingering claim to Edward. But I don't think we need to go there. Notice that both letters were addressed to their apartment in New York, where Annie would first see the mail, unlike all the other letters Priscilla sent, which always went to the Judge's office. And neither Chambers nor Priscilla seems to have been trying to conceal anything from the Judge. I think we have to assume the Judge never saw these, since there is no

mention of them—how could there be?—in the memoir, much less to us about the lost day described. Maybe he suspected their existence, or something like them, since it had to have required a pretty systematic search to undercover Annie's hidden copy of Witness. As he wrote in the memoir, he and Annie uncannily mirrored each other's subterfuges. Note the date on Priscilla's letter, only a few weeks after Chambers and the Hisses made that crazy road trip to Harry Dexter White's home, Blueberry Hill, in Fitzwilliam, New Hampshire. Not that she mentions boo about Chambers! Nor Chambers about Alger and Priscilla Hiss, as if for both, the other(s) had disappeared from memory, as they have, so it seems, from the Judge's memory as well. But then Handytown is a pretty magical place, where our better selves seem to take up residence—and linger, or at least those parts we chose to hold close.

I just discovered the letters this evening. Suddenly Martha's and Alice's cryptic remarks about Teddy at lunch take on an ominous feeling—no? Yet, how could they know, unless they were old enough to remember something—Teddy, slightly older than both of them, might have—although I sense they aren't aware of knowing anything. Perhaps I jumped the gun today at lunch with the Altmann painting, cavalierly dismissing the sketches, absolving the Judge—is that what I did, do you think? For these letters change everything, certainly the credibility of the memoir. Begging the question: Why didn't Chambers speak up at the trial when the August 1937 road trip to New Hampshire was totally disparaged by the defense as yet another figment of Chambers's warped and deceitful imagination. A trip that included Hermitage and Handytown!

The Judge has known Hiss was guilty from the get-go.

And so there it is: Weinstein's missing day—and how. Won't he be pleased!

Are you pleased? Or more than a little perplexed, as I am? I'm hanging out with Cecily if you need me.

Love, Wendy

July 15, 1951

PIPE CREEK FARM
WESTMINSTER, MD

Dear Annie,

Thank you for your kind letter of a month ago. I have been pondering
for some weeks how to best answer you, whether a phone call or a letter
would be the more secure or safer communication. I have taken the
precaution of having my wife post this to you while doing an errand
in town, so as to avoid the possibility of its being intercepted from our
mailbox or hazarding the postman's being waylaid.

First, let me offer you my most heartfelt condolences on the loss
of your beloved Teddy. As the father of a son, I cannot even begin
to comprehend the agony of your loss, for which there is no rem-
edy in the human heart, except to know his soul rests in the kind
hands of his Maker, while his memory will forever burn as a luminous
presence in the hearts of all those who knew him and loved him. I
realize my thoughts are probably no consolation (even as your spiritual reflections along the lines of Bunyan's *Pilgrim's Progress* remain
a stirring memory), but I truly believe that he died for a righteous
cause, fighting against one of the greatest tyrannies ever conceived
in the seething brain of man. A boy, even in the short hours I knew
him, with such a free spirit, born of generations of freedom-loving
people, could not remain indifferent to the sin of communism. Of
this, I have no doubt. In my brief acquaintance with Teddy as a child,
I was immediately and indelibly struck by his curiosity and intrepid
love of the natural world, recalling to me the better instincts of my
own youth, when I, too, found myself entranced by the wonders of
the avian world.

Which, even now, I am reminded of by a family of bluebirds who
have taken up residence in a massive two-hundred-year-old elm
beyond my office window, a most pleasing distraction from the labors
of my memoir. What sweet consolations in those flashes of blue living
light, recalling as if yesterday, how Teddy—was he four or five?—
immediately took the lead of our party as we made our way to that
sylvan glade in your woods where we were serenaded by an angelic
host of wood thrush, only to have our eyes dazzled by a flock of scarlet tanagers, the likes of which—such a conclave of holy orders—I

have never witnessed before or since. I shall never forget young Teddy, the light shining in his golden locks, a bald eagle feather stuck in his Indian headband, as he rushed ahead, arms outstretched, as if to hurry our party forward to meet with some dazzling invisible destiny. As, indeed, it was for me, confirming my too-long-delayed plans to break with the Soviet underground and save what remained of my life. Emboldened, as well, by your inspiring thoughts on performing Mozart and delving into Proust—things of the heart and soul that make us most fully human. Freeing us, as I believe you put it, quoting Blake, from the tyranny of our "mind-forged manacles."

A liberty of soul forever emblazoned in my mind by a young intrepid Hawkeye, free and alive to his glorious youth.

But I must admit that I'm troubled and perplexed by the apologies I found in your letter, almost in a tone of agonized repentance for what you described as the sins of your husband. "Edward's sins against you—unforgivable on both a professional and human level. For which we have both now paid the full price." Is this your Puritan soul seeking out sin where there is no sin to be found? That you, of all people, should ask for my forgiveness. Forgiveness for what? I presume your letter was referring to Edward's defamation of my character in the Hiss trial. I will not attempt any explanation, at least not here, not in written form. But you can stand assured there is nothing that he or you need to be forgiven for. Nor should you perturb yourself about it. Edward was simply doing his job—a job that he may have had less choice in carrying out than any of us care to imagine. I hold no grudges or ill feeling on this score. Nor should you. And I will tell you that I have been exploring the circumstances of my life and times leading up the Hiss trial in excruciating—sometimes harrowing—detail for my memoir, which is close to being done, and should be published next year. Nowhere in its pages will your name or your husband's be found. I hope that will tell you all you need to know. Because I have borne witness to the horror and evil that metastasized in our midst over the last decades, I have spared no one, including myself, when the truth needed telling.

It is unlikely for various reasons that we shall ever meet again, for the dangers are hardly passed. But you should know that I will never forget your kind, engaging spirit and warm hospitality to an utter stranger arriving out of the blue in your sanctuary—a sanctuary I have tried to re-create on my farm, and a blessing of God's infinite mercy. Besides, I feel that some part of you will always remain with me: I find great solace in one of your early recordings of the Chopin Etudes. Perhaps if you return to the New York concert stage—or perhaps appear in Baltimore—you may find me in your audience. I have even begun to delve deeply, in my limited reading time these days, into your beloved Proust, which never caught my fancy in terms of his social commentary and exploration of Gallic snobbism. Though, in his descriptions of the natural world, as you once suggested on our walk, I do find a strange affinity, almost an Emersonian translucency in the way he embodies the human spirit in certain places, where time and fond memory have merged into the rarest glories of sight and sound, and so affirming the undying affections of the human heart. As you and your darling Teddy have in mine.

Yours sincerely,
Whittaker Chambers

September 27, 1937

Dear Annie and Edward,

I feel remiss in having delayed so long in getting off a thank-you note for our sudden and uninvited descent upon you a few weeks back. Your Catskill retreat, your Hermitage, especially Handytown, is divine beyond words. Hopefully, Alger and I will have the chance one day to visit the Saint Petersburg version, although your ship's keel ceiling surely is an irreplaceable wonder unto itself. I remember as a college girl falling completely under its spell—a fierce Diana with bow drawn something of an inspiration, I fear! In truth, as you must have suspected, I was being rather reckless that day, for there was a lot of tension in our marriage right about then having to do with the prospects of having a child of our own, and various other anxieties. Given Alger's busy career and the looming disquietude of the world these days, the thought of another child, our own child, to go along with Alger's stepson, was bewildering. And yet that flying—rash!—visit, seeing the two of you in your beautiful home—such a lovely and loving couple, surrounded by your three children—confirmed for me—a leap of faith perhaps—and for Alger later, that there was a place and time for that child in our life, our own flesh and blood to bond our marriage. A miracle of faith that followed in the wake of our hike to Handytown: that we—that Alger and I—that the four of us—had all made the right choices in our lives.

That realization unfolded for me like snatches of memory from a dream as we walked to Handytown with you both and your son—your handsome little Teddy, your wild Indian. And crystalized for me the moment we entered that marvelous glade beneath the pine and oaks boughs—Handytown. I forget the story you told us about those first settlers except for their grit and determination to build a life in the wilderness. But the image of Teddy raising his arms to hush our steps remains indelible in my mind, how suddenly a pair or three or even four hermit thrush began an antiphonal response, only to usher in a choir of scarlet tanagers to regale our spirits! And then there was that ancient spring in the midst of the woods from which we all drank—a blue antique ironware cup that Teddy filled for each of us—as if from some fountain of youth. A Communion cup to celebrate our queer little band of seekers. I felt as if I had drifted outside of myself and inhabited some other realm, a better place and better time, intimation of that better—timeless—world we all aspire to. A crazy thing for sure. But you see, I found my love for Alger there, or, more to the point, found confirmation in what we were, and felt proud to be a part of his life—as I am sure both of you feel about each other. And it endowed me with the strength and inspiration to have our own child.

Isn't that what you always accused me of in our early days at Yale, Edward, and later walking the promenade in Riverside Park, that I was always too status-conscious? That I turned up my nose at dowdy Baltimore? Wasn't it you who always insisted that we must be proud, not of who we are and where we come from, but in what we do? And I was happy for you both, as well, that, even if we had taken different paths, we all managed to end up at Handytown together.

And a special note of thanks to you Annie, for accepting our abrupt rude incursion on your privacy with such grace and charm. And most especially for the impromptu concert you regaled us with that evening in such a breathtaking star crowned setting. We were utterly spellbound and the following week I went right out and bought all your recordings as a special present for Alger.

So I have you both to thank for being who you are, and so allowing Alger and me to be all of what we are: all of us children of light.

I still dream of Handytown—filled with that inner light, where I was happy and freed from doubt. Thank you both for indulging us and allowing us that wild moment of freedom from a harried life. And you, Edward, for all your always gracious concerns for my welfare.

I will always think of you both at Hermitage, at Handytown, but more especially try to keep the memory and spirit of Handytown alive wherever I go.

Love to you both,
Pross

—

George read the letters over twice, then a third time, his hands trembling at the very feel of the decades-old stationery and faded ink that seemed to resonate in every nerve ending in his body, only to set his brain afire. He carefully replaced the letters in their envelopes, and the envelopes in the volume of Proust—glancing at Annie's extensive underlining and commentaries in French—and then replaced the book in its approximate place on the shelf where it had harmlessly lived for so many years. Genie back in the bottle, he half hoped. But moments later, the familiar data feedback loop began cranking at full tilt in his mind as the new facts further added to the disequilibrium caused by the appearance of Ben Wright at the boathouse.

Oddly enough, this panicked recalibration passed almost as quickly as it had arrived, replaced by a feeling of unaccustomed serenity (lingering, perhaps, from Nancy's youthful joy and wonder), as if out of the maelstrom of the moment something of his own youth had been returned to him, even as scene after reedited scene began playing before his eyes, drawing him to the window—there to get a lay of the land—or rather the teasing bewitchment of the lunar-white lake, the familiar moon now resting in the steepled boughs of a distant pine, a cosmos more than ever reflecting the mythic intimacies of the ship's keel ceiling, peopled with the fateful wanderings of the planets and stars, where the mischief-making gods could only do their worst, perhaps daring him to add yet another cruel tale to theirs, that ineffable continuum of tales in which he, thankfully, was only an minor actor. Stories not so much lost as rediscovered generation after generation, seeding memory before it was memory, as starlight from before he was born—vivid as heat lightening, in the soul all compact. Other lives, previous lives merging with his and so buoying all on eternity. Freeing him at the last to feel again with a child's curiosity.

To reach out hands across time, as Ben Wright had reached with his dripping oar.

Defeated yet born to victory.

He placed a palm against the glass, as if in solidarity, seeing his boyish face against that woodland dream, familiar, comforting—and Handytown, that sanctum sanctorum glimpsed in the guise of a four-year-old wild Indian with a bald eagle–feather headdress, a hand held up for silence . . . a silence enveloping the five adults, prelude to the sweet sad song of the hermit thrush, that pregnant moment outside of time, transforming their lives as it now transformed his.

Finally, safely cloaked in night's felicities, he turned from his secret sharer and moved to the Bunce painting and the luminous lagoon, where his grandparents still walked in the Giardini as they contemplated names and places to come, and so the world as he'd found it.

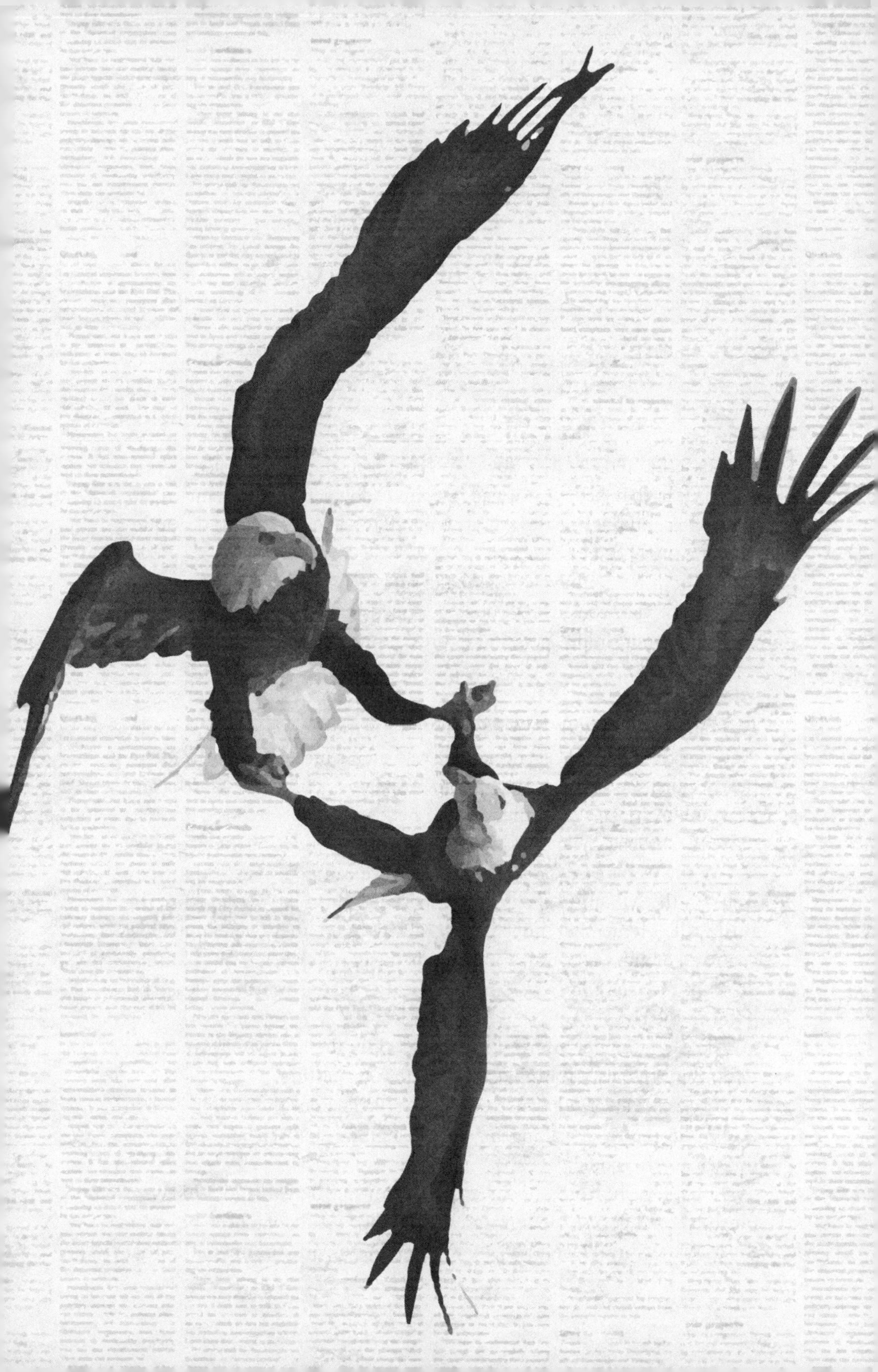

66

Tumbling from Heaven's Gate

WHEN GEORGE CAME down to breakfast, the Judge made it perfectly clear that he was to lead the hike down the mountain to the Neversink and the Roebling abutments that had once carried the aqueduct for the D & H Canal.

"Most importantly, you must make sure Nancy hears the stories from your lips or your cousins'. A youngster needs to have these things made alive to her, not simply facts and figures in one ear and out the other."

—

At first, the sisters weren't going to attempt the arduous descent to the Neversink, but then Alice, because it was such a nice day in the mid-fifties, decided she and Stan could do it, or part of it. That got Martha and Theo on board, and even Jim, despite his bad leg, decided he'd give it a try with Cordelia's help (so as not be left with the Judge by the fireplace).

"In the worst case," assured Martha, "we can go as far as the stone walls on the Mount Hope and Lumberland Turnpike overlooking the Bush Kill—remember how Daddy always said they were the most beautiful of all?—and wait for the kids to return or just go back. But I do want to reach the Neversink for Teddy's sake; I want to release his letter to the river."

Alice, choosing a hiking stick, said, "Why the hell would you want to do that? Such a—so unlike you—romantic gesture."

"It was his favorite place. He always talked about the feeling he had wading in the river, casting his line, imagining himself journeying to the sea and beyond."

"Each—yeah, Korea—to their own, but maybe you should keep it for the record, in case George and his shadow—still not a peep between those two at breakfast—try something funny with the memoir. That

part about criticizing Daddy and the trial is a pretty powerful indictment, although nothing new—certainly intriguing. What people
arriving at Hermitage did he mean? Could Teddy have known something we didn't—when we were kids?"

"I suppose we could press the Judge on the matter, but I don't have
the heart for it anymore, digging up ancient history—the day's just
too beautiful."

"You've got to at least call Daisy Wright and let her know about
the letter."

—

George, too, found the warm pine-scented late-autumn day too beautiful to be fretting about anything. He no longer cared about what
people thought—of him or anything else, or stepping on toes, only
that Nancy would have a good time, that she'd get caught up on the
lore of Hermitage—and find at least one rusted spike (a family tradition) in the rotted railway ties that littered the embankment of what
had once been the roadbed of the Port Jervis & Monticello Railroad.
They drove two cars to the head of the trail for the older folks, and
then, with George, Erich, and Nancy in the vanguard, bushwhacked
into the overgrown remnant of the Mount Hope and Lumberland
Turnpike, frothy with timothy and meadow fescue and barberry
bushes, until they gained the ghostly nave of the defunct railroad
bed, overhung with hemlock, black birch, and bedraggled maple and
looming oaks, which led down the mountain along the Bush Kill
until it merged with the Neversink two miles below. Wendy, Karen,
and Cecily—an all-girls contingent, laughing and cutting up—followed a hundred yards back, Karen and Cecily competing to tell
stories of their own misspent youth in the woods. The six older adults
happily made up the baggage train, dressed in scavenged fleeces and
wool coats of uncertain vintage and mysterious ownership. All were
equipped with knobby hickory and walnut hiking poles from a large
collection by the door of the mudroom.

George pointed out the carved D in Nancy's hiking staff and recited
almost verbatim, "The miracle of his trade, so he always said, was chlo-
roform; the curse, inoperable cancer. He honed his skills in the abattoirs
of the Civil War surgical stations. And made his trade treating the wives
of New York's wealthy, delivering their million-dollar babies and tending
their female complaints. He didn't suffer fools gladly, and charlatans not

at all. He refused to have grace recited at his dinner table—saying to one perturbed guest, 'Where was grace during the Wilderness?' He invariably ordered his guests to eat when served, before their food got cold. He loved to hike and bird-watch and fish—hunting he'd lost all taste for after the war. He never turned down a charity case. He treated gratis the denizens of these woods—the few left—and canal men when medical emergencies arrived at his doorstep."

As he spoke, he often gazed down the steep hillside at the Bush Kill rushing pell-mell in its boulder-strewn course, its rising tones seeming to offer a comforting counterpoint to the old stories, yet another voice in his, translating the oft-told tales into memories that seemed more and more his own, a siren call ceaselessly spiriting him back whence he'd come.

Nancy, decked out in all her brand-new hiking regalia—Filson mossy oak camo pants, leather bomber jacket, and orange baseball cap—wielded an old hatchet-claw hammer with DIMOCK burned into the ash handle, hungrily eyeing the gullies on either side of the gravel and cinder roadbed, where rotted ties were tumbled like green felt pick-up sticks.

—

"You seem happy," said Jim, limping along beside Cordelia as well as he could, now lagging behind Alice and Stan, Martha and Theo. "Must be that ravishing little ditty your big sis was playing this morning—catchy as hell."

"Strange—hypnotic, how that tune, whatever it is, keeps running through my mind, like maybe I just dreamed it up. You see, I was dreaming last night about my ballet days, for the first time in a long time. Funny, I keep seeing the faces of a couple of ballet masters who always took such interest in me, a kindness they rarely showed to the others. One even kept writing long after my injury, after Annie died, asking how I was doing and saying how much he missed my mother. I don't even know—how sad is that—if he's still alive."

"You always had men at your beck and call."

"Remember how the Judge—you're first time up to Hermitage—made you put on someone's old boots and hiked you down here for three hours? I was nervous as hell waiting back at the house, worried that he might do you in and hide the body."

"Fifth degree. He offered me a bribe not to marry you. And I don't think my feet ever recovered from the blisters."

"You should've taken the money and run. He said you were a dreamer and a ladies' man, and he was right."

"Yeah, but you can't argue with the good sex."

"Jesus, I hope you never told him *that*?"

"Oh, he knew . . . he knew." His mustache bristling, he grinned wickedly as he took her hand. "Your sex drive can't have come only from your mother."

At this, she smiled serenely, a spotlit stage, thrilling to contemplate, a new spring in her step sparking a girlish scintillation in her blue eyes as she turned to gaze upon the foaming telltale waters of the Bush Kill in the valley below.

—

Martha, walking with Alice, paused, as if to get a reaction out of her husband, who was too far behind to hear. She waited, winded, leaning on her walking stick. The murmur of the Bush Kill rose to them from its crooked banks, now clearly visible through the leafless trees.

Theo raised an eyebrow at the sound of his wife's voice and then returned his pensive gaze to the doglegs of the Bush Kill below, his baggy gray eyes taking on a bleary sheen.

"I had a father and a brother back in Poland," he said to Stan, ignoring the waiting sisters farther down the line. "In the summers before the Soviets and Nazis invaded, we had our vacations in Szklarska Poreba, a hilly pine country west of Warsaw with beautiful wandering streams, each with a distinctive sound. How much the sound of the water was like this place. Funny, it had never quite occurred to me before this moment. Why is that, do you suppose? Perhaps because in summer the leaves obscure the view and muffle the sound."

Stan, too, looked perplexed. "Yeah, there's something about the view I can't quite put my finger on."

"Maybe it's that piece your wife was playing this morning—a thing of rare beauty, quite entrancing. Not unlike the *Trout Quintet*, the andante."

"Me, I wouldn't know. But lovely, something her mother wrote. Unearthed it just yesterday. It's nice to have her playing again."

—

"What was that you were playing this morning?" asked Martha. "It was quite fetching, quite mesmerizing."

"Oh, that," said Alice. "Something Mom was struggling with. Just fragments really, which I kind of wove together, riffing here and there—you might say: improvisations on a theme."

"Sounded a little like Satie."

"Yes, I suppose, something like the *Trois Gymnopédies*. Haunting, sad really, it's kind of taken me over."

Martha looked impatiently up the hill at Theodore with a dismissive toss of her brown curls. "Did you know that Theo used to shave twice a day like Humbert Humbert in *Lolita*?" She pulled Teddy's letter out of her pocket with a lost expression and shook her head. "The years . . . the years. When you spend your life dealing with other people's disasters every day, you begin to stop recognizing your own. I look in the mirror and I hardly recognize the old woman there. You think because people consider you so omnipotent, so normal, so competent, life will never happen to you, that you have some special dispensation to master human nature."

Alice, exasperated, raised her woolen jacket sleeve to her nose, noting the distinct smell of mothballs. "Oh, Martha, human nature is such a crock of shit. People believe the last thing told them in a convincing and authoritative way." She held out her hand. "Here, let me see that letter again before you deep-six it."

"Alice, I can't tell you how much I miss Teddy. I can almost see him scampering down the embankment and manhandling a tie out of the dirt to see if there was still a spike embedded."

Alice smiled. "He'd put them in the pockets of his fishing jacket until he rattled like the Tin Woodsman . . . Not to mention the garter snakes and toads."

"Hermitage lost something for me when he didn't return from Korea. His shining spirit—the magic gone. Like a part of me, something . . . somehow, I've never managed to get back."

Alice sighed in sympathy and closed her eyes, staring blindly at the Bush Kill where it glittered so familiarly below. "Oh, Martha . . . try losing your son."

Martha laid a hand on her sister's shoulder and adjusted the collar of her moth-eaten coat.

"Forgive me, dear, of course . . . you and Daddy. How selfish of me. I know I should count myself lucky with Erich and Karen. And *now* you have Cecily back home."

"Let's take a look at that letter one last time."

Alice opened the two pages of crumpled yellowed paper scrawled in pencil, and the sisters sat together on a bluestone wall, a mosaic interlaced with mustard and olive lichen, while the Bush Kill's incantation played in their ears.

"You read it to me, Alice."

Alice, not a little spellbound, dug out her reading glasses.

November 28, 1950

Dear Martha:

Pardon my handwriting, I'm writing to you lying up against a rock on my back in the snow with my gloves on, not that my handwriting was ever as fine as yours, as you always let me know. Our squad has formed a skirmish line behind a ridge, mostly stumps and boulders, facing the distant snow-clad hills, which are exceptionally beautiful, with hazy tree lines running up and down in the most delicate patterns, except those hills are crawling with Chinese, who now seem to have us in artillery range.

Well, we thought we had this thing won; we pushed the Commies back to the Yalu, but nobody thought the Chinese were going to come in. They did, though, and now we're in a fix. Up until that moment, MacArthur seemed a tactical genius, now we're in full retreat and, to be frank, things aren't looking so good. The men are freezing to death and can't understand why we don't just drop a few atom bombs on the bastards and get them off our backs.

So I figured this might be as good a time as any to get a few things off my chest, just in case. If anybody in our family can understand why I enlisted it's probably you, although Dad and Mom know perfectly well, even if they can't, or won't, admit it. The Hiss trial was a sham from start to finish, among other things, because Dad always knew the truth, that at least on one count of perjury, Hiss was guilty as hell. My God, those people visited Hermitage. I remember when they arrived, although you wouldn't, as you were too young at the time.

(Two hours later) We've just been in a firefight; we lost one fellow, another wounded. Frostbite is endemic, and it's only getting colder. Batteries run down in the jeeps; even the firing pins of our weapons sometimes don't function. I'm peering at my scrawls through my frozen breath. And I seem to have lost my train of thought as well. Jesus, it's cold, and I thought I knew cold in the Catskills, but this is biting and relentless—and no cozy fire in the great room to retreat to. Where was I? So, it's not that I don't perfectly understand the role of a defense lawyer. How many times did Dad knock it into my head about our adversarial system of justice—the glories of the common law, that a man is innocent until proven guilty by a jury of his peers. How every man has a right to the best defense possible. That's why I still plan on going to Harvard Law if I get out of this mess and finish at Yale. But, to be frank—and please don't mention it to him—Dad's work on the defense team sent shivers of horror down my spine. It was bad enough that a man like Hiss, and all his Commie pals, could have so completely infiltrated our government and wreaked God knows how much damage on the country. But I just couldn't shake the feeling that somewhere along the line Hiss had hoodwinked Dad, or had some kind of hold—a spell—over him, to so drag him down into that mire of deception—not to mention the perverse tactics the defense used.

It was clear that the only realistic hope to get Hiss off was to destroy Chambers—the one witness in all this who Dad, of all people, had to have known was telling the truth! Worse, using voodoo Freudian theories to try to discredit him in front of a gullible jury—thank God they didn't fall for it. And Dad was made a laughingstock in the press and the profession. How could he have called those two charlatans, Binger and Murray, as expert witnesses? Imagine any well-run court allowing the introduction of such mumbo jumbo, hearsay, and thirdhand speculations about that poor man's character. Any first-year law student with half a brain would have known better, and the prosecution's cross-examination made mincemeat of Binger and Murray as expert witnesses. Even the pro-Hiss press was embarrassed. Judge Goddard, an experienced man, should have ruled against the introduction of such tainted rantings about Chambers's private life, much less the employment of such oblique character assassination based on the witness's writings and so-called unconscious motivation. (Surely, you don't believe in such nonsense!) Why did Dad let it happen? Allow the defense to pillory Chambers in such an unprofessional and uncouth manner? Against everything he ever taught us? It's the very same torturous technique of twisted half-truths, lies, character assassination, and fallacious propaganda the Communists use here and everywhere to their odious ends. It just turned my stomach. Many of my closest friends at Yale disowned me.

Frankly, I don't understand how Dad's judgment and sense of fair play, much less professional integrity, could have so let him down. And

I don't see his reputation recovering anytime soon. How can any self-respecting lawyer defend a man on a count of perjury when he personally has firsthand knowledge that the indictment is true?

If I were Dad, I couldn't live with myself.

Well, that's about it. The light is going, my fingers are stiff, and I long to be back with you at Hermitage—I missed being there for Thanksgiving. A nice big hunk of warm turkey would suit me just fine right now. When I turn my head to the wintery hills, fading behind mist, I think of late-autumn days at Hermitage. How I ache for the smell of wood smoke and pine and the clean fresh smell of the Neversink rushing past my waders. I yearn, too, for you to be my little coxie once again, so you can guide me out on the lake like you used to when we were kids, and we can make up silly songs that echo endlessly from shore to shore. Did I ever tell you what a lovely smile you have? That secret smile when you forget for a moment about being so serious, when you leave your teeming brain ashore and begin to laugh at this crazy, beautiful world. When you are truly yourself. At Handytown, too, of course.

So keep me in your thoughts, and keep that smile going. You can even try a prayer or two, or at least touch wood for luck—the wooden head of our skyward-gazing angel by the fireplace would do. Write to me about Thanksgiving at Hermitage. And yes, wish Mom and Dad and Alice a Merry Christmas from me.

Signing off, your loving brother,
Teddy

P.S. I've been thinking a lot recently of those mating bald eagles over the lake, talons locked, white wheeling flames through space, like sunlit angels tumbling from heaven's gate. Oh the magic of it, the beauty, that God created such a thing.

And by the way, do one very important favor for me: Ask Daisy to forgive me. Tell her I love her. That I miss her. That I'll be back. Just mention: "The Dalliance of the Eagles," by Whitman. She'll understand.

———

Alice put her protective arms around her sister and hugged her as Martha wiped tears on her coat sleeve.

"Can you believe he was killed two days later?"

"What," Alice asked, "do you suppose he meant . . . 'Dad always knew the truth'?"

"You're the defense lawyer—don't you always know the truth about your client? Whatever the case."

"And who were 'those people'?"

"Your guess is as good as mine."

"Why didn't you ever share it with Daddy?"

"How could I—the last letter from his son? He'd have been devastated—at least right away. I was going to show it to him someday, so I stuck it in my organic chemistry text, but then I forgot where I'd put it."

"Come on, Martha, you were thrilled at sixteen and seventeen with Freud, with Dad's expert witnesses. Didn't you take Binger's course at Harvard? You hid that letter because it embarrassed you."

To this, Martha remained silent.

"You've got to show this to Daisy Wright." Alice looked at Martha directly in the eye. "That's really why he wrote the letter. I know how Teddy's mind worked. The last line was the thing that really mattered, the excuse for everything else."

"I'm sure she seduced him."

"Oh come now, Martha, you, of all people, know better than that."

Alice put her arm through her sister's and led her out onto the gravel roadbed to resume their hike. Suddenly, she paused, her eyes widening with wonder.

"Oh my God, do you remember when Teddy picked up that timber rattler!"

———

Theodore pointed once again to the Bush Kill with the stem of his meerschaum pipe. "Beautiful, isn't it? The feel of flowing water, the lullaby of sound. You see, it got me thinking about my older brother, Stanislaw, how much he loved fishing in the river in Szklarska Poreba before the war. Summers with my father. Just the boys. My mother didn't care for the woods. The quiet frightened her. Spiders, too. She was a city girl." He knocked his pipe against the bluestone wall and began to refill it. "You see, Stanislaw was murdered, along with over twenty thousand of his fellow officers, by the KGB in a beautiful place called the Katyn Forest. They have a memorial there now for Stalin's victims. Black marble, with a huge granite boulder at the center on which there is a memorial plaque to the murdered. At the top of the boulder, affixed there, is a bronze bird—a dove, I suppose—with outstretched wings, as if about to lift off and fly away. A symbol of the soul perhaps, or peace . . . who knows. In 1990, after the fall of the Berlin Wall, I returned to Poland for the first time to pay my respects. The memorial is in a shaded grove, a place of much serenity, where slender young pines reach to the sky. Very much like it is here. You see, I think it's been at least twenty years since I've been back here, since our wives accused their old man." He lit his pipe and closed his eyes for a moment, then again stood gazing at the meandering Bush Kill through the lazy gray-blue pipe smoke. "Well, now, you see, I find myself returned to the Szklarska Poreba of my boyhood. And you understand, when I returned to Poland after all my years of, well . . . exile, I suppose, I was moved to tears. I realized how completely I'd dispensed with memories of my family by becoming a hotshot academic in New York—so much admired, especially by all the young women. Surely you know how it is—those kids, reminding you of the happy youth you never had. And yet, strange to say, that day, standing by the Katyn memorial, the old prayers came back to me, things I barely remembered from childhood. As you know, I'm not a religious man. But I prayed to God that the last thing Stanislaw saw, his last glimpse of life, so to speak, was of those tall pine trees, his last memory of our childhood joys before the executioner fired. Dumped into that pit with thousands of Poland's finest."

"Jesus, Theo, that's just awful. You never said boo to me before."

Theo reached out and touched Stan's arm in a tender gesture of brotherhood.

"How come you never told me much about your family, Stan, or where your Jews came from?"

"Oh, they got out before the First World War, Czarist pogroms, while the going was still good, I guess. They made money like it was nothing."

"Land of milk and honey, eh."

"I was just thinking how the Judge dragged me down here when he got wind of the fact that Alice and I were going to get hitched. Not pleased she planned to marry a Communist, or at least someone who had pleaded the Fifth in a congressional hearing and served time, and so might as well be a Communist. Not someone he wished for his daughter, especially after all the shit he took for defending Alger Hiss. He took my arm—probably someplace right around here—and looked me straight in the eye. 'So, I've had quite enough Communists for one lifetime, professionally and otherwise.'" Stan smiled at the memory and his reply. "And

I told him, 'Sir, so have I . . . so have I. You have my assurance that I will not try to subvert, much less convert, your daughter.'"

Theo smiled in recognition of a shared experience.

"Ah, yes . . . the talk. I was already a big shot at Columbia—professor, you know—so he went easy on me."

"But here's the thing, Theo." Stan took his brother-in-law by the arm and they continued to walk, slowly ambling behind the women, who were now continuing on their descent of the Bush Kill.

"It's been bugging me for the last hour, the view—like you say—a childhood memory. I couldn't have been more than five—the late twenties, it must have been. Every summer we took the train to the mountains, a fancy hotel in Monticello. And, well, I just suddenly realized it had to have been this railroad, the Port Jervis & Monticello, that we rode when I was a little kid. Imagine that! All these years and I didn't put it together. And get this, what I really remember like yesterday was when the train slowed and ascended Rose's Point—so it was called—from the valley of the Neversink . . . Oh, the old engine would shudder and the cars bang in their couplings, and out the window, as far as the eye could see, white and pink, pink and white—everywhere, like it had snowed strawberry shortcake. You see, it must have been the chestnut trees in bloom—like out of a dream. Imagine that, seeing the valley full of the last of those magnificent trees, before the blight took every last one."

Stan squeezed Theo's arm, excited at the memory.

"Sad, how they're all gone, like all the great hotels in the mountains—the Concord and Grossinger's—the Borscht Belt—all gone, back when we Jews hung out together and laughed at ourselves, made fun of ourselves, so glad we'd gotten away from Europe, that some of our families had survived. And now we're top dogs—big shots. We own it all, and nobody cares anymore where you came from; nobody laughs the way we did when we were kids."

"You're a lucky man, Stan. When I returned to Poland, our Jews were all gone, not a member of my family survived, except for a few distant cousins in Israel. No Communists, either, of course; they had all disappeared, as well."

"Welcome—mazel tov, Theo—to America, where we wipe the slate clean generation after generation."

———

George, while relating the Judge's tales to Nancy, found the cascading voice of the Bush Kill soothing as the slope steepened, greeting the travelers with an eager refrain as they closed in on the point where the meandering stream merged with the Neversink. Oddly, the melody of the rushing water reminded him of the piece that Alice had been playing on the piano before breakfast. Just a little phrase or two—spry but haunting, evocative of memories beyond recall. He stopped to listen, all his senses attuned to the stream below, the voice, the Bush Kill fed by the same springs that fed their lake at Hermitage—the flow, gravity's free energy, as he now imagined it, moving the little band from a world of low entropy to high, from a tranquil, ordered present into the messy disorder of the coming unknown.

The hikers were spreading out along the roadbed, drifting farther and farther apart, their ranks thinning, as if indeed prey to the second law of thermodynamics, especially for the elder group, whose pace was slowing as they took breaks to linger and rest. Entropy, thought George, sighing: the archenemy of structure and coherence, much less the generation of new information. This realization saddened him as he witnessed time's dissolution in his aunts and uncles, even his once sprightly mother, all content to harbor their energy, to share their stories out of their comingled past and so sustain a fleeting happiness as the moments rushed them on. He recognized, too, the Neversink hike (the Judge's Way, so he now thought of it) for what it was: his family's lifeline, a way replete with storied memories conjured from the past. As Annie had always intimated, quoting Proust—if the Judge's memoir was to be believed—"The only truth of life is in art."

Prompted by such musings, George pointed to a clearing where an old cellar hole and the tumbled remnants of a bluestone wall now called out to him.

"When your great-great-grandfather arrived in the 1880s, the nearest neighbors were the Davises, although the Dimocks seldom saw them." George had to smile at the echo of the Judge's voice in his, the rhythm and cadence with its uncanny likeness to the hurrying Bush Kill in its eagerness to join the chorus of the Neversink. "They lived on what had once been the Mount Hope and Lumberland Turnpike, pretty much defunct even in their day, which then became the roadbed for the Port Jervis & Monticello. The Davises were dirt-poor. The old man's name was Prosper, and his wife's name was Iantha. Theirs was a large family of boys and at least one girl. The names of all the boys except one began with an *E*. There was Elijah and Elisha and Enoch and Ezekiel. The laborers building the railroad saw human tracks in the snow and found a barefoot child looking at them from behind a tree.

They asked him where his boots were, and he said that Prosper had gotten up first and taken the boots."

"That's so sad," said Nancy, "how there's nothing left of those people, Elijah and Elisha and . . ."

"Enoch and Ezckiel," added Erich, laughing, as if about to launch into a rap lyric.

George could now hear the distinct roar of the Neversink ahead.

"I feel sorry, Dad, for the Judge just sitting there by the fire all alone."

"He's cool," said Erich. "He's glad that we're taking his favorite hike."

"You see, it's the stories that keep them alive," George explained. "Whenever you say those names now, whenever you pass this way again, they will come alive, bare feet and all in the snow."

"Can we get to Handytown from here?"

George let her Dad answer.

"No. Look at that fancy compass of yours. Handytown's in the opposite direction; it's a very different kind of walk, remember, a very different kind of place."

"Tell me that story again."

Erich bowed out to George, who closed his eyes for a moment to the locomotive roar of the Neversink, now just in view ahead of them as a broad expanse of white water surging around a bend from the high Catskills in a cacophony of eager voices.

"Once a year, David Handy would load up his oxcart with the cedar shingles he'd cut, then make the slow, ponderous eighty-mile journey by cart track down the mountain to Newark, where he'd sell his shingles and get all the goods that he needed, the things he couldn't produce on his farm. Then he made the long journey home up those endless hills. The Handy graves are still there. David Handy erected huge tombstones for himself and his family selected from the flagstone quarries of the neighborhood. Or, as the Judge used to recite from Quinlan's *History of Sullivan Country*: 'They are exactly as nature formed them; but their neatness will strike the eye of even a person who is weary of monumental magnificence.'"

Cecily came running up, breathless. "Look—you missed it!" She pointed down the embankment, where, in the gloom of a stand of mountain laurel, the outline of a railroad tie was barely visible in the earth. "A virgin tie—what think you, Jedi?"

"Go for it," said George, "I'll wait here with Erich."

"Let's give it a try," said Cecily. "You game, girl?"

"I'm in," said Nancy.

Quickly joined by Wendy and Karen, the girls scrambled down the embankment to the tumbled tie lying upside down in the loamy leaf-strewn earth. Grabbing one end, they strained to lift the moss green tie and flip it over, which took the strength of all four, until they toppled it over with a dull thump.

"Wow," said Nancy, spying a rusted bit of iron still embedded in the rotted wood.

"Eureka," said Wendy. "Grab it before somebody else does."

Nancy began to bang away at the side of the spike with her hatchet-claw hammer.

"Amazing," said Karen. "I think I only found two or three in my whole life."

The three sisters, now drawing closer, spotted the activity and hurried forward. First Alice yelled, then Martha.

"Use the hatchet," shouted Alice, making a chopping motion.

"You've got to chop on either side of the spike to loosen it," shouted Martha. "That's how Teddy always managed it."

Nancy swiveled the tool and began to chop with both hands at the rotted tie. A minute later, she grabbed the rusty iron spike and pulled it free.

"Yippee," she shouted, and held her prize high in the air, displaying her find to Erich and walking it up the embankment to show the older folk.

Wendy and George, Erich and Cecily and Karen exchanged high fives and waved everyone on. Martha and Alice crowded around to congratulate Nancy.

"Oh, dear," said Martha, kissing Nancy, "Teddy would be so proud."

"The hell," said Alice. "He'd be pissed that Nancy beat him to it."

———

By the time they reached Rose's Point, the turn up the Neversink valley into the mountains, where the abandoned roadbed of the Port Jervis & Monticello and the overgrown ditch that had once been the Delaware and Hudson Canal intersected, the party was down to the younger generation: George, Wendy, Cecily, Nancy, Karen, and Erich. The three sisters, along with Stan, Theo, and Jim, had turned back for Hermitage.

Karen now carried Teddy's letter for her mother, with instructions that upon reaching the banks of the Neversink, she was to kiss the pages, say a prayer—"any kind of prayer will do, sweetie"—and release the two pages to float downstream.

"That's crazy," said Wendy, eyeing the two creased pages in Karen's hand. "It's a historical document, a family heirloom, a part of Teddy."

"I know, but she has this idea in her head that Teddy would want her to do it, that he would have preferred to have his ashes scattered on the Neversink instead of having a headstone in Arlington National Cemetery. I don't think they even recovered his body. So this is as close as she can manage it." Karen surveyed the shoreline for a good spot from atop the steep bank. Wendy took her hand to steady her footing as they picked their way down through the brambles to the shoreline. "No way she was going to make it down this embankment and back," said Karen, giggling nervously once they gained the river.

"Well, you could just tell her you did it and keep the letter for yourself, for Max."

"I get the sense she doesn't want what's in the letter to be known, probably because it would hurt the Judge's feelings or something."

"Have you read it?"

"Yes, I was there when she found it in an old science textbook the other day."

"And?"

"He's kind of hard on the Judge about the Hiss trial—but then everybody seems hard on him about that trial. Goes with the territory in this family."

"Tell you what: Why don't I photograph it on my cell and then I can send you the jpegs."

"Good idea."

Karen found an inlet with good, if uneven, footing and knelt on a flat rock above the surging current of the Neversink. She hesitated, unnerved at the roar in this narrow bottleneck, as Wendy knelt beside her and placed a comforting hand on her shoulder. Then she shrugged, spoke some words to herself, brought the letter to her lips, and gently let one page and then the other float down to the tea-stained glitter and her pebbly reflection. Instantly, the pages were snatched away and carried off, riding a frothy roller coaster, sucked into a series of low rapids, spinning and jittering, only to wink out of sight, out of mind in a torrent of white water about ten yards out.

Karen suddenly turned on Wendy, as she'd been an unwanted accomplice. "You know, you're so damned secretive about your own mother, while you watch us all like a hawk."

"What do you want to know?"

"What any woman wonders about: how much you're like her."

"That depends on whom you talk to. In her world of alpine climbing, and this was years ago, a woman paid a price for being stronger or smarter—better at things—than the men. Meaning, she always carried more than her share, going faster, taking risks that even the hotshot guys weren't willing to take. At high altitudes, she had more stamina and strength. She'd insist on taking the lead on the hardest, most dangerous ice shelves. And when they didn't let her . . . on Everest, she slept with a Sherpa just to fuck with the all-male members of the expedition, including my father. But she made the summit team. The men hated her and desired her for everything they admired in themselves: independence, ambition, assertiveness, *and* competitiveness—something I think women are worse about than men, especially among themselves . . . know what I mean? Competitiveness is a cancer that I try to cut out of my soul every day." She smiled weakly and squeezed Karen's shoulder. "A work of delicate surgery still in progress."

———

The moment George reached the Roebling abutment on the west shore of the Neversink, he felt suddenly drained, worn out, less from the hike than from the weight of expectations that had been laid on him by the Judge. Perhaps a delayed reaction to the mind-scrambling implications of the two letters from the night before. All of which found him overcome by sadness at the ruins of a once-monumental grandeur, that archaic feat of engineering that was no more, especially absent the Judge at his elbow to infuse his gaze with the wonder passed down four generations. He felt a fraud, a fumbling ineptitude at the pretense of imparting an enthusiasm to Nancy now languishing in himself. He pointed out to her the six massive iron loops still anchored in the concrete and stone of the abutment, which had once carried the nine-inch cables supporting the 170-foot span of Roebling's aqueduct. But he sensed her attention waning, as indeed it might for a young woman used to skyscrapers and mile-long bridges spanning huge rivers. So he let Karen, Cecily, and Wendy take over.

He sat and stared down at the river, his mind wandering. Some instinct in him recognized that the old abutments marked the vague transition point from the intimacies and timeless certainties of Hermitage to the wider world beyond. On the swirling surface of the river below he detected the monstrous powers that ruled the earth, fields of gravitational energy set free in earnest, as time was set free, in the flow of a river inexorably yearning for the release of the sea, and so rudely elbowing the landscapes it passed to join its waters with the vastness beyond. Free energy carving and channeling millions of geologic byways to shape a world. A single-mindedness harnessed by man in technology ancient and modern as humankind enabled the movement of greater and greater masses of energy, whether coal barges to tidewater or the space shuttle into orbit, the combustion engine or the electric grid or nuclear fission, creating and merging and evolving more and various sources of power to change the face of the planet, and so fueling knowledge and the movement of people and ideas to create wealth unimaginable, enough to reach out to the stars and beyond.

And yet he found such an awe-inspiring journey, given all its pitfalls, somehow deflating without a faith—without love—to guide him, leaving him desolate at the prospect of a curious nature that only led to more questions than answers. He yearned for something he couldn't name, for certainties—yes, for the peace and serenity of a mind at rest, for the sure thing. He breathed deeply, concentrating on his breath (a meditation technique Wendy had taught him), as his thoughts retreated from the vastness of creation to a more circumspect survey of the best upstream fishing holes of youth, remembering how the Judge had offered patient instruction from the stony ramparts of the abutment. A memory bolstered by all the familiar scents that rose as one to his flaring nostrils: of mossy rocks, and sere leaves and rich leaf mold, and the wafting aroma of hemlock and pine and the wintergreen of black birch, and that purest of pure essences—mineral-rich rushing water, which now returned to him the nasal drone of the Judge's voice as he'd once known it, calling out from above, guiding the casts of a young boy wading below, absorbed in the arcane art of fly-fishing. With his walking stick, he'd point out glittering silent pools in the lee of the current, there to cast his line, there where the trout were surely poised and waiting for just the right fly, offered with just the right twitch of the wrist. And he saw himself as he once had been, a young teenager on the river—wearing Teddy's fishing vest over his *Star Wars* T-shirt, and Teddy's old waders, even using some of his hand-tied flies—alive to the stillness in motion of the river's current, to the timeless buzzing of bees along the wooded shore, to the elegant swoop of a kingfisher, to the pickerelweed crowned with blue spires, as safe and happy and free and present in mind and spirit (Woodstock High a distant dismal memory) as he'd ever been, even as the flow of gravity and time that powered the destruction and formation of worlds whispered ceaselessly past his knees.

And in that moment, as man and boy, he knew he'd seen a ghost at the boathouse the night before, a sweaty teenager with a handsome chin and rugged nose, the spitting image of a young Teddy resting on his oars.

Through his tears he heard Cecily's voice somewhere behind him.

"Nancy, I bet George left out the best part, the folks who made it all happen. You see, Nancy, each lock had to have a lock keeper and each lock keeper had his home on the canal, and some of the lock keepers built stores or had inns for travelers. And the first of those locks, once you crossed the Neversink, over there past the stone abutment on the east shore, was called the 'Pie Lock.' The reason it was called that was because Mary Casey, who worked for the store owner, Moses Van Inwegen—don't you love that name?—was a fabulous baker. Mary made the most mouthwatering bread—famous up and down the length of the canal. It was so good that the canal men waited in line to buy her baked goods, especially her rice custard pies for fifteen cents. You see, everybody wanted her pies. And she also made special little pies for the children, which she gave away to the poorest of them, especially those on the canalboats, and many of those folks really were poor. And you see, your great-great-grandfather, my great, Dr. Dimock, would hike down here on his Saturdays when he was in residence at Hermitage, and he would treat the poor folks on the canalboats who needed his help, everything from concussions due to falls, broken bones, snake bites, and many awful diseases, like TB and scarlet fever. Don't you think that's cool? I sure do . . . makes me just a little proud. Why I always wanted to be a doctor."

Erich, who had been making his own reconnaissance of the abutment and its archaic technology, lost in his own dreams of canal transport and vast trade routes of the Venetians spanning faraway seas, wandered back and turned to his daughter as if suddenly coming to.

"Oh, and next spring we can come down here and I'll teach you how to fly-fish."

"You do that, Erich," said Cecily. "You weren't too bad, if memory serves."

Erich shrugged. "Yeah, but Billy was a whiz."

Cecily laughed, touched a fingertip to her cousin's nose, and sang out, "'When you're hot, you're hot/ And when you're not, you're not.'" They all laughed as a buzzing sound erupted from the back pocket of

Nancy's camo hiking pants. She let out a little yelp at the unexpected noise and reached for her cell phone.

"Oh my God, it's Max, texting me," said Nancy.

"What did he say?" asked Karen, rushing over from where she'd been sitting, dangling her feet and daydreaming.

"'Football, really boring. Where r u?'"

"Hey," cried Erich, taking out his phone, "three bars."

"What do I tell him, Aunt Karen?"

"Tell him you're floating down the Delaware and Hudson Canal and life is but a dream."

Nancy tapped away ". . . life is but a dream."

"Tell him to get his butt . . ." Karen paused as Wendy signaled to her and pulled out her phone and asked for Max's number.

"Hey, Max, it's Wendy. How you doin' my man? . . . Good, good . . . Hey, I wanted to tell you that the Judge bought a whole closetful of really cool gear for you—camo pants and a leather Filson jacket, hunting knives, pocketknives, Nikon binoculars, a super flashlight—Nancy is over the moon with all her new stuff—like Christmas at Macy's. And listen, here's the best news of all: The Judge has invited Nancy down to his palatial condo on the beach in Florida for spring break, two weeks in the sun and surf with all the college girls in their bikinis—should be quite the rockin' scene . . . Yeah, sure he'll invite you, but I think he needs to at least meet you first—*Lo entiendes, mi amigo*? So here's the deal: I can have a limo meet you in half an hour, and in another two hours you're joining us for a fabulous dinner with Nancy and all your aunts and uncles—the whole crew—and you're a made man with all the fab new clothes and gear—and your spring break is in the bag for a rockin' great time . . . Way to go, man—now half an hour, be ready and waiting at the front door."

67
Deny Everything—Never Confess

IN THE WEEKS after Thanksgiving, before the time set aside to drive the Judge to Siesta Key for Christmas, George found himself increasingly perplexed as he faced the disheartening prospect of radical revisions to the Judge's memoir, prompted by the stunning revelations in the newly uncovered letters from Priscilla Hiss, Whittaker Chambers, and that of Teddy, retrieved in the nick of time from the Neversink by the miracle of digital technology. The implications of these missives slipped from the pages of the past were made clear in a flurry of e-mails from Allen Weinstein, a paroxysm of alarm mixed with introspection and, finally, exasperated wonder. All this occurred during the busiest weeks for George's gallery at the height of the Christmas season, not to mention e-mails and calls from curators at major museums asking to view privately what might be available from the Altmann estate. The oddness and randomness of it all sometimes left him reeling and sleepless, emotionally drained (unable to regain the state of grace momentarily his while looking out the window at the lake after first reading the letters). Especially the uncanny inverse function between the apotheosis of one grandfather and the looming threats to the once-formidable reputation of the other, one rising from obscurity to fame while the other foundered as the Judge faced possible scandal, accusations of bad faith, or at best a quixotic and unhappy footnote in the history of the Hiss trial and the Red thirties and forties once his memoir was published.

And what if his aunt Alice got wind of the two letters that would clarify Teddy's?

As Weinstein made it abundantly clear, the letters not only confirmed the visit to Hermitage in August 1937 by the Hisses and Chambers on the way back from Fitzwilliam but also that the Judge knew all along that on one perjury count—Alger Hiss had claimed to have seen nothing of Chambers, whom he admitted to knowing only as George Crosley, after January 1937—Hiss was guilty. And perhaps more to the point, Priscilla and Alger Hiss were well aware that Edward Dimock and Annie, and possibly young Teddy, knew from that same visit to Hermitage with Chambers that Hiss was lying and that they could potentially be called to testify to that effect. Weinstein had first wondered out loud in a phone conversation if Priscilla Hiss had initially even remembered writing the thank-you note from more than ten years before, or if she had even mentioned it to her husband and the defense team before the first trial. If she had, Hiss and his lawyers would have been forced to assume the letter was still in Annie and the Judge's possession, which, if introduced in the trial along with their testimony, would have gone a long way to substantiating Chambers's claim about the trip to Fitzwilliam, New Hampshire, to retrieve the document on Soviet monetary reform from Harry Dexter White. If the prosecution had gotten wind of the existence of that letter, both Edward and Annie Dimock could then have been called as witnesses under oath to explain Priscilla's letter, its whereabouts, and whether or not Chambers had indeed arrived at Hermitage with the Hisses.

There had been a long, pregnant pause on the phone line from Washington while George stared out his gallery window as both pondered the devastating implications. "She must have waited until after the first trial ended in a hung jury," said Weinstein. "Maybe she didn't want to involve Edward and Annie Dimock. The Handytown—her letter is touching, don't you think?—she described was a sacred shared moment in her mind; she may have trusted that they would hold their tongues. Maybe she'd never even mentioned the letter to Alger, fearing how it could potentially corroborate Chambers's testimony about their trip to Fitzwilliam, which turned out to be the weakest part of his testimony."

In the days and weeks before Christmas, George and Weinstein tried to hash out the imponderables by phone and e-mail. Why had Chambers remained silent? He'd said nothing about the visit to Hermitage before, during, or after the first trial—or the second! The Dimocks as witnesses, given their stature, would have substantiated his accusations against Hiss and upheld one of the counts of perjury. Apart from Chambers and his wife, during the entire trial, the prosecution only turned up a single witness who could or was willing to place the Hisses and Chambers in the same company after

January 1937: That was the Hisses' black maid, Claudia Catlett, who remembered Mr. and Mrs. Chambers visiting at the Hisses' residence on Volta Place, a woman who required a prodigious beating of the bushes by the FBI to find.

Why had Chambers chosen to remain silent?

As George showed curators around the storage facility in Brooklyn where the Altmann estate now resided, this puzzling fact played havoc with his mind. And with it, a nagging sense of betrayal by the one man he had loved. He began dreading the drive to Siesta Key.

As the days grew colder and the time approached to pick up the Judge, the e-mails from Weinstein began coming at odd times of day, often late at night, after leaving the National Archives or a dinner reception, or first thing in the morning, as the new information was reevaluated in light of a career spent tilting with the subject of Hiss's guilt or innocence. A man who had been vilified by many from the milieu of his upbringing for betraying Hiss, Weinstein combed through his research notes, searching for overlooked clues to what he now referred to as the "missing day" at Hermitage.

Clearly after the hung jury of the first trial, Hiss and his defense team were desperate; the mood of the country was changing with the testing of the first Soviet atom bomb and Communist regimes installed in Poland, Czechoslovakia, and China. The second trial loomed ominously as the mood of the jury pool grew more skeptical about the machinations of the Soviet Union. If Priscilla Hiss hadn't spoken up before about her letter, she probably did then. That might have been enough to spur the Hiss defense team to bring Edward Dimock on board. First, to test his position on the matter of the Hermitage visit (perhaps feel him out about Priscilla's letter) or at the very least to sound out his "loyalty" to Priscilla and Alger. Second, to test Chambers's loyalty to the Dimocks. Chambers hadn't brought up the Hermitage visit in the first trial, but who was to say he wouldn't "spring it on the jury" in the second if things didn't go his way? Surely he'd shared this fact with his personal attorney even if he might have refused to let the government prosecution use it against Hiss, presumably to protect the Dimocks. Might not the federal prosecutors have tried to convince him to testify about Hermitage in the second trial—if need be? Would having Edward Dimock confronting him in the witness box have kept him silent or opened the floodgates? This, speculated Weinstein, would have been a calculated risk on the part of Hiss and the defense team: that Chambers, due to some misbegotten loyalty, didn't wish to bring the Dimocks on as witnesses. "It boggles the mind," was how Weinstein ended one e-mail at two in the morning. "Chambers—you have to respect his integrity—never wanted to harm the innocent."

The upside of this risky strategy was that once on the defense team, Edward Dimock was, in theory, safe from being called by the prosecution to testify, even if the government had gotten wind of the Hermitage visit. But why would Dimock have done it? Both George and Weinstein agreed that the Judge had most likely not known of the existence of Priscilla's thank-you note; otherwise, he'd probably have hunted it out either before or after Annie's death and destroyed it. And why had Annie always kept it to herself? Had the letter, at least in 1937, moved her to feel sympathy for Priscilla and her husband? Or, more likely, with the man she'd then known only as Carl. And how had Edward Dimock justified himself to his wife in taking on the Hiss defense job when she knew the truth, or when the truth had dawned on her—that Carl was Chambers? Presumably over the course of the first trial, if not before. Had Dimock made the case to his wife that whatever Hiss had done back in the thirties didn't amount to much and he deserved a fair and vigorous defense as much as any accused man? Did he offer the excuse that all in all it would raise his profile in the legal world and open the door for a judgeship? Did husband and wife discuss the matter, squabble over the guilt or innocence of Hiss, the treatment of Chambers by the defense team (certainly in the margins of her copy of Witness)? Where was Annie in all this? Was her brusque dismissal of Altmann's gift of the charcoal sketch at the end of the trial's first day a demonstration of her fury and disgust?

"She must have been a supporter of Chambers," said George in a late-night phone conversation. "Chambers's letter to her, the inscribed copy of the book, her annotation in the pages all point to her championing his cause."

"Okay, then it really comes down to the third question: Did Edward Dimock share with her his concerns about their safety and his strategy, the subterfuge he had in mind?"

"The subterfuge he *and* Chambers had in mind?"

George would obsess over these imponderables. He desperately tried to put himself in the Judge's shoes, imagining the tricky position in which the Judge had found himself in late 1949, facing subtle and not so subtle threats from Hiss in their preliminary meetings—threats George now kept detecting between the lines of his grandfather's account, and that echoed out of their conversations in the great room, the tremor in his grandfather's voice, his glassy-eyed inward gaze, the old man's anxious body language as they sat together before the fire at Hermitage.

Weinstein remained less forgiving, more unsparing, rational, factual, and academic in his approach—unflinching as he enumerated the possibilities.

Could Dimock have considered the second perjury charge unimportant, a slip of the tongue or memory, perhaps a classic case of a perjury trap set by the prosecution team and so not warranting prosecution? Possibly, like most defense councils, Dimock felt duty-bound to defend his client even as he knew the truth, even a truth that might have thrown an unfavorable light on his own relationship with Alger and Priscilla Hiss, who had so blithely, so rudely broached his sanctum sanctorum at Hermitage on that blissful August day in 1937. For that matter, why had he not spoken up in the first place, offered to testify in the first Hiss trial and bring down the man he'd once advised Priscilla not to marry? Why had he remained silent?

Over George's objections, Weinstein moved the conversation to places where George was unwilling to go.

Did Edward Dimock take the defense job in spite of the truth because he believed in Hiss's cause—that is, he was either a fellow traveler with the Communist Party or even part of Chambers's apparatus himself, and so under orders to protect and defend Hiss at any and all costs? Had he and William Remington been in cahoots? He wouldn't have been alone, since some members of Hiss's defense team were undoubtedly past or present Party members or working directly for the Party or Soviet intelligence. Thankfully, Weinstein dismissed these scenarios as quickly as he brought them up. Although the Judge's less than passing mention in the memoir of William Remington, when both worked on the War Production Board, still gave him pause. During those war years, Dimock would have been in possession of top-secret information that William Remington may well have passed on to his Soviet handlers. A relationship with both Alger and Priscilla Hiss and perhaps an even closer professional relationship with William Remington would not have looked good during the Red Scare of the fifties. But as George pointed out in an e-mail and Weinstein refuted, in late 1949, when the Judge first viewed the Altmann sketches, Remington's spying had not yet been uncovered by the FBI.

"Yes, but if Edward Dimock had known or even suspected William Remington of spying during the war, then finding that sketch of Remington with the others would, at the very least, have been an unpleasant shock. After all, Harry Dexter White, Laurence Duggan, and Noel Field had all been accused of spying by late 1949, and, of course, Hiss. Yet another reason he might not have wanted those Altmann sketches to see the light of day once he was on the Hiss defense team—or later, for that matter."

While the first winter snowstorm hit the Catskills, George and Weinstein kept circling the most impenetrable mystery of all facing them every day: why Chambers in his letter to Annie and, by extension, the Judge, encouraged her not to blame her husband for how he'd treated him in the trial, assuring her as well that he wouldn't mention their names in his forthcoming book, *Witness*? Why was he so intent on protecting his hosts at Hermitage way back in August 1937? Chambers may have been the kindest of souls, but he could be unsparing of enemies when required. Clearly, he was very taken with Annie, both on their walk and in conversation, and presumably when she played for him and the Hisses later that evening in the great room. The best Weinstein and George could come up with as the drive to Siesta Key loomed was that Chambers and Dimock had had some kind of understanding, probably unstated. He pointed out to George that the psychiatric accusations Dimock leveled against Chambers, certainly as they considered it in the present, had elements of opera buffa, they were so absurd—as the jury had quickly decided, as well. Did Chambers and Dimock, in effect, silently conspire to let the psychiatric attack play itself out, the attack insisted on by Alger Hiss, because both figured the absurd strategy would blow up in the defense's face—as indeed it did? Did Dimock bow to Hiss's pressure and subtle threats because his better judgment told him that the Hiss strategy, fatally flawed as it was desperate, even laughable, would most likely end in disaster for his client?

If Chambers and Dimock had indeed colluded in some manner, it was unlikely either would have ever revealed it, not given the long, vindictive memory of the KGB. Certainly not Dimock, for professional reasons, not to mention offering Hiss an opening to petition for a mistrial on the basis of collusion between one of his attorneys and the star witness for the prosecution. A strategy or act of collusion barely intimated in Chambers's letter to Annie, but just enough that it might well have prompted her to hide his letter, possibly encouraging second thoughts about her husband, and so preserving her rocky marriage, now with the blessing of a new daughter, Cordelia, as she struggled to find forgiveness after the death of Teddy. And so a letter to be kept close, hidden, reread over the years, pondered, paired with Priscilla Hiss's letter recounting the same moment in time, out of time, out of mind—perhaps an evening when her playing for her guests had made the rafters of the great room sing with a celestial harmony and brought tears to her rapt audience.

Whereas once Annie had been just a name to George, more an emanation of the Judge and Hermitage, now his grandmother began to seem more real to him, as her original recordings of Mozart and Chopin, transferred and remastered to CDs by Wendy, began to cast a far different spell, invoking rumination as to the workings of her mind and soul, which began to interweave with his: her doubts, her joys, her moments of bliss, her love of her daughter. Her music, even her beloved Proust, a yet unturned key in his imagination.

Looming in the background of all the exchanges between George and Weinstein was the bizarre role of the Altmann sketches—which had passed the FBI forensics with "flying colors"—in the saga of the Hiss trial.

Only in the days leading up to the drive to Siesta Key and Christmas, when George would spend almost a week with the Judge, and the planned "review" of the memoir for publication, did George and Weinstein fully grapple with the issue. They both agreed that Altmann, too, must have been feeling the pressure between the first and second trials, either from the KGB or the FBI, or both, and so decided to try to protect himself the best way he knew how, by opting to turn over the sketches to the Hiss defense team as opposed to the prosecution. He might have already lied or cut corners on the truth when speaking to the FBI. To cooperate and testify for the government, to turn over the sketches to the FBI, to squeal on his old comrades would, in his mind, have ended his career as an artist, if not resulted in a death sentence. Perhaps he had contemplated turning over the sketches at the opening of the first trial but hadn't been able to summon the nerve. Then with the second trial, after Altmann's having been again interviewed by the FBI, the newspapers reported that Edward Dimock, husband of the pianist Annie Davenport Dimock, had joined the defense team. Had it really been the artist's infatuation with the Soyer portrait of Annie, and the inspiration provided by her music, that had prompted the handover? Sheer serendipity? Had pure sentiment been the deciding factor? Did the artist naïvely assume that Annie's husband had to be a likeminded sympathetic and sensitive soul who would be the person best placed on the defense team to dispose of the sketches—presumably to guarantee their destruction—and so demonstrate he was no threat, thus keeping him and his family safe?

Had the panicked artist misplaced his faith in Edward Dimock: a man who would do the right thing? How could he possibly have known that the first of the sketches in the envelope, that exquisitely rendered portrait of Priscilla Hiss (with whom the artist, too, might have been infatuated) might well have touched a chord either of nostalgia or a lingering vague attachment in Edward Dimock's heart, and so cause him to put the sketches aside momentarily, and later, as he stated in the memoir, simply deposit them in the defense files for further examination and evaluation and so fail to alert Hiss or the defense team?

Then came Weinstein's bombshell.

"Except, and I hate to tell you this, George, I've come to the conclusion that Edward Dimock never deposited the sketches in the defense files in the first place."

"No fucking way . . ."

This part of the Judge's story had always rung false for Weinstein: Something didn't quite add up. Over the months since their first meeting in Washington, Weinstein had been diligently exploring the matter. Law firms have elaborate protocols and safeguards in place to prevent just such cases of interested parties purloining important evidence. Edward Dimock was no friend of the law firm in question and would have been hard-pressed to cut some special deal to access those files, especially as a sitting federal judge. Nor did he have Alger Hiss's permission to do so, a critical permission exclusively obtained by Weinstein thirty years before to access those very same files. And there was no memory or record of Dimock's having even made a request or overture for special consideration among the surviving firm partners Weinstein had contacted. Decisively, all the defense files in the Hiss case had been meticulously archived and cataloged. And nowhere in any archive or catalog listings was Weinstein able to find a record of the nine Altmann sketches.

In the days before George was to drive to Hermitage to pick up the Judge, consumed with logistics and frantic calls from Felicity about what needed to be packed, including scores of books insisted on by the Judge, he and Weinstein tried to wrestle the anomalies down to a few key questions.

"Why would Edward Dimock lie to you, and in his official memoir lie to posterity, about how he'd come by the sketches in the first place and how he'd disposed of them? Why would a sitting federal judge lie, in writing, admit to breaking the law—to illegally having removed the Altmann drawings from the defense files, when, in fact, they must have remained in his possession for over fifty years? And then turn them over to you at the eleventh hour once his nemesis, Alger Hiss, was dead—and, I suppose, coming to the end of his own road?"

George, flustered, immediately sought to make the case for his grandfather.

"What was the Judge supposed to think when a court reporter, out of the blue, thrust an envelope into his hands containing sketches of top-ranking government officials, including his client Alger Hiss, along with his wife, Priscilla, and two who had died violently within the year? Was George Altmann a friend or foe? Was Altmann a member of the Communist Party? A stool pigeon? Had he been put up to this gambit by the KGB to test Dimock's loyalty to the defense? For all he knew, he was being tested or warned by the defense team or the KGB—even Alger Hiss—because he was the one person who knew for certain that Chambers and Hiss knew each other in 1937. Maybe the Judge was thoroughly confounded—frozen in place. Christ, who wouldn't be!"

Weinstein paused, a ruminating reply. "What if Hiss never told any other members of the defense team about the visit to Hermitage in August 1937? Kept it to himself and Priscilla, like so much else he must have kept back from his minions."

"So only Alger and Priscilla would have been aware that the Judge and Chambers might have some kind of understanding—what do we call it, a modus vivendi, silent pact of some kind, a kind of truce?"

"Hiss preserved his credibility among his team and still maintained his hold over Edward Dimock."

"So the Judge felt no compunction to turn the sketches over to Hiss or the defense team because . . . because it wouldn't look good, because it might suggest some kind of previous relationship (friends, conspirators—what have you) with George Altmann that would be hard, if impossible, to explain. And yet my grandfather Altmann was brutally murdered on Christmas Eve. Then, suddenly, horribly, those sketches must've taken on a very different complexion."

George thought he detected a pensive, agonized sigh on the phone.

"So we're down to this: Edward Dimock preferred to admit to a crime he never committed—stealing the sketches from the firm files—to cover up for an act of incompetence—or misapprehension, or perhaps, at least in his mind, cowardice in not sharing the sketches with the defense team, and so inoculating George Altmann from retribution. George, it certainly won't do his posthumous reputation any good to have this lie or oversight—not to mention the Handytown cover-up—however you choose to dignify it, much less the irregularities surrounding this whole mess, recorded in his memoir."

"I can't help wondering what Chambers thought about the murder of Altmann—if he even knew about it. Of course, he never mentioned it in his memoir, either. What would he have thought had he seen those sketches of Alger and Priscilla Hiss and the others in the Volta Place cell when he was their spy master, faces so full of hope and fervent expectations?"

"He ran only Hiss and White," said Weinstein. "The spy handler in him would've been aghast."

George found himself nodding, breathing deeply as he stared out the window of his apartment at the snow-covered gingkoes. Then he put his cell phone to his ear again. "A conspiracy of silence that bound the Judge and Chambers—and Annie—over all the years."

"And Priscilla Hiss . . . abandoned in the end by her husband, who followed Kim Philby's admonition to the letter: 'Deny everything; never confess. Young man, you've got your work cut out for you.'"

George agreed he would try to bring up the matter over Christmas, that he might even delicately try to flesh out that long-ago visit to Hermitage by Alger and Priscilla Hiss and Whittaker Chambers. But he was in no mood to press his grandfather on tender subjects. He wanted the Judge to get away from the harsh winter weather that hit a week after Thanksgiving; he wanted the old man to have a chance to relax in the sun by the sea, away from the disturbing issue of the memoir and so, hopefully, dwell on happier times.

"Who knows how much time he has left."

After hanging up with Weinstein, George realized he had barely spoken to Wendy in weeks. What conversations they'd had concerned logistics on her upcoming show in February. But he decided now that she should accompany him and Cecily and the Judge on the drive to Siesta Key. How could he not invite her to go with them? Without her, the three letters would not have been turned up and in the case of Teddy's letter, survived.

68
Votive Flames

THE OLD MAN stood on the piazza in the ten-degree cold and stinging flurries and gazed upon the world as he'd known it. He was supported on his right arm by his grandson. For ten minutes, he insisted on standing there, wobbly-kneed, shaking with cold, as he gazed out at the icy desert of the lake, replete with windblown snow dunes. Swollen flakes adhered to his wool hat and earflaps, dusting the shoulders of his faded red plaid hunter's coat. His lips turning purple, he moved his leather-gloved hands to wipe away the stray motes of white that settled on his flaring eyebrows. His blue eyes, red-rimmed, bleary, blinking rapidly, continued to blaze outward. There, swaying before the steps and the pair of granite snubbing posts and the waiting Tahoe, he surveyed his realm. He swiveled his gaze to right and left like a wizened owl from its sheltered perch, determined to pack in tight the denizens of memory as he'd known them since childhood—here, in this very place, where his older brother, Jack, had said good-bye as he returned from flight training on Long Island and headed off to France; where Annie had sat in her favorite wicker rocker with her Proust and binoculars; and where Teddy, a blur of intrepid energy, had vaulted off the snubbing posts to vanish into the outdoors, the woodlands that even in his ninety plus years—a single lifetime—had grown tall and thick, crowned by the white pine lording it over God's creation. All of it now safely tucked under the palest of pale dust sheets—the world as he'd found it, hibernating for another long Catskill winter. Then he raised his gloved hand and signaled to be helped down the salted steps to the waiting Tahoe, saying simply: "It's time . . ."

—

"Petersburg," said the Judge from the shotgun seat, a few seconds after the green-and-white sign floated by on 95 South. "Anybody in this automobile know what happened at Petersburg?"

"Ah," said Cecily from the backseat, where she and Wendy sat, "I do believe an educational moment is at hand."

The Judge explained to them in some detail about the Battle of the Crater at Petersburg and the sad fate of Justice Holmes's Harvard classmate Brigadier General William Francis Bartlett, who led the attack and was captured at the bottom of the crater with black troops, most of whom were shot on the spot, while Bartlett, minus his wooden leg, was paraded the following day through Richmond on a donkey and spat upon by the populace.

"Holmes kept a photograph of Bartlett on his desk. 'The bravest man I ever knew,' he called him, 'my intrepid general.' He gave a moving eulogy for his friend—who was the youngest Union general—at Bartlett's funeral. There is a very fine marble bust of Bartlett by Daniel Chester French in Memorial Hall."

"I remember," said George. "A Princeton-Harvard game. Memorial Hall has been turned into a freshman dining hall."

"Dr. Dimock treated Bartlett in his last illness. He spent the time left to him trying to promote reconciliation between the North and South."

"Right, letting those motherfucking KKKers lynch my people for another century—some kind of reconciliation." Cecily patted the Judge's shoulder.

"Cecily, dear, welcome to the human race. We're all sinners. I, first and foremost. But my life has been dedicated to the law in the hopes of giving people a better life by setting and enforcing rules of procedure and standards of conduct, while protecting our constitutional freedoms—not that that's any guarantee against sin. But it's a start. The rest, I'll leave to the human heart."

Cecily snorted. "That's your system, not necessarily my system."

"There you go again, just like your mother."

Cecily grinned in appreciation of the riposte, as did the Judge.

"Your judicial system killed my father."

To this, the Judge made no reply, but continued a keen watch of the signage as it drifted by for the Petersburg Battlefield National Park and various tourist attractions hosted by the likes of Burger King and McDonald's. The Judge muttered to himself and drifted off, occasionally coming to, suddenly launching into a subject he'd either been mulling over or dreaming about.

"Of course, I've been down to Florida dozens of times for conferences and meetings, but I never drove there—through old Dixie, that is. I don't know that I like the look of this countryside much. Too many lost Union battles, the Wilderness being one of the worst. I remember my father telling me he got more practice on traumatic wounds in these parts than anywhere else."

"Ha," announced Cecily, "your Dr. Dimock—now, he's my main man."

"Did I ever tell you, George and Cecily, that Dr. Dimock, when he was in his nineties, wintered in Palm Beach. Once he was old and enfeebled, he became increasingly angry and embittered, even with all his accomplishments. He'd invented dozens of medical instruments, many named after him, but by the time of his death, the *New York Times* obituary didn't deem such things worthy of mention—they'd all been superseded by new technology. Worst of all, he felt useless as a healer. As a doctor, he understood his own demise too well. He predicted he'd die of kidney failure, and he did."

"Judge, do you need a pit stop?" asked Wendy. "There's a Dunkin' Donuts in fifteen miles."

"Uh-oh," said George, "I do believe there's a sugar high coming on fast. Judge, when was the last time you had a glazed cinnamon swirl coffee roll?"

The Judge's mind was elsewhere.

"My sense of the sea," said the Judge, "of a beach, was somehow set in stone all those many years ago when I clerked for Justice Holmes, when I spent those three months at his place in Beverly Farms. We were never beyond the call of the sea . . . something I associate with bracing conversations and, of course, Annie's Chopin."

"Your condo is going to be right on the beach, where you can hear the waves. And there is a small Steinway grand, just delivered, and we've arranged for a top student from the Sarasota Music Conservatory to come in three afternoons a week to practice and play."

"Where's Felicity?" asked the Judge for at least the tenth time, an edge of anxiety in his voice. "She's my reader."

"She's packing her bikini—so you're forewarned—and will be with you when we have to go back after New Year's. Mom's planning to come down for Christmas and in February for a couple of weeks. Nancy and Max will be down for a visit over spring break."

"My, that Max is a handsome boy; he's got Teddy's eyes and chin."

"A ladies' man, too," said Cecily, laughing.

"Of course, I first met Annie at Beverly Farms . . . We walked the beach."

"Yes, she wore a blue dress with yellow shoes," said Wendy, smiling at George in the rearview mirror.

"I think she loved Jane Austen then . . . Monsieur Proust, later. That is my only real regret: that Annie didn't live to see her grandchildren as adults. Although I often wonder if she could have stood the world as it has become, filled with all these new gadgets—phones in your pocket that rule your life. She relished quiet, 'the universe between the notes,' as she put it. She believed that art, music, and poetry could make the world a better place, 'one human soul at a time.' She always said, 'I want to raise musicians and readers, and so give them wings to fly free.' That was the Unitarian Universalist in her."

Cecily looked up from her phone. "Hey, I won the Chopin prize—I hope Annie approves."

"Annie did believe in the immortal soul, as her friend Chambers wrote. Not that I fear death—far from it. But my soul, Annie's soul . . . well, who knows."

"Were you never tempted"—George winced inwardly at broaching the subject directly—"well, after the trial, I mean, to meet up with Chambers again?"

"Chambers was a Quaker, George." The Judge sighed, nodding, a ruminative side-step. "There was something very appealing in his humility, his quiet and unassuming blue eyes . . . an inner light . . . Annie liked that in him—Priscilla, too, I suppose—the kind of quest for truth and understanding that was always central to her Unitarian faith."

"Did Annie ever meet Chambers?" asked Wendy.

At this, George turned to the Judge's pensive face with some apprehension.

"Perhaps my children would have been happier for a more organized religious upbringing. Annie did take them to Unitarian services. And she insisted that Teddy at least take confirmation classes at Groton."

"My ex came from a Bible-thumpin' family of Southern Baptist preachers and it never stopped him from cultivating all the white pussy he could muster. And he wasn't even that good a lover."

George, in a quick side glance, thought he saw a smile crack the Judge's lips.

"For Dr. Dimock and Holmes, the slaughter of the Civil War destroyed what was left of their old New England religion. When Annie and I said our good-byes, we knew it was for good."

For a few minutes more, the rolling hills of the Virginia countryside presided upon their reveries, a passing blur of muddy, frost-encrusted meadows dotted with copses of gesticulating barren trees. Then Wendy quite suddenly spoke up in a strange searching tone, more dreamlike than real.

"When my parents died, I was taken in hand by some very nice people from our local Methodist church in Houston—St. Paul's, very upscale, very Pugin Gothic—who helped me through the shock, burial service, and the years of grieving. My mother had occasionally taken me to St. Paul's at Easter or for Christmas carol services, about as much pomp and circumstance at the Methodists go in for. My father, never . . . always the geologist. Evolution was his religion, Darwin his patron saint. When we climbed together—always father and daughter, as Mom never took me up herself—all we talked about was geology and time and fossils. When I was climbing with him, it was like the mountains opened a storybook of time travel, his husky voice a magic carpet ride drifting over the ages of the earth, sedimentary layer after layer, his eye attuned to the slightest variation in color or tone in the rock. He was spellbinding, unbound by gravity, leading me ever sky-ward. Of course, that's how he made his living; he was responsible for some of the most productive oil fields in West Texas.

"During the funeral service, seeing those two large oak coffins with brass handles set at the front of the nave, side by side, gleaming in the sunlight streaming down from the stained-glass windows, I couldn't believe he could ever be confined like that, so earthbound, so trapped. Their coffins almost touched: a perfect pair with a beautiful honey gold finish under that prismatic glow from the stained glass—a color so unlike anything found in the mountains. They had kept the coffins closed at the viewing because the bodies had been pretty broken up from the impacts on the rocks. I somehow couldn't believe they were really there. I thought that maybe it was all a big fake—something that my mother, who liked practical jokes, had concocted, while she was really off somewhere smoking her Virginia Slims on the sly and laugh-ing at all the ado about nothing. But I was in shock and confused, only thirteen, so I went along with things and tried to believe in everything I heard and was told. The big idea, so the pastor repeated: If I could believe in Christ and his forgiveness for my sins, I would be reunited with my parents in paradise, and everything would be made clear about God's plan. During the service, the minister assured us that because my parents were such fantastic people, God had called them home sooner rather than later. They had spent their lives climbing high, trying to touch the face of God, and now, so I was assured, they had managed it. I remember their mountain-climbing fraternity, seated in the first two rows, rolling their eyes at that. It certainly didn't answer my question: Why had they left me? It all made me feel very small and very alone.

"Over the following years, when I lived with my crazy aunt in a rural slum of Houston, I attended Sunday services at St. Paul's—without her, as she would have nothing to do with fancy, rich oil people. I tried to get closer to God, too, hoping I'd feel less lonely, less estranged from my parents—somehow learn to put up with my aunt. I wanted to go climbing in the worst way, but none of my parents' friends or climbing instructors would take me . . . nobody would dare. My aunt forbade me to ever think about such things. I worked out in the gym, on climbing walls, doing as best I could on my own. I worked on my art, doing still life studies of my rock collection, which I'd assembled when climbing with Dad. And I studied like mad to make sure I could get as far away from my aunt and later my senile grandmother and Houston as possible.

"Only when I went away to Yale was I really able to start seriously climbing again, first with student groups, then with professionals, as I had with my Dad years before. I knew I could never return to Houston. I kind of fell in love with my instructor, who, of course, was a married man. But when I was climbing, the higher I got, I did feel that I was getting closer to my parents, that at least some answers were out there, waiting on the distant horizon. And that's when I began asking around . . . people in the fraternity who had climbed with them, who knew them as I had never known them. When I finished Yale undergrad and went into the graduate painting program for my MFA, when I turned twenty-one, when I got my father's stock portfolio of company shares, and the life insurance money, I arranged to have their coffins dug up from the graveyard outside Houston and their remains cremated. The crematorium asked me how I wanted the remains packaged and if I wanted to pick them up or have them sent via FedEx. They had a catalog of beautiful handmade urns. I told them to put them into two plain cardboard boxes, to keep it as light as possible. When the cardboard boxes arrived by FedEx, I put them side by side on the mantel of my apartment in New Haven. Every day when I got home from the studio, I'd check on them, sometimes moving the boxes farther apart, sometimes closer together, sometimes touching.

"Then one weekend, I put the two boxes into my backpack and drove to New Hampshire and the White Mountains. I had always wanted to climb Mount Washington—I'd been saving it for a special occasion. It was spring and warm and the trees were golden green with their first buds. I hiked up the most difficult route available, the Huntington Ravine trail, which required a little technical climbing. I wanted to go fast, and I made it in about six hours, all six thousand two hundred and eighty-eight feet. I felt good and strong, even if winded, and I could feel my body come alive as the view expanded, as the circle of the horizon, full of pale azures and avocado greens, began to engulf me, like an albatross riding the updrafts. I hiked around to find a private spot on the summit away from the tourists who came up by car and the cog railway. On a granite outcropping, I carefully placed the two identical boxes side by side, inscribed with the names of my mother and father. I sat observing them for a while, the oblong pale Morandi shadows on the veined granite slipping longer and longer as the sun arced lower and lower, as the day was gathering in. The wind began to pick up, not cold, but cool and refreshing. Like a faraway whisper. Then I took my father's box and carefully removed the tape and the cover and opened the plastic bag and held it out to the wind and tipped it, watching as the ashes and bits of bone were whipped away and dispersed. I think I smiled. Then I picked up my mother's, but I couldn't open it; I just couldn't do it. I'd been hanging out in climbing circles by then and I knew probably more than I should have known about her and the circumstances of the accident. About how she behaved on Everest, when trust and confidence in the team means the difference between success and failure, life and death. And so I found myself walking back to where the little cogwheel railway takes passengers up and down the mountain, and sat and waited for the last down train to depart. When it arrived to pick up everyone left on the summit, I first got in the car and put the box on my lap, but a minute later, just before the doors closed, I stepped off and dropped the box of my mother's ashes into the platform recycling bin full of fast-food wrappers and Styrofoam containers. I cried all the way down, but once I got to my car and was driving home, radio blaring, I felt a lot better. Knowing . . . it was just Dad and me."

Cecily let out a long exclamation. "Woo—ee, girl!" She put her arm around Wendy and drew her head to her breast. "Talk about getting stuff off your chest. I think you done us all proud. Better still, we done earned ourselves a visit to Mr. Dunkin' D." She wiped Wendy's wet cheeks with the sleeve of her sweatshirt. "Driver, this is your exit—time for our sugar high."

—

The last thirty miles of North Carolina passed in near silence after George remarked on the turnoff for Camp Lejeune.

"Bet those marines are busy preparing for Iraq."

He knew the Judge had seen the sign, because he had a map open on his lap and his finger had silently slipped down Interstate 40 to Route 24 and Jacksonville, where on an evening in September of 1950, Annie had dinner with their son, a last conversation that echoed down the wind for the remainder of their marriage.

As they crossed into South Carolina, the clouds parted and luxurious sunlight flickered over the swampy lowlands on either side of 95. The air was warming mile by mile, even as the dusk began to settle in. For an hour, everyone kept silent, as if a little in awe of the oncoming evening. Then an exit sign appeared that listed tourist attractions for the Charleston area, including the Fort Wagner Battlefield Monument.

"Of course," said the Judge, seemingly out of the blue, "Holmes had been very close to the 'Shaw boy,' as he called him. Holmes gave a dedication address at the Robert Gould Shaw monument by Saint-Gaudens, in 1897, before he became a Supreme Court judge."

"What's this?" asked Cecily. "Not another dead white hero. Seems like it's Harvard roadkill all the way down Ninety-five."

He raised a tentative finger, as if reminding himself of something he had always believed. "It's important to know who you are and where you came from and what your people stood for."

"Here we go again," scolded Cecily. "Easy for you to say."

The Judge seemed to give this some thought.

"I've often wondered if your mother told your father that her great-grandfather was killed at Antietam."

This brought conversation to a halt for a few tense moments.

"So," said Cecily, "you've known all along about George Jackson?"

"My dear, my career has been in the judicial system; by the nature of the beast, things filter up."

"You never said anything to me. Does Mother Alice know you know?"

"Why do you think she managed that outrage in the first place? . . . She knew when word got out that it would scuttle my chances for a Supreme Court appointment."

Cecily slammed the back of the Judge's seat with her fist.

"Hey," said George.

"It's okay, CeCe," said Wendy, putting a hand on Cecily's knee.

"It's not fucking okay. It's always something—always."

"My apologies," said the Judge. "That was a low blow, even if accurate. And it's not my place to criticize. If your mother had wanted to tell me, she would have."

"How does it make you feel to know you've got some Black Panther blood in your family . . . a cold-blooded killer at that?"

"My dear, life is a long haul, in case these battle-scarred landscapes don't remind you of the fact. The cause of justice is even longer. Just ask the Irish and Italians, the Poles and Chinese and Jews, the Indians— the Trail of Tears began somewhere around here . . . Yes, a long, long haul. We are lucky to see the races learning to live in harmony, to see the country heal its wounds, a chance to remember and honor your people's plight, and the evils of slavery, without which, by the way, your world wouldn't even exist. Isn't that right, George, since you're the expert on alternate universes?"

"A world where slavery had never happened, you mean?"

After a minute of silence, the Judge responded in his way.

"The curse of slavery goes back well before the Greeks. I sometimes think about Emerson's stirring words and I wonder how the Civil War happened, why we got ourselves into the First World War—why good and stirring words never seem to be enough. Well, Annie's people were abolitionists to the bone, with a taste for freedom and art . . . Well, let's hope the Degas sells well in the spring."

"The Monet," said Wendy, correcting him.

"Yes, Giverny."

With that, he slipped into a long nap.

———

After a night at a Hampton Inn south of Charleston (Cecily, acting as nurse practitioner, rooming with the Judge), the following day turned out like magic. No sooner had they crossed the Georgia state line than the sunlight seemed to intensify and the landscape became radiant with soft earth tones merging one with another. Occasionally, the Judge would nod to himself, as if waking from a daydream, or perhaps dreaming he'd already returned to Beverly Farms. He stared out his side window at the low-lying prongs of a palm grove. Every mile seemed to stir forth more concoctions of basswoods and black gums blushing with lemon light as the air freshened with scents of newly thawed earth. The Judge breathed deeply and closed his eyes. George slipped in a CD of Annie playing the Chopin Etudes and turned the volume down low.

As he did so, he glanced in the rearview mirror and caught Wendy's eye; she nodded in the affirmative.

"Judge, Wendy and I were remarking to one another this morning how your description of that surprise visit from Alger and Priscilla Hiss to Hermitage is one of the most vivid passages in your memoir."

At first, the Judge didn't seem to register, as if perhaps he'd nodded off. Then he raised his head, gazing out the window, as if unsure where he was. His map had slipped to the floor as a finger on his knee kept time to the music.

"Alger and Priscilla at Hermitage?"

"You know, the day they arrived out of the blue and you all walked to Handytown."

"With a friend of theirs," added Wendy.

"Oh yes, Annie played for them that evening. Is that in my memoir?"

"As big as life," echoed Wendy from the backseat. "All three of them, and you and Annie . . . and Teddy led the way, wearing an Indian headband with a bald eagle's feather stuck in it."

"Oh, that Indian headband . . . the beadwork of horses."

"He couldn't have been more than four or so in 1937," noted George. George gripped the wheel, his eyes flashing to Wendy's in the mirror. "I wrote about *that*, did I?"

"Vividly," exclaimed Wendy, "beautifully . . . about the hermit thrush and a flock of scarlet tanagers!"

"Oh, yes . . . the tanagers. It was a day—time out of mind . . . Handytown . . . just cast a spell, you see."

"Well, that explains it," said George. "When was it again, exactly?"

"Oh, goodness, how am I supposed to remember that? But let me see . . . well, it had to be August, summer vacation, since we were all there. Annie and I were sitting on the piazza with our binoculars, and Teddy was there—yes, of course he was . . . he must have been about five that summer, just learning his birds."

"He was four; it was the summer of 1937, according to your memoir," said Wendy from the backseat, a notepad open on her lap.

Cecily gave her an odd look.

"Teddy, you see, was obsessed with red-tailed hawks and the bald eagles nesting on the lake," the Judge said. "We'd catch sunnies and leave them on the shore for the bald eagles, and he'd hide just yards away to watch them swoop and grab the flopping fish. It was all we could do to dissuade him from trying to trap them, like the Indians did. Yes, he was right there at his little table with his collection of bird feathers."

"Where were Alice and Martha?" asked George. "I don't believe you mentioned them in the memoir."

"The girls were with their nanny, an Irish girl, pretty brunette with curls dancing on her forehead. It was early afternoon, and this Ford roadster turned the corner of the lake and roared to a stop in front of where we sat on the piazza. A woman's hand reached from the driver's window and waved. A moment later, Priscilla stepped out, to be followed by Alger, and a more portly man from the back. I was stunned; Annie was stunned to have the Hisses turn up unannounced and uninvited on our doorstep, to shatter the tranquility of our most private hideaway. Of course, back then, there was no telephone, even if they might have tried to communicate. Priscilla's appearance brought back to me a spring weekend of many years before, when I'd been a Yale freshman and had brought Priscilla up to Hermitage after a crew race in New Haven. When I had lost . . . well, let's just say it was a first for me on that very piazza—on the porch swing, as a matter of fact, while the house slept. Perhaps it was the same for Priscilla, then a senior at Bryn Mawr, but I tend to doubt it. Although never a great beauty, she was always way ahead on that score. Of course, Annie knew we'd been lovers; we held no secrets back when we married. Nevertheless, Annie did bristle . . . She was not amused."

"I'd bristle, too," said Wendy.

"Priscilla was wearing a blue-print summer dress that showed off her shapely legs, and the men wore business suits and white shirts with open collars."

"Men," said George, catching Wendy's eye again, "so they *did* have someone with them? I don't believe you mentioned his name in your memoir."

"Oh, yes . . . nice fella. But they, the men were not happy—not happy at all. I could tell by their faces, especially the disgruntled look on Alger's—a snarl, as if he were about to bite off Pross's head. Those boys were not at all pleased to be there, as if they'd been hoodwinked, kidnapped. Priscilla's expression of forced gaiety led me to immediately suspect her of having precipitated things. One of her impetuous jokes. Without waiting on the others, she lunged up the steps to the piazza with guileless familiarity and threw herself upon our hospitality. She greeted me with a chaste kiss and gave Annie a hug. Then, spying our binoculars, she began spouting some story about how they'd been out and about bird-watching north of Milford, in the Poconos, and since they were in the vicinity had thought to stop by and say hello. It was a foolish lie, since none of them was dressed for birding, though they did have binoculars with them. And by Alger's irritation, I could tell he was thoroughly put out, even as he sought to make things copacetic by confirming Priscilla's cover story, pointing out a swooping red-tailed hawk to their traveling companion and exclaiming, 'Ah, she stoops to conquer.'"

"Who was their friend?"

"They introduced him as Carl. Overweight, bad teeth, ill-fitting suit, lumpy fedora. Alger said he was a fellow 'amateur ornithologist,' said it with a kind of smirking showmanship, like a self-conscious carnival barker, as if, once resigned to this theater of the absurd, he was going to embrace their oddball companion. Alger was always quick like that, able to blend into the requirements of the moment. We shook hands with Carl—with a C, I believe—who was a tad morose and spoke softly, with a hint of a foreign accent. When he smiled, his hideous teeth showed, which may have explained the rather dour, saturnine expression he habituated. But his blue eyes were intelligent and quick to take the measure of things. Of course, Teddy had immediately pricked up his ears when he heard mention of bird-watching. And after being introduced, Carl immediately gravitated to Teddy, showing much interest in my son's collection of bird feathers, which he was mounting in an album. Carl picked up Teddy's feathers, one after another, and named them all, as if perfectly accommodating Alger's little white lie."

"Judge," said George, "are you telling us that in the summer of 1937—"

"Go on, Judge," interjected Wendy, glancing at George in the mirror with a sharp look.

"I don't mean to repeat myself, if it's already in the memoir."

"Not at all," said George, nodding. "Tell us while it's so fresh in your mind." He shrugged at Wendy. "Maybe we can add a little color in the editing."

"Well . . . we offered refreshments and the gentlemen took off their jackets and rolled up their sleeves and took their seats on the piazza. It had been a hot drive. When Annie handed Priscilla her glass of iced tea, she put the car keys on the side table. Alger immediately snatched them and put them in his pocket. We sat and talked for a few minutes. Carl seemed uneasy and soon went over to the far side of the piazza and began entertaining Teddy with stories about falcons—how falconry was so pervasive in the seventeenth century that a man walking around with a falcon on his fist would not have been deemed unusual. Or that was how Teddy explained it to me later, making a little gloved fist to demonstrate as he strutted around. Alger was impatient and hinted more than once that they needed to be on their way for some obscure meeting in Scranton, but Priscilla dismissed his concerns and said it would be a shame not to at least get a little bird-watching in. 'Edward has the most marvelous bunch of hermit thrush at his beck and call,' she announced in a playful voice. This was her only allusion to the fact that she'd visited Hermitage in the past—although I caught her more than once eyeing the porch swing—when we had indeed spent a late afternoon listening for the song of the hermit thrush, impatient for the privacy of nightfall. As you know, George, the hermit thrush is peculiarly abundant in our corner of the Catskills. Thus prompting Dr. Dimock's naming of Hermitage. I was perfectly prepared to take our party on a brief birding excursion, but I warned that it was August and the thrush had pretty much gone silent. At which, Teddy piped up and said, 'Oh, no, there's always some singing at Handytown.'

"So off we went to the Handytown spring, an easy excursion for the men dressed in work trousers and city shoes, although Priscilla may have borrowed a pair of Annie's tennis sneakers. The two girls, Alice and Martha, were too young for the hike and so were left with the Irish girl and the cook, who was preparing the children's dinner. But Teddy said he wasn't hungry and insisted on going with us, wearing his favorite Indian headdress, typically taking the lead, as if only he knew the way to Handytown. I walked with Priscilla, who seemed to be making an effort to be convivial and chatty, if I remember, talking about the child by her first husband, a boy she was worried about, given the rocky relationship with his father. Alger, looking fit and tanned, walked behind us, just out of earshot, oblivious of our conversation, but seemingly in a better mood as he borrowed my field glasses, avidly pausing to point out a sighting for the rest of us. Annie and Carl lingered behind in fervent conversation.

"Something—some mood—seemed to shift among the five adults, perhaps initiated by Priscilla's gaiety—she was prone to sudden emotional swings—or the serene weather. I had a sense that her impromptu visit had been about testing herself, testing the waters, touching on some aspect of our early relationship, only to have the elusive thing come clear in her mind. As the sun dipped and the mauve-emerald shadows lengthened, she began to wave her arms with animation and tell me in excited snatches how splendidly Alger was getting on in Washington, especially now that he was working in the State Department under Assistant Secretary Francis Sayre. She was quite proud of the fact that Sayre was Woodrow Wilson's son-in-law. She let me know, for my benefit or Alger's, that she didn't even miss New York. Almost as if to say—and Priscilla was always very status-conscious—See, Edward, this shabby Baltimore boy I married has gone on to have a splendid career, and, yes, we are going to change the world. Of course, I am only seeing that now, in retrospect."

"And what about Annie and Carl?" prompted Wendy from the backseat, feverishly taking notes.

"You two," scolded Cecily, but in good humor.

"Carl, our lugubrious guest, lumbered along behind with Annie, the cuffs of his trousers almost touching the ground, so that when we returned, he had to pick fern leaves and burs out of them. What I think struck me, from what I could overhear and from what Annie told me later, was the spirited literary conversation that passed between them along the trail to and from Handytown. They talked of Keats and Shelley and even Emerson. Carl and Annie were so caught up in their banter that they remained almost oblivious of Alger's sightings."

"Did you ever catch a last name for Carl?" asked George. "That would be important for the memoir."

The Judge did not seem to hear as his voice rose with a hint of mystic rapture.

"And then, you see, the most marvelous thing happened. We entered the overgrown glade of Handytown with its sparkling spring beneath a massive oak and mossy bluestone outcropping. There, in pensive shadow, were the Handy family's hand-worked bluestone grave monuments standing bold and tall. And, of course, the boulder-ringed cellar hole, out of which a stand of silver birch grew like a naiad's fountain. Teddy flew around like a feathered wood sprite, showing off the sites: the fieldstone walls lapped by purple steeplebush and goldenrod and

barberry. As you know, the place has the feel of a sylvan chapel, especially then, with this delicate azure light—it fairly made one's heart
pause. And as if on cue, Teddy raised his hand for silence and pointed.
The hermit thrush began to sing, an entire family of five or six, their
eerie, transcendent voices filtering down out of the canopy of oak and
pine like some avian choir, antiphonal responses echoing and fading,
only to be caught up again and traded around, as if we were supplicants
at heaven's gate. We all just froze in place, staring skyward, as if struck
dumb by some invisible force of nature.

"And I remember Teddy—even my whirlwind little wood sprite
struck dumb—standing there amid the sweet fern—oh, the ambrosia
of their perfume—and raising his arms like a conductor with a radiant
smile, as if he were the Toscanini of this celestial performance. But it
wasn't just the thrush he was signaling, but the fantails of silver birch
from David Handy's cellar hole. There, hung in the wispy branches
like Christmas decorations, was a flock of about twenty or even thirty
scarlet tanagers. It was as if the birch had erupted into votive flames, a
flickering mobile mass of royal reds, glittering and rising, flocking and
settling, as if enchanted, too, by the sweet, sad music of the thrush. We
five adults and one golden-haired youth were so mesmerized that we
remained speechless for many minutes. Then, as if some unseen breeze
had swept through an open window, the flock of tanagers leapt free of
the birch, almost as one, and vanished like fiery smoke into the yellow
sky. We looked at each other, starstruck children. None of us had ever
seen anything quite like that—never. Priscilla had tears in her eyes and
bowed her head into Alger's shoulder, like a sentimental image out of
Bouguereau. For a brief moment, time stood still, and the harsh realities
of the Great Depression and our own insignificance fled our minds."

George drove slowly, both hands fixed on the steering wheel, trying
to keep the Tahoe dead steady between the lane markers, flashing brief
glances at the Judge and then at Wendy in the mirror as she frantically
transcribed. All the while, he was struggling to hear each and every last
word voiced above the slipstream. He fought an inchoate panic at this
data download that threatened everything.

Wendy, unperturbable, looked up, her face lit with delight.

"And Teddy, as you wrote, Teddy handed around that blue ironware cup . . ."

The Judge's face broke into a broad smile.

"Ah, like a last Communion from our spring of eternal youth."

"Ponce de León," added George. "Realms of gold . . ."

"You see, I've always known it to be so . . . the beauty of birds; it's not just for survival's sake, for purposes of adaptation . . . but a thing in and of itself, for the pure delight of the female, for our delight. Beauty and the appreciation of beauty is the art of our very existence, even for our living, breathing, sinful selves."

"Aha, your true religion," said Wendy. "We've ferreted you out. Along with Carl, Annie's literary companion."

"Oh, that's why she couldn't let them go. She insisted our guests stay for dinner, stay the night. She played an impromptu concert of all her favorites in the great room, as well as she ever played. There were tears all around as the company listened, gazing upward into the blue imperium of the ship's keel ceiling. Later Annie huddled with her soulful friend Carl around the fire into the wee hours, with our dour angels listening in on their conversation. Then they were gone at the crack of dawn. Didn't even stay for breakfast. And not even a thank-you note."

"Did Annie or you ever keep up with Carl, or see him again?" asked George.

Wendy signaled with her hands from the back seat to end the conversation.

"Why would we do that, a man with only a first name? I thought I'd made it clear in the memoir that it was a singular moment—a fable never to be repeated, like a shooting star, more an apparition than real."

At this his head nodded with the effort of conversation, and in moments he was fast asleep.

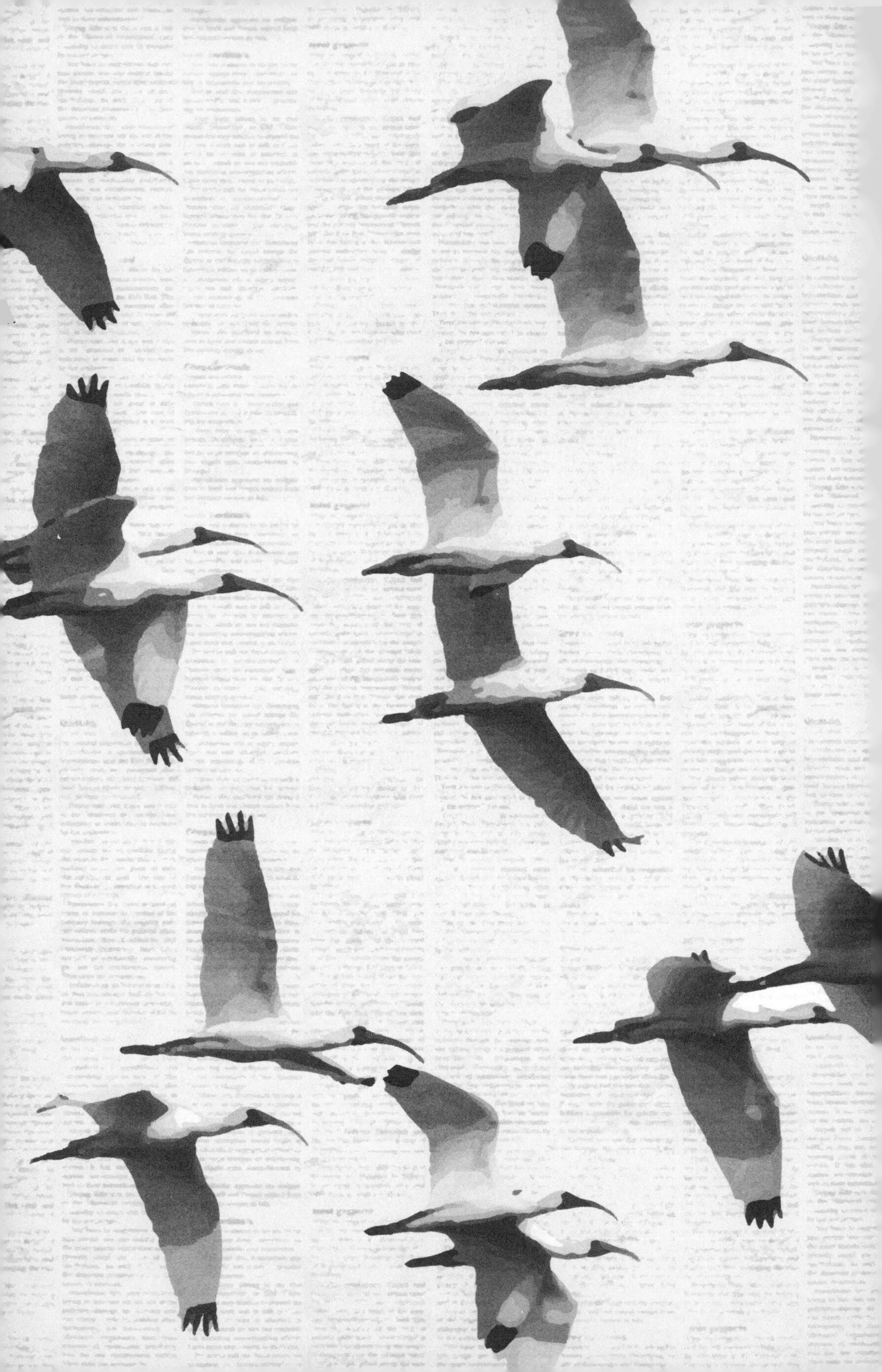

69

Love's Sad Satiety

HE LAY BACK on the lounger, too tired to talk, to comment or complain or even offer unwanted advice, but alive, nonetheless, to the soft, humid-scented voice of the sea. Made it back to Beverly Farms—imagine! . . . To Annie. He tried to keep his eyes open as best he could to catch the running lights of the sailboats returning to harbor, drawing electric arcs across the lavender-streaked clouds, trailing pinafores of gulls, flanked in turn by the returning squads of Mesozoic pelicans . . . soaring, rising, stalling, diving like wrecked hulks for a last shot at a herring or two . . . just as they used to when he and Annie walked the beach . . . for how many millions of years?

Something weighed on him, something said, or thought, or even dreamed—so many dreams. Something about Teddy, his little Indian sporting that bald eagle's feather.

He breathed deeply, deeper than deep, of sweet time itself limned in his weary gaze by bowing palm fronds fronting the low dunes, where the oat grass shouldered the west wind. And beyond, where the foam-crowned breakers nudged the fading horizon, touched here and there by the artist with lovely passages of translucent orange fading to hints of Delft blue. Surely, dear, an inspiration for our William Gedney Bunce, even absent a campanile or stalwart pali or two. He struggled to keep his eyes open, to remember what worrisome story he'd told, the one with Teddy as pathfinder. But the splendor of the sea soothed any last worries, as did the comforting presence of his granddaughter sitting nearby, absorbed in her organic chemistry textbook, headphones connected to some kind of bright yellow gadget, listening to God knows what kind of crazy music. So like Annie of all the grandchildren, with her talented hands, kind hands, which delved regularly for his still-beating heart. Annie, Annie, listen, dear. But she did not stir or hear. Listen, dear, to the sounds of the earth rolling, rolling along, the world refreshing itself moment after moment, wave after wave, one moment merging forever with the next.

Ah . . . a flight of white ibis . . . most elegant birds in flight, he and Annie had always agreed, pink bowsprit trailing pink legs with an undulant, supple white line—black tipped wings, like a dancer leaping into her lover's arms, or so Annie had put it to him once.

A tune kept drifting through his mind that Cecily had played for him on the piano before dinner, a Christmas present from Alice, theme and variation on something Annie had composed, just a few phrases, but enchanting—"Annie's Theme," Cecily called it.

Oh, Annie . . . The tune kept repeating, now as delicate and fugitive as memory, the sorrow and pity of the thing like a shadow softening and blurring, an iridescent bubble floating in sunlight, glistening, perfect, speaking wordlessly to his soul.

Eyes closed, he felt the pull of her hand in his, the sand crunching between their toes, and, in the salty caress of the breeze, her voice in his. "What would Uncle Ollie say about your conduct?" The scolding tone returned him to Justice Holmes's sunporch and the granite outcroppings in the yard dotted with lilacs and hydrangea, where the old man presided in majesty, propped up by threadbare cushions in his high fan-backed wicker chair, where a young whippersnapper fresh out of Harvard Law read to his mentor from Austen and Gibbon, Emerson and Wordsworth.

Sir, it's like this . . .

But he could no longer remember the case at issue, or what prodigies of data (his grandson's words) required throwing into the scales of justice, or the nudge of conscience to save one's soul.

Dear Edward, that just doesn't wash . . . *non lavabit* . . . no, not at all.

A verdict for what infraction? He found himself imploring that white-whiskered solonic face and those twinkling eyes. God will not hold me responsible for the few dull books I have birthed in this life, Edward, perhaps for a bad opinion or two. Or will it be the dissents, do you think, that will stand the test of time? Yours, too, no doubt. Not to worry, not to worry, my dear Edward. I erred in *Debs v. United States*, upholding that abomination, the Sedition Act, to my eternal shame, though making amends later with my Abrams dissent, upholding the right to freedom of speech. So a long life affords both contrition and making amends. Like you, I am a little swirl of electrons in the cosmos, and someday the swirl will dissolve. No more, no less, no matter, son. On the battlefield of life, a man has to do what he has to do in the moment, with eternity as his only judge.

He struggled to open his eyes, rise once more from the dock, just enough to see again the swaying palms silhouetted by fading wisps of fiery red, now nuzzled by a pale gibbous moon, as if insolently shouldering her way onstage.

And now I am even older than Holmes. Imagine that, Annie.

He turned his head to the blur of his lovely helpmeet seated nearby, absorbed in her studies, who did not seem to hear him or seem to care about contrition or amends.

But just in case you ever doubt yourself, if a steady hand is required, well, there's somebody I've been wanting you to meet.

Through half-shuttered eyes, he gazed out at the gathering darkness flecked with shards of flamingo pink . . . and then to his onetime companion, bent to the book in her lap. He wanted to cry out to her, Look, look, look . . . Annie, while you can, dear!

Remember, dear, in the early years, the happy years, when the children arrived, and Teddy tore up and down Hermitage in the summers like a human cyclone, and Alice practiced like a demon, and Martha holed up in the boathouse with her books? He blinked, straining to keep his eyes open as his companion smiled at something on the page, her lovely nose and tapering chin undulating to the music . . . underlining in her book with quick, determined strokes. And a gentle crash of waves, there, and again, between the notes as her hands rose from the keyboard of the old Chickering & Sons piano in Holmes's parlor, pausing for the waves to fill the telltale silence between the phrasing—the thing she always told the children: Listen, dears, to the quietude between the notes, for that's part of the music, too. And sitting in her favorite chair by the lake, she would lift her arm for silence, raising her glad eyes skyward into the canopy of green against the fading blue . . . There, the hermit thrush . . . Hush, children. Hear him? And there's his mate. Hear her? Hush, Teddy, hush . . . listen . . . Alice, Martha, Cordelia . . . learn to listen to the silence between your heartbeats, where the birds sing . . . *oh, holy, holy, ah purity, purity eeh, sweetly sweetly.*

Again the tune came back to him, the repeating phrase, "Annie's Theme," so like the thrush, of joy and faith ecstatic.

And there, too, in the rhythm of the sea, the murmur of her young sweaty heart beneath the softness of her full breasts, the skin so soft, her lips soft as they had been on that first night walking on the beach, and their first kisses soft as dusk . . . where the old crooked dock posts marched out into the bay like a column of bent and harrowed veterans at a last regimental reunion.

Annie, Annie, dear, do you hear the waves? . . . Almost as beautiful as your playing.

I will not judge you, Edward; only Ollie and your God can do that. But as you always tell the children, the only moral course that matters is doing the right thing when nobody but you will ever know the difference.

—

This discordant voice woke some last righteous plea in his fading soul—there among the first blush of stars, in the form of a shadow of a face he barely knew, had never known, yet which knew him. Or was it Annie he knew? There, standing with his family amid the commotion at the end of the trial's first day, he was approached by a ragged stranger in a dark beret, fingers smeared with charcoal dust, clutching an envelope—a fearful look left and right—to be wordlessly thrust into his hands, their eyes meeting for barely an instant, those dark, red-rimmed, sleepless but acute, all-seeing eyes burning into his, and on into some cavern of dark foreboding. The smell of whiskey on the man's heated breath as his lips pressed close to his ear, a whisper imparted in haste, a warning, or was it a plea . . . something? Then a knowing nod and then an adoring smile turned on Annie, who coldly rejected his offer of a charcoal sketch, which he then presented to Alice, a signed souvenir of what was supposedly a triumphant day for her papa. Then evaporating into that baying crowd, that scrum of jostling, shouting reporters.

Out of nowhere nine faces, nine shades who refused all pleas as to their fate when first examined in his study that evening, and forever more—even a young starry-eyed Priscilla—no matter the blood libations poured out in his research, much less his unsettled dreams at their sad fates and pleas for justice, like Alger proclaiming their innocence to the end.

What words had been whispered in that whiskey breath? Had he heard clearly with all the commotion, or simply forgotten?

And suddenly, miraculously, there they were, come back to him in the slow, rolling cadence of the waves. Was it a plea or warning that had prompted him to hold the sketches close—to save them from time?

Do what you need to do with these. To save me, to save yourself, to save your soul, if nothing more.

The hoarse voice, mingled with that of the waves, conjured once again Annie's skeptical stare.

"Yes, dear, yes—but I was truly blindsided—truly knocked for a loop. And the only right thing, the only necessary thing a man is duty-bound to do, whatever it takes, is to save his family."

But she, as usual, had the final say where she had underlined in Chambers's book on the necessity of witness to be fully human: "For it frees them from the trap of irreversible Fate at the point at which it whispers to them that each soul is individually responsible, and out of man's weakness will come strength, out of his corruption incorruption, out of his evil good, and out of what is false invulnerable truth."

He wanted to open his eyes to the stars and so receive her forgiving smile—perhaps that of the artist, as well—but was too exhausted, even for thought. And so he let his mind slip under the sound of the waves and somewhere deep, deep within the darkness, the song of the hermit thrush—tallying song of his soul—trailing away into the dusk like some sylvan flute played by irreverent Pan to the healing sky, at Handytown, where Teddy halted them for silence, where the sweet fern grew and the laurel and lilacs bloomed and the spring water sparkled with a lustral grace, as Dr. Dimock had always told him: ambrosia of the gods, son, the elixir to whatever ails a man's soul.

Annie's way, where her ashes were scattered . . . Thou lovest—but ne'er knew love's sad satiety.

The waves were more distant now, a song lovely and inviting, consoling, like a Chopin nocturne laving the ship's keel ceiling, where the careless gods whispered their suspect tales of love and malice among the infinite stars.

70

If Winter Comes, Can Spring Be Far Behind?

GEORGE AND WENDY walked in silence back and forth along the moonlit beach, keeping the porch lights of the condo in view at all times (screened just off to the side by a magnificent stand of royal palms), as if somehow fearful of straying too far. The three-quarter moon, a pebbly alloy of pewter and vermillion-gold, rode the two-foot-high breakers that poured onto the beach of white—almost blindingly white—sand (the whitest sand anywhere, so the brochure for the condo had assured). The air was warm and moist, as if the radiant heat of the day was stirred to life by their searching footsteps as they navigated the tide line. They took comfort in leaving crusty barefoot imprints to mark their return. The smell of brine and sea bracken infused the sucking, seething air. He kept looking back at the lighted porch just off the low dunes, where a recumbent figure was silhouetted by the interior light, while another figure sat nearby, wearing earphones, a heavy textbook open on her lap.

They did not hold hands as they walked, did not even touch hands; they had not made love since before Thanksgiving. For three weeks, they had corresponded mostly about her upcoming show. Only on the first day of their drive to Siesta Key did he share his e-mail correspondence with Allen Weinstein.

"Relax," she ordered, "we'll get him a Christmas tree tomorrow."

"He looked so exhausted."

"You're exhausted; we should've shared the driving. You need to learn to stop worrying about stuff you can't change."

"But that's the problem: It keeps changing."

She picked up a fan-shaped shell and playfully held it up to his ear, like a child, taking delight in the reticulated concave surface. "Besides, I thought he came through the long drive just fine—wow, and how." She laughed self-consciously, a tad guilty. "Cecily is wonderful with him; she took his blood pressure before dinner and said it was only a little elevated."

He glanced at her moonlit face beside him, her blond hair pinned up to the back of her head, so that her long neck showed to good advantage above the vee of her sports bra. When she raised her arms to breathe deeply, every muscle stood out like carved alabaster—white against white. Her khaki shorts showed off her muscular legs. He could barely restrain the temptation to once again indulge in the comfort of her body.

"I don't think she really cares about any of this." He lightly caressed her shoulder.

"Well," she replied, smiling, relieved and glad for his touch, "she doesn't *really* have skin in *this* game. Trust me, she's got plenty of skin in her own to fully preoccupy her." She smacked his butt. "And that little piece she was playing before dinner, I can't get the tune out of my mind."

"'Annie's Theme.' Something Aunt Alice concocted as a Christmas present for the Judge, from notes Annie left for a Balanchine ballet she never finished. Full of tenderness—don't you think?—and passion, as if floating out of some different world."

"Another universe. Of all things . . . perhaps, Handytown."

He shook his head, perplexed, as if hearing the melody line once more in counterpoint to the waves.

"What blew my mind is how he so guilelessly put it out there—Carl and everything. Like he was saying, So what else is new? As if he really didn't make the connection between the mysterious friend of Annie's and Chambers. As if the Chambers—Carl—of Handytown and the Chambers he tried to destroy in court were two different people."

"Maybe they are, at least in his mind (the spy and the witness), at least now—you're the big expert on parallel universes." She threw this out almost hopefully, patting his hand. "He's simply parked his conscience in a convenient limbo between two realities—one of your Lagrange points."

"Unless, he and Chambers had it all worked out before the trial."

"You really believe that or is that Weinstein's theory?"

"How can I trust him again, trust anything he's written? He's so still there . . . and not."

"Listen, tomorrow, when he's rested and relaxed, when the time is right, we just continue a casual conversation about editing the memoir, pointing out that the one glaring anomaly is his description of Carl and Priscilla and Alger visiting Hermitage, and—well, what happened in the trial. We can put it to him directly: 'You do realize that Carl and Whittaker Chambers are one and the same, don't you? Because, well, people will wonder if you just forgot or were trying to cover up something.' And we'll see where he takes it."

"I hate doing this to him, pressing him, deceiving him, telling him it's in the memoir when it isn't."

"But it is, now, because now you have to include it."

"Says you."

"It's your call." She shrugged.

"The hell. Now you have the evidence, too. I presume you photographed the Chambers and Priscilla Hiss letters, along with Teddy's."

She gave the sand a kick—along with a guilty shrug, so he thought—then watched the white—a shower of diamond points—anoint the foamy breakers.

"Blackmail to add to my sins." She stared off a moment at the dim stars, nodding to herself. "Did I ever tell you my father used to always recite Shelley's 'Ode to the West Wind' when we summited, pointing out the constellations. He wanted to be a poet in high school, even studied poetry at MIT, if you can believe it. He loved the last bit." And she recited a few lines in a girlish tone, as if desirous of drawing nearer to a thirteen-year-old fading to memory:

> Drive my dead thoughts over the universe
> Like wither'd leaves to quicken a new birth!
> And, by the incantation of this verse,
> Scatter, as from an unextinguish'd hearth
> Ashes and sparks, my words among mankind!
> Be through my lips to unawaken'd Earth
> The trumpet of a prophecy!

Again, like that teenager, she kicked up another blizzard of whiteness. "He'd put his arm around my shoulder and give me a hug. 'Wendo,' he'd say, 'the falling leaves, see, are like the stars, don't you think?'"

She took his hand, but his mind seemed elsewhere, or maybe not.

"Cecily says when your heart gets weaker like that, the brain is getting less blood. I don't think he quite realizes what he's saying, as if he's just resigned now to let the memoir stand as is."

"It's lovely, George, how he trusts you. You've given him peace."

"His voice had such a serenity, like I've never heard, as if he were just relating a fairytale."

"Maybe he was."

"You don't seem to care that he's been lying the whole time, to us, maybe to himself—his family, to the whole fucking world, for all we know."

She grabbed his arm, fed up with his doubt, and squeezed hard. "Okay, so, we lied to him, too. But he confessed on his own terms about Carl—Chambers's underground GRU pseudonym. If anything, he did it for you: to give you the choice to make things right." She touched his cheek. "There's something sweet, deeply moving in the relationship between Annie and Chambers, a recognition of some human faith or frailty that caused them both to keep their silence. Call it an act of grace. Priscilla, as well."

They stood silently for a minute, watching the stars bleed through the veils of ashy azure, vying for the moon's circumspect limelight.

"And how exactly am I to do that, edit what happened, or didn't, at Handytown—the trial? It's more like a fable, a child's bedtime story."

She laid her forehead against his chest for a moment, as if listening there, listening above the murmur of the sea . . . the yet unfathomed thing.

"How do we talk to him about Daisy Wright?" she asked. "Do we show him Teddy's letter—all of it? Put it under the tree as a present for him to open? Or do we just gently clue him in around the edges, yet another story of Teddy's exploits? Perhaps wait until he can meet with Daisy and Captain Wright and young Ben on the piazza at Hermitage in the spring—call it a family reunion?"

At this prospect, he seemed even more confounded, sighing painfully.

"That was the strangest feeling sitting there on the dock with Nancy and having Ben appear like that—talk about ghosts."

"I only wish I'd been there. And talk about feeling—didn't you find it eerie, hearing him reminisce in the car about that walk to Handytown? It was like an echo of Chambers's and Priscilla Hiss's letters, like a shared memory, like one wave of sensation following another . . . Like our first time at Handytown when you described what it's like in spring, in summer—like we'd been there with them." She nodded to herself. "Well, one thing's for sure: What happened at Handytown certainly changed all their lives."

He laughed with a cynical note of exasperation. "What happens in Handytown stays in Handytown." He picked up a pebble and threw it far out, watching for a moment the spreading ripples. "Listen, dream or daydream, it doesn't change the fact that, if true, the Judge and Annie, and even little Teddy, were witnesses to the fact—just like Allen wrote—that Alger and Priscilla Hiss and Whittaker Chambers were friends and had indeed made that trip to Fitzwilliam, New Hampshire, in the summer of 1937 to pick up Harry Dexter White's plan for the reform of Soviet monetary policy." He frowned at his recitation of such boilerplate, the shaky facts, perplexed, trying to see it clearly as he went on. "And stopped at Hermitage on the way back—Allen Weinstein's missing day, yet another clincher for his scholarship on the trial. You don't think that's not going to come out someday? Which means the Judge's role as defense attorney in the Hiss trial will be revealed as bogus from the get-go. He knew that Hiss knew Chambers as Carl and that they along with Priscilla were hanging out together in August 1937. He knew Hiss was lying; he knew, all along, his client was guilty."

"But—how many times have you said it?—that's what defense attorneys *do*; even Teddy wrote as much: They defend their client, guilty or not guilty—hell or high water. Goes with the territory. Of course, Chambers knew, too, so maybe they never even had to exchange a word? They simply intuited each other."

He stopped and looked back again toward the condo on the beach. "That's a stretch, even for the Judge." Squinting, he passed a hand through his hair and rubbed the back of his neck.

She reached to his free hand. "Unless, unless, Annie and Chambers had . . ."

"Yes?"

"Talked."

"Talked? Before the trial?"

"Oh my God." She squeezed his hand, segueing from a defensive tone to one of mild alarm. "If she had acted as a go-between, it would have put them all in danger—just like Allen suggested—like George Altmann, anyone who could testify that Hiss *had* known Chambers in 1937—or *had* been part of the Communist underground. Even years later when Chambers took such care in posting his letter to Annie."

He now clutched her hand, his voice hollow. "Annie . . . but it doesn't make sense." He kicked at the sand as had she. "Why would Hiss have suggested his old Harvard Law School classmate for his defense team since he knew the Judge knew the crucial truth about him and Chambers? It would be like bringing a Trojan horse into the defense team."

At this, they stared into each other's eyes, their faces only inches apart.

Again she caressed his cheek, less a sensuous gesture than the reflex of conspirators. "Hiss knew Chambers well, intimately, for years. Some part of him bet on Handytown, bet on Chambers's inner decency not to expose Annie and the Judge—once Edward Dimock was his defense attorney."

"No way . . ."

"Hey, you're the Judge's grandson; he practically raised you. What do your instincts tell you? Was your grandfather a Hiss ally or was he in on that bet, while defending himself and his family? It's your call, George."

Again he peered up at the star clusters forming above the bruised-peach horizon, struggling to read something there. "So, you hire a potential witness for the prosecution, put him on your defense team . . . and he's immune—immediately covered by attorney-client privilege. Even if the government prosecutors found out, they couldn't call one of Hiss's own defense attorneys to testify against his client—nor his wife or son, for that matter—checkmate—fucking brilliant."

"Brilliant, sure, but George"—her eager face darkened with uncertainty—"why *would* the Judge agree? One, even if not technically unethical, it makes a mockery of the law and his fabled integrity; and two, if it was revealed . . . sooner or later, it could be enough to destroy his reputation and career. Certainly why he left it out of his memoir."

"My God, no wonder Annie was so against it . . . so aghast at the whole thing—so, so anguished in her split loyalties—especially if she'd been drawn in, that she hid those letters and kept them to herself."

"Like you said, another reason to put the Judge on the defense team: Neither he nor Chambers was going to pull Annie into that mess." She slipped her fingers between his. "Unless, of course, she already was."

"Teddy knew his father better than any of us, knew Hiss had a chokehold of some kind." George squeezed her fingers, breathing heavily, pondering Virgo as it slowly deliquesced to the southwest. "Either they were, in effect, buying his silence or—"

She grabbed his arm in both hands, his feet sinking in the sand. "Or even if Annie wasn't caught up in the mess they *must* have threatened him."

"No," he shot back, shaking his head with a sudden shiver of terror. "They were too expert for that. Hiss never threatened Chambers in so many words, but Chambers knew, absolutely, that if the opportunity presented itself, Hiss would let the KGB or the GRU kill him . . . or members of his family."

She released her grip, relieved but wary. "George, are you sure, now, after everything, we want to do this, go to this place?" Again she laid her ear against his chest, trying to fathom the unstated, murmuring, "He can't last much longer. You've got the memoir safely copied and scanned and the original typescript locked away in the Chase bank vault. It's in your hands . . . Hermitage." And she scooped up a handful of white sand and let it fall away like a last trickle in an hourglass.

At this, they continued walking, as if sobered, even relieved, staring out to sea. He squinted again and again, brow furrowed, as he raised his eyes higher above the cooling ashy horizon to the incipient glitter.

"It's not that I want to confront him tomorrow or ever."

"Then don't . . . leave it, Handytown and all: their parallel universe. Let Captain Wright and Ben Wright be your Christmas present— what's more beautiful than that? We'll wrap up the photograph of father and son standing on the bridge of the destroyer and leave it under the tree."

He turned on her, head tilted, eyes squinting, as if catching her out: his co-conspirator, perhaps again deftly playing him.

"Let's just call it a thought experiment, okay? If you're Hiss and you're going over the evidence with your lawyers—and probably a KGB man at your elbow—and you're making a list of potential witnesses for the prosecution, anyone who could confirm Chambers's story that you and he had been friends—close friends, for years, part of the Soviet underground, an agent for Soviet military intelligence until at least 1938, per the grand jury indictment—who's on that list?"

"All it takes is just one believable corroborative witness to back up Chambers."

"Just one," he repeated. "And as Allen pointed out, the Hiss's black maid, Claudia Catlett, helped sink Hiss with the jury when she testified she'd seen Chambers with Alger at Volta Place."

"George," she said, trying to stifle the alarm in her voice, "George Altmann and the sketches would have been the clincher on a guilty verdict."

"And then," he continued, "out of the blue, he was handed the nine sketches by George Altmann, incriminating evidence, putting him in even more potential jeopardy with the Hiss camp. And there, right on top, is the lovely portrait of Priscilla, which must have terrified him the moment he slid it out of the envelope, touched some lurking doubt in his mind, confounding him—or confounding his plans to throw the trial to the prosecution with limited collateral damage."

"The others would know."

Wendy put an arm around him as if to steady herself.

"If the Judge had shown the sketches to the rest of the defense teams, those who really believed in Hiss's innocence, the old Harvard boys, they'd have known that Hiss had been guilty all along—and Priscilla. Many already thought Priscilla might be the guilty one and Alger only loyally covering for her. Maybe as Weinstein suggested, Priscilla never admitted the existence of the thank-you letter she wrote, or anything about a visit to Hermitage in 1937."

"So it must have been she who insisted on bringing the Judge onto the defense team."

"And he wasn't going to blow her cover—or Alger's—by showing the rest of the defense team the Altmann sketches, which might have resulted in many of them quitting in disgust, while putting himself in even greater jeopardy."

Wendy let out a cry of joy at this imaginative leap. "Ever the romantic!"

"Me?"

"Yes, you," she said, laughing, "who wanted to save Princess Leia when you were eight years old."

"Okay, say it *was* Priscilla. Put yourself in her shoes—something you seem to relish. If you wanted to save Edward Dimock—save your soul—how would you do it?"

"I'd keep my mouth shut about the thank-you letter but get my husband to put Edward Dimock on his defense team, make a case to hire him, think up an excuse—'he'll do it for me, dear; and keep his mouth shut,' but say nothing touching on the dark side, so to speak, of my reasons." She closed her eyes tight, nodding to herself. "No . . . no, I'd definitely not mention my Handytown thank-you note to Alger."

"So, Hiss makes his case to his team: Edward Dimock is known for his integrity, a progressive, a man of the establishment—the perfect figure to attack the credibility of that slimy ex-Communist Chambers, who has emerged from the sewers, that rotten psychopathic liar. He wouldn't even have to have admitted to his defense team that Edward Dimock was a threat—that he knew all about his friendship with Chambers."

She shivered and caught his arm.

"Yes, yes, but there's still that unanswered: Why would the Judge have agreed—a man not apt to give in if threatened?"

George nodded up at the night sky, his chin canted left and right, so that a stranger might have thought he was simply counting the emergent stars. Then he laughed unconvincingly, as if a little desperate to ignore the supernova blowing up in his face, yet unable to avoid the devastating shock waves.

"They're both superb lawyers. All Hiss would have had to do would be to invite the Judge to his lawyer's office, just the two of them; he wouldn't even have had to mention that day—Handytown, and Annie and Teddy—in the same breath. I can almost see Hiss smile as he alluded to it across the table—maybe he went to the Judge's downtown twenty-second-floor office, to be alone—the oak paneling, the portraits of the founding partners. Then just a vague allusion to Handytown, the song of the hermit thrush, a jocular reference to that all-male confab of scarlet tanagers come to entertain little Teddy with his Indian headdress; a smile, a wistful look. And of course, Carl, the baleful Carl: 'He tried to get me entangled in things I should have known better to avoid . . . entrapment is what it was; Priscilla's doing, mostly—you know how careless she can be.'" George squinted again, swallowing hard at the conjured voice. "And perhaps the clincher, a veiled comment about the sad end a year before of one of his colleagues at State, Laurence Duggan, who had mysteriously plunged sixteen stories to his untimely death . . . a smile, a glance out the window high above the city streets."

"Leave it at that George—no more where he came from," she pleaded. "An offer he couldn't refuse—that's all we need."

"But you have such a high regard for the old boy, or is it just unblemished Hermitage?"

"That's unfair." She put her arms around him and held him tight. "I love you."

She moved a pleading hand to his face, his lips, as if, just possibly, aghast such a confession had slipped out.

"Love—us?" he cried.

"Yes, love," she repeated not without a hint of sarcasm, changing tack. "Do you really think love, loyalty, integrity—call it what you will, was enough to stop Whittaker Chambers under cross-examination from pointing a finger at his relentless accuser and announcing to the jury that Edward Dimock was a fraud, a liar, that the defense counsel had first met him, Whittaker Chambers, when he and Alger and Priscilla Hiss had arrived at Dimock's vacation home in the Catskills in August of 1937 on the way back from New Hampshire and a meeting with Harry Dexter White, when he'd met Dimock's wife, Annie, and her son. Given his penchant for the telling detail, Chambers would have included the monumental gravestones at Handytown, the thrush, the scarlet tanagers, Annie's concert in the great room under the stars of the ship's keel ceiling, certainly to the jury, if not later in his book." She paused for breath. "Is that what you and Weinstein are saying: his decency and love were really enough?"

George laughed as if in relief at being able to refute such romantic fantasies, if not his own, tugging on her arm, needing to be under way once again, to feel the soft sand between his toes.

"And you?"

"Of course," she laughed, "love is never enough without the imagination to see the truth—your telltale stars." She skipped in the sand beside him. "Silly, because it didn't happen."

"What didn't happen?"

"Handytown."

"Handytown?"

"Like the Judge said: Like time stood still—out of time, out of mind." She touched his chin, his lips, as if urging his rejoinder to hers.

"Yes, yes, Priscilla wrote to him, something about another realm, a better world . . . that *something* out of time, when their insignificant lives didn't matter."

"Go on," she again urged.

"You see"—George squinted, as if trying to decipher that unscripted past risen above the horizon—"Chambers didn't need to mention it . . . didn't want to mention it. What's not in his letter: the folly of the psychiatric defense that would utterly discredit the defense in the eyes of the jurors." With that, he looked down into her glittering eyes and held her shoulders, forcing her back a few inches, as if to properly take in the meaning writ there, her possibly hopeful expression outlined against the expanse of white. "They must have had an understanding, like Allen suggested."

"No, *you* suggested. That Chambers and Edward Dimock were . . ."

"And Annie: secret sharers."

She nodded eagerly. "Yes, Chambers had discussed Conrad and Proust long into the night with his wife, Annie; he'd helped Teddy identify his collection of feathers."

"Chambers was a Christian, a Quaker, attuned to an inner light; he always tried to spare people who'd been ensnared by the same evil that had ensnared him."

"Even as Edward Dimock viciously cross-examined him as a pathological liar, bringing up all that ridiculous and humiliating stuff from his childhood and adolescence? His brother's suicide. The implied homosexuality and deviant behavior?"

George smiled, first with relief, then with what turned into a devilish grin. "A brilliant counterintuitive stroke: Chambers and the prosecution made mincemeat of Edward Dimock and both expert witness psychiatrists. It was a turning point. The defense lost all credibility when their gambit to destroy Chambers failed."

"So you see"—she laughed triumphantly—"the fix was in all along."

"When Alger Hiss bent over that table in Edward Dimock's office and alluded to Handytown, to Teddy, to Laurence Duggan and Marvin Smith, the Judge knew instantly he'd have to destroy Hiss and how he—he and Chambers were going to do it . . . with his own petard."

"George," she laughed again, hugging him, "and this isn't even astrophysics—one of your parallel universes?"

"Oh, deep—as deep as it gets." George bent and gave Wendy a joyous kiss of relief. "Annie had seen into Chambers's heart and he into hers. Enough that Chambers believed in the man Annie had married."

"As did George Altmann when he handed the sketches to the Judge with Annie standing right beside him, even if she rejected his gift of a charcoal sketch of the handsome defense counsel."

"George Altmann had her recording . . ."

She laughed yet again but this time it rang hollow, her voice faltering. "Ah, the path to Handytown."

"Your Shelley and royal falconry . . . I think we can leave it there: the old fox. No need to press it further—it's Christmas anyway."

They both smiled uneasily and turned again to the distant lights of the condo and nodded in tandem. George swung her around and she let out a scream of delight as a wave caught her feet. Slowly, longingly, leaning on each other, they began walking back. Then he paused, turning to the sea as if suddenly made aware of its vastness, the sound of the waves, the timeless bewitchment . . . waiting.

"What?" she finally said.

"If space were visible, this is what it would look like, the gravitational field rippling across an infinite curving ocean." He shook his head in wonder. "It's all interaction . . . including the Altmann sketches."

She leaned her head into his shoulder and bit him, like Eve the apple, gently on the flesh of his upper arm.

"But," she snorted, as if to dismiss her question, "if your story is right, George, and the Judge and Chambers managed to sabotage Hiss's defense, why the obsession over all the years with the sketches, much less getting you involved?"

George stared, looking down at their joined moon shadows on the white sand, where the cooling sea washed over their feet, erasing their footsteps as they went along, as if they'd never been. They both took a deep breath, anything to hold back the tide, looking off toward the house above the dunes, where the last living link to their proposed narrative still resided, even as their footprints dissolved into nothing.

George groaned. "Shit, oh shit . . . yes, the Altmann sketches."

She grabbed hold of his arm to stop him, to steady herself. "You mean the collateral damage. His conscience finally got to him."

"Why else would he take the risk of raiding the defense files for those sketches? Or at least writing as much in his memoir." George closed his eyes, wiping at his perspiring brow.

Her eyes turned to a line of battered and broken wooden pilings marching out beyond the surf, remnants of what had once been a jetty.

"And if Weinstein is right and he was never able to access the defense files?"

George sighed, struggling to see the thing clear. "If he understood the danger . . . then when George Altmann handed him the manila envelope with the sketches of a Communist cell on the first day of the trial, he had to have known that Altmann, too, was in dire danger, and desperately seeking a way out."

"So he never buried them in the defense files. Just another lie, and blatantly lying about an illegal act in his memoir."

"If he really wanted to save Altmann and protect himself—save Priscilla, he'd have been better off sticking the sketches in his briefcase, taking them home, and destroying them. When turning them over to the defense team could have blown up everything."

"He's a romantic, like you, George. Saving the two women who meant the most to him in his life." She shrugged as if barely believing her own words, a hint of despair in her faltering footsteps. "Or at least keeping the sketches—can we call them masterpieces?—in a safe place, a life preserver, in case things turned against him."

"Certainly the smart thing, if not the right thing." He squinted, desperate to see the specters that rose before him. "Do you suppose somebody on the defense team spotted Altmann handing over the envelope and got suspicious—and Altmann was probably being watched by the KGB—of the Trojan horse on the defense team?"

She grabbed his arm as if to pull him back from the brink of the sea.

"You weren't there; I wasn't there. We have no right to go there—let's not go there. The memoir is safe with us." And she waved at the ungainly line of rotted pilings illuminated in the moonlight, muttering something to herself, as if satisfied to let the ruined jetty make her point.

"What?" he asked.

"Lonely sentries . . ."

He shook his head in exasperation and instead turned his eyes to the heavens, to the broken constellations shedding the past like so many sloughed-off skins . . . countless, endless, eternal.

"He's had me wrapped up for years, his nemesis, Banquo's ghost, the namesake of George Altmann: the living reminder of the murdered man whose life he failed to save, to save his own."

She put a hand to his cheek. "It's all right, George."

"Fuck you."

"Look at it this way, baby, from the moment you were born, from the moment he ever laid eyes on his grandson, his flesh and blood, he knew, some part of him knew, that he had the blood of your grandfather George Altmann on his hands. Not burying the damn sketches deep enough, not sharing them with the defense team, keeping them to himself—to save himself. Not having the guts to return them to the son of the man he'd failed—sending his daughter instead. How would you—a man like him—live with that?"

"The son of a bitch." He sank, trembling, to his knees.

She turned again to the line of barnacled piles swept by the tide, as if remembering, or reassured by some image summoned to mind. Then bent to his face, her breath warm against his cheek as she tried to console him.

"No, no . . . he kept the sketches in reserve in case he lost the case, to be deployed against Hiss if he was found not-guilty. That was the risk he took. The sketches were his insurance in the event Hiss ever threatened him or his family, or might have been successful in turning over the verdict on appeal. Or if the matter of his guilt, some day, was ever thrown gravely in doubt. That was the role he's bequeathed to you, the role he's been preparing you to play all your life. Why your aunt Alice is probably right: why he kept you and Cordelia in Woodstock. Why he came around to funding your gallery—penance for sins of omission, perhaps."

She now bent to one knee, putting her comforting arms around him, her sandy face next to his as they stared out at the waves, the silver breakers moving gently, tirelessly, to erase their fugitive tracks. They remained like that for a long time, clinging together like marooned shipwrecks, as if some invisible current had swept them up and left them naked on that dreaded shore of endless doubt. A doubt, neither more nor less, but changed from only moments before. As were the stars, the universe . . . subject, too, to the randomness of time and memory.

At last, she sighed. "You released him, George." She touched his chin and eased up his face to meet hers. "Soothed his agonizing doubts, I guess. You gave him room for witness . . . set him free. What more could you do? And now, now it can all be safely explained away in the memoir. Hermitage is safe. You're safe, here with me." She pulled up her bra and pressed his face to her breast, then reached to his crotch, his breath quickening in the salty taste of her.

For an instant, he grabbed her face in his hands and stared intently into her cat-like eyes.

"And Cecily?"

"You silly, lovable baby." She pulled him to her breast again. "She can't get pregnant, and I am."

Moments later, as if her seductive words had indeed nudged that cosmic pendulum, they became aware of a distant cry and then another, their names like an echo. They picked themselves up and turned back to the lights of the condo, where a woman stood silhouetted against the palm fronds, waving frantically, calling out their names over the murmuring sea.

Dear George and Wendy,

I can't thank you enough for your kindness in sending the copy of Teddy's last letter from Korea. Like a missive of love from heaven's gate, it has filled my heart with joy and wonder. I have passed the letter on to my son, Captain Benjamin Wright, now on deployment in the Gulf. He writes back to me that Teddy's stirring words written while in harm's way on a Korean battlefield have strengthened and fortified him in the difficult duties he faces. He says he feels a love inexpressible, as do I. As does Ben, his son, who immediately called me and shouted with joy and wonder and a million questions that I fear I can never answer. But I will—I will try with all my heart and soul as soon as he's back from school.

I must tell you, when Benjie arrived back from rowing on the lake Thanksgiving night, that boy had stars in his eyes and enchantment in his voice as he told us about a lovely girl he'd met at your boathouse, your niece, Nancy, I believe. A boathouse long abandoned and not a little spooky in his childhood memory. Clearly, something very special happened that night, certainly for our family, as if Teddy's letter appeared out of some rare celestial crossing—in some infinite constellation of love beyond our wildest dreams!

And we must surely meet on the piazza of Hermitage in the spring—perhaps the whole family this summer if Ben senior's deployment is over—and spend time together going over the many things that must be on all our minds. What a blessing to still have your grandfather with us. He was always a wise and wonderful man—witty and kind and full of poignant stories about our woods—and I always admired him greatly in the old days, as, of course, did Teddy.

And to answer your kind concerns: I don't hold it against Teddy. My pregnancy struck him in his most vulnerable part: his sense of absolute freedom and joy in the world. He simply wasn't ready. He was confounded. He was afraid of his parents' disapproval. And so he headed for the hills, where duty called him, where he thought he might find safety from the things he was not ready for. His weakness was his strength. For one glorious summer, I came alive in his arms, sharing all nature's splendors through his eyes, as I do to this day, as I have shared with my son and grandson. Now I know his love for me and my son was absolutely real—finally real. And his duty done, I'm sure he would've returned to us. He has returned. I feel him now in my heart in every moment. And that love will keep my boys safe. I know—I just know it.

Bless you and your family for returning him to me—what an extraordinary Christmas present!

Love to you all,
Daisy Wright

P.S. We watched those mating bald eagles for an entire afternoon, while Teddy recited Whitman's "Dalliance of the Eagles." Yes, like angels tumbling from heaven's gate—oh, how we watched them!

Acknowledgments

TO MY WIFE, Patricia, who for over thirty years has stood by my side: always encouraging, always offering helpful advice on things literary and otherwise. Without her steadfast support and love none of my books would have been possible. And to my two sons, Carter and Christopher, who grew up loving great books and so inspired their dad to keep writing them. My gratitude and love are boundless.

To Allen Peacock, my editor of record, who forced me to go back to the drawing board and get this novel right, and then gave me the confidence, once I'd gotten it right, to move it to yet a higher plane. Allen, you are still the master of the editor's craft: thank you. And to Sally Arteseros, another masterful editor, who in early drafts helped me to see where the book was headed. Thank you, Sally, for your forbearance in an industry that discourages long novels. And once again—three books we've worked on together!—my thanks to my copy editor, Carol Edwards, for her uncanny eye—not just for issues of syntax and usage, but for prose that does the important work and what doesn't. Carol, you are still the best of the best. Many thanks to Anne Sanow, at Greenleaf, our superb proofreader who so expertly combed the manuscript for errors and so barred the door to errors of fact or fiction that had been overlooked. And Erin Brown, my lead editor on the Greenleaf team, a pro's pro, who so ably shepherded the book though proofing and design, carefully bringing all the parts together. Endless thanks to Drew Stevens, our talented interior designer, who produced our chapter-starts and the interior design. And to the incomparable Jason Booher, our cover designer, who came through with yet another fabulous cover. And to the whole Greenleaf team, Tyler LeBleu, Chelsea Richards, Cameron Stein, and our dazzling publicity team, Wunderkind's Tanya Farrell and Elena Stokes, who have worked tirelessly to get *Gods of Deception* into the hands of reviewers and readers who would discover a rich universe within.

Gods of Deception is a work of fiction about a time and place that already seems infinitely remote, even if the history that came out of that long ago era still weighs on our lives in the guise of various total-itarian ideologies and a resurgent Russia headed by an ex-KGB agent. Haunting the pages of the novel are two historical figures who also play larger-than-life roles in the fictional world of the Dimock family: Alger Hiss and Whittaker Chambers, a spy and his spy master, a con-victed perjurer and the witness who sent his onetime friend to jail. Both are extraordinary characters, fictional or otherwise. Alger Hiss remains a mystery wrapped in an enigma, while Whittaker Chambers has emerged in the twenty-first century as largely vindicated, his once-con-troversial memoir about his life as a Soviet spy-handler, *Witness*, now rightly understood as both offering an invaluable insight into the shad-owy world of Stalin's penetration of the U.S. government, and a literary masterpiece to go along with the likes of Arthur Koestler's *Darkness at Noon*, narrating one man's escape from the toils of a brutal system of deception and mind-control. Sam Tanenhaus's biography *Whittaker Chambers* also provided excellent insights into the Hiss trial and the life of Chambers.

I have drawn on many historical sources for the background of *Gods of Deception*. The historian Allen Weinstein (also a fictional character herein) provided crucial insights in his seminal work on the Hiss trial, *Perjury*, and his later history (with Alexander Vassiliev) of Soviet spying, *The Haunted Wood*. The uncovering and still unravel-ling tale of Stalin and the KGB's penetration of the U.S. government during the 1930s and 1940s is the result of many scholars exploiting the decoded Venona transcripts (Soviet cable traffic from the Second World War years later); these would include Herbert Romerstein and Eric Breindel's *The Venona Secrets*; Jerrold and Leona Schechter's *Sacred Secrets*; and the indispensable *Spies, The Rise and Fall of the KGB in America* by John Earl Haynes, Harvey Klehr, and Alexander Vassiliev, which also draws upon material from Soviet era intelligence files that, for a short time during the Yeltsin era, were made available to Alexander Vassiliev. H. Stanton Evans's *Stalin's Secret Agents: The Subversion of Roosevelt's Government* also proved insightful. On Yalta, S. M. Plokhy's *Yalta: The Price of Peace* remains an indispensable guide. John Koster's *Operation Snow* (which provided a translation of a part of Vitalli Pavlov's memoir, *Operation Snow: Half a Century at KGB Foreign Intelligence*) is the most authoritative account of Harry Dexter White's collusion with Soviet intelligence to undermine U.S. interests from Pearl Harbor to postwar Europe and Asia. I also drew upon countless contemporary accounts in various newspaper archives now available online. In the end, *Gods of Deception* is and remains a work of fiction—guided and directed as much as possible by the historical record as it has come down to us.

About the Author

DAVID ADAMS CLEVELAND is a novelist and art historian. His previous novel, *Time's Betrayal*, was awarded Best Historical Novel of 2017 by Reading the Past. Pulitzer Prize–winning author Robert Olen Butler called *Time's Betrayal* "a vast, rich, endlessly absorbing novel engaging with the great and enduring theme of literary art, the quest for identity." Bruce Olds, two-time Pulitzer-nominated author, described *Time's Betrayal* as a "monumental work . . . in a league of its own and class by itself . . . a large-hearted American epic that deserves the widest possible, most discriminating of readerships." In summer 2014, his second novel, *Love's Attraction*, became the top-selling hardback fiction for Barnes & Noble in New England. Fictionalcities.co.uk included *Love's Attraction* on its list of top novels for 2013. His first novel, *With a Gemlike Flame*, drew wide praise for its evocation of Venice and the hunt for a lost masterpiece by Raphael.

His pathbreaking art history book, *A History of American Tonalism 1880 – 1920, Crucible of American Modernism*, has just been published in a third edition with a new sixty-page introduction by Abbeville Press; this best-selling book in American art history won the Silver Medal in Art History in the Book of the Year Awards, 2010, and Outstanding Academic Title 2011, from the American Library Association. David was a regular reviewer for *ARTnews* and has written for *The Magazine Antiques*, the *American Art Review*, and *Dance Magazine*. For almost a decade, he was the arts editor at Voice of America. He worked with his son, Carter Cleveland, founder of Artsy.net, to build Artsy into the leading art platform in the world for discovering, buying, and selling fine art.

He and his wife split their time between the Catskills and Siesta Key, Florida. More about David and his publications can be found on his author site: davidadamscleveland.com.